I0610850

Books by Ron Mueller

The Taelo Series-Prehistory America
 Taelo: The Early Years
 Taelo: The Golden Feather
 Taelo: Journey of Discovery
 Taelo: Dangerous Passage
 Taelo: Condor Clan Slingers
 Taelo: Circumvention
 Taelo: The Journey of Sages
 Taelo: Collection

The Alex Evercrest Series-Detective
 The River Front
 The Girl on the Grill
 Missing
 Maggot
 Racist
 Votive Candles
 Windy City
 Country Road
 Pool of Blood
 Sins of the Daughter

The Door Series-Science Fiction
 The Door

The Savitar Series-Science Fiction
 Journey's End
 Savitar
 Confluence

Bram Nielson Series-Science Fiction
 The Fold
 The Message
 Fold Wormhole
 Negative Fold
 Ripples in Time

A Taelo Story
 The Name of the Child
 White Swan and Quiet Pheasant
 Broken Spear
 Floating Cloud
 Quiet Rabbit
 Busy Bee
 Little Otter& Talking Wren
 Burley Bear & Meadow Flower

A Feather-in-the-Wind Story
 The Eastern Elk Clan

The Problem Solver Series-Secret Agent
 The Beginning
 Drug Lords
 Border Crosser

Current Past and Future-Science Fiction
Event Survivors-Science Fiction
The Door-Science Fiction
Viajante 7-Science Fiction
Imagination by Courtney Huynh and Chloe Parker

<u>Taelo Collection</u>

By Ron Mueller

Around the World Publishing LLC
4914 Cooper Road Suite 144
Cincinnati, Ohio 45242-9998

This book is a work of fiction. Names, characters, places, and incidents either are products of the author's imagination or are used fictitiously. Any resemblance to actual events or locales or persons, living or dead, is entirely coincidental.

Taelo Collection Copyright © 2023

All rights reserved, including the right of reproduction, in whole or in part in any form.

ISBN 13: 978-1-68223-406-8
ISBN 10: 1-68223-406-1

Distributed by Ingram
Cover Picture By: Hien Mueller
Eagle by Teekaygee - Dreamstime.com
Cover Design By: Ron Mueller

Ron Mueller

Table of Content

Taelo The Journey of Sages... **845**

Introduction

The story of Taelo (Tā low), talon of the eagle, follows the journey of a young, exceptionally talented child and then young man. The Eagle, Taelo's totem always makes its appearance at the critical and important moments in Taelo's life. Golden Hawk, Taelo's cousin is his best friend and partner in their many adventures.

White Swan and Quiet Pheasant, their mothers are sisters who gave birth to the two on the same day. Taelo's mother, White Swan politically guides both her husband Grey Fox Running and Taelo in their interactions within the Elk Clan. She also ensured Red Oak and Quiet Pheasant transferred with them from the Elk Horn Clan to be the hunter for the main Elk Clan. She was determined her son would grow up with his cousin and best friend. The two boys each have leadership totems. The two families still talk about the boys seventh birthday when a golden hawk caught and dropped a salmon into Golden Hawk's lap as an Eagle cried and flew overhead.

All knew when an Eagle screamed from the sky, something eventful was about to happen.

The story of **Taelo**:

The Early Years begins with his naming and takes the reader through Taelo's and Golden Hawk's early years into young adulthood.

They constantly contribute to the well-being of all around them. They are known throughout all the Elk sub clans as being good luck to have around.

In **The Golden Feather,** this same team takes the next step in their development. They first travel South into the Andes of South America. They meet the people living in those areas. On their return they go into the North Coastal area where the Elk Clan originally had its home.

In **The Journey of Discovery** Taelo and Golden Hawk travel from the Pacific to the Atlantic Ocean and see the wonders of nature.

In **Dangerous Passage,** the team travels across the northern ice bridge to the origin of their race.

In **Condor Clan Slingers** the team returns to aid the Condor Clan in their battle against an aggressive Warrior Clan.

In **Circumvention** Taelo leads his team around the world and discovers the diversity it holds in both people and in animals.

In **The Journey of Sages** Taelo takes all the leaders of the clan in a journey around the Pacific.

Taelo The Early Years

Dedication:

My Thanks to:

Richard Hart,

His dedication to Taelo made Taelo into a series,

and

He insisted that the Stories be good.

Taelo The Early Years

Chapter 1: Wonders in the Stream

Soft white puffs floated across a clear blue sky. Just below the clouds a huge eagle glides effortlessly on the updraft from the valley below. The mountains surrounding the valley, still capped in snow, was a display of variations of green grasses, new leaves against the backdrop to the dark green pine trees standing like sentinels guarding the white crown above.

It was spring.

It was the Elk Clan's naming ceremony. This was when the child selected an object that was then used to give the child a name.

It was his turn.

Rougher, older hands replaced his mother's gentle ones. He was carried into the center of the circle. All the naming objects were lying on the rim of the circle surrounding him. From the beginning there was only one object of interest to him.

He made his choice immediately. Instinctively he looked up and stretched his arm to the sky. In his small hand was the claw of the eagle.

High in the sky the eagle's almost exuberant cry reverberated across the valley. Swiftly the eagle went into a silent dive. Her agile claws closed firmly on her prize. She, on strong wing strokes, rose back high into the sky and disappeared down the valley.

He remembered the quiet weeping of his mother, White Swan, her tears falling on his cheek, the strong arms of his father, Grey Fox Running, encircling them. He remembered snuggling in the middle in a feeling of warmth, safety, and contentment.

He had chosen the talon of the eagle and the eagle had chosen him.

He became Taelo (Tā low), the talon of the eagle.

His cousin had selected the wing of a golden hawk.

He was named Golden Hawk.

The cool morning air moving softly across his cheek woke Taelo from his recurring dream. He opened his eyes and through the dark grey of early morning, could barely see the trees outside the tent opening.

He crawled out and gazed up to the crumbling rocky cliffs towering above the small lazy Flint River, the rocks formed a long sloping skirt of crumbling rock down to the river at its base. The clear water of the small river gurgled down numerous small rapids and meandered down to a wide-open valley just beyond where the Clan was camped.

He gazed across the camp to the point where the cliffs ended, and the valley opened.

A quiet satisfaction warmed him against the cool morning air. The Clan was camped in one of his favorite places.

He walked to his cousin's tent. It was their naming day.

He arrived just as Golden Hawk stepped out.

Taelo hugged Golden Hawk and wished him a happy seventh naming day.

Taelo and Golden Hawk both saw the early morning fire at the Weaver's tent. The Weaver's fire was their most visited morning camp. The weaver not only told them good stories, but he also always had something for them to eat.

Golden Hawk picked up the rabbit they had skinned and hung up the previous night.

The two would trade it for a morning meal and with luck they would hear a new story from the Weaver.

This morning they saw him sitting by his small fire. The Weaver, an old warrior no longer capable of hunting was now the Clan's net maker. His many stories captivated Taelo and Golden Hawk.

"Good morning Grey Weaver, may we join you for breakfast," Taelo inquired politely.

They decided a breakfast of berries, boiled egg, and a tough, bread-like muffin, provided by the old hunter, would be just the thing.

Grey Weaver grunted his greeting and began to serve the two a morning meal. He was pleased to have them at his fire. The two were considered good luck and welcomed throughout the camp. He enjoyed their company and their attentive manner and questions when he told him about one of his many stories.

He remembered well the action of the eagle on their naming day and knew that it was still discussed every year.

Grey Weaver felt privileged to influence and develop these two. He taught them many important skills through the stories he told. The Clan had enjoyed fruitful years since the birth of these two. They seemed to bring good luck.

Taelo listened to another story from the weaver as he and Golden Hawk slowly ate their breakfast. The coolness and freshness of the air and the quiet of the camp, Golden Hawk at his side, gave him a warm complete feeling.

After breakfast Taelo returned to his own campsite and waited restlessly for his mother to pack some food for snacks and lunch.

The family was going to Taelo's and Golden Hawk's favorite swimming hole up the Flint River by a huge sandstone rock that had been washed down stream in some long-ago flood from the upstream cliffs. The two families could sit comfortably on the flat slightly sloped top of the rock and there was still enough room for Taelo and Golden Hawk to dive into the deep pool of cool clear water surrounding the flat-topped rock.

Just downstream of the rock they had tied a rope to the limb of an old tree that extended out over the water. They would dive off their rock platform, swim to the bank, climb up to the first oak limb and swing back out into the pool.

Then they would climb the rock to dive again. This round robin of diving and swinging would go on for most of the day.

The naming day family outing was a custom they all looked forward to.

When everyone was ready, he and Golden Hawk ran out ahead.

The way to the river went by an immense old rambling limbed mulberry tree.

As they approached, Golden Hawk was pulled to the tree by the large dark purple mulberries so dense they were pulling the limbs low. He and Taelo scrambled into the tree, and each claimed a low limb running parallel to the ground to stand on. They each began to eat the purple jewels of sweetness that were as big as their thumbs.

"To get the best ones, you must climb up on the branches and pick only the largest mulberries," Red Oak, Golden Hawk's father called out encouragingly.

Taelo and Golden Hawk walked fearlessly out along the large low branches using both hands to pick the succulent dark purple berries. Hundreds of mulberries at least three times the length and size than those found on the younger mulberry trees hung within reach on each side of their branch. It was the ultimate treat enjoyed only in early summer.

Taelo meticulously picked one of the long, multi-lobed berries and carefully put it in his mouth. He slowly squeezed the berry to the top of his mouth and savored the sweetness that spread across his tongue and infused his mind with sweet wonder.

He knew these mulberries were meant to be savored and enjoyed in slow motion. He closed his eyes each time he put one of the mulberries on his tongue. The sweet juice teased the taste buds and instilled him with a peaceful contentment.

Taelo watched as his mother, White Swan and his aunt, Quiet Pheasant, efficiently picked berries from the lower branches as they talked quietly. Red Oak and his father, Grey Fox Running ate a handful of berries and then sat down on the trunk of a large old tree blown down in some past storm.

Taelo heard his father, "If we are going to get any swimming done today, you better come down so we can get to the swimming rock."

This caught Taelo's attention, and he looked over to Golden Hawk.

They began to laugh at each other when they saw the purple around each other's mouths and on their hands.

"Last to the water is a turtle," Taelo called out as he scrambled down from his branch and took the lead running toward the rapids.

They were laughing merrily as they again ran ahead of the family toward the river. They were only a short distance down the trail when they spotted bushes with translucent golden ripe goose berries dangling in the morning sun. These berries were gigantic. They were about the size of a small bird's egg.

"Look at these jewels," Golden Hawk exclaimed as he popped one the size of a blue bird's egg into his mouth.

The two had been by here a few days ago and had totally missed them. Taelo held up one of the smooth golden orbs to the sun. He could almost see through the tiger striped translucent skin.

"Wow look at these beauties," Taelo commented to Golden Hawk as he dropped the large succulent orb into his mouth and carefully popped it. "They are delicious," he exclaimed.

By the time their parents caught up to them, the two had picked and eaten a handful of the delicious bubbles. Gooseberries were not quite as sweet as the mulberries, but their refreshing tangy sweet flavor was as much a treat as the mulberries.

Once again, the procession stopped. This time they all took part in picking a bag of gooseberries. After a few more gooseberries, Taelo and Golden Hawk concentrated in filling the bag White Swan had pulled out.

This time the two were first to say it was enough.

They ran off together towards the river.

They were now on the flood plain of the Flint. This area had been swept clean of its leaves and forest floor covering and except where the brush or willows had captured debris, the floor was sand swept around several old elm trees surrounded by open grass and a few smaller ones trying to reach up into the sunshine.

The two reached the bank of the small river. The clear cool water at this point tumbled lazily down a series of small rapids.

A person could cross at almost any rapid and remain dry. Here rapids punctuated the transition of the cliff's switch from the left side of the river to the right side of the river.

Across the river, the land transformed from a steep hill to the high cliffs dominating the valley for the next few miles downstream.

The cliff was punctuated with two distinctly different types of caves. One was a large room with two entrances. The opening facing the Flint was a large oblong square. The back opening slanted upward and came out on top of the cliff. The cave had a hole in the center of the roof forming a perfect chimney for the fire circle below it. This cave was used for the meetings of the elders.

The other cave was a long narrow tunnel going back into the cliff for a good two hundred spear lengths before coming to a room where half a dozen people could fit. Though the opening of this cave was very large, it quickly diminished in size to the point where only small boys like Taelo and Golden Hawk were able to crawl through the very narrow area to reach the room that was beyond.

The cave had been put off limits for the children after several became trapped and had to be rescued. However, almost all the young boys still made the journey to the back room in the cave.

Taelo and Golden Hawk regularly went back and enjoyed the solitude they found there.

Their thoughts were now on a day of playing in the river. They had been outfitted with old foot coverings intended to be used in the water. Their only other clothing were the two leather flaps tied to their waist.

The rapids before them extended up-river a good stone's throw. The water flowing through the placid pool up stream made a tumbling, gurgling journey down multiple paths to a spear deep pool of rippling but calm water that was the closest swimming hole to the camp.

At this time in the morning, they were still the first, but Taelo knew that soon the other Clan kids would be arriving to swim. The quiet they now enjoyed would be broken by the shrieks and laughter of swimmers chasing and playing in the water with each other.

He and Golden Hawk eagerly raced out into the rapids and jumped into the pool on the far side at the base of the rapids.

They jumped from a big round boulder into the four-foot-deep pool around it.

They were frolicking in this pool until the rest of the family caught up.

Grey Fox Running called to them as he waded out into the rapids and walked up stream toward the calmer waters at the top, "Today we are going to teach you how to catch crayfish."

This caught Taelo's and Golden Hawk's interest and they immediately ran up stream toward their fathers.

They were forever chasing the crawfish and catching them, so they wondered what they were going to learn.

"Follow me to the rocks upstream, where the water runs smoothly and silently passes the rocks in the stream," Grey Fox Running spoke quietly as he took out a long thin stick from his backpack. Red Oak held a similar one in his hand.

Their curiosity peaked, and they quietly followed their fathers.

Quiet Pheasant and White Swan stayed on the bank on a trail running parallel to the river. They were enjoying the sight of the fathers and sons playing together. The two sisters cherished moments like these.

Their husbands were great fathers, but they were two of the top hunters in the Clan and almost always away hunting. Times like these were rare and therefore special.

"Once those two boys learn how to capture the crayfish, we will lose them for the rest of the summer. They will relentlessly pursue their new-found skill," White Swan commented to Quiet Pheasant.

"Yes, they will work on this until a new skill or game can be added to it. They are so intense in perfecting what they learn. It sometimes scares me," Quiet Pheasant replied as she closely watched the four in the river.

"However, we will have an abundance of crayfish tails for the rest of the summer," she chuckled.

"I agree. The two learn swiftly and work together well. When they are together, they watch out for each other," Quiet Pheasant continued as the two slowly walked along to a point upstream where a fallen tree provided them a comfortable seat to sit and watch.

The two sat quietly and watched the father and son interaction as the four hunted the mighty crab.

Taelo and Golden Hawk followed and watched as their fathers walked smoothly and quietly upstream looking down into the water. Suddenly their fathers stopped. Red Oak reached slowly down into the water with the hand holding the thin long stick. He slowly lifted the edge of a large flat stone and swiftly reached down with his other hand. He grabbed a crayfish just behind the two large claws and quickly lifted it out of the water.

As the crayfish began to reach back with its two large claws, Red Oak put the thin stick into one of the open claws and then deftly put it into the second claw. The crab instinctively closed his claws on the stick and held on.

Grey Fox Running just as quickly opened a sack and Red Oak dropped the crayfish into it. After a few shakes, the crab let go of the stick and fell to the bottom of the sack.

"We now have one very nice snack for later today," White Swan said from her seat on the bank.

Grey Fox Running opened the bag for the two boys to look in.

"Wow look how big it is," both said in unison.

"Would one of you like to try to catch the next one," Grey Fox Running asked.

"Yes, Yes," both cried out in unison.

Grey Fox Running took out two additional thin sticks about two feet long.

OK, I have been standing here quietly because there is another crab, as big as the one we just caught. Taelo and Golden Hawk, you two will work together. One of you will reach down and lift the rock up. The other must be ready to grab the crayfish by the body.

It is extremely important the two of you work together otherwise the person holding the crab will get a nasty pinch. The stick must be put into the claws of the crayfish before it can pinch the hand holding it.

Later when you get better, each of you can do it by yourself the way Red Oak just did. This time you will work together," Grey Fox Running instructed quietly.

"I will pick up the crayfish. You pick up the rock and then keep the crab from pinching me," Taelo spoke up as he stepped up to the right of his father.

Golden Hawk stepped up to Grey Fox Running's left side as he slowly stepped back to give them both more room. There at the edge of the rock the two boys could see the two claws of a very large crayfish. One claw was almost twice the size of the other.

"This one lost a claw in a fight and is now growing a new one. The small claw is more dangerous than the big one because it can reach farther back, so get that one first then engage the big one," Grey Fox Running said as he stepped back farther.

Golden Hawk bent and slowly raised the rock. A gentle swirl of sand lifted with the rock and was slowly washed away by the clear, gently moving water. The crab was exposed and waiting for the water to clear before making its getaway.

Taelo swiftly plunged his hand down into the water and grabbed the large crayfish where Red Oak had grabbed his and lifted it out of the water. He could hardly hold onto the crab as he lifted it up.

Just as he thought the crayfish was going to pinch him with the small claw, Golden Hawk put his twig in, and the crayfish bit it instead. Golden Hawk then quickly fed the end of the branch into the large claw.

Together the two boys dropped the crayfish into the bag Grey Fox Running offered. To the surprise of everyone, it was at least twice the size of the previous one.

"Congratulations, the two of you have caught one of the largest cray fish that we have ever seen," Red Oak said as he looked into the bag and passed it around for the others to look inside. He then took it over to White Swan and Quiet Pheasant.

"This is the largest crayfish I have ever seen. It's a miracle that those two were able to capture it without getting pinched," Red Oak said quietly to White Swan and Quiet Pheasant.

Even though the swimming rock was only a mile or so up the stream, it took over an hour to reach it.

Taelo and Golden Hawk were on the hunt for more crayfish. They caught six more and the group was ensured of a wonderful lunch of roasted crayfish tail. It was hard for the two boys to stop hunting. They were hooked on catching the cray fish, but they were also looking forward to a rare day of swimming and frolicking with their parents.

"There will be no safe crayfish for the rest of the summer," White Swan said in a knowing tone.

She repeated that the two would pursue their new-found skill relentlessly until they found a new skill to add to their collection.

The huge wedge of the swimming rock came into view. Its point was wedged up into the bank and its flat top leaned slightly toward the water.

Just upstream a small clear stream ran into the river. This was water from a spring just past the other bank of the Flint. Its source was a natural spring bubbling up from the ground at the base of the cliff. They would use it to drink and would take several bags back to their camps on their return.

The steep bank of the river was rich black dirt dropped by flood waters over the years.

A slick mud slide was easily made by splashing water up on the bank.

For the rest of the day, the boys went swimming, diving from the rock, sliding down the mud slide and swinging out on a braided rawhide rope out over the water.

The mudslide kept them busy for a short period and then they took up swinging out on the rope. Then it was diving from the rock. Then the two would start the cycle all over again. This went on until a late afternoon lunch caused them all to gather on the swimming rock.

Lunch consisted of freshly roasted crayfish tail and wild onions. White Swan and Quiet Pheasant had used the gooseberries, onions, and mulberries to make a seasoning to go with the freshly caught crayfish. They put this on the crayfish as they roasted them over the hot coals of the small fire.

They also had a snack of fresh mulberries and gooseberries. All of this was washed down with some crystal-clear spring water.

Taelo savored the succulent crayfish tail. It was one large piece of white meat. The magic taste his mother had crated did not escape him.

"This is unbelievably delicious. I have never had anything so good," Taelo complimented his mother and aunt.

"This is absolutely wonderful. I did not think that we would eat so well today," Red Oak commented as he finished his second helping.

Everyone chimed in their agreement.

Everyone was sitting on the swimming rock relaxing and drying off in the late afternoon sun. Quiet Pheasant was just going to announce the time to go home, when high in the sky a loud piercing scream reached her ear.

Everyone looked up at a huge bald eagle. It let out a loud second cry and then turned upriver.

Everyone silently watched the grand sight.

Again, Quite Pheasant was about to speak, when a different and much closer cry reached her ear.

Coming up the river was a golden hawk. It dove toward the water at the edge of the swimming area and pulled up a large trout.

As it went over the rock, it dropped the fish.

Golden Hawk was astonished as the fish dropped between his legs.

There was a moment of stunned silence. This was just not real.

Golden Hawk and Taelo gave a cry of surprise and then scramble about as they captured the large trout and together were holding up their prize. It was large enough to be a meal for all of them.

"This is truly a sign that our sons have strong totems watching out for them. Their totems have come by and wished them well and even left a gift.

Let's go home and enjoy the gift given to Golden Hawk," Red Oak spoke up as the adults looked at each other and up at the sky as the two totems flew out of sight.

No one spoke of the impossibility of such an event.

The trip back home went rather quickly. The two boys ran ahead down along the trail on the bank of the stream as the two couples followed at a normal pace. They talked quietly about what had just transpired.

For the rest of the summer the two boys spent their days playing in the rivers and streams of the various valley's through which the Clan traveled. Taelo and Golden Hawk would roam the streams and rivers catching their crayfish lunch and then bringing the extra home for White Swan to cook in soups and other dishes.

That first season, Taelo and Golden Hawk became known for supplying the camp with crayfish. They always returned from the rivers and streams carrying a bag of crayfish. They were generous and repaid their many morning breakfast providers and gave some to everyone in the camp.

White Swan and Quiet Pheasant never turned down the boy's offering. If there was too much food for the day, they would season and smoke the meat. The crayfish would be welcome treats in the coming winter.

Chapter 2: Talking to Cave Bears

Taelo learned from his father about the dangers of bears. Bears were constant competitors when the salmon made their run. The bears were always given the rapids they chose.

The bears were also very territorial and when the Clan wandered into a bear's territory, they would leave it as quickly as possible.

Taelo and Golden Hawk listened to the Weaver tell stories of how a bear should be handled.

The Weaver advised that the best way to handle a bear was to let the bear have what they wanted. But if you had to face the bear, then it was best not to run away because the bear, despite its size, was very fast. It was best to slowly move away into the thick dense part of the forest that provided a thick dense cover that would make it difficult for the bear to get through.

Hunting a bear was a recognized way for a young man to transition from boyhood into manhood. Even then, they were only hunted if the Clan thought they needed the meat and the hide. The hide provided the best cold weather covering and jackets.

Taelo and Golden Hawk went out one day and tracked one of the Giant Brown bears. They spent almost all day following the bear through the mountain pine forest.

They watched the bear as it stood and reached high up on a pine as thick as the fire ring at their lodge was wide. It clawed its mark a good foot above a previous scar on the bark of the tree.

It let out a roar and then peed on the trunk. She had declared this her territory and had left her scent.

When the bear began to sniff the air, they both immediately began a retreat. They first followed the Weavers advice but then fear gave wings to their feet, and they ran at full speed taking turns looking over their shoulders to make sure they were not being chased.

Several days later, Taelo and Golden Hawk agreed to join the group of children being organized to go out to pick blue berries. Usually, they would not have done so but both White Swan and Quiet Pheasant suggested they help watch out for the younger children.

Three Clan mothers led the kids on the hike out to the hills where the blueberry bushes were thick and loaded.

It was a pleasantly warm and sunny day, perfect for berry picking. The clouds over head were puffs of various shapes and sizes causing kids to see the heads of dogs, or a swimming fish floating by in the sky. The sun was warm but there was a light breeze making the day fresh and invigorating.

It was a fine outing with a constant flow of chatter and joking.

The kids ran about shouting and chasing butterflies, picking meadow flowers, and chasing each other. Taelo and Golden Hawk were content in following the group and talking about which berries they liked the most.

They all followed a small gurgling stream a step wider than most of the kids could jump, up a wide sloping valley to the blueberry patch on toward the top lip where the ground flattened out. It was surrounded by large trees on the approach side and many small paw-paw trees around its far side.

The many head high bushes with dark bluish leaves were loaded with dark, almost black blueberries of various sizes. Everyone was to fill their bags with these purple, bluish-black jewels.

Most of the kids that eagerly rushed into the area were shorter than the blueberry bushes and they disappeared as they scattered to pick and eat the berries. An equal number of berries went into their mouth as went into their bags. The mothers knew this would happen and were happy to see it. This saved them from picking the extra berries the youngsters were consuming.

The morning passed without incident, everyone picked and filled their bags, ate their fill and were generally enjoying the day.

Taelo and Golden Hawk spent their time keeping track of the kids who disappeared as they went ever deeper into the patch.

The sun was at its zenith when everyone gathered out in the valley for a lunch of cold goose, some bread like buns and cool water from the small gurgling spring.

Then after a short rest, the group was once again out in the middle of the blueberry bushes picking berries.

High in the sky an eagle let out a loud scream. Taelo looked at Golden Hawk and then saw the large female cave bear and her single cub coming into the same blueberry patch.

The arrival went unnoticed by the rest until the bear, upset by the chatter and the noise of the kids around her, let out an ear-splitting roar. Everyone froze where they stood. They had all heard stories of the dangers of an angry cave bear.

Instinctively the mothers nearest to the meadow, hastily led the children out away from the blueberry patch.

The bear stood on her hind legs and pawed the air as she once again let out a roar. She was at least two full spears high. She was one of the largest anyone had ever seen. This was her blueberry patch, and her angry ear-splitting roar was letting the intruders know it.

Taelo and Golden Hawk were on the opposite side of where the mothers were frantically moving the children out of the patch.

This movement and the noise being made by three crying youngsters caused the female cave bear to let out another ear shattering roar that was heard back in the camp that was almost a mile away. The giant brown bear was extremely agitated and angry. This was her territory and invaders were not to be tolerated. She was on the verge of charging at the intruders.

By now the mothers were rushing everyone they could out of the thicket and down the hill.

On the opposite side of the thicket, separated from the fleeing group were three of the younger children. Their crying made them the center of attention of the female bear.

Taelo and Golden Hawk instinctively moved to where the children were standing. Taelo quieted them down and told Golden Hawk to slowly lead them out of the patch.

Golden Hawk began to lead the children away from the bear toward the edge of the blueberry patch.

Taelo stood between them and the bear. He raised his arms high into the air as possible. He was following the Weaver's instruction on how to face down a bear. The part worrying him was about not showing any fear. He hoped the stories he had listened to were true. He did not feel very large or very brave in the presence of a bear four times taller than him.

He recognized this as the bear he and Golden Hawk had tracked. He remembered how high her mark was in the tree. He stood a mere half a spear and with his hands in the air he might reach to three quarter of a spear.

Her mark was at least two spears high.

Taelo began to speak to the bear in a loud but calm voice.

"Great mother bear we did not mean to encroach on your blueberry patch. Let me give you the wonderful blueberries I have picked. I have all I need and want to share them with you.

My mother expects me home soon. It is time for me to go. You do not want to get into a shouting match with her. When she is mad, she can roar almost as loud as you. If you were to hurt me, she would come after you. So, if you excuse me, I will quietly leave," Taelo said as he threw his bag of blueberries at the large bear and waved his arms and got her attention.

Taelo stood quietly with his arms raised and watched the giant mother bear before him. He tried to show no fear though it permeated his entire being. He wanted to run.

The bag he threw hit her in the snout. She roared and took a few steps toward Taelo who was slowly moving away from the three children as Golden Hawk led them back into the woods.

The smell of the berries distracted her. She and her cub stopped to eat them.

Taelo had counted on her eating the berries. He was not sure what he would have done if she had charged him immediately. He hoped this would calm her down and allow time for everyone to leave the area.

Golden Hawk successfully used this moment to get the children out and around the patch.

"Yes, please enjoy the berries and then follow me. I will show you the best berries so you can enjoy them with your cub," Taelo spoke confidently as he moved further into the blueberry thicket and away from the retreating group of children and mothers.

He was moving slowly toward a thick stand of small trees. These would provide him a barrier. The bear would have to break through the small trees if she decided to chase him. He would be able to easily navigate the thicket, but the bear's size would prohibit her from easily following him. At least he hoped this was the case.

One of the braver mothers had returned to the edge of the blueberry thicket and watched in wonder as the giant bear quietly followed Taelo with her cub close behind.

She found it inconceivable to think about doing what Taelo and Golden Hawk had just done. She had never witnessed such self-sacrificing courage. She knew this would be a story she would tell many times in the years to come.

Taelo kept up a calm conversation with the giant bear and pointed out the bountiful blueberries. As if understanding, the mother bear, and the cub began to eat the blueberries Taelo had pointed out.

The lone mother at the edge of the thicket could not believe the bear was doing what Taelo instructed. It was as if the bear understood his direction.

Finally, when Taelo thought he was close enough to the thick stand of small trees, he dropped down into the blueberry bushes and scurried away.

Once in the thicket of small trees he stood and slowly walked back around the blueberry patch to the other side. It was a relief for him to watch the Mother bear and her cub as they continued to eat blueberries. It was clear that the mother bear no longer had anything more on her mind.

He went down the hill to where everyone was reunited and making a hasty get away.

Everyone looked up into the sky as once again the eagle let out a scream and glided away down the long valley.

"That was an unbelievably brave thing for you to do," the mother who had observed him said as she looked at Taelo with awe and a quiet respect.

In her mind he was a warrior not a child. This was a tale, others who heard it would find hard to believe but she would tell all the elders. She would proclaim and give the credit of the bravery shown by both these two young men.

She would tell the story of Taelo talking to the mother cave bear.

Taelo tried to explain the rational of his actions.

"The mother bear, just like you, was only worried about the well-being of her cub. She was as frightened of us as we were of her. Had we shown fright or otherwise caused her more alarm she would have attacked us. She just had to be comforted and to know we meant no harm. She had to see we were not hunters. She could not understand my words, but she knew the meaning by the tone of my voice," Taelo replied.

This seemed reasonable to him, and he was glad to have listened and thought about the stories told each winter by the older hunters and by the Weaver.

He would need to thank the Weaver for his story on how to face a bear.

A few days later, Golden Hawk and Taelo were up early and once again sitting at the Weaver's breakfast fire.

The Weaver thanked Taelo for crediting him with teaching the two on how to face a bear. He laughed and said he was glad that it had worked and would have missed them for breakfast had it not.

The story of Taelo talking to the cave bear soon made the rounds of the camp and everyone once again looked at Taelo and Golden Hawk with new interest. The Weaver was especially happy to have the two boys at his fire ring for breakfast.

Golden Hawk laughed and looked at Taelo and pointed out that the Weaver had just told them that the two of them were lucky to be alive.

The Weaver laughed and asked if they wanted to hear a story on how to handle a dire wolf.

Little did he know that later his dire wolf story would once again serve to save Taelo and Golden Hawk.

Quiet Pheasant and White Swan let them know how proud they were of the bravery they had shown in rescuing the children. They both expressed concern that they not become overconfident and become a dinner for some other bear.

White Swan and Quiet Pheasant initially wanted to admonish the two for taking such a risk, but they recognized that the two had kept a level head and reacted in the most appropriate manner. Their quick action had saved the lives of the three children.

They were sure Taelo, and Golden Hawk were guided by the voices of the Ancients. There was no doubt in the hearts of the two mothers that these same Ancients had guided and watched over them and that their totem watched over them as well.

As mothers, they knew their role was to ensure these boys grew safely and were well taken care of. They were not to be limiters but enablers.

By custom, the children saved by Taelo and Golden Hawk owed them both for their lives. The families of the three children came by to thank them for saving their children and to see what they in turn could do to reward Taelo and Golden Hawk.

The two knew that they must accept some form of recompense otherwise they would shame the families.

The two boys had decided to ask for something reasonable and symbolic.

They asked each family to gift the tongue, tail, and hump of a buffalo to White Swan and Quiet Pheasant. This was the most valued pieces of meat from a buffalo, and it recognized their mothers as well.

They expressed the fact that these gifts would be enjoyed by them both and would balance their account.

That night as she lay next to Grey Fox Running, White Swan shared her concern about Taelo's fearlessness and his habit of taking immediate action.

"I was proud of both Taelo and Golden Hawk today. They accepted the praise in a modest fashion, and they found a way to have each family thank them in a way that will not be a burden.

They were very wise and understanding. However, I worry that Taelo knows no fear. You must speak to him and let him know he must be careful. As soon as possible you must also make sure you teach him how to hunt and handle weapons. You must show him how to handle himself in all dangerous situations," White Swan said quietly.

She and Quiet Pheasant had decided they would never be able to protect the two but needed to make sure they could take care of themselves.

"Yes, I will talk to him. He may be fearless, but he is wise for his age. He knew not to show the bear fear. Instead, he showed the mother bear his confidence and I am sure the bear saw a figure of immense size. His quiet voice soothed the worried heart of a protective mother. He did everything exactly as he should have. I am not sure there is anything I can teach him about how to handle such a situation. But Red Oak and I will train both boys on how to handle the tools of the hunt," Grey Fox Running replied quietly in words he felt were coming from another dimension.

Chapter 3: Herding Salmon

Taelo and Golden Hawk watched as the silvery flashes of quivering muscle propelled the fish up the rapids as they made their last swim to the place where they were born. They were the survivors returning from the sea and returning from where they had started out as small fingerlings. Now they returned to their beginning to ensure the next generation of their kind. They would lay and fertilize their eggs. There would be no sense of graciousness, no sense of virtuousness, it was all a deep life force that drove the cycle of survival.

Taelo and Golden Hawk watched the bear, the eagle, and the hawk all take their share of the persistent, seemingly endless numbers of the fish.

This year they felt they had grown strong enough to pull in the dying giants and planned to be part of the Clan members that would be called the gatherers and would pull the fish from the stream and take them to the cleaning area.

Taelo and Golden Hawk stood behind the older gathers and listened to the instructions being given. This was the start of the annual gathering. It was the most important food gathering the Clan did each year.

The Clan leaders organized the gathering into nine groups. The gathers brought the fish to the cleaners. The cleaners cleaned and passed each fish to the slicers who would cut the meat from the bones.

The slicers in turn passed the salmon steaks to the salters who rubbed them down with salt and sent it on to the skewers who in turn handed the fish on skewers to the smokers.

The smokers put the skewers over small, elongated smoking fires that were maintained by the wood gatherers.

The smoke-drying area looked like schools of headless fish swimming in unison over small smoky fires. The series of small fires over which the fish were suspended on horizontal poles slowly dried and smoked the fish. A variety of wood chips chosen for the flavor of the smoke were thrown periodically into the small fires. It took most of a day for a fish to be dried. As soon as one batch of fish was dried another batch was loaded. The drying went on around the clock.

Once dried the fish were bundled together in groups of four or five. This amount, when mixed in a stew with vegetables and greens, made a meal for a family of four. These bundles were stored in baskets hanging high in the branches of the trees to prevent the various wild animals from taking them.

The Clan made good use of the salmon. This was a key source of sustenance for the winter. The Clan thought of themselves as hunters, but fishing provided them with most of the food they consumed throughout the year, and it provided much of the currency for bartering with the other Clans.

The salted fish could be taored for the entire year. This made for a very effective way to build up a food reservoir. They could not have survived most winters without their supply of dried fish.

All these groups were supported and attended to by those distributing water and food.

The fish heads were used by the feeders to make a stew to feed the working groups throughout the day. There was no specific mealtime, instead the stew was available and eaten when one became hungry.

Taelo and Golden Hawk made their way to the stew each time they had brought in three fish.

This was a total Clan event.

Everyone worked together to keep the entire gathering running. Each worked to their level of capability.

The camp became one huge assembly line. As many as twenty long horizontal drying poles about two feet off the ground covered the smoking area and was the focal point that controlled the speed of the entire gathering.

The drying was continuous and those at night had the added task of keeping the wild animals away.

Taelo and Golden Hawk had in previous seasons worked at delivering the water, at gathering wood and as a smoker. This year they had decided to move up to gathering fish.

They knew they had been accepted on a trial basis and most thought they would drop out once they found how hard the gathering work would be.

In previous years, Taelo and Golden Hawk had observed the spearing technique, and the hand catching technique. They decided that they would hand catch.

Once started, the harvesting of the fish went on from morning until night.

They observed the older gatherers as they caught and carried the large salmon by the gills over to the cleaning area.

They tried this and found it was quite hard on their hands.

After taking in the second fish, Taelo went into his dwelling and came back with an old pair of leather mittens. He gave one mitten to Golden Hawk, and he kept one. The mitten protected their small hands as they carried the fish by the gills.

This idea worked so well that the two of them were bringing in as many fish as the older Clan members.

Several of the adults copied what the two boys had done and soon everyone was using their old gloves or mittens. This was an idea they all liked. Everyone had previously accepted the minor cuts and scrapes as part of the fishing process.

Now they were able to work faster and did not have to worry about getting cut.

Together Taelo and Golden Hawk spent hours wading in the shallows of the river and retrieving the spent salmon.

They took short stints in helping clean, steak, skewer and smoke them. This gave them a break from the strain of the gathering.

Taelo and Golden Hawk were exhausting themselves. Taelo kept asking Golden Hawk if he could think of an easier way to handle the fish. The two constantly talked about finding an easier way to catch and process the salmon.

Golden Hawks snide reply that they should ask the fish to swim over to the cleaning area triggered an idea for Taelo.

Taelo pointed to the fact that the fish were swimming in the stream. Why not get them to swim to a fixed pick-up point?

Golden Hawk said that sounded great but made the point that the fish, even though they were dying still struggled to escape and neither of them knew how to instruct the fish of where they should swim.

Taelo smiled and replied that they would just have to be politer and more persuasive in how they talked to the fish and asked them to go to the pick-up area.

During the next lunch break Taelo jumped up and shouted that he had figured it out. Everyone around the two looked over to see what was going on.

Taelo quietly shared his idea with Golden Hawk.

High in the sky an Eagle let out a scream.

This excited both of them. White Swan and Quiet Pheasant looked at each other and wondered out loud what the two might be up to.

"The fish are swimming in the stream, why don't we guide them with some sticks stuck in the sand to where we want them and then pick them up. This will save us a lot of effort." Taelo suggested to Golden Hawk.

After lunch, the two examined a location where a large shallow pool existed just upstream from the fish processing area. They measured this area by walking the shape they planned to lay out. Then they estimated the number of vertical and horizontal poles it would take to implement their idea. They cut about two hundred straight thin willow sticks.

By this time most members of the Clan noticed the two boys had stopped gathering fish and were industrially cutting and laying out the poles. Though they all kept working at their jobs, everyone had one eye on Taelo and Golden Hawk.

The small river was only about three feet deep at the deepest.

The vertical poles were about four feet long. The boys laid out the vertical poles three inches apart and parallel to each other. They then put the horizontal poles across them and lashed the shorter vertical poles to the horizontal ones.

They built two similarly sized long lengths and two shorter lengths. Finally, they built one short section.

Taelo and Golden Hawk were ready to try out their idea.

By this time everyone was curious as to what the two were building.

White Swan, Grey Fox Running, Quiet Pheasant, and Red Oak came over to where the two were struggling with their unwieldy contraptions and asked how they could help.

Taelo smiled and had them immediately help to put their fish trap into place.

Curiosity was running high as the Clan watched the shorter poles get pushed into the sand at the bottom of the stream.

One half of the guide began on the far side and came across and upstream in a shallow arc. The arc guided the large salmon going upstream toward the camp side of the river. The smaller fish swam right through the guide. A mirror image arc was put on the upstream side to guide the fish going down stream toward the camp side of the river.

The remaining two sections of poles went from the point where the upstream and downstream arcs met and guided the fish into a holding area in which they were then trapped.

As the fish swam around, trapped in the pool, a single row of polls guided the next unfortunate fish to a dead-end channel dug in the sand beach. This was the point at which the fish were picked up and taken to the cleaning area.

Even before they had completed their fish trap, the fish began to pile up. It appeared to those watching that the fish were willingly lining up to be lifted out of the water.

Taelo and Golden Hawk exhausted themselves hauling the fish out of their trap.

In short order they had caught and pulled out more fish than the entire Clan. They could not keep up with the rate the fish came into the capture area.

When the older men saw what the boys had accomplished, several of them came over and formed a line to move the fish to the processing area. Soon all the men in the camp were helping pull the fish out of the catch basin.

The processing of the fish took a huge leap in the number of fish ready for smoking. This went on all day without stopping.

As evening approached, Taelo closed the entrance to the pool and opened a way for the fish to go up or down stream.

This was easily accomplished by removing two of the vertical poles at the end of the arc just before the fish had to swim into the catch pool.

That evening the elders sat around the fire discussing what they should do with the number of fish they were capturing. The Clan had never caught so many fish in one day. Everyone knew this new way of taking in the salmon was going to provide an abundance of fish. This was a luxury of food abundance the Clan had not anticipated.

The leaders in the camp reorganized the Clan based on the new volume of fish being caught. More processing and drying were needed.

Fewer catchers were needed but more help was needed in processing the fish and in gathering wood for the fires.

The drying area was expanded.

The next day when the camp was ready for more fish, Taelo and Golden Hawk lowered the poles they had lifted, and the fish began to swim into the pool. Everyone was amazed at the ease of the harvest.

The cleaning area was moved closer to the area of the catch. This greatly reduced the distance to carry the fish.

Everyone ended up doing less work and processing more fish.

The bottle neck now became the drying. More drying racks were set up and soon the Clan had doubled the capacity of their drying process. This meant having to gather more wood.

A number of those catching fish began to gather more wood.

The Clan had a record catch of fish. Never had they been able to capture so many so quickly. They knew they had enough fish to give a bountiful share to all the other sub-Clans and still have abundance for themselves. This would put them in good stead with all the other Clans and that season they could live without the fear of hunger during the coming winter.

Taelo and Golden Hawk had revolutionized the way the Clan caught their salmon. The salmon harvesting went on for some very productive but many fewer weeks.

This year, during the fall gathering, the Elk Horn Clan would have an abundance of salmon to share beyond what they normally would have even in the best times in the memory of the Clan.

They would also tell the story of Taelo and Golden Hawk and how they had devised a new way of harvesting the salmon. This story would be the way the other Clans would learn of this new way of catching fish.

Once again, the two boys had distinguished themselves. The fact the two boys were making such a huge difference to the well-being of the Clan at such a young age did not go unnoticed by the elders.

Taelo and Golden Hawk enjoyed their notoriety, but they found it hard to accept that they had done anything so unusual.

Chapter 4: Flying with Lions

Taelo and Golden Hawk continued their fearless wandering on the challenging snow-capped rocky mountains. The chain of sky-high snowcapped mountains ran parallel to the wide area that the Clan wandered as they hunted the elk, buffalo, and other game. The mountains appeared to be nearby but the distances to their base was measured in multiple sun rises. The many valleys, small rivers, cliffs, and foothills created an environment that pulled the two into a world of adventure and discovery. The two young adventurers wandered the rivers, the valleys, and the foothills around them. Each morning they would decide what type of adventure they were seeking and then prepare themselves.

Each day they returned with enough small game to keep the family fed or to trade with their favorite storyteller the Weaver. He broadened his stories and used them to teach them survival skills, the hunting lore, and the more esoteric concepts of dealing with other people.

The Weaver tapped all his friends and Clan members for their knowledge, so he could be ready for the questions Taelo and Golden Hawk would ask. He became one or their primary teachers.

White Swan and Quiet Pheasant had worriedly watched their boys grow and develop for ten seasons. They had no other children. Like all mothers the two constantly thought about the dangerous predators traveling the same areas as their two sons. They knew trying to limit the boys would only cause them to sneak out and take more chances. They preferred to know where the two were going and what they were planning on doing.

Taelo and Golden Hawk always let them know what their adventure was to be. They had agreed that sharing that with their mothers ensured that they would know if something had gone wrong.

White Swan and Quiet Pheasant prevailed on Grey Fox Running and Red Oak to teach the two young boys how to defend themselves.

Red Oak made the two boys some fixed hunting spears and some throwing spears with the same type of stone heads the men carried. He spent a great deal of time with the flint smith to fashion some smaller but just as deadly spear heads to fit the smaller spears he was making for the two boys.

Meanwhile, every night he had the boys target practiced using spears with simple points made by burning a straight stick end in the fire. This gave the boys a chance to gain throwing experience without losing valuable flint heads. They soon were hitting the target at every throw.

Then Red Oak tied a bundle of grass to a rope and hung it in a tree. Now he began teaching the boys how to hit a moving target. This was a challenge both boys took to eagerly. Soon they were as adept at hitting their swinging target as the fixed one.

Finally, Grey Fox Running and Red Oak taught them how to use the hunting spears to protect themselves from an aggressive attacker. This last lesson was not about throwing but on how to use a spear to ward off an attacking animal. How to always keep the animal at a distance and how to back away to keep the advantage the spear provided.

The sling was a weapon the two fathers had also decided to teach the boys. Grey Fox Running made a set of slings the right size for the two. Then he and Red Oak set out to teach the boys throwing accuracy and power. They took the boys out to hunt rabbits with their slings. This was a very useful way to learn how to hit a moving object. In just a few months the boys were almost as good as their fathers.

The boys took to the use of the spear and the sling with an eagerness and natural ability that surprised both fathers.

They would go out in the morning and by the end of the day they would come back loaded with small game.

Their skill with the sling continued to improve.

Unknown to any of them the training for the two came just in time.

One morning, Taelo let his mother know that he and Golden Hawk were going to the cliffs rising high on the other side of the valley. He let her know they were going to see if there were any interesting caves and if they could find some crystal and other valuable stones. The jaunt the boys were planning was a long way but was not unusual. Both mothers urged them to be careful and to come back before dark.

Taelo showed her his spear, his flint knife, sling, and his bag of stones and reassured her that they would be back before sundown.

Taelo and Golden Hawk set out at a steady but rapid jog that most of the others their age would have found too fast but for them it was comfortable.

Taelo took in the cliffs rising several hundred feet into the air and extending for miles in a north and south direction.

Their jog quickly closed the distance and soon they were close to the foot of the cliff.

As they approached, they spotted a young mountain goat and decided to follow it upward along the cliff.

The base of the cliff had a skirt of fallen boulders and smaller stones formed when the winter freeze expanded the trapped water and crack the stones that then in the spring fell to add to the growing skirt.

The goat led the boys up the face of the cliff along an almost invisible trail.

With an expertise that would have impressed most of the hunters in the Clan, Taelo and Golden Hawk carefully trailed behind the goat. They kept it in sight but managed not to spook the shy animal.

Golden Hawk commented that the goat seemed to be following an invisible trail. They were able to find the footholds and continued to follow.

Neither had any thought of killing the goat. It was just their guide and a teacher of goat movement. The sun slowly traveled across the clear blue sky as the morning approached its zenith.

Taelo made a quiet comment to Golden Hawk wondering where they would end up by following the goat.

Back across the valley, a mother's premonition burrowed into White Swan. During the previous night she had dreamed of a mountain lion chasing the two boys. The dream had bothered her, but she had dismissed it. As the sun reached its daytime zenith, she could no longer ignore her intuition. She stopped what she was doing and talked to Quiet Pheasant.

The sight of a white swan flying overhead moved White Swan into immediate action. She told Quiet Pheasant to pick up her spear and join her in finding Taelo and Golden Hawk.

Quiet Pheasant did not ask why or what was up but took up her spear, hiking bag and joined White Swan and together they set out at a fast jog toward the distant cliffs. She too had seen the white swan as it flew quietly by.

White Swan was glad the boys had told her where they were going. The two often set out with no particular activity in mind but they always told her where.

Golden Hawk was in the lead as they followed the mountain goat along its meandering upward route. They watched what the goat ate and they themselves would try some of the leaves or berries the goat had eaten. Soon they were able to let the goat get out of sight and then find it by trailing it by the bitten leaves and broken small branches of various bushes or by the grass which had been cropped. This was a challenge in tracking that they were perfecting.

Even the best Clan trackers would have been impressed.

At one point, the trail along the face of the cliff went outward and Taelo was able to look back along the trail he and Golden Hawk had just traversed.

The two were about one hundred feet up the face of the cliff on a narrow ledge just wide enough for the goat to walk along. The footing or lack thereof made it a challenge for the two of them.

High overhead a large eagle soared. She was watching the scene below.

She let out her piercing scream.

Taelo stopped to look up to the sky and then he again looked back along the way he had just come. What he saw froze him in his tracks.

Behind them coming up the trail was a large mountain lion. The lion had not yet spotted the two boys, but it was clearly following the same trail.

Taelo's adrenaline immediately kicked in. He realized that they were in great danger. Quietly he tapped Golden Hawk on the shoulder and pointed to the lion. They were between the lion and the lion's favorite meal. This made them meals as well.

Taelo and Golden Hawk instinctively began to look for a place where they could defend themselves. As they watched the goat, they saw it turn and instantly disappear.

They quickly followed to that point on the path. Here the path made a sharp ninety degree turn back to the left around a point of rock.

This Taelo decided would be the place to make their stand.

He looked at Golden Hawk and told him that they would have to stand and fight the lion as it came around the bend.

The path was only wide enough for one.

Taelo told Golden Hawk that he would run full speed and spear the lion in the heart and try to push if over the edge to its death on the rocks below.

Golden Hawk knew they were in great trouble. He nodded in agreement and told Taelo that he would be behind and to make sure to leave enough room for him and his spear.

Both knew facing a lion that was larger than the two put together presented an overwhelming challenge. The Clan never hunted the lion or any of its kin. They had no need, and it was just too dangerous.

Taelo prepared himself to rush the lion and to drive his spear into it as it turned the corner.

"Why should you be the one that faces the lion by yourself," Golden Hawk asked in a concerned voice?

"Because I am the closest one and there is only room for one," Taelo replied since there was no other reason.

Taelo knew that his only hope would be to surprise the lion and push it off the path with his spear. He had to push with all his might.

Golden Hawk put his hand on Taelo's shoulder and asked the ancestors for their help and then stepped back.

Taelo prepared himself to attack. Surprise, speed, and the chance he would catch the lion off guard was his only hope. He also hoped he was strong enough to push the lion off the cliff. He intended to hit the lion with all the speed and weight he could muster. He took several deep, slow breaths.

Taelo heard the call of the eagle.

He knew this was a test and he was being watched.

Golden Hawk also heard the eagle and knew instinctively this was Taelo's moment.

White Swan heard the scream of the eagle. This both reassured her and frightened her. Taelo's totem was near and calling.

Something significant was going to happen. But what was the challenge Taelo and Golden Hawk were facing?

She and Quiet Pheasant began running full speed toward the cliffs ahead. They now had the mystical power and strength only worried mothers possess.

The tension was high both on the cliff and with the two mothers who were now running at full speed. They were now sure the boys were in danger. Their adrenaline was giving them the boost that would have carried them into first place in any race.

In their motherly hearts, there was no fear for themselves.

The lioness already on the alert because of the smell of human, sensed something wrong as it turned the corner. It did not expect to see the small figure rush at it with a spear. The sharp spear tip cut through the hide and drove into the lion's rib cage going between the ribs and proceeded toward its heart. The spear found its target and scored immediate success. The lioness was dead even as she reacted.

Taelo had used all his quickness to rush forward and drive his spear into the lion. However, he was now within reach of the mighty lioness. She reached out with one claw and grabbed him by the shoulder and pulled him toward her in what appeared to be an embrace. Taelo pushed with all his might, but it did not seem the lion was going to budge.

Then the eagle came hurdling down and caught the lion by the snout and pulled the beast out away from the cliff.

Instead of pulling back when the lion's huge paw clutched him tighter as Taelo lunged in with all his might and drove the spear in as far as he could.

The lion reared up as the eagle pulled on his snout.

The force Taelo was exerting was enough to send all three off the edge of the cliff.

The eagle let go of the lion. It spread it large wings and regained its flight. It rose upward and let out another piercing scream. Instinctively it knew it was done and was already departing down the valley.

As the lioness left the trail and began the quiet, almost floating descend off the cliff, her clutch pulled Taelo to her chest. Already, her life had left. The two hit the rocks some fifty feet below.

Golden Hawk was stunned by the swiftness of the events and Taelo's fall off the cliff. He was in a state of panic. He watched in horror as Taelo, the lion and the eagle left the cliff and fell to the rocks below.

To him it appeared the lion had hugged Taelo to its chest and protected him from the fall. But Taelo was not answering his call.

Golden Hawk began a frantic descend to the rocks below.

Golden Hawk took daring leaps and jumps in his descent toward his cousin down in the rocks. He risked everything to get down to Taelo. He was in fear of losing his other self.

White Swan and Quiet Pheasant were now almost to the cliffs. They had heard the eagle scream. They had witnessed its dive for the cliffs and then had seen it rise and fly away.

Both were now in a state of panic. What had happened? Were the two boys alright? What did all this mean? The eagle was gone. It had left, and this was a point of confusion and concern to the two of them.

Were the boys alright?

"I am not sure I can take it much longer," White Swan said between taking long breaths.

Quiet Pheasant only nodded her response and continued running at full speed.

To Taelo the descent was in ultra-slow motion. He looked back and saw Golden Hawk's surprised look. He looked into the pale-yellow eyes of the eagle. He thanked it for its help as they all went over the edge. The eagle seemed to blink at him and then let go of the lioness's nostril.

He had felt the claws of the lioness flex and pull him toward her chest. The impact on the rocks knocked the wind out of Taelo but the lioness below him provided the cushion keeping him from harm.

He lay quietly taking stock of himself. Everything seemed fine. He relived the last few moments and realized he had just lived through a miracle.

His totem had helped him, the lioness had held him to her chest and the landing had only knocked his breath away.

Suddenly he heard Golden Hawk calling his name and he slowly sat up.

He watched as Golden Hawk descended the cliff and across the rocks as if he were flying.

Taelo watched in amazement as Golden Hawk took his last giant leap to where he and the lioness had fallen.

"I didn't know you knew how to fly. How did you get down so fast," Taelo asked as Golden Hawk arrived in a breathless state and sat at his side?

"Unbelievable, you are alive, are you OK," Golden Hawk asked as he sat breathlessly down beside Taelo.

"You talk about me flying but you actually do it and don't even get a scratch."

They were both sitting on the chest of the lioness.

"I am fine. A little surprised at how this all turned out. I am not sure how we are going to explain the dead lioness," Taelo said as he examined his kill.

Just then the two looked down the slope of rocks and saw their mothers and heard their shouts. This surprised both of them.

"How did they get here? What made them come out this way? What are we going to tell them," Golden Hawk rapidly inquired?

"Let's not tell them about my flight down with the lioness. Let's just keep it to killing her," Taelo said quietly to Golden Hawk.

White Swan and Quiet Pheasant stopped in their tracks as they reached the spot where Taelo and Golden Hawk sat on the chest of the lioness.

They saw the spear driven into the lioness. The animal was magnificent. It was in its prime. It was at least eight feet long and more than three feet high at shoulders. The animal must have weighted five hundred pounds.

The two boys sat looking calmly at their mothers.

"We see the lioness, we heard the eagle, and we see the spear. Tell us you were not out hunting for her," White Swan said quietly as she tried to make sense out of the situation.

She was so happy to see the two that she was not really concerned about what their intensions had been.

Taelo slowly and carefully explained how they were trapped between the lioness and a mountain goat. He pointed up to the trail along the cliff and explained the situation and how the eagle had helped him as he attacked the lioness.

He purposely omitted the detail about falling with the lioness, but he credited the eagle with helping him push the lioness off the cliff.

After a few awkward moments of the two mothers just standing and taking in the situation, Quiet Pheasant spoke up.

"We will need to get help to carry this lioness back to the camp.

White Swan and I will stay here.

You two run and get enough of the young men and women to help.

Make sure they bring strong enough poles," Quiet Pheasant instructed the two.

She had never seen a lioness this large and in full prime.

Taelo and Golden Hawk were glad to get away without more questioning. They quickly set off on a fast jog to get the needed help. This also gave them a chance to talk about how to tell their story and leave out the part about falling off the cliff.

They did not want to be restricted in their activities.

"Let's go over the story another time," Taelo commented to Golden Hawk as they made their way to the camp.

"Don't worry, I have it memorized. You did all the talking so at least we have only one story," Golden Hawk replied.

"The story they just told us is too simple. I know Taelo well enough to know he is leaving something out, but I can't quite decide what it is. How do two boys kill a lioness at least eight times bigger than they are," White Swan said as she walked among the rocks trying to read the signs?

The signs she was trying to read did not exist. She soon realized this and looked up at the trail along the cliff.

"I agree with you. Did you notice Taelo did all the talking and Golden Hawk only spoke after the whole story had been told? Should we press and find out what else happened," Quiet Pheasant replied as she too could find no indication of what had happened?

"No, let's accept the miracle for what it is, a sign the two are protected and have capabilities well beyond their years. Someday, I am sure they will tell us the rest of the story," White Cloud said as she once again looked up to the trail the boys had been on.

A small goat stood on the trail looking down at her.

How had they gotten down here so quickly?

She knew they could not fly. Or could they fly with lions?

The camp came to life as the news spread about the lion. A group of eager young men and women went out to bring it into the camp. It was late evening when the lioness was brought in. Most of the camp turned out to look at the huge beast.

"You will have to tell me the real story the next time you stop for breakfast," the Weaver smiled at Taelo and Golden Hawk after the first explanation had been shared with the camp.

The older men who no longer could hunt came out to examine the lioness. They were surprised at the size and great condition of the animal. This was a prime specimen. It would have given a team of hunters a full battle. The fact two young boys had brought the animal down was astounding.

They looked at Taelo and Golden Hawk with new respect and appreciation. The elder's prediction that the two were meant for greatness in the future was indeed coming true.

The women gathered round and skinned the lioness.

They all commented to White Swan and Quiet Pheasant on how brave Taelo and Golden Hawk were and wondered how the two could let them go hunting lions at such a young age.

Both White Swan and Quiet Pheasant kept quiet. There was no way to answer such a question. Of course, they worried but they could not keep the boys from going out into the woods.

Taelo offered the lioness's skull to the medicine man. The claws were extracted and saved to make jewelry and decorations. The hide would be used by their mothers to make formal clothes for them.

In the evening around the central campfire, Taelo once again told the story of tracking the goat along the cliff side. He told of the call of the eagle and then realizing that he and Golden Hawk were themselves being tracked by the lioness. He elaborated on the part of the lion coming around the bend and how he and the eagle had worked together to catch the lioness off balance.

Many questions were asked but Taelo did not reveal he had fallen down the cliff with the lioness.

He did tell of the help from his totem, the eagle and of driving his spear into the lioness and then pushing as hard as he could to get her to go over the edge of the cliff.

He thanked the flint smith for giving his spear a sharp edge and Red Oak and his father for having taught him how to use the spear.

Taelo and Golden Hawk enjoyed the notoriety that followed but were soon looking for their next adventure.

Chapter 5: The Clan

The Clan gathering was one of Taelo's and Golden Hawk's favorite times. Their fathers and the Weaver had all told them stories about the Clan history.

His father's stories went back to a time before the Clan met in this valley. A time before the Clan became so large that it had split into sub-Clans. At that time, they lived in a valley with a giant waterfall. It was the first home of the Elk Clan after they had crossed the ice bridge from another land.

The onset of continuous cold winter weather drove the Clan leaders to move south. It was at that time they first chose to split the Clan, so each sub-Clan could have their own hunting territory.

That was long ago. Now there were five sub-Clans formed from the Elk Clan. Taelo and Golden Hawk were in the Elk Horn Clan. It was the first sub-clan. The Grazing Elk, the Shy Elk, the Swift Elk, and the Elk Hide Clan each had been formed as the clan grew through the years.

From the Weaver they learned that the Clan meeting gave the leaders a chance to balance the prosperity and the balance of the overall Clan population. If a Clan was getting too large for the area where roamed the leaders would either rebalance the Clans or periodically, they would add another Clan.

The stories of the Weaver showed the two that the Clan leaders used the gathering to ensure all the sub-Clans were prepared for and able to survive the coming winter.

The naming ceremony was always held during the gathering. Taelo often dreamt of his naming day. This he recognize was the day he had chosen the Eagle, and the Eagle chosen him.

White Swan credited the gathering as a time for finding and then choosing a mate. It was a time for new romances to begin. Normally a mate always came from another Clan. In this way the Clan's make up, strength and survivability were enhanced.

The people were of one kindred and looked forward each year to renew old friendships. This was a time to recount adventures and often to honor those lost to unfortunate accidents or hunting injuries. At this time, the histories of the elders were recalled and celebrated. It was a time of bonding and rekindling of old friendships.

The gathering place was a luxurious valley through which a small, lazy stream meandered and in one location broadened to form a small lake. The small lake boasted a few mallards and northern geese and for those energetic enough to throw their nets or go spear fishing it easily yielded a variety of fish.

It was guarded on the far side by tall dark green pine trees separating the dark hued blue water from the light blue sky that reached well beyond the valley like a blanket to embrace the far snow peaked mountains.

This was a valley Taelo, and Golden Hawk knew like the back of their hands. There was not a spot or point in the valley the two did not know by heart. They had explored every nook and cranny as they embraced and acted out the adventures their minds created.

For the last several years the Elk Horn Clan had out produced all the other Clans by a significant amount.

They had generously shared food supplies with the other sub-Clans. This year the Elk Horn Clan was loaded with an over-abundance of dried fish, elk, rabbit, moose, and other food stuffs. Their supply of leather goods, baskets, general utensils, woven cloth, various tools, fishhooks, stone ax heads and clothing made them the most prosperous members of the Clan. This abundance had so loaded them down to the point that they were the last to arrive at the meeting valley.

They stopped at the top of the hill to look out across the valley.

Below them the early morning air was still and the light wispy campfire parallel plumes of smoke from each family lodge rose like slowly undulating white worms straight into the still morning air and danced in what seemed an orchestrated performance.

The sun, rising over the far horizon seemed to give them life as they changed colors of pinks and yellows and mixed with grey.

It was a scene that caused the Elk Horn Clan to stop and appreciate the beauty of the scene that greeted them.

The grouping of campfires indicated all the other sub-Clans but theirs had already arrived and set up camp. The Elk Horn Clan would have to take the place farthest away from the river and up along the hillside.

Elk Horn Clan leader, Wise Owl, stood overlooking the valley below. The abundant wealth they were bringing to this gathering had greatly slowed them down. Now he stood contemplating what he should have his sub-Clan do.

There were no good camping spots left.

Taelo stood between his father, Grey Fox Running on his left and his mother, White Swan on his right. They were a close-knit family and Taelo felt a great love and affection toward both. He was now twelve seasons old and was beginning to grow.

He was seldom disciplined, not because his parents were lax but because Taelo was attuned to the requirements of their rigorous, demanding life. It did not escape him how hard all the elders worked to gather food and to make the clothes and equipment needed to sustain the Clan.

He and Golden Hawk often talked about this and had decided to make a purposeful effort to contribute their share.

Grey Fox Running commented that because they were late, they would be camped farthest from the lake.

We will be the sub-Clan with the most wealth, but we will be doing the most work was Wise Owl's response.

He was not looking forward to having his camp out on the fringe of the valley.

Taelo let his eyes move slowly across the valley as he listened to the adults. His eyes traveled to the flat clearing on the other side of the river opposite the camp on the far side of the lake. He, Golden Hawk, and their friends had often played on the far side of the lake. They had wondered why none of the Clans ever chose to camp there.

Now Taelo spoke up and suggested the Elk Hide Clan camp on the other side of the lake.

Wise Owl pointed out that if they camped on the other side, they would have a long walk to get to where everyone else was camped and there would be the problem of crossing the river.

"Yes, but if we camp on the hillsides on this side of the river, we will need to carry our water from the river through the various camps. And you will need to walk just as far to go to all the activities. I think the hill side will be more work for the entire Elk Hide Clan," Taelo replied.

He and Golden Hawk would be two of the boys carrying water all the time.

Taelo pointed to the rapids just upstream of the lake and said that they could move a few large stones into place and create a walk across the rapids. The Clan could have a comfortable and easy to maintain location and the distance to the other Clans would be the same.

Wise Owl, Grey Fox Running, and Red Oak all looked at each other. It was rare for Taelo to talk so openly when the adults were talking. This made them pay attention.

He immediately liked the idea and already had visions of his sub-Clan marching grandly through the camps.

"It sounds like this may be a good idea. Before we commit to it lets send a team ahead. If they can get the stones in place and provide a solid crossing, they can light a fire on the other side and our Clan can come down the valley, through all the other Clan groups and cross the river.

It would be a grand way to show our good standing this year," Wise Owl said with a twinkle in his eye and a new spirit in his voice.

He looked at Taelo and Golden Hawk and put them in charge of getting a bridge across the river and sending a signal when they had successfully done so.

He assigned four older and stronger young men to provide the muscle for the work and instructed them to travel around the camp on the ridge and do the work without being seen.

Wise Owl really wanted this idea to work.

Taelo and Golden Hawk looked at each other. They were to be in charge. They were both excited to have been assigned leadership roles for this venture. This was a new experience.

Taelo immediately sensed some resistance from the older boys. They jogged along the ridge as they went around the rim of the valley. All six carried backpacks with various items needed to prepare a place for the Elk Horn Clan to cross.

Taelo and Golden Hawk set a fast pace keeping all of them from talking too much. They arrived undetected at the rapids a short time later. They were far enough up-stream that they did not draw the attention of the nearest Clan group. The six of them studied the rapids.

Taelo used this period to get the opinions of the other four. His approach was to get them to propose how the work could be done and then to let them go do it. Leading to him did not mean controlling every action. Golden Hawk shared the same feeling, so it was obvious to him what Taelo was doing by getting the other four to define the work. When it was as Taelo wanted nothing was said and the work proceeded. Taelo only commented when subtle adjustments needed to be made.

Taelo and the rest discussed how they could create a bridge across the gap. They decided to cut some small trees and make a walk to span the middle of the rapids. The remaining crossing could be improved by moving stones to strategic positions.

They found a series of stones providing an almost continuous path across. Only in the middle was there a large gap.

The plans were made for the middle span. Taelo and Golden Hawk undertook the job of finding the main beams for the bridge while the older and stronger members moved the large river stones into place.

This arrangement had been reached among all of them in what seemed to be an open discussion, though Taelo had quietly guided it to achieve the outcome he desired. Even at this young age Taelo already had the leadership skills needed to influence and guide the older boys.

Golden Hawk and Taelo found the trees they needed and after cutting them down they began to prepare the bridge. They used three small tree trunks for the bottom walk of the bridge and then lashed smaller willow branches across the three tree trunks. This made a strong three, foot wide section.

The four older members of the team carried and positioned the bridge across the center span of the rapids. Then a low railing was added to provide stability for those walking across.

When all was done, the group made the journey to the far side of the river. They collected enough wood for a good fire and cut some green limbs with leaves on them to make the smoke.

Once all was ready, they lit their signal fire and put some green wood and leaves to make a white smoke that could easily be seen.

They had achieved their goal in the early morning and as their fire sent up the white smoke the sun was directly above them.

Wise Owl and the rest of the Elk Horn Clan had waited until the sun was at its zenith before starting down into the valley. If their young men were successful, they would proceed through the valley and across the river. Meanwhile, however, they would proceed toward the rest of the Clan and keep an eye out for the signal fire.

All the Elk Horn Clan members were now aware of the game they were playing. When the white smoke was spotted a small cheer went through the group.

It had been a very good year for them, and they wanted to show off a little and they did not want to do extra work because they were coming with generous gifts. There was always some competition going on between the various sub-Clans. They prized the chance to show off. Camping on the other side seemed like a great idea.

This walk through the camps would be a moment all the Elk Horn Clan members would relish. They had changed into their best dress and had put some of their best work on display. All added a light swagger to their walk. Today they would show off their good fortune.

Silent Hawk watched as the Elk Horn Clan walked into the camp. It was clear to all the other Clans that the Elk Horn Clan had done very well. They were all healthy and were loaded down with their supplies and goods. It was good to see that one of the Clans had done so well.

The rest of the Clan would seek to learn the secret of how this had been accomplished. Silent Hawk, eldest Clan leader and leader of the main Elk Clan, felt some pride for he had helped get the Elk Hide Clan started.

Several of his personal friends had gone with this sub clan.

The current leader, Wise Owl, was one of his best and brightest pupils who Silent Hawk had supported in getting the leaders role.

The lead hunter, Grey Fox Running, was the son of one of his best friends.

Silent Hawk felt a strong connection with this sub clan.

There was cheer and good tidings being shared but the Elk Horn Clan continued to move steadily toward the river. Several of the other Clan members kept telling them there was no room to set up camp in the direction of the lake.

But the Elk Horn Clan members paid no attention.

To everyone's surprise the Elk Horn Clan proceeded to the bank of the river and turned upstream and continued their march. There was a sudden puzzled hush in the main camp area.

It was then Silent Hawk saw the span of bridge across the center of the rapids.

He wondered when the Elk Horn Clan had built the bridge.

Now, he understood the smug look Wise Owl had when they greeted each other.

The Elk Horn Clan was showing off. They would have a place on the riverbank and a way across the river.

Silent Hawk let out a chuckle. It was good to see such spirit.

His pupil Wise Owl had become an exceptional leader. He would be someone to watch.

The Elk Horn Clan continued their march to set up their camp across the river from the rest of the other sub-clans. The crossing and the bridge set up by Taelo's and Golden Hawk's team worked perfectly.

The room they had available was more than they would have had if they had stayed on the other side of the river.

The Elk Horn Clan was late and had been awaited, for several days.

The leaders from each of the other sub-clans came across the river and congratulated the Elk Horn Clan for being so ingenious. There were the general greetings among old friends but also the official ones. They shared the planned schedule of leadership meetings to take place starting the following day.

Without exception the leaders of the other clans all eyed the goods the Elk Horn Clan had on display. It was clear to all that this sub clan had exceeded all of them in the past year.

It was the custom of the Elk Clan to gather and have the elders meet to discuss the appropriate division of the surplus food, goods and even families. They were careful not to strip too much away from any successful group. There was sharing, but each sub clan was expected to feed their own.

This balancing allowed for the unforeseen accident of a key hunter. It allowed for a bad season in a specific part of the Clan's domain. It was also used to recognize the contributors and to encourage the less fortunate to try harder. If the same clan came up short more than once, the elders discussed the potential for a leadership change or the addition of a key hunter to the ailing clan.

This year the main Elk Clan was suffering from the loss of several key hunters. In the previous year, the establishment of the Elk Hide Clan had left the main Elk Clan weaker than desired. However, at that time they thought they would be able to make do. They had been heavily loaded with older members but expected these members to still be productive. Events had not unfolded as had been expected. It seemed everything that could have gone wrong did go wrong.

Their main hunting party had been out running down a deer when they surprised a woolly rhino. The rhino reacted by attacking the group. Two members were gored, and the rhino broke the leg of a third before the brave hunters brought it down.

The lead hunter died from the goring he received as he defended the first injured hunter. Before dying he requested his funeral fire be out on the grassy plain where he died.

The other hunters had struggled to return to the main camp and those injured were still recovering.

Having three key hunters put out of commission was beyond what the Elk Clan could manage. The remaining older hunters had tried to help but had done poorly. The Elk Clan was living hand to mouth, hunt to hunt. Winter was close at hand and the Elk Clan had no reserves of food.

Silent Hawk felt his age and felt the pressure of the dismal condition of the Elk Clan. The Elk Clan was at risk of not being able to survive the coming winter.

The hunter that died was to have been elevated to be the Elk leader at this gathering.

Silver Hawk would seek the counseling and help of Wise Owl.

Chapter 6: The Meeting

The composite Clan leadership was made up of three representatives from each of the sub clans. One member was the overall leader. Each sub clan was independent except for changes and agreements made during the meeting each autumn that won a majority of the vote. Currently with six sub-clans there were eighteen representatives. The overall leader had one vote if there was a tie.

A talking staff controlled the flow of presentations and discussion. The speaker from each Clan stood in the center of the gathering and reported the condition of their Clan and identified any issues that needed to be addressed by the entire Clan leadership.

Silent Hawk, Leader of the Elk Clan was the senior member and overall leader of the composite leadership team. He sat at the northern position on the circle.

In reverse order of their establishment, the Grazing Elk, the Shy Elk, the Swift Elk, the Elk Hide and the Elk Horn Clan each reported on the events of the past year.

Wise Owl elaborated on the wealth the Elk Horn Clan had to share with the all the rest. He reported on a new way of trapping fish that had led to this abundance. It was clear to all that the Elk Horn Clan had prospered and had out done all the other clans.

Most sub-Clans would face the winter in a challenging but acceptable condition. The help that the Elk Horn Clan offered appeared to be the margin that would allow all of them to return in good stead the following year.

The sun was reaching its zenith by the time Silent Hawk stood to take his place in the center of the circle and report on the condition of the parent Elk Clan.

He shared the story of losing his main hunter and next in line for the Elk Clan leadership. He continued with the fact that the injured Elk Clan hunters were still in recovery. He painted a bleak picture of the condition of the main Elk Clan.

Silent Hawk admitted that the Elk Clan needed very specific and dramatic help. It needed a lead hunter and at least one additional experienced hunter. It needed much food. He was sure it was more food than he thought the Elk Horn Clan would be able to share.

He let the other Clans know that the Elk Clan had nothing to pay with for this help that he was asking for.

He made the point that the Elk Clan was requesting all the help the other clans could extend.

Even as he made his request, he knew he was sharing only the minimum amount of information. It was even worse than he was reporting.

It was hard for him to stand before this group and show them that he had failed. He had no choice. He swallowed his pride to make the request and hoped the other sub clans would help in some way.

Having heard the condition of the other Clans, he knew most were not in position to give much help and he did not have much hope. The Elk Clan would have to look out for themselves. It would be a miracle if the Elk Clan could get the type of help it needed.

All the sub clans had been heard from and now it was time to see how they could help each other.

Silent Hawk's report and request had put a chill in the proceedings of the meeting.

One after another, the leaders of the various sub-clans made their excuse for not providing the manpower requested by the Elk Clan. Each did offer some small amount of food or some materials to help but backed away from giving up any key members. They had fared only a little better and were not able to give up any hunters nor could they provide much food.

Wise Owl listened and knew he would make an offer that would help. He had the resources and the reserves that would make the difference.

Wise Owl remembered how Silent Hawk had supported him in establishing the Elk Horn sub-clan. Silent Hawk had made sure the sub-clan had the necessary manpower to be successful. Wise Owl now watched as Silent Hawk sat stoically and listened to each subsequent sub-Clan reject the original Elk Clan's request for help.

It was hard for Wise Owl to watch his mentor in such distress. Silent Hawk was too good of a person and the main Clan too important to let it suffer a potentially hard winter without food.

Wise Owl concluded he could and would provide the support needed.

Finally, it was his turn.

Wise Owl stood to make his proposal for support.

"The Elk Horn Clan has had a very good year. We will generously share food and we offer Gray Fox Running to take the position of lead hunter."

A hush fell across the circle of leaders. Everyone knew Gray Fox Running was the lead hunter in the Elk Horn Clan and next in line to become a Clan leader. He was in fact thought of as one of the best hunters in the whole of all the Clans.

Wise Owl continued, "He is my best hunter and leader. He has ambitions of being a Clan leader. The offer is to have his family join the Elk Clan and next year upon his successful contributions to your well-being, you Silent Hawk shall become an elder and let him lead."

The conditions of the offer surprised everyone.

Wise Owl was offering one of the best but stipulating a very tough condition in effect putting Silent Hawk to pasture. It was almost an insult, but all knew Wise Owl was a supporter of Silent Hawk.

What was afoot? What was Wise Owl up to?

Wise Owl was trying to help Gray Fox Running achieve his own personal goal of becoming a Clan leader. Grey Fox Running would not be able to move into a Clan leadership position for many years to come in his current position. This situation offered the opportunity and Wise Owl saw a way to help two people at the same time.

Everyone in the meeting was quiet. Gray Fox Running was known to all of them. His skill and ability to provide was known throughout the Clan. All the other Clans were amazed Wise Owl would offer him up.

Would Silent Hawk agree to such a condition?

Wise Owl figured the leaders around the fire thought him a little daft. However, Gray Fox Running and Red Oak were such good trainers, Wise Owl was confident even his youngest hunters could provide enough food to take them through the coming winter.

The Elk Horn Clan currently had enough food to take them through the hardest of winters without the need of any additional hunting. It was a small risk on his part and a way to solve two problems.

This was the only way he knew Gray Fox Running could quickly become a clan leader.

He also sensed his good friend Silent Hawk was about ready to step aside.

Silent Hawk thought about the offer. He knew it was a very good offer. He was tired. It would be a relief from the constant worry of ensuring the success of the Elk Clan.

When he stepped down from being the Elk Clan leader, Wise Owl would become a senior Clan leader and leader of the overall Clan assembly. He would have the North seat.

He, Silent Hawk would become a junior elder. Still on the council but not its leader. He marveled at his protégé's cleverness as well as his generosity. He understood and accepted the situation.

Wise Owl was indeed true to his name, and he was truly generous in his offer. It was a little hard for Silent Hawk to initially accept but he knew it was the thing to do.

"My friend, thank you for such a generous offer. I will certainly accept Gray Fox Running and the condition you stipulate," he replied in a strong, quiet voice.

There were tears of relief and hope in his eyes as he sat quietly down. He hoped this would be enough. He had not told the whole story of just how desperate the Elk Clan was.

Later in the day, Wise Owl presented the opportunity to Gray Fox Running. The Elk Clan wished him to become the lead hunter. In the following season he would most likely ascend to be the leader of the Elk Clan.

"Think about this. It accelerates your rise to Clan Leader. Discuss it with White Swan and let me know tomorrow morning of your decision," Wise Owl said as the two approached the river.

He knew Gray Fox Running would accept the position. It was not an opportunity to be turned down.

Normally this would have been a great honor, immediately seized upon. However, Gray Fox Running was alarmed at the condition of the Elk Clan. Even if all the food was to be split up evenly, there would not be enough to carry the Elk Clan through even a mild winter.

If the coming winter were a hard one, many members of the Elk Clan would be lost.

He was honored for himself and bothered and fearful for the well-being of his own family. He indeed would need to talk this out with White Swan. He needed her consul, her support and most importantly he knew she would provide her observations from a very different perspective. She had been his teacher in the way he now hunted. She was extremely adept at seeing the whole and positioning actions in an aggressive but fair manner.

He discussed this with her long into the night. They both knew he would accept the offer.

Taelo listened in even though they thought he was asleep. He was immediately alert to every word being spoken. He wanted to speak up, but he knew better. Then his mother spoke the words he was thinking.

White Swan made a suggestion that seemed to pop into her mind from nowhere.

"You must become the Clan leader immediately and you must bring Red Oak with you as the lead hunter. Only then will you have the influence and power to save the Elk Clan.

She suggested that Silent Hawk become an elder now.

The injured hunters should come over to the Elk Horn Clan. This would immediately lighten the load of the Elk Clan," White Swan said confidently.

She was as surprised at the suggestion she was making and could see from the look on Grey Fox Running's face that he was too. White Swan continued to share her thinking and plan. She said that she recognized the danger of the situation of moving into the Elk Clan and that her protective instincts were guiding her thinking. She was determined to ensure her family did not suffer from this situation.

White Swan was also thinking of the bond shared between Golden Hawk and their son Taelo. She wanted to ensure that bond remained intact and the only way to do that led to her suggestion.

Wide awake, Taelo listened to his parents discuss the situation late into the night. He did not remember falling asleep. However, the next morning he was immediately out and talking to Golden Hawk and sharing the situation as he understood it.

The two watched as Red Oak and Gray Fox Running went for a walk together. They quietly followed the two to a large boulder and hid behind it where they could overhear their two fathers talk.

"White Swan and I have talked all night. I have been offered to the Elk Clan as a lead hunter. Next year I will become the Elk Clan leader," Gray Fox Running began.

A feeling of loss and despair passed through Red Oak as he congratulated his best friend.

"There is more, the Elk Clan is in a very distressful situation. I believe it will take more than just me to save the Clan from devastation this coming winter. I would like you to go with me," Gray Fox Running said as he watched the expression on his friend's face.

"I would be honored to go with you my old friend. However, will Wise Owl let this happen," Red Oak replied?

"He will certainly not be pleased but I believe he will. He knows the Elk Clan needs this help. Silent Hawk is his mentor and dear friend. I will talk first with Silent Hawk and then with Wise Owl. I will ask Silent Hawk to send all the wounded hunters and their families to the Elk Horn Clan.

The Elk Horn Clan has enough food. Additional hunting will not be needed until spring. By then the injured hunters will have healed. In this way the Elk Horn Clan will have a strong hunting group this coming spring," Grey Fox Running continued.

Taelo and Golden Hawk quietly left their hiding place and went out to roam the valley. They were excited about the new adventure they were about to embark on. Both were ecstatic they would remain together.

"There goes the other reason I am asking you to come with me," Gray Fox Running said as he pointed out the two boys disappearing into the forest.

"They would be lost without each other. They are more than friends, they are true kindred spirits meant to roam this world together," Gray Fox Running continued.

Red Oak grunted his agreement. He and Gray Fox Running shared very much the same relationship. They had even married sisters.

Grey Fox Running went to Silent Hawk and asked him to walk with him. He told him how honored he was to come to the Elk Clan and to learn how highly Silent Hawk thought of him. He shared that he and White Swan had discussed this for most of the night.

Then Grey Fox Running pointed out that very dramatic action would be needed to save the Elk Clan from starvation. This action would need to be carried out without question or resistance. To make this happen Grey Fox Running needed to be the Elk Clan leader and Red Oak his lead hunter.

Silent Hawk would serve as his coach and guide.

He stopped talking and looked directly at into Silent Hawk's eyes.

Silent Hawk was surprised and somewhat taken aback but immediately recognized the leadership abilities Grey Fox Running possessed. He recalled a similar trait in Gray Fox Running's father. He saw the same and perhaps sharper mind.

"Your father would be proud of you. You have his leadership skill. I appreciate the honesty and forthright way you have approached me." Silent Hawk replied.

Silent Hawk thought ahead to the situation the Elk Clan faced and decided what Gray Fox Running was proposing was indeed best for the Clan.

He knew the situation was even worse than he had so far shared, and the fact that Gray Fox Running had made such a clear assessment of the Elk Clan's situation did not escape Silent Hawk.

This knowledge and Gray Fox Running's clarity and strong leadership convinced Silent Hawk to accept the proposal.

"I see you have developed into a determined and forthright person. Your father and I were best friends. I was sorry to hear of his passing two seasons ago. If you agree to come over to the Elk Clan, I will do as you ask. I will step aside and let you lead. Sending the three wounded hunters to the Elk Horn Clan is an excellent suggestion. In this way they will not be a burden to us. Have you shared this with anyone else yet?" Silent Hawk asked.

"No, if you had not agreed with this proposal, I would have honored Wise Owl's proposal.

I have talked only to Red Oak to see if he would consider coming with me but to no one else.

I do not wish to hurt your position in the Clan, I am very aware of your great talent, but I am very concerned about this situation," Grey Fox Running said as he continued to look into Silent Hawks dark brown eyes.

As Silent Hawk thought about the power and leadership Gray Fox Running displayed, a confidence rose up inside of him. It all felt right. Here was the leader needed at this moment to ensure the Elk Clan survived through the winter. He felt relieved someone such as Grey Fox Running was available in this time of need.

Silent Hawk decided that he would help this young man as he took the mantle of leadership. He would hold his own pride in check and take the right action for the sake of the Elk Clan members.

Silent Hawk looked at Grey Fox Running and nodded his head. I will go with you to each of the Clan leaders and tell them that you and I have come to this agreement.

He realized Grey Fox Running was the only hope for the Elk Clan and without his open and public consent to this change, it would not happen.

Together the two made the rounds of the other Clan leaders and got their agreement and support. They began with Wise Owl who immediately felt the sting of this arrangement but agreed to it.

"Grey Fox Running, you drive a hard bargain. I hate to lose both you and Red Oak. However, I can see your logic. You have trained our other hunters well and the Elk Clan will give us their three recovering hunters who will be available when the next great hunting season begins.

I also see White Swan's hand in keeping Taelo and Golden Hawk together as well and I agree with her as well. Tell her that as always, she has great vision.

It must really have been a hard year if you, Silent Hawk, agree to step down," Wise Owl said as he looked into the eyes of his old mentor and nodded agreement to Gray Fox Running's request.

To Wise Owl, Grey Fox Running explained that the Elk Clan was in a desperate situation that needed immediate and drastic action. His respect for Silent Hawk was unquestionable and he wanted his guidance, but he wanted the direct control that only by being the Elk Clan leader would give him. He was sure he and Red Oak together could save the Elk Clan from certain starvation.

Grey Fox Running ended by saying that he looked to Wise Owl for support to make it happen and to Silent Hawk's coaching to make him a great clan leader.

Wise Owl put his hand on Grey Fox Running Running's shoulder and expressed his support.

Grey Fox Running was happy this meeting with Wise Owl had gone the way he had hoped. He would have to thank White Swan for sharing her insight on how to make this happen and let her know that Wise Owl had seen her design in keeping the two boys together.

That afternoon he and Silent Hawk visited with each of the other Clan leaders and let them know of the new situation.

All were surprised and shocked that Wise Owl had accepted the proposal but understood the logic of the change.

White Swan was proud of her husband's ability to negotiate the change in leadership.

She was also relieved he had been able to get agreement to include Red Oak as part of the trade.

Wise Owl's read on this confirmed her positive assessment of his keen mind and power of observation.

She was pleased that this would keep Taelo and Golden Hawk growing up together. This was as important to her as was Grey Fox Running's rise to leadership.

Taelo and Golden Hawk went running out of the camp to their favorite lookout across the valley. There they sat on the huge boulder with a view of the entire valley. They talked late into the afternoon about how they would contribute to the well-being of their new Clan, the Elk Clan. They were relieved to be going together into this new adventure.

The agreement to the leadership change was shared in a council meeting and the decision to make the change when the clans split to go their own ways was decided.

The clan celebrations could not lift the weight of concern from Gray Fox Running. He discussed the situation with Silent Hawk and Red Oak. Silent Hawk let them know that the situation of the Elk Clan was much worse than had been shared. The Elk Clan was celebrating with the last of its food stores. They did not have any food in reserve. Silent Hawk confirmed even with the generosity of the other Clans, there would not be sufficient stores for a mild winter.

Elk Clan mothers were already in fear for their youngest children. The young always suffered first when food was in short supply. The eldest members of the tribe would sacrifice themselves by not eating. This had been on the minds of all the Elk Clan members. They had not spoken of this with each other, and no one had shared this with the other sub-Clans.

They knew the basic survival was each individual clan's responsibility. They knew each sub clan would share what was possible without risking starvation. In their memory, there had never been a time when the Elk Clan had been in such a clear and dangerous situation. No one in the Elk Clan could conceive of anything but suffering and death in the coming winter.

Gray Fox Running and Red Oak came to understand how dire the situation was. They knew full well they would have to take extra ordinary action to ensure the survival of the Elk Clan.

Their days were spent discussing this with each other, with their mates, and with a few other leaders and hunters they respected. Together they were on a mission to create a plan leading the Elk Clan away from the edge of disaster and away from the precipice of death.

They knew they would have to do something different. They needed a miracle to save the Elk Clan and they knew the ancestors had no way to send them real food. They would need to do something extraordinary to get the Clan through the coming winter.

A week later the Clan gathering came to an end. The day of departure arrived, and the various Clans packed their belongings and departed to their wintering grounds.

The Elk Horn Clan broke camp and got ready to go back to their territory and their winter homes.

Red Oak and Grey Fox Running remained behind on the far side of the river as the Elk Horn Clan took leave. Red Oak and Gray Fox Running were rich in food and goods.

They would add much to the Elk Clan's stores. The food they brought with them was probably as much as the rest of the Elk Clan had in total.

As each family of the Elk Horn Clan was about to depart, they stopped by to wish Taelo's and Golden Hawk's family good fortune. Every family provided an extra gift of food. They too had seen the terrible condition of the Elk Clan.

The Elk Horn members all expressed their best wishes and that they would miss the two boys running around their camp.

The Weaver stopped by and gave his food directly to Taelo and Golden Hawk. He gave each a big hug and invited them to his campfire whenever they wished.

All the Elk Horn Clan wished the two well and that they would bring the same luck to the Elk Clan they had brought to the Elk Horn Clan.

"Well, my friends, I wish you well. We leave the best of the Elk Horn Clan behind. May you bring luck to the Elk Clan. I will miss all of you but especially Taelo and Golden Hawk. They have been an inspiration and have brought good luck to the Elk Horn Clan. May they do the same for the Elk Clan," Wise Owl said as he departed.

Taelo and Golden Hawk waved as their friends both young and old proceeded across the river and up the valley back the way they had come.

Their departure had less swagger than their arrival, but they left in confidence as they returned to face the winter with a good reserve of food.

Chapter 7: Survival Plans

The grey cloud covered sky, a cool breeze, and the knowledge that they were in dire trouble dampened the spirits of the Elk Clan members as they waved to the last departing clan.

The valley seemed foreboding in the quiet of the grey morning and the threat of snow.

They were now alone. They had a new leader, but they faced the grim fact that many of them might not see the warmth of another spring.

The cool wind rose and with it the fear of hunger and starvation that winter would bring became more real.

The elder leaders of the Elk Clan gathered around in a circle with Gray Fox Running in the center. The rest of the Clan surrounded them.

In a clear, loud confident voice, Gray Fox Running, asked that everyone, men, women, and children speak and suggest what each could do to ensure they all survived the winter.

There was silence.

The expectation had been that Grey Fox Running would tell them what they had to do to survive.

This behavior in a leader was new to the Elk Clan members. It was very different.

A grumbling murmur could be heard as Grey Fox Running stood in silence.

Silent Hawk worried about how the Elk Clan would take to this new style of leadership, but he held back and did not interfere.

Taelo shouted out that he would hunt enough rabbits each day to feed five.

Golden Hawk joined in and said the two together would feed ten.

Next to him stood Floating Cloud and her granddaughter Quite Rabbit. They had asked to join the Elk Clan because they had just lost Quiet Rabbit's mother and father and did not want to return with the Elk Hide Clan.

Floating Cloud pointed to the large amount of food that they had accumulated and declared that she and Quiet Rabbit would share their personal food wealth with all Elk Clan members.

This broke the ice and soon the talking stick was being passed around to each person to control the flow of ideas.

As the talking stick was passed from member to member and each member shared what needed to be done, the general framework for survival began to take shape. It had a natural and inclusive feel to it.

It was as Gray Fox Running had envisioned.

But rather than trying to force hard times upon the Elk Clan and be the person blamed for the suffering, the clan members themselves described the necessary survival actions. They prescribed the necessary medicine enabling the clan to survive through the coming winter. Each speaker in turn shared additional ideas and refinements in how the clan should govern and prepare for the hard times ahead.

The elders in the tribe immediately saw what was occurring and appreciated Gray Fox Running's respect for their situation. They saw that he listened and his comments on the input showed confidence. It became clear to them that he would lead them to overcome this dire situation. They also saw he allowed the clan members full voice and input.

As Silent Hawk watched Gray Fox Running in action, he knew he had made the right decision. His leadership style was different, but it allowed each person to voice their own opinion and see that their opinion counted.

An eagle and a golden hawk circled silently overhead.

White Swan and Quiet Pheasant exchanged quiet words as they saw the totems of their sons.

This was an important sign for them.

White Swan wondered whether Gray Fox Running had seen the two birds high in the sky.

Though Taelo and Golden Hawk were young, Gray Fox Running and Red Oak had wanted them to understand the situation firsthand. They wanted the two young men to understand the serious nature of the situation. They knew the two would understand and would contribute greatly to the benefit of the Clan.

The two totems in the sky did not go unnoticed by Gray Fox Running and Red Oak.

It brought comfort to both, to know the totems of their sons were present on this serious occasion. They knew that somehow the two boys would play a key role in helping the Elk Clan.

Already the two had been the catalysts to get the clan talking. Grey Fox Running and Red Oak knew that somehow the two were as important as they themselves were to the survival of the clan.

Their totems were clearly on Taelo and Golden Hawk Hawk's minds. They commented that the two totems showing up at the same time was unusual. They were at full alert as they listened to their fathers.

Taelo pointed out to the lake. On the far side, near the yellowing cat tails swam a great white swan.

This was a surprise.

He walked over to his mother and turned her, so she could see her totem.

The swan on the lake surprised White Swam. Its presence made her realize that she too had been singled out as a person who would contribute to the recovery of the Elk Clan. It signaled to her that she would take positive but forceful action.

After all the discussion had run its course and everyone who had wanted to say something had been given a chance, Gray Fox Running and Red Oak called for all the families to bring out their food supplies.

This was a surprise to all the Clan members, but they complied.

The two leaders went about examining the food supplies the Clan had. Grey Fox Running and Red Oak realized their two families and Floating Cloud had more food and supplies then the entire Clan put together.

Some of the families must already have been on short rations.

They talked quietly to White Swan and Quiet Pheasant and Floating Cloud and asked them to redistribute the food, so each family had about the same amount. The three warned each family this food would need to be rationed to ensure the clan would survive.

It was obvious to all that the new members from the Elk Hide Clan were being very generous with their own supplies and were sharing equally with all.

This increased the respect for Gray Fox Running and Red Oak. They and their family would face the same perils as the rest of the Elk Clan. This made the Elk Clan one large family.

Gray Fox Running announced the clan would immediately go on short rations.

He spelled out specific actions for every member of the Clan. Everyone was to go out every day and gather anything that was eatable.

The older members were to fish and dry meat.

The youngsters were to go out to set snares and to use their slings to bring down birds and small game.

The younger women would gather nuts, berries, and edible roots. While the older women would prepare the food that was gathered.

One communal meal would be prepared each day.

Every member would be put to work to ensure the survival of the Clan. The care of youngest children was given over to the eldest Clan members.

Everyone would need to contribute if the Clan was to make it through the winter.

Gray Fox Running took another precaution. The entire clan would move southward toward the warmer climate by the sea. This was outside of Elk Clan domain and held some risk but the area the Elk Clan had always occupied was stressed from years of hunting and the weather change had caused the animals to move southward.

Winter and starvation held the greater risk, so they would go to a new area and risk infringing on someone else's territory.

Grey Fox Running sent out runners to the each of the other sub clans to let them know of this change in territory.

The planning was detailed and meticulous.

Silent Hawk would lead the main body, made up of the women, children, and the elderly southward toward the sea.

Advance scouts, young men too young to go on the long hunt, would be sent out to find appropriate shelter several days ahead.

The elders would then move with the young children toward the new shelter. They would set up the new camp.

The older boys would move ahead with their slings gathering the game along the way. The women would explore in all directions for potentially fruitful areas to gather nuts, berries, and roots. Those fishing would stay in a good spot until another fishing spot was found.

Gray Fox Running then surprised the Clan once again by calling for additional long hunts.

This late of a hunt was unprecedented but both Gray Fox Running and Red Oak thought it necessary for the survival of the Elk Clan. The long hunts were usually held at the end of the summer to prepare for the coming winter. It was during the long hunt this year when the Elk Clan had lost its lead hunter.

Gray Fox Running proposed a different approach to the long hunt. Instead of one large group going out together for the long hunt, three groups of six to eight hunters would go in different directions.

Each would hunt long enough to accumulate every bit of meat they could drag back. Early kill of significant size would be brought back to sustain the travels of the clan.

One group led by Gray Fox Running would go to the south and would travel the longest distance, be the farthest away and return last.

The other led by Red Oak would go to the southwest. They would remain closer to the Clan since it was in the general direction of the Clans travel. Red Oaks group would return second.

The third group, led by the most experienced remaining Elk Clan hunter, Brave Deer, would go ahead of the Clan and leave the catch for the Clan to find. His return would be based on when his team hunted the area that ended at seaside.

The long hunters were to come back to the Clan at different times.
Brave Deer would be back first in time to help set up winter camp.
Red Oak would be back second just before the winter solstice.
Gray Fox Running would return last well into the heart of winter.

In this way Gray Fox Running hoped to guide the Clan to survive the winter. The hunters would fend for themselves thus lightening the burden on the Clan. They would send back extra food and they would return at different and critical times into the long winter.

The mix of hunters also surprised the Clan. Each group would have a few of the older hunters, a few of the very young men and just a couple of hunters in their prime. This allowed for enough hunters to make up three teams.

Gray Fox Running and Red Oak had carefully plotted their hunting strategy. They anticipated the Clan would take some forty to sixty days to travel the long distance to the sea. They also knew the Clan had or would have enough food to make the trek if the short rations were maintained and the third hunting party, out in front were moderately successful.

They discussed the skill of each hunter with Silent Hawk and Brave Deer. Brave Deer would be given the more developed and seasoned hunters. The youngest and swiftest hunters were teamed up with Gray Fox Running. Red Oak took everyone else and had the largest team but the one that had the older and slower men among the hunters.

Silent Hawk voiced his concern on behalf of Red Oak.

"It seems Red Oak will have the weakest hunting team. Shouldn't we balance the teams a little better? Perhaps some of those young hunters with Gray Fox Running should be put with Red Oak," he said with some concern.

It seemed apparent to him an imbalance existed.

He was surprised but somewhat relieved by Red Oak's amused response.

"This is the only way Gray Fox Running can hope to match my team's kill. Do not worry. My team will match the output of the other two teams. Grey Fox Running will be traveling at least twice as far as any of us. He will need to have the swiftest and the youngest. He will need to condition and train them to a new way of hunting, and he will need all his luck to out hunt us," was Red Oak's confident reply.

It was obvious these two had worked together before and they were following a strategy they had agreed upon. They both were confident in the design and the deployment of the hunters.

Silent Hawk looked at the two and said no more. He knew they had been very successful hunters for the Elk Horn Clan. He hoped they would continue this success now.

Grey Fox Running and Red Oak's plan was to gather enough meat to load a travois that two men could pull. The men chosen for this chore would be the strongest and youngest of each hunting party. It would be up to them to move fast enough to catch up with the Clan. This would ensure the Clan had enough food to reach the sea and set up the winter quarters.

The primary burden for the initial supply of food was on Brave Deer and his forward team.

Grey Fox Running brought all the long hunters together in the presence of the Elders and Silent Hawk.

Gray Fox Running and Red Oak took turns describing what lay ahead. These two had hunted and traveled like this before. They were the reason the Elk Horn Clan ate well throughout the hardest winter.

"We will all jog throughout the hunt. We will jog to get into position and during all our travels," Grey Fox Running shared with the hunters.

"When a hunting party has enough for one travois, that travois will be pulled back to the Elk Clan," Red Oak continued.

"No matter how successful a hunting party has been, they will send back what they have after the passing of the first moon," Grey Fox Running resumed.

"We will go out with no food. It is up to us as we jog to kill the occasional rabbit or ground hog. If we are lucky, we will surprise a deer and eat very well," Red Oak continued the instruction to the hunting teams.

This caught the hunters and their families by surprise. Never in the memory of the Clan had a hunting party left with no food to carry them through the hunt.

All the hunters grumbled about this.

Red Oak ignored the grumbling and continued the explanations about how each major kill would be handled and how the meat would be processed. The hunters would salt and dry enough meat for cold meals for the next several weeks. At other major kills, the meat would be salted and dried over fires.

If the short supply of salt ran out the meat was to be dried without salt. When winter became cold enough the meat would be left on the animal and brought back that way.

Red Oak and Gray Fox Running took Taelo and Golden Hawk aside and told them they expected the two of them to be the right and left hand for Silent Hawk. They were to obey and help Silent Hawk lead the Elk Clan to their new home.

"Silent Hawk is a very good leader. He has had some bad luck. He has much to teach you and he has much to gain from you two. There will be a few older boys in the camp, but I am sure you two will be the best at hunting and finding food.

Red Oak and I are counting on you two to make a significant contribution to the well-being of this Clan," Gray Fox Running solemnly instructed the two of them.

Both fathers were still concerned for the well-being of their families. They would be gone for a long time. Any mishap no matter how small, could be the undoing of all they planned.

Taelo and Golden Hawk assured their fathers that they would listen and learn from Silent Hawk, and they would contribute significantly to the well-being of the Clan.

The next day, Taelo and Golden Hawk were up early. The grey morning sky was giving way to a clear blue cloudless day.

The two watched the white swan on the lake stretch its long neck straight as it awoke. Moments later it began a long flapping run across the water and slowly lifted itself off the water and began a long gentle rise.

Their totems had departed the day before after broadcasting a series of cries. The departure of the white swan seemed to signal the beginning of their role in helping their new clan.

Golden Hawk commented that he already missed the Weaver's breakfast hearth. Taelo gave him a cold piece of rabbit they had captured and cooked the previous night.

The two had gone out hunting and had returned with a dozen rabbits that they had skinned and roasted.

They cut up the rabbits so that each of the long hunters would have one piece of meat for their morning meal before they departed.

The hunting parties each gathered together and prepared to depart the camp. They talked about leaving with no food.

Those remaining behind watched as the line of silent men, jogged out of the camp.

The Clan let their good-byes ring out. Wives, children, mothers, and fathers all wished them good hunting, the blessings of the spirits.

Everyone worried that the hunters were taking no food with them.

Taelo and Golden Hawk handed each hunter a piece of rabbit wrapped in a hide as they went past and wished the hunter's luck. This surprised the hunters and pleased Grey Fox Running and Red Oak.

A cheer went up from the Clan members when they realized what Taelo, and Golden Hawk were doing.

All knew the hunters would face many trials and dangers before their return and they knew the future of the clan lay in the success of these hunters.

So began the Clan's great journey for survival.

Taelo and Golden Hawk immediately began to meet their father's challenge.

They caught rabbits, squirrels ground hogs and a few wild boar.

They gathered nuts.

They found and brought in anything eatable.

Their actions and their success began to have a positive impact on the clan as it moved slowly westward.

Taelo and Golden Hawk stopped and admired the giant oak dominating the small dimple of a valley they were entering. Its leafless branches reached high up like thousands of tendrils floating to catch the white puffy clouds floating above in the crystal blue sky. Its trunk was as wide as Golden Hawk was tall.

A huge crack that ran the full length of the trunk drew them for a closer look. In some past lightning storm, the heavens had struck the tree and wrenched a giant crack down one side. Ants and termites had eaten much of the inner wood and created a hollow interior.

The buzzing of thousands of bees created a crescendo of sound that immediately peaked their interest. The tree was now filled with a giant beehive. They approached cautiously and looked up into the crack that extended at least a spear length above their head.

They were amazed to see the layers and rows of light and dark golden honeycombs covered with bees.

Taelo reached in and carefully brushed aside the bees, cut one section of honey cone, and slowly pulled it out. After each had enjoyed a small portion of the honeycomb, Golden Hawk wrapped the remaining cone in a piece of leather. They knew they had found a priceless treasure.

They returned to the Elk Clan and displayed the honeycomb. Silver Hawk immediately called a halt to the travel when he learned of the size of the hive. This was a treasure the Elk Clan needed to leverage.

Taelo and Golden Hawk led the way to the huge knurled old Oak tree.

The older Clan members marveled at the size of the hive.

The find reaffirmed to the Elk Clan the stories shared by the Elk Horn Clan members about the strong positive omen Taelo and Golden Hawk represented.

The honey was a treasure of unmentionable value.

The Clan stopped for an extra day to weave containers and to gather the honey. It was a stop all welcomed. They had been on the trail for nine days.

The amount of honey was a great fortune for the Clan. The quantity put up by the bees also told of a hard winter ahead.

The Clan left enough honey to ensure the hive would survive. This would be a place the Elk Clan planned to come every year. It was one of the few sources of sweetening and it provided a healing balm used to heal wounds. Honey was one of the most valuable commodities the Clan could have access to.

Clan members now looked upon Taelo and Golden Hawk with new respect. The two had provided the first sign of hope to a Clan down on its luck and low on its emotional stock.

Luck seemed to be changing for the better.

And luck continued to improve. Four young warriors chanting the pull song that Red Oak had taught them were heard as they approached the Clan. They were pulling a travois loaded with the meat of one buffalo, two boar, a deer and four elk. This did not count the numerous small game, rabbits and ground hogs that was mixed in.

The Clan heard the chanting and looked back to see the approaching young men. A cheer rose up and the four pulling the travois increased their pace and the volume of their chant.

That evening after a meal of honey coated grilled buffalo the four told the story of Red Oak and his uncanny strategy of moving the game into a center area to maximize the kill.

They talked in awe about Red Oak's speed and ability to take down the buffalo. They talked about the dusk to dawn jogging hunting style.

They thanked the cooks of their honey coated dinner but told of how well all the hunters were eating.

They were eager to return to their hunting team and the following morning they took up their jogging chant and went back the way they had come.

Taelo and Golden Hawk had listened intently. They knew how their fathers hunted and were surprised at the awe that the Elk Clan hunters expressed.

From these stories and the load of meat, the Elk Clan gained even more hope. Silent Hawk noted this encouragement came from the hunting party with the weakest, slowest and oldest set of hunters. He shared this with the remaining elders in the camp.

Silent Hawk and the Clan now began to believe survival was possible.

Now the advance scouts each carried large honey containers on their backs and pulled a travois with dry or drying meat.

Several of the older men pulled a travois loaded with honey and the remainder of the meat wrapped in the scraped and salted hides. Later, the hides would be properly treated or eaten if the food supply ran low.

Periodically they came upon the game left behind by the hunting party out ahead of them. The going became slower as the Clan gathered more and more sustenance. Soon half the Clan was employed pulling food laden travois.

They all welcomed this burden of hope.

Though now the travel was slower than before, Silent Hawk was pleased the food problem was becoming less of a concern.

Now the matter of good shelter was becoming the primary issue.

Taelo and Golden Hawk now had new visions and hunting games to keep them busy. They began to practice the jogging and hunting on the run.

To their amazement and more so to the Clan's they became the source of most of the daily food gathered by the Clan. Every day they provided the food for at least half of the camp.

Silent Hawk took note and praised them for their contribution. He also made sure each Clan family recognized the contribution the two were making.

Chapter 8: Dire Wolves

Day after day the Clan slowly moved west and southwest. Their course took them through the mighty mountains and through the passes laden with snow. One narrow passage had the Clan proceeding single file. Silent Hawk, now less worried about food, worried about the Clan's ability to make the coast as planned. The mountains were a much greater challenge than anticipated.

He had also noticed that the wolves and other prey animals were beginning to follow the Clan. It was the lions and dire wolves that worried him most.

Taelo and Golden Hawk ranged wider and wider in their hunting. They began carrying their spears and stone headed clubs to supplement their slings. They did this quietly so as not to worry their mothers. The two made excellent hunting partners. They operated together with a harmony developed from years of running and playing together.

White Swan and Quiet Pheasant of course noticed that the two were now going out with spears and stone headed clubs. They wondered why but the two agreed they felt better about them going out with more protection. Like all mothers, they worried about the well-being of their offspring.

One morning, the two boys left after a hearty breakfast and set out to make the rounds. They set out jogging and looking for sign of any game. About an hour out of camp they spotted the tracks of an elk and followed it up the valley breaking away to the right. Neither thought they would find the elk, but they planned to follow the tracks a short distance up the valley cross over and then come back on the other side. They were expecting to find rabbits and other small game.

They were jogging along enjoying the scenery when they both spotted what looked like a wonderful tree to climb. It was a grand old leafless maple tree with horizontal limbs growing out parallel to the ground.

This tree commanded a small clearing between the valley sides. It was similar in size to the old oak honeybee tree they had discovered a few days before, but this tree was enticing and calling versus the bee tree that had been towering and imposing.

It stood out by itself in the middle of a snow-covered valley that surrounded it like the white feathers of a swan. Its leafless branches reached out like a mother's fingers reaching for her young. Its appeal was like a lovers look making you want to take them in your arms.

They jogged over to it jumped up on the first low limb and swung up into the second limb. They did this several times for fun. As they played and frolicked, they could have easily been mistaken for their cousins the ape. They were able to swing up between their arms and pull themselves into a sitting position on the first limb and then pull themselves up and into the second limb. They did this several times in pure enjoyment of having found the perfect climbing tree.

Taelo commented that it was too bad the Clan was just passing through and they would never be able to see this tree with its leaves gracing the valley.

After enjoying themselves, they decided to continue up the valley for a few more miles. Together they once again set off.

Just as they crested the hill beyond "their" tree, they surprised three huge dire wolves. These were the largest wolves that either of two had ever seen.

The wolves stood almost a spear high at the shoulders and were almost a half spear wide and as long as the length of the elk on the ground. The elk looked more like a small deer as it lay dead.

There was mutual surprise for both the dire wolves and the two young hunters. Time froze as the two adversaries and competitors looked momentarily at each other in surprise.

Taelo knew immediately that he and Golden Hawk were in mortal danger. The dark black eyes, more likened to pools of deep fury, of the largest wolf, burned into Taelo's mind as he shouted, "back to the tree."

In unison Taelo and Golden Hawk turned and at top speed sprinted back to the tree.

The wolves took up the chase.

Taelo's quick decision and action put the two far enough ahead of the three wolves to give them time to scramble up into the tree. This time they scrambled up with all their gear. They were standing on the second limb when the wolves arrived at the base of the tree.

The growling wolves circled the base of the tree and looked up to where the two stood.

Taelo looked down at what he thought of as three giant wolf hides and wondered how he might take them as trophies back to the Clan.

He pointed out to Golden Hawk that if they could kill the three wolves, they would be able to have a whole elk and some trophy wolf hides.

Golden Hawk looked down at the three growling wolves that were prowling around and trying to figure out how to get up to them, gave a small laugh and asked about the crazy idea Taelo had in mind.

"I wonder if they can jump as high as the first branch," Taelo conjectured.

"What are you thinking," Golden Hawk asked?

"If we tie ourselves by the waist to this top limb and have just enough length to stand on the next limb down, we may be able to tease the wolves to jump up at us. As they jump up, we could spear them and club them," Taelo explained.

"Sounds exciting, will we be able to get all three," Golden Hawk inquired as he got his length of hide rope ready?

"Well, it's worth a try," Taelo said as he tied his leather rope to the top limb.

They tied their backpacks to the limb above them and then got everything ready.

When the two were prepared, they lowered themselves down at the same time to the limb below. Immediately the wolves reacted, and the largest one jumped up to attack Taelo. The speed of his reaction surprised Taelo and he almost lost his concentration.

High overhead, the cry of an eagle pierced the morning quiet.

Taelo's attention was on the leaping wolf, and he did not hear it but out at the mouth of the valley where the Elk Clan had just arrived, White Swan heard the cry.

"We must stop. Some major event involving Taelo, and Golden Hawk is taking place. We must be ready to help if help is needed," she informed Silent Hawk.

This pressure from White Swan, Quiet Pheasant and Floating Cloud was new to Silent Hawk. Confidence and leadership seemed to run in these two families, and he noted that they always had support from those that knew the two.

Silent Hawk was surprised by the insistence of both White Swan and Quiet Pheasant. He knew the eagle was Taelo's sign. He hesitated for a few moments but then called a halt.

High overhead the eagle cried out again.

Taelo and Golden Hawk were on the first limb when the first of the wolves charged and jumped up at Taelo. The height he achieved surprised both Taelo and Golden Hawk. The wolf was going to clear the limb they were standing on!

Taelo had his spear up and drove the spear into the open mouth of the wolf. The weight and the velocity of the wolf caused the spear to go in almost the length of the wolf's body.

He hit Taelo and then the two spun around. Taelo held on to his spear with both hands and as they spun, the wolf cleared the limb and fell on the other side. Taelo lost his balance for a moment but the leather rope, up to the next limb allowed him to regain his footing and he pulled himself back upright on the limb.

The second wolf attacked Golden Hawk almost simultaneously. He too had driven his spear down into the wolf's mouth. This wolf did not clear the limb but instead hit it full force and fell to a crumpled heap below.

The impact knocked both Taelo and Golden Hawk off the branch.

The remaining wolf made several snarling, snapping jumps as the two regained their perch on the limb. It seemed confused about what had just taken place. He checked out his two dead companions.

Both Taelo and Golden Hawk jumped down and pelted him with rocks from their sling. The rocks were not enough to inflict any major damage, but they did hurt. The wolf backed away and then turned and went trotting up the valley away from them.

Taelo and Golden Hawk took stock of the situation. The event from beginning to end had only taken a few minutes. They decided to first ensure both dire wolves were dead. Then they went cautiously to the crest of the hill to verify the three wolves had indeed been the only ones at the elk kill and they wanted to make sure the third wolf had left the area.

They were now the proud owners of the dead elk and two large dire wolves.

Taelo and Golden Hawk now heard the cry of the eagle overhead and watched as it flew out of sight.

White Swan looked at Quiet Pheasant, "Well whatever those two were up to, it must be done. Taelo's totem has departed. I wish I could be sure all was well. In the past the eagle has always left after one of Taelo's successes. I hope that this is the case now."

Taelo and Golden Hawk looked at each other as the eagle's cry reached them.

"I think this was a test and we passed it," Taelo said looking at Golden Hawk. "However now we must sweat at getting the prize back to the Clan," he continued.

The wolves measured almost seven feet long and three feet high at the shoulders. They were larger than either Taelo or Golden Hawk had expected and certainly larger than they had ever heard about.

They then gutted the Elk and kept the heart, liver, and kidneys.

They skinned the wolves and kept the heads.

They carried the bodies of the wolves up the valley away from the elk. And then took the entrails to another location. They wanted this decoy spread out in case other wolves returned.

As quickly as they could they cut down two tall slender trees and used them to make a travois. They made the poles extra-long. This gave them the leverage to pull the extra heavy load. They put the weight of the elk as far to the back on the travois as possible. The elk's large rack was tied to the travois poles, and several cross poles supported the body. The legs stuck up into the air.

The two wolf hides and heads were put across the body of the elk. The travois poles went a good six feet beyond the elk's head. Even with this extra leverage the two could barely pull the load.

Luckily, the journey back out of the valley was slightly downhill.

For the remaining part of the day and well into dusk, the two pulled their load slowly back to the main trail.

They were almost exhausted and had talked about spending the night away from the camp, when up ahead they saw the campfires. Their energy level picked up and they continued to drag their large load.

Had the Clan not stopped when White Swan had asked, the boys would never have been able to catch up that day.

White Swan and Quiet Pheasant had been on the lookout for them. At first, they thought it was one of the hunting parties bringing in more food. Then they realized how small the two individuals pulling the large load looked.

Both let out a yell and the whole camp came to life. Several people ran out to help the two.

White Swan was in the lead. She first saw the elk and then she saw the dire wolf skins. She hugged both Taelo and Golden Hawk. Quiet Pheasant duplicated her hugs. Then the two mothers once again took in the sight of the two dire wolf hides and the large elk.

"Why don't we go to the central campfire? You can tell the story of your great hunt, while I prepare you some dinner," White Swan suggested.

She was overwhelmed with relief.

A combination of the older boys and a few of the elders pulled the heavy travois into the camp.

Taelo and Golden Hawk enjoyed the attention. They told of the events of the day. How they had first found and played on the tree they found so interesting.

How their play on the limbs had prepared them for their later use of the tree. How they had surprised the three large dire wolves and had bolted like lightening back to their tree.

They told of their stand and defeat of the very aggressive wolves.

The elders knew how dangerous dire wolves could be and were amazed at how the two boys had decided to kill them. Their success could not be denied but the danger had been overwhelming.

The size of the wolves put them among the largest the Clan elders had ever seen. There was no doubt that these two young men had faced and defeated an enemy often a challenge for the most developed hunting parties.

This was a story to be told many times during the coming cold winter nights.

White Swan and Quiet Pheasant wanted to put limits on the hunting of the two boys. The elders joked the two women were protecting the wolves, but they knew a pack of dire wolves could devastate even a party of many hunters. The fact the two boys had gotten the better of three of the giant dire wolves amazed everyone.

Silent Hawk took the boys aside and cautioned them about going too far from the rest of the Clan or tangling with dire wolves.

"You must be careful. As the winter takes hold these animals become more aggressive. Their hunger drives them to do what normally they would be afraid of. You have shown you are smarter than they are. You must use their hunger to make them fight each other and forget about you," Silent Hawk shared the hunting stories of old and how hunters had been able to outwit large packs of wolves.

His stories would later prove very valuable to Taelo in his own actions.

Silent Hawk, however, did not put any restraints on the two boys. How could he? When they left the protection of the camp, they were the ones out on their own. They had shown they could protect themselves as well as any of his other hunters.

He would give them advice and teach them, but he would not put any limits on what they should or should not do.

On the twentieth day, two hunters from Gray Fox Running's party were spotted ahead of the Clan. They brought with them a travois heavily loaded with some fresh but mostly dried meat.

They told of the new way of hunting they were learning, how they never walked but jogged from morning to night, of Gray Fox Running's great skill and his ability to find game. He was described as the greatest person they had ever known. They described his kill of a bull elk and cow with awe. How single handily Gray Fox Running had brought down both animals while over taking them from behind. They now knew why he was called Gray Fox Running.

He was the fastest runner among all the hunters. The stay of these two hunters was as short as the previous four.

The hunters heard of the success of the other hunters.

They learned of Taelo and Golden Hawk's triumph against the dire wolves.

It was clear to all the Clan members that they were going to survive. The hunters were eager to get back to the hunt with their new leader and share with him the improving status of the Clan. The wisdom of his leadership was already being lauded.

Taelo and Golden Hawk sat among the elders to listen. These two were now accepted as one of them. The two had an aura and intensity about them and after they brought in the elk and wolf hides, they were treated more like warriors then young boys. When these two played, those watching always learned something new. These two were indeed good luck for the Clan. Their fathers were out working to save the Clan. These two should listen and learn.

Silent Hawk was reaffirmed about his decision to step down to allow Gray Fox Running to lead. Even in absence, this new leader was inspiring the Clan. His decisions were already having positive impacts. Hope was on the rise. Survival was now all but assured.

The food supply was now enough to last to the winter solstice. However, all members except for the younger children maintained their short rations. Though now once every other day a full meal was prepared and enjoyed by all.

This treat was complements of Taelo and Golden Hawk. Their elk was used for these feasts.

The journey and the food gathering continued. Taelo and Golden Hawk continued their hunting and bringing in of small game. The Clan was entertained many times as the boys ran down a rabbit with only a stick.

This technique was used when the boys would spot the tracks of a rabbit. If it had stopped at a point that a tuft of grass formed a shelter the two would approach the hiding spot from the downwind side. When they were within jumping distance of the hiding spot they would jump forward and as the rabbit finally bolted, they would hit it on the head with their club.

The other boys in the Clan began to use this technique to catch rabbits as well.

One late evening the Clan watched in amazement as the two boys ran down a deer. The two sprinted along each side of the deer and knocked it off its feet. Once down the deer was quickly dispatched. The entire Clan again enjoyed a feast.

The going was now more routine, less stressful. But the food expected from the third hunting party led by Brave Deer was no longer found. Something had gone seriously wrong. It would not do for the poorly defended Clan to be surprised. Silent Hawk discussed defense with the Clan Elders and quietly established sentries to closely watch the surrounding territory. He recruited some of the women to stand guard.

He put his two young runners up to a new task. Taelo and Golden Hawk were to go out away from the Clan as far as they could but still see the main body. Then they were to circle around and look for anything strange or signs of someone watching them. They were not to be seen or heard by anyone.

Taelo and Golden Hawk were excited. After each meal of the day, they would go out for their mission. They imagined themselves full warriors in defense of their Clan and so they were. Even with this added responsibility, the game they brought in from these jaunts was enough to feed their families and several others.

Chapter 9: First Kill

Grey Fox Running and his team were the lead team when they departed the Elk Clan. He traveled westward for a day before turning and leading his team in a path that the sun would cross almost directly from his left.

This was new territory for him and all his team members. The snow-covered mountains, dark green sentinel pines and bare oak and maple tree covering their sides, rose to meet the sky on both sides of the wide broad valley he and his team entered. Pine, willow and many old oak and elm trees grew along the banks of a river flowing lazily down the middle of the Valley.

The team made their first camp on its snowy banks. The evening meal was light because Grey Fox Running was the main contributor of small game. The rest of the team had observed his skill at killing small game but had yet to learn be as successful.

He and Red Oak had put the fastest, lightest and the youngest Elk Clan hunters on his team.

The pace Gray Fox Running set was grueling but the men in the hunting parties were in good spirits. They quickly learned to kill small game as they jogged. They began to eat and drink well.

Grey Fox Running knew they needed to eat well to accomplish the nearly impossible task of being successful at this long hunt held in the dead of winter.

They needed to hunt well enough to get the quantity of food needed by the thirty families of the Clan. His team needed to deliver the food that would take the Clan from the solstice through to spring.

Early each morning the hunting team would rise before the sun, eat a cold morning meal prepared the day before and then set out for a day of hunting. As they traveled, they would scout around in search of game. Small game was killed using a sling. The small game was cleaned as the men jogged. This was the food for the next meal.

Smaller valleys periodically breaking off roughly ninety degrees to each side were explored and often yielded substantial kills. Once a small side valley was explored the team would once again proceed down the main valley.

When the sun was at its zenith, they stopped and prepared a meal larger than they would need. The extra food was packed and would serve as the evening meal and the breakfast for the following morning. This allowed them to hunt right up until the sun sank below the mountains rising high to their left.

After the hunt they ate a hearty but cold meal. They prepared any small game needed for breakfast and then fell asleep.

On the third day after leaving the Clan, as the line of hunters came over a rise leading to a shallow side valley, Gray Fox Running spotted a bull elk and two cows.

This was the first test of his hunting team. He barked out his single command of "Hunt" and took off after the three animals.

The team's reaction speed was mixed but they all dropped their packs and carrying two spears they followed Grey Fox Running.

They fanned out in a line behind him. One cow broke off and scrambled up a rocky slope and escaped. The bull and one cow began a run down the valley.

Grey Fox Running surged forward and moved ahead of the cow and placed the butt of his spear onto the ground and the tip of the spear on her chest. The cow was immediately skewered on the spear and dropped as Grey Fox Running surged forward to catch up to the bull and drive his second spear deep into the bull, behind the left front leg.

Grey Fox Running stopped and one of the younger hunters continued on to help bring down the mortally wounded beast.

The team gathered round the two elk and thanked the spirits of the elk for providing this abundance to the Clan. They then cut open the animals. The liver was symbolically offered to the spirits of the departed clan members. It was then sliced up and eaten raw as they continued to clean the animals.

The hunters were excited about such a good outcome. They had only been gone a few days and already they had enough meat to take back to the clan.

Grey Fox Running's speed and skill strengthened his position as their new Elk Clan leader. It was an absolute demonstration of the meaning of his name.

The next morning Grey Fox Running left two of the hunters behind to prepare the meat that would go to the Clan. He and four others went out to hunt for additional game.

He sent three team members jogging ahead for several miles along the side of the valley. He and the remaining member proceeded to move up the valley. The part of the team jogging out ahead, fanned out across the valley and then proceeded back toward Grey Fox Running and the other hunter. This created an area with hunters coming together from two directions.

The team killed a buffalo, two elk, a deer, and a young boar.

This extremely successful hunt meant the team would spend the remainder of the day building a travois and then taking the meat laden travois back to the processing area.

Grey Fox Running carried the young boar back to the camp while the rest of the team worked at bringing the remainder of the hunt back. He skinned and salted the boar and put it on a spit. He stuffed the inside with tubers and other greens he found near the riverbanks and then put it to roast over the open fire.

He assigned one of the hunters to periodically turn the roasting boar.

He was following White Swan's instructions on how to best cook over a fire.

He periodically brushed salt and water as the meat began to bake and the smell of the cooking meat drew every hunter over to look at the feast they would soon enjoy.

They gathered together for their first of many celebration dinners. The young boar would provide an evening feast and tasty meals for the next few days.

Gray Fox Running took this time to let his men talk about the hunt and any other topics on their minds. Up until this time he had kept the talk to a minimum. He knew his men were wary and had many questions about his leadership.

They had never experienced this kind of travel and hunting. In two days, they had traveled almost eighty miles and had their first load of meat to be sent back to the Clan.

It was time for Grey Fox Running to have his team foster the mind set of success.

The men discussed their initial concerns about leaving the camp with no food supply. They were surprised at how many small game they had learned to catch on the run.

Though their muscles were still sore from the pace they were setting, they were amazed at how good they felt.

To a man they praised Grey Fox Running for leading them and promised to follow him in whatever lay ahead.

Grey Fox Running was pleased but he knew they didn't know what their promise might mean in the coming winter and the days beyond.

The next day Grey Fox Running left two additional men to prepare the meat for travel.

He and the two remaining hunters went out for the hunt. He would continue in this fashion until all the hunters were needed to process the kill. He knew he had several days before he needed to send his catch back. This re-supply of the Elk Clan would need to carry them until the solstice.

The location they had chosen to process the meat was near a small clear stream coming down from one of the mountains into the main river that ran down between the two ranges. Each morning the part of the team assigned to hunt would leave in the direction of the next side valley to be hunted. They used their travois to bring back their kill to the location by the stream.

The hunt and meat processing continued successfully for ten days. Much of the meat was dried using a fire drying technique. The team did not have enough salt to properly season the drying meat. This meant the meat dried with little flavor.

The hunters would long be teased by their wives, mothers, and spouses to be, about the lack of quality of their drying technique. They in turn would recall their own growth in confidence that the Clan would survive because of their efforts.

Grey Fox Running Running's team had the longest distance to travel to take the meat. He wanted to keep as many hunters as possible hunting versus pulling the load of frozen meat back to the Clan. His drying approach was effective in quickly reducing tons of meat into what could be brought back by two strong hunters using a travois.

Finally, all the meat was ready and properly bundled. These bundles were arranged on a large travois.

Gray Fox Running and the remaining hunters continued on. The two young hunters were told the general direction the hunting party would travel and how to proceed back from the Clan.

He also gave them directions on how to cross the valley and the mountains to intersect the path the Elk Clan was traveling.

Gray Fox Running and the remaining hunters would leave a trail of stone piles marking their trail and they would light a smoking fire each morning and evening to aid the returning hunters. He instructed the two pulling the travois to mark their trail frequently to ensure they would not get lost.

Navigation in the vast expanse of the mountains and valleys they were traveling was a huge challenge. The hunters all had practical travel capabilities, but it was very easy to get disoriented. Such a mistake could be a deadly one this late into the winter season. The mountain nights were very cold. Getting lost meant death.

Grey Fox Running made a point of impressing this on the younger hunters and on coaching them on how to navigate using the sun, key mountain peaks and the evening stars and moon. His teachings were greatly increasing the survival capabilities of his team.

Earlier, Red Oak had waved to Grey Fox Running as he led his team past the first team's turn off point. His team would travel in a more westerly direction than Grey Fox Running. His team did not have as natural of a path as Grey Fox Running's team. They were crossing the foothills to the west of the mountain range Grey Fox Running was in and they would cross the mountains to the west.

This meant Red Oak was traveling up and down from one valley to the next. His team would exert much more effort during their travels.

Red Oak paced his team allowing them to acclimate to the strenuous travel they would experience.

He set a pace and kept a routine similar to Grey Fox Running and his team. He used a different but as successful hunting technique. At each promising valley in his direction of travel, he would stop and send two-thirds of his party on ahead along the ridge. Two and three hours out, two hunters would stop and position themselves on each side of the valley. Four hours out, the remaining hunters spread themselves in a semicircle across the valley and proceeded to march back up the valley.

The group left behind also spread themselves in a semicircle across the valley. They proceeded slowly up the valley. Small game was brought down using slings and processed as the group marched on. A deer or elk was quickly gutted and hung up away from predators. It was left as close to the kill point as possible. Once the hunters gutted and hung up an animal, they would run back to join the remaining group.

The net of hunters slowly and continuously closed in toward each other. Each kill being handled by a few while the rest maintained the hunting line across the valley.

A good valley would yield several elk and deer. Occasionally the team also bagged a buffalo.

The kill from the first valley was so large, four hunters were needed to pull back the load to the Elk Clan.

The scene at the campfire the evening of the first major valley harvest was filled with excited hunters sharing their adventures. They sat by a small river around the fire and discussed the hunting they were doing and the fact they now felt the Elk Clan would survive the winter.

Red Oak had instructed the hunters to only kill the male deer, or elk. Yearling males and females were also fair game. This approach allowed the valley to stay fertile while ensuring an abundant take for the hunters. This approach was discussed in length among the group.

Some thought they should take all the animals, but the rest sided with Red Oak especially since they were already taking a record amount.

The entire group was impressed with Red Oak's hunting ability. He was the fastest among them. His keen insight seemed to make the difference in the outcome of the hunt. He was always at the right spot at the right time.

His men began to watch and to respond to Red Oak's leadership.

The processing of the meat took all of them almost a week. Since his team was closer to the Clan, his team was taking much of the meat back fresh. Red Oak picked four of his strongest young men and sent them on their way back to the Clan with the kill that they had taken.

He and Grey Fox Running had strategically loaded his team with the slower but stronger men. This allowed Red Oak to send back heavier loads to the Clan and allowed Red Oak's group to send back fresh meat. Fresh meat weighed significantly more than dried.

It would be delivered earlier to the Clan and ensure their intermediate food needs.

This approach maximized the contribution of the slower and stronger members without slowing down or hampering the hunting of the fastest group. By working together in this fashion, the kill was maximized and the energy to make the kill dramatically reduced. Red Oak and Grey Fox Running had discussed and agreed on this approach.

Red Oak's group would travel half the distance of Grey Fox Running's group. They could travel more slowly, hunt very effectively and compete with the faster moving team Grey Fox Running led. By fitting the speed profile in this manner each team was designed to make the maximum hunting contribution.

The men on Red Oak's team were as inspired by him as those with Grey Fox Running were of their leader. They had never been led on a hunt by better leaders and they had never enjoyed the hunting success they were currently experiencing.

Grey Fox Running and Red Oak knew they had the right survival strategy. The hunting success of their teams assured the success of the strategy.

Their only remaining worry was about the winter quarters the Elk Clan needed to survive the coming winter months. They had left this in the hands of Silent Hawk, White Swan, and Quiet Pheasant.

Chapter 10: Fight for Survival

Brave Deer watched as Grey Fox Running and then Red Oak led their team in the south and southwest directions. He and his team traveled almost directly westward on the path the Elk Clan would follow. He led the group of older seasoned hunters.

They had all been instructed on how to travel and gather food as they jogged but they lacked the confidence and hands-on capability that Red Oak and Grey Fox Running provided to the other two hunting teams, and they did not fare as well.

They did succeed in killing several elk that they hung up in a tree and left for the Elk Clan that would follow their tracks. This also gave them enough meat to carry with them for their daily food needs.

They left a trail of food for the Clan and felt very good about their performance. On the tenth cycle of the sun, they came to a promising valley, and they turned and followed its northwest direction. They hoped to take down some elk or deer and return to the main valley they had been following.

They surprised a large rhinoceros and were chased by it farther up into the valley in the opposite direction they wanted to travel.

After their escape Brave Deer called a halt and the team set up camp for the night in an out cropping of rock that gave them a defensive position.

Several of them had been members of the team that had faced a similar surprise by a rhino. Their leader had been gored and died. They did not want to go directly back down the valley and face this rhino again.

The next morning the hunting party continued to travel up through the valley. They were hunting both for game and for a way out toward the west. The hunting was strangely sparse and the forest ominously silent. It seemed this valley had already been hunted out. They wondered if some other group was ahead of them.

On the third day into the valley, they ran into their competition.

A large dire wolf pack had hunted this territory clean. The dire wolves were hungry and were fighting with each other. The lead wolf was ready to lead the group from the valley.

He had brought his growing pack down from the cold northern territories. His success and the overpowering of the packs whose territories he invaded had continuously grown his pack.

The only problem facing this very large pack was finding enough food. The leader of the pack was ready to move on when a fresh and new scent worth following came to him. The pack spotted their quarry ahead of them. This was a new animal to this dire wolf leader. The quarry was large but seemed defenseless. The pack would eat well this day.

Brave Deer had been following a game trail when the rear scout shouted a warning. Quickly, the hunting party formed a circle ready for defense. This surprised their oncoming enemy and bought the time needed for Brave Deer to move his men to a more defendable location. Ahead along the trail he spotted a large boulder. There was abundant dead wood all around.

Brave Deer deployed the men to gather wood and to move some stones up closer to the large boulder.

He made sure there was no other way to the top of the boulder.

The gathered wood was placed in a semi-circle around in front of the boulder. Additional wood was taken to the top of the boulder.

He continued to have the men gather wood.

He counted more than fifty dire wolves. This was the largest pack he had ever heard of, and they seemed unusually brave. The wolf pack surrounded the boulder and sat on their haunches watching the hunters.

"They must be desperately hungry to stalk us," Brave Deer shared with his team.

"Did you see the size of these wolves? Their leader seems to be twice the normal size," one of the hunters replied.

There was much discussion and concern about the bold action on the part of this pack of wolves.

They did not seem to know the humans as a threat.

"Let's get ready for the night. We will take turns keeping the fires going. We will keep watch in pairs. Be careful when you put the wood on the fire. They may be brave enough to rush you when you go to the edge of the camp.

The leader of the wolf pack circled the camp. The smell of food had him drooling. These creatures were different from any other game he had led his very successful pack in hunting. They were able to defend themselves with a power he did not know how to overcome. All night long he continued to circle the camp. He tested the perimeter but there was no way in.

Brave Deer awoke the next morning to find the wolves still gathered around the camp. He led a small group out to gather additional wood. They had not gone far before they were challenged and had to fight their way back to the camp. They had gotten enough wood for the next day, but the hunters knew they could not stay in their present location and survive.

From the vantage of the large boulder, a cliff could be seen about a half a mile away. It appeared there was a crack running up the cliff.

"See that crack going up the cliff? We are going to make a break and run for our lives. Once there we will climb into the crack, move up, and defend ourselves against this pack of wolves," Brave Deer shared his plan with his men.

"When it gets dark, we will light a fire on the valley floor. The moon will provide us enough light to run through the forest. We will need to jump through the fire and get out ahead of it," Brave Deer continued to coach his team.

The wind was blowing in the right direction. The moon rose and when it was at its height, they lit the underbrush and watched as the flames began to travel in the direction they needed to go. Carefully the hunting party followed closely behind the flames. They knew as soon as the wolves got behind the flames, they would quickly follow the scent of the group.

The leader of the dire wolves was caught by surprise. The flames posed a serious threat. His pack moved away from the flame. He led them back around the flame to where he expected his prey to be. They were gone! Quickly he followed their scent. It led to the ashes where the fire had been started. Faintly he caught their scent among the ashes. They were following the flames! He would trap them between his pack and the flames. He let out a howl of anticipation.

The howl was what Brave Deer had been waiting for.

"Now let's move through the flames and get out ahead of it. We will need to run for our lives. It will either be the flames or the wolves if we are not fast enough," he shouted as he dashed through a low point in the flames ahead of him.

No one wanted to be left behind and all quickly followed Brave Deer through the flames. Everyone experienced a few burns but all of them were quickly out in front of the fire and running for their lives toward the cliff ahead and the crack in its face.

The pack caught up with the flames just in time to see the last of their prey leap into the flames and disappear.

This was more than the leader could handle. He turned away from the flames and led his pack to the stream they had been using as their base.

Brave Deer was the first to reach the crack in the cliff. He turned to look behind and was relieved to see the dire wolves were not following. The trick with the fire had worked. He checked all his hunters and other then a few minor burns and cuts all seemed to be in good condition. They took a few minutes to scan the cliff and decided to take a trail leading up the face.

"As we go up this cliff trail let's put some brush barriers to prevent the wolves from following us," Brave Deer instructed as he led the team up the trail.

They hiked slowly up the steep trail throughout the night. By early morning they were at the top of the cliff. They decided to jog along the ridge in what they thought was a westerly direction.

By late afternoon they realized the ridge had taken them more north then west.

An elk was spotted, and the team surrounded it and then closed in to take it down. The elk's reaction was too late, and it met two spears as it tried to make an escape.

They pulled the elk over to a series of boulders that provided a place to set up a defensible camp.

They had just completed skinning the elk and sectioning it so they could transport it when the wolf pack was spotted by one of the team who shouted a warning.

The wolf pack had followed the scent of their quarry and then they had picked up the scent of the blood of the elk.

Brave Deer had his men threw out the entrails and scrap pieces of the elk. The pack found the entrails, fought over the scraps, and discarded parts. This delayed the pack long enough for Brave Deer and his team to prepare to defend themselves.

The leader of the dire wolf pack could smell the blood of the recently killed elk as he circled the camp. He could smell the remainder of the carcass inside the ring of the camp. He moved in toward the camp. This time he ignored the fires and attacked immediately.

Brave Deer shouted a warning as the wolf leader ignored the fire ring around the camp and led the wolf pack directly at his quarry.

Brave Deer called for a tight fighting ring and for the team to fight for their lives.

He led the team in a loud vocal roar that slowed the wolves down a little.

He shouted for his men to kill as many as they could with their spears. Then using clubs and hand knifes they continued following his instruction as the wolves charged the team. They stood in a ring and fought the wolves from all sides.

The battle was unbelievably fierce. The majority of the first wave of wolves died as the flint pointed spears pierced through their chest and cut through their hearts. But the second wave made it past the spears, and it was a hand to wolf fight.

The fact the wolves would dare to attack a group of hunters was unthinkable.

There were wolves laying stunned, wounded and dead all around the circle of hunters.

The growling and snarling, the howling and grunting came from both groups.

Several of the hunters had been severely wounded. They retreated into the center of their fighting circle. They cared for their wounds as quickly as possible and then rejoined the fight.

The leader of the wolf pack watched to see which one was the leader of these strange creatures. He finally made his move and attacked Brave Deer. The timing of his attack came as Brave Deer delivered a fatal blow to another wolf.

Brave Deer's swift reaction of deflecting the wolf's leap with his left arm saved his life. Instead of the targeted throat, the wolf clamped down on Brave Deer's shoulder.

As Brave Deer fell backwards, he drove his spear into the huge body above him. He could hear the bone in his arm crack.

Sharp Beaver, the warrior standing next to Brave Deer clubbed the wolf with his war club. A third hunter drove a second spear in from above and through the wolf's body.

The giant dire wolf leader collapsed on top of Brave Deer but did not let go of his prey.

The fight went on with Brave Deer trapped below the dying wolf. He could see the light going out in the eyes of the giant wolf.

The remainder of the pack backed away from the fight. Their leader was missing and most of their pack was dead. Their leader was dead. They backed away from the circle of fighters and away from the circle of fire. Several of the wolves were carrying the burns they had received during the fight.

The remaining wolves stayed in the forest surrounding the camp.

Several team members freed Brave Deer from the giant wolf's mouth.

Still in a stunned and disoriented state, Brave Deer instructed the team to feed a quarter of the elk in several chunks to the remaining wolves.

He had the wolf hides and what was left of the elk distributed among the team as he had them prepare to retreat southwest toward the coast.

Brave Deer had a deep cut on his face, a bite on his left forearm where he had protected himself and his right collar bone was broken where the wolf had clamped down with his first bite.

Brave Deer could not use his left arm. He had his shoulders strapped to a two-finger thick limb to hold his shoulders square so it would give the broken collar bone, that he personally set for himself, a chance to heal.

Sharp Beaver stitched the gash on Brave Deer's face and cleaned and closed the wound on his forearm.

Another hunter had his left leg broken just below his knee. Brave Deer supervised the setting and splinting of the hunter with the broken leg bones. A travois was made for him to ride on. He would ride with the wolf hides and elk meat.

Everyone had suffered bites on their arms or legs. They all carried the marks of the fierce battle that was fought.

Brave Deer knew their only hope was to escape the wolves.

There were twenty-seven dead wolves including the giant leader.

The able team members skinned the dead wolves and threw the carcasses out around the camp as instructed.

He would not be able to carry his belongings on his shoulders and would need to pull a small travois with his belongings and the hide behind him. He had this travois strapped to his waist.

Brave Deer thanked the team for saving his life and made the point he could not have killed the wolf pack leader by himself, but he was claiming the giant hide.

"I will wear his hide with pleasure. This wolf cost us all our hunting success and he led this pack in a way that threatened all of us," Brave Deer said as he watched the hide put on the travois he would be pulling.

When everyone was ready to travel, several of the team threw parts of the elk as far away as they could and in the opposite direction they planned to travel.

Once this was done and the remainder of the wolf pack began to fight over the meat, the hunting party hurried westward toward the coast.

Brave Deer led the way and moved as fast as he could. He put the three healthiest hunters behind the hunting party as their rear guard in case the wolves continued the chase.

The travel was down the mountain, through a long valley toward the sea. The team could not move very fast. They continued to worry about the wolves, but they did not encounter them again.

Brave Deer and his team took almost two weeks to make it to the coast. The team was exhausted, and he called a halt to their travels, and they spent the several days camped in recovery by the seashore.

They would have a difficult story to tell the elders, but they felt lucky that they were all returning.

Brave Deer and the rest of his team knew they had been lucky and were happy to begin the travel southward down the coast in search of the Elk Clan.

Chapter 11: Winter Camp

 The continuing winter snows and the challenging terrain as they crossed through the thick pine forest that towered over them often blocking the little sun the day offered made their travel frustratingly slow.

Silent Hawk was growing more concerned as the days became increasingly colder. He made sure everyone had protection from the cold and the snow. The Clan needed to find a good winter home.

The Elk Clan members knew their fate, whatever it would be was quickly descending upon them. They had traveled for fifty-eight cycles of the sun.

The mountains were finally growing shorter on the horizon behind them, but the snow-covered hills and thick brush and trees slowed their progress.

Taelo and Golden Hawk ranged far and wide. They out distanced the lead scouts and were first to reach the ocean. They arrived as a storm rolled in from the sea. They marveled at the thunder of the waves sweeping into shore. They waded in waist deep and experienced the strong surge and freezing cold of the saltwater waves. The water was cold but warmer than the air. They wanted to feel the power that accompanied the thunderous sound.

They left as the advance scouts reached the beach and were back in time to receive these same scouts back to camp.

When the scouts reported they had reached the sea, Silver Hawk called the council of elders together to discuss how to go about finding the winter quarters for the Clan.

He suggested that two scouting groups would go in search of suitable winter quarters for the Clan. There would be at least three persons in each group. They would travel along the coast until suitable quarters were found or for three days. Then each group would return.

The Clan would move immediately to the first suitable quarters found. If a team returned to find the Clan gone, they knew to follow to the area where suitable quarters had been found.

Silver Hawk was worried about the fact that Brave Deer and his party had not returned. He was afraid the clan might face an enemy and did not want to leave the Elk Clan unguarded.

To ensure he would have enough able warriors to protect the camp, he took the unusual action of asking White Swan to take the lead of one of the scouting groups in search of a suitable place for the winter camp.

She confidently accepted and asked Soft Down, a young woman in the Clan, to accompany her and Quiet Pheasant. White Swan had watched Soft Down on their trip to the coast and wanted to give her recognition if front of the Clan.

Silent Hawk would lead a second group toward the northwest.

Taelo and Golden Hawk were two of the young men he was leaving behind. He instructed them on keeping watch while he was gone.

Taelo and Golden Hawk were to continue their surveillance of the surroundings and they were to report any suspicious activity to the Clan elders.

Taelo and Golden Hawk was proud that their mothers had been selected to lead the search for the Clan winter home. He and Golden Hawk watched as the two and Soft Down left the beach camp toward the south jogging alone the water's edge.

He and Golden Hawk followed their progress as they traveled parallel through the forest on their surveillance route. They stopped when they reached their limit and watched the three continue on their way. Then they dutifully turned into the forest on their route around the camp.

White Swan, Quiet Pheasant, and Soft Down jogged mile after mile along the beach looking for the Clan's winter home. The dark green tops of the towering pines touching the blue sky on their left blocked the view of the white snow-covered mountains that lay beyond them. Ahead they could see the cliffs that might offer a coveted cave or outcropping that could serve as the shelter the Clan would need.

They jogged all day until almost sundown and then found a place up in the woods where they could shelter for the night. They shared their warmth as they huddled in a single buffalo hide for the night.

The next day seagulls flying inland gave them hope. They continued and found a small cove protected from the sea by a long finger like spit of high rocky cliffs running out to sea and then hooking back around the beach. This formed a protected cove with rocks on the beach to break up any waves making their way in around the finger.

They carefully searched along the cliff lining the shore on the land side of the cove. A small tumbling stream of fresh water falling down a large crack in the cliff formed a short freshwater canal that ran into the cove.

The broad area below the cliff running out to the shore provided the space needed for a lodge and individual habitats needed for the Clan. There were enough stones of various sizes that White Swan knew a clan lodge and the individual homes for families could be built.

There was no cave, so they would need to exert their labor to make this into a suitable place to winter.

They all gave a prayer to the good mother. With some hard work, this would be a good home for the Elk Clan.

The three talked through what needed to get done as they set a swift pace back that brought them back on their third day.

The journey of the two search parties was a contrast in speed and style.

Silent Hawk moved cautiously west and along the forest line. Fearing the sea and its storms, he was looking for a place in among the trees.

His team traveled out for three days and found nothing.

Taelo and Golden Hawk had explored a fair distance in both directions along the coast. They were sure White Swan, and her team would find the best winter quarters.

They were the first to see White Swan returning along the beach and ran back to alert those waiting in camp.

White Swan, Quiet Pheasant and Soft Down shared the description of the cove and beach area.

White Swan then requested that everyone follow her down to the Clan's winter home.

A significant part of the Clan wanted to wait until Silent Hawk returned, or the missing hunters returned before committing to the area White Swan had described.

White Swan quietly but firmly pointed out it could be several days before Silent Hawk's return.

The appropriate action for the Clan to take had already been agreed upon before he had left. The time could best be used to set up the winter camp and gather wood and water.

White Swan signaled Quiet Pheasant and Soft Down and they gathered their belongings.

"We will lead you to your new winter homes. It is a beautiful place. You must be brave, and you must act if you wish to survive this winter. We have little time for arguments. They keep us from building our winter homes. Follow me now," White Swan spoke calmly but forcefully.

Taelo called loudly to Golden Hawk to follow Silent Hawk's directive and to follow White Swan down the beach.

Floating Cloud and Quiet Rabbit stood up and declared they were going to go to their new home.

Busy Bee and her parents were next.

She was followed by Talking Wren and her parents.

Quiet Rabbit, Busy Bee and Talking Wren had become close friends that had been taught by Taelo and Golden Hawk to hunt with the sling and other weapons and they were huge admirers of White Swan and Quiet Pheasant.

White Swan turned and set off. She did not look back. Slowly, grudgingly the Clan members began to follow.

White Swan, Quiet Pheasant and Soft Down exchanged a look of pride and gave each other a hug as they continued down the beach to their new winter home.

"I am amazed the Elk Clan elders have granted you so much respect," Soft Down said as she followed the two and saw the rest of the Clan was doing the same.

"Leadership is something you must demonstrate. When you do it properly, then few can stand in its way and most will follow," White Swan replied over the thunder of the breaking waves.

Taelo and Golden Hawk exchanged looks with each other. They were extremely proud of their mothers and openly showed it.

The Clan set out along the beach. White Swan and Quiet Pheasant were in the lead. Soft Down and her family quickly caught up.

Taelo and Golden Hawk explored the forest sides of the beach as the Clan proceeded.

White Swan was discussing with Quiet Pheasant, Soft Down and Floating Cloud the work required in setting up the winter camp. In her mind she divided up the work.

White Swan was in a continuous dialogue with her three supporters. They evaluated everyone's capability and organized the work assignments. They planned to have the camp functional and be able to provide the minimum survival shelter needed by the Elk Clan in a seven-sun cycle.

Then weather permitting, the comfort features and additional individual shelters could be built.

As the Clan proceeded eastward along the beach, White Swan spent the time moving among the older men and women discussing what needed to be done. She was establishing the relationships that would allow everyone to work together with as little friction as possible. She did not want any head-on conflicts with the Elders.

By the time they arrived at the inlet to the cove, everyone knew what to do and all were anxiously looking forward to getting their winter quarters built.

The cove presented itself like a person leaning forward and holding their arm above their face to ward off the worst of a rain or a blowing wind. The Clan stopped and took in the towering cliffs, the stone arch extending out to sea to form the cove and the stream falling down the waterfall to the stream below.

They now appreciated what White Swan had said.

The sea would provide a way to get salt and fish. The cliffs and the hooked spit of land would shield the site from the worst of the winter storms.

Quickly and efficiently the Clan went to work.

There was general agreement that White Swan had been right to push them to follow her.

White Swan was now recognized and listened to as a leader in her own right. She quietly went about ensuring the work proceeded smoothly, harmoniously, and efficiently. The first order of business would be to build the main lodge.

The cove area was heaven, to Taelo and Golden Hawk. They climbed the cliffs. They followed the small stream above the waterfall and found the spring where it vigorously ran out below a section of the cliff.

They went above the camp and rolled down stones from the top to help in building the lodge.

This action quickly led the planners to move the camp away from the base of the cliff beyond where a person could throw a large stone. They did not want to put themselves at the mercy of attackers coming in from the cliffs.

Taelo and Golden Hawk became the primary explores of the area surrounding the camp.

White Swan became the supervisor directing the building of the main lodge. This building was designed so half to two thirds was built into the ground. Several of the older men knowledgeable on the procedure to properly build and drain this structure supervised the selection and layout of the site.

The Clan members, supervised by these elders, then set out to excavate the dirt and rocks. A thirty-foot wide and fifty-foot-long area situated on high ground was marked off. A trench about three feet wide and four feet deep was dug around the perimeter of the area that would hold the building structure.

The dirt was carefully laid up along the outside of the trench. Stones of the size of a head or larger were put to the inside area of the building for use in building the lower part of the walls. The smaller stones were piled in one area and would be used as fill between the larger stones.

The digging was hard cumbersome work. Building the main lodge was usually the responsibility of the men of the Clan. Since most of the able-bodied men were hunting, it was now being done mostly by the women with the help of a couple of older men and many of the children. This main building would be the pride of the women both young and old, of the old men rejuvenated by the need of the clan, and of the young boys inspired by being needed.

The trench was dug in three cycle of the sun. This was a record, but everyone was working as hard as they could from sunrise to the setting of the sun. They knew they needed to have a warm place to escape the cold.

The stones required to build a retaining wall around the entire compound were gathered up from the beach, the campsite area and from the cliffs.

Everyone carried, dragged, and rolled the stones needed to build the wall.

The retaining wall came up and the digging continued. Basket-after-basket was passed down the line toward the outside perimeter. The dirt piled up on the outside would be pushed up against the wall that would extend above the ground. The lower wall would be stone, and the top third would be made of woven small branches covered with the dirt being piled up. The dirt would provide insulation from the winter cold.

The materials to make the roof and interior were obtained from the surrounding forest and Clan supplies.

The roof structure was made up of logs anchored on the stone wall and tied together with raw hide. It was first covered with a series of mats made of small branches woven into larger long slender branches. This was then covered with several layers of hide.

Strategic vents to control the comfort of the interior were positioned along the circular wall and in the roof structure.

All the hides of the Clan were gathered. Unless the long hunters brought back additional hides to replace the ones being used, the Clan would spend the winter as a group inside of the gathering house because there were no additional materials for the individual huts.

All usable hides were needed to make the covering of the large central lodge.

The Clan had been at the site for about seven cycles of the sun when Silent Fox returned from his search. He had not found any acceptable place. He was surprised that the main lodge structure was up and already provided significant protection from the weather.

He was pleased with the progress of the Clan and openly thanked White Swan for her excellent leadership.

"It is good we have made so much progress in getting ready for winter. The signs are for a storm at any moment. We will need the long hunters to bring in more hides and meat," the medicine man informed the group.

He was openly voicing what everyone had already realized.

The final touches were just being made to the great lodge when a lookout at the top of the cliff spotted a hunting party returning.

Brave Deer, still pulling his personal travois was leading his ragtag group of hunters.

The local game and fishing had increased the Clan's food supply to the point White Swan had suggested it was time to celebrate so the Clan prepared a welcome home dinner in anticipation of the first returning hunting team.

As Silent Hawk led the long hunters up to the lodge, a hush went through the Clan.

Brave Deer, limping as he came in, now had a fresh scar healing on the side of his face and had one arm still in a sling. He was greeted by his partner and Busy Bee his daughter. The three hugged and tears could be seen in the eyes of all three.

The hunters looked grim. Each had a visible wound or scar.

Wives with tears in their eyes approached their husbands. Children at first afraid of their long absent fathers were quickly held in hugs.

This was not the triumphant return Brave Deer had wanted but he was relieved to be back and that all his hunters were back with him.

The Clan's medicine man quickly began to examine and treat the wounded hunters.

White Swan organized the women, and the Great Lodge was prepared for its first use.

It would hold all the Clan members as they celebrated the return of the first of the long hunters.

Tonight, the story of Brave Deer and his men would be heard.

A well bandaged but severely wounded Brave Deer stood before the Clan to tell the story of his group of hunters.

"Our hunting went well when we first began. As you know we left the game from these first successes for you to find. Then we turned up a promising valley.

We traveled north just beyond a huge old maple tree commanding an area just up from the entrance of the valley. There we surprised a woolly rhino. We were in his territory. He chased us farther up into the valley. The valley seemed to have been thoroughly hunted out. We wondered if we had encroached on another Clan's hunting grounds. Then to our surprise we became the hunted. A pack of very aggressive and surprisingly aggressive dire wolves attacked us," Brave Deer began his story.

Taelo and Golden Hawk looked at each other as they heard Brave Deer describe "their" tree and the place the two of them had confronted the dire wolves. They commented that they had been lucky not to have run into the wooly rhinoceros.

"Brave Deer's knowledge and wisdom saved all of us from the most aggressive pack of wolves I have ever experienced or heard about. The pack was at least sixty strong. The leader of the pack, the skin which is now being held up was the largest wolf that I have ever seen," one of the season hunters continued.

White Swan commented to Quite Pheasant, "Taelo and Golden Hawk have the same size hides. It indeed was a miracle the two did not end up like Brave Deer's team."

"After being surrounded for two days by this large pack of wolves, Brave Deer had us light a ground fire. The wind was blowing toward a cliff about a mile away. Brave Deer had us follow, the flames.

When the wolves began their attack, Brave Deer led us through the fire, and we all ran for our lives toward the cliffs. We thought we had lost the wolf pack," Sharp Beaver continued the story.

"The next day we cornered and killed an elk and were just getting it butchered when the wolf pack showed up again.

Even though we were inside a ring of fires, the pack leader did not hesitate but attacked immediately. The battle was intense and we almost lost," Wild Raven picked up the story.

"Then the giant wolf leader directly lunged at and caught Brave Deer by the shoulder. Brave Deer survived only by his quick reaction and the act of driving his spear through the wolf. The wolf died on top of Brave Deer and even in death would not let go. We had to pry his mouth loose to get Brave Deer free.

We killed two thirds of the pack. When the leader was killed the remainder of the pack backed away," Wild Raven stood and silently looked around at those listening before sitting down.

"Even though he was sorely wounded, Brave Deer organized us to move out and come home. Many of us were wounded. Standing Buffalo, who bravely fought and killed many of wolves was bitten several times in the leg and could not walk. We thought his leg was broken but found out later that it was not. We are thinking of changing his name for making us pull him while he sat comfortably on the travois.

His new name is Sitting Buffalo one of the team said quietly and got a laugh from the listening Clan members.

Brave Deer pulled a small travois attached to his waist with his possessions and the dire wolf leaders hide on it. We made a ragtag group coming down from the mountains to the sea. We fed the remaining wolves more than half of the elk. Luckily, they no longer followed us. I do not think we could have fought them off again," Sharp Beaver continued the story.

"I apologize for our poor performance. We are pleased to be here and happy that even though we failed in our long hunt, the others have been successful, and you have found such a good winter camp. As we recover, we will do all we can to contribute to the clan," Brave Deer finished the story.

"Brave Deer, the food you first left us made a big difference. It came at just the right time. It gave the Elk Clan hope. Your return is a gift in itself. We all recognize your accomplishment. We understand your disappointment in the hunt.

Your clan has been doing its share and together we will survive the winter. You will be able to help us catch the fish in the cove and finish building our winter homes.

Do not dwell on your hunt but at being here with your families," Silent Fox spoke elegantly.

The Clan gave a loud cheer.

All the Clan members vigorously pounded the lodge floor and gave a loud hurrah.

The Elk Clan now had two more long hunt teams to welcome home in the near future.

Chapter 12: .Long Hunt Success

The drying rack fires were burning low, and he watched two hunters go out to gather wood. The camp had been busy drying meat since they had arrived. Burley Bear had been watching them for several cycles of the sun. He wondered how they had accumulated so much meat.

The bitter cold reached into his sleeping hide and rudely poked its cold fingers to awaken a weary Red Oak. An inner sense urged him awake. He had dreamed of a raid on his team. Without moving or indicating he was awake; he silently studied the area around the campsite.

The fires were burning low. This immediately alerted him and brought him fully awake.

He could not locate any of the night watch. He quietly prodded awake the hunter in front of him with the tip of his spear. He left the tip of his spear on the base of the hunter's neck. As expected, the hunter was quickly alert and did not move.

Red Oak signaled the hunter to do the same to the next in line. Quickly the entire party was awake and alert. Silently they withdrew into the woods and began to circle around toward the stream.

The quiet morning air seemed especially unfriendly. A disturbing silence hung in the cold gray morning.

He and his hunters had now been out for almost two months. Winter had launched its army of freezing winds, extremely cold nights, and blustery snow.

The successful hunting team was now headed back to the Clan. Red Oak and his hunters had camped at this place for the past week. A small stream provided water and the surrounding forest yielded an abundance of firewood.

With relief, Red Oak surprised the two sentries who had the early morning watch. They were returning with more wood for the campfires.

Most leaders would have assumed the fires had run low because of the lack of wood and gone back to the camp. However, for the last several days Red Oak had felt someone watching. Red Oak's senses were still on edge.

He told his men to prepare for a fight and that something or someone was close at hand and was watching them. He sent three of his hunters to look around the edge of the camp to see if they could find any sign of someone watching the camp.

High on the hill on a rocky outcropping, Burley Bear quietly backed away from the edge of the boulder he was lying on. He did not know how the leader sensed his presence, but it was obvious he knew he was being watched.

Burley Bear had found this camp of new ones a few sun cycles before and had decided to quietly observe them.

His Clan was on short rations and on the verge of running out of food. He was on the way back after an unsuccessful hunt. He would now go and inform his Clan members these hunters seemed to have enough food to feed them for the entire winter.

Since it meant survival, a raid on these hunters was worth the risk.

He made sure he left no tracks as he departed the area. It would not do to alert the group below. They looked quite capable, and they must be good with their weapons to have killed so much game.

When Red Oak's hunters passed by the place Burley Bear had been, he was already gone. He had used his skill well and his sign was not detected.

The hunters returned to Red Oak and reported there was no one around.

Red Oak's team had been very successful. Success meant the team had slowly become more pack mules then hunters. The load was heavy enough that he decided to dry as much of their meat that they could salt. This would lighten their load and allow them to make better time on the trek home.

The men were now getting restless. They were ready to get home to their families. The respect the team had gained for Red Oak over the last several grueling weeks kept the team from revolting.

Red Oak in his thoroughness carefully processed all the game killed. He made sure the meat was well salted and dried slowly over the fires. This meant around the clock watches.

The huge supply of meat they were now carrying proved to be as trying as if they had been unsuccessful.

Red Fox had announced the day before that they would load up and move out on the following day. By Red Oak's reckoning the hunters were no more than a seven sun cycles from the Clan's location.

He had led the hunt south and southwest. He should be no more than a two sun cycles march from the sea. The team should be able to go southward along the coast at a good pace and locate the Clan's winter quarters.

Red Oak had his men prepare the travois in a special manner. Two travois were set up in the woods out of sight. All the meat would be loaded on them. Two empty travois were put on top of the heavily loaded ones. Four men were assigned to pull the two travois slowly through the forest.

In the camp four additional travois were loaded with wood and stones with some minor amount of meat placed on the top layer to cover the wood. Someone watching their progress would see four travois set out for the last leg to the sea. The travois heading to the beach would be the ones loaded with the wood.

Red Oak anticipated an attack either as the group was approaching the beach or when they were on the beach.

He sent the strongest four men he had with the meat loaded travois up over the ridge to the south. He told them to protect the load of meat with their lives and to immediately send someone for help if they were attacked.

Red Oak and the remaining eight hunters pulled their decoy loads toward the sea.

Red Oak's actions put his hunters on edge. Only their successful hunting experience with Red Oak made them do as he asked. No one had seen or heard anything warranting the precautions Red Oak was suddenly taking.

Never-the-less they did as he asked. After all, he had worked miracles on the hunt. His leadership was not to be questioned easily.

His hunters had decided to humor him as far as the beach.

When the stream finally approached the sea, Red Oak began to go southward. The team had gone about a mile down the beach, when a group of about thirty warriors of the Others burst out from the forest just ahead of them and began to run toward them.

Red Oak and his men burst into a high-speed run. This caught the advancing group of Others by surprise. Red Oak and his men were able to run past the group and leave them behind. The months of running was now paying off. The load however slowed Red Oak and his men down enough to allow the oncoming group of Others to close the gap.

When spears began to fly, Red Oak gave the signal to cut and run.

A few of the group pursued Red Oak and his men for a short distance but it was obvious they would not catch up to the men running away.

The hurrah from those converging around the four travois quickly drew those chasing Red Oak back.

As Red Oak and his men ran into the forest, he looked back to see the travois being hauled off up the beach to the North. The warriors were clearly members of the people the Elk Clan called the old ones or the Others. He hoped they would not inspect the whole load until they reached their camp. He also hoped their camp was several days away.

He was laughing so hard he could barely run. His ruse had worked. He hoped to be back to the Elk Clan before his attackers found out they had been duped. He was glad he had acted on his premonition even though his hunters thought he was a little touched.

They caught up with the other four hunters.

Quickly they redistributed the load into four travois and then attached themselves like sled dogs and began a forced jog home. They came out of the forest some five miles down from where they had been attacked.

Red Oak made sure all tracks made coming down onto the beach were erased. He knew that anyone seriously tracking them would quickly figure out the direction they were going but Red Oak wanted to make it hard on anyone following him.

Then he and his men jogged along the water line pulling the four travois. Each travois followed directly behind the other. The rising tide would erase all traces of their having gone this way.

Except for brief rests to drink and eat, Red Oak kept the men in harness the remainder of the day, throughout the night and throughout the following two days.

There were no complaints. The men now had total confidence in Red Oak.

How he had known they were being watched and would be attacked was a mystery to all of them. None of the members of this team would ever doubt or question his leadership again.

After three days of moving south Red Oak was beginning to question whether they might have missed the camp and jogged by it. He did not think so.

On the third day just after sunset and just before he was going to halt, an armed party emerged out in front on them.

Under his breath, Red Oak made some disparaging remarks to the spirits. He then turned his men in among the rocks and prepared to fight. He went out alone to meet the oncoming group of warriors.

At twenty paces, Red Oak's war cry stopped the oncoming group.

"If you are of the Elk Clan or friend you are welcome," Silent Hawk replied.

Red Oaks heart soared. Yet he needed to make sure.

"I am Red Oak of the Elk Clan. Who is the Elk Clan leader's wife," Red Oak inquired?

"None other than me, White Swan," White Swan replied.

The tension broke and Golden Hawk followed by Taelo ran out to greet the returning hunters. After a quick greeting out on the beach, the returning hunters were escorted into the camp.

The travois loaded with meat were pulled over to the edge of the great lodge and left.

Once again wives, children and parents greeted the returning men. When the villagers saw Red Oak and his men up close, they knew they had used all their strength to bring back the bounty that would tide the Clan over a few more months. The load now in front of the Clan's main building provided another boost to the moral of the Clan.

The memory of starvation was now replaced with hope and a growing confidence that the Elk Clan would survive the winter.

The men were exhausted and needed a good night's rest. Everyone was still staying in the great lodge since there were not enough hides to cover the individual shelters.

After a good meal Red Oak declared it was time for his team to get a good night's rest. His men followed their leader and without exception retired for the night.

Silver Hawk was somewhat amazed and commented to White Swan and Swift Deer as they watched the hunters leave the central fire, "It seems Red Oak's men have the ultimate respect for him. They are not going to allow us to get information from them until they are all together to share their tale."

The next day was spent preparing for an evening feast. The great lodge would now hear the stories of the second group of long hunters. Clan members tried to get the hunters to talk. None of the hunters would divulge their story until they were all together around the evening meeting fire.

Quiet Pheasant spent the day preparing Red Oak's favorite dishes.

Golden Hawk and Taelo followed Red Oak around as he surveyed the camp and the surrounding area.

"This is a very nice winter's quarter. It is well situated and will provide for early fishing. The Clan has done well in getting the main building up. We must use the additional hides my team just brought back and cover additional living quarters. Then we can build more living quarters and plan to use the hides Grey Fox Running will bring," Red Oak commented to the two boys.

He listened to the two tell of their journey to the winter quarter, of White Swan having led them to this location, of having helped in digging and getting rocks and timbers.

"You two have done well. You each have grown a good hand in height. I am proud of your contribution to the Clan," Red Oak reaffirmed them as he gave them a hug.

He was impressed with the way the two acted and carried themselves. He was a proud father and uncle.

The evening was spent in the telling of the travels and hunting of Red Oak's team. Each team member spontaneously contributed to the telling, and all were especially vocal about crediting Red Oak on his hunting and leadership abilities.

Silver Hawk was impressed with the camaraderie this team had established.

Red Oak finally got to the part of the story when the team was being watched.

He had the team make eight travois. They loaded four travois with wood and stone covered with a thin layer of meat. These travois were left in plain sight in the middle of the camp.

Two travois loaded with all the meat were out of sight.

He then told of being attacked by a group of about thirty warriors of the Others as they began their trek down the beach and how they had abandoned the four decoys, travois and saved the main load of the kill from their long hunt.

The last part of the tale was the best, but it was also the one that most concerned everyone. There was great laughter about the trick the hunters had pulled on their attackers.

He shared his concern that the Others might pose a threat to their winter camp.

Two days later, after his team had enjoyed the triumph of their return and he had time to rest from the grueling days preceding. He voiced is concern that somewhere to the north the Others needed food and were desperate enough to attack them. It was very likely the need for food would cause a fight between the two groups.

The threat of the Others finding and attacking the Elk Clan's winter quarters greatly concerned Red Oak. He felt he needed to send out a runner to warn Gray Fox Running and to get him to return as soon as possible.

Since Grey Fox Running was not due back for another two months, Red Oak decided he would go out and replace him as hunt leader. He discussed this with Silver Hawk and the elders and after much discussion they agreed with him.

Red Oak stayed a few more days to allow for a thorough recovery and to prepare to once again, go out for a few months.

"I really hate to go out again but Grey Fox Running needs to return and take up leading the Elk Clan," Red Oak commented quietly to Quiet Pheasant.

Then with one other warrior he set out to find Grey Fox Running.

Chapter 13: Battle for the Beach

White Swan held a different view of what needed to be done to address the presence of the Others. She had listened to the stories that Grey Fox Running had told of friendly interactions he and his family had with the Others.

The Elk Clan was struggling for survival and had feared starvation. The Clan of Others might be in the same situation. A hungry desperate Clan would be a danger to them. Perhaps help given early would prevent a later battle with desperately hungry people.

White Swan had kept quite when Red Oak talked of the coming battle. She had a very different idea in mind. She had her own plan she wanted to try.

She talked to Quiet Pheasant about her idea. She wanted to try friendship and aid as a way to approach and find out what the Others needed.

The two decided in the absence of their two best warriors, their husbands, they should take the initiative and try a non-threatening approach. If it did not work, then when Grey Fox Running returned, he would know what action to take.

She convinced Silent Hawk the worst that could come from trying her approach was rejection on the part of the Others. Such information would be invaluable for the Elk Clan to have.

White Swan asked Silent Hawk to call the council of elders together to convince them of the appropriateness of the action.

White Swan took the council talking spear, with the Elk teeth and a variety of decorative feathers, from Silent Hawk and turned slowly to look at each of the old warriors who served on the council. She understood she had to overcome Elk Clan culture and biases. She had carefully thought through the argument she faced and the points she would need to win to get her way.

Her approach was to reach out to the Others with the offer of help and friendship. A small amount of food and small gifts would provide a way for the Elk Clan to better understand the situation faced by the Others and the risk to the Elk Clan. The worst outcome would be that they found out the Others were hostile and Grey Fox Running would know he needed to lead a war party when he returned.

After much discussion and the quiet supportive guidance of Silent Hawk the council reluctantly agreed to the plan. They were hesitant to deny the wife of the new leader of the Clan.

White Swan thanked the council for their approval and assured them they would be positively rewarded for this important decision.

She openly praised Silent Hawk for his continued leadership of the Elk Clan.

Taelo approached his mother and informed her that she was not going to go see the Others by herself.

White Swan was on the verge of telling him that he would stay in the Elk Camp when an eagle scream from high overhead stopped her in mid-sentence. Instead, she smiled, gave Taelo a hug and told him he and Golden Hawk would be welcome.

She looked to see Quiet Pheasant smile and nod in agreement.

Two days after Red Oak left, White Swan, Quiet Pheasant, Taelo and Golden Hawk waved to Silent Hawk as they set off up the wintry beach.

The tumultuous waves crashing violently up onto the beach and the gusting wind blowing in from the ocean created a white haze of freezing salt spray sweeping across the beach like a miniature snowstorm.

The four of them proceeded as close to the tree line as possible in an attempt to skirt the worst of it. Even then their hair was soon encrusted in a coating of ice, and they laughed at how wild they looked.

Taelo and Golden Hawk pulled a travois with some fresh fish, dried meat, some frozen meat, some honey, and some salt. It was a substantial amount and would probably feed thirty people for several sun cycles. They also had a few freshly worked leather pieces, some headbands, some gloves, and some shoes. Taelo and Golden Hawk had contributed some delicate seashell necklaces.

The idea had been half accepted and half rejected but White Swan had insisted they try a peaceful way before they tried a more forceful way. This was a matter of principle to her. She was not going to accept a battle until she was sure all other means had been exhausted.

White Swan had been raised to believe goodness given was always rewarded.

"Taelo, Golden Hawk, if anything goes wrong or the people are unfriendly, you and Golden Hawk run as fast as you can," White Swan instructed as they continued their walk northward up the coast.

She was sure the two boys could outrun any of the Others. She was not worried about herself but as she thought about the situation, she worried about Taelo. Perhaps she should have insisted he stay home.

Silent Hawk had insisted Taelo, and Golden Hawk accompany them.

Taelo and Golden Hawk looked at each other as if their mothers were a little daft. They both knew without speaking neither one would ever leave their mothers behind. If anything were to happen, they would all leave together.

"Mother, if anything goes wrong you had better be running ahead of me or we will both be standing together," Taelo replied.

"Yes," was all that Golden Hawk added.

White Swan looked over at Quiet Pheasant who just smiled back at her and raised her right eyebrow to show her support of Taelo's response.

Quiet Pheasant looked back and commented that such a plan would work because both she and White Swan could outrun the two them.

After walking all day, they all sat down and had their dinner and arranged a small camp for the night. They had moved into the woods and found a small depression to protect them from the ocean winds. Taelo and Golden Hawk scouted around and came back with some fresh water.

On the evening of the third day, Taelo climbed a tall pine tree on the edge of the beach. To the north he could see some campfires. The fires were off the beach and back at the edge of the forest. The camp was probably a day's walk.

He came down and shared what he had seen with the rest of the group. They settled down for a small dinner.

Taelo and Golden Hawk cleared the snow from an area large enough for all four of them to lie down on and got some pine needles from under one of the pines. Then they lay out one large bear skin for all four of them. They each had a smaller one to cover up with. They set up an elk hide lean-to over their heads.

Once everyone had crawled into sleep, the edges of the larger lower hide were folded over them all the way around. This made for a very warm bed, and it provided cover over their heads.

The next morning after a breakfast of hot fish soup the four set out once again.

After walking most of the day, they saw the tendrils of smoke rising above the camp site of the Others.

Several of the camp's warriors came toward them as they slowly made their way up the beach.

The Others were rather short but powerfully built broad shouldered, hairy men. Several of them walked toward White Swan. It was clear to her that they were being very cautious but did not seem to be too concerned.

The initial interaction was awkward since they did not speak the same language. However, White Swan spoke softly and indicated they had come as friends and had gifts for the camp.

The men were suspicious, but they could see no other people back along the trail. They were not worried about two women and two young boys. The ones standing before them seemed weak.

It was clear to White Swan that they were being accepted. She had counted on just this attitude.

One of the Others took the lead and two followed behind as they all went into the camp and were quickly surrounded by the entire camp membership.

A huge burly young man came out and spoke loud and roughly to White Swan and Quiet Pheasant.

Taelo immediately moved around to the giant's side. Golden Hawk saw Taelo's move and put himself in front of Quiet Pheasant.

White Swan indicated they came in friendship, and they had gifts of food and other items for the women. She picked up a headband and gave it to the burly man. She then picked up some fish and gave it to a woman standing close by.

Immediately the camp members crowded in close.

White Swan was surprised when the burly man grabbed her roughly by the arm and began speaking loudly to her. He seemed to be exceedingly rude and rough. He was unaware of the movement around him.

Taelo had been watching this situation and decided to act. Suddenly, he let out a loud cry, ran forward, used the man's body to launch himself into the air and hit him across the head with his oak club.

The man grunted, sank down on his knees, and fell flat on his face.

Taelo stood over him as the camp stopped in a stunned silence.

Taelo held his club in the air and pointed it to the surrounding members of the Others.

"Be kind and gentle to my mother." Taelo said as he pointed to his mother.

"We come to give you gifts, but we are warriors of the Elk Clan. We harbor no ill will to any person who treats us well. We eliminate those who do us harm," Taelo spoke evenly as he stood over the large warrior at least three times his size and let his hand swing smoothly in an arc and take in the people around him.

The silence was suddenly filled with a loud whooping from several of the older warriors as they came forward and raised Taelo high into the air just as an eagle swooped down from the mountains and let its cry be heard over the camp.

All eyes looked upward. The members of the Elk Clan knew this was Taelo's totem. Now the members of the old ones saw his totem and reacted as well.

"It is as the omen said. A young eagle will overcome the bear. This young boy is a future leader of men. See even the eagle sends him congratulations at his victory.

Let's celebrate this visit and enjoy the food being shared with us.

Move Burly Bear into his tent and keep him calm for the rest of the day. We will have enough problems this winter without antagonizing a group of well fed and well clothed new ones," one of the older warriors said.

"What is your name," the leader of the camp asked Taelo and used sign language to make his request clear.

Taelo explained his name was the claw of the eagle. He drew the eagle in the sand and pointed to the sky. He then drew the claw.

A hush descended on the camp.

The mood of the camp changed and Taelo was seated at the right side of the leader.

Golden Hawk had stood ready to defend himself, his mother, and his aunt. The three of them watched as Taelo became the center of attention.

White Swan recovered from her initial alarm and proceeded as if nothing had happened.

She was somewhat amazed by what Taelo had just done but she had long ago learned he was full of surprises. She was not sure what had caused the sudden change in the camps atmosphere.

She presented the leader's wife with a shell necklace Taelo had made.

"This is from my young warrior, Taelo," White Swan indicated as she presented the necklace.

The necklace was made of tiny shells strung on fine elk gut cord. In the front center was a blue crystal woven skillfully into a holder.

"I call it the Eye of the Sea," Taelo said quietly as he drew the picture into the sand.

"I am Little Doe, thank you Taelo, for this wonderful necklace. I will proudly wear this "Eye of the Sea," the leader's wife said quietly.

Everyone came around to look at the necklace.

They all looked at it and then to Taelo. He was the center of attention of the camp.

"They are of the old people we call the Others. They are a large Clan, but they are running low on supplies. They do not seem to have good hunters though they have many men," White Swan said in a low voice to Quiet Pheasant.

"Yes, they need help if they are to survive the winter. It will be difficult to keep them from attacking us when they get desperately hungry," Quiet Pheasant replied.

Taelo listened to the exchange between the two and looked around at the Clan of Others.

"Why do your men not fish the food from the sea," Taelo suddenly asked as he looked around the camp.

He drew his question out in the sand. A hush again fell on the camp. This boy was talking to the leader and the elders and was asking why the camp seemed to need food.

"Boys can fish, girls and women can fish, and everyone can eat. Hunters can go to the mountains for meat. There is no reason to go hungry," Taelo said as he drew out his words in the sand.

"Golden Hawk and I can teach you to fish, to hunt rabbits and to find herbs. I am sure my mother, the mate of the Elk Clan's leader can let us stay and teach you," Taelo said as he continued to draw his message.

"Taelo, where did you get such an idea, and how do you know I will agree to let you stay," White Swan said in shocked surprise?

Taelo looked calmly at his mother and asked if she had a better idea.

She saw the wisdom in his approach, and she did not have any other ideas on how to resolve the problem.

"There is little choice. Either we show them how to get food or in a short time they will be attacking us for our food supply," Taelo replied astutely.

Suddenly, there was a roar in the camp and Burley Bear came roaring out of one of the huts.

"Where is the warrior who attacked me without warning?" Burley Bear shouted looking around for his attacker. He was expecting a grown man.

"Burly Bear, I am Taelo. The scream of the eagle, the claw that strikes," Taelo said as he stood up and extended his hand to Burly Bear.

Just then everyone heard the eagle scream as it again flew back across the camp. Even Burly Bear looked up into the sky.

"It is an omen, the sign we have been awaiting," the leader, Quiet Fox, said to Burley Bear.

Burley Bear looked around, "Are you telling me this stump of a lad was the one that put out my lights?"

"Yes, he is the one and he is holding out his hand in friendship. You made the mistake of handling his mother too roughly," Quiet Fox continued.

Burley Bear let out a loud laugh.

"This is great. I have fought and beaten every warrior in this camp. Now I come face to face with, Taelo, "The scream of the eagle, the claw that strikes," and I have my lights put out.

Well done my small friend," Burley Bear said as he took Taelo's small hand and shook it vigorously.

"I am at your service, and I apologize to you mother," he continued.

"Burley Bear, I am glad you feel that way. Taelo has agreed to stay here to teach us how to fish and to find small game. I believe his young friend will stay with him. I am putting them both in your care. See nothing happens to them." Quiet Fox said with a smile.

He was glad to have this out of the way. He had wondered how he would handle the mountain sized, over strengthened, burley young man.

White Swan and Quiet Pheasant talked quietly and decided Taelo really had provided the best option.

"We will send a few Elk Clan members to teach you how to set the sea traps and how to efficiently make salt, is there anything that you need immediately," White Swan asked?

"Thank you for the offer of help. However, do not send anyone else. We have all the people we need. We know how to do all these things. We were waiting for a signal prophesied by our seer. A young eagle was to come and show us the way. Taelo, I believe is the person we have been waiting for," Quiet Fox replied.

"Mother, before you leave, I need to ask you for some advice," Taelo said after the gifts had all been given and the food distributed.

"Well, now my young man needs advice. And what advice do you need," White Swan said as she held him by the shoulders and looked into his eyes?

"Well, I have been looking around this camp. It seems to me they are so vulnerable to the weather here. Shouldn't they be farther up the beach into the woods and away from the surge of the sea?" Taelo asked.

"Yes, this place is very vulnerable to a large sea storm. It would be good to scout out a better location farther away from the beach. However, it will be difficult in this weather for them to move.

The day came to a close and after a grilled meat dinner, they all spent the night in one of the huts.

The next morning White Swan and Quiet Pheasant walked back down the beach toward the south toward their own camp. They were uncomfortable leaving their sons at this camp. However, they knew this was the best course of action.

They also saw Taelo, and Golden Hawk were being treated like royalty. The clan of Others looked to Taelo to guide them. The two mothers waved back to Taelo and Golden Hawk who were standing on the edge of the camp.

It was clear the camp needed a lot of help.

"Let us hope Taelo and Golden Hawk can inspire the camp to self-survival. These are the old ones. They know how to survive but for some reason they have not chosen to do so. The boys can learn as much from this Clan as they will teach them," White Swan said as she and Quite Pheasant marched south to the Elk Clan's winter quarters.

So, the battle for the beach ended peacefully. If all went well, there would be no bloodshed. More than likely there would be harmony and friendship.

Later, White Swan would see her actions reaffirmed over and over.

Chapter 14: Taelo's Guidance

Burley Bear had stayed with them on the beach. He was impressed with the two young men.

"These two are as one. They have strength and yet they have much passion. They are young but fearless and brave. These are leaders of men," Burley Bear observed to himself.

Taelo and Golden Hawk waved goodbye as they watched their mothers fade in the distance. The sea was calm, the rays of the morning sun was burning away a light haze that lay over the camp.

The two turned toward the camp and slowly took in the situation. It was poorly arranged and very susceptible to the wind and an ocean surge. They stood quietly talking and agreed that their first task was to find a better location for the Clan of Others. They would need to act immediately to change the situation. They slowly walked back up from the beach exchanging ideas about what to do.

Burley Bear listened to the two exchange ideas. It was clear to him they were discussing the situation they were in. He was impressed at their focus and earnestness.

Taelo made the point to Golden Hawk that the Elk Clan had just finished its march for survival and a search for a winter home. They should do what the Elk Clan had done and see if it would work for the Others.

"The first thing we should do is to see if we can find a winter worthy place to make camp. We will send one group back into the mountains toward the east, another group toward the north. You and I will search up the coast in hope we can find another spot similar to what was found for the Elk Clan," Taelo said to Golden Hawk.

Taelo and Golden Hawk walked back to the group of elders standing awaiting their return. The two looked around at the grizzled group of worn veterans.

"They must know ten times what we know. Why have they not taken better care of themselves," Taelo quietly asked Golden Hawk? "I feel a little out of my league but let's get the action going," he continued.

"These two young men seem to be very self-confident and self-reliant. Let's see what they are thinking," the oldest of the group of Others said to those around him.

Taelo began talking and drawing his thoughts about the vulnerability of the camp.

He sketched out the three groups going out for three days and then returning. Each group would do two things; first they were to look for a better camp for the clan, second, they would hunt and bring back all the food they could.

The group of elders talked among themselves.

"This young one is the one sent to show us the way. We were to wait on the beach until we received guidance. Even though it comes from someone so young from the new ones, we are being given direction," Quiet Fox expressed his thoughts.

"Broken Spear says he is the one. He wants to see what this young man does before meeting with him. He did not realize from his visions he would be from the new ones and be so young. Many years ago, Broken Spear watched through the eyes of the eagle as it took the claw from his small hand," another of the elders shared.

"It is a reasonable and well thought out plan. We will act on this and organize the three groups to go out in the morning," another of the elders summarized.

Taelo and Golden Hawk listened to the exchange even though they could not understand any of the guttural language the old ones used.

"We need to learn some of their words so we can communicate more clearly with them," Golden Hawk said as he listened to the conversation of the leaders.

"Well, they seem to be agreeing to the search for a better camp and food. Let's hope we are as successful in finding them winter quarters as good as our Clan has found," Taelo observed.

Several of the women brought food to the group and took the new information back to the rest of the clan. They were buoyed by the fact better quarters would be sought.

"Let's walk around the camp and see what the situation is in more detail," Taelo suggested to Golden Hawk.

Burly Bear followed the two around during the inspection tour. He observed the two as they walked around taking in the living conditions. It became obvious to him the two were concerned about the condition of the camp. Burly Bear became concerned as well. How had he missed the poor condition the camp was in? He felt a degree of shame for having been so preoccupied with himself and to have missed what now was becoming so obvious.

Taelo and Golden Hawk noticed a disturbing fact they had not noticed before.

There were no young children. The youngest were almost young adults. What had happened to this Clan?

After dinner one of the women approached them and motioned for them to follow. The two were shown into one of the shelters and pointed to their beds. They were in the shelter next to Burly Bear's.

Darkness was quickly drawing over the camp and preparations were being made for everyone to sleep.

"We may as well get a good nights' sleep. We will have a full day tomorrow," Golden Hawk suggested to Taelo.

The two walked down to the beach, stripped their clothes off and waded knee keep into the cold water. It was too cold to go any farther in. They used a piece of leather hide to wash themselves off.

They turned and waved for Burley Bear to join them, but he shook his head and sat down.

Afterwards the two took in the camp one more time before retiring to their beds.

In the morning, Taelo was up early and had gone around the camp once again to see its condition.

"It is as if they have stopped growing, stopped having children. They seem so cowed and remorseful. They have lost their will to survive. We will have to find out what is happening in this Clan," Taelo said to Golden Hawk.

After a light breakfast, Taelo went to the center of the camp. He found the group of elders organizing the three groups.

Quiet Fox was organizing each team. Burly Bear and one other warrior would accompany Taelo and Golden Hawk. The two other groups were each made up of three young warriors.

Taelo quietly inspected the packs of each search team member. He took out two thirds of the food and put it aside on a separate pile. He made a point of giving the now much smaller packs to each of the hunters.

"You will all hunt as you go. Any large find of food will be brought back to the camp by one of the team members. This is a search for better shelter and a search for more food.

As you travel, you will kill any rabbits, squirrels, groundhogs, fox, or deer you encounter. The small game will be your daily food, the larger game will be brought back to the camp," Taelo explained as he drew pictures of what he was saying.

"This young man is a tough leader. He expects you to find food as you go. The food from here is only for emergencies. Now we know why his Clan was able to give us so much food as a gift," Quiet Fox said to the group as he looked at Taelo and Golden Hawk with new respect.

If these young men represented the new ones, he could see why they were doing so well.

Taelo saw each of the two groups off as they set out.

"Look carefully for a home with water, shelter, and access to food. Hunt carefully, feed yourselves well, send much food back to the Clan," Taelo said to each of the members of the search party.

Golden Hawk and Taelo made a point of looking each member in their eyes as they put their hand on the shoulder of each and wished them good luck on their quest.

The leadership these two young men displayed impressed the elders of the Clan. Never had such direct contact between the new ones and themselves occurred.

Quiet Fox immediately saw the impact Taelo, and Golden Hawk's manner and actions had in challenging each team to do their best. He was impressed with these young men of the new people. They had high expectations of those around them and they communicated these expectations well even with a language barrier.

After the second team left the camp, Taelo engaged Quiet Fox and the leadership team. He wanted those staying at the camp to hunt for small game around the immediate area. He also wanted the beach combed for any food that might have washed up. His final request was that some fishing be done.

Quiet Fox smiled and agreed to organize the Clan members to do what Taelo was requesting.

Golden Hawk and he were ready to depart. Taelo looked at Burley Bear and another warrior called Rolling Stone. Taelo had prepared their packs in public so all could see that his team had no more food than those who had already left.

He and Golden Hawk set off on a brisk jogging pace. Taelo knew the beach was not going to be a very good place to hunt. He hoped they would be lucky and find a small stream for fresh water and maybe some fish.

On their second day Taelo saw what looked like a huge boulder in the waves. As the team drew nearer the size of the boulder grew and he realized it was a small, beached whale.

It appeared to be a very recent event because there was no damage to the whale. The cold weather had kept it in good shape and the wild animals had not yet found it.

This was a huge treasure for the Clan of Others. They would be able to live off this for the rest of the winter. The team needed to get this whale anchored and then processed.

Taelo led the way into the woods to find some stakes with which to anchor the whale.

Burley Bear carried a stone the size of his head and used it to pound the three stakes brought back to the beach.

Taelo realized they had no rope to tie the whale to their stakes. Golden Hawk suggested they drive the stakes through the jaw of the whale into the sand below it. This worked well, and Burley Bear put a stake through each side fin as well.

"Tonight, we will eat well. Early in the morning Rolling Stone will return to the Clan. The Clan must send a team, so we can immediately process the whale. Burley Bear, you will stay here and guard the whale carcass.

Golden Hawk and I will go on to look for shelter. I see high cliffs up ahead along the beach. Perhaps we can find a cave big enough for the Clan.

We will spend the rest of the day to gather wood for fires to ward off the animals. We will need enough to last for the next several days," Taelo explained to the other three.

They gathered and brought wood out to the beach, set up a camp for Burley Bear.

They drove some additional stakes where the fins met the body and another two in the whale's mouth.   Taelo was worried about losing the whale to the sea or to scavengers from the land.

Taelo hoped the Clan would arrive in time to recover most of the meat and fat from the whale.

The temperature was dropping and the sky to the west looked as if a storm might be approaching.

The next morning after a hearty breakfast of whale tongue soup, Rolling Stone started out on a brisk trot back to the camp of Others. He was excited by the find. He knew it was another sign Taelo was the one chosen to show them the way. He would use all his energy to return rapidly to the Clan.

Taelo and Golden Hawk went the opposite direction.

Burley Bear watched as Taelo disappeared along the coast.

"He is the omen we have waited for. The gods have sent up a whale to keep us fed for the winter. He is of the new ones, but he has a good heart and a sharp mind. I am sure he is being led by the ancients," Burley Bear thought as he watched Taelo and Golden Hawk running swiftly up the beach.

He began to set up the drying racks and continued to gather wood and bring it to the edge of the beach. He would begin the preparation for the processing while he awaited the arrival of the Clan.

Taelo and Golden Hawk were now able to travel faster. The Others were much more powerful than the two of them, but they were much slower.

The cliffs Taelo had seen were a good two days away and much larger than he had imagined them. As they approached it became clear they would need to find shelter before they got there, or they would run out of beach. The cliffs ran right out to the edge of the sea.

They could see the end of the beach when they came to a small stream cutting through the beach to the sea.

"Let's follow this upstream and see if there are any likely camps and any good fishing holes," Taelo commented to Golden Hawk as they continued up the creek away from the beach.

They had gone about a mile when the stream ended at the base of a high cliff.

"Well, why don't we set up camp here? This looks like a good place to try to catch some fish. I will look around and see what I can find," Taelo suggested.

"I will set up our camp and try my hand at fishing. Don't get lost out there. Try to make it back for the fish dinner," Golden Hawk replied as he started to set up camp.

Taelo left the camp with only his bow and quiver of arrows and a flask of water. He approached an extremely high and solid cliff with no indication of any caves. His eyes traveled up the dark, almost brown, smooth stone to the point where the light blue of the sky made it appear someone had etched a jagged line outlining the cliffs top.

He began to follow a game trail to the right, away from the stream. He had not gone more than a quarter mile when he spotted a huge Elk stag and his three cows. Taelo had his arrow in his bow and was moving silently toward them. Suddenly the group ran and to Taelo's surprise disappeared in front of his eyes.

Taelo went forward to the spot where the Elk had disappeared. There he found an opening in the cliff. Had it not been for the Elk he would very likely have walked by without seeing it.

From high above, Taelo heard the cry of the eagle.

The cry let Taelo know the path taken by the elk would lead to the shelter the Others needed for the winter.

The elk was his tribal sign, and the eagle was his totem. Both were letting him know the way. He was being guided. He knew that he did not walk alone.

Carefully, Taelo went through the fracture in the face of the cliff.

As he came out the other side, he saw a gentle slope leading to a wide-open valley surrounded by dark green tree covered white capped mountains.

The overhang he was standing under ran to his right for several hundred yards. The overhang to the left tapered in to where a waterfall was tumbling down into a steaming pool. Water from this pool went down to another pool at the base of the cliff and disappeared into the ground.

With a little work, this area would make an excellent shelter for the Clan.

The overhang to the right was ideally arranged to allow for the building of a wall, a full spear high, to protect the cave from the valley outside.

The cooler lower pool of water kept the surrounding area warm enough preventing any snow from accumulating.

Taelo returned as the sunset and the evening darkness set over the small camp Golden Hawk had set up. Long before he arrived at the camp the smell of cooking fish made him hungry.

Golden Hawk had been successful in his quest.

"I heard the cry of the eagle. Has it been guiding you again?" Golden Hawk asked as Taelo came into camp.

"Yes, the eagle and our friend the elk guided me to a place I wish the Elk Clan could winter. However, this Clan of Others needs it worse than we do. Perhaps the richness of their new home and the valley it overlooks will spill over into the fertility and growth for their number," Taelo replied.

"From what I understand, this Clan is made up of all that is left of several Clans. It seems they have not had children in several years," Golden Hawk shared.

At about the same time they were enjoying the trout, Rolling Stone arrived at the camp of the Others and delivered the good news about the beached whale. This news energized the Clan.

It was noted that the team led by Taelo along the beach was the one finding the food needed by the Clan. This was taken as confirmation of the omen.

The elders acted immediately and prepared to send a crew out at the break of dawn. The camp would be packed, and the rest would follow with all their belongings by evening.

The eagle had visited Burley Bear, during the late afternoon. Its screams had inspired the large, powerful young warrior.

"Are you letting me know Taelo has found us a home?" Burley Bear said as he looked up into the crisp blue sky and watched the graceful flight of the eagle.

He knew in his heart his young friend had succeeded.

Burley Bear worked tirelessly throughout that day and the next. He made a dozen drying racks and gathered enough wood to dry most of the meat.

He checked the stakes holding the whale and added several more. He did not want high tide to take this from his clan.

His last act was to wrap himself in his large sleeping hide, put his back to one of the stakes holding the small whale and fall asleep.

The next morning, Taelo and Golden Hawk came swiftly down the coast. They were not hunting or looking for anything. They were running at a constant pace along the very edge of the sea. It had taken them two days to reach the point where they had found the shelter.

They were determined to make it back in one.

As the sun was setting on the third day, Burley Bear was sitting and watching the ocean when he spotted the two runners. He marveled at their sleekness and grace. None of his kind could run like those two. The two looked as if their feet were not touching the ground but were instead flying along the edge of the sea.

He went down to the beach to greet the two young runners.

They ran up to him and gave him a bear hug in greeting.

This surprised Burley Bear. He was taken aback by their exuberance and friendliness.

"We have found the ideal place for the Clan of Others. With this food and the shelter, we have found, your clan will enjoy many seasons of comfort and prosperity," Golden Hawk shared.

"Well, my bear of a friend, you have really been busy," Taelo said as he looked at all the wood and the drying racks.

"Tomorrow we will begin to process the whale. We will begin to move the meat up the shore. I hope your clan will arrive soon," Taelo said.

The next morning Taelo tied a cutting flint on the end of a long pole and went up to the whale and made a cut down from the backbone to the ground.

He moved half the length of the pole and made another cut. Then he went up on the whale and made a cut along the backbone connecting the two vertical cuts. Soon he had the skin and about four inches of fat rolling down the side toward the ground.

Golden Hawk knew what Taelo was doing. The two had listened to the stories of the Weaver about how to process a whale.

Burley Bear watched in puzzlement but when he saw the skin and fat rolling down toward the ground, he got the idea. When the skin and fat was about halfway down, he and Golden Hawk were able to reach it and guide it.

Taelo had instructed them in setting up a grid of logs to lay the slab of fat and skin on to keep it off the sand. Cross members had been laid and lashed down with strips of willow bark.

Now as the slab of fat came down toward them, Burley Bear and Golden Hawk pulled it across the platform. After the first slab had been cut off the three pulled the sled across the beach and up to the edge of the woods.

They set up another sled and cut a similar piece off the opposite side of the whale. By the end of the day, they had stripped the carcass of its layer of fat.

After each trip they gathered around a large fire and to thaw out. Taelo had never been so cold.

"If we are not careful, we will all turn into chunks of ice," Golden Hawk commented.

They went to sleep totally exhausted. They had eaten some of their food from their backpacks and collapsed into their sleeping hides.

Burley Bear made sure all the fires were lit and then he too fell asleep.

Just before dawn, Taelo awoke to the grunting of a giant brown bear. He watched as the bear helped herself to a portion of the whale fat laid out at the edge of the woods.

He noticed a pack of wolves sitting on their haunches just beyond the giant bear. He was glad they were not dire wolves. It was clear they were waiting for the bear to leave before they came in for their share.

"Well, mighty bear. It seems you are hungry. Please help yourself but earn your meal by staying long enough to keep the wolves away," Taelo said quietly to the giant.

The bear looked at him and grunted and continued to eat her helping. She was out between sleeps and was extremely hungry. She did not know what had roused her, but the fat was a luxury that she could not pass up.

Taelo went quietly about putting wood on the fires. All the while he carried on a quiet conversation with the giant female bear.

The bear seemed to answer with grunts and low growls as she went about helping herself to a full stomach of whale blubber.

Taelo went out to the beach and started the fires around the whale. He knew the wolves would soon find the carcass on the beach and he wanted to be ready to defend it.

Golden Hawk had quietly gotten up and gone out to where Taelo was lighting the beach fires.

"Are we going to be able to defend this carcass against the wolves," he asked Taelo?

"Not tonight. You must run down the beach and bring a troop of warriors on the run. Come back immediately. You must be here by sundown, or we will be in big trouble. Our bear protector will not be out to help us tonight," Taelo replied.

Burley Bear quietly watched the entire interaction between the bear and Taelo. He was in awe at the bravery of the young man who talked to a grown female cave bear and walked confidently around and stoked the fires to keep the wolves out.

He crawled out to the beach so as not to aggravate the feasting bear. He was not sure she would be as kind to him as she was to Taelo.

Once out on the beach he saw Taelo was lighting the fires to prevent the wolves from making an early morning raid on the meat of the whale carcass. He also saw the dim form of Golden Hawk running swiftly down the beach toward the location of the Clan.

The bear took her time eating. Taelo and Burley Bear agreed she was welcome to whatever she wanted. The bear, as much as the two of them, was keeping the wolves at bay.

Taelo cut some flesh off the whale and was putting it on sticks. He remembered the advice of the Weaver about how to distract wolves. He planned to toss pieces of the meat out among the wolves to keep them back and fighting among themselves. He showed Burley Bear what he had in mind. Burley Bear was impressed with Taelo's thinking.

The giant bear gave a grunt and stood up and gave a roar and seemed to wave at Taelo and Burley Bear.

Taelo immediately advanced back into the camp and threw more wood on the fires around the camp.

The wolves were making ready to rush in, but Taelo strategically threw out some pieces of meat to scatter and break up the pack. Instead of coming forward they were fighting among themselves for the pieces of meat Taelo was throwing out.

"I will share the bounty with you my wolf brothers. But you must retreat after you have had your breakfast," Taelo instructed them as he went about tossing out the food.

He made sure every wolf got some meat, but he always threw the stick, so the wolf pack was scattered and moved away from the area.

Burley Bear went back out to the carcass and made some more of the throwing sticks. He was amazed at Taelo's approach to managing the crisis. He talked to the bear and fed the wolves. Both chose to mind him.

Finally, the sun broke through and the day began to warm. The wolves seemed to be satisfied with the meal they had been given and they retreated from the humans.

By late afternoon, the two had brought in more wood and had established a perimeter of small fires spots around the camp. They would be lit to keep the wolves away. What they needed was some help. It would be impossible for them to keep the wolves away on their own.

A splendid red, yellow, and purple sunset was painting the sky to the west when the chanting of running warriors came to them. This immediately cheered them. Taelo gave Burley Bear a big hug.

Sharp Blade led the jogging warriors in. He surveyed the scene and saw all the preparation and defensive work.

"Well, Burley Bear, we thought we might find your carcass, instead we see you have protected this whale very well," Sharp Blade said in greeting.

"You speak to the wrong person. Young Taelo awoke this morning to talk with a giant female brown bear. He greeted her and thanked her for helping keep the wolves at bay. When she had eaten her fill and the sun was just rising, she thanked him and waved goodbye, so Taelo had time to get the campfires burning.

Taelo fed the wolves and told them they could have what they needed but they were not to come into the camp.

He has found us enough food for the entire winter and has also located our winter quarters. He indeed is the messenger sent to guide us," Burley Bear replied in greeting.

Everyone was amazed at such a long speech from Burley Bear. He was known not to speak more than a few words in multiple cycles of the sun.

Sharp Blade conversed with Taelo and Burley Bear for a few more minutes and then took charge of the camp. He assigned warriors around the perimeter and set up a rotation to cover the entire night. He could see Taelo, Burley Bear and Golden Hawk were asleep on their feet. He thanked all three and told them to get a good night's sleep.

Taelo was asleep as soon as his head hit his sleeping pad.

The next morning went without incident. Taelo instructed the warriors in how to strip the carcass of its meat. This he knew from listening to the Weaver's stories.

He also knew most of the entrails should be washed and used to encase the meat and to use as storage for the rendered fat.

The warriors were making good progress when up the beach came a group of the younger women. They were jogging along singing some ancient song. All the warriors sang back in unison.

Taelo took in the scene and marveled at the camaraderie taking place. It was good to see the hopes of these people rise.

Taelo went about telling the women what they should be doing.

Golden Hawk had gone out with a few of the warriors and collected some additional flat stones to be used to melt the fat. Several melting stations were set up to melt and catch the fat in bags made from the entrails of the whale. The bags of oil were hung in the trees well away from the wolves and out of the reach of the bear.

The merriment and happy chatter could be heard everywhere. The story of Taelo talking to the bear and feeding the wolves was added to the other stories of the tribe. It would be repeated for years to come as the Clan sat around the fire and marveled about the young boy sent to guide them.

Quickly the great whale was reduced to bone. Even these would be kept and used for a variety of purposes. The Ivory of the teeth would be carved into figures and bartered for various other products from Clans all around them.

The remainder of the day was used to continue the processing of the whale. First to arrive were the younger half of the Clan.

Finally late in the afternoon the remainder of the Clan came up the beach dragging all their belongings on travois. Everyone ran down the beach and helped the elders bring their belongings into the camp.

In the evening Taelo sat with the elders and told them of the fine camp he had found. In the morning he would lead the elders to this place, so they could begin to prepare it.

Burley Bear sat with the Elders and in their tongue again shared the tale of Taelo and the Bear. The Bear continued to grow in size and the number of wolves was now in the hundreds.

Everyone enjoyed the story, and they all were amazed at the change in Burley Bear. He was starting to be fun to be around.

They joked that this change in Burley Bear was the best present Taelo had given the camp.

Chapter 15: New Home, New Hope, New Beginning

As the sun rose, the morning shadow receded up the beach to where Taelo was sitting. Today, for the first time, he would meet the Other's Clan medicine man. He was not sure why he had not met with him before, and he was curious about the man they called Broken Spear. Broken Spear had been carried up the beach the night before by four of the younger warriors.

Taelo knew that it was he who had predicted an eagle would come to show the clan the way.

"This is Broken Spear. He was our leading warrior and hunter until he was injured and almost died when his group surprised a mother brown bear. She killed two other hunters and left our proud Sure Spear, broken. Since then, he has had visions and has guided our Clan," Quiet Fox introduced Taelo to the medicine man.

There was a twinkle in the eyes of this old warrior as he shook Taelo's hand, and his eyes seemed to penetrate the very being of what Taelo thought was his inner self.

"I have heard much about you. I expected a giant and here standing in front of my eyes is a normal young man of the new ones. You must indeed have strong magic guiding you to have done so much. In only two weeks you have brought more hope to our clan then we have had for years.

Burley Bear has told us about you talking to the giant brown bear. I wonder did the bear have a notch cut from her left ear," Broken Spear asked?

It took Taelo several moments and some drawing in the sand by Broken Spear until he understood the question.

"Yes, this bear did have a notch missing in her left ear. Is she a bear you know?" Taelo replied in surprise.

"Yes, it was she who almost killed me. I see the ancients have used her again, this time to help us," Broken Spear replied.

"Let us proceed to the new home you have found for us. Tell me did the eagle scream when you found this new home," Broken Spear asked Taelo?

"Yes, the ancients showed me the place by using the Elk, the sign of my clan. Once I had found the opening, the eagle screamed. I took it as a sign this was the place I was seeking," Taelo responded.

Just before they were ready to leave, one of the other two groups out seeking better shelter returned. They were in good health and had an abundance of small game but had not found any shelter for the clan.

The three were in awe at all the food and looked at Taelo with new respect when they heard the stories of the last few days.

The elders, the older women and a selected group of warriors and younger women were to be part of the journey to the new home. They would bring every bit of food they could carry. About two thirds of the Clan of Others was left on the beach to process the remainder of the whale and melt the fat into oil.

Golden Hawk and Burly Bear stayed behind at the beach to help in completing the processing of the whale. Taelo led the remainder of the group up the beach toward the Clan's new home.

It took three additional days to guide this larger and slower group to the opening in the cliff. Like before, the opening was unnoticed until Taelo took the group around an outcrop of stone.

Quiet Fox stopped the procession and told them to wait until Broken Spear and Taelo went ahead and blessed their new home.

Broken Spear and Taelo walked in together. Broken Spear used Taelo like a crutch and the two, one from the past and one for the future, hobbled in together.

Tears were in the old man's eyes as he beheld the pool of hot water, the valley below and the living area to the right. After years of suffering and decline, here was a place where the Clan should prosper. The weight on Taelo's shoulder lightened ever so lightly. Broken Spear's heart had soared and lifted him to new hope.

They had been mistreated by many of the new ones, but it was something else that had been causing the Clans decline.

Broken Spear was sure the ancients and spirits were ending the time of the Others.

He chanted thanks to the ancestors and blessed this as their new home. Broken Spear sat down and sent Taelo back to lead the rest of the Clan in.

There was an immediate hush as the group beheld their new home. This was an unbelievably rich and comfortable place. The Clan members spread out and began to examine the layout of the cave. There was excited talking and pointing as they grasped the richness of their surroundings.

Quite Fox took charge. He and the group of elders walked around the entire overhang area. They quietly discussed how to lay the place out.

Taelo guided them to a place he had selected to be the latrine and another where he indicated waste should be collected during the winter and then moved out for the summer. Taelo was focused on improving the hygiene of the Clan. He had been a little appalled at their current practices.

Taelo was hoping to add a couple of new habits. In his home each day they would sit by a steaming pot of water and wash. Bathing was one thing he had not seen this Clan do. In the evening he invited the group of elders to the hot pool.

He went to the edge and sat to one side of where the water ran out. Here the water was pleasingly warm. He took off all his clothes and stepped into the pool. He lowered himself into and under the luxuriously hot water. He came back to the surface and washed his hair. He washed his entire body and then rubbed it down with some crushed pine needles he had prepared before getting in. He also rubbed some whale oil scented with pine needles into his hair. He then rinsed his hair one last time and stepped out of the hot water and dried himself off with a leather drying cloth.

The Elders watched in wonder. They were afraid to sit in the water.

Taelo indicated that they should do the same. Broken Spear knew it was up to him to overcome this fear. Bathing had been a Clan custom until the last great illness. He took off his clothes and joined Taelo.

Taelo helped Broken Spear into the hot water and helped him to sit on a large stone. This provided a convenient place to sit and wash. Taelo helped Broken Spear wash off. The rest of the elders slowly followed and soon they were enjoying the warmth of the hot pool.

Taelo left the group for a few moments and returned with a large skin full of whale oil. He poured some of the oil into a cooking skin and put in some cooking rocks. He added the crushed pine needles to the oil and let it cook for a while. The oil from the pine needles mixed with the whale oil and provided a lightly scented concoction.

Taelo again rubbed some of this hot scented oil on his skin and put a small amount in his hair. Finally, he dried himself off with one of his leather drying clothes. Everyone watching got the idea and copied what Taelo had done.

For the first time in days Taelo felt clean and comfortable.

Taelo noticed the lice and fleas floating away in the hot water. He and Golden Hawk had talked about this problem and the fact they were getting infested.

Taelo pointed to the dead lice, and fleas and commented to Quiet Fox and Broken Spear, "You must bathe each day and keep doing so until there are no more small animals living on you. Then you must do this at least once every two or three days. Then the Clan will be healthy, and all will feel better."

"He speaks like the medicine men of old. They taught us how to prepare various oils with the smell of flowers, and other plants. This lost favor many moons ago because people thought the water and the oils were causing members to get sick and die. He is telling us to do what the elders told us. It is as if they are using Taelo to awaken the memory of the Clan," Broken Spear spoke to the rest of the elders.

The rest of the Clan had watched in silence and awe as the elders all shed their clothes and got into the water with Taelo. Then came the bigger surprise, they were instructed to get into the water and wash as Broken Spear instructed. Soon they were enjoying themselves in the warm water and the new feeling of being clean.

Everyone in the camp enjoyed the hot water and the chatter indicated that they were enjoying the feeling of getting clean and of the luxurious scented oil on their skin.

Taelo stood back and watched as the entire group took a communal bath. He sat down on his rabbit skin blanket and enjoyed the festive nature of the communal bath. For the first time in several weeks, he was clean, comfortable, and warm. He fell asleep sitting on his rabbit skin blanket as he watched the group in the pool.

The Clan left him by the warm pool and proceeded to make dinner. One of the women brought him some whale meat cooked in salt water and gently woke him up.

Taelo took a few bites and then walked over to where he had put his things and climbed onto his sleeping hide. He was very tired and fell asleep immediately.

He dreamed of the Clan. They were to prosper here. They would live in this valley for years to come. He would visit them often, yet they would slowly decline in number. They would have children and they would be around until he was an old man. He had tears in his eyes when he awoke.

He felt someone's hand and looked into the eyes of Broken Spear.

"Now you know the fate of this Clan. We are of the old way. You are of the new. We will soon be gone. I have told no one of our future but you should know so you will know we are of no threat to you," Broken Spear said quietly as he sat by Taelo's side.

Taelo immediately realized it had not been a dream. Not in the sense of other dreams. He was sure Broken Spear had in some fashion spoken directly to his mind. He was surprised at this feat.

"Can all old ones do what you just did," Taelo asked.

"No, not all, all can hear the ancient ones. All have visions but they do not understand them. When the bear injured me, she caused much damage to my head and body. Whatever she broke caused me to be more sensitive to the ancient ones and to the other spirits surrounding us. There are many animal spirits I can feel. I can feel and sense the spirit of your totem, the eagle. I know when it is coming. I have seen through its eyes," Broken Spear shared with Taelo.

"Your mind has many places I cannot see. I sense your general spirit but can't see details. I can send it my thoughts and you receive it well, but you block any other probing I do. Your mind is quite interesting," Broke Spear confessed.

Taelo was not sure what to make of this exchange other than the fact he often wished he and Golden Hawk could exchange thoughts. The fact the old ones had such power did not surprise him and it confirmed the stories his father had told him.

The work in the camp went quickly. Stones were gathered, and walls built and held together with mud mixed with grass. The outer wall went up first.

This insured the Clan would be able to defend themselves from any predators. The individual quarters were decided next and communal fires and cooking areas allocated.

Taelo had little to do with the majority of what was now going on. He had all the tribal clothes and sleeping blankets washed and processed. There was an immediate change in the energy of everyone in camp. Unknown to any of them including Taelo, the camp had been suffering a continuous fever due to the lice and fleas.

The entire smell of the camp became more favorable.

On the fifth day Golden Hawk brought another group loaded with dried meat, fresh meat, bags of oil and processed whale skin, ivory, bone, and gut. The group was welcomed, and the food put into the communal pantry area prepared for it.

The final search group had found them on the beach, and they were back helping the processing of the food.

Amazingly the first group took the new arrivals to the hot pool and had them take a bath before letting them into the camp.

This caught Golden Hawk by surprise. "What have you done to this Clan," he shouted to Taelo as he plunged into the warm pool and showed the others how to bathe.

Afterwards, Taelo talked to Golden Hawk, and they agreed on how many trips it would take to bring in all the food. They discussed this with the Elders and plans were put into place to bring in the remainder of the food.

Taelo interjected a sense of urgency. He told them his Clan was preparing for a very long and cold winter. They would need to get all their goods in and be prepared for the cold.

Taelo thought how lucky this group was to have a hot spring to provide them with a warm cave and hot bathes. He knew his mother was bathing using water carried in from the stream and then heated by stones.

Thinking of his mother made Taelo decide it was time for him to return to the Elk Clan. In the evening he sat with the elders and let them know as soon as the rest of the food was brought in, he and Golden Hawk would return to their own Clan.

It was close to the Winter Solstice. The Elk Clan always celebrated the solstice with a night of eating telling stories and drinking a special brew the women prepared.

Taelo discovered the Others also celebrated the Winter Solstice with a similar ceremony. The Elders decided to hold the celebration a few days early so they could host and honor their new friend and young leader. The event was planned and when the last of the food was brought in the party was to be held.

A few days later the last of the whale was brought to the cave.

The remaining members of the Clan were indoctrinated into the new bathing ritual and then allowed into the camp.

In the evening, a celebration was held. All night the elders told stories of days past and the feats of heroes of old. Taelo and Golden Hawk felt the presence of these old ones and it seemed they walked among them.

It was surprising how many of the stories about heroes were similar to the ones told by his people.

Toward the morning the elders added the stories of Taelo and Golden Hawk and the scream of the eagle in with the rest of the Clan's history. This embarrassed Taelo and Golden Hawk, but the Clan considered them their honorary new ones.

The two told the elders they were not worthy but honored that they were included in the Other's history.

The elders all invited Taelo and Golden Hawk to stay longer, though they understood their wish to return to their own Clan. They, however, decided the two should be escorted back by Burly Bear and at least three other warriors. It would not do for the messenger sent by the ancients and ancestors to befall any harm.

The next morning a well-provisioned Taelo and Golden Hawk jogged down the beach. They ran just ahead of the four young warriors of the old ones. Someone watching might have mistaken the scene for two slender people being chased by four burly, rough looking attackers.

Chapter 16: Return Home

The fire warmed Gray Fox Running as he sat by the coals of the night fire and quietly discussed the progress of the hunt with his team of hunters. Their harvest was abundant. Most of the meat was dried. They were now fully loaded. Grey Fox Running was ready to return to the Clan earlier than planned. The team had performed beyond expectations and had sent back two previous loads. There was enough dry meat to sustain the Clan until spring. They were finishing drying the huge amount of meat from the large mastodon they had taken down.

This last excursion had been a great success but one of the warriors had his leg broken when the mastodon fell on him at the end.

Grey Fox Running had set the warrior's broken leg and he was doing well. To the injured hunter's chagrin, the other hunters had renamed him Falling Mastodon. This tale would grow in its telling and Falling Mastodon knew his new name was his and would always be so.

This injury put the team short of people to pull all the travois of meat and the tusks of the mastodon.

Grey Fox Running was deep in thought when one of the warriors called in a warning.

Two people were coming across the valley toward them. This was empty territory, so Grey Fox Running went out to see who was coming. Looking out across the wide, snow covered plain below, Grey Fox Running, recognized Red Oak's red feather flying from the top of his spear.

The sight of Red Oak brought immediate apprehension to Grey Fox Running. Something was wrong otherwise Red Oak would not have come. He went out to meet him. The two were the best of friends and were always happy to see each other.

After their initial greetings Grey Fox Running asked," What brings you out to find us?"

"When I returned from my long hunt, I was attacked by a large group of Others. I tricked them and gave them mostly stones and wood, though they got about ten percent of what I had hunted. We lured them with a decoy and then ran away ahead of them to where four of our strongest hunters were pulling two very heavily loaded travois. This allowed us to get most of the food to our Clan.

The Clan has found a very good place to spend the winter, but I am afraid the Others will attack. They are a much larger group than our Clan and you know how strong and fierce they are.

I came as soon as I could. It has taken me ten days to find you. I think we should return as soon as possible. Perhaps you should go ahead, and I will bring the hunters back as soon as possible," Red Oak hurriedly told his story.

"No, we will all go back together. We have enough food and the two of you are exactly what we need. Now we have enough muscle to pull our load home.

The Others usually do not attack us. It is usually we who attack the Others.

Yes, they are very strong, and they are unusually hairy and fierce looking, but I have lived with them, and they are reasonable. They are unusually wise and seem to be able to do things with their minds of which we have no knowledge.

I will heed your warning and we shall proceed back quickly. However, I will be surprised if they have attacked," Grey Fox Running replied.

Grey Fox Running recalled how his father had befriended a group of old ones and had lived with them for several years. This was before they had joined the Elk Clan.

"Let's get the others ready to return home," Red Oak replied not feeling as confident as Grey Fox Running.

He wanted to return as soon as possible.

It took the hunters two days to pack up all the food and position it on a travois each would pull. Falling Mastodon had a crutch, but he would ride one of the travois along with some of the food. It was too soon for him to travel on his bad leg.

It would take them a good fifteen to twenty sun cycles to make the journey home. Red Oak had marked the trail on his way out and knew if any danger was to befall the Clan's winter quarters a runner could quickly find them.

The fact no runner came was somewhat reassuring.

The hunting on the way home was only for their daily meals. It consisted of a few unlucky rabbits or deer surprised by the slowly moving procession of heavily weight travois each pulled by two warriors.

Now with the hunt over, Grey Fox Running and Red Oak were eager to return to the Elk Clan. They set a grueling pace and marched for at least ten hours a day. This was a dawn to dusk march.

They only had one small, heated meal prepared hastily in the evening. No one had time to enjoy the beautiful but cold vista of mountain valley's and streams. They were now into the heart of winter and eager to get back to the Clan.

The cold was deep and bit through their clothing and coats.

This was truly a breathtaking country. The long valleys held abundant game. The various thickets showed signs of blackberries and dewberries.

Red Oak and Grey Fox Running shared what they had learned about the country around them with each other and agreed this land offered the Clan a bountiful territory in which to take up their residence. Hopefully, they would not run into any other people claiming this area.

They hoped to enjoy this abundance and keep the Elk Clan well fed.

After almost two weeks of travel, they finally were headed down the valley leading to the sea. Red Oak figured they would make the main camp in about three sun cycles.

They had targeted to make it home by the winter solstice, so they could all celebrate the shortest sun cycle and the lengthening of sunlight afterwards. They looked forward to the feasting and the celebration which would take place.

They moved out onto the beach at about the same place Red Oak had before. Red Oak was wary but there did not seem to be anyone about. He wondered where the Others were, but he was pleased not to have to deal with them.

On the third day they were moving down the beach as the sun set far out to sea. A far away golden glow, with gray and purple shining from the clouds greeted them to the beach. The loud crashing of the waves made casual talk almost impossible. The sight of the sun's rays painting the clouds a pink, grey and golden yellow, caused Grey Fox Running to call a rest halt so all of them could enjoy the beauty.

The winter quarters are just about a mile down the coast from here," Red Oak informed the group as they were enjoying the sunset.

Not far down the beach Taelo, Golden Hawk, Burley Bear and the other three warriors accompanying them were sitting down enjoying the same sunset.

"There are other people on the beach just north of here," Burly Bear said as he drew his message in the sand.

"Now how does he know such a thing," wondered Taelo out loud to Golden Hawk?

"Let's move over to that log and see who it is," Golden Hawk said as he looked around for some shelter.

The six of them moved to a large log located on the beach and lay down behind it.

As the sun dipped rapidly below the horizon, Grey Fox Running Running's group set out with new energy. Their legs were strengthened by the fact they were close to their new home. All were looking forward to seeing their families and loved ones.

Suddenly an eagle cried out and the cry of the hawk followed.

Red Oak and Grey Fox Running looked at each other. They knew these calls. Grey Fox Running returned the call of the eagle and Red Oak did the same for the cry of the hawk

Up ahead they saw two bodies stand up from behind a large log. The two ran out toward the oncoming group. It was Taelo and Golden Hawk.

Behind them came four strangers. As they drew closer, Grey Fox Running recognized them as some of the Others. He wondered if they had indeed attacked. The Others stopped a good distance away and were not making any moves to come any closer.

The two boys rushed to their fathers.

"It's very nice of you two to come out to greet us," Grey Fox Running said as he hugged Taelo. He noticed Taelo had grown a good hand in height.

"No, it is you who are greeting us. We are just returning from several weeks at the camp of the Others. We would have made it to our Clan's winter camp if we had not stopped to enjoy the beauty of the sunset," Taelo replied.

Just then, from down the beach came the cry on the eagle. Taelo eagerly replied since he recognized his mother's version of his cry.

"Well, this is a great home coming. I don't know who is greeting whom, but it is nice to be back," Red Oak said.

White Swan, Quiet Pheasant and three of the Elk Clans warriors met the group. There were hugs and quiet rejoicing.

White Swan was a little overwhelmed to have the two men in her life back home at the same time.

Quiet Pheasant had the same feelings as she greeted Red Oak and Golden Hawk.

Burley Bear sat down cross-legged on the beach as he watched the two groups. He quietly talked to the three other three warriors.

"Look at the amount of food this hunting party is bringing home. This Clan will eat as well as ours. It seems that these new ones have a gift for gathering food," Burley Bear said to the three younger warriors.

"Look at how they care for each other. They are just like us in so many ways. I wonder why we have not been friends," Burly Bear asked but he was not addressing anyone?

"Who are your new friends? And what are their names," Grey Fox Running asked?

He walked toward the Others and the rest of the Elk warriors followed him.

The two groups came together.

He knew that though Taelo had helped his Clan, most of the new ones were usually afraid of the Others. The new ones looked very frail, but they were very fast and agile. The Others were much stronger and muscular but as Burly Bear knew they were slower.

Gray Fox Running approached, Burley Bear and extended his hand in friendship.

Burley Bear stood up and returned the handshake. This was the first time one of the new ones other than Taelo and Golden Hawk had approached him in a friendly manner.

"You must be the father of the great one we call, Taelo the scream of the eagle," Burley Bear said to Grey Fox Running.

To his surprise, Grey Fox Running replied in rough but understandable language of the Others.

"Yes, Taelo is my son. I hope he has provided your people the help he promised," Gray Fox Running replied as both groups looked at him in amazement.

Only White Swan knew Grey Fox Running had this talent. It was because of the stories he had told her, that she had been so certain her actions were the right ones to take in trying friendship first.

"We were sent to escort Taelo and Golden Hawk home to ensure their safety," Burley Bear explained his presence and of the other three warriors.

"Well let's get to the camp and see if there is a decent meal for all of us," Grey Fox Running continued speaking in Burley Bear's language.

Taelo was surprised by Grey Fox Running's ability to speak Burley Bear's language. He and Golden Hawk had been practicing and had picked up quite a few words, but neither could fully understand what Grey Fox Running had just said.

After repeating himself in the language of the Clan, Grey Fox Running with White Swan, at his side, led the way toward the village. Gray Fox Running took in the work done in making the camp winter worthy. The main shelter had been finished. Down near where the water fell from the cliff, he could see a fire pit that he would later learn was the one personal lodge put up by Floating Cloud the mother of his good friend Fast Skimmer, who he had lost during his last long hunt.

Several cooking areas had been set up outside of the main lodge. A few separate quarters had been completed and the frames for most of the other quarters had been erected but remained uncovered.

Grey Fox Running figured the shortage of hides was the reason. His return would solve most of this problem.

Silent Hawk greeted both Grey Fox Running and Red Oak.

They all listened to the account Taelo brought back to them about finding food and relocating the old ones to the cave with hot springs. Everyone commented the perhaps they should have sent Taelo out to find them winter quarters with a hot spring.

White Swan moaned and acted hurt about such a comment, but she smiled as she did so. She complemented Taelo and Golden Hawk for having done so well.

Taelo and Golden Hawk thanked White Swan for the kind comments and in turn introduced their friend Burley Bear and the three other warriors.

Burley Bear stood as he was introduced. He was a good head taller than Grey Fox Running and at least twice as wide. His smile looked like that of a snarling wolf to many in the Clan.

Even though there was a language barrier, it was Burley Bear who told the story of Taelo and the whale. He told his account of Taelo finding the whale, of talking to the huge female brown bear, of feeding the wolves and finally of finding the new dwelling with a heated spring. The surprise for everyone was that Grey Fox Running translated this account to the entire Elk Clan as Burley Bear told it. The Clan in turn sat quietly taking in every word of the story.

Taelo became even more mysterious and symbolic to the Clan than before.

Taelo sat quietly by White Swan. Golden Hawk sat next to him with Quiet Pheasant and Red Oak.

It was clear to both he and Golden Hawk that they needed to get away from all the attention they were getting from both Clans.

Chapter 17: Winter Takes Hold

The days got progressively colder and the storms coming in from the sea more powerful. Even with the protection shielding of the spit of land, the camp was buffeted by powerful storms and became coated with a salty ice. It was good the camp had been built up away from the beach, for the beach disappeared under the surging sea.

The main shelter stood the weather well. Its construction had been thorough and solid. The earth bank on the outside kept the cold winds at bay. The movable sections of the roof allowed for easy temperature control.

Only a few families were now without their own family shelter. The Clan was still short on the materials to make all of them individual family shelters. Grey Fox Running had made all the additional family shelters in the same way as the main building. This provided each with good insulation against the cold. A small fire in the center of each building provided all the warmth needed.

During these brutally cold days, everyone busied themselves inside with the preparation of the few leather hides not used for shelter, carving on the ivory of the elk or the teeth of the black rhino.

Taelo had brought back several ivory teeth from the beached whale he had found. He was intricately carving the scene of the beach on one tooth and on the other he was carving a picture of the Clan's camp. He would work on his pieces for a while and then do something else for a while before continuing. He figured it would take him most of the winter to finish his two pieces.

Burley Bear had chosen to stay with Taelo and had sent the other warriors back north to their new home. Burley Bear felt a kindred spirit in this young man called Taelo and felt it was his role to protect him. He would accompany Taelo and talk with him wherever they went.

Taelo and Golden Hawk were quickly picking up the language of the Others. They would sit around and practice with Burley Bear and then try their new learning on Grey Fox Running.

The camp members soon accepted this burley young warrior from the Others as just another Elk Clan member. He looked very different, and it was clear he was covered with enough hair to make his name appropriate. He worked hard and he seemed always at Taelo's side.

Even if they had wanted to, none of the other boys Taelo's age would have dared confront him. His own bodyguard looking like a wild bear usually shadowed him.

After a few weeks of fixing his clothes, his shoes, his weapons, and anything else seeming to need repair, Taelo grew restless. He and Golden Hawk decided to climb the cliff behind the camp and see what was on the other side and beyond. They talked it over and decided not to say anything to anyone. They prepared everything in secret.

Early one morning they left.

They prepared themselves for the extreme cold they expected to face and carried plenty of warm clothes. They were not sure hunting would provide enough food at this time of year, so they carried a supply of dried foods.

Long before dawn, Taelo and Golden Hawk quietly left the comfort of their beds and started up the cliff. They were climbing the cliff just as dawn broke. It was slow going up the steep cliff face, but they made good progress.

Once on top they followed a trail they had found when they first arrived. By the time the camp began to stir, they were almost to the top of the cliff. By the time Burley Bear began to look for Taelo, the two boys were over the top of the cliff and on their way along the ridge leading eastward away from the beach. They took off trotting in their normal traveling gait.

The timing of the two could not have been worse. A cold front came in during the day and the temperature took a steep drop and the wind steadily increased. A severe winter storm was blowing in from the west.

On the backside of the cliff, away from the sea, the turn of the weather was not immediately noticeable to Taelo and Golden Hawk. The air was noticeably colder, but the wind had not yet started to blow. They were trotting along a ridge going inland away from the sea. The wind was at their back.

They had left a message for their parents not to worry and were quite satisfied they would not be missed. The self-confidence they had in themselves and each other shielded them from any concern they might have had.

The weather continued to get colder, and the wind picked up. This became noticeable to both Taelo and Golden Hawk and they began looking for a place to shelter. They had slowed to a walk along an old animal trail when they heard the sound of a waterfall. The trail went around a huge wall of stone and seemed to disappear down the mountain on the other side. It was a sheer drop down the narrowest of trails. The sun was making its final descent and the trail would be impossible to follow.

Taelo turned back to where they had first heard the waterfall. He found a crack in the rocks and followed it. He found himself looking into a large cave with a steaming pool of water inside. From a crack in the rocks on the other side, cold wind was blowing in and pushing the air through the crack where he was standing. There was a flat area all the way around the pool and what looked like benches around the edge of the pool area.

"Look at this place. If we can close the opening on the other side, we will have a warm winter home," Taelo exclaimed to Golden Hawk.

"Let's find some timbers and get the opening closed. I think we are going to need a good place to escape from this cold winter storm," Golden Hawk replied as he looked around for the wood he wanted.

The two found the timber they needed in the forest they had been jogging through. They also found some stones they could use to help close the far gap as well as the entrance gap. They brought all the materials to the cave and set about closing the far opening. They determined the final closing could best be accomplished with the use of some of the hides they were carrying. Together they closed the opening with a thick buffalo hide. It would allow them to open it to let light in during the day.

Taelo closed the cracks on entrance to the cave in such a manner that he created a cold area to the left side of the entrance. This would be a great place to keep meat and other food. This was separated by stone from the warm area surrounding the pool. They gathered enough stones to close the entrance opening.

This greatly reduced the airflow through the cave. Immediately the cave began to warm.

Using the hide, they had put across the top of the crack in the cave closest to the waterfall, they were able to control the air flow so a small fire could be placed on a flat stone. The smoke went up and out through the crack in the roof.

They did not need the fire for warmth, only for cooking. The heated pool provided all the warmth needed. This kept the air in the cave very fresh.

The two had spent most of the day working on making the cave fit for use and they had not spent much time worrying about the weather. By now the storm was beginning to be a serious raging storm. They, however, were in warm, comfortable quarters. The evening brought the storm, and the temperature outside took a steep dive.

Back at the Elk Clan camp White Swan worried about the two getting caught unprepared by the incoming bad weather. To her surprise it was Burly Bear who seemed the most worried. He had been caught off guard. He had not sensed or anticipated this event. He immediately prepared his belongings and was going to follow the two.

Grey Fox Running and Red Oak thought it would be a good idea for Burley Bear to find the two young adventurers. They figured he would find them and help keep them safe. They loaded the young warrior down with extra dried meat and other food that would travel well. Finally, they gave him a great bearskin to carry with him.

Even if caught outside Burley Bear and the two adventures would have a warm place to sleep. Burley Bear's pack was almost as large as he.

The camp watched somewhat amazed when Burley Bear climbed the cliff with the load he had on his back. All the Clan members found it strange to have this warrior from the Others so attached to Taelo and Golden Hawk.

"In his short time, Taelo has made strong friends who are willing to risk their lives for him. Let's hope our young man does not overextend himself in his adventures," Grey Fox Running said as he held White Swan to him.

Together they watched Burley Bear's progress up the steep cliff.

"I am not too worried about Taelo, but it is comforting to know he has such strong friends who will risk themselves to know he is alright. I am sure Taelo will again surprise us," White Swan said as she returned Gray Fox Running's hug.

She sensed this was another of Taelo and Golden Hawk's adventures where they would distinguish themselves.

Burly Bear struggled as he climbed up the cliff. He wondered how Taelo and Golden Hawk had made this climb. The capability and resilience of the two were constantly surprising him. Their daring and capability seemed to overcome all obstacles put in front of them. He finally made the summit and after taking some time to recover from the climb he began a constant gait as he followed their trail.

Thank goodness they had followed the ridge and taken a fairly level, somewhat downhill path. Burley Bear figured he would catch up to them by noon. Noon came and passed. He continued at a constant jog as he chewed on some of the dried meat sent with him. He realized he had greatly underestimated the speed at which the two traveled. He had previously watched them seemingly and effortlessly glided across the ground as they jogged along. He now was personally experiencing just how fast the two moved.

Finally, as dusk was falling, Burley Bear came to the end of the trail he was following. The weather by now was biting through his clothes and he was worried he would have to stop and prepare a camp. Snow was falling heavily. Where had the two disappeared? For the third time Burley Bear read the tracks. The tracks all lead to a huge stone and disappeared.

"Could Taelo walk through stone," Burley Bear thought to himself?

"Taelo, Taelo, where are you," Burley Bear shouted repeatedly as loud as he could?

Inside the warm cave, both Taelo and Golden Hawk heard the bellowing of what they thought was a bear calling Taelo's name.

"Is our friend, Burley Bear shouting your name," Golden Hawk said in surprise?

"We had better go out and look otherwise if he is, he will freeze in such weather," Taelo replied.

The two carefully removed the stones they had put in the entrance fissure and stepped out to greet Burley Bear.

"On the spirits of the Ancients, you can walk through stone," Burley Bear stepped back in amazement, as it seemed to him the two literally stepped out of the stone!

"Now what is going on with you," Taelo said as he stepped forward and gave the much bigger warrior a hug and pulled him toward the opening in the stone.

The cold by this time was bitter and was immediately going through the light clothes the two had stripped down to.

Burley Bear at first hesitated but the bitter cold urged him to follow. Then he noticed the fissure he had previously missed and realized the two had closed it with a series of well-placed boulders to close the gap.

It was a tight squeeze for him to enter and his height meant that he had to lower his head as he crossed to where they were sitting.

Once closed, the snow quickly covered the stones. From outside the face of the stones seemed solid. A few moments after they stepped inside, anyone approaching the fissure would not recognize it as an opening. This was a perfect hiding place.

Burley Bear took in the work the two young warriors had already put into the place. He was impressed with their capability. The place was very comfortable. He noticed the heated pool and marveled at Taelo's ability to find such places.

The big bearskin he was carrying was a perfect finish for the cave. It provided a sleeping area allowing all three to lie down in comfort and with their own lighter sleeping hides be comfortable in the warmth of the cave.

Back on the beach the storm raged and the waves from the sea crashed up against the base of the camp. It was by far the worst storm to have come at the camp up to this time.

"I hope Burley Bear has found Taelo and Golden Hawk. Now I am more worried about him than the other two," White Swan said quietly to Grey Fox Running as the two lay by each other enjoying the warmth they shared as they listened to the storm outside.

Not far away, Red Oak and Quite Pheasant were exchanging similar words.

"As long as Golden Hawk and Taelo are together, I do not worry too much. The two complement each other and together they seem able to accomplish anything they set their minds to. I believe this is their naming journey. It is early but these two do everything ahead of their time," Quite Pheasant shared with Red Oak.

"You are probably right. I will bring this up to the council tomorrow when we meet," Red Oak replied.

He hoped the two had found a good place to make camp and that Burley Bear had found them.

The winter seemed to take a dive into temperatures that made a bearskin coat seem to be made of thin grass. A person could only stay out a few moments and then be in peril.

Everyone gathered close to the campfires and tried to stay warm as the weather continued to stay cold. The storms seemed to come unabated. The cold literally crept through every crevice and came across the floor and grabbed a person at the ankles or any part of the body close to the ground.

The gathering of firewood became a dangerous effort. It was the only work to take anyone outside.

North, up the beach, where the Others were passing the winter in their warm and relatively comfortable cave, Broken Spear shared a vision with the Clan.

"Last night, I saw Taelo, Golden Hawk and our very own Burley Bear. They are on a journey together.

This is Taelo's journey into adulthood. He has gone out in the middle of winter on a call from his ancestors. He does not hear them as we do but he responds to their call none-the-less.

He will find the food to carry his Clan through the spring and a prosperous place for his Clan to live. He will return at the end of the winter with the food the Clan needs to make it through the final days of winter.

We will see him in the spring when he comes to greet us and invite us to live in the same valley as the Elk Clan," Broken Spear shared with the others sitting by the fire.

The Others all understood what Broken Spear had seen would come to pass, as had all his visions.

They began to discuss what it would be like to live with the new ones.

Taelo awakened to the constants roar of the waterfall and the light coming in from the opening nearest the waterfall. He walked to the opening and looked down into the valley below. The snow of the night before had stopped falling.

The morning was crisp, the view was crystal clear. He could see far into the distance.

Below the earth seem to move and undulate. It took Taelo a moment to realize a huge herd of Bison stretching as far as the eye could see were digging through the snow and eating the grass bent below it.

"Golden Hawk, Burley Bear, come see a most spectacular sight," Taelo said in both languages.

As the three stood watching, a lone eagle soared over the valley and let out a long, lonely cry. A shiver ran down Taelo's back. Once again, he had been led to a place and been given a sign.

Once the storm had subsided, he would go down into the valley and explore it.

Chapter 18: Valley of Plenty

Taelo took one last look to the valley below and marveled at the dark brown sea of buffalo undulating like the waves of the ocean. He tied down the hide to securely close the opening and turned and looked around the shelter with its warm water pool and the small stream flowing by his feet out to join the rest of the water coming down the fall to the pool far below.

Golden Hawk and Burley Bear were waiting for him at the exit. They were ready to close the entrance once he was out. They had left some dried food hanging out over the warm water pool to keep it safe from the rodents. They had talked about coming back to their personal hot water pool when they wanted to get away from everyone.

The mountain snow was deep and the downward path treacherous. They made their way slowly and carefully down the trail to the valley below. Working together they were able to descent the steep, icy dangerous path down the face of an almost vertical grade.

The valley floor seemed to move and crawl on its own. The sight of a sea of buffalo greeting them was overwhelming and astounding. Never had any of them seen so many buffalo in one place. The undulating mass of buffalo extended as far as the eye could see. The motion of this mass seemed scripted and harmonized as it slowly undulated with the movement of buffalo foraging for food.

The three kept just into the edge of the forest as they progressed down the valley. They did not want the herd to be frightened. The large number of buffalo would make it extremely dangerous to hunt them.

They traveled three days down the valley and still the herd had not broken. Had they wanted to cross the valley to the other side they would have had to risk going through the herd.

After traveling for four days, they came to the end of the valley and the end of the herd.

The small stream meandering down the valley from the waterfall ended at a bend of a medium sized river. The herd of Buffalo ended on the bank of the same small river.

Taelo, Golden Hawk and Burley Bear decided to travel down the river to see where it led.

Burley Bear pulled three dried wooden logs to the river where they made a raft on which they could float and keep dry. From this platform they were able to spear fish and catch the food they needed. Several rabbits met their fate as did a fat ground hog. All became a meal for the three.

They saved the dried meat Burley Bear had brought for the times when nothing presented itself to them.

The three had every intension of hunting the herd of Bison but they decided to wait until they were returning to the Clan. They figured to come back and harvest a few buffalo to take back to the Clan.

The trip down the river was uneventful. It led to a large harbor, and they followed the western shore until they came to the opening to the ocean. The three had followed the valley south and the river west. They had traced an arc leading them back to the ocean. Though the three did not know it exactly, the range of travel put them some twenty-one sun cycles travel south of where the Clan had its camp.

They finally decided to return to the valley of plenty, secure a sizeable amount of buffalo meat and then find a short cut to the ocean and return from the south along the seashore, back to the Clan.

Winter was still testing their tolerance of the cold. The large sleeping hide Burley Bear carried provided them ample warmth each night.

The three would sleep side by side with Burley Bear in the middle. Half the hide would be the bottom and they would fold the other half over the top. They then used a lighter hide to cover their heads.

The snowfall was unusually heavy and fell steadily as they made their way back to the valley. The going became a test of their stamina. They reached the mouth of the river and found they could not effectively push upstream. They figured to use it again, so they beached their raft and pulled it up on the bank and into the forest where together they stood it on end to keep the logs from decaying.

Burley Bear surprised Taelo and Golden Hawk by stopping by a willow stand as they struggled to make their way back to the valley. He cut several small willow trees and bent them into teardrop shapes. He used the bark to tie them and then used the smaller branches to create a crisscrossed pattern. He then tied them to his feet and demonstrated his ability to walk more easily across the top of the snow.

Taelo and Golden Hawk immediately copied him and made a set for themselves. From then on, the three made better time as they proceeded back to the valley.

Burley Bear cut several more willows and carried a large bundle of them on his back.

"What are the willow branches for," Taelo inquired

"You will find out later. It is a surprise," he replied in a smug secretive manner.

This time they stayed to the western side of the valley. About halfway up the valley, the three found what appeared to be a westward way out of valley. However, to reach the cut leading toward the sea they would have to climb about halfway up the mountainside.

It would be a challenge, but they decided it was probably the best way they would find. After some scouting and consideration, they decided they would have to make several trips up the mountain to haul up the meat they planned to take back to the village.

On the evening before their hunt, Taelo, Golden Hawk and Burley Bear sang their praises to the ancients and the ancestors. They asked for guidance and for accuracy in the use of their weapons. Using hot stones and their cooking pack they prepared and ate a hearty meal made from the dried meat cooked into a stew.

Burley Bear appreciated the cooking talent the two displayed.

They agreed Taelo and Golden Hawk would try and take down two young bulls. They would stay to the edge of the herd and separate their quarry from the rest of the herd. They desperately wanted to avoid a stampede.

The buffalo meat would be their return present to the Clan.

Early the next morning the two left Burley Bear at the edge of the forest and slowly approached the herd.

They each were covered with a buffalo skin and were moving very slowly toward the edge of the herd. It took them a full hour to get close to the herd.

Taelo slowly began to edge a young male yearling away from the herd.

Golden Hawk was doing the same with a second young bull.

The bulls nervously moved away from the herd toward the edge of the forest.

Suddenly, Taelo dropped the skin he was using as a cover. He dashed out toward the young bull. The bull immediately began to run toward the forest.

Taelo ran alongside of the bull until they were near the edge of the forest then he put on a burst of speed and dashed ahead of the young bull. He planted the butt of his spear in the ground as he had seen his father do and put the spear tip in the middle of the young bull's chest.

Immediately the spear was driven almost half of the way into the young bull. The young bull stopped and staggered a few steps and then collapsed. Taelo looked around and saw Golden Hawk had accomplished the same feat.

Burley Bear stood in amazement at the edge of the forest. He had never seen such a feat. His people could not run fast enough. They would guide their quarry into traps where the warriors would take down the buffalo.

This would be a story he was going to love to tell the Others. It would be hard for his listeners to believe, and they would probably think he was just embellishing the story.

But he would tell this story many times.

The rest of the herd continued grazing as if nothing had happened. This was exactly what Taelo had hoped. He had worried the herd would stampede. He wanted the herd to stay in place so the Clan members could come to the valley to hunt more of the buffalo.

Taelo, Golden Hawk and Burley Bear pulled the young bulls into the edge of the forest.

This was where Burley Bear's size made a huge difference. His strength made it possible for the bulls to be pulled up into the trees and there the three gutted and skinned them. When they were through with the skinning, they cut the bulls into transportable sections and moved them about a quarter mile away from the point of the butchering and pulled the sections up into the trees.

They made their camp a few yards away.

In the afternoon, Burley Bear began to assemble a device neither Taelo nor Golden Hawk had seen before. Burley Bear patiently warmed the young willow saplings over the fire and then bent them into sled runners.

Then he tied a straight willow section between the two curved ends of the willow. Next, he began to link the two runners together with X braces and some straight braces. This made a floor for the sled. The device took shape as both Taelo and Golden Hawk finished their work of butchering and moving the meat into the trees where they could protect it.

They bundled the heart, tongue, liver, kidneys, and the tail into one section of hide. All of these were special gifts to be given to the elders. The hump of each young bull was carefully wrapped and would be a gift to each of their mothers.

It was not until they had finished their grueling work when Taelo and Golden Hawk finally had a chance to study what Burly Bear had been making. His device was about two spears long and had curled ends. The sled could be pulled in either direction. But the end with the largest curled end was definitely the front.

When Burley Bear demonstrated the sled by using it to slide down the slope away from the campfire, both Taelo and Golden Hawk let out a whoop and got excited.

"This is unbelievable. This device will let us transport the meat out in a much faster way," Taelo pointed out to Golden Hawk.

"Yes, it will also let us pull much more weight than we could with a travois," Golden Hawk replied as he pulled Burley Bear back into the camp.

The two stood looking at a smug Burley Bear.

"See, we of the Others, still can teach you something," Burley Bear said with a fair amount of pride.

Taelo took a slice of meat from each of the bison humps and presented it to Burley Bear.

"To our brother Burley Bear, thank you for sharing this new tool with us. It will allow us to transport the meat we have harvested," Taelo said as he put the meat on a spit.

He spread some of the precious salt on the meat and then held it over the fire. He presented the cooked meat to a proud Burley Bear.

They all sat around the fire talking, roasting pieces of fresh meat and sharing their vision of the future. It was hard for Burley Bear to remember he came from a tribe which was shrinking. His two brothers of the new people had so much enthusiasm and dreams of the future. Their enthusiasm carried over into his soul.

The next day was spent slowly moving the meat up the mountainside to the higher exit leading out of the valley and down to the sea. The sled was easy enough to carry up to the beginning of the valley. They used the hide of one young bull to cover the bottom of the sled.

They then carried, pulled, and generally manhandled each section up the steep mountainside to where the sled was positioned. They put the sections on the sled and used the second hide to cover the load from the top.

They tied the bundle securely to the sled.

Each of them tied on to the sled with a pull line and slowly began to pull the load along the valley floor. By this time, it was late afternoon. They immediately began looking for a defendable place to spend the fast-approaching night.

They had gone a little more than a mile when they found a huge tree that had blown over. The roots had pulled out and left a shallow depression. The roots themselves offered a backdrop and a defendable shelter. The same tree provided an abundance of wood for a fire.

The three of them worked the sled up against the tree roots and then made three small fires out around the periphery of the root depression. They hoped they would not need to fight off any hungry wolves.

They had another hearty evening meal of fresh roasted meat and a few boiled roots. Then they pulled out their giant bearskin and the three huddled in the middle with the skin pulled around them.

They took turns sleeping. One of them was always awake to feed the wood into the fire throughout the night. Their sled provided a backdrop to lean against. The night was uneventful, and no animals bothered them.

It took them two days to slowly descend to the sea. The sled Burley Bear constructed allowed them to make the journey in record time. They were all glad when they saw the ocean spread out before them.

The three turned and headed northward toward the Elk Clan's winter quarters. They found that by staying close to the forest, the snow on the ground allowed them to pull the sled.

Almost two months had passed. During this time, the supplies for the Clan was slowly depleted.

"I had hoped we would catch more fish, but the storms have kept us away from our fish traps," White Swan bemoaned her frustration at not being able to stretch her supplies.

"We will need to send out a hunting party to see if they can find some game to tide us over into late spring," Grey Fox Running replied as he thought how frustrated spring often made him feel.

The weather would improve but food was hard to find and many a Clan lost their members to hunger just as summer began to promise riches.

A lookout scout came in with the news that three people were coming up the beach from the south. They were pulling a strange contraption behind them.

Grey Fox Running, Red Oak and several of the younger men went out to see who was coming and what they were pulling. From the top of the peak of the rocky cliffs making up the spit out to sea, the two friends smiled when they saw the three figures pulling an unbelievably large load behind them.

"I am not sure what those three are bringing home but if it was not for the figure in the middle, I don't think that load would move," Grey Fox Running said with a chuckle to Red Oak.

"Truly that has to be Burley Bear in the middle. No other person we know looks so much like a bear," Red Oak replied.

"Let's get down there and see if we can help them bring in what I hope is a supply of food," Grey Fox Running instructed the group of young men around him.

The Elk Clan members descended and met a jubilant but very tired trio. They had pulled two thousand pounds of meat for more than fifty miles up the coast.

Now six fresh young men harnessed themselves to the sled and pulled it the rest of the way to the village. It had been almost two moon cycles since the two had climbed up the cliff behind the village.

They had ventured out and made their own way across the mountains and had arrived with a load of meat just as the stores of the Clan was running low.

Taelo and Golden Hawk presented their gifts to the elders and finally they presented the richest gifts to their mothers.

To Grey Fox Running and Red Oak, the two presented the spears with which they had each killed their first bison.

Grey Fox Running accepted the spear and for the first time told the story of having learned to hunt the buffalo in this manner form his mate White Swan and Quiet Pheasant on the hunt they had gone on together and where White Swan had extracted his request that she be his mate.

In a joking manner, Red Oak added that not only did they show them how to hunt in a new manner. The two also captured the best-looking men of the Clan.

Taelo and Golden Hawk looked over at their mothers, raised their eyebrows, and winked.

During the evening Clan dinner, they told the story of Burley Bear teaching them to walk on the snow and showed them their snowshoes.

The sled was another story. Burley Bear now had his story intertwined with the Elk Clan's stories. He sat proudly as various members of the Clan thanked him and patted him on the back.

Two different peoples, despite their differences, were learning from one another.

Taelo had marked the way into the valley and hunters would be sent to gather more bison. The well-being of the Clan was ensured. Several trips would be made to harvest more meat and hides.

The weather seemed to take its cue from the return of the three adventures. It began to warm up and spring descended on the beach.

Fishing once again became feasible, and the Clan emerged renewed and reinvigorated after surviving what they had anticipated as the winter of their demise.

Chapter 19: Spring on the Beach

Taelo and Golden Hawk stood on the top of the tooth spit that protruded out into the opening of the protected cove in front of the Clan village. The top of the cove's jaw was the rocky arm of the mountains running in a semicircle three quarters of the way around the beach on the seaward side. This protected the beach, and it attracted a variety of fish that fed on the seaweed growing abundantly in the cove. Large green turtles also frequented the cove to feed on the algae and seaweed.

Across from the Head rock thousands of birds nested in the steep cliffs.

The two discussed how they would set up a way to guide fish into an area where they could easily be speared. Some fish would be guided to shallow pools where they could be picked up by hand.

They were reapplying the same idea that they had devised to catch salmon when they were in the Elk Hide Clan. Building the fish trap in the cove was a huge undertaking as compared to the small trap they had built in the river a few years ago.

They located the position for a series of vertical poles to guide fish into a trap where they could more easily be speared.

Taelo and Golden Hawk tied large stones to the bottom of straight three-inch poles about twenty feet long or longer. The poles needed to stick out of the water, so a narrow walkway could be built along the top of the poles. The poles were positioned about six feet apart and formed a cone that narrowed to about a two-foot opening.

Some small, curved willow limbs were tied at a ninety-degree angle to the last two poles. They acted like whiskers allowing the fish to easily enter but were an obstruction for those fish trying to swim out. Woven mats of willow limbs filled in the six-foot sections between the main polls.

Taelo and Golden Hawk enrolled everyone in the camp in some fashion.

Red Oak and Grey Fox Running were impressed with the planning capability of the two. Several of the Elk elders had expressed some doubt about the value of such an effort.

Taelo and Golden Hawk managed the many different groups putting together the various parts of this huge fish trap. They hoped it would work as well as the trap the two had built in the river.

Taelo had pointed the end of the cone into a round shallow area about three feet deep.

Here, standing on the walkways built on vertical poles, it would be extremely easy to spear the fish once they had been guided into this area.

Opposite the entrance was one more opening were the water was only a foot deep. The fish going into this area were usually smaller, they could be scooped out with pronged sticks and thrown up on the beach.

There was some skepticism about doing all this work for a few fish. Grey Fox Running however continued to encourage the members to participate and help Taelo and Golden Hawk.

Once the mouth of the cone was opened and the fish began to come in, it became obvious the Clan would enjoy an abundance of fish, an abundance beyond what they could imagine.

The number of fish captured kept everyone busy throughout the spring and early summer. Thousands of fish were dried. The Clan prospered, and everyone was well fed and healthy.

Burley Bear made a trip back to his Clan to invite them to a fishing festival that he, Taelo and Golden Hawk had devised.

They knew this would be a way for the two Clans to learn about each other.

White Swan and Quiet Pheasant knew that salt was critical to processing all the fish and other meats. She recruited several of the women and a few of the older warriors and created a broad flat pool that could be repeatedly filled and sundried. It was on the far side of the cove's tooth stone where the sun beat down through the entire day.

The salt production could barely keep up with the demand. Many fish were dried with no salt on them.

Once the salt processing area was functioning, White Swan turned its operation over to several of the older hunters whose job became that of repeated filling of the evaporation pools until the salt was thick enough to scrape off the flat rocks where the salt accumulated.

The salt was used in drying the fish but also in processing hides and for the normal cooking of the Clan's meals.

Taelo and Golden Hawk explored the cliffs along the spit and were constantly bringing back a wide variety of berries, sea conches and sea plants.

Taelo and Golden Hawk came home from one trip loaded with eggs they had gathered along the cliffs. They passed out the eggs to all the families.

Their generosity was one of the things which made the two stand out. It always seemed to take the Clan members by surprise.

White Swan and Quiet Pheasant led a band of young women to the area described by Taelo and gathered enough for a special dinner for the whole Clan.

One day there was shouting and a great deal of commotion from the cove. Taelo, Golden Hawk and Burley Bear found that a huge shark had become trapped. It was at least twenty-five feet long and seemed to take up the entire shallow area.

They speared the beast and the three fought with it for more than an hour as they worked to pull it ashore.

Burley Bear repeatedly hit the shark in the head with his stone headed war club until the shark finally died.

Taelo and Golden Hawk erected a tripod from which they hung the huge shark.

The sharkskin would be a rare and valuable item.

Taelo and Golden Hawk gutted the shark. Then they carefully skinned the shark and peeled the skin from the tail to the head.

The shark skin would be processed to make shark skin leather.

Taelo and Golden Hawk presented this very valuable leather to their mothers.

Burley Bear planned to do this as well.

Then they cut the meat off from each side. Two thirds of the meat was divided equally with all the families in the Elk Clan.

One third was for Burley Bear to take to the Clan of Others.

The shark teeth were carefully removed. There were at least fifty full size razor teeth and many smaller ones in the formation stage. These would make good spear tips and about one hundred more could be used for arrows and various cutting tools.

Taelo and Golden Hawk gave the best teeth to Grey Fox Running, Red Oak and to Silent Hawk.

Burley Bear became the keeper of one third of the shark teeth. He would share them with the Clan of Others.

Taelo, Golden Hawk and Burley Bear each kept half a dozen teeth for themselves and then gave each of the other young men in the Elk Clan several teeth.

They made a special presentation to three of the young women who had been most active in guiding the construction of the fish trap.

These were Quiet Rabbit, Busy Bee, and Talking Wren.

Little did either Taelo or Golden Hawk realize the significant role these three would play in the near future.

The shark teeth were one of the most valuable items one could possess. Their sharp edges and piercing points made the best and sharpest spear tips. This treasure could make a young man rich in their society.

This unselfish sharing of such a valuable treasure again surprised the Elk Clan members. No one had expected such generosity.

Grey Fox Running, Red Oak, White Swan, and Quiet Pheasant took pride in the character of their young warriors.

Burley Bear also took note of the character of the two. Their equal recognition of the Others and their generosity toward them fused his spirit to theirs. He filed yet another story to tell his Clan upon his return. The tales of Taelo and Golden Hawk were beginning to add up.

Silent Hawk spoke to the elders of the Clan, "These young men have repeatedly shown they deserve to be considered as full adult members of the Clan. It is time we honored them as they have honored us. Let us give them their adult names and make them full members of the Clan."

There was little debate about the merits of the recommendation. There was considerable discussion about their age but in the end everyone agreed. They would be the youngest members of the Clan's adult council.

Most of the discussion had been about what the other Clan leaders would say when the entire Clan met in the fall. However, the Elk Clan figured they could face any of those concerns at the time of the Clan gathering. There might be a few questions, but no one would be able to refute the contribution the two had made to the well-being of the Elk Clan. It was the right of the elders of the Elk Clan to decide.

The council picked a date about a full moon away to induct the two as full adult Clan members.

Taelo and Golden Eagle spoke about this to White Swan and Quiet Pheasant. They always approached their mothers when it concerned the politics of the Clan.

"We would like to invite the old ones to this ceremony. They are part of our story, part of who we are and who we will be. We would like them to attend," both confided in their mothers.

They knew if these two were supportive, then their fathers would also be supportive. Then they could face the rest of the Clan with full confidence in their request.

"That is an excellent idea. It will be a good way to bring the two people together. I will speak with Grey Fox Running about it," White Swan replied.

The fishing get together had worked very well, and this would extend the interaction between the two Clan's.

The discussion on the topic of inviting the Others to the ceremony was not as harmonious as the one agreeing to have the Others attend the fishing festival or the one to induce the two young men.

This would be an unprecedented event. It was a time when the ancestors were called. A time of deep ceremony.

The discussions went back and forth and, in the end, Grey Fox Running with the support of Silent Hawk and Red Oak used his clout as leader to push through an agreement.

A few days later Taelo, Golden Hawk and Burley Bear began their journey up the beach to the home of the Others.

They were making the trip to invite them to the ceremony.

Burley Bear seemed to have new energy in his step and did a fine job keeping up with the two younger members who seemed to have wings on their feet. Even then it took more than a week for them to travel up the coast to the stream leading back to the living area of the old ones.

To their surprise, the entire Clan was awaiting their arrival and had planned an evening's celebration of their return.

"Tell us about your winter's journey, through the mountains and the valley of the Buffalo," Broken Spear asked with a gleam in his eyes.

Taelo never ceased being surprised at the knowledge the old ones seemed to have. He was not sure how they did it but somehow, they could glean information from one's mind.

Taelo surprised the old ones by telling the story in their language. He carefully recited the story of their travels and unselfishly embellished Burley Bear's part of the story.

Burley Bear not only walked on the snow in his snowshoes, but they were so well made that he left no prints in the snow where he walked.

The Clan of Others began hooting and stomping the ground.

When he made the sled, he went down the mountain side so fast that he ran into two buffalo. They flew up in the air and on the way down he skinned them and loaded them on the sled before returning to his campfire.

Golden Hawk and I were so mad that we made him pull that sled for three days all the way back to the Elk Clan on his own.

This brought the Clan to their feet as they continued their hooting in appreciation of the story Taelo was telling.

Taelo held up his hand and asked the gathering to listen to one more feat of the Burley Bear.

On our return to the Elk Clan, Burley Bear was swimming in the water by the beach. A giant shark was attracted by his thrashing about. When it came to investigate the noise, it got so disoriented by the sight of Burley Bear in the water that it swam up onto the beach to where Golden Hawk and I were standing.

At the same time Burley Bear, seeing the size of the great shark ran out of the water screaming in fear.

The scream was so loud that it brought the entire Elk Clan to the beach but even more amazing the scream was so powerful that the shark died of fear.

Who in his right mind would want to face and fight someone so large and ugly?

By this time, the hooting and the stomping of feet made it impossible for Taelo to continue.

Burley Bear was standing and laughing, the Clan of Others went wild.

Golden Hawk spread a dozen buffalo hides out in front of Burley Bear, placed the shark skin on top of them and then spread the shark teeth for everyone to see. They had given the jaw of the large shark to Burley Bear and had left the smaller teeth embedded.

The entire Clan stopped and looked on in disbelief as they took in the prize Burley Bear had brought back with him.

The elders had enjoyed the stories, and all passed food or drink to Burley Bear. It was clear they were proud of his accomplishments and the fact he was so well accepted by the New Ones.

His status was now of a hero among the Clan of Others.

Burley Bear stood up and waved a finger at Taelo. He was a little overwhelmed by the stories Taelo had shared.

It was his turn, and he could tell stories as good as or better than Taelo.

He had the Clan on their feet when he told of Taelo walking through solid rock.

They were hooting and stomping in appreciation when he told about Taelo and Golden Hawk running down their buffalo and letting the buffalo run into and spear. His insistence that this was true and the way the two hunted only made the hooting louder.

Burley Bear really had become quite a good speaker and storyteller.

The evening was a great reunion and at its close, Taelo extended his invitation to the Others to attend the Elk Clan induction ceremony for him and Golden Hawk.

A hush fell over the Clan of Others. Never in their history had they been invited to such a ceremony. There was no Clan memory to guide them in making this decision.

Broken Spear had warned them of such an invitation and still they were shocked.

"We are honored by your invitation. You must give us a few days to discuss this. We have no Clan memory to address this situation," Broken Spear replied with a certain look of confusion.

He knew other members of the Clan were reacting in a similar fashion.

This was a similar reaction to the invitation Burley Bear had made for them to fish in the cove, but it was much more important and held a meaning far beyond fishing on the beach.

"Well, I think we have surprised them. We will need to talk with Burley Bear and see if he can talk to them. He has gotten use to our brash and forward ways," Taelo shared with Golden Hawk.

After the story telling broke up, the two cornered Burley Bear and asked him to talk with the Clan elders and make certain they understood that both of them wanted them present at the ceremony. Burley Bear agreed to do so and to make sure the elders understood the importance of the Others being there.

The elders told Taelo and Golden Hawk of their plans to induce Burley Bear into the circle of adults.

This was great news to all three of the young men. They went out on a walk to enjoy the good news and discuss their good fortune.

A month later, members of the Others and the members of new ones, met on the beach and for the first time in the history of either Clan, they sat together to usher Taelo, Golden Hawk and Burley Bear into the council of elders.

Each Clan gave the three, membership in each other's circle of adults.

"Tonight, each Clan has induced these three into the circle of adults leading their Clan. This makes us kindred Clans and makes it a responsibility for each to look out for the other. I believe the three have already demonstrated that by doing so everyone receives benefit. I propose we become partners and help each other weather the storms and any hard times we may face," Gray Fox Running said standing in front of both councils and giving his message in both tongues.

Broken Spear stood up and called forward a young woman and her new child.

"This is the first child born to our Clan in more than ten springs. Most of us cannot remember the cry of a child. When it was born an eagle screamed overhead. Tonight, we are naming this child Scream of the Eagle in honor of Taelo who has guided this Clan to a new life.

We know our time is short, but we are honored to join you as partners for the remaining time we the Clan of Others have," Broken Spear spoke.

To everyone's surprise, Burley Bear translated the speech into the tongue of the new ones. Though it was clear Burley Bear's throat struggled, the words were clear and understandable. By this act his stature, in the Clan of Others and in the Elk Clan as well, went up dramatically.

Each of the young men was led into the circle of elders where their contributions were described, and they were praised for their good work. They were honored for their leadership and for their support of the two Clans. The old ones followed a similar ceremony.

Taelo was given the added name meaning to guide or leader of men. Golden Hawk was given a name meaning brother to Taelo. Burley Bear was given the extra name of protector. Each Clan gave the same name though there were different words in each language.

Taelo was taken a little by surprise since he never thought of his feats as unusual. He was always himself. This genuine self-effacing quality is what made him so effective and unknowingly powerful. The ceremony went on all night until the crack of dawn.

Taelo, Golden Hawk and Burley Bear walked along the beach watching the sun come up over the mountains to the east.

"Life has been kind to us. We must be thankful our two Clans have chosen to work together. Let us vow to always chose to do what is honorable, just, and fair to all concerned," Taelo proposed as they stood looking out to sea.

Chapter 20: Golden Harvest

Grey Fox Running, Silent Hawk, Red Oak, Broken Spear and Quiet Fox spent a full week in discussions on the relationship between the two peoples. This experience was new to both Clans.

Broken Spear and Quiet Fox explained how hard it was for the Others to accept change because they were regulated more by their memory of what was done before.

Grey Fox Running explained how the Elk Clan members had to overcome the fears based on the stories of how fierce the old ones were in battle.

Both sides knew they were more alike than different. Both groups were focused on the wellbeing of the Clan and its families. Both wanted only to be prosperous enough not to suffer cold and hunger each winter. Both peoples were guided by similar principles.

This understanding bound them and led them to the agreement to work together.

"It is time we shook up all the other Elk sub-clans. I would like to extend an invitation to the Others to attend our fall Elk Clan meeting," Grey Fox Running invited the leaders of the Others.

Grey Fox Running had talked this over with all the Elk Clan elders for quite a while before making such an offer. The elders of the Elk Clan felt that having the Others attend would indeed shake up the overall Elk Clan leadership and refresh their way into the future.

Broken Spear discussed this with the Clan of Others. It was Burley Bear who encouraged the Clan leadership to accept and after a long discussion they decided they would attend the meeting. This was unprecedented for both Clans.

For the rest of the summer the two Clans shared their knowledge and many of their Clan secrets. It was surprising how many things the old ones knew but did not use because they found it hard to accept doing things differently or because they had decided to stop doing something. And yet many of these things the Others had stopped doing were of tremendous value to the Elk Clan.

The Others were especially good at processing and treating leather. They were able to soften it and make the leather smooth and pliable. However, they kept secret of how to get the leather a brilliant white color.

Many of the Elk Clan members brought their raw leather to get treated by the Others so they could have pieces of white leather with which to work.

The payment for this was half of the leather and the meat that could be wrapped with it.

This was reasonable because the Elk Clan had a valley full of buffalo as the source of their leather.

Burley Bear, Taelo and Golden Hawk inseparable before, now worked with new energy, harmony, and purpose. They led a hunting party into the valley of the buffalo. Most had moved out but throughout the summer some stayed and provided a substantial bounty for both Clans.

Neither Clan would suffer any hunger in the coming winter. The summer hunting alone had provided the necessary reserves.

There was a huge amount of leather being harvested because of the abundance of the Buffalo. New clothing was made for everyone. Extra outfits were made in anticipation of the trade with the other Clans in the fall.

The sea provided colorful stones and seashells with which to decorate the jackets and dress clothing. Every afternoon the women would sit looking out to the sea and make and decorate the clothing. Their designs were intricate and inspired by the brilliant country around them.

The stones, shells and pieces of antler were expertly used to make buttons and patterns. They also mixed the leather of various animals to create textured shirts and jackets.

The fish trap continued to supply an abundant number of fish. The construct fascinated the members of the old ones. This was a new capability for which there was no memory for the Others. They wondered how Taelo, and Golden Hawk had thought of and constructed such a huge fish trap. They, however, had no trouble in participating in the spearing of the fish in the trap.

The production of dried fish took on the feel of a well-designed production system

From morning until noon fish were speared from the fish trap.

Then the fish were cleaned and staked out so they could be put out to dry. The steaks of fish were rubbed with salt and when thoroughly dried were tied together with fiber twine, in bundles of four.

The fishing went on throughout the summer and the supply of fish was so plentiful the Clan would be taking a great amount to share with the other Clans.

Salt was in constant production. A shallow flat area, covered with flat rocks, had been doubled in size. This was filled with seawater and allowed to dry. The salt was then carefully scraped off and put in woven fiber bags. This was tedious work but until the Clan found a salt quarry it was the only way to get salt. Though this was hard work, it provided an abundant supply of salt.

This salt would also be valuable in the fall trading.

Blueberry bushes covered the ridges on the spit. When they got ripe the entire Clan went out and gathered blueberries.

These were eaten fresh. They were also cooked and mixed with other greens to make a relish to put on the meat and finally they were dried so they could be used throughout the rest of the year.

Once again, the abundance surprised the older members of the Clan. This was a time of plenty. No one could remember having such good times.

Periodically, Taelo, Golden Hawk and Burley Bear would disappear for a few days. No one knew where the three went but they would appear a few days later fresh and relaxed.

The three had kept the cave with the warm water a secret. They periodically retreated to their cave to relax.

They planned to share it with their parents in the coming winter but until then, they would enjoy it as a retreat for themselves. They always took a good supply of food and relaxed in the hot pool, looked out over the valley of plenty and discussed different philosophical ideas.

"Those three have a secret place they periodically retreat to. It seems to do them good. I wonder where this place is and what is there," Grey Fox Running said one day to Red Oak?

"Well, I would say they deserve it. Those three have made a huge difference in the well-being of the Clans. They have brought two very different people peacefully together, have found a supply of meat, they have developed a way of fishing so effective we have to stop fishing, or we catch too many," Red Oak replied.

"I agree. Those three have indeed provided the Clan with a new way of living," Silent Hawk added.

The summer and early fall became a rhythm of gathering food, making various implements, fishing, diving along the cliff for various sea animals. Life for both Clans was enjoyable and prosperous. The hot springs at the Others became a favorite place for families to go to enjoy a few days of relaxation. This interchange of members of the Clans brought the two Clans even closer together.

The two Clans would go to the Clan meeting with more goods and food to share than ever before. They had decided everything they took to the Clan meeting would be left for the Clan to divide. They would leave all their winter stores behind and have it guarded by a few warriors.

Taelo, Golden Hawk and Burly Bear explored the valley below the residence of the Others and found it had an abundant supply of dewberries and blackberries. They led various members out to these patches so the berries could be harvested.

Burley Bear made the discovery of a large honey tree. This was marked for harvesting later in the season after the bees had a chance to collect the late harvest blooms. The Others had come to enjoy bathing in their hot water spring. They recalled the Clan had in the past made a variety of bath oils.

The making of scented oils was re-introduced to the Clan membership by Broken Spear.

Soon a variety of these bath oils were being made. It became somewhat of a contest to see who could make the oil with the best aroma. They presented a generous amount of these oils to Taelo and Golden Hawk to bring back to their family and Elk Clan members. They also prepared enough to trade in the fall meeting.

Taelo especially liked this specialty of the Others. After a hot bath he loved to rub on the various scented oils. He, Golden Hawk and Burley Bear took a supply to their hide away to use when they retreated there.

Chapter 21: The Hunting Team

*C*hange was in the air for the Elk Clan. The leadership of the Clan took on a new flavor as the women exerted their influence. They had observed how the women of the Others had the same and sometimes the more commanding positions in the leadership council. They were not yet in the position nor had they the experience to take on those positions, but they were extremely active in the matters of the Elk Clan.

When Taelo suggested the Valley of Plenty might make a better home for the Clan, the women were the ones to decide the current site should be their spring and summer quarters to complement the fishing and making of salt and the winter quarters would be made in the valley.

A group made up of women and men went to the valley to locate the best place to make their winter camp.

A large lake was located at the entrance to the valley. It was just a small distance away from the river.

The higher ground on the western side was where they decided to put the main lodge. The individual lodges would be built toward the mountains rising above the valley to the west.

The small river or stream feeding the lake ran from the warm water cave Taelo, Golden Hawk and Burley Bear had used as their personal hide out. They had taken their families to the cave and shared the location with the rest of the Elk Clan.

From the vantage point out the opening of the hot water cave, White Swan was able to see the entire area and make small adjustments to the plans for the village. She was able to place all the homes and the main lodge well above the flood plains that were very recognizable from above.

The valley would be a secure winter home for the Elk Clan.

Though the valley seemed to promise a bountiful supply of buffalo, the Elk Clan members were still sensitive to the fact that they had just faced a possible winter of starvation. It would send out its long-hunt teams to secure their winter meat supply as they had done in the past.

The hunting teams were organized and sent their various directions. The Elk Clan and the Others split up the territory, so they would not hunt against each other.

Burly Bear joined Taelo's group and a few of the more adventuresome young men of the Elk Clan joined the Others in their hunt. Taelo had encouraged this with some of his young friends saying they would learn a lot from the Others.

Another interesting situation came up when several of the young women spoke up and wanted to go out with the hunting parties. This was hotly debated by some of the elders.

It was one of the women from the Oothers who finally swayed the group. Through Burley Bear, who had become the interpreter between the two peoples, she explained many women of her clan hunted and they also fought in any attack on the Clan's camp. This was known and few dared attack their camps because the women were especially fierce in defending their children.

She went on to point out that, it made the men feel better when like now they went away on the necessary long hunts. They felt confident their women were well equipped to protect themselves and the camp.

Women did not always go on the hunts but all of them had done so one time or another to learn the ways and to toughen themselves to the rigor of the hunt and prepare themselves as leaders in the Clan.

After this session, several young women who were brave enough to do so, joined the same group Taelo and Golden Hawk were in. The leader of this hunting party, Little Otter, looked at his group, Taelo, Golden Hawk, Burly Bear and three young women, Quiet Rabbit, Talking Wren, and Busy Bee and let out a small groan. With this team, he figured his hunting chances were as dead as a cold rabbit.

A few of the doubting elders had talked to Little Otter and had let him know not much game was expected from his hunting party. However, it was his task to keep them safe.

Though Taelo, Golden Hawk and Burley Bear had repeatedly proven themselves as hunters, there was still some doubt among some members of the Clan and with the women on the hunting team they felt the team would not do well. Some thought Taelo and Golden Hawk were always lucky and were not sure what they would produce when out on a regular hunt.

Grey Fox Running had discussed this dissension among the leadership with White Swan.

"Make sure the young women do not get dissuaded but go with Taelo. I think the Clan will be surprised with the outcome of this hunt. I know Taelo and Golden Hawk well enough and trust they will guide their hunt leader to new heights of achievement," White Swan advised Grey Fox Running.

Grey Fox Running had no doubt and both he and Red Oak made sure the memberships of the hunting parties were as White Swan had advised.

White Swan took Taelo aside and explained the politics and the doubts being discussed. She had made a habit of informing him of the politics of the various situations throughout the Clan. She was always amazed at Taelo's measured and mature responses or advice. It was no different this time.

"I have raced with these young women as we grew up. They are almost as fast as I when it comes to running. I will teach them to bring down the buffalo as you taught Grey Fox Running. They know the sling and we will gather small game while we run and play. We will account for ourselves as good as the rest and my goal is to be much better," Taelo replied.

Taelo discussed this with his team.

"The elders do not expect us to catch much game. Little Otter has been told the only thing expected from this team is for him to keep us safe.

I think we should set a goal to outhunt all the other teams and from the first week and every week we should send more game home than anyone else," Taelo said as he talked to the group.

There was general agreement from all the team members. The young women in the group felt a special kindred with Taelo for his confident attitude and his respect for their ability.

The day arrived for the teams to leave, and Little Otter led his team out in the direction they had been given. Taelo immediately recognized it as the least desirable area for hunting. Burley Bear, being the slowest runner was in the lead. Taelo caught up with him and shared the bad news with him.

"If we go northward, we will come by the far end of the valley where your Clan is situated. Perhaps we can visit for a day and then go east of the valley. The hunting there may be better than where we have been sent," Taelo shared with Burley Bear.

Taelo had spoken all of this in Burley Bear's language. He was better at it than Burley Bear was with the language of the Elk Clan. Having this command of a second language was useful, as now when he could talk to Burley Bear without worrying about Little Otter overhearing.

Taelo next jogged along with Little Otter, who in contrast to his name was quite large. He was as large as Burley Bear but was hairless as compared to him.

Little Otter was the name given him as a child and no one had given him a better name yet.

Taelo conversed with him and let him know the team knew not much was expected from them. He let Little Otter know the team wanted to prove the elders wrong. He also shared with him the area they had been given to hunt was sparse in game since it was more desert than anything else.

Finally, he suggested they alter the hunting area a little and go farther north and east than had been assigned. This would take them beyond the desert to a range of mountains Taelo and Golden Hawk had seen but had not yet visited.

Little Otter was a little overwhelmed with his team. They were not the meek and mild group he had been led to think they would be. Instead, they were active and assertive and needed little guidance. He found if he was to remain in charge, he would need to change the way he had intended to lead this team.

He knew they had the worst hunting grounds and personally resented being given this poor area. The idea of visiting a rich hunting ground and doing well attracted him.

He had also heard so much about the camp of the Others. Visiting them was an attraction he could not pass up.

He agreed to Taelo's suggestion.

Little Otter and Burley Bear were about the same size and running was not their strongest suite. The two traded the lead back and forth.

Taelo and Golden Hawk taught the use of the sling to bring down small game as the team jogged along. Soon the women in the group were hitting the rabbits almost as well as Taelo.

Every evening they ate well.

The women were much better cooks than the young men. They taught their skills on how to cook the rabbits and other small game.

Taelo made sure that those who did not cook helped before and after the meal.

Little Otter was taken at how well the team functioned. He began to think that perhaps they could do better than expected.

On their third day out and close to the home of the Others, Taelo spotted an elk and immediately signaled Golden Hawk and the two dashed out. Golden Hawk went the opposite direction to Taelo. The rest of the team did not even notice the two disappear until they were gone.

Suddenly, the elk jumped across the trail ahead of the jogging team and almost immediately Taelo crossed behind it. He drove the elk to where he hoped Golden Hawk was waiting.

As the elk jump over a fallen log, Golden Hawk drove his spear in from below.

The two let out a whooping war cry and the rest of the party came to where the two were celebrating.

The team spent the rest of the afternoon skinning and preparing the elk. This was their first large kill. The liver, heart and tongue were wrapped and kept in a cool place.

The remainder of the carcass was cut up into sections and then wrapped in the hide and put on a travois.

Early the next morning the group set out to the camp of the Others. They were considerably slowed by the travois. They arrived at a waiting group of Others. The camp had been warned by Broken Spear of the hunting party's arrival.

Taelo greeted Quiet Fox and presented the Clan with a gift of the elk meat. This and the team membership impressed the Clan leadership.

Taelo introduced Little Otter as the hunting party leader and made it clear he was in charge of the hunting party.

"I see your Clan has adopted our way in how you organize your hunting party. Each of you has a female partner. We will see if there is someone to accompany Burly Bear," Quiet Fox said as he took in the hunting party.

This interpretation caught Taelo by surprise and he looked again at the young women members of the hunting party. Taelo did not want to correct Silent Fox's assumption about the relationship of the team members.

Instead, he said, "That is up to Burley Bear. We have come by to see you and then to proceed east of your valley in hopes we find some good hunting. If we are successful, we will send some food your way. How does your hunting go this year?"

"Our hunting teams are out and have been sending back a steady supply of meat. There are two groups who are hunting our own valley and doing very well. There is one group north of here and another East of here. You may encounter them if you go that way," Quiet Fox replied.

"We will look for them as we travel, perhaps we can celebrate by hunting together if we meet," Taelo continued as the hunting party was led into the Clan's quarters.

Broken Spear greeted him and asked him to sit with him for a while. After everyone had gone away, he spoke from his seat by the heated spring.

"I dreamed of your coming. Your team will do well this year. You will find our hunting team and save them from some danger which I can't see clearly nor understand.

There is a disturbed spirit I can't grasp or understand. Be careful this danger will be a threat to you personally. When confronted with this danger you must act quickly and decisively. If I understand more, I will let you know," Broken Spear said quietly as he looked at Taelo with concern in his eyes.

"Thank you for this information. I will look out for the hunters and to their well-being. I will make sure my actions are swift and focused," Taelo replied in the tongue of the Others.

"I see Burley Bear has become a teacher as well as guardian. His relationship with you has saved him from becoming a bully and pest of the tribe. It was a good day when you hit him on the head," Broken Spear said with a chuckle.

"He indeed is a good friend. His strength has become the talk of our Clan. However, his wit and intelligence has also been recognized," Taelo said fondly as he thought of his large friend.

Burley Bear guided the rest of the team to the campfire designated for their stay. He and Little Otter, who except for the lack of hair was the same size as Burley Bear, gave out the gifts of meat. The tribe was impressed by the matching size of the two.

Except for their looks they could have been brothers. The two worked well together and both were smiling and talking to the Clan members as they distributed the elk meat.

"What were the two of you speaking about," Little Otter asked in curiosity when Taelo joined the group?

"Broken Spear is the seer of this Clan. We don't have anyone like him in our Clan. He sees into the future. He was sharing with me that we will run into a dangerous situation. When it occurs, we must act swiftly, and we will overcome it. Broken Spear, however, could not tell me exactly what the danger we face might be," Taelo shared with the entire team.

Quiet Rabbit, Talking Wren and Busy Bee were amazed at the cave of the Others. The fact they had a hot spring was something to envy.

"You found this place for this Clan," they asked Taelo?

"Yes, I was shown the way by my elk ancestors and an eagle in the sky," Taelo replied.

"I am going down to the hot spring to bathe, everyone better enjoy the evening and get a good night sleep. We begin a long journey tomorrow," Taelo said as he took his things and went down to the spring.

"Can we come with you," Talking Wren asked trying to embarrass Taelo?

"Everyone is certainly welcome. The more the merrier," Taelo replied with a grin.

He turned and walked confidently to the pool where he stripped down and entered the warm water.

The next morning the warming rays of the sun shining into the overhang awakened the visitors. The young Elk Clan women were envious of the excellent location Taelo had found for the Others. They would dream of the warm water spring and luxurious bath they enjoyed the evening before. This place was an ideal home.

Quiet Fox came over to the group and introduced a robust and good-looking young woman of the Others.

He looked at Little Otter and said, "I would like you to accept Meadow Flower as another member to your hunting party. I know you feel your team has been organized in such a way you will fail. Instead, Broken Spear foresees your party being the most successful. Meadow Flower is strong of heart, strong of body and she is to be Burly Bear's partner someday."

Taelo translated this to Little Otter, who let out a small groan. He was not yet sure this was going to be a good hunting trip, but he figured one more woman would make little difference.

"I am pleased to have her with us. I hope she can be ready to leave in short order," Little Otter replied with a forced smile.

His heart was heavy with the burden of having what he thought would be the weakest hunting team.

After Taelo had replied to Quiet Fox that he was pleased with the arrangements, he began to get his things ready to depart. He was just getting everything completed when Burly Bear came by and told him Broken Spear wanted to talk to him.

"We are about ready to leave, hurry up so we can get under way," an irritated Little Otter called after him.

Taelo left the group and went to see Broken Spear.

Broken Spear was sitting out in the early morning sun, and he spoke as Taelo approached.

"In my dreams, I saw you in great danger. You were trapped and were trying to get out of some cave or hole full of water. You must go in the opposite direction. It will seem to be the wrong way, but it is the way to save your life. Go down in the water, it will lead you to another opening where you can get out.

One last thing, there may be someone with you. You must take immediate action if they fight you. It was a very confusing vision. The spirit is deranged. It is not a normal predator. I cannot see what it is." Broken Spear informed Taelo.

Taelo thanked Broke Spear. He told him he would use this information and do the best he could to protect the rest of the team from this threat.

He then returned to the hunting team just in time to take up his things and say farewell to the various members of the Clan.

Burly Bear's parents were present, and a self-conscience Burly Bear was giving his mother and father a hug before joining the group.

"What a softy, the biggest among us is the one whose mother worries most about his well-being," Taelo, teased Burley Bear as they began their jog away from the camp.

Chapter 22: The Hunt

The team set out with Burley Bear setting the pace. Meadow Flower turned out to be faster than both Burly Bear and Little Otter. She kept up very well and presented no problem.

The other three women began to teach her their language and they began to pick up the language of the Others.

The three Elk Clan women had seen the special treatment and respect the Others gave Taelo and Golden Hawk. They wanted to be able to understand this Clan directly versus having the language interpreted. Each day as they were running or picking berries, they would learn a few words and bantered back and forth.

Meadow Flower had a good sense of humor and she and the other women were soon joking with each other as they tried to learn each other's language.

Each day when they stopped, Little Otter would be surprised at the amount of small game the group had caught as it traveled. There was always enough for a good dinner and leftovers to serve for breakfast.

He was beginning to enjoy his team and was beginning to feel they would do well. At least they would do better than he had at first feared.

On the fourth day of travel, they were going along a ridge when they spotted three mastodons coming up the valley. Little Otter wanted to hunt them immediately, but Burly Bear objected.

"They are only three. Broken Spear says soon they will all be gone.

Broken Spear has told us to enjoy seeing them and only hunt them from the larger herds. We should not hunt this small herd," Burley Bear explained.

The hunting party watched as the three mastodons, a male, a female, and a young cow, went past below them. The male let out a blast as if to thank them for letting them go.

Little Otter was a little put out, but Taelo explained if Broken Spear had seen the end of the mastodons, then they should heed his words and enjoy seeing the animals as they journeyed on their way.

Little Otter looked at his hunting party and decided he was in charge in name only and only the Elk Clan elders thought he was in charge.

The hunting party continued their travel along the ridge they were on toward the east. They traveled another day and then as they came over a crest of the trail a huge lake surrounded on the top side with a stand of tall green pine mixed with an occasional towering oak and a wide valley bending around it to the east and then going north met.

Taelo commented on the grandeur of the area and pointed to a small stream just in front of them that trickled down the mountain side.

They began following the small stream. It seemed to be leading them to the lake they had seen. Periodically other small streams would join into the one they were following.

Soon they were traveling along a small river. At a bend, where the river made a pleasant pool and several large trees dominated a flat spot on the bank, Taelo stopped.

"This is our first hunting camp. I recognize it from my dream last night. Tomorrow morning, we will kill three bison when their herd comes down to the lake. We shall make our camp under that big tree and sleep up in the limbs. I will show you how to make a hammock sleeping place in the trees," Taelo announced.

He felt a shiver go down his spine because he had also dreamed a saber tooth lioness would trap him and he would have an adventure whose end he could not see.

The hunting party went about gathering wood, arranging their camp, and watching as Taelo took some green willow saplings from the riverbank and made a flat sleeping spot between two limbs, about twenty feet above the ground.

"Why are we making our sleeping place up in the tree," Burly Bear asked?

"That is a great question," Little Otter said patting Burley Bear on the back as Golden Hawk translated.

"In my dream, a large bear will come and greet us. She will be followed by a pack of wolves. A saber tooth lioness will follow the wolves. The lioness will chase me to a cave not far from here.

In the cave I will run into the mother bear, she will chase off the lioness but will trap me in the cave. We are sleeping in the tree so we can survive this group of predators. Do any of you object," Taelo said with a grin?

After Golden Hawk had translated, they all began gathering the willow branches and making their beds.

"Is Taelo pulling our leg," Meadow Flower asked Burly Bear.

"Maybe a little, but Broken Spear warned Taelo of some danger on this trip," Burly Bear replied as he worked at making something strong enough to hold him safely in the tree.

He was taking Taelo seriously.

Quiet Rabbit, Talking Wren and Busy Bee were having a similar conversation and asking Golden Hawk if what Taelo had said was true.

"Well, if anything, Taelo has left out the more dangerous or worrisome parts. Make sure you make your sleeping area strong and able to withstand wind and storm," Golden Hawk replied.

He was worried about what Taelo had said and would talk with his friend later. He wanted to be ready to help when the crisis arose.

All of them watched as Taelo made his sleeping area and copied the way he brought his leather cover over the top from one side. This left one side partially open but made the whole sleeping structure rainproof.

Taelo had pointed out the various branches with potential to make good sleeping areas. He made sure the four women had the higher locations and Golden Hawk, Burly Bear and Little Otter were spread evenly around the tree on the lower limbs.

Any predator climbing up the tree would face this first level from each side.

Taelo was nervous about his dream and about Broken Spear's warning. He was worried about the hunting party members.

In his dream several of them were in trouble and what happened to them was not clear. The order of things also was jumbled.

Additionally, there were other members of old ones. The dream just did not make sense.

Taelo suggested each of them should keep their spears up in the tree with them. He himself had all his belongings hung up in the tree around his bed area. He had tied a rope to his limb and used it to climb down from his perch.

The evening dinner consisted of fish from the river, rabbit stew and a few greens which were found along the riverbank. The banter was light, and the discussion turned to their hunt. All of them were eager to begin hunting in earnest. It would be the first time for the young women, and they were nervous.

The night passed without incident and early the next morning Taelo was up before everyone. The sun was yet to come up. He took a bath in the river and then started the fire to warm up and get the camp ready for a quick breakfast.

He went out to scout the area around the lake. When he returned the camp was bustling and everyone was finishing breakfast.

"We should be able to bring down several buffalo today. There is a large herd on the far side of the lake," Taelo shared with the other members.

Taelo asked who had hunted the buffalo before. He knew that the young women had not. He asked because he wanted the team to openly discuss the hunt.

He suggested Little Otter take charge and split the group up into two teams.

He was sensitive to the fact Little Otter was supposed to lead the party, but he was not going to leave anything to chance.

Little Otter appreciated Taelo passing the lead over to him.

"I would like to put the fastest of the women with Taelo. Then I will put the next fastest with Golden Hawk.

The last two will match up with Burly Bear and me. We know we are the slowest.

We will match a fast team with a slow team. The job of the fast team is to mortally wound the buffalo. The slower team will run down the wounded animal and finish it.

Both jobs are critical and dangerous.

The slow team must be careful the wounded animal does not turn and attack them," Little Otter counseled.

He was pleased Taelo had turned the matter over to him. He had been afraid Taelo would try to take over. Little Otter now saw why Taelo was so highly thought of by all who associated with him.

Taelo could have just as easily have said what had just been said but he turned it over to him.

"Let's have a race to that far tree and back to see how we will assign you women," Little Otter continued.

The four women lined up and on Little Otter's signal they raced to the tree and back.

Quiet Rabbit was a full ten yards ahead by the time she got back to the camp. She had wanted to hunt with Taelo and had used every ounce of speed she had.

Busy Bee was second, and Talking Wren was next by several yards and was almost passed by Meadow Flower as they neared the end of the course.

"OK, Quiet Rabbit, you are with Taelo.

Busy Bee you will be with Golden Hawk.

I would like to have Meadow Flower with me but until we can communicate better it is too dangerous. So, Meadow Flower you will go with Burly Bear and Talking Wren will go with me.

Burley Bear will back up Taelo and I will back up Golden Hawk. This should give us a well-balanced approach.

Let's get our gear and get to the hunt.

Each team will discuss what is about to happen and how they will handle different situations.

Before we leave, we will need to cut two small trees to form the main part of a travois and smaller willow branches to make the carrying platform," Little Otter instructed as he thought how much he would have preferred the quieter Meadow Flower with him.

He would have to listen to Talking Wren all day long and he knew she would talk.

Once each team had the material for their travois and they had organized the tools and other things needed to skin the animals and to prepare the meat, they set out along their side of the lake.

Taelo and Burley Bear went around the south part of the lake.

As they walked, Taelo explained what would happen and how he planned to bring down the buffalo, "We will first work together to split two or three young buffalo from the herd. Once they are away and out to the side, I will run up alongside them and place my spear to their chest and the ground at the same time.

This will cause the buffalo to plunge the spear deeply into themselves. If we are lucky and get two or three the first time, our hunt will be over for the day. If we only get one, then we will try for another.

Once the animal is wounded it will be the job of Burley Bear and Meadow Flower to make sure the animal is brought down.

We will need to be aware of what the other teams are doing so we do not interfere with them.

Quiet Rabbit, this time your job will be to carry two spears for me. You must keep up with me and be ready to give me the spears.

Perhaps the next time you will want to place the spears. However, we will need to practice this together before you try it on a buffalo. I practiced with my father for over a year before he allowed me to try the first time. I was very young and not strong enough earlier. We will know how long it will take you once I see how you do in practice.

Do not worry. Golden Hawk will have the same speech for Busy Bee."

Taelo explained this in both languages so there would be no confusion. Burley Bear understood and had hunted with Taelo before. He explained to Meadow Flower that she would see an amazing way of hunting the buffalo.

"Only because of Taelo's speed will we be able to hunt so easily. I think that Little Otter will be amazed at what Golden Hawk will do. He has not seen the skill of these two amazing individuals," Burley Bear shared with Meadow Flower.

A similar discussion was going on in the other team as Golden Hawk explained how the hunt would be organized.

Little Otter thought Golden Hawk was just trying to show off. He had not seen anyone do what Golden Hawk had just described.

It was not long before they came out on the far end of the Lake where the herd was grazing in the early morning sun. The wind was blowing from the herd toward the two groups of hunters. This made their approach easier.

"We are the second team. We will work the buffalo we select away from the herd, but we will wait for Golden Hawk to make the first attack. Then we will follow. In this way we will keep from running into the other hunting party," Taelo explained.

Slowly, Taelo worked four young animals away from the rest of the herd. He was able to get the animals well away from the herd before they saw Golden Hawk begin his sprint toward the group of buffalo he had culled out.

Taelo nudged Quiet Rabbit and began his run at the nearest young bull. The bull jumped and was just getting to his top speed when Taelo placed the spear. The bull went down almost immediately.

Taelo was already bearing down on the second animal, a young cow. He repeated the act of placing the spear and having the animal spear itself.

The remaining two young bulls had now reached full speed. Quiet Rabbit, running as fast as she had ever run and was struggling to keep up with Taelo.

He grabbed the two spears from her and then to her amazement he accelerated to catch up with the two young bulls.

Quiet Rabbit continued to run as fast as she could, but she could not keep up.

Taelo reached the third young bull and repeated the placement of the spear and immediately sprinted on ahead.

He was now on a personal mission. He raced on to catch up to the fourth animal. It had now become a contest of will and Taelo wanted to get this last animal. It had turned and was running up hill for the tree line.

Taelo knew he had him. He waited until the bull was just reaching the tree line and then rushed forward and placed the spear. The bull fell just shy of the edge of the forest.

Taelo checked to make sure the bull was dead and then turned to look back along the trail of fallen animals.

Quiet Rabbit came staggering up and then she too looked back along the trail of the fallen animals with Taelo.

She bent over and then went to her knees as she worked to catch her breath.

"What an unbelievable run. How could you run so fast and then still have energy to place the spears," Quiet Rabbit said between breaths as she bent over trying not to be sick as she sucked in every searing breath.

She now understood Taelo's apprehension of having her try to spear one of the animals. She was not sure she could have gotten the first one and she knew she would never have been able to get four.

She got up and followed as Taelo slowly walked back along the path he had just finished running.

"It became a contest of wills. I was determined to use all four spears.

Usually when Golden Hawk and I go out we take turns bringing down the animals. Sharing the load makes it a little easier.

I hope in practice you will pick up this skill quickly, then we can let you take the first one or two and I will concentrate on the last animals," Taelo explained.

"Having seen how it is done, I can appreciate why I must practice. I was a little upset when you first told me I would have to wait," Quiet Rabbit confessed.

Now she was not sure she would be able to do it.

By the time, the two made it back to the second bull where Meadow Flower was waiting, Taelo saw Burly Bear assembling the travois.

Taelo looked up the valley where the hunters on the other team were doing the same thing. He could see three animals Golden Hawk had downed. He wondered if there was a fourth. He knew Golden Hawk had culled four out.

The two teams had agreed to meet halfway between them. This would allow for the least amount of work for the hunting parties.

The last bull Taelo had killed was almost at the perfect spot.

"Now the hard work begins. We must drag the animals up to the tree line, gut them, skin them, and then prepare the meat. We need to get them up into the trees before dark," Taelo explained to Quiet Rabbit.

Taelo arranged a pulling harness for each of the four. It was an arduous pull to the edge of the forest. They brought their second bull up to the edge of the forest and pulled it to where Taelo thought would be a good spot to hang him. The other hunting group soon brought their first animal up.

Little Otter was overwhelmed at the kill. "I have never seen anything like it. Golden Hawk brought down four buffalo," he said to no one in particular.

He was excited and agitated. He now felt they had a chance to match up to the other parties.

When you have your animals up here please begin. Don't wait for us, we have four, yes four of them to drag up here," Little Otter gave instructions to Taelo's team.

Taelo walked over to Golden Hawk and clapped him on the back and congratulated him on his four kills.

Meadow Flower quietly asked Burly Bear why Taelo did not tell everyone he too had taken down four buffalo.

"I think because it will be a surprise when the rest realize we have eight animals," Burly Bear replied, "He will not boast about his skills, but he never lacks in confidence."

With Burly Bear and Meadow Flower's superior strength, Taelo's team worked faster than Golden Hawk's team. They had their four carcasses quickly hanging in the trees before Golden Hawk's team had brought up their fourth kill.

They were cleaning up the livers, hearts, and kidneys and cutting up the intestines they would keep.

They had also brought out wood for the fires they would need for the night. Meadow Flower had already started to cook a late afternoon lunch.

Talking Wren, who noticed the four hanging animals quietly, joined in the preparation of the lunch. She knew this would be a surprise for Little Otter and she was waiting to see his reaction. This was one time she would be quiet and enjoy the surprise.

It was obvious, Quiet Rabbit and Busy Bee were exhausted from the hunting run.

"Perhaps some of you could begin to help us, after all we have four animals to skin," Little Otter began, and then he noticed there were already four buffalo hanging in the trees. He looked around and realized there were four more still to be gutted and hung.

Golden Hawk laughed, "Well, my friend it seems you too have had a good day and you have yours already gutted. I suppose now your team will take a nap, while we get our animals ready."

"No, we will help, but seriously, look at the herd. Notice the large bull toward the middle. Now look at the cow just this side of him. See the late calf. The wolves will have it in the next day or two.

I am going out and bring it up here for us to celebrate with," Taelo said with a wink at Quiet Rabbit.

"Who on my team wants to go with me," Taelo asked?

"I will go with you," Quiet Rabbit spoke up quickly. She was tired but she wanted to experience the thrill of the hunt again, besides, she wanted to hunt with Taelo again.

"I think she has her eyes on him," Meadow Flower said quietly to Burly Bear, who just grunted in response.

Taelo prepared two spears. Put a short length of rope around his neck and then grabbed two small square pieces of leather, he gave one to Quiet Rabbit. He also carried a coil of rope.

As they walked down toward the herd, Taelo explained to Quiet Rabbit the spears were only for an emergency. They would catch the young calf and tie his legs together. Then they would use the rope and lead it back to camp, so they would not need to carry it.

Near a lone tree, Taelo dropped the coil of rope, and he had Quiet Rabbit leave her spear. Taelo put the leather over his shoulders and began to crawl out toward the mother and her young calf. He could tell the calf was about four months old and he knew it would be culled out by wolves in no time. He was surprised it hadn't already happened.

The going was slow. The afternoon sun was nearing the horizon before Taelo had worked his way out to the calf. He then began to move the mother and calf out toward the edge of the herd.

The group on the hill had a perfect view of the herd and even though they knew the target of Taelo's hunt they often could not see him. They were impressed with how subtle and precise his action and movement were.

Taelo used his spear with a rabbit hide tied to the end to signal the cow the way to the edge of the herd. Once he got her there, the cow immediately sensed danger and wanted to move inward, but Taelo kept moving the calf away from the herd. The mother followed as Taelo got the calf clear of the herd.

Taelo suddenly jumped up, leaving his spear behind and ran straight at the calf. The calf had just started to react when Taelo caught its head, twisted it, and brought the calf down. He immediately caught a hind leg and a front leg and tied them together with the rope around his neck.

The mother buffalo looked on, began her attack but backed away when Quiet Rabbit came up and shouted and waved the leather she was carrying.

"Well, done Quiet Rabbit, you probably saved me from having to either run for a tree or kill the cow," Taelo praise her.

Quiet Rabbit was pleased. She had been afraid of the cow and had acted on instinct. Taelo's approval relieved her. Quite Rabbit ran over to the tree and retrieved the extra spear and the rope.

Taelo made a simple head harness from the rope and put it on the calf. He then untied the legs of the calf and immediately began leading it toward the edge of the forest. The calf tried several times to run but finally settled down and followed Taelo.

"What in the world is Taelo up to," Little Otter exclaimed as he first watched the calf being taken down and then the harness being put on.

"Well knowing Taelo, he will have the calf talking to him and probably its mother giving him her blessings," Burley Bear said as he too wondered what his friend was up to.

"This calf is fairly large, perhaps it can help us transport the meat back to the Clan," Taelo said thoughtfully as they walked up the hill toward where the hunters were processing the eight buffalo they had killed.

Taelo shared his idea with Little Otter. "It sounds a little crazy to me, but if you can get it to pull one of the travois, I am all for it.

Because of his size, Little Otter was always being asked to pull a travois and the idea of not having to do it excited him.

All afternoon they processed the meat and then moved the carcasses halfway back to the original camp. The calf helped a little, but he was a little too jittery to be useful. Taelo took him the rest of the way to camp and built a small pen to keep him in.

The team went to their main camp and feasted on grilled buffalo tongue. This was a treat they all enjoyed.

Taelo fortified the enclosure for the calf and then went up to his sleeping quarters and fell immediately to sleep. The rest of the group very quickly followed his example. They knew the next day held a full day of getting the meat prepared for smoking and drying.

The night passed uneventfully and the next morning the group was up early and discussing how to proceed.

It seemed all was well.

A few days later the entire load of hides, semi dried meat and some fresh meat was loaded on a larger than usual travois and attached to the young buffalo. Little Otter and Talking Wren would return with the load of meat to the two Clans. Once they had delivered it, they would return with the young buffalo. They planned to use him again for the next load.

The journey home took Little Otter and Talking Wren fourteen sun cycles. Talking Wren lived up to her name and Little Otter thought his second name should be Little Otter the Deaf.

He was amazed at the strength of the young buffalo and fed and treated it well. When they finally made the beach and were walking along the water the young calf seemed to get new energy and they made excellent time. As they approached the camp the Elk Clan members came out to greet them.

"The camp has moved into Taelo's valley. We are here to make salt to take to the main camp. However, we will take your meat and process it, so it is ready for winter. Then we will transport it down to the main camp when we take the salt down.

We go once every fourteen sun cycles with the salt," explained one of the elder warriors as he took in the strange sight.

Everyone marveled at the calf, and they were amazed this team had brought in so much meat. They told Little Otter and Talking Wren no other team had sent back any meat so far.

Little Otter thought about the members of his team and realized he had the best hunting team in of the Elk Clan.

Chapter 23: The Rescue

Taelo and the rest of the team decided to rest for a couple of days before going back on the hunt.

The warning by Broken Spear had not materialized. Taelo was nervous about the fact nothing out of the ordinary had occurred. He would remain vigilant.

On the last day of their declared rest period, three members of a hunting group of the others straggled into camp. They were exhausted and desperate. They explained they had been hunting when they came across an overly aggressive saber tooth. It attacked part of the party. It then stalked them as they were trying to clear its territory. The three had left the wounded hunters in a cave.

They had fought the saber tooth all the way back to Taelo's Camp. It was somewhere in the area close by. Taelo made sure the three hunters had a good dinner and then helped them make their beds up in the tree. The tiger might be able to climb, but if he was as big as the hunters claimed, then it probably could not climb very well.

Taelo made sure anyone going to the edge of the camp was escorted. The entire team was on alert.

They stoked the fires and then climbed up to their beds.

Taelo had set a watch and each person would sit awake for three hours and pass the watch to the next person.

He climbed into his enclosure and went to sleep.

In the dark of the moonless night, a putrid odor awoke Taelo. He heard nothing but sensed danger close at hand. Swiftly and silently, he moved into a fighting crouch.

Deadly claws whisked through the space he had just vacated. Uncharacteristically, the saber tooth had climbed silently up the tree.

Taelo automatically thrust the spear into the tiger's mouth. The angry roar was heard for miles around.

The occupants in the tree were all immediately awake. They were not sure where their adversary was.

Suddenly, pushed off balance, Taelo and the tiger fell from the tree.

Both lay stunned for a moment.

Taelo recovered first and jumped up and ran toward the lake. He knew he was at a disadvantage on the ground. In the lake he would have a fighting chance. He also wanted to get the tiger away from the camp to ensure the safety of the team. He would make his stand near the edge of the cliffs towering above the lake on the mountain side.

This would give him the option to dive off to escape the tiger.

The saber tooth was rapidly closing the distance. Even Taelo's speed was not enough. Taelo realized when he reached his destination, he would need to turn immediately and fight the tiger.

He dug deep and came up with one more surge of energy and speed.

Burly Bear jumped out of the tree and shouted at the top of his voice and threw a spear toward the tiger.

The tiger hesitated for a moment but then took up the chase after Taelo. This hesitation gave Taelo a slight margin.

Burly Bear picked up his spear and shouting at the top of his voice was chasing behind the tiger trying to distract the animal.

What he would do if he succeeded had not crossed his mind.

Confusion reigned in the camp. The various camp members were trying to sort out what had happened and what was going on.

Quiet Rabbit had seen Taelo running out of the camp with Burley Bear close behind. She grabbed her spear and ran after Burley Bear. She quickly caught up with him and then went out in front.

She picked up the shout and was making almost as much noise as Burley Bear. She was quickly a hundred yards ahead of Burley Bear. Her only thought was to help Taelo.

She was running faster than she had ever run before. What she would do when she caught up to the tiger and Taelo had not crossed her mind. She just knew she had to help Taelo.

She heard the roar of the tiger somewhere ahead and then there was only a still silence. She found more speed and ran fearlessly toward where the sound had come from.

Burley Bear soon joined her. The two tried to find the trail but there was nothing. They both shouted for Taelo but there was no reply. They went along the edge of the cliff that overlooked the lake but saw no sign of either the tiger or of Taelo.

At the last moment just as the tiger pounced, Taelo turned and brought his spear up. Taelo's spear found its mark in the center of the tiger's chest.

He was not sure this action was going to be enough to save his life. In reflex the tiger was reaching out with her sharp claws.

Suddenly the ground gave way and both he and tiger were falling. Even as he was falling, Taelo instinctively used his spear to position himself above the tiger. He looked into the eyes of the maddened animal.

The black at the bottom of the fall came into view. He hoped it was the water that the seer had mentioned. Then the impact took his breath away.

The impact of the water drove the spear all the way through the tiger.

Taelo hit the tiger and then fell into the water and went down into it for what seemed like eternity. He came up with his, shark tipped hand spear ready to fight the tiger. However, the impact and his hunting spear had done its job. The tiger was floating dead on the water.

Taelo looked up the chimney that had saved his life. The walls were smooth, with no visible foot or handholds. He could barely make out the opening high above him.

He was alive and trapped.

Taelo relaxed and took in his surroundings. The faint light from the opening at the top gave just enough illumination to let him see in the tunnel. He let his eyes adjust to the relative darkness. He knew he was in trouble unless he could figure a way out.

The tiger was still floating with Taelo's spear through its body. The spear seemed to provide just enough buoyancy to keep the body afloat.

It was too bad he would have to leave the carcass here. He would have loved to have the skin. Perhaps if he got out quickly, he would be able to lower himself down from the top and haul the tiger out. It was huge; it probably outweighed him by several hundred pounds.

He then recalled Broken Spears guidance about going down to another passage.

Golden Hawk and the remaining hunters had arrived at the cliffs and were scouting around and calling Taelo's name. But there was no sign of him, and no one found the new hole opening into blackness and the water below.

"I am sure he is alright," Burly Bear said as he continued to look for Taelo. He was sure Taelo was close by. He could feel his presence.

Taelo remembered Broken Spear's words. The way out is under the water. He had failed to tell Taelo there would be some thirty feet of water. Taelo took several deep breaths and then dived into the water.

The visibility was poor, but using his hands, he found an opening near the bottom leading out of the funnel. He went along a horizontal tunnel until there was light from above. He was fighting for air as he rose through the water expecting to come out in the lake.

Instead, he came out in a pool located in a large cavern. The opening of the cavern was about twenty feet above the lake.

As Taelo was about ready to get out of the water when he a roar caused him to freeze. There on a shelf above the water lay the huge mother bear who had visited Taelo on the beach.

"It is good to see that you are well," Taelo said in a conversational tone. He went to the far side of the pool and slowly got out. He was hoping the bear would let him out of the cave.

"I only need passage out of your cave. I did not mean to disturb you and will leave you alone once I have left," Taelo continued his banter as he backed slowly to the edge of the cave opening.

The big bear gave one more roar and then lay her head down in disinterest.

Taelo turned and walked out along a trail leading from the cave. He made his was upward and headed up the cliff.

The members of the hunting party were spread out along the cliff still trying to locate Taelo. Quiet Rabbit was calling his name in desperation.

Taelo walked up behind her and quietly answered her.

Quiet Rabbit turned and gave Taelo a hug.

"What happened? Where did you go? Are you alright," she asked Taelo in rapid fire.

She called out to the rest of the hunting party.

The whole group returned and exploded with questions.

"I learned from an old medicine man if you grab the teeth of a saber tooth and pull them sideways out of its mouth, it will leave you alone. I remembered this as I ran. I turned and waited for the saber tooth to catch up and grabbed the teeth one in each hand. I am sure you all heard the roar of pain as I pulled the teeth from her head," Taelo said as he looked at his teammates.

"Then, since I was a little sweaty, I walked to the edge of the cliff and dove off and went for a swim. I swam across the lake and back and here I am," he said with a bow.

Burley Bear started laughing when he realized Taelo was telling them a tale.

Quiet Rabbit wiped the tears from her eyes. She was not sure whether they were tears of joy or whether she was mad at Taelo for making light of such a serious situation.

"Who would like to help me bring this tiger into camp," Taelo asked?

The entire camp followed him to the hole at the top of the chimney. The group realized they had all walked by the top of the tunnel several times. However, unless one climbed up the slight rise surrounding the chimney it was not visible.

Quiet Rabbit looked down the deep hole. It seemed very frightening, but she volunteered to be lowered into the tunnel to tie the rope to the tiger.

When she got down to the water, she saw the huge tiger still floating. Its size was unbelievable. Quiet Rabbit tied the rope around the tiger and then tugged on the rope.

The tiger was slowly raised.

Quiet Rabbit stayed to the edge of the pool. She realized how isolated she felt and wondered how Taelo had gotten out of this situation. It was obvious he had not climbed out.

It took a good hour of pulling, holding, and pulling some more to get the tiger to the top of the chimney. It must have weighed five hundred pounds. Finally, the group was able to pull the tiger clear of the hole.

This feat would not have been possible without the help of the members of the Others.

Taelo immediately dropped the rope down for Quiet Rabbit. Burly Bear made pulling Quiet Rabbit seem easy. She was light as a feather in comparison to the tiger.

"That was brave. Thank you for going down so I could have the tiger hide and head," Taelo said as Quiet Rabbit was lifted from the hole.

"How did you get out," Quiet Rabbit asked in a low voice?

Everyone stopped to hear Taelo's explanation.

"When I saw I had killed the tiger, my spirit soared. Before I knew it, my feet were on the ground" Taelo replied with the same twinkle he had earlier.

"Yes, and if we look closely, we will see wings on your feet," Burly Bear said gruffly as he and several others picked up the pole to which they had tied the tiger.

That morning after a good meal. The three hunters from the other hunting party were given food and supplies. Burly Bear, Meadow Flower and Quiet Rabbit went with them to help and to tend to the wounded.

"Return to us as soon as possible. If the one injured can no longer hunt, bring those who can hunt back to our camp. They can hunt with us, and we will make sure they are able to contribute their part to the Clan," Little Otter commented.

Little Otter took his hunting party father east and there in a large valley they found many elk. Hunting elk took more skill then running down the buffalo but within three days, the group had several elk hung in the trees. They were processing the meat as fast as they could.

They were able to pull back all the meat on a large travois pulled by the young buffalo that had become a constant companion of Little Otter. It followed Little Otter everywhere he went.

They had just returned when Quiet Rabbit followed by Burley Bear, Quiet Meadow and four hunters from the Others walked into camp.

Burley Bear was pulling a travois with one of the hunters laying on it.

Taelo greeted them and guided them to the area around the campfire. He recognized Rolling Stone who had been one of the warriors on the beach when they had found the whale.

Burley Bear let everyone know that Rolling Stone's new name was Saber Scar.

Saber Scar smiled and pointed to Quiet Rabbit. He recalled that he was delirious by the time Quiet Rabbit arrived. He was sure he was on his death bed and just wanted to be left alone but she proceeded to wash his wounds that went to the bone and in several areas to the other side.

He pointed to the neat stitches that closed the gashes across his chest. There are more than two hundred stiches on the outside and she tells me there are as any on the inside.

I hope to tell my children about the miracle lady of the Elk Clan.

"We were just getting ready to take our next load of meat back to the Clan," Little Otter commented.

"I will take this load back. I can take them back to our cave and then take the load on south to the Elk Camp," Burly Bear volunteered.

Little Otter suggested Burley Bear take the entire load of meat to the Clan of Others. The Load of meat would make up for the loss of one hunting party.

He was glad to have the opportunity to do some more hunting with the team.

He now had the confidence that his team would show themselves quiet well.

"By the time you return we should have another load to take south," Little Otter said in closing.

The next morning the hunting party loaded the travois up with most of the meat they had hunted.

"When you return, come by here. We will leave our kill here and then travel a few more days east," Little Otter spoke up.

His hunting party was doing much better then he would ever have imagined. He was learning how to lead them and proud of being with this team.

Taelo commented to Golden Hawk that Little Otter had found his confidence and was becoming a good leader.

Chapter 24: Return to the Valley

The Hunting continued to be bountiful. Taelo suggested to Little Otter that the team move south as they hunted.

Golden Hawk made the point that they should end their long hunt and return home.

Talking Wren added that their team had already sent more meat home than any other hunting team. Three large loads of meat had been sent back to each of the two Clans.

Burley Bear stopped at the top of the hill that they were all coming up and stated that he thought their hunt was at an end.

The rest of the team came up to where he had stopped. At first it was hard to register the sight. The far mountains silhouetted by the light blue sky and snow caps formed the frame with the dark green of forest tops rising above an undulating mass of dark brown forms that seemed to have worms wiggling randomly above curved white spears.

Little Otter was the first to speak and ask Burley Bear if this was a big enough herd for them to hunt.

Quiet Rabbit suggested they take one young male as she made the point that one would be more meat than they had sent back to the Elk Clan so far.

Taelo and Golden Hawk agreed with Quiet Rabbit and decided they would travel down along the herd and look for a place they could make a trap for such an animal.

"Let's see if there is a narrow valley or canyon somewhere ahead where we can drive one into. We will tell the rest of the team to follow along the ridge and we will scout ahead for the place where we can trap the animal," Taelo said to Little Otter.

"May I accompany the two of you," Quiet Rabbit asked when she heard what they were going to do?

"Yes, you may. I just want you to know we will be running almost the entire day," Taelo replied. "Does anyone else want to come along," he asked?

There were no takers. They all knew they would not be able to keep up.

The three set off running along the side of the herd. It was early afternoon before they found a suitable valley or canyon. Golden Hawk spotted a short, narrow passage that came to a dead-end after one bend. It was perfect if they could guide a mastodon to go into it.

Taelo and Golden Hawk decided to spend some time preparing the narrow passage to trap the mastodon.

He asked Quiet Rabbit to go back to the hunting party and guide them to this place as quickly as possible.

He stated that he and Golden Hawk would spend the rest of the afternoon preparing the trap. They would be ready to trap a mastodon and would do so if the right one wanders into their trap area.

Quiet Rabbit left immediately with the promise of getting the team back before sunset. She made Taelo promise not to do anything too dangerous.

Taelo and Golden Hawk cut about twenty long poles and cut a point into one end. They put these with one end in the ground and the other end pointing up into the passage. The mastodon would be able to walk past them going into the passage but would not be able to walk back if it tried to turn back out of the passage.

They put two poles on one side and a matching pair on the opposite side of the passage. These poles were just far enough apart so the mastodon could pass between them. They put five sets of four about ten feet distance from each other.

After the entrance, they set up a series of poles about half the height they estimated the mastodon to be and put in poles with sharpened points so the animal would not be able to move forward, sideward, or backward. This would be the point where two or three of the hunters would drive spears into the mastodon from the sides.

By the time they were done the late afternoon sun was casting long shadows. The herd was still making its way slowly past them as it seemed to flow up the valley.

Together the two went down the valley to decide which animal to cull out. They spotted one of the younger, smaller bulls at the edge of the herd and decided to try to slowly move him out away from the rest.

They approached him from behind and waved a piece of leather to move the young mastodon to the edge of the herd. Then at the critical moment, when the passage was close at hand, Golden Hawk moved up between the bull and the herd.

The young bull reacted exactly as Golden Hawk desired him to and moved toward the entrance to the passage.

The two got the young bull past the first set of guide poles and stopped. They were not going to push the animal any farther until the rest of the hunting team arrived.

Quiet Rabbit was the first to arrive. She had alerted the team and they were coming behind her, but she knew that Taelo and Golden Hawk would act before the sun began to set.

She told the two that the team would arrive just as dusk was setting in.

"We will stay here across the end of the crevasse. Hopefully, the mastodon will move slowly into the trap and will not try to back out. If he tries to escape, we will try to wound him to keep him from escaping. We need to be very careful. These animals are powerful and when frightened they can cause unbelievable damage and harm.

The spearing will require great strength. We will let Burly Bear and Little Otter do the initial spearing to bring down the mastodon.

The rest of us will try to distract the animal so the two can get a good throw and follow through," Taelo explained to Quiet Rabbit.

His explanation comforted Quiet Rabbit, since she was worried about Taelo and Golden Hawk acting on their own to down the mastodon.

She had run back to keep them from taking any hasty action against the animal. She had underestimated Taelo's and Golden Hawk's level and logical thinking. They were very careful and serious.

The young bull mastodon moved slowly up the crevasse. Every time he tried to back up the pointed poles would poke him. He slowly moved forward only to find he was more constricted than before. Finally, he was in the main trap with spears poking him in every direction he tried to move. He stood still and seemed content to just stand in place.

Taelo, Golden Hawk and Quiet Rabbit had been moving slowly up the crevasse and moving the pairs of pointed spears up into position behind the mastodon. Should it somehow be able to turn around, the mastodon would face a wall of spears blocking his escape

The rest of the team arrived as the evening was taking on that grey black appearance where nothing seemed exactly real. It was hard to see.

Taelo decided it would be too dangerous for the team to try to take down the animal so late in the day.

Burley Bear, Little Otter and the rest of the team agreed.

They decided a camp at the top of a small knoll would be a safe location.

Taelo sat for a long time looking at the stars twinkling in the black fabric of the night sky. He welcomed the presence of Quiet Rabbit who true to her name sat by silently by his side.

He looked around and found that the rest of the members of the team were doing the same.

He knew that hunting together had bonded them to each other and he saw that each had found the one they wanted to sit with.

The next morning Taelo explained who on the team should spear the mastodon. Burly Bear and Little Otter agreed with the two of them driving the spears in from the side. Burley Bear would spear for the heart and Little Otter from the other side for the lung.

They each sharpened a spear. They approached the mastodon from the side.

Taelo and the rest of the team distracted the bull by getting out in front of it and waving small pieces of leather.

The mastodon tried to back up but was trapped by the extra pointed poles behind him. These poles caused him to panic, and he lunged forward into the pole in front. At the same time both Burly Bear and Little Otter ran their spears full force into the mastodon from the side.

Little Otter's spear glanced off a rib. His forward momentum put him in danger of falling into the pit when Talking Wren grabbed him by the hair and pulled him back up hill.

Little Otter let out what sounded like a war scream as he fell back uphill on his butt.

Talking Wren's action had saved his life. He looked at her and holding the top of his head where it felt like his hair had been ripped out, he thanked her for saving his life.

"Perhaps, she was not so bad a person to partner with," he thought to himself.

Meanwhile Burly Bear's spear found its mark, went between two ribs and into the heart. The mastodon gave out one more cry and collapsed.

Taelo let out a cry of victory and thanked the ancients for giving the young bull a quick and painless death.

Except for the incident with Little Otter the kill had been easy and very clean.

Taelo pointed at Talking Wren and shouted praise for her quick and decisive action.

The kill represented three times the amount of meat the team had sent back so far. Two thirds would go to the Elk camp and one third to the Others.

The skinning and preparation of the meat took two weeks. At the end of this time one travois, pulled by hunters from the Others' camp took a load of meat to their camp. A much larger travois, to be pulled by the now, almost tame bull was loaded with the meat to pull to the Elk Clan camp.

Even then there were four other smaller travois, each loaded with a variety of meat, hides and other foods the hunters had gathered. These other foods included some fish, and many plants and roots.

Taelo, Golden Hawk, Little Otter and Burly Bear sat over the evening meal to discuss the best way to go back to the valley along the river. Taelo thought if they continued down the valley they were in, they would hit the river and then be able to travel west. They decided two hunters would always scout out ahead of the party and mark the best way the loaded party should travel.

Burley Bear would follow the valley in the direction the Mastodons were traveling and then close to where they had hunted the first buffalo around the lake he would turn to the west.

In the morning they each went their separate ways. They planned to get back together once they had delivered their hunting spoils.

Golden Hawk and Busy Bee went out as scouts first. The going south followed the natural direction of the valley. It was the westerly direction Little Otter was worried about. They had several tons of meat to transport. This would make a climb up any mountains extremely challenging.

The first day they only made ten miles down the valley. Golden Hawk and Busy Bee came back and let the party know the valley proceeded for another ten miles beyond.

Taelo and Quiet Rabbit went out the next day and proceeded south, southwest in search of a way out of the valley or to the river. They moved in a steady jogging rhythm. They were well matched in stamina and carried on a conversation as they moved along.

Quiet Rabbit had learned a tremendous amount of hunting lore and the two practiced some of the skills Taelo described.

The two practiced the language of the Old ones and Taelo shared his belief the old ones were dying out and Broken Spear had foreseen their demise.

Taelo on the other hand learned a few additional things about plants and even if he knew about them, he would listen politely to Quiet Rabbit give her explanation. He had learned that the art of listening gave him the ability to think through what he heard and allowed him to encourage others. It also caused the people with him to talk more and share more of their perspectives.

A tall cliff closed the end of the valley. However, there to its right was a gradual rise and then it went down to another small valley. This valley was the beginning of a spring flowing to join a small creek. They would be able to follow these small streams down and hopefully they would come to the river.

The two returned to the camp late into the night with the good news.

The hunting team traveled for almost a week on a south, southeast course. The streams did flow together to form the river and the river was heading west. This convinced Taelo it was the same river he; Golden Hawk and Burley Bear had followed the winter before.

Golden Hawk and Busy Bee came back to camp one day with the news they had found the Elk Clan camp. The hunting party was only two days away.

When they were one day out, a scout from the Elk Clan camp found and greeted them. He was amazed at the amount of meat and other things to eat the hunting party was bringing in. The other hunting parties had returned but they had only done marginally well. The first two loads of meat Little Otter's party had brought back, were about the equivalent to what all the others had brought in. What he saw now dwarfed the others.

The scout stayed with them for the remainder of the day and then went ahead of the party to let the camp know the last group was returning. He was excited to let them know how much this last team was bringing in.

A loud round of welcomes came from the members of the Elk Clan as the team pulled in the main travois and the four auxiliary ones. They had come back as the best party of the four sent out.

"Little Otter, you have done extremely well. You will be known as a great hunt leader," one of the elders said.

"I am the weakest hunter of this team. It was the teamwork that made it possible for us to bring home such a harvest. Every member has become a top hunter and someone who I would want by my side in case of trouble.

Both Golden Hawk and Taelo are superb hunters and fearless leaders.

Burley Bear is the strongest of us and knows no fear.

Taelo, the speaker to bears and the slayer of saber tooth tigers performs magic when he hunts.

"You have brought in the safety margin for our Clan this coming year. We will be able to share with the rest of the larger Elk sub-clans and still enjoy our margin of safety. If the buffalo return to the valley then we will indeed be a wealthy Clan. Tonight, and tomorrow night we will celebrate your return and listen to the stories each of you must tell," Grey Fox Running announced to the entire camp.

He and White Swan exchanged a hug of pride as they watched Taelo, Golden Hawk and the rest of the team move into the center of the camp.

The early fall passed at a comfortable pace until it was time for all the sub-Clans of the Elk Clan to get together once again.

Chapter 25: Meeting of the Clan

Grey Fox Running and Red Oak led the Elk Clan members up the beach away from their camp. The Clan was getting an early start and planned to be the first to arrive at the valley for the Clan meeting. He wanted to claim the area on the far side of the lake. That area would provide the space for both the Elk Clan and the Clan of Others.

He knew that all the other Elk sub-Clans would have an initial negative reaction about having the Clan of Others as part of their meeting and wanted to control the interactions of the two cultures.

Taelo, Golden Hawk and Burley Bear went out ahead as the Elk Clan and the Clan of Others met and came together on the beach. They would turn to go northwest toward the meeting valley.

The two clans were coming together at the location where Burley Bear had chased after Red Oak and his team only a few moons before.

Burley Bear made the point of walking over to Red Oak to thank him for being such a good leader. They both had a good laugh as they recalled that chase event.

Silent Hawk, the leader that had stepped aside to put Grey Fox Running in the leadership position of the Elk Clan leader, had been selected to lead the two Clans back to the Elk clan meeting valley. This journey was one of renewal for the Elk Clan. They had left the valley on starvation rations and were now returning early because they were now so rich in goods that they were slowed by them.

A few days later, the Elk Clan came to the valley where Taelo and Golden Hawk had killed their giant dire wolves and Brave Deer and his hunters had fought the rest of the dire wolves in hand-to-hand combat.

Brave Deer and his team and Taelo and Golden Hawk stood together as they recalled their experiences.

This time the two stood with Burley Bear their new friend from the Others. He was impressed by the size of the dire wolf hides that Red Oak, Taelo and Golden Hawk held up.

Busy Bee, Brave Deer's daughter, commented to her two closest friends, Quiet Rabbit, and Talking Wren that she now had a much greater appreciation of Taelo's and Golden Hawks capabilities and that the night they had returned with the two giant dire wolf hides now meant so much more than it did at that time.

Silent Hawk commented on the dramatic change the Elk Clan had experienced in such a short time.

Later they stopped at the Honey Tree and collected enough honey that every family of both Clans had two small bags.

The sharing of the honey was a continuing sign of how close both Clans had become.

The procession was a strange sight. Tall smooth skinned people walked with an easy gait alongside of the broad, hairy people walking with an awkward somewhat stiff one. This was a contrast in human design.

Though different in appearance and some customs, it had become apparent to all in both groups they were more the same than different. They embraced their common beliefs and foundational principles.

Both clans brought a huge amount of extra food and other valuable supplies. They had baskets, leather goods, tools, spears, clothing, and specialty foods, such as mastodon meat, to trade with the other clans. The leather work of the old ones was unique and intricate in design.

Taelo, Golden Hawk and Burley Bear had come with a supply of their own things to trade and share. They had made several sleds and snowshoes. They had speared several more sharks and had a supply of arrows made with the teeth. Additionally, they had used several of the larger teeth to make the spears for trade purposes.

The three young men were the only single males doing this kind of work and were looked upon curiously by some. However, Taelo and Golden Hawk knew there would be items at the clan meeting that they would want, and they planned to have the currency to be able to get these items. They enrolled Burley Bear who immediately joined them in the preparation for trading.

Secretly the three had also created as series of carvings designed to be stacked one on top of the other. There was a base representing mother earth. On top of it stood a large Bear with a notch cut on the ear, a Deer, a Fox and together an Eagle and Hawk. This made a very impressive totem.

The three were going to present this totem to the entire Clan. For both people it represented the unity of nature. This had been a project they had spent their time on when they went to their hide away.

They had made a large travois to pull it to the meeting center. Little Otter and what everyone now thought of as his buffalo, had been recruited to pull the travois. The journey convinced them the totem would permanently stay in the valley.

They certainly were not going to pull it back.

The entire procession stopped and took in the valley. The dark green pines stood like sentinels holding the far snow-capped mountains at bay from the long oval dark blue lake at their backs.

The yellowing cat tails on the far-left bank shielded the far side of the lake where they planned to camp from the rest of the flat valley floor on the other side of the lake.

And in the distance, they could follow the tumbling path of the small river as in entered the valley to feed the lake.

The light blue sky, large tumulus clouds slowly drifting by, and the gentle breeze of the early afternoon seemed to pull the two clans forward.

Grey Fox Running was pleased that they were the first to arrive and they would have the place he had planned.

Taelo, Golden Hawk and Burley Bear cleaned up the area where the council always had their seat. They set up their totem and covered it with a large hide. They would unveil it as a surprise gift to all the sub-Clans. They had kept the entire effort secret from everyone. Only the three of them knew what it was.

Wise Owl brought in the Elk Horn Clan two days after the arrival of the Elk Clan and the Clan of Others. He saw that the area on the far side of the lake had already been taken. He chuckled at having been displaced. He was early enough to have a place down by the lake just across from those on the other side.

He went over to greet Grey Fox Running and see how the Elk Clan had fared. He was greeted by Grey Fox Running, Red Oak, and Silent Hawk at the point where the small bridge sat in the middle of the river. There he was introduced to Quiet Fox, leader of the Others.

Wise Owl was surprised to see that the Elk Clan had brought a group of Others as large as their own group. He understood immediately why they had chosen to be on this side of the river.

He also noted all were healthy and they had an enormous amount of food and goods on display. It was apparent Grey Fox Running and Red Oak had performed the magic they had been sent to do.

"It is good to see the Elk Clan has done so well. Who are the friends you bring with you," Wise Owl said as he greeted Grey Fox Running, Red Oak, Silent Hawk and Quiet Fox of the Others? He was intrigued by the situation and was very interested in how it had all come about. He was sure this was going to be an interesting and historic gathering for all the Elk sub-clans.

"It is good to see you my friend. I would like to introduce you to Quiet Fox of the Others. We have joined our two Clans in friendship and bring them with us to introduce them to the rest of the Elk sub-clans," Grey Fox Running said and then repeated the introduction to Quiet Fox.

"I am honored to meet Wise Owl. Taelo and Golden Hawk have told me many stories of the Elk Horn Clan and its wise leader," Quiet Fox spoke in Wise Owl's language.

This surprised Grey Fox Running who did not know Quiet Fox had been getting lessons from Taelo, Golden Hawk and Burley Bear.

The three were standing on the bank of the river beaming with pride. Quiet Fox was their pet project.

"I would ask you to help in the introduction of the Others to the rest of the sub-Clans. We have prospered and done well by working together. We have invited the Others to this meeting as a sign of friendship. They have brought gifts to share and goods to trade," Grey Fox Running continued the introduction.

"You have my support. This should be one of the more interesting gatherings we have held for as long as I can recall," Wise Owl said with a chuckle.

Gray Fox Running instructed each family to prominently show the wares they had brought so all could see.

Broken Spear and Quiet Fox had given similar advice to the group of Others. Their pure white leather with its intricate bead work was especially of interest.

Each arriving sub-clan had a different but surprised reaction. The entire Clan was speechless. A silence had fallen as each sub-clan understood there were Others among them.

There was a rise in the acrimony felt toward the main Elk Clan. Representatives from each of the other sub-clans came forward.

"What is the meaning of this? Why have you brought this group of Others with you," one of the elders from one of the sub-clans asked?

"They have become honorary Elk Clan members at our invitation. They attended my son's induction into adulthood and named the first child born to their Clan in over ten summers after Taelo. They have worked hard with us to reap the bounty the ancestors have sent to us. They are our brothers, and we honor them so," Grey Fox Running replied slowly and eloquently to the leaders who had come across the river to confront him.

"We have brought the best of our stores to share with you. We could not carry all we have. What we have brought will be shared with all. We have much excess food if it is needed. We wish our brothers and sisters of the other sub-clans only good tidings, but you must honor our friends as your friends," Silent Hawk spoke in support.

There was some grumbling among the group from the other sub-clans, but it was obvious the Elk Clan which had left in desperation and on the verge of starvation had returned with an abundance none of the other sub-clans could match.

They were accepted more from an inability to provide a counter proposal as to why the Others could not participate.

At the Elk Clan leadership welcome meeting, Wise Owl stood up and spoke in support of Gray Fox Running and pointed out to all, when the Elk Clan left the valley last season, most thought the Clan had little chance at survival.

Now the Elk Clan has returned seemingly the richest among all of them. This turn in fortune and their newly found friends all pointed to the Clan being led by the ancestors.

There was some grumbling, but the representatives returned to their sub-clans with the news of the wealth displayed by the Elk Clan and the fact the Others were friends and would stay.

As was the custom, the elders and leaders from each sub-clan came together for their first business meeting on the following evening. The Elk Clan continued its assault on tradition. It arrived with its group of elders now consisting of both male and female members. Including the Others in the Clan leadership circle by itself would have been enough but having women in the leadership circle was an additional challenge.

"Are there any other surprises you plan to pull on us?" a member of the Elk Hide Clan asked in a tone of disgust as he stood and looked over the arriving group.

"Brother, have I offended you in some way. Please accept my offering of young buffalo hump, the tongue and heart of the same animal prepared with salt from the sea and cooked together on a flat stone in the way of the Others," Gray Fox Running said in a loud and proud voice as Taelo, Golden Hawk and Burley Bear carried the cooked items on thin flat slate slabs in for all to share.

They put the items on tripods as the Others had shown them to make.

This surprised all in attendance, but all came forward to try the food whose aroma and flavor seemed to tease their palates. Several of the elders commented that they had never tasted anything so wonderful.

Taelo, Golden Hawk and Burley Bear then crouched in the shadows outside the circle of elders.

Broken Spear could feel their presence and was enjoying the discomfort felt by some of the elders from the other sub-clans. It was interesting to notice that women were not welcomed or accepted in the circle of elders of the new ones.

This was strange to Broken Spear since women were the primary leaders of elders in the circle of the Others. They usually lived longer then the men and were around many more years. It made sense to have the women provide this continuity on a leadership team.

"And why are women included in your circle of elders?" another representative asked loudly.

"This is something we learned from the Others. In the Clan of Others, women hold equal power with the men. They have more members on the council of elders. We are learning from them and have found the women add a balance previously missing in our planning discussions. We have changed our meetings to include our women elders," Grey Fox Running replied.

A murmur went through the group of elders. How would such a situation be addressed? If they acted against the Elk Clan, they would face their own angry women. If they accepted this change then the women of all the sub-clans would want similar privileges.

Why had this happened?

Who had given the Elk Clan the right to turn the world on its head?

The elder men quickly realized there was but one solution. In frightening rapidity, the world around them was crumbling. This day, the Elk Clan had walked in and turned the world as it had been known and lived for so long, upside down. The stability the Clans had known for an unknown period was on its head and change was thrust unceremoniously upon them all.

The word spread rapidly throughout the sub-clans.

The food turned out to be a good idea. Its preparation had been purposely planned and the cooking had been very meticulous. This was the best food the Elk Clan and the Clan of Others knew how to prepare. The women had made the point that it was hard to argue after a good meal.

"Let us take a moment, share the food, and drink we have brought. Then let us sit down and talk about the coming year and what must be done to ensure we all prosper," Grey Fox Running proposed.

"I agree with my good friend and look forward to these new ideas. It is clear the Elk Clan, the first clan, has been renewed, refreshed, and enriched. The rest of us should listen and learn from them.

Let's finish enjoying this delicious smelling food and then conduct business," Wise Owl of the Elk Horn Clan said as he put his arms around Grey Fox Running's shoulders.

"Was that the kind of help you were looking for," Wise Owl said quietly to Grey Fox Running.

"Yes, thank you for speaking up. I do not want to create a permanent problem. I do want change to take place," Grey Fox Running replied.

From the dark surrounding the Council of elders, Taelo, Golden Hawk and Burley Bear enjoyed the moment. They had been instrumental in bringing this change to the Elk Clan and now to all its sub-clans.

Both Grey Fox Running and White Swan sat looking at each other proud in their knowledge of Taelo, Golden Hawk and Burley, sitting in the dark sharing this moment of change, being the fuel and instruments of this historic moment.

Grey Fox Running spoke to the entire gathering of Clan leaders and repeated something Taelo had shared with the Elk Clan when he was induced to the Elk Clan as an adult, "Change is important if we are to grow as a people. In our lives only, change is certain. Without change we cannot grow or prosper. To feel comfortable with change we must all be humble learners. Humble learners handle the discomfort of change in a positive way."

After everyone had something to eat, Grey Fox Running stood and announced Taelo, Golden Hawk and Burley Bear had each been inducted into the circle of full adults and warriors. He shared all the adventures and contributions the three had made.

He closed by pointing to the mysterious item covered with a hide.

"Taelo, Golden Hawk and Burley Bear have made a gift to all the Clans. They have done this in secret. Even I have not seen this. They will now unveil their gift and present it to the council of elders," Grey Fox Running said in closing.

Taelo, Golden Hawk and Burley Bear came forward.

"It has been our pleasure to work on this gift to all the Clans and to the council of elders. It represents the union of the people, the animals, and our mother earth. It shows we are the same in thought, the same in heart, the same in spirit," Burley Bear spoke in the language of the new ones as Taelo, and Golden Hawk pulled the covering from the totem carving they had made.

There was a general murmur of appreciation and wonder at the quality of the work.

"The base represents the mother earth. You see the waves of the sea, the mountains, the trees, and sky," Golden Hawk continued in the tongue of the Others as Taelo translated to the language of the new ones.

"Next is the bear. This is a powerful totem for both peoples. Notice this one has a piece missing from its ear. This is the bear who created Broken Spear," Burley Bear spoke in his own language and Golden Hawk translated.

This same bear visited and spoke to Taelo on the beach this past year as it protected him from a pack of sixty wolves.

"Above him are our fox and wolf brothers. They are both our competitors and as we can see by looking around, they are becoming our companions. One is my father and the other is the leader of the Others," Taelo said in the language of the old ones and Burley Bear translated to the language of the new ones. They had rehearsed their speech and cross translation. They wanted to make the point that both peoples were equal.

"Above are the birds of the sky, a swan, a pheasant, a hawk and at the top an eagle. The lion is the one Taelo and the eagle flew with several years ago. They are all connected," Golden Hawk finished. The eagle at the top had its claws in the nose of a mountain lion and the hawk, the swan and the pheasant were carved in a spiral up the side of the lion. A spear protruded from the side of the lion.

The leaders gathered around the tall totem pole standing at least three spears high. The work was very well done. It was unlike anything seen before by anyone in either of any of the Clans.

This was taken as a sign by all the leaders they were being sent a message from the ancestors.

"The leaders of the future speak to us of the past and present. They are adventurers, they are inventors, and they are the masters of change. I speak to you as one who is old and who was broken so I would be able to see and understand. This is a symbol of unity and of the wholeness of nature," Broken Spear said in the language of the new ones.

This was a surprise to everyone but especially to Taelo, Golden Hawk and Burly Bear. They were very close to Broken Spear, and he had not let them know he was learning the language of the new ones. Broken Spear looked at the three with a twinkle in his eyes and winked at them.

After the first meeting, things proceeded in a more normal way. Trade among the various sub-clans went on in a vigorous manner.

Taelo, Golden Hawk and Burley Bear each did a brisk business in trading their shark teeth and shark teeth arrows and spears for various articles they desired.

When it came the time to share and redistribute the food supply, the Elk Clan had food to give to all the other sub-Clans. This was the final sign the partnership with the Others was valuable and would continue.

And so Taelo, Golden Hawk and Burley Bear began a long and enduring friendship. They were young men, who were recognized for their leadership, their ingenuity, and their honesty. The new stories added to the collection of both Clans included their many adventures. The stories told were memorable and the stories yet to come would continue to build on the solid accomplishments already achieved.

The End

The Golden Feather

Dedication:

To the best sons one could have.
They listened to many similar stories at bedtime.
I wish I had written those stories down at that time.

The Golden Feather

Chapter 1: Spring by the Sea

Taelo, Golden Hawk and Burley Bear accompanied the Elk Clan and the Clan of Others back from the first combined and very successful meeting of all the Elk Sub clans and the Clan of Others.

The three were the prime motivators of the cultural change taking place in both peoples. The Elk Clan and all the sub clans now had women on the Council of Elders. This was an adoption from the practice of the Clan of Others where women made up the majority of the membership in their Council of Elders.

Taelo was pleased that both White Swan, his mother and Quiet Pheasant, Golden Hawk's mother were members of the Council of Elders. His father, Grey Fox Running, the leader of the Elk Clan joked about the fact that he now had to take direction on how to manage the Elk Clan and how to behave in his personal lodge from the same woman.

The bond among the team that had been led by Little Otter on the first Elk Clan mixed gender long hunt continued to strengthen and grow.

They often retreated to the hot water pool at the cave by the top of the cascading water fall that fell several hundred feet into the Valley of Plenty.

The team operated as a unit.

They were bonded by the mutual respect and the experience of looking out for each other during one of the most successful long hunts in the Elk Clan's memory.

They were to learn they were bonded by language, by principle, by their capabilities and as predicted by Broken Spear, the seer of the Others, by a bond that would carry them through their lives.

Taelo's and Golden Hawk's accomplishments and unselfish sharing of the wealth they could have accumulated for themselves was woven into the stories now told by the Elk Clan and the Clan of Others. They openly shared the most prolific honey tree with the entire Elk Clan. They generously shared the shark's teeth taken from a huge shark they and Burley Bear fought and killed.

The young buffalo bull Taelo rescued became Little Otter's constant companion and the first draft animal the clan had ever utilized. He was the reason Little Otter's team was able to pull two thirds of a Mastodon killed during the long hunt back into the Valley of Plenty.

They guided the Clan of Others to a new home and the food they needed to survive the first winter. Burley Bear, a member of the Others, with the looks of and almost as large as the giant brown cave bear, became their best friend, protector, and partner. He was the older brother both Taelo and Golden Hawk looked up to both physically and intellectually.

The past winter the three had made their joint journey into adulthood. Taelo and Golden Hawk were the youngest members of the Elk Clan to be given the honor of being called hunter and warrior.

Their induction to this position was a joint ceremony between the Elk Clan and the Clan of Others. Burley Bear, Golden Hawk and Taelo were inducted by both Clans to the position of hunter and warrior.

The first newborn to the Clan of Others in almost ten winter cycles was named, Scream of the Eagle, in honor of Taelo.

The two clans had speakers that had learned the language of both Clans. Taelo's team as they were referred to all spoke both languages and were equally welcome and accepted in both Clans.

Taelo, the source of change once again surprised the Clan by rescuing and raising a wolf pup he found wandering lost in the forest. The wolf now almost full size, named Lasher, followed him everywhere. The bond between the two was immediate and mutual.

Taelo had spent much of his time bonding with and training Lasher. The two were inseparable. At night Lasher slept next to Taelo. The wolves had previously become familiar, but they always stayed on the periphery of the camp. Now there was one among them.

Golden Hawk and Taelo were walking slowly along the beach. The two friends were on the way to meet the rest of their group for their weekly dinner by the sea.

They and the rest of the team had recounted, retold, and polished their hunting stories more times than they cared to think about. They had contributed their fair share of the work to keep the clan fed and clothed throughout the winter.

The early spring breeze promised warmth and brought the fragrance of flowers from the cliffs above the bay.

Taelo, Golden Hawk and their hunting team friends had endured the winter in the Valley of Plenty and the hot spring cave at the top of the falls. This spring the move to the beach camp was an effort they had spearheaded and led.

They surprised the entire clan by cleaning all the beach side lodges and the main lodge prior to everyone's arrival.

They had also set up the fish trap in the bay and caught one large fish for every home. These events always caught the clan by surprise because Taelo's whole team seemed to do as they pleased. They, however, always ended up contributing in some significant way to the clan.

The team had also become more then friends. They had paired off and were young lovers. After a long winter they were all ready for some new adventure. Their long hunting experience had changed all of them. They were more daring, more confident, and restless.

Red Oak and Grey Fox Running, fathers, and uncles to Taelo and Golden Hawk sat in front of the main lodge of the beach summer camp.

"Look at those two. They are inseparable. I think they will come up with an excuse to leave us for the season," Grey Fox Running shared his observation with his best friend Red Oak.

"I think you are right. Golden Hawk has been restless. Quiet Pheasant has been worried about what the entire hunting group is up to," Red Oak continued.

Grey Fox Running and Red Oak were lifelong friends. Together they had pulled the Elk Clan back from the edge of disaster and ensured the clan had food for the winter. They had brought it from near starvation to become one of the wealthiest clans of the Elk Clan group.

Taelo and Golden Hawk were their sons and were just as close friends as the two of them.

"Look how Taelo's wolf follows the two everywhere. Taelo has an uncanny way of making animals work for him.

Last fall it was taming the young buffalo calf and putting it to work pulling a travois.

Now he has trained the wolf to hunt with him and obey signals as well as voice commands," Red Oak commented on the strange new feature in the camp.

The two commented that they would help their two young hunters in every way they could.

In another part of the camp, Quiet Pheasant was talking to her older sister, White Swan.

The two had some very different and interesting observations.

"Taelo and Golden Hawk are discussing some new journey. This time they will end up taking their friends with them. Have you noticed how tightly the hunting team has bonded," Quiet Pheasant commented?

"Yes, and it is clear to me that I have already lost my son to Quiet Rabbit, and you have lost yours to Busy Bee. The four of them are always together. They seem perfectly matched," White Swan said wistfully.

Floating Cloud, grandmother of Quiet Rabbit added, "Isn't the outcome what the two of you worked to arrange? And did it not work out exactly as you planned?"

White Swan was quite pleased with the outcome of the match making that she and Quiet Pheasant had arranged.

"It turned out just as we planned. So why the sigh," Quiet Pheasant said.

She felt exactly the same way.

The two had maneuvered the young women and ensured their placement on the hunting team. It had all worked out exactly as planned. Now as mothers they were feeling the loss of their young men.

"You know the surprise is the bond between Little Otter and Talking Wren. That is the odd couple. I would never have made that match," White Swan said with a chuckle.

"Well, I enjoyed the fact the Others assumed they were all matched pairs and immediately added Meadow Flower as another hunting partner. They wanted Burley Bear's mate to hunt along with the rest of the team," Quiet Pheasant replied.

She too was happy with the outcome.

"The Others seemed to have been right in their assessment," White Swan said putting down the blouse she had been decorating as she looked down the beach to where Taelo and Golden Hawk were just joining the rest of their team out on the large tooth boulder.

From above, the small harbor looked like a saber tooth tiger lying on the beach with its mouth slightly open. The head and upper jaw was formed by high rocky cliffs jutting out into the sea. The cliffs were green in their fern and thick moss covering. Blueberry bushes added a smoothing texture to the rocky cliffs. Millions of sea gulls nested on the cliffs to hatch their young.

The saber tooth was a large, long boulder jutting up from the beach pointing toward the upper jaw formed by the rocky cliffs.

The combination provided a perfect shield against the large waves crashing against it on the ocean side. The inner harbor side was the favorite swimming hole for all the youngsters and the source of an endless supply of fish.

"What a contrast. The waves on the right crash against the rock on the seaside. The pool on the left of the rock is smooth and quiet. Out in front are the green covered cliffs. They provide us a bounty of bird's eggs in the spring and our summer blueberries. The harbor itself is the magnet for fish," Taelo spoke quietly as he joined the rest of his friends.

At the moment he was enjoying the beauty and pleasant atmosphere of the bay.

He was thinking ahead to the next adventure but had yet to break the subject with his friends.

Lasher walked along the edge of the rock and seemed to follow the fish swimming around below. He looked around at the humans around him and quietly settled down near Taelo.

"Yes, it is beautiful and serene," Quiet Rabbit said as she sat down next to Taelo.

She was the only one allowed to sit so close to Taelo without getting a growl from Lasher.

The team met once a week on the rock to sit, enjoy the sunset and share their evening meal. The meal was usually simple but each week the responsibility to feed the team rotated to another team member. A small contest on who could serve the most unique dish became the norm. Today was Taelo's turn, and it appeared to the team that he was showing up empty handed.

Well, I wonder if we are going to get any dinner tonight," Burley Bear loudly asked Meadow Flower.

"Yes, it appears someone forgot his turn," Talking Wren spoke up.

She was looking around to see how Taelo was going to get out of this situation. She figured something was up. It was not Taelo's nature to forget anything.

"Whose turn is it anyway," Taelo played along as he started the fire under a giant clay pot and emptied a small bag of spices into the water.

He put one lone polished stone into the pot.

"The stone is all I have to put in the pot.

Well, I hope whoever is supposed to bring us food will do so by the time the water heats up.

Meanwhile, I think I will sit and enjoy the last rays of the sun with a drink of honey wine," Taelo said as he pulled out two large bags.

He gave one to Burley Bear. He passed his bag to Quiet Rabbit and soon everyone was enjoying the drink.

When steam began rising from the water, Taelo walked over to a long crack in the rock where four sticks were wedged.

"Well look what I have found," Taelo said as he pulled up a bag with three rabbits. He made a point of displaying each rabbit as he cut and dropped the pieces into the water.

"There seems to be more here," he said as he pulled up a bag of eggs and expertly cracked and dropped the eggs into the water he was stirring. He tossed one to Lasher who caught it in his mouth and seemed to swallow it.

"You spoil that wolf," Golden Hawk said as he watched Lasher run his tongue around the edges of his mouth.

"Well, I don't know who left all this here but look at this salmon," Taelo said as he removed the large salmon and showed it to everyone before cutting it into sections and dropping it into the stew.

Next Taelo pulled up a bag full of wet seed sprouts.

The next cord had several large birds each skewered to a Y shaped split end stick.

"Well, it looks as if someone left all of us another great treat," Taelo commented as he gave a stick with a bird to each person.

"And look they even have two for Little Otter and Burley Bear," Taelo joked as he handed the two their second birds.

The birds had been pre-grilled and only needed warming.

"Each of you will need to warm your grilled bird. When they are ready you will be offered a bowl of soup," Taelo instructed as he finished handing out the skewered birds.

He pulled the last line up with the soup bowls, and spoons. Each bowl was lined with flat bread. The bowls were a new addition to the team's experience. Taelo and Golden Hawk had carved the bowls out of oak. The grain of the wood was beautifully displayed.

By this time, the soup was beginning to steam. Everyone had gathered around the fire. They were slowly turning their birds to warm them.

The bowls of soup with fish and rabbit was served and all sat around enjoying the best meal served out on the rock to date.

Taelo looked across the tooth rock to see his parents and his aunt and uncle walking casually toward the team.

Silent Pheasant commented that the four of them were following their noses and wondered what smelled so good.

"Well, I hope Taelo hasn't given too much of this food to his wolf friend and that there is still enough for us," White Swan said as they arrived.

"Well, it all depends on Little Otter and Burley Bear. They usually take care of any extra," Golden Hawk joked.

He then refilled his soup bowl and offered it to his parents.

"Hey, don't put us on the spot," Little Otter exclaimed as he handed his extra bird to Grey Fox Running.

Burley Bear followed suit and gave his second bird to Red Oak.

There was plenty of rabbit and salmon soup.

After a few moments it was obvious the group of young people were being quiet and respectful to their elders.

Quiet Pheasant spoke up, "Well Red Oak, we were on a beach walk. I think we should finish our walk and relax at our own lodge."

With that both couples thanked the group and went walking on down the beach.

The talk of the team turned to what they were going to do for the spring and throughout the summer. Both Taelo and Golden Hawk were unusually silent.

Taelo was crouching by Lasher giving him a bowl of the soup and some cooked rabbit.

"OK, what are the two of you not telling us," Burley Bear finally spoke up.

Just then an eagle and a hawk flew across the cove. The eagle let out a long cry.

Back in the camp and along the beach all eyes turned to the sky.

The eagle and hawk flew out toward the sunset and in unison gracefully turned and headed back across the cove. The eagle let out another cry.

Lasher let out a small howl.

"Whatever the two have planned, the eagle and hawk have just verified it. I am sure the two of them will be going on some challenging adventure," White Swan said as she shielded her eyes and followed the eagle's flight until it disappeared above the cliffs.

Out on the rock all eyes turned to Taelo and Golden Hawk.

"Yes, what is it the two of you are holding back and the eagle and hawk have blessed," Busy Bee spoke up.

Taelo looked at Golden Hawk and gave him a nod. For some time, the two had been discussing a journey of discovery. Golden Hawk had dubbed it a *"journey of the heart"* because it really had no other purpose than satisfying what the two were wishing for.

"We have been discussing a trip south. A trip of discovery, a journey of the heart," Golden Hawk replied.

Taelo then explained that the journey would be to the south and would most likely last more than twelve cycles of the moon.

"Who would be going with you," Burley Bear inquired?

Taelo sat down next to Quiet Rabbit and said that anyone wishing to go would be welcome.

Quiet Rabbit smiled and stated that with both Golden Hawk's and Taelo's signaling that the adventure was being watched by the ancients all of them should go.

Busy Bee had energy in her voice as she pointed out that they had all been wondering what the team should do for their next adventure.

The silence from the team caused Golden Hawk concern. Maybe it had not been such a good idea.

"How far south," Burley Bear asked?

"We are not sure. Until we can't go any farther or we decide we have gone far enough," Golden Hawk replied.

"I would love to take such a trek," Talking Wren volunteered as she gave Little Otter a neck massage.

"How about the rest of you," Busy Bee asked?

"The question that comes to mind is, will the Elk Clan leadership let all of us leave at this time," Little Otter asked?

"If all of us are interested, I will discuss this with my mother and ask her advice on how to present this to the leadership," Taelo volunteered.

"If she agrees and decides to help us, we should also plan to visit my Clan and talk to Broken Spear," Burley Bear suggested.

He was very interested and knew Broken Spear would have good advice about this journey.

"Well, it sounds as if we all want to go. Once we have agreement, we will plan our next steps," Golden Hawk said.

Taelo, Quiet Rabbit, Golden Hawk and Busy Bee walked along the beach back toward the camp. They were a common foursome often joined by Burley Bear, Meadow Flower, Little Otter, and Talking Wren.

This evening the talk was about their upcoming adventure and how they should prepare for the trek.

Later that evening Taelo approached White Swan.

Taelo was quietly talking to White Swan as they sat in front of their lodge looking at the sunset behind the spit on the far side of the bay.

Lasher sat quietly between the two.

As White Swan slowly scratched Lasher on the head, she listened as Taelo described the trek he and Golden Hawk were planning. She had seen and heard their totems and knew that this trek was going to happen. She knew Taelo was engaging her to ensure it would be approved by the clan council.

She asked who was going and was not surprised when Taelo said it was the entire team. She felt good that they were all going together. There was something to be said about taking care of each other.

The length of time Taelo planned on being gone surprised her. Twelve moons was a long time.

"So, you think the clan leadership will let all of us go," Taelo pressed his inquiry.

"Well, they will balk at having such a large number of their young people traversing across the country but in the end you will all go with their acceptance.

The Valley of Plenty will easily support us without any major hunting parties needing to go out. So, they will have no reason to keep you. How far do you plan to go?" White Swan asked.

She was pleased Taelo had come to her. She knew Taelo was not asking permission but asking advice on how to maneuver through the politics of the Clan. She knew he was going. It was just a matter of how to best position such a trek.

She would help and she would make sure the team went well equipped.

"Yes, all of the team wants to go," Taelo said as he got up gave his mother a hug and walked down toward the beach.

He knew Quiet Rabbit would be out on her favorite rock with her feet in the water.

Golden Hawk and Busy Bee joined Taelo and Quiet Rabbit.

"Well, what did your mother say," Golden Hawk asked.

"She says we will get grudging support, but we should plan on going," Taelo shared.

"This trek is the event that will separate Taelo and Golden Hawk from the normal Elk Clan progression of leaders," Grey Fox Running said quietly as he sat down next to White Swan.

He was watching Taelo walk down to the bay to the figure sitting out on the rock. Grey Fox Running warmly recalled courting White Swan. He was as madly in love and infatuated with her now as he had been those many years ago. He put his arm around White Swan and gave her a hug.

"Yes, I know. There is something pulling Taelo, and he must follow and discover what it is. I have no doubt our ancestors are guiding his moves. I am pleased he and Golden Hawk are doing this together. I am also happy each has found their mate." White Swan replied.

Chapter 2: Preparation

𝒜 few days later Taelo and Golden Hawk stood at the center of the leadership council. They had just finished explaining their desire to go on the trek south. They identified their team that would go with them.

They then stood by as the discussion or more often the argument between the different leaders transpired. Several of the elders were less than positive but slowly and grudgingly gave into the leaders White Swan had aligned in support. Finally, the council agreed to the team's request.

"We recognize the opportunity the Clan leadership is giving us. We understand this leaves you shorthanded. Perhaps there will be some way those of us on the trek can repay you. Until then, please accept our most sincere thank you," Taelo said as he looked around after the grudging agreement was reached.

The advice of the Others about leading with food would always be in Taelo's mind.

He had watched a group of negative Elk Clan leaders relax and reach the right decisions about allowing the Others to be part of the clan after eating the most extravagant meal the Others could prepare.

Even as he spoke the rest of his team was delivering food to each of the leader's homes. The entire team had gone hunting and returned with three elk, two boar and four deer. They had again caught one large salmon for every household. The largest salmon were delivered to each leader's home along with the choice pieces of the elk, boar, and deer.

The members of the clan were surprised by the team. Their way of saying thank you endeared them to the entire clan.

"I certainly am glad that I did not prevail," one of the older clan leaders, who had spoken against the trek, commented to a colleague.

He recognized the support Taelo's team had created with the approach they had taken in saying thank you. The hunting team was elevated in his estimation.

Red Oak and Grey Fox Running had talked about Taelo's and Golden Hawk's trek. They knew their two sons well enough to know they would go. They were enthusiastic in supporting their sons. They had made a similar trek when they were young. Taelo's and Golden Hawk's trek was much more ambitious. They were planning on going much farther, for a longer time, with their entire team.

The two sought to support their sons and the team and to make sure the team had thought through the entire trip and the obstacles they might face.

Red Oak made a shark toothed spear for Golden Hawk and Busy Bee.

The long hunt and the change her parents had seen in Busy Bee made them strong supporters of this new adventure. They visited with Quiet Pheasant and quickly understood the strong support that Golden Hawk had from his family.

They were happy with Busy Bee's choice of Golden Hawk as her mate. Busy Bee's family had come by to check with Quiet Pheasant and her reaction to the trek. The trek was a concern they had not expected. It took some adjusting for them to become supporters, but the team's actions had always made them proud.

They came expecting to get support to oppose the trek but left with the realization they needed to strongly support Busy Bee's decision.

Quiet Rabbit had lost her parents when she was young. Her father died from a wound he got in a hunting accident. Her mother died from a fall while fetching the water for the day.

Her grandmother told the story that the fall only gave her mother an excuse to join the person she loved.

Quiet Rabbit had been raised by her grandmother.

"Grandmother, I know this is different than in your day. But I wish to go everywhere Taelo goes," Quite Rabbit said as she hugged her grandmother.

"It is not that different. I ran away with your grandfather when I was told I would be mated with another. He and I went to another of the Elk Clan, and it was only years later that I made up with my parents," her grandmother shared a part of the family history Quiet Rabbit had never known.

She was fascinated and spent the rest of the evening asking questions and talking to her grandmother. She went to sleep with a deeper appreciation of both her grandmother and her mother and father.

Little Otter's parents had watched the transformation of their son with pleasure. He had gone out on last season's long hunt with the mixed gender team expecting to be humiliated. He was unsure of himself and negative about those who would be on his team. His growth and maturity shot up immeasurably in the month he spent on the long hunt.

His strong friendship with Burley Bear and his unabashed admiration of both Taelo and Golden Hawk spoke to a new level of maturity and a personal self-confidence.

They were surprised about his relationship with Talking Wren. This at first seemed like an unusual bond but when looked at carefully the two were very compatible. Little Otter was very shy, and Talking Wren was an extrovert. Together they made a perfectly balanced pair.

They became ardent supporters of every member who had been on the long hunt, and they began to enjoy Talking Wren and her constant witty and sometimes sharp banter.

Talking Wren had earned her name and still maintained it daily. Her spirit was always positive and always vocal. She spoke what she saw and thought. She was always had a running commentary about every topic, person, current or past event. If she were quiet those around suspected, she was ill. Though vocal she was fun to have around.

Her parents had long ago realized Talking Wren did what Talking Wren decided to do. They were pleased at how things were turning out and always supported their vocal daughter.

Quiet Rabbit looked around at the team sitting together on the bay's giant tooth rock.

She looked at Meadow Flower as she named her the best at treating wounds and the medicine woman for the trek.

She pointed to Burley Bear and declared him the most sensitive and skillful at guiding the way and named him chief guide.

She looked at the rest of the team and declared everyone as capable hunters and that was what they would do as they traveled.

Then she pointed to Taelo and Golden Hawk and declared them the dreamers of the team, a skill that gave them nothing useful to do for the rest of the trek.

Taelo and Golden Hawk both laughed. Taelo responded that he and Golden Hawk dreamed of making a travois they could ride on while being pulled by Quiet Rabbit and Busy Bee.

"Yes, I think we can have them done first thing in the morning," Golden Hawk replied with a chuckle.

"In your dreams," both Quiet Rabbit and Busy Bee chimed.

Both knew Taelo and Golden Hawk would be what would make this trek fun, interesting and successful.

White Swan, Quiet Pheasant, and the other parents of Taelo's trek team worked together in giving the team a beach front departure dinner.

Grey Fox Running gave a brief departure speech that lauded the best hunt team in the memory of the Elk Clan.

Red Oak presented a shark tipped spear to each of the team. He and Grey Fox Running had carved a figure of each of the animals the team had killed during their long hunt.

Burley Bear was specifically recognized for being a strong friend and protector of Taelo and Golden Hawk. He was given a special spear with the largest shark's tooth that was available.

Burley Bear was touched by the recognition that was given to him. He thanked the entire team for helping him grow and promised his spear would be used to keep the team safe and well fed.

The next morning the team bade their farewells and began their trek by going north along the shore. Burley Bear was in the lead as they headed for his home.

Lasher ran along the edge of the water and periodically tried to catch a fish or crab.

The journey took them past the spot where the beached whale had been found by Taelo almost two years before. Someone had made a large stone arrangement from all the stones collected for the fire rings and for melting the fat.

"It was here that Taelo spoke to the bear, and she replied by protecting us from the wolves," Burly Bear explained.

He still vividly remembered Taelo and Golden Hawk running along the beach. He recalled the way it appeared they were flying down the beach on their return from finding a new home for the Clan of Others.

The team continued north for the rest of the afternoon.

Broken Spear had foreseen their arrival and the entire Clan of Others were waiting for Taelo's team. Everyone on the team was known and befriended by someone in the Clan of Others. The team's exploits were now part of the stories told around the campfires of the Others.

"Welcome, Burley Bear, it is good to have you home," Quiet Fox said as he officially greeted him.

Burley Bear's mother clearly just half his size gave him a big hug.

She knew Burley Bear always took a ribbing about her passionate display of affection, but she did not care. Though he was the biggest member of the clan, he was still her little boy.

The entire clan looked silently on as Taelo approached with Lasher at his side.

"This is my new companion. He obeys my command and will not harm any of you. Please do not try to touch him," Taelo instructed those around.

He, however, took Broken Spear's hand and brought it to Lasher's nose.

"This is Broken Spear. He is the wise man I have told you so much about. He is a friend," Taelo said as if Lasher understood the human language.

Lasher gently licked the back of Broken Spear's hand.

"Well, that is the closest I have been to a living wolf without a spear in my hand," Broken Spear said as he happily withdrew his hand.

He was impressed with Taelo's ability to make friends with almost any animal.

Their afternoon arrival allowed them to relax and bathe prior to the evening dinner and of course the story telling that would inevitably follow afterwards. The clan members loved to listen to the stories both Burly Bear and Little Otter told.

Taelo took Lasher into the heated pool with him and washed him down. Lasher seemed to enjoy the warm water and kept chomping at it. Once Taelo had thoroughly washed him he pushed Lasher out of the pool. After shaking off all the water Lasher lay down on a leather skin Taelo had put out for him.

"You really spoil that wolf," Golden Hawk said once again. He was sitting with only his head above water higher up in the pool.

"I guess I do spoil him. However, he is extremely loyal to me and will defend me with his life," Taelo said as walked up to where Golden Hawk was sitting.

A few moments later as Taelo exited the heated pool, he was approached by a messenger. Broken Spear wanted to talk with him.

Taelo had hoped to spend time with Broken Spear. The guidance he had received prior to the hunt last season had saved his life. He trusted Broken Spear to give him key insights and valuable advice.

"Thank you for speaking with me," Taelo said as he sat down with Broken Spear.

He knew that it was an honor for anyone to sit and talk with the Seer.

"It is good to see my favorite of the New Ones," Broken Spear replied.

He had a deep respect for the young man. He had learned much from one so young.

Each of them was speaking in the other person's language. It was their way of paying respect to each other.

"You know of the trek we are about to take. I seek your council and advice," Taelo said quietly.

"Yes, I have seen parts of your journey. But as you know by now, I cannot see all and what I see can be changed by the people taking slightly different actions. I have flown with the eagle, and I do know you should not take the coast down. The coast is like the thumb of your hand; it goes down and then you must come back up the other side and then go south again. You must stay to the mountains and go down the middle," Broken Spear commented.

"Somewhere beyond where the thumb takes off, you will be surprised by a group of young warriors out to raid their neighbors. They will out-number you three to one and believe they can take your food and your women. Be alert for their ambush. They will not talk but try a surprise attack," Broken Spear went on.

"You will meet people far to the south. There you will find a people similar in beliefs to yours. They have a powerful clan. Their domain is in the mountains. They will treat you well. There is much to learn from them. They are builders.

On your return you will meet a fierce clan near the other coast. They are powerful warriors, but they have lost their way by looking inward too long. They fight each other more than other clans. You will befriend one side and be the enemy of the other.

There will be a moment in which you must act without thinking and slay your attacker. It is crucial you keep your defense high at all times when you meet these people," Broken Spear shared his vision.

Taelo remained silent as he took in what he had been told.

"Will any of the team be in any danger I should know about," Taelo asked.

"Yes, the leader of the clan I just spoke about will want one of the women to be his. This is what the confrontation will be about," Broken Spear continued.

"When you return, you must come to see me before you return to the Elk Clan. Your trek will be only halfway done. I have not seen the second part of your trek. I have only been allowed to know you will have additional travel and work ahead of you before this trek is over.

Taelo was surprised about this last part. He now wondered what the second part of the trek would be. He was now beginning a trek that had a mysterious ending.

That evening around the campfire he shared what he had learned with his team. He left out a few of the points about the conflict on the return. He had learned that too much information sometimes caused others to take actions that made situations more difficult.

Chapter 3: Journey South

They had originally planned to go back south along the coast, instead, they went eastward to the valley they had hunted two seasons ago and followed that valley. Its course went slightly eastward as they went south.

This time the team took in the expanse of the plain they were jogging. Burley Bear or Little Otter were usually in the lead. Their pace was a comfortable pace for the team.

The high snow-white peaks jutting high into the sky and often rising above the clouds surrounded them as they traveled.

Lasher was either at Taelo's side or periodically he would be making quick hunting excursions.

Burley Bear commented that Taelo's wolf fed him well as Taelo gave Lasher a pat on the head when he returned with a ground hog.

"Well, any time you bring me a rabbit or other small game, I will scratch you behind the ears as well," Taelo joked with his large friend.

The team was armed the way they normally were for a hunt. Their long spears were bundled, and Burley Bear carried them on his back. Each team member had their bone knifes and a hand club.

On their first stop after leaving the camp of the Others, Taelo opened several of the bundles he and Golden Hawk had been carrying.

The two had previously been asked about the contents of the bundles and had refused to tell the team what the bundles contained.

Taelo and Golden Hawk had made weapons for the entire team. These hand weapons were smooth flat pieces of red oak. They had scrapped and polished the carefully selected oak wood to highlight its grain. Each grip was rounded to a smooth oval and sized to fit the user's hand. Shark's teeth were embedded and tied in with elk gut on both edges of the flat blade. The length of each blade varied from weapon to weapon based on the size of the grip. Burley Bear's weapon was the largest at almost four feet long.

"We want each of you to carry these for personal protection. They are light but very effective if we need to protect ourselves," Golden Hawk explained as he presented the gift to each team member.

"This is a beautiful weapon. I have never seen anything like it," Burley Bear said as he tested his new prize as he swung it through the air.

His was not only the longest but the thickest and heaviest of the weapons. He commented how good it felt in his hand.

Each weapon had been made with the user in mind and each of the team members was having the same surprised reaction.

"When did the two of you find time to make all of these," Talking Wren commented as she studied the detail of her weapon.

"It feels like this was made especially for me," Busy Bee said as she took several swings through the air.

Lasher had a low rumble coming from his throat.

"Easy boy, there is nothing threatening us," Taelo reassured him.

"The two of you have out done yourselves," Quiet Rabbit said as she gave Taelo a hug.

"Taelo and I thought about the team needing immediate protection. We must be prepared to defend ourselves. Most of our weapons are for hunting and Burley Bear is carrying those.

We have also made smaller spears for the same purpose. Each spear has a shark's tooth point. Each has a different decoration. Please pick out the one you like.

Taelo and Golden Hawk stood by as the team members looked and selected one of the shorter spears.

"I suppose you would like us to practice using them," Meadow Flower guessed as she fingered the tips of the shark's teeth on her weapon.

"Yes, we have thought through how we might face an attack. Our backpacks will be used as shields. Each of you will need to sew on the leather straps as Golden Hawk and I have done. This will allow you to slip your arm through them. You can then shield yourself holding the backpack. The hand through the straps will hold the spear. The other hand will use the new weapon you have just been presented," Taelo demonstrated what he was saying.

If attacked the person pulling the travois will stand it on end, stand behind it and use it as a shield. The team will gather in a circle with the travois facing the rear. We will alternate gender around the circle. Anyone getting seriously injured will back into the center of the circle and it will close to provide protection," Taelo replied to the question.

When the team began its first practice, Lasher ran about looking for the offending attackers and then began barking and growling at the various team members.

"Easy boy, we are all friends. You will know the enemy when they attack. Then you will know what to do," Taelo said as he calmed Lasher.

The team maintained a brisk but casual pace southward. They often jogged. The weather was hot and dry. Fewer mountains had snow at their peaks. They followed a river leading through canyons and huge gorges. At times they were so far down the sun did not touch the riverbed.

"So far this has been an enjoyable trek," Talking Wren said as they called it a day.

Taelo insisted they set up their camp high up on the bank along the canyon wall.

"Why do you want us so far from the riverbank?" Busy Bee asked.

"Have you noticed the gorges we have come through? If there is a large rain upstream somewhere there is no place for the water to spread out. So down here the water will rise quickly even if it is not raining here," Taelo replied.

"Where did you learn such a thing?" Little Otter said looking up from the work he was doing.

"I wish I could claim it as my thinking, but Broken Spear is the one who warned me. He claims to have seen it through the eyes of the eagle," Taelo replied.

A few days later, on a clear sunny morning, as the team hiked along the top of the canyon area, they observed firsthand as the water below swelled and filled up the canyon to the very walls.

"Now I know why you listen so closely to the guidance Broken Spear gives," Talking Wren said as they all looked down to the roaring waters below.

Several days later they came out to a body of water. It looked like a sea and had waves like a sea. When they tested the water, they were sure they had arrived at the crook of the thumb Broken Spear had described.

The team spent several days relaxing and enjoying the bounty the sea brought them. The fish, clams, and mussels all enhanced their meals. They frolicked in the water and generally enjoyed the great weather.

Lasher loved to retrieve the sticks that Taelo, or Quiet Rabbit threw out into the waves for him. He had acclimated to the team's weapons practice but always ran around the outside of the ring barking.

"The last few days have been great. Tomorrow we continue along the inner coast.

Just south of here we will be attacked. At night we will take turns at watch. In the morning we will practice our defense. Let's pack our backpacks with an extra hide so they provide better protection. Anything that does not fit will be on the travois," Taelo announced after the evening meal.

"So, this was the reason for the weapons and our practice," Quiet Rabbit said quietly but so the entire team could hear.

"No, the weapons were made before Broken Spear let me know about the attack," Taelo replied.

He had dreamed about the weapons and how to make them in a dream many moon cycles before the trip had been planned.

"I will keep a sharp eye on the trail ahead. We should make sure we do not get too far apart. Meadow Flower, please use your keen hearing to listen. Listen for the absence of sound as well as for the quiet talk of someone hiding," Burley Bear said as they were getting ready to continue their journey.

The team traveled in a fixed arrow formation, Burly Bear at point, Golden Hawk to the left, Little Otter to the right, Meadow Flower immediately behind the point, Talking Wren on the travois behind Meadow Flower, Quiet Rabbit to the left side of the travois, Busy Bee to the right and Taelo at the rear. The travois pulling rotation was always in action, but everyone would return to their assigned position after their turn pulling.

The exception was Burly Bear and Little Otter. They exchanged the lead between them throughout the day.

They traveled along in this formation and periodically either the lead or Meadow Flower would call for an attack. They had agreed to practice on a random basis at least once a day.

They were traveling southward about a mile from the beach to get around the rough coastline when Meadow Flower quietly announced, "I hear something up ahead."

Taelo relinquished the travois to Talking Wren and took up his position in the rear. The entire team was at full alert.

Lasher at Taelo's side immediately let out an almost imperceptible rumble from his throat.

An eagle cry came from high above. The team familiar with Taelo's totem immediately put their back packs on their arms and their weapons in their hands. They knew this was the time for the attack.

Suddenly thirty young warriors surrounded them. There was no talk. The thirty came in rapidly in a full-scale attack. The attackers intended to take what they wanted.

The team closed ranks and stood silently as they had practiced.

When the attackers were almost upon them the entire team stomped their feet and exploded in a giant roar. The noise surprised and momentarily stopped the attackers.

Lasher surprised the team by running around through the oncoming warriors and biting them on their calves. He never stopped long enough to do any serious damage, but it destroyed the composure of the fighters who danced to keep from getting bitten.

The team's stance and formation proved to be extremely effective. The team was outnumbered three to one. They threw back the initial charge. The attackers could not take advantage of their superior number because of the tightness of the group.

Taelo and the team inflicted significant injury while only receiving minor cuts. Their shark edged weapons were brutally efficient at inflicting painful but not fatal wounds. Their short spears were deadly for any attacker that got in too close. The initial charge lasted only a few moments though the intensity of the fight made it seemed forever.

As the attackers backed off the team again exploded in another giant roar. Lasher let out a loud howl in accompaniment.

Burly Bear led the team in unison to a rise in the trail. The next attack was more determined, but it was obvious there were fewer attackers.

The team followed the same routine of letting out a tremendous roar just before the enemy reached them. It had the wanted effect. At the same time Lasher went into his attack mode.

The first blows on contact came from the team. After a ferocious fight, the attackers were repelled. Almost half of the attackers had serious wounds and had to be helped in their retreat.

Taelo and Lasher ran after them for a short distance. Taelo let out a roar and Lasher a loud howl.

The attackers hastened their retreat. The eagle cry overhead greeted his return to the team.

"What was that last display for," Talking Wren asked as she rearranged the load on the travois?

"They heard the roar each time they attacked. They paid a dear price for not listening. I wanted them to hear it again as they retreated. It will make them think twice about attacking us again," Taelo replied with a smile.

He knelt down and hugged Lasher, "Good boy," You knew exactly what to do."

"I would not have believed it, but I saw how effective he was at disrupting the warriors. They spent half their time worrying about being bitten," Meadow Flower said.

"Will he let me pet him," she asked.

"Sure, bring a small piece of dried meat and I will introduce you," Taelo replied.

The whole team lined up to make friends with Lasher. In the past they had periodically tried to make friends, but Lasher would have none of it. Now he accepted them with a small lick to their hands.

"What are our wounds," Taelo asked looking around.

Little Otter spoke up as he showed the team the wound on the side of his torso, "I think it is probably me. I did not twist away from a spear thrust fast enough. I think I need to lose weight. I make too large of a target."

"Here let me fix that immediately," Meadow Flower said as she took out a needle and some cat gut. After three stitches she rubbed what looked like fat on the wound.

"What is that awful smelling stuff you just put on," Little Otter complained.

"You don't want to know. I will tell you it works wonders," Burley Bear said with a chuckle as he gave Little Otter a pat on his shoulder.

"Well, it's time to get going. Busy Bee and Quiet Rabbit, please pull the travois. We will jog for the rest of the day. This will put a good distance between us and the attack group. It's no use tempting them by sticking around," Taelo said as he got the team reorganized.

The team had inflicted many wounds but as agreed they did not try to fatally wound any of the attackers. They knew they would need to return through this territory on the way back.

They rotated positions pulling the travois. This determined the speed of progress for the team. Whenever the pair pulling the travois seemed to slow or falter Taelo would call for a switch. He and Golden Hawk took the last turn. Together they moved the team almost as fast as if they were jogging without the travois.

"I think you two are just showing off," Burley Bear complained as he struggled to stay ahead in the lead.

For the next two days the team repeated the day long jog but not at the intensity they had done on the first day.

The weather got continually warmer until it was always hot and humid. The mountains no longer had snow caps but had areas where the forest was sparse.

Quiet Rabbit pointed out that they were all losing weight even though they ate well.

"We all better take it easy until we get use to this weather," Taelo commented as they stopped by a river and sat down at its bank.

They had stopped sitting around a fire as they often had done in camps in their home territory. The weather was just too hot and humid. It was more comfortable to sit by the edge of the river with their feet in the shallow water.

The animal noises were loud and strange. They continued to post a watch throughout the night.

Lasher became an important part of the watch. His growling often gave them early warning about some animal that was poking about.

"My only worry is if we cross paths with a lion. I am not sure what kind of animals we will find this far south. We have not seen any of the large animals we know," Golden Hawk commented as they sat at the edge of their camp at the edge of river.

After a full moon's travel Taelo pointed out a mighty mountain.

"We are going to climb to the top. I believe we are at the point Broken Spear said we would be able to watch the sunrise on one sea and the watch it set in the other," Taelo shared with the team.

"I would ask how he would know such a thing, but I already know the answer," Burly Bear said with a grunt and said in a voice mimicking Broken Spear, "I have seen it through the eyes of the eagle."

"Well let's do it. The only path I see seems to be made by a mountain goat. I think we will need to distribute all our gear and carry them on our backs," Talking Wren spoke up as she began to arrange their various goods to be packed.

Taelo took the lead as the team made its ascent. He stopped at the peak to look down into the mouth of a quiet but visibly active volcano.

"Look at the pool of fire," he said pointing to the red bubbling lava.

He guided the team to a point where the black surface was clear, and the wind was blowing toward the volcano.

The air was cool and noticeably thinner.

High above an eagle let out its cry.

"I think we are where we are supposed to be," Quiet Rabbit said as the team all watched the eagle fly.

It went out as far as they could see. It returned and flew the other way until it disappeared.

They set up their camp for the evening. The stars in the sky were different from the ones they knew but they were clear, intense, and humbling in the numbers they represented.

"There are so many lights in the sky. Are they really our ancestors looking down at us," Busy Bee asked as they all lay and looked up?

"I do not know what the lights are but remembering our ancestors and believing they look down on us and guide us is a wonderful way to think about our night sky," Taelo replied as Quiet Rabbit nestled in his arm.

The feel of her warmth and having her nestle in the crook of his arm was the best feeling he could ever have imagined. He gave her a gentle hug.

The following morning was clear. The entire team watched the sunrise over one sea. The sky was clear, and they could just barely make out what they thought was the other sea.

Through the day they watched and monitored the progress of the sun. In the late afternoon they were able to see the sun touch the water on the other sea. *

*This is possible from the top of a volcano in Panama.

"I would not have believed such a story. I will be laughed at when I tell this to our Clan," Burley Bear said quietly.

"Yes, we will all be laughed at, but we are here, and we have seen this wonderful sight. We will tell it to our grandchildren if we are that lucky," Talking Wren commented in a hushed tone.

They all stood as the sun slowly set into the far waters. Finally, the sky turned into a mix of red, purple, and grey when the sun was below the horizon.

Taelo was now ready to continue the journey to the south.

The team made its way down the mountain and continued their journey south.

Chapter 4: Mountain Kingdom

Their easy jog ate up the miles and they made rapid progress. They had traveled another full moon cycle when they found a trail leading slightly to the east and upward.

The mountains were more thickly forested with a mix of trees new to the team. Often the clouds floated below the white peaks of the highest ones. There was a change in the temperature and the air seemed thinner.

Burley Bear stopped to point out the sign of people traveling a trail that led upward to a ridge above.

Taelo express his desire that they greet anyone they met in a friendly manner.

"Our last greeting was not so friendly," Little Otter spoke up.

"Yes, but Broken Spear has said we will meet a friendly clan down in this area," Taelo replied.

The team proceeded in their normal formation. The trail up the mountain was narrow, and the arrow formation collapsed into a single line. Each of the team members again carried their load in their back packs.

This time Taelo took the lead.

The team agreed Burley Bear appeared to be an attack all by himself and would seem threatening.

"Yeah, put me in the back carrying all the heavy stuff," Burley Bear whined as he carried the travois beams.

He agreed with the team. He understood and was just keeping the chatter going.

They traveled the trail for almost three days when in the far distance they saw what appeared to be a village.

Once again high in the sky an eagle cried.

When the team looked up, they saw it was flying with a bird almost twice its size as the two flew overhead.

"Your eagle has been the largest bird I have seen until today. This huge creature is unbelievable," Golden Hawk exclaimed as the team stood and watched both the eagle and the new giant bird.

"It must be the totem of the region," Quiet Rabbit said.

"Yes, it probably is. We will need to find out the name of this huge bird," Taelo said as he once again led the team onward.

The next day, far in the distance, they saw what appeared to be a gathering as large as their yearly clan meeting.

"This is a very large clan of people. Let's put on our best dress and prepare to meet them," Taelo said as they reached a crest in the trail.

"We should also prepare our gifts," Golden Hawk said as he opened his pack and took out two weapons like the ones, they all carried.

Each of the team members had some little gift.

Meadow Flower had several beautifully decorated white leather vests.

Taelo had several intricate necklaces of seashell, crystal, and sharks' teeth. He also carried one huge black sharks' tooth as a separate gift.

The rest had wrist bands, head bands and several decorated spears.

Once dressed in their best, the team once again proceeded onward.

They had traveled about an hour when they spotted a procession coming toward them.

"It is time for our greeting song," Taelo said and together the team sang a song wishing the oncoming group well.

They raised both hands to the air to show they had no weapons and continued their song as they walked along.

"Look, the group meeting us has taken up a song as well and has raised their hands as we have done. I think this is a sign of welcome," Little Otter exclaimed.

"Yes, it is a very good sign, but I want all of us to feel our weapons on our backs. It is always wise to be friendly but to be prepared for the unexpected," Taelo replied.

When the two groups were about a long spear throw apart Taelo stopped his team.

"I will go forward by myself. If things do not work out as we plan you will need to run for your lives," Taelo said as he proceeded to go forward.

Lasher was at his heal.

"Where does he think we can run?" Burly Bear said quietly to Meadow Flower.

"I don't think anyone will be harming Taelo if Lasher has anything to say about it," Golden Hawk interjected.

"Well, it is comforting to see they are not carrying weapons in their hands, and they are a mix of men and women," Quiet Rabbit pointed out.

The team watched as a single person came forward from the other group. Taelo and the other person met about halfway between the two groups.

It was interesting to see that both raised their right hands and then extended them to the others shoulder.

Lasher sat on his haunches to one side.

"Welcome to the Mountain Kingdom. We have come to greet you. Our Seer said an eagle would cry and a condor would fly across the sky together when you came. We saw them yesterday," Bold Walker greeted Taelo as he drew his welcome in the dirt.

"Our Seer did not tell me that you also walk with the wolf," Bold Walker said pointing to Lasher.

"We are pleased to be here. We come from the north to learn from you. Broken Spear has seen your land through the eyes of the eagle and speaks highly of you," Taelo replied as he drew the team's journey from the north to their current location.

He had drawn out six moons to indicate the time it had taken the team.

"Lasher is a gift from the spirits. Let me introduce you to him Taelo said taking Bold Walkers hand and bring it to Lasher's nose.

Lasher gave the hand a little lick.

Bold Walker repeated Lasher's name and sat for a few minutes taking in the rather large wolf.

"Let's return to the city where you will be officially greeted," Bold Walker said as he got up from the squatted position both had assumed.

Taelo stood and waved his team forward. The two groups merged and greeted each other. Together the two groups walked back down the trail toward the city. Each of the team members was escorted by two of the people they had just met.

The team proceeded until they came to a deep crack in the earth. A very narrow bridge was suspended across what seemed to be a bottomless abyss.

"I think I am ready to go back home," Little Otter said meekly as he looked down. "I can't see the bottom."

"I hope the bridge is strong enough to hold my weight," Burley Bear joined in.

The whole team walked to the edge of what seemed like a bottomless crack in the earth and looked down.

Lasher let out a low growl.

"I wonder how they ever managed to get the bridge built," Taelo said out loud.

Taelo took a deep breath and followed Bold Walker onto the bridge. It would be single file across the bridge.

"I wonder what happens if we meet someone crossing the other way," Quiet Rabbit said as she followed closely behind Taelo?

She had jumped ahead of her guide because she wanted to remain as close to Taelo as possible.

Lasher was staying as close to Quiet Rabbit as she was staying to Taelo. If he could have spoken, he would have probably objected as much as the rest of the team.

The wind blowing across the bridge added an additional challenge.

"I just want to make it across," Taelo replied as he kept his eyes on Bold Walker.

"I think I will wait here on this side," Little Otter called out as he hesitated to get on the bridge.

"Come on. Follow me," Talking Wren said as she stepped onto the bridge. Little Otter let a couple of the escorts pass him by and then hesitantly followed.

Burley Bear watched the proceedings. He was not sure about bringing the poles for the travois across with him. His hosts solved his concern by taking the long poles from him and carrying them across.

"I guess for them this is just another crossing," Meadow Flower said as she followed.

Burley Bear was the last of the team to come across. He was the largest of them all. He stopped in the middle of the bridge and dropped a stone the size if his hand. After a few moments, a little sound echoed up as it hit bottom.

"I would not want to slip off this bridge," Burley Bear commented as he reached solid ground.

"This must be a very large clan. Look at all their living areas. They are built into the sides of the mountain and the little cliffs," Taelo commented to his team as they were escorted farther into the village.

They were led into a wide green grassy bowel. A rocky cliff rose on one side and over the lip of the other side was a view of a huge valley stretching out as far as the eye could see. High snow-capped mountains formed the border on the far side.

Taelo followed Bold Walker toward a raised stone area where a person with a headdress with a feather plumage was sitting.

"This is our leader, Star Leaper," Bold Walker introduced the person.

"Please come up," Star Leaper said and indicated the invitation with a sweep of his hand and a beckoning hand motion.

"I believe we are invited up onto the flat platform," Taelo said to his team.

Together they all climbed up the stone steps. This was the first time any of them had seen such construction.

Lasher hesitantly followed Taelo up the steps.

"Look how all the stone fits perfectly together," Golden Hawk observed.

"We will learn much from these people," Taelo replied as he closely inspected the stonework.

From this height the valley beyond the edge of the bowl was visible.

The team stopped and took in the scene from the top. Lasher walked slowly around the edge of the platform.

"This is another unforgettable view. It is almost as good as seeing the two waters" Busy Bee observed.

"We are from far to the north. This is Golden Hawk and Busy Bee. This is Burley Bear and Meadow Flower. This is Little Otter and Talking Wren. This is Quiet Rabbit, and I am Taelo, and my wolf is called Lasher" Taelo spoke slowly and drew the symbol of each person on the sand he found on a flat stone.

"I am Star Leaper, leader of the Mountain Kingdom. Our Seer predicted your coming. He said the eagle would fly with the condor. "He forgot to tell me that you would walk with the wolf."

"You are Taelo, the claw of the eagle. You are the leader of your people. We have looked forward to meeting you," Star Leaper said as he stepped forward and shook hands with Taelo. He then proceeded to do the same with each of the team members.

"These two are different from you," Star Leaper said as he pointed to Burley Bear and Meadow Flower.

"This is my friend and his partner. They are members of the Others. We share the same territory with Burley Bear's people.

Yes, I sense he will be leader of his people as you will be of yours," Star Leaper continued as he looked up at Burley Bear and put his hand on his shoulder.

Burley Bear returned the gesture.

We have prepared a feast to celebrate your arrival. Please sit and make yourself comfortable. We will enjoy dinner and then show you where you can stay. We hope you will stay and share what you have seen on your travels here.

During the dinner Golden Hawk presented Star Leaper the gift of one of the shark tooth edged weapons. To Star Leapers wife Taelo presented a necklace made from a crystal.

Little Otter presented Bold Walker the other shark edged weapon.

The rest of the team presented their various little gifts to their hosts. The gift giving broke the ice. The chatter and communicative hand gestures was continuous, and the laughter was heard often as the two sides tried their best to communicate.

Almost immediately the team began to pick up words and phrases. They were keen to learn from this clan and had talked about quickly learning the language. The team's interactions with each other and in the past and having learned each other's language prepared them well for learning yet another language.

Chapter 5: Stone Village and Condors

Taelo and the rest of the team were content to relax and wander about the village taking in the way these new people worked and interacted.

After a few days of rest and getting to know their hosts better, Taelo and Golden Hawk stood watching some stones being prepared for use. The stones were selected and expertly broken into the desired shape. They were then matched to one another. The procedure was to then place a little sand, water between the stones, and slide them back and forth on top of one another until the surfaces matched. It was slow tedious work, but the stones then were close to a perfect fit to each other.

The stones were then moved to the area where they were to be used. Since the stones needed to overlap to interlock with each other, the same procedure to match the stones was used by those making the wall.

The sand used to mate the stones was left in place. On the last cycle of mating the stones, some clay was added. When this dried, the stones were locked in place by the thin layer of dried mud and sand.

"I wonder how they figured out how to do this," Golden Hawk commented as he and Taelo followed the construction of one of the buildings. They had spent almost ten sun cycles observing the work being done to build a new home.

"I have no clue, but we will most certainly use this knowledge to improve the way we build our next lodge," Taelo replied.

"We do not have as many people to do this work so I am not sure we will be able to build such elaborate structures," he continued.

Not far away Busy Bee, Quiet Rabbit, Talking Wren, and Meadow Flower were helping in the preparation of the lunch meal. The meat was from an animal they had only seen in the area around the mountain. Some of the spices were new as well.

"It's interesting to learn how to cook some new dishes. We will have to take some of these spices back with us when we return home," Talking Wren commented.

"Perhaps some will grow for us if we plant their seeds," Quiet Rabbit commented.

"There is so much to see and learn here," Busy Bee said from where she was stirring food in a clay dish new to her.

Quiet Rabbit took in the behaviors of the female members of this Mountain Clan. They dressed in a material that she had never seen. She and Busy Bee wanted to learn about this material for future use.

Out in the valley Burley Bear and Little Otter were walking with several of the younger men who tended the herd of strange animals.

"They are tame like the buffalo Taelo captured for us to use." Little Otter observed.

"By managing these animals, they have little need to hunt," Burley Bear replied.

"I guess having to climb up and down these mountains caused them to tame these animals. I know I would never be able to hunt here the way we do back home," Little Otter continued the line of thought.

Burley Bear and Little Otter were exhausted by the time they returned to the village for dinner.

In the late afternoon, the team gathered on the terrace outside of their stone lodge. They shared their learning with each other.

"It really is amazing all the things we are learning from our new friends," Golden Hawk commented.

As had become the practice, Bold Walker stopped by to talk to them about the day. This evening he had a special treat to offer.

"Star Leaper suggested I take you to go see the nest of a Condor. There are several nests only a few days away from here. Are you interested?" Bold Walker asked.

There was an almost simultaneous positive response from the entire team.

"Yes, we would love to see where the Great Condor lives," Taelo officially accepted the invitation for the team.

"I will arrange for the food and the camps. All you need to do is bring your personal items you want for yourselves. We will leave in one sun cycle from now. It will take us about six sun cycles to go and then return. I will also show you the roots of a giant river that runs many moons to the far seas in the east," Bold Walker informed them.

"These people are quite advanced. They are skilled in what they do. They control the territory in which they live. They overcome the challenges of the land," Taelo commented after Bold Walker had left.

"Yes, and they are friendly to us. They have warned me of the people just to the north. They periodically fight with them in defense of their territory," Little Otter joined in.

"The group that attacked us must have been from that clan," Golden Hawk conjectured.

"Well, I am excited about seeing the home of the Condor," Talking Wren said as she tried to guide the discussion back to the upcoming trip.

"It seems we will be taken care of and only need to carry a little pack," Quiet Rabbit joined in.

The team spent the next day continuing their observation of the work in the village. They were interested in how the water for the village had been guided into the center and had several side distribution channels throughout the village. All refuse was gathered and put in a location away from the water.

This attention to how waste was managed did not escape Taelo. This practice supported his belief that the waste was the source of not only bad smells but the cause of problems with how the clan members felt.

Bold Walker gathered the team and took the lead up the mountain. Golden Hawk and the rest of the team followed behind him. There were about a dozen heavily loaded people carrying the food and camping supplies following immediately behind them.

Lasher followed behind Taelo or was often at his side.

"I am certainly pleased that we are being treated so well. It is hard to breathe just hiking along the trail. I am not sure how long I would last if I had to carry the load the people behind us are carrying," Little Otter commented.

"They probably figured we wouldn't have the endurance and gave us a break," Taelo said with a chuckle as he thought about Little Otter, one of the strongest among them, worrying about having the stamina to keep up.

"We can certainly help with some of the load being carried up the mountain for us," Taelo volunteered to Bold Walker.

"Thank you for your offer. Those carrying our camp and food are very happy to do so. Seeing the nest of a condor is a reward for their good work and contribution to the clan. They volunteered and are eager to carry the load they have," Bold Walker replied.

Their trail took them above the tree line and continued an upward course through green grasses and rock edged trails. They were often walking along cliff sides where the drop was hundreds of feet down to sharp rocks below.

Scattered tumulus clouds dotted the clear blue sky. Soon they were walking above the clouds. A strong wind pushed or at times seemed to pull them along the trail.

At these times it was clear to Taelo that Lasher was hugging the cliff wall.

"This is so beautiful. Every turn of the trail rewards us with another breath-taking view," Quiet Rabbit observed.

"It makes me feel so little but so happy," Busy Bee replied.

"The area on top of those rocks, isolated at end of this ridge, is where the home of our clan's condor is located," Bold Walker said as he stopped the team and pointed to the location he was talking about.

"We will set up our camp here. Tomorrow I will take each of you one at a time to see the nest and if you are lucky, you will see the condor and maybe a young one," he continued.

"I am not sure about taking Lasher up with us," he said looking at Taelo.

"Lasher will be as behaved as any of your people," Taelo reassured Bold Walker as he scratched Lasher behind his ears.

The next morning Bold Walker took Taelo and Quiet Rabbit to the nest of the condor. On the return from the first visit, they were all smiling and talking about the activity at the nesting site.

"I was surprised at how well Lasher behaved. He crawled up just like the rest of us to look," Bold Walker said as he prepared to take Golden Hawk and Busy Bee up to the nest.

"There are two younger condors and a very large mother condor at the nest," Quiet Rabbit explained to the rest.

The trips to the nest continued for the rest of the day. The sun made its way up and across the mountain range. The jubilant chatter of the group continued throughout the day. By evening all had made the journey to the nesting site.

Night brought a steep drop in the temperature. The team sat around one of several small fires. Each team member was snuggling in one of their new woolly coats given them by the Clan of the Condor.

Lasher was under his hide and only his nose stuck out.

"Their animals are as good as and perhaps better than our buffalo. They give them meat, milk, fiber to weave and the hides make such warm coats, boots, and gloves," Quiet Rabbit said as she leaned into Taelo's arm.

"We have learned and have seen so much here. It has been worth the journey. I think we are close to the time we should leave and go back home," Taelo announced.

"Yes, I agree. It will be good to get back to our own lands," Burley Bear replied.

The next morning Bold Walker announced, "We will travel along this ridge heading to the east."

There was a panoramic view in every direction. Many small streams could be seen flowing to the east and repeatedly joining together to form a larger river. The mountains stretched north as far as the eye could see. There was a continuous fall toward the west and beyond the littler mountains it appeared there was a sea.

"No, you cannot see the sea but there is one there," Bold Walker replied when asked. "What you see is the sky beyond the mountains."

They hiked until the sun was low behind them and until the trail came to the edge of a cliff. The bottom was hidden by clouds, but a green forest spread out as far out to the east as the eye could see. The blue of little rivers could be seen repeatedly coming together to form an ever-larger ones. At the farthest point the little rivers seemed to come together to form just one large river.

"See the rivers beyond. They continue to merge together to form a giant river that flows many moons to the east. I have made this trek and followed these waters, from the condor's nest to the far sea.

My friend and I were gone for almost three seasons.

There are fierce fish in the river, animals that will eat you, snakes longer than three people and almost as large around.

We found no people.

When we returned, we each received the names we now carry. I am now Bold Walker, and my friend was named Trail Blazer. He was killed in a battle with our enemy to the north," Bold Walker shared as they all stood or sat on boulders looking out toward the east.

"Thank you for bringing us here to see such a wonder. Our team is on a similar trek as you took. Each of us already has earned our names but we will carry these visions and add your people to the stories of our Clan. We are lucky to have found The Clan of the Condor," Taelo replied quietly.

"We call our trek a Journey of the Heart."

The return trip down the mountain was as wondrous as the journey up. It was easier, and it was quicker.

Chapter 6: Sacrifice and Departure

Bold Walker told the story of the Condor Clan's totem. The Condor was their primary link to their ancestors. For hundreds of seasons the Clan of the Condor had celebrated this link with a ceremony lasting seven sun cycles. It ended with a maiden being given to the Condor as his mate.

It was an honor to be chosen as the most beautiful maiden to be sacrificed. This was the part of the ceremony that both his father, he and his family disagreed with. A young girl is sacrificed. She is taken to a cave at the very top of the mountain. The peak is higher than where we went to see the Condor. There she is left as an offering to the spirits of our ancestors and the spirit of the Condor.

He invited the team to stay for this celebration.

A silence fell across the team. A human sacrifice was something beyond their experience.

Taelo accepted the invitation to stay.

The team spent a great deal of time discussing and arguing the concept of a human sacrifice to the ancestors or to a Condor totem.

None of them could overcome the mixed feeling they had about this ceremony. The team's principles guided them to be absolutely against such a practice.

On their next meeting with Bold Walker the issue became a personal challenge to them.

Bold Walker came to the team and asked for their help. His sister of thirteen seasons had been given the honor to be the sacrifice at this celebration.

He asked for the team's help.

Taelo looked at each of the team members. He knew without asking that they would all agree to help but he approached each and quietly asked what the team should do.

"How can we be of help," Quiet Rabbit inquired of Bold Walker?

"During the ceremony, the sacrifice is given food and drink. Then she is taken by one of the high priests to the Cave of the Condor at the highest point of this mountain. Up there the snow never melts. It is always winter. The snow and ice stay the year around. She is left there with nothing but her clothes. No coat or covering. She will freeze and join the other sacrifices there. Only the high priests ever go to this cave. Anyone else would be killed for going there," Bold Walker replied.

"You however are not bound by our tradition. Once Feather-in-the-Wind is left in the cave the ceremony is over. If she were to be rescued, she could leave with you and live among you," Bold Walker said in a matter-of-fact way as he contained his emotion.

"We will help, let's talk about our departure and how we will do it," Taelo replied.

This was unexpected and they needed to think carefully on how to help. It was a big responsibility and the team needed to understand how their actions might be interpreted if they were caught.

After much discussion they decided, Busy Bee and Quiet Rabbit would take a warm coat and some food up to the cave and hide it away.

Feather-in-the-Wind would then be rescued as soon as possible. When the team was about to leave, they would bring Feather-in-the-Wind down from the peak and hide her on the travois to be pulled by Burley Bear and Little Otter.

In the following days, Busy Bee and Quiet Rabbit made a point of taking several long-extended hikes.

On one of these they hiked up to the top of the mountain to the cave described by Bold Walker.

The two walked into the cave and stopped in their tracks.

"They look like they were just placed here recently," Busy Bee said in a hushed tone.

"Each has been moved into their current position. One of the medicine men must come up and arrange them after they die," Quiet Rabbit said as she slowly walked toward the back of the cave.

It was clear to her the bodies of the beautiful sacrifices were in order of the time they were brought to the cave. The ones in the back were showing signs of drying out.

"This is unbelievable. There must be at least one hundred," Busy Bee said as she followed Quiet Rabbit to the back of the cave.

There seemed to be no place to hide the bear skin coat they had brought up with them. As they were walking out, they noticed a dark hole to the right of the cave opening. It was an empty bubble deformation near the mouth of the cave. It was hard to see. The bear skin coat disappeared when it was put in. You had to reach in and touch it to realize it was there.

"I think this is a perfect place to hide the coat. I hope Feather-in-the-Wind will be able to find it and get into it," Quiet Rabbit said as she stood back to examine the hiding place.

The two jogged back down the mountain. It was late when they re-entered the village.

"We were getting worried about you," Golden Hawk commented as he and Taelo greeted the two.

"We made the trip as quickly as possible. It took us longer than we thought to find a hiding place for the coat. There are a least one hundred sacrifices in the cave," Quiet Rabbit shared.

"This is a sad custom for this clan to have. I wonder how it ever started," Busy Bee said.

The next morning Bold Walker learned the coat was in the cave. He said he would let Feather-in-the-Wind know where it was hidden.

He thanked them for this help.

"Your hospitality has been phenomenal. All of us have learned so much from you and we want to thank you. We have agreed that our departure should be the day after the Condor ceremony. In this way we can take Feather-in-the-Wind away immediately," Taelo shared.

A few days later Taelo informed Star Walker, "Our Clans are spread out through a vast territory but come together once a cycle to re-unite and make sure each part of the clan is doing well. Your visit at such a meeting would be an honor."

"We have enjoyed your stay and I am sure some of us will travel to your lands in the future. My Seer lets me know that you have great integrity and a good sense of justice and fairness.

Be very careful with the warriors to the north. There are two competing leaders. The one called Sharp Stone is the one always wanting war. The other, Tough Hide is the more reasonable. Make friends with Tough Hide but do not fully trust him either. Their clan has different beliefs about the use of power," Star Leaper said quietly.

Thank you for your consul. I will heed your advice. I have also been warned by Burly Bear's Clan Seer, Broken Spear, and what action I must take. I will be ready," Taelo replied.

The Condor ceremony was a three-sun cycle celebration of eating, drinking and storytelling. The celebrations built in intensity toward the last part of the ceremony. Then Feather-in-the-Wind was brought to the same raised platform where the team had earlier been greeted.

Feather-in-the-Wind was dressed in a beautifully decorated outfit and her hair was braided in backward sweeping rows.

"She is indeed beautiful. I can see why she was selected," Talking Wren said to the team.

"Oh, great Condor, see the beautiful prize we sacrifice to your honor. She will reside in your cave for eons to come. We take her now to you," the medicine man said in a strong clear voice as he gave Feather-in-the-Wind a bowl of liquid to drink. Her beautiful outfit was taken off. She was led totally nude off the platform and up the mountain path. It was clear she was totally inebriated and did not seem to notice a thing.

"One long sip of that drink will cause a man to forget the night. The bowl she drank will knock her totally out. I told her to pretend to drink but to drink as little as possible, but I am worried," Bold Walker confided to Taelo and the team.

"The sun will be down by the time they get to the cave. What is the procedure once they arrive," Taelo asked?

"I have quietly asked around about this. It seems the medicine man will take her to the cave and seat her next to the last sacrifice and lay her down. I was told usually the sacrifice just falls asleep in the position they were placed and never awaken," Bold Walker shared.

"Does the medicine man stay or leave," Quiet Rabbit asked worriedly?

"It seems they return immediately to allow the spirit of the Condor to come into the cave," Bold Walker commented.

The team decided they needed to act immediately. Quiet Rabbit and Busy Bee set out on their night hike to the cave. They jogged slowly up the path. They each carried their spear. They planned to let the medicine man pass by them on his way down the mountain. They would then proceed as quickly as possible to the cave. The thin air tried their stamina, but they continued their fast pace up the mountain.

They were about three quarters of the way to the cave when Quiet Rabbit sensed someone coming down the path. Silently she and Busy Bee climbed up into a crack in the rocks above the trail. There they waited until the crunching of gravel went by them. After what seemed like a very long wait but was probably only a few moments the two came down to the trail and proceeded on a fast jog up toward the cave.

"I hope she was able to find the coat. We are jogging and even with my coat on I am freezing," Busy Bee commented quietly.

The temperature on the mountain was dropping very fast as they jogged up toward the cave.

"There it is," Quiet Rabbit said as the moonlight outlined the opening of the cave.

They found Feather-in-the-Wind passed out but laying beneath her coat. She had found the coat but had passed out before she had been able to get in. She looked a little blue, but she was breathing.

"Let's all get into the coat together. I have brought some strong black drink this clan is so fond of. I have also brought some meat broth," Quiet Rabbit instructed as she opened the bear skin coat and put Feather-in-the-Wind into it.

They all got into the coat. The two held Feather-in-the-Wind between them and gave her the hot liquid and food.

A small moan from Feather-in-the-Wind let the two know she was alright. The potent drink had probably saved her from the cold. Now all she needed was warmth. After a short time, Quiet Rabbit decided it was time to begin the journey down.

"Let's hook the jacket to the spears and get back as quickly as possible." Busy Bees said as she pushed her spear through the hoops on one side while Quiet Rabbit did the same on the other side.

The two lifted Feather-in-the-Wind's sleeping body and proceeded down the trail at a slow jog.

"Her name is appropriate. I am glad she was not named like Little Otter. She is as light as a feather," Quiet Rabbit commented as they jogged effortlessly down the trail.

Bold Walker met them and guided them to a trail leading to the bridge.

"I will carry her across and put her in your travois. Burly Bear and Meadow Flower are sleeping there tonight. They will take care of her," he commented as the spears were withdrawn from the coat and he put Feather-in-the-Wind over his shoulders like a sack of food.

"Thank you again," he said as he walked away.

"Let's get back to our camp before someone notices we are missing," Quiet Rabbit said as she led the way back into the village.

"It's good to have the two of you back," Golden Hawk and Taelo said as they greeted the two.

It appeared all had gone as planned.

The next morning the entire village was out to see the team off.

"We will escort you to the edge of the valley to where we first met you. Then you are off on your own once again. I will plan on coming to see you soon," Bold Walker said before leading the way across the bridge.

"My Seer says you take a part of us with you. It will be a great story for our clan. The Condor has finally accepted our gift and we will not need to sacrifice any more of our beautiful young women," Star Leaper said quietly into Taelo's ear.

"Thank you"

Taelo looked steadily into Star Leaper's eyes and replied loud enough for all to hear.

"The beauty of these mountains, the power of the Condor and the richness of the people will be with us for our lifetime. We welcome you to the North and we look to you as our friends to the South.

He then put his hands onto Star Leaper's shoulders and mouthed, "You are Welcome,"

He then turned and followed Bold Walker across the bridge.

Chapter 7: Feather-in-the-Wind

The team had come down the mountain trail on the side that would take them along the waters on the opposite side from the one they had come down.

Quiet Rabbit and Busy Bee took turns checking on the condition of their new member. They were amazed at the potency of the drink that made her pass out. They had made her drink some of the soup stock that Meadow Flower gave them.

Bold Walker had given them a pouch of personal belongings and gifts from her mother, father, and him. The contents were remembrances that had little practical value but were a link to her family. Busy Bee had placed that next to Feather-in-the-Wind.

They were halfway down the mountain on their way to the sea when Feather-in-the-Wind awoke. She was totally disoriented and wondered where she was.

Lasher gave a low growl as she asked where she was. This was a new person and one he had not yet been introduced to by Taelo.

Meadow Flower was the first to notice Feather-in-the-Wind was awake. She called out as she helped Feather-in-the-Wind to stand up.

Taelo informed her that she was now a member of the Elk Clan and was traveling with them toward Elk Clan territory.

She looked around at each of the team members. She was very much aware of each of them. She and her friends had followed the women around on a constant basis. They had traveled from the far north for many moons. To make such a trek was the dream of many of the young women.

She looked at Burley Bear and smiled. The stories about him and how fierce he must be was the constant talk of all the young men. And Meadow Flower his mate was deemed number two in *the to be feared* category.

Little Otter and Talking Wren were fun to watch. She was always laughing, talking to everyone. To everyone's surprise she spent her time learning about the water distribution and the layout of the village. The interactions between the relatively tiny woman and the huge man called Little Otter reminded her mother of numerous Clan stories about how opposite behaviors often are compatible.

Taelo and Golden Hawk were admired for their thorough observations and study of the Condor Clan workers doing the building and repair work around the village. Bold Walker often walked and talked in detail with them. She knew by the way he talked about them to their father that he admired the two.

Her favorites were Quiet Rabbit and Busy Bee. Her friends and her all wanted to have the same relationship with their mates that these two seemed to have. It seemed each was the other half to the mate they had chosen. Their confidence and the fact that they had their own weapons equivalent to the men made them heroines in her circle of friends.

The world she knew with her friends and was living in just a few Sun cycles ago had all crashed in on her when she had been selected to be the Condor Queen. She had never thought of herself as a candidate for that honor and was shocked when she had learned of it.

Her mother, though she was supposed to be honored by this selection, spent her time crying each time they were together. Her father, who usually had some word addressing her unconventional behavior with her friends, now greeted her pleasantly. She liked him better when he was trying to correct her. Bold Walker said nothing. It seemed he was mad at her.

Feather-in-the-Wind now knew each was handling the fact that her selection was the same as her death to them. She loved each of them more now that she understood.

Bold Walker had acted to save her. Her father got the alignment of the Clan Seer. Her mother quit crying.

It was the bravery of her heroines, Quiet Rabbit and Busy Bee risking their lives to rescue her that she now thought about.

"Won't they come looking for me," Feather-in-the-Wind inquired?

"No, your disappearance will mean the Condor finally found the Queen he was looking for and took her to his palace. This frees your clan from the promise of offering their most beautiful virgin to the Condor. You are the last sacrifice to the Condor," Taelo explained.

"Oh, Bold Walker tried to explain to me, but I was not sure how everything would work. I don't remember getting into the coat," Feather-in-the-Wind said as she looked around at the team.

"Let's set up camp and enjoy a good meal," Taelo continued.

Taelo announced that the team would once again practice their defensive formation.

"What position will Feather-in-the-Wind assume," Little Otter asked?

"Let's talk about that later. Right now, I am ready for a nice hot broth and a piece of llama," Burley Bear commented as he began setting up camp and arranging for a central fire.

Feather-in-the-Wind sat down on one of the stones and watched as the team automatically got the camp set up.

Taelo watched as Lasher sat down at her feet and let her scratch the top of his head.

He quietly pointed this out to the rest of the team. Lasher, usually the last to accept someone new to the team had immediately accepted Feather-in-the-Wind.

During dinner, the talk turned to the clan to the north.

"We will need to be on high alert at all times. Broken Spear has told me that we will be in great danger. There will come a time when we will be confronted and must act decisively," Taelo shared with the rest of the team.

"Tough Hide is the leader Star Leaper said is the most trustworthy and fair. Sharp Stone is the leader he gave warning about. We will need to be very careful as we pass through their territory," Taelo continued.

"Should we just try to go past their camp and keep going," Golden Hawk inquired?

"Yes, that is actually a very good idea. If we are lucky, we will do just that. However, Broken Spear has seen us in their camp. This means we will not be so fortunate and must be prepared," Taelo continue.

Things had changed. Broken Spear had not seen the situation with Feather-in-the-Wind. He had not mentioned the Condor.

Taelo felt a difference in the situation. He would need to martial all his senses in the upcoming meeting with this aggressive clan.

The team fell into harmony almost immediately. Feather-in-the-Wind was given a position directly behind the point person. She was overshadowed by either Burly Bear or Little Otter. Her role would always be in the center of the triangle. She would aid any of the fighters needing help. It became her duty to call for random attack simulations.

Feather-in-the-Wind joked about those in front of her falling backwards and crushing her.

Taelo decided that the best position for her was to remain in the center of the defensive circle and serve as aid to anyone that was hurt. Once she was weapon trained and demonstrated her fighting capability this role would be re-evaluated.

He had voiced his concern about putting her anywhere else.

"You put her into a useful position and out of harm's way. Busy Bee and I will teach her how to use all the weapons," Quiet Rabbit replied to Taelo as they walked along.

"I have no doubt she will do well with you two teaching her," Taelo said just as Feather-in-the-Wind called for her first simulated attack.

Lasher assumed a position in the center of the circle next to Feather-in-the-Wind.

They continued their journey northward at a crisp pace. Once again Meadow Flower assumed her role as listener.

Seven sun cycles past before the team reached the sea. They then traveled northward for another four sun cycles.

This time it was Burley Bear who signaled someone was approaching.

They came around a bend in the trail and ahead of them were three warriors in full fighting gear. They stood and waited for the team to approach.

"They seem to be the only ones. I do not hear or sense anyone near them" Meadow Flower said quietly.

Taelo told the team to stay in their defensive position. If their interaction went badly, they would fight.

Taelo, Golden Hawk and Burley Bear and Lasher went forward together to meet the three warriors.

Taelo walked confidently toward the three. He approached to an arm's length and took one shorter step. He did not want to encroach on the warrior's personal space.

"I am Taelo, these are my brothers Golden Hawk and Burley Bear, and this is Lasher," Taelo made the introductions.

"I am Tough Hide, and these are my two sons Strong Sinew and Storm Wind," Tough Hide responded in his own language.

Taelo was able to understand almost immediately.

Taelo fount it was surprisingly like the language of the Clan of the Condor that they had just left.

"I am here to greet you and to escort you into our home village. You will have to leave your weapons with me," Tough Hide explained as he drew symbols on the ground in front of him.

Taelo replied in the language he had just learned, "In that case our visit to your village is over. We yield our weapons to no one and give them up only on our death."

There was a moment of silence from Tough Hide as he processed the message and the fact Taelo was speaking to him in his own language.

Lasher sat on his haunch with a continuous low rumble sounding like it emanated from his chest.

"I now understand the stories of the fierce group of warriors where the women were more dangerous than the men. And a wolf engaged in the battle. We thought it was just a story made up by thirty of our warriors who were exaggerating because they came back so wounded and defeated," Tough Hide said with a smile.

He had not believed a small group of people could have faced his warriors. The added piece of a wolf also fighting in the battle had been too much to accept. Now here was the fighting group in front of him and he saw extreme confidence in the leader.

"Our small team fears no one. Even your army waiting over the hill will not be enough should you chose to engage us," Taelo said quietly.

He was watching the reaction of the Tough Hide closely.

Tough Hide was surprised that Taelo had correctly placed his small army and had challenged him directly.

"I think we will get along. I like your directness. One of the women would not by any chance be your mother," Tough Hide said with a smile?

"No but you are right to fear her. Just ask Burley Bear what happens when you mess with her," Taelo said as he looked to Burley Bear.

"Yes, I know firsthand, those who do not treat her well are lucky to wake up at all," Burley Bear said with his smile that looked more like a grimace.

Tough Hide took in the giant of a man. He was different but clearly a member of this team and not someone he would want to fight.

"Well, then let's get back to the Clan of the Warrior and celebrate your arrival," Tough Hide said as he put his hand on Taelo's shoulder.

"Yes, that will really be welcomed," Taelo said as he returned the greeting.

As they walked back to the team Golden Hawk asked, "How did you know that he had his warriors beyond the hill?"

"It was purely a guess. He is in a struggle for power with Sharp Stone. He was dressed for battle. He probably travels with his warriors wherever he goes," Taelo replied.

"Let's be super vigilant while we are here. Do not go anywhere alone. Let's go in together and leave together," Taelo said as the team marched forward in formation.

Taelo rearranged the team so that Burley Bear was in back and Little Otter was in front. He and Golden Hawk were in the middle. Their escort split with half behind the team and half in front.

Taelo did not like this arrangement but decided to accept it.

Chapter 8: War Seekers

The countryside was brush heavy, with wind twisted trees leaning toward the west. Large, flat branched limbs like the shark toothed weapon on Taelo's back, topped with dark red flowers were interspersed around the trees. Some stood as high or higher than the trees around them.

The village grew in stature and size as the procession approached. A circular wall as tall as Burley Bear surrounded stone buildings that were built around a central area dominated by a huge four-sided, stone covered hill that had a flat top similar to but larger than the area that Star Leaper had greeted the team on their arrival to the Condor Clan.

Unlike that friendly greeting, their arrival to the Warrior Clan seemed more like being prisoners on display to the mass of people that came to watch their arrival.

Taelo was talking continuously to the team as they were led to a large area that was clearly the meeting area for this clan. At one end was the four-sided stone cover hill at the other end was a large open area that had been excavated and had seating all the way around.

Another group of warriors, led by a thin person half the size of Tough Hide, approached the procession from the other side of the field.

Tough Hide introduced Sharp Stone, co-leader of the Clan.

It was clear to the team that there was no love lost between the two.

What immediately caught the team's attention was the way Sharp Stone looked at them and then seemed to dismiss them. He also did not greet Taelo or anyone else on the team in the manner Tough Hide had done.

Taelo did not miss this intended insult but also did not take the bait being placed before him.

Sharp Stone seemed to notice Feather-in-the-Wind and focused on her. As he stepped toward her, Lasher assumed a position between Sharp Stone and Feather-in-the-Wind.

"What is the meaning of this animal threatening me," Sharp Stone spoke up loudly, but he stopped walking.

Taelo made the point of thanking Lasher for his vigilance and following his orders.

"This is Lasher, assigned to protect and defend anyone on the team he feels is threatened. Your actions so far have caused him to believe you are a threat," Taelo said casually.

"Tough Hide is vouching for you, so welcome to our village. He says you are the ones our warriors faced several months back. You are returning from the land of our enemies, and I wonder about your intentions," Sharp Stone said in an oratory fashion so everyone around could hear him.

It was clear to Taelo that Sharp Stone was speaking for the benefit of those around listening. He decided he would put Sharp Stone in his place by taking a public approach.

"I thank Tough Hide for a gracious and warm welcome. We are from the North on a journey of discovery and a journey of the heart. We seek to learn from all and we are happy to share our knowledge.

We would have stopped here first on our journey to the south except for the unfortunate interaction with your warriors. Their pride may have been hurt but recall, all wives and mothers were able to hug their warriors when they returned home. You must understand the return of all your warriors was no accident but truly a gift from my team. My team could as well have sent each and every one of them to see their ancestors. There was not a single warrior on which my team did not count coup.

Your warriors are brave and fought well. We salute them. We would like to present them with a symbolic gift of friendship. It is a leather wristband with the symbols of each of my team members," Taelo spoke slowly and clearly as he held up one of the wristbands the team had made from the leather of the Llama and the dark black and red of the seeds found in the south.

They had talked about how to engage the people of this clan and had decided to leverage their battle with the group of young warriors. Now they would find out if their approach would work.

"I will speak for my warriors and thank you for thinking of them. This is a clear gesture of friendship. Let's all enjoy a great meal together," Tough Hide said as he took the wristband and put it on the wrist of one of his son's. He had wondered about the condition of the warriors on their return. Now he knew it had been no accident.

Sharp Stone examined the wristband. It became clear to Taelo why he was in the position he held.

"You seem to have an extra member on your return trip," Sharp Stone commented as he examined and counted the symbols on the wristband.

"Yes, we are accompanied by Feather-in-the-Wind. She, Quiet Rabbit, and Busy Bee have become good friends. They arranged for her to travel with us to the North," Taelo responded with all true statements.

This Taelo knew immediately was where Broken Spear's description of coming events took a new turn.

"Interesting," was all Sharp Stone said.

The team was settled in an open area adjacent to the meeting area. They were invited to an evening of celebration. The evening went well, and the tensions seemed to have lessened.

Sharp Stone was quiet and seemed ill at ease with the women sitting around the fire with the warriors.

Lasher's presence at Feather-in-the-Wind's feet seemed to bother him the most.

"Do your women hunt with you?" he inquired.

"Yes, but it is something new to us. We learned it from Burley Bear and his Clan," Talking Wren replied.

"Our women have always hunted and fought at our side," Burly Bear explained. "They often outnumber the men on the leader's council."

"Our clan has learned from the Others and women now serve on our highest council in equal numbers to the men," Quiet Rabbit added.

It seemed to Taelo that Sharp Stone was surprised to get his reply from the other team members since he looked only at Taelo during this period.

"Interesting," was all Sharp Stone said.

Taelo decided that Sharp Stone was so self-centered that he could not envision any of the aspects of the Elk Clan or the Clan of Others culture.

In the following days, the team was escorted about by Tough Hide or one of his two sons. They each wore the wristband gift the team had given them. Storm Wind, the youngest of the two, was the lighthearted one. He was always in conversation with Meadow Flower. It seemed he was curious about the Others. He had never known anyone as large as Burley Bear. He observed the fact that both ate twice as much as the rest of their team.

"Yes, you are right. "We eat almost twice what my other team members do. And we are almost twice as strong, but we are not as fast," Meadow Flower responded as she chatted with him.

She liked the approach that the young warrior took to their interactions.

The team went about the village together. They were especially interested in the four-sided hill the clan built for their priests. The steps up the sides were steep.

Tough Hide explained the high priest held ceremonies to the gods, the ancestors and to the stars. The priests were the highest authority of the clan.

He and Sharp Stone were responsible for the protection of the clan and the warriors answered to them but they in turn answered to the high priests.

"This is very different from our clan's approach to leadership," was Taelo's way of not engaging in the conversation any farther.

He knew it would do no good to talk of a different way or different culture.

Taelo noticed they were always observed by the warriors loyal to Sharp Stone.

Sharp Stone would periodically appear. Everyday Sharp Stone made it a point to meet the team. He made it a point to speak to and give a gift to Feather-in-the-Wind.

He tried to no avail to make friends with Lasher. The team knew whenever Sharp Stone was approaching because Lasher began his deep low rumbling growl.

"I don't think Lasher likes Sharp Stone," Quiet Rabbit observed.

"I don't like Sharp Stone's focus on Feather-in-the-Wind," Busy Bee spoke up at dinner a few evenings later. "It will be a problem when we get ready to leave."

"I don't like his focus on me either. He does not seem to be a good person. I don't like him, and he frightens me," Feather-in-the-Wind added as she lightly scratched behind Lasher's ear.

She had become one of the few on the team to be able to touch Lasher anytime she felt like it.

"You must speak your mind truthfully if you are asked. We will protect you," Taelo told her.

He knew a confrontation was coming.

Little Otter made the point that it was time to leave and that he felt the longer they stayed the harder it would be for them to depart.

"Yes, I agree with you. Let's talk to Tough Hide and let him know that we are ready to continue on our journey," Golden Hawk added.

Taelo took the responsibility to talk with Tough Hide and let him know.

A few days later, Taelo informed the team, "I have spoken to Tough Hide and let him know our team is ready to continue our journey. He was gracious and said that it was good to have met and that he wished us a good journey."

"Well, given the tension and the politics here, it is none too soon," Golden Hawk added.

"I agree, we don't want to be in the middle between Sharp Stone and Tough Hide they seem destined to fight each other," Talking Wren chimed in.

The next day the team organized their equipment and set about packing.

"I am sorry you will be leaving so soon," Strong Wind said as he examined their handy work.

"It has been a good visit and we invite you to come North to visit us," Meadow Flower responded.

"We are not builders of ceremonial hills, or of living areas as complex and rich as you do. The cycle of the weather is our master, and we travel widely throughout our territory to ensure we survive each year to repeat the pattern."

Taelo listened to the conversation between Meadow Flower and Tough Hide, but he was worried about the ability of the team to leave the Warrior Clan stronghold.

The next morning as they were breaking down their camp a group of warriors surrounded them.

Taelo had expected Tough Hide and his warriors to be the escort out of the area. He saw none of Tough Hide's warriors.

"We will need to make sure you are not taking any of our religious objects and it is also customary that guests leave a significant gift," Sharp Stone commented as he walked toward Taelo.

The hair on Lashers back was standing straight up and a low rumble came from his chest. Taelo knew he was poised to attack.

"Feather-in-the-Wind is not of your clan. She shall become part of the Warrior Clan. I accept her as your departure gift," Sharp Stone continued and smiled at Taelo.

It was clear this was the moment Taelo had been warned about. The focus of the problem was not Quiet Rabbit as Broken Spear had described the situation. It had changed because of the actions the team had taken on saving Feather-in-the-Wind.

It did not matter.

Taelo knew what he must do.

Everything went into slow motion.

Taelo's eyes never left Sharp Stone's. "Battle formation," he spoke out loudly and clearly.

The team immediately formed their fighting triangle with Taelo at the point.

Lasher assumed his position in the center next to Feather-in-the-Wind.

"What is this? Do you dare to threaten us with your few warriors and half of them women," Sharp Stone said as he stopped?

"I am a chief in my clan. Any woman would be honored to be selected as my mate. Let Feather-in-the-Wind speak for herself," Sharp Stone said as he stopped confidently in front of Taelo.

"I am honored by your proposal, but I am a member of the Elk Clan and on a journey of discovery of the heart with my team," Feather-in-the-Wind replied quietly but clearly so all could hear.

Her face was white, and it was clear she was frightened as she stood rigidly in the center of the team's triangle.

Quiet Rabbit and Busy Bee both rested their hands onto Feather-in-the-Wind's shoulders. They had both discussed such a proposal by Sharp Stone and reassured her that the team would not leave her behind.

What happened next was as Broken Spear had predicted and it happened in the blink of an eye.

Sharp Stone's face went an angry white. He drew his knife and lunged at Taelo without saying a word.

Taelo heard Feather-in-the-Wind say, "Kill."

Lasher became a blur as he moved to protect Taelo.

Taelo let out his battle roar and the team did the same. He took a full step back as he pulled his shark edged weapon from its holder on his back.

The team moved in unison with Taelo's motion and again let out a roar.

"This team is crazy," Sharp Stone thought as he continued his attack.

His knife was halfway to Taelo's heart when he sensed something was wrong. His wrist was in the mouth of the wolf, and he could hear his wrist bones cracking.

The weapon in Taelo's hand flashed swiftly and he watched as the shark teeth ripped through Sharp Stone's skull and ended the attack.

Lasher released the wrist and went back to Feather-in-the-Wind's side.

"Warriors of Sharp Stone, you are now under my command," Taelo spoke out immediately. He had learned that any warrior could challenge a leader to a fight. If he beat the leader, he would gain the leadership position.

The warriors surrounding them were stunned and unsure what to do. They stopped their attack at Taelo's declaration. They indeed knew this custom. Many of them had also participated in the fight with this team and did not look forward to doing it again.

Just then Tough Hide and his warriors appeared.

"I see you have just defeated Sharp Stone," Tough Hide said as he took in the scene.

He had been diverted by a rouse perpetrated by Sharp Stone and had been angry and afraid of what he would find. He now hoped it would work out to his advantage.

"You have earned the right to lead Sharp Stone's warriors and claim his position. What is your intention," Tough Hide asked?

This was a situation Tough Hide had not anticipated. He was pleased to see his longtime adversary eliminated. He hoped he did not have a new one.

"My intention is to continue on my journey. I believe you will make an excellent leader for Sharp Stone's warriors. Lead them well. When you come north to visit, come as a friend leave your army at home," Taelo said quietly as he extended his hand to Tough Hide's shoulder.

"Warriors, for a moment I was your leader, but I am not of your Clan or your customs. Tough Hide deserves your loyalty. Let me hear the battle roar as a sign of acceptance of your new leader, Tough Hide," Taelo commanded as he looked at a group of warriors who looked defeated.

Sharp Stone's warriors let out a resounding roar.

"Yes, as a friend," Tough Hide responded as he put his hand to Taelo's shoulder.

Tough Hide ordered the body of Sharp Stone be moved to the base of the four-sided hill. He was aware that most of the Clan had gathered when they heard Taelo's team battle roar and knew first-hand what had happened, but he would have the high priest make the official announcement of the leadership change.

Please accept my two sons as escorts for a day or two. This will prevent anyone from seeking revenge," Tough Hide said as he gave the command to pick up the body.

Taelo immediately led the team out of the village. The team took up their familiar formation and jogged in unison for the entire day.

"No wonder you are all in such good shape," an exhausted Strong Sinew said as they finally stopped at the end of the first day.

"Yes, even on a raiding party we don't travel at such a pace," Storm Wind added.

"In one day, you have gone almost as far as we normally travel in three. Doesn't the heat bother you," Strong Wind continued?

"Yes, we are in great shape and yes the heat does bother us. We would have gone twice as far in cooler weather," Meadow Flower joked.

"I suggest after a morning meal tomorrow, the two of you can begin your journey back to your clan. We will be safe enough and will be cautious as we return," Taelo said as the evening camp was set up.

"We will continue at the same pace tomorrow. Tonight, we will take turns on watch. Let's get a good night's rest," Taelo continued as he watched as the team prepared for the night.

He had set a grueling pace and the team had followed. They were as shocked at the morning's event as he. He knew they were exhausted, but no one complained about the pace or the heat.

"You did what needed to be done. He would not have let us leave with Feather-in-the-Wind," Quiet Rabbit said as she nestled into Taelo's arm.

"Yes, I know. It could only have been different if Sharp Stone had acted differently. There was only one outcome for that situation," Taelo said as he lay looking up at the stars.

"I will have to tell Broken Spear about the change in what he saw. It really speaks to how the future does change based on the actions each of us take," Taelo thought to himself.

He knew his actions had been guided by the warning Broken Spear had given and that it had saved the lives of the entire team. He thanked his ancestors for providing him a guiding hand and then fell asleep.

He also reached out and lightly scratched Lasher.

"Thank you for your help," Taelo said quietly.

Lasher replied with a lick on Taelo's hand.

Chapter 9 :Home to the Others

The next morning the team said goodbye to Strong Sinew and Storm Wind. They had taken Taelo's advice and were returning to their clan. They figured it would take two days to return home at a normal pace.

The team headed Northwest with Burley Bear back in the point position. The pace was closer to their normal pace versus the one Taelo had set the day before. He and Taelo had discussed the need to set a pace that would be more sustainable by the entire team.

Their path took them across multiple ridges of mountains and the up and down elevation was challenging.

"It will be good to get home," Busy Bee said as they jogged along.

"Our journey will not end quite yet," Taelo replied.

He decided this was the time to let the team know about the second half of their journey.

"Broken Spear asked that we come back to him to learn what the second half of our journey is to be. He knows we have a second half, but he was unable to tell me what it was," Taelo continued.

"If anyone wants to call it quits and return to their Clan it is OK. I plan to go and see if Broken Spear has seen what the second half of our journey is to be," Taelo went on.

"Wow, winter is coming on and we are heading North. I think we got our journey backwards," Talking Wren said jokingly.

"I'm in for the second half of the journey," Golden Hawk spoke up.

A "me too" came from all the rest of the team.

"Great, I didn't mention this before because I wanted us all to be going home before we contemplated an addition to our journey. Our trip has been a little different than Broken Spear told me. This is another reason I waited until now to tell you about the second half," Taelo continued.

He was feeling somewhat defensive.

"I understand. I have been guided by Broken Spear all my life and I still wonder how he knows what he knows. I am always hesitant to share his guidance too openly," Burley Bear spoke up as he sensed Taelo's unease.

The way back toward the Clan of Others was longer than the path they had taken South. Taelo was using the stars of the night sky and the position of the sun to estimate the direction they should travel. Finally, the snow-capped peaks became familiar, and they found the long valley they had traveled on their way South.

They were now in more familiar terrain. Their steady jogging pace ate up the distance and they were soon passing the river leading to the Valley of Plenty.

Taelo called a stop and asked the team if they should all stop by and let the Elk Clan Members know of their return.

The team felt that such a stop would complicate their journey and though everyone wanted to see their family, they knew that to leave immediately after being gone for so long would be hard and it would get them a negative reaction.

Burley Bear suggested that they send a messenger down from the Clan of Others after they left there.

"I am now really curious what the second part of our journey will be," Quiet Rabbit spoke up as they once again took up their steady jog.

"I am only thinking about a warm pool of water and a comfortable bath," Busy Bee shot back.

"I have heard so much and I am very curious about this place Taelo found for the Others," Feather-in-the-Wind joined in.

"You will be amazed at the richness of the valley and the wonder of our main encampment but the main attraction for everyone is the warm water spring. It is a comfort worth dreaming about," Meadow Flower added.

The next day they turned to the West and approached the Clan of Others from the East. They climbed down into the valley on a seldom used trail.

They had decided to surprise the clan. It did not work. Broken Spear sat on a large hide with Quiet Fox next to him. The entire clan stood behind them.

"Welcome back. We are pleased to see you are all well. I see you have come back with a treasure from the South," Quiet Fox said as he took note of Feather-in-the-Wind.

"Yes, we have had a wonderful trip and learned much. We have seen mountains higher than ours, a bird twice the size of our eagle and rivers that are larger and longer. We have learned from the people to the far South, and we have fought with other people as we made our journey. We have seen the sun rise on one sea and set on another. We have many stories to tell," Burley Bear replied.

"We are eager to hear of your journey. We have prepared for a night of feasting and listening to your stories. We hope you don't exaggerate too much," Quiet Fox went on.

The entire clan was looking forward to listening to Burley Bear and to Little Otter. The two always told such good stories.

"I will let Taelo tell about the most outrageous ones otherwise you will not believe they are true," Burley Bear replied defensively.

He enjoyed telling his stories and he often exaggerated to make them more interesting. Now he had stories that needed no exaggeration, but his audience would believe he was exaggerating.

"Let's go in and get situated. I am ready for the hot springs," Meadow Flower nudged Burley Bear and led the way to the hot spring.

The evening meal consisted of slices of salted grilled buffalo meat, some roots cooked in the coals of the fire and a honey wine drink. The entire clan continued to grill and eat as the stories began.

Everyone was comfortable and relaxed.

"It's great to be home where we don't need to be on guard," Quiet Rabbit said as she enjoyed a sip of honey wine.

"Yes, and the clan is really into listening to our stories," Busy Bee noted as the entire clan burst into hooting at the story Taelo was telling about watching the sun rise from one sea and standing in the same spot to watch it set in the other sea.

Burley Bear's story about the battle with the thirty warriors of the War Seekers, first caused a hushed response then a loud hurrah when he told how the team had counted coup on all the attacking warriors and had not killed anyone. This was an amazing accomplishment for a team of only eight.

Meadow Flower told of the strange new animal, the Llama, and showed everyone some of the hide and clothing made from it. The samples were passed around and it was clear from the compliments that everyone seemed impressed with the work.

"This may be Llama hide but it has been prepared in the secret way of our clan. You did not give that away?" one of the women asked.

"No, our secret is still ours. I did give away many vests and jackets prepared in this way," Meadow Flower replied.

Every team member told one story. Then Burley Bear and Little Otter took turns embellishing even the minor events of the team's travel.

Then Broken Spear asked Feather-in-the-Wind to tell her story.

"I only know half of my story. I must ask Quiet Rabbit and Busy Bee to help me with the half I don't remember.

She turned to her audience and in the language of the Elk Clan she told her story.

She was the last virgin sacrifice to the great Condor, the giant bird Burley Bear told you about in his stories," Feather-in-the-Wind began talking to an almost silent clan.

They were hanging on every one of her quiet but steady words. She had learned most of the language of Elk Clan and only knew a few words in the more guttural language of the Others. She mixed both languages as she used her words well.

She held the attention of the entire clan for the rest of the night as she, Quiet Rabbit and Busy Bee shared the story and told of the hundred frozen virgins in the cave.

The night ended with the entire Clan of Others slapping the ground and giving a great bellow in appreciation.

Taelo joined broken spear at his morning fire. Broken Spear complimented him and the team on the strength they had when they worked together. He was pleased Taelo had successfully prevailed in facing the attack from Sharp Stone.

Taelo thanked Broken Spear for the warning and told him that knowing of the threat helped in taking immediate and deadly action.

He then shared how Feather-in-the-Wind changed the situation in the meeting with Sharp Stone.

"Yes, that may be my fault. I saw a beautiful young woman you were to protect. I just thought it was Quiet Rabbit," Broken Spear replied. "However, you took the right action."

"I have been looking at the second part of your journey. You will help many people and will set up a new branch of the Elk Clan. You and your team will go North and find a valley where you will build a lodge for the new clan," Broken Spear continued.

"It will be a hard winter and you must hurry to establish your compound. It will take hard work by your entire team. Burley Bear will go with you one more time.

He will soon be called on to lead our clan. He has grown to be a leader who is looked up to by all the Clan members. It was a good day when you hit him on the head," Broken Spear said with a chuckle.

Taelo recalled the day Burley Bear had been rough with his mother, White Swan. He had knocked out Burley Bear with his war club. Later he and Burley Bear became the close friends they were to this day.

"It is now hard to imagine me doing what I did," Taelo replied with a grin.

Taelo left Broken Spear and joined the rest of the team that by now was sitting and eating their morning meal.

"You have got to be kidding," Little Otter said as Taelo shared what the second part of their journey was to be.

"It sounds exciting but cold," Feather-in-the-Wind spoke up from inside her bearskin blanket.

"It is late in the season. We will need to work like crazy to set up a lodge and other buildings. We don't even have a location for our new home," Golden Hawk added.

"Yes, it is crazy but think of the good we will do," Burley Bear said as he thought about establishing a totally new clan.

He was becoming more flexible and accepting of doing new things. This was very different from the rest of the members in his clan.

"Well, it really doesn't matter to me. We will end up fighting through the winter in some camp somewhere. It might as well be one that we made for ourselves," Talking Wren added her perspective.

Winter was always a hard season for her. It was the season of being trapped by the weather, worried about food and too few people to talk too.

"When do we go North and where are we going?" both Quiet Rabbit and Busy Bee asked almost in unison.

"I thought we would rest for another few days and prepare ourselves. Let's think through what we should take with us and what we will need to have to be successful. We may be able to put our learning from our trip to the South to help in the establishment of this new sub clan," Taelo commented.

Chapter 10: Northern Valley

Taelo and the team spent the next two sun cycles preparing for the next part of their journey. They knew they would be needing to build their winter lodge and they would need enough food for the winter.

Talking Wren was the star planner of the team and became a key organizer for the team. The back and forth, between Little Otter and her, was also a source of amusement on the team.

On the morning of their departure, Taelo thanked the Others for their hospitality and generosity in outfitting the team.

Once again Burley Bear was teased about the affection his mother always displayed.

"I would never have believed anyone would publicly claim you as their little boy," Taelo joked.

"Yeah, Yeah, have your fun. I have seen how your mother always treats you like a soft puff ball," Burley Bear rebutted.

He secretly enjoyed the public attention his mother gave him.

"Well, I hope the eagle helps us locate a good home. I have no idea how we should find the right place. A good hot spring would be nice but there are only so many around," Golden Hawk chimed in.

"Broken Spear has given us a clue on how to find the valley where we are to set up our camp," Taelo replied as the team walked along in their now familiar formation.

This time there were four travois to carry all their food and supplies.

"The setting sun will outline two mountains to our left and right. We must then proceed straight ahead until we reach a river. We are to turn upriver until we reach its first branch. We are to take the left branch. It will lead into a narrow opening and then spread out into a long wide valley. The valley runs toward the northwest."

"That description certainly makes the journey so much easier," Talking Wren spoke up in a sarcastic tone.

"I am sure we will recognize the signs," Quiet Rabbit countered.

"The wise man of my clan is very much like Broken Spear. He predicted your arrival. I wonder if he saw my escape," Feather-in-the-Wind asked?

"Yes, I believe he did," Taelo responded as he thought about the departure from her village.

"Well, I am with Golden Hawk in hoping the eagle shows up to show us the way," Little Otter piped in.

The team continued northward along the coast for almost two days before turning in a northeasterly direction. They were making very good time since they were traveling in their normal jogging rate. Exactly as foretold, a week later in the late afternoon two mountains seemed to frame the way ahead of them. Their twin snow peaks capping the dark green of soldier like forest pines stood out brightly in the afternoon sun that was now behind the team.

Meadow Flower pointed to the two peaks as she stopped to comment as how obvious they were.

"We will know soon enough. There should be a river just beyond them," Taelo responded.

They were in new territory for the team. The Elk Clan had migrated south from this area many generations ago.

Taelo and Golden Hawk had both listened to Grey Fox Running and Red Oak tell them stories about the original grand valley the Elk Clan had lived in. They had been told stories about the salt gathers. Stories about the cave of elders where they enjoyed the hot rain.

The late afternoon sun was beginning to drop behind the mountains to the west when the team stopped at a point midway between the two mountains.

"This looks like a good place," Burley Bear spoke up as the team jogged up to a small clear blue lake.

Quiet Rabbit took in the small circular lake with willow trees along its bank bending over the water in graceful like bows of deference. The frogs were singing their deep throaty greeting of the evening or perhaps they were trying to attract the slowly twinkling fireflies.

She agreed that it was a good place to stop.

Little Otter, spear in hand, carefully followed his ears toward the deep almost cavernous croaking at the edge of lake. He was intent on augmenting his dinner with some fresh roasted frog legs.

Golden Hawk followed Little Otter and they began slowly going along the bank.

"It looks like we will have at least one frog," Busy Bee said as she watched Little Otter drop something into a bag Golden Hawk was holding.

The rest of the team began to set up camp for the night. Once most of the work of setting up the camp was done Taelo, and Burley Bear went out to the lake and proceeded in the opposite direction.

"Let's see if we can get something for dinner," Burley Bear commented.

"We have been doing a fairly good job of killing enough game as we travel. Usually by the time we stop for the evening we have enough for a good dinner," Taelo responded.

All day they had traveled along some very rough terrain and had seen almost no game. The few rabbits were able to scamper to safety among the rocks before anyone could react.

Even Lasher had come up empty handed.

Now two rabbits made the mistake of crossing their path and in an amazing burst of speed Taelo leaped forward and thrust his spear into one before it had the chance to react.

Laser had the second one in one long leap.

"I don't know about getting something at the lake but here is at least a start at getting a full meal," Taelo said as he removed the head and skinned the two rabbits.

"Yes, you will get one all for yourself," he told Lasher as he hung the rabbits on a carrying stick.

By the time, the two met up with Little Otter and Golden Hawk, they did have enough for dinner. There would be frog legs, roast rabbit and three fish.

"Well, this will make a great dinner," Busy Bee said as the four handed over their catch.

"We will even have enough for a light breakfast meal. If anyone gets up early a few more fish would round out breakfast," Quiet Rabbit said as she skewered the fish and put them on the fire.

"I have learned more on this journey with you than I had learned at home. My mother tried to teach me to cook but I wasn't very interested. It seemed boring. Now I am always hungry and eager to cook," Feather-in-the-Wind said as she rubbed the rabbit with salt and began roasting it on the fire.

Lasher lay watching his rabbit being roasted.

"I think Lasher is making sure no one takes his rabbit," Feather-in-the-Wind said as she watched him.

"Hunger is a great teacher," Burley Bear said simply.

Taelo and Golden Hawk got up early the next morning and caught several fish. Breakfast was complete and everyone was in a good mood when once again they set out.

"River ahead," Little Otter called out from his point position in the lead.

The team jogged down to the riverbank and without stopping turned and proceeded upriver. By late afternoon they reached the first major river branch. It came in from the northwest.

High overhead an eagle flew a lazy circle.

"We must have arrived," Burley Bear said as he pointed to the eagle.

Dinner once again became the focus for the remainder of the afternoon. The rapids just upstream from the camp proved to be a great place to find and capture some crawfish. Taelo and Golden Hawk laughed as they recalled the summer their fathers had taught them how to catch crawfish.

"We caught so many crawfish we gave them to every family of the clan," Golden Hawk recalled.

"We were asked to stop so there would be some for the next season," Taelo added.

"Will you teach me how to do it," Feather-in-the-Wind asked.

"I am so happy we were able to rescue her from her fate as a sacrifice to the Condor," Busy Bee commented as she listened to the excited squeals and laughter coming downstream from Feather-in-the-Wind as she learned to catch the crawfish.

"Yes, she really is enjoyable to have around. She is like the young sister I never had," Quiet Rabbit commented.

It was not long before an excited Feather-in-the-Wind led the way into camp talking about the number of crabs she had caught.

Lasher had walked around looking puzzled but then he spotted a fish just upstream of the rapids. He proudly returned with a trout in his mouth.

"Well, I see you two are still able to catch these beasts without getting bitten," Quiet Rabbit commented as she took the bag.

"Yes, and I see you have the water hot and ready to put them in," Taelo replied. The smell of the spices cooking in the water already had him hungry.

Taelo took the time to filet the fish Lasher had caught. He warmed it over the fire and then cut it into pieces for Lasher.

"That is the most fun I have ever had," Feather-in-the-Wind said excitedly.

She had wanted to continue catching more crawfish but had been overruled by both Taelo and Golden Hawk who laughed as they recalled their own enthusiasm when they were young.

The next morning the team crossed the river and proceeded up the valley.

"Wow look at this valley. And look at the giant waterfall in the distance," Talking Wren said in a hushed tone as they rounded a bend leading into the valley.

The river cut up the center of the valley's wide plain toward a distant white crowned mountain towering high above the clouds.

A large flat expansive grass covered plain lay as far as the eye could see on the western side of the river. Halfway across the valley the river turned toward the north and then followed the bottom of a long continuous barren rock cliff. The waterfall, from a point just below the cloud line, fed a small lake that was the source of the river water.

The team was no longer in their normal formation but walking in a parallel line as they all took in the immensity and the grandeur of the area around them.

"Let's follow this up toward its source," Taelo said as he knelt and felt the warm water in a stream cutting across their current path into the valley. He was hoping for a warm water spring.

"Taelo, you seem to have a knack at finding hot springs," Golden Hawk said as they jogged up an incline. A pool of water with what looked to be a lite mist rising from it took up about a third of the area at the top of the rise.

High above an eagle let out a loud cry.

"Well, I believe we have arrived at the designated spot," Burley Bear said as he once again pointed up into the sky.

"It is just like our Condor. Only your totem follows you," Feather-in-the-Wind said as she looked up.

"Yes, I believe we have arrived," Taelo said as he sat down on a large stone and surveyed the area.

The large stones scattered about gave him an idea of how to lay out the area. This would make a great place to put a large central lodge. Smaller personal homes would then be placed out around the base of the rise.

"Let's make camp here. Tomorrow we will all work together to design our central lodge.

Chapter 11: Winter Preparation

The next morning Talking Wren suggested the team do a quick tour of the valley before considering the design of the lodge. She pointed out that the team could get a better understanding of the valley and the resources it held.

She pushed Little Otter down the slope leading toward the river and the rest of the team followed.

Soon they were jogging along the bank of a river respectfully wide running briskly over many rapids but one that could be crossed in five or six long leaps.

Taelo and Golden Hawk followed at the rear of the team chatting and taking in the wide expanse of the valley as they noted the light grey clay banks on the opposite side. The layers of thin flat stone was the next resource they both noted.

Quiet Rabbit and Busy Bee looked ahead to where the water fall left the cliff and turned into a cloud of mist as the wind blew across the falling water on its way to the roiling, turbulent, churn in the lake below.

The roar of the water seemed to emanate from the surface of the lake itself. The team stopped to look up and were immediately soaked by the mist spraying up from the impact of the falling water. This would be a favorite spot in the heat of summer, but it was cold this late into the season.

Burly Bear led the team across the valley away from the falls to the edge of the pine forest whose height blocked the view of the snow-capped mountains behind them. Less dominant maples and oak periodically broke the endless rank of pine and claimed areas where they shared the ground with grasses and other smaller brush.

The team jogged all day and into early evening. The valley had been larger than any of them had anticipated, and they were happy to see the rise with the warm water spring come into sight as the valley light dimmed and turned into an evening grey.

Taelo listened as Busy Bee identified the need to gather enough food to hold the team through the winter and Quiet Rabbit made the point, they needed a lodge or similar structure as a place the team could live.

Little Otter made the point they would need to hurry if they were going to beat the coming winter weather.

"I have been thinking about how to get everything done in time," Taelo spoke up.

"Little Otter, Quiet Rabbit, Feather-in-the-Wind and Busy Bee should go out hunting for elk or deer. Talking Wren and Meadow flower will explore the valley and find any late plants and herbs we can use for food, spicing and medicines.

They will additionally bring back a travois full of wood each day. Burley Bear, Golden Hawk and I will begin building the main lodge," Taelo shared how he thought the work should be divided.

"Should we be hunting as if we are on a long hunt," Quiet Rabbit asked?

The answer would decide whether they would try to return to the camp at night or not return until they had gathered all the meat they could transport.

"A long hunt approach will make it easier for you to stop wherever you are rather than to return to this location. However, since the territory of the valley is new to all of us, you will decide and do what you believe is best," Taelo replied.

Little Otter confidently organized the team as they prepared a travois with their personal effects and a contingency of dried meat to take with them. This time he knew his team comprised of three women and himself would do well.

The next morning Taelo and the remainder of the team wished the hunting party good luck and watched as the four followed the river up the valley.

Taelo encouraged the four members of the team to remain behind. He recognized Talking Wren as an expert planner, but she also had an eye for structure and layout. He and Golden Hawk has spent many sun cycles studying the construction of the lodges in the Condor Clan.

Building this lodge was an opportunity to utilize their learning and their skills.

The hot water spring by the falls above the Valley of Plenty where the Elk Clan currently made their winter home gave Taelo the idea of building this new lodge with the hot spring located inside of the lodge. This would warm the lodge as well as make the water easily available.

The way the Condor Clan channeled and directed the flow of water in the village gave Taelo the idea to guide the hot water in a snake-like channel below the lodge floor. This would evenly distribute its heat throughout the lodge.

He shared this with the team and got some surprising push back. Talking Wren got excited and was enthusiastic about it but pointed out there were only five of them to do the work.

Golden Hawk wanted to know where all the material would come from.

Burley Bear looked at Taelo, shook his head and pointed at Taelo and told the rest of the team they might as well get to work because they were the army that was going to accomplish this impossible task.

Meadow Flower took up Burley Bear's suggestion and suggested they do an initial layout, mark the area out and get a better idea of the quantity of stone, timber, and other materials they would need.

Taelo was pleased with the input and reaction of the team. He knew his ideas sounded impossible, but he felt confident that they could build the lodge he described.

Talking Wren used her spear to mark the overall oval for the lodge. Meadow Flower suggested a longer layout would better fit the terrain. After this adjustment Talking Wren marked out the path to be dug, that would guide the hot water under the floor.

Golden Hawk put a fist sized stone down ever two feet or so to clearly mark this path.

The time between discussion and action had been almost immediate.

The team stood at the front of the lodge where the water came out and admired their work.

Taelo was pleased and thanked the team for this quick action.

He made one more suggestion to make a stone pit for the water to run into before being guided back to its original path down the slope toward the river. This pit would be where the clan members could bathe.

Talking Wren applauded this idea and suggested that a second much larger one could be built later at the base of the hill to serve a larger clan membership in the future.

Meadow Flower and Talking Wren discussed their role in the recent lodge design. They highlighted how valued they felt by having been pulled into the planning by Taelo. He had shared the good part of the work. Now they were out and about doing the harder more mundane work of gathering herbs, small game, and firewood. They were at the same time locating and gathering the critical materials for building the lodge.

Talking Wren knew that Taelo's behavior was no fluke. He constantly sought to empower the people around him.

Meadow Flower knew she had been selected to be part of the lodge building team because of her strength but she had been listened to during the lodge design.

She was impressed with Taelo's easy way of distributing the load and getting everyone engaged in the work.

She and Talking Wren discussed the team culture and environment and were surprised how aligned they were in their evaluation and in their support for Taelo.

It bonded them more closely and they embraced their role.

Taelo knew that getting the materials and having the time to do the work were both monumental challenges.

There was plenty of stone and clay down by the river. Transporting the stone and clay back to the hot springs would be a staggering task.

Taelo asked Burley Bear to dig the holes for the main lodge poles. He and Golden Hawk went down to the river to locate the stones and clay for the walls.

Burley Bear struggled to dig the twelve holes for the main lodge wall support poles. He used a large flat oblong stone to dig a hole the depth of his leg. By the time he got to that depth the top of the hole was about as wide as it was deep. During the first sun cycle he was able to dig only three holes.

He resigned himself to the drudgery of the digging and sang the teams travel jogging song.

Taelo and Golden Hawk located the stone and clay down by the creek.

They located several small trees and made three travois. One for each of them and one for Lasher. They decided to first transport the stones for the lodge floor. This would provide Burley Bear with the material to cover the water channel as he created it.

They also located some thin layered stone to be used to make sides for the hot spring inside the lodge and the stones to be used to make the exterior walls of the lodge.

They made several trips gathering and delivering the lodge floor covering stone. They soon realized the two of them would not be enough to gather the stone needed for the walls.

Meadow Flower and Talking Wren returned as the sun was setting with enough small game, firewood, and tubers to sustain the team for several days.

They complemented their three teammates in the amount of work that had been accomplished but were aware that is would not be enough.

Taelo's request for their help in gathering stone, dry grasses and clay was quickly accepted. It was clear to them that extra effort was needed to get the lodge up.

Talking Wren shared that she and Meadow flower had located and marked twelve pine trees of equal size that would serve as the vertical wall pillars. She volunteered to cut them down and prepare them to be pulled in by the team.

Counting Lasher, five travois made continuous trips delivering stones to the top of the hill for three sun cycles.

Golden Hawk looked at the ten piles of smooth, round edged, oblong stones about the length of his forearm and about half as wide.

The team had been selective, and the stones seemed to be duplicates of each other. Each pile represented one section of the lodge wall.

He was very happy to be done with dragging stone up from the river. He knew there would be more trips but that would come after the lodge was complete.

During this time Burley Bear dug the holes for the main lodge poles.

The evening of the third cycle, Taelo called for a day of rest.

Everyone would go out the next day and gather dry grasses and bring that back to the compound.

Burley Bear laughed at the day of rest but said it was ten times better than digging another hole.

The grass gathering did turn out to be less stressful and the team bagged an abundance of rabbits and several ground hogs to replenish their food supply.

During their forays out gathering grass Talking Wren took the team to each of the trees she had selected.

The next step was to get them cut down.

During the next twelve sun cycles, the trench for the hot water was dug and covered. The hot water pool area was constructed. A center cooking area was designed and the materials to build it was accumulated.

The main timbers were prepared by Meadow Flower and Talking Wren and then pulled in and erected by all five team members. The lodge exterior wall was knee high all around the lodge.

The prize possession of the lodge, its hot water stream had been enhanced. Taelo and Golden Hawk had hauled layers of thin flat stone to build a wall around the stream and form a holding pool.

They were able to spread the smooth white clay between each layer of stone to create a seal that did not leak. The pool was a spear and a half-length long and a spear wide. An opening that the top could be adjusted to hold the water at the height desired.

Taelo commented to the team that he had never experienced Talking Wren being so quiet. This worried him and he suggested they all get into the hot water pool and enjoy its comfort and sooth their aching bodies.

The rest of the team agreed, and they spent most of the early evening relaxing and talking about the work they had each been doing.

Burley Bear said little, but his moans of appreciation said a lot. Talking Wren recovered her persona and once again began to lead the conversation.

Taelo thanked them for the hard work.

"Let's thank the ancestors we are nearly done with it. It has been a monumental effort for all of us.

He commented that he hoped the hunting team was having the same success.

Out on the hunt, Little Otter concluded that the valley seemed to be depleted in the number of deer and elk. The team had bagged some rabbits and they had one boar on their travois.

"Yes, we may have competitors. We need to be watchful for wolves or mountain lions. Let's hope there are no dire wolves in this territory," Quiet Rabbit replied.

She had been the most successful and had been the one to run down the boar.

"Where did you learn to hunt like this," Feather-in-the-Wind asked after having observed Quiet Rabbit's feat of running down the boar.

"Taelo and Golden Hawk taught all of us how to hunt in this fashion," Little Otter replied.

"Quiet Rabbit was Taelo's hunting partner during our long hunt. On that hunt Taelo and Golden Hawk each ran down four buffalo in a row. Their hunting partners were required to carry the extra spears and be ready to give them the spears as needed," he continued.

"That first time, I thought I was going to die. I could not believe anyone could run so fast for so long. After I gave Taelo his fourth spear he accelerated away from me to bring down the fourth buffalo," Quiet Rabbit recalled.

"Yes, and at the same time I was having the exact experience with Golden Hawk," Busy Bee said as she recalled the exhilaration of hunting with Golden Hawk.

"I think it is probably wolves. I have seen many tracks," Busy Bee added.

"Well, my personal observation is the two of you also caught what you were hunting," Feather-in-the-Wind said slyly.

The four had been out for seven sun cycles. They were now pulling a travois loaded with meat of mostly small game. They had dutifully skinned each animal and carefully field prepared the hides. Each evening they had cooked the meat.

"We are doing fine on the quantity of meat we are gathering. It would be nice to get an elk so we could get back to the camp," Little Otter commented.

The next morning Quiet Rabbit called the team over to show them eight little wolf pups she had found wandering outside of a burrow.

"Oh, they are so cute," Feather-in-the-Wind said as she moved forward.

"It seems their mother is missing," Busy Bee observed as she looked around.

"I believe she may have met her end. I smell something dead," Little Otter said as he walked in the direction his nose was leading him.

"Yes, here is the mother. By the looks of her wounds, she must have met up with a mountain lion," Little Otter commented.

"Let's gather up the pups and take them back to our camp," Quiet Rabbit suggested.

"I guess Lasher will expand his clan with this group," Quiet Rabbit said as she threw out little pieces of meat to attract the young wolves.

"I am sure Taelo will find a way to put these pups to use," Little Otter said as he threw a few pieces of meat out to the pups.

The wolf pups were very hungry. By feeding them individually by hand the team was able to get the young pups to follow them.

"I will keep track of the pups," Feather-in-the-Wind volunteered.

She found she was still very clumsy in her ability to hunt and often felt she had caused some game to get away.

"Well, let's take the meat we have back to camp. We can leave the wolf pups there and then hunt the rest of the valley," Quiet Rabbit suggested.

The team agreed. They were all curious what the lodge builders had accomplished.

Chapter 12: The Lodge and Compound

Taelo and Golden Hawk had become the stone layers. They built the huge oval footings for the lodge. They left an opening where the hot water stream went out the front part of the lodge. Just outside of the lodge they made a round stone lined pool.

"This lodge will be as good a place as the cave with the heated pool you found for our Clan," Meadow Flower commented as she arrived with another load of stone for the outer perimeter walls.

When the walls of the lodge were just above the height of Burley Bear, they stopped.

"Now we need to place the timbers for the roof," Taelo declared as he stood looking with a great degree of satisfaction at the work they had done.

A few sun cycles later, the stone walled lodge and the initial roof timbers were finally in place. The opening at each end of the lodge needed to be finished. The spaces of the carefully placed stone floor had been filled with a mixture of clay and sand. They had copied this technique from the Condor Clan.

Taelo and Golden Hawk had discussed their lack of hides to cover the roof. They knew the hunting team, even if they were very successful would not return with enough hides to make the roof.

The area inside the lodge was already being kept warm at night by the hot pool and the water running below the stone slabs.

Talking Wren and Meadow Flower had opted to build the cooking area themselves. They utilized the stone used for the hot pool and some thicker slabs they found along the cliffs near the river and were in the process of building a flat fire area and a stone box used to cook meat and other food without fire as they had learned from their southern Condor Clan friends.

Taelo had engaged the entire team to roll some large boulders up the slope of the mound. Each time Taelo, Meadow Flower and Burley Bear moved the stone up the slope, Talking Wren and Golden Hawk would put a log on the downhill side to lock it in place until the next move. The team had moved more than fifteen boulders up to the top of the rise.

The stones were positioned around the periphery of the compound area with the six largest boulders setting the points of the uneven oblong compound with the largest area to the right of the lodges main entrance.

To Golden Hawk's dismay, he realized that the smaller stones to build a wall between these boulders were still in the river and would all need to be brought up by travois.

"Look at what the rest of the team has been doing," Quiet Rabbit commented as the lodge came into view.

"It looks as if a whole Clan has been working on it," Little Otter replied.

"I wonder how they managed to roll all those boulders up to the top of the mound," Busy Bee added as they all came to a stop to look at the compound ahead and looked at the large perimeter boulders. Primary timbers for an entrance were already in position.

The stone walls of the main lodge came into view and again the returning team were amazed.

"I can't wait to see how far everything has come along," Quiet Rabbit commented as she continued the walk back to the compound.

"I see the hunting team returning," Burley Bear said as he pointed to some specks in the distance.

"You have excellent vision," Golden Hawk said as he shielded his eyes from the sun so he could see what Burley Bear was pointing to.

The team arrived and walked around admiring the work that had been done on the lodge.

"You have done the work of an entire Clan," Little Otter said as he walked around the outer edges of the compound.

He stood at the outside of the lodge at one section of the wall that had been constructed. He was intrigued by the way the stone was bonded to each other and the entire wall was sealed.

I see you have brought us some new members," Taelo commented as he walked over to where the young wolf pups were gathered around Feather-in-the-Wind.

Lasher followed on Taelo's heals. There was a low growl deep in his throat.

"Easy boy, these pups will be our friends. You will be their leader," Taelo said and gave Lasher a scratch behind his ear.

Taelo had Feather-in-the-Wind hold each you wolf pup up to Lasher as he gave each a name.

Quiet Rabbit knew he was doing this so Lasher would accept them.

"I see you have been successful in your hunt, but no elk or buffalo," Golden Hawk commented.

He tried not to show his disappointment. He had hoped they would find an abundance of one or the other.

"We saw neither animal," Quiet Rabbit commented.

We will go out one more time, but we felt it was important to bring the young wolves in before proceeding.

Busy Bee was standing in front of the cook area. She recognized it as a design they had used when they cooked with the Condor Clan.

She complimented Talking Wren and Meadow Flower in the skill that the construction showed.

"Well, I guess we will be able to cook in the manner Feather-in-the-Wind did in the south," she commented.

"Not the way I cooked. But certainly, the way my mother cooked," Feather-in-the-Wind replied as she looked over the work done by the team.

"You have a very good memory. This is almost exactly what we had in our cooking area at home."

"I am glad you are back. We could use your help for the next few days. We need to bring a tremendous amount of stone back from the cliffs. We can pile them close to where they will be used.

We need enough stone for the compound perimeter wall, the external washing pool, and some miscellaneous work inside the lodge." Taelo informed the four returning hunters.

"I knew it would be a mistake to come back," Little Otter replied with a fake groan as if he were objecting.

He was glad to be doing something that would give him immediate feedback for his work. The hunting had been very disappointing, and he felt bad about it.

"Taelo has worn us out. Even when he called for a day off, he takes us out to collect grass and into the forest selecting and marking timbers for the lodge," Talking Wren piped in.

She had never worked so hard in her life. Even the hard jogging they had done when traveling did not compare to how hard they had been working.

"We will certainly do our part," Busy Bee said as she took in the scope of work still needing to be done before winter set in.

The nights were already getting very cold.

It took them twelve sun cycles before enough stone had been brought back to the compound area.

The morning after the last load of stone had been brought in Taelo announced that there should be one more hunt and that a message would be sent to the Elk Clan to let them know the team was doing well.

He and the team had discussed this the evening before so there was no surprise. The team had decided that Quiet Rabbit, Busy Bee, and Feather-in-the-Wind would be the three to deliver the message.

"I don't suppose you will let me go so I can relax a little," Talking Wren had piped in.

She really didn't want to go. She knew it would be a fast, exhausting jog in both directions.

"You were high on the list of candidates, but you have become so good at selecting rocks to match each other that we decided you could not be spared," Taelo joked back.

Little Otter, Meadow Flower and you will go on the hunt," Taelo said addressing Talking Wren.

"Yes, a break from hauling and handling stone all day," Talking Wren said doing a little dance in a circle.

"Burley Bear, Golden Hawk and I will continue to build the compound. There is only one thing needed before the hunters depart." Taelo said with a tone of anticipation.

"Oh, I knew it was too good to be true," Talking Wren said as she stopped her dance.

"Yes, there is the matter of hauling up enough clay from the clay bank by the river. Let's do that for about three sun cycles and then the hunters can go out," Taelo said catching Talking Wren to keep her from falling down in her exaggerated reaction.

The next morning Busy Bee, Quiet Rabbit and Feather-in-the-Wind put on their back packs and set out down the river south to the Elk Clan. They carried enough provisions to get them to the cave of the Others.

There they would rest and then continue south to the Valley of Plenty.

"I am so excited about meeting the rest of the Elk Clan," Feather-in-the-Wind said as they jogged along.

She was in the best condition of her life and could easily keep up. Her brother, Bold Walker, would be surprised at how his younger, spoiled sister was turning out.

"You will be a surprise to all of them and they will quickly accept you as one of us. We will need to protect you from all the young men who are going to pursue you," Busy Bee joked.

She knew this would in fact be the case. Feather-in-the-Wind was by far the best-looking young lady in the clan.

"Well, there go the best-looking ladies in our clan, Taelo said quietly to Golden Hawk as the two stood and watched the three jogging away from the camp.

"Well, our mothers might argue that point," Golden Hawk joked back.

"Hey, are you two going to help in getting these roof timbers into place," Burley Bear called as he stood and held one of the four center posts of the lodge?

By evening the main timbers for the roof were in place. These would be covered with thinner cross limbs to form a frame to hold the hides. They had talked about putting grass across the limbs as they had learned from their neighbors to the south, but they realized there was not a large enough grass supply for the task. They were also faced with the fact they did not have enough hides.

"Well let's concentrate on the perimeter wall. Perhaps our hunters will come back with an abundant supply of hides," Taelo said.

He had an idea about the roof that wouldn't quite come clear to him.

The walls for the perimeter went up quickly. They used Burly Bear as the measure of how high to build the wall.

The main gate was a work of art. They had learned how to make it by studying the gate of the Warrior Clan. They built the frame and then put in vertical timbers. Then the frame was positioned and pinned.

The vertical timbers had the bottom pointed into a blunt spike. The cross timber at the top had a cone shaped hole.

A cone shaped hole in a large flat stone was positioned at the bottom of the gate. The entire supporting frame was bound together at the corners by leather rope.

They adjusted the gate to swing easily in by positioning the bottom stone so that one person could open and close the gate.

"Now we have only the roof to complete," Taelo said one evening almost a full cycle of the moon later.

The nights had now become cold, and the sky was threatening snow.

"Well, we don't have enough material to cover the roof," Golden Hawk said as he roasted a rabbit, they had caught that day.

He was frustrated about having done so much and yet they had not solved the problem of how to cover the roof.

"I don't think our hunters will bring back enough hide," Burley Bear added.

"Do you remember the roofs they were putting on the homes when we were with the Warrior Clan," Taelo asked?

"Yes, they were using flat pieces of clay they had hardened," Golden Hawk commented.

"It would take us all winter to make enough clay pieces to cover the roof," Burley Bear commented as he devoured his rabbit.

"I agree, but I recall seeing a huge amount of thin flat stone by the cliff where we got our stone for our hot water well and our bathing tub. It was too thin for that use but if we are careful, we can use it to cover the roof. I think it is time to go and look again," Taelo suggested.

"That's a great idea. Are the beams of our roof strong enough to hold up the weight," Golden Hawk asked as he looked up at the long runs of the main roof timbers.

"Good point, we will need to add in vertical supports about halfway on each main roof beam," Taelo suggested.

Each evening Taelo had been having the young wolves and Lasher pull a log in the area around the lodged.

"What are you doing," Burley Bear asked as he watched Taelo and the wolves?

"I am training them to pull together. They now can pull a log around and follow the commands I give them," Taelo replied.

"Later after you build me a large sled, I will have them pull it for me," Taelo went on as he made his request for a sled.

"I see you have been waiting until I got into the trap," Burly Bear grunted as he realized Taelo had been waiting for his question.

"Our wolves will earn their keep this winter by providing us a means of traveling in the snow. Lasher is strong enough to be the lead. The others will quickly gain strength and pull their share of the load," Taelo went on with his explanation.

Why don't we put a little travois on each young wolf and have them help us bring the stone for the roof of the lodge," Burley Bear suggested.

"That is an excellent idea. I will work with the wolves to bring the stone up to you and Golden Hawk. You two can put the stone on the roof," Taelo said eagerly.

Burley Bear seemed to always surprise him with his excellent ideas.

The next day the three went back to the cliff and located the stone Taelo had mentioned. There was an abundance of the thin flat stone.

The three examined the thin stone sheets and decided it would make an excellent roof.

They loaded the travois for each of the wolves and then they loaded their own. The first load would keep Golden Hawk and Burley Bear busy for the rest of the day. Taelo continued making trips back and forth.

"I think we better change roles," Burley Bear said after the initial few rows of stone had been put on the roof. "I am too large to be crawling on the roof to place the stone." he volunteered.

"I hadn't thought of that," Taelo admitted.

Burley Bear was at least four times heavier than any of them.

"Please tell Lasher not to bite me," Burley Bear said as he got ready to take the wolves back for another load.

The slabs of stone were easy to position and were easy to lay across the webbed wood lattice work. A thin layer of clay spread across the top third of each stone slab allowed the next row to bond and seal. Ten sun cycles later the roof was finished.

The roof had an opening in the center above the cooking area. It had a large hide that went over a grid of solid oak timbers. This hide could be pulled back to allow the smoke and heat of cooking to escape. It could be pulled closed once the cooking was done.

"I think we are done. There may be some work needed to make the inside more comfortable, but the lodge has solid walls, a very fine roof, and a heated floor," Taelo said as the three stood in front of the lodge and admired their handiwork.

It had taken them three moons to complete their task.

Our hunters should be returning anytime and our three ladies who traveled to the clan should also be returning shortly. Once everyone returns, we will celebrate," Taelo said as he sat on one of several extra stones, they had rolled to the front of the lodge to be used for such a purpose.

"I especially like the door you built for the lodge," Golden Hawk complemented Burley Bear.

"Even the Others can learn new things," Burley Bear said proudly.

He had been impressed with the concept of a door in their visit to the Condor Clan. He had built the door in secret and had brought it in from the woods after he had it done.

It was a huge door large enough for him and it had interlocking timbers so that it was a solid mass. It was more than his hand in thickness. No one would ever be able to break it down. He had also made the pivot points at both the bottom and the top. This enabled the door to pivot smoothly in the V cone at the top and bottom.

The snow began falling the next day. They had beat old man winter.

Chapter 13: The Elk Clan

Quiet Rabbit, Busy Bee and Feather-in-the-Wind jogged away from the compound in an easy going, distance eating pace. They were the first to travel back along their original path north.

Feather-in-the-Wind asked how they would recognize their way back if it snowed.

Busy Bee praised her for asking the question. She and Quiet Rabbit looked at each other in the realization that they had not thought about the answer.

Let's put up markers as we go. We will put a pole up with a black feather tied to it or we will tie a black feather to a tree branch or small tree along the path.

"Why a black feather," Feather-in-the-Wind asked?

"Because that dead black bird at the side of the trail will provide all the feathers we need," Quiet Rabbit replied as bent to pick out as many as she could.

The valley was completely covered by pine trees with trunks as wide as Little Otter or Burley Bear and at least twenty spear lengths tall. The trail made its way through these silent sentinels as it slowly ascended to the top the ridge leading to the seaward side of the range.

Busy Bee reminded her two companions to keep their spear ready in case they surprised a bear or a wild boar.

"I think I am much better with the sling than any other weapon," Feather-in-the-Wind replied as she whirled her sling and let a rock go.

It hit a little tree next to the trail. A few moments later a rabbit jumped up in front of them and Feather-in-the-Wind brought it down.

"Well, I am impressed. You can use your sling while jogging. You really are very good," Quiet Rabbit said as she picked up the rabbit and handed it to Feather-in-the-Wind.

Feather-in-the-Wind felt an immediate surge of pride and energy from the praise.

The three proceeded throughout the day at a fast jog. They finally stopped as they got to the top of the trail leading away from the two mountains.

There was one point at the crest of the trail where they could look back down into the valley and see each of the two snow-capped peaks of the twin mountains.

They tied a black feather to a small pine just getting its roots sunk into a crack on the side of the rock outcropping.

They jogged through the forest on the seaward side of the mountains, along a ridge that provided a steady slowly declining path.

Quite Rabbit was surprised that they did not see deer or elk as they made their way down. Perhaps they were making just enough noise to scare them away from the trail.

The periodic rabbit suffered the fate of being hit by one of Feather-in-the-Wind's stones coming from her sling.

They continued the jogging and camping each evening for another eight sun cycles before the sea became visible on their right.

Busy Bee made the point that they would need to go down to the beach and go around the face of the cliff to get to the entrance of the cave of the Others.

"I see someone on the trail ahead," Quiet Rabbit said as she saw what appeared to be a warrior of the Others.

They slowed but approached the single warrior without hesitation.

"Do you recall me from the long hunt? You saved my life in the cave after we had been attacked by the crazy saber tooth tiger. I am now called Saber Scar." the warrior said as he showed the long scar across his chest.

"Broken Spear sent me to guide you to the cave," he continued.

"Yes, I remember you well. Even when you were wounded you first helped your fellow hunters and saved their lives. Thank you for coming to guide us to the cave," Quiet Rabbit said putting her hand to his shoulder as he did the same to her.

"It healed well," she said as she traced the scar across his chest.

"I think the Seer of the Others is better than the one we had in my clan," Feather-in-the-Wind said quietly to Busy Bee.

"Yes, he has an uncanny ability to sense the coming and going of the people around him. He seems especially connected to Taelo," Busy Bee replied.

"I am ready for a hot water bath and a good night's sleep," Quiet Rabbit said as the three followed Saber Scar back to the cave of the Others.

"I am pleased to see you. You have made excellent time. I just sent out the warrior this morning and explained to him you would be by in the next several days. You must have wings on your feet as Burley Bear claims," Broken Spear said from his seat by the entrance.

He was always attended to by several of the older women. They made sure he was always taken care of.

"We are keeping a fast pace. We need to return before the winter fully sets in," Quite Rabbit replied.

She was honored to have Broken Spear talking to her and replied in his language.

"Yes, you will make it. Tonight, you can eat well and relax. Tomorrow you can fly down the beach to the south. The Elk Clan has moved into the Valley of Plenty for the winter so you will need to travel a little farther down the coast.

Do not go by the way of Taelo's hot water cave. There is some danger there that I could not see but that would cost one of you your life. Go down the coast and across the pass Taelo, Burley Bear and Golden Hawk used," Broken Spear said solemnly as the three sat in front of him.

"We will heed your warning," Quiet Rabbit replied.

She wondered what the danger might be.

"Let's get a nice hot water bath and then get something to eat before we go to bed. We have been pushing ourselves and this is a rare opportunity to enjoy ourselves," Busy Bee said leading the way to the pool.

"I would love to accompany you to the Elk Clan, but I do not have wings on my feet," Saber Scar said the next morning after escorting them to the beach.

"Why do they keep talking about wings on our feet," Feather-in-the-Wind asked as the three set off on a fast jog.

"Because the Others cannot run as fast as we jog. Their endurance is unbelievable, but they are not fast. They see us running and claim we can do so because we have wings on our feet," Quiet Rabbit explained as the three, ran side-by-side down the beach.

"Oh, I get it," Feather-in-the-Wind said as she realized how fast they were moving.

Five sun cycles later the three approached the Elk Clan's summer ocean side quarters.

"This is where we began our journey of the heart," Quiet Rabbit said as they approached the compound. "We will stay here for the night. Tomorrow we will make it to the Valley of Plenty," she said as she approached the main lodge.

"This is a beautiful place, the Valley of Plenty must have much to offer to make the clan move there for the winter," Feather-in-the-Wind said as she looked around at the lodge and the many separate huts around the perimeter.

"Yes, there is a hot spring and there is a herd of buffalo that winters there. This gives the clan food and heat throughout the bitterest winter," Busy Bee replied.

"And was it Taelo, Golden Hawk and Burley Bear that found the valley," Feather-in-the-Wind asked though she had heard the story before?

"Yes, and still the elders would not recognize the three as full warriors. They thought them to be just lucky and too young. It was the long hunt that finally made a difference," Quiet Rabbit added.

"It's such a great story," Feather- in-the-Wind said as she lay out her sleeping hide.

"We will have Burley Bear and Little Otter tell all the stories of our clans this winter. By spring you will be ready for new adventures just so you will not need to listen to the old stories," Busy Bee said with a chuckle.

She enjoyed the changes the stories took depending on the mood Burley Bear or Little Otter were in.

The next morning, they crossed over the rocky spit to the beach on the far side and again jogged along the beach down the coast. They reached the path leading to the east through the gap in the mountain range. High in the sky an eagle let out a cry and flew above the path leading to the valley.

"We will have a greeting committee when we get there but let's be careful. The eagle may be warning us of danger," Quiet Rabbit said as she turned and jogged east.

Busy Bee stopped short and gave warning about the three dire wolves coming toward them.

Feather-in-the-Wind stepped toward the wolves and released a rapid fire of stones from her sling. Every sling found its mark.

The wolves stopped in their tracks as did the three of them.

Feather-in-the-Wind continued her barrage of stones. The stones caused the wolves to back away and head into the forest.

"Well, let's move and take advantage of Feather-in-the-Wind's very quick reaction," Quiet Rabbit said as she led the three on a full run through the cut in the mountains.

"I don't have wings on my feet," Feather- in-the-Wind said when she was looking down into the Valley.

She was breathing heavily, and her lungs burned.

"Let's get down to the valley. I see our escort waiting," Busy Bee said as she led the way down.

She was moving just as fast as Quiet Rabbit had done. She knew the power of the three predators and that the wolves might decide to come back for them.

Up ahead was safety.

"Who is the beautiful lady in white," Feather in the Wind asked as they slowed down to more dignified walk.

"That is Taelo's mother, I am sure she saw the eagle and was expecting to see Taelo," Quiet Rabbit answered as she greeted White Swan.

"Greetings, I must first warn you we have been running ahead of some dire wolves," Quiet Rabbit said quickly.

The warriors immediately set up a wall on the forest side of the group.

"Let's hasten back to the compound and then we can talk more casually," White Swan said as she took in the three exhausted looking young women.

She had been expecting Taelo after seeing the eagle.

"Let me introduce Feather-in-the-Wind. She is the most beautiful of young women in her clan and was the sacrifice to the great Condor. This is a bird about three times larger than our eagle.

Busy Bee and I rescued her from her sure death in a remote ice cave. Today she repaid the debt by single handedly attacking and discouraging three giant dire wolves. Her sling shot out a rapid series of stones so accurately that every stone found its mark on the snouts of the wolves. The wolves retreated into the forest, and we ran as fast as we could to get to the valley. This is the first time I have seen dire wolves back away from a confrontation with us," Quiet Rabbit elaborated.

"We are pleased to have such a brave member join the Elk Clan," Grey Fox Running said as he greeted the three.

The entire leadership was present. They all had been expecting Taelo and the entire team back. He could hardly contain himself as he waited to let the three tell their story.

"Broken Spear told our team; that our journey had two parts. The first was to the south where we met two very different peoples. Feather-in-the-Wind's Condor Clan was very friendly, and we learned many new things from them," Quiet Rabbit began the story.

"On the way down, we faced and fought about thirty warriors and counted coup on all of them. Taelo had coached us on not hurting them too badly or killing any of the warriors. This is one of the weapons Golden Hawk and Taelo made for each of us," Busy Bee said as she stood and pulled the weapon from its holder on her back.

The entire group present leaned forward to get a better view of the weapon.

"This is a new weapon to us," Red Oak said as he accepted the weapon from Busy Bee. Quiet Rabbit took hers and passed it to Grey Fox Running.

"I will let Taelo, and Golden Hawk tell the tales of seeing the sun rise on one sea and watching it set in another," Quiet Rabbit went on and received some laughter about her comments.

"We continued south until Taelo's totem flew over us with a bird three times its size. Later we learned it was the Condor. It is the totem of Feather-in-the-Wind's Condor Clan and she is the Condor Queen, the last of the virgin sacrifices to their totem.

"We got a very friendly reception and enjoyed a full moon cycle there. We have seen the nest of the great Condor and later we were present for the sacrifice of the most beautiful virgin to the Condor," Busy Bee took up the story.

"I must speak for my protectors. Busy Bee and Quiet Feather rescued me from the ice cave. Later Taelo protected me from the leader of the people my clan has fought with for many years. Taelo killed him in a hand-to-hand battle.

It was over so fast the fifty warriors facing us did not know what to do. Taelo claimed command of them as was the custom of their clan, and they stopped immediately.

Taelo could have become a powerful leader in the Warrior Clan but chose instead to give his army over to the second leader who earlier had befriended us. It was at that moment, I knew I was proud to be a member of the Elk Clan," Feather in the Wind said in her quiet but steady voice.

"So where is Taelo, Golden Hawk and the rest of the team," White Swan finally asked when she could wait no longer.

"Taelo said you might worry since we are going into winter. He wanted all of you to know about the second half of our journey. Our team is in a valley more than a full moon cycle to the North of the Others cave," Quiet Rabbit replied.

There was a sudden quiet in the lodge.

"What in the world are you doing so far North and how do you plan to survive," Silver Arrow, one of the elders of the clan asked?

"I am eager to return. When we left, the team was building a lodge you can only dream of. It has a hot water spring, and the floor is heated. By now the roof should be on. The compound is about twice the size of the one here and it will have a stone wall all the way around.

"How is that possible? You are so few and three of you are here," Silver Arrow continued.

"You have known Taelo as long as I. You know when he sets his mind to do something, it gets done," Quiet Rabbit replied.

"Are you three planning to return immediately," Quiet Pheasant asked.

"Who is she," Feather-in-the-Wind whispered her question.

"Let me introduce you to Golden Hawk's mother," Busy Bee replied bringing Feather-in-the- Wind forward.

"I am sure we will all enjoy the stories by Burley Bear, Little Otter, Taelo and Golden Hawk," Red Oak said to the entire assembly. "Let's get these warriors fed and give them a chance to get some rest.

"Thank you for making the journey to let us know where you are located and what the team is doing. It will be hard on all of us to wait until spring to come and visit you," Grey Fox Running said as he indicated the meeting was over.

"We are so pleased you are all safe. I know Taelo and Golden Hawk will get you through the winter. Is there more we should know," White Swan asked as she guided the three to a sleeping area?

"Yes, Broken Spear has predicted Taelo will establish a new sub clan with people he rescues this winter," Quiet Rabbit said in a quiet tone.

She did not want to let anyone else know.

"Ah, another interesting clan gathering coming up after the hunting season," White Swan said as she took in the magnitude of the teams' activities.

No sub clan had ever been established in this manner.

"Leave it to those two to make our lives interesting," Quiet Pheasant said.

The three enjoyed the morning meal and the tour of the Valley of Plenty. They shared the warning Broken Spear had given about the cave at the top of the falls. They were now sure it was associated with the dire wolves they had met.

Finally, on the morning on which they were leaving, White Swan led out the tamed buffalo loaded with warm sleeping furs, coats, boots and a large supply of dried meats and fish.

Quiet Rabbit thanked White Swan and the Elk Clan members for their generosity and made the comment that they would be thanking them many times throughout the winter.

"I look at the warm furs and I thank you now. My blood is growing thicker, but I grew up in warm weather," Feather-in-the-Wind said as she ran her hand into the furs.

"I will thank you for Little Otter. Throughout our journey he has worried about his buffalo. He will have a much better winter as he struggles to keep it fed," Busy Bee said as she looked over the treasure they were being given.

"There is one more item. We would like to send a litter of wolves back with you. I have kept them alive and well fed but I do not know how to train them the way Taelo trained Lasher," Grey Fox Running said as he brought forward ten young wolves.

"I have loaded enough food for each in the packs on their backs," he pointed out as he brought the rather large young wolves forward.

Feather-in-the-Wind approached the young wolves and made individual contact with each. She talked to them and told them that they would mind her as she gave each a scratch between the ears and a pat on their haunches. She was copying what Taelo had done with the eight wolves Quiet Rabbit had brought to him.

She then took the ten thin leather ropes and followed behind Quite Rabbit and Busy Bee who led the way with the buffalo that had no name.

Chapter 14: In for the Winter

The trio and their wolf pack left the Valley of Plenty and followed the coast northward toward the Clan of Others. Their gifts would slow them down considerably. Quiet Rabbit was now concerned about making it back to the lodge before any major snowstorm.

In the far north, Little Otter was returning to the lodge after a long hunt with a large supply of meat. It was mostly ground hogs, rabbits, mountain goats and one elk. He was disappointed that he had seen no buffalo.

"We got the elk on our last day," Little Otter said as the team pulled in three heavily loaded travois.

Talking Wren was amazed by the work that had been completed at the lodge. She walked around admiring the floor, the hot pool of steaming water and watched as Burley Bear proudly showed Meadow Flower the door to the lodge.

She walked to the door and opened and closed it several times as Burley Bear continued to describe how it was all put together so that it would open and close freely.

The larger, two spears wide by three spears long, hot tub for bathing that was located several spears lengths away from door attracted her and she decided it was time to wash off the smells of the hunt.

Meadow Flower complimented Burley Bear on the huge door.

Golden Hawk carried some of the meat to a cool storage room they had made to store their meat. He and Taelo had thought about this from their experience at the hot springs above the Valley of Plenty.

The roof was the item that caught Little Otters attention. Clearly it was not covered with hide because the team had exactly three of them from two elk and a deer.

The two elk hides were above the cooking area and could be moved aside to open the area above it. He kept opening and closing them as he thought about their use.

Meanwhile Talking Wren and Meadow Flower were walking around the cooking area that now had a smooth stone floor and a work surface built around the oven and cooking surface they had built.

The entire lodge was at a comfortable temperature and Taelo was demonstrating the opening and closing of four hinged roof openings that could be raised or lowered to control the warmth in the lodge.

"Is this where we bathe," Meadow Flower asked as she sat on the rock rim put up around the hot water spring?

"No, we have built the bathing area just outside of the lodge. This will make sure all the water in the lodge is clean," Burley Bear explained.

He was very proud of the stream of heated water running back and forth under the floor of the lodge. He made it a point of showing the returning hunters how it worked.

"I was worried about how we would survive the winter. I am now ready to enjoy my stay here," Little Otter said as he sat down and relaxed.

Well don't get too comfortable there is much still to get done. Burley Bear has done a fine job on our lodge doors. I want him to improve our main gate the same way. We are still missing the cross timbers for the top of the compound wall. Finally, we only have a little portion of the wood we will need to cook with and possibly to heat with during the winter," Taelo said as he sat across from Little Otter.

"Maybe we should go out one more time on a long hunt," Little Otter joked.

He was not worried about the work. The comfort of such a lodge would make up for all the hard work.

"I think I will take that hot bath, have some dinner, and call it a day. Tomorrow I will do whatever you ask," Little Otter said.

Where do I sleep?

"Well, that is another thing we have not finished. Just pick a place. Perhaps tomorrow we can lay out the interior of the lodge and decide where each of us will sleep," Golden Hawk said as he pointed out where he was currently sleeping.

"Why is Taelo pulling a log with Lasher and the young wolves," Meadow Flower asked a few days later as she stood watching?

"He is training them to pull a sled that I need to make for him," Burley Bear replied.

"I guess I should go find the wood to make it," he went on.

"Perhaps you should get enough wood to make several sleds. I will help you. Knowing Taelo I am sure we will harness more wolves if it works," Little Otter commented from his seat on a stone.

"You and I can go get the framing timber for the main gate. While we are out, we can scout out the materials for the sleds," Burley Bear said replying to Little Otter's suggestion.

"I think we should also get enough of the clay from the river so we can try our hand at making the clay pots the way they did in the Condor Clan," Talking Wren suggested.

As I recall, they mixed a little amount of fine sand with the clay, shaped the clay pots and dishes, put them in an oven and heated them for three days.

"Why don't the two of us go to the river today and get the materials. I would like to make our pots in the evenings. When we have enough, we can put them in the oven of our cooking stand," Meadow Flower said to Talking Wren.

"I guess that leaves Taelo and me to do as we please," Golden Hawk spoke up from where he had been quietly sitting and listening in on the conversations.

The four turned and in unison replied, "Yes, the two of you can do as you please."

To the south, Quiet Rabbit, Busy Bee, and Feather-in-the-Wind made good time in reaching the cave of the Others.

They were eager to get back to the team in the north but a short stay and a bath in the hot springs was something the three had been talking about as they traveled.

"I see you return with a large load of furs. The litter of wolves Feather-in-the-Wind is leading is a surprise. I knew she would be taking wolves back to Taelo because Saber Scar rescued a litter and has been raising them. It is his gift to Taelo.

So, you will have two sets of wolves to take up. We will add dried meats, herbs, and some of our scented soap. It is good you have your tame buffalo to carry all of this for you," Broken Spear said in his greeting.

He noticed each young wolf also carried a pack.

"What do your wolves carry," he inquired?

"They each carry their own food for the trip," Feather-in-the-Wind said as she took a handful out and showed it to those around.

"I will outfit my young wolves the same way," Saber Scar said as he rounded up several of his buddies to make the back packs to carry food.

The next day Saber Scar once again was the person to guide the three up to the top of the cliffs and wish them well on their journey to their lodge.

"Let Burley Bear know Broken Spear has put him up to be leader when he returns," Saber Scar said as he was wishing them well on their continuing journey.

"That will be surprising news for Burley Bear. I am sure he will make a fine leader, but it is not something he has ever spoken of," Quiet Rabbit commented to Busy Bee.

"Yes, the time is coming when Taelo and Golden Hawk too will be called upon," Busy Bee replied.

"I don't think they are ready for that yet. Taelo and Golden Hawk are talking about a journey to the east. Taelo has discussed this with Broken Spear," Quiet Rabbit replied.

The three jogged on in silence for the rest of the day. With her sling always at the ready, Feather-in-the-Wind turned out to be the best at killing the small game they scared up as they traveled.

"I may never be able to run down a buffalo and put the spear into its chest as you have described Taelo and Golden Hawk doing but I will be one of the best at hitting what I see with the rock from my sling," Feather-in-the-Wind said proudly as she picked up her third rabbit of the day.

"I am fine with fresh rabbit for dinner," Busy Bee said as they continued their jog northward.

They stopped at their marker where they could see the two mountains framing the way to the river. They were within three days of the valley.

That evening the first snow of the season came down.

"I am really happy to have such a nice thick bear hide to keep me warm," Feather-in-the-Wind said as she poked her face out of the fur wrapped around her.

Both Quiet Rabbit and Busy Bee were sitting on their furs with just light jackets on. The three were sitting below a makeshift lean-to covered with pine branches. A small fire provided some meager warmth.

The young wolves, having adopted Feather-in-the-Wind as their mother, gathered around her. The buffalo was tied off enjoying some dry grass and nibbling on some fresh grass nearby.

"Let's all get a good night's sleep. Tomorrow I want to push through to the compound," Quite Rabbit said as she rolled into her sleeping hide.

Not far away, sitting comfortably in the hot water of the bathing pool, Taelo and Golden Hawk were watching the first hard snow of winter as it came down on them.

Taelo expressed his concern about Quiet Rabbit, Busy Bee, and Feather-in-the-Wind.

"If they don't make it in a day or two, I will go down trail to find them," Golden Hawk replied.

He hoped the snow along the trail was no worse than what was falling on them, but he knew how the snows in the mountain could be treacherous in some places even when most places were not experiencing any unusual amounts of snow.

The next morning the snow was a solid cover but no more than a hand deep.

"Are we ready for the day," Quiet Rabbit said as she got ready for the last part of their journey.

They set out at the fastest pace they could manage. The young buffalo easily kept up with the pace they were setting.

"The wolves seem to enjoy our jog each day," Feather-in-the-Wind said from her position in the rear.

The realization of how lucky she had been to have been rescued from her certain death by Quiet Rabbit and Busy Bee renewed her energy.

The three began singing a welcome song as they turned up the river leading to their valley and lodge.

"I think I hear Quiet Rabbit and Busy Bee," Meadow Flower said getting up from forming a clay pot.

She was only fifty percent successful in her trials at making the pottery. Talking Wren had gone down to the river to get additional sand to mix with the clay. They had decided they were either putting too little sand or too much sand into their clay. They were lost and trying different amounts.

Meadow Flower walked out to the wall of the compound where she expected to see Quiet Rabbit coming.

"What are you looking for," Burley Bear asked from where he was working on the frame for the main gate?

He and Little Otter had built a new stronger frame for the gate and were in the process of locking the pivot points in place.

Taelo and Golden Hawk were in the forest retrieving wood and the long slender tree trunks they were using to finish the top of the compound wall.

After a moment Meadow Flower said, "I can hear Busy Bee singing but I cannot see them yet. Let's get ready to greet our returning members."

Little Otter picked up a horn of a buffalo and blew into the hole on the end. He had learned this from the Condor Clan. They used it to signal across the great valleys they roamed.

The blast could be heard through most of the valley.

"Well, I think Little Otter is letting us know our travelers have returned. Let's get back to the compound and greet them," Golden Hawk said as he heard the blast.

"What in the world was that" Quiet Rabbit said in surprise.

"It is the sound of a horn," Feather-in-the-Wind said as she heard the familiar sound.

"They know we are coming and have let everyone else know." she continued with certainty.

Just then the compound came into view.

"Oh, my," Quite Rabbit said as she stopped and then took up a slow walk.

"How did they get all of this done," Busy Bee said taking in the size and overwhelming look of the compound?

"Look at the doors of the main gate," Feather-in-the-Wind said as she took in the two massive gate doors. They rival the gates of the Warrior Clan village.

How was it possible for them to get so much done? How long were we gone," Quiet Rabbit asked?

Just then Taelo and Golden Hawk jogged in from the opposite direction. Talking Wren made her appearance from the direction of the river. Burley Bear and Little Otter were walking down the incline of the hill.

"They have returned with my buffalo," Little Otter said as he jogged down the slope.

"They have also brought a pack of wolves with them," Burley Bear commented to Meadow Flower.

"I wonder where they got them," she replied.

"Another day or two and we would have come looking for you," Taelo said as he held Quiet Rabbit in his arms.

"Who gave you all these wolves," Taelo went on as he took in the pack surrounding Feather-in-the-Wind?

"They were given to us by each clan. And no, I do not want my name changed to Wolf Woman," Feather-in-the-Wind said as she brought the wolves forward.

Taelo took the time to introduce Lasher to each of the new wolf pups.

"It looks as if your clan is getting populated faster than ours," Taelo said speaking to Lasher.

"I am glad I collected extra materials to make the sleds," Burley Bear commented.

"Come on let's get you into the lodge and get you something to eat. You can then clean up and relax," Talking Wren said as she took the rope tied to the young buffalo and handed it to Little Otter.

She turned and led the way up to the main gate of the compound.

"What is covering the roof of the lodge," Quiet Rabbit asked as she took in the compound and the lodge? She had not imagined such a solid structure.

"Some thin flat sheets of stone gathered from the cliffs," Golden Hawk replied.

Busy Bee picked up a cracked clay bowl from a pile of broke objects and asked Talking Wren what she was looking at.

The explanation was that it was Meadow Flower's pile of failed attempts at creating some clay pottery like what the team had seen being used by the Condor Clan.

Chapter 15: The Missing Ingredient

"Too much sand in the clay causes it to crack," Feather-in-the-Wind was explaining to her group of pottery students.

She was so happy to have found something she could excel in and teach the members of her new clan.

"I knew I was doing something wrong," Meadow Flower said as she formed her clay bowl.

"Well, my mother was constantly talking about putting in just the right amount of sand into the clay.

"Too much or too little and your pot is no good" she was constantly saying," Feather-is-the-Wind mimicked her mother. *"Just a pinch will do it."*

"Also, you need to fire your object twice if you want a glaze on the outside. Once you have a good clay pot on the first firing you put on a light coating of sand and fire it a second time.

My mother considered losing three out of ten a good first firing. If she lost only one on her second firing, she felt she had a good firing. I saw her really mad a few times when she lost most of a firing," Feather-in-the-Wind said as she made a thin-walled drinking cup.

Back home this had been her specialty even though success with thin cups was only fifty-fifty.

"Back home! I am home," she thought as she looked around at the comfortable lodge she was in and the friends surrounding her.

"From Ice Princess to pot maker," she chuckled to herself as she got up to put her cup in the oven.

Taelo selected the largest wolves of the pack and attached them to a central rope tied to the sled Burley Bear had made. Lasher was the lead wolf and the other end of the rope tied to his harness. Eight wolves were positioned behind him and attached to the pull rope. Taelo called out to Lasher to get him to pull and to run to the left or the right. He would keep calling out right, right, right, enough times to get Lasher to turn as hard as he desired.

He spent several days training his new team. The sled Burley Bear had made was the length of a long spear and just wider than the distance from the ground to his knee. The bottom runners extended back a little more than the length of his foot. Once he had Lasher into a full run he would step on the runners and ride the sled.

He came back in and praised Burley Bear for the great work he had done on its construction.

"Your skill has increased tremendously since the first sled you made when we were bringing the meat home from the Valley of Plenty," Taelo complemented Burly Bear.as he wiped the sled down and leaned it against the lodge wall.

"This time I had more time and the hot water of our spring helped soften the wood so I could more easily bend the various sections. I also learned how to apply the tree sap from our friends of the Condor Clan. This helps seal the wood.

Each time you bring the sled in from a long run, the runners should be treated with a mixture of sap and grease," Burley Bear replied.

He was proud at the quality of his new sled. He had paid close attention to the wood workers of the Condor Clan.

The pivot for the doors was learned from the less friendly people of the Warrior Clan on the way back.

Taelo took the time to praise each member of the wolf team and made a point of giving each a treat of elk meat.

Feather-in-the-Wind joined him and together they named each of the team.

Along with Golden Hawk they selected the next two teams that would be trained to pull a sled.

Feather-in-the-Wind suggested they watch how the wolves interacted and then team up the wolves that had already selected each other. She thought this approach would make for teams that got along together with each other.

Their starting point would be to have them pull a log the way Taelo had initially trained the wolfs Quiet Rabbit had brought back.

"Have any of you noticed we are missing a critical ingredient," Taelo asked the team during the morning meal.

Outside high in the sky an eagle let out a loud cry.

Everyone stopped what they were doing and looked at Taelo.

Taelo was as surprised as the rest of the team as he looked at the eagle in the sky.

"What is the ingredient we are missing," Quiet Rabbit asked.

She was confused but knew this was another pivotal moment for the team.

"Salt," was Taelo's reply as he continued to look skyward.

"Salt, the eagle screams because we have no salt," Talking Wren said from where she was decorating a bowl for the second firing!

"Well, the eagle is a surprise for me. But yes salt.

I am told there is a salt pit near the coast north from here" Taelo continued.

He was now wondering what the call of the eagle meant in all of this.

"I don't suppose we know who told you about the salt," Burley Bear asked?

Everyone already knew the answer, but he had to voice the question to bring it out in the open.

"Well, I was surprised that knowing where to get salt would be important enough for Broken Spear to say something, but he did. I always pay attention to what he says," Taelo went on.

"He also told me that wolves would lead the way. I didn't see how the pups you found in the valley would be strong enough to pull the sled, but the ones sent up by Saber Scar are older and stronger. He must have been training them or they are just natural sled wolves. In a few months all the wolves will be able to pull a sled. We will be able to go out in the winter and travel as we desire."

"Salt," Quite Rabbit repeated. "You are not leaving out any important information? Are you?"

"Honest, the salt connection is a mystery to me," Taelo said.

He really did not have a clue what it all meant. He just knew he would need to go to the coast where he would find the salt. He was not sure what else the journey would hold.

"How long will you be gone and how can we help," Golden Hawk asked?

He knew his friend would make the journey to find the salt. His role would be to give him support. He felt this was indeed a pivotal moment for the team.

It was like the time on the mountain trail when they had found out that a lioness was tracking them. Taelo had to take the action and he was in support.

"Given the season and the poor hunting we have had in the valley I will need to leave with enough provision for the entire trip. Before I leave, I would like all of us to go up to the waterfall and explore the area around it," Taelo replied.

"What will we be looking for," Little Otter asked.

He was looking forward to this excursion to the waterfall. They had visited it earlier when they entered the area and its impressive height and the mysterious appearance the mist the falling water created.

"Golden Hawk and I found the warm water cave at the top of the water fall above the Valley of Plenty." It would be great to find another cave like that. However, I am really just curious about the size and height of this waterfall," Taelo replied.

"Does anyone object to a little side adventure before I go find salt," Taelo asked looking around.

A general murmur of agreement from all made him feel better.

The next morning the entire team left the compound. There were twenty-eight wolves and nine humans.

"How are we going to climb to the top of this monster waterfall," Burley Bear said as they approached.

"I think I see a way up to the left of the waterfall," Taelo said.

"I think I see as way up the right side," Golden Hawk replied.

"The two of us will go up the front face, the rest of you take a look around and see if there are any more accessible paths up to the top," Taelo said to the team.

He and Golden Hawk took off up the face on either side of the fall.

"Well let's quit watching them and find an easy path to the top," Little Otter said as he pulled his eyes away from the cliff face.

It was Lasher that found an almost invisible trail along the side of the cliff. It rose away from the water fall to the left. About halfway up the trail vanished into the face of the cliff.

"Well, the mystery is solved," Burly Bear said as he pointed to a long crack in the face of the cliff. The trail continued in this crack and went gently upward. By early afternoon they had set up camp by the river at the top of the falls.

"Well, I wonder what our two climbers have found. Let's locate a place where Golden Hawk can safely cross the river," Burley Bear suggested.

Meanwhile, Taelo and Golden Hawk made slow but steady progress up the face of the cliff. Over the eons the water of the river had eroded the cliff, so it formed a V on either side of the falls. Taelo could often see Golden Hawk as they climbed. Periodically the mist of the river spray would hide the climbers from each other.

Taelo took his time as he moved from one foot and hand hold to the next. His arm and leg muscles could feel the strain as he pulled himself up.

He was almost at the top when he found a huge opening behind the falls. He climbed in and slowly walked behind the falls to the side Golden Hawk was climbing. To his left was a dark cavern too dark to see how large it might be, but he could feel a breeze coming out toward him.

"Hello, my friend it seems we have found yet another great cave. This one is much larger than any except for the Clan of the Others," Taelo said as he helped Golden Hawk up onto the ledge leading into the cave.

"Let's explore back as far as we can. I feel a breeze in my face as I go into the cave. There must be an opening not too far away," Golden Hawk said as he led the way back into the darkening cave.

They used the wall as a guide through the dark.

"Look," Taelo said as he saw a light not too far ahead.

The light came through an opening out to a large boulder that Burley Bear would be able to move and use as a door to the cave.

The cave opened on the right hand, up stream of the falls. It was shaped like a large buffalo horn with the wide opening at the falls and the point where they were stepping out.

"It looks like we are upstream from the falls. Let's go down to the falls and see if we can spot the rest of the team.

"Yo, the climbers," Burley Bear called just as the two were getting started.

"Well, you found a trail up the cliff," Taelo replied.

"Yes, we were just finding a good place for Golden Hawk to cross over. How did both of you get on the same side," Burley Bear asked?

"Come on over and we will show you. Let's get some material for some torches. It is very dark in this cave," Taelo replied.

"Let me go get the rest of the team. They will be mad at us if we leave them out," Little Otter called back.

Quite Rabbit suggested they prepare themselves with some torches so they could better explore this new cave. They quickly collected some dry grasses and some fat from the boar meat they had with them and made each of them three torches.

By late afternoon, the team was ready to go back into the cave.

Each now carried a torch as they climbed into the cave opening.

Suddenly Quite Rabbit said, "Look" as she held her torch close to the wall.

There on the wall was a drawing of a hunter spearing an elk.

"This must be the home of the first Elk Clan," Golden Hawk exclaimed in a hushed tone.

Our fathers have often told stories of the valley in the north and the sacred cave where the elders held their meetings and decided the direction of the Elk Clan.

The team found a series of drawings that seemed to document the hunting seasons and gave an accounting of the success or failure of the hunt.

The figures were simple, but it was clear that one was throwing a spear, the elk with the spear sticking in its side, the skinner skinning the Elk. And with each scene a series of marks to indicate how many elk had been killed.

There were also scenes of battling with the dire wolves and one where six hunters fought with a giant bear.

Busy Bee verbalized each scene as the rest of the team looked and listened.

The sleeping area was a ledge to the back of the cave.

The cooking area still had the blackened stones in a circle and the remains of two Y pieces of wood.

Taelo walked over to a large boulder. He moved it aside and pulled a smaller one from the wall. A stream of water began to run down an ancient channel.

"It is exactly as in the story Grey Fox Running told us," Taelo said as he looked at Golden Hawk.

He felt the ancients touch him and a rush of warmth went through his body.

He had always thought them to be only stories but now he knew the stories were rooted in truth.

"Feel the water," Golden Hawk said to the rest of the team.

"It is warm," Feather-in-the-Wind said in surprise.

"Yes, that was the miracle of the cave. It is located below a river and has a warm water spring inside. If we follow the stream, we will find a large pool where the elders would bath and relax during the cold winter months.

Taelo pointed to an old cracked hollow log that he was sure was the guide for the hot water stream. It would take the water to the distribution ring. See there is what remains of the hollow log and over the pool we should find what remains of the distribution ring.

They found the pool out close to waterfall just below the overhang.

The cave projected its ancient roots and the tremendous period of time since it was last occupied.

"Did Broken Spear tell of this," Quiet Rabbit asked.

"No, he said there was something important about the falls, but he did not know what. I decided we should check it out before I answered the eagle's call or perhaps this was the reason of the eagle's call. Salt may have nothing to do with it," Taelo said somewhat confused.

He was overwhelmed by finding the place where many of his imaginations had taken place as he listened to the stories of his father. All the stories were now running in rapid succession through his head.

"Let's spend the night here, enjoy the heated pool and study the history of our ancestors," Taelo said as he took in the scene with Lasher and all the wolves sitting around the pool looking out at the waterfall.

"Salt" was the last thing Taelo remembered as he fell asleep.

Chapter 16: Salt

The next morning, the team sitting to the right-hand side of the falls could see the twin snow-capped mountains in the far distance. The dark green of the predominant pines appeared like standing waves of a green ocean. The darker, almost black color generated by the deeper valleys played off the lighter sunlit green of the small mountain tops that looked like the white foam in a storm.

The valley emanating from the foot of the cliff ran at an angle to the southeast and spread out into a wide carpet of waving grasses and smaller trees.

The willow bordered river went along the base of the cliff and then tumbled and gurgled down continuous rapids as it flowed briskly and seemingly joyfully down the left side of the valley.

From their vantage point they could see their lodge looking more like a small pebble than the enormous structure they all knew it was. The pebble was located where the valley narrowed and ended. The river made its escape and went on to join another coming in from the north.

When it was time to leave, Burley Bear led the team out of the cave.

Taelo looked around and got Golden Hawk to help him close the cave opening with the boulders they found outside on the ground. It seemed to him that these were the same that had been used hundreds of seasons before.

Burley Bear and Quite Meadow took the lead as they returned to the valley floor.

The heavy snow began as they reached the valley floor and were about a third of the way back to the lodge.

"You will need to use the sled and wolves," Golden Hawk said as they arrived at the compound.

The two had discussed the other stories their fathers had told about the cave.

The team had decided to re-furbish the cave and put it into service.

"You go find the salt mine in the stories our fathers told us. I will work with Burley Bear and Little Otter to get the pipe and shower set up at the pool. We will celebrate upon your return by having a ceremony at the cave," Golden Hawk announced to the team and Taelo.

The second part of their journey was now becoming clearer. They did not know how Broken Spear had guided them to this valley of discovery, but they were convinced it was part of their development.

"Be careful and don't take any chances," Quiet Rabbit said a few days later as she gave Taelo a hug as he was about to depart.

There was a thick layer of newly fallen snow. The valley was a white wonderland where nothing seemed to be moving. Far to the northwest was the trail Little Otter had told Taelo about. It left the valley and went up to a ridge that seemingly ran to the coast.

"I think it is the same ridge that ends up at the top of the falls," Little Otter said as he pointed to the location of the trail.

Seeing it from the compound made it clear it was the same ridge.

"I will plan to come back by the same trail as I leave but in case of an emergency or other problem, I will signal from the cave. I will use the same code we always used as kids. Look for it at night or early morning," Taelo told Golden Hawk in one of their private conversations.

"Broken Spear warned me about meeting some evil warriors. I will not bring them to our valley or allow them to threaten our clan," Taelo told Golden Hawk in one of their conversations.

The journey across the valley was exhilarating. The wolves yelped in seeming enjoyment and were easily pulling the sled swiftly behind them.

Taelo stood on the runners and enjoyed the cold air hitting his cheeks as it rushed past him.

Good job Lasher," Taelo called out as he alternated riding on the sled and jogging along beside it.

At this point, the sled only carried his sleeping and cold weather gear, dried food, and enough other food to feed the wolves through the trip. As always, he planned to kill enough game as he traveled to prepare his evening meal.

He was holding a new sling with a stone in it for just that purpose. The sling was a gift from Feather-in-the-Wind. She had become better, with a sling, than anyone of the team had ever seen. One day she brought down a goose when the flock flew over the compound. She had hit the goose squarely on the head. Other similar feats finally convinced everyone they had a champion slinger in their midst.

By the time he crossed the valley he had bagged three rabbits. They seemed to be the only abundant game in the valley.

The snow seemed to clarify the trail. As Taelo came closer the trail appeared as a white passage bordered with dark green pine.

"The snow has made it easier to see the trail," Taelo thought as the sled began its climb to the top of the ridge.

"Keep it up boys," Taelo encourage his team.

He jogged along behind the sled even pushing it a little to help his team as they went upward. At the top he jumped back on as the team picked up speed. They were now traveling across an almost level ridge.

A large bull elk stood looking at the strange procession until the team was almost upon him and then he only moved far enough away to let them pass.

"It seems you know I am on the way out and do not want to be loaded down. Thank you for your interest and I hope you are verifying this is the right way to the salt mine," Taelo called out as if the elk would understand.

Taelo was proud of Lasher's ability to concentrate on pulling the sled versus chasing after the elk.

"All the training time in the valley paid off," Taelo thought to himself.

"I know I have traveled farther today than I have ever done before in this amount of time," Taelo thought as he called for a stop.

He had spotted a spring bubbling up from the ground. The area around the trail was wide at this point and would make a good place to camp.

"Well done, Lasher," Taelo said as he released him and rubbed him behind the ears.

He also gave him a large treat of dried meat soaked in water. Lasher ran off to check out the place.

Taelo released each of the wolves and gave each a treat and individual praise. Each wolf had a different reaction, but each eagerly took the treat. They were soon following Lasher on his exploratory round.

Taelo went about setting up the camp. He had arranged the sled so a leather hide could form the top of a shelter and another leather hide would form the bottom of the shelter. The sled would then be totally enclosed in the shelter and act as a main wall. This meant he could make camp without unloading the sled.

"Well boys let's eat our meals and get a goodnights sleep," Taelo said out loud as he salted one of the rabbits for himself and left the rest unsalted for the wolves.

They were all fast asleep when the sun set, and the moon rose into the night sky.

A few days later Taelo stopped the sled as the ridge came to an end.

Taelo could see a dark blue strip project from the dark green of the pine treetops that he figured was the ocean and then join the light blue sky at the point where a sharp line seemed to separate the two.

He walked to the head of the wolves and released Lasher and gave him a small treat.

"Stay" he said to the remaining eight wolves, and they sat down on their haunches.

He went down the line giving each a treat.

"Let's go find the trail down," he said to Lasher as he walked up ahead where the ridge clearly ended in a cliff down to a narrow valley below.

"I wish I remembered this part of the story better," Taelo said as he looked to his left and then to his right.

He walked out to the very edge of the cliff and stopped when the vertigo almost overcame his balance. From this vantage he could see a ridge to the left sloping down and connecting to another lower ridge going toward the sea.

"Thanks for worrying about me," Taelo said in response to Lasher's continued deep growl that had started when Taelo stepped out to the edge of the cliff.

Taelo found the trail to the left. He had missed it because the trail turned at a large boulder. As soon as he saw it, he recalled this part of the story. In Grey Fox Running's stories, he told of the ancestors moving the boulder to its current spot to mark the trail.

"I wish I had Golden Hawk with me. He probably would have recalled this part of the story," Taelo thought to himself as he stopped and looked for any markings on the boulder.

In the story the salt gatherers put a mark for each load of salt they brought back to the clan.

"My gosh! Here they are," Taelo exclaimed as he ran his hand across the white scratches put their eons ago.

He counted several hundred scratches. As far as Taelo could figure they were organized into seasons and the number of loads gathered each season. The clan had stayed in this area for almost a hundred years.

"I will add a new mark when we return with yet another load of salt for the Elk Clan," Taelo spoke out loud as he patted Lasher.

Lasher seemed to understand and gave Taelo a push with his snout.

Taelo returned to the sled and tied Lasher back into the lead position.

The team turned the corner around the boulder and then headed across a short connecting ridge and then turned back toward the west. They were now traveling slowly downward as they proceeded along the ridge. As they got down lower, they were constantly crossing from one ridge to another. There were marker boulders at every turn.

"I am glad I remembered this part of the story. Without the boulders it would be impossible to find the way. Even if you saw the boulders, without understanding what they signaled it would be impossible to find the way," Taelo said to himself as they rounded yet another boulder.

He had been counting the boulders and after the tenth one he looked for the small lake he had been told about in the story. It was there!

"Well let's stop, see if we can catch a fish and eat our dinner," Taelo said as he guided the team to the edge of the lake.

In the stories every salt gatherer stopped and ate fish caught in the lake. Taelo saw the fishing stone and with his spear jumped out to it and stood patiently as he looked into the clear water. A short time later a large trout came swimming by. In one swift movement Taelo plunged his spear into the water and gracefully flipped the fish onto the shore.

Lasher took it in his mouth and carried the still wiggling fish to the sled and put it down. He growled at the other wolves when they came to investigate, and they retreated. The scene was repeated five more times before Taelo came up and prepared the fish.

He had a few pieces of raw trout for each of the wolves.

"You my friend get the most," Taelo said as he generously fed Lasher.

Finally, he was down to the smallest trout which he put on a slender sapling, rubbed it with salt, and cooked it over the fire. This one was his.

The stories of my father are coming to life," Taelo thought to himself.

The story about fishing in the lake had been used to teach he and Golden Hawk about the parallax water caused when you looked down into it. One had to thrust the spear below where the fish appeared to be.

The salt gathers were usually the older hunters who could no longer see well enough or move fast to hunt. Their success at spearing a fish was an indicator of their wellbeing. When they could no longer spear the fish even their salt gathering days were over.

"We are only a day away from the salt mine," Taelo said as he gave Lasher a gentle rub down.

"You will come down from the ridge run and then go up a narrow valley along a cold-water stream running opposite to your direction. Suddenly to your right will be a stone spear, pointing to the sky. The salt mine is at the base of the stone spear point." Taelo recited the line he and Golden Hawk had played out over and over again as kids.

"Lasher this trip causes me to lose the sense of time, place, and identity," Taelo said as if Lasher could understand.

"I am the salt gatherer of old. I am my ancestor on a journey in the present. I am Taelo one moment and some ancestor the next," Taelo said quietly as he slowly fell asleep.

In his dream the eagle came down and took the eagle claw from his hand.

The next day the team was moving at a fast clip up the valley when suddenly the stone spear pointing to the sky came into view.

Taelo stopped the team immediately. He had wondered whether he would recognize the spear, but it was impossible to miss it. He released the team from their harness while praising each wolf as he gave each a snack. It was a bonding ritual repeated every day.

"Let's go find the mine and see if the story about cutting out the salt in blocks is true," Taelo said to Lasher.

After about an hour of looking for the opening Taelo let out a loud groan.

"I must have forgotten part of the story," he said to himself.

"Hold your spear vertically at your arms full reach. Spear tip to spear tip. Equal distance left and equal distance right. Six paces forward, six to your right," suddenly flashed through his mind.

He had forgotten this as part of the salt gathering story. He and Golden Hawk never did figure out what spear tip to spear tip meant. Now Taelo finally understood.

"I just hope we still make the standard spear the same length and that I am the right height," Taelo thought to himself as he held his spear at arm's length and positioned himself to look over his spear tip and aligned it with the tip of the stone needle pointing into the sky.

He took the steps as directed and stood looking. He was looking at a long crack in the face of the stone. He walked forward and into the crack. About halfway back he found a large opening to a completely black interior. He went back to the sled and retrieved several torches he had prepared for this part of his journey.

The shaft went back horizontally about six spear lengths and at that point opened into a large cavern.

"Look at all the salt," Taelo said to Lasher who was following at his heal.

The blocks that had been removed by his ancestors provided Taelo with a clue of the amount of salt each salt gatherer carried back to the valley.

The blocks were knee high squares. They were heavy enough that Taelo found it difficult to carry out of the cave.

"They must still have been in fairly good shape to carry so much salt," Taelo thought to himself as he put the fourth and final block on the sled.

Each of these blocks would have been carried on a person's back. It would have been a grueling trip back up to the main ridge and then across to the valley. A travois would most likely have been used for the last part of the trip to the valley.

It was time to return to the valley.

He was still not sure what the eagle cry that had started him on the trip was about. The salt was important but was the salt the reason for his trip? He had learned a lot about his ancestors. Was that the purpose of the trip?

Taelo was ready to return to the valley but there were still questions on his mind.

Chapter 17: The Heated Cave

The salt from the mine was a heavy load to pull back up to the top of the ridge. The sled was loaded to full capacity with salt, the dry food, several rabbits, and some frozen fish. The wolves were pulling at a good steady but slow pace.

He wanted to make it to the point in the trail where it went down into the valley. He knew Golden Hawk and the rest were expecting him back soon.

The black clouds coming in from the west darkened the ocean waters and made the dark green of the pines seem like a reflection of the sky. It came speeding at Taelo with winds that at times seemed to be on the verge of tilting the salt laden sled.

He quickly realized that he would not make the valley in the next few days.

Two grey plumes of smoke rose in stark contrast to the black background of the sky. One was far to the northwest close to the coast. The other near enough for him to smell, was just below him in a small valley.

He quietly stopped Lasher and the team of wolves. He walked up the line giving each a treat and released Lasher. Together they crawled to the edge of a small cliff that overlooked the valley.

To call it a camp was an over statement. There was something strange about its arrangement. There was a makeshift shelter up against a large boulder. A small fire burnt at the entrance to the shelter. There was no one in the opening to the shelter.

Thinking that perhaps they had heard him, he kept very still and observed the surrounding slopes and forest.

Night was falling swiftly, and the black sky made it impossible to see anything. The snow was now coming down so thick the camp was fading from view.

Taelo knew he was within a long day's run to the cave at the top of the falls. He would not go there until he could learn what was going on. He was not going to chance leading someone to it.

He decided to wait until morning to investigate the camp below and determine what his action would be.

He returned to his sled that had almost disappeared in the snow. His wolf team curled into balls that looked like white snow-covered boulders.

He wondered about the smoke by the sea, who were they and when had they arrived? Were these the people that Broken Spear had said he would rescue?

He undid the bundle holding his giant bear skin. This was his emergency shelter.

He brushed the snow off the sled cand quickly tied one edge of the hide along the far side of the sled along the side bars. He then pulled the hide over the sled and out about three feet and made a tunnel by looping the hide back around on top of the snow.

He closed each end of the tube, so he had a warm refuge from the storm. He put up stakes and used a long pole to hold the hide up.

He then crawled out and walked along the line of wolves. He gave each some food and water. Each had already made a comfortable hole in the snow, and they were ready to sleep.

Darkness and snow hid the entire surroundings. He could not see the sled from Lasher's lead position. Slowly he made his way along the line of wolves back to the sled. Each wolf greeted him on his way back but stayed curled in his hole. Lasher was the only one loose. He was following close behind.

The bearskin hung off the side of the sled like a loose layer of skin. After relieving himself, Taelo crawled inside making sure to keep as much of the snow as possible out of the pouch. He wanted a dry shelter for the night. Lasher crawled in with him.

He had access to the entire content of the sled. This allowed Taelo to easily get to the food and water.

"Well, it was a good run today. Let's see what tomorrow brings." he talked quietly to Lasher.

He ate some dried fish and took a drink of water. It had been a long journey from the coast to this location. For three days he had been moving south, southeast.

He was now running the main ridge leading to the waterfall above the valley. His goal had been the compound and a hot water bath.

Now he was unsure of what he should do next.

The smoke on the far horizon created uncertainty. Was there another clan in the region? Taelo and his team had arrived in this territory and for the last eight months found no other humans.

Long ago it had been the origin of the Elk Clan. The Clan had chosen to move south as the winters got more severe. He now knew of a group of people behind him along the ocean shore.

He had just left the area close to where the smoke seemed to be. There was also a group immediately below him.

A group living up in this area was a surprise. How had they gotten here? He was sure that they had not been there on his way down to the salt mine.

He hoped for a friendly meeting, but he would be carrying his shark toothed weapon on his back. New members would be a welcomed addition to the Northern Elk Clan.

He decided morning would be soon enough for him to unravel this mystery.

He felt grimy and would have loved to take a bath in the hot springs. He was looking forward to doing that tomorrow.

The wind picked up and the temperature was taking a dramatic dive. He could feel the cold penetrating through the bearskin.

He put up several small poles to hold up the bear skin but realized the snow was getting so thick that the skin was slowly being pushed down. He put up several more poles with interconnecting rods.

Finally, he decided to bring the other wolves in so that they would not suffocate in their holes.

Stay, he told Lasher and crawled out to release each of the other wolves. The wolves indeed were in distress. He undid their harness and guided them back to the bearskin and let them in. Each wolf found a comfortable location and curled up. He gave each wolf some more food and talked to them.

"Well, boys, it looks like this is going to be a very cold night. You are all welcome to gather round and sleep with me.

Throughout the night Taelo got up and brushed off the snow that was piling up over the sled. There was at least two feet of snow above the sled and the makeshift tent. His quick set up and the supporting poles had guaranteed him a warm secure alcove.

He wondered if the people below had been as well prepared.

The biggest challenge was to keep the inside of his shelter from getting too hot from the body heat from he and the wolves.

He had managed a few hours of sleep, but he felt exhausted. The sun was not yet coming up. He was relieved the snowfall had ceased. It was going to be a clear, cold day.

He was not sure how he would get the sled out of the spot it was in. The sled had disappeared under the snow. It and his shelter blended in with the hillside and was invisible and seemed just to be a mound of snow.

However, the first thing on his mind was the camp below. He crawled back out to the edge of the cliff.

There was no sign of life below, no smoke, no movement. In fact, he wondered if he had really seen the camp below. But yes, there was the large boulder where the lean-to had been. Now the boulder was barely above the snow.

He thought about moving on but instinctively he knew the people below needed his help. He decided he would go down and see what shape they were in.

He used his body to create a channel along the pulling rope that he kept between his legs as he pushed himself to the end of the rope.

He then turned left and went down the incline of the hill. The snow on the hill was only knee high and the going was easier.

Before going down he created several paths for the wolves to use to relieve themselves.

He warmed some snow over a small fire just outside of the shelter. He kept melting this into a bag until he had enough water for all of them to share.

The salty fish had made him thirsty, and he figured the wolves would be feeling thirsty as well.

He thought about the camp below and put some items into a bag to take with him.

He got out his teardrop shaped, leather webbed snowshoes that he had patiently made in preparation for just such an event. He gathered the other items on his list and put them into his backpack.

He again fed the wolf team and told them to behave until he returned. They all wagged their tails as he spoke to them as if they knew perfectly what he had just said. They all loved him, and he loved his wolves. This trip had made them his team.

Then he prepared himself to meet the people below.

The day was coming to life in a grey, yellow hue. The sun was hidden behind thick grey clouds. Taelo expected snow by early afternoon.

He walked to the front where he had broken out of the deep snow. He put on his snowshoes and then hoisted his backpack onto his back. He never went anywhere without this pack. It contained some medicines, splints, blankets, food, rope, a stone ax, and some miscellaneous things that he had thrown in.

The forest was silent. The quiet worried Taelo. When the animals were quiet there was either an enemy about or the weather was going to turn worse.

"Probably both," Taelo thought.

He made a cautious approach from the uphill side of the boulder. This was the opposite side from the lean to.

It was very cold, and the fallen snow was dry and powdery. Taelo sunk down to his knees in the snow. The going was slow. Going downhill was a difficult task. The quiet of the morning made each step sound loud to Taelo.

All was quiet.

"Too quiet," Taelo thought.

He could see where someone under the snow had poked a hole in the snow to let out the heat and let in the air. This at least let him know, whoever they were, they were still alive.

He called down into the hole. A weak voice answered from below.

Throughout the night Lily had stayed up and poked the air hole open. The lean-to they had made the night before was slowly breaking down. Blessedly the snow had sealed them in, and their body heat had been enough to ward off the numbing cold of the night and kept them from freezing to death.

Lily had stopped in exhaustion the previous night. She had barely managed to build the lean-to before the snowfall overwhelmed them.

They were too weak to go on. The two younger women did not seem to be aware that this was going to be their deathbed. The two children were in shock. Their parents were still captives back at the camp they had just escaped. Lily was sure they were being pursued.

Now a strange voice was calling down to her from above. She could not understand the person, but she knew he was not of the evil ones. She answered back weakly, and hope surged up from her soul. Perhaps they would survive. There were other people in this land. Perhaps they would be able to fight the fierce warriors who had overcome her clan.

She gave another call-in response to whomever was outside.

Taelo knew he had to get the group out of their current location and up to the cave. Another snow like last night would make their current camp a tomb.

He began to dig around the boulder. He was using one of his snowshoes as a shovel to scoop the snow aside. Slowly he made his way around to the lean-to. It was in shambles. The snow had formed an arch. This was the only reason the group had not been buried and suffocated.

Taelo uncovered five in all; three women and two children. One was a boy about twelve and the other was a girl perhaps a few years younger. They all looked frightened, exhausted, cold, and hungry. They looked like they had not eaten in days. None were dressed for this kind of weather.

Taelo concluded they were on the run.

"Hello and what are you doing out here without any food and clothing for this type of weather," Taelo said as he went back and got the pack that held his supplies.

He immediately registered their desperate condition. It appeared they had been horribly treated.

He passed around the bag of water that was eagerly consumed. He handed out about a mouthful of dried fish to each. He wanted them to have enough energy to hike up the steep hill but if they were in as bad shape as they seemed to be, he did not want to feed them too much and make them sick.

The stench coming from the five was overpowering. They all needed a bath much worse than he. They smelled like they had not washed in months and there was an odder of death to them.

He passed out another mouth full of dried fish and more water. He decided how he would share the blankets that he had brought. He gave each of the younger women a blanket. He then gave his light jacket to the children. He took off his outer jacket and then took off his inner shirt made from rabbit skins and gave this to the older woman and then wrapped the remains of the blanket that was in the lean-to over her shoulders.

He could see tears in the eyes of all three women. He did not know what their plight might be, but he knew that they had run away from something, and they probably had expected to die in this makeshift hut.

"Let's go find some warm water to wash the lot of you so that I can stand to talk to you," Taelo said politely.

With that he put on his jacket. He signaled them to follow him out and around the boulder.

The temperature was falling, and the wind was beginning to blow the dry snow. The weather was quickly getting worse.

Taelo stopped several times to allow the group to regain their energy. Each time he stopped he back tracked and hid their trail as best as he could.

"This man seems to know we are being tracked. He is working to hide our trail," Lily commented to the other four.

She sensed his strength and wisdom.

Taelo hoped a heavy snow in the afternoon would cover up the tracks. He suspected these women were being hunted.

He knew for sure that they were running.

The uphill climb would have been a challenge without the snow. It took until noon before they were back on the ridge. Taelo looked at the five and knew they were exhausted. He made a small fire and heated some water in a leather bag by dropping hot stones into it. He put some raw rabbit meat, some salt, a few dried onions, and other dried ingredients. By rotating his heating stones, he soon had a large quantity of hot rabbit soup.

"Look at this man. He cooks for us. He knows how to cook a wonderful stew. He has abundant food. It is hard to be polite when we are as hungry as we are," Mayflower spoke quietly to the other four.

The aroma was overwhelming.

Taelo only had two wooden bowls. When it was apparent the group did not know what the bowls were for, Taelo demonstrated the use of the bowl. The five had no problem in understanding and in sharing the two bowls. The soup worked a miracle on the group's behavior and energy.

They seemed to have new hope and they jabbered away as they watched him.

Taelo decided they were in good enough shape to help him get his sled loose and up to the cave. He estimated they had a full day's pull ahead. However, they were going to have to work fast and hard to make it before the next snow began.

He led the group back to where his sled was buried.

The wolves raced out toward him. The five people following him froze in their tracks.

Taelo got down on his knees and greeted the wolves in his arms. They were rested and were excited to see him return.

The group he had just rescued looked at him like he was a genie or a mad man.

"Look, the wolves greet him like he is their master. He must be a wolf man. That would explain why he is out and how he could survive in such weather. I have never seen wolves treat a human in this fashion," Lily observed.

Taelo went about clearing the snow from his lean-to and putting away his bear hide. He then cleared a path just a little wider than the sled.

Finally, when he had an open path and a way to guide the sled to a place where the snow was not as deep, he hitched the wolves up to the sled.

"The wolves work for him," Lily continued her comments to the rest.

It was clear to Taelo that the cave was much farther away than he had hoped.

Taelo positioned the bewildered women and the young boy around the sled to help push it out and then got the wolves to start pulling. The five understood what Taelo wanted them to do and pushed as hard as they could.

The sled broke free and slowly began moving up the ridge to where the snow was not as deep. Suddenly, the sled was up and out of the snow and back on top. The wolves were eager and ready to go.

Taelo spent another precious half hour covering his tracks as best he could and then put one of the women and the two children on the sled. He put the other two back on the extended runners. He got the nine wolves pulling. The sled started out slowly.

Taelo pushed and ran along behind until the momentum of the sled seemed to reach a critical point and the wolves were off and running at a good speed.

"Good job Lasher. Take us to the cave," Taelo spoke to his team as they pulled the heavy load.

He knew the wolves would love their hot baths when they got to the cave. He laughed to himself and received the puzzled look of those he had just rescued.

"This is a wild but generous man. I hope he is not mad," laughed one of the younger women. They were enjoying their ride.

The wolf team made much better time than Taelo had expected.

They passed by the trail leading down into the valley and continued to the top of the waterfall.

By the time they arrived at the river, the day had grown a deep dark gray and the snow had started falling in earnest. Taelo figured it would be another heavy snowfall.

It would be a race to unload all his supplies and get the group into cave before the snow once again covered the world.

He was pleased as he thought about the tracks behind him being covered by the snow.

The group he had just rescued stood around and looked at the river a little bewildered. There was no obvious shelter in sight.

"I hope our wolf man has not rescued us from one cold hole just to let us freeze out here in the open," the Lily spoke up again.

As they watched, Taelo walked across the rapids to a large rock. He began to remove some key boulders. Soon Taelo disappeared into the opening.

He went into the cave and lit the lamps around the entrance area.

It was clear Golden Hawk, Burley Bear and Little Otter had returned to clean and fix up the long unused cave. There was wood for a fire and the water pipe and shower had been repaired.

Taelo knew immediately that he was going to enjoy himself that evening.

He exited to greet the confused group he had just rescued.

Taelo wanted to get his supplies stored in the entrance to the cave

He praised the wolves and gave each a treat as he let them loose. Lasher led the way as he made a beeline for the cave. Lasher knew he was in for a warm night.

Taelo signaled the women to follow him.

"This man keeps surprising me with his ways and the wealth he has. Let's see what is inside his shelter," Lily commented to the other younger women.

"He has enough food to feed twenty people for the winter. I wonder where all the people are and if they will accept us," one of the younger women commented hopefully.

The warmth inside and the spacious surroundings caused all of them to stop and stare.

Taelo got the women to help him bring in the food. He stacked most of it in the cool area at the entrance to the cave.

Taelo unloaded the salt. He folded the sides of his sled flat and then took it inside as well. He carefully backtracked and covered all the tracks leading up to the cave and then arranged the stones so that he could put them up from inside. This effectively closed the crack and as the snow fell it looked as if no one had ever been there.

The women were surprised by the size and warmth of the cave.

The wolves had all found comfortable spots and were watching the scene around them.

Taelo collected all the clothes that he had given to the group. He took stock of what was needed to outfit them. They would be properly outfitted once they were down in the valley.

However, the first thing they needed was a bath. He walked over and pulled the plug stone from the hot water spring. The warm water flowed down the trench to the pool area.

"It is like magic. The water is warm," White Pearl said

Taelo always hated the smell of dried fish, but these people had the stench of death on them.

Taelo took some of the pine soap he found in the cave and took off his clothes and waded into the warm water pool. The group was standing around watching him and wondering what was going on. Taelo signaled for the young boy to come to him.

The young boy was in awe. First at the man standing by the pool and second by the steam rising from the water. However, he understood he was being called and walked hesitantly out into the pool.

The warm water felt pleasant against his skin. At first it was hot but then it just felt good. He reached down and splashed some water up on his chest.

Taelo lowered himself all the way to the point the water was over his head and then came back up. He indicated for the young boy to do the same. He could see fear in the boy's eyes. The boy, however, copied what he had just seen.

"Good, now let's get some of this soap into your hair and that grim off your body," Taelo said as he lathered up his own hair and then gave the ball of soap to the boy.

Taelo got out and put the channel logs into position. The hot water was rerouted through the channel logs to the mesh above the spring.

He then got back into the pool to enjoy the shower of water cascading down from above.

"Look he has made warm water rain," Lily said as she shed her clothes and waded into the pool.

Soon everyone was in the pool bathing. They all passed the soap around. The scent of pine and a faint smell of flowers replaced the stench that had been on them before.

Taelo gathered all the clothes that had been taken off and showed the women how he wanted them washed. The clothes were tattered, but it was too early to throw them out.

"The women are gaunt though they will be fairly good looking once they are fattened up a little," Taelo thought.

It looked like they had not eaten well in months.

Taelo used the young man to show the group how to use the facilities. There was one spot were some water was side streamed and a body could perch above it. The excrement was then washed out of the cave into the waterfall. This allowed the cave to remain clean. Taelo showed Lasher how to do this at another place by the outgoing stream. The other wolves learned to use this place as well. Taelo then washed their mess into the side stream.

"This is very strange," Gentle Fern, one of the young women commented.

"Yes, but it keeps us from having to go out in the cold and it makes this location almost impossible to smell out," White Pearl, the other young woman commented.

"You are right. When we were in front of the cave, we could not tell it was here. Usually, you can smell our caves from a great distance," Lily joined in.

The wolves were all on one side of the cave. They had gathered below a ledge.

Taelo went about preparing dinner for the wolves. He had killed several rabbits the day before. He now cooked up some of the meat and made sure each wolf got a good portion.

"Look, he feeds the wolves' better food than what we have eaten in months. I hope there is enough for us," Gentle Fern commented as she thought of going up to the wolves and fighting for the food.

"He has enough food for all of us. It is good to see that he takes care of the animals that serve him. I am sure he has enough food for all of us. We will need to learn how to prepare the food the way he likes it. We should plan to take care of ourselves and not wait for him to do all the work," the Lily said to the group around her.

Earlier Taelo had fed the rescued group lightly because they looked undernourished. He was afraid to give them too much too soon. Now he decided to cook bread in the bread bowl and cook another soup with pieces of rabbit and deer. He soon had all the ingredients in a large clay bowl and placed the bowl over the hot coals. The smell made all of them hungry.

This time there were enough bowls for all of them. Taelo passed the full bowls of stew out with a large piece of bread. He could tell the bread was something new to all of them. He enjoyed their surprise and their enthusiasm for it. There was no doubt about their hunger.

An animated discussion in a strange language exploded between the rescued women. Taelo could not understand one word.

"We should teach our men to cook," Lily commented as she went to the water and washed her bowl as she had just seen Taelo doing.

The others did the same and placed them on the ledge where Taelo had put his.

Taelo walked to the edge of the cave just to the right of the waterfall. The snow was falling heavily. There was still some grey daylight left and it allowed all to see the magnificent view down into the valley and out to where the river disappeared from view. It was hard to tell how high they were above the valley.

Taelo looked out. He imagined he could see the river at the other end and into the compound where Quiet Rabbit, Golden Hawk, Busy Bee, Burley Bear, Meadow Flower, Little Otter, and Talking Wren all were awaiting his return.

The rescued women and the two young children gathered around to look out into the valley. They were awe struck.

"What a beautiful place. The view out is one of the most magnificent that I have ever seen," Gentle Fern said quietly.

Yet it does not seem that this is his home.

It seemed that all Gentle Fern could remember was the fear, the hunger, and the atrocities she had seen and experienced for the last few weeks.

Taelo was very curious about their story but knew it had been a long day for all of them. He was ready for a good sleep. He showed them where they could each sleep and provided them with the hides and blankets Golden Hawk, Burley Bear and Little Otter had left in the cave.

Taelo would thank the three the next time he saw them.

He talked to each of his wolves. To Lasher, he said, "Keep an eye on these new people. Do not let them near me."

He was sure these strangers would not bother him, but he also did not want to be surprised if he was making a mistake in his judgment of them.

"Look he talks to his wolves. I am sure none of us could get near him without the wolves attacking us. He seems to be kind and generous enough. He has much wealth even though he has some peculiar ways. His cooking is better than most I have experienced, and the food is very good though strange. Let's all get a good night sleep," Mayflower spoke to the rest.

Everyone immediately found a comfortable place.

Taelo walked around and snuffed out the various torches around the cave.

He went to the cave opening and lit a small fire. He sent a signal to Quiet Rabbit who he knew would be watching for his safe return to the cave.

"He is signaling others," Lily observed as she relaxed for the first time in weeks and fell almost instantly asleep.

Chapter 18: The Cannibals

*T*aelo woke early as the grey of dawn was pushing the pitch black of the night westward toward oblivion. The two snow covered peaks to the southwest were two beacons of white above a black and dark green skirt surrounding them. He worked at starting the beacon fire and felt the same relief he always did when the heat hit his cheeks.

He sent the cryptic message that he had found new good, people and some bad people. He was going to investigate and would let the team know what he found out.

He was relieved to see a response acknowledgement. He said no to the question of sending help.

It was time for a good breakfast, so he cooked some boar and made some more bread.

By this time, it was light outside. And the light was enough that only a few torches were needed.

The smell of breakfast caused all to awaken. Taelo passed out the food and indicated that there was more.

He gave each of the wolves some food and then opened the exit and told Lasher to go have some fun. He walked to the river to make sure no one had been about.

He went back into the cave where the rescued group were washing their breakfast utensils.

They were conversing and looking about. Taelo took this as a sign that they were recovering and ready for him to learn what had happened to them and what they were running from.

Taelo gathered the group around him. He made a point of letting them know his name.

"I am Taelo," he said pointing his finger at his nose and chest.

They all understood.

The oldest spoke for them.

"I am Lily, this is Gentle Fern, next to her sits White Pearl. The children are Little Pearl and Running Stag. Their parents are being held captive by the cannibals," Lily rattled off.

Taelo understood the names and repeated each as he pointed to the person. He did this several times since he had never been good at remembering names.

Then Taelo took a stick and drew on the smooth dry powdery soil of the floor. He drew the camp where he had found them. He then drew a trail away from it back to where he had seen the plume of smoke.

He got a reaction from Lily. He handed the drawing stick to her.

Lily understood what was being asked. She drew the picture of a group of stick figures attacking a village. She then showed the villagers being herded into an enclosure.

The last scene was about one of the villagers being taken away. She enacted the process of the person being eaten as she drew the scene.

Taelo verified what he thought he understood. The hair on the back of his neck rose as a chill went down his back. He had heard stories that such people existed but had never met or talked to anyone that had met them.

Taelo showed the five of them running away and then drew a few people in the enclosure and pointed at it.

Lily drew five figures and then two more very lightly.

Taelo drew a picture of himself and one other person going back to the camp where the group had run from and then looked around at the five in front of him.

"Who will go back with me to rescue the ones still being held captive," Taelo inquired?

Taelo drew a picture of himself and one other person going back to the camp where the group had run from and then looked around at the five in front of him.

He asked if they would go back with him to rescue the remaining captives?

Lily understood the request and explained it to the group. The young women let out a moan and dropped their heads and indicated they would not go back. For them those in that camp were already dead.

Running Stag got up and came to Taelo. He was afraid of going back, but his mother and father were still in the camp. He was afraid but he would help. Running Stag drew a picture of a woman and a man in the enclosure and put his hand on his heart, to let Taelo know.

Taelo understood immediately that Running Stag's parents were the ones left behind.

Taelo drew a picture of Running Stag and then another much larger. He pointed to it and to Running Stag and then to his eyes to let him know how brave Taelo thought he was.

He stood up and walked to where the signal fire had now died out. He would leave tomorrow morning. He took time to prepare the signal fire and make it ready for use that night.

He would alert his team to the situation and let them know he was taking action against an enemy.

Throughout the day he worked on his weapons. He had a bow and two dozen arrows, a spear, a battle ax or hammer, and a cutting ax. The flat shark edged weapon he had made for each of his team members was his final weapon.

Taelo thought through how he and a willing but inexperienced boy could execute the rescue against a large group of cannibals.

He went out and found a limb with which to make as small bow for Running Stag.

Running Stag quickly grasped how to use this new weapon.

Next Taelo prepared a series of meals. He prepared enough food for the rescued people and himself to eat on the run without stopping.

Taelo had no doubt that the smoke on the coast came from the cannibal's camp.

He calculated six sun cycles to the coast and six sun cycles back

Throughout the day Taelo went to the part of the cave overlooking the valley. He could not afford to have a raiding group of cannibalistic people on the loose.

If he had the opportunity, he would annihilate all the cannibals. This thought bothered him, but he did not have the luxury to allow such a group of people to roam and hunt in the same territory as he and his clan.

He steeled himself to the grim decision he had reached with the cloak of the memories of his joyous youth and the vision of the life he wanted for his children.

By evening he had a plan. He and Running Stag would approach the camp from a downwind position and observe the camp.

Using his bow, Taelo would silently kill as many of those in the camp as possible.

When discovered, he would draw them out and move about so he could take them on one at a time.

Running Stag would stay to the edge of the camp and protect Taelo from side attacks. He would have only a few arrows and the cutting ax.

Lasher and the other wolves would stay with Running Stag and would be released when the battle became overwhelming.

Throughout the afternoon, Taelo had Running Stag practicing with the bow. He was not expecting much help from him, but he felt that the young man should have some sort of self-protection. He also knew that in the one-sided attack he was planning, any help would be welcome.

Perhaps some of the captives could help him as well.

Taelo rehearsed the upcoming battle and made mental adjustments to the variations he could think of.

Lily and the others stayed away. They were ashamed for not having the courage to volunteer.

Taelo did not hold that against them. It was clear they had already been brutalized and abused.

By late afternoon, he called them to him and explained as best he could about where the food was and how to prepare it. Then he indicated that he would be gone for fourteen sun cycles.

He went about finalizing the preparations. He would take as many warm clothes as possible. He took enough food for ten people. He organized all the materials in front of the opening leading out of the cave.

Afterwards he and Running Stag took a long hot bath. They dried off, had a snack of dried meat, and then went to bed.

Early in the morning, with the sun just touching the white tops of the twin mountains. Taelo was at the ledge lighting his signal fire.

He saw a distant twinkle at the far end of the valley that let him know the team was watching.

He sent a good morning signal and received a reply.

Slowly, Taelo told those below about the cannibal enemy. He let them know he would kill the enemy.

There was no signal he knew to describe a cannibal. He signaled, "enemy."

High above, up in the rays of the early morning sun that had not yet robbed the dark from the valley, an eagle let out a long cry and flew toward Taelo. From his vantage point it appeared to Taelo he was looking eye to eye at the eagle.

"Well, my friend, I hope you are signaling my success and not my demise," Taelo spoke quietly to his totem.

The reply from the valley asked him to wait for some more help.

It would take them at least another day to get to the cave. He didn't believe he had that much time.

Taelo signaled as best he could that he wanted no help. The team should prepare to house ten to twelve more people.

He had the help that surprise, cunning, and ruthlessness would provide.

He would take no prisoners.

"Well, it seems Taelo is off to face a major test. Golden Hawk, please go to the cave and prepare for his return. We can take care of our defense here if it comes to that. Meanwhile the group Taelo has brought to the cave is alone," Quiet Rabbit commented.

"Yes, that is a good plan. We will meet him halfway. You will stay here and prepare for the entire group. I will go to the cave. That way he will have some help when he returns," Golden Hawk said agreeing to Quiet Rabbit's request.

He knew he could not stay in camp. He needed to get to where he could be of some help.

They all agreed that this would be the best plan. Golden Hawk got out his wolf sled. This would be the first real use of this new way of getting about. His wolves were eager to go. They loved to be out in this weather. It would be at least a day's travel to the base of the trail up to the cave. He would spend the night at the foot of the cliff and then take the trail up the next day.

So as Taelo pulled away from the cave, Golden Hawk was preparing to go up the valley. He would have a smooth trip until he got to the end of the valley.

Taelo took the ridges back across the mountains. The day went swiftly by as he let the wolves run at their own pace. The sled was relatively light, and they made excellent time.

He wanted to cross the stone arch before the sunset. This crossing was tricky because the wind from the valley whipped through the gap between the two mountain ridges.

The arch was at least five hundred feet above the valley floor. Even on a good day it was a frightening crossing. As he approached the arch the snow had started coming down heavily and a cross wind was creating a snow curtain making it hard to see the other side. He chose not to think about it and started his run from the far-left side toward the opposite far-right side.

The wolf team was running at top speed and at first seemed to be doing fine. Then Taelo saw Lasher blown off his feet.

Taelo yelled at his team and at the same time jumped off the sled and pushed it with all his might toward the far side.

Lasher recovered almost instantaneously and was once again up and pulling but the wind was slowly pushing the sled toward the left edge of the bridge.

Suddenly the wind was cut off by the peaks on the opposite side. Taelo, the wolves and sled all collided with the side of the mountain.

Taelo was immediately up and calling for his wolves to pull. The sled shot out and around the side of the mountain. Up ahead was a stand of pine. Taelo called for a stop and pushed the sled into the center of the group of pines.

He quickly checked the team and thanked them for their effort as he gave them each a treat and let them loose. The wolves sat on their haunches. They seemed to know how close that call had been. They all gathered around Taelo and enjoyed his praise and licked his cheeks.

Taelo sat and enjoyed the attention of the wolf team. He hugged Lasher and thanked him for leading the team.

Taelo showed Running Stag how to put up the sled tent. This provided an immediate shelter and with the two of them and the wolves inside, it was soon warm enough to take off most of their outer winter clothing.

Taelo talked quietly to the wolves and shared their names with Running Stag.

They had made tremendous time across the mountains. The way had been mostly level to downhill and the wind had been at their back or at least neutral.

After the evening's dinner and other rituals, the group was ready for a good night's sleep. This came immediately to all of them.

Early, in the morning just prior to daylight, Lasher's deep throated growl awakened Taelo. Immediately Taelo was on alert.

This was Lasher growl when he felt a threat to Taelo.

Taelo awakened Running Stag and indicated for him to get dressed but to be quiet.

After slipping on his boots, snow pants, jacket, and gloves, Taelo crawled out on his hands and knees and slowly stood up next to one of the pine trees.

Lasher was at his side.

Taelo gave the command for Lasher to stop growling.

He looked down into a camp of six lodges and one large cooking area.

The pine stand that he was in was almost directly above the Cannibal's camp. It appeared as if the camp had been hastily put up. Those below had probably been traveling up the valley when the weather closed in.

Taelo watched for a good hour. He counted twenty warriors and ten females. He had seen only two younger women carrying babies.

He was surprised at the small stature of the people below. They were all about two thirds of a spear high. They were powerful looking people. The warriors appeared to be almost as wide as they were tall.

He concluded that he would face a very dangerous enemy and he had no room for error. He had not expected fewer warriors.

He returned to the tent to let Running Stag know of the situation. He was pleased to see the young man had gotten dressed and had laid out all the weapons.

Taelo increased the number of arrows he had to twenty-four. This left Running Stag with only two.

"You will come with me until we get just above the camp. Your job will be to shoot any person trying to run out of the camp. You will have five of the wolves to help you. When an enemy runs out of camp you tell the wolves to kill. Can you say kill," Taelo asked as he finished drawing out the role the young boy would play?

Kill," Running Stag replied.

"Very good, now I want you to be very quiet as we go down. We will wait until after lunch before we attack," Taelo said as they finished their breakfast.

Taelo made sure they each had a solid breakfast.

He approached the camp from the down-wind side. The small pine and the brush in that area provided him cover for his sneak attack.

The boulders and evergreens provided enough cover for them to get down within accurate arrow range. Taelo could hear the camp members speak to each other. Several times they pointed up the valley. He would have to be careful in case there was a group out ahead of the main party. He estimated that with a clan this large the group out ahead would probably number five or six.

Suddenly there was a clamor from one of the makeshift shelters. Several warriors were dragging a tall male out and toward a pole. It appeared he would be the next victim to be killed and eaten.

Taelo decided this would be the time to start his attack. He determined the order in which he would shoot. He targeted the rearmost warrior. The arrow hit home, and the warrior was down without a sound. The next three arrows were off and hit home before anyone noticed.

Even then no one reacted other than to raise their spears and look around. It appeared this group had never seen an arrow.

Standing behind his evergreen blind, Taelo continued to pick off the warriors in the order he had selected. He was methodical and deadly in his shots. He had downed sixteen warriors before they figured out where he was. Then the remaining group charged the evergreen blind.

Taelo quietly called out to Running Stag to tell the wolves to kill as he stepped out from behind the pines.

Lasher and the attacking wolves caused additional confusion and slowed the warriors down.

By the time the warriors recovered there were only three standing, and the wolves were on them and taking them down.

Taelo stepped in with his war hammer and crushed the skulls of the remaining warriors. He did the same with every warrior that he approached. Most were severely wounded, but he showed no mercy.

Some of the women took up spears and attacked Taelo, but they were no match for his might and swiftness. In no time the eight of them were dead.

Taelo approached the first hut and sent one of his wolves in. They surrounded a young woman and her two small children.

"I am sorry little mother but only your children will live this day," Taelo said.

She seemed to understand and handed him the infants. At the last moment she lunged at him with a knife. She was growling with hatred in her eyes.

Taelo stepped back and his war hammer found the side of her skull and brought her eyes to peace.

As Taelo stepped out with a child in each arm, he was met by a single warrior.

"Well, you must have been late getting up today. I didn't count you. I don't suppose you will let me set the children down," Taelo said pleasantly with a smile on his face.

This calm reaction confused the warrior and caused him to hesitate.

Suddenly an arrow struck the warrior in the leg. This distraction was all Taelo needed. He dropped the two children in the snow and pulled his shark tipped weapon from its holder on his back and he split the warrior's skull.

The camp was now quiet, but Taelo knew that he was short two cannibal women and maybe some children. He sent Lasher out.

"Find," Taelo shouted and circled his fingers around the camp.

Immediately Lasher and the wolves began a spiral run around the camp. A few minutes later they had their quarry just beyond the edge of the camp.

"Running Stag help free your people," Taelo signaled his young ally as he walked out to carry out the cruel but necessary task.

When Taelo returned, he held one more cannibal infant.

Running Stag was standing by a woman Taelo guessed was his mother. It appeared that the man that had been dragged out was his father. His legs had been broken. This was often a method used during battle to incapacitate an enemy before torturing and killing him. Taelo guessed the cannibals used this method to maintain control over the most dangerous victims. It allowed them to keep them alive until they were to be the dinner menu.

There was also another half dozen women and children. It appeared they had been kept alive while the more dangerous warriors had been dealt with.

Taelo pointed up the hill to where the sled was and instructed Running Stag to bring down the bag with food and the bag with his emergency supplies.

Running Stag shook his head in affirmation and raced up the slope.

Taelo selected the three women who seemed to be in the best shape and had them pull all the bodies to the center of the camp. Taelo gathered all the weapons that were of any value and lay them aside. Next, he began to layer wood and bodies. He used all the materials in the camp. The group saw what he was doing and helped. Soon everything was ready.

Later, Taelo would light the pile and send the dead to the next world.

There was a whoop from the mountain side, and he could see the sled and Running Stag come sailing down the mountain side together.

Taelo ran out to meet the bullet coming down the slope. He hoped that neither the young man nor the sled would incur permanent damage. He caught each with a hand and they all went down together.

Taelo stood up and looked down at the thoroughly frightened young man.

"Well, you conquered your enemy, saved my life and then you try to commit suicide. I suppose you have a good reason for your actions," Taelo said as he helped Running Stag to get up.

"Thanks for bringing the sled down," Taelo said as he set it up right and began to distribute the individual bags of food.

It was clear that they all had little to eat in their captivity.

Taelo approached the only surviving male of the group. He was still on the ground and his wife; Golden Flower was trying to feed him.

Taelo stopped her from feeding him.

"Let him have something to drink," Taelo said giving her a bag of water.

Taelo removed the man's tattered leggings and examined the breaks. They were bad. He was not sure he would be able to set them.

He brought out his soap and water and carefully cleaned the man's legs.

Taelo went back to the sled and took out his splint kit and the ceramic bottle of almost pure alcohol.

He handed the bottle to Golden Flower and told her to give it to her husband to drink. Meanwhile he picked out two of the other women and drew pictures of what he wanted them to do.

When he returned to the man, Taelo was pleased to see that he had consumed about half the bottle and had passed out.

"Well, the amount he drank should keep him out for at least a day," Taelo said as he picked up the ceramic bottle and felt how much was left.

This would give Taelo the time to set the bones in the man's legs.

He had Golden Flower sit on her husband's hips. The two younger women pulled on the ankle. Taelo carefully moved the bones into position. He probed the bones with his fingers and lined them up as best he could. He could feel the pieces as they clicked into place. Then with the help of Running Stag he put splints on the leg. They repeated this on the second leg and then Taelo showed Golden Flower how to finish giving her husband a washcloth bath.

Once her husband was clean Taelo gave Golden Flower a warm hide to wrap him. When this was accomplished, he and Running Stag put his father into the sled to sleep.

Taelo had each of the women and the two additional children all bathe and clean up. After each was done, they were given clean warm hides. The day was quickly passing and Taelo wanted to move away from the camp.

He gathered the group at the center of the camp and ignited the funeral pyre. He gave thanks to the powers above for their help and asked their forgiveness for his lack of mercy. Several members of the group said something, and they all cried.

Taelo led his band up the hill away from the funeral pyre. They would make camp by a rock walled area he recalled that was up along the ridge.

He put the infants and children in the sled with Golden Flower and another woman. This left three women, Running Stag and Taelo outside. He positioned the three on the back of the sled. He and Running Stag ran along the side of the sled.

They moved at a jogging speed for about three hours. They only stopped periodically to get a little breather and then proceeded on.

The full moon was up and night well on its way when Taelo recognized the area where he planned to stay. The distance had been farther than he had expected.

Chapter 19: Golden Hawk's Rescue

He was exhausted. It was clear those he had rescued were exhausted. He handed out some dry food for each of them to eat.

He enrolled Running Stag to help him set up the camp. He moved the sled a spear's length distance out from and parallel to a vertical rock wall. The wall provided shelter from the cold night wind. He extended the bearskin and attached it to crevices in the rock to create a large and comfortable sleeping area.

He put out several hides that could be used to sleep on and he had the group collect some dry pine droppings to create a warm surface to lay on.

The missing group of cannibals made him feel uneasy and he did not want to be surprised.

He went out with the wolves to scout the surrounding area. He picked out a place above the camp where he and Running Stag would spend the night.

Taelo told him to get some sleep and that he would get the early morning watch.

The night went by quietly. Taelo thought he saw a far-off fire but was not sure. When he looked back, he could not locate it.

He woke Running Stag and caught a quick nap before sunrise.

A rejuvenated Golden Flower took control of the rescued group and instructed them on taking down the camp and putting everything back on the sled. She was determined to help the person who had taken such an extreme risk to rescue them.

She still could not believe that her young son and one warrior could have defeated the cannibal warriors.

Taelo harnessed the wolves to pull the sled up the mountain side. Wise Council was now awake but with two broken legs. All he could do was to watch. His legs ached but the pain was at a level he could manage.

Taelo put Running Stag at the point and told him to get to the top where the ridge ran flat to the left.

Meanwhile Taelo erased all possible signs of the camp. He then followed the trail up the mountain side erasing all the tell-tale signs he could. If another snow occurred, all traces of their passing would be erased.

They reached the ridge leading to the cave as the sun reached its zenith.

Taelo had seen no sign of the cannibal warriors and his apprehension and concern increased as the sun traveled its course. He decided to stop the group when they came to a stand of pines that provided a fair shelter.

They were a short distance from the cave and Taelo decided to go by foot so he could scout the trail and be prepared to meet the group that he thought would be ahead of him.

He distributed the captured weapons to the women and through some pictures explained that he and Running Stag would scout ahead and would return by nightfall.

If they were not back by tomorrow, then the group should proceed cautiously up the trail until they reached the top of the mountain.

Taelo and Running Stag left with their weapons and an emergency backpack. Taelo was sure somewhere ahead they would meet the remaining cannibal warriors.

As the sun traveled slowly across the sky toward the horizon, Taelo traveled a long lazy zig-zag path toward the cave.

He had Running Stag maintain a slow steady pace up the trail. He had indicated to Running Stag that if the warriors came into view, he should race back to Taelo.

Taelo realized that they were almost to the cave.

Had the cannibals found the cave?

They arrived at the bank of the river opposite of the cave. He guided Running Stag around to the left and away from the entrance to the cave. He was looking for signs of the warriors. He was just about to turn the corner around a boulder when he heard someone speaking.

He and Running Stag froze in their tracks. Slowly he backed up and went into the brush. He knew that he needed the element of surprise. He wanted to reduce the number of able warriors to one or two before he faced them head on.

He took out his bow and loosened the arrows in the carrying sheaf. This time he and Running Stag had the same number of arrows.

They would both be shooting when the fray started.

One of the warriors came around the boulder looking for a place to relieve himself. He must have smelled something in the air because he became very still and began to look around. Taelo stood still but his arm pulled back the arrow to its full length. When the warrior looked directly at him, Taelo let the arrow fly. The arrow entered the front just below the diaphragm and stuck out of the warrior's back. A second arrow almost simultaneously went through the warrior's throat.

Taelo would have to ask Running Stag if the throat had been the target.

Taelo and Running Stag quickly moved through the brush around to the front side of the boulder.

There were five more warriors squatting around an open fire.

Tied to a pole and stripped to his waist was Golden Hawk. He had a cut on his forehead but other than that did not seem to be hurt.

The spear end burning in the fire made it look like the warriors were getting ready to torture Golden Hawk.

One of the warriors called over his shoulder to the missing companion that had gone around the rock. He then got up and walked to the boulder and began to go around. As he spun around to warn the rest of his team, Taelo's arrow entered the warrior's throat and went out the back of his neck. The force of the arrow caused him to fall back behind the boulder out of sight.

Golden Hawk was the only one who had seen what had just transpired. He had been resolved to die a warrior's death but now he got ready to protect himself. The pole he was tied to was loose in the ground. He figured he could pull it out and knock over one of the warriors if he got the opportunity.

A third warrior got up to see what was going on behind the boulder. He had taken only a few steps when he spun around to warn the rest and was met with the same fate as the last warrior.

The remaining two warriors stood up to see what had happened and Taelo and Running Stag both let their arrows fly.

Taelo's arrow went through the diaphragm and out the back. Running Stag's arrow did not have the punch and stopped about a third of the way in. This warrior staggered toward Taelo who finished him off with the war hammer.

Taelo cut Golden Hawk loose and chided him for not listening to his instructions, but he gave him a great bear hug.

Golden Hawk looked at both and thanked them for saving his life.

Taelo introduced Running Stag as an up-and-coming young warrior of the Northern Elk Clan.

"Thank you, Running Stag for coming to my aid and saving my skin," Golden Hawk said extending his hand and shaking hands.

"This young man has earned a high place in our family. Yesterday he saved me during the battle at the cannibal's base camp and now he participates in saving you. Later we will have to have a ceremony making him an official warrior," Taelo said to Golden Hawk.

"Let's clean up this mess and then get into the cave," Taelo said as he looked around.

They arranged the bodies that they would latter move out into the forest. They then collected the weapons, retrieved the unbroken arrows, and recouped the arrow heads and feathers from the broken ones.

"Running Stag, run back to the sled and tell the group to get up here as quickly as possible," Taelo instructed in both words and pictures.

Running Stag set off on a fast jog and was soon out of sight.

Running Stag's energy carried him swiftly along the trail. He had been praised by Taelo and had met Taelo's friend. He replayed his own part in the last two battles and felt proud of his bravery. His mother and father had been saved. He felt sad for, White Pearl and Gentle Fern since one had lost her father and the other had lost both mother and father.

He was running almost full speed when he saw the sled ahead in the brush. After some animated chatter as he explained the brief battle, the group got ready to get under way. Running Stag stood next to the wolf line trying to remember what Taelo said to get the wolves running.

"Come on Lasher, let's get this team running for home," Running Stag mouthed the words he did not understand and was pleased to see the wolves begin to pull the sled.

The wolves recognized the cave entrance and stopped on their own.

By the looks of it the cannibal warriors had walked right up to the cave entrance and not recognized it as such. Taelo had put a lot of snow on the rocks at the entrance and it looked just like some rock pile.

"Hello, the cave, this is Taelo," Taelo called out as he pulled the stones out.

He was greeted by four women holding spears pointed at his chest.

"Very good, I am glad that you are willing to fight for this territory. But now please put them away," Taelo said with a grin as he pushed the spear points aside.

The women began to jabber when Golden Hawk stepped in behind Taelo.

"Ladies this is Golden Hawk. He is my best friend and fellow clan leader" Taelo said in introduction.

Taelo organized the women to make dinner for a total of seventeen people. He and Golden Hawk put the young boar Taelo had killed on a spit and put it over the fire.

Taelo asked Lily to manage the cooking. He placed some sweet potatoes in the coals of the fire.

Golden Hawk explained that he had left his sled down at the foot of the cliff and had come up the crack by foot. He excused himself and said he would return with his sled and team of wolves.

The sky had gone dark as the sled with those Taelo had rescued arrived.

Taelo came out to greet the group and helped carry Wise Council into the cave. He put Wise Council on the only flat place in the cave. This was the place Taelo had slept.

There was a silence when those in the cave realized that only one grown man was left alive.

Gentle Fern and White Pearl both let out a cry and White Pearl fell to her knees and hugged Lily's waist as she let out a moan and continued to cry.

"Lily, please help this group take a bath and after they have bathed, we can get them dressed in clean clothing. Gentle Fern, White Pearl, and Running Stag, please wash the clothing that has been used and then hang them to dry.

Golden Hawk and his team of wolves arrived, and the cave had two wolf teams and nineteen people.

"We seem to have doubled the size of the Northern Elk Clan. Soon we will be as big and strong as any of the other Elk Clans," Golden Hawk conjectured.

"Well don't celebrate too soon. They will soon become used to us and then they will begin to demand things their way. I am sure there will be a constant battle as we learn to be one clan," Taelo said as he looked over the group.

The three young babies, the only survivors from the fight against the cannibals were passed around among the women.

Once everyone was bathed and clean, dinner was served. Everyone had a large appetite, and the boar and sweet potato dinner was a tremendous hit. The entire group had been starved for so long that they could not get over the abundance of food.

Taelo took all of them to the cave where it overlooked the valley.

"I am sorry for your anguish. I cannot replace your loved ones, but I can offer you a warm home where you will find kindness and love in the valley below," Taelo said in a voice that exuded sadness and kindness.

"Tonight, we will tell stories of our friends and loved ones and we will escort them to their resting place with the ancestors," Taelo said and drew the message out in the dirt floor.

After dinner, Taelo poured some cider into a large cup and began to pass it around. Each person who it came to was required to tell a story before they were allowed to drink.

Taelo started it off by telling the group about his surprise at finding the first group of women. Even though they could not understand each other directly, the stories began to come forth and when it was important for the group to understand each other, pictures were drawn until the story was understood.

This got everyone in a good mood and soon there was some laughter. There were also tears when certain stories were told about those who had died.

Taelo knew that it was important to remember both the good and the bad.

By the time the cup came back to him, Taelo decided it was time to get the group to bed. He made one more prayer to the ancestors who watched over them.

"Our enemy was cruel. They killed and ate our brethren. This is wrong and they have been punished. However, take their spirits, correct their behavior, and make them understand that they must treat the souls of mankind differently then they treat animals. I ask you to forgive my cold and cruel approach to this problem, but I acted as I thought I must," Taelo finished and put the cup down.

"Someday this group may understand what you just said but I know you did the right thing and I thank you," Golden Hawk said as he gave Taelo a hug.

Everyone else but Wise Council did the same thing and then the group broke up and each went to a chosen location to sleep. Taelo decided to sleep near the opening of the cave where it overlooked the valley. He wrapped himself up in his favorite sheepskin blankets and sat down.

Golden Hawk chose to sleep by his side.

They talked about the events of the day and finally fell asleep.

Taelo slept an extremely deep sleep. He had exerted himself in the last few days and now the danger was over. He slept long after the sun had come up. No one dared to bother him.

Golden Hawk had gotten up early and sent a message to those in the valley. He had sent the number of people and the fact the enemy had been eliminated.

He began the breakfast fire and was cooking up some eggs, bread, and tea when some of the women gathered around to help him.

"The men of this clan all seem able to clean and cook. They must have very strong mothers," Lily commented to the young women around her.

By the time Taelo woke up almost the entire group had been fed. He got up and thanked Golden Hawk for the cup of tea that he was given.

Taelo went over to Wise Council and checked on his splint. The skin looked healthy, and the binding did not seem too tight. He and Golden Hawk carried Wise Council to the edge of the hot springs and showed Golden Flower how to wash Wise Council down.

The group was not use to daily washing in water, but they were quickly getting use to this strange way and were even enjoying the good feeling it gave them. It also got rid of the fleas that usually infested them.

Taelo and Golden Hawk decided they would take their new Clan members down to the lodge.

They directed everyone in cleaning the cave and then took the sleds out of the cave and loaded them up.

They would be at the lodge by the time the sun went down behind the sentinel pines and the sky darkened to show the multitude of stars that studded the winter sky.

Chapter 20: Down to the Valley

The hot water cave was washed cleaned and straightened out. A minimum of supplies and goods were left behind for emergencies or for someone stopping in as they had.

The fish, meats, and salt Taelo had stored in the cave was put on Golden Hawk's sled. Wise Council was carefully put on Taelo's sled. By late afternoon they had reached the valley floor and were heading across the valley toward the compound. Taelo pushed the group on throughout the day and into the full moon lit night.

With two sleds and the extra wolf team, the trip down into the valley went smoothly.

They made brief nature breaks and ate lunch on the go. The sky was gray and heavy with snow and the wind was once again howling and whistling through the forest at the sides of the valley.

Taelo and Golden Hawk both spotted the signal fire while they were still a few miles away. The day was just past, but the fire provided an excellent homing beacon, and the wolves were pulling hard to get home to their beds.

Golden Hawk had the lead sled and came roaring up to the opening of the compound and ran ahead to give Busy Bee a hug for a greeting.

Taelo followed immediately after. Quiet Rabbit ran into Taelo's arms.

They stood and looked over the group that was now getting out of the sleds.

"These seem to be good people. We were wondering how to get started as a new clan. I think we have been given the answer. Let's get unloaded and get this group in and fed," Taelo said.

Burly Bear came out and let out a roar of a welcome. Everyone stopped in their tracks. Taelo went up to him and gave him a hug as well.

"Well, my friend, what is all the noise for," Taelo asked?

"How could you leave me out of such a glorious battle," Burly Bear asked.

He and Taelo went around and released all the wolves from their harness. The wolves knew what to do and were soon inside the compound at their places and eating the food put out for them.

By the time the humans had the sleds unloaded most of the wolves were curled up sleeping. The only one still awake was Lasher and he was half asleep, but he always slept at Taelo's side. He was waiting for his master to go to his bed.

Taelo closed the compound's gate with the help of Burley Bear. Burley Bear took control of the group and led them inside the compound and into the living quarters. There were curtains to make six sleeping areas.

Meadow Flower had grilled some elk and made a stew with some of the vegetables brought back from the Valley of Plenty.

Busy Bee, Meadow Flower, Talking Wren, and Quiet Rabbit served the entire group in wooden bowls and wooden plates. This new group got its first experience using a spoon and chopsticks. There was much laughing and joking as they watched Golden Hawk skillfully eat his food and then someone would try to copy what he was doing.

Feather-in-the-Wind quietly showed Running Stag how to use the chopsticks.

After the eating was done, Busy Bee organized a cleanup crew and supervised them until the place was clean and ready for the next day. The new group was impressed by the organization and the cleanliness of their hosts. There were many things that the new group seemed clueless about. This was especially true about the washing procedure. They had not used bowls and wooden platters in their clan.

Before bedtime Taelo went out to the hot springs and washed up. He had Burly Bear bring Wise Council out with him and helped him wash himself.

He watched as Golden Flower came out with Gentle Fern. The two quietly took a bath prior to going to bed. The hot water and the cool night air were invigorating and very enjoyable.

"Well, I no longer have the position of being the newest member of the clan," Feather-in-the-Wind said as she came out from the lodge and joined Burley Bear, Taelo and Golden Hawk.

Lily brought out White Pearl and washed up. Running Stag washed up likewise.

Once this group was done, they went in, and the other women came out and all took a bath.

Taelo was pleased the young women all got together to bath the three small infants and watched as they then took them to bed.

He would organize the group tomorrow and give them each a role and duties to contribute to the work running of their new clan.

The clan needed a name. He would hold a contest to determine what it would be. Taelo fell asleep, as he often did, thinking about the future. Quiet Rabbit was on his left and with his right hand he absent-mindedly scratched Lasher behind the ears.

Taelo and Golden Hawk were up and walking the stream to the river long before anyone else was up. They were discussing how to organize their new group. They knew the compound needed to be reorganized and the group needed to spread out.

They decided the compound would be reserved for group activities and individual living quarters would be built around the base of the mound. They looked back and discussed the new arrangements. Their plan meant more flat stone needed to be brought from the cliffs to the compound. Additionally, timbers and boulders would need to be brought in from the forest.

The preparation of materials could go on throughout the winter. In the spring when the weather warmed, they would be ready for some serious building.

The two discussed how the group should be governed. In their journey to the south and the interaction with the people there they had learned a great deal about how they ruled the people in their territory. Some of these rules made sense.

However, the Elk Clan managed their area with fewer rules and more freedom. They did not have need for the entire system, but they could use some of the organizational structure they had learned about to better guide this new clan.

The new members would need to be educated so they could be tapped for some of the leadership roles.

This brought the two to the education of the group. They decided this education was the priority. They needed to be able to converse and to talk through ideas if they were going to form a true clan.

Taelo turned and looked up the valley and recalled the time he, Golden Hawk, and Burley Bear had made the trip to a similar valley. It was at that time they had earned their full status in the clan. They had bonded into lifelong friends and now they were together forming a clan of their own.

He recalled his life's love, Quiet Rabbit. How they had hunted together and come together in realization they were meant for each other. There was not a day in which she was not in his heart.

Taelo and Golden Hawk were discussing how the village should be organized when Lasher's deep growl instantly stopped their discussion.

About thirty dire wolves were between them and the compound. The dire wolves were about twice the size of Lasher and his kind.

Lasher was much faster but in a head-on fight like this he didn't stand a chance.

Taelo instantly let out a piercing whistle. His only hope would be to have his entire set of wolves attack the dire wolf pack from behind.

Golden Hawk immediately understood and called his own wolves out. Each of them pulled their war club from their back and let out a war cry and attacked head on. The wolves from the compound came rushing silently out.

Taelo and Golden Hawk gave a series of loud battle cries.

Burley Bear heard the battle cries and immediately took up his spears and war club and ran out of the building. The women and Running Stag did not know what was happening, but they all took up their weapons and ran out behind Burley Bear.

The head on attack surprised the dire wolf pack. They were not used to being challenged. They were just starting to engage the two wild men and the lone wolf when they were attacked by about thirty of their wolf enemies from behind.

Burley Bear came in yelling his frightening rendition of a battle cry. He was followed by wild women with spears.

The dire pack tried to retreat but their wolf enemies hit them full on. The rest of the Clan all mixed into the fight.

The powerful dire wolves put up a fierce fight but, in the end, only a few managed to escape the carnage.

"Well, your morning walks certainly attract strange visitors," Burly Bear commented as they all stood together.

"Thank you all for coming to our aid," Taelo said holding his bloody club in the air.

They had lost three of their wolves. Many of their wolves were seriously wounded. One of the women had a broken arm where she had been bitten. Almost everyone had some cut or minor injury.

"Let's get everyone taken care of. Then let's treat the wolves," Taelo said as he carried Lasher back to the compound.

"Thank you, my faithful wolf," Taelo said to Lasher.

Lasher had saved Taelo several times during the battle.

Lasher had his leg broken when he knocked down a dire wolf as it attacked Taelo from behind. The fallen dire wolf clamped down on Lasher's leg and broke it. Even in that condition Lasher clamped down on the dire wolf's throat and suffocated the larger animal.

Everyone noticed Taelo carrying Lasher into the compound.

"He treats his animals better than we treat each other," Lily pointed out to Wise Council and Golden Flower.

"Yes, and the animals would all give their lives to save him," Golden Flower observed.

Burley Bear went around the battle area and made sure all the dire wolves were indeed dead. He then organized the skinning of the wolves. The hides would make great winter coats.

Taelo instructed Running Stag to take the three dead sled wolves and bury them by the forest. They had earned their way to the next world.

Feather-in-the-Wind helped Running Stag bury the three dead wolves. She had been close to all the wolves. She was touched and saddened by the loss of the wolves she had brought to the valley. She realized she had become the wolf woman she joked about. She loved her wolves.

The battle with the dire wolves had served to bond the two groups into one. They had fought for their lives together and had moved to a new level. Taelo thought about this as he set the splint on Lasher's leg. To Taelo's relief, Quiet Rabbit had come through the battle unscathed. She had been one of the most vocal and swiftly moving fighters. She was patiently giving Lasher some water. She then attended to one of several gashes Taelo had received in the battle.

"There is something about you that seems to attract the dire wolves," Quiet Rabbit said.

"Yes, they are jealous of me having someone as beautiful as you as my mate," Taelo said as he brushed her cheek with the back of his hand.

The battle with the dire wolves brought the different members closer together and there seemed to be a new energy in the group.

Chapter 21: The Others

The next moon cycle passed quietly. The days grew colder but there was no snow. The lodge was now fully functional, and the smells of cooking filled the air. The camaraderie continued to build as the members talked with each other and began to learn about each other.

Taelo spent many hours with Burley Bear and Golden Hawk talking about the Elk Clan ancestors that had lived here for so long. They had found some drawings of Others in the cave so they must also have lived in this area.

One morning Burly Bear informed Taelo that he had been having visions calling him to come home to the cave of the Others. Taelo knew that this calling was very strong in the Others.

The next morning at breakfast Taelo announced that Burley Bear and Meadow Flower were going to journey home.

Golden Hawk commented that they had been planning on the visit in the spring.

"Yes, I thought so too, but Burley Bear and Meadow Flower cannot wait that long," Taelo replied.

Taelo asked Little Otter if he and Talking Wren would consider working with Wise Council to manage the home site while he, Quite Rabbit, Busy Bee, and Golden Hawk accompanied Burley Bear.

Little Otter and Talking Wren knew this was a considerate way for Taelo to ask them to stay behind to take care of the camp.

They replied that it would be their pleasure to work with Wise Council to guide the camp while you are gone.

Taelo walked over to Wise Council and asked Lily over and explained to them as clearly as he could about the trip. He pointed to Little Otter and Talking Wren and indicated they should all work together.

"I believe Taelo is telling us to help run the camp while he and the others go and visit another group of people," Lily said to Wise Council.

"It is the middle of winter, and he is willing to go out into the cold to visit friends. He is very different than anyone we have ever met. I wish we had run into him before we met the cannibal warriors. Our loved ones would still be alive," Wise Council replied.

"Yes, he acts very quickly. He is fair. He really knows how to get the best from me. I will be pleased to help keep the camp in good shape," Running Stag volunteered from where he was sitting.

The word spread and everyone immediately voiced their support of helping keep the camp orderly and safe.

Taelo was not sure what had just been shared by his new clan members, but all seemed supportive of his visit to the Others.

"You know, I think they love you," Little Otter said as he gave his friend a pat on the back.

"What else could one do when in almost every case, Taelo acts selflessly for the good of those needing him," Talking Wren thought.

Early the next morning Taelo led the way down river and to the pass between the two mountains.

"Burley Bear do you recall a similar pass where the three of us carried three buffalo on our way home from our wandering journey," Taelo asked as they looked up between the mountains to the trail beyond?

"Yes, Burley Bear taught us how to make a sled to carry the load. The wolf sleds we have today were fashioned after the sled he made for us that day," Golden Hawk chimed in.

"We pulled that sled down to the coast and up to the village by the sea," Taelo shared with the group.

Lasher was the only wolf accompanying them and he walked as if listening to the story. He still had a splint on his leg, but it had healed, and he was doing well.

"Yes, we have wonderful memories and perhaps we will create more of them for the future," Taelo said as he led the way up the trail.

All six trotted smoothly along the trail for the rest of the afternoon. Lasher moved smoothly at an even trot.

Taelo stopped and looked around.

"Up ahead are the mountains just north of the Others camp. We will need to get wet to get around the short way or we will need to climb over the mountain," Taelo observed.

They decided to pitch camp and proceed on the next morning. They set up a simple camp along the edge of the beach. An outcropping of stone shielded them from the cold wind and their small fire yielded just enough warmth to keep them comfortable.

The night sky was pitch black and the stars overwhelmed their imagination. Several shooting stars dashed across the deep black sky putting on a splendid show. Each couple sat wrapped in their sleeping hides and talked quietly about their journey and about their continuing friendship.

"Ah, my Quiet Rabbit it is such a pleasure sitting here with you," Taelo whispered in her ear. "You are the spirit that supports me."

Quiet Rabbit snuggled a little closer to Taelo. She had known he was her soul mate the day she ran after the crazed saber tooth tiger that was chasing Taelo.

She, not the tiger, had caught him. Their bond had continually grown stronger.

In their travels the group had learned to make tea from a variety of ingredients. Taelo was up and heated some water for the tea made from a variety of flowers and grasses that they had collected on their return. This was a habit they had picked up in their travels to the Condor Clan to the south.

They had also learned to drink a more potent black drink from a bean grown by trees. The tea was easy to concoct from the various plants they found in the wild. The black drink could only be made with the beans, and they had long ago run out of them.

"Today we will arrive to the camp of the Others. I am looking forward to learning how they have been doing. I think they are expecting Burly Bear and Meadow Flower," Taelo said over the morning fire.

All six of them followed a narrow trail along the face of the cliff as they went around to the beach on the other side.

There they were met by their friend Saber Scar of the Others. "Broken Spear said you would be arriving today. I am here to guide you to the cave.

They were soon at the opening of the cave.

As they entered, they were greeted with a chant by the entire population. They finished their greeting by stomping their feet and letting a loud yell.

Broken Spear was supported by two young men, but he was sitting upright near the pool.

"It is good to see you one more time before, I go to see my ancestors," Broken Spear said as Taelo walked over to him.

Taelo took Broken Spear's hand and put it to his forehead, "Read my thoughts about, you and your people; feel the warmth of my memories; feel the comfort knowing you, has given me; feel the strength you have bestowed," Taelo said quietly.

He could see Broken Spear was giving him the ultimate respect by using all his strength to greet him.

Quiet Rabbit stood at Taelo's side. She knew the respect Taelo had for Broken Spear.

Broken Spear was surprised at the energy he felt. He had experienced this only once before on the day he tried to read Taelo's mind so long ago. It was the same now but only stronger. Broken Spear could feel the intensity of an energy surge. He could feel energy flowing into him!

This time Taelo was giving it. Taelo knew. Did he know then?

Later after the dinner Broken Spear started the story telling by making a request, "You must tell us the story of the attack on the cannibal warriors."

"How did he know about that," Golden Hawk asked.

"Either he already knew it, or he learned of it when I touched him," Taelo whispered.

"Yes, I knew of this before you touched me," Broken Spear said from across the fire.

"And it does no good to whisper," Taelo said with a smile.

"The cannibals had a run in with a few of our warriors, but they left without attacking us. Even our young warriors were too fierce for their liking," Broken Spear offered. "It seems they made a mistake in fighting with you."

"I will share the story with you but there is no pride in this story. It is a sad story. It is the story of offering no mercy for man or woman," Taelo began as he stood in the center of the group.

He knew it would do him good to let the grey spirits that haunted him loose, as he told the story. He felt each of the spirits float free as he told of the battle with the cannibals.

"In the deep of winter, I found a group of frightened, dying women and children, who had run away into the cold with no clothes. They had left behind their loved ones. They were ashamed to have abandoned them.

Once I got this group to safety and learned what had happened, I knew my actions must be swift, must be just and my actions would need to ensure that no cannibals would be in our region.

I needed help.

The women were too afraid to go back with me. One young man, Running Stag, really nothing more than a boy with the group was brave enough to help me. He had never seen battle. He had never shot an arrow or held a war club in his hand. I gave him training for a short time before we left the cave.

My warriors were the weather, my wolves, and the boy Running Stag. My battle plan was surprise, speed, and no mercy. My arrows, my war club, my wolves, and a cold heart were my weapons.

I counted twenty warriors. I shot twenty arrows. It was not a battle. I gave them no chance. It was an execution. And it mattered not if you were a warrior or a woman of the tribe. My battle club silenced the women. My wolves know my kill command and they did their work. Only three babies were spared. They are in our camp being raised as one of us.

Only one warrior had the chance to fight me. I had miscounted. I had one baby in each hand. He had a war club on its way to my head.

But my small warrior, Running Stag, shot an arrow through the warrior's leg. Instantly I dropped the babies, and my war club found its target.

Running Stag later admitted he was so scared his arms were shaking. He had intended to shoot the warrior through the heart. He was apologizing to me, the man he had saved," Taelo stopped for a moment to let the story sink in.

Everyone was silent.

"As I said, it is a sad story. The only captive male left alive was Running Stag's father. He was being dragged out to the killing post when I attacked. Both his legs were broken. I gave him some of the drink I learned to make on my journey to the Condor Clan. He was soon out cold. Together with the women we reset the bones in his legs.

Yes, Broken Spear, with what I have learned, I could have fixed your legs when the bear broke your body. I wish I could have been there then.

There was one more battle where Running Stag rescued Golden Hawk from five of the cannibals. I will let Golden Hawk share the story of being saved by this brave young man.

Golden Hawk rose and told the story of being surprised and captured by the five cannibals. He had approached the river and was about to cross when he was surrounded by the five. They tied him to a stake and started a small fire. It was clear they were going to torture him.

It was then he saw the first of their warriors go down behind the rock. Taelo and Running Stag shot three of them before those remaining by the fire knew what had happened.

Running Stag has my support when his time comes to be called a warrior of the clan.

Burley Bear stood and spoke.

"Taelo took the right action. His actions saved us many battles and lives."

"Let me tell you about the battle of Taelo's new Clan and the dire wolves. They surprised Taelo a few days after his return from the battle with the cannibals. The entire camp and all our wolves were partners in this battle. The dire wolves were powerful but no match for the new Clan and its wolf partners. They were soundly defeated and only a few escaped.

It was during this battle that I realized it was time for me to come back to my Clan. I have heard my calling and it is to be here for our new spring. Taelo found us this home and it keeps us warm. He taught us to hunt differently, and we have been able to continue the hunt. There is enough for us here. This is our valley and I want to make sure we continue to prosper here," Burly Bear said to a quiet crowd.

Broken Spear spoke quietly, "It is good you have returned. My time is nearly over. I have been waiting for your return. Tonight, our ancestors celebrate your return and soon you will celebrate my departure. Taelo has been our guide to this our new home, and he will be our guide and friend to the end of our days."

The stars were out and yet, everyone heard the eagle's cry, ring out.

"My totem has spoken. I will stand by you as a friend and as a member of this clan," Taelo said as he stood and looked around at his clan of Others.

Chapter 22: Broken Spear's Vision

The light rays slowly lit the valley with individual golden streams of light as the sun rose slowly above the mountains to the east. The valley went from a dark grey to a valley adorned with a brilliant white blanket. The air moving slowly as the sun warmed and made it rise was crisp and clear.

Taelo, Quiet Rabbit, Busy Bee and Golden Hawk sat around their small fire quietly watching the morning come to life.

"That was an intense evening. I was surprised to hear the eagle cry so late at night," Golden Hawk commented.

He looked over at the steaming water of the pool.

"I think I will take a dip in the pool and relax," he continued.

The eagle cry had been there the day Taelo had rejected the demands of the fierce leader in the south. The leader had attacked. Taelo's war club had magically appeared and delivered instant death. He could have ruled that clan. Instead Taelo gave the leadership over to Tough Hide the leader who he had befriended. Each time something significant happened the eagle's cry was there.

Taelo walked over to Broken Spear's living area. Two older women were taking care of the Seer.

"You sent word you would like to speak to me," Taelo greeted him in the language of the Others.

"Yes, sit, have some warm soup," Broken Spear said in the language of the new ones.

Taelo knew this was a sign of respect and something important was to be shared. He sat and waited patiently as Broken Spear ate his soup.

"I have flown with the eagle. It has taken me to a place north of here. There a group of people are slowly starving. They will not make it through the winter. There are twenty-three men, women, and children. The eagle screamed over their encampment. You know what that means," Broken Spear said.

"I will need to take my wolf sled and go see who these people are," Taelo replied.

Another twenty-three people; this would increase the population of his clan to more than fifty.

"I have seen your future. It is good. You will travel across this land to the other sea," Broken Spear spoke softly in his language. "You will want to see me once more before you begin that journey."

The meeting ended and Taelo left and returned to his team.

The rest of the day was spent talking with Burley Bear and Meadow Flower. They would be staying with their Clan for the rest of the winter.

It was clear to Taelo that Burley Bear would be the next leader of the Clan of Others.

The next morning Taelo, Quite Rabbit, Golden Hawk, and Busy Bee said goodbye to the Clan.

Taelo assured Burley Bear he would stay in contact and would be back before going east.

The four made their way back to the valley as rapidly as possible. They knew that they needed to move as quickly as possible before the winter weather became more hostile.

Little Otter and Talking Wren and the rest of their new clan members greeted them warmly on their return.

Wise Council, who by this time was able to walk but was still weak from his ordeal, was pacing around the lodge. He was working the muscles in his legs.

"Do you think you will be able to make it through the mountains in this weather? Would it be better to wait a few weeks," Wise Council asked?

He knew Taelo and Golden Hawk would choose to go. He had watched Taelo closely and recognized the determination in his eyes.

"Yes, it will be a challenge. If we wait, we will find only the bodies. Broken Spear said we only have a short time. He is seldom wrong. We must go immediately," Taelo replied.

"I have checked each of our wolves. All the women are cutting and making coverings for their feet as Taelo has requested. We should be ready by the end of the day tomorrow," Golden Hawk contributed

"You must make the entire trip in your mind. You must imagine everything that could go wrong, and you must see how to overcome the wrong," Taelo shared with young Running Stag.

Feather-in-the-Wind sat quietly nearby. She felt comfortable and at home when she was near Quiet Rabbit and Taelo. She also liked to learn from Taelo.

Taelo had talked Running Stag through the entire trip and together they had imagined all the challenges. Running Stag constantly shadowed Taelo and Golden Hawk as the two went about their work. He had not yet filled out as a man, but he had demonstrated his willingness to contribute and fight like a man. Running Stag had asked to go but Taelo had kindly said no.

"Running Stag, you have proven yourself worthy. There are only three sleds, and we need to carry as much food as possible. You must remain here. Wise Council can now walk but he is still not fully recovered. In a crisis he will need to rely on you for swift action.

So, I ask you to take on the responsibility of being his aid while the rest of us are gone," Taelo said to Running Stag.

Running Stag understood this was final. He knew it was the right thing. He still wished he could go but he accepted the decision. He would earnestly put all his effort in helping in the preparation.

"Thank you for being so kind in the way you said no," Running Stag's mother Golden Flower said quietly. "I know he will contribute and be a great man, but he must learn from you for a few more seasons," she continued.

The next morning after a hearty breakfast Taelo, Golden Hawk and Little Otter donned their winter weather clothes. They had triple layer boots with rabbit fur lining on the inside. The mittens, their leggings and jackets were of similar construction. In addition, they each had a full-length outer bear skin coat.

The three got hugs from their three mates and then they went off northward into the cold winter weather under a dark grey cloud covered sky.

Chapter 23: Rescue Trail

The sky was clear, the air was cold, and a light breeze was blowing at their backs. The wolves were eagerly running and pulling the sleds with ease. Their training had been thorough, and each wolf had built a bond with their human partners. They recognized Taelo, Golden Hawk and Little Otter as their leaders.

Taelo closed his eyes and let the feeling of the cold clear air penetrate his mind. He felt the connection with the forest, the mountains, and the world that surrounded him.

Lasher was leading the pack. He listened intently for Taelo's voice and reacted by either going left, right or continuing straight ahead. His many experiences in both his lead position or as Taelo's companion had created and cemented a bond that would only break if one of the two died.

Taelo was in the lead and Golden Hawk brought up the rear. They had discussed their travel and had agreed to rotate the order each day. The lead would choose the best path ahead. This would be a challenge since they were heading into new territory.

They had agreed if the leader had any doubt about direction, they would all stop and decide together how to proceed.

Taelo stopped three times and they decided together on the direction they should take. He could have made the choice himself, but he wanted to lead by example.

The stops also served to give the wolves a break. They were each given a snack and their paws were inspected. The well-being of the wolves was critical to the success of the rescue mission.

The sun was rapidly descending behind the mountains when Taelo stopped his sled near a small stream cutting across the valley they had just descended into. They positioned the three sleds to form a U and were quickly able to put a cover across over the top. A pole in the center held the cover up so they could stand. A small fire at the open end of the U provided a place to cook and heated the inside enough that they were able to remove their outer coats.

After getting the camp arranged and a small fire going, Taelo, Golden Hawk, and Little Otter always examined the wolves' paws and rubbed them with some whale oil. They talked to each and fed them. After all the wolves were fed and resting, the three would cook a dinner over the fire.

The three talked about their Condor Clan friends to the south and how much they had learned from them and how they wished they were there where they had experienced the warm summer months of that region.

Little Otter smiled whenever the conversation carried him back to their journey south. He and Talking Wren had truly fallen in love on their trip to the southern lands.

"Yes, it was the group in the middle that still scares me. They were very productive, but the leaders were cruel to their people. Your quick action was the only thing that saved us," Little Otter said as he recalled the surprisingly swift and dramatic action Taelo had taken when threatened by the dejected Sharp Stone.

"It was a miracle we weren't all killed on the spot," Taelo replied.

He recalled his confrontation. He had slain the leader on the spot. Expecting a charge by the other warriors. He had then turned and growled like a puma as loud as he could and claimed the right of leadership. The Sharp Stone's warriors remained rooted where they stood.

"Yes, it was good that Tough Hide and his warriors arrived at that moment," Golden Hawk added to the story.

I think the fact Taelo had made friends with Tough Hide the co-leader of the clan and then turned the total control over to him got us out of there. If Taelo had tried to take control, as was their custom, our skeletons would be tied to stakes outside their compound," Golden Hawk reflected.

Taelo smiled at the conversation they were having. The fact that they were comfortably sitting by a warm fire surrounded by their wolf teams was a gift the ancients must have given them. There was no other answer to their good fortune.

The next morning the snow began to fall. It snowed steadily for the next four sun cycles. The travel routine and attention to the wellbeing of the wolves and themselves paid off. They were all in good shape. They had now been gone from their valley for seven sun cycles.

"We should be close to where Broken Spear said we would find the group," Taelo said as they broke camp and got ready for the day's run.

Little Otter was in the lead and Taelo was in back as they left the camp. At midday, Little Otter stopped as they were about to descend into a valley with a small river. Three separate valleys opened before them.

"Well, I have no idea which way to go," Little Otter said as he pointed out the three openings in the mountains ahead.

Three small streams converged to form the small river flowing past them in the valley below.

Suddenly the three heard an eagle's cry. Their eyes turned upward and followed the eagle as it flew up the left-hand valley. It let out another cry and continued its flight.

"I think we should take the left-hand valley," Little Otter said as he turned with a smile to Taelo.

"Yes, I agree with you," Taelo said as he turned to go back to his sled.

They followed the small stream up into the left valley. The snow seemed to deepen as they went up the valley. They were traveling across the snow at a tree top level.

"I think there must be three spear lengths of snow below us Taelo commented as they stopped for the evening. "We will need to make sure we don't slowly sink during the night.

That night they moved three times in order not to sink too far into the snow.

In the morning it was Taelo's turn in the lead. He was just about ready to stop when the eagle cry was heard once more. It flew up the right branch of the valley and then circled in the sky.

The three stood by their sleds looking at where the eagle had circled. They did not see any signs of life.

Taelo called to Lasher and his sled moved forward. The sun was just starting its descent when they arrived in the spot the eagle had circled.

"We would never have found them," Golden Hawk commented as he stood at the tip of a tall pine tree looking down into an area where five buffalo could have stood end to end.

"Hello, can we be of help," Taelo called down.

Taelo's voice had the effect of freezing all movement in the camp below. The entire camp came out and stood looking up at Taelo, Golden Hawk and Little Otter. A man and a woman stepped forward.

"I am Semper, and this is Wan. We are the leaders of this group," Semper introduced himself.

He hoped the three strangers could understand him.

"Did you understand anything they said," Taelo said looking at Golden Hawk and Little Otter.

"No but I think the man might be Semper and the woman, Wan because he pointed to himself and the woman when he said those words," Golden Hawk spoke up.

Taelo always looked to Golden Hawk when it came to understanding new languages. Taelo thought Golden Hawk's abilities came from his ability to observe what people were doing.

"Semper, Wan; I am Taelo, this is Golden Hawk, and this is Little Otter," Taelo pointed to each of them as he responded with introductions.

"Let's throw down some food so they get the idea we are here to help. Then we need to cut some steps down to their level," Taelo suggested as he turned to his sled and picked out some dried fish and a cured deer leg.

They carried the food to the edge and lowered it down.

"They offer food. We must remain vigilant, but they seem to offer help," Semper said as he turned and talked to the rest.

The entire camp knew that they were in desperate need. The fact that the three men looking down at them seemed prepared to help brought new hope to them.

"I think it would be quicker to use a rope to get down. It will be easy to bring everything they have up the same way. This will save us time," Little Otter suggested.

"What do you think," Taelo asked looking at Golden Hawk?

"Well let's get the rope secured to a tree close to the edge otherwise the rope will sink down into the snow and when you wish to climb out it will be of no use," Golden Hawk said as he looked for a tree no more than three of four feet from the edge.

"I didn't think of that," Little Otter said a little humbled.

He had started with a superior mental state and realized he had missed in understanding the conditions.

"Why don't the two of you set up camp and get the wolves out of their harness and fed. I will go down the rope and make contact with our new clan members," Taelo suggested.

Taelo removed his bear skin coat. He then went swiftly down the rope.

It was clear the group had been very hungry. The dry fish had already been dropped into several cooking bags and the cured deer meat was being chewed by everyone.

"I am Taelo," Taelo said as he stepped forward toward Semper.

"I am Semper," Semper said pointing at himself and extending his right hand to Taelo's shoulder.

Taelo responded likewise. This seemed to be a universal sign. He had experienced this in almost all his encounters with other people. Open hand, no weapon, and a direct look at the other.

It took the rest of the late afternoon to communicate the intention of taking the entire group out of the valley.

"He wants us all to go with him. What do each of you think," Semper turned to the rest of the camp and asked for comment.

Taelo climbed back up the rope and from a strategic branch of the tree stepped back onto the snow at the top.

"Well, I think I explained the intention of taking them out of this valley. They are talking about it. I will go down in the morning to see what they have decided," Taelo said as he noticed their camp was set up so they could head out of the valley.

Chapter 24: Home to the Valley

Taelo came awake while the sun was slowly making its climb over the tops of the snow-covered mountains to the east. The cold air stood still but penetrated the bearskin he was under and made him shiver. The blue of the sky above belied the fact that he could see the dark grey clouds moving down from the northwest. He stood and pulled on his leg covering and the warm rabbit lined vest Quiet Rabbit had made for him.

He walked over to the flat piece of stone Little Otter had found so they could make a small fire. They were on top of almost three spear lengths of snow and were in constant risk of sinking down into it. Taelo had moved three times during the night to get out of the trench his body heat made as he slept. Now he started a small fire to warm some of the stew Golden Hawk had made the evening before.

Taelo looked over to where his closest friend was still sleeping. They had grown up together and it seemed to Taelo that they would go through life together.

He turned to look at the deep hole where some twenty-six people were stranded. It was time to get everyone back to the lodge.

Taelo woke up Little Otter and Golden Hawk and after greeting them and offering them some warm stew he suggested they get back to the lodge with the people as quickly as possible.

Taelo turned and walked over to the tree to which the rope to climb down into the snow pit where the people were trapped.

He looked down to see that their leader was up and waiting for him. Taelo climbed down and greeted him.

"Before we agree to go, some of our members want to know how you found us," Semper asked.

Taelo drew a broken spear and a figure of a man and connected the two. He then drew the picture of a bird and pointed to the sky. He connected the two drawings and gestured to the camp.

"He says a man named Broken Spear or broken arrow and an eagle pointed the way to our camp," Semper translated to the camp members.

At that moment, an eagle cry was heard. High overhead it could be seen circling.

"He is indeed sent by the ancestors and is to be trusted," Semper said to the rest of those present in the camp as he pointed to the eagle in the sky.

Golden Hawk and Little Otter looked to the sky.

"Let's get these sleds reorganized. Going home will be much slower. I wonder how we will get all of these people back safely," Little Otter commented.

"Hey, we imagined this together. Did you forget to imagine the way back? What are you wondering about," Golden Hawk replied joking with Little Otter?

As was his nature, Little Otter was seeing things in a negative light.

Little Otter suggested that one sled could take five people back as swiftly as possible and return for five more. They could keep doing this until the three sleds could bring the remainder back in one trip. He was trying to think of the fastest way to get everyone back to the lodge as quickly as possible.

Golden Hawk thought about the problem for a moment and suggested that they engage Taelo in determining the best way to get everyone back.

Once engaged, Taelo agreed with the idea of getting one sled back as quickly as possible. He suggested taking as many of the youngest members as possible back first.

Then we can determine who is in the next group by who is most at risk.

Taelo announced that he would take the single runs since Lasher and his team was the fastest.

"Taelo always takes the action he thinks is of the highest risk. We need to watch out for him as much as he worries about us," Golden Hawk commented quietly to Little Otter.

"Yeh," was all Little Otter said.

Taelo went back down into the pit and explained the plan as best he could to Semper. He pointed out six of the younger children and one young woman with her infant.

Semper turned and explained what he understood of Taelo's request.

"Golden Hawk, Little Otter, get ready to haul up the smaller children. I will tie them to the rope. You two pull them up," Taelo called up to them.

"Here we go," Little Otter commented as he walked over to the tree.

He and Golden Hawk had agreed they would each take turns while the other stood by to help. The six came up easily. Then the infant was sent up.

"You look good holding the child, but I am going to need your help in pulling up the mother," Golden Hawk teased Little Otter. Together the two easily pulled the young mother up.

The sled was loaded with the mother sitting with her back to the back of the sled. Everyone was sitting on a large buffalo hide.

The children sat side-by-side down the sled. Each was given a small hide as a blanket and then the buffalo hide was brought back over them and tied so each could stick their head out or they could hide below in the warmth.

"Make sure everyone has done their duty before getting into the sled. You show the young boys and ask the mother to show the two young girls," Taelo had instructed.

Taelo left all the snowshoes and extra food behind with Golden Hawk and Little Otter. He had just enough food to get his group back to the lodge and only be hungry. He wanted to travel fast, which meant as light as possible. He would push while his wolves pulled. His sled had four extra wolves. They had taken two from each of the other two sleds. The darkening sky declared that speed was of issue.

"Get the rest of the folks up and packed by tomorrow morning. I will be back as soon as possible. You get them started back to the valley. Everyone will be on snowshoes. If you make five miles a day you will be lucky," Taelo said as he looked worriedly at the sky.

It looked like snow.

Miles away sitting in the heated pool Broken Spear announced to Burley Bear, "Taelo has found the people and has started back to his new home valley. He will need to hurry for the full winter fury is about to unfold."

"Sometimes, I wish I had the ability to see what Broken Spear sees," Burley Bear thought to himself.

Out loud he said, "I hope he makes it in time."

He already missed being with Taelo.

Taelo kept the sled moving at top speed. He jogged behind and pushed when he could.

The wolves seemed to know he was in a hurry. Lasher kept the reins pulled tight.

Taelo praised Lasher who responded by keeping the pack pulling at full strength.

Taelo signaled the young mother to feed everyone on the sled, but he kept the sled moving. He did not plan to stop. Lunch and dinner were on the go.

Just before sunset Taelo stopped. He fed the wolves and checked their feet. Then he had everyone take a nature break. It was back on the sled. He roused the sleeping wolves and once again they were off.

The moon was full and Taelo decided he would go as long as it was easy to see.

The motion of the sled was hypnotizing. Lani the young mother held her young daughter in her arms. Periodically she would ride with her face exposed and take in the scenery of the white valleys and snow-covered mountains. Other than getting a numb behind, the ride was comfortable.

When night finally called her to sleep, she was able to curl up in the sled with her little one on her chest and several of the children sharing the space for her legs.

She came awake when the sled stopped. She poked her head up and saw Taelo talking to and feeding the first wolf in line. It was strange to see a man talk to a wolf and have the wolf lick the man on the cheek.

"What kind of magic does this man have," Lani wondered. She began to prepare and sort out the morning food for the children.

The grey of dawn was just breaking. The sun was painting a thin light line across the edges of the mountains to the east. Lani got out of the sled and led the girls to the edge of the pine forest.

Taelo decided a morning break would be for the best. He looked back along the line of wolves to the sled and saw the young mother get out and go to the bush. As he continued to tend to the team, he was pleased to see her wake and take each one of the children to the bush as well. She was then giving them food.

"Thank you for doing your part," Taelo praised her.

He knew she would not understand his words, but he gestured to indicate she had done well.

"Please wake me when the sun gets to the top of that tree," Taelo indicated to her.

Taelo had been awake and guiding the sled for almost two straight sun cycles. He was exhausted. He took his blanket and lay down behind the sled and went instantly to sleep.

Lani made sure the children were all warm in their blankets. Most of them went back to sleep. She looked down at the man behind the sled. He had come to save them. She had not met anyone like him before.

Taelo followed the same routine the next few sun cycles. Early one morning Lasher recognized the valley, and the team sprinted the last few miles at breakneck speed.

Running Stag heard the wolves coming. He ran to the compound gate and opened it up. The sled had a ghostly appearance as it raced toward him in the early morning light.

"One of the sleds is back," Running Stag called into the main building.

Wise Council and Golden Flower rose and began to prepare. Golden Flower heated some water and prepared some stew. She was not sure how many would arrive on the sled. Wise Council went about getting everyone up. He figured there would be something for everyone to do.

Quiet Rabbit recognized Taelo as soon as the sled was in sight.

"I wonder why they have decided to bring some people in fast," Talking Wren commented to Busy Bee and Quiet Rabbit.

"These will be the youngest and most vulnerable," Quite Rabbit replied.

She knew how Taelo thought. He would have decided on a strategy that would save all the people but the most vulnerable would be saved first.

Lani came awake when the wolves started to consistently yelp as if they were cheering. She poked her head out and saw the compound ahead. She was impressed at the stature of the place. The wolves pulled swiftly up the steep slope to the flat part on top. The sled stopped suddenly as it left the snow and hit the clean stone surface of the compound.

Running Stag ran out and gave Taelo a big hug and helped him out of his full-length jacket. Several women ran out and opened the cover on the sled and began chattering to each other as they guided the children into the main building. Lani was helped out. Her young daughter became an instant magnet for the other women in the compound.

Taelo walked up to the front of his wolf team petting each one, giving a treat and thanking them for doing a good job. When he got to Lasher he got down on his knees and gave the wolf a hug as he took off his harness.

"Please feed the team, wash their feet, and put salve on them. Then give them food and let them sleep," Taelo instructed two of the younger boys.

Wise Council knew exactly what Taelo had asked and instructed the boys again.

He could tell Taelo was tired.

Quiet Rabbit led Taelo inside. She could see he had pushed himself hard.

It was twelve sun cycles since his departure. Quiet Rabbit had no clue that it had taken seven days to find these people, one day to get the first group ready to come back and then the intense dash back in four days.

Taelo went into the compound to his living area. He went out to the hot tub in front of the lodge and quickly cleaned up and went back into the lodge. The warmth of the lodge and his extreme exhaustion made it hard for him to stay awake.

Quiet Rabbit brought him a piece of rabbit and some hot broth. He talked to Quiet Rabbit and asked her to wake him up at noon.

He would then head back to get another load.

Far to the North, Golden Hawk and Little Otter pushed their group of people. They went until it was almost too dark to see well. Then they pulled out enough hides to make a good cover over the snow. After everyone was fed, it was time to rest.

Little Otter and Golden Hawk made sure their wolves were fed and in good shape and then they went immediately to sleep.

"These men are good leaders. They push us to the limit. We are lucky to have been rescued by such as these," Semper said to Wan as they fell asleep.

"We were foolish to try to make the passage so close to winter. We would have made it if the weather would have held a few more days. We are lucky," Wan said as she fell asleep.

The second day the weather started to turn colder, and the wind picked up.

"Let's hope it holds off a couple more days," Golden Hawk said to Little Otter as they got ready to start out.

Golden Hawk inspected all the people following him and then led the way forward.

Taelo saw the same sky as he got up just before lunch. He would be riding an empty sled back to the oncoming group. He planned to return as fast as possible.

He was sure there would not be time for another trip.

Taelo thought the problem through and concluded he needed help. He asked Running Stag if he would help bring in the remainder of the rescued people.

Running Stag was surprised and elated. He had accepted not being able to participate now he was being asked to help.

"Yes, of course I would like to help," he replied to Taelo.

"Get all your warm gear. You will bring Lasher and my sled back. I will bring in the heartiest of this group back on foot. We will need to leave immediately."

"You have made us proud of our son and I know he will do well," Wise Council said to Taelo as they were getting ready to go.

"You have a brave son. He is why we are all here today. He has earned his participation," Taelo replied.

"It was an arrow that missed the mark, but it was an arrow that saved my life," Taelo thought as he looked at Running Stag gathering his things.

He had earned the opportunity by the bravery he had displayed.

Taelo also noted that Feather-in-the-Wind was quietly helping Running Stag.

The two set off sharing the runners on the back of the sled. Taelo would jog along while Running Stag stood on the runners. Then Running Stag would jog.

Running Stag was soon worn out. He wondered how Taelo could keep running for so long. As the day passed, he spent more and more time on the runner and Taelo jogged longer. Running Stag had expected to stop but after a brief stop and getting something to eat Taelo surprised him.

"Running Stag, you get in the sled and get some rest. We are going to continue through the night. When you wake up you will take my place and we will continue our journey with you on the runner and I will take my turn in the sled," Taelo informed him.

Taelo walked the line of wolves. He fed each. Then Taelo checked out the condition of their feet and put new leather booties on each. Each wolf wagged their tail and seemed to enjoy Taelo's attention.

Running Stag followed Taelo and talked to each of the wolves as well. At times he was surprised as one growled at him. This was the first time he had mustered the courage to get near the wolves. He had observed them in battle and knew they could kill.

"Don't let their growls bother you. They are just nervous because they don't know you. Just give them an extra treat. Soon you will be accepted as one of the team," Taelo said patting Running Stag on the shoulder.

When they got to Lasher, Taelo introduced Running Stag by holding his hand in his and letting Lasher smell

"This is Running Stag. He is our friend. Please treat him well," Taelo said as if Lasher could understand him.

Lasher wagged his tail and licked both hands.

"Now give him his food and pet him," Taelo instructed as he stepped back and walked back to the sled.

"Thank you, Lasher, for accepting me," Running Stag said and scratched Lasher behind the ear as he had observed Taelo doing. He was rewarded by Lasher's wagging tail. He followed Taelo to the sled and climbed in and under the buffalo skin covering. The sled lurched forward, and he was soon asleep.

Taelo guided the sled at top speed throughout the night. The team was in great shape and running well. The weather was getting colder, but the sky was still clear and the moon full.

He altered between jogging while holding the handle of the sled and riding by standing on top of the runners. The miles evaporated behind him.

The morning sun was just clearing the mountains to the east when he decided to stop. He began his routine of feeding each wolf, checking their feet, and talking to each one. He was almost up to Lasher when he observed Running Stag get up and go to the tree line.

"Well Lasher old buddy, how are you doing? Have you got a few more miles left," Taelo asked?

He knew he was pushing his team hard. He stopped only to feed them and let them drink. They would probably sleep for a week when this was over.

By the time he was walking to the sled, Running Stag had gotten himself organized and ready to guide the sled.

"I'm sorry I did not wake to help with the wolves. I have never run so much in my life. How do you do it?" he commented.

"Oh, I imagine I have wings on my feet, and they get lighter and faster. I imagine that they are not touching the ground and the way gets easier," Taelo joked with Running Stag.

He was ready to ride in the sled for most of the day. He climbed in and told Running Stag to go.

Coming in the other direction, Golden Hawk and Little Otter pushed their group throughout the second day and instead of stopping for the night they told everyone to get a few moments rest. Then they would continue. There was silence from the group, but they were also aware of how cold it was getting.

"We should check their feet. Those who have wet feet must get them dry," Golden Hawk said as he was checking the feet of his wolves.

"Whose feet are you talking about," Little Otter called from his sled where he was checking the condition and feet of his wolf team.

Golden Hawk stopped what he was doing and called Semper and Wan over. He showed them what he was doing with the wolves and pointed to Semper's and Wan's feet and then the rest of the group.

"I believe he just told us to check on the condition of all of our people's feet," Semper said to Wan as they walked back to the rest of the group.

On inspection it was clear two people were in danger of getting frost bite. Many people changed their foot covering with new dry skins. The two people in jeopardy were each put on one of the sleds.

The extra weight would normally have slowed down the sled, but they were moving at a rather slow pace.

"It is better to keep them from getting frost bite then to have to care for them later," Little Otter said to no one in particular.

He was just justifying having two people ride while the rest continued to walk.

It was early afternoon when in the distance they could see an approaching sled.

"Either our Taelo has shrunk in size or that is Running Stag guiding the team," Golden Hawk commented when he saw it.

"Well, I do hope Taelo is sleeping in the sled and not back at the lodge," Little Otter replied.

"Oh, I am sure he will be. Lasher would not run for anyone else," Golden Hawk replied.

The clouds had been closing and as Taelo's sled met the other two, snow began to fall.

Taelo got up as the sled stopped. He was well rested. He knew he would need all his reserves for the next part of the trip.

Taelo greeted Golden Hawk and Little Otter and then addressed the group. He told them that as many people as possible would ride back on the sleds. He would select those that would return with him.

He had the four wolves that he had borrowed returned to their sled teams.

He looked at Semper and Wan and explained what he wanted the group to do and that he would select those he would lead back.

"How are you planning to bring them home." Little Otter asked?

"We will jog back. Once you make the valley you will return and meet us. We will make it as far as we are able. However, I do not want you to return if the snow is so heavy you cannot see your lead wolf. If the weather is that bad, trust me to bring my group in safely," Taelo replied.

Semper volunteered to go with Taelo.

"You are a good leader and of course you would want to bring in those behind, but you are not on my list. I want only the younger men and women," Taelo bluntly replied.

Taelo looked over the group and selected nine of them, six men and three women. He knew this group might face some extreme conditions.

After the selection he talked to Lasher and had Running Stag feed Lasher again.

"Take my sled back to the Valley. Listen to Running Stag," Taelo said quietly to Lasher.

The sleds left with Lasher in the lead.

Each of those left with Taelo had a large backpack. The packs contained a sleeping hide, food, and extra foot coverings.

Each person also had an extra coat. These had been taken from those on the sleds.

Taelo talked to each person, checked each of the group, and made sure they had their snowshoes on securely.

He then set off at a steady slow walk. Once he observed the entire group seemed to have the hang of walking on the snowshoes, Taelo increased the pace to an easy jog. He kept up the pace for the entire day.

The snowfall kept getting heavier. Soon Taelo could barely see the trail. He stopped to make sure everyone was still in good shape.

He had them eat some of the food they had brought with them.

He attached a rope around each of the group member's waist. He then tied the rope around his waist and slowly began the jog again.

He took up the chant he and Golden Hawk used when they were jogging. Soon the entire group joined in the chant.

The hours passed as Taelo led the group onward. It was hard for him to see the trail.

He knew there would not be a sled coming back to get them. He listened to make sure the group continued the chant.

Golden Hawk, Little Otter and Running Stag let the teams run as fast as they possibly could go. By the end of the fourth day, it was hard to see where they were going.

Golden Hawk stopped the sleds. He walked to the back to talk to Running Stag.

"You must take the lead. Our only hope is to tell Lasher to take us home and let him go his way. Will he listen to you?" Golden Hawk asked Running Stag.

"I will tell him he must," Running Stag said earnestly.

He walked back with Golden Hawk to where Lasher was resting.

Golden Hawk watched as Running Stag gave Lasher a treat, scratched him behind his ears. He continued and checked each of his four feet.

"We need your help. You must take us home," Running Stag said firmly in Taelo's language.

Golden Hawk was surprised as Lasher wagged his tail and licked Running Stag's hand. He had never seen Lasher this friendly with anyone but Taelo.

"Well, our young warrior has made friends with Lasher. Are you friends with Lasher," Golden Hawk asked Little Otter?

"No, I didn't think Lasher liked anyone but Taelo," Little Otter quipped back, "I hope he understands our young friend."

Running Stag took his team around the other two and took the lead. They stopped long enough to let Golden Hawk tie the three sleds together.

Golden Hawk tied a rope to the lead sled and then tied it to Little Otter's lead wolf. He did the same from Little Otter's sled to his own lead wolf.

After lightly feeding and checking his team, Running Stag called out to Lasher, "Take us home, take us to the valley."

On Running Stag's loud command all three sleds moved out together.

"Did you see how well these three work together? The oldest two put the youngest one in the lead. This shows an unusual trust. But it seems they all talked mostly to the lead wolf," Semper commented to Wan who was sitting in front of him.

They were riding in Running Stag's sled.

Running Stag could no longer see Lasher. He let his reins hang loose and he lightened the load by running at the side of the sled. He would trust Lasher to get them home.

Little Otter and Golden Hawk kept their wolves running at the same pace as Lasher was setting. They too were running blind only the rope kept them all together.

Miles behind, Taelo continued his chant and kept his band moving. He had no idea what time of day or night it might be. It did not matter. He was not stopping as long as the rope around his waist let him know everyone was keeping up. He could no longer see the last in line, but he could distinguish all their voices.

Periodically he would add a new phrase to the chant. In this way he could check that everyone was still lucid. He was leading by instinct and by keeping between the tracks made by the sleds.

Back in the lodge, Wise Council heard the wolves. He could see nothing. It was dark and the snow was so thick he could not see out to the gate. He went out with several of the younger women and opened the gates.

Quiet Rabbit knew Taelo would not be in this group. He had explained his plan to her. She hoped he was making good time. She roused Feather-in-the-Wind, Busy Bee and Talking Wren and they prepared to feed and manage the new people coming in.

Wise Council could hear the wolves getting closer. Then suddenly the first sled burst through the gate. It continued past him and almost crashed at the other end. The other two sleds came in just as wildly. It was then Wise Council saw the lines tying all of them together.

He quickly escorted the people from the sleds into the main building.

"Look at this place. It is spacious. It is warm. And the smell of the food is wonderful," Wan commented as she was escorted in and greeted by those inside.

Lani came forward to greet them.

"This is the place Taelo built. I am beginning to understand the people who are here. Taelo rescued them too. Where is he and where is my husband and where is my brother," Lani asked when she realized they were not with the group.

"Taelo is bringing them on foot," Semper replied.

By the looks of the storm and the amount of falling snow Semper was not sure the last group would make it, but he was not going to say this to any of his clan.

He returned to the gate and with some help closed them. He hoped he was not closing the gate on the ten people he was sure were struggling through the snow, wind and cold in hopes of making the lodge.

Chapter 25: Lasher's Rescue

Semper retuned to the lodge as Golden Hawk, Little Otter and Running Stag entered. The three had taken their wolves out of their harness and fed them. Each wolf had received special attention and praise. Their booties were removed, and their paws dried and oiled.

This was the first time Running Stag had performed the task of taking care of Taelo's wolf team. Lasher had stayed with him as he attended each of the wolves. When one of the wolves seemed to act up, Lasher would growl, and the wolf allowed Running Stag to take off the booties and clean his paws.

Lasher helped Running Stag and then followed him into the lodge.

"Lasher, follows you," Wise Council commented in surprise!

He knew Lasher followed no one but Taelo.

Even Quiet Rabbit was surprised. She went to Lasher and gave him a hug. Until now she had been the only other person allowed by Lasher to hold or pet him.

"No, it is I who follow Lasher," Running Stag knelt down to scratch Lasher behind the ears, "He brought us through the snow. We came in blind. I did not realize we had come through the gate until I went by the lodge door."

Lasher took Running Stag's wrist in his mouth and went back toward the door.

"I think you should follow him," Golden Hawk advised as he watched Lasher.

He knew Lasher could easily crush Running Stag's wrist.

At the door Lasher let Running Stag go and scratched at the door.

"I believe he wants out," Little Otter commented.

"Bring me some food, water, and some new boots for his feet. Also give me a hide to put around his body," Running Stag requested with a voice of substantial authority.

Quiet Rabbit brought some water. Talking Wren came over with the food. Golden Hawk brought over a new set of booties and Feather-in-the-Wind found the right size piece of bear skin hide to put around Lasher's body.

Lasher seemed to know Running Stag was preparing to let him out. He patiently allowed Running Stag to give him the food and water. He gave a little growl as Talking Wren removed his wet booties but was quiet as Running Stag cleaned his feet, put some ointment on them and then put dry booties on.

"Go to Taelo and guide him home," Running Stag said quietly to Lasher.

Lasher let out a deep growl and licked Running Stag on the cheek. He disappeared as soon as the door opened. Running Stag ran out and opened the outer gate. When he returned, he was shivering and totally covered in snow.

"I can't believe how cold it is getting," he commented as he wiped the snow off and stood by the fire.

Feather-in-the-Wind brought Running Stag a bowl of soup. She was impressed by Running Stag's actions. Taelo had praised him for his courage, and he had trusted him with Lasher and his other wolves. She did not miss that this was the highest praise Taelo could give.

Out in the now full blowing and howling snowstorm, Lasher was back tracking the faint scent of the wolves. He was running as fast as his nose allowed him to keep the scent. The snow was so thick that all he could see was a white wall of snow.

Taelo meanwhile had stopped and walked back and talked to each of the members tied to his rope. The last person in the line was the oldest of the group but was having no problem keeping up. Everyone was tired. They were also scared because of the weather. They were all totally coated with a layer of snow.

Taelo gathered them all around.

"We are continuing on. We will go a little slower because I must make sure we stay on the right path. The snow has erased all traces of the sleds. I am now going on instinct. Can everyone continue?"

It was clear they did not understand all of what he had asked but they seemed to nod ascent when the person bringing up the rear talked to them. Taelo did a quick inspection of each person then retied them closer together. He wanted to hear them as they moved forward.

The slow but steady jog continued through the night. The break of dawn brought a gray light, but it was still impossible to see beyond the length of a spear. Taelo continued the slow forward progress. He was afraid it would get even colder when the snow stopped. If it did, he would be forced to stop and dig in. He was not sure this group would survive such an ordeal. They were already weakened, and the additional cold would take its toll. He continued on for another cycle of light to dark.

He called a halt to let everyone get a quick rest, a bite to eat and to take a nature break. He was examining each of the group when Lasher almost knocked him down.

Taelo deflected the spear of one of the group members.

"This is my wolf Lasher. He has come to save you. Don't spear your rescuer," Taelo said as he looked at the group.

"You look like some spirit monster," Taelo said as he hugged Lasher.

"I see they out fitted you for the cold. Your boots are still in good shape Taelo said as he inspected Lasher's paws. Are we close to home," he casually talked to Lasher?

He took a length of line and tied it to the hide on Lasher's back.

"Take us home," Taelo commanded.

The little group once again began a slow jog through the snow.

Taelo took up the chant and the rest joined in. Hour after hour they chanted. The gray light of day gave way to the pitch black of night.

"I am sure these young men will be telling this story to their grandchildren," Taelo thought as he fell into an automatic rhythm that needed none of his attention.

His mind was already planning his next trip that he planned to take to the east. They went on this way for another gray sun cycle and into the black of night.

Suddenly, Lasher increased his pace. The jerk on the rope tied to his wrist brought Taelo back to the present.

"How long had they been going," Taelo wondered? Lasher was now barking loudly and Taelo heard all the other wolves respond. Suddenly the gate was in front of him and swinging open.

The group staggered in. They were each helped into the lodge. Everyone collapsed once they got inside. They had made it. They knew it was a miracle.

Taelo watched as the other rescued members greeted those who had just arrived and who had collapsed in exhaustion.

Quiet Rabbit came over to him, helped him out of his frozen outer covering and led him over to their sleeping area.

Golden Hawk came over and greeted Taelo and jokingly asked him what had taken him so long. He was pleased that once again Taelo had done the impossible.

Talking Wren for once was quiet as she watched Quiet Rabbit get an exhausted Taelo out of his clothing. This time Little Otter jokingly commented on Taelo not having him along to guide him but having to rely on Lasher.

"I think we have enough people for the Northern Clan. No more rescues this season," Busy Bee added as she pointed around at almost ninety people crowded into what now seemed to be a small lodge.

Those rescued were inside. They had made it. They knew it was a miracle.

Chapter 26: The First Season

Three groups of people were now living together. There was Taelo, Quiet Rabbit, Golden Hawk, Busy Bee, Little Otter, Talking Wren, and Feather-in-the-Wind of the Elk Clan.

There was Lily, Wise Council, Golden Flower, Running Stag, and four others rescued from the cannibals.

Now Semper, Wan and thirty-six more people.

Taelo immediately realized that getting everyone to understand each other was going to be a big challenge. Putting up with each other was also going to be a challenge.

"This is a great way to get all of us to understand each other," Taelo commented several days after his return.

"Yes, we will certainly know each other very well by spring," Quiet Rabbit replied with a smile.

"Well, I will certainly enjoy getting out of this crowd. I hope I survive until spring," Golden Hawk continued.

Taelo looked around at his immediate team and reminded them that when they led this new Northern Elk Clan to the Elk Clan meeting in the fall, they would need to be a successful clan. A clan that had goods to trade, one whose members all spoke the same language and who were willing to move to other clans and integrate into the Elk Clan.

We will need to come in as the most successful, rich, and sharing sub-Clan any of them has ever seen," Taelo proclaimed.

Little Otter let out a small groan. Even after all his time with Taelo, he still approached events from the negative side. His groan though minor put him in the spotlight.

"I have been thinking you could teach all the young men and women how to use their weapons. I would like to make sure they are all proficient with the sling, the spear, and the bow.

Would you and Talking Wren be willing to do this," Taelo said looking over at Little Otter and Talking Wren.

"Oh, that would be wonderful," Talking Wren replied immediately.

Little Otter just let out another small groan. Taelo just gave him a smile across the fire. He knew that Talking Wren would organize the entire event.

"Golden Hawk would you and Busy Bee give language classes?" Taelo asked.

He was playing to Golden Hawk's strength and knew he would do a great job.

"Sure, I would love to do so. What will you do?" Golden Hawk inquired.

"I am going to work with all of you and the leaders from the two groups that have joined us to set up our leadership council and set up the rules by which we will all abide," Taelo replied.

"I would like to organize all the cooking and have everyone experience each other's styles. I think we could become a source of new ways of cooking for the Elk Clan," Quiet Rabbit volunteered.

The clan slowly came together as one group. There were the normal disagreements. There were those that liked each other and those that did not. But allegiances and friendships slowly realigned across the boundaries of their original groups. It slowly became one group.

The language classes slowly lowered the communication barriers.

Having all the young adults, practice with the weapons and become proficient in how to use them to hunt created another bond.

Getting the leaders to discuss and align how the new Clan was to be governed provided yet another level of alignment.

The surprise activity contributing the most to the new alignment and cohesion of the clan was Quiet Rabbit's cooking classes. Once a week the clan shared a common meal.

Quiet Rabbit had established a schedule for the remainder of the winter. A unique dinner was selected, discussed and everyone participated in preparing the dinner.

Anyone could participate. Taelo made a point of participating in the preparation of one of the early dinners and he challenged each of the leaders to do the same. This broke the ice and there was competition from young and old to participate in the preparation of each special weekly meal.

The clan was far enough north that winter hunting was a challenge. The fish in the river provided the main source of food for the clan.

Taelo chose a core group to gather the fish from the trap once a week. Each week he would take the core group to the river to operate the trap. Working the fish trap was cold wet hard work. Taelo made both young and old experienced this work. He would always pull in a few new participants on this task.

The fishing never stopped.

During the break from the fishing Taelo would demonstrate how to make an arrow or how to set a shark's tooth to tip the end of a spear.

He made sure everyone understood that in the coming meeting of the clan there would be clothing and other goods that could be traded for. Each member of the Northern Elk Clan would want to have enough goods with which to barter.

Salt, fish, and weapons were always in demand. Decorative shirts, skirts, and shoes were also in demand.

More and more often the meals were eaten out in the compound as the days grew warmer. The snow receded up the mountain side and the valley grew green.

"Why don't we send a gift to the Others and the Elk Clan and let them all know of our newly established clan," Taelo suggested one morning.

"That is a great idea," Little Otter spoke up.

Everyone looked at him in surprise.

"Why is everyone looking at me," he questioned when he realized everyone was looking his way.

I am glad you like the idea. Would you lead a small group on this journey," Taelo asked?

"Yes, that would be great," Little Otter replied.

He was tired of the fishing and training all the young adults how to use their weapons for defense and to hunt. A trip was very attractive.

"The leader of each group, Running Stag and a few others or about six people should go with you," Taelo continued.

The planning for the trip triggered an enthusiastic discussion throughout the lodge.

Running Stag became an instant celebrity. Everyone wanted to know why he had been chosen.

Little Otter told the story of Running Stag's fighting the cannibals. In his version Running Stag faced the last warrior on his own and Taelo just happened to help.

Then he told the most recent story of his participation in saving Semper's crew. In this version Taelo slept all the way back to get the last group of people and then single handedly, Running Stag led Golden Hawk and he back to the compound.

"That's the way I remember it," Little Otter concluded as the entire lodge roared in laughter.

It was clear to Taelo that Little Otter had stepped in to fill the story telling vacuum created when Burley Bear stayed with the Others.

A few days later Little Otter led his small band out. They were loaded with salt, dried fish, and a few other gifts for specific Elk Clan members.

Taelo turned to Golden Hawk, "It's time we got started on the building of individual living huts. You and I talked through the general design but now we need to get specific."

"Talking Wren, Wan, Busy Bee and I have been talking this topic for a few weeks now. We would like to suggest a layout for the individual living quarters," Quiet Rabbit interjected herself into the discussion.

Golden Hawk raised his right eyebrow and smiled at Taelo, "I believe the problem has a team already addressing the situation. I think we should listen and get ready to execute."

For the rest of the morning Quiet Rabbit, Talking Wren, Wan, Lily and Busy Bee walked around the outside of the compound laying stones out to mark the various homes and cooking areas. Their lay out was radically different than the one Taelo and Golden Hawk had been discussing when the dire wolves attacked. It was also clear Talking Wren was the leader of the layout team.

"I guess our ancestors sent the wolves as a means to distract us from making a really horrible mistake," Golden Hawk joked with Taelo as they relaxed against the main gate of the compound.

"I am going to take a group down to the river to plant the seeds for our wheat. Would you like to come along and help," Taelo said as he got up and walked inside?

"I guess Taelo got bored watching us lay out the village," Quiet Rabbit commented as she watched almost the entire members of the camp following Taelo toward the river.

"What is he up to," Lily inquired. She had come to expect the unexpected from Taelo. She had also come to respect his judgment and admire the way he brought people together.

"He is taking them to the river to plant the wheat used to make our bread," Busy Bee commented.

"Do you mind if I go watch," Lily commented as she got ready to follow the crowd.

"I would like to go too," Wan said as she followed Lily.

"Well, I guess we are done with the layout. We will explain this to the clan tonight and then tomorrow we can organize the clan to gather the materials needed to begin the building of what we have proposed," Talking Wren commented as all of them followed the rest of the clan to the river

Out to the southwest, Little Otter was enjoying the walk along the ocean. The group with him was in a good mood and the weather was co-operating. They would make the cave of the Others in about seven sun cycles.

Along the way Little Otter was recounting his various adventures with Taelo. No one believed him when he told them about Taelo and Golden Hawk running down the buffalo and placing a spear in front of them and letting the buffalo spear themselves. The laughter only got louder as he kept proclaiming it was true.

When he told the story of the crazed saber tooth tiger chasing Taelo down, the team again roared in laughter. The team began to believe Little Otter was the best storyteller any of them had ever listened to.

"Fine, when we get to the cave of the Others, ask Burley Bear about my stories," Little Otter said as they arrived on the other side of the cliffs just a few miles from the cave.

They were met by Burley Bear himself. Semper had never met Burley Bear. He suddenly realized he was looking at one of the Others. His father had told stories about them, but he had never seen one of them himself.

"Are we safe here," he asked Little Otter.

At the same time Running Stag was out ahead running toward Burley Bear. The two had become friends in the short time they had known each other.

"This is the clan Taelo, and Golden Hawk helped many years ago. Until a few months ago Burley Bear and his mate Meadow Flower were living with us helping build our compound. They helped us build everything you have seen back there," Little Otter commented as he put his arms around Semper and guided him forward.

"Welcome Little Otter, we have been waiting for your arrival. Meadow Flower has prepared your favorite buffalo tongue dinner," Burley Bear said in his own language as he gave Little Otter a hug.

"I was so hoping she would do something like that," Little Otter replied in the language of the Others.

Semper stood by watching in amazement.

"Maybe some of the stories Little Otter told were true," he commented to Wise Council.

The entire group was led to the cave. They were all impressed with the size, layout, and the large warm water pool.

Everyone was invited to clean up in the pool and invited to dinner and to an around the campfire talk afterwards.

Wise Council was impressed with the luxurious home of the Others. He had heard the story of how Taelo had found the cave and hot springs and helped the Others move in. Seeing it all firsthand made an overwhelming impression on him.

He would always credit Taelo with giving him his life and his legs back. His feelings about Taelo just kept getting more positive and stronger.

It seemed every story that came up included some brave deed or generous act Taelo had performed.

Burley Bear stood in the center and began telling Taelo Stories.

"The first time I watched Taelo and Golden Hawk running down the beach toward me, I was sure they had wings on their feet.

Then when I hunted with them, and they ran down the buffalo and let the buffalo spear themselves I truly thought they could fly. Then the day came when Taelo speared four buffaloes in a row one after the other; I knew he could fly. Golden Hawk had done the same as he hunted with Little Otter.

The only persons who could keep up with Taelo were Golden Hawk and Quiet Rabbit.

Quiet Rabbit was there the day the crazed saber tooth attacked our camp. The saber tooth tiger was after Taelo. He made a dash toward the lake with the tiger hard on his heal. I tried to distract the tiger by shouting at the top of my voice as I chased after.

Suddenly someone shouting louder and running twice as fast passed by me as if I were standing still. It was Quiet Rabbit. She was carrying her spear and gaining on the tiger. I wondered what would happen to the tiger when it was caught from behind.

Well, we all know Taelo got the better of the saber tooth tiger when he turned and pulled its teeth out sideward.

Burley Bear ended his story as the entire audience shouted for more.

"He didn't really pull the teeth out. Did he," Running Stag shouted in the language of the Others?

Burley Bear stopped in surprise and looked at Running Stag. A murmur could be heard going through the entire clan.

"He might be a young Taelo," Burley Bear thought.

"That is a good question. Let me finish the story of the crazy tiger so you know the magic that Taelo does possess," Burley Bear said as he turned to the audience and continued the story to its real end.

"I have the two teeth we took from the saber tooth tiger" Burley Bear reached down and held them high. "I am saving them for Taelo."

The next day after a hearty breakfast the six set out with their full travois. They had arrived with two but the gifts they brought for the Others reduced the load down to one. They had a few gifts from the Others for White Swan and Grey Fox Running and for Red Oak and Quiet Pheasant.

The trip down the coast took them by the place where the whale had been discovered and where the bear had come to eat her fill of blubber.

Little Otter once again was telling Taelo and Golden Hawk stories. This time everyone was paying closer attention. They now believed him much more than before. This let him expand and elaborate on the actual details of the stories.

"Burley Bear has created new space for my story telling," Little Otter thought to himself with a smile.

Little Otter was not sure what to expect as they approached the coast village. He let out an eagle's cry. There was no response. They came into the village, but it was obvious no one was present.

"The clan now winters in the Valley of Plenty. This is their late spring and summer quarters. We will stay here the night and then go down to the valley in the morning," Little Otter announced.

Once they had straightened out the main lodge, Little Otter walked along the beach and examined the fish trap. Most of it had been pulled out and stored back up on the beach.

He was standing looking out over the water when Semper, Wise Counsel, Running Stag, Lani, and Golden Flower came down to where he was standing.

"This seems to be such a fine location. Why would the clan leave it unattended? Are they not afraid to lose it to some other clan," Golden Flower asked?

This trip was opening her mind beyond what she had ever dreamed possible.

"Yes, this is a great place. It was here where Taelo and Golden Hawk captured a giant shark. They had so many shark teeth they would have been the richest young men in the clan. They gave shark teeth to the entire clan. They gave the biggest ones to Silent Hawk our old chief and to Burley Bear. They then gave some to all the rest of us. They made special spears for their fathers.

The elders were surprised by their generosity but still suspicious of Taelo. Even I had my doubts at the time. I believe I was just jealous of anyone able to be so generous," Little Otter commented.

After a moment of silence, he continued, "But you asked about the other camp, "Taelo, Golden Hawk and Burley Bear made their transition journey into manhood together.

They wandered to the east and then to the south. Some of you have been in the heated cave up north where we live. Taelo found a similar one not far from here. The waterfall here is much smaller than the one up north but falls into a valley now called the Valley of Plenty.

The buffalo come into the valley for the winter months. Taelo, Golden Hawk and Burley Bear returned pulling a sled carrying three buffalo. Their return was in early spring, and the clan was almost out of food. Their story about the herd was at first thought to be an exaggeration but was soon verified. They suggested the clan follow the lead of the buffalo and winter in the valley and spend the late spring, summer, and early fall here by the sea. And that is what the clan now does." Little Otter explained.

The next morning, they left the camp in order and proceeded down the coast to the cut through the mountains. A day later they entered the valley and saw the slow undulating sea of buffalo.

"Such riches," Semper exclaimed as they all stopped in wonder.

"Why has Taelo set up a camp so far north if there is so much here," Lani asked?

"You have met Broken Spear of the Others. He is a seer. He saw people needing help and shared this with Taelo. He guided Taelo to be there to help all of you," Little Otter replied.

The cave at the top of the falls in the valley up north is the cave in the legend of our clan. Taelo has gone to the salt mine used by our clan in ancient times.

The group was silent for the rest of the day as they walked down the valley toward the river where the village was located.

This time when he let out the call of the eagle there was the echo of a similar cry as White Swan, Taelo's mother replied.

White Swan heard the call of the eagle. She knew it was not Taelo but one of the team with him.

Grey Fox Running and Red Oak were out hunting. She and Quiet Pheasant were running the camp. They and a small following of curious members came out of the compound to see who was approaching.

"Well, there are only two people of that stature," Quiet Pheasant commented as she recognized Little Otter.

"I do not recognize any of the others. Taelo seems to have found new people," White Swan commented.

Little Otter increased his pace and let out the family whoop when he saw his mother coming out of the compound. Little Otter seemed to crash into the group coming out of the compound. His following was standing back feeling a little hesitant.

White Swan turned her attention to the five new people. It seemed obvious to her they came from two separate clans. She was eager to hear their stories.

"I am White Swan of the Elk Clan, mother of Taelo," she declared as she greeted the new people.

"I am Running Stag, Taelo saved my life," the youngest of the group spoke up.

Let me introduce the members of the Northern Elk Clan," Little Otter said in a formal manner. He was now assuming the role of clan representative. Taelo had asked him to announce the new clan's name.

"Oh, I didn't know that we had a Northern Elk Clan," Quiet Pheasant replied in faked surprise.

"Have you ever heard of someone setting up their own Elk clan," she asked White Swan.

"No this is unprecedented and will need much discussion. Let's welcome our new acquaintances and invite them in for discussions," White Swan replied.

The two sisters were joking with each other but even Little Otter appeared to be worried.

Semper and Wise Council look worriedly at each other.

"This does not appear to be what Little Otter was expecting," Lani said quietly to Golden Flower.

The group followed White Swan in. They were taken to an area in the main building where they could put their things.

"Once you get settled and cleaned up from your travels, please join the rest of us for dinner. We would like to hear about our new clan," White Swan said in a formal voice.

A runner was sent out to Grey Fox Running and Red Oak. They arrived back in the early afternoon. They did not have a need to hunt but they were out scouting the surrounding territory. They were glad to hear Little Otter had come with visitors.

"Our son and Golden Hawk are once again challenging the norms of the Elk Clan," White Swan began as Grey Fox Running cleaned up and got ready for dinner.

"The two have found some ninety people in various forms of distress and have brought them all together. They have given themselves the name of the Northern Elk Clan. I am sure Taelo has thought this through and figured this was the easiest way for the Elk Clan to deal with so many needy people showing up at the same time," White Swan informed Grey Fox Running.

"Well good for him. I wish I would have thought of becoming a clan leader in such a direct fashion," Grey Fox Running joked with White Swan.

"This will make this coming clan meeting extremely interesting. It should be as good or better than when we arrived with the Others a few years ago," Grey Fox Running continued.

"Are we in trouble," Semper asked Little Otter as they unpacked their travois and brought their gifts into the central hall.

"No, I don't think so. Just relax and enjoy the evening. Let everyone know the parents of Taelo and Golden Hawk are the leaders of the Elk Clan. They will help us, but they will also have their fun with us. Just enjoy the evening," Little Otter replied with more confidence than he was personally feeling.

His explanation to Semper served to put him at ease. Taelo would not have sent him in harm's way without warning and coaching.

Back in the north, Taelo and Golden Hawk led the entire village to the riverbank and guided the planting of the wheat seeds. This would be their first attempt at growing the wheat as they had learned to do from Feather-in-the-Wind's clan, the Clan of the Condor. They had brought with them the knowledge of putting the remains of the fish they had cleaned down in the soil before putting the seeds into the ground. This they had learned would feed the seeds and grow healthy plants.

They assigned guardianship to the various sections of the planted seeds.

Golden Hawk demonstrated watering and the weeding each section owner needed to do daily.

"There are three owners for each section because you will need to guard the wheat all day and all night," Talking Wren spoke up.

"Each of you is trained to use the sling, the bow and arrow and the spear. You will be responsible to maintain your weapons and replace any lost or broken arrows. That is why I prefer the sling," Quiet Rabbit informed the owners of each wheat plot.

"You can get lessons on the sling from Feather-in-the-Wind who is the best among us. All of us will own a part of the wheat. There are no exceptions. And all will continue to participate in fishing," Golden Hawk spoke next.

"Well, this is getting to be a major clan meeting," Taelo said quietly.

"I did not mean for it to get so serious. The more exciting event will be the building of our new living quarters. This will happen in the next few moon cycles. Let's listen to our leaders who have spent the morning laying out our new village," Taelo said as he turned to Quiet Rabbit.

"We spent the morning laying out homes for each of you. There will be individual living areas for all of you.

The layout is around the main compound. Each home will have a stream of water, an oven, and a cooking area.

Each home will be of about the same size. Every fourth home will be larger. This will allow for a larger family.

The building will begin tomorrow with the first two on either side of the gate. When the first two are complete the building of the next two will begin. We will continue building until all the homes are up. The finishing touches will be provided by the new occupants," Talking Wren explained to the entire clan.

"I see you selected the vocal one to speak to the clan," Golden Hawk whispered to Busy Bee.

She just smiled back and replied, "We each have our talents."

The building began in earnest. Timbers were brought in from the forest. The flat stone for each home was gathered and put near where it would be used. The main structure for each unit was rapidly built and within a moon cycle everyone had a unit for themselves. The finishing work would go on for most of the summer.

The wheat was growing and those defending their wheat plots were adding rabbit, ground hog, many deer, and a variety of bird to the clan meat supply. The wheat seemed to be a strong attraction for all types of animals. At the rate, the meat supply was growing a long hunt might not be necessary.

Chapter 27: Threat from the North

The lush lighter green grasses were bordered by the dark green of the sentinel pine forest surrounding the valley. The falls on the far end of the valley began the early morning shrouded in grey mist until the sun's rays dispersed them in a turmoil soup of flashing colors. Such mornings were wondrous displays that made early morning a favorite for all the clan members.

The wheat was growing well, the fishing was plentiful, and it seemed that the animals such as deer and elk were returning to the valley.

Taelo surmised that the dire wolf population that they had almost extinguished during their battle at the beginning of winter had been the reason the larger game had been missing for most of the winter.

Taelo and Golden Hawk decided it was time for them to go north along the coast and determine if there were any other people living in this northern region.

He shared this news with the team as they finished their evening dinner.

"I was wondering how long you would last in our calm valley," Quiet Rabbit said quietly.

She and Busy Bee had talked about something like this coming up soon. They knew their two spouses well.

A few days later Little Otter and his band returned.

"Grey Fox Running and White Swan send you, their greetings. They have sent you an eagle feather for the spear of the Northern Clan Leader," Little Otter announced as he was greeted.

"Well, I believe they may be premature in their assessment," Taelo said quietly so only Quiet Rabbit and Golden Hawk could hear.

The next day Taelo and Golden Hawk left the valley heading northwest and out to the coast.

"Do you want to be the Clan Leader," Taelo asked Golden Hawk?

"No, I don't, do you," Golden Hawk replied?

"No, I only plan to bring a new clan into the Elk Clan," I figure I will let the clan leadership decide who should be the new clan leader," Taelo replied.

"Well, it should be an interesting meeting," Golden Hawk chuckled.

The two had crossed the ridges and descended to the beach and were now jogging effortlessly north along the coast. They were looking for smoke or any other sign of other people in the area.

Lasher was easily keeping pace and periodically would run into the water after a fish or crab.

Taelo spotted an eagle flying toward a mountain peak that was northeast from their current location.

"Let's head for that high peak up ahead and see if we can see any indication of other people. Remember there is one group of people that are extremely dangerous. I want to make sure if there are more of them that we deal with them carefully," Taelo said as they veered slightly to their right toward the peak.

The change in direction proved to be fortuitous. Just north of where Taelo and Golden Hawk turned toward the mountains a group of predatory beings were planning an attack on a quiet group of people just north along the beach.

Back in the Cave of the Others, Broken Spear awoke from his dream in a cold sweat. He called Burley Bear to him.

"Taelo and Golden Hawk need your help. You must lead a dozen of our warriors north along the coast. You must hurry. Leave immediately or it will be too late. Let your feet have wings," Broken Spear said as he almost collapsed.

Burly Bear acted immediately within the hour he and his best fighters left the cave. He led them at a fast jog up the beach.

Quiet Rabbit awoke to the cry of the eagle. She went out and looked up and saw the eagle flying toward the north. Her instincts immediately cried out "danger." Taelo was in potential danger.

She woke up Busy Bee and shared her concern.

They gathered their weapons and let Little Otter know they were leaving to help Taelo. Running Stag overheard them and gathered his things. He let his father and Feather-in-the-Wind know he was going with Quite Rabbit.

Quiet Rabbit, Busy Bee and with Running Stag trailing just far enough behind to not be immediately discovered headed north along the coast.

Coming up behind them was Burley Bear and his team.

All were responding to Taelo's totem, the eagle.

Meanwhile Golden Hawk had just spotted the fires of a group of people north of where they had stopped on the mountain side.

"I have the campfires of a group of people. There are five fires, so it is at least twenty or so," Golden Hawk commented to Taelo.

"Let's go down and quietly check it out," Taelo said as he left everything but his weapons in their current location.

Golden Hawk did the same. He could tell Taelo expected a major battle.

They went silently around the camp and saw a group of people with their children cooking their evening meal and chatting quietly.

"There are others nearby. I feel them," Taelo whispered to Golden Hawk.

He signaled for them to move silently toward the beach area.

Taelo led them south through the trees. The attack group was making its way silently through the woods. There were about thirty warriors. They were short and stocky like the group of warriors Taelo had fought the previous winter.

They would arrive at the camp in about an hour.

Taelo led Golden Hawk to the edge of the forest, and they set out at a fast run back to the camp they had just left. They burst into the camp and in the three languages Taelo had just learned he slowly repeated one phrase, "Take up your weapons, your enemies are on their way."

All the weapons did indeed come out, but they were aimed at Taelo and Golden Hawk.

Taelo slowly backed into the forest and the men of the camp followed in pursuit.

"This will do," Taelo muttered to himself.

Loud piercing battle cries came out of the forest to the south of them. The women and children still in the camp came screaming into the woods where men had followed Taelo.

Taelo again spoke in three languages and in a commanding voice said, "Turn and fight for your lives. Your bravery will determine your fate."

He and Golden Hawk gave their battle cry at the top of their voices as they went out and met the on-rushing warriors. Each had a war hammer in one hand and their smaller multi-edged shark tooth club in the other. They went in cutting down warriors in rapid succession. Their onslaught gave the men behind them a chance to get into the battle.

The attack was blunted but the battle was going against Taelo and Golden Hawk.

"We are in trouble unless we get a small miracle," Taelo shouted to Golden Hawk.

Coming at full speed up the beach, Quiet Rabbit and Busy Bee heard Taelo's battle cry. They increased the speed of their running. Running Stag was surprised at their ability to speed up, but he was determined to close the distance.

He was almost up to them when both Quiet Rabbit and Busy Bee let out battle cries that almost stopped him in his tracks.

They had arrived at the back of the attacking cannibal warriors. They kept up their battle cry as they charged in and began cutting down the warriors from behind.

Running Stag followed their lead and hacked away with his ax and his small spear.

Taelo recognized Quiet Rabbit's and Busy Bee's war cry. Golden Hawk had the same realization. They both let out their battle cry as both seemed to get new energy. They doubled the damage they were causing. The attacking warriors faded back into the woods in disarray.

"Let's get ready for their return," Taelo said as he took stock of the situation. About half of their number was wounded.

Golden Hawk and he had only minor cuts.

"Running Stag, what are you doing here," Taelo inquired as he gave Quiet Rabbit a hug.

"I followed Quite Rabbit and Busy Bee. I wanted to make sure they would be alright. Little did I know," he replied flippantly.

"Let's retreat to our camp up on the ridge. Then they will need to come up toward us. This will give us a better fighting chance," Taelo began repeating in three languages, but Running Stag stopped him.

"It is my language, these are my people," he said and gave instructions to the camp members.

They immediately responded to him.

"Are you the son of Wise Council?" one of the older members inquired.

"Yes, this brave young man has been instrumental in saving me and many of your people. Now let's move fast," Taelo interrupted.

They moved as fast as they could but about half of the camp was wounded. They left the dead behind.

They had just reached Taelo and Golden Hawk's camp when the attacking warriors came up at them through the forest. Taelo had showed some of the members how to roll down some of the bigger boulders on the steep ridge.

Taelo let out his battle cry. At this signal about half a dozen boulders went down the slope. The crunching of bone and the screams that followed signaled their success. It served to slow the attack.

Burley Bear heard the battle cry out by the ridge. This was followed by the rumbling of rolling rocks and screams.

"Let's swing around and approach from the side. I don't want to face any boulders being rolled down on me by Taelo," he instructed his warrior.

"Keep silent. This will give us the advantage of surprise," Burly Bear continued as he led his warriors up the open side of the ridge. The other side was a sheer cliff. He knew the attackers would try to come around in this direction. They would be in for a surprise when they did.

High above in the sky an eagle screamed.

Taelo knew his totem was giving him a signal.

"Three of you stay here and randomly roll the rocks down the slope. Running Stag, you stay here and command this position. Keep your eye out to the right in case a few attackers have decided to come up and surprise us.

Call for help if the attackers are making it up the slope. The rest of you spread out to the left. The main force will be coming at us from that direction," Taelo commanded.

When Burley Bear heard the eagle, he spoke quietly to his warriors. "The eagle has visited. When we hear Taelo's war cry we will attack from the rear. Show no mercy. Fight bravely and protect each other."

The attackers were trying to sneak in but when Taelo spotted them he let out his war cry and moved his warriors forward. The Others moved in from the rear with every warrior giving their clans war cry.

"It is the Others," Quiet Rabbit called out.

"They are our friends, do not harm them," Busy Bee cried out to her set of fighters.

Running Stag thought he had been given his role because Taelo was trying to protect him but suddenly he and his three fighters had their hands full with those trying to come up the slope. When two warriors came at him from his right, he let out his own war cry and attacked.

The two warriors were not expecting to fight someone so young and small. Running Stag ran at them and just before he got to them, he slid on the ground past them and cut across their Achilles tendon. The two warriors fell face down. They never had a chance as Running Stag's war hammer found their skulls.

The three older warriors on his side, busy rolling stones down the hill side called for help. They had witnessed the fight Running Stag had just put up. They were losing their own battle as more of the attackers came up the steep grade.

Quiet Rabbit heard Running Stag's war cry and knew he needed help. She sent six of her warriors to the ridge.

The battle was in full swing on all fronts. The attack of the Others from behind was devastating to the attackers. They were soon trying to retreat but the only way out was cut off. Their only hope was if their attack up the slope could succeed.

Running Stag and his reinforcements took on the attackers coming up the grade. Luckily, they were able to face them singly or in pairs. There was no way for the attackers to form a cohesive fighting unit. Running Stag's small stature and quick nimble movement caused consternation among the stronger but slower attackers.

Busy Bee arrived with all her fighters and the ridge battle was soon over.

Burley Bear's fighters were down hunting the few remaining attackers.

"Thank you, my friend, for coming to our aid," Taelo said as he gave Burley Bear a hug.

"I am Kamil, leader of these people. I thank all of you. How did you know of the attack?"

"I fought a similar group of warriors last winter. They had attacked a group of your people coming into this land. I felt uneasy and came to check the coast. Do you know Wise Council," Taelo asked?

"Yes, he left earlier with many of our people," Kamil recalled.

The people of the camp had not been so lucky. They were not warriors. They were brave and had fought gallantly but several had been killed and many were wounded.

Running Stag came forward.

Busy Bee had already stitched up the cut across his back

"Kamil, I am Running Stag, son of Wise Council, I remember you from the grand council meeting two years ago," he said as he joined the group and gave Burley Bear a big hug.

"Thank you for saving us," he said to his favorite giant.

"What brought the three of you," Golden Hawk asked Busy Bee as he wrapped his arm around her shoulder?

"The three of you saved us in the attack down below. Your unexpected rear attack and the strength of Quiet Rabbit's and Busy Bee's war cry made it sound as if all of Burley Bear's warriors were with you. It gave us the time to reorganize and move up here. We all need to thank you as well," Golden Hawk commented.

"Quiet Rabbit reacted to the eagle's cry over the valley. She took up her weapons and some food and was ready to leave the valley on her own. I was not about to let her go by herself, so I joined her. I recalled how she got her name as we ran up the beach.

When she let out her war cry, I remembered the day she chased after the saber tooth attacking Taelo. I knew the warriors in her path faced certain death. I stayed in her shadow and finished off the warriors she wounded. We make an excellent fighting team," Busy Bee recounted.

"And why were you following us," both Busy Bee and Quiet Rabbit asked Running Stag in unison.

"Because Taelo told me to watch out for Quiet Rabbit while he was gone," Running Stag replied.

Burley Bear let out a loud laugh and patted Running Stag on the shoulder.

"As always, we are in this trouble because of Taelo," he went on with a chuckle.

"Kamil have your people treat all the wounded. My warriors will clear up the battlefield and pull all the dead attackers to one location.

Quiet Rabbit it would be great if we could prepare a meal for everyone. I know my warriors are starving. I have sent several of them back to get our supplies.

Then we could all use some sleep," Burley Bear said as he turned to one of his men and gave orders.

Taelo quietly walked among the new people. He spoke quietly to them, giving condolences to those who had lost a loved one and thanking each of them for their bravery in battle.

He was pleased with Burley Bear's leadership. It was clear Burley Bear had matured to be the leader of his people.

"You are welcome to come to the Valley for a visit," Taelo said to Burley Bear the next day as they were about to part and go their separate ways.

"Thank you for the invitation. I will see you this fall at the meeting of the Elk Clan. It should be as much fun as when Grey Fox Running brought the Others to the meeting. You are bringing a whole new clan. We will be bringing a fine supply of our white leather, dress vests and shirts and a wide variety of scented soap. Be prepared to pay dearly for them," Burley Bear said as he gave Taelo and Golden Hawk goodbye hugs.

Running Stag gave Burley Bear a big hug and then took the lead on the trail west up the river to their valley.

Taelo pulled Running Stag aside and thanked him for taking him seriously about watching out for Quiet Rabbit. Then he sent him ahead of the group to let Little Otter know that they were returning with another thirty people.

When Taelo arrived at the valley, Little Otter came out to meet the arriving group.

The integration of all these people into the Elk Clan was a topic Taelo brought up to all the leaders. There were two distinct new peoples. They sought to join the Elk Clan.

Taelo proposed a way to make the integration rapid and permanent. This was to distribute family units throughout the various Elk Clans and to accept new families into the Northern Elk Clan. Taelo listed those he saw as the potential leader of the Northern Elk Clan; Semper, Kamil and Wise Council, Little Otter, and Talking Wren.

Me," Talking Wren exclaimed in surprise!

"Yes, you have demonstrated all the critical skills of leading the clan. You have been instrumental in designing and executing the building of the village. You have shown your skill as a hunter. Why not as the leader of the clan," Golden Hawk recounted.

"What about you and Golden Hawk," Wise Council inquired.

"We have other plans," was all Taelo would say.

The following months were spent on finishing the building of homes, minding the wheat crop, fishing, mining the salt and transporting it back to the valley. This was all in preparation for the clan meeting and of course the coming winter.

Golden Hawk and Busy Bee continued the language lessons, and everyone became fluent in several languages.

Talking Wren had taken over as the construction leader and made sure there would be plenty of homes and that all the features they had planned were constructed to her standards.

"You know we are going to cause a major upheaval in the clan's proceedings. Remember the coaching the elders of the Others gave Grey Fox Running; lead with the food and warm the stomach, then talk business," Taelo said to Quite Rabbit, Golden Hawk, Busy Bee, Little Otter, and Talking Wren.

"Let's plan on getting to the valley early. We will help each arriving clan set up camp and feed them an arrival feast. Then at the first council meeting we will present the best of the best food before we talk business," Taelo finished.

Semper, Wise Council and Kamil had all been listening. They were still trying to get use to the equal stature of the women and the men.

Golden Flower and Wan were now showing the same independence.

The men sympathized with the elders of the Elk Clan.

Let me plan the dinners," Feather-in-the-Wind said to Quiet Rabbit.

"That is a great idea. You organize what will be prepared for each of the arriving clans," Quiet Rabbit replied.

The summer months melted into fall. The hunting and fishing went well. The evenings were spent preparing goods for trade. Weapons were fashioned, vests made, jewelry fashioned. Each person making what they knew how or learning new skills when they needed to.

Hunting brought in the needed supplies and hides. Fishing was extremely successful. Taelo led a team to gather extra salt. The salt would be used as gifts and to barter for the more expensive items. The Northern Elk Clan resources were abundant. They were going to make a good presentation during the clan meeting.

Chapter 28: Elk Clan Meeting

Taelo led the Northern Elk Clan to the ridge and stopped in the same place that only a few years before he had first suggested using the space on the other side of the lake.

This time he was leading a now unified mix of people who were seeing the valley with a long lake bordered with weeping willow whose yellowing leaves signaled the coming winter. The tall, dark green pine with their lighter brown bark were crowned by the white tops of the tall mountains to the east.

A few ducks and geese were lazily swimming along the cattails periodically dipping their heads into the water to claim some prize food below the surface. Most wildflowers were dried on their stalks, but a few purple or yellow blossoms dotted the valley floor.

Taelo led the way to the lake and took the number one spot by the lakefront. They would not be missed. They left the far side for the Elk Clan and the Others.

They were in the spot Wise Owl normally used.

Everyone had worked hard to execute the plan Taelo, and the rest had devised.

Feather-in-the-Wind had given every family their cooking assignment. Scouts were out around the valley looking for the incoming clans. The new families had each been interviewed. Almost all were willing to go into the other clans if they could keep their family together. There were many young women who had lost their husbands. And there were the single women who were looking for husbands. The population of the Northern Elk Clan was skewed to almost two thirds being young women.

Golden Flower, Busy Bee, Wan and Quiet Rabbit made sure all these single women accumulated a rich supply of salt, food, and leather goods. They also made sure they would be wearing their best outfits during the clan meeting. They were working on nature's way of integrating the clan. They worked with each young lady to build up their self-confidence when meeting young men. Running Stag became the focus of this practice. He was on the young side but he in turn learned how to deal with young women.

Only Feather-in-the-Wind seemed to mind all the attention Running Stag received.

A white swan cried out as it landed on the lake. Shortly after that a runner came in and reported a larger group of people coming in from the southwest.

Taelo sent some workers to set the bridge up across the stream and to make sure all was ready on the other side.

As Grey Fox Running and Red Oak came into the valley, they could see the white smoke coming up from across the lake.

They knew Golden Hawk and Taelo were already in the valley and had sent up the white smoke in memory of the first time they had selected to stay on the far side.

They were surprised Taelo had selected the prime position by the main side of the lake. They and the Others came to the camp and after greetings proceeded across the bridge to the other side of the lake. There they were surprised by the feast awaiting them. They were helped in getting their goods arranged and then escorted to an arrival dinner.

"I am Semper of the Northern Elk Clan. We welcome you to the clan meeting and wish all of you well," he said as the food was served to all the new arrivals.

Taelo was getting a hug from White Swan when another runner came in.

"Your totem is out on the lake. It let me know you were on the way. I think the next group to arrive will be Wise Owl and the Elk Horn Clan. Let's talk later this evening when we get a chance," Taelo said as he left for the other side of the lake.

He wanted to get White Swan's reaction to his plan. She was a wizard at tuning the political instrument.

Wise Owl realized the two best spots had already been taken. He proceeded up to the spot he had anticipated putting his group. He saw Taelo coming forward to greet him. It was clear Taelo had reached full manhood. His eyes already had the look of wisdom.

"Welcome Wise Owl. Please let my team help you get situated and then serve you dinner," Taelo greeted Wise Owl and walked with him to the number two site along the lake.

The Elk Horn Clan members were surprised about the help they were getting. They let out a cheer when they were escorted to an eating area and given a dinner they had not been expecting.

"I see you learn fast about using food to change the mind," Wise Owl let out a chuckle, "Good for you. It works every time."

He wasn't sure what Taelo had planned but he already was swayed to support him. The many young women helping and serving did not escape him either. This was a well-planned, full-scale assault on the Elk sub clans.

Taelo made a surprise proposal to Wise Owl.

"Really, your logic is impeccable and with the changes that are coming about this would be a good time to do what you propose. I am surprised by who you have not included. I will consider it and see how it holds up with the council of elders," Wise Owl replied.

The novelty and the power of Taelo's suggestion surprised him.

"This is an interesting proposal you bring forward. I am surprised that after your personal effort in all this you would be making it," Wise Owl replied.

For the next three days the scene was repeated as the sub clans came into the valley. The Northern Elk Clan was the talk of the valley. They had fed everyone a unique and delicious arrival meal.

They had tremendous wealth on display. Even though the people were different they all spoke the language of the clan.

It was also obvious to all the mothers of the single young men that the Northern Elk Clan also had some very good-looking young women with their own apparent wealth.

The first council meeting was called by Wise Owl. Busy Bee and Quiet Rabbit had asked him to serve dinner before the meeting. The dinner was served as the sunset and the evening darkness arrived. There was an oil fire in a clam shell on each of the thin flat stone dinner platters. This was a new experience for all the clan members. They marveled at the oil fires as they were served not only their traditional dishes but several new dishes as well.

"I hope our leaders don't fall asleep after such a feast. I would like them to take up the business of the new sub clan as the first item of business," Wise Owl said.

He too was impressed not only with the dinner but the oil lights as well.

"I am the son of White Swan and Grey Fox Running of the Elk Clan. The people who you have met in the last three days are new to this land. They were escaping some very fierce and cruel warriors who eat people. Together with the help of Burley Bear of the Others we faced, defeated, and killed these warriors in a fierce battle. The tale of our hero's will be told later around our council fire.

I introduce the people of the Northern Elk Clan. The clan is ninety in size. It is larger than all the other clans.

The Northern Elk Clan is prepared to move one family to each of the other clans and to accept families from the other clans. This will insure a smooth integration of these new people.

You the council of elders must chose the leader for the Northern Elk Clan. I would like you to consider the following potential leaders, but you may have others that you are considering. The names I am putting forward are Little Otter and Talking Wren both previously of the Elk Clan; Semper of the people of the north; Wise Counsel, Lily and Kamil of the people pursued by the cannibals. We will await your direction. Thank you," Taelo concluded and sat down.

"Why are not Golden Hawk and your name on the list," Wise Owl asked?

"Neither of us desires the position," Golden Hawk replied.

There was a silence of surprise around the council circle. The council members had expected Taelo to lay claim to the leadership position.

White Swan rose to speak. She had spoken to Taelo and was aware he did not want to lead the Northern Elk Clan.

"We have been given a great opportunity to invigorate our clan with new blood, new ideas and as all of you experienced, new ways of preparing and serving food. We were all worried how this new clan would behave. They are showing us the way for a smooth transition.

I like the idea of moving families across the clan boundaries. I have experienced this in the recent past. If done with consideration it is a wonderful experience."

Each of the clan leaders rose to speak. Most were positive and all agreed to family exchanges to create a clan wide integration.

"I propose we table the discussion of who should lead this new clan until we have a chance to agree to the list of potential candidates and interview each of them," Wise Owl said as he took control of the meeting.

In the following days, the families of the Northern Elk Clan made a point of visiting each of the other clans. Busy Bee was to guide the placement of the families. She worked with White Swan and Quiet Pheasant to match families with clans and to select families from the clans to move into the Northern Elk Clan.

The night before the announcement of who was to be the leader of the new Northern Elk Clan, Broken Spear invited Taelo, Quite Rabbit, Golden Hawk and Busy Bee to his camp. Burley Bear, Meadow Flower, Little Otter, and Talking Wren were also present.

Since Burley Bear now sat on the council as the leader of the Others, he knew what the announcement was to be.

"Tomorrow you will get a pleasant surprise. I have seen through the eyes of the eagle, and it will be here to herald the announcement of the leaders of the new Northern Elk Clan. The eagle will cry, and the white swan will fly from the lake. I am pleased with what the council has done. Each of your recommended leaders will be sent to separate clans as lead hunters. Let them know this is an honor.

They must not misunderstand. The Northern Elk Clan must also understand they have been given the best," Broken Spear said in his slow deep voice.

"So, my good friend you withhold such valuable information from your two best friends and just sit there with a smile on your face," Taelo teased Burley Bear.

"Yes, this is a once in a lifetime opportunity to know something before you do," Burley Bear said with a smile.

As they were getting ready to go to sleep Quiet Rabbit asked, "You seem relaxed. Do you know what the announcement will be?"

"Yes of course I do. Broken Spear told us. It is so good that I will let it remain a surprise until tomorrow evening," Taelo said with a smile as he hugged Quiet Rabbit.

The only point he was not sure about was which would be named the leader, and which would be named lead hunter.

The next day seemed to drag by slowly. Several of the young women of the Northern Elk Clan had attracted suitors and could be seen walking and talking with them. The mothers of the clan worked quickly and were very good at match making. The various families were still making their introductory rounds and then sharing their preferences with Busy Bee and Quiet Rabbit. The two were in turn talking to White Swan.

Finally, the council meeting was convened. Taelo and Golden Hawk were invited for the final discussion and announcement.

Busy Bee and Quiet Rabbit made the announcements of which families in the Northern Elk Clan would be moving to other clans and which clans they were going to. They then announced which new families would be joining the Northern Elk Clan. There was one family from each of the sub clans coming to the Northern Elk Clan.

There were about two families leaving the Northern Elk Clan and going to each of the other clans. So, all the other clans would gain in population.

The Northern Elk Clan would become smaller but equal in size to all the other sub clans. This two for one redistribution resulted in an almost balanced distribution among the clans.

Then Wise Owl stood up to make the leadership change announcement.

"Let me begin with the change in leadership of the Elk Clan." This statement caused everyone to become quiet.

"Red Oak will become the new leader of the Elk Clan and his main hunters will be Little Otter and Talking Wren. Let's congratulate these three." Wise Owl paused to let the pounding of the spear butts against the ground subside.

"The Leader of the new Northern Elk Clan will be …. and Wise Owl paused and looked around, "none other than our own White Swan.

Just then everyone could hear the white swan on the lake calling and running on the water as she took off. High in the sky an eagle let out a cry. The white swan circled the valley in a low flight over the camp, while high above the eagle flew the counter circle.

Everyone watched in silence. This made White Swan the first woman leader of one of the Elk Clans.

"The main hunter for the Northern Elk Clan will be Wise Council," Wise Owl continued.

This again surprised everyone since they were expecting Grey Fox Running to be the main hunter.

"Grey Fox Running will become an elder."

Semper and Kamil will become co-hunters for the Elk Hide Clan. This will allow them to become familiar with our traditions. Next year we will re-assign lead hunters.

A murmur was going around the leadership circle. "Why would Grey Fox Running be made an elder so soon?"

Golden Hawk and Taelo will be named to new positions of warriors at large. I give them each a spear with their totem feather and a golden feather.

Over the years these two have continually enriched the clan. The golden feather is a symbol of their membership in all the clans.

In the future, they will also have the privilege of attending council meetings. This time the spear butts hitting the floor was deafening and continued for a long time.

In the next two days the changes just announced will take place and the clans reorganized," Wise Owl concluded.

Taelo went up to his mother and congratulated her. He handed her a ceremonial spear with one white swan feather at the top and the eagle feather that she had sent him just below it.

"This is for you. I believe it is customary for the clan leader to have the symbol of their totem on their ceremonial spear.

"Who better than you to bring a new clan into existence," Taelo said as he gave her a hug.

Taelo was pleased that the seed he had planted on the first evening of Wise Owl's arrival had taken root. He would thank Wise Owl later.

He had also talked to Grey Fox Running, "I want to invite you to go with Golden Hawk and me on a long trek across to another sea. Broken Spear has flown with the eagle to the far sea. He says the ancestors are calling for me to go."

"It's a great invitation. However, it would be very hard for me to leave White Swan for so long. I will be staying to support her in her new leadership role." Grey Fox Running replied knowing he would not be going.

Chapter 29: Journey to the East

The Clan meetings came to an end and each clan left with their new members. Several of the young Northern Elk Clan women were mated with young men in the other clans and went with them to the clan of their new mate.

Busy Bee, Quiet Rabbit said goodbye to Talking Wren.

"Your design of the living area around the compound was unique. You will have to do something similar for the Elk Clan," both said as the Elk Clan and the Others left the valley.

"Come by and visit Broken Spear before you wander to the East," Burley Bear said as he gave Taelo a hug.

"I certainly will. I will want his guidance and any other insights he may have," Taelo responded.

Semper and Kamil came by together to thank Taelo for his help and guidance.

"Wise Owl says you spoke highly of us and recommended us as leaders of the clan. Thank you. We look forward to your next contributions to the Elk Clan," the two shared as they were getting ready to leave with Wise Owl and the Elk Hide Clan.

"As always, you have enriched the clan. I look forward to your continued contributions to our wellbeing," Wise Owl said as he led his clan out of the valley.

"Thank you for acting on my suggestion," Taelo replied as they parted.

The Northern Elk Clan and its new members waited until all the rest left the camp.

"We the Northern Elk Clan, have the greatest change in the families that make up our clan. We will stay here a few days longer and listen to the history of each family. We will talk to each other and extend our celebration of being the newest Elk sub clan. We are truly a mix of all our history. I am new to this role. My main hunter, Wise Council is new to the Elk Clan. Together we will seek to make this clan the best of all the clans," White Swan spoke to all of the new Northern Elk Clan members.

"We have followed the lead of Taelo and Golden Hawk for the past season and we are prepared for the winter. We have the best shelter I have ever known. We have an abundance of food. We need only to learn to work together to continue our wellbeing," Wise Council said as he spoke next.

Taelo and Golden Hawk walked out to the two large boulders where many years ago Taelo overheard his father talking to Red Oak about getting promoted to be the leader of the main Elk Clan.

Grey Fox Running had taken over from Silver Hawk.

Taelo was relieved when he learned he and Golden Hawk would remain together.

Now he and Golden Hawk were sitting in the same spot talking about their future.

"I can't think of anything more interesting than going East to the other ocean. We went south and found an interesting land, people and so many good things to eat. I wonder what we will find to the East," Taelo conjectured.

"It is the journey with a good friend that makes it enjoyable. The four of us make a good team. We should have as much fun on this coming journey as we did in our journey south.

I think we will miss Burley Bear and Little Otter. One has a quiet helpful partner, the other has a partner that never stops talking. The two always balanced out.

Our journey north has yielded an interesting result but think about how much work it has been," Golden Hawk replied.

"Yes, those who journey together grow bonds and become close. I have been asked by two young adventures if they can come with us," Taelo share with Golden Hawk.

"Who would they be," Golden Hawk asked.

He thought he knew who the two would be.

"Running Stag and Feather-in-the-Wind each asked. Running Stag asked me, and Feather-in-the-Wind asked Quiet Rabbit," Taelo responded.

"I think they would make great traveling companions. It is fine with me," Golden Hawk responded.

The two sat quietly and watched the sun slowly set. High above an eagle circled quietly. There was no need for an eagle cry.

The Northern Elk Clan returned to the valley in the north.

"I never thought I would be living this far north again," White Swan commented to Grey Fox Running.

They had stopped to admire the compound built on a small hill, surrounded by a stone wall and that featured a massive wooden gate. Individual living quarters also build of stone were organized around the base of the mound.

"It looks as if Taelo and his team built the most elaborate compound of all the clans," Grey Fox Running commented.

"Yes, we will benefit greatly from this unique home," White Swan replied as she walked around inspecting the facility.

Taelo and Golden Hawk had chosen to travel about a day behind the rest of the clan. They wanted White Swan to establish her role and leadership without interference.

"Hey, would you mess with your mother in this situation," Taelo responded when asked why he was hanging back.

"Not I," replied Golden Hawk.

"It was a surprise to me that Wise Owl supported White Swan for the leadership position," Busy Bee commented.

"Wise Owl has the unique capability to see change coming and act to get ahead of it," Quiet Rabbit replied.

"It also helps when someone makes a direct suggestion," Golden Hawk said jokingly as he gave Taelo a pat on the back.

"I think Wise Owl is really good at selling his position and ensuring the support he needs from the other leaders is in hand before he asks for agreement," Taelo responded.

The four talked and decided that they would leave on their next journey before winter. They would visit the Others and then travel to the winter quarters of the eastern most Elk sub clan. The Grazing Elk were on the eastern side of the mountains.

Feather-in-the-Wind was walking with Running Stag behind the four.

"The Journey East sounds so exciting," Feather-in-the-Wind said quietly to Running Stag.

"We will arrive to their location sometime in the middle of winter or early spring. This will give us a head start in our Journey to the East," Taelo said as they reached the bend in the river leading to the compound.

There was one more surprise feast awaiting them as they walked up the rise to the gate.

The End

Journey of Discovery

Dedicated to all who seek, share, and utilize
knowledge to help society.

Journey of Discovery

Chapter 1: Salt and Preparation

The far cliff tops at the far end of the valley, blurred and hidden at the top
by the mist from the water making its long descent to the river pool below,
glowed red, yellow, and orange as the sun rose above the towering white
snow-covered mountains to the east.

The dark green sentinel pines in their rigid rows formed a green skirt from
midway on the mountains down to the valley floor. The valley was an almost
long perfect oval with the pool at the base of the falls at its far end.

The river ran toward the Clan lodge along the foot of the cliffs that slowly
descended to the left side of the valley.

Taelo and his mate Quiet Rabbit stood together enjoying the quiet of the
morning and listening as the valley creatures awakened. This was always an
enjoyable peaceful moment.

This was the valley where long ago the original Elk Clan was established.
The Elk Clan had abandoned the Valley hundreds of years ago as the cold
made living harder. The history of that time had become no more than stories
parents and grandparents told to children.

Taelo and his team, Golden Hawk and Busy Bee, Little Otter and Talking
Wren, Burley Bear and Meadow Flower, Feather-In-the-Wind had
rediscovered the Valley, built a unique and remarkable warm water heated
lodge, populated the new Northern Elk Clan with two different groups of
people rescued from the edge of peril.

This team developed the new people and took them to the annual Elk Clan
gathering. There, Taelo guided the exchange of families to smoothly integrate
Northern Elk Clan families into the other Elk sub clans. Taelo secretly and
successfully pushed for his mother White Swan to become the leader of the
Northern Elk Clan.

Wise Council was now her lead hunter.

She relied heavily on her mate, Grey Fox Running for guidance on how
the clan should be managed. Until her selection to lead the Northern Elk Clan,
he had been the leader of the main and original Elk sub-clan. He had chosen
to retire and become an elder to support her in her role as the first woman
leading one of the Elk sub-clans.

It was early winter, and the snows were once again beginning to cover the
mountains in white.

This was the day Taelo would take White Swan, Grey Fox Running, Quiet
Rabbit, Golden Hawk and Busy Bee to the ancient salt mine to the Northwest
of the Valley.

Up to this time he had been the only one to visit the salt mine.

It took most of the sun cycle for the three sleds pulled by their trained
wolves to cross the valley and pull up the slope to the ridge running almost
due west.

The group spent the evening enjoying roasted rabbit for dinner and
engaging in the normal family chatter.

The next day they reached the cliff where the Talley Stone marked a sharp turn toward another ridge. It was at this point where Taelo stopped to show everyone the Talley Stone and all the marking on it.

"This is the Talley Stone in the story you told me as a child," Taelo said to Grey Fox Running, as he pointed to the scratches on the stone.

"These marks account for all the salt brought up from the salt mine. The last four marks are mine," he continued.

"The stories were told to me by my Father. I never really knew if they were true. A deep emotional feeling that I don't know how to describe is going through me as we stand here," Grey Fox Running replied as he let his hand slide gently down the row of scratch marks.

He was quietly remembering his mother and father who had passed just a few seasons ago. He wished they could have known the truth in the stories they told.

White Swan came over and touched the marks as well. She too had listened to her parents tell the stories.

Everyone in all the Elk Clans had heard the stories at some time since they were stories that were told at in almost every fall gathering.

The group stood around the rock absorbing the ghosts of all the ancient salt gatherers that had left their mark on the stone.

"Is there really a small fishing lake to test the salt gatherer's physical condition," White Swan inquired.

She had heard all the stories and was now amazed to find out they were true. She was taken back to the stories she had listened to as she grew up.

"We will stop by the lake for the night and all of us can take a turn standing on the fishing stone to determine if you are fit to gather salt.

Lasher will gather the fish that get tossed to shore," Taelo said with a chuckle as he scratched Lasher, his wolf companion behind his ears.

Taelo, put Lasher back in harness at the lead position of the team of sled wolves and proceeded down the ridge toward the lake.

The ridge joined a small, high, flat valley formed by two co-joined mountains. The lake took up most of the valley area. Windblown, scraggily pine gave the valley the appearance of slopping toward the West when in fact it was almost perfectly flat.

"So, this is the fishing lake where each salt gatherer had to prove he was still fit," Busy Bee commented as the group set up camp.

It was still early afternoon, and they were all eager to try their hand at spearing a fish.

"Remember the lesson on spearing fish in the water," Taelo counseled as the group prepared to try their hand.

"It's not even a challenge for you," White Swan commented as Grey Fox Running flipped his fish onto the bank. "We will let you carry the most salt."

Taelo sat at the center of camp and dutifully gutted the fish Lasher carried over to him. Everyone had speared a fish.

A short time later they all sat around the fire roasting their fish.

"Well, we all qualify to gather salt," Grey Fox Running commented.

He was again thinking of his father and the stories he told him about the spearing of the fish.

"Tomorrow you will all be put to the test to see if you can find the salt mine. You told Golden Hawk and me the story of how to find it.

Tomorrow you can tell the story again and see who is first to understand it. I will tell you it took me a full morning to finally remember the words of the story and take the right action," Taelo commented.

He remembered how difficult it had been for him to take the right action based on his memory of the story Grey Fox Running had told.

"I can't wait. I want to see if I understood the story right," Golden Hawk said as he ate his fish.

"No, I told all of you how I finally solved the problem," Taelo said as he pointed his roasting stick at Busy Bee, Quiet Rabbit, and Golden Hawk.

White Swan and Grey Fox Running get to solve the riddle by themselves," Taelo countered as he smiled at his parents.

The trail away from the valley with the lake was barely visible in the early morning light as the two sleds went down the trail toward the west.

The sun was almost at its zenith when they stopped at a small merrily gurgling stream where the water fell merrily down into a small pool.

"This is where we are to turn left and proceed to the spear rock," Grey Fox Running said as he recognized the scenery from the stories his father had told him and he in turn had told Taelo.

"You've got it. I doubted myself all the way. It seemed too easy," Taelo replied

After a cold meal, the two sleds turned and went up stream on the ancient path now almost overrun by nature but periodically still visible as a well-used path.

Not much later Grey Fox Running called for a stop as the black Spear Rock stood out in stark contrast to the light blue sky behind it.

"And here is the Spear Rock just as my father described it," Grey Fox Running said as he walked toward it.

He commented on the shiver that had just run through his body as he thought back to the time when he as a small boy had listened to the stories his father had told him.

He reached out and gave White Swan a hug. She in turn pulled Taelo to her side.

"I too listened to this story many times," White Swan said as she gave both of them a hug.

She had always wondered if any of the stories were true.

Now here she stood in front of the Spear Rock.

It took Grey Fox Running and White Swan almost as long as it had taken Taelo to solve the mystery of where the salt mine was located.

They voiced the words of the ditty numerous times.

"Hold your spear vertically at your arms full reach. Spear tip to spear tip. Equal distance left and equal distance right. Six paces forward, six to your right,"

The two were entertaining to watch. Taelo, Quiet Rabbit, Golden Hawk and Busy Bee sat around enjoying White Swan and Grey Fox Running discuss and argue about what the story meant.

Grey Fox Running finally held his spear at arm's length and positioned himself to look over his spear tip and aligned it with the tip of stone needle pointing into the sky.

He took the steps as directed and stood looking. He looked at a long crack in the face of the stone. He walked forward and into the crack.

A cheer went up when the riddle of "spear tip to spear tip, eye to the sky, equal distance left and equal distance to right, six paces forward, six to your right" was finally solved.

They gathered the salt as it had been done for centuries before them. There was a long stick with a sharp stone at one end and a crook on the other end.

The holes were repeatedly drilled back into the salt. The salt drilled out of the hole was put into leather bags. The holes were drilled close together all the way around the block. When the walls between the holes along the bottom of the block were broken, the entire block broke loose.

"It took me a while to figure out how this was done, and I had to stop to make some bags to hold the loose salt," Taelo admitted.

Each of the two sleds carried two large salt blocks. Taelo had brought back four on his previous trip, but this time enough room was needed in the sleds for people to ride.

"It is better to gather salt in the winter using the sled and a team of wolves. I can only imagine the effort it took to carry the blocks back up by hand," Taelo commented as they traveled back toward the lake in the valley above them.

Two sun cycles later the team stood at the top of the cliff overlooking the valley.

"We will stop and spend the night at the original Elk Clan Ceremonial Cave. This is where I brought the survivors who had escaped their cannibal captors. Golden Hawk and I found the cave when we climbed the face of the cliff on each side of the waterfall," Taelo commented as he removed the entrance stones.

It was evident that no one had been to the cave since they had last closed it up a few moon cycles ago.

"Let me show you the drawings I discovered when we first came in," Quiet Rabbit said as she held her torch to the drawings on the cave's wall.

Everyone gathered around and studied the drawings.

"All the stories my father told me were true. I can't believe I have been given this chance to rediscover the past history of our Elk Clan," Grey Fox Running said as he took in the cave.

"Does it have hot water rain from above," he asked as he walked around the cave.

Golden Hawk removed the stones blocking the hot water spring and the water followed the groove to the pool. Once it had filled, he put the hollowed log into place and the water was diverted to create the "hot water rain" from above the pool.

"I find it hard to believe that you were able to solve all these riddles and to return the clan to the point the Elk Clan began their journey," White Swan said as she stood beneath the hot water falling down from above.

She instinctively knew Taelo had been guided by the ancestors.

"I guess this is a good time to let you know about our next journey," Taelo replied after they had all enjoyed a warm shower and were sitting around the fire looking out of the cave and into the star filled night sky.

"Yes, tell us about your plans and who you are planning to take along," White Swan replied.

We are planning a trip to the East. This one may take longer than our trip to the South," Taelo began.

He shared the vision Broken Spear had told him and the fact that the ancestors were calling for him.

"We were thinking of leaving once we return from this salt gathering," Quiet Rabbit continued. "Feather-in-the-Wind would like to travel with us."

"Running Stag also wants to travel with us," Taelo continued.

"Busy Bee and I are planning to go," Golden Hawk spoke up next.

"Well, it sounds like this will be another journey of adventure and discovery. Do your parents know of this journey," Grey Fox Running asked in reply as he looked at Golden Hawk.

"Not specifically. At the end of the Elk Clan gathering, they invited us to come back to the Valley of Plenty. We declined because we were planning a new trip. They wished us well on our next adventure," Golden Hawk replied.

"My grandmother told me to have fun and enjoy the trip," Quiet Rabbit added.

Her grandmother had raised her, and they shared a very close relationship.

"Follow your dream," had been her advice.

In the last year, the two had become closer than they had ever been before. Quiet Rabbit was following a path in life similar to her grandmother who had left her original clan to be mate to the one she loved.

"My parents really have changed. They have been impressed with what our team has accomplished, "Have fun but be careful were their parting words," Busy Bee continued.

"Well as usual, you are not asking permission but politely letting us know your plans," White Swan said with smile. "I am sure the entire Northern Elk Clan will want to help you. Please don't take them all with you."

She would have loved to have Taelo stay but she knew he was already on his next adventure.

It took the team longer than they expected to get ready. A moon cycle later the team stood outside the lodge next to their sleds. Taelo, Quiet Rabbit and Running Stag were by one sled and Golden Hawk, Busy Bee and Feather-in-the-Wind were by the other sled. Their wolves knew something new was about to happen and were eager to go.

The entire lodge was out to wish the travelers well.

An eagle was flying silent circles overhead. Then it let out a loud scream and flew down the valley away from the waterfalls.

It was time to go.

Golden Hawk talked to his wolf team and took the lead. Taelo and his team followed. Soon they were traveling between the twin Marker Mountains on the way to the cave of the Others.

"I must stop and meet with Broken Spear before we go East," Taelo had informed the rest of the team.

He had heard the Seer, Broken Spear in his mind requesting that he come by.

They stayed to the ridge as they approached the cave of the Others.

Up ahead of them they spied a member of the Others.

"Welcome," Saber Scar said as he stood in the path before them.

"The Clan has been expecting you. I am to escort you in."

"It is good to see you again," Quite Rabbit replied.

She had sewn up the tiger scars across Saber Scar's chest.

He had been beside her in the battle against the cannibals. They were now close friends. He greeted Quiet Rabbit with special attention. He was forever in her debt.

The entire Clan greeted them at the valley entrance to their cave.

Burley Bear's mother came out and gave Taelo a big hug.

Burley Bear and Meadow Flower gave everyone a hug and escorted them into the cave.

"I told her you were jealous of me always getting a hug from her and that this time she should give you one," Burly Bear said as he enjoyed the scene.

"I am really jealous of this new trip you are taking without me," Burley Bear continued in Taelo's language.

"And I will miss you greatly," Taelo replied in the language of the Others.

Burley Bear was more like an older brother, certainly more than just a friend. They had trekked together to become warriors and had brought their two clans together.

Burley Bear and Meadow Flower were on the team that had trekked south in the journey of the heart. They were more like family than friends.

"Later I will talk to you about some additional members for your team," Burley Bear said quietly so only Taelo, and Quiet Rabbit could hear him.

"After you have had a chance to bathe, eat and relax, Broken Spear would like to spend time with you this evening. He seems more excited about this trip than he was about the last. He has invited Quiet Rabbit, Golden Hawk and Busy Bee. I invited myself and Meadow Flower and was surprised when he agreed," Burley Bear shared in one of his lengthier exchanges.

"I can't wait to hear what he has to say. I am pleased he felt comfortable enough to invite everyone," Taelo replied.

"Yes, you are all invited," Taelo said as he sat in the hot spring talking to Quiet Rabbit, Golden Hawk and Busy Bee.

"Wow, I would love to listen in on what Broken Spear will tell them," Feather-in-the-Wind said to Running Stag as the two sat on the other side with their feet in the pool.

"I feel so lucky that we were allowed to come along that I really don't mind," Running Stag replied.

"Yes, I agree. But Broken Spear seems to know so much. How does he do it? How does he see what will happen," Feather-in-the-Wind continued quietly?

"I don't know how I do it," a quiet voice said from behind them.

The two turned and went quiet when they realized Broken Spear was sitting behind them.

"When and how had he gotten there," flashed through Feather-in-the-Winds mind?

"I am pleased that the two of you are going on this journey. You will see and learn a great many things. You will contribute and be very valuable members of the team. In time you will lead a clan back to those far shores. Pay close attention and learn all you can. This is for you only to know. So now you have talked to Broken Spear and have received his message," Broken Spear said and then went silent as if he was asleep.

A few minutes later he was helped back to his personal area by two older women.

"Can you believe what just happened," Feather-in-the-Wind said as she held Running Stag by the arm. She was shaking as she thought about the message, he had given them.

"He came and talked to us. This is unbelievable," Running Stag said as a shiver ran down his back.

"Did you just see what happened across the pool," Taelo asked Quiet Rabbit.

"No, I was talking with Busy Bee," Quiet Rabbit replied.

"I saw it. It seems our two young companions just got some guidance from Broken Spear," Golden Hawk replied. "They seem stunned," he continued.

"I would be if Broken Spear came and talked to me," both Quiet Rabbit and Busy Bee spoke up almost in unison.

They had never talked to Broken Spear directly.

A short while later they all sat around Broken Spear.

"I am pleased that you have stopped by to talk and listen to this old man," Broken Spear began.

No reply was expected, and all remained silent.

"I have flown with the eagle on many parts of your coming journey. This will be a journey of wonder. There will be danger, but you will work together to outwit or overcome your adversaries.

On the other side of the Mountains in the area of the Grazing Elk Clan you will find a river going east. Follow the river east, southeast until you reach a giant river running south. Follow the giant river only a short distance and then follow the other big river to the east into the eastern mountains.

Follow the mountains north, northeast until you reach the ocean. Once you reach the ocean and rest for a brief period you should turn south and seek the warmth.

What you find and how you use what you find will make your trip much faster than you expect it to be.

Leave your sled wolves with the Grazing Elk Clan. You can collect them on your return.

I know each of you have your own personal wolves. Take them with you. They are not only your companions but guards against danger. They will tell you when to run or when to fight.

Burley Bear thinks he is asking a favor for a pair of Others to join you on your journey. I insist they go. They will make the difference in the battle of the river monster. Burley Bear please introduce our team members," Broken Spear spoke, and each word and phrase was given time to float and be absorbed by the listeners.

Saber Scar and his mate have been training for months. I have personally made them a sled and they have trained their wolves to pull it. I have made them the flat weapon with sharks teeth. They have learned to use the sling. I am sure Feather-in-the-Wind will be able to improve their ability. They are strong and they are fast. No wings on their feet but they will keep up," Burley Bear said quietly.

"I am so pleased it is Saber Scar," Quiet Rabbit replied. "Who is his mate?"

"She is Marigold, sister of Meadow Flower," Burley Bear replied

"We are pleased to have them along. Saber Scar was a key warrior when we defeated the cannibals. He gave me my wolf sled team," Taelo said as a good feeling came to him about the arrangement.

The trip east would have a diverse team. The two were also powerful people to have on the team.

"This," Taelo thought, "is good."

He knew how tough the people of the Others were. To have them along would make their trip safer.

"They are indeed welcome. I know they will make our trip much safer," Taelo said out loud to the group.

A few days later Taelo took the lead as three sleds left the valley of the Others toward the East. Golden Hawk brought up the rear. All the teams were eager to run.

Chapter 2: Into the Valley

Shortly after leaving the valley of the Others, they went up into the mountains to the east. The mountain pass was already heavily covered in snow and only the fact that they were traveling with sleds made their passage possible. The path they followed took them out to an open plain beyond.

Dark clouds threatened more snow, and a brutally cold frozen wind blew the snow on the ground up into the air.

The entire team was overwhelmed by the fierce storm battering them as they crossed the open expanse. This was more than any one of them anticipated. Finally, they came upon an uneven part of the plain where jagged rock ridges rose up to break the flat plain.

"Look up by the ridge. There seems to be an overhang. This may be a place where we can get away from this cold wind," Saber Scar yelled out to the other two sleds.

He turned toward it as Taelo and Golden Hawk both gave him a signal indicating they agreed. The wind was howling and blowing the snow in their faces. Those in the sled were hiding under their hide.

"This has been a long trip," Taelo commented as he maneuvered his sled so it would be almost in place behind Saber Scar's sled.

He immediately began checking his wolves. Both Golden Hawk and Saber Scar were doing the same. They had been traveling for eight sunrises and on this last leg they had come down into either a very large valley or they were on the Eastern side of the mountains.

"Feather-in-the-Wind and Running Stag, please go out and gather enough wood for our fire," Quiet Rabbit asked as she began to unload the food to prepare the evening meal.

"I will put the sleeping hides out. Any specific spot you want," Busy Bee inquired.

"Anyplace to the back of the overhang will be fine. Let me brush the snow out before you bring back the sleeping hides," Marigold replied as she broke off a pine branch from a small scrub cedar pine and began to clear the area of snow.

"I think you have set a record for setting up camp and getting a hot meal ready," Golden Hawk commented as he pulled the last of the meat off his roasted rabbit leg.

He knew how tired he was and was sure the rest of the team was just as exhausted. Every one of them had taken their turn at the back of the sled or had run alongside when the going got rough.

"The weather is too cold to do anything slowly. I want to get under the sleeping fur and get warm," Quiet Rabbit replied.

"Are we on the East side of the mountains? Does anyone know where the Grazing Elk Clan camp might be," Running Stag asked.

He was sure Taelo knew exactly how to get there.

"I asked the Grazing Elk Clan leader how to find their camp. We must look back to the West and find the tallest mountain. We must then follow a straight line to the morning sunrise with the mountain at our back. Their camp is about five sunrise cycles away," Taelo explained.

He thought he had spotted the tallest mountain as the sun was setting but he had been busy guiding is sled. He hoped the directions would be clear when the sun came up in the morning.

"I am sure everything will be clear in the morning. I am ready for a good night sleep," Feather-in-the-Wind said from under her bearskin hide.

She had quickly helped clean up and put everything away and now she was under her sleeping hide. She was toasty warm, and her eyes were already hard to hold open.

The fire died slowly. Only Quiet Rabbit and Taelo, cozily wrapped in a warm buffalo hide, still sat up.

"There is something on your mind. I have seen this look before," Quiet Rabbit said as she snuggled next to Taelo.

"Yes, Broken Spear described an animal that will help speed up our journey.

I have never seen such an animal. He said we would find them in large herds once we were to the East side of the mountains. However, none of the people in the Grazing Elk Clan have ever mentioned them," Taelo replied. "So, are they to the eastern side of the mountains?"

A few moments later, they both crawled under their sleeping hide and quickly fell asleep.

The storm ran its course during the night and the team woke to a cold, crisp morning.

"Look at that single mountain standing above the rest," Marigold said pointing it out to the rest of the team.

Breakfast had been served and they were all cleaning camp items that had been taken from the sleds and then neatly storing them in their place.

"Yes, I believe that is the mountain. But if you look East, you can see another set of mountains," Saber Scar replied.

"Ah, you have the eyesight of an Other," Taelo said as he put his arm across Saber Scar's back.

He squinted to see what Saber Scar was pointing out. He could barely see the gray ridge in the far distance.

"No wonder that the Grazing Elk Clan members did not mention that range," Golden Hawk joined in as he too squinted to make out the distant mountains.

"We are close. We do not want to show up empty handed. Let's use this camp as a base hunting camp. We will go out as two hunting teams and see what we can find," Taelo suggested to the rest of the team.

"I agree. Marigold will you join Busy Bee, Feather-in-the-Wind, and me," Golden Hawk said.

"I would really like that," Marigold replied as she pulled her spear out from the side of the sled.

"That puts you on our party," Taelo addressed Saber Scar.

The two teams went out and took parallel paths going south. They were traveling just within sight of each other.

"Look, a small herd of buffalo," Saber Scar said as he pointed to a herd just within his sight.

"We need to get around in front of them otherwise they will run away from us," Quite Rabbit said.

"I will go out with Golden Hawk. We will run ahead and around them and turn them toward you. Once that is accomplished, we will want to bring down three young buffaloes," Taelo replied.

"May I come with you," Running Stag asked when he heard the plan.

"You two find a large boulder or tree to hide behind. We will bring the herd back to you," Taelo said to Quiet Rabbit and Saber Scar as he pointed out what seemed to be a good boulder.

"Here comes Taelo, Running Stag and Lasher and Arrow. I am sure his team has seen the buffalo ahead. He must have some plan," Golden Hawk commented as he saw the two approaching figures and the two wolves.

"Walker and I want to go with you," Feather-in-the-Wind said as she heard the plan to run around to the front of the herd and turn them back to the North.

"Alright, Feather-in- the-Wind you will be on the right edge and Running Stag you will be on the left edge. Keep the buffalo headed straight North.

Golden Hawk and I will take the middle. Our job will be to turn the herd. Your job will be to keep the herd grouped together by pushing the ones on the edge back toward the center," Taelo instructed.

He hoped the two would have the stamina to keep up. Lasher, Walker, and Arrow each followed their masters.

"Feather-in-the-Wind you come with me on the right side of the herd. Running Stag, you go with Golden Hawk down the left.

You two find a good boulder to protect you. We will bring the herd to you," Taelo repeated the final instruction to Busy Bee and Marigold.

The four left at a fast jog as each went to their side of the herd. Each was carrying only a large square of leather hide. Lasher ran easily at Taelo's side.

Feather-in-the-Wind and Walker were easily keeping pace.

They all got ahead of the herd and then turned back toward them.

"Yee ha, Yee ha," both Taelo and Golden Hawk screamed at the top of their voices as they waved their hides and ran back towards the lead animals in the herd. Echoes of this call could be heard both on the right and left as Feather-in-the-Wind and Running Stag imitated the two.

Lasher ran up toward the lead buffalo growling and then turned and ran back and forth behind the herd.

The herd turned slowly. It was going toward Feather- in-the-Wind.

Yee ha, Yee ha," she screamed as loud as she could and ran back and forth waving her hide in front of the oncoming herd.

Walker ran growling at the lead animals.

"Yee HA, Yee HA," Taelo joined in as he sped around to help her.

Golden Hawk and Running Stag rotated around and the four managed to get the herd running back toward the other four hunters.

Lasher and Walker were running back and forth in front of Feather-in-the-Wind turning the oncoming buffalo away from her.

"We need to shift our position to be in front of the herd," Quite Rabbit said as she waved to Busy Bee for them to come towards her.

The two teams moved and positioned themselves to where they anticipated the herd was going.

Taelo and Golden Hawk were running near their top speed.

Out on the edges Running Stag and Feather-in-the-Wind were both keeping up. They were both doing as instructed.

A few members of the herd broke off, but most were going straight North toward the waiting hunters.

"This may be a small herd but there must be a thousand animals," Quiet Rabbit said as she saw the oncoming herd.

"I will bring down two. You make sure they stay down. Use your war hammer," Quiet Rabbit instructed as she prepared her two spears. Similar words were being shared by Busy Bee.

"Here they come," Quiet Rabbit screamed over the thunderous roar of the hooves of the oncoming herd.

She was holding her spear with her two hands as she looked out around the boulder. She now wished they had picked a bigger boulder.

"Hi Ya," she screamed as she momentarily stepped out from behind the rock.

She was directly in front of a young bull racing full speed at her. She planted the butt of the spear in the ground and pointed it at the bull's chest and then as the tip touched the bull's chest she rolled behind the stone.

She immediately grabbed her second spear, rolled over Saber Scar, looked quickly around on the other side of the boulder, and repeated the act once again.

She was sitting with her back to the boulder as Saber Scar pulled closer and farther behind the boulder.

"I don't think I want to do this another time," Saber Scar yelled over the noise of the buffalo going past.

The two bulls, one on each side of the boulder protected them as the rest of the herd thundered by.

Not far from them a similar feat had been repeated by Busy Bee and Marigold.

"You should see Marigold wield her war hammer," Busy Bee commented later as the two teams met in the middle after the herd had passed.

Both teams were exuberant about their success.

"You four look like you could use a bath and a rest," Quiet Rabbit commented with a laugh as Taelo, Golden Hawk, Feather-in-the-Wind and Running Stag approached.

The four were covered is mud and whatever else the hoofs of the herd had flung up from the ground. Only their eyes showed up clearly in their faces. Lasher, Walker, and Arrow were the only ones that looked normal. They had been rolling in the snow to clean off the mud that had accumulated on them.

"I will stay here and guard our kill and begin getting them ready to be moved. Bring two of the sleds back so we can move our kill to the stream," Saber Scar spoke up.

He could see that he would need to take over this part of the hunt.

"Good job by everyone. Saber Scar seems to have this in control. The four of us will go get cleaned up," Taelo said as he chuckled at how muck covered all four of them.

They had run without their winter clothing on, and it was now getting cold. Taelo was already feeling the cold seeping in through his dirt covered clothing.

"I am putting on my outer coat," Feather-in-the-Wind said as she pulled on the coat she had left behind when she had set off for the run.

"I don't have any heat reserve. I will clean my coat later," she continued.

"Let's go," Taelo said as he led off at a slow jog.

About an hour later, Marigold commented, "Look at those four. Sound asleep and probably dreaming of running."

"We have our four animals hanging up in the trees. I am ready to join them," Saber Scar said as he grabbed a piece of meat Quiet Rabbit had been roasting and was holding out to him.

"Yes, we can finish our work tomorrow," Busy Bee continued as she looked at the four skinned carcasses in the trees. The hides had each been stretched out between two trees.

The four were now probably as tired as the four who were sleeping. They had moved, hung, and skinned the four buffalo. They had fed the wolves and were now exhausted.

The next morning Taelo and Golden Hawk marveled at the four animals and hides hanging up at the edge of the camp.

"Wow, I thought we had worked hard yesterday but look at what the rest of the team did while we slept. Let's fix them all a large breakfast," Golden Hawk suggested as he watched Taelo kneel and blow on the red coals to get the fire started.

"Let's make a stew with some of the dried roots, some of the wheat seeds and pieces of buffalo tongue and tail joints. That should really go well, "Taelo suggested as the fire came to life.

The smells of the cooking stew awoke the rest of the team. They quickly gathered around the warm fire to enjoy a warm breakfast stew.

"That was one of the best meals I have had," Feather-in-the-Wind commented as she stood to go and rinse her bowl.

"I agree. You two should cook more often," Busy Bee said as she followed Feather-in-the-Wind to the small stream.

"Well, I wish the work was done but we now need to prepare the buffalo so we can carry it into the Grazing Elk Clan as a gift," Taelo said as he took out his cutting blade.

It took the team two full cycles of the sun for the team to process and pack all of the buffalo. Marigold did the initial processing of the hides. She wanted the hides to be presentable. These would also be given as gifts.

"Let's go find the clan and then we can decide whether we continue on or stay a few moon cycles," Taelo said as he took the lead on his sled.

He, Running Stag and Quite Rabbit took almost equal turns on the sled runners. Taelo would jog along and talk to Quiet Rabbit when she was on the sled runners. Running Stag would often fall back and jog with Feather-in-the-Wind.

The sleds were fully loaded with the meat and travel was now a little slower.

"Have you seen how easily Feather-in-the-Wind jogs alongside of the sled. Busy Bee says she may be the fastest among all of us," Quiet Rabbit commented to Taelo.

"She can outrun me," Running Stag commented as he jogged alongside of Taelo.

"We will have to test her speed," Taelo said as he looked back to where Feather-in-the-Wind was running up alongside of the wolves and apparently petting each as she went up the line toward the leader.

"She may not want to be called wolf woman, but she has the best rapport of any of us with the wolves," Taelo continued.

The thin almost invisible trail behind the sleds left deep but almost invisible cuts in the snow of the valley. Finally, far in the distance ahead of them they could see smoke rising into the sky.

An eagle cry caused everyone to look up. There in the distance an eagle glided smoothly out ahead of them.

"It is always reassuring when Taelo's totem verifies our actions," Golden Hawk commented to Busy Bee and Feather- in-the-Wind.

"It is magic. There was nothing in the sky a moment ago. Now the eagle screams," Feather-in-the-Wind said as she shielded her eyes to look up at the giant bird flying out ahead of them.

She jumped up and out of the sled and began an easy but fast jog.

Life here is so good. I am with the people I belong with," she thought to herself and envisioned giving the message to her mother.

She was unconsciously running along the wolves and petting them as they pulled the sled.

"Look at Feather-in-the-Wind. She does not have wings on her feet. She is a flying bird," Marigold commented to Saber Scar.

"She is indeed Feather-in-the-Wind," Saber Scar commented.

He knew both of them were thinking about the stories Burley Bear had told to the entire clan about Taelo and Golden Hawk.

"This is already a great adventure to share when we return, and we have just started on this journey. I could not believe how Quite Rabbit stepped out in front of a charging buffalo, planted her spear, and then rolled back behind the boulder. I was barely able to swing my war hammer to finish them off and then join her behind the boulder," Saber Scar commented.

"Yes, it was the same with Busy Bee," Marigold replied.

She had been amazed at the courage and the speed she saw displayed.

"We will have our own stories to add when we next sit around our Clan meeting area," Saber Scar continued.

Taelo brought his sled to a stop by a small stream.

"Let's stop here and make camp. We can rest up. Get cleaned up. Tomorrow we will go into the Grazing Elk Clan camp."

"Let's plan on a display of our team. The people of the Grazing Elk have not seen the use of the wolf sleds. We can show off a little for their amusement and entertainment," Golden Hawk suggested.

"I like that idea," Quiet Rabbit said in support.

"Me too," was echoed by the rest of the team.

Chapter 3: The Grazing Elk Clan

Taelo looked back at the towering white peaked mountain to the West. He turned and looked at the sun rising in the East. Dimly on the far horizon he saw yet another range of snow-capped mountains. He knew that the Grazing Elk were between two mountain ranges and not on the far plain Broken Spear had described.

The circling eagle had not gone unnoticed. Taelo had watched his totem arrive at the break of dawn. He was pleased when the eagle descended to take a fresh piece of buffalo meat from the end of a spear, he had planted in the snow out away from the camp.

Once back up in the sky with the meat held firmly in his claws, the eagle let out a piercing cry.

The team now dressed in their best clothing, looked up into the sky as the eagle's piercing cry reached their ears.

Lily, now living with the Grazing Elk Clan immediately roused all those around her.

"The scream of the eagle, Taelo is nearby," Lily called out to those around her.

She, Gentle Fern, and White Pearl had been rescued by Taelo from the cannibals. They had agreed to stay together and except for Lily had found mates in the Grazing Elk Clan. The three younger women felt lucky to be courted and chosen as mates. They wanted to be as far from the scene of their horrible experience as possible.

"It will be good to see Taelo again," Gentle Fern commented to White Pearl.

The two of them were inseparable. They had both lost their previous mates to the cannibals. Their bond was forged and welded tight by those months of suffering as they watched their brethren being killed and devoured. That was a nightmare that they would live with for the rest of their lives.

They were now at peace with their feelings though they would never get over that time or lose the horror of those memories.

"Let's get everyone ready to greet them. I was not expecting them until spring, but they are always welcome," Fierce Badger, the leader of the Grazing Elk Clan, announced.

Golden Hawk was in the lead as the three sleds sped toward the Grazing Elk Clan.

"Look at how fast they move. We will need to learn to build these devices and to tame wolves to pull them," Fierce Badger commented to those around him.

Everyone was dressed in their best outfits.

Additional living areas had been set up and were ready for the incoming visitors.

"Let's circle the perimeter of the village and then come back around and stop in front of Fierce Badger," Taelo called out as they approached.

The three sleds, one behind the other went smoothly past those waiting for them and went around the camp.

Everyone turned around and watched the three sleds. They were amazed at the ease of the journey around. This was something totally new to them.

The sleds came to a side by side stop in front of Fierce Badger. Once stopped, the sled team members walked up and stood by their lead wolf.

Each member of the team had similar jackets that they chose to wear. This really made them look like the team they were.

"It is good to see all of you again. Thank you for coming out to meet us," Taelo began.

"We have brought a few personal gifts," Marigold, Quiet Rabbit, Busy Bee, and Feather-in-the-Wind said loudly in unison.

Saber Scar, Golden Hawk, and Running Stag loudly called out one after the other.

"My sled has a buffalo for all of you,"

"My sled has a buffalo for all of you,"

"My sled has a buffalo for all of you,"

"Thank you for your generosity. This gift is very timely and welcome. Please, let me show you to the living areas prepared for you," Fierce Badger replied as he greeted each with a hand on the shoulder.

Lily, White Pearl, and Gentle Fern ran forward and gave everyone a hug. Running Stag got a group hug from all three. The four of them walked off toward the center of the village talking together quietly.

"Come, I will lead the way to your quarters," Fierce Badger said as he turned and walked toward the other side of the village.

"We will take the sleds to the center of the village. The wolf teams will not let anyone else do it," Taelo replied as he watched Busy Bee, Quiet Rabbit, Marigold, and Feather-in-the-Wind follow Fierce Badger.

Taelo, Golden Hawk and Saber Scar moved their sleds to a central area.

They then went through the process of taking the wolves out of their harness. They first removed the leather foot covering from each wolf, praised the wolf for his or her work, gave them a treat and then released them from their harness.

The wolves gathered around their masters and then joined together as one large pack and ran off to play and to enjoy themselves.

Lasher and two other wolves remained behind. Lasher was Taelo's shadow. The two other wolves; Arrow and Walker, ran and found Running Stag and Feather-in-the-Wind.

Running Stag had named his wolf Arrow in memory of the arrow he had first shot when he helped Taelo defeat the cannibals.

Feather-in-the-Wind had named her wolf after her brother Bold Walker.

"Every time I pet him, I think of my brother," Feather-in-the-Wind shared when asked about the name.

Feather-in-the-Wind missed her family, but she was comforted by the fact that she had such good friends, and she already knew Running Stag was special to her.

"Let's get our personal items unloaded from the sleds. Afterwards, the meat and other items can be unloaded," Quiet Rabbit suggested.

The entire clan helped them, and everything was soon unloaded and moved into their respective lodging.

"This is a great amount of meat. It will allow us to postpone our next hunt," Fierce Badger commented as he managed the unloading and distribution of the meat.

He made sure his guests had some of the best cuts. Food was always a key concern for him. The amount of food needed by the oncoming guests had been the first thought that had crossed his mind. He was now more relaxed and impressed with Taelo's team. They had come into camp with great fanfare, but they had delivered more than a month of food for the entire Grazing Elk Clan.

"It is clear to me that the Grazing Elk Clan is not on the Eastern side of the mountains but somewhere in between," Saber Scar said a few days later as he, Golden Hawk and Taelo walked away from the camp along the small river.

I agree. I can now clearly see the next tall ridge of mountains to the east," Taelo replied.

"It is beyond that ridge that Broken Spear has seen a new animal that will become central to our travels," Taelo shared with the two.

"What are we going to do while we wait for spring," Golden Hawk asked?

"Well, first let's find three warriors willing to keep our wolf teams. We can then spend a few days training them to handle the wolves and the sleds. Finally, we will take them on a hunt with us so they can experience using the sleds," Taelo replied.

"Tomorrow evening there is a clan gathering. We will be asked to tell our stories. The gathering will be a good time to find out who would be willing to keep the wolf teams," Saber Scar responded.

"Great idea," Golden Hawk added.

The three walked along enjoying the warmth of the morning sun.

In the following weeks, the keepers of the wolf teams were identified and trained in the handling and caring of the wolf teams.

These three were then taken on a hunt. The idea was to show how useful the sleds were in bringing back the animals.

Taelo, Golden Hawk and Saber Scar took the three volunteers hunting and two days later returned with three large buffalo. There was one in each sled.

The buffalo were hung up and skinned in the center of the village. That evening a feast followed, and the three Grazing Elk members told their story of hunting with Taelo and Golden Hawk.

"If we learn to hunt like Taelo and Golden Hawk, we will have more meat then we will know how to use," the three commented when they told the story of how Taelo and Golden Hawk had run down their two buffalo.

"You have been more than just guests. You have contributed hugely to the wellbeing of the clan. You are welcome to stay until spring," Fierce Badger said when Taelo let him know the team was planning to continue their journey East.

"It is time we were continuing with our journey," Taelo said as his team sat around an evening fire.

It was still winter. Spring was challenging the cold but had yet to defeat it and take hold.

"I agree. I am getting restless and bored. I am ready to continue our journey," Golden Hawk replied from the other side of the circle.

"We are all probably ready. I just hope winter does not have some nasty surprise for us," Meadow Flower said as she poked the fire with a stick and watched the sparks fly up into the air.

"I don't think I can do one more session in how to use the sling," Feather-in-the-Wind interjected.

She had provided almost continuous training in the use of the sling. All the young boys and girls and about half of the women had taken up the sling and taken lessons. This weapon had become the favorite of the entire clan.

Running Stag patted Feather-in-the-Wind on the shoulders and sarcastically said, "Poor princess."

"We can prepare everything tomorrow and be ready to leave on the day after," Quiet Rabbit added.

She and Busy Bee knew the signals from their mates and had talked about being ready to continue on their journey for several sun cycles.

Chapter 4: Passage

The morning was crisp. The morning sun arrived with a clear blue sky replacing the early morning gray. The winter wind from the northern regions reminded everyone that the warmth of spring was not yet to be enjoyed.

The camp was put back into the condition they had received it.

The team had a new team member.

"I would like to journey with you. I am a single "old" woman and there are no likely mates in this clan," Lily had announced the morning of their departure. "I can provide help in cooking and in the work around the camp."

She had come to this decision after talking with White Pearl and Gentle Fern. She hoped Taelo would accept her.

I think that would be great. I know that all of us prefer to hunt overstaying in the camp," Quiet Rabbit had replied, and everyone had grunted their agreements.

She had already commented to Busy Bee and Marigold that Lily seemed to be living by herself. This would give her a purpose and later she would return with them to the Elk Clan meeting.

Perhaps at that time she would meet her mate.

"Thank you all for accepting me. I am pleased to be back with you. I will try to have the courage you expect of me," Lily replied as she looked at Taelo.

"I have no doubts about your courage," Taelo replied as he recalled the time after he had rescued Lily and the others from the cannibals.

It had been obvious that the three women had been in a state of shock from their experiences as captives. He had seen the haunted look in their eyes and could not imagine what it would have been like to have watched someone eat your friend or mate. He had never held their refusal to go back with him as a sign of their weakness. They were in shock.

"We wish you a good journey," Fierce Badger said as Taelo and the rest of the travelers each picked up their backpacks and their two travois.

The team fell into their normal arrow formation. The travois pulled one after the other formed the shaft of the arrow.

On their previous journey of the heart, Burly Bear and Little Otter had always rotated into the lead position. They were the slowest of the team.

On this journey, everyone rotated into the lead position and all other positions equally.

"This team has a different balance and flavor, but it is a solid, talented team," Taelo thought to himself.

Each day they found a stream or body of water toward the late afternoon and set up camp. The repeating travel pattern went on thirty sun cycles. The mountains ahead loomed ever larger.

"No wonder the Grazing Elk Clan members thought they were east of the mountains," Golden Hawk commented as they set up camp at the edge of the foothills leading up into the ridge of mountains before them.

"Our timing seems good. The weather is growing warmer, and the leaves are beginning to show on the trees," Lily commented as she tended to the handful of rabbits, she was grilling over the hot cooking embers.

"This camp seems a good place to stop while we find a way through the mountains," Taelo continued as he sat on the top of the largest boulder at the edge of their camp.

"Golden Hawk and I have a small gift for all," Taelo said as he unrolled a hide that held a set of digging tools. "We have made a set of digging tools. Each of you can have one of our sharks tooth digging sticks. We also have a few flint stone tipped ones as well."

"Tomorrow we will split up into teams of two and go out to see if there is a reasonable path through the mountains," Taelo continued.

"Feather-in-the-Wind and I will make up one team," Quiet Rabbit said from where she was sitting.

"Running Stag and I will make up another team," Taelo echoed as he took a grilled rabbit from Lily.

"Busy Bee and I will go as a team," Golden Hawk said as he took a rabbit.

"I wonder who I should go with," Marigold asked from where she was sitting.

"Unless one of the teams needs me, I will stay with our equipment in the camp," Lily added as she handed the last rabbit to Saber Scar.

As the sun rose the next morning all teams headed toward their designated opening in the mountains. The mountain foliage was thick and the only paths available were those made by deer or other similar animals.

"Well, that is the third rabbit you have bagged this morning," Quiet Rabbit commented as Feather-in-the-Wind picked up and beheaded her latest kill.

"One more and I will put my sling away," Feather-in-the-Wind replied as she dropped the rabbit into her hunting pouch.

She then turned and caught up with Quiet Rabbit and the two took up the steady jog they had been keeping.

"Look, there is a stream flowing in the direction we want to go," Quiet Rabbit said as she stopped to point down into a valley ahead of them.

"It's time we find a place to make camp," she continued.

"That huge rock outcropping looks like a good place," Feather-in-the-Wind said as she veered slightly left toward it.

They spent the next sun cycle finding a reasonable path down to the stream. They would have easily made it to the stream if they took a direct path down, but they were thinking about the two heavily loaded travois.

"Well, we have finally made it. The stream seems to be going in the direction we want to go. This will make a fine passage through the mountains," Quiet Rabbit said from the top of a large boulder.

"I wonder if any of the other teams have found a path," Feather-in-the-Wind said as she looked along the stream for a place to make camp.

"We are lucky to find this stream. There may be others. In the morning we will find a way down to the stream and get a better understanding of how it flows through the mountains," Quiet Rabbit replied.

She was happy to find the stream, but she wanted to verify it was as good a passage as it looked to be.

The next morning it was Feather-in-the-Wind that found the way down from the high ridge they had come in on.

"Here is the way down," Feather-in-the-Wind said excitedly from her position in the lead. "It is wide enough for our travois and it seems to be clear all the way down to the stream," she continued as she broke into a full run down to the stream.

"Be careful, keep your eyes open for any wolves or lions," Quiet Rabbit called out as she picked up her pace.

This was the reason she had taken Feather-in-the-Wind with her. She wanted to keep this young lady safe.

Oh, look at the rapids. I think we are in for a fine dinner of crayfish tonight," Feather-in-the-Wind exclaimed as she prepared a willow stick with which to capture the crayfish.

"I will snatch up the crayfish, you put in the stick," Feather-in-the-Wind said handing the stick to Quiet Rabbit.

"Well, this will end the day on a great note," Quiet Rabbit thought to herself as she took the stick from Feather-in-the-Wind.

The next day after a breakfast of fish Quiet Rabbit asked, "What is your assessment of this route across the mountains?"

A warm feeling went through Feather-in-the-Wind as she answered, "To this point the way is passable and only the way down to this stream will be challenging. I do not know the way ahead, but the small river means the way is open."

She knew Quiet Rabbit didn't need to ask for her opinion.

"I agree with your assessment. Let's head for the camp," Quiet Rabbit said as she arranged her pack for travel.

The journey back took another sun cycle.

"It's good to have you back. We hope you came back last because you were successful in finding a way through the mountains," Taelo said as he gave Quiet Rabbit a hug.

"The rest of us failed to find a way through and have been out doing some hunting while we waited for your return.

"Yes, I will let Feather-in-the-Wind describe our experience," Quiet Rabbit said for everyone to hear as she sat down next to Taelo around the fire.

"Thank you. Our exploration took us to a small river that cuts through the mountains. It is going almost exactly where we need to go," Feather-in-the-Wind began.

She was nervous because she realized Quite Rabbit had elevated her to an equal position to all the older members in the journey team.

This she recognized as a big step for her.

Chapter 5: Paradise

The water bubbling up from a large spring brought the clear water up from some unseen underground flow. The plateau to which it rose was well above its final destination hundreds of miles away. The stream it produced would be joined along the way by countless other small streams to form a small river and finally it would join a giant river.

In the millions of sun cycles of its existence, the river had cut its way through the mountain as the earth's mantle had pushed high into the air. Its waters had found a path through and had maintained its downward flow. It had prevailed and won the battle.

Now populated with crayfish, trout, carp, blue gill, and a host of other fish, the stream sustained a population of turtles, birds, and bears. Deer, buffalo, elk, all came to its banks to drink its clear water.

Taelo and the team followed Feather-in-the-Wind to the point just before the stream began its journey through the mountains.

The towering mountains, with their snow-covered peaks and now greening grasses and meadow flowers forming a gay skirt to the more serious greens of the dominant pines and the occasional lighter green oak higher on the mountain side, presented a formidable barrier to the land beyond.

By the seventh sun cycle, Taelo and the team believed these were truly the mountains described by Broken Spear.

The small stream grew in stature as it progressed through the mountains and finally exited as a small river on the eastern side.

The travois loaded with their possessions were cumbersome and were constantly having to be unloaded and then reloaded as they made their way through the passage. When it became apparent that the stream had become a small river, they found some logs and built two rafts to float down the river.

This made traveling much smoother and easier.

They floated along at the pace the river provided. Periodically scouts were sent out to jog ahead and locate camps and check for any waterfalls that might endanger the team.

"I think Lasher likes riding the lead raft," Quiet Rabbit commented to Busy Bee.

"Yes, all three of our wolves seem to enjoy riding the river," Busy Bee replied.

The weather was now warm, and summer was coming into full bloom. The digging tools were put to good use to dig tubers, roots, and bulbs. Everyone participated in gathering these food items to add flavor and a variation of taste to their meals.

Taelo and Golden Hawk went out ahead of the rest of the team to scout for their next stop and to better understand this new region they were passing through. They left the edge of the river and jogged up to the top of the hill to the north.

They both stopped and took in the animals in the valley on the other side of the hill.

Look at those animals," Taelo said quietly to Golden Hawk.

"I have never seen anything like them," Golden Hawk replied.

"Look at their tracks. They have only one hoof," Taelo said as he crouched down and traced the outline of the hoof print.

"Let's go get a closer look at them," Golden Hawk continued.

The two went slowly down toward the newly discovered herd of animals.

Their presence did not seem to alarm the animals. The two were able to get within five spear lengths. This allowed them to closely examine their find.

"They are really beautiful animals. Look at their size and their smooth and graceful movement," Taelo said at a whisper level.

"I think this is the animal Broken Spear described to me. He said we would be able to use them to make out trip faster and easier," Taelo continued.

High above them an eagle let out a scream.

"I believe your totem has answered the question," Golden Hawk said as he lay down on his back and watched the eagle make a graceful flight up the valley.

"Let's find a good location where we can set up our camp," Golden Hawk suggested.

"We will need one where we can hold the animals we select to use," Taelo replied.

"Let's get back to the team. We can stop this afternoon and organize a hunt for a good longer-term campsite," Golden Hawk added.

Taelo and Golden Hawk returned to the river and stopped the team where they met them.

The team stopped and set up camp.

They were all curious about the new animals and were excited that they would be looking for a good long-term site where they could bring the new animals.

"Broken Spear said we would find these animals and they would serve us. We will ride on their backs, and they will carry our things," Taelo shared with all the team members.

"Let's all go out and take a look at these magnificent animals," Golden Hawk suggested to the team.

"I can't wait to see them," Feather-in-the-Wind said excitedly.

The jog back to the spot looking down into the valley took only a short time.

"Oh my, what wonderful animals," Meadow Flower commented to Saber Scar.

"I see the animal I want to have," Saber Scar replied as he pointed out a young but very large black male animal with three scars on its chest.

"He has my sign on his chest."

"Tomorrow two teams will go out to find a camp where we can keep the animals we capture. The rest of us will begin to prepare the materials we will need to make these animals our friends and helpers," Taelo said as he scanned the herd.

"We will need to capture the younger ones. I think it will be similar to Lasher. Once they bond to us, they will be our friends," Taelo continued as he petted Lasher.

After they had returned to camp, Taelo asked, "What shall we call these animals?"

"They will carry us. So perhaps their name should have that meaning," Meadow Flower volunteered.

"We will get on and sit on their backs. So perhaps the name should have that meaning," Feather-in-the-Wind continued.

"They move smoothly, with power and are very fast," Quiet Rabbit said from where she sat.

"So here is what I have heard; strider, mount and carter," Taelo summarized the suggestions.

After much discussion and several more suggestions Busy Bee stood up and gave each of the team two stones. On the ground she clearly put the symbol of the top three suggested names.

"You each have two stones. There are three names. You can put two stones on one name, or you can put each stone on a different name. The name with the most stones will be the one we give to the animal," she instructed.

A few moments later Golden Hawk observed, "the name "Mount" clearly has the most stones,."

"Well, I am glad that we have given them a name. Now we will need to capture about fourteen mounts and train them to do what we want. We will need a place to hold our new friends," Taelo continued.

"Tomorrow we will send out two teams to find a suitable location to set up such a camp."

"I would like to go out with Busy Bee," Quiet Rabbit volunteered.

"Yes, I would like that," Busy Bee added.

"That sounds good. How about if Running Stag and Feather-in-the-Wind go out as the other team," Taelo said looking at the two.

"We would love to," Running Stag quickly accepted.

He immediately recognized the trust Taelo was extending to Feather-in-the-Wind and him.

"You two scout the north side of the river. Quite Rabbit and I will scout the south side of the river," Busy Bee said as the two teams got ready to leave the next morning.

Feather-in-the-Wind and Running stag jogged out of the camp with their two wolves, Walker, and Arrow trotting at their sides.

"Take Lasher with you," Taelo said to Quiet Rabbit and Busy Bee.

"Watch out for these two," Taelo said to Lasher as he petted him and gave him a push toward the two.

He and Golden Hawk stood and watched the two teams jogging east along each side of the river.

"Look at how smoothly and fast those two youngsters move," Golden Hawk observed.

"What equipment do we need to prepare," Saber Scar asked as the two turned back to camp.

"We will want one animal for each of us and about four or five extra. We will need a guide rope for each one.

Little Otter made a head harness for his buffalo that slipped over the nose and the back of the head. I will show you how to make it," Taelo began.

"We will need to cut many hides into thin strips and then weave them to make enough rope," Golden Hawk spoke next.

The work in the camp got underway.

Feather-in-the-Wind and Running Stag approached a small river about half the size of the one they were currently following.

The willows growing along the riverbank made a smooth turn and continued upstream following the banks of the new river. It seemed to be a natural choice to turn upstream of this smaller river to find a convenient point to crossover.

The way toward the north was in the same direction as they had taken when they went to observe the mounts.

Together they turned and followed the small river northward.

"Well, there go our two young warriors and their loyal wolves. Their rhythm seems to be of the wind," Quiet Rabbit said as she, Busy Bee and Lasher continued on along the south side of the river.

"I hope they have good luck in finding something because our side seems to be getting flatter, and dryer with fewer trees," Busy Bee said after a short time.

Feather-in-the-Wind stopped to take in the fall as it fell down fifty feet across a series of step like shelves with the last shelf dropping the water some three spear lengths into a pool bordered on the right side by a sandy beach. The beach led up to a finger of the cliff that extended out from the falls and disappeared smoothly into the ground on the eastern side.

Running Stag commented that it appeared someone had tilted the ground causing the angle and allowing the water to pour down the falls as it buried a long finger of stone into the ground.

They both noted that on the left side of the pool three eerily smooth flat layers seemed to have been pulled out from the base of the cliff. The bottom most layer was about three spear lengths wide and about one-half spear length above the pool.

Each layer above it was about half that of the one below it. The top two layers were covered by the stone cliff overhang coming straight out above them.

The flat bottom layers seemed to flow together as they disappeared behind the waterfalls.

The two stood silently and took in the entire scene framed by the dark green of the pine sentinel trees and thick light green grass along the banks of the stream.

The crystal clear light blue cloudless sky provided a strong contrast to the dark blue waters in the basin below the falls.

The picturesque site caused the two to stand silently next to each other.

"Oh!" was all they said as they took in the scene.

The two wolves, Walker, and Arrow went on ahead. They were checking out the area and seemed not to find anything threatening.

"I think we have found a small piece of paradise," Feather-in-the-Wind said as she slowly walked onto the lowest platform and walked toward the falls.

"The rapids below the pool, provide a way across and connect both sides. We can be on one side and the mounts can be on the other," Running Stag said as he picked his way on stones across to the green grass on the opposite bank.

"It even has a natural fire area," Feather-in-the-Wind called out as she waved for Running Stag to come back over to her.

"We can sleep along this highest layer with the stone cliff as the back wall and the overhang can be a roof," Running Stag said as he took off his backpack and put his flat weapon down on the top layer.

"I am going out to gather some wood for a fire. We should stay here for the night and return tomorrow. We have found our camp," Feather-in-the-Wind said as she put down her pack and scratched Walker behind the ears.

"We will go gather wood together. We may not be the only ones who like this paradise," Running Stag said as he put his flat weapon back on his back.

The fact that both wolves seemed relaxed eased Running Stag's concern, but he did not want to be surprised.

Feather-in-the-Wind's sling took down four rabbits as they collected the wood for a fire.

"I'll clean the rabbits, if you grill them," she said as she carried the rabbits to a point downstream from the pool.

"Sound like a deal to me," Running Stag said as he worked to light the fire.

Walker and Arrow each chewed away at their rabbit. They usually chewed on the bones and cracked them and often ate most of them as well.

After dinner they both went for a swim in the pool.

"This is the most relaxed I have been on this journey," Running Stag said as he floated on his back.

The ice-cold water quickly drove them back to the bank where they took in the warmth of their fire.

The sun had set, and the night was taking hold as the two sat on the rock at the side of the pool.

"I am constantly reminded of how lucky I am" Feather-in-the-Wind replied as she moved closer to Running Stag.

"Look at all of our ancestors in the sky," Feather-in-the-Wind said as she lay next to Running Stag looking up into the pitch-black night sky.

The full moon was low in the east and made the spray of the waterfall shimmer.

"This is an evening I will always remember. I am in paradise with a princess," Running Stag said as he brushed Feather-in-the-Wind's hair back from her face. He knew that he would repeat these words many times as he grew older.

Chapter 6: .Preparation

The sun's rays streamed as it rose above the horizon to the east. Running Stag started the fire and went to the rapids below the waterfall pool to see what he could find to cook for a morning meal.

The rapids provide several large crayfish, and he was able to spear one trout. He cleaned the fish and cut several small willow branches to serve as cooking spits.

Feather-in-the-Wind was up and took over the cooking. She rubbed salt on the fish and the crayfish tails to bring out the unique and delicious flavor of each.

They talked about a swim but decided against it when they recalled how cold the water had been.

They spent a few moments straightening out the area and then began their jog back to the camp where the rest of the team was staying.

I see Quiet Rabbit and Busy Bee returning," Meadow Flower commented as she hung up the mount harness she had just completed.

"What did you find," Golden Hawk asked as he greeted Busy Bee and Quite Rabbit on their return?

"We turned back late this afternoon. The river continues on, and the land is made up of rolling hills, trees, and grass. There were many places that were good for a short stay, but none offered a place to contain the mounts," Busy Bee reported.

"Let's hope our young warriors have better luck than Busy Bee and I had," Quiet Rabbit said.

"The fact that they are not here means they will come back in the morning with good news," Saber Scar conjectured.

"We work together very efficiently. We have our harnesses for fourteen mounts ready. Now I am ready for a good night's sleep," Lily said as she retired into her sleeping hide.

"I am going to the river to wash the dust off," Quiet Rabbit said as she and Busy Bee headed for the river.

Lasher followed Quiet Rabbit to the river.

"We will keep an eye out for you," Golden Hawk offered as he and Taelo followed the two to the riverbank.

Taelo and Golden Hawk took some of the evening meal of fish and rabbit for Quiet Rabbit and Busy Bee and waited for them to wash up.

The water was cold enough that they knew it would not be a long wait.

Sunrise the next morning found the team warming some of the leftover meal from the night before.

"Let's pack up and get ourselves to the other side of the river. We will go down to the river as far as the stream where Feather-in-the-Wind and Running Stag turned," Taelo suggested in the morning.

He was keen on getting setup so they could capture their mounts.

Later in the afternoon Meadow Flower called out, "Look at our young warriors as they fly on winged feet. Their wolves seem to be running at full speed."

"How did you know to come," Running Stag asked as he stopped?

"Did you find a suitable place," Lily asked as she gave him a hug. She thought of him as the son she had lost long ago.

"Yes, it is a wonderful place with a water fall and a deep pool, a place to hold the mounts and a wonderful place for us to sleep and live-in comfort. If we were not on a trek, we would choose to live there," Feather-in-the-Wind said with enthusiasm.

Well lead us to this idyllic location," Taelo said as he turned Feather-in-the-Wind around by the shoulders as he gave her a congratulatory pat on the back.

"Do you have a snack we could eat," Feather-in-the-Wind asked.

"Yes, I packed some grilled fish and meat left over from breakfast," Lily said as she opened up a bag and un-wrapped the food she had described.

She had several bags she had made from elk and buffalo intestine that served to carry such food.

"Take a moment and eat. How long will it take us to reach the location of these falls," Taelo inquired.

"We left at sunrise and jogged at our normal travel pace until we met you. If we return at the pace we travel with our travois we will get there in the dark after the sunset," Running Stag replied.

"Well let's see if we can get there by late evening," Taelo said as he led the team forward at an ambitious jogging pace.

They arrived in the early evening. Taelo, Golden Hawk and Saber Scar had taken turns pulling the travois at the ambitious pace so that they could make good time.

"Well, this place is all you said it would be," Meadow Flower commented as she lit the fire.

The full moon provided enough light to let them set up the camp in a leisurely fashion.

The moonlight added a magical touch to the beautiful sight of the water mist rising in the air from the surface where the falls hit the still water of the pool.

"This place has a magical air about it," Busy Bee commented as she unwrapped her sleeping hide.

"Let's all settle in and get a good night sleep. I will take the first watch, Saber Scar the second, and Golden Hawk the third. Tomorrow we will each assume specific camp duties for the time we are here," Taelo said as he walked to the location on the upper tier that Quiet Rabbit had selected.

The early morning sun came in from across the pool and just made it onto the top shelf where everyone slept. Later in the day the top shelf was in the shade and remained cool.

"This would make a perfect home for a small group like us," Busy Bee said as she ate the fish speared by Taelo, Golden Hawk and Saber Scar.

"The herd of mounts must be upstream and perhaps a little south from here. I would like to have Running Stag and Feather-in-the-Wind locate the herd while we prepare the holding area and get the other preparation completed," Taelo commented.

"Thank you for giving us the fun part of the work," Feather-in-the-Wind said as she prepared her backpack.

She knew the work of getting the holding area ready would be a lot of hard work.

Taelo and Golden Hawk had briefly talked about this and though they would have loved to go out themselves the camp needed some additional preparation. The campsite would benefit by building a wall from the cliff to the edge of the water to guard against any night prowlers.

The side where the mounts would be kept needed a containment wall from the cliff to the edge of the water as well. Additionally, they would put in a temporary wall along the water's edge to keep the mounts from jumping if they were panicked and tried to swim out of their compound.

"Who wants to volunteer to make a wall woven from the willow branches for our living area," Taelo asked.

"Lily, Busy Bee and I will make the wall," Quiet Rabbit volunteered.

She knew Marigold and Saber Scar would be more useful in building the heavier wall needed for the mounts. They were the strongest members on the team. They could move objects such as stones and logs that most of the rest of the team would think unmovable. Marigold was strong and Saber Scar even stronger.

The only person Quiet Rabbit knew who was even stronger was Burley Bear who was twice the size of Saber Scar. In the battle against the cannibals, she had witnessed Burly Bear hurling the bodies of the cannibals at least ten spear lengths.

It was in that battle that a very young Running Stag had earned her ultimate respect. Running Stag had followed her because Taelo had casually told the young boy to protect her. He followed her into the fierce battle and had become a warrior. After the battle, she had stitched the cut on his back and noted that he made no sound even though she knew how much it must have hurt.

"Let's layout the spacing for the vertical posts and then we will know the length for the cross members and finally how much willow we will need," Busy Bee said as she began to walk the line where the wall would be.

"Let's walk the layout for the wall for the mounts," Marigold said as she led the way across to the other side of the stream.

She understood why she was going to work with the men on building the wall for the mounts. She was stronger than either Taelo or Golden Hawk. Only Saber Scar was stronger.

Taelo, Golden Hawk and Saber Scar followed Marigold across to the other side of the stream and began the work of collecting the stones required.

For most of the morning Running Stag and Feather-in-the-Wind jogged westward and a little to the south.

"We should be getting close to where we saw the herd of mounts," Running Stag said as Feather-in-the-Wind and he kept an easy jog.

"I think we will find them in the next valley. Let's spend a little time and pick out the mount we each want. Even the young ones are strong enough to carry us," Feather-in-the-Wind said in return.

"Yes, certainly carry you. I could carry you. But Saber Scar will need a large and strong one," Running Stag replied.

A few moments later they were laying on the ground on a rise above the valley they had earlier seen the mounts.

Walker and Arrow lay beside them quietly wagging their tails. Feather-in-the-Wind was scratching Walker behind his ears.

"Most of them are tan, some have dark brown spots, and they all seem to have black hair along the top of their necks. I like the looks of the one that has the white on its leg," Feather-in-the-Wind said as she pointed out what she thought was a female mount.

"There is the one with the scar on its chest that Saber Scar wants. I will like anyone of them," Running Stag said as he took in the beauty of the mounts.

They all seemed to have long hair above their hooves.

"Let's put up some markers on the way back to the camp. We better start back now so we can help in getting the camp ready for the mounts," Running Stag continued.

I am wondering how we will capture the mounts," Feather-in-the-Wind said as they piled up some stone to make their first marker.

"I bet Taelo will run them down," Running Stag said with a sense of certainty.

They set up the first marker and then jogged away until they could barely see it. Then they stopped and put up another marker. For the rest of the day, they repeated this process until they got back to camp.

"We have found the mounts. We saw Saber Scar's mount again and we have each picked our own mounts out," Feather-in-the-Wind announced as the two jogged into camp.

Chapter 7: The Amazing Mount

The sun rising in the East provided the perfect morning wakeup call. Taelo and Golden Hawk spent a few moments capturing some crayfish and some slow morning rabbits and had them roasting on the rekindled fire when the rest of the team got up.

The team was eager to go and capture the mounts. They left camp immediately after having a light morning meal.

"You did a great job marking the trail. It will be easy to come back and forth," Taelo praised Running Stag and Feather-in-the-Wind.

The two had not only made simple stone markers but they had added a tall pole with a strip of hide on it. The trail was easily followed and would stand out even in a deep snow.

"We will begin by capturing the mount Saber Scar has picked," Taelo continued.

"Many of the mounts looked the same so it is hard to decide which one to pick. In the end it probably doesn't matter," Taelo thought to himself.

He would keep an eye out for the one he would select for himself.

"We will have two small capture teams. Busy Bee, Golden Hawk and Saber Scar will make up one capture team.

Quiet Rabbit, Marigold and I will make up the second capture team.

We will also have a hold team made up of Lily, Feather-in-the-Wind and Running Stag. The hold team must calm the captured mount and make sure it does not escape," Taelo explained to everyone.

"We will decide whether to capture four mounts today after we see whether we can hold them.

Quiet Rabbit and Busy Bee will cull out the target mount and bring them toward where Golden Hawk and I are located.

Golden Hawk and I will put two loops over the mount's head.

Then Marigold and Saber Scar will aid in holding and then moving the mount to the holding location. I am counting on Marigold and Saber Scar's strength to help us bring the mount in after we capture it," Taelo explained.

"The herd is grazing and at ease. I see the mount Saber Scar has selected on this side of the herd. I will jog out ahead of the herd.

Saber Scar you should go out even farther than where I stop. Busy Bee will move in behind the mount and slowly ease him away and toward me. I will stay hidden as long as possible. Then I will make my try once the mount either sees me or is close to where I am," Golden Hawk instructed his team.

"We will do the same but on the other side of herd. Quiet Rabbit will select the mount she wants and move it toward me. Marigold, I am counting on you to make sure we make the capture," Taelo said following Golden Hawk's instruction.

"We have four strong trees here in the holding area. These animals are very large and probably stronger than the ropes we have made. The three of you must make sure they calm down and then stay calm," Taelo went on to encourage the holders.

A short time later Feather-in-the-Wind pointed out Busy Bee's location, "Look it is easy to find the mount with the scar, but I have only been able to see Busy Bee once. I just saw her wave her stick with a small piece of hide on it. I am not sure where to find Golden Hawk or Saber Scar."

Suddenly Golden Hawk sprang forward. The mount and he were immediately running full speed.

"He is taking the mount away from the herd. Look at them run.

This is unbelievable. I have never seen anyone run so fast. He has the two loops over the mounts head," Running Stag was shouting as he ran back and forth on the rise, he, Feather-in-the-Wind and Lily were standing and excitedly watching the scene.

"Look, Saber Scar just jumped up and has grabbed one of the ropes," Lily was shouting with enthusiasm.

"Hold him," Golden Hawk shouted as he held on to the other rope and was pulled into the air.

"I am trying but he is a strong one," Saber Scar shouted back.

"Let me help," Busy Bee said as she grabbed onto the rope Golden Hawk was holding.

"Let's run him back to the holding area. Busy Bee, take Saber Scar's rope. The two of us will run Saber Scar's mount back to the holding area," Golden Hawk called out.

It was clear the mount wanted to run so Golden Hawk was going to let him run.

"Let's get ready. Golden Hawk and Busy Bee are bringing the mount toward us at full speed. I'm not sure they are running with the mount or being pulled by it," Lily said.

"I think we should each put on another set of ropes," Feather-in-the-Wind suggested.

"Saber Scar is coming in at full speed, but he is far behind. I hope he gets here quickly," Running Stag said as he gave a rope to Lily.

"What about me," Feather-in-the-Wind asked.

"You talk to the mount and tell him everything will be fine," Running Stag suggested as he turned to the oncoming mount.

"All right let's start holding him back," Golden Hawk shouted to Busy Bee.

Running Stag and Lily came out and put two more ropes on as the mount came into the holding area. The four were still struggling to hold on when Saber Scar arrived. His strength made the difference, but it was clear the mount was not yet convinced to stay.

"Be calm, it is safe, your life is full of grace, your mother will look out for you, Be calm, life is good, you have friends who like you, Be calm, you will find you like all of us, Be calm, Be calm Be calm," Feather-in-the-Wind sang softly as she walked with her hand out to the mount.

She slowly repeated the song her mother had sung to her.

As if by magic the mount settled down. He only pulled back when Feather-in-the-Wind put her hand on his nose. Then he stood still as she continued to pet him on the nose and sing to him.

"Well, I was not sure how our holders would hold the mounts. I am glad your mother taught you such a nice song and that you sing so well," Golden Hawk said as he tied his rope to the tree,"

"Busy Bee tie your rope to the second tree.

Feather-in-the-Wind, see if he will let you remove the other two ropes," Golden Hawk said quietly.

Feather-in-the-Wind continued to sing softly. She knew many songs. She quietly sang each one.

Saber Scar brought some green grass he had pulled up and placed it where the mount could eat it.

"Look, there is Quiet Rabbit bringing in a mount all by herself. I don't see Marigold or Taelo," Busy Bee said pointing to where Quiet Rabbit was slowly walking toward the holding area.

"There in the distance is Marigold leading another," Saber Scar pointed out.

"Where is Taelo, and what magic do they have on their side," Golden Hawk asked as he picked up two ropes and ran out toward the two on coming mounts.

He knew Taelo had gone out with only two ropes and figured there was one more mount that Taelo was either watching or following in hopes of capture.

"I see you anticipated Taelo's request for more ropes," Quiet Rabbit said just loud enough for Golden Hawk to hear.

"He is about halfway up on the other side of the herd. There is a white mount he would like to capture. He is culling it out and bringing it this way. He is counting on one of us to be out in front for the capture."

"I understand. I will position myself and when he comes by, I will capture the mount," Golden Hawk replied as he continued his jog across the valley.

"It always amazing what my cousin manages to pull off," Golden Hawk thought to himself.

A few moments later he saw Taelo patiently and slowly guiding the white mount toward him.

"It appears the mother is following," Golden Hawk observed to himself. "I will give one rope to Taelo, and I will capture the mother."

Golden Hawk stayed hidden until Taelo drew abreast then he slowly joined Taelo.

"Here is your rope. I will capture the mother," he said quietly to Taelo. Taelo just nodded and the said, "Now."

He and Golden Hawk sprang forward and made their capture.

"Look, I can see both Taelo and Golden Hawk. They have captured two more mounts. It looks like Golden Hawk could use some help," Running Stag said as he watched Golden Hawk flying through the air holding on to the rope that was around a very large mount

Busy Bee picked up a rope and ran at top speed toward Golden Hawk. Quiet Rabbit and Running Stag were hot on her heals.

"Thanks for the help," Golden Hawk said as they all held on to the three ropes around the mother mount.

Quiet Rabbit was singing a lullaby and the two mounts settled down and allowed themselves to be led.

"I believe these animals like songs," Golden Hawk stated his observation.

"Let's take these five back to the camp. I would like to see how they act in their new home," Taelo said once all the mounts were secure.

Quiet Rabbit, Feather-in-the-Wind and Busy sang lullaby's all the way back to the camp.

"I can't wait to tell White Swan that the songs she sang to me to keep me happy as a child are the ones that make these wild animals calm," Taelo said as they approached the camp.

A new problem arose when they tried to take the mounts across the creek.

"Wait a moment and let me find a calm spot where they can cross," Feather-in-the-Wind spoke up. She was leading Scar, Saber Scar's mount.

The two walked down stream until Feather-in-the-Wind found a calm flow that was about a foot deep. She slowly walked out into the stream and quietly talked to Scar.

"It's Ok, the water is calm, and the footing is fine," she explained to the mount as if it would understand.

The two went slowly across and up the other side.

Quiet Rabbit took her mount to the same spot, but it did not want to follow her.

"Here let me try again," Feather-in-the-Wind said as she put her hand on the mounts nose and petted it.

"Feather-in-the-Wind has a magic touch with these animals," Marigold said as she gave the rope to her mount over to Feather-in-the-Wind.

"Magic touch indeed," Taelo said as he gave Feather-in-the-Wind the rope to the white mount. Its mother followed with no additional coaxing.

"It seems the five mounts are accepting the holding area. Let's have three sentries along our barrier for the night. Tomorrow one of us must stay and watch the mounts," Taelo said to the team.

"I will stay tomorrow," Running Stag volunteered.

He and Lily were the only two who seemed not to be critical during the capture.

"I will stay the following day so Running Stag can select his mount. I like the mother of the white. May I claim her as my mount," Lily spoke up.

"Yes, I don't believe anyone has spoken for her," Taelo said with a questioning inflection.

"Well, it seems you have your mount," Taelo concluded.

"We will continue capturing mounts in the next few days.

Tomorrow we will capture at least four more. I would like to capture more if the mounts are not too hard to handle.

We will all need to learn our lullaby songs again," Taelo concluded with a chuckle.

Chapter 8: Training

℺ily and Running Stag stayed back in camp as the teams went out the next morning. They went along the stream, collected the tall grasses, and put them along the base of the retaining wall for the mounts to eat.

The mounts seemed satisfied with their holding area, the grass, and the pool of water.

The rest of the team was out capturing the next set of mounts. They were not so lucky and came back with only three.

It took three more sun cycles to capture all fifteen mounts.

Taelo selected and captured his mount. It had a white streak in its dark brown mane.

Golden Hawk selected one with a white spot on one leg.

On the third outing, Running Stag selected a black with a notch out of its ear.

They now had all fifteen mounts they planned to capture.

"The mounts seem to have accepted their containment. Today we will lay out the training area and prepare to train each mount to carry us," Taelo said as everyone gathered for the breakfast meal.

"How will we train them to carry us," Running Stag asked.

"First we will train them to carry two heavy logs hanging on each side from a hide that goes over their backs. After they get use to the logs, we will mount them ourselves. We will need to find a location where the grass is high and the landing is soft," Taelo explained.

"We trained our Llamas in a similar way. We had to tie a band around the Llama's mouth so it could not turn and bite us," Feather-in-the-Wind explained.

"That is a good idea. We will do something similar. I would not want to be bitten by any of these mounts. They would create a serious wound," Golden Hawk commented.

"We taught the Llamas to turn in two different ways. Some learned to turn when you put your knee into their side and leaned in the direction you wanted to go," Feather-in-the-Wind said as she displayed the move on the stone she was straddling.

"The other way was to put a rope around their snout and have two ropes coming around each side of their neck. This was easier for the Llama to learn and for the rider as well," Feather-in-the-Wind continued.

"Well, not only is Feather-in-the-Wind the best with a sling and the teacher on how to make clay pottery but now she has become a mount trainer. Who knew when we accepted her into our clan that she would be so valuable," Quiet Rabbit commented to the team.

It pleased her to see Feather-in-the-Wind gain her confidence and grow in her interaction with the team.

"Yes, who knew," Busy Bee, Taelo and Golden Hawk echoed.

"Is there anything else we should be aware of," Taelo asked Feather-in-the-Wind.

"Yes, the mounts act very much like the Llama. Whenever something is behind them, the Llama kicks. We should not walk around behind the mount or even to the side behind the mount," Feather-in-the-Wind replied.

"When it comes time for the Llamas to be ridden, the Llama, the rider and one holder is in the center of a ring of people. The ring of people is there to catch the rider should the Llama bolt from the center. The holder stays close to the Llama and the rider and if the rider gets thrown off, he catches the rider if possible," Feather-in-the-Wind continued.

She was surprised at how much she had learned from her previous experiences at home. It made her appreciate her parents and brother and how they had helped her grow.

"Again, thank you for sharing your experience. I think I now have a clear idea of how we will organize ourselves when we get ready to try and ride our mounts.

Golden Hawk and I will be the two persons who will be the holders. Everyone else but the rider will stand in a circle. Since there are so few of us the circle will be closed by having a guide rope going from person to person. In this way perhaps we can hold the mount and provide some support for the rider. Does everyone understand what I am suggesting," Taelo finished with a question?

"Who will be the first rider," Lily asked?

"I think we should see which mount seems to be the most calm and stable. Let's watch each one closely as we get them to accept a load. The owner of the calmest mount will be the first rider," Golden Hawk suggested.

"That seems like a good way of determining the first rider," Marigold commented.

"Well let's begin to train them to carry a load," Saber Scar said as he got up and proceeded across the river.

He considered himself brave, but these mounts frightened him. They were large, powerful, and fast. He was strong but felt very slow when he was around the mounts. He hoped he could get on his mount and stay on him.

It took much longer than expected to get the mounts to accept the carrying a load on their backs.

"It has been fourteen sun cycles and we are finally getting done with having each mount carry a load. Tomorrow we will have the first person try to ride their mount," Taelo said as the team gathered around the evening fire.

"Who is the first rider," Running Stag inquired. He knew he would not be first. His mount was one of the most difficult ones.

"Quiet Rabbit, Lily or Feather-in-the-Wind will be first," Golden Hawk replied.

"I would like to volunteer to be first, but I would like to ride Lily's mount. She is the mother of my mount, Condor, and is the gentlest. I have done this with Llamas. For me it is just a larger mount," Feather-in-the-Wind spoke up.

"Are you sure you want to be first," Busy Bee asked in surprise?

"Feather-in-the-Wind has become fearless," she thought to herself.

"This is actually a good idea. Feather-in-the-Wind is lighter than the loads the mounts have learned to accept. This may be a way to introduce a live person on their back," Taelo said out loud what was going through his mind.

The last few weeks had proven how right Feather-in-the-Wind had been in how the mounts would act.

"Well let's go set up our circle while Taelo and Golden Hawk brings out Mother," Quiet Rabbit said as she got up and began handing out a lead rope to each of the team.

Lily was walking across the creek quietly talking to Feather-in-the-Wind.

"Are you sure you really want to do this," Lily asked.

She was relieved to have Feather-in-the-Wind ride her mount first, but she was feeling guilty at her own fear.

"I am a little nervous, but I feel confident that Taelo or Golden Hawk will catch me if I get thrown off. I am hoping Mother is gentle enough and will let me ride her without putting up a big fight," Feather-in-the-Wind said as she went up the bank on the far side of the creek.

The circle was formed in a clear area with a tall stand of grasses.

"Let's make sure there are no rocks or logs that would cause a problem," Marigold suggested.

Mother was led to the center of the circle. Mother had the leather strap on so she could not bite.

"Well Mother, I would like to ask you to allow me to ride on your back," Feather-in-the-Wind said quietly as she stroked Mother on the snout. She continued to talk to her softly and sang a lullaby as she had done every day with all the mounts. Mother was standing perfectly still and seemed relaxed.

"I will help you get on," Taelo said as he cupped his hands together for Feather-in-the-Wind to step on.

Feather-in-the-Wind slipped smoothly onto Mother's back.

Golden Hawk began to lead Mother around in a circle.

Mother turned her head back to look at her rider but otherwise had almost no reaction.

"I did not think it would be so easy," Lily said from her position in the circle.

"Well let's not celebrate yet. You will need to duplicate what Feather-in-the-Wind just did," Quiet Rabbit responded.

"Yes Lily, come on out and get ready to take your turn," Golden Hawk said.

Feather-in-the-Wind slid off to the ground and then stroked Mother on the snout.

"You are a fine mount. Please let Lily ride you as you let me ride," Feather-in-the-Wind said.

"Yes, please let me ride as easily as you just let Feather-in-the-Wind ride," Lily said as she began to hum the lullaby, she always sang to Mother.

Taelo helped Lily swing up onto Mother's back.

Mother immediately responded to Lily's weight on her back.

Taelo and Golden Hawk held the ropes tight as Mother reared up. Lily was hanging onto the ropes around Mother's snout. She sang her lullaby louder and talked to Mother as well. After a few times more of rearing up, Taelo and Golden Hawk managed to get her to walk around in the circle. A short time later Taelo declared victory.

"I think Mother and Lily have it. Let's take the control ropes off and let Lily guide Mother around the circle," he continued.

Lily guided Mother around the circle once and then turned her and went in the other direction.

"Well let's bring Condor into the circle next. Lily just keep riding Mother," Taelo instructed.

Saber Scar brought Condor into the circle. Condor was a little more nervous than Mother until Feather-in-the-Wind began to talk to him and to sing her lullaby.

"Let's take the two holding ropes off. He will be less nervous," Feather-in-the-Wind addressed Taelo and Golden Hawk.

She reached up and pulled the two ropes off before either of them could object. She then grabbed Condor's mane and with a light leap threw her leg over his shoulder. Condor reared up once and Feather-in-the-Wind held onto his mane with one hand and used the guide ropes to get him to trot around the circle. It was as if the two had practiced together.

"Say hello to your mother," Feather-in-the-Wind said as she pulled Condor to a stop in front of Lily and jumped down.

"I think we should bring out Notch. I will ride first again if you wish," Feather-in-the-Wind volunteered.

"I think Notch will let me ride with only a little struggle. Save yourself for the other mounts who will indeed put up a fight," Quiet Rabbit replied

It turned out Notch was not as gentle as Quiet Rabbit expected. She went flying off immediately after she mounted.

"I'm glad you're not any heavier," Golden Hawk commented as he caught Quiet Rabbit and broke her fall.

Quiet Rabbit petted Notch on the snout and said, "that's no way to treat me. I am your friend."

She then grabbed his mane and leaped back on his back as she had seen Feather-in-the-Wind do. This time she held on for the first few bucks and then took control as Notch settled down.

Let's break for lunch and then continue with the next mounts," Taelo called out loudly so everyone could hear him.

Both Busy Bee and Running Stag had Feather-in-the-Wind ride their mounts first. The arrangement seemed to work well. She was thrown off twice but each time either Taelo or Golden Hawk caught her or broke her fall. By late afternoon they had work through six mounts.

"Tomorrow morning, we will exercise all six mounts that made it in the circle today. We will ride them all at the same time. Then we will work on the remaining mounts," Taelo said as they finished up.

Everyone was tired. It had been an enjoyable day but one that constantly cycled from everything being normal to points of high tension.

Feather-in-the-Wind had become one of the leading figures on the team. Her ability to ride the mounts impressed everyone.

"I am exhausted. I am going to swim in the pool, have dinner and get right to sleep," Feather-in-the-Wind said as she draped her lead rope on the limb next to the other ones.

She was not about to admit it to anyone but every muscle in her body seemed to be hurting.

"You were awesome today," Running Stag paid her a compliment as the two swam in the pool and went under the waterfall.

"Thanks, I really enjoyed the riding. I am looking forward to traveling on the mounts on our journey," Feather-in-the-Wind replied.

She said nothing about how exhausted she was. The water and the spray from the falls refreshed her and she was ready to eat.

Feather-in-the-Wind was the first to leave the evening campfire and climb under her sleeping hide.

"Running Stag, bring Walker and Arrow. We will take our usual walk and examine the mounts," Taelo said as he stood up and began to walk with Lasher to the other side of the stream to the mount holding area.

He had made it a point to take a daily walk through the holding area with the three wolves. He wanted to get the mounts use to the wolves and the wolves use to the mounts. The familiarity seemed to have lessened the nervous response of the mounts.

"Today we will continue with the last four mounts. Thanks to Feather-in-the-Wind this phase of the training of our mounts has been accelerated. It will still take us the next few weeks to complete," Taelo commented the next morning. "However, we also need to go hunting soon."

"There seems to be plenty of game about. There are many deer tracks along the stream," Saber Scar commented.

The work with the remaining mounts followed the same routine that the team had become use to. Feather-in-the-Wind was the lead rider followed by the owner of the mount.

Finally, a few cycles later, the time for their first hunting excursion was at hand.

"I was thinking of going hunting on our mounts," Taelo replied.

"That should be a fun adventure," Busy Bee replied as she tried to imagine throwing a spear from the back of her mount.

"Will any of us be able to throw our spear from the backs of our mounts," Quiet Rabbit asked as the same though crossed her mind?

"Yes, this is really interesting. We will need to learn a different way of hunting and of using our weapons. We may need to modify our weapons. I had not thought of this before," Golden Hawk joined in.

"I think we will need a lighter spear and we will want to utilize the bow and arrow more," Running Stag conjectured.

He had been imagining hunting from his mount.

"Perhaps we should practice shooting our bow and throwing our spear from our mounts before we go out hunting," Quiet Rabbit suggested.

"That is a great idea. We can set up a practice area out where we have been training our mounts," Busy Bee replied.

After several sun cycles of practice, it was clear that the spears were too heavy. The bows worked if shooting out to the side but hitting the target while the mount was running was extremely difficult.

"Well, I think Taelo is the only one that will hit anything from a moving mount," Golden Hawk declared in frustration at the end of a practice run.

"I have figured out that you must release your arrow as the mount begins to push with his hind legs. There is a moment of stability when your release is steady," Taelo said in response.

"Let's all give this a try and see if any of us will be able to hit anything at all," Running Stag said as he leaped on his mount and rode out to the practice area.

"Well, that simple advice has made a significant difference in our ability to hit the targets," Lily said a short time later as she returned from her run.

"Yes, once you get the rhythm it becomes much easier to hit the target," Golden Hawk replied.

He now could hit the target consistently.

"I wonder how much harder it will become when the target is moving," Saber Scar commented.

He had found he could usually hit the target but really wondered if he would be able to hunt in this manner.

"Since few of us can run as fast as Taelo and Golden Hawk, I think in the open the mounts will be very useful to run down our prey. However, I feel that in the heavy woods we will be better off hunting on foot and moving our prey into pre-arranged areas," Quiet Rabbit commented.

"I know that my current sling skill is almost useless on the mount. I think I can change how to use my sling from my mount, but I will need to practice it before I feel good about it," Feather-in-the-Wind added.

"What direction should we go to do some open field hunting," Taelo put the question to the team as they finished their evening meal?

"Quiet Rabbit and I came across the tracks of what we believed to be buffalo or something similar. The herd crossed the river and was heading north," Busy Bee replied.

"We should ride northeast from here," Quiet Rabbit continued.

"Let's get ourselves ready for our first hunt from our mounts. We will take all the mounts along. If we do take down a buffalo, we will bring the meat back on our mounts," Taelo said to the rest.

Chapter 9: First Hunt

Bags the size of small bodies were suspended from high branches around the edge of the camp. The team's personal possessions, all dried foods, extra sleeping hides and any item the team was trying to protect from a wide variety of animals were in the storage bags.

The camp was getting its final cleaning before they left for the hunt.

They were carrying their sleeping hides and other personal items. They were planning to stay gone for several days.

All the mounts were going with them as well. This left the site they were all now calling Paradise empty and unattended, and the team prided itself in leaving it clean.

"Well, we seem to be ready to leave," Taelo said the next morning as he looked around at everyone.

"Let's see if the mounts make a difference in how successful we are in hunting," Golden Hawk said as he led the group toward the northeast.

On really steep climbs, Saber Scar and Marigold would both drop off their mount and walk up ahead of them.

"I can feel when my mount is struggling with my weight," Saber Scar commented when asked about it.

He was much heavier than anyone else on the team. He knew he was the strongest as well.

He had watched Taelo in battle and had no illusion about who would be best in a fight. Taelo's speed and fighting ability was the talk among the Other's warriors. They had never seen anyone moved so fast and be so deadly.

Burley Bear commented how Taelo had gotten the best of him. Since Burley Bear was the best among them, they knew Taelo was even better.

"We will watch you and do the same," Taelo commented.

"I don't think any of the rest of the team presents the same load as Golden Hawk, Saber Scar, Marigold and I do," he continued.

He liked the practice that Saber Scar had demonstrated to the rest of the team.

"Look at the animals of this herd," Busy Bee commented as she led the team to a point looking down into a wide valley almost fully cover with a humped woolly animal similar to their buffalo but very different in how it looked.

"I don't think our arrows will penetrate the wooly hide these animals have," Golden Hawk commented as he looked down into the valley.

"I agree. Let's try something a little different.

We will only want to kill two young animals. One we will dry and the other we will cook to carry with us. Let's pair up into two teams of four and five.

Golden Hawk will lead team one.

I will lead team two.

Let's dismount and I will draw out how we will take down each animal," Taelo said as he thought out how to utilize the mounts they were riding.

Taelo found an area where he could lay out a series of sticks and stones.

"Before you begin, what are we going to call this animal," Quiet Rabbit asked?

"Bison. It is different from our buffalo but similar," Busy Bee suggested.

"Sounds good to me," Feather-in-the-Wind said almost immediately.

Everyone else agreed. They had spent a longtime to name their mounts and did not want to go through it again for the new discovery.

"OK, this stone is the bison.

The two sticks on either side are two mounts and the riders who will do the primary spearing to bring the Bison down.

These two sticks behind are the follow up support riders. They will kill the downed Bison.

If the first two riders do not bring down the Bison, they will move out away from the Bison and the follow up riders will move forward and spear the Bison as well.

The two back riders will always be the ones that ensure the kill," Taelo explained as he pointed and moved the sticks around the Bison.

"Any questions," Taelo conclude his description.

"Where shall we guide the Bison we select," Saber Scar asked?

"We should select the animal we want and then guide them away, or ahead of the herd. We will want a long open, clear area," Taelo replied.

"Have you selected who will be throwing the first spears," Quiet Rabbit asked.

She knew Taelo would have thought through this, and she wanted to give him a chance to move into this naturally.

"As I mentioned, we will break into two teams. Golden Hawk and Saber Scar will be the two primary hunters of team one.

Meadow Flower and I will be the two primary hunters of team two.

Quiet Rabbit and Running Stag will back up Golden Hawk and Saber Scar.

Busy Bee and Lily will back Meadow Flower and me.

"Feather-in-the-Wind will go out with each back up and be a third back up if something more is needed," Taelo conclude the role assignments.

"Golden Hawk's team will have the honor of the first try. My team will observe and see if we need to do something different," Taelo finished with a grin.

He knew Golden Hawk had been itching to go first. He was not going to disappoint him, and he really wanted to see how the action would take place.

"I will take the inner position. You take the outer position," Golden Hawk said to Saber Scar.

"OK, use your hand to wave me out if you want me to let the bison to go out more rapidly," Saber Scar said as he used his hand to show the motion he would be looking for.

"What about our positioning," Quite Rabbit asked?

"Don't come too close. I think we will down the bison. You will need to dismount and kill it by hitting it in the head with a war club," Golden Hawk replied.

"We will need to be very careful about our approach," Quiet Rabbit said to Running Stag.

"I would like to try to stun the bison with my war club but do it from the back of the mount," Running Stag replied.

"Show me how you would do that," Golden Hawk slowed his mount to come parallel with Running Stag.

"I would need to ride in from the left. I would then hold onto my mount's mane and swing my war club like this," Running Stag urged his mount forward and demonstrated the swing.

"OK, you ride on the left behind Saber Scar and give it a try," Golden Hawk said after seeing what Running Stag had in mind.

Quiet Rabbit said nothing, but she was planning to follow Running Stag and after his hammer swing, she was planning to dismount from the left side of the mount. She would drive her spear through the heart of the bison.

"Golden Hawk has selected a bison and is angling it away from the herd," Taelo voiced what everyone was observing.

"Quiet Rabbit is either out of position or they have decided to do something a little different than we discussed," Taelo commented to Busy Bee.

"Yes, she is following just behind and to the right of Running Stag and not behind Golden Hawk. It appears that Feather-in-the-Wind is filling in behind Golden Hawk," Busy Bee confirmed that she was wondering about the change too.

Feather-in-the-Wind was leading two additional mounts out. They would be used to bring back the dead bison.

Each of the two horses carried one travois log.

They seem to be easily moving the bison away from the herd," Marigold added.

She was happy to be observing and that Taelo had selected her to be one of the first to use the spear from the back of the mount.

"Let's spear him now," Golden Hawk cried out to Saber Scar.

He followed his cry with as strong a throw of his spear that he could muster.

He was not sure the spear made it through the hide until he saw some blood on the bison's leg.

He saw that Saber Scar's spear had gone deeper.

The bison did not seem to have slowed down very much.

"I am coming in for my hammer swing," Running Stag called out and surged forward and brought his hammer through a full swing and caught the bison in the middle of the forehead.

The bison went down to its front knees and slid to a stop.

Quiet Rabbit jumped down from her mount and smoothly plunged her spear through the side ribs. This immediately killed the bison.

"OK team, we will try something a little different from the first team," Taelo said as he observed what had just happened.

"I will do as Running Stag just demonstrated and hit the bison in the head.

Meadow Flower you will do what Quiet Rabbit just demonstrated and plunge your spear through the side and into the heart.

We may not need any additional help but both Busy Bee and Lily will be ready to drive their spears into the bison if needed," Taelo commented as he watched Saber Scar gut the bison and get ready to put it on the travois.

The second team waited until the first team had their young bison back to the camp.

"Good job. We learned a lot by observing you. Any suggestions," Taelo praised the first team.

"Yes, the spears in the shoulder did not have as significant an impact as we thought it would. Perhaps the hind quarters would be a better target," Golden Hawk replied.

"The spear to the heart was easy to administrate," Quiet Rabbit added.

"The second team will take your comments and adjust what we do. You can observe us and afterwards we can decide how and what to do on our next hunt," Taelo said as he went to his mount.

He gave his spear to Lily. "Please carry this out for me just in case we need it.

"I can see that they are going to do something different from what we did," Golden Hawk commented as he saw that Taelo was not carrying his spear.

"They are going to use the same run that we did," Saber Scar commented as he watched Marigold and Taelo slowly move the bison they had select away from the herd.

"Taelo is using my hammer attack," Running Stag said excitedly as he watched Taelo deliver a blow he thought he could hear from where he stood.

The bison went down to its knees in a long slide.

"Look at Marigold's dismount and the way she has plunged her spear in," Quiet Rabbit commented as she watched the spear penetrate deep into the chest cavity.

It seemed that Marigold had barely used her strength.

"Well that certainly seemed smoother than what we did. They are almost in the same spot as we ended up.

"What is Feather-in-the-Wind doing," Saber Scar said as he suddenly noticed Feather-in-the-Wind drop the ropes to the horses she was leading and take her bow off her shoulders.

"Lion," Feather-in-the-Wind cried out as she saw the lion or tiger.

Taelo immediately guided his mount to Lily and took his spear from her. He turned and rode over to where Marigold was trying to recover her spear.

"Here take my spear. Lily, please lend me yours," Taelo said reaching over to Lily.

"Keep the bison between you and the lion. Ride away if we are losing the fight," Taelo instructed and turned back toward the direction of the lion.

In the distance he could see four mounts coming at full gallop. This gave him encouragement.

"There are at least two stripped lions, and they are much larger than the ones we know in our mountains, or the saber tooth tigers I have seen," Marigold said from her mount as she pointed out the location of the second lion.

The two lions were now approaching as if they expected no resistance from the mounts and the people on them.

"Easy boy, easy Streak, easy boy" Taelo said to his mount.

Lasher was standing nearby letting a slow rumble come out of his throat.

Feather-in-the-Wind began singing a lullaby to her mount and Walker was silently standing nearby.

"I have my arrow ready to fly," Feather-in-the-Wind said from where she was to Taelo's left.

"Let's all retreat," Taelo called from his mount as he spotted another two tigers.

"Look, Taelo and his team are retreating from their kill," Quiet Rabbit said as she slowed her mount to a slow trot.

She watched the lions stop as they reached the downed bison. There seemed to be six of them. Soon they were followed by younger tigers.

High above an eagle let out a cry.

"There is an entire clan of tigers," Saber Scar commented as Taelo, and his team reached them.

They all sat on their mounts looking at the tigers rip through the tough hide and begin to feast on the bison.

"These tigers are huge and see how easily they tear through the bison's hide," Busy Bee commented.

"Are we going to do anything about them," Running Stag asked. He hoped not.

"No, we will go back and finish processing the bison we have in our camp area. These tigers will eat well today. They will not bother us for at least a couple of days and by then we will want to be somewhere else," Taelo replied.

He looked up at the eagle flying a slow circle over the valley. He heeded the support for his decision.

"Feather-in-the-Wind and I will take first watch to make sure none of the tigers are coming this way," Running Stag volunteered.

"That's a good idea," Golden Hawk commented as he looked back to the area where the tigers were.

There were now large birds circling in the sky.

"There seem to be vultures arriving to get their share of the bison," Marigold commented.

"Let's take the hide off and do a quick initial scraping of the hide. We can cut the meat off the bone and leave the bones here. Let's wrap the meat in the hide and then depart for our camp," Taelo suggested.

"I like that idea," Saber Scar commented as he began to skin the hide off the carcass.

"We will want to leave here by early afternoon," Quiet Rabbit commented as she began to skin the hide off the front quarter of the animal.

Her flint blade easily took the hide from the flesh.

"Let's roll the bison over to the side we have already skinned and begin on the other side," Busy Bee said as she stepped back away from the bison.

"The processing has gone very rapidly," Lily commented a few hours later as she cut what appeared to be the last meat from the bones of the bison.

Lasher, Arrow, and Walker were all stretched out on the ground and chewing on some bones they had been given. They seemed to be enjoying the outcome of the hunt.

"I have the four pack mounts ready. It appears the four carrying pouches that Quiet Rabbit and Busy Bee made will be enough to carry our meat back to camp," Feather-in-the-Wind commented.

She had spent most of the afternoon watching the tigers and worrying about them coming to where the team was processing the buffalo.

She also observed some other animals challenging the tigers for the food. She was fascinated that there were animals that would challenge the tigers. It was clear these other animals worked together in larger numbers than there were tigers.

"There is a major fight going on between the tigers and what appear to be wolves," Saber Scar said as he cupped his hand above his eyes.

"I am sure they will find our pile of bones. Let's hope the bones will keep them from following us," Marigold commented as she put the last of the meat into the side pouch of the pack mount.

"Taelo and I will drop pine branches across our trail to hide the scent of our mounts. I am hoping to delay running into the pack of wolves," Golden Hawk said as the team left the site where they had processed the bison.

It was well into the night by the time they got back to the waterfall and their main camp.

"Let's hang the meat in the trees outside of our camp. We will set up a watch throughout the night," Taelo instructed as they dismounted near the trees where the meat was to be hung.

"Running Stag, Feather-in-the-Wind and I can begin to clean the mounts in the stream and take them to their holding area. We should plan on having someone watch them through the night as well," Quiet Rabbit said as she led Taelo's and her mount toward the stream.

Once there she stopped with them in the middle of the stream and splashed them with water. Then beginning from the top, she brushed the water off with a square piece of hide. Running Stag and Feather-in-the-Wind were each doing something similar.

"The meat I have been grilling is ready," Lily called out to the team.

She noted that those not already on watch were swimming in the pool. Those in the pool would replace the ones on watch once they had eaten dinner.

The following days were spent on processing the meat they had brought back. The team continued their around the clock watch for any dangerous predators. The size of the lions and the pack of wolf like animals had heightened their awareness to the dangers around them.

"Well, it has taken us a full seven cycles to dry our meat and get ready to continue our journey," Taelo commented a few days later.

He felt lucky that neither the wolves nor the lions had followed them to their camp.

Everyone on the team had contributed to a charcoal drawing of their first hunt of bison using their mounts. It showed the hunter killing the bison and the lions and wolves taking over one of the downed bison. The drawing was done on the cliff just above the sleeping area.

"When the next group of people come here, they will see the story of our first hunt of bison on our newly trained mounts," Quite Rabbit commented as she and the team cleaned up the camp in preparation to leave.

"It really is a great drawing. We have Feather-in-the-Wind to thank for initially doing an overall layout of the drawing," Busy Bee added.

"I may have done the initial layout but each of you put in the detail," Feather-in-the-Wind joined in.

"I agree, my part of the drawing is especially good," Running Stag commented and bowed.

"Well, I do believe that Saber Scar and Marigold have the best drawings," Golden Hawk said as he took in the entire drawing.

"Well, everything is packed. The camp is cleaned. The holding area is open. All our belongings are loaded on our mounts. We are ready to ride on in our journey of discovery," Taelo said as he guided his mount south along the edge of the creek.

Chapter 10: Mammoths

The river ran through a land of low hills that resembled low widely spaced undulating waves in the sea. The undulating green grasses of the open expanse were bordered by trees hugging the banks of many small tributaries to the river leading East, Southeast.

The expanse was hard to take in. It met the sky on the far horizon that appeared to fuse together where the light blue met the light green of the plain. There seemed to be nothing between the observer and the infinite beyond.

Then the endless sea of bison mixed with accompanying mastodons traveling in the opposite direction came into view and the magnitude of the terrain and the miniscule size of the observers came into perspective. They could not see across the herd that blocked their way.

They traveled along the bank of the river that had grown from a multitude of small streams merging and growing to the point it was one of the largest rivers the team had experienced.

It became the source of the fresh food for the team. Turtles, crayfish, trout, bass, and sunfish were all abundant.

The campsites were all easy to find and establish.

"Traveling on these mounts makes the journey rather easy," Quiet Rabbit said to no one in particular.

"Yes, after I got use to riding for this long, I am able to nap as I rock back and forth on my mount," Feather-in-the-Wind replied.

"Well, my joints are still trying to get use to sitting in this position for so long. My butt is bruised. I am now putting an extra hide on my mount's back for padding," Busy Bee joined in on the conversation.

"I agree with all of you. Think how far we have come in just a few cycles of the sun. It would have taken us at least three times as long to get this far on foot," Marigold interjected.

"We must be getting close to the very large river Broken Spear told me about. He said that we would be talking about how large the rivers were and then we would come to the really large river," Taelo said as he rocked comfortably along.

He had watched how Feather-in-the-Wind rode her mount and had tried to copy her easy movement in rhythm with her mount. It immediately eased all his strained muscles. He shared his observation with Quiet Rabbit who had also copied Feather-in-the-Wind.

"The beauty of the land is hard to take in. And look at what we have in the valley ahead," Saber Scar said.

He was in the lead and had just come to the crest of the hill that overlooked a long wide valley.

The valley below was undulating in a sea of moving mastodons mixed with twice as many bison.

"Let's make camp here and just observe the valley ahead. We will not be able to cross until the majority of these animals get passed this point," Taelo said to the team as he dismounted and sat down on a large log.

For the rest of the afternoon the team sat and watched the slowly moving mass below. They saw wolves marching alongside the massive herd. It was clear they were looking for the weak, injured or the unwise ones that wandered too far from the herd.

"Well, if there are wolves, we must also think there will be lions or tigers," Golden Hawk commented when Running Stag pointed out the wolves.

"Well, if you see something a little smaller than a bison, buffalo or mastodon it may be wise to kill one, this is the last of the fresh meat," Lily said from where she was roasting a series of bison meat strips.

Even though Lily was only a few years older than the rest, she had become their surrogate mother figure.

"Who wants to go out and see if we can find a deer or some other small game," Taelo asked?

"I think I will go out and get some rabbits and other small game with my sling," Feather-in-the-Wind said as she stood up from where she had been sitting and leaning against a boulder.

She and Running Stag had been quietly talking and watching the valley below. Walker was content lying next to her and Arrow was sitting next to Running Stag.

"I will go with Feather-in-the-Wind," Running Stag got up and took up his bow.

Arrow followed at his heels.

"Wait, I just finished grilling some meat. Get a bite to eat before you go," Lily said to everyone.

"I will go with the two of you," Saber Scar said as he got up.

"I will stay here in camp with Lily," Marigold spoke up.

"I guess the four of us will hunt together," Quiet Rabbit said as she took her things to the spot, she figured she would sleep that evening.

"You did a great job on this meat. How is our salt supply holding out," Taelo asked?

He had been looking for signs of salt as they traveled but had not found any so far.

"We have used up more than half of our salt," Lily replied.

"Let me remind everyone that we will need to find some before long," Taelo continued.

"If we do not find any we will need to stop and make some from the sea," Busy Bee added.

They all knew that this would be time consuming.

"We are going to go along the river. We will take our mounts. Feather-in-the-Wind is hunting from the ground, but we will take her mount with us. We will most probably scare game up the hill away from it," Running Stag announced once the three of them had discussed where they were going to go.

"Marigold and I are going to fish after we get the camp set up. We will find a place to keep the mounts by the river," Lily announced.

"I think the riverside of this ridge will be where the small game will be. They are probably waiting for the herd to pass just like us. Let's spread out and see if we can intercept anything going away from the river. I will take the ridge," Golden Hawk said.

They had decided to hunt on foot since the terrain was very uneven and the brush was thick.

"I will take the lowest position. That leaves the middle positions for the two of you," Taelo said addressing Quiet Rabbit and Busy Bee.

"Let's stay within sight of each other," Taelo said as he picked up his spear and followed Saber Scar out of the camp.

Lily and Marigold proceeded to the river to better situate their camp and find a place to tether the mounts.

Marigold was walking beside her with her spear, when suddenly she threw it at something moving in the brush. There was a grunt and some rustling and then silence.

"What did you see," Lily asked as the two of them rushed forward.

Lily still held her spear in a defensive position.

"Look what we found right near out camp," Marigold said as she pulled her spear from a small boar.

"It will be a welcome treat for everyone," Lily said.

She would also gather all the fat drippings as they roasted it. This would give her some fat to be used to flavor some other dishes.

"Good eye and ear let's get the mounts located down here by the river and then we can begin to roast that prize," Lily said as the two of them pulled the boar to the edge of the river where they would be able to gut and clean it more easily.

The two of them tied off the mounts so they would be able to drink from the river. Each mount had a long rope so they could graze on the ample grass that was growing nearby.

"I have found some wild onions that we can use when we roast the boar," Lily said as she displayed her prize.

She had about a dozen egg sized onions.

"Well, I have scrapped the hair off, gutted the boar and cut off its hooves. Help me put a spit through it and then we can carry it up to the fire," Marigold continued their running dialogue.

Meanwhile downstream of the two, Feather-in-the-Wind was putting up a demonstration of her acumen with the sling. The team had almost a dozen large rabbits, several squirrels and one groundhog.

"I am beginning to feel cheated. I have not had a chance to even think about throwing my spear or shooting my bow," Running Stag teased.

"I can't even register the animal before Feather-in-the-Wind kills it," Saber Scar joined in.

He had come with the two at Marigold's urging. She wanted him to go to ensure the safety of the two. He was now beginning to think he needed to protect the small game in the area.

Suddenly Feather-in-the-Wind raised her hand in a gesture of silence. She pointed up ahead and swiped her hand like a claw across the air in front of her. She was quietly backing away when a roar shattered the quiet.

That was a roar of a lion or tiger," Taelo called up to Busy Bee who in turn passed the message up to Quiet Rabbit who then passed it on.

"Let's gather together here," Taelo continued.

The four were together almost instantly.

"It came from the river where Running Stag, Saber Scar and Feather-in-the-Wind are hunting. Let's go down slowly and carefully. I do not want to engage with the lion or tiger if we can avoid it.

The tiger was a huge male. It spotted Feather-in-the-Wind and saw a nice meal and was immediately on the attack. It did not recognize the mounts and the people on them as potential threats.

"No," Running Stag shouted as he let multiple arrows fly from his bow as the tiger leaped through the air at Feather-in-the-Wind!

He was sure the tiger had her.

Saber Scar jumped down from his mount so he could use his spear. He ran forward shouting at the top of his lungs.

Feather-in-the-Wind let one final stone fly from her sling. As it hit the tiger on the nose, she ran forward and dived under the leaping animal and plunged her knife in from below and rolled out behind it. She was now weaponless and could only look on.

The knife was still stuck in the tiger's ribs and seemed to have little effect. The tiger was now charging Saber Scar. There were at least four arrows sticking out of the lion, but it seemed to be unfazed and had Saber Scar as its current focus.

The tiger was almost twice the size of Saber Scar. At the last moment Saber Scar knelt down, placed the butt end of his spear in the ground and pointed the tip at the tiger's chest.

The tiger managed to knock the spear tip aside and received only a gash on its front leg. It had its prey in its grasp.

Suddenly the lion was hit from the side by some flying object. The tigers slashing claw cut across Saber Scar's chest. Saber Scar ducked his head under the gapping jaws and reached in for the knife that was still stuck in the tiger's chest. He rolled it around, pulled it out and stabbed once again but closer to where he thought the heart would be.

Running Stag drove his spear into the tiger's chest.

The tiger went down, twitched, and then lay still.

The gash on Saber Scar's chest was bleeding profusely.

High above and Eagle scream could be heard.

"I've got Saber Scar. Check on the rest," Quiet Rabbit called out as the four arrived on the scene.

"I'm alright," a badly shaken Feather-in-the-Wind said as she slowly stood up and then sat back down.

She was not as alright as she had thought. She was holding her side.

"Let me check," Busy Bee said as she reached Feather-in-the-Wind.

"I don't believe what just happened," Running Stag said as he stood taking in the scene.

He had his flat shark's blade weapon Taelo had made for him, in his hand. The arrows seemed to have had little impact. He had driven in Saber Scar's spear and then drawn his last weapon and smashed it across the tiger's head.

Taelo took the weapon out of Running Stag's shaking hands.

"How is Saber Scar," Taelo asked Quiet Rabbit.

"Please give me the stitching kit. I will need to sew him up once again. From now on I am just going to call him Scar," Quiet Rabbit said.

She had taken her leather vest, folded it, and used it to apply pressure to the wound that ran at the opposite angle from his previous scars.

Saber Scar was now breathing smoothly but he had his eyes closed.

"What do lions and tigers have against me," Saber Scar said in almost a whisper.

He was just now beginning to feel the pain.

"Here, this will make you feel better," Taelo said as he took a small clay jug from his emergency bag.

It was the clear liquid that Feather-in-the-Wind's clan had taught him to make. It was the same drink Feather-in-the-Wind had swallowed before she was led up the mountain as a sacrifice to the great Condor.

Saber Scar drank.

"Thank you," he said quietly.

He watched as Quiet Rabbit threaded the needle with some threat he knew was made from the gut of a lion.

"I want to thank Feather-in-the-Wind for saving my life," Saber Scar said as Quiet Rabbit began to stitch the gash on his chest.

"If she had not used herself as a weapon, I would be dead," Saber Scar continued.

He was trying to take his mind off the stitching that Quiet Rabbit was carefully doing.

"Feather-in-the-Wind probably has a cracked or broken rib. Everything seems in place, but she is in pain when she breathes," Busy Bee reported.

"Let's skin the tiger and leave its body here. We will drape the hide over one of the mounts. We will put Saber Scar on another mount. Busy Bee and Feather-in-the-Wind will ride back together," Taelo instructed.

"Just lean back against me and relax," Busy Bee said as she helped Feather-in-the-Wind sit down in front of her.

She turned the mount and began a slow walk back to the camp.

Running Stag was following on his mount. He was carrying the tiger's hide and the bag of small game Feather-in-the-Wind had killed. His mount had been nervous but had now settled down.

Taelo was riding with Saber Scar holding him as they rode.

Golden Hawk and Quiet Rabbit were carrying the extra spears and weapons.

"We saw and heard the eagle cry and now look, something is wrong, they are all returning together," Lily called over to Marigold.

The two stood up and looked at the approaching group.

"Saber Scar is hurt," Marigold said as she ran toward the oncoming group.

"I will live but will now have another scar on my chest," Saber Scar said weakly from his mount as Taelo jumped down.

Taelo and Marigold helped Saber Scar dismount and then guided him to where Marigold had set up their sleeping area.

"What smells so good," Saber Scar asked as he let out a deep breath and relaxed.

"Here, eat some warm boar's meat," Lily said giving him a big chunk.

Quiet Rabbit helped Feather-in-the-Wind get down from her mount and then over to where Lily had set up a sleeping area for her.

"Lie down and find a comfortable position. I am going to wrap some straps around your chest to hold the ribs in place. You will be in pain for at least one cycle of the moon," Quiet Rabbit instructed.

"Well, Running Stag, you were to hunt small game not tiger. What happened," Taelo asked as he handed a piece of boar to the clearly shaken and concerned young man.

"It all happened so quickly. Saber Scar and I were lamenting the fact that Feather-in-the-Wind was taking down all the animals with her sling.

Suddenly, Feather-in-the-Wind stopped and began to back up as she tried to warn us. I think Saber Scar saw the tiger first as it attacked Feather-in-the-Wind. She used her sling and hit the tiger with a stone to the nose. Then she ran toward it and rolled under and plunged her knife into the tiger's chest. She rolled out behind the tiger.

The tiger then focused on Saber Scar. I shot the tiger with at least four arrows before jumping off to try and help Saber Scar.

The tiger knocked Saber Scar's spear to the side and just as I thought it would tear Saber Scar in half, Feather-in-the-Wind hurled herself at full speed into the tiger's side and moved it away from Saber Scar. The tiger slashed across Saber Scar's chest as it fell to the side.

Saber Scar used the knife Feather-in-the-Wind had plunged into the tiger's chest to repeatedly stab it.

I picked up Saber Scar's spear and drove it into the chest of the tiger. Saber Scar managed to kill the tiger with a second stab that must have hit the tiger's heart.

It all happened so fast. I just can't believe we all survived it," Running Stag recounted.

His hand was still shaking as he brought the boar meat to his mouth.

"Well, all of your quick thinking and working together saved the day.

This tiger was as tall at the shoulder as Feather-in-the-Wind.

It is the biggest I have ever seen or heard of. I want to recognize all of you for your bravery and complement you on how well you fight together," Taelo said as he helped Lily pass out her delicious roast boar and cooked onions.

"Well, the tiger's presence explains why we didn't see any large game on the hill side. I hope he was a lone male," Golden Hawk spoke.

"We will need to stay for a few cycles of the sun. We should make this camp a little safer if possible," Quiet Rabbit said as she got done attending to her two patients.

"There are many willow trees along the river. We can cut them and make a spiked perimeter barrier," Marigold said as she carried in the twelve rabbits, three squirrels and two ground hogs Feather-in-the-Wind had killed.

She had carefully skinned the rabbits and planned to make a vest from the fur for Feather-in-the-Wind. She knew Feather-in-the-Wind 's actions had saved Saber Scar and for that Feather-in-the-Wind would always have her support.

She also planned to make Feather-in-the-Wind a tiger skin vest.

"I don't recall of any stories where three people fought a tiger or saber tooth and won. Only Taelo fought a saber tooth single handed and lived to tell about it," Golden Hawk said as he sat and thought about what happened.

He was still processing the scene of the unbelievably large dead tiger and the three surviving team members.

"The eagle screamed at your success. That is really important," Quiet Rabbit commented. This was one of the first times the eagle had screamed for someone else.

"I am going down to cut some small trees so we can make a barrier around the camp," Golden Hawk said as he stood up.

"I am going with you," Busy Bee said joining him.

"So am I," Marigold said as she joined Busy Bee.

"I will lay out the perimeter and make the fire pits to keep the animals away," Taelo said as he began to survey the camp perimeter.

"I will gather more wood for the fires," Lily said.

"Perhaps, Running Stag and I should join in on the wood gathering," Quiet Rabbit added as she continued to think upon the significance of the eagle's scream.

She was sure it had something to do with Feather-in-the-Wind.

Both Saber Scar and Feather-in-the-Wind seemed to be asleep. It would be dark soon and Taelo wanted everyone behind the barrier once it got dark. He decided on a tight perimeter, but it needed to be large enough to hold the mounts. He began to carry and roll stones into place.

Wherever possible he incorporated the boulders and trees that were already in place. There was only one weak location on the perimeter. It was a large boulder that could easily be climbed up on from the uphill side.

Taelo brought the perimeter away from the boulder and planned for spiked poles to be placed below the boulder. The stakes would be placed around the stone perimeter. They would slant the stakes at an angle outward away from the center. The stakes would be tied to each other with the leather ropes.

The fire pits would be on the inside of the perimeters and could be fed safely by the persons on night watch.

"We have many stakes," Golden Hawk said as he dropped the first load on the ground.

It was clear Taelo had been busy. The camp was now circled in small boulders. The mounts had already been moved into the inside of where the perimeter would be.

"Where did you find all of these stones," Golden Haw asked as he began to lay out the stakes as Taelo instructed.

"Here are the rest that we have cut," Marigold and Busy Bee said as they dropped their load and began to distribute them around the perimeter.

They ended up with a few extra stakes.

"Take them over to the large boulder. We will use them to eliminate the boulder as a weak spot," Taelo instructed. He now knew how to make that part of the perimeter more secure.

"The mounts seem calm enough," Quiet Rabbit observed.

"Yes, they will be good alarms if dangerous animals come near. However, we must keep them calm, so they do not break loose," Taelo said as he thought about how powerful the mounts were.

"Marigold, can you take the first watch," Taelo asked.

"Golden Hawk can take the middle watch and I will take the early morning watch," Taelo continued. He was not really asking but assigning.

"Let's sit down for a moment and go over what we will do during the watch," Taelo ended.

"I will sit up a while and see how my patients are doing," Quiet Rabbit said.

She was planning on keeping Marigold company for most of her watch. She knew how difficult it was for Marigold. She was obviously worried about Saber Scar's condition. He was sleeping but periodically moaning.

Taelo went around and got each of the small perimeter fires going before he lay down to get some sleep. He looked over at the tiger hide and thanked the ancestors for looking over the three hunters.

Chapter 11: In the Valley of the Others

Grudgingly the snow had receded as it yielded to the sun's spring warming rays. The falls thundered down at full strength and the mist constantly replenished itself and sparklingly sent twinkling rays across the valley.

The valley was still sparse in animal life, but it seemed to be increasing. The battle between the clan members and the dire wolves the season before, when more than thirty dire wolves had been killed, had tipped the balance back to the deer and small game.

The planting of the wheat had already taken place and each plot along the river was growing well. The sentinels assigned to guard the plantings from the deer and other animals provided a constant supply of deer, boar, rabbit, and groundhog.

The Northern Elk Clan had come through the winter in fine form. Their main lodge with a hot spring and water heated floors and a central baking area made their life pleasant. The hot water bathing pool just outside of the lodge gave everyone a sense of living a life of luxury.

The compound provided the sense of security from the outside forces of nature that every member of the clan had always dreamed of.

Every family enjoyed an individual home around the base of the main lodge. Water from the spring was delivered via small channels to each home.

White Swan was talking to her leadership team about the ease of leading a clan that had the luxuries they enjoyed and that they needed to remain humble and not forget that they needed to think ahead and prepare for the bad times as well as enjoying the good ones.

She introduced the messenger who had come with an invitation from Broken Spear of the Others. Broken Spear was extending an invitation to the Northern Elk Clan to attend a summer gathering one moon cycle from now.

It was clear the runner, though fluid in the language of the clan, seemed a bit overwhelmed when he addressed White Swan. To him she was a legend whose stories he had listened to around the evening campfire.

White Swan sent back an acceptance message thanking the Others.

"Let Broken Spear and Burley Bear know that I welcome and look forward to seeing them in a moon cycle from today," White Swan replied.

She knew Broken Spear must have had a vision of what Taelo and his team was experiencing. It must be good news since he was willing to wait for a moon cycle.

Six cycles of the moon had passed since Taelo's departure.

"Who should go to this event and what should we take as a gift," White Swan asked as she sat in the hot water pool in front of the main lodge.

"Well one thing we have plenty of is salt. It always makes a good gift. However, we should come up with something special for Broken Spear," Grey Fox Running replied.

He was glad he had stepped down as leader of main Elk Clan. Watching White Swan's leadership style was a rounding education for him. She nurtured her leadership team and got them to agree with her even when some at first opposed her position. It was a lesson in a different style of leading.

"I will discuss this with everyone and see who can come up with a new idea for a gift to the clan of Others," White Swan replied.

A moon cycle later a group thirty strong from the Northern Elk Clan came marching and singing into the valley of the Others. They brought with them a gift of salt and a surprise.

"I think this will be a surprise even to Broken Spear," White Swan said when the idea was proposed by one of the clan members.

"It is good to see you. We have been looking forward to hosting you," Burley Bear came forward and gave White Swan a hug.

"We have been eager to come. The hard work you did to build the lodge really makes life easy. The heated floor is a miracle. The massive entry door is a work of art as are the gates for the compound," White Swan praised the work she knew Burley Bear had done.

"I am happy to hear you enjoy the lodge and compound. Everyone on the team contributed hard work to get it done. The design was Taelo's, and he was the force that drove us to work beyond our capability," Burley Bear replied.

He was pleased to be recognized for his contribution.

"It is a pleasure to have you," Meadow Flower said as she gave White Swan a hug.

She missed being with Taelo and Quiet Rabbit. She wished she and Burley Bear could have gone along.

The entire procession proceeded to the main cave area. There Broken Spear sat on a large bear skin mat.

"It is my pleasure to be able to greet you," Broke Spear said but stayed seated.

He was now some ninety seasons old. He thought the last few seasons were his last, but each time Taelo returned their meeting re-energized him.

In their last meeting he had felt the energy flow from Taelo into him when Taelo had taken his hand and placed it on his forehead. There was a strange power associated with Taelo that even Taelo did not understand but that he was willing to share.

"We will let you get your things arranged and then we will have a dinner meal. However, the celebration will be when Red Oak and Quiet Pheasant arrive. My scouts tell me they will arrive tomorrow," Burley Bear announced.

"Oh, what a wonderful surprise, it will be so good to see the two. How many of them are coming. Perhaps we should go out and hunt, so we have enough for everyone," White Swan replied.

"Do not worry about the food. We have learned much from Taelo, and we have an abundance of meat and fish," Meadow Flower interjected.

"Very well, we will spend tomorrow preparing the main gift to your clan," White Swan replied.

She had thought about bringing more food but had decided that their gifts would suffice.

"As to who is coming, we are not sure, but we know that Little Otter is one of them and where he is I am sure you will find Talking Wren," Burley Bear replied.

"This is turning into something of a family reunion," Grey Fox Running commented to White Swan.

"Yes, it's such a great plan. I wonder who came up with the idea," White Swan wondered.

"Well, the clan of the Others is well positioned to play the host location," Grey Fox Running observed.

"I am going to go out and make sure all of the parts for the rain maker are properly positioned so we can get it assembled tomorrow. I want to make sure my recollection of the elevation is correct," Grey Fox Running said as he went over to the ten members who were carrying the logs and other parts.

He spent the rest of the afternoon supervising the placement of the materials and the gathering of some boulders and other stones to be used for the project.

The next morning Burley Bear sat watching Grey Fox Running and his crew of workers as they built some sort of device in the hot spring.

"I think I know what they are building. It always amazes me at the ability of the new ones to change their environment to suite them. I have seen this device and never thought of building it for our hot springs," Burley Bear commented to Meadow Flower.

"I know, I have the same reaction but, Oh, how I will enjoy the feeling of the hot rain," Meadow Flower said as she gave Burley Bear a hug.

They were the only two who understood what the contraption being built would do. There was a crowd around the hot springs watching and wondering what was being built.

The other gift was an entire block of salt. It remained covered and was placed against the wall in the sleeping area. The block had been pulled on a travois. It would be carried in and be presented to the clan of Others during the official greeting ceremony.

In the early afternoon runners arrived with the news that the Elk Clan was coming up from the beach. Everything came to a stop, and everyone went out to greet them.

The greetings were warm and cordial and soon everyone was back inside the cave and pool area.

The formal dinner would be that evening. The rest of the afternoon was spent settling in for the visit. The Others were busy preparing the food and getting everything ready for the gathering.

Later, before dinner the formal greetings between the clans began.

"We have brought you the meat of two young buffalo, the hide of a dozen buffalo and the two travois of dried fish," Red Oak said as each gift was brought out and presented to Burley Bear.

"You are too generous. We were not expecting such generosity," Burley Bear gave his formal reply.

He was pleased especially with the amount of dried fish. It was a treasure when the winter went long. The hides were always a welcome gift.

"We only have a few symbolic gifts. For you and Quiet Pheasant we have our white Llama leather vests, inlaid with the shells from our shores and a few precious stones we brought back from our Journey of the Heart," Burley Bear said as Meadow Flower brought out the vests and helped Red Oak and Quiet Pheasant put them on. "For everyone else we have a small sack of honey for your enjoyment."

"We of the Northern Elk Clan bring you the salt for the meat you have been given," White Swan said as the block of salt was carried in.

There was an ooh! From almost the entire clan when they saw the size of the block and the amount of salt.

"We also have a unique gift. Please look out at your hot springs and a few of our young members will demonstrate a new way for you to enjoy your home," White Swan said as she gave the signal to open up the flow.

A cheer went up from the clan as they understood how the shower worked. Some of the younger members ran out and joined in on using the shower.

"Well, the White Swan from the north will long be remembered for this gift," Burley Bear said as he watched the younger members frolic in the hot rain.

"Finally, a personal gift to Meadow Flower from Quiet Rabbit and Busy Bee we present a series of clay pots and bowls for her use in cooking. They made these with the help of Feather-in-the-Wind," White Swan said as the pots were taken from the bags stuffed with grass.

"For each of you we also have the Llama vests, and the honey for enjoyment," Burley Bear continued the greeting ceremony.

He had not expected the overwhelming generosity of both Elk Clans.

"Let's all enjoy the dinner and then we will listen to Broken Spear tell what he knows of Taelo's journey East," Burley Bear closed the official greeting ceremony.

The dinner of fish, rabbit, buffalo, pigeon, and groundhog mixed with a variety roasted onions and tubers was a true treat.

The drink was a honey water mixture.

"Please gather around and listen. Broken Spear will share what he knows of the journey of our friends, in their Journey of Discovery," Burley Bear announced.

Everyone gathered around and sat down in semi-circle with Broken Spear in the center. He was supported on each side by two women.

"We all know Taelo.

We remember the first time we met him when as a young lad when he knocked out our own Burley Bear for being rude and rough to White Swan.

We remember how he found the whale that fed all of us for the winter.

We remember how he talked to the bear that gave me the name Broken Spear and asked her to keep the wolves away until our warriors could arrive.

We remember how he found our cave and gave us this home.

You have heard of the story of Taelo and the crazed saber tooth tiger. This was the same tiger that gave Saber Scar his name. Taelo faced it and killed it even as the tiger and he fell down into a water filled hole.

It was Quiet Rabbit that treated Saber Scar and sewed up his wound.

You have heard the stories of Quiet Rabbit and Busy Bee attacking the cannibals from behind. Two brave warriors that turned the tide of the first battle.

You have heard the stories of Running Stag and his bravery as a warrior long before it was time for him to be so brave. He carries a scar on his back that he received from one of the cannibal warriors. Those that faced him all perished. He was only following Taelo's command to watch over and protect Quiet Rabbit.

You have met the princess, Feather-in-the-Wind, and learned the sling from her. Quiet Rabbit and Busy Bee rescued her from the cave of the Condor where a hundred other frozen princesses lay in death.

Taelo protected her and killed the leader of the Warrior Clan and could have become their leader, but he chose to come back to all of us.

Together with our own Burley Bear and Meadow Flower the Northern Elk Clan came to be.

Together they built the best home anyone could wish for. Together they developed a way to travel on the white rain and taught the wild wolf to be their servant.

Over and over, you have heard the stories of Taelo, of Quiet Rabbit, of Busy Bee, of Running Stag, of Feather-in-the-Wind and you have heard of the stories of our own Burley Bear and Meadow Flower.

These are all stories we enjoy and have told many times. They are all a part of us," Broken Spear paused in his slow recital of the adventures of Taelo and the rest of his friends.

There was total silence as everyone strained to hear every word uttered by Broken Spear. He seldom talked so long at clan gatherings. This night he was telling a story everyone wanted to hear.

"Now let me tell you about this latest journey.

This is a journey of discovery. Taelo and his team have discovered a new animal to serve them.

The team has tamed this animal and ride on their backs. It is the same concept as Little Otter's buffalo. They have hunted a cousin of our buffalo using these animals.

During this hunt they met a new tiger larger than our saber tooth tiger. This was not an animal Taelo wanted to fight on the open plain. He gave up the buffalo he had just killed.

The tigers were happy with the offering and left the team alone.

The team was stopped by a herd of these new buffalo and a herd of Mastodons. The combined herd would fill the beach from here all the way to the valley of the Elk Clan.

The team stopped to make camp and went on a hunt for food.

Saber Scar, Running Stag and Feather-in-the-Wind met and fought to the end with a monstrous tiger.

The tiger was as tall at the shoulder as Feather-in-the-Wind. It was as long as our buffalo. The tiger attacked Feather-in-the-Wind as she tried to back away from it. Once attacked she ran, not away from but toward the lion. She slid on her knees under it and drove a knife into its chest.

Saber Scar tried to spear it with the ground spear technique, but the tiger swept the spear aside and would have ripped Saber Scar in half, but Feather-in-the-Wind, now weaponless, ran with all her strength and used her body to hit the tiger on his side.

Her body was her weapon. This gave a gravely wounded Saber Scar the opportunity to use her knife still buried in the tiger's chest to repeatedly stab it in the heart.

I believe that Quiet Rabbit has suggested changing his name to Scar.

Running Stag finished the tiger with a spear and the use of his shoulder weapon. The tiger had six of Running Stag's arrows in its body.

The three survived because they knew how to fight together as they had been trained to do by Taelo.

The eagle screamed when he saw this victory. The eagle has become the totem for all those who travel with Taelo.

Now the team is once again proceeding east. They are now at the great river and will soon find another river coming from the east," Broken Spear finished.

The silence held for what seemed eternity then the cave thundered with palms slapping the floor.

"Thank you for sharing such a fine story. I am much relieved and look forward to another such meeting in the near future," White Swan said quietly to Broken Spear.

"I try to fly with the eagle every day, but it will not always let me. I will let you know about this journey as often as possible," Broken Spear replied

Chapter 12: The Mighty River

The camp site was eerily bright under the bright yellow full moon. Taelo was feeding and talking to a pack of wolves that had found their campsite.

"We have nothing against our brothers. As you see Lasher is my companion. Here have something to eat. Once you have your fill please move on and allow us to stay here in peace," Taelo carried on his conversation with the wolves.

The barrier around the campsite had been improved by a head high woven willow mesh that went around the entire campsite and was attached to the closely placed vertical poles.

Taelo sat on a small boulder feeding the pack of wolves that had found the compound and had been trying to get in.

"Sometimes I worry about my cousin," Golden Hawk commented to the rest of the team.

"It does seem strange, but did you notice the pack left after they each had a bite to eat," Busy Bee came to Taelo's defense.

"You misunderstand my conversation. It is not my words; it is the tone and my manner. Wolves run in packs and have a leader. The leader is the dominant wolf. I learned this in setting up my wolf sled team. Tonight, I have established myself as the dominant wolf," Taelo explained.

The evening visits continued for most of the time they remained in the camp. One evening a lone lion happened to come into sight while the wolves were being fed.

"I think it is time you earned the food I have been feeding you. Please chase this lion from my camp area," Taelo commanded.

As if they understood him the wolf pack turned on the lion and began to harass it until the lion decided it had enough and turned and left the area. The wolf pack followed and could be heard harassing the lion until they got out of hearing range.

"Ok, I take it back, you can talk to any animal you want, and I will back you up," Golden Hawk commented when he saw what had just occurred.

High above an eagle screamed. Once again Taelo's action had been the correct one. He had chosen not to confront the first group of tigers and had befriended the wolves and used them to prevent the lion from trying to get into the camp.

"Feather-in-the-Wind's rib is not fully healed but the pain has subsided. Saber Scar's new addition to his chest has healed well enough to travel. Our camp is becoming an attraction to the wildlife. I think it is time for us to continue our journey," Taelo announced to the team.

"I am ready to go. I need to do something other than sit in this camp," Saber Scar said from across the fire.

He was restless. He had been sitting for the last few cycles while his scar healed. He still could not lift any weight without feeling the scar stretch but he knew it was time to test it and rebuild the muscle in that area.

"I am ready to go also," Feather-in-the-Wind joined in.

She and Saber Scar had shared their restless feelings. Her rib still hurt but it was different from the piercing pain it had been only a few cycles earlier.

Saber Scar had a new appreciation for Feather-in-the-Wind. He now knew she was fearless and knew how to immediately take action. She was the smallest among them and the most fragile in appearance, but she had power within that was as large as anyone on their team. Her quick thinking and action had saved his life.

"Tomorrow we will spend the time getting ready. We will want to leave this area free of our presence. Early on the next sunrise we will continue our journey east," Taelo declared.

"Golden Hawk would you and Running Stag plan on scouting ahead and find the best path for us to follow. The rest of us will stay and get ready to travel," Taelo continued.

The breaking of the camp went smoothly and the following morning the team set out on the path with Golden Hawk and Running Stag in the lead.

"We have picked up some traveling companions," Taelo noted as he spotted the wolf pack he had befriended following along on both sides of the trail. He noted that Lasher and the other two wolves seemed to accept the pack with no sign of a problem.

This let Taelo relax.

When the team came down from the ridge to the lower land next to the river, the wolf pack became visible. They were following along behind on either side of where the mounts were traveling.

"Well, I hope they think you are the dominant leader," Quiet Rabbit commented.

She was always amazed at the reaction wild animals had to Taelo's interactions. The animals sensed something about Taelo that instilled trust.

The terrain was grand in its expanse and in the wildlife that was present. An abundance of various birds and small game made it easy for the team members to gather small game for the evening meal.

Scattered bison groups and a few families of mastodon were also present. One group was bathing, and the young were playing in the river and seemed to take little notice of their passing.

They were able to gather both onion and garlic growing along the riverbed. The digging sticks that Taelo and Golden Hawk had made for everyone were always in use.

The blueberries and dewberries were ripening. There were many blackberries, but they were still green and would not be ripe for another moon cycle.

"This is a rich land," Busy Bee commented as she dropped down from her mount to gather some ripe dewberries.

She was thinking about using them to season the evening meal of mostly rabbit and the one groundhog Feather-in-the-Wind had killed.

"Feather-in-the-Wind seems to be our daily meal provider," Saber Scar commented as once again Feather-in-the-Wind let her sling bring down another flying pigeon.

Feather-in-the-Wind usually would get more than a dozen pigeons as she rode along. The pigeons usually served as individually roasted snacks while the main dish was being prepared. Everyone made sure she always had plenty of stones.

Her accuracy from the back of her mount now matched the accuracy she had when she was on the ground. She had shortened the length of her sling for use on her mount. It therefore had a shorter range, but it made little difference on most occasions.

"Yes, we are all getting spoiled at the easy time we have as we travel," Taelo commented as he trotted alongside of his mount.

He had come to the conclusion he needed to keep up his stamina by running alongside for at least half of the day. Even though he had said nothing to the rest of the team, they began following the same practice.

The mounts were now getting use to their riders and had become more relaxed. Each rider paid special attention to their mount and made sure it got plenty to eat. Besides the grasses there were a few roots that the mounts seemed to like.

It turned out one purple root with multiple green leaves also became a favorite for the team to use with the meats they prepared.

The colored water from the mashed root was something Marigold was experimenting with. She took some of her pure white leather and soaked it in the purple water and heated the mix. The leather took on a light pale purple color.

She kept this experiment to herself until she was satisfied, she had something that worked to permanently color the leather. Now she would have regular leather, pure white leather, and a light purple leather to offer for trade.

One evening Marigold brought out a lightweight leather vest.

"This is a present for Feather-in-the-Wind," she said as she held up a lavender vest decorated with small black beads and trimmed with black rabbit fur.

"Oh, this is so beautiful. Why for me," Feather-in-the-Wind said as Marigold helped her put the vest on?

"So, you have developed another leather tanning skill," Quiet Rabbit said as she examined the fine work done on the vest. "Will you teach us this one?"

"Yes, you can all join in with my experiments. I am now trying this with other colors from the plants around us," Marigold replied with a sense of pride.

The next day the river they were following met a much larger and wider river. They had come to the mighty river Broken Spear had said would run north and south.

High above the eagle scream pierced the air.

"I believe we have arrived at the halfway point of our journey," Busy Bee said as she took in the river.

"We will need to plan our crossing. There will be no place to ride across. All of us and our mounts must swim with the current and make our way to the other side," Taelo commented as he sat and looked across to the other side.

He looked both upstream and down. He was trying to see if there was some launch site that would be the best in reaching the other side safely.

"Let's ride upstream along the bank and see if there is a place that seems the easiest to make a crossing," Taelo commented as he turned his mount northward.

"Here are some islands in the middle of the river. I think we should cross to the islands and then go across the wider area. This will give us a chance to recover if it gets too rough for us," Golden Hawk pointed out.

"I wonder how well our mounts swim," Saber Scar interjected.

He was also worried about himself and Marigold. They would sink like a rock unless they worked at staying afloat. He was looking around for some solid logs they could use to float across.

"The current is fairly swift. Let's measure how fast it flows so we know how far up stream we need to be to make it to the island," Quiet Rabbit suggested as she threw a stick in and watched it move swiftly downstream.

"This seems far enough upstream. Let's make camp here and plan on how we can all get safely across," Taelo announced as he dismounted in an opening surrounded by large trees.

He noted that his wolf pack had gathered just into the woods. He walked out to where he could see them. He was ready for anything, but he seemed sure the pack was not a threat. In fact, they might even serve as a protection against the more dangerous predators such as the tigers and other cats that seemed to be present in this area.

"Well, my fellow wolves. It is good to have you with us," he said as he reached into the bag, he had carried out with him.

Lasher, Walker, and Arrow were sitting quietly at his side. He gave each a piece of meat and then threw pieces out to the each of the wolves. When he had given each a helping of the meat, he instructed them, "now go out and hunt for your evening meal so you will feel full and have a good night without bothering us."

"Well, our wolf leader is out talking to his wolf clan," Golden Hawk observed as the camp was being set up.

"I guess the pack will leave us alone. I actually feel more comfortable with them around since they will alert us to other more dangerous enemies."

"It still seems strange to me, but Taelo is the one that killed the saber tooth that marked me. I will believe anything Taelo does," Saber Scar commented as he observed Taelo talking to the wolf pack.

"Marigold and I will ride these two logs we have bound together. We will float ahead of our mounts and guide them. Our belongings will fit behind us on the platform made of woven willows," Saber Scar was explaining to the rest of the team about how he planned to cross.

"That seems to be a good design. We should all make similar rafts. Then we can cross in pairs. That way we can help each other," Quiet Rabbit commented.

There was a slight problem with the plan since there were nine members.

"I agree with the design of the rafts however, I suggest a slightly different pairing," Taelo spoke up.

"Golden Hawk, Running Stag and I will each cross by ourselves. We will take the extra mounts and any other possessions that don't fit on the other rafts.

Quiet Rabbit and Feather-in-the-Wind will go together, and Lily and Busy Bee will go together," Taelo suggested.

"We need a flat piece of wood like our battle weapons to help us guide our rafts," Quiet Rabbit said as she looked about for such a piece.

It took almost seven cycles of the sun for the team to make the crossing preparations.

It took some time to get enough older logs and the right wood to make the paddles. The logs were placed parallel to each other, and willow branches were used to join them together and to make a platform to carry the goods.

The platform took up almost half of the length of the logs.

The other half would be where the riders would sit.

They worked together to build and test the first one. Marigold and Saber Scar were the riders for the test raft.

They had been chosen because they were the heaviest members of the team.

They sat on the two logs, and each had a paddle to help guide the raft. A rope was attached to the back of their raft, and they paddled out into the river.

"It appears this design is working well. It is time to build the rest," Lily commented as she sat and watched the test.

She was pleased to have a raft to ride since she was not a very good swimmer.

Each day, each of the mounts were taken into the water so they would get accustomed to floating in the water. They seemed to have little concern about the water and appeared to enjoy swimming.

Taelo and Golden Hawk swam over to the island and tested how far up stream they need to begin the journey across in order to hit the island. The swim across had been leisurely. They determined the starting spot and about where on the island they would try to land.

They had scouted out the way to the other side of the island and decided that the first leg would be done on one day and then they would go across the second part of the river on the following day.

"Well, it's time to make our way across the river," Taelo said as he got ready to lead the way.

He was leading his mount and two of the pack mounts. He pushed his raft out into the stream and pulled the mounts out into the water. Once they were all floating down river, Taelo got on the upstream log of his raft and began to paddle across. The mounts were floating along behind him and seemed to be having no problems as they crossed.

Saber Scar and Running Stag were asked to be responsible to get all the rafts pulled across to the east side of the island. The river was wider on the other side of the island, and they would all travel downstream about twice as far on the second day.

"I will bring up the rear. We will cross one raft at a time. Taelo will help each team land on the island and pull their raft to shore," Golden Hawk instructed the group.

Everyone was watching Taelo's progress as he floated slowly across to the island. Taelo appeared to struggle as he tried to land his raft. He was able to tie the raft off to a tree limb and once he had the mounts on the island, he was able to use them to pull his raft ashore.

"Ok, Quiet Rabbit and Feather-in-the-Wind it is your turn," Golden Hawk said as he helped lead their mounts into the water.

They were taking an extra pack mount across as well.

The crossings continued throughout the day with no mishaps. Golden Hawk was the last to cross. By the time he landed Saber Scar had most of the other rafts pulled across the island.

"Well, so far, so good," Lily said as the last raft was positioned along the shore for the next morning's journey.

She was busy cooking the evening meal. It was an appropriate meal in the sense it was roast fish. She had one skewered fish per person. She also had a stew she had prepared with dried bison meat. She figured Marigold and Saber Scar would need more than one fish a piece.

Busy Bee and Quite Rabbit had found a treasure of mushrooms that they grilled with a sprinkling of salt. This added a delicious touch to the fish.

"I think we should relax tomorrow and plan to go across beginning early the following morning," Golden Hawk suggested.

He was thinking about the long swim the horses would have on the next part of the crossing.

The evening was relaxing, and all seemed well. Then in the early morning a heavy rain began to fall. Everything they were carrying was getting soaked.

There was no way to cook. Breakfast was the leftovers of the evening meal.

"I am afraid if we wait the river will rise and we will find the crossing even more difficult than it is now or we will find this island underwater," Taelo commented as he looked at the clouds and the torrent that was pouring.

"Let's pack up and go now. We will tie each raft to the one in front and we will go across together. When we get to the other side, I will tie my raft off to a tree and we will let the river current swing each of you to shore.

As you get your raft to shore you must immediately tie your raft to a tree. Make sure your mounts are on the down river side of the rope. When you are close to shore let them get out of the water on their own."

They launched immediately after getting everything on their rafts.

"I can barely see the raft ahead," Quiet Rabbit commented to Feather-in-the-Wind.

The rain was now coming down even harder.

Walker lay with his head between his legs on the mound of personal gear tied to platform at the back of the raft.

"The mounts seem to be keeping up with our progress, but we are going fast enough that it may be hard for them to get out of the water. When we get to the far shore, you tie us off and I will get to shore and help the mounts out of the water," Saber Scar commented to Marigold.

The rafts in front of Golden Hawk were progressing slowly across the river but the entire team was speeding down river faster than he had expected to be moving. The force of the river was much more than anyone had anticipated.

It was going to be critical for each raft to tie off immediately on reaching the other side otherwise the strain on the ropes would be too great and they would snap.

Taelo reached the far side and guided his raft to a low hanging tree and tied his raft off. Lasher jumped into the water and struggled to get up on the bank.

Taelo immediately got his mounts out of the water. He saw Quiet Rabbit and Feather-in-the-Wind swinging swiftly in toward shore. It was obvious that they would not have a good place to tie off their raft.

Taelo took the rope off one of his mounts and raced downstream to help. He watched as Feather-in-the-Wind jumped off the raft and for a moment disappeared under the water.

"We will not be able to tie off. You get the mounts to shore," Quiet Rabbit called out through the rain.

She watched Feather-in-the-Wind slip into the water and swim for the shore. She and the mounts were being propelled downstream. Walker was on the bank running back and forth trying to figure out what was happening to Feather-in-the-Wind.

Busy Bee looked ahead and found a place to tie the raft off, but the tree was down stream of where her raft was coming in.

"Get the mounts to shore," she shouted to Lily as she tried to adjust to the situation.

The rope to Quiet Rabbits raft was singing and then a sharp bang could be heard.

Busy Bee threw her rope over the low hanging branch and quickly tied it off. Her raft was swinging in toward shore and she was afraid she was going to hit the mounts who were struggling to get out of the river.

"Hi eee, Hi eee," she shouted at the top of her voice.

The screams seemed to have the desired effect and the mounts lunged ashore. They pulled Lily up on the bank with them.

"Watch out, I am going to hit you," Quiet Rabbit was shouting as loud as she could.

Instinctively Busy Bee jumped away from Quiet Rabbit's voice. She plunged into the river and was propelled downstream. She was struggling to get oriented when suddenly an iron grip caught her by the shoulder and lifted her out of the water.

"I think it's too dangerous to go swimming in water like this," Saber Scar commented as he put her down on the bank and moved swiftly up stream to where Quiet Rabbit was tying her raft to the one Busy Bee had been riding.

He watched as Quiet Rabbit tied her raft to the same limb used by Busy Bee.

Golden Hawk looked on helplessly as he passed swiftly by on his raft. He was now looking ahead and trying to determine if Running Stag or he would have a similar problem.

Arrow jumped off the raft and was swept downstream, but it looked like he would make it to shore.

Taelo ran along the bank taking in the situation. He saw that Saber Scar was helping Quite Rabbit and had the situation in hand. He continued running downstream to where Running Stag was coming in with the two mounts he was guiding across.

"Let the mounts go. I will help them ashore," he shouted to Running Stag.

Running Stag saw he would have one chance to tie off, but he would have to be swift. He immediately let go of the ropes holding the mounts and concentrated on throwing his rope over a fairly small tree bending close to the water. He hoped the force would not pull the tree out by the roots.

Golden Hawk realized he had no tie off point. He decided to untie the rope leading to Running Stag's raft. This would let him go downstream to find a tree or other tie off point. His mounts were slowly pulling him toward the shore. He decided to tie them more securely to the raft. The three mounts found their footing and he found himself and the raft being pulled up onto the bank.

"Whoa," he shouted to the mounts as they backed away from the river pulling the raft further up the bank.

He managed to get to them and settle them down.

Golden Hawk looked upstream and could see that everyone was busy trying to help each other to shore. He jumped on his mount and rode along the top of the bank and gathered all the loose mounts and tied them off to various small trees.

Saber Scar was the muscle that saved the day. He was able to pull the rafts close up to the bank and out of the swift river current.

"Well, that was exciting," Busy Bee said as she stood in the rain torrent and washed the mud from her body. She was still trying to get over the fact that she had almost been swept downstream.

"Tie Quiet Rabbit's raft to this rope and I will pull it ashore," Golden Hawk called out.

He repeated this with the other rafts and soon had all of them up by the area where the mounts were tied off.

"Where is Taelo," Quiet Rabbit asked as she looked around at everyone standing in the intense rain.

There was a thunder roll and lightening so bright that the area stood out in clear contrast to the black of the clouds above.

For a moment she had a sinking feeling but then she saw that Taelo's mount and Lasher were also missing.

Taelo had taken a quick look at the situation and realized the team needed a shelter to get out of the rain and to recover. He rode into the forest hoping to find a cave or some cliff overhang.

He did not appreciate the size of the trees until suddenly before him there was a tree that appeared to have a cave in it. He dropped from his mount and walk cautiously toward the opening. Once he was standing on the ground he could see into the rather dark opening. He realized the entire group could fit comfortably into it.

"The team will not believe it," he thought to himself as he finished examining the interior.

He turned and quickly made his way to where Golden Hawk had tied off the mounts.

"How was your ride in the rain," Golden Hawk inquired when Taelo returned to the rest of the team.

"Bring all your personal gear, I have found a place where we can get out of the rain. Bring several of the larger hides. We will be able to use them to make the space more useful," Taelo replied.

He turned and quickly made his way to where Golden Hawk had tied off the mounts.

He led the way back to the tree he had found.

Later the fire that Lily had started was trying to stay alive.

Lily was patiently feeding it dry chips she had gathered from inside of the hollow tree. Feather-in-the-Wind was carefully stacking pieces of wood so they would dry and could later be used to fuel the fire.

The skin hides were stretched and held up with some poles. The rain played its tune on the hides and water ran freely to the ground.

"I will gather enough wood for the night," Running Stag volunteered.

He was already soaked. He couldn't get any wetter.

"We will tie the mounts around the edge of this opening," Taelo suggested as he drove a stake into the ground with a large stone.

"I found a large growth of grass," Saber Scar commented as he dropped a huge hide full of wet grass to the ground. He proceeded to divide it up, so each mount had some to chew on.

"It seems to be late at night, but it must only be around noon," Quiet Rabbit said as she sat by the opening in the tree trunk.

She had changed into something that was almost dry. Everyone had unpacked their belongings and spread them around in the inside of the tree. Everything was damp.

"I have brought up some saplings from the riverbank to make several drying racks," Marigold said as she stood and let the water drip off of her.

"It is lucky we made it across. The river is already halfway up to the flat area were we tied off the mounts," she continued. She had never experienced such rain or a river with such force.

The rain continued through the night and for the next four days. Everyone relaxed and worked at drying their belongings on Marigold's drying racks.

"It was lucky we crossed immediately when it began to rain," Golden Hawk observed as he and Taelo walked through the rain along the river. It was now almost twice as wide, and the flow of the water was a roiling torrent.

"If the rain doesn't stop, we will need to move our camp," Taelo observed.

The water was now up to the point where they had put their rafts.

Chapter 13: Giants

The sun rising in the East spread its rays that were split by the thick foliage and branches of the gigantic oak tree the team had taken refuge in. The water of the mighty river had come within throwing distance but was now slowly receding.

The forest around was a mix of giant old oak and maple trees surrounded by smaller versions of themselves and a mix of tall pine reaching eagerly for their share of the sun.

The underbrush was light, but the blackberries and dewberries were numerous.

The land seemed to defend itself from the mighty river by rising into the hill riddled with body sized boulders and a mix of smaller cousin rocks. These smaller rocks were held in place by a variety of wildflowers whose roots embraced the stones and reached beyond into the fertile earth below them.

The sun shining in from the east woke Feather-in-the-Wind. Everyone else was sleeping peacefully. She quietly exited the camp and went out to explore the forest around the camp. She took her sling and her shark toothed weapon and walked up the hill to the East of the camp.

Feather-in-the-Wind went like a bee from flower to flower. She used her digging stick to gather a few small onions and garlic cloves. It was early in the season, and she was pleased to be able to find them.

Walker followed at her heals and seemed to enjoy smelling the flowers almost as much as she did.

"It feels so refreshing. The air is so clear and clean. The early morning sun so welcoming," Feather-in-the-Wind thought.

The morning dew was still on the golden dewberries she found as she wandered quietly up the hillside.

She downed a sleepy rabbit with a stone from her sling. She placed the rabbit into her hunting pouch, picked up her stone and continued her hike.

She had no direction or purpose and was just enjoying the warm sunshine.

She came to a large blackberry patch. There were only a few berries that were ripe.

She bagged another rabbit as she got to the edge of the patch. The first berry proved to be sweeter than she anticipated. She began to eat and pick the few other berries for later.

The birds were singing, and the morning forest was coming awake.

An eerie quiet caused Feather-in-the-Wind to stop and cautiously look around. For once Walker was silent. What she saw made her heart stop.

A bear like creature but so large that it was hard to describe, was across the blackberry patch. He was sniffing the air.

Feather-in-the-Wind stood very still but slowly turned her head looking for a place of refuge.

A large, tall pine with limbs she could quickly climb was about two hundred yards away on the far side of the clearing. She turned and ran as fast as her legs would carry her. Her swift and immediate action put her just a few feet ahead of the giant bear that took up pursuit.

She was surprised something so large could move so fast. Walker was running with her but stopped and turned to face the bear. His bravery in her defense gave Feather-in-the-Wind just enough time to reach the tree.

"Keep running she shouted at Walker," as she scurried up the tree.

The bear rushed forward and stood on its hind legs and almost got her.

"Go to the camp," Feather-in-the-Wind shouted to Walker as she climbed higher into tree.

The bear was trying to climb but its weight broke the lower branches. He ignored Walker's growling. His total attention was on the animal in the tree.

"Where is Feather-in-the-Wind," Running Stag asked as he finished his morning meal.

He had been expecting her to show up at any moment.

"I haven't seen her this morning," Lily replied.

"Does anyone know where she is," Running Stag said as he got up to check inside.

Taelo had been listening and was getting concerned. Walker's arrival at the camp cause Taelo immediate concern. He knew that Walker was very similar to Lasher in his loyalty.

At the same time the scream of the eagle gave a piercing wake up call.

"Let's go find Feather-in-the-Wind," Taelo announced to the camp.

"The rain has made it easy to follow her tracks. Usually her walk is almost invisible," Saber Scar said as he tracked Feather-in-the-Wind.

"I think Walker will guide us back directly," Golden Hawk commented as Walker veered to the right of where the tracks were leading.

"Everyone stop and be absolutely quiet," Taelo said as he watched Lasher, Walker, and Arrow stop.

A low rumble could be heard from Lasher's throat.

A huge animal was sitting at the base of a tall pine. It looked like a bear but was about three times larger than any Taelo had ever seen. It appeared to be as large as three of their mounts. It stood more than two of him tall and was one of him wide.

"Well, hello father of all bears," Taelo said quietly as the bear noticed the new arrivals. Taelo stepped forward and away from the rest of the team.

"The rest of you find a tree you can quickly climb if you need to escape," Taelo said quietly. To the bear he said, "It is a beautiful morning, and we have no desire to hurt you. Please go your way. We have only come to bring Feather-in-the-Wind home."

He was slowly walking across in front of the bear so it would face away from the rest of the team.

Golden Hawk recalled the time, a much younger Taelo had talked to an angry mother bear. His courage then as a young boy had saved three of the children of their clan. This bear made Taelo look the same size as when he had been just a boy.

"Is there anything I can do," Golden Hawk asked quietly?

"No, this father of all bears will either choose to leave or it will die here," Taelo replied as he readied his spear and long blade knife.

"You should go back to the blackberry patch and enjoy yourself. To stay here is to die," Taelo said in a calm steady voice.

The bear was now on all four. He seemed to be listening. He then started toward Taelo.

Taelo raised his hands high above his head and let out a loud roar that mimicked a bear.

The bear stopped in front of him and stood on its hind legs and raised his paws up and let out an unbelievably loud roar in return.

This was the moment Taelo had been waiting for. He stepped forward and in a swift movement he drove his spear up and through the throat of the bear into its skull. At the same time, he stepped in and drove his knife in just below the ribs and up into the heart cavity.

The bear brought his front legs together and pulled Taelo tightly to his chest. The two fell over and only a powerful twist on Taelo's part kept him from being crushed beneath the weight of the bear.

As the two met the ground Taelo could feel the bear claws sink into the muscles of his back. The pain was instantaneous and extremely painful. He felt sick inside. His leg was trapped under the bear. It did not feel broken, but he could not free himself. The claws remained in his back.

Feather-in-the-Wind had witnessed the surreal scene from above. Her image of Taelo had always been of a large man but at that moment he looked little standing in front of the giant bear.

The entire team rushed forward, and Feather-in-the-Wind scurried down from her perch.

"Are you alright," a very worried and strained Quiet Rabbit said as she reached Taelo.

Golden Hawk and Saber Scar were trying to get Taelo's leg out from under the bear.

"Are you alright," Running Stag asked the same question of Feather-in-the-Wind.

Everyone stood around the bear as Saber Scar positioned a stone so he could use a limb to lift the bear off of Taelo's leg.

Marigold, Saber Scar and Golden Hawk pushed a good-sized log under the chest of the giant bear. Together they pushed down on the log and lifted the bear.

Quiet Rabbit, Busy Bee and Lily pulled one front leg out. The claws came out of Taelo's back and blood flowed freely out. They rolled Taelo over to remove the other four claws.

Taelo sat up to rub his leg while Quiet Rabbit remove his vest and began to attend to the eight holes on either side of his backbone. They were bleeding but it seemed that all but two were slowly coagulating.

"You have eight deep piercings in your back from the bear claws. I will need to wash them out and stitch each one closed. Let's go over by the tree so you can lay down flat. We need to get the bleeding stopped," Quiet Rabbit said as she examined the wounds.

She was worried about the depth of the bear claws wounds.

"We will need to be very cautious not to get into any other bear's territory," Taelo said as he rubbed his leg and moved toward Quiet Rabbit.

"I think we have our meat supply for the rest of the journey," Lily said as she took in the size of the animal.

"I know how to skin a bear, but this is almost like working on the whale Taelo found on the beach. I still remember climbing on it to help cut off the fat. We will need to work on half of this bear at a time. We will end up using his hide as the ground cover to cut up the meat," Saber Scar commented.

He knew Quiet Rabbit would take care of Taelo. He had decided to take charge of processing the bear.

"Well, let's get started. We will need the camp prepared to dry most of this meat. That means a supply of wood and the making of drying racks," Golden Hawk organized the team.

He was amazed at how easily Taelo had handled the giant.

Making it stand up and then stepping in had been the trick that gave Taelo the advantage. He was not sure he would have thought of doing something similar.

"I think the bear claws went all the way in," Taelo said. He felt feint and nauseous and then realized the world was closing in on him.

The last he heard was an eagle scream in the sky.

Taelo seemed to come awake in a strange place. The elders were sitting around the fire talking to each other about him.

"It is not yet his time. He has many more miles to travel. He has many more things to learn. There is the journey to the north and to the west. He has yet to learn of those in the other lands," an elder that looked a lot like Broken Spear spoke up.

He came over to where Taelo lay and put his hand on his forehead.

"Yes, it is I Broken Spear. I am now speaking to you through the world of the ancestors. Be calm, your wounds will heal, and you will travel on. Your bravery has been noted by the ancestors. They give you many more years to learn, travel and grow old. You will be a Seer for your people," Broken Spear said quietly to Taelo.

It seemed like time was standing still. Taelo could only understand some things but most of it was confusing. He tried to make sense of what was around him but each time he thought he understood the scene changed and he lost the context of his situation. He seemed to be going in circles. Periodically Broken Spear would encourage him and Taelo felt refreshed.

"Now drink this magic potion and get well," Broke Spear said holding a gourd with a dark thick fluid in it.

Taelo opened his eyes and looked into Quiet Rabbit's worried face.

"Well, you certainly look much prettier than Broken Spear," Taelo said as he took a sip of the broth Quiet Rabbit was trying to get him to swallow.

The broth warmed his throat and felt good as he sipped on each helping that Quiet Rabbit offered.

"Well, I am happy to see you back in this world," Quiet Rabbit said as she put her cheek to his.

She was trying to hold back tears of joy. For many sun cycles she had attended him almost constantly.

Everyone had come by and relieved her so that she could cook or prepare the water to wash the wound on Taelo's back. Several of the wounds slowly oozed blood. The remainder seemed to heal quickly. She had washed out the wounds that were oozing the blood and had stitched the others shut.

Lasher gave Taelo a nose to the other cheek. Lasher had refused to leave Taelo's side except for periodic forays into the woods. It was clear he was happy to have Taelo scratch him behind his ears.

"I hope you have gotten your rest and are ready to travel," Golden Hawk said as he looked down at Taelo's rather pale face.

He had been very worried about the fate of his cousin and best friend.

"How is the bear," Taelo asked.

All he could remember was driving his spear upward and his knife inward.

"He is mostly dried meat now. Marigold has been working for more than six sun cycles on his hide. She insisted the head be left with the hide. It is the largest hide I have ever seen," Golden Hawk continued the conversation.

He was overjoyed to see his cousin recovering from his injury.

"Six sun cycles! Have I been out for that long," Taelo said in surprise.

He did not feel refreshed. He felt hot and nauseous.

"Yes, we carried you back and Quiet Rabbit and Marigold have been taking care of you both night and day. You were so much work that I think I overheard them planning to continue the journey without you," Saber Scar joked.

He and Marigold had both been very worried about Taelo.

Taelo slowly sat up. He was stiff and his back still ached. He was very thirsty. He felt nauseous as he sat up.

"I have a treat of bear roast wrapped in fatty boar strips with a little salt," Lily said she gave Taelo a small bite sized piece of meat.

She had saved what she thought was one of the best cuts of meat from the bear to give to Taelo. She was going to give him a little at a time.

"Thank you that was great. May I have some water," Taelo asked.

"I am sorry to have caused so much trouble," Feather-in-the-Wind said as she gave Taelo a gourd full of water.

Every day she had sat and told him stories her mother had taught her. Her mother said a person was always listening.

"So, it was you who called the bear," Taelo said after he had taken a long drink.

"No, the bear found me," Feather-in-the-Wind exclaimed!

She had been blaming herself for what happened to Taelo. If she had stayed in camp, then maybe the bear would not have bothered them.

"In the future, we must travel in pairs at all times. The bear is only one of many dangers. We must always be prepared to help each other," Taelo replied.

"It is time for us to continue our journey east. I will walk around and see how I feel but I believe we should plan on continuing our journey," Taelo said as he took Golden Hawk's offered hand and pulled himself up.

Chapter 14: River East

The shadow of the giant oak was deep and blocked most of the bright warming sun. The mounts had been moved toward the river where the grasses were flourishing from the silt left behind by the mighty river.

They had been under the watchful eye of Running Stag, Feather-in-the-wind, Arrow, and Walker.

The two wolves were the main watchers as Feather-in-the-Wind pursued the mushroom hunt that challenged her. She would go looking along the riverbank and just when she was about to give up, she would look back along the path she had just taken and be surprised at seeing the mushrooms she had missed.

The team relished the mushrooms and were always pleased when Feather-in-the-Wind brought a batch that could be grilled with the meat or put into a stew. The grilled mushrooms with a sprinkle of salt by themselves was always a treat.

During Taelo's recovery, the team had settled into a routine of fishing, gathering young onions and other plants used for cooking and flavoring the food and hunting for small game to provide variation. They had more bear meat than they knew how to use.

Now it was time to straighten out the camp, pack their goods and get back on their journey.

It was clear to Taelo that he was not fully healed. He rode his mount for the first few sun cycles. He was often dizzy and nauseous. He would fall asleep as he rode.

Quiet Rabbit and one of the other team members would each ride along side of Taelo's mount.

"I am worried about Taelo," Quite Rabbit confided in Busy Bee.

"Luckily, the mounts provide an easier way to travel otherwise we would need to wait for Taelo to fully heal," Busy Bee replied.

She mentioned the concern to Golden Hawk, and he had told her they would stop early each sun cycle.

You keep an eye on Taelo and see that he eats well," Golden Hawk replied.

He was sure the bear had created a deep internal wound. It seemed to be healing more slowly than the outer wounds.

"We have arrived at the river flowing in from the east," Saber Scar announced from his lead position.

"Let's stop here and make camp," Golden Hawk announced.

It was still early but he was going to make sure Taelo got a chance to rest.

He noted that Taelo dismounted, tied his mount off, fed the mount, then fed himself. He then took his sleeping hide to lie down.

Lasher lay down quietly beside him.

"I think Lasher will tell us when Taelo is fully healed," Golden Hawk said to a worried Quiet Rabbit.

"Thank you for the early stop," Quiet Rabbit said as she went about preparing her and Taelo's area.

Lily warmed some soup and brought it over. "Here is some soup. He needs both food and sleep. Make sure Taelo eats it all before he goes to sleep."

"The ancestors have been talking to me for the last few cycles. It is hard for me to understand them, but Broken Spear is with them, and he comes to me and explains what is being discussed. They talk about a journey to the north and a journey to the west.

Feather-in-the-Wind will lead the first people to live in the East.

You and I will have two boys that will become great leaders in our clan. It is very disorienting and tiring as I listen to the elders," Taelo said as he ate the soup Quite Rabbit was giving him.

He was exhausted. He had planned to do some jogging to get back into shape but found that just staying on his mount was a challenge.

"I am relieved to hear about the future. I am worried about your survival right now," Quiet Rabbit said as she ran her hand through his hair.

Taelo fell asleep and slept through the entire night with no mumbling or moaning

He was surprised to find it was morning or maybe later in the day. he got up feeling well. He walked toward the river with Lasher at his side. There he saw Golden Hawk, Saber Scar and Running Stag lifting fish from a fish trap they had set up.

I think Taelo is finally getting well. Last night was the first time he slept quietly since facing the bear," Quiet Rabbit said to Busy Bee as she watched Taelo walking toward the river.

"Perhaps the movement on the mount did some good. Let's hope he is now recovering his stamina," Busy Bee replied.

"It's good to see you up and about," Golden Hawk said.

He noted that Lasher was wagging his tail. At long last Taelo must be on the road to recovery. Golden Hawk had decided to keep the team at this place for the extra day.

"Look at this new fish we have captured," he continued as he brought the fish over to where Taelo was standing.

"It is a good-looking fish. What about that giant that is slowly entering the trap," Taelo said as he pointed to something that almost looked like a small log.

"I saw it earlier, but I thought it was a piece of wood floating down river. Then it disappeared," Running Stag commented.

"Stand back. I will spear it and throw it up onto the bank," Saber Scar said as he picked up his spear and waded out into the water to where the fish had entered the trap.

The giant fish did not cooperate. The spear glanced off the thick scales.

"My spear did not go through," Saber Scar yelled out in surprise.

His second try into the side of the beast was successful. The sudden fury of the fish threw Saber Scar down into the water.

Golden Hawk and Running Stag grabbed their spears and joined in.

"Wow the scales on this fish are unbelievably thick," Running Stag commented as he tried for the third time to drive his spear into the fish.

In the end all three were using their spears to push the monster up on the rocky bank.

"What in the world is all the noise about," Busy Bee said as the remainder of the group gathered around.

The giant fish was trying to get back to water but Saber Scar was sitting on its body.

"What a hideous looking creature," Feather-in-the-Wind commented as she watched Saber Scar take a large stone and whack the monster on the head.

"I bet those teeth will make some great needles," she continued as she walked out on the stony bank and carefully poked them with a small branch.

"This will feed all of us tonight. Clean it. Put it on a spit and bring it up to the camp. I will get ready to roast it. Don't fight the scales. The fire will take care of them," Lily instructed.

"The fish is cooking well," Lily commented as she scrapped off the scales as the fire cause them to wrinkle and bend.

The only objection from the rest of the team was the smell the scales made as they burned.

Lily patiently put small cuts in the skin and put salt into the cuts. The aroma had the entire team sitting around eager to try some of it.

"This is a great feast. The food is delicious. I think Lily has become one of the best cooks in the Elk Clan," Taelo praised.

He felt new energy as he sat comfortably with his back against the log behind him. The fish and the honey water made him feel warm and generally satisfied.

The next morning the team packed up, cleaned up their camp and proceeded on their journey east. The terrain was now heavily forested, and the going was slower as they worked their way upstream along the river.

Taelo once again started to jog alongside of his mount. He was still not fully recovered. He would begin to sweat after only few moments of jogging. He would then get back on his mount.

"Woe, there is a monster ahead of us," Feather-in-the-Wind said from her lead position.

She was backing her mount away from the huge animal ahead. It was an animal that she could never have imagined, and it looked fierce and dangerous. She automatically had her sling out and loaded. She chuckled to herself about the futility of the action.

The giant, as large, perhaps slightly larger than a bison was pulling some branches from a young tree and eating the leaves. Its movements were slow and deliberate. Its front claws were large and very long. Its tongue would come out and wrap around the leaves it pulled towards its mouth with the claws.

"Let's spend some time and observe it. It does not appear to be alarmed by our presence nor interested in us," Taelo said as he took a position next to Feather-in-the-Wind.

Soon everyone was gathered around and watching. A second ground sloth emerged from the thick woods and joined the first. They both proceeded across the team's path. The two sloths were heading toward the river side. Their slow deliberate pace gave the impression of total relaxation.

"They do not appear to have any enemies," Golden Hawk observed.

"Their claws are so large they cannot walk on their feet," Lily observed. The giants seemed to be walking on the sides of their feet.

The two giants stopped directly in front of the team and pulled down another helping of leaves.

"They seem not to care about our presence and are not interested in us," Busy Bee noted with some relief.

She did not want to experience another dangerous confrontation such as the one they just had with the bear.

"They might not be interested but the two lions and their young seem to have taken an interest in us," Lily said.

She had observed the hair on Lasher's neck standing up and she had felt they were being watched. She had turned her mount around to look behind in the direction Lasher was looking and had spotted the two female lions creeping forward as if to attack. Her sling immediately went into action even as she was giving warning.

She was not as accurate as Feather-in-the-Wind who immediately hit both females on the nose with her barrage of throws. Quiet Rabbit, Busy Bee, and Marigold all joined in. There was a constant stream of stones hitting the lions.

Instead of a charge, the lions, after a moment of confusion turned and trotted away in the opposite direction.

"That was unbelievable. All of you saved us from a certain attack," Taelo said as he watched the lion's retreat.

He had been surprised at the effect the stones had on the lions. He also was aware of how unprepared the team had been for the situation.

"All of us should learn to use a sling from the back of our mounts," Golden Hawk added.

"I will collect stones for you at the next stream we come to," Saber Scar added.

He too had been surprised at the effectiveness of the combined barrage.

"I guess the sling is more useful than just rabbit hunting," Running Stag said.

He and Feather-in-the-Wind previously had a conversation about the usefulness of the sling. This was his way of letting her know he conceded to her argument. He gave her a waving hand gesture to let her know.

"When did all of you learn to use the sling from the back of a mount," Taelo asked in surprise.

"We needed something to do while you slept the cycles away," Busy Bee replied with a smile.

"Well, I am now ready to take lessons from Feather-in-the-Wind. The next time I meet a bear I will first try to talk to it but then I will unleash a barrage of stones to see if it will decide to run away," Taelo replied in return.

"Let's ride on and get out of the lion's hunting territory. I will take the rear position first," Taelo commented.

They rode at a crisp trot for the remainder of the day. Their only stop was at a small stream where they had lunch and collected a new supply of stones for their slings.

Chapter 15 Eastern Mountains

The moon was once again full as Taelo sat and talked with the team. They were at a fork of the river and a decision needed to be made.

The terrain was becoming more challenging. The river was still substantial but wandered snake like around every foot hill and small mountain. The banks were no longer smooth, level, and easy to follow.

The river had cut through stone and created deep gorges that narrowed at their base and created a torrent of water on its way through.

The mountains, with the oak, maple and pine trees offered a better environment.

These mountains were not as large as the mountains they were familiar with in the Elk Clan's home territory. The forest covering the mountains was dense and formed an overhead canopy.

The team decided it was time to abandon the river and follow the sun and the moon.

Keeping track of direction proved to be challenging. Each sun cycle, the team took note of the position of the rising sun and the setting moon. The two provided a general calibration of direction.

Their mounts proved to be the edge they needed to make progress toward their goal of reaching the sea.

A few sun cycles after their decision to follow the sun and the moon, a bee caught Taelo's attention. It had been attracted to something on his mount. It landed on his arm and then flew off in the direction of a clump of trees.

Taelo followed it for as long as he could and then rode in the general direction the bee had taken.

"Where are we going," a curious Golden Hawk asked?

It became apparent Taelo was going off in a tangent direction.

"I am hoping for a sweet reward," Taelo replied as he continued to keep a sharp eye on the flying bee.

Everyone else was curious as well and they all followed behind and watched Taelo's strange behavior.

About halfway up a huge tree was a hole with honeybees surrounding it.

"Let's see if we can collect some honey and celebrate our progress with some sweet drinks and some honey baked bear," Taelo said as he dismounted.

"Why don't we make camp along the stream just ahead," Lily suggested as she took in the surroundings.

There seemed to be a convenient spot where everyone could gather and later find a place to sleep.

"Let me climb up and see if there is an easy way to extract some of the honey," Feather-in-the-Wind volunteered.

She was eager to satisfy her sweet tooth.

The hive had another opening above the one seen from the ground. It was about the distance of Feather-in-the-Wind's standing height.

"It must be hollow between these two openings," Taelo surmised as he stood on a limb near Feather-in-the-Wind.

"Let's carefully cut a section out here," Taelo pointed as he tapped the side of the tree.

"Let me do it," Running Stag volunteered.

He was still worried about Taelo's condition and also wanted to be of help.

"Thanks, your help is welcome. Make the hole about this large," Taelo indicated by stretching out his hand and going from thumb to little finger.

"Cut the hole as carefully as you can. We will want to seal it so the hive can remain," Taelo instructed.

He was already thinking about how to seal it using the material from the hole, some pegs, and some beeswax.

The camp was set up. Everyone was enjoying the early stop and were relaxing. Lily was salting some of the bear meat while Quiet Rabbit and Busy Bee walked along the small stream.

"We found some wild onions and caught a half dozen large crayfish," Quiet Rabbit announced as the two walked back into the camp.

"We seem to be going into the mountains. We have been going north, northeast," Golden Hawk commented.

"I think we will reach the ocean at the very northern part of our journey," Taelo replied.

"The hole is cut through," Running Stag called excitedly from his perch in the tree.

He was holding the block in place because the bees had become agitated by his actions.

"Let's go collect some honey and then we will get back to discussing our journey," Taelo responded as he picked up the gut lined bags he had prepared and walked away toward the honey tree.

Once up in the tree, Taelo carefully removed the section of the tree that had been carved out. He waited as the bees checked the opening and flew around him. He kept calm even when several bees landed on him. They were flicking their stingers, but they were not stinging him. He waited for several moments while the bees calmed down.

"Why don't they sting him," Feather-in-the-Wind asked Quiet Rabbit.

"Taelo has done this many times when we were growing up. He always seems to find the hives. He learned that if you stay relaxed, even if you get stung, then the bees don't see you as a threat. In the past he has used smoke to neutralize the bees.

In this case it would be very difficult to do that, so he is taking the chance of getting stung as he collects the honey," Quiet Rabbit replied.

She just hoped Taelo was back in full health. She was not sure how strong his recovery was at this point.

Taelo was able to see the honey laden sections of honeycomb just inside the opening. He carefully took the thinnest blade he possessed and cut a square just smaller than the opening and carefully pulled it out. He brushed off the bees crawling on its surface and then put the section in one of the bags. He soon had extracted enough honeycombs to fill the three bags he had prepared. The bags were each lowered to those on the ground one at a time.

"Drill some holes in the tree; here, here and here," Taelo instructed Running Stag as he pointed to the spots.

Meanwhile Taelo drilled holes in the wood that had been cut from the tree. He put two hardwood pegs into one side and the single on the other side. The single hole was deeper than the other two and the peg went almost all the way in. The two other pegs went in halfway.

Taelo matched the two protruding pegs to the two holes Running Stag had bored out. He then carefully worked the single peg out and into the third hole that had been bored out.

The final trick was the small hole Taelo had drilled from the outside. He was able to lock the single pin in place by pushing in a fourth peg from outside.

The patch was an almost a perfect fix.

"We will come back later and seal the opening with beeswax. This will seal the opening shut. We want the hive to be protected," Taelo said as he climbed down from the tree.

Lily took the first bag and returned to the camp and immediately began to glaze the bear roast. She was as eager for this treat as everyone else. She slowly roasted the onions on a stone by the fire. She put both honey and salt on the waiting crayfish. These would be roasted at the last moment.

"So, you were saying, you thought we were coming out on the northern part of our journey," Saber Scar brought the conversation back to their journey.

He was eager to reach the ocean.

"Yes, the river we have followed toward the east was also going toward the north. If we continue in the same general direction, we should be at the top end of our circle," Taelo replied.

He was not totally sure of where they would come out, but the season was getting late, and they would soon need to go into warmer climate. He knew the point that they reached the ocean would be the northernmost point they would reach on this journey.

Taelo collected the honeycomb material that was left over from the honey that had been used and let it melt across a hot flat stone. He collected the melted wax and formed it into a round lump. He had a ball about the size of his palm.

"Let's go seal the honey tree," he said to Running Stag and Feather-in-the-Wind.

"This will stay sealed for years. The bees will seal it from the inside, and nothing will get in or out this way," Taelo said as he got done with his handy work.

"Why are you so careful with these bees," Feather-in-the-Wind asked.

She knew that Taelo always took action based on a reason.

"The bees worked hard to collect their food. They have stored extra but we may have taken what they planned to have in case of a hard winter. We enjoyed their honey and will for weeks to come. We owe them the courtesy of not making it even harder for them by leaving their nest in jeopardy," Taelo replied.

"We have now traveled for almost one cycle of the moon in this direction, and we are still traveling through these low mountains," Saber Scar commented as he rode alongside of Taelo.

The honey tree seemed now to be memory.

"It has taken us longer in crossing these mountains than I had anticipated. I think we are traveling along the range as much as we are traveling through it," Taelo continued.

For the last two sun cycles he had been watching the eagle flying above them. He was sure everyone else had seen it, but no one had mentioned it.

"Do you think we are almost to the coast," Quiet Rabbit asked him a little later.

"I think we are near. We will know when the eagle screams," Taelo replied with a smiled.

He wondered and hoped Broken Spear was seeing them through the eyes of the eagle.

Chapter 16: The Ocean

The smell of the air changed and brought the familiar aromas of the sea. The birds rode the air and smoothly led the way east on the rising warm air and seemed to call and encourage the team to follow.

The foothills continued to the east but now they flowed smoothly and gently, and the trees once again thickened into dense forest with a high thick dome.

The three wolves dutifully retrieved the small game the team consistently hit with their slings. To the detriment of squirrels, rabbits, ground hogs and even an occasional pigeon or dove, they had all become proficient mount riding sling hunters.

The ocean was in the air and they all gained new energy in anticipation of reaching their most eastern goal.

"We will continue toward the east until we see the waves washing the shore," Golden Hawk said from his lead position.

Then in a magical moment, ahead of them they could see the water and hear it washing up on the beach.

Lasher, Walker, and Arrow ran to the water and swam out into the waves.

High overhead the eagle let out a cry as it flew out over the ocean.

"That was our official notification that we have arrived at our most eastern destination," Taelo called out to the team as he rode his mount into the waves.

On the left was a small island just off of the shore. The sandy beach was bound on each side by large rocky outcropping that fell into the sea.

"Let's find a good place to camp on top of the rocks to the right," Taelo suggested as he looked around.

He dismounted and waded into the ocean up to his waist. He then led his mount in the direction of the rocks.

Short windblown trees ran along the top of the rocky area. They provided excellent support for hides put over the individual sleeping areas.

"I think I can see forever," Quiet Rabbit said as she stopped from the work of setting up the camp and gazed out to sea.

There were white puffy clouds high in the sky and the afternoon sun was turning them hues of yellow and orange. The breeze was blowing lightly in from the sea, lifting a few waves that then broke into white tops as they proceeded in toward the shore.

"This is a beautiful area. I am going down along the rocks to see if there is something good to eat. Does anyone want to come along," Taelo asked as he got done unloading and putting his belongings safely into the limbs of the trees.

His rule was to put everything out of reach of the animals and bears.

"At least regular sized bears," Taelo thought to himself recalling the last bear he had faced. He then jumped down from the limb he had been standing on.

Everyone followed Taelo to the water's edge. They had mimicked Taelo and picked up one of their light spears.

"What are we looking for," Running Stag asked?

"Anything that we can eat; fish, crab, small sharks," Taelo replied.

"Oh, Oh, how about a giant crayfish," Feather-in-the-Wind said as she pointed into the water to show Busy Bee.

"I don't think you catch that thing with two small sticks. It looks much meaner and better armored than the small crayfish we find in the rivers and streams," Busy Bee said as she readied her spear.

"You spear it through its tail, and I will drive my spear in just behind the head armor," Busy Bee said as she got into position.

The two got into position and executed as they had planned. They both fell into the water.

"Look at the size of this saltwater crayfish," Busy Bee said triumphantly as she stood waist deep in the water and held her spear up with the huge animal speared through its head.

"Let's see how many of those we can find," Running Stag said enthusiastically as he sought out another one.

"I am going into the water to see if there are any sea plants that we can use to cook our prizes," Taelo said laying down his spear and diving in.

He had seen what looked like long leaves waving in the water. He cut several of the wide seaweeds and brought them to shore.

"I think we can at least use them to wrap the crayfish in as we cook them," Lily said as she picked up the seaweed and carried it up to the camp.

She had set up a drying rack and chose to hang the seaweed from it.

The team was laughing and enjoying their hunt for the giant saltwater crayfish.

Golden Hawk surprised everyone by diving down into the water and coming up with a crab large enough that he called out for help.

"Here, bite this," Saber Scar said as he lay his spear into the large claws.

The crab bit down on the spear shaft and the two brought it out of the water to the shore.

Quiet Rabbit had been out ahead of the rest. She carefully approached the edge of a large crack in the rocky face that went down into the water. There she saw a large fish eating at the green mossy growth on the rocks.

"I think this will round out our dinner for tonight," she thought as she slowly raised her spear and then with lightning speed thrust it into the water.

Marigold had been following just behind and ran quickly forward. As Quiet Rabbit pulled the fish to the surface, Marigold reached down and picked it up by the gills.

"This is a huge fish," Marigold exclaimed as she strained to pull it up onto the ledge.

"I would not have been able to get it up on the rocks without your help," Quiet Rabbit said as the two fought with the fish.

It was at least half the length of Quiet Rabbit.

"Let's clean it here and perhaps it will be easier to carry it up to the camp," Marigold suggested.

"Even if we don't get more crab, we won't go hungry tonight," Feather-in-Wind said as she took in the size of the fish.

"How in the world did you ever catch anything that large with a spear," she continued.

Lily was busy building the cooking fire. She had gathered stones to form a circle and had unpacked the Y stakes on which she placed the poles for holding the meat. She pulled out one of the poles she had made to use as a skewer.

"Here I have just the tool to get that fish ready to eat," she said as she put the tip of the pointed skewer into the fish's mouth and guided it through the flesh along the spine.

"Rotate it a couple of times over the flames to get the scales to flake off. Then put it over here and I will put some salt under the skin," Lily instructed.

The lobster, crab and fish cooked with salt and wrapped in seaweed turned into an unexpected feast.

"I think this is one of the best meals we have had in many cycles," Golden Hawk said as he cracked open one of the legs of his crab.

"The fish was exceptional," Feather-in-the-Wind commented as she ate another chunk of the tasty white meat.

"I especially like the taste of the dried seaweed," Running Stag added.

"I do too, especially with a little salt on it," Lily said as she ate a piece.

"I think the three wolves prefer the rabbit that we gave them and the mounts certainly like the grasses in the field we found farther back from the shore.

"We still need to watch our mounts. Who still has enough energy to stay awake with them until early morning," Taelo asked.

He listened to the groan of the other members of the team.

"OK, I understand. I will take the watch tonight. Then we will rotate in the following order," Taelo said as he called out the order of the watch.

Later Taelo and Quiet Rabbit were comfortably sitting with a hide around their shoulders as they watched the lights in the blackness of the night sky.

"Our journeys have been so interesting and wonderful.

We have gone south to find people more advanced than us. We rescued Feather-in-the-Wind and now she travels with us.

We went northward and established a new clan.

Now we have come eastward and have discovered an animal that we can ride. We now know that the land is very large and there is a sea on each side. There are lions and bears the size of our mounts and that is frightening.

One almost got you. We are lucky to have experienced so much in our short time," Quiet Rabbit said as she gazed at the points of light in the dark night sky.

"Yes, I have enjoyed experiencing the learning of new things but what means the most to me is doing this with you," Taelo said quietly as he gave Quiet Rabbit a hug and ran his hand slowly through her hair.

There was no mistaking the chill of the night. It was now late summer, and the days were getting shorter.

Taelo walked the perimeter of where he had tethered the mounts to make sure nothing was bothering them.

"Well Lasher, you are a great companion," Taelo said as he sat in the dark scratching him behind the ear.

Lasher responded by poking his nose into Taelo's side.

Quiet Rabbit was sleeping on the ground a short distance away.

"The ancients keep talking to me. They tell me things I do not understand. We have reached another great body of water.

They tell me there is more beyond.

The world is large, and we humans are few.

It is our destiny to be in all the places on this world," Taelo talked quietly to Lasher as he watched a meteor shower flash strips of light across the night sky.

The next morning Feather-in-the-Wind watched as Walker dug a hole in the sand and uncovered a host of small clams.

She had awakened early and had taken a stroll down the beach.

"Good wolf," Feather-in-the-Wind praised him as she dug up the clams and filled her collection bag with the small clams.

She brought them back to camp.

"We can have a clam broth for our breakfast," She exclaimed as she showed Lily her treasure.

"That is a good idea. I will take the scraps of fish, sea crayfish and crab and put them in to the mix. This will make a quick meal for everyone to begin the day," Lily replied.

"Let's go to the other side of the rocks. There is a long beach in that direction and another rocky shore beyond," Running Stag suggested.

"I would like to go out onto the small island just to the North of this cove," Busy Bee suggested.

"I am for going to the island today," Marigold said in support of Busy Bee.

Traveling down the long beach to another cliff did not seem interesting.

"Well, as long as we go out in two or three, we can each do what we wish," Taelo said as he sipped the broth of seaweed and water and ate the small clams.

"I am going to get some sleep while it is cool."

"I will stay in camp until Taelo gets up," Lily volunteered.

"Then I will go with Marigold and Busy Bee," Quiet Rabbit responded.

Saber Scar said he would go with Feather-in-the-Wind and Running Stag but that he would ride his mount.

Golden Hawk was going to wait until Lily was done working around the camp, then he would go down to get more seaweed while she watched from the cliffs.

Everyone got ready and then went to their selected destinations.

Taelo and Golden Hawk sat looking out to sea and talked quietly.

"This is a great place to relax but I can feel the weather changing," Golden Hawk commented.

You are right. I think we can stay a few more sun cycles but then we should go south to a warmer climate. We will continue south and then turn back to the west and begin our journey home," Taelo replied as he laid out his sleeping hide in the shade of the tree and went to sleep.

In his sleep, Taelo was once again visiting with the ancients. They were asking him if he was learning the ways of the land. From far away he heard his name being called.

Taelo woke up to Lily's screams of, "Taelo, Taelo, Shark, Shark!"

He jumped up and ran over to where Lily was pointing into the bay. He turned and picked up his spear and went running for the cliffs.

Golden Hawk could see Lily waving and screaming something, but he could not hear what she was saying.

Out on the Island Quiet Rabbit saw the waving and then froze as she looked from her vantage point down to where Golden Hawk was swimming. A huge shark at least four times as big as Golden Hawk was swimming toward him.

High in the Sky an eagle let out a cry. The cry seemed to put everyone into slow motion.

"Oh, no, noooo…" Busy Bee cried out as she saw the shark and sank to her knees.

She was sure Golden Hawk was going to die.

The eagle's cry immediately put Golden Hawk on the alert. He looked around and saw the huge fin of the shark coming toward him. He dropped the bag of seaweed he had been struggling to get to shore and prepared to do battle with his spear. From the size of the fin coming toward him, he knew his efforts would be useless.

On the far beach both Running Stag and Feather-in-the-Wind looked to the eagle in the sky and stopped what they were doing and immediately began to run toward camp. They knew something was happening.

"Thank the ancestors that I rode my mount," Saber Scar said to himself as he went full speed toward the camp.

Out on the Island, Marigold pointed to Taelo running for the cliff just above where Golden Hawk and the shark were in the water.

"Taelo is running for the cliff. I think he is going to dive in," Marigold pointed Taelo out to the other two just as he launched himself into the air.

Taelo ran faster than he had ever done before. He knew he would have one chance to save his cousin.

He had imaged this jump the evening before and it had been in his dream a few moments ago.

He felt every muscle in his body tense and release as he launched himself off the cliff. The point of his jump was a good ten spear lengths above the water.

He instantly calculated the movement of the shark, his speed, and the distance he had to achieve.

He had his arms spread to allow him to adjust his trajectory. He gripped his spear with both hands just before hitting the water.

He went into the water just short of the shark. His momentum drove his spear through the side of the shark just behind its head. He slammed into the body of the shark and found himself on its back.

Golden Hawk did not see Taelo's dive. He was just thrusting his spear into the giant shark's mouth when Taelo's spear went through the shark. Golden Hawk's spear went down the throat. The shark was thrashing in the water.

Both of them disappeared in the splashing water created by the sharks thrashing.

Taelo drove his knife through the sharks head and wrapped his legs around its body as if he were riding a mount.

Golden Hawk was holding his spear and trying not to drown. The shark bit through the spear shaft. This left Golden Hawk with half of his spear. He drove this through the shark's left eye.

This put him only a foot away from the giant shark's teeth.

When his feet hit bottom, he slowly turned and moved the still thrashing shark toward shore. Taelo let go of the knife handle and dropped into the water and used his spear to help Golden Hawk push the giant toward the shore. There was blood in the water, and he hoped it was all coming from the shark.

Lily came running into the water with her spear and drove it through the shark near the tail.

The three of them had the shark on the shallow rocky beach when Saber Scar arrived on his mount. He ran out and tied a rope onto the shark's tail and used his mount to pull the shark the rest of the way out of the water.

Running Stag, Feather-in-the-Wind, Quiet Rabbit, and Busy Bee all arrived within moments of each other.

They were breathless and somewhat shocked as they saw the size of the shark.

Both Taelo and Golden Hawk were bleeding from various cuts they had received during the brief battle.

The eagle let out another scream and took a lazy circle around the small inlet and flew off into the West.

"Well, my friend, you certainly attracted the largest shark I have ever seen," Taelo said as he put his arm around Golden Hawk and checked him out for any serious wounds.

"I am only glad that you know how to fly. You must teach me," Golden Hawk said as he put his hand on Taelo's chest.

He was still not sure how Taelo had achieved the jump from the cliff. Taelo had to have jumped outward at least seven spear lengths to reach him. Such a feat was just unimaginable.

"I was sure you would kill yourself on the dive," Quiet Rabbit said as she gave Taelo a hug.

She quickly examined all of Taelo's scratches that were bleeding. The blood made Taelo look as if he had received a major injury.

She was still soaking wet from her swim back to shore from the island. She and Busy Bee had immediately jumped in and swam back to the mainland.

Marigold, who was more like a rock in the water brought their raft back.

"Look at the size of this monster," Running Stag said as he used his spear to measure its length.

"A little over four spears long," Feather-in-the-Wind declared as Running Stag flipped his spear for the third time.

Saber Scar approached with his war hammer. He took out Taelo's knife from behind the head and then hit the shark several time in the head.

"I think we can hang it on the cliff by putting a stake in the crack in the rocks above," Saber Scar pointed to the place he was proposing.

"Look at those teeth. I think they are even bigger than the ones you gave to Burley Bear," he said as he used his spear tip to touch the teeth.

"You two are rich in shark's teeth," Lily said as she climbed up to place the stake to hold the shark up on the cliff.

"We are all rich in shark's teeth," Golden Hawk declared from a rock he had chosen to sit on.

"We will all share evenly, except for the biggest three that will belong to Taelo. I only want one of the biggest to wear around my neck," Golden Hawk replied.

"I am going to recover my bag of seaweed that I dropped. Does anyone want to go swimming with me," Golden Hawk said as he stood up and walked back along the shore to where the battle with the shark had started.

"Do you need to get it back just now," a worried Busy Bee said as she followed him?

"How can he go back in the water after having faced such a beast," Feather-in-the-Wind wondered out loud.

"How can you go out on your walks by yourself after being chased up a tree by a bear," Taelo replied in a reflective tone, and he smiled as Quiet Rabbit washed the blood off his chest.

The shark was quickly pulled up on the side of the cliff. Everyone took part in its preparation.

Lily set up her drying racks and began to salt the strips brought up to her by Feather-in-the-Wind and Running Stag.

Marigold set up her hide stretching rack and soon had the giant shark skin stretched on the frame. She immediately gave it the first scrapping.

She was the preparer of most of the hides the team was now carrying along. The four mounts were slowly being loaded with hides. There were two buffalo hides, several bundles of rabbit hides, the giant bear skin and skull, the tiger skin, several deer, and a bundle of hides from various other animals.

If they continued to gather hides at their current rate, they would be pulling them back on several more travois.

Taelo and Quiet Rabbit walked along the shore to where Golden Hawk was bringing in the large bag of seaweed he had been collecting.

"Let's sit here a moment and enjoy the ocean," Taelo suggested.

The four friends sat quietly each in their own thoughts as the sun turned a bright red behind them and the clouds out over the ocean turned reddish orange with a yellow edging on their bottom.

"I will always remember you flying through the air using your arms to adjust your trajectory. You went into the water with almost no splash. Both of you disappeared underwater," Quiet Rabbit broke the silence.

"My eyes were on the water. All I saw was the shark moving in for the kill and Golden Hawk going underwater to face it. It did not seem like the shark could be stopped. Then there was a pool of red," Busy Bee continued.

"Well, I saw the shark open its mouth and I was sure I would fit in with no problem. Just when I was about to follow my spear into this mouth, the shark took a sudden surge to the side. At that moment it bit through my spear. I was stunned but I did the only thing I could to keep those teeth away from me. I plunged what remained of my spear into the shark's eye and pushed it away," Golden Hawk continued.

"Well, I was lucky. I did not realize how hard the impact with the water was going to be.

The only thought I had was a flashback to the time we went to gather salt. You recall how each of us had to spear a fish from the fishing stone. You had to spear below the fish to actually hit the fish.

Well as I flew through the air, I aimed below the fish, but when I hit the water, I realized there would be no parallax if I was in the water.

I was lucky because I was able to raise my spear enough to drive it through just behind its head. I hit with such force that the shark was driven sideways.

I think I got the scratches on my chest from my own spear. I was stunned to find myself on the sharks back and I drove my knife into its head so I could hang on as it started to thrash.

That is when I finally saw Golden Hawk so close to the giant's mouth that I was not sure he would survive," Taelo added quietly.

"I was very aware of those teeth. Your spear through the side gave each of us a place to hold and move him to shore.

We will have to thank Lily for her courage and quick action in helping us get the beast to the shallow water.

Saber Scar's use of the mount to pull it up onto the shore closed what could have been a deadly fight in the shallows," Golden Hawk pointed out.

"I hear Lily calling. Let's go enjoy some of that shark meat," Quiet Rabbit said as she stood up and led the way back to camp.

The next day they all worked together to make some additional drying racks and put the strips of salted shark meat on the racks to dry. It was a good feeling to know they had enough food to carry them through the remainder of their journey.

The shark was the highlight of their stop by the seashore. They stayed almost a full moon cycle. Finally, they broke camp and continued their journey.

They were lazily moving down the coast when the sand beneath them started to sing. Or at least that was what Feather-in-the-Wind declared. She jumped off her mount and went dancing around.

"The sand sings to you as you walk," Feather-in-the-Wind declared as she laughed and danced about.

"I am not sure if it is singing or crying in pain," Quiet Rabbit said as she joined Feather-in-the-Wind.

The sand would squeak and make noise with each step. The mounts hooves make a louder noise.

Lasher, Walker, and Arrow were running around and barking. They would dash into the water to escape the squeaking sand and then return and run around the others walking and running in the sand.

Taelo sat on his mount and watched in wonder as the team frolicked on the beach.

"The land really does talk to you," he thought to himself.

Though he could feel the chill in the air, he was thoroughly warm inside.

He quietly watched the lone eagle flying inland and then South. He knew he would be taking the same trail.

Chapter 17: Southward, Into the Warmth

The ocean breeze was soon cutoff by the towering forest and thick canopy created by the interlocking limbs of the giant old oak and maple trees. Curious squirrels seemed to be able to follow them continuously as they jumped from one limb to the next.

The rolling hills and the abundant mix of small game once again greeted the team as they traveled west, southwest.

The atmosphere was relaxed and for twelve sun cycles the going was at an easy enjoyable pace. The many wandering streams provided good places to camp and yielded the favorite crayfish, fish, and the occasional turtle.

The only question was the direction that the team was traveling.

"Why are we going so far inland and away from the coast," a curious Running Stag asked?

"The coast has many inlets and bays. It would take us a considerable amount of wandering to follow the coast. It will be simpler to keep the mountain ridge to one side and the rising sun to the other," Taelo said as he pointed to the mountains to their west.

Broken Spear had told him about this portion of the trip and the coastline. It made sense to follow the mountains and the long valley formed on its eastern side.

"We will return to the coast once we have reached our most southern point," Taelo continued.

He hoped he would know where that point was when they got there.

"We have been making good progress, let's hope things continue to go smoothly," Taelo commented to the team.

The next morning as they continued south, Saber Scar came riding back in from a scouting run.

"We have a pack of wolves following us," Saber Scar said as he rode in from a circular ride around the group.

"This explains the low growling coming from Lasher. What kind of wolves are they," Taelo inquired?

He had been looking carefully around ever since Lasher started his growling.

"I am not sure, but their tracks are very large," Saber Scar replied.

"Let's find a good place to stop where we can defend ourselves and our mounts," Taelo said to everyone.

"Let's see if we can find a place where we can collect enough poles to build a solid perimeter around our camp."

"I'll scout ahead for a good place," Golden Hawk spoke up as he took the lead and rode ahead at a brisk pace.

"I will ride with Golden Hawk," Running Stag said as he urged his mount forward.

Arrow ran alongside.

"Lasher's constant growl tells me these will not be wolves or animals that I will be able to talk too," Taelo said to the rest of the team.

A short time later Running Stag came riding back.

"There is a very good place on a small island in the middle of a small river. Golden Hawk has started to cut the poles. I left Arrow there to make sure Golden Hawk is warned if any of the wolves show up unexpectedly," Running Stag announced as he brought his mount to a stop in front of the team.

Let's get to the island as quickly as possible. I think it will be critical to get our compound built immediately," Taelo said as he urged his mount forward at an energetic trot.

A short time later they arrived at the small river and crossed over to the island. The water was only an elbow to hand deep. The island rose several feet above the river level.

Taelo agreed with Golden Hawks assessment about the island making a good place to put their compound.

"Lily and Feather-in-the-Wind please secure the mounts in one spot there in the middle of the island.

Saber Scar and Marigold, you come with me.

The rest of you collect as many poles as you can and spread them out around the area where the mounts are located," Taelo issued a series of instructions.

"The three of us will collect as many boulders as possible and place them in a circle to form the perimeter of our compound," Taelo said as he pointed out the boulders, he wanted collected.

The rest of the afternoon was a flurry of activity.

Boulders were carried and positioned in a large oval to form the perimeter of the compound. The poles came in and were spread around the perimeter.

Fire pits were made in between each perimeter boulder.

"Feather-in-the-Wind and I have staked all the mounts out in the center, and we have made fire pits around the perimeter," Lily said as she and Feather-in-the-Wind began spacing the poles around the perimeter of boulders.

"Great job, thanks for getting the poles into place," Taelo said as he placed another boulder on the perimeter.

The perimeter now had boulders located about a spear length apart from each other.

"Let's finish getting the poles placed around the perimeter.

Feather-in-the-Wind and Lily please get all our ropes out and put them toward the upstream part of the perimeter," Taelo continued to instruct the team as he hurried them to complete the compound perimeter.

He was sure they would have visitors in a short time.

"Please drop your poles into position as you get them back here and then begin tying them together," Taelo called out to Busy Bee and Quiet Rabbit as they brought their next load to the compound.

"Saber Scar and Marigold please go for the next load of poles.

Lily, Feather-in-the-Wind please weave the ropes around the bottoms of the poles.

Quiet Rabbit, Busy Bee we will begin to stand the poles up and weave the rope in the middle section. To do this we will need to tie ropes to hold the poles up as we go around the perimeter.

The perimeter poles were about halfway up when Golden Hawk, Saber Scar and Marigold brought in the last load of poles.

"Golden Hawk, thanks for the poles.

Please work with Quiet Rabbit, Busy Bee, and continue to stand the poles up.

Saber Scar and Marigold please gather as much wood for our fires as you can.

Running Stag please help Lily and Feather-in-the-Wind with weaving rope along the bottom of the poles," Taelo instructed as he began to tie the bottom of poles to the boulders.

He wanted the entire perimeter anchored to the boulders.

"I saw a large fallen tree when we rode our mounts in. Let's take our pack mounts with their carrying bags back to that tree and get as much of the dead wood as we can," Marigold suggested.

She and Saber Scar rode their mounts and took the four pack mounts with them.

Feather-in-the-Wind looked around as her team finished putting the rope around the bottom of the poles. She was trying to anticipate the next piece of work.

"Let's pound in the stakes for Golden Hawk and his team. It will speed up the pace of getting the perimeter raised.

Lily why don't you help Taelo tie the stakes to the boulders," Feather-in-the-Wind said as they tied the bottom rope to the last stake and finished their job.

Finally, the perimeter poles were all in place. Taelo was still tying poles to the boulders.

The gate poles were positioned, and three cross poles were tied to hold them together. A rope was tied across the top of the perimeter poles at the gate area and the gate was put into position.

"Alright we have the basic perimeter set up. Now we need to put stiffening and reinforcement poles into position," Taelo said as he stood up from tying a pole to the boulder.

"Feather-in-the-Wind, Running Stag good work in getting the stakes put in. Let me ask you to finish tying the perimeter stakes to the boulders.

Quiet Rabbit, Busy Bee please figure out the best place to put the mounts in toward the center.

Then get our hides up for a rainy night. It looks like it will start to rain at any moment.

Lily how about working your magic with the fire pit and get some food prepared for all of us. Keep it simple and light.

Golden Hawk and I will reinforce the perimeter," Taelo redeployed the team in the preparation of the compound.

Every third boulder Taelo and Golden Hawk tied a pole to the perimeter pole and anchored it to a boulder about a spear length back from the wall. Then they would tie a pole across the perimeter poles at angle. A zigzag pattern took form all the way around the perimeter.

"Well, the dead tree was a good call. We have enough wood to last the night," Marigold said as she put another chunk of wood into the side pouch.

All the mounts were now fully loaded.

"I think we better ride hard for the compound. I hope they are done because I see the pack of wolfs approaching. They must be the big cousins of the dire wolf," Saber Scar said as he jumped onto his mount.

The two urged their mounts to a fast trot. The load of wood slowed them down. The on-coming pack of wolves was rapidly closing the distance.

"It is going to be a close race. Take all four pack mounts and ride hard for the compound. Get the team ready for a major battle. I am going to try and slow down these wolves," Saber Scar yelled to Marigold.

"Don't do anything crazy," Marigold yelled as she thought he already was doing something crazy.

"Open the gate, I see Marigold coming in as fast as she can ride. She is bringing in four loaded pack mounts. I don't see Saber Scar," Feather-in-the-Wind said from where she was tying a stake to its anchor boulder.

Saber Scar rode his mount back toward the oncoming wolves.

"Scar I hope you have the speed to outrun these wolves," Saber Scar talked to his mount.

"I hope I am half as accurate as Feather-in-the-Wind," Saber Scar said to himself as he loaded a stone into his sling and let it fly at the oncoming lead wolf. He immediately reloaded his sling and let another fly at the same wolf.

The stones had the desired effect as they both found their mark. The entire wolf pack came to a stop.

"Thank you, Feather-in-the-Wind," Saber Scar said to himself as he continued to pelt the wolves with stones.

The wolves were now milling around in confusion.

"It's time we ride like the wind," Saber Scar said with a chuckle.

He just hoped they would ride fast enough.

"Keep the gate open until Saber Scar shows up.

Marigold you, Golden Hawk and Running Stag stand by the gate. I am going to check the condition of the perimeter.

The rest of you please unload the wood and tie all the mounts to their stakes," Taelo instructed.

Taelo walked around adjusting the stakes and making sure there were no places that a wolf would be able to come through.

He knew the team had just accomplished the impossible. He was now worried about the integrity of all the work.

A steady solid rain began to fall from the dark grey sky above. It was the type of rain that would last the remainder of the day and probably through the evening.

"Here comes Saber Scar and he is just ahead of a huge pack of wolves," Golden Hawk called out.

"Let's get ready to put the gate in place as soon as Saber Scar rides in," Golden Hawk said to Marigold and Running Stag.

Taelo ran over and gave a hand putting the gate into place as Saber Scar rode in at full speed.

Feather-in-the-Wind, Quiet Rabbit, and Busy Bee all let stones fly from their slings in a coordinated continuous barrage. The wolves came to a stop and backed up away from compound. The stop lasted only a short time.

"That was quick thinking. It has given us the chance to secure the gate," Taelo said as he finished tying the cross poles to the vertical ones.

He looked out at the wolves.

"Let's get our weapons ready. I don't think they plan to stop," Taelo called out to the team.

The wolves came at the compound as if there was no barrier. They hit the barrier, and some came almost halfway through. They were snarling and snapping as they tried to push all the way in.

The war hammers were in constant motion. As soon as a wolf put his head between the poles a hammer smashed it. Slowly the perimeter had dead wolves between almost every pole and the live ones still kept attacking.

They seemed to lack the understanding that their prey was fighting back and winning.

The rain was a constant companion and soaked everything.

"I am not sure what is driving these beasts. They must never have met an enemy they did not defeat," Taelo yelled as his war hammer came down on yet another wolf.

"Someone help me hold the perimeter wall down," Golden Hawk yelled as the perimeter wall was lifted above one of the anchor stones by several wolves hitting the barrier at the same time.

Saber Scar threw a rope over the top of a pole and pulled it down. His weight pulled the perimeter wall almost back into place.

Taelo did the same with another rope.

Lily pounded a stake into the ground for them to tie their ropes to.

"Good move, and thanks," Taelo said to Saber Scar and Lily and then picked up his war hammer and walked up to the three wolves at a point of the perimeter.

One wolf had made it through under the perimeter wall.

Lasher, Walker, and Arrow attacked the intruding wolf. It was bigger than the three put together.

"Let him go," Running Stag commanded, and Lasher and the other two wolves stopped their attack as Running Stag stepped in toward the giant wolf.

The wolf made a leap forward toward Running Stag. Running Stag took a swift step to the side as he spun and aimed his war hammer to the side of the giant wolf's head. The loud crack made everyone look. The wolf landed and never moved.

"That was a very brave move," Taelo said from his position on the perimeter.

After what seemed like an eternity the attack subsided. At least half the pack lay dead around the perimeter. Apparently, the lead wolf had finally been killed and the pack backed away in confusion.

The rain and the dying light of the day added to the eerie atmosphere in the compound. There were close to fifty dead wolves with their heads through the perimeter wall.

A large number of wolves were lurking just across the small river. Everyone was soaking wet with water dripping down their noses. They were all exhausted.

"We were lucky to have had the perimeter up in time," Taelo said as he walked around the compound.

"Luck had little to do with getting the compound up and built. It was due to Taelo the slave driver," Golden Hawk said with a tone of humor in his voice.

"And we still have had nothing to eat for the whole day."

"I am sorry about the meal. The wolves came before I was able to get something together for all of us," Lily spoke up as she rummaged through the supplies to get something for them to eat.

She brought out her supply of dried salty shark meat and gave everyone some to chew on.

"Let's open the gate and skin the wolves. We will throw their bodies to the other side of the river," Taelo said as he walked up to the gate.

Taelo asked Saber Scar to throw the wolf carcasses across the river to where the other wolves were still lurking.

"You and Running Stag keep an eye on the remainder of the wolf pack. The rest of us will skin them and bring the carcass to you.

Running Stag took his bow to the edge of the river and each time one of the wolves showed themselves he let an arrow fly. He shot at least a dozen arrows, but he could count only one wolf killed. It had fallen in plain view.

"I hope we can retrieve those twelve arrows. I know how hard you have worked to make them and that they are tipped with the teeth of the giant shark we killed," Saber Scar commented as Running Stag shot yet another wolf.

The wolf skinning went on for most of the night. The pile of carcasses built up on the far side of the river. Running Stag could no longer see to shoot at the wolves.

He now concentrated on listening for any of them coming across the water.

The steady dreary rain continued to soak all of them.

The central fire was burning, and the good smell of some food cooking attracted all of them.

Lily had used some of the extra poles to make a rain cover over her fire pit. That made it possible to keep a small fire burning.

"Here is the last carcass. Toss it over and then let's retreat into our compound for the rest of the night," Quiet Rabbit said as she and Busy Bee pulled the carcass over to Saber Scar.

"I want to complement everyone. We came through this because we worked together. I know I am soaking wet, hungry, and exhausted. I don't know whether to eat or sleep," Taelo said as he and Golden Hawk secured the gate.

"I will take first watch," Lily said as she put stew into one of her carved wooden bowls and handed it out.

"I will be up with the fire anyway," she concluded.

There was no argument from anyone. Lily kept watch for the remainder of the night.

The steady rain was still falling when Feather-in-the-Wind awoke. She was always the early riser. The heavy grey sky made it look like evening. She could not tell what time in the morning it might be.

"Good morning," she said to a very tired looking Lily.

"Good morning. I have a fish stew ready for anyone who wants something simple but warm," Lily replied. "I give you the watch and I am going to sleep."

"Thank you, I will take the watch and the fish stew," Feather-in-the-Wind said as she sat down out of the rain, near the fire.

Later after the team had all awakened, eaten and were once again functioning, Taelo went cautiously out to look across the river at the pile of wolf carcasses and to see where the wolves might be.

"We need to find out if the wolves are still around or where they might be. We cannot face them in the open and I don't want us to travel in constant fear. I am going to go across to see if they are around.

Golden Hawk would you stay here and have the camp ready for another attack. Leave the gate open so we can ride in if necessary.

Running Stag bring your bow and arrows and accompany me. The rest of you relax where you can stay dry and enjoy this rainy morning," Taelo said as he prepared his mount.

Running Stag always felt a surge of energy and pride when Taelo called on him. He eagerly gathered his things and got on his mount to accompany Taelo.

"It looks clear across the river. I can't see any of the wolves but if they attack, we will retreat immediately and run for the compound," Taelo instructed.

"That makes twelve dead wolves with arrows through their chest," Taelo commented as he watched Running Stag retrieve his arrows.

The two pulled the wolves into a row.

"The next time I will just put you on the river's edge and make sure you don't run out of arrows. How many did you shoot," Taelo finished with a question.

"I am four arrows short," Running Stag replied.

He was overjoyed at the success of his arrows.

Taelo sent Running Stag back across the river to let the team know about another twelve wolves to skin.

They then tracked the remaining pack of wolves. They were retreating to the mountains. They came across three more dead wolves and the fourth arrow.

They skinned the three wolves.

"That was good use of the shark's teeth, and you were able to retrieve all of them. This will make a fine story for the evening fire. I wish Burly Bear or Little Otter were with us. They are fine story builders and finer story tellers. This story will make you legendary by the time they get done with it," Taelo said to Running Stag.

On their return to the compound the steady rain stopped and the sky to the west began to clear.

"The wolves seem to have retreated. I believe we killed more than two thirds of them. Running Stag can claim more than sixteen kills. His arrows took out fifteen and we all saw him kill number sixteen with his war hammer. How many did you kill at the perimeter," Taelo finished with a question.

Quite Rabbit responded that there were seventy hides.

"If you all help, we can use the perimeter as the place to stretch out the hides. We can then scrap and clean them and get them ready for travel," Marigold said as they talked about what to do next.

"Let's move the wolf carcasses well away from this location. They will start to smell by this afternoon," Saber Scar suggested.

He and Running Stag went out together. They tied several of the carcasses together and pulled them away into the valley not far from the river. Soon the vultures could be seen circling the sky where they had put the carcasses.

For the next twelve sun cycles the team was busy scrapping, washing, drying, and oiling the hides slowly. The hides could not be folded and made ready to travel until they were finally dry and pliable. Even then the hides they carried needed to be periodically opened and lightly oiled to keep them in good shape. They now had another seventy wolf hides to add to their growing collection.

They finally broke camp. They dismantled the compound in order to retrieve their rope. It was too valuable to leave behind. They piled the stakes neatly in case anyone might ever return to this spot. The carrying bags of the pack mounts were close to being full. Any additional trophies would require them to start pulling travois with the mounts they rode.

Chapter 18: Westward along the coast

The weather cycled consistently with sunshine in the morning and most of the afternoon. Then a steady rain fell for a short time and a clear cool evening followed.

The mountains slowly receded toward the west as the team was going more to the southeast.

The forest thinned and the underbrush became more prevalent.

The sea birds once again greeted the team and the air spoke of the odor of the sea. The rhythm of the wave was similar to their last encounter and the team looked forward to one more visit.

The land leading to the ocean was very different from their experience to the North. It was low and flat covered in low foliage and was heavily populated by tall limbless trees with a burst of long leaves at their tops. Closer examination also revealed a fruit that grew in clusters hanging down from between the leaves.

Feather-in-the-Wind climbed one of these trees and cut the entire stem of hanging fruits down. These proved to have a thick husk that once removed, exposed a hard nut. Three dark spots on one end were easily penetrated and a delicate and refreshing liquid was enjoyed by the entire team.

Most of the ground water the team experienced was brackish. They decided to make camp by a spring that had cold sweet water bubbling up from below.

The spring formed a small stream that followed into a large brackish swamp area. Feather-in-the-Wind jumped in and slowly let herself float along the stream.

Taelo declared that they had found their camp for their stay in this area. The sea was a short ride away, their spring water was fresh and cool, and the air warm and enjoyable.

Quiet Rabbit commented that the ancestors in the sky had different homes in the night sky from those they had grown up with.

Taelo pointed out a few familiar patterns, but they clearly were joined by those they had seen when they had taken their Journey of the Heart to the southern lands of the Condor.

I agree with Taelo. I think the ancestors each have their own place to live. We are only able to see a part of their home at a time. What you see depends on where you are," Feather-in-the-Wind joined the conversation.

"Why do some have brighter light and other so dim," Busy Bee inquired?

I think some live far away and some live closer to us. It is just like our campfire. If we are far away it looks dim and small. If we are close it looks large," Golden Hawk replied.

"We believe the ancestors live in a dark cave with a fire at its center. They watch what we do and try to guide us," Saber Scar added from where he sat.

"So, you don't think the lights in the night sky are the ancestors," Feather-in-the-Wind asked?

"I don't know what the lights in the sky are. They could be the fires of the ancestors but there are so many, and we are so few. How could that be," Marigold joined in?

"It does not matter what they are. The beauty draws us. The number awes us. The questions they raise cause us to improve," Quiet Rabbit said softly.

The next morning Taelo was up early. He walked around the camp.

Lily got up shortly after and began to get the cookfire started. Everyone else was still sleeping.

The mounts were quietly cropping the grasses around them.

"We have ridden south for a moon cycle. The weather remains warm, but I know it is now the time for the clan gathering. Is it time to begin our journey back to the west," Taelo thought?

Taelo looked up into the sky and was surprised to see his totem fly silently high above him.

"So, you have come to help. Thank you. Is this the time to turn to the west," Taelo spoke quietly?

Lily observed Taelo as he walked around the perimeter of the camp. When he looked up, her eyes followed his gaze. She saw the eagle flying silently overhead.

"It comes to guide us. I see Taelo speaking to it. The ancestors watch over us," Lily thought to herself.

The eagle turned and flew effortless to the west.

"It is time to return," Taelo said to himself.

Taelo moved the stakes of each of the mounts so they could reach fresh grass and then returned to the camp.

"Lily tells us it is time to go westward," Golden Hawk commented as Taelo returned to the center of camp.

He was teasing his cousin and Taelo caught on immediately.

"Yes, Lily is a wise woman, and she is right. Today we will turn and proceed westward," Taelo responded so the entire team could hear.

"I thought we would go to the sea once more," Running Stag commented.

"Perhaps we will but only if we find it to the west," Taelo replied.

The journey proceeded westward with a slightly southern direction. A few cycles later Taelo turned directly south. He had been watching the sea birds and decided to follow them.

"Where are we going," Busy Bee inquired.

She had been riding along almost asleep. There had been little excitement.

Feather-in-the-Wind continued her assault on the small game. She would challenge someone on the team to see who could get the most game in a certain distance. Once in a while someone would beat her but seldom.

They always had an ample supply of ground hog, squirrel, rabbit, and a few pigeons.

Everyone kept a watch out for plants that would add flavor to the food. The digging sticks given out by Taelo and Golden Hawk had made a huge difference. One of the team was always jumping off their mount to dig up a tuber or pull up some wild onions or garlic.

Taelo insisted that everyone declare their riding partner each day. This partner would stop while the digging was going on.

"We have been surprised several times. We must protect each other," Taelo had insisted.

The sea birds led them to the sea.

"We will need to cross this small strip of water to get to the sea," Saber Scar commented as he looked across the water to the grassy backed sand dunes on the other side.

"The water here does not look deep. It is salty so it is connected to the sea," Golden Hawk added.

"Let me ride across first," Feather-in-the-Wind volunteered.

She knew she was the lightest load for the mounts and her mount did exactly what she wanted.

"Running Stag, please cross with Feather-in-the-Wind," Taelo requested.

"You spoil those two," Quiet Rabbit said quietly to Taelo.

"Yes, but they both have earned their treatment," Taelo said with a chuckle.

He was not that much older than the two, but he felt like their father. He was very protective and proud of them as was the rest of the team.

Lily had taken on the role of mother to both of them.

"The water is slowly getting deeper but there is no current," Feather-in-the-Wind commented as she guided her mount out into the water.

When she was halfway across the mount began to swim but only a short moment later it found footage. After that both Running Stag and Feather-in-the-Wind made good time to the other side.

They rode up the sandy incline, stopped at the top, and looked south away from the team.

"It is the sea, but it looks different from the one we just left," Running Stag called across to the team.

"Golden Hawk, Busy Bee, Saber Scar, and I will stay and build a raft to carry our supplies. We need to keep everything as dry as possible.

The rest of you, cross over and find a good place to make camp," Taelo instructed.

"Golden Hawk you're the master at harvesting poles. See if you can find enough to make a decent camp. We won't be putting up a perimeter, but we will want enough to make a floor for the raft and to keep everything off the ground.

Busy Bee you are Golden Hawk's partner today so keep an eye out for him.

Saber Scar you and I need to find several logs with which to make a sturdy raft," Taelo handed out the assignments.

"Well, here are your poles. Busy Bee and I think we just saw a monster, but it disappeared into the water, and we did not see it again. It has a large mouth with many teeth and eyes at the top of a long snout. It was fresh water so maybe it does not live out here," Golden Hawk reported.

"We will need to be careful. There is no telling what it might be or how dangerous it is," Taelo replied as he began to tie the poles across the logs to form a platform.

A short time later the four of them came across with the raft behind them. Their mounts were able to pull the raft as they swam toward the other side.

"Look," Quiet Rabbit said as she pointed back into the clear water of the channel they had just crossed.

The four of them looked back and saw some very large fish. They had a peculiar head.

"Their head looks almost like a war hammer only more stretched out," Saber Scar commented.

"They swim like the shark, and they look about the same size as the shark that attacked Golden Hawk," Taelo added.

"Well, we are now at this side. I don't plan to cross here again," Golden Hawk said as he thought about his encounter with the shark.

"We were lucky today. We will want to be very cautious when we get ready to cross back," Taelo said as he turned his mount and followed Quiet Rabbit back to where the rest had set up camp.

Taelo rode his mount along the top of the sand dune. There the grasses were thick enough for the mounts to get a good grip on the ground.

The only other place to ride was at the water's edge where the sand became firm. The white sand in between was soft and pliable. This made it slow going for the mounts.

The sand was a brilliant white. The inner waterway was calm and there were several shallow inlets. The water in these inlets was only thigh deep.

"Who wants to go fishing and seeking other things to eat in the shallow bay," Taelo returned to the camp and inquired.

About half of the team wanted to go.

"Saber Scar, you have the best eyesight, would you be willing to be our look out," Taelo asked as they sat overlooking the small cove on the inland waterway.

"Especially give us warning if you see those war headed sharks."

"Yes, I think I like my role up here on the top of this sand hill," Saber Scar said as he thought about trying to get out of the water if one of the sharks did show up.

"OK, no one goes in over their waist. I will take the outer most position. Golden Hawk will take the next. Then it is up to each of you to choose where you will be with the exception of Feather-in-the-Wind who will take the position closest to the shore," Taelo said as he dismounted and left his mount on the mound where it could graze.

"I will lead. Everyone wait until the person on the outward side is two spears ahead of you. In this way the fish will swim in toward Feather-in-the-Wind and the shallower water," Taelo instructed.

Everyone had a gathering bag and a spear. They formed a perfectly angled line across the small cove.

"Hey, I just picked up what I stepped on and it is a clam just like we ate in the far northern shore," Quite Rabbit said loudly so everyone could hear her.

"Shuffle your feet along and see if you can find some," She continued.

She already had four of them.

Taelo's spear flashed, and he came up with a flat fish with an eye on the top side and one on the bottom side.

"These fish lay flat in the sand at the bottom. Look for their eye," he called out as he showed everyone a very unusual fish.

It was about four of his palms in size.

Saber Scar was feeling the hot sun, but his focus did not falter. He was keeping a sharp eye out for the strange shark they had seen.

Suddenly, Feather-in-the-Wind let out a shriek, started to run and then turned and plunged her spear into the water.

She was half laughing and half crying as she held her spear to the air to show everyone her prize.

It was a baby war hammer shark.

"It was sleeping in the sand. I stepped on it, and it took off. My first reaction was to run but then I decided it was easier to spear it so it couldn't bite me," Feather-in-the-Wind explained.

"I am done fishing for now. I don't want the mother war hammer shark coming after me," Feather-in-the-Wind said as she carried her prize in.

"Let's all turn in and work our way to shore," Taelo said from his position.

He agreed with Feather-in-the-Wind's thinking.

"Well, I think Saber Scar was testing your courage. He didn't warn you about this war hammer shark," Taelo joked as they all gathered around to look at it.

"I have good eyes but this one was already there before we started, and it is little. It might have eaten Feather-in-the-Wind, but it would hardly be able to take a bite of anyone else," Saber Scar said defensively.

He knew he was being teased.

"When I stepped on it and saw what it was, my heart stopped. I really had to fight the desire to just turn and run across the water. My first move in the water made me realize I had no chance by trying to run. I think now I know how Golden Hawk felt when he saw his shark," Feather-in-the-Wind said as she tied a cord to the tail of the now dead shark and got ready to carry it to the camp.

"Well, this was a fruitful adventure. We have four bags of oysters, six large flat fish and one small war hammer shark," Golden Hawk commented as he gathered everything together to be carried back to camp.

"I would like to study the shark before we gut and skin it," he continued. He was interested in the location of the eyes.

Later as they sat around the night campfire, listening to the gentle action of the waves, and looking up into the star studded, sky Golden Hawk started the discussion with his observation of the war hammer shark.

"I think the eyes allow it to see everything up and down and in front. It is very much how our eyes work. It amazes me at the different shapes of the animals we keep learning about. How did all of these animals get to be," he threw out the open question?

"I don't know but the monster we saw when you were collecting the poles will make me run if we meet it again. It scares me more than any snake or lion," Busy Bee said in reply.

"I am still replaying my reaction to having stepped on the small war hammer shark," Feather-in-the-Wind continued.

"Well, I am happy I stayed with Lily to help get the camp organized. The work went smoothly. We even had time for a swim in the sea. Then we found the small clams in the sand so we will have a wonderful breakfast stew," Marigold added.

"We will continue to travel along the shore as long as we can. Tomorrow we will break camp after breakfast and travel westward," Taelo announced.

Chapter 19: Clan Meeting

↋ack in the Far Northwest the black of night was punctured by countless points of light. Once more all the Elk sub-clans would travel across the endless, snow-capped mountains. They would gather in the gentle valley with its oblong lake bordered by yellowing willows overhanging the now bursting cattails. The gentle green grasses were now yellowing, and the numerous flowers of summer were shadowy husks of their former bright color and beauty.

Three clans, the Elk Clan, the Northern Elk Clan, and the Clan of Others had traveled together. They were the first to arrive and had agreed to share the far side of the lake. Their past twelve moon cycles had bonded the three clans to the point they felt as one.

The three clans arrived at the same spot that long ago, Wise Owl had stopped the Elk Horn Clan and sent Taelo and Golden Hawk to get the far side of the creek set up. It had been a historic moment.

Suddenly, to the surprise of everyone, the white smoke signal was seen rising from the far side of the lake as it had done so long ago.

"I am not sure how Taelo arranged this, but this certainly looks like his handiwork," White Swan said with a smile as she looked over at a beaming Burley Bear.

Taelo had asked Burley Bear to recreate the white smoke signal event in case the journey east took longer than one season. Burley Bear had sent two of the younger members of the Others to carry out this wish.

The two that had been selected were ecstatic to replicate a Taelo adventure.

"This will be the first clan gathering without Taelo and Golden Hawk that I can remember," Quiet Pheasant said as she cleared the tears from her eyes.

"Yes, but Broken Spear has told me that he will tell of Taelo's and his team's adventures as clearly as he has been able to follow through the eyes of the eagle," Burley Bear shared with those around.

They continued and set up their camps on the far side of the lake. In the following days, the other five sub clans arrived.

"It is good to see you. I see you have all decided to make camp on the far side of the lake. This is a good idea. It keeps the layout the same as it always was for the other sub clans," Wise Owl said as he came across the lake to greet everyone.

The Elk Horn Clan had arrived during the night and spent their time setting up their camp. They were in the number one position that Wise Owl liked to have. He had been surprised about the clans on the other side of the lake.

He had planned to be first.

The Shy Elk, the Swift Elk and the Elk Hide Clan were the next to come in that day.

A day later the Grazing Elk from the eastern most area of the clan territory arrived.

This year the Northern Elk Clan had prepared a gift of salt for each of the other sub clan leaders.

The Elk Clan had brought buffalo hides for each leader and later they would share a substantial supply of dried meat with all the clans.

The Clan of Others had brought a bag of honey for each of the clan leaders.

"Where are you getting all this honey," White Swan had asked Burley Bear.

"Taelo taught us to give homes to the bees.

Several of our younger members have been spreading these homes out and now have many of them throughout our valley. You will have to talk to them and see if they will take some of their bees to the northern valley," Burley Bear proudly shared the success they had in getting the honey trees established.

It appeared that all the clans were experiencing a good season. This was sometimes hard to tell because of the pride each sub clan had. It was only at the time of sharing that the exact details would be exposed.

The meetings had all been very interesting for many years. It had started with the change of leadership of the Elk Clan, when it appeared they were headed toward starvation in the coming winter. None of the other clans could give help and Grey Fox Running became the leader. The following year the Elk Clan returned as one of the richest of all the clans.

Later the Others were invited to join the Elk Clan. Women shared equal status in the Clan of Others. This action put the entire culture of the Elk Clan on its head.

Women became members of the leadership group.

The next big change was when Taelo established the Northern Elk Clan with newly arrived people he had rescued. The Northern Elk Clan introduction was highlighted by Taelo introducing the Northern Elk Clan's flat slate plates and with small oil lights to illuminate the plate.

It was a surprise when White Swan became the first woman clan leader of this Northern Elk Clan.

Most of the leaders had assumed Taelo would claim the role as leader.

There were many additional smaller surprises that were all talked about.

With Taelo missing, everyone was wondering what the surprise would be this year.

This meeting Burley Bear and Little Otter supervised the erection of the clan totem. This was the totem Taelo, and his entire team had made for the meeting two seasons ago.

As always, the trading of goods was the highlight of the gathering.

Old friends visited with each other. Those that had passed on were remembered.

The mothers of available young women made a point of seeking out potential young men. It was the same with the mothers of the available young men. The two sets of mothers met and arranged for the young people to meet and get to know each other.

Every year a significant number of couples were set up in this way.

The meetings to evaluate the health status of the clan started several cycles after the arrival of the Grazing Elk Clan.

"The meeting of the Elk Clan leaders will now come to order. Remember you must have the talking staff before you will be allowed to address this group," Wise Owl opened the meeting.

This he knew would be one of the easier sessions in recent years. All the clans seemed to have fared well and seemed ready for the coming cold season.

The clans reported in the order they had been established. Red Oak now leader of the original Elk Clan was the first to report.

"The Elk Clan has enjoyed a very fruitful season. We arrive with an abundance of goods and food to share with all the clans. We will make these goods available in a coordinated offering arranged between us, the Others, and the Northern Elk Clan," Red Oak announced.

A murmur went around the room at this announcement. This was the first time such an arrangement had been practiced. Each subsequent clan announced that they were in relative, good shape for the coming cold season.

"We of the Elk Horn Clan have had a good season. The hunters taught by Red Oak and Grey Fox Running have matured. They are very good hunters and have supplied us well. The Elk Horn Clan is in good shape for the coming cold season," Wise Owl said briefly before passing the talking staff onto the Grazing Elk leader.

"We of the Grazing Elk Clan have learned a new way of hunting.

Taelo came to us in the dead of winter with three wolf drawn sleds loaded with the bison of our region. He left his sleds and wolf teams after teaching us how to care for the wolves and handle the sleds. We were able to hunt and bring back abundant loads of meat. We will be sharing our abundance with each of the other clans.

We have also collected our own young wolves and have started teaching them how to pull a sled.

We will be trading with the Others to be taught how to build the sleds," Fierce Badger made his report.

The reports from the Shy Elk, the Swift Elk and the Elk Hide Clan were that they were doing fine and would get by in the coming cold season. They were not as positive as the first three clans. Finally, the Talking Staff was passed to Burley Bear.

"We of the Others will gladly teach the Grazing Elk and any of the other clans how to make the sleds. Send your students to our valley for a season and we will return them with new skills that will serve each clan well.

We also have a new skill of bee tending that you may be interested in and of course there is the soap making we excel in.

Only our technique of how we create the whitest of leather will remain secret.

Our valley, our home, the hunting techniques we have learned and the art of tending the honeybee are all gifts that Taelo gave us. You will all get a taste of this honey later when Broken Spear tells of Taelo and Golden Hawk's travels to the east.

We of the Others are proud to be members of the Elk Clan," Burley Bear said and then passed the talking staff to White Swan.

"Let me begin by telling you how much I have learned as a leader of the newest sub clan. I have new respect for all the leaders of the other clans.

Grey Fox Running has coached me and helped me tremendously. Even in good times this is a hard job.

Thank you all for having given me this opportunity.

The Northern Elk Clan has had a tremendous year.

Burley Bear and his mate Meadow Flower, Little Otter and his mate Talking Wren and the rest of Taelo's team built a compound that you must all come to see.

I extend an invitation to each of you.

We have a hot spring that heats the main lodge. The Lodge has a floor warmed by this same hot spring. Outside of the lodge is a bathing area filed with the hot water from this spring.

Around the hill on which the lodge is built are the individual homes of the clan members. Each home has a stream of water from the hot spring.

This was designed by no other than Talking Wren. I understand from Red Oak that she is transforming the Valley of Plenty.

Taelo also taught the Northern Elk Clan to grow the grain that gives us a new source of food. It is tedious and hard to deal with. The animals and birds are attracted to it. We don't hunt deer. They come to get the grain. We don't hunt pigeons. They come to get the grain.

With the sling taught to us by Feather-in-the-Wind and the arrow taught to us by Running Stag our supply of meat is overflowing.

Finally, the grain gives us a new food that we grind and mix with water and cook on a flat stone. You will all get a taste of it when Broken Spear tells his story.

We of the Northern Elk Clan together with the Others and the Elk Clan will offer each of the other clans the support as desired and selected by each clan.

This will allow each clan to get exactly what they need. This season no clan should fear the winter. We have plenty and wish to openly share it with the rest," White Swan slowly and carefully spoke her words.

"This is a most generous offer from these three clans. I know I will see what the offering is and make sure the Elk Horn Clan leaves the valley with a buffer for the coming cold season.

Thank you and I will come to visit the Northern Elk Clan before the cold season closes in. I would now like to close this meeting," Wise Owl said as he hit the talking staff to the ground.

There was a pounding of palms on the ground as all those in attendance signaled their acceptance.

The meeting attendees mingled and talked informally for a few moments and then dispersed.

That was one of the most positive meetings we have held for years. I am sorry that Taelo and Golden Hawk were not here to see how well everyone is doing," White Swan said to Grey Fox Running, Red Oak, and Quiet Pheasant.

"They must be having a grand adventure. I know they will bring back a wealth of knowledge as well as goods. The last stories by Broken Spear were inspirational. I can't wait until tomorrow afternoon," Quiet Pheasant replied.

"Yes, I am looking forward to listening to Broken Spear. I understand he has asked Burley Bear, Meadow Flower, Little Otter, and Talking Wren to help him," Red Oak informed the others.

"What are the four to do," White Swan said somewhat surprised.

"I think they are to be his voice. He will speak softly, and they will repeat in a loud voice for those listening to hear. He called them all together earlier. Burley Bear came to the leaders meeting straight from his practice," Red Oak went on.

The next morning a white swan flew once around the valley and then landed on the lake.

"Your totem has arrived," Grey Fox Running informed, White Swan.

"Well, I wonder what it means," White Swan wondered.

Then high in the sky she saw the eagle gliding smoothly around the rim of the valley.

"I think they have come to listen to Broke Spear's story," Quiet Pheasant offered.

"I agree with her," Red Oak added.

"Well, let's get the treat we promised to everyone ready. This will be a big event," White Swan said as she stood up.

"You know that it has all been taken care of and there is nothing you need to do. Meadow Flower, Little Otter, and Talking Wren have it all organized and ready," Grey Fox Running commented.

He had checked with them, and they had enough volunteers to hand out the treats.

"The grilling of the meat from the Valley of Plenty, the baking of the flatbread, and the square cuts of honeycomb are all organized. We have workers at the selected positions. They will do the grilling and hand out the treats. They will serve the entire clan with no problem," Meadow Flower assured White Swan.

She and Talking Wren had organized this part of the afternoon event together and she had executed on the plan.

Talking Wren was busy with the rest practicing with Broken Spear.

The loud reverberation of the pole beat on the hollow log signaled the beginning of the story telling. It was being held at the end of the lake.

The hillside was covered by the members of the various clans.

Broken Spear sat on a fur covered log with his back to a large boulder.

Burley Bear was on his right and Meadow Flower on his left. Talking Wren was next to Burley Bear and Little Otter.

"Clan members let me introduce Broken Spear the Seer of the Others and those that will be his voice so you can all hear," Wise Owl said as he gave a slight bow to Broken Spear as he handed him the talking staff.

"Thank you for the introduction. This afternoon I will tell you the story of Taelo," Broken Spear said quietly and then passed the talking staff to Burley Bear who repeated what Broken Spear had just said.

"Before we begin, let me tell you about the stations with food that are all around you. Please help yourself to as many grilled pieces of meat that you desire. It has been flavored with the bark of a tree that gives meat a very good flavor.

There will be flatbread with a piece of honey for each of you. Please take only one of these. We wish we could offer more but there is a limited amount of both the honey and the flatbread," Burley Bear said in a booming voice.

"Now we will begin the stories of Taelo as told by Broken Spear," Burley Bear continued.

He would be the lead in the story telling. Then each of the others would take a part as they had practiced.

"Everyone knows the stories of Taelo.

We of the Others have a special relationship with him. Many years ago, we were told to await the coming of the man of the eagle. We were to travel to a new land and there he would find us.

One day two beautiful princesses and two young boys came to us as we waited. It was near winter, and we were waiting by the sea," Burley Bear ended his part and Marigold took over.

"The two princesses had brought food and other gifts and were being friendly. However, our giant Burley Bear was rude and rough with one.

Suddenly one of the young boys let out a war cry, ran forward, used Burley Bear's body to launch himself into the air and hit Burley Bear across the head with his oak war club.

Burley Bear grunted, sank down on his knees, and fell flat on his face.

Taelo stood over him as the camp stopped in a stunned silence," Marigold ended her piece and Talking Wren spoke next.

"Be kind and gentle to my mother,"

"We come to give you gifts, but we are warriors of the Elk Clan. We harbor no ill will to any person who treats us well. We eliminate those who do us harm,"

An eagle swooped down from the mountains and let his scream be heard over the camp.

All eyes looked upward.

The members of the Elk Clan know this is Taelo's totem.

The members of the old ones saw his totem and reacted as well.

"It is as the omen said. A young eagle will overcome the bear. This young boy is a future leader of men. See even the eagle sends him congratulations at his victory.

Taelo explained his name was the claw of the eagle. He drew the eagle in the sand and pointed to the sky. He then drew the claw.

That day a hush descended on the camp.

The mood of the camp changed and Taelo was seated at Quiet Fox's right side."

Little Otter took over repeating the narrative as Broken Spear continued.

"Taelo and Golden Hawk examined the camp and asked, "Why do your men not fish the food from the sea."

Taelo drew his question out in the sand. A hush again fell on the camp. This boy was talking to the leader and the elders and was asking why the camp seemed to need food.

"Boys can fish, girls and women can fish, and everyone can eat. Hunters can go to the mountains for meat. There is no reason to go hungry,"

"Golden Hawk and I can teach you to fish, to hunt rabbits and to,"

Suddenly, there was a roar in the camp and Burley Bear came roaring out of one of the huts.

"Where is the warrior who attacked me without warning.

He was looking for a giant.

"Burly Bear, I am Taelo. The scream of the eagle, the claw that strikes," Taelo said as he stood up and extended his hand to Burly Bear.

Everyone heard the eagle scream as it again flew back across the camp.

"It is an omen, the sign we have been awaiting," Quiet Fox, said to Burley Bear.

Burley Bear let out a loud laugh.

"This is great. I have fought and beaten every warrior in this camp. Now I come face to face with, Taelo, "The scream of the eagle, the claw that strikes," and I have my lights put out. Well done my small friend," Burley Bear said as he took Taelo's small hand and shook it.

"I am at your service, and I apologize to your mother.

Meadow Flower took over the narration. This was one of her favorite parts.

"And so, Burley Bear became Taelo's protector and friend. Taelo sent hunters out to find meat for the clan.

Burley Bear and Rolling Stone, now called Saber Scar went with Taelo northward up the beach. There they found a small whale. Taelo had the team anchored the whale to the beach. Rolling Stone was sent back to get help so the whale could be harvested.

Taelo and Golden Hawk continued up the beach. Taelo followed the elk and the cry of the eagle to our current home by the hot springs.

The two returned to Burley Bear a few days later. Burley Bear says to this day they were moving so fast as they ran along the beach that he thought they had wings on their feet.

That night the bear that gave me my name, Broken Spear, came to feast on some whale meat. Taelo talked to her and asked her for help in keeping a pack of wolves away. She seemed to agree with him. She ate her fill and gave him warning when she was going to leave.

Taelo wisely fed the hungry wolves and asked them to leave. They seemed to understand and when the sun came up, they departed back into the woods.

Taelo, Golden Hawk and Burley Bear went everywhere together. The three returned to the Elk Clan as the season cycles shrank to its shortest point. They stayed a few days but then Taelo was called by the ancestors. He and Golden Hawk climbed the cliff above the village and went to their secret cave.

Worried parents sent Burley Bear to find them. The snows came in full fury. Burley Bear was at the point where he was sure he had lost Taelo.

Then before him he saw Taelo walk out of the huge stone. It was not magic. It was Taelo and Golden Hawk's secret cave with a hot spring. It looked out over the Valley of Plenty that is now the home of the Elk Clan.

The three took their warriors journey together. It was the dead of winter. They supported each other.

It was on this trip that both Taelo and Golden Hawk demonstrated how fast they were. Each ran down a buffalo and put a spear in front of it and let the buffalo run the spear through itself.

Burley Bear built his first sled and the three brought back three buffalo as an offering to the Elk Clan leaders.

Burley Bear took over the narration.

You know of this and other stories.

You know of the first hunt led by Little Otter. You know of the success of the hunt.

I am sure you have seen the young buffalo that Taelo tamed. Little Otter became its keeper.

You have heard of the crazed saber tooth tiger. This tiger gave Rolling Stone the name of Saber Scar. Quiet Rabbit saved Rolling Stone's life by sewing up the wounds on his chest and taking care of him until his fever passed.

When the saber tooth attacked Taelo, Quiet Rabbit went after the tiger. She is a fearless young warrior of the Elk Clan.

Later in the following spring, Taelo and Golden Hawk decided they would take a long trip to the south. Taelo made everyone the flat shark toothed weapon. He trained the team for self-defense.

On his trip South, the team of eight defeated a band of young warriors thirty strong.

The team climbed the highest mountain and from that point they were able to see the eagle fly from one sea to the other.

Taelo and his team found friendly people to the south where the eagle met the condor. The condor is a bird four times larger than the eagle.

These people build their homes of smooth surface matched stone. The roof is a covering of flat dried and oven baked clay.

The people in that area climb the mountains like we walk the flat plain.

Each season they sacrificed their most beautiful young woman as a gift to the condor. Feather-in-the-Wind was the sacrifice. Her brother, the son of the leader asked for Taelo's help to rescue her from her sure death.

It was Quiet Rabbit and Busy Bee who took a bearskin to the cave of the frozen princesses. There they found more than one hundred frozen beauties that had been sacrificed to the condor.

Taelo and the team prepared to leave. Feather-in-the-Wind was carried down from the mountain by Quiet Rabbit and Busy Bee and hidden in one of their travois. She would be the last sacrifice. The clan would believe the condor had at last accepted their sacrifice.

Later, on the way home, the team met a fierce warrior clan. They had defeated the warriors of this clan on their way south. Now they met them again on the way north. This time they were invited peacefully into the village.

However, two separate powers were in a contest with each other to rule the warrior clan.

One leader wanted Feather-in-the-Wind for himself. He was determined to take her by force when Taelo was ready to leave. With his thirty warriors backing him, he approached Taelo with his knife drawn.

It appeared Taelo was unarmed.

However, as the leader lunged forward with his knife, Taelo reached and pulled the flat shark toothed weapon off his back and killed the leader.

Taelo had earned the right to lead the defeated leader's warriors and could have stayed and become one of the rulers in that clan.

Taelo chose to take his team home. He knew the travels of the team were only half over.

Talking Wren took the next part of the story as Broken Spear continued to tell the story.

Taelo and his team went north. He was guided to a valley by his totem. There he found a hot spring and built a lodge.

This was the valley in the legends of the Elk Clan. There the team discovered the ancestors of the Elk Clan. They learned that the childhood stories each had been told by their parents were true.

Taelo designed a lodge like no other. Burley Bear was one of the builders. He has talked many times about the heated floor of this lodge and about the stone roof.

It was during this time that the dire wolves attacked, and the entire team fought and defeated more than thirty dire wolves.

A short time later Taelo went to collect salt.

On his return he rescued three women and a young boy. He learned they had escaped from cannibals. Some of their clan members were still held captive. Taelo returned with the young boy, Running Stag, and freed his parents and several others.

Today the rescued sit here with you to hear this story. They are now part of the Elk Clan.

There was a second peoples saved from freezing to death in the winter weather.

Running Stag had earned Taelo's respect by his bravery in facing the cannibals. This time Taelo let him lead the wolf team led by Lasher. Running Stag led the three rescue sleds back to the compound through a howling, blinding blizzard.

Taelo came back on foot leading the people that did not fit on the sleds. They were in the blizzard, unable to see, but Taelo kept them going.

It was Lasher, his trusty wolf, who came back for him. He led them all back to the compound.

These were the people that became the Northern Elk Clan. Never before has a clan been formed in this way. The clan was more than ninety in size. Taelo brought the new "Northern Elk" clan to the end of the season overall clan gathering.

Many expected Taelo to seek to be the leader of this new Northern Elk Clan.

Instead Taelo suggested a list of people to Wise Owl. His name is Wise Owl because he is indeed wise. He chose wisely and nominated White Swan to lead the Northern Elk Clan.

Taelo and Golden Hawk were made Elk Clan leaders at large and given a golden feather. This is in recognition to their continued contribution to all the clans.

Taelo, Golden Hawk, Quiet Rabbit, Busy Bee, Saber Scar, Marigold, Feather-in-the-Wind, Running Stag and Lily are now all on a journey to the east.

They have found and tamed a new animal that they ride on.

It was during this time they discovered a huge tiger larger than the saber tooth. This tiger attacked Feather-in-the-Wind, Saber Scar and Running Stag.

The three together killed the tiger but not before it gave Saber Scar yet more scars on his chest. He was saved by Feather-in-the-Wind's fearless barehanded attack when she launched herself like a spear at the tiger's side. Saber Scar managed to repeatedly stab the tiger through its chest and Running Stag ran a spear through its body.

A moon cycle later, the team met a huge bear bigger than any seen before. It attacked Feather-in-the-Wind and would not leave when Taelo asked it to leave. Single handedly Taelo killed this monster of a bear.

But Taelo was seriously wounded. For many sun cycles he was in the land of the ancestors. There I was able to talk to and comfort him. He has a powerful mind and is able to hear the ancestors as they talk.

Taelo recovered and the team reached the far sea. There Golden Hawk faced certain death when a giant shark attacked him. Taelo ran and jumped from a high cliff and at the last moment speared the shark. Together they killed the shark.

This time Lily showed her courage by joining them as they brought in the wounded shark."

Burley Bear had been talking a long time and it was clear his voice was failing. He passed the Talking Stick to Meadow Flower.

The team has continued their journey. They have gone south.

During this southern travel, a large pack of giant wolves began to follow them. Taelo and his team set up a compound on an island in the middle of a small river. There they faced a pack of more than one hundred wolves.

They killed more than half of the pack before the wolves left. Every team member fought valiantly during the battle. The hastily built compound saved them from certain death.

Running Stag and his bow killed more than a dozen. Taelo has joked about changing his name to Wolf Slayer.

The team is now traveling back toward the west along the southern sea. There they have discovered a new shark. They call it the war hammer shark because of the shape of its head. Feather-in-the-Wind is the first to kill such a shark.

The team is well and on their way home. The eagle watches. Periodically I will continue to look through its eyes to see what the team is doing," Broken Spear said as he concluded the story telling.

"The story telling is over. But follow your noses to the great smell of roasting meat and help yourself. This treat is the compliment of the Elk, the Northern Elk, and the Clan of Others," Burley Bear conclude in a loud voice.

"There were a couple of surprises for me," White Swan said as she and Grey Fox Running sat near Broken Spear eating a snack.

"Yes, Taelo always does surprising things," Broken Spear said with a smile.

He knew this was the first time White Swan realized that it was Taelo that had put Wise Owl up to nominating her as the leader of the Northern Elk clan.

"I did not realize Quiet Rabbit had been so active in all these travels," Quiet Rabbit's grandmother joined in on the conversation.

She had raised Quiet Rabbit after both of her parents had died.

"Yes, her name may imply gentleness, but she is as hard and as sharp as the head of a spear. She is a powerful partner to Taelo," Broken Spear replied.

Chapter 20: Busy Bee's Monster

The bright white sands created a sharp clear line far into the horizon along the clear aqua green water pushed up on the beach by a northward blowing breeze. At times, Taelo took the white sands for a rippling snow drift one would experience after a wind-blown snowstorm.

The sun's warmth in the morning quickly dispelled any thought of the cold of a snowstorm and by the time it was at is zenith the air was warm, and the sea breeze a welcome respite.

The occasional rabbit, the many heron, the graceful pelicans smoothly gliding a few feet above the sea, and the host of seagulls each provided a moment to be absorbed and appreciated.

No major predator seemed to be out on the long island providing a leisurely way that ran due west.

Each day the team would move their camp down the coast to a new spot on the beach.

"This is the most relaxed I have been," Busy Bee said as they rode their mounts along the top of the sand hill where the grasses provided better footing.

The alternate place to ride was right at the water's edge. On a random basis the team alternated their choice throughout the day.

"As relaxed as we all are, we will continue having someone stay up for the night watch," Taelo replied.

He had insisted that at least one of them take this duty.

Busy Bee had been the night watch on the previous night.

On the sixth cycle of the sun, they rode up to a break of the long sandy beach.

At this point, the inner waterway linked back to the sea.

"Let's put together our raft for our hides and other things we want to keep dry and then go across to the other side. I will ride across first to see how deep the water gets," Taelo said as the team came to a stop. It was just after the suns peak for the day.

The sun was at its daily zenith as the team stopped to prepare to cross to the other shore.

"I will keep an eye out for any sharks," Golden Hawk said as he rode up to the edge of the water.

To everyone's relief, the crossing went smoothly and was uneventful. This time they had not seen any sharks.

They regrouped on the other side and continued on until time to make camp.

Two cycles later their procession arrived at another area they would need to cross.

"This time we will cross tand go toward the north Taelo said as he watched his totem turn and head in the northward direction.

It had been flying gracefully along parallel to them for most of the morning.

"How close do you think we are to the great river," Golden Hawk asked after they had made the crossing.

"I am not sure. Ask Quiet Rabbit. She has been keeping track of our travels on her travel hide," Taelo responded.

That evening Quiet Rabbit shared the pictures she had been drawing. The hide had the drawings she had been doing since the beginning of their journey. Busy Bee had been the only other person she had shared it with. She tried to space the various drawings out based on the time it took them to travel.

"I drew the circle of our journey on the hide when we first began. Busy Bee and I did this while we were still at the Northern Elk Clan lodge.

We did not know the distance we would travel or what we would see but we estimated we would travel more than one full cycle of seasons in each direction.

Each event that we have experienced has a picture on the hide," Quiet Rabbit explained as she unrolled the hide.

Taelo and Golden Hawk held up the hide while Quiet Rabbit pointed to the events the team had experienced.

A black line started on the upper left corner, went across the hide to the right, turned and went down and now was heading back along the bottom.

The scenes and events were intricately drawn out.

"I began marking each travel period and have estimated how far apart each event occurred," Quiet Rabbit continued.

"I believe that in the next handful of sun cycles we will be close to the great river," Quiet Rabbit finished.

"This is a wonderful way for us to remember this journey. Where did you learn to do this," Lily said as she carefully traced the journey with her finger?

"I watched some craftsmen put their mark in the clay of the lodges they were building when we were down in the land where Feather-in-the-Wind comes from. I thought about how this could be used, and this idea came to me.

Busy Bee helped me get it started and has done some of the sketches," Quite Rabbit replied.

She was very proud of the work the two had done on the hide.

"What is this one," Running Stag asked as he pointed to a particular sketch just a few cycles in the past?

"That is the monster I saw when Golden Hawk and I were gathering the stakes for the raft to cross over to the white sand beach," Busy Bee replied.

"There can't be such an animal," Running Stag said as he thought about its size and look.

For the next several cycles they traveled in a north, northwest direction. They were going along a body of water that extended toward the north. They proceeded until they reached a river running into the body of water they had been following.

"We will turn toward the west, but it looks like we will be traveling in a very marshy area. We will want to be very cautious as we travel," Taelo said as he looked across the river before him.

They were just above an island where the river was at its narrowest.

"Running Stag see how deep the water is here and if we can get across without building a raft," Taelo requested.

"It's not deep but it is muddy. The land on this side is low and wet" Running Stag called back as he rode across to the other side.

"Let's make camp here. We will get a fresh start with the sunrise," Taelo continued.

Taelo set up a fish trap and caught a few fish.

The prize of the afternoon was the frogs Golden Hawk and Saber Scar speared as they walked the bank of the river. They had gone looking for some rapids where they were hoping to catch some crayfish. Instead, they kept spearing the frogs that seemed to be half asleep in the late afternoon sun.

The two efforts yielded an abundant dinner of fish and frog legs for the team.

"I really enjoy preparing food for this team. We always seem to eat well, and we always have something new and unique," Lily said as she turned the spits holding the frog legs and the fish.

Feather-in-the-Wind had used her sling and a fat young groundhog met his fate and now was slowly roasting over the fire on its own spit.

"I know Saber Scar is fond of the groundhog. I am sure it will not go to waste," Marigold said as she turned it slowly on its spit.

Early the next morning they crossed over the river. The ground on the other side was indeed wet and soft. The mount's hoofs sank a good hand into the soft ground. There were many small streams flowing through the area they were crossing.

The team had only traveled for a short period when they came to a slightly smaller river to cross. The land had continued to get wetter and tall reeds where growing along the edges of the river.

Golden Hawk was in the lead. Suddenly his mount reared up and turned. There in the water was Busy Bee's monster.

"It looks as mean as any animal I have ever seen," Saber Scar commented as the entire team stopped well back from the enormous animal.

"It seems to be asleep," Running Stag said as he stared at the beast.

"Would you like me to wake it with my sling," Feather-in-the-Wind asked?

"Let's see if there is a way around it. Let's make sure we don't meet one of these in the water," Taelo said as he led the team upstream of the beast.

"We must be in the home area of these beasts. I see two more on the other side of the river," Marigold said as she pointed to where they were.

As soon as the mounts went into the river and made splashing noises, the beasts seemed to come to life. They turned and slowly went toward the water.

"Let's get to the other side as fast as possible," Busy Bee said as she urged her mount forward.

"They are faster than I thought they would be," Quiet Rabbit yelled as she followed Busy Bee.

The entire team raced to get across the small river ahead of the monsters.

Lily who was guiding the pack mounts and was last in line was barely ahead of one of the monsters.

It came out of the water and was racing after the last mount.

Taelo and Golden Hawk jumped off their mounts and rushed back, spear in hand to protect the mounts.

The beast did not stop but came straight at them.

"Let's step to opposite sides and drive our spear in just above its front legs," Taelo said as he got ready for the impact.

The two took their positions and moved slightly apart.

The beast chose Golden Hawk as its target and was quickly closing the distance.

Suddenly there was a yell from the side and Saber Scar came running forward with his spear and war hammer. He ran in from the side and drove his spear down into the beast just behind its head.

The beast's tail caught him and sent him flying through the air.

The impact of Saber Scar's landing made a dramatically loud "wham" sound.

Taelo and Golden Hawk utilized the diversion to plunge their spears in and then quickly backed away.

The beast had three spears in its body and was still trying to attack.

Busy Bee ran forward and drove her spear into the beast just behind its left leg.

She leaped over the beast. The tail almost caught her, but she was just fast enough to escape.

Quiet Rabbit raced in and drove her spear into the same area. She stopped and pushed both spears in farther.

The tail would have caught her, but Taelo leaped across and pulled her away to safety.

The beast was done. It was still swinging its tail, but it was no longer able to run.

Marigold came in with Saber Scar's war hammer and repeatedly smashed the monster between its eyes. It was clear she wanted revenge for the hurt it had given to Saber Scar.

"Well, let's make sure we never make her mad at us," Busy Bee said as she stood back and admired the beast.

Taelo and Golden Hawk helped Saber Scar to his feet.

"Are you alright," Golden Hawk asked as he checked for any injuries as he helped a wobbly Saber Scar stand up.

"What happened," Saber Scar asked as he finally walked on his own.

He was taking in the monster. His spear had gone all the way through and pinned the beast to the ground.

"You saved our lives," Taelo replied as he put his arms around Saber Scar's shoulders.

"It seems the other beasts have left the area," Busy Bee said.

She had quickly scouted the area to make sure that other members of this animal would not be coordinating an attack.

"They seem to work alone," Feather-in-the-Wind commented from where she sat on her mount.

She had stayed on her mount the entire time. She had launched many stones at the beast but this time the stones had no effect. She realized there were few stones in this area, so she got down from her mount and proceeded to pick them up.

"Let's quickly skin the beast and take any useful meat with us. We can process the hide later when we get across this area," Taelo said as he took out his knife to begin the skinning.

"You go sit down and relax," Golden Hawk said to Saber Scar as he joined Taelo.

Lily helped in the skinning. She cut the meat off the tail and put it in one of her carrying pouches. The rest of the team tended to Saber Scar and snacked on dried fish. They were all surprised that after flying through the air for more than six spear lengths, he had no broken bones or other injuries.

"Let's get across. Once we are on normal ground, we will find a good place to camp," Taelo said after the meat and hide were loaded.

A short time later they made it out of the marshy area and found a small clear stream where they could camp for the night.

"This is the tail of the beast. It is a meat almost like a fish, but it has no bones. It is quite tasty with a little salt and a roasted onion," Lily explained as she passed out some for everyone to try.

"Well, I will have as much as you cook," a recovered Saber Scar said after he had his first bite.

Chapter 21: Armored Animal

The sun seemed to take on a new intensity and the air now still was laden with moisture. The team was heralded by lush vegetation and an abundance of small game. Once again only the sun provided a way to navigate through the dense growth that surrounded them.

A few cycles later they came to the mighty river.

"Let's hope we don't find any of those beasts in these waters when we are crossing," Lily said as she looked to the other side.

They had carried the materials from their last raft as they traveled. The main logs served as a place to sit, and the various stakes were used in holding up their night cover.

Now they stopped to assemble these items into the raft to be used to go back across the mighty river.

According to Quiet Rabbits drawing, the team had reached their three-quarter point of their journey.

"Find a third log to add to our raft," Golden Hawk requested as he organized the assembly of the raft.

"Golden Hawk, Running Stag and I will swim with our mounts. Marigold, Saber Scar, and the rest of you will ride on the raft. The wolves can ride up on the platform with our dry goods," Taelo instructed.

"Let's take it easy. We will lead with the mounts. Give us a chance to get about halfway across. Then launch the raft," Taelo continued.

"I will swim with you and lead three of the pack mounts. This will make it easier on all of us," Lily volunteered.

"Ok, let's get organized. Then we can decide whether to cross now or whether we wait until morning," Taelo replied.

The team had become proficient in assembling the raft and in making water crossings. They immediately went to work and before long they were ready.

"I think we are ready to cross, and we should do it now," Saber Scar said as he positioned the raft in the water.

Taelo led his mounts in and soon the entire team was swimming or rafting across the mighty river. Their speed downstream was once again a multiple of the speed across the river. The mounts found footing on the far side and pulled their handlers up onto the bank.

"Lily, Running Stag, take the mounts and secure them. Golden Hawk and I are going to help get the raft to shore. When you have the mounts secure, bring one to help in dragging the raft out of the water," Taelo instructed as he and Golden Hawk estimated where the raft would come to shore.

They would have to make their way downstream to where the raft would come to shore. The woods were thick, and it was difficult to move down stream. By the time they arrived Saber Scar was up on the bank tying off the rope holding the raft.

Lasher, Walker, and Arrow were scouting about around the area.

Running Stag arrived with one of the pack mounts at about the same time.

"That was a smooth ride across," Quiet Rabbit said as she took various bundles from Busy Bee and put them up on the bank.

Suddenly the wolves were snarling, growling, and chasing some pure black animal. They cornered it by a fallen tree. The entire team immediately took up their spears and ran toward the wolves.

"Easy Lasher," Taelo said as he looked at the black animal. It was like a tiger but pure black. It was long and sleek and was as large as the three wolves combined.

The yellow eyes looked around and the tiger snarled.

"You are a beautiful animal, and we would value your hide, but it is a beautiful day, and I would like to let you go on your way," Taelo said quietly as he got the wolves to quiet down and move back.

"Go on your way. Do not come back tonight or you will be a hide I sleep on," Taelo continued his dialogue with the tiger.

The tiger seemed to understand. It hissed quietly and walked away from the group.

"Well, you did it again. You talked to a wild animal and convinced it to do as you instructed. You forgot to ask me if I wanted its hide," Golden Hawk joked as the tiger disappeared.

"I am glad it decided to listen. I have done enough for today. I would like to have a relaxed evening," Marigold defended Taelo.

"That was one of the most beautiful animals I have seen. I am glad you sent it on its way," Feather-in-the-Wind said as the team turned back to the river to get their goods ashore.

Quiet Rabbit, Busy Bee and Feather-in-the-Wind went out with their slings and a short time later returned with their bags full. Several rabbits, and squirrels were in the bag, and they had found an ample supply of onions and garlic plants.

Saber Scar and Running Stag had gone along the riverbank and had speared a number of frogs.

Taelo and Golden Hawk had rubbed down all the mounts with grass to clean and dry them.

Meanwhile Lily and Marigold arranged the camp and set up a cooking area.

They all came together to clean the animals and to prepare their evening dinner. The team shared the work naturally.

They had now traveled for eleven cycles of the moon.

"We may make it back for the solstice celebration," Quiet Rabbit said as she finished the drawings of Busy Bee's monster and the black tiger.

"That would be great timing," Busy Bee replied.

"Well, let's see how it goes, I would like to take a few extra mounts back as gifts. That would take a few cycles to get done," Taelo commented.

He had been thinking about getting back for the solstice, but he really wanted to have six extra mounts. He wanted four for the Elk Clan, and two for each of the other two clans.

"How much farther west will we go before going toward the north," Running Stag asked.

"That is an excellent question for which I do not have an answer. Let's talk it over and decide" Taelo replied.

"I think that we should turn northwest now," Quiet Rabbit spoke up as she looked at the hide with her drawing.

"It would be wonderful to get back to the same place where we tamed our mounts," Feather-in-the-Wind joined in.

"I support Quiet Rabbit. We should journey in a northwest direction," Golden Hawk said as he angled his hand across Quiet Rabbit's hide.

"It seems we will be going northwest," Taelo said as he looked at the hide.

"Let's spend a sun cycle or two here and dry out all our hides. We can repack and get everything organized for going north. We will be getting into colder temperature and need to make sure we are prepared," Taelo suggested.

"I agree, this will let me get the hide of our monster finished and all the other hides can be rubbed down. There is enough work to keep all of us busy," Marigold spoke up.

She had become the unofficial manager of the over abundant bundles of hides.

After several of sun cycles, the team was ready to continue their journey to the northwest. They rode at an easy pace.

Running Stag was out in front finding the way. They came to a river running in the direction they were going and decided to follow it. It was not long after when Running Stag came galloping back toward them.

"There is a new animal just up the ahead. It is by the river drinking water. It does not look to be aggressive, but it is very different," Running Stag said excitedly.

"Let's go on foot and see what Running Stag found," Taelo said as he tied his mount off and led the way toward the spot Running Stag had pointed out.

"This animal is huge, and it seems to have armor like the tail of a lobster," Saber Scar commented as he looked at a curved armored animal as tall as himself.

The head was close to the ground and the snout was long and pointed. A long tongue flicked in and out as if it was trying to get something off of it.

Taelo approached it from behind and touched the armor. It felt solid like that of a turtle. He retreated and each of the team members followed his example.

"The only way to kill this animal would be to knock it over and attack it at its belly," Lily commented.

Lasher, Walker, and Arrow were finally allowed to go and investigate the huge, armored animal. They sniffed around its feet.

The giant seemed to ignore all of them and lumbered off away from the river. It was clear it was not worried about the three wolves.

"It is an amazing find. I will add it to the drawings on my hide," Quiet Rabbit commented as she studied the animal.

The team continued up the river for several more cycles until the river turned due west. They crossed over and followed a smaller tributary toward the northwest.

"I think we need to go directly north from here," Quiet Rabbit commented one evening as she studied her drawing.

"Due north it is," Taelo said as he looked at Quiet Rabbits drawing.

They traveled north and slowly the weather grew colder. It was clear they were moving into the winter.

"I wish the weather here was as nice as along our trip along the white beach," Feather-in-the-Wind said from deep inside her rabbit fur lined parka.

She had made a pair of leather leg coverings similar to her parka to keep her legs warm and her boot went up to her knees.

"I have never seen anyone who hides from the cold like you do. It is a wonder you can stay on your mount," Quiet Rabbit teased.

Even with all her gear, Feather-in-the-Wind was one of the best riders. She could ride standing on the mount's back. She could do side dismounts and remounts as they rode along. She had also demonstrated a flying leap up onto the mount that only she could perform.

"I believe this is the river we followed east. Which way is our camp by the waterfall," Golden Hawk asked a few cycles later?

"I believe we should follow it up stream. This looks like the territory Quiet Rabbit, and I explored," Busy Bee spoke up.

"Running Stag would you go up the river and scout it out. I would like to get to our camp by the waterfall before that grey sky to the north dumps snow on us," Taelo said as he pointed out the dark clouds to the north.

"We should all continue up the river. We are close and perhaps we can make camp there tonight," Taelo continued.

A short time later an excited Running Stag returned with the news that he had found the tributary leading to the waterfalls.

Chapter 22: Mount Falls

The setting sun burnt a red edge on the lower front edge of the dark black clouds approaching from the northwest. This fiery edge evoked the image of a hot blade ready to cut the flesh. Its fast movement threatened the watchers who rode their mounts with more urgency in hopes of reaching a safe haven.

The falls appeared before them and were as stunning as ever. This was a place of good experiences and memories.

The setting sun to the south hit the water spray and created a mix of colors almost like a rainbow only in pink, gray and yellow.

Taelo took in the scene and made a quick decision of how to best face the oncoming weather.

"I think the side where we put the mounts is the best place for a warm lodge. We will need to build it fast," Taelo shared with the team as they stopped to take in the scene.

"We have most of the material we need already cut. We will only need green poles to bend for the roof," Quiet Rabbit continued as the team crossed over to that side of the river.

"I will keep an eye out for the longer poles we need," Saber Scar replied as he took his mount out to gather the tall slender willows.

"We have enough hide to cover any frame," Marigold contributed.

"We need some large flat digging stones," Busy Bee said as she thought about the task of digging a large base for the lodge.

"Oh, I know exactly where to get those," Feather-in-the-Wind said as she recalled the layer of loose stone at the edge of the pool.

"I will make sure we have a good cooking fire and will keep you all well fed," Lily shouted from the rear of the procession where she was leading four of the loaded pack mounts.

"Let's sleep on this side tonight. Tomorrow we will join our mounts on the other side," Taelo announced as he dismounted.

The sky was now pure black, the air was clearly getting colder.

The next morning Taelo and Golden Hawk marked out the area for the lodge and the digging started in earnest. Once the frozen top layer was penetrated the digging got easier.

Lily located her cooking area very close by, but far enough away to keep the smoke out of the lodge.

There would be a small fire in the center of the lodge with the purpose of keeping out the chill and would only be used for cooking in an emergency.

The slope of the land meant that half of the lodge would be under the ground except for the roof. The dirt removed for that half would be used to cover the walls of the bottom half of the front walls.

Running Stag and Feather-in-the-Wind were bringing stones to make the primary wall for the exposed part of the lodge. They positioned the stones and closed the gaps with a mixture of mud and grass.

The cold made all of the work exceptionally difficult.

Lily was continually bringing some hot soup for each of the team to drink and get warm.

"Keep working your small miracle," Running Stag commented as he drank down some of the hot broth.

"Here are the poles for the roof," Saber Scar called out as he and Marigold returned from their pole gathering journey along the riverbank.

"If we continue at this pace, we may have our small lodge complete by sundown," Taelo commented as he began to push the loose soil back around the wall closest to the cliff.

"The hides for the roof are pulling in smoothly," Busy Bee commented as she and Quite Rabbit worked on bending the poles across and getting the hides pulled tight along the bent poles.

The team worked steadily. They worked through their normal lunch and dinner period.

The snow started to fall as the last hide for the roof was pulled into place.

Marigold and Saber Scare were positioning the front wall and door.

Golden Hawk and Taelo immediately built up the exterior stone wall and moved dirt around to insulate the bottom half of the wall.

Lily's cooking area was only a short distance to the side of the door.

Feather-in-the-Wind and Running Stag collected wood from the surrounding area. They put the pile to the side of the lodge so it would be easily accessible for both the internal warming fire and the external cooking fire.

The lodge was in the same enclosure as the mounts. They had spent the day eating the grasses and curiously watching what their human friends were doing.

Lasher, Walker, and Arrow had roamed around the area along the river and found their own dinner.

"We are done just in time. Let's get all our belongings stowed inside," Taelo said as the snow began falling in earnest.

The inside of the lodge still needed to be organized.

"Let's put all the extra hides and other supplies up to the front. We will arrange our sleeping area to the back where it will be warmer," Marigold said as she took over getting things arranged.

The small central fire was doing a good job of keeping the temperature in the lodge at a comfortable level. Everyone was able to get out of their heavy jackets and boots.

"Here is a treat for each of you," Lily commented as she distributed pieces of grilled deer and rabbit.

"We must all have been hungry," Quiet Rabbit commented after a several moments of silence.

"I was not only hungry. I am also exhausted. I have just enough energy to arrange my sleeping area and crawl in," Busy Bee replied.

The heat from the small fire kept the opening in the roof free of snow but the entire lodge was under the snow by morning.

Taelo and Golden Hawk had gone out several times to keep the mounts from getting buried. They had continually worked to clear an area for all fifteen mounts. This area was surrounded by snow as deep as the height of the mounts.

Lily had stayed up to help by giving them hot broth and keeping her cooking area cleared. She had also kept a trail clear down to the river so she could get water, and everyone could get to a latrine area farther down the riverbank.

"Thanks for helping. The hot broth is the only thing that seems to keep us from freezing," Golden Hawk commented on one of their breaks from moving snow out from around the front of the lodge and mount holding area.

"This is the most snow I have seen since the time Taelo saved us from the cannibals," Lily commented.

The memory of that horrible time was still fresh as she thought about all the good that had happened since then.

"The amount of snow that we are getting is going to make staying here long enough to capture and train mounts impossible," Golden Hawk commented to Taelo.

"We will need to go to the Grazing Elk Clan and see if we can stay there. I would still like to capture the mounts if we can," Taelo replied.

The next morning the team sat around the small warm fire in the lodge talking about their situation.

"A few of us should go and see if we can find our way to the valley of the mounts," Saber Scar suggested.

"That is a good idea. Wait until the snow stops before you go. Golden Hawk and I are going to get some sleep," Taelo replied.

It was late afternoon when the snow finally stopped, and the sky became clear.

"Let's get the far bank cleared so we can cross the mounts and get out of the water," Saber Scar said as he led the way across and began to pull the snow down from the bank.

He was standing in the cold water, and it was not long before he was back by the fire taking off his wet boots and warming his feet.

"Well, you cleared enough so we can ride across on the mounts and get up the on the other side. Tomorrow we will cross and continue to clear a path out toward the valley of the mounts," Taelo said as he patted Saber Scar on the back.

"Let's make sure we dry the mounts legs off after we get them on the other side. It is really cold out there," Saber Scar commented as he put his bare feet toward the fire.

"While we find our way out, the rest of the team can prepare to leave our lodge. We will leave the lodge standing. This means we will have a lighter load. I would like each of us to carry our own sleeping hides and a part of the other hides or goods we have. The pack mounts will all be better off with a lighter load and if we are lucky, we will be leading a set of wild mounts," Taelo informed the team.

Taelo, Golden Hawk and Running Stag rode across the river to the far bank. They soon ran into a wall of snow. Their progress was slow. They were literally digging their way forward. Finally, at the top of the rise of the hill leading away from the river the snow was only as deep as the bellies of the mounts. They were able to slowly ride forward. They constantly traded the lead position so the mounts would not wear out.

"Look out ahead and tell me what you see," Taelo said to Running Stag.

"I see the tops of the trail markers that Feather-in-the-Wind and I made last season," Running Stag said as he looked ahead as far as he could see and spotted the poles with the piece of leather blowing in the wind.

"Well, I think we should return and get ready to bring the rest of the team out tomorrow," Golden Hawk suggested.

Later after they had returned to the Mount Falls Lodge Taelo commented, "The excellent work done by Feather-in-the-Wind and Running Stag last season to mark the trail to the valley of the mounts is now going to save us much time. Their leather flags on top of their marker poles go out as far as the eye can see.

Both Feather-in-the-Wind and Running Stag beamed at the praise. They had wanted to make trail markers that would be there for a long time and now their work was going to help the team get out of a tough situation.

The sky was clear, but the weather was a piercing cold that crept in through their thick coats as they rode through the deep snow toward the west.

"I think I could use two more bear skin coats," Feather-in-the-Wind commented. She had on all the warm clothing she could possibly put on and she was still cold.

"It is cold so make sure your feet don't get wet or frozen," Marigold contributed.

By early afternoon, the team came to the end of the trail markers. This put them at a point overlooking the valley of the mounts. At first there seemed to be no valley. It was completely covered in a deep layer of snow. Just to the right of the point where the team had stopped there seemed to be a large hole with steam rising out of the center.

"What do you make of that," Golden Hawk asked as he pointed to the scene.

"I think we have found our wild mounts. Let's make camp here. I will put on my snowshoes and see if I can get to the edge of that hole," Taelo replied.

Even with their snowshoes on, Taelo and Golden Hawk sank almost to their waist into the snow.

"We need to be very careful near the edge of the hole. You stay back and hold the rope," Taelo commented as he tied a rope around his waist.

"I am going to go just far enough to look down into the hole and verify there are mounts below."

"I will hold firm," Golden Hawk replied as he tied his end around his waist and slowly fed out the rope as Taelo went forward.

"I can't see all the mounts but there are, at least a dozen that I can see. I don't think I can get any closer to the edge," Taelo called back as he felt the snow below him seem to give.

"Let's go back and talk this over. The mounts trapped down there are doomed if they don't get out. The only way we can help is to dig a path down to them," Golden Hawk commented.

"Our flat shark toothed weapons make good shovels," Feather-in-the-Wind commented later when they were talking about digging through the snow.

"Yes, and I brought several of the flat digging stones along to use when cooking," Lily volunteered.

"Alright, we will give it a try. The path Golden Hawk and I took to the edge of the hole is where we will dig through the snow. We will need to get it wide enough, so it does not cave in on top of us," Taelo commented.

"We will work in teams of three and rotate frequently so we will not get overcome by the cold," Golden Hawk added.

"One team will be made up of Saber Scar, Quiet Rabbit, and Running Stag.

The other team will be made up of Marigold, Busy Bee, and Feather-in-the-Wind.

Taelo, Lily and I will make up the third team.

Two teams will always be digging while the third team is drying out, eating, and warming up."

"The snow will need to be pulled back and moved away. Perhaps we can load a large hide on the ground with snow and have the mounts pull the snow out to a dump area," Quiet Rabbit suggested.

"That is a great suggestion," Busy Bee replied.

"Let's get everything ready to start the first thing in the morning," Taelo said as he prepared several of his boots for the following day.

The snow removed to make the path grew into a small mountain. Quiet Rabbit's suggestion of pulling the snow out and away on a large hide worked exceptionally well. Even then it took two cycles of the sun to get the path opened.

"We have broken through," Saber Scar cried excitedly on their third sun cycle of work.

"Let's keep the opening small. We will move the mounts to the opening. We will keep the ones we want here. In the morning we will put lead ropes on them. The rest we will let go to find their way as best they can," Taelo instructed.

There were about forty mounts trapped and he was pleased they would be able to get as many mounts as the team could lead.

The released mounts followed their leader away from the team.

Sixteen mounts were culled out. The team spent the next few cycles getting the wild mounts calm enough to be led. Then it was time to move on. Lily led the four pack mounts and each of the other team members were now leading two of the newly captured mounts.

The mounts seemed to accept the situation more quickly than the original first group. Perhaps it was that they were in a worn-out condition, or the tamed mounts provided a calming effect.

"The weather seems to be holding. It is the coldest weather I have experienced," Taelo said as the team moved westward toward the Grazing Elk Clan's winter quarter.

"I can't hear you," Feather-in-the-Wind called out.

She was on her mount and had pulled an additional hide around her over her heavy winter parka.

"We can't see you," Quiet Rabbit replied jokingly.

"There seems to be something out ahead of us," Saber Scar called out from his lead position.

"I think it may be a small group of bison," Golden Hawk added.

"Yes, there seem to be about a dozen animals," Marigold observed.

"We could use some additional fresh meat. It would be good to take as much as we can into the Grazing Elk Camp. We cannot expect them to feed us," Lily said as she pulled to a stop.

"I will go around to the far side.

Running Stag, you take the right with Quiet Rabbit.

Golden Hawk you take the left with Saber Scar.

I will move them back in this direction.

Lily, Marigold, Busy Bee, and Feather-in-the-Wind will stay here.

Golden Hawk, Saber Scar and I will each try for one of the buffalo. Let's see if we can drop them here close to camp," Taelo instructed.

Moving the bison in the deep snow was more difficult than expected but Taelo and Golden Hawk did each get their buffalo.

"I would have taken mine as well, but my mount slipped and we both went sliding through the snow," Saber Scar was explaining to the team.

He had been launched through air and his fall was cushioned when he hit the side of the bison he was seeking to spear.

"You were supposed to throw the spear at the bison, not be a Feather-in-the-Wind," Taelo joked with him.

He knew the team had been lucky that Saber Scar was so tough. Any other team member would probably have suffered some broken bones.

"You almost succeeded. Your bison was down for a few moments. I ran out to kill it, but it got up and ran away. I think it was laughing," Marigold joined in.

She had run out concerned about Saber Scar and was overjoyed to see him get up unhurt.

"Well let's get these animals skinned and cut up. I will grill some meat for us to enjoy," Lily said as she pulled the tongue out of each bison and cut it off.

She returned to the cooking fire she had set up and began to grill the first round of meat. The team would eat well on this evening.

"Some wolves have found us," Taelo commented a short time later as he calmed Lasher who was letting out a low growl.

"Give me some of the meat scraps we have. I will go out and see if I can get them to have a small meal and move on," Taelo said as he gathered the scraps.

"I will come with you just in case these are not friendly wolves," Golden Hawk volunteered.

"We should all be ready just in case," Saber Scar said as he gathered his weapons and followed.

"Welcome fellow travelers," Taelo called out to the pack of wolves.

They had been attracted by the smell of the blood and were examining the remains of the bison. He threw each of them a piece of meat.

Lasher kept a low rumble in his throat.

Walker and Arrow sat quietly on their haunches and watched as Taelo talked to the wolf pack and made sure each wolf got some meat.

The wolves remained wary but seemed to accept Taelo who kept at an easy throwing distance. This was a pack of about a dozen. He talked quietly to them and made sure each wolf had something to eat.

"Well, that went well. I wish all wolves listened to Taelo," Quiet Rabbit said after the pack had moved on.

The next day the team broke camp and continued their journey to the Grazing Elk Clan. The weather was once again getting colder, and the sky was a threatening gray. Four sun cycles later they could see smoke rising in the far distance.

"We will make it to the Grazing Elk Clan camp by late afternoon," Golden Hawk commented.

"It will be good to have a place to stay for a short time and rest before we move on," Taelo said as he thought ahead to the hot water at the warm springs of the Northern Elk Clan lodge.

"Welcome," Fierce Badger greeted them as he took in the thirty mounts and the packs they carried.

He was not prepared to feed another nine people with the meager supplies of food he currently possessed. He hoped they had brought their own food.

"We are happy to return to your camp. We would like to stay for a few moon cycles before moving on to return to the Northern Elk Clan," Taelo said in greeting.

He sensed a tension in their greeting.

"Where would you like us to put the two bison we have brought," Quiet Rabbit spoke up.

She had seen the concern in Fierce Badger's eyes. She knew that at this time of year food was always the issue.

"Thank you for bringing so much to us," Fierce Badger said as he took in the amount of meat before him.

"We have been expecting our hunters to return but they are long overdue. I am worried about them," Fierce Badger continued as he guided the team to their quarters.

The places prepared for them in the previous season had been maintained and only needed some quick cleanup to be fully functional.

"I will clean up before we bring things in," Lily volunteered.

"Where did your hunters go," Taelo inquired?

"They went to the north where they expected to find a herd of bison. I have been hesitating and was just getting ready to send a couple of young hunters out to see if they could find them." Fierce Badger replied.

"We will go out at sunrise and find them," Taelo replied.

"I would greatly appreciate it," Fierce Badger said with a sense of relief.

"Who would like to go to find the hunters," Taelo asked the team as they sat around the fire together.

Everyone wanted to go.

"Alright, I think I asked the wrong question. Who is willing to stay and take care of our mounts," Taelo rephrased his question?

"I will stay with our mounts. It will give me some time to catch up with Gentle Fern and White Pearl," Lily volunteered.

She planned to continue her travel with Taelo, and this would give her a chance to see her two friends.

"Alright, the rest of us will need to take our cold weather gear, enough food to last us about five sun cycles and our weapons. We will go in the direction the hunters went but there will be no trail because they left before the snow hit," Taelo informed the team.

"We will look for the bison herd and if we find them, we will look around for the hunters. I am concerned they have met with some catastrophe otherwise they would have sent someone back if they had been delayed," Taelo continued.

The sun was just rising the over the mountains to the east as Taelo and the rest of the team departed.

"Thank you for going out in search," Fierce Badger called out.

The snow was still deep, and the temperature was brutally cold. The entire team was in full winter gear, and they wore eye slits to keep from going snow blind.

"I thought the mountains where I grew up got cold, but it was never like this," Feather-in-the-Wind said from behind the face covering she had pulled down from the hood of her thickly lined buffalo hide coat.

"This is the coldest weather I have ever been in," Quiet Rabbit agreed.

"Let's hope we find the hunters before the weather gets worse," Taelo said from his lead position.

He was looking at the dark gray clouds moving in from the northwest.

"I have found the trail of the bison," Saber Scar said as he rode in from his search out to the northeast.

"What direction were they moving," Taelo inquired?

"They are coming from the northwest and going toward the southeast," Saber Scar replied.

"Then we should intersect their travels if we continue going north," Taelo said as he urged his mount forward. He picked up the pace slightly. He wanted to make camp after finding the path of the herd.

By late afternoon they intersected the path the herd had taken. Close inspection of the trail gave them an estimate of the speed the bison were traveling.

"Tomorrow we will spread out and travel back toward the northwest where the bison came from.

Golden Hawk and I will be on each side of the trail.

Marigold and Saber Scar will travel out beyond the trail and the rest of you will come up the middle.

All of us will be on the lookout for any sign of the hunters" Taelo instructed the team.

The next morning the team traveled back along the bison's path. The path was wide enough that the far side was barely visible from the nearside. Nothing had been discovered by the time the sun was at its zenith.

Taelo signaled the team to the middle of the bison path.

"Let's continue after we have something to eat. How is everyone doing with the cold," he inquired.

"I am fine," Feather-in-the-Wind spoke up.

Everyone else grunted their agreement.

"Marigold, Saber Scar, keep an eye out for a good place to camp. Look for a place with water and that can easily be protected," Taelo continued.

It was late afternoon when Quiet Rabbit jumped down from her mount. She had found a broken spear and it still had its stone tip in place.

"I have found a spear," she called out.

"Whoever used this spear did not have time to retrieve it. It appears that the spear was broken by the bison stepping on it. So, it was used prior to the herd arriving at this point," Saber Scar said as he assessed the scene.

He tried to read the trail, but he could only see the hooves of the bison.

"Let's go back to each side of the trail and see if we can find any additional sign. Remember it has snowed about a half a spear length so obvious sign will not be visible," Golden Hawk added.

"If I were under duress, where would I go from here," Taelo conjectured out loud as he looked out over the terrain.

"I would go where there was some sort of shelter, stream, or trees. Perhaps a hill or cliff as well," Busy Bee replied.

She too was looking out beyond the trail.

"There seem to be some trees on the far side of the trail just before you reach the mountains," Marigold said as she pointed toward the northwest.

"I believe you even though I can't see that far," Running Stag said as he tried to make out what Marigold was pointing to.

"All right let's ride over there and see if we can find anything," Taelo said as he took the lead.

"Don't see any tracks," Running Stag commented as he rode along the edge of the bison trail. The snow cover there was at least waist deep.

"Yes, but someone climbed that tree," Golden Hawk commented as he rode closer to get a better look.

"Look at Lasher," Quiet Rabbit said as she watched him digging in the snow.

Taelo dismounted and walked to where Lasher had partially exposed the body of a dire wolf. It was at least twice the size of Lasher.

"This wolf met his end from this spear," Taelo said as he pulled it out and held it up. "The wolf is totally covered in the snow, so it was killed just before it began to snow."

"It looks as if the wolves chased the hunters into these trees. At least three people climbed this one. They later jumped to make a run to some other location," Golden Hawk added as he looked around the tree.

"We need to proceed cautiously. The wolves may still be about. I do not want to ride the mounts into this area. The snow is too deep, and they will most probably be frightened of the wolves.

Running Stag, I would like you and Feather-in-the-Wind to hold our mounts out in the middle of the bison path. If any dire wolves show up, you two, ride toward the herd. Keep going if they pursue. Ride into the bison herd and let the bison protect you.

The rest of us will proceed on foot and see if we can find the hunters. We will want to be out of this area by dark," Taelo instructed.

"I will take point.

Marigold and Saber Scar will be the sides.

Golden Hawk will bring up the rear.

Quiet Rabbit you will be behind me, and Busy Bee will be in front of Golden Hawk.

If we are attacked, we will form a circle. Anyone who is hurt will move into the center of the circle," Taelo continued giving instructions.

The team had practiced this hundreds of times on their journey.

Running Stag and Feather-in-the-Wind moved the mounts out toward the center of the bison pathway. A short time later Feather-in-the-Wind pointed to two very large animals coming toward them.

"I think the wolves have found us," Feather-in-the-Wind said as she pointed to the oncoming wolves.

"Let's get ready to ride. I want to get a couple of arrows into them before we turn and run," Running Stag said as he dismounted and got his bow ready.

His first arrow found its mark and went at least halfway in. The second also found its mark on the second oncoming wolf. Two more shots put two more arrows into the coming wolves.

"I am going to shoot for their mouths," Running Stag shouted as he let two more arrows fly.

The last two arrows had the effect he had hoped for, and the two wolves came sliding forward on the ground. His war hammer smashed into their skulls with deadly accuracy.

"Well so much for following instructions and riding for the herd," Feather-in-the-Wind said in a relieved voice.

"Well, I wanted to slow them down. They looked as if they could run as fast as we could ride," Running Stag defended his actions.

"Keep an eye out for more of them," Running Stag said as he pulled out his arrows and cleaned them.

He then took out his knife and proceeded to skin the two wolves.

Back in the stand of trees the rest of the team moved slowly through thigh deep snow. They were looking for some sign of the hunters.

Suddenly from on top of the rise to their left two dire wolves appeared and launched themselves at the team. They were dead before they reached their intended target. Each had two spears through their bodies and their skulls smashed.

"Great teamwork. Keep your eyes out for more of them," Taelo said as he removed his spear.

"Let's keep moving forward, stay close," Taelo said as he once again began to move toward the area where some huge boulders were located.

"I see smoke up ahead. Keep your eyes out for wolves," Taelo said as he looked around. He was watching and listening to Lasher.

Lasher had turned away from the boulder area to a section the woods to their left.

"I think we are clear toward the rocks. Let's move quickly," Taelo said quietly and went forward at a rapid jog.

The team followed in a tight formation.

The wolves appeared from the area pointed out by Lasher.

As the team approached the space between the rocks, they saw the barricade being opened up.

"We are very happy to see you," the young hunter said as he closed the barricade behind the team.

"What is your name and what is the situation," Taelo asked as he looked around. Four of the hunters were obviously wounded and laying on the ground. The two that seemed to be in the best shape had wounds as well.

"I am called Whistling Wind. We have been slowly recovering but we are out of food. We have melted the snow for water. We must be in the dire wolf's territory. They do not leave this area. We released our wolves and used the sleds to make the barricade that is protecting us."

"We fought our way here. Our wolves helped us, but they are no match for the dire wolves. They saved us but, in the end, they had to retreat and run, or they would all have been killed.

We almost did not make it, but we held them off here and were able to use our sleds to close the entrances to this area. Most of our wounds came from holding this area," Whistling Wind continued.

"Their wounds are extensive," Quiet Rabbit said after she and Busy Bee examined everyone.

"We need to figure out how to lure the wolves away from this area," Saber Scar commented.

"Golden Hawk and I will do that and then we will come back with the mounts. I am not sure how long it will be before we return with the mounts but all of you must be ready to ride," Taelo said as he opened up one of the packs and removed some bison meat.

He cut them into chunks and put them in two small bags.

"I always like the way you get us into these exciting adventures," Golden Hawk said as he took his bag.

He did not need to be told what the meat was for.

High in the sky an eagle let out a long cry.

"I am not sure what the eagle cry is for but let's be ready to ride or to give help," Feather-in-the-Wind said as she looked up into the sky.

Running Stag had just finished skinning the two dire wolves.

"Let's drag these two to the edge of the trail. Perhaps it will give the others a second thought," Running Stag said as he tied the rope to the back legs of the skinned wolves.

Taelo and Golden Hawk ran out full speed toward the trail they had come in. The dire wolves seemed to hesitate before taking up the chase. It was clear they were very fast.

"Alright let's hope they are hungry enough to stop to pick up the meat," Golden Hawk said as he sped up and past Taelo.

"You know the old joke. You only have to outrun me," Taelo said as he pulled up even.

The dire wolves were distracted by the pieces of meat as Taelo had counted on. Each time they began to close the gap Taelo, or Golden Hawk would drop pieces of meat and accelerate away.

The two flew out onto the bison trail and saw Running Stag standing with his bow ready. Feather-in-the-Wind had the mounts ready to ride and two spears to hand out.

Running Stag Stood and rapidly shot his arrows at the oncoming wolves. This time he shot for the wolves mouths. The arrows hit their mark and the arrow went through and cut the spine. The wolves dropped in their tracks.

Running Stag had six kills before Taelo, and Golden Hawk turned with spears in hand.

Suddenly there was a loud cry and Feather-in-the-Wind rode in from the side and bashed two of the wolves in the head with her war hammer. She had removed her coat and was riding with no hands on her mount.

The battle continued for only a short period. Taelo and Golden Hawk used their spears and war hammers to kill several of the wolves, but it was Running Stag and Feather-in-the-Wind that made the difference.

"You two make a deadly pair," Taelo said as he helped Running Stag retrieve his arrows.

"We need to move fast and go back and bring the hunting team out. There are more dire wolves between us and where the hunters have been holding up. Let's refill our meat bags. The trick worked on the way out. This time we will need to hold off any of the attackers as we load up and ride out," Taelo said as he got on his mount.

"Running Stag, you ride point and kill any wolf that comes toward us. Golden Hawk and I will be to either side of you.

Feather-in-the-Wind get the mounts into the center area. We will try to hold the wolves at bay" Taelo said to the two.

This time he did not cut the meat into small chunks. He was planning to feed the wolves as much meat as he had on hand.

The four came riding full speed into the clearing where the three stones formed a barricade.

"Here comes Taelo and the rest of the team. Let's get ready to move," Saber Scar called out as he saw Running Stag riding toward him.

Whistling Wind opened the gate and let Running Stag ride in. He was followed by Feather-in-the-Wind and the mounts she was leading.

Taelo and Golden Hawk dismounted and pushed their mounts into the center area. They turned and threw the meat from their bags out at the approaching dire wolves.

Taelo walked toward the wolves and continued to strategically throw the meat among the wolves.

"You can all live long lives if you leave us alone," he said as he continued to feed them.

Lasher was growling as he stood next to Taelo.

"It is time to ride," Golden Hawk called out as he watched Taelo's performance.

"Bring my mount to me," Taelo replied without taking his eyes off the dire wolves.

He knew he would need to move swiftly.

As he was mounting to ride, one of the wolves moved forward. Suddenly an arrow went through the wolf's eye and out the back of his head.

"Thank you, Running Stag," Taelo called out as he followed the team out of the area.

He continued to drop pieces of meat as he rode out behind the team.

When the team reached the bison trail, they turned and rode full speed away from the area. Taelo dropped the remaining meat he had and rode away.

Running Stag, Golden Hawk and he brought up the rear. The wolves did not pursue.

"I guess we were in their territory," Golden Hawk commented as he looked back and saw there was no pursuit.

"Or all the dead wolves had an impact on them," Taelo replied.

"All I know is that I am about six arrows short," Running Stag added.

"I will personally make you two handfuls, with the best shark's teeth I have," Taelo replied.

Chapter 23: Return to the Coast.

The dark grey clouds that had threatened snow turned the threat into a blinding, whirling full winter blizzard. The snow became invisible as the light of day disappeared behind the black of the clouds. The outstretched hand disappeared from view into the thick falling snow.

Taelo guided the team to a slight depression where they made camp for the night. There they sheltered and fed their mounts. Their large elk skin cover, held up with all their spears, provided a comfortable shelter where Quiet Rabbit and Busy Bee tended to the wounded hunters.

Marigold grilled some salted meat and fed them all a simple but delicious dinner. The Grazing Elk hunters welcomed the stop and celebrated the food they were eating.

There was a clear sky on the following sunrise and the team made their triumphant return to the Grazing Elk Clan. Their return with all the hunters was highly celebrated.

Many in the clan had feared the worst and were overwhelmed in their relief. An impromptu celebration in honor of Taelo and his team occurred.

"I can tell you that the stories of the hunter's trials, their belief that they were doomed, and your teams incredibly brave rescue will be told to all this coming clan gathering," Lily commented the day after the celebration.

"Two of the hunters are Gentle Fern and White Pearl's mates. They now are both grateful to you not only for saving their lives but also the lives of their mates." They commented that they will be at your service whenever you ask.

"Our success was due to our ability to work together and to each act individually when it was needed.

Running Stag's decision to kill the two dire wolves instead of running meant he and Feather-in-the-Wind were there to help when Golden Hawk and I ran out ahead of the pack chasing us.

Feather-in-the-Wind's unbelievable riding skills and courage again was a key action that ended the pursuit.

Running Stag's accuracy with his bow saved the day.

The rest of the team got the wounded hunters ready to ride.

The strength of Saber Scar made it possible for the wounded hunters to be put on the mounts.

Each hunter had to be held as we escaped the chase of the remaining dire wolves.

After our return Marigold, Quiet Rabbit and Busy Bee have tended to the wounded hunters.

Let them tell the story of their recovery.

Make sure the team gets credit in the stories that will be told," Taelo extemporized so all could hear.

"This is why everyone follows Taelo. He gives all of those around him equal credit," Golden Hawk said quietly to Busy Bee.

In the following several cycles the team went out hunting and brought back, another count of one hand of, bison. This ensured the Grazing Elk Clan would have food well into early summer.

By then key hunters would once again be able to hunt for the Grazing Elk Clan.

"I would now like to go on to the Northern Elk Clan," Taelo said when they had returned from their hunt.

"We are still in the grip of winter, but we know our way and should be able make the journey by the southern route to the sea and then north along the coast.

This will be a longer return journey, but it has its advantages," Taelo brought up the subject of continuing their journey.

"And what would these advantages be," Golden Hawk asked as he leaned forward to get closer to the fire.

"We could deliver the mounts we are taking to each clan and have a brief visit. The Elk Clan would be the first stop, the Clan of the Others the second stop and the Northern Elk Clan the third stop.

This would also be an opportunity to visit for a longer period with parents and other friends," Taelo pointed out.

"I like the idea. I would like to spend time at the Elk Clan with my grandmother," Quiet Rabbit said as she thought about the suggestion.

"Yes, and in the spring the team could gather for a celebration at our clan location," Marigold added as she thought about getting home and sharing her experiences with Meadow Flower and her parents.

"Well let's get the team ready to travel," Taelo said as he went into his lodge with Quiet Rabbit.

"So, I gather you have been thinking about spending time with your grandmother? She could ride with us to the Northern Elk Clan," Taelo suggested.

He had realized that Quiet Rabbit would stay with the Elk Clan if her grandmother did not come with them.

"I like that idea. Let's see if she is willing to ride a mount and come along," Quiet Rabbit replied.

She hoped her grandmother still had the adventurous spirit she had talked about.

For the next few cycles, Taelo and team spent time with members of the Grazing Elk Clan on training the mounts they had brought with them.

The younger Grazing Elk Clan members were eager to participate. The older hunters were in no shape to help, and it was an opportunity for the younger members to do something exciting.

"We will teach you how to capture and tame these wonderful creatures. There is a price. You must deliver six pairs of male and female mounts to the Northern Elk Clan, and you must bring one mount for each clan leader to the next gathering of the clan," Taelo explained when he offered to train the Grazing Elk Clan in how to tame the mounts.

Feather-in-the-Wind put on a show with the first few mounts and all the young women of the Grazing Elk Clan lined up to take part.

Lasher, Walker, and Arrow returned from one of their many outings with many of the wolves from the sled teams. Taelo carried treats out to the edge of the village to greet the returning wolves.

"Welcome back," he said as he crouched down and gave each of the wolves a small piece of meat.

Soon the entire team came out to greet the wolves.

"I am really pleased to get my team back," Taelo said as he thought about the next trip he was planning.

He and Golden Hawk had discussed their next adventure and had worried about their missing wolf sled teams. Now most of the wolves of all three teams had returned and would be available for that trip.

"I am so happy to have my wolf team back," Saber Scar said as he greeted them and joined in giving them treats.

He had worked for almost twenty-four moon cycles to train them. His missing team had been on his mind since the rescue of the Grazing Elk hunters.

"We will take them with us when we return home," Taelo said as he led them to the three lodges being used by his team.

A few days later the team was ready to continue on their way to the western coast.

"Thank you for all you have done for the Grazing Elk Clan. May your travels be smooth. Your lodges here will always be available to you," Fierce Badger said as the team got ready to ride out.

"We look forward to this coming gathering. Bring many extra mounts. You will have many wanting to trade for these wonderful animals," Golden Hawk said as he got on his mount.

The trail south proved to be relatively easy, and the miles melted away rapidly. It was only one cycle of the moon later when the eagle cried out as it flew over the Valley of Plenty.

"We should get ready. Taelo and Golden Hawk are near," Red Oak said as he and Quiet Pheasant looked up into the sky.

Late that afternoon scouts sent out to locate Taelo and Golden Hawk returned. They were jabbering about monsters coming toward the valley.

"I think our scouts have seen the team riding the animals Broken Spear told us about," Red Oak said with a chuckle as he discussed this with Little Otter and Talking Wren.

"I am so excited. I wonder why they chose to come here at this time," Talking Wren pondered?

"That they are coming is all I care. It will be so good to see them," Quiet Pheasant said as she thought through the arrangements for a celebration.

The greetings, hugs, the celebrations all followed in quick succession after the team arrived.

Soon Golden Hawk had Red Oak taking a ride on the mount he had brought as a gift.

"What an unbelievable feeling," Red Oak said as he returned from his first ride.

"It is the most fantastic feeling I have ever had," Talking Wren said excitedly as she turned her mount and rode off for another ride up the valley.

"I would love to follow her, but I think my mount would like a break," Little Otter said as he dismounted and watched as Quiet Pheasant followed Talking Wren up the valley.

His butt already hurt from his first ride.

The surprise was Quiet Rabbit's grandmother, Floating Cloud. She was eager to ride one of the mounts and she turned out to have a natural talent. She looked as if she had been riding all her life.

"This is one of the best days of my long life," Floating Cloud, who had just celebrated her fiftieth winter, said after returning from her ride with Quiet Rabbit.

A few sun cycles later when Taelo suggested they continue to the Clan of the Others, Golden Hawk explained that he and Busy Bee would stay in the Valley of Plenty until spring. This would give both of them a chance to spend time with their families before the next adventure.

"It is a good idea. I would have stayed but my grandmother is coming with us to the Northern Elk Clan. I will miss both of you," Quiet Rabbit said to the two of them.

"I know I promised to mind your fire and cook for this entire journey, but I have been asked by a handsome hunter to stay. He lost his mate and has been so impressed with my ability to ride that he is overlooking how old I am," Lily said quietly.

She knew this would be her last chance at finding a mate. This was the first she had let anyone know about her getting courted by one of the Elk Clan hunters.

"This calls for a celebration," Golden Hawk said as he realized what Lily was sharing with the team.

"I will arrange for a celebration of this event."

"Well, this old woman will be pleased to mind the fire and cook for the rest of the journey. Perhaps you will consider me for the next journey," Floating Cloud volunteered when she heard the news.

She wanted to travel with the team and wanted to be a contributing member. She was old but felt the same adventuresome spirit she had always carried within her. She had run away with her mate when her parents objected to the mate she had selected. She and her mate had lived by themselves for two cycles of seasons. They were accepted by the Elk Horn Clan after one of the gatherings and lived with them after that. After losing both her daughter and her mate, she had raised Quiet Rabbit. She had followed her friends, White Swan, and Quiet Pheasant when they moved to the Elk Clan.

"We are pleased you are coming with us, and I know the team will eat well around your fire," Taelo greeted the offer.

Floating Cloud's success would mean the team would have one of the best cooks in the clan guiding their cooking and Quiet Rabbit would have her only living relative with her.

A jubilant Lily accepted the generous gifts of hides and shark's teeth given her by the team.

"You will have more time to work on these hides and turn them into useful items," Busy Bee said as Lily commented about the generosity of team.

Lily, like the rest of the team, had come back with an abundance of hides, shark teeth and a few teeth of the monster from the swamp that they had never named.

She was by clan standards considered to be well to do.

And her independent spirit made her an influential entity in the clan.

"You are leaving us a well-developed member. I remember meeting Lily in the first clan meeting when she went to join the Grazing Elk Clan. She was very unsure of herself. Now she comes to us as a confident individual and leader," Red Oak said to Taelo and Golden Hawk.

Yes, she has grown since then. She kept up with all of us and displayed her true courage many times. It is nice to know you recognize her growth." Taelo said as he thought back about her rescue from the cannibals and her fear at the time.

A few sun cycles later the team left the Valley of Plenty and crossed over to the coast.

"I am looking forward to sitting in the hot spring and just thinking back on our travels," Marigold said as she rode along the edge of the water.

Broken Spear is sure to see our return. We will be telling stories of our travels for the first few evenings," Saber Scar replied.

He had a good feeling about this return. He knew he had grown and though he was sure to be kidded about the new scars across his chest, he would also be looked upon as a full member of the clan.

"It is good to have you visit us. Broken Spear has told about some of your travels, but he said he would let you tell of the last part of your travels," Burley Bear greeted the arriving team.

He wished he could have been on the journey with Taelo, but he was now the leader of the Clan of Others.

"As always we look forward to our visit and we bring with us a unique gift," Taelo said as Marigold and Saber Scar brought forward the gift mounts.

"I hope I don't break the poor animals back," Burley Bear said as he took the rope holding his mount.

The team had selected the largest mount in the herd for Burley Bear but next to him it did not seem as large as they had thought it to be.

"My mount is beautiful, and I know I will enjoy riding," Meadow Flower said as she gave Quiet Rabbit a hug.

"I am not sure I will be able to ride mine," Broken Spear said as he touched the nose of his mount.

"I will ride with you on your first ride," Taelo replied.

He had thought about Broken Spear's condition and had an idea of how to make it easier for him to ride.

As it turned out Broken Spear was easy to hold. He loved the ride and asked Taelo to teach the two women who took care of him how to ride. They would be able to hold him on the mount. This was a better idea than the one Taelo originally had thought about.

The hot spring and the rain from above was a hit with the entire team. They sat the rest of the afternoon enjoying the pool.

That evening they were called upon to tell their story for the rest of the Clan of Others.

"I do not tell stories as well as Burley Bear. And I can't tell them as good as Little Otter. I have been told of the stories Broken Spear shared about me and all those on our journey," Taelo began the stories after dinner had been eaten.

"But has he told you the stories of Saber Scar and Marigold?

"Saber Scar stand up and show your clan your new chest scars," Taelo continued as he made a point of turning Saber Scar around so everyone could see the new scars.

The clan let out a loud, "Oh" as they saw the new scars.

"Saber Scar now has the scars of the saber tooth and the scars of the giant tiger of the plains.

Team bring out the hide and the claws of the tiger," Taelo continued.

Again, Taelo waited for the response of the clan members.

The hide was the largest tiger hide anyone had ever seen.

"See the size of this beast. It was as tall as one of the mounts we have brought to you and longer by half.

Feather-in-the-Wind also faced this beast and was the first to put her knife into its chest.

Running Stag shot it with five arrows.

Then the beast charged Saber Scar. He stood his ground and lunged forward with his spear. But the tiger deflected the spear and would have killed Saber Scar.

Suddenly there was a loud war cry and an object hit the tiger on its side and knocked him down.

Saber Scar bravely jumped in toward the tiger.

Feather-in-the-Wind's blade was still in the tiger's ribs. Saber Scar pulled it out and repeatedly stabbed the tiger.

Running Stag lunged in and hit the tiger in the head with his war hammer. Together the three killed the tiger.

The tiger had marked Saber Scar with new scars.

It was Feather-in-the-Wind that the hit the tiger in the side. She used herself as a weapon. In doing so she broke some ribs, but she saved Saber Scar.

Saber Scar saved all three because of his strength and his focus. He lasted long enough to kill the tiger with multiple stabs to the heart.

Saber Scar collapsed immediately after the tiger was dead.

It took Saber Scar and Feather-in-the-Wind fourteen sun cycles to recover enough to travel," Taelo said as he looked around at his audience.

He had them in his spell.

"But if you think Saber Scar is brave, you should have been there when Marigold saved me from the river monster," Taelo began on his next story.

"Team bring out the hide of the river monster so everyone can see its size," Taelo called out.

The clan members let out a long OOH as Marigold, Running Stag, Quiet Rabbit, and Feather-in-the-Wind pulled the hide into the center. It was as long as three spears and as wide as one. It almost covered the giant tiger hide that was already in the center.

"This monster came out of the river and chased us. Golden Hawk and I faced this beast.

Saber Scar's spear pinned it to the ground but with its tail the monster hurled Saber Scar through the air into the marsh.

Busy Bee and Quiet Rabbit both put spears into its side but that was not enough.

An angry Marigold came out and pushed both spears farther into the beast and then she proceeded to bash the animal in the head with her war hammer. We all learned that it was not wise to make Marigold angry," Taelo said with a chuckle.

There was loud vocal agreement in, "Don't make Marigold mad," from the entire clan.

They were enjoying the stories Taelo was telling.

"Now I would like to let Marigold and Saber Scar tell the stories they remember," Taelo said as he waved the two forward.

"We must tell you about Taelo and the Bear, the Bees and the Shark," Saber Scar continued the story telling.

The story telling went on long into the night but finally the time came when everyone retired for the night.

The next day Taelo had a private session with Broken Spear.

"You know your travels keep me active and alive," Broke Spear began the discussion.

"What you tell me keeps me from being killed," Taelo replied.

"I did not tell you about the shark, or about the river monster and you seem to have handled that quiet well," Broken Spear continued.

"Your wisdom and vision have helped me since I was a young boy. It is always something I seek," Taelo continued.

He was not sure where this meeting was going.

"Your next trip will be to the north. It will not be as long as the other two trips, but it will be more dangerous.

You will fight the cold.

A bear as big or bigger as the one you killed and that is more territorial will hunt your team.

Finally, you will face a clan of people who have slaves. They are different than the cannibals in that they do not eat those they conquer but they enslave them.

You must not confront them directly but sequentially attack, retreat, and draw them out until you have worn them down. I will see who from our clan should accompany you," Broken Spear said quietly.

"I trust your guidance. Saber Scar and Marigold were a bed rock of support. My stories were not exaggerations of their contribution. I hope they can accompany us," Taelo replied.

He had not questioned that they would accompany him.

"Yes, I am sure they will want to go with you. I was thinking of perhaps two more," Broke Spear said with a chuckle.

He had seen the battles and knew more help would be needed.

Chapter 24: Home to the White Feather

The twin snow covered mountains, their green skirts of dark green pine interspersed with white spots where dominant oak or maple held their ground during the warmer months greeted the travelers on their return. Only previous experience let them rediscover the small frozen lake totally covered by a thick layer of snow.

Always a favorite place, it once again served as the point to stop and prepare for the next short leg of the trip up the river to the branch leading back to the valley and the lodge of the Northern Elk Clan.

The team was now down to two pack mounts and six gift mounts. Floating Cloud insisted she take care of the pack mounts.

"It will be good to return to the Northern Elk Clan," Quiet Rabbit said.

She realized she now thought of it as her home.

"Yes, I want to ride the valley and experience it in a new way," Feather-in-the-Wind added.

The distance between the various clan homes had in the past been measured in four to five handfuls of sun cycles of the sun for the three western clans. Now on the mounts it was just short of two handfuls.

"I have heard so much about the valley of the Northern Elk Clan. I also grew up with the stories of gathering salt and the cave of the elders and the hot rain. I now know the stories were real. I hope I get a chance to see if I can still spear the fish and qualify to carry salt," Floating Cloud said.

"We will stay here tonight. Let's prepare for our arrival," Taelo said as the team reached the point in between the mountain twins where the team stayed on the first trip into the valley.

True to her word Floating Cloud performed Lily's duty of preparing the cooking fire.

Taelo and Running Stag went to the lake to catch some fish. They dug down into the snow of the fully covered lake and cut a hole in the ice.

Quiet Rabbit and Feather-in-the-Wind tended to the mounts. Afterwards the two took their slings and hunted for rabbit.

"This team does not even discuss what they are going to do. They just work together in harmony," Floating Cloud thought as she went about the duties Lily had so carefully instructed her about.

"I can see why she was so disorientated as to whether she wanted to accept a new mate or just come with the team."

"I hope Lily recruits her mate to accompany her on the next journey as I suggested," Floating Cloud continued her personal thoughts.

If she was accepted by the team, she would personally like to have Lily as well. It would make taking care of such a large team much easier.

There was only one large fish. Luckily, or maybe just because the two best people with a sling hunted together, there were two rabbits for each of them.

"Does this team eat so well each time it stops," Floating Cloud asked as she tended to the roasting rabbits with the rest of the team.

"Only when Feather-in-the-Wind and Quiet Rabbit hunt together," Running Stag replied with a smile.

He was remembering his complaint about Feather-in-the-Wind getting all the game and then having to watch in fear as the tiger attacked her.

"Yes, in this whole journey, I do not recall a time when the team did not have a good to great dinner," Taelo replied.

"Oh, what about the times you cooked," Quiet Rabbit teased.

Taelo was one of the best cooks on the team and always came up with some new twist in his cooking. He and Lily had often collaborated in the meal preparation.

One of the best meals had been after the shark attack. They had eaten shark, small clams, oysters, and seaweed on the side.

"Yes, I suppose you could blame me for some of the poorer dinners. Luckily, we had Lily there to save the day," Taelo replied with a coy smile.

The way the team always ate his meals gave him confidence in his cooking ability.

"Well, I will be pleased to try to fill Lily's place on the next journey. I did suggest that she recruit her mate to join. So maybe there will be two of us around the cooking fire," Floating Cloud floated her idea.

"That is a great idea. I really hope Lily follows your advice," Taelo said as he smiled at Quiet Rabbit.

He now knew Lily had gotten the same advice from at least three of them.

The next day after cleaning up the camp and leaving it ready for the next visit, the team took up the last part of their journey.

From high in the sky came an eagle cry. It flew out ahead of them and later gave the same cry over the valley of the Northern Elk Clan.

"Oh, that is such a wonderful sound," White Swan said as she looked up to see the eagle flying in up the small river and into the valley.

"I am looking forward to meeting my grown son," Wise Council replied as he thought about Running Stag.

He knew the trip was the transition from a boy to a full man.

"He is so lucky to have taken this trip with a young woman like Feather-in-the-Wind," Golden Flower said as she thought about her son and Feather-in-the-Wind.

She was sure the two were meant to be mates.

"I am sure everyone grew. These trips have opened the world to all of us," Grey Fox Running joined the conversation.

"We know that to the South there are people who came before us. We know new people are coming from the North. Now we will learn what is to the East," he continued.

"Here is our river into the valley," Running Stag said as they reached the juncture of the small river from the valley joining the larger one.

"I hear the eagle cry. They will be ready when we arrive," Quiet Rabbit said as she pointed to the eagle high above.

"Well, it appears the whole clan is out to greet us," Taelo said as he held up his spear with the golden feather.

White Swan saw the spear being hoisted and raised her own with her white swan feather.

"These animals they ride are beautiful," she commented as she took in those arriving.

"I do not see Golden Hawk and I do not recognize the fifth rider. They must have gone to the Valley of Plenty first," Grey Fox Running said as he looked over the team.

"The fifth rider is Quiet Rabbit's grandmother, but she looks much younger as she rides her mount," White Swan replied.

"Look at the wolf pack that is following the team. I do not see any sleds. I wonder what happened to them," Grey Fox Running continued.

"Well so much for official protocol," Wise Council said as both White Swan and Golden Flower rushed out to greet the on-coming team.

Everyone else followed but held back away from the mounts.

Lasher led the wolf pack up to his familiar area in the compound. This was his home.

"We have brought special gifts.

From the Elk Clan and the Valley of Plenty and Red Oak and Quiet Pheasant, we bring four mounts loaded with meat.

For White Swan and Gray Fox Running we have a mount each," Taelo said as he stepped back from hugs of both White Swan and Gray Fox Running.

Quiet Rabbit handed the ropes of each mount to White Swan and Gray Fox Running. She had worked hard at taming each mount.

"And for my favorite parents, I bring you each a mount," Running Stag said as he handed over the ropes to the two mounts he had been leading.

"And for all the rest of you to learn to ride, I bring two more mounts," Feather-in-the-Wind said from where she was standing on her mount.

The thought had just magically appeared. She had been struggling as to who she would give her mounts.

A cheer went up from the entire Northern Elk Clan.

"Well, I see our Feather-in-the-Wind has gained another new skill," White Swan commented as she watched the young woman ride standing on her mount around the edge of the ring formed by the clan members.

"Yes, she is the best rider on the team," Quiet Rabbit said as she gave hugs all around.

"Let's get all of you on your mounts. We will take you out on your maiden ride. We can unpack later," Taelo suggested.

"I will take care of the pack mounts and get them unloaded," Floating Cloud volunteered.

"I will give short rides to any person wanting to try," Feather-in-the-Wind volunteered as Taelo helped White Swan get mounted.

The rest of the afternoon was spent riding and watching as each of the clan members took turns riding. Once the pack mounts were unloaded, they became available and there were eight mounts for the clan members to ride.

"This clan has seen many things. The only other activity that brought them together like this one was the fight against the dire wolves. This one is much more fun," Wise Council commented later as the team sat outside the lodge watching Feather-in-the-Wind and Floating Cloud giving rides.

"Yes, and I remember many activities Taelo, and Golden Hawk initiated that brought the Elk Clan as a whole closer together," White Swan added.

"What is the next adventure you have planned," Grey Fox Running asked Taelo who was sitting with Quiet Rabbit in the hot water pool.

The two were relaxing and enjoying the hot water and the cold air.

"The team has discussed a journey to the north. We will set out later this spring," Taelo replied as he watched the sun slowly set behind the mountains.

He was home where the White Feather ruled over a peaceful valley.

The End

Taelo: Dangerous Passage

Dedication:

To My Daughter and Sons who constantly inspire me.

Chapter 1: Uneasy Feeling

Much of the water falling from its mighty height turned into a fine mist and then as it fell the cold air froze the mist and it landed gently on the valley below as a fine delicate snowflake. Each flake formed its unique and delicate beautiful pattern. It would drift down and land on top of the ever-growing mound below.

The water not turned into mist cascaded down from its height into the ice-covered pool, open where the water from above kept it from freezing over. The water left the pool below a layer of ice into the small river that ran along the cliffs past the compound to join another stream and then flow on toward the sea to the west.

Taelo stood in the compound outside of the main lodge and watched the early morning sun turn the mist into a mix of pink, grey and then a glowing yellow. Briefly a section of rainbow graced the sky. It was a cold, frozen display of the beauty of winter.

He had heard the call. He and the team would head North and backtrack the path Semper, and his followers had traveled.

The Journey of the Heart had been to the South. The Journey of Discovery had been to the East. This coming journey was a journey he was being called to go on by the ancients. There was an ominous nature to this call that he could not quite grasp. He would consult Broken Spear, the Seer of the Others to get a better understanding.

That afternoon as he and Quiet Rabbit sat in the hot water pool Grey Fox Running asked about the next journey. He and White Swan knew their son would soon take his next journey and had conjectured if it would be to the North.

"When the weather begins to warm, we will set out on a journey to the North. This journey may be the hardest and the least enjoyable. Semper and his followers came down from the North and stayed to the valley between two mountain ranges.

Unlike those we rescued from the cannibals, Semper and his followers were migrating here in hopes of finding a better area. He was keeping track as best he could of the places he traveled through.

Running Stag had been listening to the conversation and shared his memories.

"I remember traveling along the coast. My father had been warned about the inland route. Huge bears would hunt people down. He said it was too dangerous to go that way. The journey down the coast was very difficult. We kept going out on a point and then had to come back to almost where we had started.

Then we ran into the cannibals. You saved us and you know the rest of the story," Running Stag shared as he talked about his journey from the North.

He and his group had fought with and lost a battle with the cannibals. The cannibals immediately broke the legs of all the warriors. They were to be eaten first.

All of the older members were kept in a compound unless they were brought out to do work. The women were made to the work around the camp.

The younger members were ignored unless they somehow caught someone's attention and then a nasty beating normally occurred.

Running Stag had been rescued by Taelo and together they had gone back and freed the few people left alive. Two of those people were Running Stag's mother and father.

Taelo had spent time with all the members he had rescued that were still residing in the Northern Elk Clan. From them Taelo began to understand the environment and the potential dangers that the journey to the North would pose.

Taelo had already discussed this with Golden Hawk, Busy Bee, and Quiet Rabbit. The four of them were deep into the planning and preparation for the upcoming journey.

"I am glad we took the other journey's first. This will be a very challenging journey for all of us," Taelo shared with the group around him.

"Yes, it may be dangerous and challenging, but I have been talking to all the team members and they are eager to go on this journey.

Even my grandmother is ready. She has been riding the mounts and working with the wolves. She plans to be a leading member of the team," Quiet Rabbit replied.

She too was ready to travel with Taelo.

Their previous journeys had made all of them grow and appreciate the world around them. They had returned from every journey with newfound knowledge that helped the Elk Clan enjoy a richer life.

There was no shortage of additional volunteers.

A few weeks later, Lily and her new mate arrived.

"I was afraid if we waited too long, we would miss your next journey. You know Slow Runner my mate and you know he is not so slow," Lily said on her arrival as she proudly highlighted her mate.

She felt so lucky to find someone of Slow Runner's stature and maturity. He was truly her second soul mate.

She had lost the first to the battles with the cannibals.

"We are pleased you came. Taelo has told us many tales of your bravery but many more about your cooking ability. I am sure he will be pleased to have you on the team for the journey to the north," White Swan said in greeting the two as they led their mounts through the gate.

"It is good that you chose to come. I was feeling challenged to prepare for the journey to the north. You will know what you need to pull together to make the journey easier," Floating Cloud said when greeting Lily.

"This will be a very hard journey for me. It will bring back terrible memories of suffering, pain, and loss. Taelo rescued me and knows how hard this will be," Lily replied.

The memory of watching her first mate being tortured and devoured in a wild feast by the cannibals, made her feel faint.

Slow Runner quietly supported her as he noticed. He too remembered the horror they had all lived through.

"The team's Journey of Discovery gave me a chance to grow and to learn to manage my pain and loss. Taelo's courage became my courage. Taelo's vision has become my vision," Lily continued after a brief pause.

Those around her were surprised at her emotional reply.

"I know how she feels. Taelo has been my hero since the time he returned and freed my mother and father. I was very lucky. I know the pain and sorrow that Lily speaks of. It will be a tough trip for me as well," Running Stag said quietly to Feather-in-the-Wind.

"I am beginning to understand why Wise Owl created and gave the title of warriors at large to both Taelo and Golden Hawk. They have given each of us a second life.

I too understand the loss of family. Mine live on, but I can never return to the condor and the mountains to the south. But I have new purpose and I will follow Taelo and Quiet Rabbit anywhere they wish to go," Feather-in-the-Wind replied to Running Stag.

The smell of spring was in the air, but the snow had not yet yielded the valley to the flowers and the grass.

The river still had ice along its banks.

The promise was only in the air, not yet in the strength of the sun. The valley and all within were coming awaked after a long cold winter.

Taelo's core team had continued their tradition of having a meal together once a week. They had found a comfortable location down by the river where they could sit and watch the sunset.

Once again it was Taelo's turn to cook. This time he was showboating. He had been out and had been lucky enough to bag a young boar. He and Lasher had run it down and brought it back for this occasion.

He had sought out both Lily and Floating Cloud for cooking guidance and had carefully followed their advice.

"Well, both of you will know if I followed your detailed instructions well enough," he said as he turned away from the fire.

The coals had slowly cooked the young boar. The aroma was tantalizing. Everyone was eager to get a piece.

All the members of the team were present. There was Lily and Slow Runner, Floating Cloud, Quiet Rabbit's grandmother sitting next to Quiet Rabbit, Golden Hawk and Busy Bee, Running Stag and Feather-in-the-Wind.

Saber Scar and Marigold were not present because they had returned to their own clan for a short visit before the next journey.

"Tonight, we will discuss the upcoming journey and how to prepare for it. I have talked to everyone who has recently come from the north.

Golden Hawk has agreed to work with each of you to organize what will be needed and each of our responsibilities," Taelo announced as he began to cut and pass out the sizzling boar's meat.

"Each of you has suggested items that we will need. We will leave with more supplies for this trip than we did for other trips. What we have learned from talking with those who have recently arrived is to expect it to remain cold and that we may not find the food we need.

Hunting will also be hard. All of your input is useful," Golden Hawk added.

"I have an uneasy feeling about this journey. I think that a trip to the old ones and a visit with Broken Spear is in order. When do you think we should go," Taelo asked Golden Hawk?

"As soon as possible," the entire team spoke at once.

They all had the same vision of sitting in the hot spring pool located in the cave of the Others.

___Chapter 2: Visit to the Others___

Spring was threatening to warm the air and to turn the valley green. The melting snows had greatly increased the flow over the fall at the far end of the valley and the cold water flowing energetically past the lodge area, no longer supported ice on the banks.

The change of weather immediately energized the team to act.

They would go and visit the Others and seek Broken Spear's consul.

"It is a beautiful day for you to start your trip to the home of the Other's. Have a good visit. We will organize all the food and goods we will need for our trip," Floating Cloud said.

She, Lily, and Slow Runner were staying behind. They had volunteered to get all the gear that had been identified collected, organized, and ready for the trip.

"Thank you for volunteering for this thankless but very important task," Taelo said addressing the three.

The trip south through the Marker Mountains, down to the sea went smoothly. Lasher, Arrow, and Walker were the only wolves accompanying the team. Each walked beside their owner.

Lasher and Taelo were inseparable.

Arrow had a similar relationship with Running Stag and Walker was devoted to Feather-in-the-Wind.

"It will be good to visit with Burley Bear and Meadow Flower," Quiet Rabbit commented as they came out on the coast to the thundering spring waves.

"Yes, and I will enjoy bathing in the warm water pool," Busy Bee said as she dashed to the edge of the ocean.

They all walked to the edge of the water and dipped their hands into the water.

"The water is still very, very cold, but even in the summer it remains cold," Busy Bee noted.

"Yes, the sea currents are from the north and remain cool throughout the summer months," Golden Hawk added as he joined the rest of the team as they walked skirting the waves.

The beach ended and the team walked single file along the base of the cliff. This approach would bring them to the small stream that made its way to the sea from the cave of the others.

"Look ahead and you will see our friend Burley Bear," Running Stag commented as he bolted ahead.

Both Burley Bear and Meadow Flower were waiting.

Besides them were two other familiar friends, Saber Scar and Marigold.

"I am honored that the leader of the Others personally came out to greet me," Taelo said as he gave Burley Bear a hug.

He turned and gave Meadow Flower one as well.

"I hope you and Marigold had a good visit with your clan," Taelo continued as he greeted the other two who had also become very close friends.

"Yes, we have enjoyed our time here, but we are ready for our next journey with you," Saber Scar replied.

"Your scars make you look as fierce as I know you are," Quiet Rabbit said putting her hand on Saber Scar's chest.

The two of them had a special relationship.

Quiet Rabbit was the one who had stitched every one of the scars on Saber Scar's chest. He had one set of scars from a saber-tooth tiger that attacked Taelo and one set of scars from the lion he, Feather-in-the-Wind and Running Stag had killed during the Journey of Discovery.

"Your arrival is timely, and the entire clan is waiting to share the evening meal and to listen to the tales you will be asked to tell," Burley Bear said as he turned and led the way back to the entrance of the cave.

Broken Spear, the seer of the Others sat at the entrance of the cave. As always, he was attended by two of the older women of the clan.

He was by this time an ancient and most revered figure.

"We have been waiting for your visit. Tonight, we eat well. You will be asked to tell more stories of your many travels. Tomorrow you and I will talk about your journey North," Broken Spear said in greeting.

Taelo was his personal inspiration. He had first seen Taelo through the eyes of an eagle during Taelo's naming ceremony.

At that time Broken Spear had not known he was seeing one of the new ones.

Quiet Fox and Little Doe were standing behind Broken Spear. Quiet Fox had stepped aside and put Burley Bear into the clan's leadership position.

"It is good to see our Eagle return. We look forward to this evening and to many more visits," Quiet Fox said in greeting.

"Well, I am sure we will learn what is up. There is something in the air that says we will be surprised by something the clan has decided," Taelo said to Quiet Rabbit as they were led into the clan's living area.

This was the first time they had been so formally greeted.

After they had been shown the area where they would stay and given a few moments to put their things down, they were led to the central area.

There they were served a variety of meats, cooked roots, and barley.

The cooking of the Others was similar to their own, but the salting and spicing was unique. It was always a surprise at the flavors that were different but very enjoyable.

"I always look forward to the meals here," Feather-in-the-Wind commented as she ate her second piece of meat.

"I don't know where you put all the food that you eat," Running Stag commented in a jealous tone.

He could never eat as much as Feather-in-the-Wind and yet she was half his size.

"Let the story telling begin," Burley Bear announced once he saw that Taelo and his team had finished eating.

"I will begin with the story of how I met Taelo."

Several people had previously told the story of Burley Bear's first encounter with Taelo. This was the first time Burley Bear was going to tell his own version.

It was clear he had matured to a higher level of self-confidence.

The ground slapping response of his audience also signaled that this was a special event.

"This will be interesting," Taelo whispered to Quiet Rabbit.

"I begin with the trickery the Elk Clan displayed the first time we encountered them. Our food shortage was severe. I was out hunting for deer or elk. Then I smelled the odor of smoking meat. I followed my nose to the edge of a cliff. Carefully I peered over the edge of the cliff at a hunting party of the new ones below.

They were drying strips of meat.

My mouth watered.

I am the largest among us, but you all know I am a ghost when I want to spy on someone. No one but Broken Spear has ever been able to see me coming.

Somehow the leader of the new ones sensed he was being watched. He sent out several scouts to determine if there was someone watching.

I quickly retreated back to our camp on the beach.

We all knew our camp was not in a good location, but Broken Spear had declared this was the location we would meet the person who would lead us on a new path.

We would meet the man of the Eagle.

On my return to camp, I organized a raiding party. I was determined we would get the meat this hunting party possessed.

Quiet Fox was not supportive of this venture, but he knew the clan was on the verge of starvation. He considered the alternatives and allowed me to take a team to see if we could steal the meat.

He gave strict orders not to kill anyone or even injure them.

This was a tough challenge for a raiding party.

We were brash and brave and knew we would come home with all the meat and be seen as heroes. We found a place down the beach and waited for the hunting party to appear.

"YES," we all whispered when the loaded travois being pulled by four warriors appeared. We waited until they had committed to their direction and then we came swooping out of the forest.

What a surprise. Even with the loaded travois the warriors were close to out running us. Slowly we gained on the travois they were pulling. When we were a spear's throw away, the four dropped the travois and accelerated and disappeared into the woods.

We triumphantly turned the travois and hastily pulled them back to camp.

We were triumphant and were loud and brash in our boasting. We were thoroughly embarrassed when we took the cover off the load and realized the load was almost all wood with only a thin covering of meat.

Instead of being treated like heroes, we were greeted with laughter. The old warriors had their day pointing out to us the difference between a piece of wood and buffalo meat.

"Well, it seems you have met your match in trickery," Quiet Fox publicly praised me.

"Though I was angry, even I had a good laugh. Such trickery can only be admired.

I now know Red Oak the current leader of the Elk Clan was the person who planned the trick. We have laughed together, several times, about that evening.

He has told me about how hard he found it to keep running while laughing to the point he had tears in his eyes. He and his men stopped at the edge of the woods and collapsed in laughter.

He told me that if we had been able to keep up with them, they would have surrendered in laughter.

The audience all let out a light whooping in appreciation of the story.

"So, you can understand how I felt later when two beautiful women and two scraggly boys trying to be warriors approached our camp. I looked up and down the beach and into the forest.

I knew this was another trick. I just could not figure out what kind of trick it might be.

Why would the new ones come to us with gifts?

Never before had any of the new ones even acknowledged our existence. The best treatment we ever received was to be left alone.

What possibly could they be up to?

I kept looking up the beach and into the forest. Something was up.

Immediately I knew these two were trying to find out what we were doing. They were spying.

I reached for the one that seemed to be in charge.

I was just going to get her attention.

Then.... Well then...," Burley Bear stopped and looked slowly around, "...then the lights went out."

The whooping of the clan members was thunderous.

Burley Bear raised his hands into the air and slowly turned a circle.

"I woke up in my lodge. It took me a moment to recall where I was and who I was. I was furious. I came roaring out of my lodge ready to kill the warrior that had blind-sided me.

As all of you know, no one in the clan has ever beaten me in combat. What did I find?

There sitting next to Quiet Fox was a small, barely above my waist, boy.

Where was the warrior that had turned out the lights, I angrily shouted?

The boy stood up and put out his hand and said, "I am Taelo, claw of the eagle, the claw that strikes,"

Burley Bear clawed the air in an exaggerated motion and slowly turned with a grimace on his face.

The clan members were whooping as they watched Burley Bear.

"Then high in the sky, an eagle cried, and I realized that Broken Spear's prediction that the "Man of the Eagle" would come to guide the clan. His prediction had come true!"

I stopped in my tracks. At that moment I realized Taelo was to lead us to our new home.

You all know that Taelo made me see. He made me see new possibilities. He made me see new ways of doing things. He made me see a new future for our clan.

He found us our cave, he found us the whale and he has given us new purpose.

The audience was slapping the ground and whooping in appreciation of the story.

And now a story by Taelo, the claw that strikes," Burly Bear said as he sat down and urged Taelo to stand up.

Taelo waited for the thunderous hand slapping on the floor to subside. The audience continued to give Burley Bear feedback to his great story. This by far was the best version they had ever heard.

"Well, done. You have truly become the leader of the clan," Broken Spear quietly gave his praise to Burley Bear.

Taelo stood up after the clan quieted down. He walked slowly around the circle made by the clan members.

"I will not try to match the Burley Bear's story telling talent.

You all know he can grow a story from a small fish to the size of a whale," Taelo said as he watched the clan members.

"The story I will tell is a new story. It is about a hero.   It is about a hero that has saved my life many times.

No, it is not about Burley Bear who is a hero that has saved my life.

No, it is not about Meadow Flower, Saber Scar or Marigold who have also saved my life.

It is not about Golden Hawk, Busy Bee or Quiet Rabbit nor is it about Feather-in-the-Wind or Running Stag.

You now know that I am constantly in need of saving," Taelo began his introduction.

The clan members were listening intently.

This hero walks among you, and you do not recognize him but instead fear him.

He is here this evening and you do not see him," Taelo said slowly in a hushed tone.

He had everyone leaning in to listen to him.

"When the moon is full, you will hear his brethren and cousins. When you are on a hunt you are often challenged by his brothers.

Look around you. Do you see this hero," Taelo asked almost in a whisper?

The audience was quiet. They were looking around for the hero. They were puzzled.

"Enemy" Taelo said in a loud commanding voice.

Lasher sprang to Taelo's side as he let out a deep growl through his snarling lip raised mouth.

The hair stood up on the back of his neck and he slowly turned his head as his snarl continued.

The front row of clan members froze where they sat.

"Friend" Taelo said in the same voice.

Lasher sat down at his side. He acted as if there was no one around him.

"This is the hero I have just described," Taelo said as he reached down and scratched Lasher behind his ear.

Lasher was there when we were attacked by the thirty warriors on our Journey of the Heart. He attacked and caused total confusion and fear in those young warriors. But he only bit them on their legs and was not out to kill.

On our return it was Lasher that stopped the knife meant for my heart. He crushed the wrist of the attacker and gave me time to finish the battle.

His purpose was to protect Feather-in-the-Wind, but he had sensed the danger and had attacked immediately.

When Broken Spear sent us to rescue the people coming from the north, it was Lasher that guided the three sleds through the blinding snow back to the compound.

Once in the camp, his behavior and actions let Running Stag know that he wanted to go back into the storm.

He came through the blinding storm to find me.

The storm was overwhelming, and I was lost when suddenly I was knocked over by Lasher. Those around me raised their spears trying to defend me.

"He is the reason we will live," I declared as I pushed aside the spears.

Taelo was acting in slow motion as he told his story.

I tied a line to Lasher and the other end to my wrist.

For the rest of the trip, we all blindly followed Lasher. Many hours later we heard the barking and howling of his partners as they called Lasher back to the compound.

He is the reason I am here to tell his tale.

He is my hero.

But his story continues.

When the dire wolves attacked outside of our Northern camp the leader of the pack attacked me, but Lasher clamped down on the dire wolf leader's throat. He would not let go even when his leg was broken. The dire wolf, three times larger than Lasher, lost his life to him.

Once again, Lasher saved my life.

He is my hero.

Look at this hero. Come meet him if you are brave enough," Taelo finished his story, and he crouched down to hug Lasher.

The hand beating on the floor was a respectable response. It was not as thunderous as Burley Bear's earlier story.

This was a different story than the clan had expected but the younger members came forward to greet the new hero that had been introduced to them.

Chapter 3: Broken Spear's Guidance

The yellow flowers growing from the roots of the large green leaves floating in the water at the lower end of the pool reminded Taelo of the mountain lake to the South where the team had found them covering almost all the water. The weather there had been warm and most of the plants they found growing there did not survive in this northern clime.

Meadow Flower had brought a ball of roots back and had successfully established them in the cooler water at the end of the pool. The plant had flourished and produced large yellow blooms and the center of the flower produced multiple seeds that when roasted had a delicate, nutty taste.

She now served them as the team sat around the evening fire and chatted. She added to the experience by also having a warm honey water drink.

The following morning Taelo watched as a mount with three riders was slowly making its way back to the cave.

It was Broken Spear. He was sandwiched between his two attendants on what looked like a leather bundle. This allowed him to see over the person in front of him.

"Good Morning. I see that you have been waiting in my morning meeting area," Broken Spear said in greeting as the three arrived.

Taelo watched as the rider in back slid off and helped Broken Spear dismount. She then helped him to slowly walk to the edge of the pool.

"Good Morning, I hope I am not on your rock," Taelo replied.

"Good Morning, may I join both of you," Golden Hawk said as he approached from the caves common area.

Taelo came to the edge and together the three made their way to the center of the pool and sat down in the warm water.

"I must thank you again for giving me this mount. She is large enough to carry the three of us.

I take a ride the first thing every morning.

Then on special evenings we go out again for a sunset ride.

It has changed my life.

My two companions love it as much as I do. I am beginning to believe they take better care of the mount then they do me," Broken Spear said with a chuckle.

"I understand how the mount can change one's life. We could not have traveled as far as we did on our *Journey of Discovery*.

It also allowed the team to travel even when one of us was hurt," Taelo replied as he thought about riding his mount while still weak from his recovery from the wounds inflicted by the giant brown bear.

The bear had grasped him and driven her claws through his back muscles and had damaged something deep inside.

What followed was a period of time when he had spent many sun cycles in discussion with the ancestors. He was told that it was not yet his time.

"On your journey to the North, you will need both your mounts and your wolf teams. But even more important you will need a bigger team," Broken Spear spoke quietly.

"Have you had your morning meal," Taelo asked.

"No. Let's go have it together," Broken Spear replied.

"I see that Golden Hawk, Taelo and Broken Spear are coming toward us," Quiet Rabbit commented to Busy Bee.

"I am sure they are after something to eat," Busy Bee replied as she stirred the coals and put a spit through a salt lathered fish they had prepared.

"Come sit with us and share the breakfast conversation," Broken Spear said as he stopped at the spot he had prepared for the meeting.

Burley Bear and Meadow Flower, Saber Scar and Marigold and Sharp Blade and his partner Single Leaf came over as if signaled.

"I see this has been planned," Golden Hawk said as Busy Bee sat beside him.

Taelo waved and signaled to Feather-in-the-Wind and Running Stag. They came quietly over and found a place to sit.

"Yes, this is of my doing. I wanted to talk to all of you at once. I have flown with the Eagle and have seen much of what is in your journey to the North.

On your *Journey of Discovery* to the East I spent many troubling days with the ancients during the time Taelo visited with them.

They know that on each of these journeys Taelo must deal with a life and death situation. If he deals with it correctly, he lives.

If he deals with it poorly, he is likely to die," Broken Spear began.

"Our very first meal at this cave, with Taelo, was whale meat. I saved some dried whale meat for these many seasons. We will have a morning whale meat stew with seeds from Meadow Flower's yellow flower and some milk from my own mount. The meal has been seasoned and prepared by our best cooks," Broken Spear said as he signaled his cooking team into action.

"Please have them rescue the fish I have roasting over the fire," Quiet Rabbit said pointing over to where the fish could be seen steaming.

"Yes, that will surely complement the stew," Broken Spear replied as he signaled to his cooks.

The aroma of the fish was very appealing to him.

"I have not been able to see the most dangerous part of the journey to the North. However, the situation was discussed among the ancients.

You must understand that though I was there in my mind, it was very hard to directly converse with them.

Taelo was there as well and often spoke to them. Do you remember your discussions with them," Broken Spear said looking at Taelo.

"This is something I have shared only with Quiet Rabbit," Taelo began as he looked around.

He absent-mindedly scratched Lasher behind his ears.

"Even then I have only shared a small portion of the discussions I had with the Ancients.

"I knew if I shared even a small part of my discussions with the Ancients, Golden Hawk would have had me bound to my mount for the remainder of the journey," Taelo said with a smile and a nod to his friend.

"Yes, I did discuss and argue the appropriate actions to take for many situations that they posed to me. It seemed to be a test of some sort. I was trying to make sense of it all when I awoke to Quiet Rabbit trying to feed me some of Lily's stew. I figured I had passed the test," Taelo continued

"Yes, indeed it was a test of sorts.

Once you left, I was locked out as well. They told me to enjoy my time with the Eagle.

I still wonder whether they meant the one I often fly with or the brash young warrior that enriches my life," Broken Spear continued with a smile and a grunt.

In a rare moment of emotion, he had tears in his eyes.

High in the sky above the valley an Eagle let out a loud cry.

Just then the breakfast stew was served. Pieces of the fish were also placed on a leaf for each person.

The timing allowed Broken Spear to regain his composure.

"The danger on this journey comes at several different locations.

The danger from other humans comes at the point in the journey when you decide to return home.

On the way home there will be an ultimate trial and it includes Quiet Rabbit.

The other danger will be faced twice, and this danger is once again from a bear," Broken Spear continued.

"This bear will not be talked to. It is the largest bear in existence, and it controls its territory against all trespassers. It is a bear that hunts down its prey and humans are just another animal to hunt," Broken Spear said as he looked at each of the members sitting around.

"I suggested sending thirty of our warriors to accompany you on the journey.

Burly Bear pointed out the logistical problems of having a small army accompany you. So, I suggested sending the most powerful warriors. And here they sit. Here are our team members for the journey to the North," Broken Spear concluded as he pointed to each of the couples sitting around for breakfast.

"Burley Bear, are you and Meadow Flower coming with us," Golden Hawk asked as Broken Spear's message hit home?

"Yes, Quiet Fox has agreed to lead the clan in my absence. Meadow Flower and I are very excited to again make a journey with the team.

"This is wonderful," both Busy Bee and Quiet Rabbit spoke in unison.

"I am sure with Burley Bear in the lead, even the dangerous bear you have warned us about will see us and give way," Taelo said as he went to Burly Bear and gave him a hug.

He then turned to Sharp Blade and Single Leaf and welcomed them to the team.

"It is time for me to take my morning walk," Broken Spear said as he got up and was immediately attended to by his two helpers.

"I am sure he will have more to tell me later and if not, I will have several questions to discuss with him," Taelo said as he watched Broken Spear begin his walk.

"Follow me. We have been preparing for this journey ever since Saber Scar and Marigold returned to us. We listened to Broken Spear's description of the conditions of the journey, and we have prepared our equipment to match the challenge," Burley Bear said as he led the way across the compound.

They approached what appeared to be a huge circular object covered by a large hide. Saber Scar and Sharp Blade crawled under and raised a pole at its center. The hide went up and eight sleds were now visible.

"Look at each sled. Each is larger than the ones we made before. There is always room for one person to sleep under the sled covering. The sleds hook together to form a tight wall and the hide serving as the roof can be quickly attached to each sled," Burley Bear began the explanation.

"Here is a really exciting feature. The sleds have been matched to travois poles. See the grooves in the poles. The sled runners match the grooves.

They can be mounted on the travois and pulled by the mounts," Saber Scar talked rapidly as he and Sharp Blade strapped one of the sleds to the travois poles.

Single Leaf brought in a mount and the travois was attached to a shoulder harness designed for the mount.

"This is amazing. How did you decide on nine sleds," Feather-in-the-Wind asked as she went to each one and took in the intricate work?

"Broken Spear gave us the number of sleds we needed. Did he miss someone," Burley Bear said looking at Taelo.

"No, I am sure he is right about the number. I am wondering about the wolves to pull these sleds. Where do we get them," Taelo said as he walked around and took in the work that had been done.

"And who participated in getting all this work done," Taelo asked?

"Everyone in the clan contributed time to this effort. It brought all of us closer together.

Our winter months have been extremely busy and the wood softening in the hot pool took up much of the space there," Meadow Flower chimed in.

She had been a key organizer of the sled building, wood bending and binding. The sleds were her prime accomplishment.

"Where will we get all the wolves we need for this venture," Quiet Rabbit inquired?

Burley Bear stood up. "Let me count. I know you have three teams. White Swan promised me two more teams so that makes five. We have three that makes eight. The Elk Clan sent up two teams, so we have enough wolves for ten regular teams.

These sleds are larger than the ones you already have so we have designed the wolf harness to have ten wolves per sled. So, we have a wolf army with us."

"Where will we get the food to feed this army," Running Stag inquired?

"Little Otter and Talking Wren send their greetings. They also sent enough dried buffalo meat to fill every sled. That is the stack over in the corner," Burley Bear said as he pointed to stacked bundles of goods wrapped in leather.

"It seems everyone in the three clans has been working together in getting our team ready to travel on this next journey," Taelo said as he took in the team and the equipment.

"Yes, this trip like no other has brought all of us closer together. Broken Spear has spoken with each of the clan leadership and has highlighted how our fortunes have improved with each journey. He says he got his new energy from you. He has challenged all of us to contribute to the continued improvement of the clan," Burley Bear said as he put his arm around Taelo's shoulder.

Chapter 4: Departure from the Others

*C*arrying the food for sixty wolves, twenty-four mounts and eighteen people alone posed a monumental challenge. Then there was the rope, harness, hides and other ancillary materials that took up additional space.

The nine sleds, nine travois to carry the sleds, the mounts to pull the travois and the team gathered around the cave opening as they prepared to make their departure.

Golden Hawk looked at the team and commented that the biggest challenge they faced was keeping this small army fed.

Feather-in-the-Wind agreed as she looked at the huge pack of wolves around her.

"These sleds tied to the travois provide a really great way to carry all our goods. And even when tied to the travois the circle of sleds can be achieved and the living area established," Running Stag commented.

He had learned that it had been Burley Bear that had come up with the idea of the combination of sled and travois.

It was ingenious.

Taelo spent most of the day in private conversation with Broken Spear.

"We have come to know each other very well in the last few seasons," Broken Spear began his dialogue.

"As you travel, you will need to follow the valley beyond the mountains. The coast is full of inlets and the coast curls around to the west much farther than you would expect.

Far to the north, the plain you travel will narrow and you will reach a point when you can barely see across a deep valley. A river runs through this valley. Follow the river up the valley. You will be forced upward toward the snow cap. Keep a brisk pace and pass through this area at mid-season. Any later and you will face brutal snowstorms.

It is on the northern side of these mountains where you will face the giant bear. When possible, just run away. You are in their territory.

If you must fight them, fight them like Running Stag fought the cannibals or Feather-in-the-Wind faced the lion. Fight below and behind them.

They are swift. Our clan warriors cannot outrun them," Broken Spear spoke this in short statements with long pauses in between.

"Your guidance has always proven valuable. I am listening and repeating all you say," Taelo commented as Broken Spear seemed to take a break.

"The next part you must remember and adjust based on what you see and what is happening around you.

It is the part where you will face hostile humans.

They are not like you and not like me. They have eyes, the color of the sky.

This group is brutal. They were driven out of their land by their own more reasonable clan members. They desire to conquer and suppress the people around them. Do not trust them and if one approaches you in an apparent show of peace, be ready for his attack," Broken Spear resumed his counseling.

As always, Taelo listened carefully. He would review the comments and think about them, discuss them with Quiet Rabbit and Golden Hawk and the rest of the team, as he traveled.

"That is the longest time Broken Spear has ever spent with Taelo. It must mean there are many perils we will need to face on this journey," Burley Bear commented to the team around him.

"I know Broken Spear is very worried. I had to talk Broken Spear out of sending almost all of our young warriors. That is when he insisted, I go," Burley Bear continued.

"I am sure there will be challenges but after having looked into the mouth of a giant shark, I find it hard to be afraid of any challenge.

Taelo found a way to help me when it seemed impossible and I have the ultimate confidence that he will guide us safely through," Golden Hawk replied.

"And what is worse than a saber-tooth that leaves its mark on your chest," Saber Scar said and then halted for a moment before going on.

"Oh, yes a lion that adds an opposite crossing mark of its own across the same area," Saber Scar joked with the team.

"We have faced many problems together. Taelo has told me he is worried about this journey. It appears Broken Spear agrees.

Be prepared to practice our self-defense and our attack formations often," Quiet Rabbit spoke up from where she was arranging her sled.

She too was worried about the dangers of this journey, but she too had confidence in Taelo and in all the team members.

"Feather-in-the-Wind and I have been getting acquainted with our army of wolves. We will need to train them to fight our enemies like Lasher did. He was a great equalizer when we fought the thirty warriors on our *Journey of the Heart*," Busy Bee added.

"We need to get our mounts use to facing both the bear and humans with weapons. I think having Burley Bear act the part of the giant bear would be appropriate," Feather-in-the-Wind said jokingly.

"Yes, I will be the practice bear," Burley Bear said as he let out a roar and pretended to attack Feather-in-the-Wind.

Just then a runner came in with the news that someone was approaching along the coast. He thought it might be from the Elk Clan because there was someone almost the size of Burley Bear riding a mount.

"Ha, he did make it on time," Burley Bear said as he turned to follow the runner out of the cave.

"I see you will have two more members of your team to accompany you," Broken Spear said with a smile.

"And who would that be," Taelo said in surprise?

"Hello, the team," Small Otter called out as he was led to the preparation area by Burley Bear.

"Oh, I am so happy we made it on time," Talking Wren said as she went about greeting everyone.

She was as animated as everyone remembered.

"We won't need to worry about Burley Bear not talking enough.

We now have Talking Wren," Saber Scar said quietly to Marigold after he had received an enthusiastic hug.

"I heard that, and I will get even," Talking Wren said from where she was carefully giving Feather-in-the-Wind a hug.

"How did you arrange to get away from your duties as a hunter," Golden Hawk asked?

"Oh, it was not so hard when I pointed out how useful I could be in protecting a certain son of Quiet Pheasant," Little Otter replied with a smile as he nodded to Golden Hawk.

"You know as well as I, that with the herd of buffalo making their home in the Valley of Plenty, we hunt only for the special meats like boar, goat, or deer," Little Otter said in a more serious reply.

"Besides, Broken Spear made a point of inviting us to join the team," Little Otter pointed out.

Red Oak had been surprised when the messenger arrived with the request. Red Oak immediately called Little Otter and Talking Wren to his quarters and asked if the two would be interested in such a trip.

"Interested, we would love to go on another journey with Taelo," Talking Wren had replied excitedly.

"Then it is settled. You will be the Elk Clan representatives on this journey. Let's send a gift of our buffalo to both the Others and the Northern Elk Clan," Red Oak had announced.

"You have made those two very happy. I am also happy because there will be two more members to help protect the team and our own Golden Hawk," Quiet Pheasant said as she watched the two rush to their quarters.

"We brought two travois of fresh meat as a gift to the clan of the Others, and we also have two travois of fresh meat for the Northern Elk Clan," Talking Wren announced as the travois appeared at the entrance to the cave.

"The hides of the animals are included on the travois. We look forward to trading back for them when they are white," Talking Wren said in the language of the Others.

"I see Red Oak and Quiet Pheasant sent you to help us. It appears we will have at least one more journey as a team. I am pleased to see you," Taelo said as he came over to greet Little Otter and Talking Wren.

"Yes, we are the official representatives of the Elk Clan. This makes this journey a three-clan adventure," Talking Wren joined in the bantering.

The next morning the team attached the travois to each of the mounts.

Feather-in-the-Wind was walking behind the eleven mounts with Walker, Arrow and Lasher and the rest of the wolf pack.

It was clear Lasher had asserted his dominance.

Feather-in-the-Wind had again demonstrated her keen ability to have the wolves mind her.

"Would you have imagined such a scene when we waited for the man of the Eagle to guide us," Broken Spear said to Quiet Fox as they stood together watching the departing team?

"How could we have known what a difference he would make on our lives," Quiet Fox replied as he slowly waved a goodbye.

Chapter 5:Team Shelter

The twin peaks on the way north to the lodge of the Northern Elk Clan graced the afternoon sky. The sun setting to cast its last rays on the snow cap of the Eastern most peak turned it almost a pure yellow. The edges of the snow cape turned almost black where the dark green of the sentinel pines created its dark skirt.

This was the point in all returning trips that the travelers on the trail looked forward to stopping to enjoy the bounty of the small lake surrounded by willows and edged by a few cattails and surrounding area.

The abundance of the rabbits, squirrels' other small game and the frog and fish population of the small lake assured the traveler of a good meal and a comfortable evening stay.

"It is good to see the twin peaks. We will camp here tonight. Tomorrow we will reach the Northern Elk Clan and be greeted by the White Feather," Golden Hawk said as their caravan came slowly down the path to the lake.

White Swan's new nickname had become the White Feather. Her leadership spear was adorned with the feather of a White Swan.

Her position as the only woman clan leader had elevated her to an almost reverent position.

"It is good that the weather is still cold. It means our meat will not spoil," Talking Wren chimed in.

She was leading two mounts each pulling a travois with the meat of three buffalo each. This was about the limit for the mounts to pull.

"Your gift will be very welcome. The hunting in this northern area is not as bountiful as in the areas around the Valley of Plenty.

I am sure the Elk Clan will receive many gifts of salt from the Northern Elk Clan," Taelo added.

"Let's practice setting up our lodging. Burley Bear, will you please guide us in getting this setup properly," Taelo continued as they arrived at the lake.

Taelo wanted the team to be able to quickly set up their shelter. This was a good place for the team to get their first practice.

Burley Bear moved each of the team members into the position where they belonged. The travois with the sleds mounted on them were easily pulled into position by the mounts. The mounts ended up on the outside of the circle formed by the positioning of the sleds.

The rider of each mount dismounted and together with their partner proceeded to detach the travois from the mount.

It took both persons on each travois to lower the travois to the ground. It was clear that several of the team pairs were not strong enough for this task.

"I need a stronger partner to help lower this travois," Feather-in-the-Wind said loudly after she and Running Stag basically dropped their travois.

"Let's put this travois back up and then see if we can use the rope to lower it to the ground," Running Stag suggested.

"We will help you," Saber Scar said as he and Sharp Blade came over.

Running Stag tied one end of the rope for the travois onto the mount harness. He then had Saber Scar and Sharp Blade lift the travois up. He secured the travois to the harness.

"Let me show you how to lower the travois by loosening the travois ropes and letting it slide around the travois shaft," Running Stag said to Feather-in-the-Wind.

The two easily lowered the travois.

"Any of us can lower the travois in this manner," Running Stag commented, "raising it up to tie off is another matter.

"We will need to think about how each of us can raise the travois into place. Either we come up with a way to do it or Saber Scar and Sharp Blade will be very busy each time we get ready to move on," Running Stag pointed out.

Once all the travois were lowered, the mounts were led away to their holding area.

"Good work, we have an almost perfect circle," Little Otter commented as he walked around the inside of the sled circle.

He was tying the sleds together as Burley Bear continued his instructions.

Meadow Flower, Sharp Blade, Single Leaf, Saber Scar and Marigold positioned the ten poles to be used to hold up the outside edges of the cover. These poles went up on the inside perimeter of the sleds.

There was a holding loop the pole would be tied to once it was in place. The leather top was large enough to cover the sleds and then be tied off at the base of each sled.

This created a closed enclosure. A section was cut in such a way as to form a doorway between two sleds. The door could be closed by moving the sled into position so that it connected the first and last sleds.

Meadow Flower placed the longest pole in the center of the circle. She and Saber Scar then positioned and rolled out the hide that made up the cover of their shelter.

"This is the tricky part. One person from each sled must attach their pole to the loop hanging down inside of the cover. The other from that sled must anchor the pole to a stake driven deeply into the ground on the far side of the sled. We must all do this together.

One person must stand in the middle and push up the center pole," Meadow Flower said as she got the covering positioned.

"Let me show each of you the loop and how the pole, the loop and the tie off rope must be positioned," Meadow Flower continued her instruction.

"I will be the center," Burley Bear volunteered.

"The strongest person at each sled must be the one pulling the poles up and anchoring it," Burley Bear continued.

"I guess I will let Quiet Rabbit pull up our pole.

I know she is the strongest, of the two of us," Taelo joked as he attached the tie line to the top of the pole at his sled.

He was not sure he would be strong enough for this effort.

They were also missing three of their team. This meant two of the sleds did not have anyone to pull up the poles.

After much straining and with Marigold, Meadow Flower, Saber Scar, Sharp Blade, and Single Leaf running around to help each of the other members the cover was up.

It was clear to Taelo that the team did not have the required strength to do this every evening.

"We should use our mounts to pull up the cover for our shelter. Your clan members are at least twice as strong as the rest of us and had no problem, but we are exhausted by this effort," Running Stag said as he sat down.

He felt a little dejected. He was not used to feeling so weak and vulnerable.

"My pole would not have gone up if Marigold had not come over and helped me," Running Stag continued.

He was not strong enough on his own to pull up the weight of the cover.

"Using the mounts is a very good idea. If we put a loop in the line being pulled by the mount, we can guide the mount away from the center of the shelter. When the pole is up the loop can be dropped over the ground post," Taelo commented.

"Yes, and the person inside the circle can tie off the pole," Feather-in-the-Wind added.

"There is enough time. Let's practice that now," Feather-in-the-Wind suggested.

"Do we really need to do it now," Little Otter said as he looked up at the covering above him.

He was one of the stronger ones and he was already tired.

"I think this is the perfect time," Talking Wren spoke from where she sat next to Little Otter and gave him a punch in the shoulder.

Everyone knew that they would indeed try it at least one more time.

"Everyone take a break and maybe have something to eat while Burley Bear and I mark each line, so we know where to put the loop," Taelo announced.

"Running Stag has come up with two good ideas. I hope he figures out how to raise the travois onto the mounts. He is right about the fact that most of the team cannot raise the travois up. Quiet Rabbit and I cannot lift it," Taelo shared with Burley Bear.

"Busy Bee and I cannot do it either," Golden Hawk added.

"We did not realize how weak you new ones are," Burley Bear said as he gave Taelo a shoulder hug.

He felt bad about having missed the fact that the team would not have the strength to carry out some of these critical skills.

Taelo and Burley Bear marked each of the lines so they would know where to put the holding loops.

This took enough time, so the rest of the team had a chance to recover.

"Everyone get in your places and get ready to lower the cover," Burley Bear announced.

Once everyone was in place, the cover was lowered.

It took almost as much effort to lower it as to raise it.

The lowering looked more like an uncontrolled collapse then a lowering.

"I am glad we did this. It was just as hard to take the covering down as it was to put it up. We will want to use the mounts on both occasions," Busy Bee said.

"It was somewhat difficult when we practiced it with the clan members, but it is obvious that the team needs to use the mounts," Sharp Blade added.

It was clear to him that using the mounts would be a great improvement. The team would need to raise the covering many times in the coming journey.

The experience the team just had would not be something they would want to repeat.

"How did we miss the idea of using the mounts or on using the rope to lower the travois," Single Leaf said to Sharp Blade as they watched Taelo and Burley Bear marking the lines.

"The new ones may be weaker physically, but they make it up by having a stronger imagination," Saber Scar commented.

"Together we make a formidable team."

"Let's go get the mounts and put them in position," Meadow Flower said loud enough for the whole team to hear.

The team went out and brought the mounts and positioned them around the circle.

The shoulder harness used to attach the travois was easily adapted so the pull line could be connected.

"Burley Bear, Golden Hawk and I will show the other team members how to connect the pull lines to the mount's harness and then how to lower the loop on to the ground stake," Taelo announced to the team.

Once everyone was clear on how the pull lines were to be handled, it was time to raise the covering again.

"This time it was really easy. Let's take it down and do it again," Little Otter joked as the covering went smoothly up.

"That is a great idea," Running Stag said.

"I was just joking," Little Otter replied with a verbal groan.

But the rest of the team agreed with Running Stag.

"It really did get easier," Talking Wren commented as the covering came up for the third time."

Feather-in-the-Wind jumped up and ran out of the compound.

"I don't know where she is going or what she is doing. I will go see if I can be of help," Running Stag commented as he got up.

"I will go with you," Single Leaf said as she followed Running Stag out.

"I think we now know how to raise and lower the covering. And I believe we can do it with only half of the team.

We are making great progress. Is everyone ready for something to eat?

If Little Otter would be so kind as to share a few pieces of fresh meat, we could all sit around and grill our own dinner.

Otherwise, we may need to practice one more time," Taelo said as he sat down on the edge of his sled.

"Come and help yourself to the piece that meets your desire," Little Otter said as he un-wrapped a bundle on his sled.

He was indeed happy to have everyone grill their own meat.

He knew he was ready to do so.

A short time later Feather-in-the-Wind, Running Stag and Single Leaf returned.

Feather-in-the-Wind was carrying two stout but slender poles about the height of her shoulders that were tied close to one end. She spread the two poles and a small V formed at the top.

Single Leaf lowered the pole she was carrying into the V. This pole was about the thickness of Taelo's forearm.

Running Stag also had two stout poles that were tied in the middle and opened to make an X.

The three walked over to Feather-in-the-Wind's sled.

Single Leaf set up the tall poles with the V at the top at about the middle of the distance between the sled and the end of the travois. Feather-in-the-Wind put the thick pole into the V and the end under the front cross member of the travois. Running Stag has his X opened and positioned between the main pole that would do the raising and the travois cross member.

Single Leaf held the main lever pole and the pivot point. Feather-in-the-Wind reached up to grasp the end of the pole. It was at the limit of her reach. She pulled down on pole and the travois came smoothly up.

When it was high enough, Running Stag put the X frame under the main travois cross member. It had a slight lean toward the back of the travois.

The three then stepped back and the travois stayed in the raised position.

"Once we get the travois into this position, the mount can be carefully backed in and hooked up. Once the harness is secure you can back the mount up slightly and remove the X member.

We demonstrated this with three people but the three of us have already figured out how one person can do it," Feather-in-the-Wind proudly shared the procedure she had thought up.

"I am so impressed that I have grilled each of you a choice piece of meat," Little Otter said as he brought each of them a seasoned and grilled piece of meat.

He knew that this idea would save everyone a tremendous amount of work.

"I will help you finish your design and get it ready for each of the travois," Meadow Flower volunteered.

Chapter 6: Northern Elk Clan Departure

The dark of early morning after a solid night's sleep greeted Taelo and let him slowly absorb the comfort of the warmth of the hide over him and that of Quite Rabbit snuggled up to his side.

He knew his movement would wake her. She as always, would wake up with a smile and lightly touch his cheek as she opened her eyes and looked into his. It was a moment that always reached into his chest and made his breath stop. This was a feeling he wanted to preserve for a lifetime.

Once up he grudgingly rolled out from under the hide and closed it back over Quiet Rabbit who once again would be curled up to get a few more moments of sleep.

He walked out to the fire ring and stirred the coals to restart the fire. Golden Hawk joined him and the two sipped on the broth of the stew left in the bag by the fire.

They watched the sunrise over the peak of the eastern twin.

This morning the two were uncharacteristically stiff. Their workout with the shelter had stretched even their physical condition. Taelo commented on this fact and suggested they let the team sleep in as long as possible since they had only a short trip to the lodge.

It was a significantly long period before the entire team was up and about. Feather-in-the-Wind was one of the last to rise. Walker had finally started to lick her cheek in concern.

"Here, I think I am waking to an eager mate and find myself looking into the eyes of a wolf," she mumbled as she wiped off her face.

Running Stag brought over a bowl of stew and sat down beside her.

He touched her cheek and just smiled. He knew better than to say anything.

Taelo called for the cover to be brought down. The team rallied and together utilizing the mounts and the covering came down smoothly.

Taelo praised everyone for the smooth execution. He was very pleased with how well they had lowered and stored the covering.

Feather-in-the-Wind, Single leaf and Running Stag supervised each team in lifting and attaching the travois to the mounts.

Little Otter volunteered to lead the making of a lifting rig for each of the travois.

The pole, line and ground stake for the covering was stored on each sled. This would in the future make it easier to position and raise the covering.

It took three team members to fold and roll the cover. By rolling it, the three were able to roll in onto Meadow Flower's sled.

"Congratulation, we seem to have mastered setting up and taking down our camp," Taelo commented as the team made ready to leave.

"Now all we need to do is pick up our two master cooks and be on our way," Golden Hawk added.

"We will be staying at the Northern Elk Clan for a few sun cycles.

Let's plan on setting up our camp in the open yard outside of the lodge. Let's show the clan our new capability and the grand gift from Burley Bear, Meadow Flower, and the rest of the Others," Taelo said as the team readied to leave the lake.

"Little Otter and Talking Wren will take the lead. They will present their gifts. Burley Bear and Meadow Flower will follow and present their gifts. The rest of us will follow," Taelo commented a few hours later as they crossed the river and started up the tributary leading to the Northern Elk Clan lodge.

"I have heard the stories about this lodge from Burley Bear and Meadow Flower. I thought they were exaggerating. But look at the size and height of it," Sharp Blade commented.

"Does it really have a heated stone floor," Single Leaf added as she took in the structure.

"All the individual homes have been completed. I hope they are working out as we planned, they would," Talking Wren said as they rode passed them.

"They are and the clan loves the layout design you provided. You will certainly be taken on multiple tours by the happy families that live in each of them," Quiet Rabbit said.

Taelo and Golden Hawk rode side by side with their golden feathers hanging from their upright spears.

The team with its eighteen mounts, eleven travois and a sixty-member wolf pack following behind them made a formidable sight.

"You left on four mounts with three wolves. You return with a full clan behind you," White Swan said as she gave both Taelo and Golden Hawk a hug.

"And the two of you look as strong as ever," she continued as she hugged Burley Bear and Meadow Flower.

"I know from all the stories and our brief meeting that you are Saber Scar and Marigold," White Swan continued down the line giving her hugs.

"It eases my mind when two more of you join the team. I know now this team is equipped for all problems," White Swan said when greeting Sharp Blade and Single Leaf.

"Each of us has brought you a small gift.

Sharp Blade and Single Leaf have three bags of scented oil.

Saber Scar and Marigold have a set of scrapping and cutting blades.

And Burley Bear and I have brought matching white, rabbit lined, leather jackets for you and Grey Fox Running," Meadow Flower said as each gift was presented.

White Swan immediately put on her jacket and thanked them for their gifts.

"And here is the famous Talking Wren and her Little Otter. I had no idea you would be joining. How is Red Oak and Quiet Pheasant," White Swan continued her greetings.

"They both send their regards and they have sent these two travois with the meat of six buffalo as greeting," Talking Wren replied as Little Otter handed the reins of the mounts to White Swan.

Again, White Swan accepted the gift with a thank you. She passed the reigns off and continued her greetings.

"It is good to have all my daughters return safely.

I see my youngest has returned once again as the wolf woman," White Swan continued her greeting and comments as she gave each of the three a hug.

She had purposely called them all her daughters signaling a status elevation to the rest of the clan.

"I am honored to be your "youngest" daughter. I want my "older sisters" to take note," Feather-in-the-Wind said as she winked at Quiet Rabbit and Busy Bee.

"Now I know why I love to be with this team so much," Feather-in-the-Wind thought to herself. She had just been rewarded by being called a daughter.

"If you permit us, we will set up camp in the green area of the compound. We will put the wolves and mounts out in the far field," Taelo asked quietly to White Swan and Grey Fox Running.

"That would solve the problem of where to put all of you. Yes of course you may," White Swan replied.

She was relieved that she did not need to host all of them in the main lodge. She had just removed all the individual living spaces and transformed the lodge into a large open area where the whole clan could gather.

Alright team let's see how fast we can erect our lodge," Burley Bear called out and led the team up the ramp and through the open gate.

All the Northern Clan members stood and watched in amazement as the team placed the travois and sleds in a circle. They noted the ease of lowering the travois to the ground.

The use of the mounts to raise the covering was another feature that everyone commented on. The speed and precision of the team was also clearly astonishing.

"This is Burley Bear's invention. We learned how to make sleds from the Others and now we have learned how to make a lodge in the amount of time it takes to run from here to the river and back," Golden Hawk said so everyone around could hear.

"This is really amazing; I see everyone is assigned to a sled. Where are we assigned," Floating Cloud inquired from where she, Lily and Slow Runner were standing?

"We have missed you. Let us show you the travois and sleds that will be your home in the coming journey," Quiet Rabbit said as she gave each a hug and led them to the sleds that would be theirs.

Quiet Rabbit and Taelo had talked about getting one more person from the clan to accompany Floating Cloud. This would ensure two persons per sled and travois. They were sure they could get enough people to volunteer but they wanted someone who would fit in with the rest of the team.

"I have the perfect person for you," White Swan said after the evening meal as they sat by the warm water pool enjoying the contrast of the pool's warmth and the brisk evening chill.

"She is one of the older young women you rescued. Her mate was killed in the battle with the cannibals. She has had no suitors, but she is very industrious and helpful. Shall I call her over," White Swan asked?

"No, let's wait and let Floating Cloud talk with her. The two will need to like each other for this to work," Quiet Rabbit said.

She wanted to give her grandmother the opportunity to make the choice.

"Well, then I think it will work out that way. I have observed Floating Cloud and Bashful Lark taking a walk to the river almost every evening during your absence," Grey Fox Running commented.

"What are your plans," Grey Fox Running inquired of Taelo.

"Once we have organized and loaded the material Lily and Floating Cloud have arranged and have made a few additional adjustments to the equipment used to raise and lower our cover we will depart.

Broken Spear has warned us to get through the northern mountain passage by the middle of the warm period. We need to be on the northern plain before the cold. There we will be able to shelter from the extreme cold," Taelo replied.

The next day Quiet Rabbit talked with Floating Cloud about having a partner for the journey.

"Do you have someone you would choose," Quiet Rabbit asked?

"Yes, I do. You have solved a problem for me. I wanted to ask about such a possibility. I would like a young lady that I have come to know well, Bashful Lark to come with us," Floating Cloud replied.

"Let's go see her and make sure she wants to come. If she does, we can move her things to your sled.

Then I want to spend some time training both of you on how to manage your mounts, travois, and your role in setting up and taking down our shelter," Quiet Rabbit said as she gave her grandmother a hug.

"Oh, what an honor to be asked to go, yes of course I wish to join you," Bashful Lark responded when she was asked.

"I am so happy Bashful Lark will join us. She and I have been friends since we were young. She has suffered a similar fate to me. I hope she is lucky enough to find someone like Slow Runner," Lily commented when she was told.

She knew how devastating it was to lose one's mate. Afterward, it was almost impossible to find another.

"It's time to go. The wolves are going to eat all their food before we even begin the journey," Feather-in-the-Wind announced a few evenings later after coming back in from feeding them.

"Tomorrow we organize and check all our gear. We have a good supply of everything we can think of needing," Taelo said from the log he was sitting on.

Every member of the clan brought some key item for them to take with them. These were mostly small items, but on a long journey very useful ones. The one item each clan member brought was a small bag of salt for each of them. This was a symbolic sign of friendship and good tiding.

"We need to make sure we have enough salt for our journey. In fact, my suggestion is to go by the salt mine and take enough that we could leave some along the way. On the way back we will be glad we did," Floating Cloud suggested.

"That is one of the best ideas I have heard so far," Busy Bee responded.

"Yes, taking the salt is a good idea but we cannot get to the salt mine with these travois," Quiet Rabbit noted.

"Let me see what I can arrange," Taelo said.

He would see if he could get the salt from White Swan and arrange for several of the clan members to retrieve more from the mine if needed.

"Salt," was the last thing that went through Taelo's mind as he fell asleep with his arms around Quiet Rabbit.

The next morning at breakfast Taelo made his request for salt.

"You know we would leave immediately if only we had half a block of salt," he announced to White Swan.

"Well in that case you will have it at your camp right after you eat," White Swan responded.

"I told you that he would leave only if we could figure out what he wanted," Grey Fox Running joined in the teasing.

They both knew Taelo was serious about wanting to take a half a block of salt. It also said something about how long Taelo expected the journey to last.

"Even though he will be gone a long time, he will return," Grey Fox Running said as he gave White Swan a hug.

He had seen her wiping away a tear when she turned away from the breakfast area.

"I have been thinking about the direction and the path the team should travel. Golden Hawk and I have traveled the river that makes the falls and comes across the valley. We have discussed going that way. This will give the team a chance to spend the night in the great council chamber and enjoy its hot water shower. Most of the team has been there but a few have not. This will be a great way to start the journey," Taelo announced to everyone's surprise.

Once we get upriver, we will go northeast until we cross the second ridge of mountains and arrive at the far plain. There we will turn again and then proceed to go northwest.

"May we accompany you and spend the night with you at the cave," White Swan inquired?

"It is I who is asking for permission to use the council chambers.

Of course, you are welcome and perhaps you and Grey Fox Running could tell the stories of old.

Quiet Rabbit, Busy Bee, Meadow Flower, and Marigold would like to put up drawings of, the team hunt, the *Journey of the Heart,* and the *Journey of Discovery*. They are eager to share them with you to get your approval," Taelo replied.

"Then it is set, we will all go to the great council chambers and spend an evening telling stories of the past, while new drawings get added to the chamber walls," White Feather replied.

She loved the idea of such an evening.

"I will go out and bring in the mounts," Golden Hawk said from where he sat.

"The three of us will go with you," Saber Scar said from where he, Sharp Blade and Running Stag sat.

"Well, it sounds like we will all be busy getting the sleds ready while you round up the mounts," Lily commented as she led the way back out to the camp.

The word, about the team's departure, traveled quickly through the entire clan living area. By the time the mounts were led into the compound the entire clan had gathered to watch.

"I see that Bashful Lark and Floating Cloud have practiced their part in taking the cover down," White Swan commented as she watched the two.

"Yes, the entire team seems to work together flawlessly," Grey Fox Running commented as he watched the poles come down and the cover being folded and stored on Meadow Flower's Sled.

High in the sky an eagle circled and let out a cry.

The team headed up the valley.

White Swan and Grey Fox Running followed on their mounts.

Running Stag's parents had been invited and followed on two of the clan mounts.

Chapter 7: Connection

The huge chamber shimmered in the light of the blue green translucent cascade of water. The air pulled from the far back opening dispersed as the cave widened and lightly grazed the backs of those sitting and facing the speaker standing with his back to the falls.

The sun's rays from the western settling sun cast shimmering rays that flickered in rhythm with the falling waters and the misting spray of countless volumes of water racing to reach the pool at the base of the falls.

Gray Fox Running took in the faces of the Elk Clan and of the Others, all eager to hear stories he had told to many in their younger years. He had heard the stories from his father, mother, and grandparents. These were ancient stories about the arrival to and establishment of the first Elk Clan in this valley.

He watched as Quiet Rabbit, Busy Bee, Feather-in-the-Wind, Meadow Flower, and Marigold began sketching in the scenes for new drawings being added to the ancient drawings placed there so long ago.

It was a magical meeting of the ghosts of long ago and the spirit and energy of those in the here and now. Gray Fox Running could see the ancients in the flickering light beams streaming over his shoulders as the sun, just before going down behind the mountain to the west illuminated the cave.

Slowly, the flickering of the fire and the glow of the torches was the only separation between the two periods of time. Time came much closer together and a hush came over the gathering.

"Grey Fox Running and I have tried to remember some of the stories that we were told as a child. I also asked Floating Cloud to recall stories she was told. We have combined what we remember and will each tell a different story. Grey Fox Running will begin with the Clan's early history, and he will end with telling the story of the Salt Gatherers," White Swan began.

She, Floating Cloud and Grey Fox Running were sitting in the center.

All the team put their sitting hides around the in a semi-circle facing the falls. The leader's circle was immediately in front of them. They all felt the mystical nature of the chamber. They were sitting among the ancients.

Grey Fox Running began his stories.

The people traveled south, southeast glaciers rose high to the northeast, glaciers rose to the southwest. There was only wide-open grassland between the two.

The clan was a mix of members of different clans. All the members were looking for a more fruitful life. The stories of those who went before them described a land of plenty and an ease of living sought by these adventuresome people.

Their leaders followed the path until the glaciers subsided. Then they turned to the west where they expected to find the broad waters.

Two towering ridges of snow-covered mountains and snow clogged passes challenged the entire clan.

A twenty-pronged elk, the largest any hunter had ever seen crossed in front of the traveling clan. The lead hunters immediately pursued the astounding animal with a rack the size of a full spear across.

The rest of the clan turned and followed the small river into a valley and were astounded to find it populated with a huge Elk herd.

It was now late fall and winter would soon be upon them. The falls at the far end of the valley turned a deep yellow, orange and a rainbow blossomed as the sun began its descent.

The clan had found its home.

By spring they had become the Elk Clan.

Grey Fox Running, stopped for a break in the story telling. The new sketches on the wall were taking shape. He walked over and looked at the new sketches and then took a torch to look at the stories of old sketches.

He would tell the story of the Giant Bear next, so he studied that particular story drawing.

"Good this gives me time to have the food and snacks brought in. Will a few of you please give me a hand in bringing in the food," Lily spoke up.

"This is my first time to come into the Elk Clan's council chambers. It is amazing," Floating Cloud commented quietly.

"Oh, let's give everyone a quick tour of the chamber and Busy Bee will hang the hides with the scenes we will put on the chamber wall," Quiet Rabbit replied.

After the quick tour, everyone took a helping of food and drink that had been placed near at hand. They were ready for the next story.

The battle with the giant cave bear came next.

Unknown to the new Elk Clan, they were in the territory of a very aggressive female cave bear. One early morning the bear rampaged through the Elk Clan's camp. Little was left standing or undamaged.

Most of the meat and anything edible had been consumed.

The entire clan had retreated into the woods away from the camp. They watched their handiwork reduced to rubble.

Their leaders organized an immediate hunting group to hunt and kill the bear. They tracked the bear as it left the camp back to the entrance of this very cave.

They organized themselves and then lured the bear out of the cave. Three hunters dropped a huge boulder from the top of the entrance onto the bear as it exited. This stunned the bear but even in its dazed state it put up a massive fight that injure almost half of the hunters.

One of the three hunters from above drove a spear through the bears side and another with a war hammer smashed the bear on the side of the head. Soon the team had killed the bear.

When they entered the cave, they found the hot water pool and the falls. They immediately realized the treasure they had found.

If they had not already adopted the Elk as their name, they would most certainly have selected to be the Bear Clan. The cave became the center of all Elk clan formal meetings.

Grey Fox Running stopped and turned the floor over to White Swan.

White Swan told of the finding of the same hot water spring that was now the center of the Northern Elk Clan's lodge and lifestyle. This never had the same impact on the Elk Clan as it now had on the Northern Elk Clan. The Elk Clan preferred having their lodge and individual homes around the lake.

Grey Fox Running ended the evening with the story of the Salt Gatherers.

During the story telling, Quiet Rabbit, Busy Bee, Feather-in-the-Wind, Marigold, and Meadow Flower were quietly drawing images on the cave wall.

"We are not done but you can see the scenes taking shape," Quite Rabbit said as the story telling ended.

"We will finish the drawings on our return from our travels to the north," Busy Bee continued.

"This has been one of the most memorable moments we have spent together as a team," Golden Hawk observed and shared with everyone.

The team made its way out of the council chambers to their camp along the side of the river in the open meadow. They had left their wolves around the camp during the evening dinner and the story telling. This let them utilize the council chambers for their enjoyment and now some of them would sleep in the camp and few would be in the cave.

The next morning the team cleaned the council chambers, then they broke camp. By the time the sun was beginning its departure from its eastern mountain tops the team was organized and ready to proceed.

After a round of hugs and goodbyes, Taelo finally gave the signal that drew the team forward on their way to their Northern journey.

"There goes our team of wanderers. It will be hard for that group to settle down in one area. Let's hope they always come up with another journey," Grey Fox Running comment to White Swan as he wrapped his arm around her waist.

They stood and watched until the team disappeared over a hill behind the cave.

"Let's go home and tend to our clan," White Swan replied.

"We will want to gather all we can eat as we travel," Golden Hawk commented as they traveled along the river.

He had his sling out as he walked beside his mount.

The team talked about how to manage their food supply. They carried a large amount of dried meat and fish and only a small quantity of fresh meat.

"You can relax when you are riding on the mounts. Everyone on the mounts needs to be alert for danger. Those on foot will use their slings to gather the small game. Keep your spears within easy reach on the travois in case we run into any large animals," Taelo instructed.

"We have ourselves, the mounts, and a large number of wolves to feed as well. So, we will be on the hunt every day for fresh meat," Taelo continued.

I have talked with Lasher, Walker and Arrow and told them that they are responsible to instruct their wolf brethren to find as much food as they can as we travel. They have assured me they understand and will do so," Taelo joked as he scratched Lasher behind his ears.

"I am pleased Taelo, and Golden Hawk have chosen to lead," Burley Bear commented to Meadow Flower, Little Otter, and Talking Wren as they sat listening.

Burley Bear had worried that Taelo might ask him to take the lead. He had been leading his clan and had no desire to lead the team.

"At the next break in the mountain range we will turn and go almost due east. This will keep us south of the glaciers. Once we cross the farthest range of mountains, we will begin drifting northeast looking for the passage north.

Last night we heard the story of the Elk Clan's arrival. We will be back tracking their journey. Let's hope the same passage is still open," Taelo commented.

I hope the warm weather follows us as we travel," Burley Bear said to Little Otter walking beside him.

"At least we won't be jogging for most of this journey," Little Otter replied.

"Wait until the wolves are pulling our sleds. Then we will all get our turn running," Feather-in-the-Wind said from where she rode her mount.

She remembered the beginning of their *Journey of Discovery*. She had run as much then as when the team had returned from the *Journey of the Heart*. Jogging and running was something this team was always doing.

"We will need to send out scouts to find the trail we should be following. We need to find the path where the mounts and travois can pass.

We have two spare mounts. Two scouts will be sent out. The first time one will ride out one cycle of the sun and then return. The second rider will ride for two cycles of the sun and then return.

Then every scout after that will ride out for two sun cycles. This will give us a continuous path as we travel," Taelo announced at their first camp.

"Every team member will take a turn as a scout. We will follow this cycle until the weather turns cold again. Then we will adjust and go out in two's and perhaps not go as far.

Golden Hawk, Burley Bear, Little Otter, and I have worked out the schedule so only one person per mount and travois is out at a time," Taelo continued.

"I will ride out tomorrow for the first cycle and Golden Hawk will ride out for the double cycle," Taelo continued.

The team enjoyed a large evening meal cooked over the fire by Lily and Floating Cloud. The two managed the preparation and everyone else helped by following their instruction.

The small game was cleaned, rubbed with salt, and roasted over the fire. Part of it was set aside for the morning meal and the high sun meal as they traveled.

The dinner had been a simple meal of rabbit stew and some pieces of salted buffalo.

"I am glad we did not put up the cover," Single Leaf commented as she took in the endless points of lights in the pitch-black sky above them.

"I agree, we will only put up the cover when the cold or rain makes us do it," Burley Bear said from where he lay looking up.

The team had been surprised by the abundance of small game. They had also come across the tracks of larger animals as well.

They set a constant and steady cadence of traveling from sunrise to setting sun. Their morning and high sun meals were eaten on the go.

Their evening meals were taken after camp had been set up.

They carried enough poles to make fish traps along the streams by which they would stop. Once the camp was set up the fish traps were put in place. Two of the team would clean the captured fish, rub them with salt, and roast them on the coals of the evening fire. Usually, the hot fish were snacks for the team members but most of the fish were held for the morning meal.

Half the team went about gathering grasses and other plants for the mounts to eat and staked each mount out in an area where they could eat fresh grasses.

The mounts were guarded throughout the night by two of the team.

One member of the team always helped Feather-in-the-Wind feed each of the wolves. The wolves were fed the minimum possible. This made them hungry enough to hunt for themselves. Feather-in-the-Wind made sure all the younger wolves got enough eat.

There were two new pups that at first were carried by her as they traveled. Later they followed Feather-in-the-Wind as much as their natural mother.

"It seems we have made all the work assignments necessary. Does anyone see anything we have missed," Taelo inquired after their third stop?

He had waited to discuss this until the team had set up and taken down the camp and traveled enough to get the feel of the journey.

"Yes, Lily and I would like to volunteer to erect a marker at each of our stops. We have designed our marker to have a stone base, a pole standing up in the middle and a black feather hanging from the top of the pole," Floating Cloud spoke up.

"That is a great idea. Busy Bee and I will help you with this. Why did you choose to use a black feather," Quiet Rabbit asked in curiosity?

"Oh, we chose a black feather because each of you has brought in a blackbird as part of your daily small game gathering. We have as many black feathers as we need for the entire journey," Lily replied with a laugh.

"We could also use rabbit skin, squirrel or fish tail," Floating Cloud added.

"Well team it seems we have figured out how to handle all the routing daily work. The work seems to be well balanced. It is time we began to practice out personal and camp defense," Taelo said to the team.

"Oh, and we will practice each at least three times," Little Otter and Burley Bear said in unison.

The entire team echoed what had been said.

Chapter 8: Dire Wolf Territory

The black surrounding their yellow irises and the length of teeth exposed when snarling, made these animals feared by all their prey. As tall at the shoulders as the backs of the mounts and boulder sized chests made them impossible to be faced on the ground by any of the team members.

Taelo, Golden Hawk and the team had faced the dire wolf multiple times and triumphed. Each time there was a steep price to pay.

On this journey, Taelo was wary of these competitors that were dominant in their territory. The other animal to worry about was the huge brown bear Broken Spear had warned of.

Taelo was also aware of the lions and giant tigers and the saber- tooths.

He began and continued to exercise the team in their self-defense practice he had assigned Feather-in-the-Wind to call at random times, three times each cycle.

A cycle after Taelo's return from his scouting, the team faced its first challenge.

"There is something wrong. The wolves are acting as if they are ready for a fight," Feather-in-the-Wind called out from where she was walking with the wolves. The two young wolves were close on her heals. She picked them up and put them in a sling she had made for them.

"My mount is also nervous," Single Leaf called in reply.

"Everyone be on alert. Let's close ranks. We will proceed at our normal pace. If I call for our defensive circle, make sure the mounts end up on the inside of the circle," Taelo called out so everyone could hear him.

"Burley Bear, Little Otter please get out in front and keep watch for any sign of danger. Also keep spotting the best place to create the defensive circle. Call for the circle at least once before the high sun," Taelo requested of the two.

"I see we will practice our defensive circle several more times whether we see a threat or not," Little Otter said to Burley Bear as they picked up their pace to get farther out in front.

"Yes, we will and later we will thank Taelo for having made us practice," Burley Bear said with a chuckle.

He remembered their battle practices on their *Journey of the Heart*. The team at first had questioned all the practice. Later the team of eight defeated a team of thirty young warriors and the worst wound was a cut on Little Otter's side.

"Yes, I know we will thank him. I am always amazed he thinks of it first," Little Otter replied.

"Sharp Blade and Marigold please watch each side of our line," Taelo continued getting the team on alert.

"Feather-in-the-Wind, let me know when the wolves gather tight around you," he called back to her.

"How tight do they need to be," Feather-in-the-Wind said as she looked at the pack surrounding her.

"Lasher, go to Feather-in-the-Wind," Taelo said.

Lasher immediately turned and went back to the wolf pack and Feather-in-the-Wind.

Lasher was on one side and Walker was on the other. The two were ready to defend Feather-in-the-Wind.

"Feather-in-the-Wind, bring the wolves in closer. Bring them into the center when we go into our defensive circle," Taelo called back.

"It was a poor idea to send the scouts out by themselves," Taelo thought to himself.

Quiet Rabbit was out two cycles and Golden Hawk was due back during this one. Taelo hoped both were safe.

He decided at that moment to send out pairs of scouts instead of sending them out individually.

As the sun reached its zenith, Burley Bear called for a defensive circle and indicated the area around him as the location for the circle.

Meadow Flower had the lead mount and immediately circled around him. She set the distance with Burley Bear at the center and traveled around until the last two travois where in front of her.

Feather-in-the-Wind rushed through with the wolves following behind. Meadow Flower then turned her mount to the inside of the circle. Each of those following closed the gaps as they in turn put their mounts to the inside.

The circle closed. They had missed perfection by three hand lengths.

The last travois had a small overlap with Meadow Flower's travois and had to be manually positioned.

"That was very good. Let's get something to eat and then proceed on our way," Taelo said announcing a break and praising everyone.

"Something must be threatening the team," Golden Hawk said as he rode into view of the team.

He looked all around but did not see any threat.

"I hope this is just practice," he continued his musings as he rode in.

"From now on two scouts will go out together. I am sending three of you out now. You will take turns jogging while the third one rides.

When you meet Quiet Rabbit, Busy Bee will return with her. Slow Runner and Sharp Blade will continue on," Taelo announced.

"I knew the jogging would show up sooner rather than later," Little Otter said with groan but with a grin on his face.

Though he disliked the jogging, he liked the fact that it kept him in shape. He and Burley Bear were huge but they both could keep up with all the rest. He was sure it was this constant jogging that made that possible.

"There is a very nice stream and lake ahead. If we move now, we can easily make it before the sun sets," Golden Hawk said as he finished his meal.

"Let's move," Feather-in-the-Wind said from the middle of the wolf pack that lay around her. She had quickly eaten her lunch snack and had been playing with the two wolf pups. Their mother was peacefully sleeping next to where Feather-in-the-Wind sat.

"I see that you are the safest one among us," Golden Hawk said as he took in the sight of Feather-in-the-Wind surrounded by the team's eighty wolves.

The wolves were sitting looking outward as if in formation.

"All you have to do is feed them and they love you," she replied with a nod and a smile.

As she stood up the wolves all stood up. It was clear that they saw her as their leader.

The team traveled on in full alert. The mounts were nervous, and the wolves kept close to Feather-in-the-Wind.

Lasher and Walker continued to walk at her side.

"I see you assigned Lasher to guard Feather-in-the-Wind. Do you expect trouble," Golden Hawk asked Taelo?

"Something has the mounts and the wolves on edge.

I am not sure what it is, but Feather-in-the-Wind is behind the team by herself.

Lasher is my insurance of her safety," Taelo replied.

Golden Hawk rode out and picked the position for the camp. The circle was once again made but this time the mounts were to the outer side.

The circle did not close. There was an open section.

This subtle difference caused Taelo to realize that the normal camping circle needed a smaller distance around the center.

The defensive circle needed to have a greater distance around the center. This allowed the front of the travois and the mount to fit in comfortably.

"We were lucky the first time because Meadow Flower instinctively picked the right distance for the defensive circle," Taelo commented.

"This time we have almost the same distance, but we have an open area. We need a tighter circle when the mounts are to the outside.

Let's try it again," Taelo requested.

The team practiced both the defensive circle and the normal camping circle three times.

"I believe I have the distance for each one," Meadow Flower commented after the third try.

"Yes, you do. Tomorrow I would like to have Busy Bee try her hand at setting the defensive circle and the evening circle," Taelo replied.

"We will each take a turn at setting the distance for each circle," Taelo continued.

He wanted the entire team to have this capability.

The team finished setting up camp. They had dinner and then each went to their assigned duties.

"The mounts are nervous. Let's get them together and into the compound," Talking Wren said to Single Leaf immediately after the mounts started to pull on their holding lines.

"Single Leaf is leading the mounts to the compound," Lily said as she saw the mounts coming toward her.

"Let's move the sled to let her in," Burley Bear said as he quickly jumped up and went to the entrance sled.

He was joined with Meadow Flower and the two moved the sled and travois.

Feather-in-the-Wind and Running Stag were out with the wolves.

"Let's slowly walk back toward the camp," Feather-in-the-Wind said as she picked up the two young wolves and put them in her carrying sling.

"What's wrong," Running Stag asked as he followed Feather-in-the-Wind?

"Lasher and Walker have started to growl, and the hair is standing up straight on their necks," Feather-in-the-Wind replied.

"Arrow is doing the same thing," was Running Stag's reply.

When the camp was in sight and she saw the mounts going into the camp Feather-in-the-Wind said, "Run." She turned and sprinted toward the compound.

"Keep the camp open. Feather-in-the-Wind and our wolves are on the run toward us," Taelo said as Burly Bear, Saber Scar, Little Otter, and Golden Hawk stood with their spears to either side of the opening.

"Dire wolves," Feather-in-the-Wind said as she led her wolves into the center and stopped.

She sat down and let the two wolf pups out. The pups went to their mother and snuggled in close to her.

Taelo threw wood into the two cooking rings at the entrance of the camp.

"We must be in their territory. Hopefully, they will not attack but we will need to be vigilant. We do not have enough wood to last all night or to put up additional sets of fires around the outside of our camp.

We will need to patrol from the inside.

We are carrying enough meat and other food that we must smell very good to them," Golden Hawk commented

"Two of us can guard while the rest get some sleep. Let's hope we do not need to fight with them tonight," Burley Bear said as he moved the travois to close the opening of the circle.

"And that is why no one ever confronts Burley Bear. Two of us can barely move our travois and he does it by himself," Running Stag said quietly to Feather-in-the-Wind.

"Yes, his superior strength is unquestionable.

What is even better is that he has grown in wisdom and in leadership through his friendship and devotion to Taelo and Golden Hawk.

The three of them are like brothers. They are connected," Feather-in-the-Wind replied.

"I suppose that is why Burley Bear chose to come on this journey. It makes me feel much safer to have him with us," Running Stag continued as he drew the covering over the two of them.

The next morning Marigold and Meadow Flower went around the outside of the camp reading the sign on the ground.

Burley Bear and Saber Scar followed them and were ready with their spears.

There must have been at least twenty dire wolves. This is a large pack. Hopefully, we can clear their territory today," Meadow Flower reported when they were back in the center of the camp.

Single Leaf, Talking Wren and Bashful Lark were all standing guard as Lily and Floating Cloud quickly warmed the morning food.

"We will move as fast as is possible. All of us will be on foot. We will push our mounts to a trot as we jog along besides them. We will stop only to rest the mounts.

Feather-in-the-Wind, please lead the way with your wolves. Watch Lasher and Walker. Let me know if either of them growls or has the hair on the back of their neck standing on end.

Golden Hawk and I will be out to either side of the lead mount.

Burley Bear, you and Little Otter bring up the back of our procession," Taelo instructed.

"You know the old joke about how fast you must run if you are being chased by a dire wolf," Golden Hawk could not resist teasing Little Otter who he knew always complained about jogging.

"It would be a contest he would lose," Burley Bear said with a smile as he joined in on the joking.

He was not so sure he could outrun Little Otter.

By the time the sun reached its zenith the team had traveled the same distance as they had the entire sun cycle before.

"This is working so well that I think we should do it every other cycle. The wolves out front frighten away the small game. Let's position them immediately behind the last mount.

Each of you leading a mount put yourselves so that every other mount is handled from the same side. This will allow you to use your slings on any small game you see to the sides.

Burley Bear and Little Otter move back behind the wolves," Taelo said as he reorganized the team for the rest of the cycle.

"I guess we are the dire wolf food," Little Otter joked as he and Burley Bear passed by Feather-in-the-Wind.

"Good that means they will be full by the time they get to me and won't be hungry," Feather-in-the-Wind joked back.

Taelo and Golden Hawk now jogged out in front of the entire procession. Their slings seemed to be in continuous use. Lasher was now up front with Taelo and would go out and retrieve the game and bring it to either Taelo or Golden Hawk.

"Hey, give us a chance," Running Stag called out as he watched the two in action.

"You will be up here tomorrow, and we will expect you to do the same," Taelo responded.

"Any other comments," Talking Wren said from the other side of the mounts from Running Stag.

Taelo and Golden Hawk were just getting ready to call a halt when they saw Quiet Rabbit and Busy Bee riding in on their mounts.

"Let's see what they have to say about this as a stopping spot," Golden Hawk said to Taelo.

"I would like to have more than this small stream," Taelo replied. He hoped the two would have a better spot where a good supply of fish could be gathered.

"There is a wonderful lake we can reach before the sun goes down. It will give us a place to fish and to bathe. We would both like to smell better than our mounts," Quiet Rabbit said as she gave Taelo a hug during her report.

"I agree. I think some of Meadow Flowers scented oil would make quite a difference," Taelo jokingly pushed Quiet Rabbit away.

"You heard our scouts. Let's double time to the lake," Golden Hawk called out.

Quiet Rabbit and Busy Bee got on their mounts and led the way.

Not long after they went out on what Quiet Rabbit called a wonderful swim.

The fish traps were set up where a small stream entered the lake and almost immediately was catching enough fish for the following day's journey.

"The timing of the scout's return was perfect. We will keep the mounts and the wolves in tonight and keep two guards awake to make sure we are not bothered during the night," Taelo commented after the team had eaten.

Taelo also arranged to have small fires around the outside of the circle of sleds. This meant two people would need to periodically put wood on them.

The next morning Meadow Flower and Marigold once again checked for dire wolf prints around the camp.

"We must be outside of their territory. There were no dire wolf prints around the camp," they reported as the team prepared to move.

"We will jog this entire sun cycle. On the next morning we will go on the slower pace. This will increase the distance we can travel each moon cycle and ensure we are through the northern passage before the cold arrives," Taelo informed the team.

"This time the dire wolves helped us," Taelo commented to Golden Hawk.

"Well, I suppose I will need to thank them for getting me into shape," Little Otter commented in a fake sad tone.

"No, I will thank them for you," Talking Wren said as she gave him a nudge in the side.

Chapter 9: Northern Passage Approach

The sun rising in the east highlighted the walls of ice and snow to the north. The opening for their travel north seemed like an empty riverbed whose border was made of ice and melting snow. The near border periodically cracked and boomed as a large piece of its face broke off and rumbled down into the opening the team was now traveling.

The far wall was so distant that it took on the look of a white line separating the sky from the ground below it.

The team proceeded northwest staying well away from the closest wall of ice.

The grasses and brush housed small game and birds and once the team saw a herd of buffalo.

The team kept up alternating the jogging and the walking mode of travel for the entire next moon cycle.

As the sun set behind the mountains and the ice cliffs to the west, Floating Cloud and Talking Wren returned from their scouting.

"We have seen the northern passage. It is hard to describe. The mountains rise higher than the eagle flies. They are higher than my clouds," Floating Cloud reported.

"We heard the eagle's cry" Talking Wren added.

"We believe it is the passage Broken Spear described," she continued.

"Tomorrow is our jogging cycle, so we will make the passage and perhaps get some distance in," Taelo said after the two had a chance to get something to eat.

"Let's all sleep well tonight. Tomorrow we will reach a milestone in our journey," Golden Hawk said.

Then he crawled into his sleeping hide.

Meanwhile, scouting out ahead, Quiet Rabbit and Busy Bee were the two scouts to reach the entrance to the passage and the first to travel into it.

Busy Bee suggested that since it was getting dark, they should wait until morning to return to the team.

"At the rising of the sun. Single Leaf and Bashful Lark will go out and take up where Quiet Rabbit and Busy Bee have stopped. The two of you will need to determine if we can travel through with our travois. If not, we will need to determine how to make it through," Taelo said to the two before they retired for the night.

He really did not want to take the path up the side of the mountain described by Broken Spear. It would take several trips to carry all the food and other gear along a mountain trail. This would make their passage through this area a very long one.

Single Leaf and Bashful Lark set out the next morning on their mounts.

"We are the new members of his team and yet Taelo trusts us with determining if we can make it through," Single Leaf commented to Bashful Lark.

"Yes, it puts pressure on us, but it makes me feel more a part of the team. I like the feeling," Bashful Lark replied.

The team followed a short time later after breaking camp. They proceeded at a rapid jog and by the time the sun was at its zenith they could see the way coming to an end. The mountains ahead indeed reached high into the sky. A layer of clouds hid the peaks from view.

The ice and snow walls seemed to close in toward the one location.

Suddenly a herd of animals crossed in front of them. Taelo and Golden Hawk sprinted out after the herd.

"Look at those two run," Burley Bear commented to Meadow Flower.

He moved to the front position and waited to see if the two would be able to down one of the animals.

"They look similar to our elk, but their antlers are different," Feather-in-the-Wind commented as she stood on the top of her mount and watched Taelo and Golden Hawk.

"Taelo has taken one of the animals down and it looks as if Golden Hawk will get his as well," Feather-in-the-Wind reported.

"Let's setup camp," Burley Bear called out.

The team had been following a small river coming from the high mountains ahead. Burley Bear positioned himself close enough to the river so the cooking fires would be on its bank. The camp went up in record time.

"I will take two of the mounts out to bring the elk cousins back to the camp," Running Stag volunteered.

"I will go with you to help," Saber Scar said as he turned his mount out to where Golden Hawk and Taelo had pulled the two animals.

"These are interesting antlers. They are rounder than the elk horns," Taelo commented as he helped Golden Hawk pull his animal toward the other one.

"Yes, but they are very similar to the elk. Their hide has more hair and seems thicker," Golden Hawk replied as he ran his hand across the side of the animal.

"Here comes Running Stag and Saber Scar with some mounts.

Let's gut the animals here and then take them back to the camp to skin them.

We will have fresh meat tonight," Taelo commented as he began to cut open his animal.

"Let us bring the animals back to camp. You two can return on the extra mounts," Saber Scar said as he slid off his mount and took out his blade.

"We will walk back," Taelo replied as he and Golden Hawk picked up their spears and headed back to the camp.

"The team has really come together well," Taelo said to Golden Hawk.

"Yes, this is the strongest team we have taken on a journey.

How many more journeys will we take," Golden Hawk wondered out loud?

"I have seen at least one more. It was during the time I was recovering from the bear wound and talking with the ancients," Taelo replied.

"Did you actually see and talk to them," Golden Hawk asked.

"I do not know for sure, but I did talk to Broken Spear, and he tells of talking to me. So, the ancients must somehow exist and perhaps be able to see and talk to us," Taelo continued.

This was the first time he had talked about this subject with Golden Hawk. He had shared some of it with Quiet Rabbit, but he had not gone into any detail.

The discussions with the ancients had been detailed and specific. He knew that once they went through the mountain passage ahead, he would face the first of three tests that were to happen on this journey.

This first test would once again be a bear. Only this bear would be more aggressive and much larger than any he had faced so far.

It was hard for Taelo to imagine a bear bigger than the one that had almost taken his life.

"Once we get through the pass, a giant bear, larger than the one in our *Journey of Discovery* will begin to hunt us. We will try to leave its territory, but he will continue to hunt us. Finally, we will have to face the bear. How we do that will determine if any of us gets killed," Taelo said quietly to Golden Hawk.

"Should we warn the rest of the team," Golden Hawk asked?

"Yes, let's do that once Quiet Rabbit and Busy Bee return. I want them to hear about this from us," Taelo replied.

"It looks as if Running Stag and Saber Scar will get the animals back to the camp ahead of us," Golden Hawk said as the two-rode past with the carcasses of the animals on the backs of two of the mounts.

"I hope Lily and Floating Cloud begin to roast some of the meat," Taelo said as he walked quietly on.

"I am sure they will, and you know that Lily will offer you the first piece," Golden Hawk replied.

The team was sitting around the fires. The nights had become less dark as they traveled north. The nights were cool enough that everyone had a small hide over their shoulders.

This night waves of colored lights danced across the heavens. The light dance was similar to a side winder snake going across the sands.

"What a strange sky," Lily commented.

"Is it the dancing of the spirits," Floating Cloud asked quietly?

"I do not know but its beauty tells me it is a reward to us for doing what we do," Lily put her spin on what she saw.

"I see riders coming in. It must be Quiet Rabbit and Busy Bee," Feather-in-the-Wind called out from where she was sitting with the wolves.

"They will be hungry. I will put two pieces of our fresh meat on the fire," Lily said as she went to where the two carcasses were still hanging.

She and Floating Cloud would cut up the carcasses into pieces before retiring for the night.

"We should find a place to store some of our dried meats and some salt on this side of the passage," Slow Runner suggested.

"There is a large split rock just up-stream from here where we can store what we decide to leave. We will be able to close the area with stones I saw in the area," Sharp Blade replied.

"Let's make enough room on Lily's and Floating Cloud's sleds for the fresh meat and put the dried meat taken off the sleds into storage. We will want to carry most of the salt with us so we will leave the minimum that Lily and Floating Cloud may want," Taelo replied as he got up to greet Quiet Rabbit and Busy Bee as they came in.

"The passage ahead is as inspiring as seeing the two seas from the top of the mountain when we took our *Journey of the Heart*," Quiet Rabbit said as she sat down by the fire.

She and Busy Bee were wrapped in full hides and were warming up from bathing in the icy cold river. They had talked about cleaning up and eating since the sun had started to set.

"It always feels so refreshing to wash in cold water, to dry and put on the scented oil," Busy Bee commented as she stood with her back to the fire.

"The two of us talked about making it back to camp in time to bathe and eat. We were not expecting a treat of fresh, roasted meat," Quiet Rabbit commented, as she took a bite of the hot savory meat.

"The pass ahead is awe inspiring. When you look up you see the blue of the sky as a thin blue line above you," Busy Bee continued.

"At this point we were riding in the river that runs through this passage. The river is shallow, and we can pull the travois at least to the point we reached," Quiet Rabbit added.

"The banks along the shore of the river offer places where we could camp but there is no place to put up our camping circle," Busy Bee continued.

"We will wait until Sharp Blade and Bashful Lark return before we go into the passage," Taelo said as he thought about what they would face on the other side.

"Golden Hawk and I will leave in the morning to scout the total passage," Taelo said as he decided he needed to see the entire way for himself.

Chapter 10: Northern Passage

The northeastern ice wall curved sharply southwest and embraced the eastern side of the snow-capped peak. The ice wall on the southern side curved slightly more toward the north.

A small run off river ran along its base in the opposite direction Taelo and Golden Hawk were jogging. They continued to jog together in silence as they took in the grand view of the mountains. Later in the day as the two approached the passage they saw Sharp Blade and Bashful Lark.

"Tell us what you saw," Golden Hawk said as they came together.

"It is an inspiring ride. We felt so small and fragile," Bashful Lark commented.

"There is only one place where it will be difficult to get through. The passage narrows and the river rushes through a gap between the walls of the cliffs. We could see a fine beach on the other side but decided not to take the mounts through. We were not sure they could swim against the current or that we could return the same way," Sharp Blade added.

"We will wait until early morning before we go into the passage. You two ride on. When you get to the team let them know that we will travel all the way through and return. They already know to wait for us on this side of the passage," Taelo instructed the two.

"I hope we can figure out a way to get through the narrow point of the passage," Golden Hawk commented as the narrow passage came into view.

"Let's proceed up the bank of the river and hope that we can pull the travois most of the way," Taelo said as he and Golden Hawk settled into a slow jog along the river.

The mountain sides rose sharply up into the sky and the banks of the river narrowed. Up ahead they could see the narrow blue line that seemed to barely separate the two sides of the river.

"I now understand the awe everyone has felt as they describe this passage," Golden Hawk said as he looked at the narrow blue line above them.

"We will make camp here. There is still enough room for regular circular formation at this point. See if you can come up with some fish from the river. I will run back to the point the valley meets the river and set up markers to guide the team to this point," Taelo said as he put down his travel pack.

"Stay with Golden Hawk," Taelo said to Lasher.

"Ok, hurry back for fresh fish," Golden Hawk said as he went to the riverbank with his spear.

Taelo ran back and set up the stone markers showing the way to the camp. He put down a flat stone, put a large round one on top of the flat stone and then put a small round one next to it to indicate the direction to follow. He put down his first marker and then turned upriver and put down another when he lost sight of the previous one.

A short time later he could smell fish being roasted on the fire.

"Your timing is perfect as always. The fish is just about done. Yours is the red one," Golden Hawk said jokingly since both fish had turned red when they had been heated.

"I also found a few thin poles. I put them in the ground, bent them over and covered them with our protection hides. We will be able to crawl under and stay warm and dry overnight," Golden Hawk continued.

"You have been busy. Thanks for both the fish and getting the camp set up," Taelo said appreciatively.

"How was the fishing," Taelo continued?

"Well, these fish have never been hunted. I stood on that large round stone at the edge of the river and in a short time I had four large fish up on the bank. I cut the flesh off of one and gave the meat to Lasher. I put these two on a spit and got the fire going. The largest one is hanging there in the bush," Golden Hawk said as he pointed to a fish as long as his arm.

"Very nice, we will have a good breakfast before we go up the river," Taelo said as he walked over to take a closer look at the fish.

"It must be a relative of the salmon," Taelo said as he examined the fish.

He had never seen one like it before.

"How cold is the water," Taelo asked?

"It will wake you right up," Golden Hawk chuckled.

He had been contemplating crawling into his sleeping hide and skipping the normal bathing. He followed Taelo down to the edge of the riverbank and watched as Taelo stripped down and walked into the river.

"It does not seem to get very deep," Taelo said as he walked slowly toward the center.

"It is very cold. I don't think I will stay in it very long," Taelo said as the water reached his chest.

Taelo ducked down and went totally under. He came up immediately sputtering and blowing out air.

"Wow, I hope we have plenty of wood for our fire," Taelo called out as he watched Golden Hawk come rushing into the water.

"Yes, I gathered enough dead wood to keep the fire going all night," Golden Hawk said in a chattering tone.

"I have had enough," Taelo said after letting the water run through his hair for a few moments.

He turned and led the way back to the camp. Once there he rummaged in his pack until he found his drying hide. He stood by the fire and slowly dried off.

"That certainly woke me up," Taelo commented as he slowly turned to let the heat warm him on all sides.

"Have you noticed we are finding more food along the way than what we were expecting," Golden Hawk commented.

"Yes, and those new ones, I will call them caribou, they provide some very tasty meat," Taelo responded.

"We may want to leave a good portion of the dried meat here on this side of the passage. If on the return we find ourselves short of food we will know where to get it," Golden Hawk suggested.

"We can decide that after we scout the passage. What we see on the other side may well make your suggestion a very good one," Taelo said as he wrapped his sleeping hide over his shoulders.

He sat down on one of the two round stones he had moved into place near the fire.

Lasher lay quietly at his feet.

The night sky was again putting on a show of dancing green lights.

The next morning the two cleaned up their camp before leaving and then headed into the pass. They jogged along the bank that remained wide enough for the travois.

Then the way ahead seemed to be totally blocked by a mountain that appeared to have been cut from its peak to its base. The small river rushed forcefully through a gorge no more than five spears wide.

A thin blue line appearing to the eye to be no wider that the width of a spear shaft was all of the sky that could be seen above the gorge.

The cliffs seemed to have been separated from each other by a sharp blade and the river at its base pulled the air through with the swift current of its waters.

The force of this water would be a challenge to overcome. The water was clear and the boulders gracing the bottom could be clearly seen.

This was as far as Lasher could follow them. Taelo knelt down to Lasher and instructed him to go to Quiet Rabbit.

"OK, Lasher, go to Quiet Rabbit. Let her know we are all right," Taelo said as he stood up.

Lasher gave a small bark and headed downstream.

After making sure Lasher was truly on his way, Taelo attacked the cliff in front of him. He had his travel pack on his back and his spear hanging from his shoulder on a piece of hide.

Taelo led the way along a narrow ledge on the face of the vertical gorge wall above the river. His goal was to reach the sand beach that Sharp Blade and Bashful Lark had seen when they looked upstream from the gravel bed that lay just down-stream of the opening.

He was soon at the point where he could see the other side.

"I can see the beach Sharp Blade said he saw from downstream from the middle of the river," Taelo called back over his shoulder.

"I am going to go around and look at the situation from the upstream side," Taelo called back only to find Golden Hawk at his side.

"I thought I would join you," Golden Hawk said with a smile.

He too was carrying all his belongings.

"The river takes a bend here. We can stand on the beach and look straight down the river," Golden Hawk said as he pointed downstream.

"Let's see if we can find two large logs. We can put the travois and the sleds on the logs and pull them through. We will need to get several of the mounts through so they can provide the pulling power we will need," Taelo said as he began to look for the logs he wanted.

"With two logs we can pull the first mounts upstream. Or perhaps I should say Burley Bear, Saber Scar and Sharp Blade can pull them up. We can put straps of hide under the mounts and attach them to the logs on either side of the mounts," Golden Hawk said as he thought about the logs.

"Great idea. Now let's find the logs," Taelo said as he continued going upstream.

"The valley is widening. There is enough room here to setup our regular camp," Golden Hawk commented as they continued to go upstream.

"Let's go upstream for the rest of the day," Taelo suggested.

"We have seen many smaller logs. I don't think we are going to find the large logs we hoped for," Taelo said a little later with a bit disappointment.

"I think we could tie four of the smaller logs together and the idea would still work," Golden Hawk commented.

"I was thinking the same thing. Let's pick eight matching logs and position them at the beach. We can get the team to help put this idea into action," Taelo replied.

Back on the trail Busy Bee had just gotten on her mount and saw Lasher approaching.

"Here comes Lasher," Busy Bee called out from where she sat.

The team had just arrived at the first marker left by Taelo.

"I hope there is nothing wrong," Little Otter said as he looked up from the marker he had just found.

"I think Taelo may have sent him back when they got to the point in the river where there is no bank. The two would need to get around that point and probably could not take Lasher with them," Sharp Blade volunteered.

"I agree with you," Quiet Rabbit added as she gave Lasher a hug.

It was clear to her that Lasher had been sent to her because he sat down quietly at her feet. This was Lasher's behavior when Taelo assigned Lasher to someone.

"We are to go in this direction," Burley Bear commented as he led the team upstream.

"This is the spot. They left a gift for us," Lily called out as she spotted the fish hanging on a pole at the edge of the riverbank.

"Let's set up camp and this time we will put the cover up as well. The weather is getting colder each evening," Busy Bee called out.

It was her turn to lead the setup.

Chapter 11: Through the Northern Passage

*C*he waters of the lake in the sky lay above and behind them. Directly above them cutting through the top of the mountain was a thin blue river. An almost straight vertical blue line brought the thin blue down from above to the waters that gathered from a gently flowing river into the waters that shot forcefully through the narrow gorge.

Taelo absorbed the three-dimensional visual game his eyes played with the sky, the mountain cliffs and the river gorge as morning came to life.

It was late and the sun was setting by the time he and Golden Hawk had beached the logs. They were exhausted and not sure they could safely navigate the narrow cliff path back through the gorge and had decided to stay on the upstream side for the night.

"I would not trust my arms at this point. The muscles are numb from fighting these logs up on to the shore," Taelo said in support of Golden Hawk.

"I am glad we did not attempt the cliff last night. My arms were so exhausted that I missed the first two fish that I tried for last night," Taelo admitted.

Golden Hawk admitted that he had struggled to get the fire going on the previous night, but that he felt great this morning.

Golden Hawk got the fire going while Taelo went to the rapids up stream and speared two large fish.

"After we eat, I will be ready to climb the cliff. How are you feeling," Taelo asked Golden Hawk?

"There is nothing as good as sleep to bring new life into my body," Golden Hawk replied as he devoured his fish.

Taelo and Golden Hawk took their time. After their morning meal, they navigated the narrow path along the cliff without incident. By the time the sun hit its Zenith they made it to the team's camp.

"I see you decided it was time to stay warm," Golden Hawk said as he pointed to the cover.

"Yes, it was the only way I could keep warm with you gone," Busy Bee replied as she gave Golden Hawk a hug.

"How are we going to get through the pass," Burley Bear asked the question everyone in the camp was wondering about?

"We are going to pull everyone through on logs," Taelo replied.

"And who will do the pulling," Little Otter inquired?

"Let me draw it out on the ground," Taelo said as he took a sharp pointed stick and drew a map of the river at the point of the narrows.

"I am counting on the muscle power of Burley Bear, Saber Scar and Sharp Blade. They will need to pull the first mount through and up to the beach.

The mount will be floating between two bundles of logs," Taelo continued his explanation.

"I know you think we are powerful, and we are, but I think I would like Meadow Flower, Marigold, and Single Leaf to help us with the first mount. We cannot take the chance of losing one of our mounts," Burley Bear spoke up after he understood what needed to be done.

"Do we have the logs that are needed," Quiet Rabbit asked.

"Yes, Taelo and I pulled eight logs to the beach. They will need to be strapped together. We will need four logs for each side," Golden Hawk replied.

"Let's get a work party to go and prepare the logs and the area we will pull the first mount through.

We also need to make sure we then utilize the mounts to the best advantage.

There are also eighty wolves to think about as well," Talking Wren added.

"Would you be willing to lead this work party," Taelo inquired of Talking Wren?

He knew she was the best among them in organizing and in designing how things should work.

"Yes, I am willing. We can plan on going up in the morning to evaluate the situation and to tie the logs together. I think Saber Scar, Marigold, Sharp Knife and Single Leaf, you and I would be enough," Talking Wren replied to Taelo.

"It's a deal," Golden Hawk said with a chuckle as he patted Taelo on the back. He was so happy to be able to stay in camp and relax.

"We will need most of the hide rope we have. Let's soak it in the river tonight so when we bind the logs it is already stretched," Talking Wren began immediately to think through the process of pulling everything through the pass.

"Once we have the mounts through, we will want to strap on cross members across the two sets of logs and create a platform above them.

We will then mount the travois and sleds on these cross logs. Finally, we will need some woven mats made of small saplings to make a floor for the platform that the wolves can sit on," Talking Wren continued as she thought through getting the entire team through the pass.

"Running Stag and I will begin gathering the saplings to make the floor for the wolves," Feather-in-the-Wind volunteered.

"I will help weave the mats," Floating Cloud spoke up.

"As will I," Slow Runner said.

"I will work with Golden Hawk to get the cross members," came from Busy Bee.

"I will come with you and keep all of you fed during the day," was Lily's offer.

"As always, I will do as you ask," Little Otter closed the volunteering and got a chuckle from the entire team.

"It sounds as if we will get this done as a team," Taelo said looking around.

The next day Taelo led the work party to the narrow gap in the river.

The path across the face of the cliff that formed the narrow passage required each person to carefully negotiated hand holds and foot placement.

Taelo led the way showing Talking Wren these critical hand holds and foot placement. She in turn passed this on to Burley Bear.

He had suggested they try it with nothing being carried and that they come back and get their loads and then cross with their loads.

"That was a very good idea," Talking Wren commented after the entire work party had made it through the gap.

"Let's get a lay of the land while we rest our muscles before we go back and get the material we will need.

"This boulder directly upstream from the gap will serve as the point where we secure our line," Talking Wren said as she envisioned Little Otter locking in the line between pulls.

"We need to turn and position each set of logs so two small ends and two large ends are matched.

We are in luck. One set of four are already in the desired position. Let's turn the other two logs and we will be done with positioning them," Talking Wren instructed.

Taelo went upstream while the logs were being maneuvered and speared a handful of fish. He brought these back to Lily who had started a fire.

"I will have these prepared in a few minutes," Lily said as she cut enough young willow sticks and skewered the fish.

"The rest of us will go and get all our equipment and materials and be back for something to eat. I don't want to eat and then have to negotiate the climb around the gap," Talking Wren said as she led the way back to get their things.

The preparation work took most of the sun cycle.

"It is time to get back to the camp," Taelo said calling a halt to the work. They were almost complete in getting everything ready.

"I agree. We can finish any additional work in the morning. Remind me to dig out pulling holes for our pullers so they don't slide as they pull the mounts upriver," Talking Wren said as she followed Taelo to the cliff.

"Here comes the work team. They look bushed. I have a treat for the entire team," Floating Cloud said as she put the finishing touches on her honey roasted caribou meat.

"Well, we are bushed too. The smells coming from your cooking fire have had us all salivating," Quiet Rabbit said from where she was sitting with the team weaving the floor for the wolves to ride on.

"We have cut our eight cross members and notched them so they will fit over the logs and hold them apart," Busy Bee said from where she had been creating the notches.

"Bashful Lark found some scallions that we have roasted in the coals. She also found a large number of red huckleberries that will be served fresh," Floating Cloud continued explaining her treat.

She repeated the entire description one more time as the whole team gathered around for the meal.

"So, I leave for a day and my position as the lead cook gets immediately challenged," Lily joked as she nibbled on some berries.

"It was the first time we have been allowed to cook," Floating Cloud replied truthfully.

"I like the idea of each of us taking the lead in cooking. We can set up a schedule. It will be good to share the cooking load," Lily said as she thought about it.

"Perhaps the rest of us could take part as well," Taelo added.

He liked to cook once in a while.

"Those of us who want to periodically cook the evening meal should give Lily their name and how often they would like to do so," Marigold suggested.

She had wanted to cook some of her own dishes but had not wanted to create an awkward situation by cooking it separately.

"Tomorrow we will focus on getting all the mounts through the passage.

We will move the travois as close to the gap as possible. We need to leave room for the mounts at the very front. The travois and sleds will be next. The wolves will be the last to cross so they will be behind the travois and sleds.

Taelo and the pulling crew will cross over to the upstream location we have picked out. They will float the log pairs down to us on this side of the passage.

I will instruct the loading crew on how to strap the mounts between the logs," Talking Wren explained at the end of the dinner.

"She is very good at organizing complex work," Burley Bear said quietly to Taelo.

Taelo nodded his head in agreement but said nothing.

The next morning the rising of the sun signaled the breaking of camp and the movement to the passage gap.

"Remember to dig the pulling holes. Taelo will show you what each of you has to do. I will stay on this side and organize getting things loaded," Talking Wren said in a commanding voice.

Taelo led the pulling team along the face of the cliff to the beach on the other side.

"I hope I don't have to go back today," Little Otter said as he thought about his near fall.

"The six of you get into your pull positions. Little Otter and I will push the logs into the river. Then we will get to our holding positions. We will practice letting the logs go down through the gap and then we will pull the logs back," Taelo instructed.

"Don't say it. I will say it for you. "We will do this three times and then we will be ready for our first mount," Burley Bear said with a grin.

"Indeed, you have it," Taelo replied with a wink and a smile.

"It's not too bad, with no load. I think we will have our hands full when we are pulling our first mount through the gap," Saber Scar commented later as they ended their third pull.

"Let's find out. But let's dig out two more pulling holes in case you need just a little more help," Taelo said, as he proceeded to scoop out two more, foot holes.

"Taelo and I talked it over. He can lock the pull in by himself, I can add a little more power to the direct pull," Little Otter explained.

"I am sure we will thank you," Burley Bear replied as he thought about the load a mount would put on them.

"Ok, here come the logs for the first mount. Golden Hawk, the leather straps have already been secured to the outer logs. Your job is to pass the front strap just behind the mount's front legs and the back strap just in front of the rear legs using this branch with a fork in it.

Then pass the middle strap over the mounts back. Each strap has a hole on the end for the fork to fit in.

Slow Runner your job is to pull the bottom straps up snug to the mount's belly. The top strap has a long cord on the end. Pull the cord and snug down the top strap and tie it off.

Meanwhile Running Stag and Feather-in-the-Wind will put the front cross bar in place.

Busy Bee and Quiet Rabbit will put the back cross member into place. This will secure the mount in place.

I wish we would have had the chance to have three practices," Talking Wren explained the process as the logs arrived at the loading area.

Golden Hawk waded out into the cold water until it was up over his waist.

"This water is freezing. Let's move fast or you will have to fish me out," Golden Hawk sang out as he pulled the two sets of logs apart so Slow Runner could lead the mount between them.

"Be sure to stay on the outside of the logs," Talking Wren called out when she saw Slow Runner about to enter between them.

"Feather-in-the-Wind, get that front log secured so Slow Runner can bring the mount all the way there," Talking Wren continued to instruct the team.

"What does she think I am doing," Feather-in-the-Wind mumbled to Running Stag.

"Great job you four. The front and back cross members went in faster than I thought they would," Talking Wren called out.

She knew she was nervous and perhaps being too critical.

Golden Hawk stumbled out of the freezing water onto the beach.

"My legs are numb," he said as he rubbed them down with his drying hide.

"I need to get to the other side. I think the mount will have the same problem I am having," he said to Quite Rabbit and Busy Bee.

"You stay here and let your legs and body recover," we will cross over and alert the pulling team," Quiet Rabbit said as she walked over to Talking Wren to let her know what was happening.

"I never thought about such a situation. I hope the mount will be alright," Talking Wren commented when she understood the potential problem.

"You must get the mount out of the water as fast as possible. It may have problems standing. If so all of us must help lay it on its side and pull it up on the beach," Quiet Rabbit called out as she approached the pulling team.

It was clear the team was struggling against the current that went through the gap.

"Quiet Rabbit, Busy Bee, come here and handle the position locking. I will help on the direct pull," Taelo called out.

Taelo quickly dug two more pulling holes for himself and got into the last position.

"Pull on my command, lock on my command," Taelo called out.

"Pull, ...Lock, ...Pull, ...Lock, ...Pull, ...Lock," Taelo called out in a rhythm that allowed the team to work efficiently and pull the mount toward them.

The mount made it to where it could stand but it was clear its legs were not functioning properly.

"I will cover its head with a hide," Feather-in-the-Wind said as she came running up the beach and stood by the mount's head.

"I am loosening the back brace so we can float her out and maneuver her to the beach," Running Stag said as he climbed up on the logs.

He quickly untied all the straps holding the mount to the logs.

The entire pulling team got into the water and helped the mount by holding its legs together and floating the mount to the beach. Together they were able to drag her clear of the water.

"Keep her head covered. Busy Bee and I will rub her legs down. We will keep her quiet until we think she is ready.

"That was quick thinking and quick reaction and great teamwork," Talking Wren complimented the team.

"I have Slow Runner bringing the noon meal over to this side. Is there a chance someone can get some fish to add to it," Lily said as she arrived?

"Thank you for holding her head. Your wolves are wondering where you went. And Nudge is the mount Floating Cloud and I share," Bashful Lark said as she talked quietly to her mount.

Floating Cloud had been given this mount because the mount was older than the others and the gentlest.

It was clear the mount recognized Bashful Lark's voice. It let out a snort and gave Bashful Lark a nudge.

"I think I know how you named her," Feather-in-the-Wind said as she signaled Running Stag and headed back to the gap.

The second mount was pulled up more quickly but needed similar attention on the beach.

"It is time to stop," Talking Wren called out.

She had planned to have all the mounts through, but it was clear they were all very tired and the day was quickly coming to a close.

"We will continue in the morning. With two mounts pulling we should be able to get the rest through during the next sun cycle.

"Quiet Rabbit, Busy Bee, Golden Hawk, and I will stay on this side. We will guard the mounts," Taelo volunteered as he headed to the gap.

He and Golden Hawk went back across the gap to get their sleeping gear and their weapons.

It took the next sun cycle to get all the mounts through the gap.

The travois and sleds were heavy but Burley Bear and Little Otter were able to man handle them onto the logs. The nine travois came upstream one at a time. This took another sun cycle.

On the third sun cycle it was time to bring the wolves through.

"This should prove to be very interesting," Taelo commented to Lasher as he and Lasher climbed up on the logs.

The woven floor mats had been tied on and provided a flat area to stand or lay on.

"Come," Feather-in-the-Wind said as she climbed on top the logs.

About twenty of the wolves followed her. It was clear many of the remaining wolves were going to present a challenge.

"I think we have a good first load," Taelo said as he gave the signal for the logs to be pulled up stream.

"Stay," Feather-in-the-Wind called out as several of the wolves readied to leap into the water to get to her.

"You have trained them well. I will want to enroll you in helping me handle any bears we run into," Taelo said as he thought about the confrontation that had been predicted.

"Thank you for your praise. Let me know what I can do to help," Feather-in-the-Wind said looking up from where she sat with the wolves around her.

It took four pulls to get all the wolves through the gap. Lasher proved to be the driver as the last of the reluctant wolves were being loaded. He growled and nipped at their heels and back sides of the wolves that were hesitant.

"They may see you as their human leader, but it is clear that Lasher is their wolf master. They dare not ignore him," Taelo commented to Feather-in-the-Wind as they got the last of the wolves on the logs.

"Slow Runner, Sharp Blade and I will clean up this area and then come up to the beach," Running Stag called out as the last pull began the journey through the gap.

Chapter 12: Pursued by the Great Bear

The river bounded on the far bank by the western slope of the snow- and ice-covered mountain turned sharply to the northwest.

Burley Bear selected a wide flat expanse of grass covered sand, strewn with the rubble of limbs and other debris carried by flooding waters, to setup their camp.

The scrap wood was collected and piled up near the cooking fire ring and smaller piles were located around the camp to be used for night sentinel fires.

The team would stay and rest for a few sun cycles before proceeding.

The travois were arranged in their familiar circle.

Bashful Lark had suggested the use of a guide rope held by the center person and the lead travois that assured a perfect circle. There was one length for the normal camp and there was a shorter length for the defensive circle.

This idea made it much easier and faster to setup the camp.

"Stake the mounts out just downstream and near the river. Let's put the wolves close around the camp but toward the eastern mountains," Taelo added to the handlers of each.

"We need to talk through how to react when we face one of the great bears," Taelo began.

"This is one time when we will not want to come together to defend ourselves. Instead, we will scatter. The bear will choose his or her target. Once that is clear, I will distract the bear and get him to chase me," Taelo continued.

"I will always try to get the bear to chase me toward the passage. Then I will circle back to catch up with the team.

The team will always scatter in the forward direction toward the northwest and then regroup after a cycle.

If you run into another bear while you are running, drop the travois and ride your mount at full speed toward the mountains ahead," Taelo directed the team.

"How many bears are you expecting," Burley Bear inquired?

"I am not sure, but we are in the great bear territory from here until we get close to the ice bridge," Taelo replied.

Broken Spear had talked about only one great bear encounter but during his stay with the ancients Taelo had seen several of the great bears. He was not sure what they faced ahead.

"I will need your help," Taelo said as he quietly conversed with Feather-in-the-Wind.

"You are able to run as fast as Golden Hawk and I and you have an army of wolves that you have trained. I have been thinking about how to handle the great bear," Taelo began.

"I am all ears. It is an honor to be considered," Feather-in-the-Wind replied.

She did not know what to expect but she knew she would do whatever was asked.

In the last bear encounter she had climbed high up a pine tree and had watched as Taelo fearlessly faced a huge bear. He had killed it even as the bear grasped him in its clutches. The bear almost took Taelo's life when its claws dug deep through Taelo's back.

"I will be glad to help as well," Running Stag spoke up.

"Thank you, I know your bravery and your skill, but in this case, you must ride the mount and get your travois safely out of the area. The only person I am asking to help me will be Feather-in-the-Wind," Taelo replied.

Quiet Rabbit sat quietly. She could run as fast, and she had volunteered just as eagerly as Running Stag.

"We need you to be ready to sew us up if we need it," Taelo had quietly replied as he gave her a hug.

He had made the point that he was only asking the help of Feather-in-the-Wind so the rest of the team would hear.

"You know all of us are having a hard time accepting the role of running instead of fighting together," Golden Hawk spoke up.

He, Busy Bee, Quiet Rabbit and Taelo had discussed and argued this during their night on the river beach.

The actions Taelo was asking the team to accept were foreign to all of them. The team culture was one of coming together to overcome any obstacle.

"Yes, we will be acting as a team. In the past as a team, we were the superior power. In this case we are not. We will be the hunted. But we are smarter than the hunter.

The team will win the battle because we choose to fight on our terms not the bear's term.

"Feather-in-the-Wind and her wolves will be my army. We will hound and tire the bear to exhaustion and then we will return to the team.

I hope in this manner to keep the team moving safely in the direction we desire to go," Taelo replied.

"I at least will volunteer to be the bear for our practices," Burley Bear spoke and broke the silence that followed Taelo's comments.

"And so will I," Little Otter said as he put his arm around Burley Bear.

"Great idea to practice," Taelo replied.

For once he had not thought about the practice.

"Well, I am exhausted from these practices," Quiet Rabbit said later as the team came together for the third time.

"I believe everyone has figured out a separate path to take and then how to find each other as they come back together," Floating Cloud commented as she brought her travois into position for the camp circle.

"Thank you all for the good practices," Taelo said as he helped pull up the roof of the camp.

"If we are in camp when we face the bear, let Feather-in-the-Wind and I draw the bear away, then abandon the camp and ride your mounts away in the same manner.

Once I have drawn off the bear, Golden Hawk and Burley Bear will lead you back to rescue our belongings," Taelo said in a steady voice.

"I hope we don't have to practice that this evening," Little Otter said in a tired voice.

He received a jab from Talking Wren for his comment.

"Bashful Lark and I have setup the fish trap in the river, and it already has two large fish. We need someone to clean them. We will help Lily prepare the dinner," Floating Cloud called out.

She knew everyone was tired and hungry.

"Thank You. I will go to the river and get the fish," Slow Runner said as he started for the river.

"I will help," Running Stag said and joined Slow Runner.

"Is Taelo always this thorough," Slow Runner asked as the two stood looking at the six fish that were now in the trap?

"Yes, and it has served the team well. We all groan while we are doing what he asks and then we are rejoicing when the practice saves us," Running Stag replied.

"You and the wolves did a superb job at chasing Burley Bear. You should stay away as far as possible. The bear may not run away but instead attack. In that case you turn and run.

I will then get the bear's attention and make him chase me. When he does, you must again have the wolves chase the bear. We will do this until we tire out the bear," Taelo sat discussing his strategy on how to handle an attacking bear.

"I understand and you can count on me and the wolves," Feather-in-the-Wind replied.

For the next six sun cycles, the team traveled across a wide plain. They followed a small river toward the northwest.

It was on the seventh cycle after the team had just broken camp that they ran into the bear. It came roaring out from a depression that was behind a large boulder.

"Go," Sharp Blade said as he hit the mount Single Leaf was riding.

This single action saved her and the mount. The bear knocked the sled and travois sideways. Single Leaf urged her mount forward and the travois came clear of the bear.

Sharp Blade turned and ran back toward the pack of wolves.

"Attack," Feather-in-the-Wind said as she fearlessly ran forward with her wolves.

The eighty wolves were no match for the huge beast.

Taelo turned and ran back from the front of the procession. He had his spear out and was yelling at the top of his voice.

"Do as we practiced," he shouted at the top of his voice.

"Sharp Blade, leave the area."

"Feather-in-the-Wind let's do what we said," Taelo called out as he attracted the bear.

Suddenly the bear focused on Taelo.

The chase was on.

"Come on you slow beast," Taelo called over his shoulder.

"This bear is much faster than I thought," went through Taelo's mind a few moments later.

Taelo could hear Feather-in-the-Wind urging her wolves on as they followed on the heel of the great bear.

The bear was ignoring the wolves and was focused on Taelo. Suddenly it stopped and turned.

"It's after me," Feather-in-the-Wind called out as she turned and ran.

Wolves flew in both directions as the Bear pawed aside the wolves who were trying to protect Feather-in-the-Wind.

Taelo turned and ran after the Bear from behind.

His dream was coming to life. He knew that in the next few moments what he had seen in his delusional dreams, during the recovery from his wounds, would come true. He had lived this experience once before. Now he knew the dream had been about this bear not the one that had attacked him then.

"Your skin will be my bed. Your claws will be my blade. Your meat will feed my body. You will die today," Taelo called out as he caught up with the bear and buried his spear into the side of the bear.

The bear gave a giant roar, stood on his hind legs, and turned on Taelo.

Taelo ran toward the bear and at the last moment slid past him on the ground. As he went sliding past the bear, his blade cut across the back of the bear's leg just above the paws.

The bear tried to turn but slowly lost its balance and toppled over. As it got on its other three legs, Taelo cut the tendon in the other back leg.

Feather-in-the-Wind had her wolves gathered around her. She ran back toward the bear with her spear and then retreated as the bear lunged toward her.

"Thank you. See if you can distract the bear so I can attack it with my war club," Taelo called out.

"My pleasure," Feather-in-the-Wind called out as she teased the Bear with the spear.

Taelo approached the bear from the back. He stepped on the bear's hind quarter and propelled himself in a lunge that allowed him to deliver a solid blow to the side of the bear's head just below its ear.

The crack and crunch signaled significant damage.

The loud roar and the sudden lunge toward Taelo made it clear the bear was not through.

"Hiiii eee," Feather-in-the-Wind cried out as she ran forward with all her speed and buried the spear in the bear's left side just below the front leg.

The bear swiped at her with its right paw.

Feather-in-the-Wind went sliding past the bear and immediately ran past Taelo.

"He is all yours," she said as she went past.

"I will thank you later," Taelo said as he hit the bear on the other side of its head with his war club and spun away.

The bear went down with a grunt. He was stunned but not yet dead.

Taelo jumped on its back and with a small hand weapon made of shark teeth bound between two elk jaw bones, he cut the bear's throat. He then hit it on the back of its head with all his might.

The bear was finally dead.

As he turned to share the news with Feather-in-the-Wind, Taelo saw that she was lying on the ground surrounded by her wolves.

Lasher was at her side.

"Where are you wounded," Taelo asked as he rushed to where Feather-in-the-Wind was lying?

"I think the bear cut me across my thigh," was the faint reply.

Taelo quickly examined the wound. It was bleeding in a pulsing fashion. He pulled his medicine bag from his belt and took out a piece of leather and some gum material.

"This may sting," Taelo said as he wiped the wound clean, put the gum material into the wound and bound it in tight with a wide leather strap.

"Go to Quiet Rabbit," Taelo said as he patted Lasher on the head.

Lasher ran off circled the area once and then chose a direction toward the camp.

Sometime later Burley Bear saw Lasher approaching the camp.

"Something is wrong. Lasher is coming back to camp, and I don't see Taelo or Feather-in-the-Wind," he announced to the camp.

Lasher came into camp and went straight to Quiet Rabbit. He took her wrist in his mouth and pulled her.

"Wait a moment. Let me get my things," Quiet Rabbit said as she patted Lasher on his head and took her wrist from his mouth.

Quiet Rabbit gathered her emergency kit. It had her needle and gut thread, various herbs, and absorbent materials. She was not sure who needed her help, but Lasher's presence was foreboding.

"Here is your mount. Golden Hawk and I are riding with you," Running Stag said as he and Saber Scar came to where Quiet Rabbit was standing.

"I am bringing an empty travois," Lilly said as she joined the rest.

"We will wait here and stay at this camp. Return here," Burley Bear called out.

Taelo succeeded in stopping the flow of blood from the wound in Feather-in-the-Wind's thigh. It was clear to him she had lost a lot of blood.

Her wolves were lying on the ground around her. Taelo looked around and counted three dead wolves. Several were wounded but with some care they would survive.

He went about tending to the wounded wolves as he waited for Quiet Rabbit to arrive.

"Ah, I see you succeeded in finding Quiet Rabbit," Taelo said as he greeted Lasher on his return.

"So, this time it was not you who the bear wounded," Quiet Rabbit said as she slid off her mount.

"You seem to have done a good job in stopping the bleeding. We need to get Feather-in-the-Wind back to camp. Once we are there, I will examine the wound and see if it needs to be stitched closed," Quiet Rabbit said as she examined the wound but did not take off the binding.

Feather-in-the-Wind was awake but very weak and said nothing but closed her eyes when she saw Quiet Rabbit examining her wound.

"It is a miracle the two of you survived. This is the largest bear that I have ever seen. The one that wounded you on our Journey of Discovery was huge but would have looked small next to this one," Golden Hawk commented as he took in the size of the dead bear.

"How did you manage to get him down," Running stag inquired?

"I applied the tricks you and Feather-in-the-Wind taught me," Taelo replied.

"Tricks that Feather-in-the-Wind and I taught you," Running Stag said in surprise as he helped place Feather-in-the-Wind on the travois!

"Place her feet toward the mount," Quiet Rabbit instructed as Taelo and Running Stag carefully lifted Feather-in-the-Wind and put her on the travois.

"Yes, if you remember in our battle with the cannibals, you brought down the attacking warriors by cutting the tendons on the back of their legs. That is how I got the bear on the ground.

From Feather-in-the-Wind I learned to run full speed at the attacking bear and at the last-minute slide past him.

As I did so I was able to cut the tendons on one leg of the bear," Taelo replied as he arranged a hide under Feather-in-the-Wind's head.

"I will take Feather-in-the-Wind back. I will send out a few of the team to help you with the bear.

Do you want me to take the wolves with me," Quiet Rabbit inquired?

"Let's put the three most seriously wounded wolves on the travois and take them back. We will examine all the wolves and see if others need to be treated. I think most will follow you because you have their leader in the travois," Taelo replied as he pulled a hide to cover Feather-in-the-Wind.

The wounded wolves put their heads on Feather-in-the-Wind who seemed to be sleeping. Quiet Rabbit began a slow journey back to the camp.

"I am going to go with Feather-in-the-Wind," Running Stag said as he got on his mount and followed Quiet Rabbit.

"Taelo, you seem to attract the attention of large animals with claws and an intention of hurting you," Golden Hawk commented as he began to skin the giant bear.

"I believe the last two times it was Feather-in-the-Wind that attracted the bears.

Feather-in-the-Wind is fearless. She is swift and she uses her size to the fullest. She is a giant in her bravery. She was the reason I was able to get the better of this bear," Taelo replied as he helped with the skinning.

"Let's hope she recovers fully from this attack. I know that Running Stag is worried," Lily commented as she skillfully separated the hide from the flesh.

"Yes, those two have the same relationship that Quiet Rabbit and I have with each other. We have all found mates with matching spirits. Together we are one. Apart we are less," Taelo said as he thought about the other members of the team.

"In fact, when you think about it, it seems that all our team members have the same close relationship with their mates," Golden Hawk replied.

"You're right, it seems very clear once you point this out. We have a team that embraces each other and have similar values. That is probably why we function so well," Lily offered.

In the distance four mounts were coming toward them.

Lasher got up from where he was quietly laying and let out a small growl.

"It's ok," Taelo said as he patted him on the head.

Only a few wolves remained. It was clear these were wounded and needed attention.

"Turn the skinning of the bear over to the on-coming volunteers. I want to get the wounded wolves back to camp. I am personally ready for a big meal and some rest," Taelo suggested as he began to examine the wounded wolves.

"Saber Scar, please bury the three dead wolves. They helped bring down this bear and deserve to go to their own hunting ground," Taelo requested as he took the leads to his mount and vaulted onto its back.

"Let's put the wounded wolves on the travois. I will have two more travois sent back. We will want to process the meat and then store it for our return," Taelo continued.

Back at the camp Quiet Rabbit was arranging her field hospital. "Put her close to the fire. Put up a wind break around her so the heat is trapped and will warm her," Quiet Rabbit instructed.

"Here is some hot broth for her to drink," Floating Cloud said as she put the bowl to Feather-in-the-Wind's lips.

When he returned, Taelo inquired, "How is she doing?"

Lasher went up to Feather-in-the-Wind and lay down beside her.

Walker was resting on the other side.

"She lost a lot of blood. She will be weak for several moon cycles," Quiet Rabbit replied.

"She had a little broth but now she seems to be sleeping. I think she will be fine by the morning. She will be warm here by the fire.

Lily, I and Floating Cloud will stay by her side tonight," Busy Bee added.

"I am going to clean up in the stream and then get some rest. We should plan to move on in the morning. Other bears will soon be moving into this territory. We will want to be gone when they arrive," Taelo commented as he went to the stream.

The next morning Taelo had urged the team to hasten their departure. He had the fresh bear meat put on several of the travois and would have it processed at a later time.

"It has been some time since Taelo has been this worried," Quiet Rabbit said as she and Busy Bee helped put Feather-in-the-Wind on the travois.

"I hope it was not my fault," Feather-in-the-Wind spoke up quietly.

"No, it is that we will be in bear territory for a long time. If they all act as this one did, we will be in for many encounters. He is worried about our ability to outwit them," Quiet Rabbit replied.

"We are putting four of the wounded wolves on the travois with you," Lily commented as she and Floating Cloud carried the first wolf over.

"We thought they would be more comfortable around you," Floating Cloud added.

"All the wolves were my protectors. I understand that I lost three of them," Feather-in-the-Wind said as she patted each of the wolves on the travois.

She reached over to Walker and scratched him behind his ears.

"Yes, you did lose three of your wolves. Taelo had them buried so their spirits could go to where the ancestors reside," Quiet Rabbit responded.

"Taelo has spent the morning examining and treating each of the wolves and he thanks each of them personally as if they actually understand him. Each has also been given a piece of the bear meat," Lily added.

"They do understand. Not his words but his voice. They protected me and they will do whatever Taelo tells them to do," Feather-in-the-Wind replied.

"So will all of us," Feather-in-the-Wind thought to herself.

"It is good to see that you are awake and feeling better," Taelo said as he and Golden Hawk walked along the line of travois in their inspection routine.

"We are short one wolf pack leader.

I have recruited Golden Hawk as my partner if we meet another bear. These animals are not only huge and aggressive but as you and I learned, they are fast, have endurance and in close combat they are agile," Taelo commented to Feather-in-the-Wind.

"Yes, a little faster than I expected," Feather-in-the-Wind commented.

The conversation allowed Taelo to let the rest of the team know how they would respond to the next bear.

"We are going to try distraction if we meet another of these animals. From what this animal had in its stomach it is clear they eat anything they find.

Golden Hawk and I have prepared pieces of meat and bundles of fruit. Perhaps we can distract them when they approach.

If they pursue us, we will pelt them with shards of stone with our slings.

Finally, we have decided to use our spears as we do when we run down the buffalo but in this case, we will wait until the bear is charging us and then plant the butt of our spear in the ground and let the bear run itself onto the spear," Taelo continued his explanation.

"We want each of you to have your long spears at the ready and use them as Taelo has described. If possible, always do this in twos. The bear is very likely to paw one of the spears away. The second one must be driven forward and planted," Golden Hawk added in clarification.

"And we will practice this every day," Burley Bear and Little Otter said in unison as everyone else then joined in.

Taelo and Golden Hawk rode their mounts ahead of the team. Taelo was out to the right and Golden Hawk out to the left.

Burley Bear and Little Otter rode close together, back close to the lead mount pulling the first travois. If a bear attacked, they would each lead half the team in opposite direction outwards and then later come back together up the trail.

It would be up to Golden Hawk and Taelo to get the bear to chase them.

"It is a plan that I don't like but it is the only way I know to deal with these aggressive bears," Taelo commented when Saber Scar shared his concern for the two.

"You killed the last one. Would it not be better for us to face the bear together," he had asked when the plan was shared?

"Perhaps we could share the danger more equally by taking turns riding the points," Running Stag volunteered.

"I think that is a great idea," Slow Runner said in support.

"Each of you will have that role when we split up. If either of the two halves of the team runs into a second bear one of you will need to be the one that distracts the bear," Taelo said in response.

For the next three sun cycles they proceeded slowly up the valley always going slightly way from the line the sun's path cut.

As always, their slings were busy claiming any rabbit, groundhog or squirrel that crossed their path.

On the fourth day a caribou crossed their path in hasty flight from some unseen enemy.

"The wolves are growling," Lily called out from the back of the procession.

"Prepare to execute our plan," Golden Hawk called out as his mount nervously went forward.

Out of a small depression a giant bear charged toward Taelo.

His mount reared up and fell over backwards.

Taelo pushed off and to the side, but he landed directly in front of the path of the bear.

Suddenly the bear stopped in its track as the shards of stone cut into its snout.

The roar that followed made it clear it was now in a frenzied crazed state.

"Let's run like the wind," Golden Hawk said as he pulled Taelo to his feet.

"I am with you," Taelo replied as he and Golden Hawk led the bear away from the team.

The bear took in all the movement around him and hesitated for a moment.

Suddenly he was hit again by shards of stone. This sealed his direction. He took out at full speed after the two figures in front of him.

"Golden Hawk just rescued Taelo from the bear," Feather-in-the-Wind called out from where she was sitting on the travois. She was still recovering from her wounds and was not yet ready to ride her mount.

"They are now running like the wind and the bear is keeping up," she continued her narrative as the team made its escape in the opposite direction.

Taelo and Golden Hawk were running at full speed perpendicular to the route the team would continue to travel.

The bear was in full pursuit and slowly gaining on them.

"I was not expecting this animal to be this fast," Taelo called out as he looked over his shoulder.

"I shouldn't have made it so mad," Golden Hawk said as he looked back to the bear.

Suddenly a pack of wolves led by Lasher began to harass the bear from behind.

"Our army has arrived," lets help them out Taelo said as he pulled out his sling and loaded it.

"You go left, and I'll go right. Aim for his eyes." Golden Hawk shouted as he and Taelo turned and ran out away from each other and toward the bear.

When the shards of stone hit his eyes, the bear let out a roar that carried for miles.

"Well, I think he is even madder now," Taelo called out.

The team had just recombined from their evasive maneuver when they heard the massive roar.

"I believe the two have made that bear really mad," Burley Bear commented to Little Otter.

"Yes, let's move as fast as we can and put some distance between us and that animal," Little Otter replied.

"Good job Lasher. Now follow us," Taelo commanded as the confused and temporarily blinded bear sat down on its haunch.

They continued running in a path parallel to the one they knew their team would follow.

"Ok, let's get back to the team. We will want to travel as far as we can. I do hope we get out of bear territory soon," Taelo said as he turned to his left.

"I'm with you. I am beginning to like lions and crazed saber-tooth tigers better than bears," Golden Hawk commented.

They had slowed their pace to their comfortable traveling jogging speed and the wolves were more or less walking fast just behind them.

Lasher was between Taelo and Golden Hawk.

"I am ready for a giant dinner of bear meat. I know I am going to reward Lasher with a large piece of his own. He saved the day," Golden Hawk volunteered.

"He indeed deserves it," Taelo said as he reached down and patted Lasher.

The reception back with the team was anticlimactic.

"Tell us what you did to that poor bear," Quiet Rabbit asked after she had given Taelo a hug.

"Well, Golden Hawk was running so slow that I knew he would get caught at any moment. Lasher and his pack were just too slow to catch up. So, I turned and ran back to the bear and told him to stop being a bully. That roar you heard was after I slapped him a few times for talking back to me," Taelo said in a serious voice.

Burley Bear started laughing.

"You should leave the story telling to Little Otter and me. After all, around you good story telling is the only thing we have left to call our own," Burley Bear said as he stood up and gave Taelo a hug.

"Now tell us the real story," Busy Bee said to Golden Hawk.

"Taelo was right about the bear. It was much faster than we thought. It was catching up to us. When Lasher and his pack attacked it stopped chasing us. This gave Taelo and me a chance to attack the bear with our stone shard filled slings. We went out to opposite sides and hit it in the face. The shards had an immediate effect. The bear let out a huge roar in anger and pain. It stopped its pursuit of us.

When we left, the bear was down rubbing its paws across its head and eyes. Hopefully, it will still be able to see but it allowed Taelo and I to make our escape," Golden Hawk replied as he gave Lasher another piece of meat.

"I hope we clear the territory of these bears soon. They are huge, faster, and meaner than they look," Feather-in-the-Wind said.

She was finally able to walk around on her own after more than half a moon cycle of recovery.

Chapter 13 The Northern Buffalo

It was hard to distinguish individual animals in the mass stretching out as far as the eye could see. The brown undulating surface stretched to the horizon in all directions. The ground seemed alive, and it was moving slowly toward the northeast.

Closer to the team, individual animals stood out and Taelo could make out the low head at the end of a short downward sloping neck. Thick horns came out the sides of the head and curved back toward each other. This buffalo was shorter and broader than the ones back in the Elk Clan territory, but it was a powerful looking animal.

The hair on its hide was longer and gave it an appearance of floating as it moved slowly along.

Their presence was a welcome sight. The team would be able hunt and be well prepared for the coming cold.

The team had made camp so often that in a very short time the camp was totally functional.

"I will stay at camp while the rest of you go out and enjoy this new adventure," Floating Cloud said as she got the cooking fire started.

She preferred to sit and warm herself by the fire instead of hunting.

"I will stay as well," Lily volunteered.

She knew that two people would need to remain behind. The team never left one person to be on their own. There were just too many problems that could come up.

Taelo thanked Lily as he led the rest of the team out to look more closely at these new buffalo.

"They look very similar to our buffalo but are lighter in color and have tighter horns," Busy Bee commented.

"They seem a little shorter, but they are huge," Talking Wren continued the observation.

"The herd is huge. I am not sure I can see across it," Slow Runner added.

"It is good we stopped and made camp. The herd is slowly making its way across our intended travel path. Perhaps by morning it will be clear of our route," Quiet Rabbit said from where she sat on a large boulder.

"Do we need to replenish our supply of meat," Running Stag inquired?

"Yes, we should do that. The wolves eat a huge amount of meat. We should get at least one of these beasts to make sure we have enough," Feather-in-the-Wind added.

"I would love to accompany Taelo as he brings one down," Quiet Rabbit volunteered.

"Let the four of us go out together," Busy Bee said as she leaned on Golden Hawk's shoulder.

"Alright, see the one that is the farthest from the herd toward us. Yes, you've got it. Golden Hawk and I will ride on each side. We will guide it away from the herd. When we have it away, we will dismount and you two will each give us our spears. We will then run it down from each side and let it run up onto the spears," Taelo shared his plan.

"Sounds good to me, I hope its hide is no tougher than our buffalo. Its head is lower and covers most of the spear target area," Golden Hawk observed.

"We will ride back and get our gear so we can skin the animal and get it back to camp," Meadow Flower said as she, Mayflower, Saber Scar and Slow Runner got back on their mounts.

"Let's make a fire here among these rocks where we can stay warm and watch the hunt," Talking Wren said as she began gathering some wood.

"I'll stake the mounts so they can feed," Little Otter said as he put the ropes on the mounts.

"I will go out and help bring the beast back here once we get a travois from the camp," Burley Bear commented as he helped setup a fire ring.

"It seems everyone is ready for the hunt. Let's ride out slowly so the herd does not get excited. If possible, we want to separate the animal from the herd and get it to run toward the camp," Taelo said as the four slowly rode their mounts toward the herd.

The late afternoon sun was casting long shadows as the four slowly moved the single animal away from the herd. They were able to guide it toward the area where the rest of the team sat watching.

"Let's see how close to the camp we can drop this beast," Golden Hawk threw out the challenge.

"I say we should get it close enough that we can roast the meat as we cut it," Taelo replied.

"You two are always trying to show off. It's like the time you both downed four buffalo on our long hunt," Quiet Rabbit commented.

"Or the time Taelo flew through the air to spear the shark before it ate Golden Hawk. If that was not showing off, I don't know what would qualify," Busy Bee continued.

"Taelo and I are always trying to make hard work seem more like fun," Golden Hawk continued the quiet banter.

Taelo had been quiet as he inspected the beast.

"The fur seems to be very thick on these animals. On the way back we may want to hunt them for their hides and make warm winter coats for ourselves and to trade with the rest of the Clans," Taelo said as he thought about their return.

The team had made it through the mountain pass but now the days were getting colder and soon winter would be upon them. Their food supply was good but with almost eighty wolves needing to be fed they went through a great amount of meat.

"We will take this one down today. In the morning we will let some other members of the team take one more down. This will give us a good reserve," Taelo continued.

"We seem to have made our way past the bears and now we have a new animal to feed us. We are doing very well. Feather-in-the-Wind has been making a rapid recovery. We need to continue and then move down toward a warmer area. We need to continue being vigilant and move quickly toward an area where we will be able to travel even when it is cold," Taelo replied.

"We have made it past two bears. Is that one or two challenges?

We have the Sky Eyes ahead of us and then we will need to return and go through the bears again. This journey is clearly our most dangerous," Taelo thought to himself.

The animal they were slowly herding back toward the camp finally reached a point where it wanted to return to the herd. They were about half the way back to the place where everyone was sitting around the fire watching the hunt.

"It looks like that will be about as far as they can move this animal," Little Otter commented to the watching team members.

"I am betting they will get it even closer," Burley Bear replied.

"Let's guess how close they will bring the beast to where we are. The one that is closest to the drop point does not have to help in the cleaning and skinning," Talking Wren suggested.

"I pick by the fire pit," she continued.

Everyone quickly picked a drop spot. As if it had been planned, they saw Taelo and Golden Hawk jump off their mounts and run besides the animal keeping it coming toward them.

"Do you think we can run it all the way to the camp," Golden Hawk called out after he noticed the young bull would swing back and forth between them but seemed content to go forward.

"Let's give it a try," Taelo called back.

They guided the young bull past the surprised group watching them and then past Saber Scar and the group coming back to help skin the bull.

"What in the blue moon is coming toward us," Floating Cloud said as she jumped up and grabbed her spear.

"It's one of the new animals we saw earlier," Lily cried out as she too grabbed her spear.

"Now," Taelo called out at the last moment and both he and Golden Hawk ran out ahead, planted their spear and let the young bull spear itself.

The bull fell to its front knees, slid toward the fire pit, and collapsed just a spear's length from it.

"We brought dinner to you," Golden Hawk said as he pointed to the downed animal.

Both Lily and Floating Cloud started laughing.

"I win," Taelo could hear Talking Wren say as the team came riding in behind.

"What do you mean you win? You said by the fire," Little Otter argued.

"Well tell me where the animal is. It is by the fire," Talking Wren said as she dismounted and ran as she laughed and gave Taelo a hug.

"He is right of course, I meant the other fire," she whispered to Golden Hawk as she gave him a hug.

"By the fire I said and by the fire it is," Talking Wren pointed out.

"What was the wager," Quiet Rabbit asked?

"The one who guessed the closest drop location did not have to help in the skinning and cleaning," Burley Bear replied.

"Well, it would seem that unless someone chose a location closer to this camp, Talking Wren wins no matter what fire the bull came closest to," Busy Bee said.

The entire team broke out laughing.

"Yes, we declare Talking Wren the winner and we know we will hear about this for many moon cycles," Meadow Flower and Marigold said in unison as they each gave Talking Wren a hug.

On the following sunrise Taelo sat and again looked out on the slowly moving herd. He was not planning to hunt but had led his volunteers to a point where they could select a young bull.

"It is generous of you to give us a turn," Slow Runner said as he and Running Stag prepared to cull out one more animal.

"I am so excited to accompany you," Lily said as she was handed the hunting spear for Slow Runner.

"And I am so happy to be recovered enough to go out with Running Stag," Feather-in-the-Wind almost sang her words as she was handing Running Stag his spear.

"That was a great way to get Feather-in-the-Wind back into action," Talking Wren commented, as the team watched the four ride out toward the herd.

"Everyone on this team is deserving of recognition. We all contribute and share the work equally. We succeed because of our actions," Taelo replied.

They stayed in camp for three cycles of the sun.

"Tomorrow we will continue our journey. This has been a good rest. Our Feather-in-the-Wind has been out with her sling and has brought in some interesting birds for our high sun meal. She seems to be back in good form," Taelo said as he ate the breast of the bird he had roasted.

"I am feeling very good. Let me thank all of you for taking care of me," Feather-in-the-Wind said as she looked around at the team.

The following morning began with the cry of the eagle. Everyone was up and looking at the sky at the eagle highlighted by the rising sun.

It gave out another cry and flew off into the distance.

"I think we should go that way, Little Otter, and Burley Bear both said in unison as they together pointed in the direction the eagle had flown.

The Team traveled in the direction the eagle had flown for more than twelve sun cycles. The going was quiet and once again the full range of small to large animals was all around them.

"I guess these animals stay clear of the area controlled by the giant bears," Quiet Rabbit observed.

"Yes, the woolly buffalo, the new elk, the fox and now the smaller bears all seem abundant," Burley Bear added.

Yes, and I have bagged many small rodents and rabbits as well," Feather-in-the-Wind continued the conversation.

"It appears we are coming to the point in our journey where we will need to use our sleds. Broken Spear said we would need to leave our mounts on this side of the ice bridge.

I have talked with Lily and Slow Runner. Lily would prefer to stay on this side of the ice bridge. Single Leaf and Sharp Blade have agreed to stay as well when I expressed my concern at leaving only two on this side.

We will send several teams to find a suitable place to build the winter quarters. We will also need a holding area for the mounts.

We will hunt enough meat to last them for an entire season. Then the rest of the team will proceed by sled across the ice bridge and explore the land beyond.

Broken Spear has foretold of a fierce group of people. We will face them, but he was not clear on what the danger would be. Another group of people will need our help.

Are there any questions," Taelo concluded one of his longer speeches?

The questions poured out. The team had been told most of this before. Leaving part of the team behind was new and the focus of the discussion.

"On our journey to Feather-in-the-Wind's homeland we defeated a superior force as a team. What is our plan to defend ourselves," Little Otter inquired?

"That is a good question, and we must define our defense strategy," Taelo replied.

"We have our wolves and our sleds. We could circle and defend," Feather-in-the-Wind volunteered.

"That would make a good defensive posture if we are given the time to create the circle. If we are not able to do that, I think we need to quickly release our wolves.

The team would create a fighting circle and the wolves would be outside and brought in behind the attackers if possible.

If not, then we would want the wolves in front between the attackers and ourselves," Golden Hawk elaborated.

The discussion continued until the team closed in on a series of plans based on the situation, they found themselves in.

"I am pleased with the outcome of our discussions. Tomorrow we shall go through a series of practices to clarify each scenario we have discussed. Once we feel we all understand each one, we will proceed across the ice bridge to the land beyond," Taelo commented to the team.

Later he and Golden Hawk went over each scenario that had been identified. They made key adjustments and discussed how to simulate and practice each situation.

"I think if we practice each of these scenarios and position our team members strategically, we will be able to defend against a much stronger enemy than we faced on the *Journey of the Heart*," Golden Hawk commented.

"The fact that the two of you have thoroughly reviewed all the ideas put forward by the team is impressive. Now I think we should all get some sleep," Quiet Rabbit commented as she got up and went to their sleeping hide.

Chapter 14: Ice Bridge: The Empty Land

The vast plain beyond the small river, now white in fresh knee high winter snow and interrupted only by the occasional enormous boulder, a few wind-blown knurly scruffy trees seemed to collide with the darker wall of the mountains and the greyer snow and ice blanketing them.

Taelo was awed by the expanse they were about to cross. They would now utilize their sleds and have the wolves earning their bear and buffalo meat meals.

The backs of the ten wolves, their tail in the air, the centerline out to lead wolf harmoniously separated the team as they effortlessly pulled the sled out from the campsite.

Taelo had chosen to be the last sled to depart.

He looked back at the large canopy cover nestled into the vertical semi-circle of the solid stone face of the small cliff. A stone wall half the height to the canopy roof curved around from the cliff face to the door opening.

The vertical leather of the canopy was attached along the outside bottom of the wall. The fresh snow had been pushed up along the outside of this wall and packed down to provide insulation against the cold.

A fire ring intended only for warming was just inside the leather lodge opening. The opening had a leather covered, stout wooden frame that locked into the slots at the end of the stonewalls.

A lighter frame, woven from willow branches taken from the willow trees found along the small stream running past the front of the compound area, went along the top of the stonewall and created an impenetrable wall that rose vertically a spear and a half in height to the edge of the canopy roofline. Poles ran radially out from the center pole to vertical poles located at the peripheral stonewall. These poles were in turn supported by additional vertical poles to ensure the roof would not collapse under the weight of heavy snow.

A huge pile of wood just past the fire ring ensured the four staying behind at this camp would have enough wood for most of the coming cold period.

Lily, Slow Runner, Single Leaf and Sharp Blade stood by the fire ring that was a spear length from the compound opening. They would remain behind and take care of the mounts.

They waved their goodbye.

Out beyond the four, Taelo took in the log and stone wall that enclosed the mount holding area. His personal black mount stood looking in his direction.

Taelo had mixed feelings about leaving four of the team behind but there did not seem to be a better solution.

He waved and then turned and spoke to Lasher.

"Run."

The journey to and across the ice bridge was underway.

It was clear they were slowly rising onto an ice plateau. Burley Bear stopped as he took in the endless expanse of the white.

Taelo approached his good friend to see what had caused him to stop.

"This is a challenge. We will need to guide our sleds across the ice slowly and carefully. There seem to be bottomless cracks down through the ice," Burley Bear commented.

Burley Bear pointed to one just to his left. He was worried about approaching one that he could not see.

And look out ahead. There do not seem to be any distinguishing landmarks. It is similar to going out in the desert.

Taelo agreed. The sun would be their only reference.

Taelo took in the scene and volunteered to lead. He trusted Lasher to help guide the way. Taelo organized the order and then gave Lasher his head.

Lasher would periodically choose a slightly different way and later, at Taelo's insistence would once again follow the sun's path.

"What is it that he sees," Burley Bear asked after a change in direction?

"I am not sure. It must be something in the ice. I have not figured it out," Taelo replied.

He had kept a sharp eye out for thin ice and any other danger he would think of. What Lasher sensed was not clear, but Taelo followed his lead.

"We seem to be making slow but steady progress," Golden Hawk commented to Busy Bee as they followed behind Taelo and Quiet Rabbit.

Two sun cycles later they seemed to descent toward a flat plain and then small brush and bend over wind-blown trees greeted the team.

The land was still snow covered, but the team moved into a full forest of ragged, bent, short wind-blown trees.

"Well, we will have to thank Lasher for guiding us through," Saber Scar commented as he knelt and talked to Lasher.

Let's stop here for the night," Taelo called out as he reached the edge of a small stream.

They had left their large enclosure with Lily, Slow Runner, Single Leave and Sharp Knife. They knew that it would be too difficult for the team to erect without the mounts. The team discussed this situation and decided they would circle the sleds and then use the covering hides stretched to the inside of the sleds to make individual sleeping shelters.

This would provide a protective barrier to protect them and the center beyond the individual sleeping areas would remain uncovered. The cooking fire was located in the very center.

The heat from the fire reached out as far as the sleeping areas.

"I like the simplicity of this camp design. It lets us determine the size of our camp site and whether we want our wolf teams in with us or outside our camp perimeter," Feather-in-the-Wind commented.

"I have some grilled meat and cooked roots for all of you. Come over to the fire and relax for a few moments," Floating Cloud called out as she saw that all the sled shelters were up and functional.

Since Lily had not come with them, she and Bashful Lark had taken over as the main cooks.

"We will travel in the direction that cuts across the path of the sun. This will take us through this empty land to where we will meet others that are like us. We will also meet the ones with eyes the color of the sky," Taelo shared as they sat around the fire.

This, he pointed out, would take them almost directly toward the south.

"How many suns do we have before we meet the Sky Eyes," Golden Hawk asked.

"I do not know but each sun cycle we will practice each of our defenses once.

Burley Bear, Little Otter and Saber Scar will you accept the responsibility of calling for the practice," Taelo asked?

"Of course, we will but do we really have a choice," Little Otter said with a chuckle?

For the next full moon cycle the team traveled smoothly southward through the snow.

The dark green of the forests on both sides left them traveling a smooth river of white that flowed in the direction they sought to go.

The mountains rising to the sky on both sides made them feel as insignificant as the grain of sand on a beach shore.

Several times they saw a white bear and were glad to see that it was not interested in them. They made it a point to distance themselves from them each time they spotted one.

"It seems the bear comes in all colors and sizes. This one is big but seems to prefer to leave us alone.

We must not be on its food list," Busy Bee commented.

"I don't mind it a bit," Feather-in-the-Wind replied.

"In this snow-covered land, the sleds allow us to travel farther and faster than when we are on our mounts," Quiet Rabbit commented.

"We have traveled a great distance and have not found any other people. It seems it is an empty land. There is plenty of room for many peoples and clans," Taelo observed.

"Why was your clan crossing the ice bridge," Golden Hawk asked Running Stag?

"Our clan was trying to escape a large clan of cannibals. We were fighting a losing battle as we traveled through this land and across the ice bridge in an attempt to escape. We really did not know where we were going. We were just trying to get away," Running Stag replied.

"Do you think some of the cannibals still exist," Burley Bear asked?

"Yes, most of their clan stayed behind. The ones we defeated later in the battle when we rescued the second group of my people were only a part of the cannibal clan," Running Stag continued.

"We may face them here and we are ready. However, I am more worried about meeting the Sky Eyed Clan," Saber Scar volunteered.

"The Sky Eyed Clan is the one that Broken Spear warned us about.

If we have a confrontation, we will fight a retreat and defend battle. The goal of each encounter will be to inflict deep wounds and then retreat. We will not allow them to use their superior force or fighting ability.

I want us to practice this way of fighting. One moment we will be invincible and the next we will be gone.

Our wolves will provide the distraction as we do this. Feather-in-the-Wind and Running Stag will be their commanders. They will need to be able to run as fast as the wolves.

Are you two up to this task," Taelo asked as he walked slowly around the campfire?

"Yes, I am ready. Will Lasher be part of our army," Feather-in-the-Wind inquired?

"Yes, he will join Walker and Arrow to protect the two of you," Taelo said as he petted Lasher.

I am confident in our ability to defeat a much superior force. We have devised strategies and practiced for many different situations. We will use all of our resources to defend ourselves.

My only hope is that we will do this so well that none of us are slain," Taelo voiced his greatest concern.

"I join Taelo in making sure we all protect each other and make sure we all return together to cross the ice bridge.

We are a strong team. We are a resilient team. We are a capable team. We are one team," Golden Hawk added in closing.

Chapter 15: Sky Eyed Clan

Flying Eagle stood on the banks of the northern running river that flowed through a frozen land to a frozen sea. He was presiding over a leadership meeting that was very personal to he and his family.

His apply named son, Angry Cougar, was rebelling against the current leadership. This name, as all names of individuals in the clan was earned and given based on the actions of the individual over many moon cycles of time.

It had been Flying Eagle's hope that his son would mature and mellow with good guidance and time. Instead, Angry Cougar followed a path that had now come to the point that he had demanded that he be elevated to a leadership position.

"It appears your son wants to oust you and take over the clan," Sharp Claw commented to Flying Eagle.

"Yes, but he is not ready to lead a clan the size of ours. Our clan has a team of leaders that guide all of us. We work together to keep the clan healthy.

His behavior does not fit the way of the clan. It is time to send him on his journey of passage. Perhaps it will change him. If he does not change then we will have to oust him from the clan," Flying Eagle replied.

This was hard for him to speak of, but it had to be done. His son's personality and behavior were not those of a person Flying Eagle could support as a leader.

He would not tell his mate the exact reason, but she would know why Angry Cougar was being sent out and she would know that he would need to return with a better behavior and attitude about how the clan operated.

She knew the situation even though she said nothing.

Flying Eagle called his son into the leadership meeting where he explained the decision they had come to.

"Yes, I will go but I will take all my friends with me," Angry Cougar responded when he was told he was being sent on his journey of passage.

"I am tired of listening to all of you old men on the council. We will go out and become strong. If and when we return, we will take over this clan and lead it," Angry Cougar replied in an agitated, loud voice.

He planned to return with twice as many warriors as the River Clan had. He would take over from these old men and take the River Clan to new glory.

Flying Eagle sadly watched as Angry Cougar left the River Clan with forty other young warriors. These young warriors wanted action and knew that Angry Cougar would lead them into it.

"Aren't you worried about your son," Flying Eagle's mate, Running Fox, asked as she watched her son leave the camp.

It had not escaped her that Angry Cougar had not wished either her or her mate goodbye.

"Yes, I am worried that he is not going out to learn about himself but to stir up trouble with other clans, wherever he goes," Flying Eagle replied.

"I have asked the ancients to guide him. I hope he listens to their guidance," she responded.

The eagle flying high in the sky, let out a scream and flew away in the opposite direction of the departing group of warriors.

Flying Eagle hoped for the best, but he expected this group of young warriors to come back to the tribe as potential enemies.

He would work with the leadership team to prepare for such an event. It weighed heavy on his heart, but he recognized his son as the biggest threat that currently faced the clan.

He would not let his people be overcome by a son who knew no self-control.

"Yes, we follow and look forward to the adventures you have described," Rolling Stone said as he raised his spear and let out a loud chant that was picked up by the others that were following.

The procession left the area of the River Clan and continued to go up the river. The clan they were looking for was located on this same river but two moon cycles from the River Clan's camp.

Angry Cougar planned to act almost immediately to enlist more warriors.

Only a few of the young women from the River Clan had considered accompanying these brash young warriors so he would see about enticing some more from the clan ahead.

The warm summer breeze was a refreshing relief from the winter blizzards and extreme cold that they faced every winter season.

However, it soon became clear that Angry Cougar would need to organize his band. They were lazy and made a terrible mess of the areas where they stopped.

He recruited ten of his most loyal friends and followers to be his marshals. He declared that every member would have to do certain work to make the group function more effectively. He also recognized the group needed a way to feed itself. He assigned two hunters to hunt every day. This responsibility would rotate to everyone.

Their arrival at the first village was not well received and soon things got out of hand.

"These people are worse than our clan. Let's take what we need and leave. They seem to have plenty of food. Take all of the dried fish and other dried meats," Angry Cougar said to the group he was leading.

The rampage that followed surprised Angry Cougar. The angry men of the village put up a losing battle but non-the-less wounded some of the young warriors.

The looting, rape and in some cases kidnapping that followed also surprised Angry Cougar.

Ten young women were taken from the village.

Many of villagers were wounded and at least a handful were dead.

"What are we going to do with the women that have been taken," he asked his followers?

"We need some cooks and workers. They will do that work," one of the group called out.

"Yes, and I need warmth and comfort at night. The one I have has already proven able," another called out as those around him snickered and laughed.

"Rolling Stone, organize the women into a work group. I am sure there will soon be more.

"I want two volunteers to watch behind us. The villagers may pursue us to get back their women," Angry Cougar continued.

"I will need to learn to control these men," Angry Cougar thought to himself.

He had not expected the cruel and callous behavior of his men. However, he recognized that he could use their behavior to his advantage.

He worked at organizing his followers into a unit of which he had control.

He approached the next village with a much different attitude.

He knew his small army was going to loot the place. He organized his band and marched them in fully armed.

He demanded food and pointed out the women he wanted.

"Who are you and why do you believe we will do what you ask," the village leader inquired?

Angry Cougar drove his spear through the leader 's chest in response.

"Are there any other question," He said as he looked around at the dozen or so people?

"Leave them enough food to survive for a day. Take only the young women. We leave immediately," Angry Cougar commanded.

He had calculated that this direct approach would be more effective and create fewer deaths than the approach in the previous village.

The element of surprise was a key factor in the total surrender of the small village.

"Well, that went rather smoothly," he commented to Rolling Stone.

"We now have forty warriors and fifteen women. It is getting harder to handle this group. I suggest we bring our five most trusted friends together and assign them warriors to lead and manage.

Make them responsible for the actions of their group," Rolling Stone suggested.

"That is a good idea. It will make my work much easier," Angry Cougar replied.

He was pleased with the advice and guidance his best friend Rolling Stone was providing.

The devastation of the next village occurred with no deaths.

The angry villagers pursued Angry Cougar's small army. This was a mistake on their part. The Angry Cougar's warriors eagerly engaged and killed most of those in pursuit.

"That worked to defuse our warriors and to show the women they should accept and behave," Angry Cougar commented to Rolling Stone.

"My friend is as mad as I always thought he was," Rolling Stone thought to himself.

He was beginning to doubt the wisdom of following him.

The group now had to deal with three heavily wounded fighters and many with minor wounds.

They buried the first warrior killed in battle.

"I am sure we will bury more," Rolling Stone thought to himself.

For the next two moon cycles they traveled toward the rising sun through a never-ending grass covered rolling terrain. The occasional river or stream was marked by the fringe of darker green leaves and the dark brown of the bark on twisted sinewy trunks.

There were no villages. The many small animals and the occasional herd of caribou made their hunting successful. Everyone was eating well. The wounded had healed, and morale was high.

The group had slowly coalesced into a working unit.

The women were resigned in their roles as cooks, cleaners, and companions.

The men identified with the small groups they had been assigned to and to the leader of that group.

"You have been doing a very good job at leading your smaller teams," Angry Cougar complemented his five team leaders.

"Yes, and I am at the limit of keeping them in control," Rolling Stone thought to himself as he observed the five.

Each of the five was slowly getting brasher and more demanding as they better understood how to control their warriors.

It was a moon cycle later when they met the brown eyed, black haired people. These people were very different in appearance and behavior. Their skin color was different, they all had black hair and had eyes the color of the dirt or of the night.

They were unlike the long yellow, red, or brown hair and blue eyes of the warrior group led by Angry Cougar. They were also significantly smaller.

The open and friendly way of these people was clearly a mistake on their part. The population of the village was at least two hundred.

"These people have no clue what just happened to them," Rolling Stone thought as he listened to Angry Cougar talk about exerting his control over these people.

"This will be a good place to spend the winter cycle. We can find out where there are other people and send our fighters to subdue them. Our clan can become even bigger than the one we left," Angry Cougar shared with Rolling Stone.

The brown eyed clan's leadership invited Angry Cougar and his leaders to attend a meeting session. From what was communicated via sign language and drawings on the ground it was clear they wanted to know how they could help and when Angry Cougar and the rest would be moving on.

The senior brown eyed clan leader stood in front of Angry Cougar and signed that they were welcome for the next seven sun cycles, but the clan did not have enough food to feed them beyond that.

Angry Cougar signaled his five leaders who took up their spears. The warriors for each of these leaders came into the lodge and surrounded the council.

"This is my answer as to leaving and to who is in charge," Angry Cougar said as he drove his spear up through the leader's jaw and out the top of his head.

"This is what will happen to you if you resist me. If you follow me you will live," Angry Cougar said pointing to the dead leader.

The spear had been pushed halfway through his head, blood was slowly dripping to the ground as he was being held up by two of Angry Cougar's warriors and slowly turned to show everyone what had happened.

Neither Angry Cougar nor Rolling Stone were interested in any of the women.

The rest of the warriors took who they wanted. The village was divided into five sections. Each was controlled by one of the five inner circle leaders.

The cruelty was overwhelming. The men of the village were brutalized. Soon most were driven out or died at the hands of one of the fifty.

The older women made an escape with most of the children.

"Let them go. They will be lucky to survive. This will make it easier to manage the village," Angry Cougar replied when asked if someone should go after them.

"Your father's totem cries in the sky," Rolling Stone pointed out the eagle high in the sky.

"What in the world does this signal," Rolling Stone thought as he took in the sight of the eagle crossing over the village.

"The eagle is a weak totem. It is not as powerful as my totem," Angry cougar replied.

He was not interested and did not care what the totem might mean.

Chapter 16: Sky Eye Reception

The terrain slowly changed to a wooded landscape of mixed tall straight pines and a dominant tree that provided opening to the sun above. The few yellow fan like leaves clinging pluckily to their branch identified it as a totally new kind to the team.

The snow still deep and thick was firm and the sleds sped smoothly along the top surface. The hunting had improved as they had entered this more prosperous area and the team was once again benefitting from Feather-in-the-Winds skill with her sling. Rabbits, squirrels, dove and many pigeons graced the end of a spit and got roasted over the cooking fire.

When the eagle screamed, Taelo knew that the calm before the storm was over.

He led the way into a secluded part of the forest and signaled for the team to make camp.

"I think our first confrontation with the Blue Eyes is close at hand," he said to Golden Hawk and the rest of the team.

"Let's setup our camp with our sleds side by side just far enough apart to allow two to sleep in between. I want the sleds setup so if we need to run, we can attach the wolves and go.

We will proceed from here on foot.

Running Stag and Feather-in-the-Wind you take the wolves out to our right side of the path we take. Keep out of sight.

Everyone prepare, your slings. If necessary, we will engage in full battle, but we will move forward in our defensive position. Our backpacks are our shield.

This time when we engage, we strike to kill," Taelo instructed.

"Floating Cloud you and Bashful Lark please stay with the sleds. If any strangers approach, make your escape immediately and come to us. We will come back and take care of the strangers," Taelo instructed.

"Thank you," Quiet Rabbit whispered to Taelo.

"I was not picking favorites. They are the best suited for this task. Neither has demonstrated high skill in the weapons training nor battle simulation," Taelo replied but he knew that he had also singled Floating Cloud out because of Quiet Rabbit.

"There is a band of travelers approaching the village. They do not seem to be a very large group and half seem to be women," one of the warrior scouts reported to Angry Cougar.

"Well, we will see if our village is going to grow in population. Call the warriors together. We will go out and meet these travelers," Angry Cougar instructed Rolling Stone.

"We will take out the leader and then round up the rest. Kill any of them that resist," was the simple instruction to his warriors.

Angry Cougar led the forty warriors out to meet the significantly smaller approaching party.

"Perhaps we should discuss our battle plan a little more thoroughly. We do not know the capability of those approaching," Rolling Stone commented.

"There are only a few. I will take out the leader and the rest will crumble," was Angry Cougar's reply.

He was a foot taller than any of the people in this area and he felt competent to take on anyone of them.

The eagle let out its scream as it circled in the clear sky.

"We must be close," Burley Bear called out from his lead position.

Taelo and Golden Hawk moved forward on each side of Burly Bear.

Running Stag and Feather-in-the-Wind and all the wolves were out of sight.

"Load your slings and spread out just enough to be effective," Saber Scar instructed.

Ahead, across a wide-open area, a group of about forty advanced toward them.

"I believe the large warriors with light; red and brown colored hair must be the Sky Eyed ones. It appears they have some warriors that look like us. They are all on the front line and are probably being used as shields.

Use your slings to neutralize the front line and then target the Sky Eyes," Golden Hawk said over his shoulder as Taelo signaled a halt.

"I will walk out ahead. It appears they are coming out to fight not to talk. If you see me take any aggressive action move forward and strike.

Then be ready to retreat as we practiced," Taelo said as he halted the team and walked forward.

"This is going to be so easy. Stay here. I will take care of this in short order," Angry Cougar commented as he stopped his group and walked forward by himself.

He was sure his actions would take the on-coming leader by surprise.

"I am Taelo," Taelo said with his hand raised.

He was looking up, at a very muscular person with rippled stomach muscles taller than Burley Bear.

He purposely stopped a weapon's distance away and his hand was positioned to pull out his shark toothed flat weapon.

"I am Angry Cougar," Angry Cougar said as he lunged forward with the spear, he intended to plunge through the lithe but weak looking person.

Taelo let out his loud war cry, took a measured step back and to the side and pulled his shark tooth weapon from its holder and cutoff the hand holding the spear.

The look of surprise and shock communicated the anger and hatred that Taelo had seen in the Blue Eyes of this warrior.

Taelo's entire team let out the same war cry and moved forward as Angry Cougar stumbled back holding his left hand over the stump where his right hand had been as he tried to stop the bleeding. He looked in shock at his cutoff hand that still grasped the spear.

His army rushed forward as Rolling Stone ran out and tended to Angry Cougar.

The front line of brown eyed warriors hung back.

An impenetrable wedge greeted the forty or so rushing warriors.

Burley Bear's hammer took down the first warrior to reach him. The story was much the same around the triangular wedge that slowly formed into an oval as the team retreated.

Rolling Stone took note of the actions of the battle and how well the enemy who numbered only ten had handled a much larger force.

The quick encounter had left eight of their number dead. It did not go unnoticed by Rolling Stone that all eight were blue eyed.

The brown eyed warriors all had minor wounds. He had not seen any wound inflicted on the retreating opponents.

"We have met our match. We should leave them alone," Rolling Stone said to Angry Cougar.

"I will kill him and gouge his eyes out and then torture him until he begs for mercy," was Angry Cougar's crazed reply.

"We are going out immediately and track him down," Angry Cougar commanded.

He looked at the stump at the end of his right arm and let out a scream.

Rolling Stone guided one of the women over and together they sewed the stump closed.

Angry Cougar moaned but did not cry out.

"Do we have any injuries," Taelo looked around in concern.

You were the only one in danger by staying out in front," Quiet Rabbit replied.

"I couldn't make it back to the triangle with all the warriors coming at me. It is clear they have not thought through their battle plans. They will be better organized the next time they attack," Taelo replied.

"I did not plan to take the action that I took.

The person in front of me made the mistake of looking at where he planned to strike me.

He never saw my weapon until it cut off his hand.

It is clear that he was their leader by the response of the rest of his warriors," Taelo continued explaining.

"We did not expose our wolf army, so we still have an element of surprise," Golden Hawk commented as the team continued their retreat back up the hill behind them.

"We will have to take a round-about way of returning to the sleds. These Sky Eyes may still come after us today," Burley Bear added.

"Taelo has gone out to discuss our situation with Feather-in-the-Wind and Running Stag. We will want to disrupt the next attack. It will be more organized now that they know we can fight." Golden Hawk continued.

"I have asked Running Stag to be our look out and let us know what the enemy is doing," Taelo shared on his return.

"We will use our barrage of chipped stone with our slings. The next time, I would like at least four of us to continuously deliver sharp stones to the faces of the warriors in the battle," Taelo instructed.

"Busy Bee and I are probably enough. I watched Meadow Flower and Marigold wield their hammers. They will be much more useful in that manner than trying to use a sling," Quiet Rabbit replied.

"Two it is," Taelo said with a smile. He too knew that Meadow Flower and Marigold were twice as strong as he and they were not as fast as Quiet Rabbit and Busy Bee with the sling.

"Lasher, Walker and I will manage the wolves," Feather-in-the-Wind volunteered.

"Do you think Lasher will let me be with him," Talking Wren volunteered?

"Yes, thank you that will let me signal silently for your attack. That way we can surprise them twice," Feather-in-the-Wind replied.

Across the valley, Running Stag and Arrow crept silently through the forest that surrounded the village. It was located near a small river at the end of a slender valley.

He stopped short when he spotted another person watching the village. It soon became clear to him as he watched the village that the warriors that looked like those on his team were in fact more captives than voluntary participants.

He remembered his village being taken by the cannibals.

It appeared the Blue Eyes had taken over the village.

"The person I am watching as they watch the village is probably an escaped member. I am sure he is trying to figure out what to do," Running Stag thought to himself.

When he saw the war party leave the village, he quickly retreated and made his way as fast as he could back to the team.

He reported to the team that the brown eyed warriors were being used as a front shield as Taelo had previously conjectured. The entire village was under the control of the Blue Eyes. There was another watcher, who was also watching the village.

"Can you find these other people," Taelo inquired?

"We can use their help."

"Yes, I can find them, but I am not sure how may there will be," Running Stag replied.

"We will be able to use any help we can get," Taelo predicted.

"I will leave immediately and retrace my steps. I hope I am able to communicate enough with them to get them here," Running Stag said as he gathered his gear.

He set out on a run back to where he had been and followed the tracks he found in the snow.

Chapter 17: Sky Eye Battle

The hill offered a clear view of the small valley all the way to the village located along the small winding river. The bare branches of the broadleaf trees allowed a spotty view of the camp but the density of the ever green blocked the view to the point that it was impossible to see what was transpiring.

Meadow Flower could see the turmoil and what seemed to be preparation for a return to the field by the Sky Eyed warriors.

She could not be sure but periodically she thought she saw Running Stag as he ran full speed through the thick forest. She hoped he would not be too reckless in his haste to reach the group of people that might help in the coming battle.

Her self-confidence was raised as she turned to listen to Taelo and saw him sitting in a relaxed manner on a small boulder.

Taelo was explaining to the team that they would fight from the top slope of the hill. The goal was to make the larger and stronger Sky Eyes come up to them.

Talking Wren would have half of the wolves to one side and Feather-in-the-Wind would have the other half on the other side.

If Running Stag is successful there will be an attack from the rear. That will provide for total chaos.

Taelo knew they would face a superior force. The team's weapon would be a surprise and a disruption to how the Sky Eyes normally fought battles.

He planned to delay the battle as long as possible. He needed all elements of surprise if the team was going to win the day.

Running Stag back tracked as fast as he could run. Once back to where he had seen the other watcher, he followed the tracks away from the village upriver to an area full of tumbled stones.

As he came through a narrow opening, he was faced with a small group all defensively holding their spears.

"I am here as a friend," he said in his childhood language, as he faced the group.

"How do you know our language," someone asked?

"I was born not far from here, but our clan had to flee from a group of savage cannibals," Running Stag replied.

"Yes, we had to fight them as well," one of the older warriors commented.

"I am Whistling Arrow, a hunter and warrior in my youth and now advisor to the council," Whistling Arrow introduced himself.

"I have returned here with Taelo on a Journey of Discovery. We need your help to fight the Sky Eyes. They have already lost but don't yet know it. If you join us, I will lead you back and we will attack them from the rear," Running Stag continued.

There were only nine men and six women. There were at least a dozen younger children. Several of the men were well beyond the age for running and going into battle. There were also several older women.

"We are willing to help. What do you want us to do?"

"Some of you will need to stay with the young and some of you have already done your duty in battle.

Those who can run from here to the valley beyond your village, line up and show me the best weapon you have.

All of you will be needed," Running Stag said as he took in the situation.

"You would take women into battle," Gentle Cub, one of the young women inquired?

"Yes, some of our best fighters are women," Running Stag replied.

There were sixteen viable candidates.

Running Stag led them out and ran at a slow but steady pace back toward their village. He kept dropping back and urging them on.

"When we arrive, we will attack from the back of the battle. When we attack, I want each of you to yell at the top of your voices. Cut your attackers on the back of their legs or spear them in their sides.

Those of you with stone war clubs hit your opponent on the back of his skull and then drop down and hit the next enemy on his knee.

Then jump up again," Running Stag instructed the group.

"When we get there and run forward into the battle, tell your friends to turn and fight against the Sky Eyes," Running Stag told them.

"I hope we arrive in time to make a difference," Running Stag thought as he worried about Feather-in-the-Wind.

He knew she was fearless and would take on any of the Blue Eyes.

Back on the Hill, Taelo got the team ready.

"Let's move into position on the hill. Let's sit and relax in our positions. I will give our attack yell when they are close," Taelo said as he watched Talking Wren, Lasher and Feather-in-the-Wind leave the camp.

"Stay until I say "Kill" Taelo faintly heard Feather-in-the-Wind give instruction to Lasher and Walker. Lasher lay down flat and his entire pack did likewise. Talking Wren lay beside Lasher.

"Thanks for humoring me," Talking Wren whispered to Lasher as she scratched him between the ears.

Feather-in-the-Wind disappeared down into the tall grass. Talking Wren and her part of the pack did the same.

"Truly a gifted wolf woman," Taelo said quietly as he looked out to where the Sky Eyes were coming up the valley.

He counted them to make sure that they were all coming up the valley. They had forty-two Sky Eyes and about twenty of their recruited brown eyed warriors.

This was a formidable number.

It was clear they were better organized, but it was apparent they still did not seem to have any fighting strategy.

"I think they are only familiar with head-on long, hand to hand fighting," Golden Hawk commented.

"Seven to one, I guess that gives them a fighting chance," Burley Bear grunted.

"I am in better fighting form then the last time so maybe I can keep up," Little Otter added.

"Remember, stone shards into Sky Eyes and stone shards to the hands for brown eyes," Taelo said quietly.

"I didn't know you had so much fun on your journey to the south," Saber Scar commented from where he was sitting.

"They don't seem to know we are coming," Angry Cougar commented to those around him. He was holding his right stump up above his shoulder in an attempt to keep the throbbing pain in control.

"Perhaps they are hoping they do not have to fight us. We out number them ten to one," Rolling Stone replied.

"They will get no mercy from me. I will gouge out his eyes in front of all his friends," Angry Cougar said loudly.

"Either they are blind, or they don't expect to fight us," Rolling Stone was now getting worried about what was about to happen.

He knew that Angry Cougar was now totally insane. He would exact a revenge that even he would not want to watch.

"Come down and fight, you worthless coward," Angry Cougar called out as he stopped his warriors at the base of the hill.

"Let's just relax and enjoy their frustration. The fighting will commence soon enough," Taelo said to the team.

"I wonder what they are saying about us," Busy Bee commented next.

She was surprised at how relaxed she was.

"They no doubt think we are cowards or crazy," Meadow Flower added.

"The longer we can delay them the more likely we will get some help coming with Running Stag," Golden Hawk commented from his position.

"Please be so kind as to wake me up when something is about to happen," Burly Bear said with a faked yawn.

"I hope they get mad enough to misjudge their actions. They seem to be getting frustrated by being ignored," Quiet Rabbit commented as she studied the arrangement of the warriors.

"It appears they expect us to charge them, and they don't seem to know what to do because we are just sitting here," Marigold made her observation.

"Stop, get down and be quiet. The fighting has not started," Running Stag said as his group came to the edge of the forest.

"Why are your people just sitting at top of the hill," one of the warriors asked?

"I am sure it is Taelo's way of disrupting the flow of the Sky Eyes. The Sky Eyes do not know how to act. When you are outnumbered almost ten to one you must use every trick in the book," Running Stag replied.

"Ten to one, do we even have a chance," one of the women asked?

"The Sky Eyes have already lost the battle. They just do not yet know it.

Half of them will go to their ancestors when they go up that hill.

The rest will be lucky if they get away," Running Stag commented as he let out a wolf howl.

High in the sky an eagle responded with a loud screaming reply.

"Our teammate Running Stag is in position and our eagle has given us its signal. We will soon face out next test," Taelo said quietly.

He was worried about this weird situation and about the meaning of the eagle's cry. He hoped it was praise for his current delay tactic. Perhaps it was a suggestion to do more.

"I am through waiting. These people do not know how to fight," Angry Cougar commented to Rolling Stone.

"They do not seem to take us seriously. I agree let's attack and take them out," Rolling Stone commented.

"Let's move forward slowly," Angry Cougar ordered.

Taelo surprised everyone by standing up and walking a few steps forward toward the Sky Eyes coming up the hill.

He raised his hand and, in the language Running Stag language, called out loudly, "My brown eyed brothers, the eagle is my totem, he has spoken and has given me the sign of victory, come as close as you can to us, put bravery in your hearts and help us fight the Sky Eyed people that have enslaved you. The people of your village are behind you, and they will help. This is your moment; this is the moment to be brave. When you hear my battle cry, you will know that it is your moment as well."

Taelo then turned, stepped back, and sat down with his back to the oncoming hoard of warriors.

"I think the battle plan just changed. We will put the stone shards in the Blue Eyes first. Meadow Flower and Marigold please give us a hand," Quiet Rabbit said quietly from where she sat.

"With pleasure," the two responded in unison.

"Yes, if the brown eye warriors fight with us, they will be spared the pain of your shards," Golden Hawk commented.

"Burley Bear, let me know when it is time to stand and give my war cry," Taelo said with a smile on his face.

There was a hesitation and confusion at the base of the hill.

"What did he just say? Did any of you understand any of it," Angry Cougar asked as he looked around?

"I don't have a clue, let's continue our charge," Rolling Stone replied.

The distance to the group on the hill was farther than anticipated and the warrior's cry went quiet as they focused on getting up the hill to the battle point.

Rolling Stone started the battle cry once he thought the warriors were closing to a spear throw distance.

"Now," Burley Bear said.

Taelo stood and let out the team's battle cry. The team repeated three pulsing cries in unison at the top of their voice. The volume of their war cry surprised the on-coming hoard.

The on-coming warriors almost stopped in their tracks.

"Run forward brothers and turn and fight," Taelo said in Running Stag's language as he stepped out to the front and raised his spear.

"Now," Quiet Rabbit said as she let her first sling loose and hit Angry Cougar in the Face.

His scream and reflex action of his arm with the missing hand almost knocked him out.

The disorienting impact of the barrage of sharp stone fragments in the face almost stopped the charge.

However, those in the back ran past those trying to recover. They were just getting ready to launch their first set of spears when Talking Wren stood up and Lasher led his wolves in from the left side of the Sky Eyes battle line.

The warriors had to turn and defend themselves from the oncoming pack of wolves.

One set of warriors reached the team's fighting triangle. They were focused on fighting with their war hammers and were surprised by the combination of the shark tooth weapons and the war hammer of the Others.

Burley Bear, Meadow Flower, Saber Scar and Marigold made a devastating combination. The bodies of dead Sky Eyed warriors piled up around them.

Taelo had three bodies around him. He noted that the brown eyes had turned and were fighting with them.

The battle was still on the side of the Sky Eye warriors when Feather-in-the-Wind rose from the grass and her wolf warriors charged the right side of the Sky Eye warriors.

Once again, the Blue Eye's attack was dulled and those warriors around the fighting triangle met the ultimate fate. They were no match for the synchronized action of the team.

Angry Cougar's eyes were just clearing when he saw Taelo raise is sharks tooth weapon and let out his war cry again.

The team around Taelo echoed his cry and then to Angry Cougar's surprise the cry came from behind him.

Running Stag and his team had run silently across the valley. When Taelo had let out his second battle cry, Running Stag responded, and his entire following took it up and continued the cry as they ran through the ranks of Sky Eye warriors.

Running Stag concentrated on using his sharks tooth weapon across the back of the heels of the warriors. This did not kill any of them, but it took them out of the battle. He took out more than his share as he went through the line of warriors.

Angry Cougar saw his warriors falling all around him.

"Run for the forest. Retreat so we can regroup," he called out.

"Bring the wounded with you," Rolling Stone called out.

High in the sky the eagle again let out its cry and flew effortlessly away.

Chapter 18: Recovery

⮎odies lay strewn down the hillside. The snow was now a bright red. Only a few bodies had black hair or tan skin, the rest were Blue Eyes now sightlessly looking up into the bright sun that had reached its zenith.

The team watched as the few able Sky Eyes helped their wounded away from the field of battle. They were headed into the mountains to the east.

Taelo counted ten warriors carrying ten badly wounded ones.

He watched Burley Bear, Meadow Flower and Quiet Rabbit going through the battlefield checking on the fallen.

It seemed they would be done for the day.

The fighting was over.

"Running Stag, you and Golden Hawk organize our friends and determine what we must do to get them their village back.

Quiet Rabbit, Busy Bee, Marigold, and Meadow Flower, please check each of our warriors and attend to their wounds.

Talking Wren, Feather-in-the-Wind please check out our wolves. Let Busy Bee know of your needs.

Burley Bear, Little Otter and Saber Scar please check each of the Sky Eyes that remain in the field. If they are not dead, do not kill them.

Call Quiet Rabbit to check their condition. We will see what can be done," Taelo said as he visually checked out each of his team members.

"Who is that man," one of the brown eye warriors asked?

"That is our leader, Taelo, claw of the eagle," Running Stag replied.

Floating Cloud and Bashful Lark had stayed hidden in the forest with the sleds.

"I don't mind eating our dried meat and not cooking," Floating Cloud commented as the two sat quietly on the side of one of the sleds.

"Yes, this is actually the easiest assignment one could have. Why were we chosen," Bashful Lark inquired?

"Taelo is expecting a serious battle.

We have been doing our share in helping the team, but we have been very poor performers when it comes to the use of weapons and fighting.

He asked us to stay here so he could take the best fighters. However, he knew that keeping our sleds safe was important. He chose us because he knew we would do a good job here and he would not have to worry about us during the battle," Floating Cloud replied.

"I hope everyone will be alright," Bashful Lark replied.

Later as the sun was low in the sky Bashful Lark saw Feather-in-the-Wind, Meadow Flower, Saber Scar and Marigold approaching.

"Is everyone alright," was Floating Cloud's first inquiry?

"Yes, and Quiet Rabbit would have come but she is tending to the wounded.

We faced the Sky Eyes twice. Each engagement was short, but they were fierce encounters. The Sky Eyes lost many fighters and left with many wounded.

Only Little Otter had a small wound," Saber Scar replied.

"The three Sky Eyes that Quiet Rabbit is tending are seriously wounded but will recover if they are taken care of," Meadow Flower added.

"We are taking four of the sleds into the village of the brown eyes. I think they are called the White Bear Clan," Feather-in-the-Wind shared as she began to put the wolves into their harness.

"I will take one sled to the team on the hill. Taelo asked me to tell you to continue keeping watch here. We will begin our return in the next two or three sun cycles. He wants to make sure we remain vigilant in case the Sky Eyes return sooner than he expects," Marigold volunteered.

"I am relieved that all went well. Tell Taelo that he left us with the hardest role; that of waiting and wondering," Floating Cloud said seriously as she smiled at the three.

In the mountains to the west a devastated group of fighters were trying to recover.

Rolling Stone of the Sky Eyes was trying to understand what had happened.

What kind of medicine man were they facing?

The group at the top of the hill had not seemed to be concerned about the number of warriors they were facing.

It was as if they knew they would win.

They had wolves to fight for them.

They were able to speak to the people we conquered and have them fight for them.

We should take our wounded and return to our own land," Rolling Stone commented as he went about tending to the wounded.

"I will not return home until I take vengeance against the one who leads that group. Those who want to return with you may do so. I am staying and I will have my way in this region," Angry Cougar replied.

By this time, the stump of his missing hand was throbbing, and he had to hold it high in the air to ease the pain.

"I have sent back a scout to see if we left any of our live warriors behind. We tried to bring all the living ones out," Rolling Stone said as he came back to where Angry Cougar was trying to alleviate his pain.

"They will probably kill all that are found alive. That is what I would do," Angry Cougar replied.

"Yes, you would. Let's hope our enemy is more compassionate," Rolling Stone thought to himself.

"Take the three Blue Eyed wounded warriors to that far hill. Leave them there with a small fire and enough food for three days. I will make sure they are found by their kind," Taelo instructed the team attending to the wounded.

"We were lucky and only have a few wounded wolves. The one with the broken snout was the hardest to treat but Talking Wren found a piece of wood to tie on and hold the snout until it gets a chance to heal. I will feed him personally until his jaw heals," Feather-in-the-Wind shared.

"The only wound to any of us was a slight cut on Little Otters side. The cut was parallel to the one he received in the battle we had in the *Journey of the Heart*," Busy Bee reported.

"Hey, I guess I need to improve my battle step. I have no clue when I was slightly wounded," Little Otter said defensively.

"He is always trying to get my sympathy," Talking Wren commented as she gave Little Otter a poke on the other side.

"We were all lucky. Our enemy underestimated us. Even so, they put on some pressure. If the local warriors had not understood my instruction the battle and outcome might have been very different.

"How did you know what language to speak in," Saber Scar inquired?

"I remembered some stories Running Stag and Lily shared with me about their homeland. We are in their homeland. Running Stag spent quite a bit of time teaching me his language. I figured it was worth a try," Taelo replied.

"It was an inspiration that came to me when I heard Running Stag's wolf call signal. We were about to have some of the local people attacking from the rear. Why not have another turning and fighting from the front," Taelo continued his explanation.

Running Stag and the inhabitants of the village had returned and taken control. The two Sky Eye warriors and the blue-eyed women fled when they saw the returning villagers approach.

"Something has gone wrong. We must flee and find our compatriots," they said to each other as they hastily made their escape.

"We have lost all of our elders. They refused to follow the Sky Eyes. We wish to come with you," Deer Chaser, one of the young men of the village commented.

"I will talk with Taelo and let him know your request. It is his decision," Running Stag replied.

"May a few of us come with you to plead our case," Gentle Cub, one of the women who had engaged in the battle, asked?

"Why don't the two of you organized your clan and discuss this issue. In the next few sun cycles, you can bring your request to Taelo, and a decision can be reached. That way he will know that everyone in the clan had a chance to make a choice," Running Stag suggested.

"These visitors seem so progressive. Their women fight with them in battle. They are very organized, and they trust young men like Running Stag to talk to us and guide us," Whistling Arrow said to Gentle Cub and the people standing around him.

"I would like to be guided by the leaders who are willing to engage all their people so openly," Whistling Arrow continued.

He knew how perilous the situation was for his White Bear Clan. Most of the elders were dead and only an inexperienced, lucky to have survived young group of people remained.

Of their village of two hundred, only about half had survived the encounter with the ruthless Sky Eyes.

Taelo and Golden Hawk had left the White Bear Clan village and had followed Saber Scar's direction to the camp of the Sky Eyes.

The camp looked exactly as described by Saber Scar. He had carefully scouted all around the Sky Eye camp and had located the large shoulder height boulders Taelo and Golden Hawk now stood behind.

The camp had two lookouts, but they were not expecting any attack, and were relaxed about their watch.

"You stay here. I will run through the camp and deliver the map and instructions," Taelo whispered to Golden Hawk.

Taelo ran silently toward the middle of the camp and then at the top of his voice let out his battle cry and threw the leather hide with the map at Angry Cougar. He kept running and never looked back and left just as fast as he had entered.

The entire camp was stunned. No one had time to react. They were all in shock as they realized that they could all have been taken out by a surprise attack.

"How was he allowed to enter the camp?
He could have killed me," Angry Cougar shouted.
He was quivering in anger at having been so vulnerable.

"It appears there are three survivors. If I understand his drawings, we are to come with three travois and with only three people to retrieve our wounded," Rolling Stone reported from near the fire.

He was studying the leather hide and the message.

"I am definitely going home.

This person has out maneuvered us from the beginning.

He has superior battle organization and does not fight like we do. He fights to win with the fewest losses, and he is merciful.

He is bold enough to come into our camp to let us know of our survivors. This is not a person I want to fight," Rolling Stone thought to himself as he listened to another tirade from Angry Cougar.

It had become clear to Rolling Stone that he no longer wished to be led by someone like Angry Cougar.

He would return to his clan by the River and be led by Flying Eagle. This had been his journey of discovery and he had discovered himself.

He wished to be more of a man than Angry Cougar ever could be.

The next morning the two Blue Eyed warriors and the women escaping from the brown eyed village walked into the camp.

"We retreated when the brown eyes came back with weapons and a new leader. What went wrong," one of the two asked?

"Have something to eat and then come with me to retrieve three of our wounded. The brown eyed leader delivered a message showing us where to find them.

Angry Cougar thinks it is a trap, but the message said come with only three, so I do not think that is the case," Rolling Stone instructed.

Angry Cougar was sleeping and moaning in pain on the other side of the fire pit.

"Is he going to make it," One of the warriors inquired?

"Yes, I think so. Right now, he is hot. His body is trying to adjust and heal," Rolling Stone replied.

Rolling Stone led the other two to retrieve the wounded warriors.

When they arrived, it was clear that the wounded warriors had been treated well.

"The brown eyes have been very generous. Each of the wounded has food within reach, a small fire burning, and their wounds seem to have been treated," Rolling Stone noted when they arrived to retrieve their wounded.

The three had arrived and were surprised to find their wounded comrades so well taken care of. They had even been provided with a leather hide to keep them warm.

Close by they could see the multiple graves.

"They buried our dead and marked each grave with the key belongings of the warrior. They honored them," one of the accompanying warriors noted.

"They are a worthy enemy. We are the invaders, and they are defending their land. I understand their resistance. I have little enthusiasm left for this trek," the second warrior commented.

"I am returning to the clan. Those who wish can come with me," Rolling Stone commented as they pulled the three wounded fighters back to their camp.

Rolling Stone counted the wounded that would be able to walk and those that would need assistance until they could heal. They were now only twenty-three warriors. They had lost twice as many in the two confrontations. There were ten seriously wounded fighters and four more that could walk and help the others.

"Truly this confrontation was a mistake. We did not recognize a true fighting force. We got use to overwhelming innocent villagers. This is not what I expected from our journey," Rolling Stone thought to himself.

Rolling Stone made the announcement that he was returning to their clan by the river.

"All those who wish to return to our clan are welcome to come with me," Rolling Stone announced after the group had their morning food.

"You are going to abandon our cause. Are you a coward," Angry Cougar began his tirade?

Rolling Stone leaned in and whispered, "If you stand in the way, I will put you in your grave. Now see who wants to stay with you and who wants to go with me."

These words from the only person who had been his life-long friend shocked Angry Cougar. He also knew he was now no match in a one-handed fight with Rolling Stone.

"Those who wish to stay with me, step to this side of the fire. Those who wish to return with our camp coward step to his side of the fire," Angry Cougar said in a defiant tone.

Only eight of the camp and their women came to stand behind Angry Cougar.

"We will pack up immediately and take our leave," Rolling Stone announced to the fifteen warriors and their women who were lined up on his side of the fire pit.

He knew he was in danger of a sneak attack by Angry Cougar. Their friendship had ended when he had whispered his threat into Angry Cougar's ear. Once out of camp he would make sure he had someone watching their rear.

He hoped Angry Cougar would focus on the brown eyed enemy that had cut off his hand.

"I will not see Angry Cougar again. If he pursues his goal, he will die here in this cold and frozen land," Rolling Stone thought to himself as he led his followers toward home.

He had gained immense respect of the brown eyed leader that had so handily defeated what seemed to be a superior fighting force.

"Superior in number but not in fighting strategy or action," Rolling Stone thought to himself as he replayed the battle in his mind.

Saber Scar and Burley Bear had returned from checking on the Sky Eyed camp.

"We watched as most of the Sky Eyes left the camp. There was a heated exchange between two of the leaders. The one with only one hand has stayed behind. It was clear the larger group is leaving the area. They are pulling many travois of wounded fighters. About ten warriors stayed in the camp.

We followed those leaving. Their leader stopped and waved at us and planted his spear with the point in the snow. He knew he was being watched," Saber Scar reported to Taelo a sun cycle later.

"This is good news. We will still need to worry about those that remain behind. They will now try a sneak attack of some sort. We will take our team north as planned. The villagers lost most of their elders and almost a half of their clan. They would like to come with us." Taelo responded as he felt a sense of relief.

Chapter 19: Final Encounter

The dark mind projected an anger and hatred that colored everything around him in a black hue. His thoughts constantly focused on the pain he would inflict when he next faced this puny individual that had somehow outmaneuvered him. The overwhelming throbbing pain caused him to look at the stump where once his powerful right hand had been. The taste of vengeance permeated his pallet. To him it was sweeter than honey.

The object of his hatred meanwhile was slowly walking back and forth on the bloody hillside with his lifelong friend discussing the battle. Taelo was analyzing and reliving the entire sequence of events to better understand what had transpired and what they should learn from it.

They agreed that there would be at least one more confrontation with what seemed to be an irrational and hateful Blue Eyes.

His shocking treatment of the villagers was slowly being recounted. The loss of half of them during this brutal time spoke of a broken or badly damaged mind.

It reminded Taelo of the crazed saber-tooth tiger that he had to face. The only solution was its death.

"We will begin our journey home, but we will not go back directly.

I am expecting more trouble from the Sky Eyes.

Burley Bear, Meadow Flower, Saber Scar, Quiet Rabbit, Floating Cloud and Bashful Lark and I will all go northeast into the mountains.

Running Stag and Feather-in-the-Wind, Golden Hawk and Busy Bee will stay with our new friends. Once they are sure the Sky Eyes are following us, they will lead our friends toward the ice bridge.

Half of the sleds will be left here to help in the transport of the village. Most of what the villagers have will be pulled on travois. They had plenty of food until the Sky Eyes invaded. Golden Hawk will lead them in hunting during the next moon cycle to prepare for their journey," Taelo explained over the night fire.

I have asked Feather-in-the-Wind, Running Stag, Busy Bee, Golden Hawk, Little Otter, and Talking Wren to guide the White Bear Clan back to the ice bridge," Taelo replied.

It took six sun cycles for the team to make the arrangements and to redistribute the food.

"Will we cross over the ice bridge during the cold months," Saber Scar asked?

Yes, the goal will be to spend the remainder of the winter in the camp with Lily, Slow Runner, Sharp Blade, and Single Leaf," Taelo replied.

"It was a mistake to have spared the leader of the Sky Eyes. He is a vengeful person. You should have finished him that first day," Burley Bear commented.

"It was not that I spared him. His followers drove me back. You are right. It shall not happen again," Taelo replied.

He had thought about this after the battle. The Sky Eyes were being led by a vengeful leader that wanted to conquer and control.

There was no use fighting the battle again. He would deal with the situation in the near future.

"The part of the team going north will want to be able to travel swiftly. Our mission is to draw out the Sky Eyes and eliminate them. We will only take enough food to reach the ice bridge. The rest of our food will go on the sleds that will go with the White Bear Clan," Taelo had announced.

"You are leaving a good part of the team with the White Bear Clan," Burley Bear commented.

"The White Bear Clan is in a very weak and perilous condition. Each of our team members provides a key ingredient to their successful journey. I have also selected the team going north for their special skills," Taelo replied.

"Are we the ones that look most vulnerable," Saber Scar inquired?

"No, you are the ones that can dance better than I," Little Otter commented as he put his arms over Saber Scar's shoulders.

He knew that the attack would come in some tight part of the trail and each swing would need to take out an opponent. The part of the team going north was heavily skewed to powerful hand to hand fighters.

The departure morning offered a clear blue sky and only a slight breeze. The weather remained cold.

It is a beautiful morning," Quiet Rabbit said as they began their northward journey.

Somewhere overhead she heard an eagle screamed as if in reply.

"I am going to follow Taelo and his team," Golden Hawk told Busy Bee on the evening after Taelo, and the team headed out toward the north.

"I do not have an eagle to signal me but last night I had a dream that he would need my help. I must be there when he does.

You must stay here and help Running Stag, Feather-in-the-Wind, Little Otter, and Talking Wren to lead the people to the ice bridge.

I have asked Little Otter to lead the hunt for additional meat," Golden Hawk said as he prepared his pack.

"You are taking Running Stag's bow and arrows. Is that in your dream as well," Busy Bee asked as she made sure there was plenty of food in the backpack.

"Yes, I will not be able to get to the battle scene, but my arrows will," Golden Hawk replied.

"Take care of yourself and let your aim be true," Busy Bee said as she walked to the edge of the village with Golden Hawk.

The first rays of sun came rapidly over the mountains and morning burst into full bloom. It would be a beautiful day and a day full of worry for Busy Bee.

"They are each-others keepers. I am his mate, but Taelo and he are of the same soul," Busy Bee thought as she watched Golden Hawk jog across the valley.

She knew that no one on the team ahead would know he was shadowing them.

Somewhere an eagle let out a scream. Busy Bee searched the sky but could not see it.

"Perhaps the eagle does cry out for you Golden Hawk," she thought to herself.

She walked back to her lodge relieved to have heard the eagle cry.

"We have killed and processed one elk and one deer," we have enough to last our group for a month," Sly Mink, now second in command, reported to Angry Cougar.

Sly Mink had stayed so he could move up in rank. He had no enthusiasm about their current quest. In fact, he thought it ill advised.

"Angry Cougar will not last long if he continues this quest. I will lead in a short time," Sly Mink thought to himself.

"Send a scout out to see where the coward's group is located," Angry Cougar commanded.

He was sure he would soon have his revenge.

"This trail is perfect for ambushes," Taelo commented as he, Burley Bear and Saber Scar walked to the head of the first sled. There were four sleds behind them.

"I will take the lead on foot.

Saber Scar will take the first sled with Marigold. Quiet Rabbit will be next. Floating Cloud and Bashful Lark will follow Quiet Rabbit. Burley Bear and Meadow Flower will bring up the rear sled," Taelo shared with the team.

"I anticipate that they will attack the front and rear most heavily. There will be fewer attacking the middle. We must all be prepared. It could well be different," Taelo commented.

"Make good use of your sleds as shields. Always make them come to you. Make them cross the sleds or go through the wolves," Taelo continued his coaching.

"Why are you out front," Marigold asked?

"I am the bait. They will want to isolate me. That is why the rest of the attack will be as I described. I will pull off three or four of the attackers," Taelo replied.

"I don't mind being the bait. I just hope I am up to besting them on the fight. They are powerful individuals," he thought to himself.

"It is like my dream. Taelo has chosen a trail that is across a narrow but deep crevasse from me. I can follow but I cannot get across," Golden Hawk thought to himself as made his way through the brush.

There was no trail, and he was having a hard time keeping up. It was taking every bit of his skill and speed to do so.

He crossed a shallow river, crossed a path to his left and thought about taking it but knew that then he would come up behind Taelo so he continued following on his side of the ravine as best he could.

Higher on the hill the team's travel was being tracked.

"He is really slow or dimwitted. This is perfect for my purposes," Angry Cougar said when Sly Mink reported back the location and the trail the brown eyed leader was taking.

"We will move out ahead of him and pick a good location to make our attack," Angry Cougar announced.

The six women that had stayed with them were left in the camp.

Angry Cougar led his team out ahead of Taelo to a point in the trail where it came up the ridge and then took a sharp angle downward and to the left. He personally ran back to where Taelo was to see how the group was traveling.

"He is really dimwitted. He is out in front by himself. He makes a perfect target," Angry Cougar commented on his return to his group.

"I hope he is really slow and dimwitted. This seems almost too good to be true," Sly Mink thought to himself as he continued to listen to Angry Cougar's instructions.

"Two of you will attack the rear, two will attack the middle, three will attack the front. Three of us will isolate the leader and kill him," Angry Cougar instructed.

He picked out two of the best fighters to be with him.

He was now certain he would soon be gouging out the eyes of the person that had cut off his hand.

"I don't think we are enough," Sly Mink thought to himself.

He had seen the fighting ability of those that remained at the sleds. It dawned on him that there seemed to be fewer in this group than he remembered.

"There they are," Golden Hawk thought as he ducked down behind a large fallen tree.

The root ball of the tree created when the tree fell over made a perfect hiding spot. He slowly and quietly broke a few of the roots to create a clear shooting area. He placed his arrows out in a row and patiently waited.

He noted the distance and became sensitized to the wind blowing along the crevasse.

"Ancestors of long ago guide my arrows on this day," Golden Hawk thought as he waited.

As soon as he came over the crest of the hill Taelo knew the attack would occur at this location. The cry of the attackers came immediately after he pulled his sharp toothed weapon from his shoulder and took a full round house swing.

A slow positioning dance between Taelo and his attackers began.

The attackers were slowly rotating around Taelo. They were looking for some momentary advantage. The noise of the attack on the other side of the rise in the trail could be heard.

Those attacking the sleds were not faring well.

Burley Bear and Meadow Flower had quickly dispatched the three in back. They quickly marched up opposite sides of the sleds.

Quiet Rabbit had lured her attacker toward her and had disarmed him with a hit to the arm and followed with a strike to the back of his legs.

The three at the front immediately stepped back when Saber Scar let out his war cry and launched one of them into the woods with the war hammer, he was swinging.

Marigold was approaching from the other side.

Sly Mink was one of those attacking the front. He immediately made his escape into the woods. He saw three others crawling into the woods to escape. The crushed skulls of three fallen visually communicated their fate.

He made his way up the hill to a vantage point and hid.

I am in trouble," Taelo thought to himself as he moved slowly around trying to prepare himself for the coordinated attack.

The three much larger, Sky Eyes knew how to co-ordinate their movement. It was clear they had executed such an attack before.

They believed they had ample time and were unaware of the fate their other members were facing.

Golden Hawk took in the attack. He put his first arrow into his bow and aimed it at a tree at the side of the trail. He missed it by a few inches, and he was short.

"Now let this arrow be true," he thought to himself as he made the adjustments called for by the test arrow.

The second arrow struck the left attacker in the thigh and the arrow went all the way through.

"Not what I was aiming for," Golden Hawk thought as he aimed at the next attacker.

Taelo saw the one attacker fall with an arrow through his leg. He danced to that side and ducked the hammer swing from the warrior out in front.

The second arrow went all the way through the second warrior's chest and Taelo ducked another hammer swing once again and stepped to the right.

"Not today," Taelo heard Bashful Lark say as she smashed her hammer into the skull of the warrior with the arrow in his leg. He had been ready to stab Taelo in the back.

Taelo focused on the only remaining warrior standing and delivered his single blow across the side of Angry Cougar's head. The shark teeth cut through the skull and the light left the blue eyes.

Taelo looked across the ravine to where he knew Golden Hawk would be standing and raised his hand in salute.

High in the sky an eagle let out its cry.

Sly Mink took note of the outcome.

He too took note of the eagle. To him it was a sign from Angry Cougar's father, whose totem was also the eagle.

The eagle had called Sly Mink home. He would take his pride and his wounded warriors and join Rolling Stone on the return to his own clan.

"This warrior is not dimwitted or stupid instead he is strategic, brave and has a team that supports him," Sly Mink thought as he turned from looking at where Taelo stood over Angry Cougar.

He rounded up and helped the three wound fighters back to their camp.

"Angry Cougar is no longer with us. We will leave immediately and catch up to Rolling Stone and return to our land," Sly Mink shared with the group.

Later as he led his group homeward, Sly Mink knew he was being followed. When he got to the point in the trail where he found Rolling Stone's inverted spear, Sly Mink turned, saluted, and planted his spear point down next to Rolling Stone's spear.

Each spear was a salute to a worthy adversary.

"There are two downward pointed spears on the trail to the east. The Sky Eyes have left the region," Saber Scar reported back later toward the end of the sun cycle.

"Our team is invincible when we work together. Bashful Lark gave new meaning to taking just in time action. What made you come to help," Taelo inquired as the team relaxed after eating?

"Marigold, Saber Scar and Quiet Rabbit were taking care of all the warriors. I thought perhaps you might need help so I just wandered forward to see if I could help," Bashful Lark admitted.

"Well thank you for doing so," Taelo said handing Bashful Lark a hot piece of roasted boar's meat.

"And how did you come to be in such a good position? I thought you were out leading a hunt," Taelo said as he looked across at Golden Hawk.

"The ancestors told me where to be and what to do. I am only their instrument," Golden Hawk replied with a smile.

He was relieved that the dream had come true and the outcome so positive. Taelo was right in recognizing Bashful Lark. Had it not been for her the outcome might have been different.

The fallen Sky Eyes were put into shallow graves and covered with stone. They were given a proper warriors burial.

"It's time to get back to the main part of the team," Taelo announced.

High in the sky an eagle let out its second cry and flew out of sight.

Chapter 20: In the Cave of the Others

Once again Broken Spear sat and looked out into the valley from the hot water springs. He had flown with the eagle. He had watched the travels of Taelo and Golden Hawk.

The way to the ice bridge was a river of green between two blankets of mountain high snow and ice. This green was dotted with huge boulders made by being rolled and ground by the moving layers of snow and ice as they melted moved, then froze and stopped.

Thousands of moon cycles of time and a warm southeast air current had slowly melted a northwesterly to southeastern path that connect to another land.

The eagle guided Taelo and his team into this path.

Broken Spear had periodically connected with the eagle and watched the team's progress.

Broken Spear had invited the Elk Clan leader Red Oak and Quiet Pheasant and the Northern Elk Clan leader, White Swan, and Grey Fox Running. These were now called friends and he was happy to see them once more.

He thanked them for accepting his invitation and coming and for the gift of buffalo meat from the Elk Clan and salt from the Northern Elk Clan.

Now we are ready for our feast and then we will listen to our own Broken Spear recall what he has seen," Quiet Fox made his formal opening speech.

"The Eagle's cry has been heard many times on Taelo's journey. Tonight, we gather round to hear what this old warrior has seen through the eyes of the eagle," Broken Spear spoke quietly but loud enough for the entire gathering to hear.

"The first minor encounter was when the dire wolves were tempted by the smells of food coming from the sleds and the camp. They circled the camp but were not hungry enough to attack. Those in the camp knew their enemy was outside and kept close watch throughout the night.

They moved rapidly northward to get out of the dire wolf's territory.

The team made good time and reached the river gap that opens to the north. This was a different route than the one I thought the team would take. Taelo was pushing his team to get through this area before the snows of winter. This was a challenging but a quiet part of their journey.

Immediately after getting through the narrow gap between the cliffs, the team entered the territory of the giant brown bears.

Almost immediately the eagle screamed.

The team had planned for this situation.

The team had practiced on how to evade a bear attack. They all did their part.

Taelo teased the bear to chase him.

Feather-in-the-Wind followed with her army of wolves.

The bear was very fast and closed the gap in its pursuit of Taelo.

It was then when Feather-in-the-Wind unleashed her army of wolves.

The bear turned and attacked Feather-in-the-Wind.

Taelo turned and ran back toward the bear in what seemed to be a suicide rush.

He buried his spear into the side of the bear and as he slid past, he cut the tendon on the back of the bear's hind leg. The bear turned to attack him but toppled over.

Feather-in-the-Wind then rejoined the attack. This allowed Taelo to attack the bear once more. He cut the tendon on the other leg and then leaped forward to hit the bear on the side of the head with his war hammer.

This would have killed most bears but this one was only stunned.

Feather-in-the-Wind ran forward and buried her spear into the bears side as she slid past the beast. Her attack gave Taelo the time he needed to hit the bear with his war hammer again and then cut its throat.

Feather-in-the-Wind was seriously wounded. The last I saw was Quiet Rabbit sewing the huge gash cut across Feather-in-the-Wind's thigh," Broken Spear finished the first part of the story.

"Does she still live," Someone in the audience called out?

"In a moment, I will continue telling what I have seen from the eyes of the eagle but first please bring this old warrior some of the honey brew so I can continue my story," Broken Spear replied.

He had intentionally stopped at a critical point in the story.

"He has my full attention when he tells these stories," White Swan said quietly to her sister, Quiet Pheasant.

"Yes, he has mine as well. How he knows and sees what he sees is a mystery to all of us, but it is a comfort to know that the team is doing well on their journey.

I hope Feather-in-the-Wind recovers from her injuries," Quiet Pheasant replied.

"Indeed, she lives, Feather-in-the-Wind did recover though she remained weak for many sun cycles," Broken Spear continued his story telling.

The next bear again chased Taelo. This time Golden Hawk was his partner. The two ran out ahead of the bear and Lasher led the team of wolves from behind.

Taelo had decided to try a different tactic in his battle with the bear. He and Golden Hawk used their sling and chipped stone shards to hit the bear in its eyes. Their tactic worked and the bear was temporarily blinded and the two escaped back to the rest of the team.

Their journey north continued. They have seen two new animals on this journey. One is a cousin to our elk and the other similar to our buffalo but with much thicker fur.

They reached the northern ice glacier. Their mounts and four of the team stayed on this side of the ice bridge.

They will have many thick furs to trade with us this coming clan gathering.

The rest of the team went across the ice glacier.

It was Taelo, or should I say his hero, Lasher, which led the team safely across this perilous crossing.

Once across they traveled south even as the cold of winter closed in.

There they met the Sky Eyes. These were people from a faraway land to the west.

Their leader made the mistake of miscalculating Taelo and the team. Taelo went out to the standing army of Blue Eyes to greet this Clan of Sky Eyed people. The leader of that clan came out with the intent of killing Taelo. Taelo was ready when the Sky Eye's leader lunged forward in a surprise move to kill. Taelo used the shark toothed weapon he to cut off the attacker's hand.

Taelo was immediately driven back and fought valiantly as his team took up their battle formation and drove the attackers off.

The Sky Eye leader made another attempt to conquer the team. His fifty warriors went into battle with the team's ten.

They were using their local prisoners as their front shield as they marched up to Taelo's team.

These were the people of Running Stag's family heritage. Taelo called out to them in that language and implored them to fight on his side and help to defeat the Sky Eyes.

Taelo used his wolves, a few recruited survivors, and he called on the line of the brown eyed warriors coming toward him to fight with him to get their freedom from the Sky Eyes.

The battle that followed was swift and deadly to the Sky Eyes. Only Little Otter received a minor wound. Three wolves were injured and required attention. The Sky Eyes lost more than half of their warriors and retreated with half of the remaining warriors seriously wounded.

The Sky Eye leader still wanted revenge and planned to continue his pursuit of Taelo, but more than half of his followers chose to return to their home clan. They had decided it was time to return to their own land.

Taelo sensed it was not over. He took half of his team north through the mountains to draw the Sky Eyes out.

Golden Hawk was to stay behind and help take the remainder of the rescued clan toward the ice bridge, but the ancients sent him a dream and instead he shadowed Taelo along his travels. Golden Hawk was able to help Taelo defeat the Sky Eye leader.

Bashful Lark was a surprise heroin. She downed a warrior who was attacking Taelo from behind.

Taelo then eliminated the Sky Eye leader.

This ended the threat from the Sky Eyes.

Taelo and his team still face several challenges. Each will test the team as well as Taelo and Golden Hawk.

I will continue to fly with the eagle and perhaps in the spring we can again have a gathering and hear more about the journey of our wandering team," Broken Spear closed to the slapping of the ground by his captivated listeners.

White Swan and Quiet Pheasant and Running Stags parents all thanked Broken Spear for inviting them and sharing the stories of Taelo's and Golden Hawk's travels. It was comforting to know the journey was going well.

The members of the three clans spent the rest of the evening in friendly discussions and then retired to their areas for the night. The visitors from the two clans would depart the next morning.

Chapter 21: Winter in the Outland

The earlier than usual fall snows had conditioned the team to winter hunting and making camp in the frigid cold. The dark grey of the sky warned of an impending winter storm.

The tall pines bent and swung around as the wind began its assault along the sharp ravine through the mountains.

The snow on the ground began to follow the flow of the wind and piled up against tree trunks, boulders and any obstacle that would hold the snow back.

A major blizzard fully loaded with snow from the moist warm air from the west meeting the cold air from the east was forming overhead.

The eagle cry was heard by the caravan of the White Bear Clan.

"I travel with a lighter heart," Busy Bee commented to Feather-in-the-Wind and Talking Wren.

"Yes, now we must beat the cold winter weather and get across the ice bridge and set up our winter lodge," Feather-in-the-Wind replied.

It was as if her words awoke the winter storm. From the East an almost black sky moved in with a vengeance. The sky turned a mean dark grey color, and the wind began to howl.

"I will go out ahead and find a place for us to stop," Running Stag volunteered and moved his sled into the lead.

The wind in the mountains was even stronger and the sky took on the same dark threatening grey.

"We need to find shelter, I will look ahead on the trail and see if there is a good place to make camp," Golden Hawk volunteered.

"We need to go to our right. There was a branch to the right that we passed at mid-morning. I suggest we go back and try that way. See if there is a good place to make camp in that direction," Burley Bear called out.

"You are right. I crossed that part of the trail on the way here. It looked promising. A river runs in that direction. Let's turn our sleds around and make our way back. I will scout ahead," Golden Hawk agreed.

"Back we go," Taelo said as he took the lead wolf of the back sleigh and led him around.

He was still feeling the effect the battle had on him.

This was now the second person he had intentionally slain in battle. In each case he had watched the light go out of their eyes. His shark tooth edged weapon had been the weapon of these deaths.

He wondered where the escaping spirit of the dying went and how it was received when it got there. He wished them well. He held no anger for their misguided aggression.

He was pleased to have Burley Bear and Golden Hawk lead.

Burley Bear and Saber Scar picked up the front of the sleigh and turned it around.

Soon the four sleds were moving back along the trail they had just traveled.

The trail to the right ran down to a small river. It was flowing in the direction they would travel. Golden Hawk went out ahead at a moderate jog looking for a good shelter.

"This large stone overhang where the stream bends will make a good shelter," he thought to himself as he approached.

After a quick inspection he turned and raced back up the trail. The snow was now falling thick enough that it was hard to see more than a spear's throw ahead.

"I think that is Golden Hawk returning," Burley Bear called out.

"Follow me there is a good spot just ahead. We will be able to use our hides to create a shelter under a large stone overhang," Golden Hawk shouted to all of them.

A few moments later they were at the overhang.

The sleds were backed up against the back wall with about a spear's length between each of them. This provided five separate sleeping areas and some privacy.

"We must all move some stones to form a low wall. Our hides can be used to close the main opening. Build the sides with stone all the way up to the top," Meadow Flower instructed as she took control of the shelter preparation.

Burley Bear made several trips down along the river and came back with several large poles to help hold the hides in place and a large bundle of long slender willow branches.

"I was thinking we would need snowshoes too," Taelo commented when he saw the slender branches.

"If it keeps snowing at this rate, we will need a way to float through the snow," Burley Bear responded.

Bashful Lark and Floating Cloud gathered wood along the stream and piled it up along the outside of the shelter. They then rolled some large stones into place to make a fire ring.

"Let's put a cover over the fire ring to keep the snow out," Floating Cloud suggested as she positioned some boulders to hold up supporting poles.

"Let's fill our water bags before we begin the cooking," Bashful Lark suggested.

After filling their water bags, they began to cook some of the fresh meat they had brought with them. Soon the aroma of sizzling meat permeated the camp.

"I love it when our team works together," Taelo commented later as he sat with Quiet Rabbit inside by the small warming fire inside the shelter.

He had followed instructions as the rest of the team took the lead in getting the campsite ready for the winter storm now pounding them with a whistling wind and a solid wall of snow.

"We have a comfortable spot in the middle," Quiet Rabbit said pointing to the space between two sleds.

Marigold had insisted they get the middle spot and Quiet Rabbit had no objection.

She was worn out by the events of the day and content to lean against Taelo as the group gathered around to spend a few quiet moments before turning in. She sensed Taelo was as worn out as she.

The snow outside was piling up on the wall. If it continued, they would be trapped by morning.

"This reminds me of the snow that covered us at our paradise site on our *Journey of Discovery*. We were snowed in for days. We finally dug our way out and rode our mounts out to capture more of them," Marigold commented as the fond recollection came to her.

They all watched as Burley Bear and Saber Scar worked at making a set of snowshoes by bending the warmed willow sticks into a teardrop shape and then weaving smaller willow branches to create a surface that they bound with strips of leather.

The wolves were all resting peacefully along the side wall near their opening to the outside.

Lasher was sleeping at Taelo's feet.

"Did I tell you that Lasher helped me defeat the warrior that attacked me in the middle," Quiet Rabbit commented as she gave Lasher a stroke across his head.

"That was my orders to him. He knew he would have been in a great deal of trouble with me if he let me down," Taelo joked as he put his hand on Quiet Rabbit's.

"It was a good day for all of us," Burley Bear said as he and Meadow Flower made their way to their sleeping area.

Out to the west, Running Stag in search for a place for the White Bear Clan to shelter, crossed the small river and proceeded to inspect a lager grouping of rocks near the river. He noted the stand of small trees and willows along the river.

"Let's hope we have enough time to get our shelter built," Running Stag thought to himself as he turned his wolf team around and raced back to the rest of the clan.

"This looks like a good spot," Talking Wren agreed after crossing the small river and inspecting the area.

"Put the sleds in a semi-circle around those large boulders. Get some poles between the boulders to hold the covering hides and tie the other edges to the outside of the sleds. Leave an opening for a door in the middle," Talking Wren directed.

"You six; gather all the grasses you can and fill the opening between the sleds," Feather-in-the-Wind directed as she began to cut the tall grass along the bank of the river.

"Let's fill in between the boulders with a combination of rocks and grasses. We will want to keep the wind and snow out," she continued as she led her team in getting the grasses cut and put into place.

"Let's get a fire ring made and all the wood you can find gathered and piled next to it," Running Stag directed as he led another group.

"A few of you follow me to the river. We will gather as many long poles as possible," Little Otter instructed as he walked down to the river's edge.

Soon the entire clan was working swiftly to get the shelter ready.

"Leave this open between these two sleds. This will be where the wolves will come and go," Busy Bee commented as Feather-in-the-Wind's team finished sealing the wall made by the sleds and the stonewall.

"Let's get everyone and the wolves inside. Then we can send the cooks and guards out to prepare a meal," Busy Bee instructed.

"Thanks for bring up the support timbers. Let's get them positioned to support the hide roof," Running Stag said as he indicated where to put each support pole.

"Let's hope Taelo and the rest of the team found some good shelter. They did not have as many hides or shelter material with them as we have," Running Stag commented later as he lay back and relaxed against one of the boulders.

The hide covering for the roof had a steep slope and many reinforcing timbers running from the top of the boulders to the outside edges of the sleds.

Running Stag remembered the Northern Elk Clan lodge had put vertical supporting poles in the key spots. He did the same with this structure. He was confident these poles would keep the snow from collapsing the roof.

"I am confident that Taelo and the team will find a good spot to take shelter. In fact, we will need to ask them if Taelo and Golden Hawk found another hot spring as a shelter," Busy Bee joked.

She was concerned but she instinctively knew the two would keep the other part of the team safe.

There were almost one hundred people crowded into the small area. It was tight but everyone had enough room to lie down comfortably. With so many people in such a small area, keeping the inside of the shelter cool turned out to be the challenge.

"We will not need a fire for heating. We will need it to provide a little light," Busy Bee noted as she opened a leather flap between two boulders to let out the hot air.

"We will keep a path open down to the river, so everyone has a place to relieve themselves. Down river please! Upriver will be for our water supply," Feather-in-the-Wind instructed.

"Two persons will always remain awake and working. We will take turns going out and clearing the path to the river and pulling the snow off the shelter. I have talked to the eight persons who are assigned tonight and have instructed them in their duties," Little Otter announced.

"We have made the right choice in asking to go with this team," Deer Chaser of the White Bear Clan commented.

"Yes, I agree. They seem to know exactly what to do with almost no communication between them. And notice they are unconcerned with who leads," Gentle Cub replied.

"I have seen many summers. I have never seen a group of people work so well together and know how to engage and lead those around them. Their leader seems to have created a metanoic team," Whistling Arrow commented.

"I agree and I feel confident that with them we are safe," Bubbling Brook added.

Chapter 22: Snowed In

The snowfall was a solid sheet almost as dense as water itself. Three spear lengths of snow rose above the banks of the river. The small river disappeared below this layer and though it was able to cut through and keep flowing it was inaccessible.

The pass, just beyond the overhang was closed and the snow was above the cliffs that formed the gorge through which the river flowed.

The heat from the camp had been pulled by the wind and had cut its own chimney up through the snow.

Taelo and the team had worked together throughout the night and the following three days to keep the air flowing. They had cut tunnels and paths down to the riverbank. They had kept the fire burning to keep the area above the cooking ring open.

They, however, were very much like ants keeping their hive functional and operating during heavy rains that threatened to wash them out. In their case it threatened to cut off the precious air they needed to breath and survive.

After the third sun cycle, noticeable only by a faint change in the available light, Quiet Rabbit commented on the teams struggle in keeping the air flowing.

She voiced her hope that the rest of the team and the large number of people of the White Bear Clan had found a good place to shelter.

Taelo assured her and the rest of the team that once the storm subsided, he and Golden Hawk would go out ahead and find the rest of the team.

He, Golden Hawk, Burley Bear and Saber Scar had made snowshoes for each of them.

"It is going to be a challenge to get our sleds out where we can get the wolves pulling them," Burley Bear commented.

"We may need to float them down the river," Meadow Flower suggested.

"I have been thinking the same," Golden Hawk added in support.

"When the snow stops, we will evaluate the situation. We will need enough logs to hold up the weight of a sled. In this weather I am not sure we can find what we need," Taelo weighed in.

The following sun cycle began with a clear blue cloudless sky. The day was clear but very cold.

"Golden Hawk and I will get on top of the snow and go down river to see if we can find the other half of our team," Taelo announce the next morning as he was loading his backpack.

"Saber Scar and I will see if we can find the logs, we need to get our sleds out of here. Check down river to see if there is a place where the snow is not so deep," Burley Bear requested.

The team had discussed in detail what needed to be done and each was taking on their share.

"I will take care of Lasher and the Wolves," Quiet Rabbit commented.

"And we will take care of Quiet Rabbit," Meadow Flower and Marigold chimed in.

Everyone had wanted to try the snowshoes out.

Quiet Rabbit especially had wanted to go but she was the best in keeping the wolves in line. The wolves were ready to try and leave but there was no way they would be able to make it through the snow.

Meadow Flower and Marigold both knew that they were twice as heavy as Quiet Rabbit and even with snowshoes they would sink into the snow much deeper. They were content to help get a raft ready if Burley Bear and Saber Scar found the appropriate materials.

Taelo used the stonewall at one end of the shelter to climb out to the top of the snow. It was at least three spears length deep. They were truly buried deeply in the snow.

"I hope we are light enough to stay on top," Golden Hawk said as he led the way.

It was extremely difficult to climb up with the snowshoes on.

"You two look like two ducks trying to climb a mountain," Quiet Rabbit teased from below.

"Yes, I just wish I had duck wings so I could fly to the top," Taelo responded.

"The snow is so deep at this place because it gets narrower just downstream. It will probably be better just downstream," Golden Hawk called down once he was out on the top of the snow.

"Saber Scar and I will look hard for the logs needed to float our sleds downstream," Burley Bear called up.

"Even with these oversized snowshoes, I sink in almost to my knees if I stand still," Taelo called down, "We are on our way."

The snowshoes were the only reason they could stay on top, but it took them until the sun was at its highest to reach the point where the snow was visibly going down.

"I think we are far enough away from the gap between the hills that the snow is beginning to get less deep," Golden Hawk commented.

"Yes, we can now get down to the riverbank and follow it downstream. Let's look for a good place to spend the night," Taelo said as he led the way to the river's edge.

"Did you put your fishing gear in your bag," Taelo asked as they reached the river.

"Yes, I did, did you bring yours" Golden Hawk replied.

"Yes, I was just looking ahead, and I see what seems to be an excellent place to stop. We can check it out and if those trees and rocks provide us with a good stopping point, we can catch a couple of fish and have an early dinner," Taelo replied.

The windblown trees were deformed to be permanently bent as if they were still in the wind. They were little more than tall brush, but they were at least two spears high. It was clear they were very old trees. The combination of the trees and the boulders around which they grew formed a large circle that was open in the middle.

"Let's use those four boulders to frame our camp. Our large hide will go over all four and make a tight enclosure. We will be able to stand inside if we find a vertical log to put up," Golden Hawk suggested as he swept the snow out from the area in the center of the rocks.

"I think this has been used before," Golden Hawk commented as he pointed to a center stone with a round center hole.

"We just need to find a center pole to put into that hole," Taelo commented.

"I'll prepare our fire ring just outside of the enclosure," Taelo said as he began to gather a few of the smaller stones about the size of his head.

"This will make a good place for the sleds to come up out of the river," Golden Hawk observed later as he and Taelo prepared to do some fishing.

"We better see if there are any fish willing to bite. The day seems to be getting colder and I see dark clouds on the horizon. I am not sure we are going to have any luck fishing," Taelo said as he carried his spear and his fishing line down to the river.

"Let's walk out on that sandbar and try our luck where the river runs. The fish will be sitting in the deeper water just past the end," Golden Hawk said once they were at the riverbank.

They each tied the line to the end of their spear and flicked the line along the bank. Their baited hook would sink into the water, and they would pull it slowly up stream.

Taelo saw one large fish following Golden Hawk's Line. He pulled back his spear and threw it with all his might at the fish. He lifted his spear and the fish out of the water and waded back up on the sandbar.

"Well, you got my fish, and you are soaked. We better get back to camp and get you dry," Golden Hawk said as he put two fingers through the gills and his thumb into the fish's mouth.

"I wasn't sure he was going to bite, and I wasn't going to wait any longer," Taelo said as the two jogged back to the camp.

"Look at that pole against the riverbank. It is perfect for the center of our shelter," Golden Hawk pointed.

"I will take it back with us," Taelo said as he picked it up and began a jog back to the camp.

"You change while I clean and cook this fish for our supper," Golden Hawk said as they got back to the camp.

Taelo entered the shelter and put up the pole in the center. It was the right height to lift the center of the hide so he could stand inside.

A few moments later Taelo came out with his wet boots and leggings and positioned them near the fire.

"I hope they dry out by morning. All I have are some light booties to use at night and this heavy coat," Taelo commented as he picked some meat off the fish.

"Well, it would serve you right for stealing my fish," Golden Hawk said with a chuckle.

"It appears as if we have another snowstorm headed our way. We better find some cross supports to hold up our hide," Taelo said as he stood looking toward the oncoming storm.

"We have our spears and I see a few shorter pieces of timber to make some vertical supports," Golden Hawk noted.

"I will gather a few more stones to anchor our center support and to put around the edges of the hide," Taelo added.

"Let's gather enough stone to weigh down the bottom edges all the way around. The wind is already blowing snow into our domain," Golden Hawk said as he got up and looked at the oncoming storm.

As they went about their preparation it became clear that the rocks and the camp had been used many times in the past.

"I think somebody set this camp up before. There seems to be all the right materials at hand and the center stone has a depression in it," Taelo commented as he cleared the spot to pile the stones up.

"I don't see any timbers anywhere around. They must have taken all their support timbers with them," Golden Hawk added.

"That would make sense. Good supporting timbers would be hard to find in this area," Taelo replied as he built up the center column.

"I am going to bring in all the firewood I can find. There was quite a bit along the riverbank," Taelo commented as he exited the enclosure.

The two went about preparing for the on-coming storm. The temperature was dropping rapidly.

"We were wise to bring our biggest hide for the cover. I wish we would have brought more clothes and food for ourselves," Taelo commented as he checked the progress of his drying clothes.

He decided to take the wet clothes into the enclosure and let them dry there.

"We have enough food to last for the next seven sun cycles," Golden Hawk commented as he continued positioning the stones around the base of the enclosure.

He went outside, rolled any stones he found up against the bottom of the enclosure and heaped snow up along the bottom edge and packed it down to seal the bottom.

"We will be warm enough with just our body heat, but this wood will allow us a small fire for cooking," Taelo commented as he stacked the wood to one side of the opening.

"Well let's use the remainder of our fish and some of our dried goods to make ourselves a stew for our dinner. It seems the storm has arrived at full force," Golden Hawk said as he secured the entrance and put some stones down along the bottom to keep the wind out.

"I hope Taelo, and Golden Hawk see the oncoming storm," Burly Bear commented as he pulled the last of the six logs up on the riverbank.

He, Saber Scar, Meadow Flower, and Marigold had trudged through the cold water up stream to find the logs. They were now wet, cold, tired, and concerned.

"I think we better get something to eat, get dry and warm up," I am worn out, my legs are numb from the cold, and I can't feel my hands," Marigold commented as she led the way back to the camp.

"I am with you," Saber Scar added as he followed his mate.

"You all look worn out and you look cold. I have some stew and hot buffalo ready for you," Floating Cloud said as she saw the four approaching.

"All of you go and get out of your wet clothes. We will bring the food to you," Quiet Rabbit said as she took in the expressions on their faces.

She had never seen Burley Bear look so tired.

The snow began to come down as Floating Cloud took the food off the fire.

"We seem to be in for another round of snow," Floating Cloud commented.

"Yes, and it seems to be about as strong as the previous one only the air is much colder," Bashful Lark said worriedly.

"I hope Golden Hawk and Taelo see it coming and find a good place to setup a warm camp," Quiet Rabbit replied.

She was confident the two would know what to do but this seemed to be a really cold storm.

"We will need to keep the path to the river open. I will take the first watch," Burley Bear said as he ate his meal.

The cold water had taken its toll on all four. He was exhausted but knew the danger of getting buried in the snow.

"No, you four get your rest. I will take the first watch and Floating Cloud and Bashful Lark will take the second watch. No arguments about this," Quiet Rabbit countered.

"You'll get none from us," Meadow Flower replied as she warmed her hands over the small fire.

Chapter 23: Convergence

Once again, the clouds had turned a mean gray and had surged, like a mad charging army, across the sky toward the three different campsites. The wind howled and the snow was a white blanket that swept through with such power that kept it flowing almost like a traveling wave at sea. Somewhere the snow would find refuge from the wind and become a thick layer that would last through the entire next warm cycle.

This storm was the aftershock of the first storm, but it blew a meaner cold front in that tried to grab one by the ankle as it crept along the floor through the enclosure.

Taelo and Golden Hawk were pleased with their handiwork and glad they had stopped early to make camp. Their small fire by the opening was more than enough to keep the frigged air at bay.

Quiet Rabbit during her first watch became aware of the strong wind slowly eroding the snow cover that blocked the passage through the narrow gap.

Along the river, the White Bear Clan was sitting quietly inside their enclosure.

"We will be eating a lot of our dried food," Busy Bee commented as she came in from the river. "We have another storm headed our way. Let's get everyone to go out and gather all the wood and any dried grass they can find."

"We are going to be short on food when we get a chance to move on toward the ice bridge," Running Stag commented quietly.

"Yes, I hope Quiet Rabbit, Taelo and Golden Hawk join up with us before then. They will have extra dried food though I don't think even that will be enough," Feather-in-the-Wind added.

"Let's get a few folks to go along the riverbank and gather enough small willow trees to make one of Taelo's fish traps," Busy Bee suggested.

"That is a great idea. We can spend the time during the storm to get the sticks ready and put up our fish trap immediately after the storm," Running Stag said as he got up and recruited a half a dozen young men.

"I think this is a little crazy. Here comes a mean storm and we are gathering young willow saplings," Deer Chaser commented to his assigned partner, as he slipped and fell into the river and came out with his teeth chattering.

"I am not sure about being crazy. Running Stag said this might well save our lives," replied White Bear.

"Well, I hope it's worth it to be out here as the storm hits. Let's get our bundle back to the camp before my clothes freeze in place and I can't walk," the wet and freezing Deer Chaser replied.

"Welcome back and good job," Talking Wren said handing each of the willow hunters a bowl of hot soup as they returned.

"Well, I go from being a complainer to feeling like a hero," Deer Chaser commented as he sat down with his bowl of soup.

"Thank you all for this great effort. We need to build up our food reserves. We think of ourselves as hunters, but Taelo always says that we are really fishermen.

We will prepare the saplings to build a fish trap. As soon as the storm passes, we will set up the trap. In the morning we will work together. Tonight, we will relax and let the storm howl as we sleep in our warm enclosure," Running Stag announced.

"Your mate demonstrates great leadership," Talking Wren commented to Feather-in-the-Wind.

"Yes, he is perfect, and he does exactly as I ask," Feather-in-the-Wind joked.

Again, the storm raged unabated for three cycles of the sun. The snow was not as heavy as the first snow, but the wind seemed to want to clear the landscape of all protruding elements. It blew across the landscape clearing most of the snow from the previous storm.

The snow, which had blocked the pass where Burley Bear and the rest of the team was located, was blown open.

Not too far away, Taelo and Golden Hawk had to fight the wind as it blew their area clear and tore at the protecting enclosure.

Busy Bee and the White Bear Clan members had it the worst as they fought to keep their structure from collapsing.

A work team had to constantly pull the snow off the ceiling hide.

Talking Wren had taken charge and had two people assigned to hold the cover poles in place.

"I am happy that we were able to keep our enclosure from collapsing," Golden Hawk commented as he noted the passing of the storm.

"The winds seem to have cleared the snow from this area. Let's break camp and see if we can find Busy Bee and the camp of the White Bear Clan," Taelo said as he stepped out and put on his heavy winter outer covering.

"Where do you plan to look," Golden Hawk asked as he began to pull their covering hide loose.

"We will follow this river and hope it is the one that we crossed on our way south. If we are lucky, they will have found a place close to it to ride out these storms," Taelo replied.

Meanwhile, down river, Running Stag was instructing a group to put up a fish trap.

"Each of us will take a turn wading out into the river and planting the stakes we have prepared. Once you get your stakes in place come immediately back to the fire, dry off and put on your warm clothes," Running Stag commented as he removed his coat and pants.

He waded into the water with only his loin cloth. He was already turning blue in the bitter cold. Once he got his six poles in place he came charging back out and rushed to the fire.

The rest of the fish trap team followed his lead. A short time later they all watched as the first fish began to get trapped in the shallow pit they had made on their side of the river.

A cheer from the fish trap team caused everyone to take a look.

"I would not have believed this was possible," Gentle Cub commented as she and a team of the young women began to clean the fish being brought up to them.

"I have seen many things, but this is amazing," Whistling Arrow commented.

"This will certainly help to tide us over and may be the margin of safety we need. Let's dry half of what we catch and enjoy the other half as part of our normal meals," Busy Bee commented.

"I will organize the smoking and drying of the fish," Talking Wren volunteered.

"We should stay here as long as the fish keep coming in at this rate," Feather-in-the-Wind commented.

"I will volunteer to be the taste tester of any cooked or smoked fish," Little Otter said in a serious tone.

"Now I wonder if it was so wise to go and hunt down those logs," Burley Bear commented as he took in the opening through the narrow pass.

The wind had created a narrow opening and it seemed to him it would be possible for the sleds to make their way through.

"I will jog out on my snowshoes to make certain it is clear," Quiet Rabbit volunteered.

"That would be great. I will get our wolves ready to pull," Saber Scar replied.

"The rest of us will break camp and prepare to move," Meadow Flower added.

"Let's pull those logs up under this overhang. We worked too hard to get them to let them float away. Maybe someone else can benefit from our labor," Burley Bear said as he walked down to pull them up.

The breakdown and cleanup of the camp went smoothly. In a few moon cycles it would be impossible to tell that they had been here.

"Here comes Quiet Rabbit. I am glad she volunteered to go scout ahead. She is the fastest among us," Burley Bear said as he pointed her out.

"The way is clear. There is one tight spot but once we get the first sled through the others will easily pass through. It certainly will be easier than floating down the river," Quiet Rabbit said as she was given some water by Floating Cloud.

"Let's go. I have all the sleds and wolf teams ready to pull," Saber Scar said as he put his team in the lead.

"You ride and rest. I will handle your sled and Bashful Lark will handle mine," Floating Cloud said to Quiet Rabbit.

The four sleds made good time to the point where the snow closed to a narrow opening. The team stopped and went about clearing the way. It was late afternoon by the time they were able to take the first team through.

"Let's go as far as possible and find some place along the river to make camp," Burley Bear commented as the last sled made it through the gap.

It was late in the afternoon and the sun was low on the horizon when they spotted the stand of low trees along the river.

"I think this is where Taelo and Golden Hawk camped," Meadow Flower commented as she walked around the stones and took in the area.

Far down river, Golden Hawk and Taelo were jogging casually along in their normal traveling pace. They had on their snowshoes, so their jog was a coordinated shuffle.

"I wonder if we will be able to find them today," Golden Hawk commented.

"That would be good, but I think it will take more than one day. That is if they stopped along this river," Taelo replied.

"Is that a herd of buffalo out to our left," Golden Hawk commented a few moments later?

"Let's get closer and get a better look," Taelo replied as they both turned in unison toward the herd.

"Do you think we could cull out one of them and guide it down along the river ahead of us," Golden Hawk pondered?

"Let's give it a try. We certainly can't get it to the rest of the team any other way," Taelo said as he looked over the large herd.

"Let's see how we do without using our snowshoes. We will need to be a little faster," Golden Hawk commented.

"The snow is hard. We will be able to jog without them," Taelo commented as he moved around.

The two agreed on the animal to cull out and slowly moved it away from the herd and guided it to follow along the river.

"Now we have a different problem. If we, stop we will lose our prize. We can continue jogging through the night or until we reach the camp we hope to find," Taelo called over to Golden Hawk.

"I thought of the same thing. Let's keep going and see if we can get the animal as close to the camp as possible," Golden Hawk called back.

It was the end of the second day of fishing. The trap continued to deliver fish.

"I would not have believed we could have caught so many fish. The little ones are able to go through the trap. Only the larger fish end up in the pickup area," Deer Chaser noted.

"We will plan to continue to the ice bridge on the second sun cycle from this one," Busy Bee announced.

It had been a hard decision to make but after discussion with the rest of the team they had come to the conclusion they needed to take advantage of the good weather and travel on toward the ice bridge.

"I have the camp clean up assignments and will come around today and share them with each of you," Feather-in-the-Wind added.

"Do you see what I see," Running Stag said as he pointed out what appeared to be a buffalo trotting toward them.

"Yes, and I also see Golden Hawk and Taelo," Busy Bee said as she took up her spear.

"It's time to bring this animal down," Golden Hawk said as two ran along behind the buffalo.

Taelo and Golden Hawk closed the gap to the buffalo. As anticipated, it took off at a full gallop and headed into the camp.

Both Taelo and Golden Hawk ran up ahead and simultaneously planted their spears. The young bull hit the spears and went sliding down on its knees within a spear throw of the camp's main cooking fire.

"I have never seen such skill. It is no surprise these two defeated the Sky Eyes," Deer Chaser commented to those around him.

"Yes, I have never seen anything like this," Whistling Arrow added.

Talking Wren had heard the comment and was glad that Taelo and Golden Hawk had displayed some of their many talents. This would be of great help later when the going became harder.

"It is great to see the two of you," Busy Bee commented as she gave them each a hug.

"Where is the rest of the team," Feather-in-the-Wind asked?

"They are trapped behind by the snow that closed a gap through the mountains. We will now go back and get them out. We can then join together for our trip back," Taelo replied.

"It's late so you should plan to return in the morning. Tonight, you will eat some buffalo tongue and hump meat," Gentle Cub volunteered as she led a group out to skin and prepare their new bounty.

The next morning Quiet Rabbit and Burley Bear were guiding their sleds in parallel down the river. They noted the buffalo hoofs and the two sets of footprints.

"I am hoping that our getting out through the gap will surprise Taelo and Golden Hawk," Quiet Rabbit commented to Burley Bear.

"We are making great time and should catch up to them this evening," Burley Bear replied.

He could not even see Quiet Rabbits eyes. The air was so cold that they wore their rabbit lined face masks with the slit eye covers. This helped with both the cold and protection against the glare of the bright white snow. It was even hard to talk to one another.

The four sleds were racing in side-by-side pairs down the river. They hoped for their sake and their comfort to reach the rest of their group by the evening.

The battle with the Sky Eyes and the two snowstorms had delayed their plans to cross the ice bridge.

"I think I see a plume of smoke on the horizon," Meadow Flower called out.

She by far had the best long-range eyesight of all of them.

"I'll take your word for it," Quiet Rabbit called out.

The four sleds seemed to increase their race against the setting of the sun.

Chapter 24: Ice Bridge: Back toward home

The coming together of friends is always a cause for celebration. The heart warms at seeing a friend. The joking and laughter are a universal signs of the positive impact that friends have on one another.

Taelo's arrival not only brought the relief of enough food for the White Bear Clan, but he and Golden Hawk's presence gave immediate relief of the concern the group had for the missing members.

Burley Bear's arrival with the rest of the team was a cause for celebration. The entire team was back together.

They were ready to tackle the passage across the ice bridge.

"I am certainly glad we didn't have to go back and float you down the river," Taelo commented during the evening meal.

"We can plan to move on in the next sun cycle or two," Busy Bee made a point of suggesting moving on as quickly as possible.

"I think with the added meat from the buffalo you brought with you we have enough to get across the ice bridge back to Lily, Slow Runner, Sharp Blade, and Single Leaf. They should have additional supplies to tide us over," Little Otter said in support of Busy Bee.

"I see that being cooped up in this tight arrangement has made all of you eager to move on," Golden Hawk said with a chuckle as he gave Busy Bee a nudge.

"You are probably correct in that speculation," Busy Bee replied with a pat on his cheek.

"I noted that you have setup a fish trap in the river. Has it been effective," Taelo inquired?

"Yes, we have gathered enough fish to feed the entire White Bear Clan for at least ten sun cycles and we have only eaten fish the past two sun cycles," Feather-in-the-Wind replied.

"It will take about two moon cycles to reach the ice bridge. We have more than ninety people to feed and as many wolves. The fish will help but we will need to send out two sleds to get four more buffalo," Taelo said as he shared the challenge of supplying the needs of this many people.

"I will be pleased to hunt with you," Saber Scar volunteered.

"Thank you but I think Golden Hawk, I and two of the young White Bear Clan hunters will go and run down the herd we saw on the way here. I would like Burley Bear and you to lead this clan toward the ice bridge. We will catch up to you in about ten sun cycles," Taelo responded.

"It would be an honor for us to hunt with you," Deer Chaser spoke for himself and White Bear.

"I think that some language lessons are in order as well," Running Stag commented. "I remember Busy Bee teaching me. I would love to get these lessons started."

"I will teach the use of the sling. There are many rabbits and other small game we can be bagging as we travel," Feather-in-the-Wind said.

"I would love to learn to use the sling. It was amazing how you stopped the charge of the Sky Eyes with them," Gentle Cub commented when she understood what Feather-in-the-Wind had suggested.

"And I will lead the cooking class. Every member of this clan will cook a meal for all of us as we travel," Quiet Rabbit spoke up.

"Let's prepare this clan to become productive Elk Clan members. Our return should coincide with the Elk Clan gathering. Once again, we will arrive with the equivalent of another clan. We must prepare the White Bear Clan members to be mixed with the other sub-clans," Golden Hawk added.

"We can prepare the young women and single men as we did two cycles ago. Almost all the young women found mates during the gathering," Feather-in-the-Wind volunteered as she thought of all the proposals she had received.

"I think your ideas are wonderful," Whistling Arrow replied when Running Stag shared what was being discussed.

Whistling Arrow had wondered about all the discussion.

"I especially like the idea of the language lessons. We need to be able to talk to ensure we all understand what is happening," Bending Willow added

"It is good to know that the White Bear Clan members are so willing to learn and adapt.

The Elk Clan is a large prosperous clan. You will be accepted and will be made full partners. We will target our return to coincide with the great clan meeting. At this meeting you will be brought into the Elk Clan as full members.

You will be asked to choose which clan will be your new home. As we travel, we will prepare you for your new land and your new life," Taelo spoke slowly in the language Running Stag had taught him.

"I leave it to the rest of the team to lead the White Bear Clan toward the ice bridge," Taelo said the next morning as he and Golden Hawk prepared to leave.

They were traveling light. Their two sleds were empty.

"I am excited to go with these two. I especially want to learn to drive the sleds," Deer Chaser said to White Bear.

"You indeed will learn to drive the sleds. First you will become friends with our wolf teams. When they accept you then you will be allowed to drive them," Taelo said quietly.

"I guess I should speak directly to you," Deer Chaser replied as he realized Taelo understood everything he was saying.

"Yes, that would be a good thing," Golden Hawk spoke up.

He was not as good as Taelo in their language, but he was a quick study at learning languages.

"If the two of you can run as fast as Running Stag, we will quickly bag four buffalo and be able to quickly return to the rest of the clan," Taelo added as their sleds went back up along the river.

"Why do we need to be as fast as Running Stag," White Bear asked?

"You will understand once we get to the buffalo herd," Golden Hawk replied.

"Those two are in for a thrill. I would have loved to have gone with them to hunt," Quiet Rabbit commented to Busy Bee.

"Me too, but I know it will take all of us to get everyone organized and moving and able to sustain themselves," Busy Bee replied as she turned to back to the fire.

"Let's sit down and lay out our plans," Burley Bear said as he gathered them back around their warming fire.

"Running Stag, you translate for Whistling Arrow and Bending Willow. I want them to help us get organized," Burley Bear continued.

"I would like six people assigned to our fish trap. Pick those that can take the cold water and recover quickly. They will fish at every stream. We will assign one sled to them. They will fish as we travel and will catch up or go ahead of us as is needed," Burley Bear put his request to Whistling Arrow.

"We will want all of the clan to learn to use the sling and gather small game as we travel. I will be the primary teacher, but our entire team is very good and any of us can and will teach as we travel," Feather-in-the-Wind added in Running Stag's language.

She was as fluent as Taelo and had spent many hours talking to the White Bear Clan members.

Running Stag translated to the Elk Clan language and then went on to do it in the language of the Others.

"Ok, I guess we know who will be assisting me in teaching the Elk Clan language to everyone," Busy Bee commented as she pointed to Running Stag and Feather-in-the-Wind.

"Oh, I am going to be too busy with my sling lessons," Feather-in-the-Wind bantered back.

She had already been engaged in teaching her language to a few of the young women.

Feather-in-the-Wind had spent the time in the tight quarters learning about the White Bear Clan. There were fifty young members, twenty older members, fifteen children and only an additional six paired couples.

"Many had lost a mate and the clan lost almost thirty older leaders to the cruelty of the Sky Eyes. These were brave members who refused to cow toe to them. The ones that took the children to safety survived. This was a tragedy for this clan," Busy Bee shared.

"I have talked to the younger women, and many were violated by the Sky Eyes. None carry any child," Feather-in-the-Wind added.

"We cannot repair the past. Now we must look to the future," Quiet Rabbit replied.

"You seem to know many things. How have you learned so much," Bubbling Brook asked Feather-in-the-Wind?

"On the other side of the ice bridge, our team has traveled many moons to the far south. Feather-in-the-Wind is from those southern high mountains there. She is a princess in her land.

Later on, another journey we traveled far to the east. You will see the mounts that we tamed and use to ride.

We are now on our third trip as a team. Including the White Bear Clan, we have rescued and brought in almost two hundred people into the Elk Clan.

You will be a surprise to many in the clan, but you will see how quickly you are accepted. Ask Bashful Lark about her experience. She is a survivor of the last battle we had with the cannibals. We have fought the cannibals and defeated them.

Taelo and Golden Hawk are our leaders in these adventures," Quiet Rabbit replied.

"Yes, I would follow them anywhere," Whistling Arrow replied as he understood the translation.

Those around him all nodded their agreement.

Out on the snow covered plain, the hunting team approached the herd of buffalo.

"There is the herd," Taelo pointed into the distance.

"It is amazing how fast we traveled," White Bear commented.

"We will stop early and make camp. We will practice for the hunt," Taelo commented as he pulled to stop at some large boulders by a small stream.

"Let's prepare our camp, capture a few fish first and then we will practice," Golden Hawk said as he began to unpack.

"We are good hunters. We know how to kill the buffalo," Deer Chaser said feeling somewhat discounted.

"We are not questioning your skill. We chose you because Whistling Arrow said you were the best. We need to hunt as a team. We need to practice as a team," Taelo commented.

"You will learn that Taelo makes us practice any new skill at least three times," Golden Hawk added with a chuckle.

A short time later they had eight fish skewered and ready for roasting. Since they were going to sleep two to a sled, the camp was ready in a very short time with little effort.

All right let's practice for our hunt. We will first see how fast we can run and if we have the stamina for a long run. See that boulder in the distance. We will run there and back at top speed. Afterwards we will pair up two to a team based on the order of the finish.

The race begins when the stone in my hand hits the ground," Taelo announced after gathering everyone together.

Taelo was soon in the lead with Golden Hawk at a steady pace just behind him. Both White Bear and Deer Chaser pulled ahead for a brief time, but they slowly fell back as the race continued.

They all arrived at the large boulder at about the same time. Halfway back Taelo increased the pace.

"Oh, you are a mean one," Golden Hawk grunted as he worked to keep up.

"This is not possible," White Bear commented through his heavy breathing.

He dug deep to get enough energy to keep up.

"I thought I would be in the lead," Deer Chaser thought to himself as he brought up the rear. He pushed to close the distance and passed White Bear.

Taelo could feel Golden Hawk and the other two close behind. At a spear's throw distance from the fire, he put on his last burst of speed. He took in the distance separating the four. They were tightly grouped and only a few steps behind.

"You two are good runners," Taelo commented as the four of them were catching their breath.

"I have never run so fast for so long," White Bear commented.

"We will take a break and then we will pair off and practice carrying our spears," Taelo said as he laid out four long hunting spears.

"Taelo and I will run in the lead. Each of us will carry a spear. You two will carry two spears each. Taelo and I will down the buffalo we each select. You will then give us our second spear. You will ensure that each of the first buffalo is dead. Taelo and I will down two more buffalo with the spears you have given us," Golden Hawk instructed.

"I now understand why we need to practice. We have never hunted in this manner," White Bear commented.

"To make this work you will need to cull out two buffalo for each of you," Deer Chaser said as he thought about the hunt.

"Yes, you are right. That is why we need to be able to run for so long and still have energy to speed up," Taelo said in a tone of respect.

"Deer Chaser, you will be my partner and White Bear you will be partner to Golden Hawk," Taelo announced.

"Don't worry. I always select the two slowest animals to chase down," Golden Hawk said as he gave a pat on the back of White Bear.

After they had practiced with the spears three times, they all gathered around the cooking fire as Taelo, and Golden Hawk prepared the fish for dinner.

"I won't have any problems sleeping tonight," Deer Chaser said as he sat on his sleeping hide on the sled.

"Whistling Arrow will think we are making up stories when we tell him of the way you hunt," White Bear added.

The hunt went almost as planned.

Taelo and Deer Chaser executed the hunt exactly as practiced.

The first of the buffalo Golden Hawk and White Bear were chasing went down as planned.

Golden Hawk planted the second spear, and the buffalo ran into it, but the spear split in two. Golden Hawk almost became the victim of the shattered spear. Only his quick reflexes kept him from being skewered by the broken half. The buffalo stumbled but then started to lumber away.

"White Bear, take this buffalo down," Golden Hawk called out as he lunged into the side of the animal to throw him off his pace.

White Bear ran at his top speed to get ahead of the now accelerating buffalo. He placed the spear as he had seen Golden Hawk do and then he rolled aside as the buffalo ran itself up onto the spear.

The buffalo came to its knees and toppled over.

"Very good! You have just earned the role of headhunter for the White Bear Clan," Golden Hawk said in congratulation.

"We saw what happened," Taelo said as he and Deer Chaser jogged up to the two.

"That was a close call with the broken shaft," Deer Chaser added.

"Yes, it was. Did you see how quickly White Bear recovered and how he downed the second buffalo," Golden Hawk continued in praising White Bear.

"Well, that was the fun part. Now let's get these animals gutted, skinned, and loaded on the sleds. We need to move fast before the wolves find us," Taelo said as he turned to go back to the two buffalo he had downed.

Four sun cycles later through the darkening evening, they saw the fires of the camp. The sun had just set, and they made the last push through the dark guided by the light of the moon.

Chapter 25: Thin Ice

ℒooking up from below, the sunlight created a glowing ceiling that bridged the bottomless miles long fissure in the ice. This fissure was invisible from above. It blended in with the rest of the endless white expanse bridging the land in the west to the land to the east.

Many such thin ice bridges or ceilings dotted the path across to the land on the other side. To fall through was a fall to one's doom. Throwing an object in and counting until it hit bottom was useless. The sound was never heard. That is how deep these fissures were.

Deep as death.

The sun traveled its course for another forty cycles before the group arrived at the ice bridge. It was really a wide expanse of ice and many dangerous cracks and bubbles in the ice where the periodic warming rays of the sun had melted the ice and it had sunk down. There were also large cracks made by the uneven movement of the ice.

By this time Taelo had the smaller children and some of the young women riding in the sleds that were now empty of the food they had carried.

"I would love to take more food with us on the crossing," Taelo confided to Golden Hawk as they approached the area, they called the ice bridge.

The team made camp at what they took as the beginning of the ice bridge.

"With all this snow, I am worried about our ability to find a safe passage across," Golden Hawk spoke up during their dinner.

"I will take the lead," Taelo replied.

"We need to worry about falling into some hidden crevasse. If your wolves start to fall through the snow, lay your sled down on its side and drive your spear down into the snow in front of the handles," Burley Bear instructed as he entered into the conversation.

"Thank you for that information. I hope not to use it. I will demonstrate what I heard you say," Taelo replied as he envisioned the action.

He stood up and went to his sled. The load was strapped solidly in place. He flipped it on its side and drove his spear into the ground.

"Is this what you are telling me," Taelo asked looking at Burley Bear?

"As always, you practice the actions that are needed," Burley Bear commented.

Just then the cry of the eagle was heard.

"Oh, now I am really worried," Quiet Rabbit commented as she came over to Taelo as the entire team looked into the sky.

"What does this mean," Whistling Arrow asked?

"We are never sure of the exact meaning. The cry came before we fought with the Sky Eyes. It comes before every challenge the team faces," Busy Bee replied.

"Let's have each of the sled driver's practice laying their sleds on their sides and anchoring them with their spear," Saber Scar instructed.

He was now more eager to practice this life saving maneuver.

"Yes, let's do it three times," Little Otter and Burley Bear said in unison.

This had become their habit every time the team had to practice some new action; they were all to learn.

"I am so happy to have a team that understands me so well," Taelo said with a broad smile.

That evening he shared one of his dreams with Quiet Rabbit. It was a dream from the time he was recovering from the wounds during the Journey of Discovery.

"I fell into a deep crevasse and was hanging on for my life. But I was not afraid for I had saved you and my friends were working to save me," Taelo shared his memory with Quiet Rabbit.

The next morning the journey across the ice bridge began. It had taken six cycles of the sun for their first crossing.

"We will need to be much more cautious on our way back across. The new snow covering will hide many of the crevasses that were very easy to see before," Taelo commented.

"Let's tie our sleds together. If one of them begins to go through the ice we can keep it from going down," Little Otter suggested.

He recalled the trip through the blinding snow where they had tied the sleds together during their rescue of the people from the north.

"Great idea, it saved us the last time," Running Stag said in support.

"Yes, and I brought in the rest of people by tying them together so I would not lose any. We will go across in single line formation.

Whistling Arrow let's tie a rope from each person to the one behind them. You will follow behind the last sled," Taelo added.

"Ok, I think we are now ready. The first four sleds will have our food and other materials. The other four have our young," Taelo said as he and Quiet Rabbit took the lead.

"Be careful where you walk," Taelo called up to Lasher.

The sun went slowly through its cycle. The team ate their snack for the high sun meal but kept on the move. They finally made camp as the sun kissed the far horizon.

"We made good time today," Talking Wren commented as the team finished their evening meal.

There was no wood for cooking. They were out on a pure layer of ice.

"Keep a close eye on the sled runners. If they begin to sink, we will need to move the sleds," Burley Bear said as he got ready to turn in.

"The way ahead looks more challenging than yesterday," Golden Hawk observed as they got started.

The entire caravan moved slowly across the ice. They followed Taelo as he maneuvered around several ice spikes and areas where the ice had pushed up like small mountains.

They traveled through such an area for the entire morning. Then as the sun reached its zenith they came out into a flat area for as far as the eye could see.

"I hope this is…" Taelo began and then Lasher disappeared.

Taelo felt himself go into his pure reaction mode. Everything seemed to move in slow motion. He pushed Quiet Rabbit with all his might back toward the sled behind them.

"Run, Quiet Rabbit Run," he shouted as he jumped on the sled and cut the ropes holding the load of food on the sled.

Quiet Rabbit did not have to run. Taelo's push had been so powerful that she literally flew through the air and hit Burley Bear's lead wolf.

"Lay the sleds down," Taelo heard someone shout and then realized it was his voice.

Everything was happening in slow motion. He saw wolf pair after wolf pair disappear in front of him.

He took the rope in his sled and tied it to the rope going to the sled behind him and then tied the other end to the lines going out to the wolves.

Then he felt the sled going down beneath him.

"Let's hope the tie rope can take this weight," Taelo thought to himself as he held on to it and the sled.

He watched as the load of meat from his sled tumbled past Lasher.

He felt the rope stretch and heard it sing. Miraculously the rope held. He was just about to start climbing up when two more ropes tumbled down from above.

Taelo quickly tied each to the lines going down to the wolves.

"Easy Lasher, rest and wait, I will make sure you get your feet back on the snow," he called down.

The wolves were hanging motionless from their harnesses.

"I am not sure I can pull myself all the way back to the top," Taelo thought to himself as he strained to pull himself hand over hand up the rope.

He took several breaks, but he continued to climb up. Suddenly he felt each of his wrists gripped by hands of stone. He knew immediately that Burley Bear had one wrist and Saber Scar the other.

"Well thanks for that last assist. I felt like I was flying," Taelo said as Quiet Rabbit gave him hug.

"We are ready to pull the sled up," Running Stag called out.

He, Busy Bee, and Feather-in-the-Wind had organized three teams to pull the sled back up.

"Saber Scar, Burley Bear, please join your teams," Busy Bee called out.

"I see that you have put the others and Little Otter in the back as the anchors," Taelo commented to Busy Bee as Talking Wren called out the cadence.

"Yes, but the problem will be when the sled makes it to the top. We will need Burley Bear and Saber Scar to pull it up over the edge.

"Let Whistling Arrow, Little Otter and I anchor the line," Taelo said as he took three heavy spears and ran to the back of the line.

"Plant the spear as deep into the snow as possible. Tie the line to the spear as close to the surface of the snow as possible. Then we will hold while Saber Scar and Burley Bear pull the sled over the edge.

Afterwards, Whistling Arrow and I will help each of the wolves over the edge as they get pulled up to it.

It proved to be a massive effort to get the sled up and over the edge.

"I think I have pulled my arm out of place," Burley Bear groaned after the sled was finally over the top.

"Let's get our wolves up," Taelo said as he led Whistling Arrow to the edge.

Taelo looked over the edge.

"The first pair is a spears length away. I will call for a stop when their harness is in reach. Then I will cut each wolf loose one at a time and give them to Whistling Arrow.

Whistling Arrow will pass them to Quiet Rabbit. Floating Cloud please help Quiet Rabbit. Give them a treat.

The rest of you keep away from them. They will be nervous, and I do not know how they will act," Taelo instructed as he called for the team to pull.

The sun was on the horizon when Taelo finally reached down for Lasher.

"Well, Lasher, how did you like your rest," Taelo said as he gave him a hug.

Lasher had a low rumbling growl deep in his throat.

"Yes, I know how you feel," Taelo said as he gave him another hug.

"Here is his treat," Quiet Rabbit said as she came over to give him a hug.

"Yes, I know you're mad at me for taking so long," Taelo continued his monologue with Lasher.

The sun was painting an orange and maroon against the few clouds in an otherwise clear sky when on the horizon an eagle let out a cry.

"I hope that is a cry of victory and not another cry of warning," Taelo called out as he looked up at the sky.

For most of the evening Taelo sat with his wolves talking to them and giving them treats. He knew how he felt about his drop over the edge and was sure his wolves were a queasy as he was.

"Thanks for launching me back to Burley Bear's sled.

I didn't realize what was happening until you went down with your sled and the wolves.

I have never seen Burley Bear move so fast. He actually threw me back a second time as he passed the end of his sled when he ran forward with the additional rope.

Saber Scar ran past me with another rope and joined Burley Bear. The two held their ropes until Feather-in-the-Wind and Running Stag organized the pulling teams.

I was in shock until Busy Bee pulled me out of it. Other than being bruised by having been thrown through the air twice I am just fine," Quiet Rabbit said as she sat next to Taelo also hugging and talking to the wolves.

"I can't tell you how my heart stopped when you went over the edge," Quiet Rabbit thought to herself as she once again brushed her hand across the side of Taelo's face.

Chapter 26: The Team Returns

ℒife threatening events tend to leave people in various states of shock. On a fall off a mount, the best medicine is to get back on and go riding again. On a fall through a thin sheet of ice into a bottomless crevasse and when you survive you are going to be in a state of shock.

The experience though is not one you will seek to do again.

When Taelo rescued the wolves, he had gotten to look over the edge multiple times. Each time he experienced vertigo. The light illuminating the crevasse ended in a thin black line so far down that he could not estimate the depth. The meat from two buffalo had fallen down and disappeared.

Nothing was visible but the thin black line.

"I will take the lead," Burley Bear volunteered the next morning.

Floating Cloud had arranged a small fire built on a flat stone held above the ice by two sticks with forked legs driven down into the snow. She had made a stew for Taelo and everyone that had helped in the rescue effort.

"I would like to cook for all of you but there is not enough wood," Floating Cloud announced to those watching.

No one objected. They had all seen the effort that Taelo's team had exerted to save him. They were in awe of the reaction speed and seamless coordination the team had displayed.

The one point of discussion was how easily both Taelo and Burley Bear had thrown Quiet Rabbit through the air.

"She is not that small. She is twice my size and Burley Bear threw her the length of his sled and wolf team. She must have bruises all over," Bubbling Brook commented.

"She may be bruised but she is safe," Bending Willow replied.

"Lasher and I will take the lead. We are counting on you to get us out of any other holes we fall into," Taelo replied to Burley Bear.

"I have asked Quiet Rabbit to ride with Busy Bee. Golden Hawk will partner with me. He has assured me that he will keep me from guiding my wolves into the next crevasse," Taelo added with a smile and chuckle.

He was worried that the exact situation would happen again. He did not want Quiet Rabbit to be at risk with him.

The rest of the journey took another two sun cycles. It went without incident.

"See how well I have done. Taelo has not fallen into any other crevasse," Golden Hawk joked as they saw the camp ahead.

"It seems the team here has made the cover larger. I wonder if they have any idea about the number of people we are bringing," Busy Bee observed.

"They are about to find out. I hope they have plenty of food because we are coming in empty handed. We lost half of our supplies when the sled went over the edge," Talking Wren commented.

"Let's hope the buffalo herd has its winter home in this area. Golden Hawk and Taelo will lead a hunting party to replenish our supplies," Quiet Rabbit added.

Lilly, Single Leaf and Sharp Blade and Slow Runner were out hunting. The storm that Taelo had experienced had hit them first. Now the four were out hunting the Buffalo.

Lily and Single Leaf each stood between two large boulders holding their spears at the ready. Sharp Blade and Slow Runner guided the young bull toward them. The young bull was nervous as he cantered between the two boulders, but it was the only opening he could go through.

"Now," Lily cried out as she plunged her spear into the young bull.

The young bull went down to its front knees as Single Leaf's plunge went in just behind his front leg and found his heart.

"I am glad you are so powerful," Lily commented when she realized her spear had barely penetrated into the bull.

"This will be enough for us and for the team. With the dry food left with us and this young bull we will be able to make it through the winter," Lily commented as the four of them worked together to skin and process the meat.

"I wonder how our team is doing," she commented later over the evening fire.

"I am sure they are doing well," Single Leaf replied as she practiced Lily's language.

"I am ready for their return," Sharp Blade added.

He was rested and bored. He would have loved to have gone across the ice bridge with the team.

The eagle's cry was heard only a few days later by Lily and her team.

"The eagle has called out twice. I think Taelo and the team are near," Lily commented as she and the team watched the sun go down behind the mountains.

"Let's finish our preparation for their return," Slow Runner replied.

"We have a dozen red fish hanging ready to be cooked. We have three buffalo tongue and tail ready to cook and we have at least a large basket of clams to cook as well. We can greet them with a wonderful feast," Single Leaf added.

"The mounts have been a lot of work. I think Taelo will be pleased to learn that we have three more young ones," Sharp Blade shared his thoughts.

"It has been a long cold winter for us, and they have been traveling through this weather. They will all be tired when they arrive. I have arranged the camp so the sleds can park farther apart. This will provide extra room between each sled that will provide more privacy and a comfortable sleeping space," Lily pointed out.

She and the team had increased the diameter of the lodge, so it had almost twice the space as before.

"It will be good to be back together as a team. I am sure they will have some good stories to share," Sharp Blade commented.

The sun was well in its journey to its zenith when Lily spied the team approaching.

"Welcome back. Let me guide your sleds into position," Lily called out as she ran forward and gave Taelo a hug. Lily continued down the line giving greeting hugs.

"Oh, my, I will need to recruit some help to feed all of you," Lily said loudly as she guided Taelo's sled into position.

"It is good to see that everyone is coming back in good shape," Single Leaf greeted the team.

"Well, I think everyone is in good shape. I on the other hand was man handled by Taelo and Burley Bear and am one big bruise," Quiet Rabbit gave a quiet reply to Single Leaf.

She then went on to briefly recall the incident out on the ice.

The White Bear Clan members entered the enclosure and were surprised at the size and the available space.

"So, my bruised Quiet Rabbit, do you approve of our area between the sleds," Taelo said as he stripped off his outer clothes.

"Lily, Single Leaf, Slow Runner, and Sharp Blade have done an excellent job at being ready for us.

They may not have known how many they would be feeding but they have enough fresh meat to keep us well fed for several sun cycles.

And expanding the size of the enclosure is a great accomplishment," Quiet Rabbit replied as she too took off her heavy outer clothing.

"What a wonderful lodge," Whistling Arrow commented as he walked around and noted its design.

"There is a space between each sled for the owners of the sleds to occupy. Please make your sleeping area out by each sled. There is enough room for everyone to have a comfortable sleeping area. The center of the lodge is for us to gather around the warming fire and to converse," Lily said in the tongue of the White Bear Clan.

"How is it that so many speak our language," Bending Willow wondered out loud.

"I am Lily. Taelo rescued me and several others including Running Stag from the cannibals. I come from the other side of the ice bridge," Lily replied to the question.

"Where are the cannibals now," Whistling Arrow asked?

"There are none left on this side of the ice bridge.

Taelo, Quiet Rabbit, Busy Bee, Running Stag, Golden Hawk, Burley Bear, Saber Scar, and their warriors fought and killed them. My mate and I fought them also. I lost my mate and many of my friends," Bashful Lark replied.

This trip had been her closure journey. She had wanted to see the land she had left and to remember the journey she and her mate had made across the ice bridge in their attempt to escape the cannibals. Her heart still ached with the memory of her lost mate.

She and Whistling Arrow, much older than her had a warm friendship and she hope this would lead to something more. She would wait and see what would happen at the meeting of the clan.

"We will need to increase our food reserve. Where is the buffalo herd," Golden Hawk asked as they sat around the central fire?

"The herd moves around the valley to the east. We will be able to hunt and get all the meat we need. Fishing is also very good so we should be able to setup the fish trap. We have enough hands so that we can catch and smoke many fish," Sharp Blade replied

"I will take a team out to the river to setup the fish trap in the morning," Single Leaf volunteered.

"Let my fishing team take part," Whistling Arrow requested when he heard about the fishing.

"That would be great," Single Leaf replied.

"Lily and I have already arranged for additional cooks," Floating Cloud commented as the conversation went around the team.

"I will lead the hunters out for the buffalo hunting," Saber Scar volunteered.

"We will want to prepare for the trip back.

For the next few sun cycles, we will study Quiet Rabbit's and Busy Bee's drawings of our journey. We will want to plan our travels so we can arrive for our clan meeting.

We now have many people, many wolves, and mounts to feed as we move south," Taelo commented when it seemed his turn to talk.

He liked the way each team member was taking on some critical work needing to be done.

"Yes, and we have the giant bear territory to go through. It would be wise to go through it during the time they are still asleep for the winter," Burley Bear added.

"The language classes have been making great progress. By the time we get to the clan meeting everyone will know the Elk Clan tongue," Running Stag said as he took his turn.

"We have been processing the hides and have been making clothes for each White Bear Clan member and we have also been making many to trade during the coming clan meeting," Meadow Flower shared.

"We will have slings, arrows, spearheads, some stone axes, bone needles and many more items that we have been making," Feather-in-the-Wind said as she leaned against Running Stag.

"We are bringing many people back with us. We must present ourselves as successful, industrious people that will enhance the Elk Clan," Quiet Rabbit added.

"We have never been so busy and productive. We are very impressed with how you have improved the lives of the White Bear Clan," Deer Chaser interjected.

"Yes, and we have learned an exciting way to hunt that we are looking forward in trying when we go out with Saber Scar to hunt the buffalo," White Bear said with enthusiasm.

"Splitting up and becoming members of the various Elk sub-clans is a point of concern for some of us," Bubbling Brook spoke up from behind Deer Chaser.

"This will be necessary. But we will make sure we match you with the sub-clan of your choice. For some of you it will also be a chance to find a mate.

Talk with Lily and Bashful Lark. They have each experienced this. Many of their friends are now in the various Elk sub-clans," Quite Rabbit replied.

"I just want all in the White Bear Clan to understand that our team is made up of members of three of the Elk Clan sub-clans. Some of us are from the Northern Elk Clan, some from the Clan of the Others and I and Little Otter are from the original Elk Clan.

Taelo and Golden Hawk are Golden Feather warriors and belong to all the Clans," Talking Wren volunteered.

"I will tell you that the Elk Clan and all its sub-clans will allow you to find the home you desire. The fall gathering is always the highlight where old friends reconnect, love affairs begin and where most find their mates.

Some, like me, will find it more difficult to find another mate. You will notice though that I now have my handsome Slow Runner," Lily added as she pushed Slow Runner out in front of everyone.

"There are many concerns.

All of them will have a positive resolution. No one will be asked to do something they do not wish to do.

However, we must first get back to the Elk Clan territory and we all do have something to worry about. There are giant bears, dire wolves, and saber-tooth tigers between here and the meeting valley.

In the next ten sun cycles we will practice our action for each of these challenges. Golden Hawk and I will design the actions we will take. We will get started at sunrise so let's all get a good night sleep," Taelo said as he stood and walked over to his sleeping area.

Chapter 27: Back Through Bear Country

Taelo looked ahead and commented, "the way back is really always a new way. The same distant white topped mountains, their skirts of dark green sentinel pine trees appearing to be close but almost as far away as the Ancients, grace both sides of the path back home, but it was a new way."

The world now takes on the backward look as left becomes right and right becomes left. The mind wants order, it simplifies the vision and accepts the difference. Up is still up, right, and left mean little.

Taelo had studied the way back on Quiet Rabbit's and Busy Bee's drawings. The buffalo outside of their camp was depicted in bright orange, the bear was represented in black, the gap through to the valley on the far side was in white, the long valley beyond in dark green.

Taelo, Golden Hawk and Feather-in-the-Wind discussed how to handle the giant bears.

"It has been a grueling ten sun cycles. The White Bear Clan members are wondering if all this practice and preparation is necessary," Whistling Arrow said as he finished his evening dinner.

"You will know when we face the dangers for which we have been getting you ready," Burley Bear replied.

"We all have had the same question in the past and each time the practice saved us," Little Otter added,

"We have no complaints," Deer Chaser and I have learned to hunt as Taelo and Golden Hawk hunt.

"We are constantly learning from Saber Scar and Sharp Blade, and we now feel confident to cook our own food after learning from Lily and Floating Cloud," White Bear said in defense.

"Thank you for speaking up. I will tell you from experience, each of us will need to contribute our part in making sure we protect each other. We will practice for the entire trip back to the valley of the gathering," Talking Wren spoke up.

Taelo had been listening quietly. He felt much like the rest of the team members. He was ready for action.

"I think it is time for us to begin our trip to the south," he had mentioned to Quiet Rabbit as he got up with the morning sun.

"I agree. It is time to take action. We will break camp in four sun cycles and begin our journey back to the territories of the Elk Clan and the Others," Taelo announced.

"I will manage the preparation of the camp for our departure," Meadow Flower volunteered.

"Marigold and I will organize the packing of the sleds," Lily added.

"Running Stag and I will make sure we have the food for the wolves," Feather-in-the-Wind went on.

"Saber Scar and I will make sure all the sled travois and the harnesses for the mounts are in good shape," Slow Runner added his voice.

"Busy Bee and I will work with all the families to ensure each has enough food for the trip and is prepared to move their family," Quiet Rabbit went on. "I will arrange for a traveling cooking crew that will make everyone the evening meal. Feather-in-the-Wind has continued training everyone on the use of the sling and has told them about hunting as we travel.

If everyone does their part, we should be able to have a mix of fresh meat and stews made from the meat we have dried," Floating Cloud spoke up.

"Well, I sense a great pent-up energy of anticipation. Thank you for volunteering.

I would like us to practice how to face the great bear. We have discussed this, and I have saved this to last. Golden Hawk, Feather-in-the-Wind and I have discussed several ways to deal with the great bear.

It is different than what we did on the way up. We have taken what we have learned, designed an approach that we think better fits such a large group," Taelo introduced the last practice before the departure.

"Taelo has faced many bears. His most successful encounter was when he fed the bear.

His next encounter almost cost him his life.

The first encounter on the way north almost cost me my life.

The second encounter went much better, and the bear also survived," Feather-in-the-Wind continued the explanation.

"Now on the way back we will be prepared to use everything we learned.

Taelo and I will pull travois loaded with good smelling meat. When the bear attacks, we will lure it away with the meat.

The rest of you will proceed at a full jog until one of us calls a halt. All of you have been trained in the use of the sling and each of you will carry a sack of sharp stone shards. Should we need to take a stand, we will take turns using our slings pelting the bear in the eyes. This should stun it long enough for everyone to turn and run.

Again, Taelo or I will leave a load of food near the bear," Golden Hawk added.

"We hope in this way to buy our way across the bear territory and keep the risk low to both the bear and us."

"I will organize a team of slingers that will always come to the aid of any group facing a bear. Once this group gets into position, the group that was attacked will jog away and get back to their normal position," Feather-in-the-Wind shared with everyone listening.

"Burley Bear and I have been recruited to play the attacking bears. Please do not use your slings on us," Little Otter spoke up.

"I have everyone's location in our caravan. You will maintain this order for the entire trip all the way to the valley where the Elk Clan holds its meeting," Talking Wren announced.

"It's no wonder this team defeated the Sky Eyes," Whistling Arrow commented to White Bear.

"I agree, if the bears want to live, they better follow the script," Deer Chaser replied.

"The practices have gone well. Everyone is ready and in their positions. The camp has been cleared and the area put back as close to what we found as possible. By next spring nature will have this area back to its original condition," Talking Wren reported to the rest of the team.

"My slingers are ready. Quiet Rabbit is the leader of one team. Busy Bee has another team. Bashful Lark leads a third team and Floating Cloud leads a fourth team. These teams will be dispersed along the travel line and come together at the point of attack," Feather-in-the-Wind reported next.

"Taelo, Running Stag and I have our gift tied to a travois we are pulling with our mounts. As you all know we decided that we needed one gift in the front, one in the middle and one at the back of our long line.

Thanks to Lily for preparing our pieces of meat," Golden Hawk announced.

"I will be in the lead with Taelo. Golden Hawk and Saber Scar will be in the back and Running Stag will be in the middle. We will let the one closest to the bear make the offering and lead the bear away. You have seen the practice. I hope that they can execute the delivery of the meat and have the bear stop to eat. If not, the slingers will step forward to aid in stopping the bear," Burley Bear spoke next.

The caravan began its journey. It was hard for those in the rear to see those in front. The wolves were pulling the sleds. The sleds ran in parallel pairs. The slingers were walking or jogging next to the sleds.

"We have reached the valley that marks the beginning of the Bear territory," Burley Bear called out.

The word quickly spread, and everyone started to keep a closer watch to the area around them.

"We are well into the area and so far, we have only frightened a few rabbits and scared some geese," Taelo commented to Burley Bear.

"It's time to make camp. We will need to station ourselves around the camp. We will space offering and slingers around the rest of the group. I hope these animals don't hunt in the night," Burley Bear commented.

"Well, if they are anything like the bear in our area, they indeed do hunt at night especially when there is enough light like it is in this area," Golden Hawk replied when he heard what Burley Bear had said.

The eagle cry in the sky put everyone on alert.

"Let's move our meat offering out away from the clan. Put up small fires all around the edge of our camp. Quickly gather enough wood to keep the fires going all night. Put the slinger teams at each offering location but inside the fire ring," Taelo rattled off his instruction.

It was early morning when there was a roar at the northern tail end of the camp.

Taelo, Golden Hawk and Running Stag ran to their meat offerings.

"I have him he is mine, Taelo called out as he quickly pulled the large chunk of meat toward the bear.

The slingers had done their work and stalled the bear. The smell of the meat did the trick, and the bear began to chase after Taelo. It was clear that the bear would quickly catch up to Taelo.

Suddenly another person began pulling the meat along with Taelo.

"I am not letting a giant bear catch you," Quiet Rabbit said as she ran alongside of Taelo.

"And I certainly don't want him to have you either," Taelo shouted as he accelerated with all his might.

The bear was slowly gaining. The camp was now out of sight.

"Ok let go and run with me," Taelo instructed.

"That was a crazy thing to do. Thanks, it made the difference," Taelo said as they ran around a large arc back toward the south where they would meet back with the rest of the clan.

An eagle scream came from somewhere ahead.

"Did you see the bravery of those two? Quiet Rabbit turned her concern for Taelo into an action of pure bravery," Bashful Lark commented to Long Leaper.

"Yes, they are an inspiring pair. I hope someday to have a similar mate," Long Leaper replied.

He had lost his mate to the Sky Eyes and had started to keep Bashful Lark's company.

The sun was just rising as Taelo and Quiet Rabbit caught up with the procession.

Busy Bee was riding up front pulling the next offering of meat.

Quiet Rabbit went to her position with her slinger team and Taelo ran up to where Busy Bee was and reclaimed his mount.

"Thank you for filling in for me. I am sure the bear would much prefer to be served by you," Taelo joked with Busy Bee.

"You're welcome and I am pleased to give up this honor," Busy Bee said as she dropped down and let the procession pass her by until she was with her team of slingers.

"See how naturally the team adjusts at the critical moments. The action taken by Quiet Rabbit helping Taelo and Busy Bee taking up Taelo's position were not planned action but because they had the rest of us doing what was required of us, they were able to make quick adjustments that seemed seamless and planned.

We can learn so much by just watching and learning from them," Whistling Arrow commented to White Bear.

"I have learned as much in the last few moons than all the time before," White Bear replied.

The next attack came two sun cycles later. The bear attacked the side of the column guarded by Floating Cloud and her team of slingers.

Floating Cloud let out the attack cry the team had practiced and let her shards of stone fly from her sling.

"Sling slingers sling," everyone heard her cry.

Running Stag reacted immediately and guided his mount between the slingers and the bear. He paused long enough for the bear to get the scent of the offered meat and then when the bear started to follow, Running Stag turned and led the bear away from the caravan.

"It seems to be working. Let's keep the caravan moving. Its double pace for the next few cycles" Burley Bear called back to everyone.

"Running Stag has slowed his mount to let the bear keep up easily. He is slowly taking the bear farther out. He has now dropped the meat and he has stopped a short distance away. The bear is now fully engaged in eating. Running Stag is moving away at a rapid pace," Feather-in-the-Wind announced from where she stood on her moving mount.

There is always a surprise with this team. Feather-in-the-Wind is standing on her mount as it continues moving with the column. Her entire attention is in watching what Running Stag is doing," Whistling Arrow commented.

"I know that she helped Taelo kill one of these bears on their journey up to this area. She has a long scar on her thigh from such a bear. She is known for her bravery.

She was also key in killing a giant lion on their last journey," White Bear replied.

"Where did you learn all this," Whistling Arrow asked?

"I have learned to watch and listen," White Bear said with smile.

"That is quite a change from one who normally likes to talk and talk," Deer Chaser teased.

"Both of us have grown and our recent experience has changed us.

Thanks to Taelo and his team our entire clan has survived a terrible ordeal and we seem to be on a path to a better life," Deer Chaser thought to himself.

"It seems that your idea of feeding the bear is the right one. It is good that we stored the extra food for our return. If we meet a few more bears we will end up giving them most of what we have," Golden Hawk commented to Taelo.

"It is a small price to pay. Keeping this many people safe as we travel is a major challenge. The weather is not done with us. We will want to be through the gap before the spring thaw floods the narrow channel," Taelo continued.

"High waters will indeed make it much more difficult even though we will be going with the river this time," Burley Bear added.

Chapter 28: Down through the Gap

The streams from the north joined together and soon the river, which flowed through the gorge that mirrored its path with the blue of the sky, formed. As the bear country seemed to come to an end, the river seemed to become gentler and flowed more easily.

The days though still cold gave way to the warmth of the sun. The fish trap kept the entire group well fed and the small army of slingers bagged an amount of small game that allowed everyone a selection they had rarely enjoyed.

The day came when the sleds had to be put on the travois poles and be pulled by the mounts.

As the White Bear Clan watched the transition from sleds on the ground to sleds on the travois, they were again impressed with the genius of the team that had rescued them.

Now all goods were being pulled on travois. Every mount and two dozen people were pulling the goods needed to sustain over one hundred people.

Two moon cycles later the river arrived at the gap. The water was higher than before but not yet at the flood level that the spring thaw would bring.

"How will we get through this gap? Is there another way around," Whistling Arrow asked as he stood looking at what looked like and impassable point in their journey?

"Up along the base of the cliff is our raft. We will be able to float all our goods and wolves through. We will want many of you to cross on a narrow ledge along the cliff. Those who we think are too young or may have problems with the narrow ledge will be floated down with the goods," Golden Hawk replied.

"I will organize the transit," Talking Wren commented as she entered into the conversation.

"We will set up camp on this side and plan on several sun cycles for the transit," Taelo continued.

"Talking Wren and I have agreed that Busy Bee and I will establish a second camp on the other side of the Gap in the location we used on our way up. This will let us make the transit in as many sun cycles as we need. There is not a rush other than getting through before the spring flood," Quiet Rabbit added.

"Once again this round robin of leadership amazes me," Whistling Arrow thought to himself.

It was clear to him that those around Taelo flowed naturally to do what needed to be done. They did not even seem to realize how different they were and how smooth their daily interactions were.

"Leaders normally struggle with each other to control the situation in a manner they desire. Taelo seems to encourage a flow of differing ideas and causes the team to converge in what seems a natural flow.

However, if you listen closely, you will always hear him asking the questions that bring the team to a common conclusion," Whistling Arrow shared with Deer Chaser and White Bear.

"Now that you mentioned this, it is obvious to me," Deer Chaser replied.

"I hope to learn how to do this," White Bear added as he thought how effective and efficiently Taelo's team operated.

The upstream camp was set up without the central cover. The cover, and the poles would be floated through the gap first. This would allow the second camp to be established before sending the White Bear Clan's younger children and the large amount of goods that needed to be sheltered.

The raft was reconstructed with the platform as the floor. The first load took the cover and most of the stronger young men who would follow Marigolds and Saber Scars instruction and setup the lodge.

A mix of wolves and the younger children were the next to go through the gap.

The mounts provided the holding power and letting the rafts move down stream. Even then the work of loading and unloading the raft was a strain on everyone.

Taelo and Talking Wren continually adjusted what was on the raft. They had a plan, but they were opportunistic and made sure the raft was loaded fully for each trip.

After two sun cycles the sleds were sent through the gap and then it was time to change the configuration of the raft and take the mounts through.

Bashful Lark made the suggestion that they keep the mounts out of the water by strapping them in from the beams that made up the platform. This would keep their bodies out of the cold water.

A pull line attached to the raft could be floated downstream.

The raft would be pulled up on the beach, the mounts strapped in. Then the upstream team could push the raft, while the downstream team pulled the raft until it was back in the water.

At this point, the upstream members could feed the line and let the current pull the raft and mounts down through the gap.

"Let's give this idea a try. We have enough pullers downstream and if we are successful, our mounts will not experience the freeze they did before," Taelo enthusiastically said in support.

The approach accelerated the transfer of the mounts and within two more sun cycles they were all through.

Burley Bear, Meadow Flower, Saber Scar, Marigold, Sharp Knife, Single Leaf, Little Otter, Golden Hawk, and Taelo were the members of the team that guided the last mount through the gap and then pulled the raft back up to the beach for the last time.

"This has been plain hard work," Burley Bear commented as they pulled the raft up stream for the last time.

"Yes, it has been hard. The camp at the other side is now fully operational. Tonight, we will all be sleeping in the comfort of our lodge.

Floating Cloud and Lily are preparing a special dinner for all of you.

They have the red fish ready to roast and they sent Feather-in-the-Wind and Running Stag and a few others out to hunt for a boar or some other game as well.

The dried food we left here is exactly what we needed but we will need to hunt and get more food," Talking Wren shared.

Taelo was very aware to the fact that the power of the Others was one of the reasons the transit had gone so well.

He had tried to relieve them as much as possible but as always, the strength of the Others was once again the main reason for the team's success.

Taelo had enrolled several of the White Bear Clan to help in handling the last load and had listened to their banter. White Bear and Deer Chaser were two of the most vocal.

"I agree we struggled to control letting the raft go down stream. All of us together would not be able to pull it back upstream," Deer Chaser commented.

"This young man is just trying to get on our good side," Marigold teased as she pulled to the cadence Meadow Flower was calling out.

"If he wants to be on my good side, he will come over here and take my place," Single Leaf grunted as she pulled.

"This is our last pull," Meadow Flower commented as the empty raft came back upstream.

"I am amazed that everything went so smoothly," Talking Wren commented.

"We will put the raft up as high as possible along the cliff. Perhaps someday someone will find use for it again," Burley Bear said as the team pulled the raft up on the beach.

"It does seem like a waste for it not to be used again," Taelo commented.

"We need to take care getting across the gap. I will cross first. Each of you keep watch on the person in front of you. It is not hard just a little tricky," Talking Wren said as she went across the gap.

"I will come across with Burley Bear and the pull team," Taelo said as he realized Talking Wren was crossing over.

"Let's all take a rest before we cross on the ledge," Meadow Flower suggested.

"I agree. My arm muscles are a little shaky," Little Otter replied.

"I think Talking Wren forgot that she asked me to bring over a bag of our honey drink for all of you.

She has gone ahead because the team has a special meal, they are preparing for you," Taelo said as he handed the bag to Burley Bear.

"Very nice," Burley Bear commented as he took a sip and then passed the bag to Meadow Flower.

By the time the bag went all the way around to Taelo it was empty.

High in the sky an eagle let out a cry.

"I think it just told me I should have had my share before passing the bag to Burley Bear," Taelo joked.

He hoped that the cry was just that and not a warning about a new danger.

Taelo was now at full attention. He looked around and saw nothing threatening them.

"Let's get across to the rest of the team," Burly Bear commented once they had all stopped looking at the eagle.

"What do you suppose the eagle cry was for," Busy Bee asked Quiet Rabbit?

"I am not sure, but I am going to the river to look around. Want to come with me," Quiet Rabbit replied.

"Running Stag and I are going to scout the area to the south," Feather-in-the-Wind added.

"What should the rest of us do, Deer Chaser asked?

"Just tell everyone to be alert and ready for whatever action we need to take," Talking Wren replied.

"I am going up to the crossing," she continued.

Burly Bear led the way along the ledge. Everyone was concentrating on getting across.

"I feel so out of shape," Little Otter commented when he slipped and almost fell.

"Steady, there are only a few more spear lengths," Saber Scar said as he steadied Little Otter.

Taelo took one last look behind him. The beach was empty. The pieces of raft were neatly stacked up against the cliff. The area was tranquil.

He turned and followed Single Leaf along the ledge.

"I am feeling a little dizzy," Single Leaf said quietly.

Then she seemed to let go and fall slowly backwards into the swiftly moving water shooting through the gap.

She immediately disappeared below the water. The Others were negative buoyant, and she literally went down like a rock.

Taelo immediately launched himself after her. He knew he had only moments before the cold numbed his muscles and make it impossible for him to help her or save himself.

The water was ice cold, and it was crystal clear. He immediately saw Single Leaf a short distance from where she had entered the water. Her foot was wedged between two boulders.

Taelo flipped over to go down stream feet first. He got his feet planted firmly one on each boulder as the water caused him to use all his strength to maintain his position. He could see the fear in Single Leaf's eyes.

The force of the water threatened to push him off the stone. He reached down and grabbed her ankle and pulled her upstream with all his might until he could feel the burning in his legs and the muscles in his back.

He was running out of air as he gave one mighty heave that pulled Single Leaf's foot free.

The two shot rapidly down the stream like a swiftly flying spear.

Taelo got his left arm around a now seemingly lifeless Single Leaf. He clawed for the surface as it seemed he was being held down by a rock.

His first breathe was more water than air and sent him into convulsion of coughing but he swam and staggered toward the bank on almost numb lifeless legs. The cold water was taking its toll.

He pulled Single Leaf out of the water and immediately threw her over his shoulders. His knees almost buckled under the weight.

He watched as the water ran out of her mouth.

He was doing what the Grey Weaver, storyteller of his youth, had told him do if he ever pulled someone out of the water.

"Grey Weaver never had to throw a member of the Others over his shoulder," flashed through Taelo's mind.

Every story the Grey Weaver had told him had so far been true and had guided Taelo. He had long ago realized the Grey Weaver had really been giving him guidance with his stories.

Next Taelo put Single Leaf flat on the ground and blew air into her mouth. He repeated it three times and then pushed on her chest. He continued to do this and suddenly Single Leaf began to cough and choke.

Taelo could hardly function as his body reacted to the cold.

"Speak to me," Taelo said as he realized how cold he was.

"I am very cold. Are we alive or is this the next world," Single Leaf said in her own tongue?

As cold and miserable as I feel at the moment. I hope we are alive. I want the next world to be warm and gentle," Taelo replied.

Taelo saw the entire team rushing downstream toward the two of them.

"We will soon be warm and well fed. Let's see if we can stand and help each other walk back up the river. I am sure Sharp Blade will be helping you in the next few minutes," Taelo said as he helped Single Leaf up.

"I have never seen anything like this," Burley Bear began.

"We could see down into the water from above.

Single Leaf let out a groan. Fell into the water and sank like a stone.

The water wedged her against two boulders.

She pushed up trying to get over them and one of her legs was pulled between the boulders. The swift water pulled her downstream and her leg pulled through, but her ankle got wedged.

Taelo guided his body feet first and put one foot on each boulder. He had to squat down so the water would not flip him over. He reached down between his legs and took hold of Single Leaf's ankle.

It was clear that he struggled to pull hard enough to pull Single Leaf upstream. Then when he got her ankle loose, the two shot forward like two spears in flight and disappeared downstream.

We all knew it was too late for Single Leaf. She let out the last of her air and went limp.

We thought we had lost them both until we heard Quiet Rabbit shout and point downstream," Burley Bear began the story.

"I saw Taelo jump in after Single Leaf and was sure it was the end," Talking Wren took over.

"When Quiet Rabbit pointed Taelo out, he had picked up Single Leaf on his shoulder and was bouncing her up and down. Then he laid her flat on the ground and breathed into her and then pressed on her chest. He did this several times until Single Leaf began to cough and then sat up looking around.

We all let out a cheer as we ran toward them. Sharp Blade outran all of us. We now know what can make him run as fast as any of us," Talking Wren finished.

"I must thank Taelo for saving my life. I think I saw the light of the land of the ancestors but then I heard Taelo talking to me telling me it was not yet my time. Now, I owe him a debt and must ask how to repay it," Single Leaf commented as she sat and let the fire warm her.

"In life we learn many things even when we think we are just listening to stories.

I listened to the stories told by my father and later found them to be the true stories of our ancestors.

I listened to the stories of Grey Weaver and learned many things that I have used. He talked of feeding the wolves and the bears as a way to control them. I did this first on the beach where we found the whale.

We used this approach on our way through the giant bear country and it worked better than battling the bear.

He also told me how to save someone who had drowned. He told Golden Hawk and me how to take the water out of the body of the person that was drowned and then how to blow new air into them.

So, your debt is not to me but to an old warrior named Grey Weaver. At the coming clan meeting, you will repay the debt. You and I will tell this story to the entire clan and praise his teachings. Then we will serve him the best meal we know how to prepare.

Finally, on each anniversary of this day until he goes to his ancestors you and I will visit with him," Taelo replied.

"I own him as much as you do."

"It is no wonder that all of you follow Taelo anywhere he wishes to go," Whistling Arrow commented to Bashful Lark.

"Yes, and I now understand Floating Cloud's total dedication to her granddaughter's mate," Floating Cloud thought as she dried the tears from her eyes.

It amazed her how much comfort she found in being around Taelo's team.

Chapter 29: The Others: Spring Celebration

View, perspective, and memory is different for the person experiencing a situation and those watching the situation.

Broken Spear had seen through the eyes of the eagle. His view and his perspective were unique in having seen events from above. The minor details were blurred but the grand scheme was sharper and more exact.

He had lived and relived his visions. His heart stopped in fear and concern for Taelo and others on his team, as from on high he continuously saw the impossible display of bravery and winning collaboration.

Some inner signal came to his mind when the eagle again flew to warn Taelo.

Broken Spear was sure it was more than one eagle because each presented a different challenge for him to control where it was looking. Broken Spear sought to see more on the ground than the eagle wanted to see.

He fought to move the eyes to focus on the scene below.

"Once again we have come together to listen to our Broken Spear tell of what he has seen through the eyes of the eagle.

Let me thank the generosity of our two brethren clans.

Red Oak and Quiet Pheasant have again generously given us three buffalo and White Swan and Grey Fox Running have given us another large block of salt.

We are the lucky clan in the middle that can host both of them here in our wonderful cave with our hot pool.

Let us enjoy our feast and the stories we will hear," Quiet Fox opened the celebration.

"It is a treat to be here and listen to another one of your visions of Taelo and Golden Hawk's journey.

Thank you for starting this during the last journey," White Swan said quietly to Broken Spear.

"I have no choice. I fly with the eagle because of Taelo. It is what keeps me alive. It is something I must share," Broken Spear explained.

He knew the life energy he drew was from a source beyond. He was long overdue for the world of the ancestors, but he refused to go.

Taelo had become his energy and inspiration. Broken Spear knew this when he first met Taelo.

A short time later a slow tempo of lightly pounding palms announced the fact that the clan members were ready for the stories.

"I hear you. As you recall, we ended when Taelo defeated and killed the crazed Sky Eyed warrior.

The winter blizzard followed almost immediately. Golden Hawk led the team to a stone overhand just up the bank from a small river.

The eagle flew to where Little Otter, Talking Wren, Busy Bee, Feather-in-the-Wind and Running Stag led a large number of people. Talking Wren seemed to be everywhere directing the building of the shelter. The sleds were strategically positioned among the boulders to form the outer wall of the lodge. Their supply of rawhides was used to form the roof of their camp.

Lily recruited a group and set up the cooking fire and a hide roof over it.

It was a marvel of coordinated work as they established their shelter in the middle of the boulder field.

I lost sight of them as the eagle flew away before the storm.

The eagle went back to its nest and fought for its own survival during four sun cycles of one of the fiercest blizzards I recall.

Taelo knows the eagle follows or that there is always one present. He always places a fresh piece of meat or fish up on a stake at the far edge of his camp. After the blizzard, Busy Bee took a large piece of buffalo meat and placed it on a stake.

I was with the eagle when it recovered the meat and brought it back to its nest. It allowed the eagle to recover. I was surprised at the feeling of well-being that swept through its mind.

Taelo and Golden Hawk left Burley Bear and the rest of the team where their camp and sleds were buried in the snow.

They were again hit by another fierce blizzard. This time the eagle stayed only long enough for me to see Taelo and Golden Hawk raise their shelter. From the eyes of the eagle, I could tell that where they were stopping had been used many times before. They did not find the logs left for others to use in making camp because the river's flooding had dispersed them through the plain beyond.

Once again after the blizzard, Busy Bee fed the eagle. Then we flew out to find Taelo and Golden Hawk driving a young buffalo as they followed the river toward where they hoped would be a camp of people looking for them.

The camp of people had come alive. Several groups went hunting with slings.

One group put up a fish trap that activated many helpers as the fish seemed to volunteer to be dried on the drying racks.

The buffalo running into the camp toward the cooking fire caused an instant sensation when Golden Hawk and Taelo placed their spear tips to its chest and the butt end to the ground. The buffalo stopped as it knelt and put its nose to the ground just short of the fire ring.

The eagle let out a small screech in appreciation.

The winds of the blizzard had a hidden gift as it swept the snow blocking Burley Bear and the team in. The team was able to leave their camp and follow the river as Taelo had done. They and their almost empty sleds made very good time and arrived in the camp only a short time after Taelo.

On the next day, a celebration was held. Taelo put several stakes with fresh fish out for the eagle.

I watched two young hunters fly like the wind as they hunted the buffalo with Taelo and Golden Hawk.

Golden Hawk's spear shattered, and he barely escaped being the victim of the shattered half that flew out in his direction.

His partner demonstrated the wings on his feet as he sped forward on the opposite side and planted his spear as he had seen Golden Hawk do.

He earned the praise of both Golden Hawk and Taelo.

Several moon cycles later, the team arrived at the edge of the ice bridge. This ice bridge is about four sun cycles of normal travel that can take three times as long.

The eagle flew over the terrain.

The blowing snow, the cycling of the weather and the movement of the ice bridge itself had greatly changed every feature that the team had experienced on their way coming across into the land they were now leaving.

The way across was like traveling through a maze. There was no direct way across.

At Burley Bear's suggestion, Taelo practiced laying the sled down and pinning it in place with his spear in the case the ice was breaking ahead of the sled.

From the eyes of the eagle, I could see the bubble ahead of Taelo. My two personal caretakers claim I was screaming for Taelo to stop, to watch out, to go back.

Then I saw Lasher fall through the ice. Taelo physically threw Quite Rabbit three spear lengths back where she hit Burly Bear's lead wolf. Even from the height of the eagle, I could hear Taelo giving orders as one pair of wolves after the other went through the ice.

Taelo followed Burley Bear's advice, laid down his sled and planted the spear but the weight of the wolves slowly pulled the sled toward the edge of the crevasse.

Taelo cut the lines holding the load of meat as the sled slowly fell over the edge.

You must all envision Taelo hanging onto the sled. When he looked down to where Lasher was hanging in his harness, he could not see the bottom of the crevasse. When he looked up there was one main line holding his sled. He was hanging onto the sled with one hand and one foot in the runner of the sled during this entire experience.

Taelo spent most of his time hanging by one hand so he could tie extra lines to the sled and the wolves. His foot finally found a cross member that gave him a chance to recover.

He pulled himself up the rope until both Burley Bear and Saber Scar grabbed him by the wrists and pulled him back away from the crevasse.

It was Burley Bear and Saber Scar who together pulled Taelo up.

Running Stag organized the rest of the team to help pull up the sled. The sled came up to the edge, but the team could not pull it up to safety. The weight of the wolves kept it pulled down at a ninety-degree position.

The wolves and the sled were all rescued.

First Burley Bear and Running Stag, together, lifted the sled directly upward until the sled was high enough to be pulled back from the edge.

All of you remember the weight of the sled. Now add nine wolves to that. Can any of you envision the strength Saber Scar and Burley Bear needed to lift all of that weight. Could any two of you match their power," Broken Spear pause with the question?

From my vantage point, I watched the team act in unison and together overcome the challenge. It was very much like a dance around our fire when we celebrate.

The rest of the trip was slow but anticlimactic.

The most injured person was Quite Rabbit. She was first thrown through the air by Taelo and the again by Burley Bear.

All made it safely across the ice bridge. The team and the new group of people are now on their way back.

We will see them at the fall gathering.

Recall that on the way through the bear country, Feather-in-the-Wind was nearly killed by one of the giant bears. Only Quiet Rabbits ability to sew people back together saved her.

"I am sure that Lily will claim it was her buffalo stew," Broken Spear engaged in a little humor.

Taelo and Golden Hawk came up with a different way of confronting these bears. They decided to feed them and run away. This turned out to be a very smart approach.

The next moon cycle was spent in getting this new clan of people to cross the territory of the giant brown bear.

The eagle called out twice as the bears once again threatened those traveling through their territory.

On the first call, I watched as Taelo began to lure the bear away by pulling the left quarter of a buffalo. He was quickly losing ground to the bear when suddenly Quiet Rabbit ran up and began to pull it with him.

It was a wonder to see the two gather enough speed to outrun the bear. Not just wings on their feet but power in their legs.

On the second call of the eagle, I watched Running Stag draw the giant bear away with another quarter, but pulled by his mount, that he dropped for the bear after guiding it well away from the caravan.

The team gave up one buffalo as tribute to the bears.

I flew next with the eagle when the team returned and crossed the river gap.

The transit through the river gap was flawlessly carried out. To move more than one hundred people, twenty mounts, eighty or more wolves and tons of meat and personal items was a monumental accomplishment.

The mounts made most of this possible but in the end, it was the strength of our clan leader Burley Bear and his partners that made possible the final loads taken through the gap.

I was surprised by the eagle's scream. I thought the transit was successfully over.

Then when Burly Bear, Meadow Flower, Saber Scar, Marigold, Single Leaf and Sharp Blade and Taelo were coming back across the gap the eagle screamed.

A moment later, I watched as Single Leaf fell from the narrow trail. The swift current pulled her down and her leg was caught between two boulders. She was drowning. In fact, she drowned.

I watched as Taelo immediately jumped in after her. The power of the water was so great that a bulge formed above where Taelo was braced against its push. The bulge immediately disappeared as Taelo, and a lifeless Single Leaf shot down the river like a thrown spear.

He slowly took a sip of his honey drink. He had the audience all leaning forward to hear every word he was saying. He looked slowly around and then proceeded.

Taelo guided the two of them to a sandy beach down river from the camp. There he crawled out pulling Single Leaf with him.

I watched as he picked Single Leaf up and bounce her on his shoulder with her head hanging down. It was clear he was barely able to stand.

I ask Red Oak or Grey Fox Running if they can pick up anyone the size of Single Leaf and bounce them on their shoulder.

They are shaking their heads and saying no they don't think they can.

Taelo did!

The water drained from Single Leaf's mouth. Then he laid her down and blew air into her body. He did this several times.

And life came back to her.

I am sure Single Leaf will tell us her story when she returns.

That is all I have seen," Broken Spear closed in a quiet voice.

Taelo was now even more of a legend to those around him.

He is bringing another surprise to the next gathering of the Elk Clan. We should all expect a surprise and the fun that he and Golden Hawk always bring to the meetings.

The two Golden Feathers continue to enrich all of our lives," Broken Spear closed to the continuous slapping of palms on the ground.

Chapter 30: Clan Gathering

Sunshine and calm after a storm are preferable to the calm before the storm. The late summer journey toward the southeast through terrain with an abundant mix of small game, buffalo and elk allowed Taelo's team and the people they were leading to stock up on food.

A treasure was found as Saber Scar crested the hill and spotted a herd of mounts. This was an opportunity that could not be passed up. Taelo called a halt to organize the capture of additional mounts.

Taelo and the team discussed how to capture the mounts out on the open plain.

"Why not use your fish trap idea, we could use all our members as the guides into a pen or trap," Bashful Lark suggested.

Running Stag found a suitable small cliff lined valley with an opening into the valley where the mounts were grazing.

Everyone was given a long stick with a piece of leather on it. They were assigned a location out on the plain. Together they formed a slowly converging cone that would guide the mounts into the small holding valley.

Taelo, Golden Hawk, Quiet Rabbit, Busy Bee, Feather-in-the-Wind, Running Stag and Talking Lark were the riders guiding the mounts into the opening of the cone. They moved the herd they had gathered slowly into the cone. They wanted to keep the herd from bolting in alarm.

The line slowly waved their leather top poles back and forth as they guided the slow-moving herd into the valley.

Burley Bear and his team closed the valley off once the last of the mounts trotted down into the valley.

There were enough mounts that every member of the White Bear Clan would have one mount.

Taelo and his team would have three each.

"Let's plan on traveling directly to the valley of the clan meeting. If we arrive early, we can spend some time arranging for everyone's arrival.

In the past we have been successful with the approach of feeding everyone and getting on their good side. We are bringing in enough people to make another clan and we bring enough mounts that these new members will be in good standing.

How do we want to handle this," Taelo put the question to the team?

"I come from the far south mountains where supposedly the great Condor has taken me for his bride. I came north with the team, and I made the *Journey of Discovery* to the East and swam the sea on that far side. I have now traveled north and survived the Great Bear and the Sky Eyes.

North, South, West, East, we live in a giant land with giant beasts and challenges.

I would like to take a clan to the East and establish a home in the bay where Taelo saved Golden Hawk from the giant shark. Just to the south is the singing beach. I remember walking there and laughter graced my throat," Feather-in-the-Wind spoke up.

She had shared this vision with Running Stag and was now putting it out in front of the rest of the team.

"This will be a great challenge to the Elk Clan leadership. I know of four leaders that will support such a vision. I wonder if we will have enough family members willing to travel so far away," Quiet Rabbit responded as she absorbed what Feather-in-the-Wind was proposing.

"I know every family coming from the White Bear Clan would be willing to be led by Feather-in-the-Wind," Whistling Arrow commented in support.

It was a new concept for him, but he realized that Feather-in-the-Wind was a true leader and what he said reflected what other members of the White Bear Clan believed.

"You have my support. I can think of no one better to establish the Eastern Elk Clan," Taelo answered in support.

"The legend of Feather-in-the-Wind is now beginning," Golden Hawk added as he crossed over and gave her a hug.

"I will work with Talking Wren and Quiet Rabbit to devise a winning meeting," Busy Bee said in support.

"We will also need to think about how to integrate our new members across all the clans. Once again, we arrive with more women than men and need to see about getting them mates," Talking Wren continued the conversation.

"We will need to get word to Feather-in-the-Wind's family," Taelo commented to Golden Hawk as the two rode their mounts in parallel.

"Well, I don't know of anyone available to send other than you and I. Everyone else will be engaged in running the clans. Do you think Quiet Rabbit and Busy Bee are up to a quick trip south," Golden Hawk replied?

"Well let's first get through the clan meeting. Then we can bring up the subject of a quick trip south.

The trip to the meeting valley took on the flavor of a traveling school.

Feather-in-the-Wind continued teaching anyone interested the use of the sling. She had all the younger members of the White Bear Clan in her following.

She was an adored person.

Her top student was Single Leaf who soon was as good and whose throwing range was at least fifty percent greater. A young boar made the mistake of running across in front of the caravan.

Single Leaf ran forward with her sling in full motion and hit the boar from at least ten mount lengths away. She continued running and as the boar struggle to get up she finished it with her war hammer.

She was beaming as she carried the boar back to her sled. She cleaned the boar as the caravan continued.

"Come to my campfire this evening," she invited the team members.

Later when the travois were circled and the camp setup the team gathered at Single Leaf's fire circle.

"Each of you has a boulder to sit on," Sharp Blade commented as he showed each member where to sit.

"The boar smells delicious," Quiet Rabbit commented as she took her seat.

"Today I saw my best sling student become a master. I must now claim to be almost as good as Single Leaf," Feather-in-the-Wind commented in praise.

"Perhaps you should wait a bit longer. I may just have been lucky," a beaming Single Leaf replied as she and Sharp Blade lifted the boar from the hot coals.

"This is the first chance that I have had to feed the person who saved me," Single Leaf commented as she cut the hind leg of the boar and handed it to Taelo.

"Thank you, this is much more than I can possibly eat by myself. Busy Bee, Golden Hawk please join us," Taelo commented as he accepted the leg and put it on the boulder in front of him.

"Your display with the sling surprised us all. I have never seen such accuracy at such a distance. We will keep this in mind for future encounters," Burley Bear added as he was given the other hind leg.

"Hey, is there going to be enough boar for all of us," Little Otter blurted out as Saber Scar was given a front leg.

"You should not worry so much. I am saving the tail for you," Single Leaf joked as she gave Talking Wren the other front Leg.

"To my sling teacher I present the head and the rest of us will eat from the side and back, Floating Cloud has promised that anyone still hungry is welcome to some rabbit, groundhog, or the pheasant she bagged today," Single Leaf said as she pointed to each offering.

Floating Cloud and Lily were tending to their fire adjacent to Single Leaf's fire.

Running Stag also had a following of those interested in learning to use the bow. The only limitation he made was that the target had to be in front of the caravan. It was the only way he could ensure he would not lose his precious arrows.

He demonstrated his skill by bagging several rabbits. Most of the other rabbits were safe as his students practiced their nascent skills.

Lily, Floating Cloud and Busy Bee established a round robin cooking assignment for anyone wishing to prepare some special meal.

Taelo's immediate participation opened the door to the men of the White Bear Clan. They would cook during their hunts but seldom did so while in the camp. There was a change in attitude and behavior when they saw Taelo and Golden Hawk team up to feed almost the entire clan.

Marigold, Meadow Flower, and Single Leaf gave lessons on the processing and preparation of the leather hides.

They showed the preparation of the pieces where the fur was to be left on and how to ensure the hairs would not fall out.

They demonstrated how to remove the hair from the hide that was to be bare. They also taught the process of curing the hide and making it soft.

The one process they would not let anyone see was how they managed to get the hide to become an almost pure white.

The hides were being fashioned into jackets, pants, foot covering, head covering, and gloves. Quiet Rabbit made sure every person had the hides to make what they wanted to. It would be important for the White Bear Clan to be in good stead.

"We will arrive early and will establish ourselves on the far side of the lake.

We will greet each sub-clan and help them setup camp. We have been successful at this once before. This time it will be easier, but we will want to flaunt our good standing and the industrious nature of our new members," Busy Bee commented as the team sat around the evening fire.

"Do you expect problems at the meeting because of us," Whistling Arrow inquired?

"No, the clan now expects a surprise from us every time we return from one of our journeys. It began when Grey Fox Running was promoted leader of the original Elk Clan.

Then Taelo invited the Others to become part of our clan.

Next Taelo established the Northern Elk Clan and worked behind the scene to have White Swan named as its leader. Wise Owl the leader of the group of Elk Clan Elders has been our inside supporter and seems to enjoy the surprises and twists that Taelo and Golden Hawk bring to the clan," Quiet Rabbit replied to the question.

"Is Taelo responsible for improving the role women have in the leadership of the clan," Whistling Arrow continued with a question that had been on his mind?

"No, that came from the Clan of the Others. Their women have always fought besides them and have been part of the Other's Clan of Elders.

Taelo learned that from them and with White Swan convinced the Elk Clan to allow women to hunt with them.

Busy Bee, Talking Wren and I were the ones to first hunt with Taelo, Golden Hawk and Little Otter.

After that success, women were allowed to hunt and to be part of the Elk Clan leader's council.

Then at the clan gathering when the Others were accepted into the clan, they had women as elders. This was probably the biggest change the clan has faced in as long as the clan can remember.

Adding more members and another clan was in fact easy," Quiet Rabbit replied.

"I will say that the participation of women in leadership roles is the part that the men in the White Bear Clan have talked about the most. I suppose that this is also true of all the women.

Your team's behavior has inspired all of us," Whistling Arrow replied.

"It is two moons to the time of the clan meeting.

Ahead of us is a large herd of buffalo and there are a few elk grazing with them. This is an opportunity for us to come to the clan meeting with fresh meat, hides as well as riding our mounts.

This would put us in a good position.

We propose that Running Stag and Feather-in-the-Wind lead the caravan to the valley where the meeting takes place. We will keep enough mounts and travois and then send the meat directly to the meeting area to process," Golden Hawk announced to all the members.

"Who will be allowed to stay and hunt," Bubbling Brook asked?

"Let's see if we can make this easy. Those who wish to stay and hunt step behind Burley Bear. Those who wish to go to the meeting valley step behind Feather-in-the-Wind," Quiet Rabbit suggested.

"Well, my friend, you seem to be more popular than Feather-in-the-Wind," Taelo said quietly to Burley Bear as two thirds of the caravan members got behind Burley Bear.

"It is clear that we have some young members who wish to be hunters. We are pleased with your desire but this time we will ask you to go with Feather-in-the-Wind," Busy Bee commented as she, Quiet Rabbit and Talking Wren sent each youngster to the other side.

The mothers of some of the youngsters went with them as well and in the end the split was closer to a fifty-fifty split.

"The work ahead will be challenging. We will hunt and process at a fast pace.

Each travois will carry three buffalo to the valley.

Once at the valley the team sent with the buffalo will skin and begin smoking the meat.

Lily and Floating Cloud will select the meat they want for their cooking and other preparation. Give them anything they ask for," Golden Hawk instructed those that had remained behind.

"We will begin with a race. The fastest will be taught to run down and spear the buffalo. White Bear and Deer Chaser will manage this race and assign each of you your roles.

Golden Hawk, White Bear, Deer Chaser, and I will spear the buffalo. Four of you will be chosen to carry our spears. You will watch what we do and then try it yourself. Once you have done this three times you will be allowed to be the lead hunter," Taelo continued.

"Those who end up at the back of the race, do not despair. You will be working with Saber Scar, Marigold and Meadow Flower and me. We are not fast, but we are powerful. We will have as much fun as the hunters.

Our job is to make sure the buffalo is dead. We will need to remain on alert. A wounded buffalo can be very dangerous," Burley Bear added.

He knew how much he would love to plant the spear in front of the buffalo, and he knew he would never be able to do so.

I was worried we would have too many fast runners but only a few kept up with White Bear and Deer Chaser. This will make it easier to give them each of the fastest a chance to take the lead," Golden Hawk commented to Taelo as they watched the race come to an end.

"It is good to see that there will be a few young women in that group," Taelo noted.

He noted that Bubbling Brook, Bending Willow, and Gentle Cub were among those in the front.

"We will make sure the rest get a good hunting experience," Burley Bear added.

"This will be a good event for the White Bear Clan. The young women are some of our stronger leaders. This will give them new confidence. I am glad to help you without running the race. I just want to watch how Taelo and Golden Hawk hunt. I am quite willing to do anything you ask," Whistling Arrow said to Burley Bear.

The hunt was very successful. Each of the new hunters got a chance at racing out in front of the buffalo and placing their spear.

The young women did as well as the young men.

I have never had such an exhilarating feeling," Bubbling Brook commented after her hunt.

It was unbelievable the rest of the hunters agreed.

The excitement for the hunt came the very next sun cycle as Bending Willow and Gentle Cub downed their buffalo with Golden Hawk and Taelo as their support.

High in the Sky the eagle cried.

Lasher began a low growl as a large wolf pack came toward them out of the forest.

"I believe we will lose one of our buffalo to this large wolf pack. Help me skin the buffalo and get some of the meat from the front quarter. I will go out and talk to them," Taelo spoke quietly to an alarmed Bending Willow and Gentle Cub.

Golden Hawk had already started skinning the buffalo.

"Here is your initial offering. I will bring you more if the wolves agree to your direction," Golden Hawk said as he handed Taelo some chunks of meat.

Gentle Cub and Bending Willow were anxiously working to skin the buffalo.

Nearby Saber Scar, Meadow Flower and Marigold were tying the other buffalo to a mount so they could drag it away from the area.

"We have come to watch Taelo talk to the wolves," Burley Bear said as he and Whistling Arrow arrived with their spears ready.

"Taelo talks to wolves," Gentle Cub said in surprise.

"Of course, have you not listened to Lasher, and he talk to each other," Golden Hawk replied with a smile on his face.

"Well, my friends, I see that you have come to enjoy the bounty that the mother earth has given us," Taelo said as he and Lasher walked slowly toward the oncoming pack of wolves.

Lasher's gave a slow steady growl accompanied Taelo's greetings.

"Easy Lasher, our friends only want to share some of this fine meat," Taelo continued his light banter as he threw the first piece of meat to the lead wolf.

The throw was so good that the wolf instinctively caught it in its mouth. The entire pack stopped and Taelo began throwing additional meat to the surrounding members.

"Now if you stop and enjoy this initial offering, we will leave you most of this young tender buffalo for you to enjoy," Taelo continued as he took the next load of meat from Golden Hawk.

"How are we doing in getting the rest of the buffalo ready to move," Taelo inquired?

"Saber Scar is back with another mount and travois. We will take the hide the two back quarters and remaining front quarter. We will leave the head and back minus the two tender back muscles," Golden Hawk replied.

"Let me know when I can release my wolf friends to enjoy what we leave behind," Taelo said as he targeted his throws to the few wolves that had not gotten any.

"We are departing," Golden Hawk called out as Saber Scar led the mount away with the buffalo meat on the travois.

"Well, my friends, it is time for me to guide you to your feast," Taelo continued talking as he slowly backed away from the pack of wolves.

The lead wolf slowly followed as Taelo kept throwing chunks of meat to the pack.

He and Lasher continued their backward walk even after they got past the remains of the buffalo. Once the wolf pack was full engaged with the ribs and back, Taelo turned and began a slow jog back toward the hunting camp.

High in the Sky the eagle let out its low screech as it flew toward the meeting valley.

Later that evening White Bear asked, "How did you know the wolves would listen to you?"

"Well, I asked Lasher if this was one of the well-behaved packs that would listen to me," Taelo replied with a smile in his eyes.

"Yes, I heard Lasher's reply," Bending Willow immediately joined in as she realized Taelo was joking.

"You should attend our wolf language lessons," Gentle Cub added.

"Ok, my question really has to do with the courage it takes to walk toward a wolf pack.

How does one develop it," White Bear asked?

"Yes, this is what I also want to know," Deer Chaser said in support of his friend.

"It is not a question of courage. We all have this ability.

Think about what is desired and how you can satisfy this desire," Taelo replied.

"The wolves were hungry and smelled food. They desired something to eat. If I had tried to stop them, they would have attacked me. Instead about the time the leader was ready to attack me, I gave him a piece of meat. And then I continued to feed the rest of the pack. I gave them what they were after," Taelo continued.

"Well call it what you want. I can't wait to share this story around my campfire," Whistling Arrow said from where he sat.

"On my first trip out with Taelo, on his hunt for a suitable place for my clan to live, I watched as Taelo talked to a huge cave bear. She talked back to Taelo. She kept a wolf pack back from the prized whale blubber she was eating. She then waved goodbye to let Taelo know she was leaving.

Taelo then talked to the wolves and fed them some of the whale meat. Once he had fed them, he asked them to leave because he did not want to hurt any of them.

Their leader turned and left as if he understood Taelo.

Taelo seems to know when he can talk and when he must act," Burley Bear added.

Chapter 31: Preparation

*R*eturning to a former place awakens the memories of the past. Good and bad memories are equally freed. The Elk Clan's meeting valley held very good memories for most of members of the expanded Elk Clan.

The surrounding mountain's dark green pine cover base with many that maintained a year-round white cap surrounded the long peaceful now tan and gold covered grass covered valley. The long oblong lake fed by a bubbling stream running down from the far mountains and then leaving the valley in a quite stream was surrounded by now yellowing cattails with their dark brown sausage tops and the weeping willows bending out over them was nestled at one end and to the far side.

This was the site of the autumn meeting of the clan. This was the place many love affairs had taken root. This was the place the clan re-united their common purpose and adjusted the balance of the Elk Clan.

Once again Taelo was returning from a journey and once again the Elk Clan would experience the strain of change and the reinvigoration and power it would experience.

"It is good to see the lake," Quiet Rabbit spoke as she stopped her mount on the hill overlooking the meeting valley.

"Yes, it has been an interesting journey, but it will be a pleasure to see our friends and families," Busy Bee replied.

"I agree, though I really do not look forward to returning to my Valley of Plenty," Talking Wren added as she leaned forward viewing the valley.

The entire procession had stopped and were all gazing down into the valley.

"What a grand view," Long Leaper commented to Bashful Lark.

"This is only my second time, and it feels more like home than anywhere else I have lived," Bashful Lark replied.

"I understand your feelings. The Elk Clan has become my clan and I am more attached to those around me at the moment than my dear family far to the south," Feather-in-the-Wind added.

"Let's get down there and get setup on the other side of the lake before some other clan comes in ahead of us," Running Stag said as he urged his mount forward.

The procession went down into the valley and across to the other side.

"Well, I see that you were able to get our detailed organizer to the other side of the lake so we could finish up in peace on this side," Busy Bee commented.

"She is great at getting things organized but once that is done, she begins to focus on details that drive me crazy," Floating Cloud replied.

"You should listen to her when she is discussing ideas for how to fight battles with Taelo and Golden Hawk. They listen intently and seldom argue with her. She has a keen mind. Taelo makes it a point of reviewing all her suggestions. He credits her with the idea for the shards to the eyes as a plan against a superior force," Quiet Rabbit commented.

"I can see her helping devise battle plans," Floating Cloud continued.

Talking Wren shared a layout for the campsites at the clan meeting. Normally the first arrivals to the lake would randomly setup their camp. This random arrangement usually ended up with the camps of the last arrivals being very far from the lake. Her layout would give every sub-clan almost equal access to the lake no matter their arrival time.

While the White Bear Clan settled in on the far side of the lake, Talking Wren and a small team of helpers proceeded to lay out the side of the lake where the Elk Clans would set up their camps.

First, she located the clan's central meeting place and set up the enclosure initially made by the Clan of Others that had been used on their trip north. It was located at the center of the long lake opposite the side of where all the sub-clans would set up their camp.

Once this enclosure was up, the sub-clan camp's main cooking and meeting areas were located. Seven sub-clan fire rings were located along the edge of the lake. Individual family lodgings were located behind each sub-clan main camp.

This arrangement optimized the access to the lake and gave every sub-clan almost equal access to the water and the view of the lake.

"I have positioned each campsite and made initial assignments. Our round compound covering on this side of the lake is in the center of all the camps on the other side. It will be our main meeting area. We can offer it up for the council meeting as well," Talking Wren said as she guided the setup of the sites.

"It a very good layout," Single Leaf commented as she stood at the entrance to the center lodge and looked across the lake to where all the other camps would be.

Talking Wren and Single Leaf gave a tour to all the members.

"Every clan shares the space along the lake. The cooking fire rings are all equally spaced. There is only one fire ring for each clan on the edge by the lake. This fire ring has more space around it than any of the others.

The other fire rings are spaced equally apart from each other, and they again go in a semicircle that matches the first set of fire rings. This pattern is repeated for several rows. The space between the rows allows for the sleeping tents. Also, the fire rings are staggered so there is always an open area in the row toward the lake. This layout provides the most harmonious layout possible.

We have moved the Totem to the edge of the lake just outside of the main lodge lakeside entrance. It is visible to all the clans and from the meeting area on the other side," Talking Wren proudly pointed out all the features of the camps layout.

Saber Scar and Meadow Flower took out at sizeable team and setup a holding area for the mounts. The stand of sentinel pines on the slope leading away from the river on the south side was one barrier.

Utilizing the long slender pine logs, barriers were built from the edge of the forest to the small stream and across for the length of two spear throws. Then utilizing a ridge of boulders and stone paralleling the small stream the rectangle enclosure was completed.

The mounts have plenty of grass, access to water and could move about freely.

Everyone's mount, now marked with their personal dark stain markings are in the enclosure.

There was enough room for at least the same number of mounts more.

Taelo had suggested this larger size enclosure to accommodate the mounts he anticipated the Grazing Elk Clan would bring for trade.

Talking Wren walked the entire layout and felt a surge of pride.

"I know that this goes against most of the instructions your mothers have given you," Busy Bee stated as she addressed both young women and the young men, "We are going to practice getting you paired off to a mate you desire."

"We will go to each of the clans and find out who is available and looking. We will let them know who in the White Bear Clan is available and looking.

We will arrange for a dinner here in the main camp for all of you to meet each other.

Then it will be up to you to introduce yourself to the person or persons you are interested in. Once you have made a connection, let us know and we will help you in making the final arrangements," Quiet Rabbit commented.

"A word to the older ones in the group," Lily interjected, "You may not find or be approached. I did not and was not. Later, I found Slow Runner and he found me. So don't despair if you don't succeed during the meeting. Just keep looking,"

"Each of you will be bringing your own contribution of hides, weapons, food, and the skills you have learned in hunting and fishing.

You will have good standing. Let's practice the art of conversation," Talking Wren continued, "It is the skill that will link you to your mate.

Look at me, I talk and Little Otter listens."

This brought a round of laughter from everyone sitting around as the sun disappeared behind the western hills around the valley.

Every other sun cycle another load of buffalo arrived at the camp. The meat was being smoked, the hides processed, and the horns were being turned into utensils.

The many White Bear Clan members were making the eating sticks made out of hardwood that were decorated with the buffalo horn. A few had carved the elk horn to make fancy versions of these eating sticks.

The vests and other clothing apparel were decorated with elk horn, buffalo horn, and the horn of the northern caribou.

Busy Bee and Quite Rabbit guided the making of this apparel.

The leather treatment that Marigold and Meadow Flower taught the White Bear Clan made the clothing garments among the best.

"I think we will have many bartering for these goods. I hope the other clans all bring something we will want, Quiet Rabbit said as she watched everyone doing their work.

Busy Bee was awakened by the hooting of an owl.

"I think Wise Owl and the Elk Hide Clan will be arriving today," she shared with Quiet Rabbit as they sat on the boulder, they shared every morning at the edge of the lake.

"Yes, I heard the owl this morning," Quiet Rabbit replied.

"Taelo and Golden Hawk should return soon. All the mounts are back with their loads.

They asked for the first travois to make one more trip out for them," Little Otter added from his perch on another boulder.

Late in the afternoon one of the scouts sent out by Little Otter returned with word that one clan was arriving.

"I believe Wise Owl and the Elk Horn Clan are approaching the Valley. Let's go and help them set up their camp," Talking Wren announced to her small army of recruited helpers.

"I see that another twist is being added to our clan meetings," Wise Owl commented as Talking Wren and Little Otter greeted him and led him to his camp location.

The other members of the clan were being escorted to the prepositioned campfire locations by the guides Talking Wren had trained.

"Yes, we hope that this layout will please all the clans. No matter the order in which they arrive each will have some lakefront, and all will have the same distance to the water," Talking Wren replied.

"I like it already," Wise Owl replied as he took in the arrangement and noted there seemed to be an abundant of new members that were taking part in helping the Elk Horn Clan set up camp.

"Is there some significance in the fact that our totem pole is on the other side of the lake," Wise Owl inquired?

"Yes, please come over and we will show you the proposed new meeting area for the council," Little Otter replied.

Another of the scouts arrived with the news that Taelo and the remaining hunters were returning with a heavily loaded travois and all the remaining mounts were also being brought in.

"It appears we have another clan of prosperous people camped on this side," Wise Owl commented as he took in the proposed leadership meeting enclosure and the surrounding campsites, abundant meat supply and all the goods on display.

"Yes, we will wait for Taelo and Golden Hawk's return and share some of the tales of our journey north," Quiet Rabbit said in greeting to Wise Owl.

"As always, Taelo and his team add spice to our clan meetings. I look forward to this meeting as I have now for many seasons," Wise Owl replied as he accepted a hug from each of the team.

"This meeting area and arrangement is very good. I look forward to the first meeting. Let me get back to my clan and see how they are doing," Wise Owl said as he turned to return to the other side of the lake.

"I see the first clan has arrived," Taelo commented as the remaining hunters came over the crest of the hill.

"They seem to be arranged differently than in the past," Golden Hawk observed.

"This is a beautiful valley, why is there not a permanent clan that resides here," Whistling Arrow inquired in curiosity?

"I don't believe any of us have an answer to that," Taelo replied.

It was an observation that had not crossed his mind.

"This looks like Talking Wren's doing," Golden Hawk observed as they skirted the edge of the staked-out area as they made their way to the crossover point.

"Whistling Arrow, please take our mounts and travois to the other side. Golden Hawk and I must greet Wise Owl of the Elk Horn Clan," Taelo said as they reached the crossing.

"Greetings Wise Owl," Taelo called out as he and Golden Hawk walked to where they saw Wise Owl and his leaders talking.

"Greetings, Taelo, Golden Hawk. It is good to see the two of you again. And as always you bring us all a challenge, new learning, and enough people to make up another clan," Wise Owl said as he put his hand on each of their shoulders but then gave them a hug.

These were his wonder boys grown into leaders of men.

"These are people of our ancestors. They endured much hardship and when they needed to choose their way, they wanted to be part of our clan. We will talk of this later.

Now I must take Golden Hawk across and get bathed before we offend the Elk Hide Clan with the odor of buffalo dung," Taelo joked as he gave his excuse to crossover to the other side of the lake.

"You're timing as always is impeccable. You have returned just in time to greet all the leaders," Quiet Rabbit said as she gave Taelo a hug.

"I agree with the timing, and we have an area for you two to bathe and some of Meadow Flowers scented oils that you can use," Busy Bee added as she waved her hand in front of her nose.

"It is good to know that you missed us so. I see you let loose our village planner who has rearranged the entire meeting living arrangements," Taelo commented.

"Yes, I remember a young boy complaining about how far one had to carry the water because his clan was late to the meeting," Talking Wren commented as she came over to greet the two.

"The two of us were talking about the fact that we sent the best organizers and the fact that we were out of the way probably meant this would be the most organized meeting the clan has ever had," Golden Hawk responded.

The Northern Elk Clan was the next arrival. Taelo accompanied Talking Wren and Quiet Rabbit as they greeted White Swan and showed them where to set up camp.

"Thank you, this solves the need for a clan to rush to the meeting location in fear of being crowded out to the back," Grey Fox Running said as he waved to Wise Owl.

The simultaneous arrival of the Elk Clan and the Clan of Others occurred as the sun was touching the horizon.

"Well, even when she is not in camp, our Talking Wren has a positive effect on the Elk Clan," Red Oak gave praise as the White Bear Clan members helped the Elk Clan set up their site.

Meanwhile Burley Bear, Meadow Flower, Saber Scar, Marigold, Single Leaf and Sharp Blade greeted the Clan of Others and helped them set up camp.

"Broken Spear told us this meeting would be more organized and again it would hold a surprise for all of us. He would not tell us the surprise," Quiet Fox commented in greeting.

"Thank you for giving us the leader's camp," Little Doe said in greeting.

"We thank you for freeing us to travel with Taelo. It was another journey of a lifetime," Meadow Flower responded with a hug.

The Grazing Elk Clan was last to arrive and were pleasantly surprised that they would still have a good location. Their camp was at one side of the camp layout. This made it easy for them to attend to their mounts they had brought to trade.

They were surprised at the enclosure where they could release their mounts.

"We have one prize mount for Taelo. This is a gift from two of the rescued hunters.

Look over the rest and be ready to trade," Fierce Badger the clan leader said in greeting as he pointed to twenty mounts being released into the holding area.

"Thank you for saving such a fine location for us. It is as if it was planned this way," Fierce Badger continued as the White Bear Clan members helped in setting up the camp.

"It was indeed planned by one of our best clan planners, Talking Wren. You can thank her for choosing your camp location and for its layout," Taelo responded.

And thank you for the beautiful mount. I am sure I will enjoy riding it.

Chapter 32: Fall Gathering

Family gatherings always entertain and usually allow everyone to catch up on the latest accomplishments or issues their family and friends have faced. The coming together of the nine Elk Clans was like a large family get together. It had its moments of fun, its anxious moments, its feuding moments, and the serious moments when the leadership gathered to discuss the functioning and wellbeing of each clan.

For the last few seasons, Taelo and his team made a significant impact. Even when he missed attending during two of the previous seasons, Taelo had been the center of attention. Saber Scar had shared the stories of the *Journey of Discovery* to the east and on this latest journey he had shared the Journey North.

Now Taelo and his team had once again come back with the equivalent of another sub-clan.

This would make nine Elk sub-clans and a total of ten clans counting the original Elk Clan.

What territory the new Elk Clan would get was a hot topic of discussion and speculation.

Busy Bee and Quiet Rabbit immediately visited each of the sub-clans and discussed the available young single women and men of the White Bear Clan.

"As in the past we are also looking to place families in each of the sub-clans. Please come to any of our evening meal gatherings for a wonderful feast and to meet these fine young people," Busy Bee said as she made her pitch once again.

The number of visitors to the evening meals grew significantly when word got out about the great food as well as the unattached young women and men.

"Once again you lead with the food and you succeed in your endeavor," Wise Owl said as he took part in the evening meal.

"We have an over-abundance of young, single members. This clan lost most of their older leaders. Taelo has mentioned the desire to create the Eastern Elk Clan. To do this we will want to exchange families. This needs to be one of the early decisions by the Leadership Council," Quiet Rabbit commented during her interaction with Wise Owl.

"Tomorrow will be the first meeting of the council. I will make sure this request is discussed. Are you supportive of Taelo's request as to the leader of this new sub-clan," Wise Owl inquired?

"Yes, all the people on this side of the lake are aware and supportive. This is what makes the family exchange so difficult. They all love the candidate Taelo has recommended and all wish to stay," Quiet Rabbit replied.

On the following day Wise Owl looked around the new council meeting area and then called the meeting to order.

"It is good that all the clans are having a good season," Wise Owl commented after the last clan gave its account of their preparedness for the coming winter.

"Taelo and Golden Hawk have returned from their journey to the north. They have brought us another clan worth of people and they have suggested we create another sub-clan to be called the Eastern Elk Clan. I support the establishment of this clan. Let me hear the discussion," Wise Owl announced.

"You all look to Taelo and then you look at me. This is the first I know of this suggestion. It seems to me a wise one as long as the Eastern Elk Clan settles beyond the territory of the Grazing Elk Clan," White Swan said in support.

"I too support the idea. It would be good to have a close neighbor." Fierce Badger the Grazing Elk Clan leader responded.

"Well, since I am supportive and I can count six of the nine clans are supportive as well and perhaps the other three will make this a unanimous decision, who will lead this new sub-clan," Sleek Beaver of the Elk Hide Clan asked?

"The leader I am recommending has been with me on three journeys. This person is a fearless warrior who has repeatedly demonstrated unparalleled courage, the ability to lead others and who has a commanding vision of the future.

She saved my life as together we defeated the great northern bear. I am recommending our princess from the south, Feather-in-the-Wind be named leader of the Eastern Elk Clan and that Running Stag be named lead hunter," Taelo said as he slowly turned to make eye contact with each of the leaders around the circle.

He knew that naming a second woman as a leader would stretch the limit of the council's good will.

"Please, let's discuss this in an orderly manner," Wise Owl stepped into the center and took the meeting over as the surprised leaders were talking and shouting across to each other.

"Women are weak, women should tend to the fire, they should cure the hides and mind the children," Red Oak stood up slowly recited many of the lines he had often heard.

"What is all the fuss about? Have you examined the riches of the Northern Elk Clan? None of us can match their wealth. They have furs, tusks, shark's teeth, and an abundance of food. It must just be luck because they are led by a woman," Red Oak continued.

"Do you like the new layout of our meeting valley? It must be luck because a team of women planned the layout.

Did you like the food? Well, just as many of the young men cooked as did the young women.

It is time we quit basing our initial decision on gender and focus on the capability required for success."

"Taelo has put forward a candidate and I suggest we take a vote," Red Oak said as he sat down.

"We will vote on two parts. First, we will vote on whether to set up a new clan and then we will vote on the leader," Wise Owl announced.

The vote to set up a new clan was unanimous.

The vote on the leader was six for and three against.

"Please call Feather-in-the-Wind to the meeting," Wise Owl requested of those at the edge of the meeting enclosure.

Taelo and Golden Hawk escorted Feather-in-the-Wind into the center circle.

"Welcome to the leader's circle.

You have been selected to lead the Eastern Elk Clan.

Taelo says that the wolf has selected you as the eagle selected him.

Your leader's spear has two wolves carved into it by Taelo and Golden Hawk. There is a blade carved by Saber Scar and there is a sling carved by Quiet Rabbit and Busy Bee.

The blade is a giant sharks tooth gifted by Burley Bear," Wise Owl pointed out each attribute as he presented the spear to a surprised Feather-in-the-Wind.

"I am humbled by this privilege.

The guidance of this wise council will be very important to me.

The support of my close friends will be my sustenance.

The teachings of my father and mother will be my foundation.

All the members of the Elk Clan, my clan, are always welcome at my fire ring," Feather-in-the-Wind said slowly and clearly as she looked each leader in their eyes.

There were tears in her eyes as she ran her slender hand across the carvings made in her leader's spear.

"This was my destiny to be with dear friends, my new family.

I wish my father and mother could know my happiness," Feather-in-the-Wind thought to herself as she took her seat in the ring of clan leaders.

The meeting ended shortly after, and the new clan members brought in a treat of refreshments and good food to eat.

Romance solved most of the perceived problems of integrating the White Bear Clan families into the Elk Clan. Those individuals finding mates decided on which clan they would live with. Finding families to come into the Eastern Elk Clan was somewhat more difficult.

"Would you consider escorting the Eastern Elk Clan to its new home and helping establish it," Feather-in-the-Wind asked Taelo?

"Quiet Rabbit, how do you feel about this request," Taelo said as he looked around the evening fire?

"Busy Bee and I were talking about what our next adventure would be. Is this what the eagle has agreed to," Quiet Rabbit replied?

She knew this was not what she and Taelo had discussed and figured Taelo was using her reply to broaden the conversation.

"Are you asking because of the difficulty of getting other Elk Clan families to join the Eastern Elk Clan," Taelo inquired?

"Yes, if you are a part of this then we will not have any problems getting the families to join," Feather-in-the-Wind replied truthfully.

She would have felt better to do this on her own, but she had to consider the members of her new clan.

"Then I suggest a two-step move. Your first step will be to move to our Paradise Valley for the winter. Our team will go with you there and help setup the camp for winter.

In the spring the team will help escort the Eastern Elk Clan to their new home on the far coast if that is still desired," Taelo replied.

The discussion closed with the agreement. Soon after it was time for the clans to disperse.

"Thank you for taking on the chore of keeping the main meeting cover and enclosure. You designed and made it and now you will be bringing it to the fall meetings," Wise Owl said as he addressed Burley Bear at the final council meeting.

"The families have all made their choices and the council is in agreement with the changes. I believe the mix for the Eastern Elk Clan is still not quite in balance but that will change in the future as the bonds across the clan get rearranged. They have enough hunters but are skewed to having many young single members.

Feather-in-the-Wind has assured me she is sure of the well-being of the Eastern Elk Clan," Wise Owl continued.

"Is there any other business that should be discussed before I close the meeting," Wise Owl inquired?

There was none.

"Have the Ancestors let you know what your next journey is to be," Golden Hawk asked on the last evening of the clan gathering.

"Yes, the Ancestors have talked to me. There is a journey to the South that we must make. Our help is needed.

He and Taelo discussed this journey in detail, and it was time to share it with the rest of the team. Only a select number of the team would be going on this journey.

Later they let the rest of the team know. They made the point that let them tell Feather-in-the-Wind's family know that she has gone from being a princess to becoming a queen." He got the surprised look he expected from Feather-in-the-Wind.

"You are going to the land of the Condor! I wish I could go with you, but I know I could not even if I did not have the responsibility of the Eastern Elk Clan.

Who will be going with you," Feather-in-the-Wind inquired?

"We would love all of you to go with us but Taelo, Quiet Rabbit, Busy Bee and I discussed this at length.

We extend our invitation to Saber Scar, Marigold, Single Leaf, Sharp Blade, White Bear and Deer Chaser," Golden Hawk replied.

"So, you aren't asking your only best friend to accompany you," Burley Bear replied as he acted hurt?

Taelo had let him know ahead of time and had made the invitation but had not been surprised at Burley Bear's reply that he would stay with the Clan of Others. He was their leader and would spend the winter with the clan, *"suffering in the heated pool talking with Broken Spear."*

"Now you know why Golden Hawk and I have so far declined leading any of the clans," Taelo had replied.

"Is there room for an old woman and an old man," Floating Cloud inquired?

This surprised everyone around the fire.

"Who would that be," Quiet Rabbit asked her grandmother?

"Whistling Arrow and I have decided to be companions. Traveling with Taelo and his team has given us new life. We are in the best shape of our lives. It would be a shame for us to sit around all winter and lose it," Floating Cloud replied.

"Can you run all day and keep up with the Others," Taelo asked?

"We know she can," Single Leaf responded as she gave Floating Cloud a nod of encouragement.

"Twelve moon cycles ago I would not have even thought about it. Now after the journey here, I know that I can almost keep up with those two slow runners from the White Bear Clan that you have invited," Whistling Arrow said with a wink to the two.

"So, there we have it, the team that will go South to the land of the Condor," Taelo said as he looked around the fire ring.

Feather in the Wind stood and told the team that she and Running Stag would lead the Eastern Elk Clan to Paradise. She knew that this would ensure that Taelo and his team would have a more direct route to the land of the Condor. She looked forward to their assistance once they returned from their travels.

The End.

Taelo: Condor Clan Slingers

Dedication:
To women.
They have carried more than their share in the battles of life.

Taelo: Condor Clan Slingers

Chapter 1: Journey South

Taelo sat bolt upright, wiped the sweat running down the side of his head and oriented himself. The morning was still dark. His dream was a nightmare that had plagued him for more than a moon cycle. In his dream the spear had easily pierced through the neck of the war priest as his axe came down and ripped through Quiet Rabbit's neck. His spear killed the warrior priest, but the momentum of war priest's axe took off Quiet Rabbits head. The nightmare kept resounding and echoing through his mind.

He touched Quiet Rabbit's cheek as he listened to the night voice of a distant owl, and the periodic low cronk, cronk of a bull frog in the lake. The gentle gurgle of the water flowing over the rocks and down into the lake tried to soothe his troubled mind. He listened to Quiet Rabbit's smooth even breathing. He slowly extracted himself from the sleeping hide. He left a calmly sleeping Quiet Rabbit in the warmth of their common bed.

Quiet Rabbit's death scene was always intermingled with the ancestors talking to him. They were calling to him to travel to the land of the Condor. Their call was strong, but his nightmare was stronger and very much more troubling.

He stepped out of his hutch. The cool breeze hit the sweat on his brow and sent a chill down his back. It was a relief to be awake and aware that Quiet Rabbit was safe. He shook his head and took a last look at Quiet Rabbit as he let the exit flap loose and watched it settle into place.

He walked slowly down along the lakeside to the large boulder that had become his thinking seat. Overhead the waning moon provided enough light for him to see his way. A second moon in the middle of the lake looked coolly back at him. It made him think of the cold light of death. He realized that for once he was at a loss and he was stressed about going back to the Condor Clan.

The ancestors had been talking to him about the Condor Clan, his friends to the south. This was the land of Feather-in-the-Wind who had recently been appointed as the leader of the newly formed Eastern Elk Clan.

The Condor Clan was in trouble. They faced a serious problem and needed his help. The last thing he had said to the Ancestors was that he would make the trip to the land of the Condor, but they needed to give him guidance on how to save Quiet Rabbit.

It was then when he saw Quite Rabbit on her knees, hands bound behind her back and the beheading axe in a swing towards her neck. Taelo put his head down in his hands and tried to take the scene from his mind. He had never experienced such a nightmare.

The ancestors had simply told him to think as fast as his feet could fly. He had no idea what that simple statement meant. He would need to discuss this with Broken Spear.

The sun was cresting the white topped mountains to the east when he saw Golden Hawk, his closest friend, walking toward him. The two of them were cousins but Golden Hawk was another part of himself. They often sat together in silence until the sun was fully in view.

Taelo did not share his nightmare. He shared the call from the Ancestors to go to and help the Condor Clan and discussed who should go with them.

Golden Hawk wondered out loud what peril might be facing the Condor Clan. He had made a close friend of Feather-in-the-Wind's brother. Bold Walker and his father were both great leaders.

Golden Hawk was ready to go. He immediately brought his focus on who would go with them. He suggested Saber Scar and Marigold.

Taelo agreed and added Single Leaf and Sharp Blade.

Golden Hawk added White Bear and Deer Chaser. These two young warriors who had just been rescued on the teams last journey across the ice bridge had demonstrated their capability and deserved to be included.

Taelo suggested they had the right people and the right number, and it was time to get some food.

The two looked back to the fire pit they shared and saw that Quiet Rabbit and Busy Bee were cooking over the fire.

The two stood almost in unison and walked slowly back. They both had mates that were precious to both of them.

Floating Cloud, Quiet Rabbit's grandmother, the woman who had raised her, came over from her lodge and joined the group.

Soon after, Whistling Arrow, a leader in the White Bear Clan that had survived the brutality leveled by the Sky Eyes against his clan, and who had recently become a close companion to Floating Cloud joined them as well.

Taelo shared that the Ancestors had summoned him to go south to the land of the Condor.

"Can an old woman and an old man join you," Floating Cloud inquired?

This surprised everyone around the fire.

"Who would that be," Quiet Rabbit asked her grandmother?

"Whistling Arrow and I have decided to be companions. Traveling with Taelo and his team has given us purpose. We are in the best shape of our lives. It would be a shame for us to sit around all winter and lose it," Floating Cloud replied.

"Can you run all day and keep up with the Others," Taelo asked?

"Twelve moon cycles ago I would have not even thought about it. Now after our recent journey with you, I know that I can almost keep up with everyone but the four of you," Whistling Arrow said as he pointed them out with the sweep of his hand.

The two insisted they could keep up and would be the official cook and camp managers.

There was a moment of silence then Quite Rabbit gave Floating Cloud a hug as she said she was sure that Taelo would enjoy her cooking.

With the two new additions, the team numbered twelve in all.

Later that day, Saber Scar and Marigold, Sharp Blade, and Single Leaf, both pairs from the Clan of the Others immediately accepted the invitation. White Bear and Deer Chaser jumped in joy and rushed to share their good fortune with their friends.

Broken Spear, the seer of the Others was pleased to see that four of his clan would accompany Taelo. The Others were not as fast as those of the Elk Clan, but they were by far the strongest. Broken Spear was sure they would be essential to the travel that Taelo was planning.

Broken Spear had also heard the calling of the Ancients, but he was not sure what the problem Taelo and his team would face. This uncertainty made him want to send more of his clan. Taelo thanked him but politely declined any more members to his team. He wanted to travel as fast as possible, and he wanted a team he had experience with.

Taelo shared his vision involving Quiet Rabbit and asked if Broken Spear had any guidance.

Broken Spear used almost the same words that the ancients used. The advice he had did not make sense and Taelo knew he would chew on it until he could make sense of the statement. The only thing that Broken Spear added that provided relief was that Broken Spear saw Quiet Rabbit putting a mark on someone's forehead as the team made its way back to the north.

The team immediately began preparations. They were all veterans of the *Dangerous Passage Journey,* and their bond was that of a family. A new journey energized all of them and they looked forward to the adventure.

Lasher, Taelo's wolf companion, sensed the mood and was either following closely behind him or seated beside Quiet Rabbit. He was staying close to make sure to be on the journey as well.

Learning of the trip the team was taking brought tears to Feather-in-the-Wind. She knew she could never return to the land of the Condor. All Condor Clan members had watched as she became a living sacrifice to the Condor and was led up the mountain to the Condor's cave. Her disappearance ended one hundred cycles of sacrificing a virgin to the Condor. Her disappearance had ended the tradition. Her reappearance might restart a tradition she was pleased to have ended.

She once again thanked Quiet Rabbit and Busy Bee for bringing her down the mountain from the Condor Cave.

She was now the leader of the Eastern Elk Clan. Her Eastern Elk Clan had prospered, and new family members had joined. Her clan was now balanced. She thanked all her friends and led her clan back to the place the called Paradise.

White Swan, Taelo's mother and leader of the Northern Elk clan said her goodbye and led the Northern Elk Clan from the valley.

Wise Owl, leader of the main Elk clan did likewise.

The valley slowly emptied.

Burley Bear and Meadow Flower, and Broken Spear of the Clan of Others were the last to come by and wish the team their goodbyes.

Broken Spear quietly told Taelo, "you will all return if you are swift and use your mind to determine what the outcome must be."

Taelo knew that Broken Spear had given him one more fragment of the nightmare puzzle.

Taelo and his team stayed one more sun cycle by the lake.

Taelo, Golden Hawk and Burley Bear had made each member of the team going with him, the fighting and defense tools they would need for the trip. Taelo and Golden Hawk passed them out to the team and together they spent the day practicing their defensive fighting diamond.

High above an eagle watched as the team began their long steady jog toward the south. It followed them for more than a moon cycle.

The rising wind currents let it soar effortlessly as it watched the team once again climb the mountain to the place where the team watched the sun rise from one sea and set into the far horizon of the other sea.

This had been a story Taelo had often told and described.

The new members on this journey south were in awe as they spent the day watching the sunrise, watching its transit, and then watching the giant orb sink into the western sea.

The black of night seemed to instantly engulf them as they watched the night sky go totally dark and the southern stars twinkle and fill the black with their million points of light.

For both Clans, the stars represented the spirits of those who had gone before them. It was magical, and everyone sat close together and drowned their minds as they drank in the awe-inspiring night sky.

The next morning the team proceeded down the mountain. At the bottom they reconstructed their two-person travois to carry their gear. The role of pulling the travois rotated four times during the sunlight period. Everyone took a turn at this, the hardest job on the journey.

On this journey they had made sure to avoid the Warrior Clan. They had no wish to engage in any battles. Their goal was to visit with Feather-in-the-Wind's parents and let them know that she had ascended to the leadership of her own clan and to help in whatever problem the Condor Clan faced.

The journey south progressed smoothly, and they passed the Warrior Clan territory without incident. The journey south brought back pleasant memories of their previous visit.

Every day Taelo and team diligently practiced their diamond battle formation.

The team members wore their flat shark toothed weapon on their back. Each had a short battle spear to use when in their team battle formation. Each member also had a long fighting spear. The team often jogged along in formation when the path forward had enough room. They were a force to be reckoned with.

Saber Scar or Sharp Blade were normally at point. This ensured a formidable warrior in front. Since the jogging pace of the Others was slow relative to the pace Taelo and Golden Hawk kept, it provided the proper travel pace for the entire team.

Taelo knew they were about to get involved in some significant action, but he could not clearly put his finger on what that might be. This unknown element and his nightmare involving Quiet Rabbit made him very cautious. He had the team achieve peak battle formation performance. Taelo had shared with the team that the Condor Clan needed their help but none of them knew what might be ahead.

The unknown had put a sense of urgency into the trip that every one of the team felt. They talked about this situation as they traveled.

They had traveled cautiously past the land of the Warrior Clan and afterward traveled more rapidly for a full moon cycle. They relaxed when they reached the foothills leading to the mountains and to the land of the Condor.

High above a Condor joined the Eagle that had seemed to be their escort. The two sentinels seemed to fly in a preplanned formation. Below them, the team followed a well-traveled path as they slowly ascended the mountain.

High overhead the condor and the eagle both let out a loud cry. Lasher let out a low growling rumble in accompaniment.

The eagle's piercing cry always preceded a significant event for Taelo.

The entire team became vigilant. The eagle flying with the condor was a warning they took very seriously.

They collapsed their travois, and each carried an extra backpack. They were now moving slowly up the mountain in their diamond fighting triangle formation.

Saber Scar, on point, put up his hand to indicate that everyone should be quiet. Everyone crouched down and crawled up to where he lay on the ground looking intently ahead.

Golden Hawk gazed out over the valley where thousands of warriors and their cohorts were camped. The view was a shock. The campfires, spread out across the entire valley, were too numerous to count. It was clear to the team that the warriors mingling around the various campfires were not Feather-in-the-Wind's people. These were the members of the Warrior Clan.

Taelo slowly scanned the valley below as he stroked Lasher and kept him quiet. The team was silent. Taelo signaled for them to back away from the ridge.

He then took his time as he studied the layout and the number of campsites. It was now clear to him why the ancients had reached into his mind and called him south into the mountains.

The debris, the odor and general poor condition of the valley indicated that the Warrior clan had camped for several moons. Feather-in-the-Wind's people had successfully held the Warrior Clan at bay but evidently could not drive them off.

The bridge across the bottomless crevasse was gone. There would be no way for the attacking Warrior Clan to cross over into the Condor Clan's village.

Taelo estimated that there were thirty thousand warriors spread across the valley. This was a phenomenal number and showed the seriousness of the situation. It was clear the Warrior Clan had come to conquer the Condor Clan.

The Ancients had sent him to change the situation. At the moment he had no idea how he would be able to help against such a superior number of fighters.

Taelo and Golden Hawk led the team down around the mountain toward the backdoor of the Condor Clan's village. Taelo and Golden Eagle had learned of the backdoor from Bold Walker on their previous visit.

They stayed out of sight. As evening arrived, the team stopped behind a large cluster of boulders and prepared a fireless campsite. Their evening meal would be jerky and water.

It was important they were not seen or captured.

They were only twelve. They could out fight multiple of their number, but they needed to get into the Condor Clan's land where they could determine how they could best be of help.

Taelo, Golden Hawk and Saber Scar each led a night watch team.

The high mountain night was chillingly cold. Beneath their sleeping hide, Quiet Rabbit snuggled close to Taelo. Each couple had found a sheltered place among the boulders. The camp, even in daylight, would have been invisible.

Except for the natural noises, night passed quietly and without incident. They had not expected any problems but had planned for the worst. What they had found the day before was beyond what they had expected.

After a quick morning meal, the team proceeded to the back, Condor Clan entrance. Taelo hoped that the Warrior Clan did not know about this back approach to the mountain kingdom. Taelo was pleased to see no Warrior Clan members in the area. This meant that the backdoor was still accessible.

Taelo also knew that Condor Clan warriors would be guarding this entrance.

The team proceeded with caution around the base of the mountain. They then slowly made their way up toward the point that Taelo referred to as the backdoor.

This was not an obvious way in. The bottomless crevasse was at least a spear length across. When closely examined there was a very narrow ledge on the cliff wall on the other side of the crevasse.

It was clear that the Warrior Clan had not discovered this way in.

The team peered down into what appeared to be a bottomless crack in the earth. Quiet Rabbit recalled the time Burley Bear had dropped a stone the size of his fist down into this crack. They had never heard the stone hit bottom.

Taelo told the team to wait while he went ahead to contact the Condor Clan.

Feather-in-the-Wind's brother, Bold Walker had demonstrated how to navigate the back door. It was a leap, the length of a spear to a small ledge. The trick was to leap across and thrust one hand into the crack in the wall and immediately make a fist. This provided the way to get one's balance for the walk along the narrow path.

The ledge was wide enough for a person to shuffle sideways until the path widened. The path then turned and came out into a flat open area. On the far side of the flat area the path went upward to a plateau. Once the trail surfaced on a plateau, the village was to the left and on the far side. There were several plateau's between the first one and the one that held the Condor Clan village. It took about a day to make the journey.

Taelo walked to the jump point. He told Lasher to stay and guard Quiet Rabbit. Lasher seemed to understand. Taelo wondered if Lasher remembered being carried across this crevasse.

Taelo remembered Feather-in-the-Wind's advice about ignoring the chasm below and focusing only on the crack in the stone. She had said it was kid's play. No kid had ever fallen.

He made the leap, wedged his hand in and closed it into a fist. After a deep breath he proceeded along the narrow path and around the bend to the flat area.

Taelo looked back at his team and signaled to them. He knew that his next step would be met by a group of very nervous Condor Clan fighters. He called out in their language that a friend, Taelo from the North, was about to step around the corner.

He then slowly stepped around the corner. As expected, spears were immediately on his chest. Taelo quietly gave a greeting of friendship. One of the young warriors recognized him and the spears immediately pointed up to the sky.

Taelo let out a sigh of relief.

Taelo explained that he was part of a twelve-person team. They would all need to come across to safety.

One of the Condor Clan members went back along the narrow path and set himself up as a helper. As he left the rest, he made the point that the Condor Clan could not afford to lose any friends.

Taelo positioned himself on the other side of the crack. One by one the team members made the leap and went to the flat area around the bend.

Taelo then made the leap back across and quietly talked to Lasher. He let him know that he would not have to jump. Lasher had a low rumble coming up from deep in his chest as he hung in the sling and was slowly pulled to the other side. He patiently waited until he was released. He then quickly navigated the narrow trail and disappeared around the bend.

Taelo chuckled when he saw Quiet Rabbit calming Lasher.

The team was now safe and Taelo could relax for the moment.

A runner had immediately set out to the village center. Even as Taelo's team was making their crossing into the land of the Condor Clan, the Clan leadership was learning of Taelo's arrival.

Bold Walker, brother of Feather-in-the-Wind and Neiva-of-the-Stream, her mother, set out immediately to greet Taelo and his team.

Their early arrival, the next day, was a joyful reunion. It was the first time that Neiva had a chance to thank Quiet Rabbit, Busy Bee, Golden Hawk and Taelo for saving her daughter from becoming a frozen offering to the Condor.

Feather-in-the-Wind's disappearance, from the ice-cold cave at the top of the mountain, was interpreted to mean that the Condor had finally accepted the offering of the most desirable young virgin and taken her as his queen. Future offerings would not be needed. The more than one hundred-year-old tradition came to a close. A celebration by all the families in the Condor Clan followed.

The team humbly received Neiva's thank you.

They in turn shared the many accomplishments of Feather-in-the-Wind.

Saber Scar pointed to the two paw scars that crisscrossed his chest and told the story of Feather-in-the-Wind using herself as a spear to hit the giant lion on its side knocking the lion away from him. She saved his life. She saved his life but broke several of her ribs.

Marigold added that they celebrated each major season cycle with a dinner in Feather-in-the-Wind's honor. Feather-in-the-Wind had their lifelong allegiance.

Taelo told the story of how Feather-in-the-Wind had distracted a giant brown bear. This distraction had given him a chance to kill it. She had received a life-threatening gash across her inner thigh. Her behavior during her recovery inspired everyone around her.

Quiet Rabbit and Busy Bee continued telling the stories of how popular Feather-in-the-Wind had become among all the Elk Clan members.

She had taught them how to make the clay pots and bowls that she learned by watching her mother. She had become one of the best at using the sling. She could stand on the back of a running mount and hit her target. Many of the young girls of the Elk Clan who had learned to use the sling idolized her.

Marigold told the story of how Feather-in-the-Wind had leaped into the air and speared the giant alligator into the ground. This had again saved Saber Scar and had given Marigold the chance to kill the nasty beast by smashing in its skull.

Taelo then let them know of Feather-in-the-Wind's appointment to be the Eastern Elk Clan's Leader. She was the second woman to become an Elk Clan leader. His mother White Swan had been the first.

Both Bold Walker and Neiva were in awe as they learned of Feather-in-the-Wind's many heroic actions and her ascent to Clan Leader. They remembered her as the petite and fragile young girl. It was hard for them to imagine the powerful young woman and take in all her accomplishments.

Taelo closed by pointing to Lasher and shared that Feather-in-the-Wind had a similar companion that she had named Bold Walker.

This put a smile on Bold Walker.

Neiva had tears of joy in her eyes as she once again hugged each of the team members and whispered a thank you.

Bold Walker stood and said he wished Feather-in-the-Wind could be back here to somehow change the grim situation the Condor Clan was currently facing. He spent the time to slowly explain the situation.

Taelo shared the call the Ancients made to him to make this visit. And the fact they had let him know the Condor Clan needed his help.

Taelo asked what had caused the current situation.

Bold Walker replied that an ambitious new leader killed Tough Hide the Warrior Clan Leader that Taelo had met and befriended. This new leader had decided that it was time to expand the Warrior Clan territory.

Bold Walker went on to explain that this past summer season the Warrior Clan had insisted that the Condor Clan pay tribute to the Warrior Clan or face retribution. This came as a surprise since the Condor Clan had not traded with the Warrior Clan since your last visit.

Star Leaper, leader of the Condor Clan had sent back a message to the Warrior Clan that they should remember the last time the two clans had engaged in battle and the humiliation the Warrior Clan had experienced at that time. He hoped that they would not make that mistake happen again.

A few moon cycles later the Warrior Clan arrived and set up camp in the valley beyond.

After a moment of silence, Taelo inquired about the plan to drive the Warrior Clan off the mountain.

Bold Walker expressed his frustration with the clan leaders. They could not seem to align on any confrontational actions. The Seer of the Condor Clan had announced that help from the North would arrive to solve the standoff.

Bold Walker replied that he had been waiting for Taelo to arrive.

Taelo's team discussed the situation on their walk to the village. They agreed that the entire Warrior Clan army was waiting to fight the Condor Clan. They outnumbered the Condor Clan by at least five to one and probably many times more in the warrior ranks.

The fact that the Condor Clan expected Taelo and his team to resolve the situation astounded the team. How could another twelve people and one wolf make the needed difference?

Taelo looked over at Golden Hawk and smiled. He told Golden Hawk to figure out what to do. He looked at the rest of the team and suggested they all contribute to figuring out how to guide the Condor Clan in driving the Warrior Clan off the mountain.

High above the Eagle let out a piercing cry as it followed the Condor out of sight.

Lasher gave a low growl and rubbed against Quiet Rabbit's leg.

Chapter 2: The Condor Village

The team had camped in the flat area just across the crevasse referred to as the backdoor. After a morning meal, Taelo and the rest of the team carefully cleaned up their area of the camp.

Soon after they began their journey up the trail toward the Condor Clan village.

The trail wound its way up a narrow knife cut crack in an otherwise solid vertical cliff. Additional guards along the narrow upward trail augmented the backdoor guards that remained below.

Every few yards a warrior of the Condor Clan sat or stood with spears stacked up against the stone and with a war hammer in hand. Taelo noted that there would be no backdoor surprise by the Warrior Clan, and he was certain none would survive the climb up the trail.

The trail ahead inclined and narrowed until it surfaced on a large broad flat area. To Taelo it appeared that in some ancient time a section of the mountain had collapsed and left this almost square surface perched and clinging to the mountain side.

It became obvious to Taelo and his team that the terrain ahead of them seemed similarly formed and that they were climbing from one plateau to another.

Taelo took notice that at every plateau transition a group of well-armed warriors protected the next level up. Each level would pose a major obstacle to any enemy fighters trying to make their way in.

He praised Bold Walker about the excellent way he had stationed these warriors.

Bold Walker gave the credit to his father's guidance in developing the defense strategy.

Taelo sensed Bold Walker had some issue with the current situation that the Condor Clan faced. Bold Walker had seemed reticent about talking about the current situation.

Taelo asked for Bold Walker to describe the situation starting with the time since the Warrior Clan had arrived. For the rest of the day as they made their way up to the village center Bold Walker talked and Taelo listened. He made mental notes about the situation. He had correctly sensed a misalignment of the way Bold Walker felt and about the fact that of most leaders had chosen to wait and see if the Warrior Clan would just tire of sitting across from the village entrance and choose to leave.

Bold Walker wanted to take a more aggressive approach.

Bold Walker guided them to the Condor Clan meeting square where Star Leaper, his father, and a small entourage of village leaders were waiting to greet Taelo and his team.

Taelo approached Star Leaper who stepped down from the leader's seat and gave Taelo a welcome embrace. Star Leaper then welcomed and embraced each of Taelo's team members.

Taelo noticed that Star Leaper was greatly overshadowed by the size of the Others Clan members and was of equal size to Quiet Rabbit and Busy Bee. This fact was only noticeable when he was at the same levels as the people around him.

Taelo and team could not openly share the stories about Feather-in-the-Wind with the broader leadership group. They knew that they would again get a chance when they met with just her family members.

Instead Taelo engaged the leadership in discussion of the strategy currently in use against the Warrior Clan.

It was soon clear to Taelo and his team members that there was no clear alignment to any battle strategy. Most leaders had a wait and see attitude and no energy for some counter measure against the Warrior Clan.

Their main idea was to hope for the hard winter weather to discourage the Warrior Clan.

Taelo refrained from making any suggestions, but it was clear to him why Bold Walker was frustrated with the lack of leadership action.

Bold Walker listened closely to Taelo's questions and soon realized that Taelo was sizing up each of the leaders. He noticed how Taelo's team sat quietly but sometimes asked follow-up questions from certain leaders.

A full-scale evaluation of the Condor Clan's leadership was underway giving Bold Walker new hope.

This was the first time Bold Walker realized how skillfully Taelo pulled out the information that was of interest to him. He was also impressed how the whole team interacted with the Condor Clan's leadership.

Quiet Rabbit was disarming in her gentle way of asking clarifying questions. Busy Bee came with a more energetic, charming approach. Both were able to expose a lack of depth, drive, or direction in the Condor Clan's various leaders.

Golden Hawk was the counter direction inquisitor. He seemed to be at odds with Taelo but in fact was able to solicit information that would otherwise not have surfaced. He would ask questions like; "Should we wait for the winter weather to convince the Warrior Clan to leave?"

Saber Scar and Meadow Flower did not ask questions but would make various sounds based on the conversation that was occurring. They had the effect of either supporting a response, or of putting it in doubt. Bold Walker was amazed at the information they were able to surface even though the two never said a word.

By the end of the impromptu meeting, Bold Walker knew Taelo, and his team would change the current stalemate between the two opposing Clans.

After the meeting ended, Bold Walker led the team to their quarters. They approached the same home they had used on their previous visit to the Condor Clan. From the veranda the view fell across a deep valley with a dark green forest that met the vertical face of the next mountain range at the far limit of Taelo's vision. Taelo spent many hours letting his eyes scan the valley length while his mind absorbed the enriching essence of the mist that seemed to hide secrets and encouraged the viewer to discover them.

The team set up camp in the courtyard at the side of the main structure.

Bold Walker felt invigorated with the greeting session.

When the stars began to twinkle, and the evening ended he made sure that Taelo understood that he wanted to participate in the follow up discussions that team would have.

Taelo assured him that he would be in the center of anything the team came up with.

Taelo, with Quiet Rabbit at his side stood out on the veranda looking up at the stars in the sky. He commented that the Ancestors lighting up the night were different than the ones in the sky above their home. These Ancestors must be worried about the situation they saw below them.

The night gave way to a cool morning breeze that lightly brushed across Quiet Rabbit's face. She had fallen asleep next to him out on the veranda. She savored the feel of Taelo's powerful arm around her. His warmth, his breathing rhythm encompassed her being.

She was on one side and on the other side, Lasher had his head on Taelo's chest and was looking at her.

She delayed getting up to savor the moment. She could see the rest of the camp slowly awaken and begin the morning preparations. Her grandmother looked over to her and smiled. It was clear she understood.

Taelo was aware of Quiet Rabbit's wakefulness and chose to enjoy remaining embraced with her. He knew that once awake, he would be leading an all-day long discussion on how the team would help the Condor Clan in their battle against the Warrior Clan.

Taelo turned slowly toward Quiet Rabbit and looked into her eyes. No words but a direct soul to soul connection electrified him. He had the only reward and motivation he needed for all the journeys he would make in this world.

Floating Cloud called out that the morning meal was ready. The team eagerly gathered around the courtyard area. They all knew this would be an invigorating but long day.

Taelo lightly brushed his hand across Quiet Rabbit's cheek and then lightly traced her eyebrows with his finger as he raised himself on one elbow and then stood up. He reached down to help Quiet Rabbit up.

Lasher placed himself between them and they both scratched him behind his ears.

The view across the valley was blocked by a low layer of clouds. The sun lit the cloud tops with a yellow, pink, and greyish hue. The clouds seemed to be a blanket meant to warm the far snow-covered mountains. The morning breeze slowly transformed and evolved the view to the far mountain tops. The impact on the eye and mind was that of slowly undulating waves washing up the shore and slowly wearing boulders into sand. It continually changed and challenged the mind to make sense of what the eye took in.

Taelo felt a surge of inspiration and a desire to ensure the success of the Condor Clan.

Taelo turned and hand in hand with Quiet Rabbit walked to where the rest of the team was well into their morning meal.

Golden Hawk was sitting next to Busy Bee. The two were seldom far from each other. He knew that today Taelo would determine on how to deal with the Warrior Clan.

He gave an almost invisible nod to Taelo and watched his friend respond in kind. He and Taelo were as close to each other as they were to their mates. There was nothing that would stand between them.

Before turning in for the night, Bold Walker had returned to his father and let him know that he was going to work with Taelo and his team on a battle plan for the Condor Clan. He wanted his father to support the plan then present it to the Clan leadership.

His father at first was hesitant but once Neiva interjected that this was the team who had saved their daughter and that he should support the battle plan effort. Star Leaper smiled and reassured both that he was open to Taelo and his team's battle plans.

He would be supportive but asked that he be allowed to review the plan before it was finished. He wanted the opportunity to review and input to it while the team was still open to his input.

Bold Walker agreed to that condition and thanked him, gave Neiva a hug and went to his quarters for the night.

Bold Walker woke early. He immediately left his home and walked down to the villa provided to Taelo. He was sure that Taelo's team would be up having their morning meal.

He walked into the courtyard and greeted everyone in Taelo's language. He had learned just enough to say, "good morning" and "could he join them in their morning meal." He was proud to have remembered that much since the last time Taelo had been in the village.

Taelo replied in Bold Walker's language that he certainly could.

The members in the camp all came over and greeted Bold Walker. Taelo had Bold Walker sit between he and Golden Hawk.

Taelo then began to engage the team by asking them their view of the current situation facing the Condor Clan.

The silence went on so long that Bold Walker wondered if anyone would speak.

He was just about to repeat Taelo's question when the woman he knew as Quiet Rabbit's grandmother spoke.

The fact that she was, in the view of most in the Condor Clan's culture, "too old" to be on a journey that she was engaged in, made Bold Walker listen carefully.

Floating Cloud began by pointing out that there seemed to be a very large contingent of the Warrior Clan camped out across the crevice that protected the Condor Clan village. She raised the point that the logistics for food must be very difficult. She wondered how many of the Warrior Clan were engaged in the movement of food.

This broke the ice, and the rest of the team became engaged.

Saber Scar wondered how many of the Warrior Clan members remained back at their village to protected it.

Sharp Knife suggested that disrupting delivery of food would have a significant negative effect on those camped across the crevice.

Each team member shared an observation or supported what was already shared.

After everyone had engaged in the input, Taelo invited anyone interested to join him on a jog through the village and along the edge of the plateau on which the village was situated.

He then left the courtyard knowing that Golden Hawk, Busy Bee, and Quiet Rabbit would follow. The surprise was that Floating Cloud and Whistling Arrow stood up to follow him. He knew that those of the Others would most likely not join.

Bold Walker, White Bear and Deer Chaser were the other persons who followed Taelo out of the courtyard.

Taelo and Golden Hawk had jogged the path they were on almost every day of their previous visit. They glided smoothly as they matched their steps to each other. Taelo maintained a smooth leisurely rhythm. He was out for an easy workout, and he knew they would all be watched by many of the village members.

He was right as almost the entire Condor Clan observed the nine joggers and wondered what they were doing.

Taelo and Golden Hawk were silent. Bold Walker had expected a discussion about the Condor Clan situation to occur but there was none.

White Bear and Deer Chaser were silent as well but were not surprised about Taelo's and Golden Hawk's behavior. Sometimes they had jogged behind the two and never heard a word spoken.

Taelo knew that word would have gone out to the Condor Clan population. He was jogging for his own conditioning and the conditioning of the Condor Clan population. They would see Bold Walker jogging with them. It was a visible show of unity. Bold Walker would become the focus point and be asked about what was going on.

The sun was approaching its zenith when the team returned to their villa courtyard.

Taelo did not stop but ran past the villa to the point where the bridge normally spanned the crevasse. He turned to those jogging with him and signaled for the team to give their battle cry. In unison the team gave their battle cry three times.

To Taelo's surprise two horns blew from the Condor Clan home of Star Leaper and Neiva. The long, high pitched tone engulfed the valley and echoed back from the mountains beyond.

Taelo again led the battle cry. This time it was accompanied by more horns.

The Warrior Clan camp had come to life as more than sixty of their top warriors heard the cry that they clearly recalled and that still haunted them. They remembered the last time they heard that war cry and the humiliation they had experience in trying to battle with Taelo and his team.

It was a battle cry that they had later heard again when Taelo killed their leader.

Now as they heard it again, dread went through their minds. They all still wore the wristbands of friendship they had received from Taelo and his team. They considered them badges of honor presented to them by Taelo.

In an instant, the situation changed dramatically for them. The battle was now a very personal one. The leader of the sixty that wore the band of friendship was the eldest son of the Tough Hide, who had been killed by the current leader of the Warrior Clan. He had been one of those against what was now in action.

He now felt that the odds had changed from a certainty that the Warrior Clan would win to one that somehow favored the Condor Clan.

Taelo then shouted out across the crevasse in the language of the Warrior Clan for them to go home or half of them would carry home the wounded other half and their dead. He added that this would be his only warning. His next actions would be to start sending them home to be buried.

The Warrior Clan members who knew Taelo went to their battle leaders to report that Taelo had somehow arrived and entered the Condor Clan enclave.

They advised the leaders to heed the warning.

They were listened to but ignored.

The war leaders discounted the message and deemed the warriors giving them this advice to be weak. They questioned their loyalty.

The Warrior Clan leaders decided to wait and see what would happen before they took any actions.

Taken aback by Taelo's action, Bold Walker was none the less overjoyed. He had not expected such a display. Looking around, he could tell that this was normal for Taelo's team.

For him, the bigger surprise had been the horns blowing from the veranda of his parent's home. And then the added horns from other villagers. Bold Walker was proud of this display of support.

The Condor Clan members who had been following the team jog quickly spread the word about the engagement of the Warrior Clan. The news of Star Leaper and Nieva blowing their horns in support electrified the whole village. They anticipated a change in their current situation.

Bold Walker excused himself as the team returned to the Villa courtyard for the next meal. He went immediately to his father to thank him for his show of support.

He was pleased with his father's laugh and encouragement to continue to work with Taelo. Nieva just gave him a hug. Both were eager to hear what he and Taelo's team would recommend.

Bold Walker hurried back to the Villa. He did not want to miss the discussion among Taelo's team that he expected would occur.

Taelo casually strolled back to the villa. It was time to formulate a plan and then to act. He was pleased to see that the rest of the team had prepared a succulent honey roast of llama for the zenith meal.

Saber Scar and those remaining at the villa had heard their team give the battle cry and had commented that Taelo would now be expecting the team to take action.

Taelo announced to everyone that once everyone had eaten, they would begin to plan for the removal of the Warrior Clan from the Condor mountain kingdom.

Bold Walker arrived in time to hear Taelo make the announcement. He sat down to enjoy the succulent honey glazed llama roast. It was hard for him to wait. He had waited for what seemed an eternity to take action against he the Warrior Clan.

He eagerly accepted a piece of llama roast and sat down on the low veranda wall. It was the first time in weeks that he felt relaxed. He had never eaten llama cooked in this fashion and commented on how good it tasted.

Floating Cloud thanked him for the compliment and brought over another piece.

Taelo knew the frustration of being overridden by the older clan leaders. He had learned long ago to influence and not directly confront the key leaders. Once they were convinced of the positive, these leaders in turn would normally carry his plan to the appropriate conclusion.

He surprised Bold Walker by asking about the leaders in the Condor Clan who would listen to him.

Bold Walker laughed in surprise. He had not expected to talk but to listen. He asked for a moment to think through how he would answer.

A few moments later Bold Walker began to describe the leadership situation. His father was the most powerful. However, his mother could get his father to do whatever Taelo or whatever Quiet Rabbit or Busy Bee would suggest. His mother credited them with saving her daughter and would forever support them.

Two more of the top leaders desired to take some sort of direct action against the Warrior Clan.

His father and these two, together always got their way.

The remaining members of the leadership team normally backed these three but there were two who always seemed to question what the rest of the leadership did.

Taelo nodded. This was similar to all the leadership teams that he had experienced.

He turned to Golden Hawk and asked him for his plan to attack the Warrior Clan back at their home.

The question surprised Bold Walker. Up to this time he had not heard a word about such an attack. All eyes turned to Golden Hawk.

In fact, this was a surprise to Golden Hawk, but he was prepared. The question raised by Floating Cloud and Saber Scar had made him think through how to disrupt the flow of food to the Warrior Clan.

Golden Hawk stood up and described how he would lead three fighting teams, thirty fighters in all, back to the Warrior Clan home. The teams would scout the area and determine the best means to attack the village.

The attack would be a rapid invasion and before any battle engagement could happen, they would retreat and leave the village. They would set fire to as much of the village as possible. They would pour llama urine into as many grain rooms as possible.

Golden Hawk went on to describe their continuing attacks on the supply line of food and goods being sent to the Warrior Clan. They would disrupt and if possible, stop the flow of food and supplies to the Warrior Clan on the Condor Clan territory.

Taelo smiled. Gave Golden Hawk a nod and thanked him.

He turned to Quiet Rabbit and Busy Bee. He inquired about protecting the two Condor llama herds.

This was a point that he and Quiet Rabbit had discussed.

Quiet Rabbit nodded to Busy Bee who then described how each of them would lead a fighting team to the two major Condor llama herds to protect them from the Warrior Clan. They anticipated the Warrior Clan would move to try for the herds once Golden Hawk disrupted the supply lines.

Once they were at the herd's location, they would train the herders how to fight to protect the herds. This would give each of them the equivalent of three fighting diamonds for each herd.

Taelo thanked Quiet Rabbit and Busy Bee.

Bold Walker looked around and wondered what was meant by the fighting diamonds.

He was in awe at the way Taelo guided his team.

Taelo turned to the rest of the team. He announced that each of them would train a battle team of nine fighters. They would each develop a Condor warrior to be the leader of that team.

Golden Hawk would leave immediately with three teams and train them on the way to the Warrior Clan Village.

Busy Bee and Quiet Rabbit would spend seven sun cycles working with their two teams and then move out to protect the llama herds.

Everyone else would spend the coming seven sun cycles working with their teams.

Nine fighting diamond teams would attack the Warrior Clan from the sides and rear.

The way of retreat for the Warrior Clan fighters to the top plateau area would be left open. The goal was to allow the Warrior Clan to disengage from battle.

Taelo hoped that this would encourage the Warrior Clan to choose to depart.

If a full battle took place, the Condor Clan fighters would slowly work their way up the cliff side of the valley.

Taelo stopped talking and quietly looked at each individual member of his team.

He then stood in front of Bold Walker and asked whether he could leap the crevasse as he had boasted he could and were there others who could do the same?

Bold Walker stood up and smiled. He had done just that multiple times as he grew up.

He put his hand on Taelo's shoulder let out a chuckle and slowly announced the names of the other nine people that would be on his team. He said there were many more if needed.

This response gave Taelo what he needed to make the plan work.

The villa courtyard was abuzz with discussion among the team members. Taelo turned from Bold Walker and called for attention.

He went on to declare that the goal was to wound but not kill anyone.

Bold Walker asked about the do not kill part of the fighting.

Taelo pointed out that a wounded fighter required attention. This attention required resources that could not be focused on the battle at hand. It would have a significant effect on how the enemy had to use its resources. The plan would be to attack and retreat and repeat the action as often as possible and wound as many as possible.

A war cry would precede each attack. On each retreat they would give the same battle cry.

All ten teams would act in unison.

The ten teams would space themselves evenly around the Warrior Clan. After the third battle cry the teams, if necessary, would retreat down the mountain and around to the back entrance. Taelo's team would ensure that the Warrior Clan fighters did not follow. Bold Walker would lead the rest back into the Condor village.

Taelo asked for input to the plan. The Villa courtyard was abuzz.

Quiet Rabbit and Busy Bee stepped forward. Quiet Rabbit said that they had an important suggestion. They wanted to include slingers, slinging glass shards as an integral part of the battle formation.

They recalled the effect that slingers had when the team had faced the Sky Eyes in their last journey. They suggested that these slingers be the women of the Condor Clan and that Single Leaf be the trainer for these slingers.

There was a moment of silence followed by enthusiastic support from the rest of the team. Single Leaf grunted and smiled at Quiet Rabbit and Busy Bee. She was honored. The two had taught her to sling.

Taelo let the discussions go on until he sensed a decline in volume. He agreed with the suggestion of including the glass slingers There would be one sling team associated with each of the fighting diamonds.

He then went on to highlight two rescue teams to carry off any hurt Condor Clan warriors. Also, there would be a contingent of replacement warriors that would step into the fight formation that had lost a fighter. The thought of needing rescue or additional fighters brought silence into the courtyard.

Taelo turned to Brave Walker and asked if he would take the plan for approval to the Condor Clan leadership. He indicated that it was now up to the Condor Clan to embrace the plan, supply the warriors, the slingers, and the weapons.

Brave Walker said he would return with the approval and support of the Condor Leadership.

What he did not voice was the concern about having women slingers in battle. He could not recall either of the clans that were about to battle having women on the battlefield.

This part of the plan needed his mother's absolute support. His next stop was to see her.

Chapter 3: Preparation for Battle

Taelo knew that the Condor Clan politics was similar to that of the Elk Clan or the Clan of Others. There would be those who liked the power but never liked to rock the boat. They supported the status quo. There would be those who liked to block and counter the current leadership. They sought attention to their viewpoints and used the moments of key decisions to get something they wanted. And there were those who wanted to be on the "winning" side. They evaluated the situation and whenever possible aligned with the group they thought would prevail. Finally, there was the group who acted on principle and logic and sought to take the actions that would benefit their clan.

Bold Walker had shared the battle plan with Star Leaper and Neiva.

Neiva immediately latched on to the women slingers. She immediately volunteered to lead them. This was her opportunity to elevate the status of the women in the Condor Clan and she could not, would not pass it by.

Star Leaper agreed and suggested that the women slingers be placed between each of the battle triangles. He said he really liked the logic of the plan and would make sure it got the leadership team agreement. He would talk to those who usually supported him, and he would arrange to handle those that usually opposed.

Start Leaper and Neiva returned with Bold Walker to ask Taelo to accompany the three of them to the meeting. It was time for the council to act.

They all walked up to the meeting platform. Once they were situated, Star Leaper stretched out his arms and let out the cry of the Condor. The meeting area became silent.

Star Leaper formally introduced Taelo who sat at his right with Bold Walker. His key advisor sat to his left. Neiva sat to the left of the advisor. Once the meeting area was silent, Star Leaper recounted the interaction the Condor Clan had experienced with the Warrior Clan. He made the point that the Warrior Clan had arrived and immediately attacked the Condor Clan. They had given no warning. There was no dialogue. Only the quick thinking of the Condor Clan bridge guards, who had cut the cable as the first Wave of Warriors made their way across, saved the village.

He pointed out that the Condor Clan had waited patiently in hopes that the Warrior Clan would decide to return to their own lands. But as all could see the Warrior Clan was still camped out on other side of the crevasse.

He pointed to Taelo and identified him as a good friend from the north. He went on to describe how the Ancients had asked Taelo to return to the land of the Condor Clan and help to resolve the problem.

He made the point that Taelo had not been sure what help was expected of him, but he had chosen to come. He shared how the Seer of the Clan of Others reinforced the call of the Ancients and insisted four members of the Clan of Others accompany Taelo and his team.

Star Leaper pointed to Bold Walker and said he was a key Condor Clan member working with Taelo and his team to develop a way to send the Warrior Clan back to their own lands. They all agreed that the Condor Clan did not want a full-scale battle with the Warrior Clan. They too felt that too many of the Condor Clan warriors would be injured or killed if they were to take and engage in a direct attack..

Star Leaper paused then he went on to declare that it was time to act.

He turned to Bold Walker and Taelo and asked them to share their plan to cause the Warrior Clan to want to leave. Star Leaper reinforced the fact that the plan Bold Walker was about to present focused, on no Condor Clan losses, and that the plan recognized the superior number of warriors waiting on the other side, but that it presented an approach to soundly defeat the Warrior Clan.

Star Leaper looked around at the silent gathering. He could see his opposition muttering and talking to each other. He turned and handed his staff to Brave Walker and sat slowly down on his granite seat.

Bold Walker stood and slowly walked around the platform overlooking the seated leaders. He had felt that Taelo should do the talking but Taelo had pointed out how important it was for a Condor Clan member to present the plan to the Condor Leadership.

His eyes met Taelo's as he returned to the front of the gathering. He turned to face the leadership members and slowly and clearly shared the battle strategy and the battle plan

He made the point that the plan was simple.

First, the Condor Clan would attack the Warrior Clan's home. Golden Hawk would lead three Condor Clan fighting teams to make this attack. They would leave immediately upon approval from the leadership team. This attack was designed to harass and to disrupt the flow of supplies but not to engage in battle.

After disrupting the Warrior Clan village, they would stay to the North along the supply trail and attack the Warrior Clan's supply line. The Warrior Clan would need to deploy guards to ensure the flow of goods along their supply line.

This served two purposes. First it would pull some fighters away from the battlefield. Second it would make it hard to keep the fighters fed.

Second, two fighting diamonds would go out to protect the Condor Clan's own food supply. Each would go to one of the two grazing areas. They would train the herders in the use of the fighting diamond to protect themselves. This would create three fighting diamonds to protect each of the Llama herds.

Third, a first attack by ten fighting diamonds would be launched to drive the Warrior Clan away from the crevasse bridge crossing area. They would engage in hit and run tactics and not engage in any hand-to-hand fighting. The goal would be to push the Warrior Clan away from the Crevasse up to the far end of the valley. This position conceded the higher ground to the Warrior Clan, but it then allowed the bridge across the crevasse to be rebuilt.

Finally, the Condor Clan would attack the Warrior Clan in a full-scale confrontation. Ten fighting diamonds and ten glass slinging teams would confront the Warrior Clan. The glass shard slingers would keep the Warriors at bay. The fighting diamonds would engage any Warrior Clan fighters that make it through the glass shard barrier.

Brave Walker went on to describe the approach of slowly moving forward with the glass slingers taking out the front Warrior Clan fighters. The goal was to wound the warriors facing them.

Once he had shared the plan, he immediately handed the leader's staff to Star Leaper and sat down.

Star Leaper stood and asked what a glass slinger happened to be and who would they be.

Bold Walker took the talking staff but immediately passed it Nieva.

Nieva stood and pointed to ten gourds mounted on poles at the far side of the square. She pointed at Single Leaf on other side of the square. The distance was three spear throws in distance.

Nieva let out Taelo's war cry. Single Leaf took two steps as she whirled her sling and released the shards. In rapid succession she did it nine more times. Nieva accompanied each sling with a war cry. The gourd targets exploded into blossoms as they were hit with the class shards.

Nieva stood in silence as the demonstration sunk into the leaders. Such a weapon was new to them, and its devastation was immediately obvious. It seemed to be a weapon that would change how battles would be fought.

Nieva continued to explain that women slingers would be used in the final confrontation with the Warrior Clan. They would be at the front of the Condor Clan army. She went on to boast that these Condor Clan women would be the reason for victory.

Taelo felt a surge of pride as he understood the dynamic shift in the battle plans that Quiet Rabbit and Busy Bee had suggested.

He was also enjoying the mixed reaction of the leadership team.

There was a moment of shocked silence. It was a realization that this was not a request for permission. Finally, Taelo got the sense of pride most of the leadership team was showing.

Bold Walker accepted the talking staff back from Nieva and went on to describe the process of slowly moving forward with the glass slingers taking out the front Warrior Clan fighters. The slingers would blast these fighters with glass shards before the diamond fighters could launch their spears.

The leadership team leaned forward to listen to this new wrinkle in fighting the battle.

The sling teams whether on attack or in retreat would continuously be slinging a cloud of glass shards at the Warrior Clan.

Bold Walker concluded his explanation of the plan and immediately handed the leader's staff to Star Leaper.

Star Leaper stood and in a voice of disbelief questioned having women in the front of the battle line. He stopped for a moment to take in the reaction of the leadership team. He then smiled and commented that it made so much sense. Women always won the arguments in the homes he was familiar with. He praised the concept of women slingers. He made the point that the Warrior Clan would be in for a major surprise. He gave his opinion that the slingers would be the most lethal weapon the Warrior Clan had ever faced.

He asked each leader to respond to the battle plan and having women in battle. He called out the response order of the leaders. He had his two solid supporters at the front of the response list. He passed the talking staff to his first supporter.

It became clear to Star Leaper that a close divide existed among the leadership team. The opposition was predictably led by his long-time rival known as Rolling Stone. Star Leaper thought the name very appropriate since Rolling Stone was always a stone, he had to roll aside to get things done. It became clear that Rolling Stone needed to be discredited in some way if the leadership council were to support the plan.

Star Leaper's signal to commence with his prearranged plan went un-noticed.

Suddenly a loud commotion disrupted the leadership meeting as two women came running into the meeting arena, arguing, and pointing at Rolling Stone. They made loud accusations against his character and how badly he had treated them. They were accusing him of marrying them both while he had another wife in his home. It was clear that they were agitated and very mad at him. They insisted the leadership team censure him and not allow him a voice in the decision that faced them. They made the point that he was unworthy of his position.

Star Leaper pointed at the two women and ordered them out of the meeting area. He ordered two guards to escort the two still arguing, shouting, and pointing, women out of the meeting area.

This kind of disruption had never been experienced in a leadership meeting. Everyone was watching Rolling Stone, a known womanizer, to see what he would do. Rolling Stone proceeded to loudly claim he had no clue what the women were accusing him of having done.

Star Leaper took the opportunity to act. He voiced his support of Rolling Stone and said it was not appropriate for the women to have disrupted the meeting and that he should retain his voting right.

He then called for a vote of confidence in the proposed battle plan that had been presented.

He had staged the event to distract everyone and to weaken Rolling Stone's position with those who might support his point of view.

The ruse worked. The plan was narrowly approved.

Star Leaper thanked the leadership team and assigned various leadership members specific support roles in the execution of the plan.

It was hard for Star Leaper to contain his emotions. He wanted to laugh and make fun of Rolling Stone whose womanizing behavior had made it so easy to weaken his influence.

He thanked all the leaders and ended the meeting.

Star Leaper quickly climbed down from the raised platform to accompany Bold Walker, Nieva and Taelo.

Star Leaper, Nieva, Brave Walker, Taelo walked slowly back to the villa courtyard.

Brave Walker asked if the two women had anything at all to do with Rolling Stone? He knew the two and had himself been surprised.

Star Leaper chortled and replied, that no they had nothing on Rolling Stone. They were acting on his behalf. They were young ladies that Nieva was friends with.

After arriving in the courtyard, the three shared the meeting proceedings with the rest of Taelo's team. Star Leaper admitted that he had set up the scene with the two arguing women. The women and the guards escorting them out were some of his most loyal followers.

After a good laugh, everyone gathered around for the evening meal and discussions on how to proceed.

The next morning, Bold Walker led the team out to a large grass cover field filled with young men and women. Most of the rest of the village members stood at the edge of the field and watched.

Bold Walker loudly introduced Taelo and the rest of the team.

Taelo stepped forward and in the Condor Clan language introduced his team members.

Taelo went on to describe the battle plans.

He finished by introducing the leader of the Condor Clan Slingers bold walker's mother, Nieva-of-the Stream.

A loud roar rose from those gathered in the field.

Nieva stepped forward and instructed the women to follow her, Single Leaf, Quiet Rabbit, and Busy Bee, to the other side of the field.

Taelo waited for the women to follow their leader. He then turned and gave control to Bold Walker.

Bold Walker identified himself as the leader of the Crevasse Leapers and called out nine names and presented them to Taelo as his Crevasse Leaping Fighting team.

He called out Mountain Runner and his younger brother Long Leaper and presented them to Golden Hawk. They would be the leaders of the fighting diamonds that would attack the Warrior Clan home.

He loudly introduced the rest of the gathering to Taelo and indicated that the rest were his to organize and train.

Mountain Runner and Long leaper each came up to Golden Hawk and put their hands on his shoulder and pledged they would follow his every order. Golden Hawk liked the confidence and pledge and knew he had the leaders he wanted. He asked if the two could identify the people they would want in battle with them.

They both looked around and made the point that Brave Walker had selected some of the best, but they had another eighteen that were just as good. They took ten large paces away and alternately began to call out names.

Golden Hawk watched as each warrior walked up to join the group they had been called to. He was visually evaluating them.

After all the names had been called Golden Hawk went around and talked with each of them individually. There were two warriors, on separate teams, who failed the direct look in the eyes test, but Golden Hawk decided the physical test would be the deciding factor.

Golden Hawk addressed those that had gathered around him and the two team leaders and simply said for them to follow him. He then set out at a modest running speed. Once everyone had gotten into a coordinated pace, Golden Hawk sped up. He sped up three times until he was running at his top speed.

Mountain Runner and Long Leaper easily kept the pace.

Golden Hawk told the two to keep the pace all the way around the plateau. He then dropped to the back of the runners so he could observe each one.

Golden Hawk was pleased with the selected warriors. The two he had worried about were in the front of the pack and easily keeping pace. Once he had finished his evaluation, he called for a rest.

Golden Hawk walked about and complemented each warrior for his stamina and running ability. Next, he made certain of each team membership.

Golden Hawk explained the fighting diamond formation and the position order and responsibilities. He then asked Mountain Runner and Long Leaper to put their people into the desired position.

He waited until each team had worked through the assigning of positions. Then asked the teams to form the fighting diamond.

The War Cry that he and Taelo used was next.

He had the two teams practice getting into the formation and give the war cry. Then he led them at a slow jog back toward the area where Taelo and Bold Walker were making the fighting diamond team assignments.

Golden Hawk led the two teams in a side-by-side formation. He had them quietly practice the battle cry.

He started singing a lullaby that went with their jogging pace. It had been taught to him by Feather-in-the-Wind. It was a surprise to the all the young men following him. This was the song their mothers had sung to them when they were young and Golden Hawk was singing it perfectly in their Condor language!

They instantly began to sing along.

Taelo saw the three teams returning and knew Golden Hawk would put on a display for the rest of the gathering.

He heard the lullaby and knew that Golden Hawk was in the mode of making his initial impression with his teams.

He called for everyone to turn and observe the first fighting diamonds that would soon be departing on their way north.

Golden Hawk led the fighting units into the middle of the gathering. The three teams stopped and in unison, three times in rapid succession, let out loud battle cries as they stomped their feet after giving each cry.

Those around the two teams literally jumped back in surprise. Then the entire gathering repeated the battle cry several times.

The energy level on the plateau reached a new high.

Neiva had rounded up several hundred women of all ages. The youngest were just into their fruitful years and some were grey haired grandmothers. Neiva heard Golden Hawk's fighters give their battle cry.

All of the women let out a hurrah and replied with the Condor Battle Cry that they had decided on.

These were women who were angry who wanted to participate in driving the Warrior Clan out of their territory. Every one of the women would be given a chance to qualify to be a member of one of the ten-woman team of slingers.

Busy Bee and Quiet Rabbit knew that keeping the slingers supplied with glass shards would be critical. They suggested that those that did not qualify as slingers should become be the suppliers of the glass shards to the slingers.

Busy Bee loaded her sling while Quiet Rabbit set up a head sized gourd about two spear throws away. It was clear that the gourd was simulating the head of a person.

The two had discussed how the women would be trained and deployed. The goal was to add an element of surprise and be more damaging than any other battle weapon currently in use.

Busy Bee loaded her sling and let her glass shards fly. The gourd target almost instantly sprouted a dark covering of glass shards. It was not quite as impressive as Single Leaf's demonstration to the leadership team, but it made the impression that was needed.

Almost instantaneously everyone watching understood the meaning of the display and let out another loud war battle cry.

Every one of the women were given a chance to qualify to be a member of the slingers. Busy Bee and Quiet Rabbit got every woman that did not make the slinging team to be a member of the supply team.

Gourds were set up in a long line two spear throws distance from the newly formed teams of slingers.

The practice coaching immediately improved all slingers capability. The excitement and chatter were contagious. Finally, the women were going to be able to participate in driving the Warrior Clan from the Condor Clan territory.

After a few rounds, Quiet Rabbit and Busy Bee moved the targets to the distance of three spear throws.

A groan went through the slingers. Most of them were having trouble with the two spear throws distance.

Quiet Rabbit introduced Single leaf as the best slinger she had ever known.

Single Leaf stepped up to the line and hit each of the ten targets. She let out a war cry and turned to the slingers. She let them know she would teach each one of them do the same.

The cheer the slingers gave in return was the only answer that was needed.

Neiva understood the importance for the volcanic glass shards. She also knew it would take a huge effort to gather enough shard to sustain the slingers in battle.

She sent out a request to the entire village and soon she had every able-bodied person engaged in gathering and bagging glass shards.

Old warriors barely able to walk went to the base of the volcano and began bagging the shards. They were accompanied by the young boys and girls and by all the women not on the sling teams. Several of the top leaders put in some symbolic time to show how important the glass shard gathering activity was.

This activated most of the people in the clan.

There would be no shortage of ammunition for the slingers. The baggers of the shards were as motivated as the slingers practicing hitting their gourd targets.

The bags of shards were positioned near the bridge area and would be taken across the crevasse once the area was back in the hands of the Condor fighters.

The leadership team had gathered to listen to how the new wrinkle in the battle would be executed.

Busy Bee began by introducing the leader of the Slinging Condor Warriors.

Neiva stood and shared the fact that she planned to field ten units of ten slingers. The Condor Clan women were practicing, would be qualified, and ready to participate in the main attack on the Warrior Clan. She went on to introduce the leader of each sling team.

Each sling team would be supported by three ammunition carrying Llama's led by five women. This meant that there would be one hundred fifty glass shard supply women supporting the one hundred slingers.

The sling teams whether on attack or in retreat would continuously be slinging a cloud of glass shards at the Warrior Clan.

Taelo felt a surge of pride as he understood the dynamic shift in the battle plans that Quiet Rabbit and Busy Bee had infused.

He enjoyed the mixed reaction of the leadership team.

Neiva let out the sling team battle cry that was echoed by all the slingers and their supporters who had gathered outside.

Star Leaper stood and praised the women and agreed that the Warrior Clan would be in for a big surprise. He stated that the women would be the most lethal weapon the Warrior Clan had ever faced.

Taelo stood and let out his battle cry that startled everyone.

He quietly declared that the women of the Condor Clan were going to almost single handedly drive the Warrior Clan out.

Star Leaper had arranged for a special evening gathering of the chosen warriors, their immediate family or significant other, to honor the three teams that would go north to attack the Warrior Clan's home. These teams would leave the at the next sun rise.

Star Leaper had engaged his craftsmen to duplicate the flat shark toothed weapons Taelo and Golden Hawk had given him in their earlier visit. The weapons did not have sharks' teeth but sharp black volcano glass. These weapons were an improvement on the shark tooth design.

He called each warrior up by name and gave him the flat weapon and the harness to carry it on their backs.

He thanked the families for having raised such brave sons.

He announced that every team would have similar weapons before they went out to face the warrior clan. He made it clear that every team meant the Slinger teams and their supporters as well.

This brought out a cheer from Neiva and the rest of the women.

Golden Hawk commented to Bold Walker that he felt particularly good about the Condor Clan members. There were no weak members.

He chose to arrange a departure camp for his teams at the top of the path that led to the back door. This was away from the village, and they could spend the early evening talking and sharing their first camp in a safe environment.

Golden Hawk knew that this would be the most relaxed the team would be for many moon cycles.

The next day the two teams spent time practicing and talking strategy and tactics. Golden Hawk made the point that in all engagements the goal was not to kill but to wound. Wounded fighters became a weight that needed to be attended to. The best wounds would be those that made it difficult for a warrior to stand or to walk.

As the sun set, Golden Hawk led the team down the path to the Condor Clan's back door. They were at the back door as the sun went down and the black of the moonless night began to bloom.

They left the Condor enclave and silently disappeared down the mountain and turned north.

Bold Walker followed Golden Hawks example and began to immediately work with his team on both the fighting formation and on vaulting. He presented each team member with newly crafted vaulting poles.

These poles were made by the experienced old warriors. They might be too old to fight but they were not too old to make a significant contribution. Every capable person was making poles, or the flat glass tipped blade.

Brave Walker led his team to an area in the valley where the downward slope approximated the slope leading to the edge of the crevasse. He had the team lay out flat hand sized stones to simulate the edge of the crevasse.

Next, he measured out the distance approximately equal to the distance across the crevasse and lay out a long grass rope to simulate the opposite side.

He then took an exaggerated step backward and moved the rope that additional distance away from the stones.

Star Leaper walked back up the slope. He turned and looked down the slope. He was going to demonstrate what he expected the team members to duplicate. He hoped he would make it across the rope.

He took several deep breaths, raised his pole, and ran down the slope as fast as he could. He planted his pole and was hurled up and forward through the air. At the zenith of the arc, he pushed off his pole. He barely cleared the rope. He took a forward roll and gave out the war battle cry and thanked the ancestors for their help.

The rest of the team followed his lead. Only two other team members made it across the rope marker. All took their forward roll and let out the war cry.

One team member took out his weapon during his flight and whacked it into the ground across the rope. He pulled himself across the rope before standing and giving the war cry followed by yelling "I live to fight."

Brave Walker gave him an embrace and agreed that he would live to fight but that they would practice until every one of them could clear the rope. Then each day the team would continue to move the rope out more.

Brave Walker noted that there were at least another thirty young men and several women standing and watching. He said he would have another dozen poles delivered that they could be used to practice. This resulted in a cheer from the entire gathering.

Taelo and the rest of the team established their fighting diamond teams. They selected one of the Condor Clan members to be the team leader for each of the teams.

Each member of Taelo's team followed this protocol. This would ensure the fighters were following the direction of one of their own.

Floating Cloud and Whistling Arrow both made it a point to thank Taelo for treating them as equal warriors.

Taelo joked with them that he was desperate for two more fighting diamonds when he had spotted them taking it easy on the edge of the field.

It was true he needed everyone.

Nieva, Quiet Rabbit and Busy Bee had followed a similar selection process as they set up the slingers. The formation for them was two rotating lines of five slingers in a row.

The women went through a similar and rigorous qualification process. To be a slinger they needed to be able to follow Quiet Rabbit and Busy Bee in a run around the valley. Afterwards they practiced the sling. Then they were assigned to a sling team. These sling teams were coached by Quiet Rabbit, Busy Bee, Single Leaf and Marigold.

The days of practice were long and intense. The day was spent running, forming the double sling line, simulating a fight, and then running some more.

Everyone ran together, then went to their respective areas.

Taelo kept everyone on the intense routine for seven sun cycles. Then it was time to send Quiet Rabbit and Busy Bee to protect the Llama herds.

Again, a dinner was hosted by Star Leaper and Nieva. All the team members received their flat blade, glass edged weapons.

It was the pitch of night when Taelo accompanied both teams going to protect the Llama herd to the Condor Clan's backdoor.

Taelo took Lasher back across the gap. He put him down at Quiet Rabbit's feet and instructed Lasher to protect her.

He then gave Quiet Rabbit an embrace. He did the same with Busy Bee. He instructed them to take no chances.

Quiet Rabbit and Busy Bee had discussed their assignment. It was clear to them that they were assigned to a task that Taelo thought was safe for them. They knew there would be a second battle and they planned to be in it.

Taelo stood in the dark as the two fighting diamonds disappeared into the dark. He felt an intense sense of unease.

He was sure this would keep Quiet Rabbit out of the main battle. He was trying to keep his nightmare of her beheading from coming true.

He turned and made the leap back to the Condor backdoor. He would not rest until the confrontation was over and Quiet Rabbit safely was back in his arms.

The following morning was spent getting ready for the attack on the following day. He had watched as Bold Walker's team seemed to greatly increase in size. It was also apparent that some of women had joined that group.

Taelo asked Bold Walker about all the extra team members. Bold Walker replied that if he lost anyone down into the deep divide, they would quickly be replaced by one of these eager leapers.

Taelo decided to leave well enough alone. He was pleased with the idea of backups.

The dinner for all the fighting diamonds was an affair that took on the aspect of a celebration. Star Leaper presented each team leader the flat blade weapons for their team.

Taelo and Nieva explained the plan of attack.

The slingers would not be used for this first attack. They would be a surprise for the next major and final attack.

This encounter would consist of coordinated attacks from the left, the middle and on the right rear of the Warrior Clan position. Bold Walker and his team would vault directly at the Warrior Clan Fighters. The attacks would be coordinated. There would be three attacks and three retreats. Each attack and each retreat would be preceded with the battle cry. On the third retreat all teams would descend and go around to the back door.

Taelo and his team would be last to retreat, and they would make sure they were not followed.

Taelo thanked all the Condor Clan village members for having served such a wonderful meal and for supporting the effort to oust the Warrior Clan.

He then called out for the fighters to follow him as he led the way to the back door.

The stars overhead provide the meager light that guided all the teams down the trail and out the back door.

Taelo and his team was last to cross. He turned to Bold Walker and wished him and the three teams of jumpers' luck.

Bold Walker smiled and replied that they would all make it across. They would assault the Warrior Clan and drive them back to the nine other fighting diamonds. He told Taelo to be ready.

He was surprised that Taelo had known about the increase in the number of jumpers. He had more than three fighting diamonds of jumpers. And they were all eager to take their jump.

Chapter 4: Assault on the Warrior Clan Home

Golden Hawk followed Mountain Runner as they descended in the pitch black of the night.

The boulders that appeared out of the dark, like buffalo running directly at you made the going slow and torturous. The faint twinkles of light from the distant Ancestors up in the night sky provided the only light in an otherwise sea of pitch-black. The sweet tasting smell of the night reminded him of the Valley of Plenty far to the north. This counteracted the tension he felt as he headed out of the Condor Clan territory. He was certain that his followers were in for an experience they had never imagined.

Reaching the valley floor was a blessing they all hailed. The night still made travel a challenge, but the level travel greatly reduced the effort. They all moved silently on. Golden Hawk could hear the reduction in the level of breathing. This indicated a more relaxed group.

Golden Hawk gazed up at the mountain on his right. The rising sun cast the towering mountain peaks as black silhouette spikes. It would soon be daybreak and they would need to stop their northward travel and get out of sight.

He instructed Mountain Runner to stop at the next place that would make a good camp for them to stop. They would spend the daylight time resting. Night would remain the primary time of travel for the rest of their journey. Golden Hawk did not want to encounter any of the Warrior Clan during his travel to their home. He needed the venture to be a total unexpected surprise.

At night they carefully traveled the well-worn path north. The night travel gave them an open road as long as they did not stumble on to a Warrior Clan camp. He instructed the person on point to be vigilant. The main challenge to the travel north toward the Warrior Clan home was to do it so that they would not encounter the stream of supplies going south to the Condor Clan territory.

They were constantly on the lookout for any Warrior Clan group that might be camped along the trail. When they encountered a camp, they went quietly around through the jungle.

They had to do this several times more than Golden Hawk had expected. He was surprised at the number of supply teams traveling south. This also made him aware that a similar number of teams were on the return. He assigned one team member to keep a watch to their rear.

During the day, their camp was always away from the main trail and there were no fires. The teams were on a Llama jerky and water diet.

The travel was slower then he would have liked but reaching the Warrior Clan village undetected was critical. He wanted his team positioned in a manner that gave he and the teams the advantage not only of surprise but the ability to strike and retreat like ghosts.

Scouts sent out ahead were in a constant rotation . Finally, one returned with the news that he had seen the walls of the Warrior Clan village.

Golden Hawk sent out scouts to find a defendable place in the jungle where they could set up their camp. Daylight allowed them to reevaluate and move their camp to a more secure position.

During their travel, Golden Hawk explained how they would "attack" the village. Their attack would be in the dead of night and if they were successful there would be no encounter with any Warrior Clan member. The idea was to reduce the ability of the Warrior Clan to send food supplies to the Condor Clan territory and to demoralize the Warrior Clan population that remained in village.

Golden Hawk explained that he wanted the warrior clan village to feel the threat of being attacked and being vulnerable.

He explained that he knew the village very well. During their previous visit, he and Taelo spent a good amount of time surveying the Warrior Clan village and discussing scenarios of battle and escape if their visit turned sour. Golden Hawk now thanked Taelo for having been so thorough at that time.

Golden Hawk chose to guide his team through the village to learn the layout. He took them into the village in the dead of night. He was their guide. The dark of the night allowed them to move through the village more or less in the open. They spread out and stayed in the dark but moved through at a leisurely pace so they would not attract attention. Each team located and simulated their attack of the stored food stock. He instructed them to memorize the layout.

Golden Hawk pointed out the homes of the leaders and he pointed out the various food storage buildings. The food storage buildings were the main targets. The goal was to destroy all the food. He knew it would be almost impossible to get to all the food, but he wanted to destroy enough so that the remainder would be needed by the people staying in the village.

He repeated this activity for three nights. Then Golden Hawk quizzed the three teams about their observations. The answers and the clarity he desired was missing. He was disappointed and let the teams know they had to improve their power of observation.

He told the three teams they would each repeat the tour of the village. It was imperative they be able to navigate through the village and retreat without engaging in battle. He estimated that there were at least one thousand warriors still in the village. He did not want to face a hornet's nest and take the stings that would be delivered if his teams made a mistake.

The team members were surprised at the detail Golden Hawk expected them to retain and how much he was able to tell them that they had missed.

He spent extra time with Mountain Runner and Long Leaper to reinforce the need for detailed knowledge and the stealth they would need as they set fires and destroyed the food supplies.

Three sun cycles later the three teams were again quizzed by Golden Hawk. This time their recollection was at the level that would allow the teams to make on the run adjustments if the situation required them to do so.

Golden Hawk praised the team members and told them that they would take action on the next setting of the sun.

In the late afternoon, the teams sat quietly talking through the coming nights activities. They had passed their second quiz by Golden Hawk. They now knew why Taelo had selected him to guide them. They had new respect for both of them and talked about how they would be successful.

Golden Hawk instructed the teams to break camp and clean everything up. They would depart the area immediately on their return.

Golden Hawk waited until the half-moon was well into the night sky and then led the teams into the village. He reinforced the need to not be caught on the way in or on the way out. Their success was to leave the village in total confusion and never have anyone see them.

Each team proceeded to their location. They began on the far side of the village. They carefully back tracked as they set fire to all the grain bins and the storage areas for the dried goods. Each team member had brought a bag with the material to set the fires. They each took turns in setting a specific storage area on fire. They worked quietly, efficiently and with amazing speed.

Golden Hawk went back and forth between the teams checking their progress. It was critical that the teams moved back away from their destruction in unison so they would be able to retreat and leave together. He pushed the teams to accelerate their pace so they could leave the village undetected once the discovery of what they were doing occurred.

Golden Hawk was surprised at how long it took for the fires to be discovered. Then the Warrior Clan villagers rushed toward the fires that had been set first and began to fight them. Meanwhile, undetected, his teams were continuing to set more storage bins on fire as they worked their way out away from the firefighters.

They were able to set more than two thirds of the food storage bins on fire.

Then gray of dawn began to threaten the dark night. Golden Hawk called a retreat and got the teams quickly outside of the village walls. He led them silently to their camp by a circuitous route.

Once at their camp, Golden Hawk had the teams pick up their packs.

He supervised a team to clean up and "erase" their site. Then he had several of the team leave the camp and travel toward the north. He instructed them to travel back south on the main trail toward the Condor Clan territory on the following night. This maneuver was done in the hope that if the camp were discovered the first direction the Warrior Clan trackers took would be toward the north.

Later when he regrouped with the other teams, Golden Hawk led them up to a huge squared flat stone that appeared to rise directly up from the earth. He had learned of this stone on his previous visit to the Warrior Clan area. He planned to make camp on its top surface that if needed would allow the small group that he led to hold off hundreds of attackers.

All sides were smooth dark black stone. Standing at its base the stone rose up the height of at least three warriors. The seemingly polished surface of the sides provided no means of climbing up.

Golden Hawk had the team build three ladders.

This activity made him remember the time, he and Taelo built the bridge across the stream that fed the lake in the valley where the Elk Clan held their fall gathering. That had been Taelo and his first time as leaders of an adventure. The two of them had sent a plum of white smoke to signal their clan that there was a place to set up camp near the lake.

He smiled at the memory and then he refocused on the current situation.

He led the way to the top of the rock. This was the first time he had been on the top side of the stone. He was pleased that the top was not flat but a half spear depression toward the center. He stepped down into the tub created by a lip at the edge of the stone. His team would fill the bowl created by the stone to capacity with water. They would be totally invisible from below.

He walked over to a bench like projection of the stone and set up his sleeping area. He and the team would establish this as their focal point from which to operate.

The attacks of the supply chain of food going to the Warrior Clan on the Condor Mountain would begin within a few sun cycles.

The next day Golden Hawk had the team members outfit the camp. Water from a nearby stream was carried and put into the depression at the center of the stone top. This would ensure they would have water in the event they were discovered.

He scouted out the best way to retreat and escape if they were discovered. He was leaving nothing to chance.

Several of the team began to gather wood for a cooking fire. Golden Hawk had them stop. They would not be lighting any fires. He did not want to risk having smoke lead the Warrior Clan to their camp.

Golden Hawk spent his time laying out his food supply chain attack plan. He engaged all the team members and got their input to the plan.

The primary focus would be to engage the supply teams heading toward the Condor Clan territory. Golden Hawk wanted to totally cut off of any food supplies headed to the Warrior Clan camped in the Condor Clan territory.

Their initial raids on the supply convoys began a few sun cycles later. They were very successful and fruitful. Golden Hawk did not destroy the captured food. He instead had his teams preserve the food as best they could.

This ensured they had the food and other resources to maintain their continued disruption of the supply chain.

The Warrior Clan was essentially totally cut from any food supplies. He knew that soon the teams taking food south would be protected by armed escorts.

He would disrupt for as long as possible and hope that Taelo would be successful in his efforts to drive the Warrior Clan out of Condor Clan territory.

Chapter 5: Sacrificial Offering

Quiet Rabbit and Busy Bee led their teams through the dark night. They followed their two young women guides who were members of the Llama herders. Each belonged to one of the two herds.

The brilliant points of light in the night sky seemed to merge into one continuous cream-colored splash of light spread in a twisting ribbon across the black of the sky. This ribbon and the stars and the moon overhead provided just enough light to make out the narrow path. The slope down the mountain to the right of the trail was steep enough that it qualified to be called a cliff. Quiet Rabbit understood the cautious and slow pace their guides were taking. Quiet Rabbit noticed that even Lasher seemed to be hugging the up-hill side of the trail as he walked ahead of her.

Busy Bee commented on how quiet the night seemed to be. She found it eerie to be traveling down the mountain in the pitch of night. She knew it would be morning by the time each of the teams reached their respective destination.

As the morning light was threatening the night the two teams arrived at the branch where each would go their separate way. Busy Bee would be going with her team to the lower Llama pasture.

Quiet Rabbit wished Busy Bee good luck. Quiet Rabbit would follow the young woman that was a member of the upper pasture herders.

Quiet Rabbit watched as Busy Bee and her team slowly disappeared down the trail into the morning dusk.

She was standing and thinking about the situation the team found itself in when Lasher's nose on her leg brought her back into the present.

She asked her guide to lead them on to the herd.

The terrain and the trail would not allow the diamond formation. This concerned Quiet Rabbit. They were vulnerable to attack.

She moved one of the bigger warriors up to point to improve their situation. This at least would provide a more powerful initial resistance if they were attacked.

The early morning sun was breaking over the top to the mountains on their left side when the young lady in front shouted out to a group in the camp ahead and waved.

Those around the campfire rose and waved back.

The surprised reaction of the guide gave Quiet Rabbit immediate warning that something was not right.

Lasher let out a low rumble from his throat and moved up to the guide.

Quiet Rabbit stepped into the lead and immediately let out her war cry and the fighting diamond formed in a tight formation.

The fighting diamond was of little use. At least thirty warriors with spears ready to throw stood on the upper side of the trail.

It would be a slaughter. Quiet Rabbit knelt and lay her weapon down. This was not what she wanted to do but it was the only thing she could do. If she resisted her whole team would be slaughtered. She signaled for the rest of the team to do the same.

One of the Warrior Clan fighters came at her with his war hammer raised. He had been told to kill the leader. It was apparent to him that Quiet Rabbit was leading.

Quiet Rabbit stood and was prepared to kill her attacker if he attempted to hit her with his war hammer. She had practiced the leaping kick that would allow her to do so.

She was just ready to execute her kick when Lasher leaped in from the side. He clamped down and crushed the fighter's wrist. He then proceeded to attack the next oncoming warrior. Total chaos ensued.

Lasher's attack ended when one of the warriors hit him across the skull with his war hammer.

Lasher appeared to be dead.

Lasher was thrown unceremoniously into the brush. His attack had saved Quiet Rabbit and the rest of the team.

Lasher's fate devastated Quiet Rabbit. She tried to see if he was moving but his body was not in sight. His fate remained on her mind, but she had to deal with her team and keep them as safe as she could.

She was furious about the unwarranted action of the Warrior Clan leader. If possible, she would make sure there would be retribution.

One of the warriors recognized Quite Rabbit as the mate of Taelo. Once this was understood, they quickly bound her and the rest of the team. They would be praised for having captured such a valuable person.

The team had their hands tied behind their backs and almost immediately they were marching back up the trail that they had just descended.

Quiet Rabbit's instincts told her that the Warrior clan fighters were aware of the Condor Clan's plan. How else could they have been so ready and be there ahead of them?

A similar fate awaited Busy Bee. Her team did not get the chance to form their fighting triangle and the lead Condor Clan warrior was mistaken as the leader and killed. The rest were restrained and led up the mountain trail with a rope around each of their necks. Busy Bee was not recognized.

Busy Bee was glad to be alive but felt a great deal of grief over the loss of the young man she had put up front. He had been mistaken as the leader. This was a heavy burden for her.

She was furious about the unwarranted action of the Warrior Clan leader. If possible, she would make sure there would be retribution.

Going up the mountain trail, even in the daytime, was much slower than the descent. The two teams came together at the fork where just a few hours earlier they had passed on the descent. Then all of Condor Clan members had ropes around their necks and were tied together to form a long single file chain. They then proceeded together up the mountain.

Quiet Rabbit was relieved to see that Busy Bee was alive. Busy Bee noted that Lasher was missing and wondered where he might be. She knew his absence was a bad sign.

She noted that one of the Warrior Clan warriors had his arm in a sling and wondered how that had happened.

Everyone was in a precarious position. Quiet Rabbit wondered if a chance to change the situation would present itself. She would keep herself alert to that possibility.

Her thoughts turned to Lasher and tears came to her eyes. He had saved her life but had lost his. His loss made it hard for her to concentrate on the climb up the mountain. It would be hard to see Taelo's sorrow.

Night on the mountain came quickly and the temperature drop was sharp. The cold of night damped out the beauty of the Stars.

When the climb up stopped, Quiet Rabbit had been able to position herself next to Busy Bee. The two sat back-to-back and managed to get some rest. They were able to whisper quietly and discuss their situation.

Quiet Rabbit called out to the leader in his language that unless he allowed the captives to use their sleeping hides he would wake up to a line of dead captives or at least captives unable to climb the mountain. He agreed to let them get their hides out.

The night was cold and long. Their sleeping hides saved the Condor Clan members but even then, by morning every Condor Clan team member was close to hyperthermia. They had not been fed or given water. Without food the climb up became a torture.

They were once again led up toward the camp site of the Warrior Clan. The exertion of the climb and the sun warming them allowed them to slowly recover from a frosty night they would all long remember. A few of the Condor Clan members began to stumble as they made their way along the trail.

Quiet Rabbit and Busy Bee aided those having the most problems. The other team members took note and followed their example. Soon almost everyone was leaning on someone as they made their way up the mountain to the plateau

The arrival of the two Condor fighting groups created a huge stir in the Warrior Clan Camp. Quiet Rabbit and Busy Bee were singled out when they were recognized by those Warrior Clan members who remembered them from their visit at the Warrior Clan village.

They in turn recognized several of the war leaders from their previous visit to the Warrior Clan home. Others they did not know personally. These were recognized by the way they were dressed.

Quiet Rabbit and Busy Bee were brought to the Lead War Priest. They did not know him personally but understood his role by the way he was dressed.

He inspected the Condor Clan captives. He scolded the warriors who had brought them into camp and then ordered the captives be given food and treated with respect.

He began to politely ask questions about the plans the Condor Clan might be making.

After Busy Bee and Quiet Rabbit had eaten, the questioning took on a more dire and mean tone.

The several other warrior priests came over. One of them had Quiet Rabbit tied to a pole and with a bamboo cane he began to beat her as he asked her questions about the Condor Clan plan for fighting the Warrior Clan. Though she groaned and cried as she was whipped Quiet Rabbit did not succumb to the beating. Blood ran down her backs when she was untied from the whipping post.

Busy Bee took her turn next, but she too would not be broken.

One warrior wearing a friendship wrist band given out by Taelo's team in their previous visit arrived at the scene. He was the son of Tough Hide who had been killed by the current leader of the Warrior Clan. He challenged the war priests. He asked them when had the Warrior Clan taking up the beating of women? This challenge stopped the beatings.

The high religious priest of war called for the building of sacrificial platform that would face the Condor Clan side of the crevasse. He intended to make a grand display of sacrificing the captured Condor Clan fighters. He described the sacrifices they would make to show the Condor Clan leaders what would happen to their people if they continued to resist.

Star Leaper and his chief advisor were immediately advised of the change of activities in the Warrior Camp.

The Condor Clan watched throughout the day as the platform was built. When a large square stone was placed at the center of the raised structure Star Leaper knew he was looking at a sacrificial alter.

Bold Walker listened to his father as Star Leaper wondered who was to be sacrificed at the sacrificial alter being built?

He did not know but he immediately called together all the warriors that could leap the crevasse and told them to be prepared to leap across. He would not standby when the sacrificial ceremony began. He and his teams would wreak havoc before letting that happen.

The head Warrior priest had both Quiet Rabbit and Busy Bee brought to him. Both were almost a head taller than he.

They were still in great pain, but they were quickly recovering from their beating. They remained defiant and had agreed that they were ready to meet their Ancestors.

Told to kneel, Quiet Rabbit chose instead to sit cross legged. Busy Bee did the same.

This seemed to satisfy the priest.

The priest identified himself as the Highest Priest of war and made the point that he knew they were from the Clan far to the North. He asked why they were helping the Condor Clan. He informed them that their actions made them enemies of the Warrior Clan.

He then pointed to each of them and let them know that they would be the first to be sacrificed to Mihacoti, the god of war. A platform had been built so the entire Condor Clan could watch as all their warriors would be led out to the platform. Then one at time each warrior would take their turn having their heart cut out and laid out on stones in front of the platform.

He told Quiet Rabbit and Busy Bee that they were special. They would be shown their own hearts and then would have their heads cut off and placed on the stone with their hearts.

He offered to spare them if they would let him know the war plan.

Both answered they knew nothing about a war plan.

Quiet Rabbit looked at the priest and in his own language quietly assured the priest that he would never see the sight he had just described. He would be dead long before that moment.

She told him that he would be made into an example of what happened to those that defied the guidance of the Ancestors.

The priest was taken by surprise but gave a small laugh and quietly replied that he was sure that nothing like that would happen. He was in control, and they would both see their hearts beating outside of their bodies before they died.

Quiet Rabbit looked at Busy Bee and then stood, turned, and walked away to join the rest of the Condor Warriors. Busy Bee followed.

The priest was surprised and angry. He had expected some pleading and bargaining. The calm response from Quiet Rabbit had sent a chill up his back.

What did the Condor Clan have planned?

He restrained his armed escorts as the two walked away.

He was envisioning how he would slowly insert his blade just below the left rib and slowly cut across Quiet Rabbit's mid-section. He would be talking to her in friendly manner and telling her how much he admired her. He knew he would then see fear in her eyes. He would reach in and lift her heart out to the point she could see it as it still pumped life through her. He would offer to put it back but laugh when she begged him to, and he would then cut it out and lift it for the Condor Clan to see it.

A warm feeling went through him as he absorbed the vision in his head.

The war priest turned and called for the war council to meet. They would talk through the upcoming ceremony. His confidence was as high as the sun as it reached its Zenith.

At the meeting he shared how he envisioned the sacrifice session to proceed. Each of the warrior priests would take a turn at beheading and extracting the hearts of the Condor Clan captives.

The other war priests had been reluctant about the sacrificing, but they knew that the lead war priest had a large following and wielded significant power. They had sacrificed many of their own, doing so with some Condor Clan warriors was of little consequence and it would probably create enthusiasm among the Warrior Clan fighters.

They each voiced their support for the upcoming sacrifices.

Chapter 6: Encounter

Brave Walker listened to the discussion of the Condor Clan leaders. It was clear that the action of building a sacrificial platform in the open area that had been the bridge landing on the other side of the crevasse indicated that the Warrior Clan had prisoners they planned to sacrifice.

Bold Walker knew they would make it a long and brutal display as they attempted to break the resolve of the Condor Clan population.

He counted the number of flat stones in front of the sacrificial platform and knew that at least two fighting diamonds had been captured.

He thought of Golden Hawk and his friends Mountain Runner, his brother Long Leaper and Sharp Claws.

Something had gone very wrong for those fighting diamonds.

Or could it be the Llama fighting diamonds? A shiver went down his spine as he thought about that possibility. Not only who would be sacrificed but the fact that the loss of the Condor Clan food supply would mean catastrophe.

He was not sure who had been captured but he was sure he would act before the sacrifices began.

The nine attack fighting diamonds led by Taelo were on their way to attack but Brave Walker did not believe they would get into position in time to save the captured warriors. He thought through what he could do.

He immediately gathered the remaining Condor Clan warriors. He singled out the ones that he knew could throw a spear to the opposite side of the crevasse. He asked them to identify the others they knew could do the same. The response was greater than he thought. More than half were both young and older women of the clan. He decided he would let every one of them participate. He desperately needed the spear throwers to provide the cover for the leap of his fighting diamonds.

He was now happy that he had developed so many leapers. He would need to get them all across. He calculated that he would have at least four fighting diamonds. Three of them would not have any experience fighting together but they would have adrenalin on their side.

He organized the spear throwers and arranged for each to have three spears to throw. Their goal would be to throw as far across the sacrificial platform as possible into the crowd immediately beyond it.

He hoped the spear throwers could disrupt and confuse the Warrior Clan sacrificial ceremony event and give his leaping diamond warriors the opportunity to jump the crevasse and establish a foot hold.

Star Leaper listened to Brave Walker's plan. He approved of this arrangement. He suggested having the rest of the village blast of the horns and give the Condor Clan war cry to emphasize the attack. Brave Walker thought that was a great idea.

Star Leaper sent out the word to the entire Condor Clan to bring horns to the crevasse area.

Every person in the village gathered with their horns in preparation for their participation. Star Leaper had the entire Condor Clan engaged in the coming battle. There was great concern but there was a new energy for them all.

Taelo, Single Leaf and Deer Chaser were the three teams to attack on the left Warrior camp flank. They would be in position first.

Saber Scar, Floating Cloud, and White Bear would be attacking from the back of the Warrior Clan. They would be in position second.

Sharp Knife, Whistling Arrow and Marigold would be on the right flank and would be in position last.

Taelo had all the teams jogging to their positions in a quiet but very fast pace.

The sun was nearing its zenith as Taelo's team came into sight of the Warrior Camp. He realized his team was slightly ahead of the other two teams, but he was prepared to engage.

Bold Walker organized everyone and then gave the signal to the throwers and the blowers. It was time for the action to begin.

The blast of horns caught everyone on the far side of the crevasse by surprise. The Warrior Clan leaders had gathered around the sacrificial platform. The prisoners were being brought forward. They were sure that this would break the Condor Clan's will and destroy the influence of their helpers from the North.

Taelo knew instantly that the blasts of the horns indicated a change in the attack plan. He immediately urged his fighting diamonds to run at full speed toward the Warrior Clan.

The loud blaring of the horns seemed to go on indefinitely. The warrior priests stopped to determine what was happening. Then a hail of spears hit the Warrior Clan members standing nearest to the platform. Several of the war leaders were hit.

Pandemonium broke out. The spears rained down on them in a seemingly continuous flow. The spear throwers were throwing in waves and their energy was putting almost all their throws beyond where they had thrown before. It seemed that on this day, at this moment every thrower could throw twice as far as they had ever been able to.

Then the hail of spears stopped. The desired effect of confusion had been achieved and the area around the platform had been cleared. The Warrior Clan members had been driven back.

Bold Walker and his fighting diamonds gave their war cry and sped down the slope to their launch area. Each of their vault poles had a long rope tied to the bottom of the pole. Once they made their leap, the pole could be pulled up for reuse. More fighters would make the jump.

All leaping warriors cleared the crevasse by a significant margin. Their practice had paid off. Their war cry rang out again as they came together on the far side. The second, third and additional teams made the leap and let out their war cry.

Bold Walker guided the fighting diamonds that formed. He was pleased to see that he had five fighting diamonds. One was made up totally of women fighters. Only his original team had the flat glass toothed flat blade and a war hammer. The rest of the teams had their spears and glass tipped cutting blades.

Bold Walker gave his war cry and was immediately echoed by the other fighting diamonds.

He led his, the best armed team directly across the platform to engage the Warrior Clan warriors. The other teams went around each end of the sacrificial platform.

He was able to drive the Warrior Clan farther back away from the platform area.

Quiet Rabbit and Busy Bee and her warriors watched as all action in the Warrior Clan gathering stopped. Their captures backed away from the platform as a hail of spears and stones hit the Warrior Clan members standing nearest to the platform.

The war priest came over and grabbed Quiet Rabbit by the hair and dragged her toward the fighting area. Quiet Rabbit tried to fight off the priest. Her scalp burned as the priest dragged her along. She had no idea were Busy Bee had disappeared to. All she could think about was that maybe her prediction about seeing the priest die was wrong and that it seemed she was about to die.

Taelo immediately reacted to the blast of the horns. He knew that something had changed. He had his team on a fast run toward the Warrior Clan camp.

Single Leaf and the ability of the Others to see much farther called out Quiet Rabbit's name as she pointed.

Taelo focused on the location Single Leaf had pointed to and with a surge of emotion dramatically increased his running speed. Almost instantly his fighting diamond was left behind. He was now running faster than he had ever run in his life. His nightmare was coming to life. For a moment he wanted to scream at the top of his voice.

Quiet Rabbit needed his help. He needed Quiet Rabbit.

Finally, ahead he could clearly see Quiet Rabbit being dragged forward by her hair. A figure dressed like a priest was raising his knife in a dramatic fashion to cut her throat. The priest shouted out in a loud voice. He wanted everyone to see his action. He wanted them to see him kill Quiet Rabbit.

Taelo knew he could not get to Quiet Rabbit in time. He remembered his nightmare. He remembered Broken Spear's advice to think clearly about the action he would need to take. In his dreams he had thrown his spear that went through the priest. It had not stopped the knife.

Then a light flashed in his mind. At the last moment before making his throw he spun his spear around and threw it with all his might, butt first, at the figure holding the knife. He called to the Ancestors to guide his spear.

He had leaped in the air for the throw and rolled forward when he hit the ground. He was immediately on his feet running at top speed. He knew he was experiencing the world in slow motion as he watched his spear flying toward the priest. The knife slowly made its way toward Quiet Rabbit's throat.

The spear flew true and hit the priest on the chest. The impact made the War priest release his hold on Quiet Rabbit.

At the same moment Lasher leaped through the air and clamped down and crushed the wrist holding the knife.

The impact of the spear knocked the stunned priest back onto the ground. The pain from his crushed wrist caused him to cry out.

Lasher collapsed when he impacted the ground, but the priest's crushed wrist remained clamped in his jaws.

Quiet Rabbit sensed what was happening. She let herself go limp and fell flat to the ground.

A wounded snarling, Lasher had the warrior by the wrist. The continued crushing of bone and the screaming of the war priest could be heard as he tried to get on his feet.

Taelo continued his run and as he leaped over Quiet Rabbit, he did a flip and came back to ground with his flat blade flashing down and across the priest. The head and left arm fell off as the priest's body crumbled.

A snarling Lasher was now at Quiet Rabbit's side snarling at any would be attacker. It was clear to Quiet Rabbit that Lasher was using the last of his energy to defend her. She wondered how Lasher had made it up the mountain in his wounded state.

The coordination of the attack had been shattered by the events. Bold Walker's fighting diamonds were effectively moving forward in attack. His desire to have more fighting diamonds to leap across the crevasse had proven invaluable.

Taelo's three fighting diamonds were holding back warriors around themselves.

Busy Bee had her diamond in fighting formation and weaponized. They were eager to make up for their experienced helplessness.

Quiet Rabbit picked up the badly wounded Lasher. He had saved her life twice. Though she was having trouble carrying him, she was determined to save him. She took her place in the center of her fighting diamond. She knelt and quietly talked to Lasher.

The fighting diamonds around Taelo were holding their place, and Bold Walker's fighting diamonds were on the attack from the crevasse side. Their movement had them joining and fighting together. This gave them a solid front against the unprepared Warrior Clan fighters.

The Warrior clan fighters were slowly retreating away from them up the valley.

This was what Taelo had hoped would happen.

The Warrior Clan fighters recovered and tried to mount a counterattack. They had a ten to one warrior superiority. The surprise had caught them off guard and the effectiveness of the fighting diamonds kept them from leveraging their number superiority.

Then Saber Scar, Floating Cloud, and White Bear brought their fighting diamonds up from the back side. They too knew that their plans had changed.

Their war cries and attack disrupted the Warrior Clan attempted counterattack.

Taelo had contemplated a Warrior Clan retreat.

The captured Condor warriors had responded almost immediately by forming their fighting diamonds. Their quick response had the immediate effect of holding back the superior number of Warrior Clan fighters.

The addition of Saber Scar and the other fighting diamonds with him put fourteen fighting diamonds into play.

As planned the diamonds gathered near to each other to present an impenetrable wall to the fighters of the Warrior Clan.

Floating Cloud was nearest to Taelo's fighting diamond. She saw Quiet Rabbit and Busy Bee and knew that their capture had been what had triggered the change of events.

She moved her team toward where Taelo's team fought and let out a war cry that was echoed by her team. Their arrival shifted the balance of the battle.

There was now a wall of twelve fighting diamonds spaced along the western flank of the Warrior Clan mass.

Five highly effective fighting diamonds were closing rank from the eastern side.

The Warrior Clan had more warriors, but they did not have the strategic battle advantage and were experiencing many wounded warriors falling out of action and needing help.

Sharp Knife, Whistling Arrow and Marigold heard the horns and the multiple fighting diamond war cries. They realized that battle had begun. They shortened the distance they had planned to take their teams.

The position of the battlefield had shifted, and they entered the battle exactly where they needed to be to join with the other fighting diamonds. Their arrival and their battle cries caused the superior Warrior Clan fighting force to break ranks.

The wounds inflicted by the fighting diamonds of the Condor Clan were having the intended impact. At least a third of the Warrior clan members had significant leg, arm, or body wounds. A few had been killed. This was counter to the battle plan strategy, but it was a hand-to-hand battle and not all encounters could be treated the same. Taelo noted that no Condor Clan fighter had been killed. He saw that several had been wounded.

The Warrior Clan leaders decided to retreat away from the crevasse and go up the slope to the high end of the plateau. They wanted the high ground in any continuing battle.

Taelo let out his war cry as the Warrior Clan retreated. He was pleased with the move the Warrior Clan was making. He took note of the substantial number of wounded Warrior Clan fighters.

He did not retreat toward the Condor Clan's backdoor but moved all the fighting diamonds to the sacrificial platform area.

Only the body of the war priest was left behind. His body was near the sacrificial platform and was not accessible to the retreating Warrior Clan fighters.

Taelo moved the body out toward the Warrior Clan. He then had two poles planted in the ground. He and Bold Walker stood the body up and lashed it to one pole and lashed the head and arm to the other. It was a grotesque sight.

All seventeen fighting diamonds stood in formation behind Taelo and Bold Walker.

A set of horns let out a long continuous blast and an echo returned from the far mountains.

The fighting diamonds let out their battle cry three times as they backed way.

There were no fallen Condor Clan warriors and only minor injuries.

The Warrior Clan leaders were discussing their counterattack plans when runners came in with the news that the home of the Warrior Clan had been attacked and massively damaged by fires set by warriors of the Condor Clan. The runners described the loss of most of the food designated to come to the Condor Clan battlefield.

This news and the fact that the battlefield before them was now totally empty of Condor Clan warriors caused the leaders consternation. They had been planning an immediate counter act against the much smaller number of Condor Clan fighters. The news of the attack on their home and the lack of a group to fight changed what they had been contemplating.

The first problem was the issue of food and water. They would need to move back toward the location they had just abandoned to have an easy source of water. However, their current location was superior from a fighting perspective, and they decided to stay on the high ground.

They sent runners out to the Llama herds with the message to send meat.

Neiva set up a field kitchen on the plateau where the trail from the back door came out. She knew the arriving fighters would be tired and hungry. Their wounds would be treated, and they would be fed. The women of the Condor Clan had all come out to help.

She stood at the exit of the crevasse and personally gave each fighter a flask of honey wine. She inspected each for any wounds. Those needing some care were sent over to where she had a pot of hot water and cleaning cloths.

Four fighting diamonds were not returning. Taelo and Saber Scar were leading their fighters toward the Llama herds. They knew the Warrior Clan would need to re-resupply from these herds and they were going to prevent this from happening.

At the split of the trail, Taelo wished Saber Scar and Sharp Knife luck and told them to send at least half the Warrior Clan warriors back up with wounds that would take them off the field.

He and Single leaf took their fighters down the other path.

In both cases the fighting diamonds surprised the Warrior Clan members that had taken over the Llama herds. The battles were short, and the escape route was left open.

One fighting diamond was assigned to each herd.

The Warrior Clan would get no meat from these herds.

Taelo anticipated the potential discovery of the Condor Village back door and with the help of some of the Llama herders he took about a third of the Llama herd up the mountain. He estimated this would be enough if the back door was found and blocked by the Warrior Clan.

Once back Taelo returned to the village to see how Quite Rabbit, Busy Bee and Lasher were doing in their recovery. He still had not recovered from the shock of seeing Quiet Rabbit being pulled by the hair and almost being beheaded.

The Llamas were taken across the crevasse one at a time and up to the back-door plateau. This would ensure a food supply for the Condor Village.

He assigned one fighting diamond with Condor Clan leaders and sent them to relieve the fighting teams that had stayed with the herds.

He also sent one fighting diamond to stay at the trail branch that led to the herds.

His last action was to assign spear throwers along the length of the trail with the job of throwing their spears at any Warrior Clan fighters that might come down the trail. They were to throw their spear and then escape.

He sent word that the three fighting diamonds were to come back up for the battle on the plateau.

The external fighting diamond assignments represented thirty percent of the trained teams. These assignments called for replacement fighting diamond volunteers.

There was no shortage of volunteers. Taelo tasked his team to train the new volunteers. The leaders and one additional experienced diamond fighter were in place with the new teams.

All teams were now led by an experienced Condor Clan member.

Taelo gathered his Elk team back to explain his thinking on how to move forward. They would let the Condor Clan Glass Slingers carry the weight of the battle. They would be in reserve and support any weak point that might manifest itself.

The Warrior Clan leaders had relocated their army to the high end of the plateau. Their thinking was that it would be much harder for the Condor Clan to surprise the Warrior Clan in this position and the Condor Clan, to their disadvantage, would have to fight uphill.

The plan was to rush their warriors downhill at the oncoming Condor Clan fighters and overwhelm them with their number of fighters.

Taelo asked Bold Walker if there was a way to go up the cliff at the side of the plateau?

Bold Walker described the backside of the plateau as a sheer cliff. At one point the only way to go up was to wedge one's hand into a crack and proceed out over the abyss hanging by one's hand. The climber had to follow that crack upward for at least three spear lengths. Then the climber reached a narrow ledge, were once again clinging to the various hand holds, the climber could edge along to the top. There the trail ended behind a huge black boulder.

There were only a handful of Condor Clan climbers that could do what he had described.

"Who are these climbers and are they ready to make this climb," Taelo asked?

Bold Walker gave the names of twelve members of the Condor Clan that were capable of making the climb. Eight of them were women.

Taelo asked to meet with these fighters.

Bold Walker introduced the fighters who could make the climb. Taelo looked at the group and it was clear to him why these were the successful climbers of the cliff behind the Condor Plateau. They were, as a group, thinner and smaller than the average Condor Clan members.

It was also plainly clear that one of them would not be making the climb. He walked over to greet her personally and with a smile asked when she was due. He thanked her for being willing but told her that there was a Condor Clan member that she would have to raise first.

Then he addressed the rest of them and asked if they were willing to be a fighting diamond? Their response was overwhelmingly enthusiastic. They had participated in all the training, but they had been deemed too small. Now they were ready to go.

Taelo asked them if they would follow him in a run around the training field. He did not wait but went out running at full speed. He smiled as one of the smaller women caught up with him and smiled as she accelerated past him.

He picked up the pace to match her. Behind him the remaining eleven members kept pace.

Taelo called a halt on the far side of the field. He asked if they knew the war cry of the fighting diamonds.

In unison the eleven responded with a roaring cry.

He led the team at a leisurely pace back to the initial meeting area.

Bold Walker was there and smiled as Taelo stopped and gave the war cry in unison with the eleven cliff climbing volunteers.

On Taelo's signal Star Leaper appeared with the leadership team and presented the Cliff Fighting Diamond team with flat blades, and glass sharks toothed weapons. Like all other flat blade weapons each had the name of the warrior engraved on it.

Each participant came forward to get their weapon.

Taelo presented a weapon to the pregnant volunteer and told her to keep it safe until her son or daughter became a warrior.

Taelo then returned to the veranda of the Villa were the rest of his team was waiting. Bold Walker now spent most of his time with Taelo and his team. Together they modified their harass and attack plan. This time, Neiva, and the glass slingers were to be the main weapon.

Bold Walker and his crevasse leaping teams would vault across the crevasse. Two of Bold Walker's fighting diamonds would stand guard as the third team helped re-establish the crevasse bridge.

Once the bridge was up, the Cliff Climbing fighting diamond would come across and immediately proceed along the crevassed to the back of the plateau.

Then an additional nine Condor Clan fighting diamonds would come across.

Taelo and his team would come across last.

The two fighting diamonds protecting the Llama herd would be brought up. The one fighting diamond at the trail branch would remain in their position.

This would put fifteen fighting diamonds in the plateau.

The team was in high spirits as they broke up for the night. The rise of the sun would be the catalyst for the day of battle.

The last thought Taelo had was how wonderful it felt to have a warm head on his chest.

The cool morning breeze brushed across Taelo's cheek. As always, he slowly opened his eyes to look at Quiet Rabbit whose head rested on his now numb right arm.

He was surprised to look directly at her open eyes as they watched him. She had her right arm across his chest and her hand was gently stroking Lasher as he lay beside Taelo.

It was clear to Taelo that the three of them were in a triangle love affair.

Taelo smiled and brushed his cheek across Quiet Rabbits hair. He closed his eyes and relived the events of the last few days. He relived the moment when he felt the fear of losing her. A cold shiver ran up his back and he gave a sigh. Quiet Rabbit was life to him.

The Warrior Clan treatment of Quiet Rabbit and Busy Bee enraged him. The war priest he had killed was the one who had beaten them but none of the other leaders had stopped him. He considered all of them complicit.

He knew that he would exact some sort of retribution before he went back North.

He reached back and put his hand on Lasher's chest and gently rubbed it. Lasher had taken several days to get fully back on his feet and Quiet Rabbit had made sure he was given the best treatment possible. He had saved her life two times and even when seriously wounded Lasher had put her life ahead of his.

Later, around the morning meal Taelo told his team that the Ancestors had talked with him, and that the Condor Clan would be victorious. He reaffirmed that the Condor Clan, though greatly outnumbered had a solid strategy and they would defeat the Warrior Clan.

He gave Lasher a tender piece of Llama and thanked him for twice saving Quiet Rabbit.

Busy Bee was recovering but she was feeling the anguish of having lost one of her fighters when he had been mistaken as the leader of the fighting team. She shared her anguish with the team.

Bold Walker informed her that the fighting diamonds she had led were now named after the fallen fighter in his honor and that his younger brother had joined that fighting diamond. He shared the fact that the family did not blame Busy Bee.

Taelo stood and thanked all of his team for their leadership. He turned to Busy Bee and gave her a hug.

This everyone knew was a show of the bond that Taelo had with the entire team.

He turned and declared that the Warrior Clan would lose the battle. He and the team would later deal with the Warrior Priests and war leaders.

Star Leaper, Taelo and Bold Walker approached the leadership meeting area to present the next battle plan. This was the plan to drive the Warrior Clan fighters out of the area.

The fighting diamonds would move along the right, high side of the valley. They would need to attack hard enough to drive the Warrior Clan fighters away from the cliff edge and allow the attack from that side by the Cliff Climbing fighting triangle to gain their footage and have a means of retreat if necessary.

The meeting to review the upcoming battle was the next event that Taelo attended with Star Leaper and Bold Walker. Star Leaper gave the talking staff to Bold Walker who took it, stood before the leadership, shared the battle plan, and answered a few penetrating questions.

Taelo watched each of the leadership team members. Quiet Rabbit had pointed out that someone the Condor Clan had shared the plan to protect the herds. He was now looking for a traitor or at least a spy. He took note as an attendant to one of the Condor Clan leaders left the meeting.

He and Bold Walker had discussed the possibility of a traitor or spy in their midst. Bold Walker assured Taelo that none of the Condor Clan leaders would side with the Warrior Clan. However, he arranged to have anyone leaving the meeting followed. Before the meeting he had instructed a hand full of his trusted friends to follow anyone leaving the meeting early. They would be monitoring anyone trying to leave by the back door.

Bold Walker was certain no one would be able to sneak out.

The attendant that had left the meeting was caught. She tried to tell the guards that she was going to the upper llama herd to see her brother.

The sun was setting behind the far mountains when Bold Walker arrived for the evening meal. He shared that an attendant to one of the leaders who had favored paying tribute to the Warrior Clan had been stopped at the back door as she tried to leave.

Bold Walker said that Star Leaper had immediately taken every person associated with this opposition leader into custody.

If he were found to have warned the Warrior Clan about the protection being set up for the Llama herders and perhaps informed them where the herds were located this leader would face a death sentence. His followers would no longer be Condor Clan members and would be sent out of the Condor Clan territory.

There would be no leniency. It had cost the life of at least one Condor Clan member. There seemed little doubt of guilt, but a thorough investigation was taking place. They were interrogating the messenger who faced the same sentence. She would be granted her life if she cooperated and shared the messages she had carried out on previous trips.

Taelo and the team discussed the situation and agreed that there was little to be gained getting involved in the Condor leadership issue. It was clear that that leader shared responsibility for Busy Bee and Quiet Rabbit's harsh treatment. The punishment he faced was sufficient.

Taelo specifically asked Busy Bee and Quiet Rabbit if they wanted to take any action. They agreed that the Condor Clan action would be enough.

The other members of the leadership team were shocked by thought that one of their own might have taken such action. The result was absolute support for the new battle plan.

Taelo arranged for a runner to give Golden Hawk the message that he should arrange for one of the Warrior Clan members to be captured and released with the message that Taelo was returning with ten times the number of fighters to ravage and annihilate the Warrior Clan village.

Taelo's actual message he wanted to tell Golden Hawk was not to engage the Warrior Clan members as they made their way northward out of the Condor Clan territory.

He wanted the Warrior Clan to return to their home territory. They would be returning with more than half of their fighters with some sort of serious wound. It would be a journey of pain and humiliation.

Golden Hawk should return and be part of the victory celebration.

The Condor Clan leadership had been surprised at the effectiveness of the fighting diamonds. They had clearly been impressed by those fighters leaping across the crevasse into the very face of the enemy. It was clear that the entire Condor Clan had new energy and pride. They were energized and agreed to follow the guidance of Star Leaper.

Star Leaper sent a message to Bold Walker and Taelo that he planned a grand celebration after the Warrior Clan left the Condor Clan territory.

The entire leadership team was now in his control. He decided he would take the leadership into battle in front of the Condor Clan Warriors. They would fall back as a fighting diamond and participate in helping drive out the Warrior Clan,

Chapter 7: Positioning for Battle

The new leader of the Warrior Clan, Dark Night, knew that the Warrior Clan still had more than a five to one numerical warrior advantage. He was concerned with number that had been wounded in their first encounter, but he remained confident in winning the upcoming battle.

The war priests were boasting that the result of the next battle favored their side. They would have the advantage of fighting downhill. They predicted that they would charge downhill and would mow down the Condor Clan members the same way a hawk takes out a swallow or sinks its talons into the back of a fish. It would be no contest. The war priests were sure the Warrior Clan fighters would immediately overwhelm the Condor Clan fighters.

Then the Warrior Clan would gain an entire new territory. They would be victorious if the Condor fighters worked up their nerve to come out and fight.

Dark Night was not so sure that it would be so easy. He had watched the effectiveness of the fighting style being used by the Condor clan. It was clear to him that his opponent had training that made them superior fighters.

Not long after the boasts by the battle priests, the wounded fighters who had been out guarding the Llama herds came into camp. Half of them were seriously wounded and unable to walk. They would only be a burden.

The Llama herds were now protected with Condor fighters.

Dark Night knew that the food for the Warrior clan would need to come down from their homeland. The fighters returning from the Llama herds mentioned that they had overheard that a number of fighters were on the way north to the Warrior Clan home. They went on to say how lucky they had been to fight well enough to escape with all their fighters alive.

Dark Night looked at the number of wounded fighters and wondered about the ease of the escape. He figured they had been allowed escape. He was well aware that a wounded fighter became a burden that required attention. This meant resources that were taken away from the battle.

The news about fighters going north was discounted until another warrior arrived. Breathless from having run up the mountain he explained that he had just escaped from two groups of Condor Clan fighters.

The leader was Golden Hawk. This name was known to several of the Warrior Clan members. Not too far in the past Golden Hawk and Taelo had been visitors to the Warrior Clan. That was the time Taelo had killed the Warrior Clan co-leader Sharp Knife and had declined to become a coleader with Tough Hide. Taelo could have become partner leader of the Warrior Clan. He chose to return to his own clan territory.

Dark Night was well aware of that event, and he had been impressed with the bravery and the principled behavior displayed by Taelo. Such a person was a threat to him.

Dark Night gathered the details of Golden Hawk's daring attack on the Warrior Clan home. He was concerned about the additional fighters going north and the fact that another attack would then be very probable. He knew that at least a thousand fighters were still in the village.

He had the war priests reappraise the situation. It was clear to him that immediately after their victory over the Condor Clan, half of the fighters would need to return home while the remainder would stay to control the Condor Clan region.

Dark Night wanted to engage in battle as soon as possible. Victory needed to be total and swift.

He had made the choice to wait until the Warrior Clan was the victor in the upcoming battle before sending fighters out to retake the Llama herds. He also wanted to see if any supplies would come up the mountain from the north. He had the war council focus on the upcoming battle. He needed a swift victory.

He ordered all the wounded be examined and those capable of fighting be put back into their fighting units.

He needed the Condor Clan to come across the crevasse. He sent a small group of scouts down to observe but told them not to engage. They were to alert him when the Condor Clan fighters came across.

A few days later, the Warrior Clan scouts positioned close to the crevasse, watched as more than thirty warriors vaulted across the crevasse. They were impressed at the ability of this group to easily clear the crevasse. They commented that they did not want to face that fighting group.

One runner immediately returned to the Warrior Clan camp to let the war leaders know that something was happening at the crevasse.

Dark Night looked at the Condor and Eagle flying lazily above as a signal. He took it as a sign of the Warrior Clan ancestors giving him a victory sign.

Had he known that these were Taelo's and the Condor Clan's totems, he might have reassessed his thinking.

Once across the crevasse, Bold Walker moved the thirty warriors into a defensive position. They were to protect those putting up the bridge across.

The bridge erection had been practiced multiple times by the bridge building team.

Bold Walker watched as the crew continued the erection well past the time the sun reached its zenith. The new bridge was wider and stronger than any previous bridge. It was designed to withstand Llamas loaded with bags of glass shards. The bridge was erected in record time.

Bold Walker knew that the Warrior Clan scouts would be watching. He sent out at fighting diamond to engage the scouts if they did not leave.

The women slingers came across to serve as a distraction. Nieva, Single Leaf, Quiet Rabbit, and Busy Bee were organizing the slingers for battle. Their presence gave the Sling teams the confidence they needed for their first time in battle. They took their position on their slinger group. Once Nieva had the women ready, she led them in a battle cry. This was the signal for the Cliff Fighters to cross and disappear.

The repeated war cry by the sling teams had the desired distracting effect.

All the scouts had to retreat up the hill or face the fighting triangle that was almost at their location.

Their report about women on the battlefield led to another round of discussion among the war leaders.

The Cliff Fighters moved swiftly out of sight as they headed for the back side of the plateau and the towering cliff they would need to scale. Each carried a bag full of glass shards and a sling.

They had all mastered the sling and felt empowered by this new capability. Their spears would be the clumsy item they had to carry up the cliff with them. They moved with surety and an enhanced enthusiasm they felt as they approached this climb of climbs.

Bold Walker signaled for the men in the fighting diamonds to come across the crevasse. Once in position and organized they let out an even louder war cry and pointed their spears up the valley to the Warrior Clan.

Bold Walker had put the fighting diamonds across the front of where the Slingers were preparing themselves for battle. This blocked the view of the of the rest of the preparation.

The Warrior Clan war priests relished the situation. They were certain when the Condor Clan made their march up the valley, the Warrior Clan fighters would have the downhill battle advantage. The battle would quickly be over.

Once again, Dark Night wondered about the acumen of the War Priests. He was not as sure about overrunning the Condor Clan fighters as his advisors.

Back at the bridge, Bold Walker signaled for the Llamas and the sling glass supply to be brought across.

The Llama handlers took their loads to three separate holding locations.

Every able-bodied person in the Condor Clan carried bags of glass shards to the three Llama loading locations. More glass shards were coming down the mountain side. Neiva had implored the Condor Clan population to ensure the slingers did not run out of the glass shard ammunition.

Taelo came across with his team. They too carried bags of glass shards.

Neiva had asked Quiet Rabbit, Busy Bee, and Single Leaf to help get the sling teams organized and positioned. She knew that her three northern aids presence would help to reduce the concern of the slingers.

Single Leaf's capability with her sling was already becoming legend with the slinger teams.

Single Leaf, Quiet Rabbit, and Busy Bee had several good laughs when they heard some of the amazing capabilities that had been attributed to Single Leaf. Single Leaf enjoyed the notoriety.

Neiva had requested that Quiet Rabbit, Busy Bee, and Single leaf support her in maneuvering the sling teams. She wanted to always keep the slingers just outside the range of the Warrior Clan spear throwers.

Taelo's team adjusted their roles to compensate for the loss of their three members. They would stay to the back of the Condor Clan fighters and move into support as they moved the Warrior Clan away from the cliff.

Dark Night had reacted in surprise at having women on the battlefield. He put this point up for discussion with the war priests. Their response was the women would pose no threat. They were probably meant to be a distraction to the Warrior Clan fighters.

Dark Night had the nagging feeling and was sure that the women would be much more than just a distraction. There was something he and his advisors were missing.

Star Leaper led the leadership team into the field in support of the Condor Warriors. He and the leadership team stood in front of all the Condor Clan warriors. They would lead from the front. This was not the traditional way but having women fight was also not traditional.

The leaders were as nervous as the Slingers.

Star Leaper suggested they take up the sling and participate in slinging glass shards.

Taelo complimented the leadership team and suggested that once the battle was about to commence, the leadership team should take their position outside of the last fighting diamond closest to the cliff side. He made the point that it would strengthen the move up the valley.

The position would be of help, but it also put them all out of the way.

The fighting diamond teams positioned themselves across the valley.

The slingers formed two lines of five in each line. They kept to the back of the fighting diamond formation. The objective was to keep them somewhat invisible until the battle began.

The two fighting diamonds that had been guarding the Llama herds arrived just in time for them to join on the far side away from the cliff.

Bold Walker walked out to the very front of the Condor Clan fighters. He turned and faced them and signaled for Taelo's battle cry. Then he gave the Condor Clan battle cry. He then signaled those in the field to do the same.

Dark Night was impressed by the organization of the Condor Clan. He however remained very confident in the five to one number of fighter superiority that the Warrior Clan held.

The loud war cry of the entire Condor Clan caught all the Warrior Clan members attention.

Bold Walker and Taelo slowly led the way across the plateau. They walked side by side each carrying an upright spear. Taelo's spear had a golden feather and Bold Walker had a Condor feather hanging from his. They stopped several times to lead a war cry.

The entire Condor Clan echoed their cry. The fighting diamonds followed with their deep guttural cry. Then the slingers followed with a high-pitched vibrating echo cry. Then everyone gave the war cry in unison.

The orchestration of the war cry had been the doing of Neiva, Quiet Rabbit, and Busy Bee. The impact was powerful and in its own way beautiful.

Taelo was watching the sun. He wanted to give the Cliff fighters plenty of time to make their ascent. This was a battle of nerves as well as a physical battle. He anticipated that a surprise attack from the cliff side would unnerve the Warrior Clan leadership.

The repeated Condor war cry made many of the Warrior Clan fighters nervous.

The Warrior Clan leaders were getting frustrated by the slow pace that the Condor Clan was moving into the battle.

The pace and the actions of the Condor Clan began to irritate the Warrior battle leaders. They wondered why the Condor Clan did not attack.

Dark Night listened to the arguments about attacking versus worrying about staying on the high ground that broke out among the War priests.

The more they argued the more concerned Dark Night became.

There was not one dominant Warrior Clan war priest, so the arguments continued all morning.

The repeated Condor battle cry had an emotional effect on all the Warrior Clan members.

A group of about sixty warriors gathered to the side of the battle formation. Strong Sinew and Storm Wind, the sons of Tough Hide the previous leader of the Warrior Clan that had been recently killed by Dark Night, recommended that they watch the first attack and determine the best course of action.

They all wore the band of friendship given to them by Taelo and his team. They were not sure about the current battle arrangement, but they believed that the women were there to fight.

Strong Sinew was not sure what impact the women might have but his previous experience of underestimating Taelo would not happen again.

Finally, after the sun reached its zenith, the Condor Clan fighters were just below the Warrior Clan army. They had taken as long as possible to get to this position.

Taelo and Bold Walker turned to face the Condor fighters. They gave out a loud battle cry. In silence the Condor Clan army slowly spread out and the slingers repeatedly gave their war cry as they stepped forward and took the forward battle position.

The Condor Clan leaders moved to the cliff side of the formation.

The War priests were preparing for their attack when they noted a distinct shift in the Condor Clan battle formation. It had spread out and the women stood casually just to the front of and between each fighting diamond.

The world of the Warrior Clan and the flavor of the upcoming battle took on an unexpected turn. Confusion reigned among the various Warrior Clan fighting groups.

The war priests called a meeting to discuss the situation and the meaning of the arrangement of the Condor Clan battle formation. It appeared the women were un-armed. The only reason for them to be there would be as a distraction. They were not dressed for battle but were showing bare legs and bare midriffs. They seemed to be enticing the Warrior Clan fighters. This was unheard of in the middle of a battle.

Dark Night listened impatiently as the Warrior Priests continued their argument. He kept trying to understand the fighting formation taken by the Condor Clan.

The Condor war cry made many of the Warrior fighters nervous. The positioning of the women to the front of the battle line totally disrupted their vision of a hand-to-hand battle.

Dark Night knew that he needed to take action.

After the sun reached its zenith, the Condor Clan fighters moved to just below the Warrior Clan army. They had taken as long as possible to get to this, a seemingly poor, battlefield position.

Taelo let out a battle cry and waved up to the Warrior Clan army for them to attack!

The world of the Warrior Clan and the flavor of the upcoming battle had taken several unexpected turns.

Confusion reigned among the various Warrior Clan fighting groups.

Dark Night signaled the first wave of Warrior Clan fighters to attack.

Chapter 8: The Condor Clan Battle

Star Leaper and Bold Walker stood in front of the gathered Condor Clan fighting triangles. Neiva and two of her sling leaders stood behind them. At Star Leaper's signal the entire Condor Clan fighters blasted out three roaring battle cries and began a slow but steady march up the slope. Every seven steps they stopped and roared out another battle cry. They repeated this more than seven times before they observed any reaction from the Warrior Clan.

They knew they were facing a dramatically superior number of warriors. Bold Walker spent a great deal of time encouraging all the fighters. He had demonstrated his formidable fighting capability and now had the respect of the entire Condor Clan. Since Taelo's arrival he had grown in stature and was now recognized as the top warrior in the Clan. Even so, he was worried as he anticipated the charge of a vastly superior number of Warrior Clan fighters.

He was especially worried as he looked around at all the women who had bravely come into battle with their male counter parts.

The women had been inspired and thoroughly trained by Quiet Rabbit, Busy Bee, and Single Leaf. The Condor Clan women had developed the confidence to stand in formation with their fighting male Condor Clan members. They would let the fighting triangles give their low roaring battle cry and then immediately follow with their higher octave but piercing echo of the same cry. The combination proved eerily effective in disorienting the Warrior Clan fighters.

The Warrior Clan were unnerved as they heard this synchronized and seemingly continuous battle cry. Never had they encountered such an army. Never had they faced women in battle.

It was clear to Dark Night and the other leaders of the Warrior Clan that something very unusual was happening before them.

It was immediately clear to the Warrior Clan that the formation marching slowly up the hill had the intension of a full-scale battle. This pleased them since they had at least a five to one advantage in the number of warriors, and they had the high ground.

Dark Night instructed the Warrior Clan fighters to treat the women as full warriors and show no mercy in battle. The warrior priests were as confused as all their warriors about the Condor Clan women.

The warrior priests called for the first attack wave to engage the Condor Clan. This first wave would have the same number of warriors as that of the Condor Clan. They would be closely followed by a second wave and then the rest of the Warrior Clan fighters would commence a series of hit and retreat encounters.

The plan was for a continuous rotating wave of assaults. They counted on the multiple assault waves rushing down at the Condor Clan would quickly overwhelm their opponents.

They planned on a short battle and a quick victory.

High overhead the eagle let out its cry. The eagle and condor flew together in a larger circular path.

Taelo and his team were now in position behind the Condor Clan formation. They were the reserve team. They were to support any area that was being overcome. He had added his coaching to that of Quiet Rabbit and Busy Bee on the best way for the Slingers to be utilized.

Nieva had implemented his suggestion to form two lines of slingers and have the front two rotate to the back after their sling. The next two would take two steps forward and let fly their sling. This rotation would mean that the battle line would move forward ten paces on every sling team rotation.

Taelo had decided that this crucial battle should be determined primarily by the members of the Condor Clan. He and his team had prepared and trained everyone on the battlefield. The women slingers had all been trained and qualified by Single Leaf, Quiet Rabbit, and Busy Bee. The three were certain the slingers would perform well. He was sure that the Condor Clan would carry the day.

He hoped the team climbing the cliff would be in place when the battle began. They had been instructed to come out when a single team of women would give the battle cry in a piercing impossibly high pitch.

Then it began; the first wave of Warrior Clan came rushing down the hill. They were expecting to throw their spears and then be replace by the next wave of warriors.

When they were about three spears throws away from the oncoming Condor Clan fighters, the Condor Clan women let out a battle cry and stepped forward from between the men and advanced in step toward the oncoming fighters.

The wave of fighters faltered as they took this in.

Almost in unison the Warrior Clan fighters hesitated before again proceeding forward. Their concentration in their downward rush had been broken. Before them in the open and apparently unprotected, they were facing a totally unexpected set of women warriors.

They were still two spear throw lengths away when they raised their spears in readiness. Their spears would most likely kill most of the women and they would be facing unwounded Condor Clan fighters.

They hoped the next wave of warriors would be close behind them.

Neiva stepped forward and let out her high piercing war cry. This was not only the signal to the fighting team that had climbed the cliff but to all the sling team members. Then they returned to the war cry with each of three steps they took forward. Hii ee, step, Hii ee step, Hii ee step.

The shards of glass left Nieva's sling as she finished her war cry. The sling team members all let out their war cry and began their rotating sling action. The glass shards found their mark.

The entire front of the charging Warrior Clan came to an immediate stop well short of being able to throw their spears. They were screaming in agony as shards of glass hit them in the face, upper body, and their legs.

All the male Condor Clan fighters now gave the deep background war cry. The battle line was slowly advancing up the slope.

The second wave of Warrior Clan fighters ran between their writhing fighting partners. They heard the high-pitched battle cry and were immediately hit by another round of glass shards. The slingers now took turns as they selectively picked off specifically targeted Warrior Clan fighters.

The screams of agony and the stumbling Warrior Clan fighters slowed the upward progress of the Condor Clan. They had no desire to engage in any hand-to-hand combat if at all possible. They chose instead to slow their upward movement to allow the wounded Warrior Clan fighters time to stumble back up the hill.

The group of sixty took in the carnage as the first wave crumbled and retreated. They began to understand the plan. Not so long ago they had faced something similar. They had returned to their village embarrassed by their inability to confront Taelo and Golden Hawk.

Dark Night now understood the purpose of the women. They were effectively neutralizing the advantage the Warrior Clan had in number of fighters.

The warrior clan War priests took in the scene and immediately dispatched the remaining three waves of warriors.

The slingers were now if full rhythm. Their synchronized assault of glass shards totally disrupted the Warrior Clan fighters. Not one spear had reached the slowly oncoming Condor Clan fighters.

The group of sixty noted the effectiveness of the slingers. It was clear to them that the Warrior Clan had no way to overcome the battleground advantage the slingers represented.

The Condor Fighting Triangles let out their much lower pitch but roaring battle cries and were echoed by the women slingers. They all proceeded slowly forward.

The women warriors were untouched and were leading the way slowly up the hill. They seemed relaxed and in no hurry. Their slinging attack became focused on those remaining warriors that had not yet experienced a face full of glass shards.

Strong Sinew and Storm Wind realized that no person could stand up to the synchronized glass slinging onslaught. They slowly led the group of sixty to the exit side of the battlefield. They would not sacrifice themselves to a poorly led army in a battle they should never have created. It was clear it was time to return to their own territory and hope that the Condor Clan did not seek revenge on the retreating Warrior Clan army.

Taelo had advised against taking any prisoners. Instead, if necessary, the battle front was to slowly back up and allow more fresh Warrior Clan warriors to make their approach. This would maximize the impact that the slingers would have.

Once the attackers were retreating the goal was to let them take all the wounded warriors back with them.

The Condor Cliff fighting team heard the battle cries. They had to control their desire to look out from behind the boulders. They took time to eat a quick snack. They knew they had used a great deal of energy to get up the cliff and into position.

Now they would need to attack from the cliff side and make it sound as if a group ten times their size was coming into battle.

They would be at significant risk until they could merge with the rest of the Condor Clan fighters.

The Condor Cliff fighting team leader looked carefully around the boulder. She wanted to take her team rapidly and with deadly effect down the cliff side of the battle and join the other fighting teams.

Her team was a hybrid. The women would be slinging shards of glass and the men would provide support if a hand-to-hand battle became necessary. She had no desire to get into any hand-to-hand fight with the Warrior Clan fighters.

Taelo had been waiting for the Cliff fighting team to make their appearance. Nieva let out her solo battle cry. Her single powerful voice floated across a quiet battlefield that now lacked the battle cries of the Warrior Clan and instead was filled with an eerie moaning.

The Cliff team let out their battle cry and stepped out from behind their hiding place.

Dark Night and the Warrior Clan leaders and battle priests immediately reacted by retreating away from the cliff. Their warrior guards were sent to engage the new threat. They were almost defenseless against an attack in their current formation.

Taelo and his team gave an answering cry and began an upward march along the cliff side.

He knew that the cliff team faced the greatest possibility of being overrun. They were there to demoralize the main group of Warrior Clan fighters and to shake up the Warrior Clan leaders who would be gathered there.

The reaction he observed signaled that Cliff Climbers had been effective.

There was now disarray among the battle leaders. Some were immediately moving along the open escape route. The hard-core leaders were sending yet another wave of Warrior Clan fighters to engage the Condor Clan fighters.

Their immediate Warrior Clan protectors advanced toward what appeared to be a small group of Condor Clan fighters. They were anticipating to quickly overcome this attack. Then they met the wall of glass shards. Their loud screams and inability to close the gap to the Condor Clan, cliff fighting team unnerved the War priests and other warrior clan leaders.

The Condor Clan cliff fighters proceeded to rain shards of glass and move slowly down the side of the Warrior Clan members. As they moved downward, they also moved forward. They were concerned about getting trapped and overwhelmed by the number of Warrior Clan fighters, but they moved cautiously toward their enemy.

Taelo evaluated the situation and led his team up toward the Condor Clan Cliff fighters.

The potential of the single team being overwhelmed was on his mind. The movement from below did not go unnoticed by the Warrior Clan members. They began to move toward the cliff side.

In a smooth coordinated movement, the entire Condor fighting formation moved to support Taelo's fighting diamond. Together they blocked the movement of the Warrior Clan.

Every seven steps the entire Condor Clan fighting team let out their battle cry. They were dominating the battle. They were controlling the field.

A heavily wounded Warrior Clan and their leaders were completely overcome with the battle situation. Not one Condor Clan fighter had yet been engaged. More than half of the Warrior Clan fighters were seriously wounded in the face. A few were likely to be blind.

The Warrior Clan war priests decided on a full-scale attack at the center point of the battle front. They would pierce through and then move to each side of the Condor Clan fighters. This was their solution to the glass slinging women who had so effectively defeated more than triple their number.

The muttering about the outcome and how there would be retribution for such unheard-of fighting could be heard among the leaders.

Nieva shouted to the slingers to sling in a continuous rotation. They were not to move forward. The slingers were now if full rhythm. They had gained confidence and their sling accuracy had improved. Their synchronized assault of glass shards totally disabled the oncoming Warrior Clan fighters.

The Warrior Clan assault became a route.

The battle front had rotated, and the Condor Clan now had half of the fighters with their back to the plateau cliff. The remaining fighter's positions created the shape of the downward stroke of the condor's wing.

The retreat of the Warrior Clan would take them away from the cliff and down from the plateau and the mountain.

Star Leaper and Bold Walker lead the battle front slowly forward. Their goal now was to force the Warrior Clan from their plateau position and down the mountain. Their battle cry was now echoed at every other step. Their fighting triangles had not yet been engaged. Their army of glass slingers had effectively defeated the Warrior Clan fighters.

The job of supplying the glass shards to the slingers became the most crucial position. The slingers were using their glass shards in a very efficient and focused way but consuming a large amount of glass shards. Even in this controlled fashion resupply was a big challenge.

Neiva passed the word to be more strategic with each sling. Only the lead Warrior clan fighters were to be targeted. This effectively cut the sling capacity by half. It was enough to keep the enemy at bay.

So far not one spear had made it to the fighting line. And not one Warrior Clan fighter had made it any closer than one spear's throw.

The Cliff fighting team had totally demoralized the Warrior Clan Leaders. The glass shards and damage to the warriors facing the barrage had seriously weakened the entire Warrior Clan army of fighters.

The Warrior Clan fighters protecting the leaders quickly recovered and advanced toward what appeared to be a small group of Condor Clan fighters. They were anticipating to quickly overcome this attack. Then they met the wall of glass shards. Their loud screams and inability to close the gap to the Condor Clan fighting team unnerved the fight priests and other Warrior Clan leaders. They were witnessing first-hand the deadly effect of a small team of fighters spewing glass shards. These slingers were able to totally stop a superior number of warriors.

High overhead the cry of the Eagle and the cry of the Condor pierced through the noise of the battle. Taelo and his team knew this cry well. The Condor Clan fighters responded with a continuous series of battle cries in response. Lasher standing next to Quiet Rabbit let out a loud howl.

The Eagle gave a screeching reply as it turned north and flew out of sight.

The war priests took the cries as a sign from the god of war. They looked out at the confusion and attitude of their fighters and the fact that not one of them had reached the Condor fighters as an omen. It was time to leave the battlefield and go home.

Word had come that the Condor Clan planned an attack of their city in the north. It was clear that if they were not there to defend their home, they could lose everything.

The group of sixty watched as the first wave of leaders left the plateau on the path leading down and toward the north. They knew the battle was over.

Strong Sinew knew that as a group the group of sixty now represented the strongest group among the Warrior Clan. He planned to take action when they were back at their home village.

The Condor Clan Cliff fighters proceeded to rain shards of glass and move slowly down the side of the Warrior Clan fighters. The shards of glass hitting the fighters from the side totally surprised and disheartened them.

As the Cliff fighting team moved downward, they also moved forward. They were no longer concerned about being trapped and overwhelmed by the number of Warrior Clan fighters. They realized that their movement alarmed the Warrior Clan fighters who began an upward retreat.

Nieva saw that the battle was over. She let out a warbling war cry and her slingers stepped back. They were relieved. They knew they had exceeded expectation and congratulated each other. No Warrior Clan spear had crossed the glass sling zone.

In a smooth coordinated movement, the entire Condor fighting formation moved to support Taelo's fighting diamond. Together they pushed the Warrior Clan back toward the open escape route.

The entire Condor fighting front proceeded at an even pace toward the Warrior Clan.

The Warrior Clan retreated down the mountain. At least half of their fighters were severely wounded and needed help in their retreat.

The Condor Clan kept their forward march to the speed of the retreat. It was clear they had won the day and the battle plan was a resounding success. The loss of many of the warrior's voices was the most noticeable wound the Condor Clan had suffered. Some women slingers had also suffered bloody fingertips from loading the shards of glass into their slings.

The Warrior fighting priests were relieved that the Condor fighters were not trying to destroy them during the retreat.

Star Leaper had to control his desire to follow and continue to wreak havoc. Taelo's counseling provided the basis for holding back.

The group of sixty were bringing up the rear. They had anticipated a continuing attack during their retreat. They were surprised when it did not occur. They, however, had no illusions about the situation. They had suffered a humiliating defeat.

The wounded Warrior Clan fighters would be the biggest deterrent of any future encroachment of the Condor Clan territory.

Bold Walker and a small team of fighters followed the Warrior Clan down the mountain. Every dozen or so steps they would let out a battle cry. They had no desire to engage in battle but wanted the Warrior Clan to hear the cry in their dreams.

They stopped when they came upon a wall of sixty spears planted tip down into the ground. Bold Walker was not sure what the wall meant but he collected the sixty spears and carried them back toward the crevasse and the village.

Taelo explained that the spears were a recognition of defeat and a symbol that the retreating army did not wish for any farther battle.

The Condor Clan fighters lifted the slingers to their shoulders and carried them back to the bridge crossing over to the village.

They sang songs of praise for their fighting women. It was a complete change in roles.

The male warriors cooked the ceremony meal. They had just participated in driving the Warrior Clan from their mountain kingdom and not one of them had been touched. Not one of them had to fight! No spear left their hand!

Single handed, the women slingers had carried the day. Single Leaf, Quiet Rabbit, Busy Bee and Nieva were all carried by the singing women slingers. They were all legends in the songs of praise and admiration.

The partying, singing and exchange of battle stories went on for several sun cycles. Taelo and his team members were constantly the focus in one part of the village or the next. It was clear that the people revered Taelo and his team members. They were permanently imbedded in the stories and songs of the Condor Clan.

Star Leaper, in a formal ceremony, presented each of them with the flat weapon edged with glass shards and their names inlayed in gold. The weapon was black wood with gold inlayed names and edged with black triangular glass shards. These weapons were as beautiful as they were deadly.

The Taelo's team humbly accepted their gifts and in turn praised the courage of all the Condor Clan and thanked them all for having given their trust to the team.

Taelo had never seen Golden Hawk as angry as when he found out about the capture and treatment of Busy Bee and Quiet Rabbit. Golden Hawk vowed revenge.

His bond with Bold Walker was sealed for life when he learned of Bold Walker's leap into the midst of the Warrior Clan with only four fighting diamond teams.

When he heard of Taelo's and Lasher's rescue of Quiet Rabbit and Busy Bee's fighting diamond team he gave his best friend a bear hug.

His emotions were hard to control. His reflexive expression was to hug Busy Bee and tightly hold her. He had tears in his eyes, but they were tears of anger for the Warrior Clan leaders that had whipped Busy Bee and Quiet Rabbit.

He vowed that on the trip back north he was going to stop at the Warrior Village and surprise every one of the Warrior Clan leaders and priests and mark them for life in a fashion they would not be able to hide.

The rising sun on the next day stirred the air coming up the slope of the valley. The cool morning breeze blew gently on Taelo's cheek. He was watching the sun come up over the peak on his left and looking down to his right, he was watching the black of the valley slowly turn to grey and reveal the small bushes and grasses sprinkled randomly down the rock covered slope. The darkness of the valley was retreating slowly away.

He had come awake with the call of the North. It was time for him and the team to make their departure.

Quiet Rabbit put her arms around his waist and brought her head against his chest. She too knew it was time go home. She pointed to the beauty of the scene before them and then declared she wanted to see the falls cascading down into the pool in the place they had named Paradise.

Golden Hawk and Busy Bee joined them and in unison expressed the same sentiment.

It was time to go home.

Taelo and Golden Hawk walked out of the courtyard and proceeded to the home of Star Leaper.

Neiva greeted them at the door. She took one look at them and said that it had been an honor to fight with them and she understood that it was time for them to return to their land. They and anyone from the Elk Clan would always be welcome in the land of the Condor.

Star Leaper brought them to his home's grand courtyard and offered some honey wine. As he was thanking them for their guidance, Bold Walker arrived.

He bade them a good morning and then surprised everyone when he asked to accompany Taelo to see his sister. This surprise was embraced by everyone.

The next morning the entire village sang their praise in song as they escorted them to the point in the path where Saber Scar had stopped the team on their arrival only a few moons ago.

The next stop would be the home of the Warrior Clan. There they would aid in Golden Hawk's plan of revenge.

Chapter 9: Elk Clan Gathering

Once again it was the time for all the Elk Sub clans to gather. The tall dark green, soldier-spined pines stood their guard while behind them gleaming white topped mountains rose up and away on all sides. The pines presented a dark contrast to the gleaming, white topped mountains behind them. The small oblong lake with yellowing willow trees on its banks appeared as a jewel on one's wrist.

The length of the gathering was usually for ten to fourteen sun cycles. The gathering was a time for family members to reconnect, for old friends to spend some time once again with each other and a time when mothers tried to pair their sons and daughters with good partners.

Feather-in-the-Wind looked down into the valley where all the Elk clan would gather for their annual gathering. Running Stag sat on his mount and looked back at the Eastern Elk Clan members that they were leading and the small herd of mounts they had brought as gifts.

The two had encouraged their clan members to be prepared to show wealth in goods for trade with the other Elk clans.

It had been a hard winter, but the summer months had been fruitful. All the clan members had applied themselves, worked hard and were all able to have many garments, grooming items, footwear, and mounts to trade. Every member was bringing two mounts as their primary trade item. The mounts alone made the Eastern Elk Clan an affluent group.

Feather-in-the-Wind had met her goal in getting the Eastern Elk Clan to return to the valley with as many trade items as possible. She also brought mounts as gifts to each of the other clan leaders. Even the Grazing Elk clan leaders, who she expected to also bring in mounts as gifts, would receive a mount. The gift mount to the Grazing Elk had dire wolf scars on its back-hind quarter. It was a survivor of the dire wolves. This was a mount that would have a special meaning to the Grazing Elk clan members. Their hunters would long remember their rescue by Taelo and his team. She had been part of that rescue effort.

She was bringing the Eastern Elk Clan to the meeting early. She would take the spot second closest to the coral that would hold the mounts. The Eastern Elk Clan would assemble the fencing of the corral for the mounts and then prepare the campsites for the other Elk sub-clans. She left the spot closest to the corral for the Grazing Elk clan. They would have many mounts as well.

Her clan had many single young women and men that had come back with Taelo from his journey to the North. They would be looking for compatible mates. She was also intent in getting a few more families from the other sub-clans to have a better balance of families to single members. There had been a hesitancy by many members of the other sub-clans to join her newly formed Eastern Elk Clan.

She hoped the show of wealth by the Eastern Elk Clan and their friendly gesture of helping all the clans set up their campsites and provide the first meal would also have an impact.

She knew that her selection as leader of the Eastern Elk Clan had also been a detractor to getting potential family members. She hoped to overcome this barrier.

The cleanup and preparation effort were almost complete when the Northern Elk Clan and the Clan of Others were spotted coming down into the valley. Feather-in-the-Wind signaled the cooks to prepare the arrival dinner that was planned for this event. She had expected the two clans to arrive early and arrive together. The two clans would establish camp on the other side of the lake. This had become the normal arrangement.

The Clan of Others would be bringing the large enclosure that would serve as the total Elk Clan leadership meeting area. This was the enclosure the Clan of Others had made for Taelo and his team to use on his previous journey to the north.

Once the two clans were at their campsites, Feather-in-the-Wind, with Running Stag at her side led the Eastern Elk Clan to the other side of the lake. Each member carried a food offering. They had prepared an eating area on the far side and invited the two clans to the prepared feast.

White Swan and Grey Fox Running greeted, Feather-in-the-Wind and Running Stag with hug. Burley Bear and Meadow Flower did the same. This was a gathering of friends and family.

White Swam commented on the apparent good fortune of the Eastern Elk Clan.

Feather-in-the-Wind replied that it was not fortune but the hard work of her clan members that White Swan was praising. She wanted her clan members to know that their success was being recognized.

Feather-in-the-Wind had prepared the Eastern Elk Clan members to be the hosts for the arrival of each Elk Clan sub-clan. The service and the meal were intended to show the other sub-clans the success of the Eastern Elk Clan and to highlight the available young people looking for mates. She wanted the Eastern Elk Clan to be recognized as extraordinarily successful and a great clan to be a part of.

The arrival gifts of beaver hides, rabbit hide wash skins, and a catered meal for every member of the other clans was intended to be a direct demonstration of the success of the Eastern Elk Clan. Feather-in-the-Wind was intent on getting mates for her single people and recruiting additional families from the other clans.

The astounding display of presents by the Eastern Elk Clan to all the clan leaders and each member of the respective clan had an overwhelming positive impact.

The gifts of the mounts would occur at the formal clan leadership meeting. She planned to make that a significant event.

The Eastern Elk Clan's greeting and support of each arriving Elk Clan had the positive effect she desired. At the first clan leadership meeting that followed the feast prepared by the Eastern Elk Clan, Wise Owl brought the meeting to order and thanked Feather-in-the-Wind and the Eastern Elk Clan for being such grand hosts for this season's gathering. He complimented the service and the great food that had been prepared.

Feather-in-the-Wind's interaction in the leadership meetings left no doubt among the leaders that she indeed was almost an equal to White Swan, Taelo's mother and leader of the Northern Elk Clan. They came to the conclusion that Wise Owl the current overall Clan leader had indeed made the right choice.

All the clans had experienced a good season. This meant that the needed adjustments and the sharing of food and other necessities were rapidly accomplished.

The show of prosperity and the enthusiastic and positive support for the Eastern Elk Clan by the Elk leadership resulted in a large number of requests to join the Eastern Elk Clan.

Feather-in-the-Wind had set up a selection committee to review each request and select the families that met the selection criteria that had been discussed. They wanted families that would work as hard as the rest of the clan.

On a walk along the bank of the lake, she shared her feeling of success with White Swan and Quiet Pheasant. Their positive reinforcement gave her new energy. She had arrived stressed out as she worried about her leadership of the Eastern Elk Clan. Their support meant the world to her.

At the next council meeting, Wise Owl made the point that the clan meeting would be on the short side and end early. The Clans could depart at their leisure. The official business had been taken up and addressed. The naming ceremony had been held. The one event that remained was the story telling by Broken Spear, the seer of the Others.

Feather-in-the-Wind asked for the talking staff. She looked around the meeting at the leaders of all the clans. She thanked them for having voted to select her as the leader of the Eastern Elk Clan.

She went on to make the point that the Ancestors had looked down favorably on the clan that she led, and it had been a prosperous successful year.

She then announced that she had brought a mount for each leader and their mates. On her signal a mount was brought into the meeting. She introduced the mount as Dire Wolf and had the reins handed to Fierce Badger, leader of the Grazing Elk.

Feather-in-the-Wind looked at Fierce Badger and made the point that he did not need another mount but that this mount was given as reminder to him and the Grazing Elk clan that they like this mount, Dire Wolf, had survived the attack of the dire wolves. The mount should be cared for and ridden by all the Grazing Elk clan members. This would keep alive the memory of the rescue Taelo and his team had made of the Grazing Elk hunters.

Fierce Badger stood and thanked Feather-in-the-Wind and made the point that Taelo and his team had a permanent home with the Grazing Elk whenever anyone of them needed one. Their stories were told at every gathering of the Grazing Elk members.

Feather-in-the-Wind had each mount pair brought in as she presented them to each of the sub-clan leaders. The two mounts brought in for Burley Bear and Meadow Flower were significantly larger than the previous mounts. Feather-in-the-Wind made the point that when the mount hunters returned with them, they immediately identified who the mounts should go to. Many of her team had seen how often Burley Bear had dismounted and walked with his mount. They wanted him to have a mount, of appropriate size. However, the one she was presenting him was the best that her clan could do, she joked.

Burley Bear stood and got on the mount and rode out of the meeting. His words over his shoulder were a loud thank-you.

Then a young girl led a white swan into the meeting. This had been a secret that had been hard to conceal from White Swan.

Feather-in-the-Wind explained that the swan was found floating down the river that passed by the Eastern Elk Clan home. It was pulled out and saved but it could not fly. It had a wing that had not healed properly. It had recovered and its home was at the pool at the base of the waterfall at the Paradise home of the Eastern Elk Clan.

"The swan is presented to White Swan leader of the Northern Elk Clan," Feather-in-the-Wind announced.

White Swan had a smile and tears in her eyes as she rose and gave Feather-in-the-Wind a hug.

White Swan turned to the leaders and held up the leash to the White Swan. Without speaking she led the swan out while holding the hand of the young girl that had brought it into the meeting tent.

Wise Owl took the staff from Feather-in-the-Wind and officially called the meeting to a close.

He took Feather-in-the-Wind's hand and led her out of the meeting. Along the way to the valley where the evening meal and the story telling was to take place, he praised her for her success and how she had delivered her message of the success of the Eastern Elk Clan. He made the point that her success put him in a much stronger position in any future argument.

The entire Elk clan members of all the sub-clans had gathered on the hill side as they waited for the storytelling to begin. They gazed beyond the point where Broken Spear of the Others and his helpers were preparing to share his visions of Taelo's current journey to the south.

The autumn gold and yellow-red leaves reflected off the lake doubling their effect. Behind them the dark green pine seemed to guard the way up the steep foothills to the snow peaked mountains beyond. The contrast of the darkening evening and sun's rays creating grey-reddish hue on the soft clouds above, set the mood for the story that would be told.

Most Clan members sat on elk hides and were either individually warmed by a sleeping hide or shared one with their family. Everyone in the valley was in attendance. This was an event no one wanted to miss.

The members of the Clan of Others were passing out snacks to all the Elk Clan. They were rich in honey and used it to make a variety of treats. This was their reward back to the Elk clan who had slowly embraced their membership into the Elk Clan.

The Eastern Elk Clan was distributing roast rabbit, squirrel, and ground hog. These had all been brought in by the younger members of the clan during their stay in the valley for this current meeting.

The main Elk sub-clan was distributing skewered buffalo meat. They had brought enough so they could give it as a gift to all the other sub-clans.

And the Northern Elk Clan was passing out small bags of salt to be put on the meat.

Broken Spear's sharing of stories and relating his visions of Taelo's travel had become a feature event for the annual Elk Clan meeting. It was third in importance, right below the actions of the Clan mothers arranging mates for their sons and daughters and the naming of the child ceremony. The official reason for the gathering was at the bottom of the list.

Burley Bear, Taelo's early travel companion and now the leader of the Others stood, pounded his wrist sized leaders spear on the ground and loudly announced the beginning of the evenings story telling.

Broken Spear's story would be loudly retold by one of the Other clan members. This retelling position was an honor. Burley Bear was the first re-teller. He would be replaced by his mate Meadow Flower. They would be followed by only two select individuals. The two were Feather-in-the-Wind and her mate, Running Stag.

This retelling would be about the travels to the Land of the Condor, Feather-in-the-Wind's land that was far to the south.

Each of the re-telling members understood the privilege they had been given in having the role of re-telling what Broken Spear said.

Broken Spear had now lived more than ninety Elk Clan gatherings. He was frail but the light in his eyes would rivet those he talked with. He was a Seer. He had been wounded by a giant brown bear that had mauled and crippled him.

This mauling had crippled him but had left him with the ability to foresee the future. This was not a capability that was completely in his control. It was a capability that allowed him to connect with those beyond his reach.

His recounted that his first connection to Taelo had been established on Taelo's naming ceremony day. He had been summoned by the ancestors and told to fly with the Eagle to see the person that would give new life to the Clan of Ohers.

He recounted that on that first flight, he had not been able to make the Eagle look directly at Taelo. It was only many moon cycles later when Taelo arrived to guide the Clan of Others to their current home that he learned that Taelo was a member of the new ones. He had witnessed Taelo's principled character and behavior. Taelo's bravery, even at an early age, was displayed when he dispatched Burley Bear for his bad behavior toward White Swan.

He described the ever-growing bond with Taelo with each passing season. He pointed out that Taelo had a power that Broken Spear felt but could not penetrate. Taelo's was an unconscious power but one that positively affected all people that met him.

The bond between them had grown stronger with each passing season.

The effort to fly with the eagle was overwhelming and exhausting. It was clear to Broken Spear that a day would come when he could no longer do it. He wondered if this might be his last story telling session.

He began to slowly tell the story that he had watched from the eyes of an eagle that was flying with a condor. The eagle looked down upon the gathering of the Condor Clan Fighters on the downside of the valley. They faced an overwhelming number of opposing fighters on the top slope of the valley.

He commented that when he saw the situation his heart had almost stopped. The sizes of the two armies were like one of the Elk sub clan facing all the rest of the Elk clans. It was clear to him that the Condor Clan faced impossible odds.

He was afraid to keep looking but once again the eagle would not let him have his way.

Broken Spear paused. He could tell that his audience wanted to know the outcome of the battle. He instead let his audience know that he would begin his story with Taelo and his team's arrival to Condor Clan home.

He identified each member on the team. He was proud to highlight Saber Scar, Marigold, Single Leaf and Sharp Blade who were members of the Clan of Others.

Broken Spear shared that Taelo, and his team were warmly received. He described how the team participated in generating the battle plans and in training the fighters. He shared the experience of Quite Rabbit and Busy Bee's capture and the initial experience in the hands of the Warrior Clan.

Broken Spear shared Quiet Rabbit's and Busy Bee's caning.

A loud "NO!" cry rang out across the valley.

Yes! It is so Broken Spear continued.

They were on the way to having their hearts ripped out and heads cut off. But the actions of Bold Walker and Taelo saved both Quiet Rabbit and Busy Bee.

He recounted how Taelo had raced toward where a Warrior Clan war priest was about to behead Quiet Rabbit and how at the last moment Taelo had turned his spear and threw it backwards so that it would knock the priest back rather than go through him. He went on to share that a very wounded Lasher clamped down on the War Priest's wrist that held the blade meant for Quiet Rabbit's neck. The priest died just as Quiet Rabbit had told him he would.

A cheer rose up from the listeners as Broken Spear described Taelo cutting the War Priest in two.

Broken Spear paused. He took a drink before returning to his recitation.

Broken Spear continued with the description of the battle formation made up of alternating fighting diamonds made up of the Condor Clan male warriors and the Slingers made up of Condor Clan women slingers. He proudly shared that Single Leaf of the Clan of Others was the lead trainer of the women slingers. He made the point that she had become legend to the Condor Clan members.

He then told of the multiple failed attacks of the Warrior Clan fighters. How they were stopped by the flying glass shards from the Condor Clan Slingers. He went on to highlight that the leader of these slingers was no other than the mother of our own Feather-in-the-Wind.

Feather-in-the-Wind had tears in her eyes as the story described how her mother, Nieva led the women slingers into battle. This was a side of her mother she had never seen. She was not surprised to learn that Single Leaf, Quiet Rabbit, and Busy Bee had empowered her mother and trained the slingers.

She was proud of her father's actions and his continuing acumen at humbly leading the Condor Clan.

Bold Walker's actions were what she had always expected of him. She was amazed at Bold Walker and his team vaulting across the crevasse. She knew he had done this several times, but it was a feat he had kept quiet about.

She sat down next to Broken Spear and put her head on his shoulder. The story was having a major effect on her emotions.

She was so thankful to be with the Elk Clan and yet so saddened about never being able to return to the land of the Condor.

She had tears of joy and sadness in her eyes.

She was eternally in debt to Quiet Rabbit and Busy Bee who had rescued her from the unimaginably cold cave of the Condor. It was a cave of frozen princesses supposedly rejected by the Condor.

Golden Hawk, Burley Bear and Meadow Flower had all participated in her rescue. They had saved her life by helping her escape from the freezing Condor cave where she had been placed in a drugged state as a sacrifice.

Later as they traveled North and stopped at the Warrior Clan village, Taelo had protected her from Sharp Stone, the Warrior Clan leader who insisted she become his bride. Taelo had fought and killed him and brought her to the Elk Clan.

She knew she could not function to do the retelling for Broken Spear.

Running Stag, who had been saved from the cannibals by Taelo, realized that Feather-in-the-Wind would not be able to do the retelling. He knew firsthand the emotions his mate was feeling. Many moons before he had gone with Taelo and helped save his mother and father from the main group of cannibals. He remembered the devastating feeling when Taelo had him tell what had happened to his family. He took up the re-telling duties that were having a major impact on his mate.

His part of the story was of the battle. Broken Spear's recount of battle and the rhythm of the Condor Clan advance, the coordinated war cry and the impact of the slingers captivated Broken Spear's listeners. When he shared how the women slingers had totally devastated the Warrior Clan, all the Elk Clan women in the valley stood up and gave Taelo's war cry. This was something to cheer. They too knew they would fare well in battle.

The part of the story of the departure of the Warrior Clan was anti-climactic. The valley was quiet. The listeners thought the story telling was over.

Broken Spear stopped. He took another drink of the honey water.

Burley Bear stood up as Broken Spear began to re-tell the part about the Golden Hawk's revenge visit that Taelo and Golden Hawk made on all the Warrior Clan enclave as they were traveling back North.

As he got into the recital, Burley Bear began to laugh so hard that Meadow Flower had to take over the re-telling for him. He wished he could have been there to participate in the "attack" on the Warrior priests and the other war leaders.

Burley Bear would seek a personal telling by Golden Hawk and Taelo.

The stars were twinkling, and the Cheshire moon faintly lit the night sky as the story telling came to a close.

The clan members slowly disbanded and went to their quarters. There was a chatter of appreciation.

They all knew that the next day most of them would depart and return to their individual clan territory.

Feather-in-the-Wind gave Broken Spear a hug and thanked him for sharing his vision. He responded that it was his small contribution and one that gave him great energy and gave her a hug back.

Feather-in-the-Wind was now eager to get her sub-clan back to the place they had named Paradise so they would be ready for Taelo's team return.

There would be a feast and long celebration when they returned to Paradise.

Her goals for the meeting had been achieved. She had added several new families to her clan but had been careful about selecting those who had earlier rejected her. She wanted only those who would stick with her in bad as well as in good times.

She led her Clan out of the valley and to the East across the mountains. She was eager to get back to Paradise. It had become her permanent home. She decided that her clan would go no farther east.

She planned for the Eastern Elk Clan to prepare a celebration that would be talked about for many seasons to come.

Chapter 10: Warrior Priest Revenge

The Cheshire moon barely lit the central grey granite center courtyard of the village. The guards standing at the base of the steps leading to the main meeting area of the War priests were the only persons awake or if not awake they were at least sleeping in a standing position.

The Warrior army was making a slow and somewhat painful, humiliating return from the land of the Condor. Their wounded required a large amount of assistance, and many could not walk on their own. The glass shards were almost impossible to remove entirely. They required meticulous time-consuming removal and even a small shard would continue to cut and cause a great deal of pain. These small pieces made it impossible to walk. Taelo knew that the shards would be a lifetime problem for many of the warriors.

The blind had the shards removed from their face, but they were among the worst for having glass shards over their entire body.

They were the warriors that had continued forward when hit by the first barrage of glass shards. They were perhaps the bravest but certainly the most foolish.

Taelo's entire team were standing on logs they had leaned against the village wall. They were examining the village square. They were several sun cycles ahead of the retreating Warrior Clan army. This gave them time to survey the city center and the routes to take when they carried out what they had come to call the Golden Hawk reckoning. He had devised what the team had agreed was the most appropriate way to get revenge on the Warrior Clan priests and leaders. They had each practiced this revenge on the green coconuts that were common in the area.

The moon seemed to have agreed to dim its light and the thin smile it presented in the night sky seemed to agree on the punishment. The team had all agreed that it was a fitting punishment that would be visible for the entire life of the marked person.

Carrying out the revenge would be a dangerous, daring, and a formidable challenge. They would carry out the punishment in the dead of night. Their goal was to punish every leader and war priest.

They had determined that the leader of the sixty warriors that had guarded the rear of the retreating Warrior Clan army was no other than Strong Sinew and Strong Wind the two sons of Tough Hide.

Taelo had seen them standing to the side during the battle. They would be spared the fate of the other leaders. They had planted their spears headfirst into the ground as they retreated to indicate the surrender of the Warrior Clan.

The team's camp was located by a small stream located north of the Warrior Clan village. They planned to stay only long enough to allow all the returning army to make its way back to the village. They had no intention of any direct engagement. They planned to be the ghosts that would forever haunt the Warrior Clan priests and war leaders.

They allowed themselves the luxury of a small fire hidden between three large boulders. There they slowly roasted pieces of Llama and recounted their success in the Battle with the Warrior Clan. The fact that not one Condor Clan warrior had thrown a spear was a point that continued to be talked about. The success of the Condor Clan Slingers would be legend.

Bold Walker pointed out that only the Cliff Fighting Dimond members and Taelo's team had directly confronted the Warrior Clan. He reminded Taelo that he had been told that only Condor Clan fighters would engage the Warrior Clan.

Taelo gave a small laugh and said that Saber Scar was on point and could not refrain from getting into the action. Saber Scar responded by saying he had heard Taelo's command to attack. Sharp Knife joined in and said that it had actually been Quiet Rabbit telling Taelo to be careful.

The banter continued until everyone had added their version of the events during the battle.

The next morning Taelo and the team watched the head of what would be a multiple sun cycle snake of despondent, demoralized, wounded Warrior Clan fighters hobbling home as best they could. The Warrior Clan priests, and the leaders of the fighting units were the first to return. It was clear they were traveling in haste to ensure they were back and able to take control. It was apparent to Taelo and his team that these leaders cared little for the devasting impact the battle had on their society.

The line of the wounded warriors went down the trail as far as the eye could see. The badly wounded leaned on their less wounded fighting partners. Those in the lead were the more fortunate. Most had minor wounds but were otherwise mobile.

Taelo commented on the devastation the Condor Clan Slingers had inflicted. Single leaf agreed with him but made the point that the Slingers had prevented the Condor Clan fighters from having any wounded.

The band of sixty, now led by Strong Sinew and Storm Wind were helping the wounded. Taelo and Quiet Rabbit pointed them out and noted that they all wore the friendship wrist bands given to them by the team on their previous visit. Busy Bee made the point that none of them were wounded.

It was clear to the team that Strong Sinew and Storm Wind had kept their men out of the battle. They had learned their lesson not to challenge Taelo. Bold Walker made the point that they were a force now in position to dominate the rest. Golden Hawk agreed that they and their men had earned a pass on the revenge.

The team counted the wounded and determined that more than sixty per cent of the fighters were returning with significant wounds. Most of the field fighters had some type of wound. Only the followers of Strong Sinew and Storm Wind were unscathed.

Two sun cycles later as the last of the returning Warrior Clan fighters entered the village, Taelo suggested that the best time to act would be as soon as the night's darkness descended. The leaders, tired and worn out would not be expecting any action. Taelo figured this was the best time to execute Golden Hawk's revenge.

The team spent the early evening reviewing the actions each would take. They were working in pairs. Each pair would act independently. The seven pairs would enter the village compound and move to the farthest positions. They would then move in unison back to their entry point. Bold Walker was the look out. His role was to spot anyone who might be out at night.

The moon was barely visible. The sky appeared to be a black pallet sprinkled with bright sprinkles of gold sand. It was dark enough that it would be difficult to navigate the city.

The team entered the compound via an unguarded side service gate. This was a gate that the workers used to take waste out of the village.

Working in twos, the team dispersed. They walked slowly, in the open, to the far end of the village. The homes of the Warrior Clan priests were easily recognizable by the markings on their doorways. Each of Taelo's team members carried their revenge kit of black charcoal powder, liquid red dye and a shard of black glass tied to a bone handle. These would be used to mark each person on the forehead.

Taelo quietly entered the top war priest's home. He quickly overpowered and tied the sleeping priest's hands. Quiet Rabbit did the same with the priest's mate.

The incapacitated war priest did not struggle. His face showed surprise as he recognized Quiet Rabbit as she stuffed grass in his mouth and then covered his mouth with a strip of leather.

Quite Rabbit carved the shape of the out spread condor wings on the priest's forehead. She made a series of small crisscross cuts where the wings came together. She then put black charcoal in the wing cuts and put a drop of red die in the center cuts. The finishing touch was to put a fermented juice that helped the flesh absorb the charcoal and red powder.

The look of surprise never left the priest's face. The priest's mate's eyes were wide and locked on the mark on the forehead. She had no idea why this was happening, but it was clear by her look of fear that she expected something more.

Quiet Rabbit put her hand to the mate's forehead and smiled as she stood to leave.

The revenge teams went house to house. They left their victims muffled and tied. All the Warrior Clan priests, and war leaders received the same treatment.

Black Night seemed the most surprised, but he did not flinch or make any sound. He was calculating his own revenge even as he was being marked for life.

The sun threatened its arrival as Taelo's team members arrived at the gate and exited the Warrior Clan village compound.

Their deed of revenge was done. They returned to their camp and prepared to move north. They then returned to a stand of trees that gave them a view from where they could observe the village central compound area. They wanted to witness the effect of their actions.

The sun was well on the way to its zenith before the marked Warrior Clan priests and leaders were found, released, and began gathering. They had been marked and it was clear to most that they were marked for life. They as a group were furious and wanted to immediately take a group of warriors and pursue the team from the North. They wanted to immediately send an army to attack the Elk Clan to the north. The cursing and agitated actions clearly showed how disturbed they were.

Dark Night called the priest and leaders to order.

Strong Sinew and Storm Wind and his group of sixty stood on one side of the square and declared that they were taking command of the Warrior Clan. Strong Sinew stepped forward and challenged Dark Night to a leadership battle.

Dark Night tried to dissuade Strong Sinew by making the point that he had defeated Strong Sinew's father and did not want to also kill the son.

Strong Sinew replied by calling the Dark Night a coward that had stabbed his father in the back before challenging him for the leadership position.

Dark Night had no choice. He moved in as swiftly as possible trying to get the advantage. It was clear to Taelo's team that Strong Sinew had practiced many of the moves taught to him by Taelo. He did not try to lunge in with his spear but repeatedly deflected the one thrust at him. He stepped slightly aside and then stepped in for a slash to the face. He was giving Dark Night the experience of death by small cuts and slashes.

The battle seemed to be a synchronized dance that Strong Sinew was leading. His level of confidence was clearly apparent, and his gaze seem locked on his opponent's eyes.

On each inward step he slashed a little lower. He made the point of slashing both sides of the face. He seemed relaxed and in no hurry. He was in command.

Dark Night began to be more cautious. He realized it was not going well for him.

Then Strong Sinew stepped in, and his slash found Dark Night's two main neck arteries.

Strong Sinew stepped away and to the back as two pulsing streams of blood shot out from Dark Night's throat. A moment later Dark Night lay dead on the ground.

The entire Warrior Clan fighters and village members let out a roar and then knelt and shouted their allegiance to Strong Sinew. It was a leadership transition they immediately accepted and welcomed.

Strong Sinew acted immediately. He stepped forward and claimed the position as leader of the Warrior Clan. His sixty supporters stood at the ready with their spears. The returning warriors moved to Strong Sinew's side of the open courtyard in support. Their experience had convinced them they needed better leaders.

The warrior priests had no choice. If they did not show allegiance, they would immediately be killed. Slowly they each knelt and gave their allegiance to their new leader.

Strong Sinew seemed to know he was being watched. He turned and appeared to look at Taelo's team. He and his band of sixty put their hands with the bands of friendship that had been given them by Taelo's team. They then raised their spears and pointed them down in a unified movement.

Bold Walker now understood the sixty spears he had found when the Warrior Clan fighters retreated.

Taelo lifted his gold plate and gave one reflected flash to show he was there and understood the salute.

Taelo and team picked up their belongings and Taelo led them on a steady jog north, away from the village. He was not worried about leaving tracks on the path they traveled. He was certain Strong Sinew would not allow any pursuit.

Bold Walker commented that he had never seen such a display of loyalty to a person that both the Condor Clan and the Warrior Clan considered a friend.

Chapter 11: Rest and Relaxation

The territory of Condor Clan and that of the Warrior Clan lay well behind them.

Quiet Rabbit and Busy Bee suggested they visit each of the seas between which they were traveling. There was no urgency to get back to the frigid winter to the north. They suggested spending at least a handful of sun cycles enjoying each of the seas.

The rest of the team instantly agreed. Marigold promised she would cook them the best seaside meals of fish and other sea creatures that they had ever tasted.

The mountain from which they could see both seas served them well as a landmark. They once again climbed the trail to the top. Their arrival at the top was as the sun reached its zenith. They planned to spend the next sun cycle at the top and then descend and go first to the eastern sea.

Everyone but Bold Walker knew what to expect. They all enjoyed their first evening watching the dense points of light that glowed above them. Bold Walker's and the Condor Clan's beliefs of what the points of light might be were almost duplicate of everyone's beliefs. He commented on how similar they all were.

The warmed honey water drinks and the lightly salted Llama jerky snacks gave the evening a warm and rich character. The team discussed their adventure and commented on the success of the Golden Hawk revenge.

Quiet Rabbit recounted her experience of being whipped by the Warrior priest and his threat to end her life. He had described cutting out her heart. Then when Bold Walker and his teams had jumped over the ravine and were attacking, the Warrior Priest had dragged her by the hair out to a point where he was going to cut off her head. She recounted the fact that at no time did she believe he would be successful. When she heard Taelo's war cry and saw him throw his backward spear she knew that she was saved. She knew because in the *Journey of Discovery* Taelo had shared with her that the ancients had said that she would have twin boys that would become important leaders of the Elk Clan.

Taelo let out a sigh and shared the fact that he had forgotten that key fact. He had rushed across the battlefield in total panic and fear for Quiet Rabbit's life. He gave Quiet Rabbit a hug and continued by saying that it took not only himself but Lasher to make the prophecy of the Ancients come true. For him it was a gift from the Ancients.

Busy Bee commented that she had been sure Quiet Rabbit was a dead person when the Warrior priest's blade began its descent toward her neck. She had no Ancients to tell her otherwise and she did not see either Taelo or Lasher. It was hard for her to accept as true the scene of Taelo leaping over Quiet Rabbit and cutting the War Priest in two. She said that at first, she thought it was her mind playing a trick.

"I was amazed that anyone could move as fast as Taelo did that day. When he threw his spear turned backwards, I at first thought he had given up. Then when it hit the Warrior Priest in the chest and knocked him backwards not only was I amaze by the accuracy of the throw but when I paced off the impossible distance of the throw, I knew how much he treasured Quiet Rabbit," Single Leaf commented.

Lasher gave a low growl, and everyone said they agreed. The evening came to a close.

The next day the team took in the early sunrise and then relaxed and enjoyed each other's company as they chatted about a variety of topics. They again planned to sit under the stars and spent part of the day preparing the snacks. They were on retreat and were planning to enjoy themselves.

In the early morning as the sun cleared the far horizon, Taelo led the team down the mountain and toward the rising sun. The team jogged at a leisurely pace for the remainder of the sun cycle. As the sun set behind them the team gazed out onto the gentle waves washing in from a light blue sea. At the limit of their vision the lighter color of the sea painted a line against the darker blue of the sky.

The team found a comfortable location on the beach. They built a fire ring and gathered around it for their evening meal. A light warm breeze graced their camp.

Quiet Rabbit, Busy Bee, Floating Cloud and Single Leaf walked down the beach. They found a small inlet and waded out with their spears at the ready. They were rewarded by a school of fish, and each speared what they referred to as a white fish. They returned to the camp to where Marigold waited to prepare them for the evening meal.

Bold Walker, Golden Hawk and Slow Runner had gone into the jungle and returned with a handful of squirrels.

It was Saber Scar and Sharp Knife that brought in a small boar that the team decided would be the feast for the following day. Marigold rubbed it down with salt and honey added some dried onions then wrapped it in palm leaves. She and Bold Walker dug a pit and burned wood until they had red hot charcoal left. Then they put the wrapped boar into the coals in the pit and covered it all with a layer of sand. When they finished, the dinner of white fish and squirrel was ready.

Swimming and lazing in the sun took up the next few days. Fish was easy to catch. Clams were found in several small inlets and a small shark also make the grilling spit.

The team spent much of their time walking the beach talking and finding shells, stones, and light flat white discs. They planned to use these to make decorations. They knew they would have plenty of time during the winter to use these items to make a variety of jewelry and other decorations.

By the third sun cycle the team was ready to proceed to the other sea. Rest and relaxation were fine, but it was clear to Taelo that the team liked action over the inaction of laying on the beach or taking their leisurely walks.

The team cleaned up their campsite early the morning of the fourth sun cycle and followed Taelo on a brisk jog to the other sea.

Saber Scar was in the lead. He and Sharp Knife were usually at point. They knew that their jog was slow enough that everyone could keep the pace. When the sun was at its zenith, they went past their lookout mountain.

Taelo and the team reached the western sea just before sunset. They quickly set up their camp and then gathered to watch as the sun kissed the far horizon and slowly disappeared. It seemed that the sun sent a message in the red, orange and gold painted on the bottoms of the clouds near the horizon.

Busy Bee and Quiet Rabbit drew the scene on their travel hide. They had drawn a similar hide on every journey. They later referenced to the drawings as they put the scenes on the walls of the cliff shelters or the clan caves.

The next morning the team was rewarded by the sight of several whales swimming by. The height of the breaching of several of the larger whales was the talk for most of the day.

Then the team found an enormous turtle laying its eggs up near the edge of the jungle. They stopped and watched as the turtle produced the eggs and buried them. The turtle then turned and slowly lumbered back into the sea.

As they followed the turtle to the edge of the ocean, they were surprised by the sight of fins traveling parallel to the beach. At first, they thought it was a set of sharks but soon it was clear they were seeing some other animal.

The new fish were coordinating their movement. They would group the fish and herd them into the shallow water. Each of the members of the group took a turn to come in and feed on the fish.

Taelo walked out into the water and approached what he called the pod. One of the larger members of the pod swam slowly toward Taelo.

In the background Taelo heard Quiet Rabbit shouting and asking if he were crazy.

Taelo noted the shape of the animal coming toward him. It appeared the animal was smiling. He stretched out his arm and let it slide along the top of the head and along the body. The skin was smooth and felt warm. The rest of the pod each swam toward him and let him do the same. Then they swam once around him and proceeded to swim down the beach.

Taelo explained that he had felt the power of their minds. He had entered the water sure that these animals were friendly. They were not fish but animals with powerful minds.

He walked back out of the surf. He reassured everyone that he had not randomly decided to enter the water to interact with these animals. He had heard them communicating and had heard them talk about the strange animals on the beach. They were talking about us. He declared them the Elk Clan of the Sea.

The entire team looked at Taelo now understanding that he connected with the animals around him in a manner that none of them understood, nor had the same capability.

The team gathered shrimp, scallops, crab from the sea. The days were once again calming and relaxing.

They reach an agreement to spend a significant amount of time gathering and drying shrimp and fish. Taelo, Golden Hawk and Bold Walker set up a fish trap. For Bold Walker, this was a new way of catching fish. He was amazed at how quickly fish seemed to end up in the holding pool. Two team members were constantly pulling out the fish and carrying them to be cleaned and dried. The drying process was like the one used by the Condor Clan when they wanted to get meat dried quickly. Wood was scarce at the high mountain altitudes so most often the Condor Clan relied on sun drying the meat.

Once the team had a travois worth of dried fish, they agreed it was time to begin their journey North to Paradise. Bold Walker had made the point that it was time to visit his sister.

The morning of the departure, Taelo walked once more to the shore and greeted the pod that seemed to come by each morning. He walked out and stroked each one. This time all the members of the team followed him and did the same. Taelo made the point of introducing each of his team members by name and let the pod know they were all friends.

Taelo then led the team back to shore and picked up one side of the travois as Golden Hawk picked up the other. Together they started back on their journey to Paradise.

The team formed the fighting diamond and followed Saber Scar to the North.

Chapter 12: Paradise Falls

The journey back to Paradise from the Elk clan meeting went through wonderous and breath-taking scenery. Feather-in-the-Wind drank the scenes as if it were sweet honey water wine. She left the Elk Clan meeting with new families. She had successfully matched many of her single folks with mates. Most had chosen to stay on with her and the Eastern Elk Clan.

The most wonderful sight was when she turned up the small stream and Paradise Falls came into view. She stopped and took Running Stag's hand into hers. She turned to him and asked if this was their home. If so, they would need to change the name of the Clan and call it the Paradise Falls Elk Clan.

Running Stag smiled and agreed that this was far enough east. He volunteered to lay out their permanent site above the fall. He would reapply the layout used for the layout in the Northern Elk clan's site.

The small stream leading to the falls had almost a solid rock bed. It was relatively easy to form a series of rock dams that formed a series of calm pools.

Camp sites were arranged at the edges of the pool. Small side streams were cut to allow water distribution past the back of each camp site. These streams were brought together out to the sides and went around the fall area and the flow was returned to the stream below the falls area.

A few sun cycles later, Feather-in-the-Wind complimented everyone on their excellent and speedy work. The Paradise Falls Elk Clan was now winter ready and was ready for a naming ceremony. She scheduled the celebration for the winter solstice. There was still much work to be done on almost all the living quarters, so she hoped for a mild winter.

Feather-in-the-Wind organized several fishing teams. She showed them how to make the fish traps as Taelo had shown her. The teams were to fish each morning and bring back their catch to a cleaning and drying team.

She made sure everyone involved knew the importance of their contribution.

Running Stag did something similar with the hunting teams. He had set up four teams to hunt buffalo. When a team downed a buffalo, it was to remove the intestines, save the heart liver and kidneys and then bring the buffalo back on a travois. It would be skinned and processed back in camp by another group.

He arranged for a rotation of the people so that everyone could get a chance to hunt as well as having to process the buffalo.

Hunting and bringing in the new mounts was the most popular. Running Stag's father, Wise Council, was put in charge of this activity. He had an eye for selecting the mounts that were to be tamed.

His main problem was curbing the enthusiasm of his helpers. He also was always aware that his team of mount tamers always took longer than expected to get each mount to be manageable. Then he had to have a group of handlers that would spend time each day with each mount.

Each evening Feather-in-the-Wind would review the events of the day. Each leader of the dozen or so tasks or teams would briefly give an update. This informal meeting approach worked well and kept the interrelationships clear and simple.

Feather-in-the-Wind made a point of thanking each person for doing their job. She insisted on shared labor and not loading any individual with more than their share.

The Winter Solstice and the naming ceremony arrived and passed.

Feather-in-the-Wind confided to Running Stag that she had hoped that Taelo and his team would make it for the Solstice. She was eagerly looking forward to their arrival.

Taelo and the team traveled northward at a steady pace. The return was taking longer than their trip to the south. They were loaded with dried fish, and they had added several deer, elk and a buffalo hide. The meat from all these animals was now on a second travois.

Taelo asked Quiet Rabbit and Busy Bee where they might be. The two pulled out their travel hide. They estimated that they were to the east of Paradise Falls. They predicted that soon they should see the river that flowed to the east.

Two sun cycles later, Saber Scar turned and let everyone know that there was as river ahead.

Marigold came up to him and verified that she too saw the river.

Taelo gave a small laugh and said that he could not see what they were so certain of, but they should lead the way there.

The team reached the river as the sun was setting. They would camp there for the night.

Taelo asked which direction they should take to Paradise Falls. Marigold immediately pointed upriver.

Smiling, Saber Scar immediately supported her and said she was never wrong.

The next morning the team traveled up stream.

An Eagle showed up and lazily flew in the air. This was a sign the entire team took to heart. They were close to their current destination.

When Taelo and the team reached the point where the small stream from Paradise Falls met the river flowing to the direction of the sunrise, Lasher let out a small throaty growl and rubbed his head against Taelo's leg.

Taelo gave a small laugh and announced that Lasher wanted to go ahead and let Feather-in-the-Wind know that the team was coming.

He gave Lasher a pat on the head and said go.

Lasher leaped forward and swam across the river. Once on the other side he let out a howl, then turned and disappeared up the path leading to Paradise Falls.

Feather-in-the-Wind was sitting on her favorite stone located above Paradise Falls. She had seen the eagle, but it seemed relaxed, and she was not sure that it was a signal. Her heart leaped at the sight of Lasher running up the path toward the falls.

Once he reached the falls, Lasher crossed over to the side where the mount enclosure was located. He ran up the slope of stones to the area above.

She stood and called to Running Stag. Together they gave Lasher a hug. They then turned to let the rest of the Eastern Elk Clan know of the pending arrival of Taelo and his team.

Lasher's arrival immediately caused Feather-in-the-Wind to activate the celebration preparation activities. She called everyone to the top of Paradise Falls. She was surrounded by almost every member of her clan.

Quiet Rabbit and Busy Bee led the team into the Paradise waterfall pool area. The entire Eastern Elk team stood in silhouette above the falls.

It was clear to Taelo that the clan had increased in the number of members.

Taelo let out the warbling call he and Feather-in-the-Wind had used during their run, away from the giant brown bear.

The entire Eastern Elk Clan responded in kind.

Bold Walker's Condor Clan call shocked Feather-in-the-Wind. She had heard that call all her young life. It was the call of her brother. Her composer evaporated. She ran down the trail toward the team. For the moment she was the little sister running to her idol, her big brother.

She jumped into his arms, and they stood hugging. Both had tears in their eyes.

Finally, Feather-in-the-Wind released Bold Walker. She then gave each of the team members a hug and invited them to enter the Paradise Falls Clan campsite.

As he was led through the camp, Taelo took in the organized layout. It closely resembled the layout of the Northern Elk Clan. He recalled that under the leadership of Talking Wren, both Feather-in-the-Wind and Running Stag had helped establish the living area. He concluded that they had learned well. They had also made sure that the camp remained clean

It was clear to him that the clan had established a permanent camp.

Taelo complemented Feather-in-the-Wind and Running Stag on establishing a very nice temporary camp. He asked when they wanted him to lead them to the east.

Feather-in-the-Wind laughed. She knew Taelo recognized this as a permanent camp. She recalled her last request that he, Taelo, return and guide her to the East.

She looked around and declared, "I and all the other members of this Clan have decided to live at Paradise Falls. We are renaming this clan the Paradise Falls Elk Clan."

Taelo, Quiet Rabbit, Golden Hawk, Busy Bee, and the rest of the team rested for a few days after their arrival. They discussed what each wanted to do for the rest of the winter.

Bold Walker planned to stay with Feather-in-the-Wind. The rest of the team was returning to the cave of the Others and after a short stay Taelo, Quiet Rabbit, Golden Hawk, Busy Bee, Whistling Arrow, Floating Cloud, White Bear and Dear Chaser would continue on their journey.

Chapter 13: Homeward

The sun was rising into the morning sky as Taelo, and the team guided their sleds to the edge of the cliff. They had decided to return while the winter snow allowed them to use their sleds. Taelo had assigned one member to bring their mounts behind the sleds. He had made this a rotating assignment that each team member would do.

They paused for a moment to look down at the white frothing and churning in the deep clear pool below Paradise Falls. Quiet Rabbit recalled the first time they had come upstream to the falls. Everyone had marveled at the beauty and grandeur of the falls. It had immediately been named Paradise. Busy Bee added that she was pleased with Feather-in-the-Wind's and her Clan members deciding to make Paradise Falls their home. Golden Hawk pointed out that they had a magical home to come back to and they certainly would stop there if they took any journey to the East. Saber Scar and Marigold commented on the wonderful drawing that had been made by the team on the overhang down by the falls.

Taelo called out to Lasher and his sled jumped forward. Quiet Rabbit looked back from her seat on the sled and waved to Running Stag and Feather-in-the-Wind. Taelo led out his war cry that was echoed by the rest of the team. They heard the Condor Clan war cry behind them as they quickly went out of sight.

The journey west through the valleys surrounded by the brilliantly blinding white snow had the entire team wearing their slit eye protectors. The cold also dropped down to a threatening level. Everyone alternated between riding on the runners and guiding the sled wolves and sitting snuggled under a protective buffalo hide to warm up.

The mount rider had the coldest seat. Everyone took a turn. The rider was totally covered by a bearskin and the more dexterous rode cross legs to keep their feet warm. Those who could not do this came up with leg coverings made out of a buffalo hide.

The feet of the wolves were the biggest worry. Taelo stopped often to check on the condition of the wolves. It was clear to him that the wolves were tougher than the human when it came to the handling of the freezing weather non-the-less he stopped early each sun cycle to rest the wolves and to get everyone into a warm enclosure.

The team had learned to use their sleds to make the walls for the enclosure. A space was left between two of the sleds to serve as the entrance. It was covered with a thick hide to keep out the cold.

The enclosure did not need heating. Thirty wolves and ten people kept the inside warm enough that a hole in the top of the enclosure needed periodic opening to let some of the heat out.

Their twelve mounts were put under a series of buffalo hides. The ground was cleared of snow and the mounts given a supply of grass to munch on. There were always three of the team under the hide with the mounts to make sure they remained safe.

Taelo and the team rejoiced when they passed the valley branch that went up into the valley of the Dire Wolves. It was Floating Cloud that recounted the story of how White Swan and Quiet Pheasant had pressured Silent Hawk the acting leader of the Elk clan to call a halt and make camp because the cry of the eagle indicated Taelo, and Golden Hawk were being tested.

Floating Cloud then suggested they camp at the very spot the Elk Clan had stopped. The team agreed and set up camp early. They enjoyed again hearing the story as told by both Taelo and Golden Hawk.

The weather had warmed to the point the mounts did not need the covering hides, but it still required three of the team to keep guard throughout the night.

They all shared a covering hide to keep warm.

Before the sun cleared the mountains behind the team, they broke camp, cleaned the area, and the sleds once again headed west.

The team agreed that they would all go to the Valley of Plenty. They entered from the southern riverside. They were met by Red Oak, Quiet Pheasant, Talking Wren, and Little Otter. The rest of the Elk Clan members all gave the now well-known war cry.

The team was ushered into the main lodge where after a celebration meal they were asked to recount the highlights of their journey. The story telling went on almost until the rising of the sun.

During the next sun cycle, Taelo thanked Red Oak and Quiet Pheasant for their hospitality and let them know that the team would leave with the next sunrise.

Busy Bee and Golden Hawk were remaining and planned to stay until the greening of the spring season.

Early the next morning, Golden Hawk and Busy Bee wished the rest of the team safe travels. They looked forward to seeing them again in the spring when they would travel to the Northern Elk Clan valley.

Saber Scar led the three sleds toward the north. The sleds were now more crowded. Taelo's Sled had two additional passengers. He and Slow Runners shared the runners of the sled when Quite Rabbit and Floating Cloud sat on the sled.

There were two fewer mounts. They had been able to replenish their grass supply on their stop in the Valley of Plenty. This meant they did not have that task to worry about. They planned to do the same when they got to the Cave of the Others.

The team had agreed to stop and camp at the same spot that Taelo had first come in contact with the Clan of Others. This was the spot where he had first met Burley Bear. Saber Scar had voiced the desire to tell that story after they watched the sunset.

They set up camp. They now had only three sleds.

The humans on the team commanded the front door and were able to sit looking out to the West. They sat together and watched as the sun began its descent on the far horizon. They were graced with the spectacle of the clouds turning to a greyish pink and then a deep golden yellow with tints of red.

Saber Scar began his story telling by reminding everyone that at that time his name was Rolling Stone and that he had a crazed saber tooth tiger to thank for his current name. As he remembered this was the same crazed tiger that had almost gotten the better of Taelo. But he was told that after a brief chase Taelo caught up with the saber tooth, grabbed the two saber teeth and ripped them out and the tiger died of fear.

The team had a laugh because Saber Scar was telling what happened in a reverse manner.

"That," Saber Scar continued, "is a different story. I am going to tell the story of the first meeting of Taelo and Burley Bear."

The entire team suggested that they get some snacks out so they could enjoy Saber Scar's version of the first meeting of Taelo and Burley Bear.

Saber Scar was enjoying himself immensely. He knew that this was a unique opportunity for him to tease Taelo. He was aware that this was a team that had a deep connection with each other and deep respect for Taelo. He knew that they would know that he was manipulating the truth for fun.

He decided to begin with Burley Bear and his early childhood and the effect his size had on the rest of the Clan.

"You all know Burley Bear, the close friend of Taelo and now the respected leader of the Clan of Others. All his life he was different. He was constantly either fighting to protect himself or fighting to protect his friends. I was lucky to be his friend. The real reason I was his friend was because Burly Bear was friends with Meadow Flower who had a beautiful sister Marigold," he stopped for a moment when Marigold laughed.

She joined in and went on to say that she had always felt sorry for Rolling Stone because he was such a wimp. She said that the day the crazed saber tool tiger marked Saber Scar was the day he came home looking like a true warrior and not the wimp Rolling Stone had been. It was the first time she had even considered him adequate.

It was clear to Quite Rabbit that the two might get into trouble with each other in the way the story was developing.

She laughed and commented she was not serious about Taelo either until she realized that she could outrun him. That is how I caught him.

Busy Bee let out a groan and asked Saber Scar to continue his story.

Saber Scar thanked the two for saving him and went on to tell of Burley Bear eventually subduing all his detractors. Burley Bear became the dominant person among all the young men. They began to follow his lead.

Saber Scar went on to tell how dedicated he became to being Burley Bear's supporter.

Saber Scar then pointed at Taelo and said in a deep voice, "Then up the beach came this young boy following his mother. He was barely as high as Burley Bear's waist, but it was obvious he had always gotten his own way.

He was even telling his mother how to act. When Burley Bear pointed out that he should be polite to his mother, Taelo yelled at the top of his voice and in a sudden surprise and unexpected attack was lucky with the swing of his war club and knocked Burley Bear out. This act caused our leader to sit Taelo down and ask him what in the world was he thinking.

Our leader was about to tell Taelo he should go home but just then an eagle fulfilled the prediction that the clan had been waiting for there on the beach.

The whole clan was shocked that this was the person they had been waiting for, but they could not dispute or stand in the way of the prediction Broken Spear had made many years before.

When Burley Bear awakened, he shook hands and said that never before had anyone acted so mean, but he would forget that and embraced the person Broken Spear had so often talked about.

He only hoped that there would be no more sneak attacks.

Saber Scar looked at Taelo and asked if that was how he remembered it.

Taelo laughed and said yes that it was remarkably close to the twisted truth. "Perhaps when we camp at Whale's beach you can tell the story of Burley Bear finding the whale and single handedly preparing it to feed the clan.

Saber Scar grinned and thanked Taelo for the opportunity to clarify how the whale was caught by Burley Bear and pulled out of the water to the beach.

In the next sun cycle the team reached Whale Beach too early to stop. Single Leaf pointed out where she had spent three day's melting the blubber into the bags made out of the whale intestine.

Everyone knew the story of Whale's Beach. They stopped long enough for everyone to walk around to see where the large bear had held off the wolves. The bear had given Taelo and Golden Hawk time to prepare their feeding sticks to throw out to the wolves.

The team had become familiar with Taelo's ability to talk to wolves and other animal and tell them what to do so it was easy for them to imagine him doing it to save the whale for the Clan of Others.

Far to the north the cliffs approached the sea and seemed to create a wall blocking the way. The sea on their left, spoke in its never-ending ebb and flow rhythm. The sun's slow decline toward the far horizon took on a mystical aura of light rays streaming between the clouds and striking the face of the cliff.

As the sun reached the far horizon, the team reached point on the beach where they would turn to the east to get to the Clan of Others.

They were not surprised to see a large gathering of Clan members out to greet them and escort them to the Clan's cave. Burley Bear and Meadow Flower were in front and the greeted the whole team with hugs and suggested they get out of the cold and into nice hot water.

They proceeded to the entrance to the cave of the Others. Broken Spear sat at the entrance where many moons ago, he and Taelo had first entered the Cave. Once again, they briefly sat together as Broken Spear welcomed the team back.

Steam was wafting up from the warm water pool beyond the entrance. The stream flowing away from the pool cut the white of the snow and seemed to split the valley in two. The dark green of the pine made dark pepper spots on the distant white peaked mountains.

The sun's reflection forced Taelo to squint as he admired the view. He had found this place with the help of an exceptionally large buck elk. The cry of the eagle had confirmed the find.

The Others living in this place for more than fifty moon cycles had taken meticulous care of the valley and it remained almost the same as when they had first entered.

Once again Taelo and Broken spear walked in together and went to the hot pool that now had the Norther Elk Clan rain maker functioning. The two entered the pool together. They were talking quietly.

The rest of the team joined them and gathered around. Together with Burley Bear and Meadow Flower they all listened to Taelo thank Broken Spear for having provided Taelo with the guidance that helped him keep every member of the team safe. He especially thanked him for putting his idea of acting differently when Quiet Rabbit's life was on the line. It was this one message that had caused him to throw his spear backwards.

The fact that Broken Spear had provided the key puzzle part to Taelo was noted by all the team members.

As the dark of night crept into the valley, they were all notified that the evening meal was ready to be served.

After the evening meal Taelo and Lasher stood in the center of the Clan of Others telling stories of the journey to the land of the Condor.

He had designated each of the team to tell a portion of the story.

Quiet Rabbit's and Busy Bee's story of their capture and later being tied to a post and beaten with a cane by the lead warrior priest resulted in a common gasp from their audience. The gasp was followed by total silence as the audience waited for the story to continue.

Busy Bee described the thrill she felt as she watched Bold Walker and his follower leap the crevasse that protected the Condor Clan village. His bravery saved both she and Quiet Rabbit. She went on to describe how the warrior priest grabbed Quiet Rabbit by the hair and dragged her out. He intended to cut her head off to shock the attackers.

Again, there was a gasp by all the listeners.

Quiet Rabbit took up the story. She told of her total faith in being saved. She shared that Taelo in their *Journey of Discovery* had suffered a severe injury. With the help of Broken Spear, Taelo had talked with the Ancestors. They told him that he would have twin sons that would become great Elk Clan leaders.

This she said gave her great strength. She had told the War Priest that he was about to die. To her surprise a backward thrown spear hit the priest on the chest and knocked him backwards as at the same time Lasher crushed the wrist that held the blade that was going to cut her head off. She told of her surprise at Lasher's appearance. She was sure she had seen his lifeless body thrown into the brush. His miraculous recovery and again saving her as the Warrior Clan War priest was about to behead her was a startling but very pleasant surprise.

She did not see Taelo, but she fell to the ground to escape the war priest.

She went on to tell how Taelo seemed come down out of the sky and cut the war priest in two from right shoulder to his left side at the waist.

The listeners were all leaning forward waiting for Quiet Rabbit to go on.

She chided Taelo for being so slow to arrive, but she said she fell in love with Lasher and to this day she does not know who she loves more Lasher or her slow running Taelo.

The listeners all let out a hoot and pounded the ground in appreciation of the story.

Taelo pounded the ground as well. It was a story well told.

He knew he and Quiet Rabbit were now closer than they had been before. There was a deep understanding at how close a call the incident with the war priest had been.

The story telling ended as the grey of dawn broke the black of the valley. Broken Spear called for the end, and everyone slapped the ground praising the story tellers.

Taelo and the rest crawled into their sleeping hides and slept through most of the day.

Later the team sat in the pool almost hidden from each other by the rising steam as they enjoyed the warmth. Their conversation focused on the final leg of their long journey.

In the familiar pattern of leaving as the sun cleared the far mountains, Taelo and the rest of the team bade goodbye to Single Leaf, Sharp Blade, Saber Scar and Marigold. Burley Bear and Meadow Flower were part of the group of Other's wishing the team adieu.

Broken Spear walked with Taelo and urged him to come back before the next journey. Taelo embraced Broke Spear and put his forehead on Broken Spear's forehead. Broken Spear felt new energy flow in as the two stood in silence. His mind cleared and his energy surged. He knew he would live long enough to experience Taelo's next venture.

The team was down to he, Quiet Rabbit, Floating Cloud and Whistling Arrow. The four would go as far as the twin mountains and the jewel like lake between them.

Chapter 14: White Feather's Hearth

Taelo guided the single sled northward. Behind him Quiet Rabbit was riding her mount and leading the three other mounts. Floating Cloud would be the next person to lead and manage the mounts. Whistling Arrow had immediately fallen asleep. He had enjoyed the story telling but now he was exhausted.

Taelo was relaxed and enjoying the smooth ride through the pass as he let Lasher run at an easy pace. He felt no hurry. He planned to stay at least two sun cycles at the lake between the twin peaks. He was sure of the fish and in the past Quiet Rabbit had taken her sling and made sure that the evening meal was well supplied with rabbit, squirrel and occasionally a fat ground hog.

A sun cycle later, Whistling Arrow was on the sled runners. Taelo was leading the mounts when the sled rounded the bend, and the twin peaks dominated the scene ahead. Floating Cloud and Quiet Rabbit were each dozing, but they came alive and commented that they planned to enjoy their stay by the lake.

Taelo rode past the sled and went on ahead to select the camp location. He had a stand of pine that shielded a triangular area that he felt would make for a comfortable camp. He wanted an easy camp to set up and maintain.

Floating Cloud and Quiet Rabbit went out with their slings while Taelo and Whistling Arrow set up their camp.

Taelo positioned a stone to serve as center of a shelter. He remembered the shelter he and Golden Hawk had put up when they faced the fierce winter storm during their journey North. Here he had all the materials to make the shelter larger and higher. It would easily house the four of them and their sled wolves.

On the next sun cycle an eagle circling in the sky above the Northern Elk Clan, caught White Swan's eye. This was Taelo's totem. She was sure it signaled his return.

Taelo and Quiet Rabbit had been gone more than twelve moon cycles. She was eager to have Taelo and the rest of the team return and enjoy the coming of spring.

She pointed to the eagle as Gray Fox Running joined her at their sitting stone in the courtyard built by Taelo, Golden Hawk and Burly Bear.

They agreed that a welcome home feast should be made ready.

Taelo saw the eagle at about the same time that White Swan saw it.

He called up to it that it was early. He was going to do some fishing and relax for one or two more sun cycles.

The fish he and Whistling arrow had caught and the several rabbits that Quiet Rabbit and Floating Cloud had contributed made for a wonderful evening meal.

A small dear had been brought down and the wolves were also enjoying a great evening meal.

Taelo looked around and decided to let everyone know about the next journey the ancients had been calling for him to take. As he described where they would travel, he let them know that a point of confusion existed. The Ancients kept talking about the fact that the children would slow this journey, but they would make it much more enjoyable for everyone.

He looked around and asked if there was something that he was unaware of.

Quiet Rabbit laughed and commented that it was unfair that Taelo had Ancients that were giving him a glimpse of the future.

She put her hands to her midsection and commented that she was sure her twins were on the way.

Taelo gave Quiet Rabbit a hug and commented that he would be eagerly waiting for their arrival.

Floating Cloud gave her a hug as well and said that on the next trip she would tend to her great grandchildren and that the team would need to make sure that Lily and Slow Walker accompanied them.

Quiet Rabbit let those around the campfire know that Busy Bee would also be having a child.

Taelo commented that taking it easy on the beaches of two seas must have been the cause for this situation.

At the next sunrise, the team broke camp, cleaned up the area and headed to the Northern Elk Clan valley.

Taelo looked up as the eagle let out a cry and flew into the valley ahead of the fast-moving sled. The wolves were as eager to get back as the people for whom they pulled the sled.

The End

Taelo: Circumvention

Dedication:

To those who venture beyond the normal borders.

Taelo: Circumvention

Chapter 1: A team of Veterans

The journey south to the Condor Clan was now a distant memory. The return had been blessed with both Quiet Rabbit and Busy Bee finding out that they were with child. They both gave birth on the same day. His mother reminded Taelo that he and Golden Hawk had both been born on the same day. The difference was that Quiet Rabbit had twin boys and Busy Bee had a daughter.

Taelo and Golden Hawk were both amazed at the change in their daily lives. Sleeping all night became a luxury. But they were both overjoyed.

Quiet Rabbit and Busy Bee recovered quickly and were both radiant and cuddling their children.

Taelo and Golden Hawk decided that when the children were old enough to ride a mount and travel on a long journey they would consider their next travel adventure.

They chose instead to leverage their privilege as Golden Feather warriors and the fact they were members of all the Elk sub clans. They set up residence in each of the subclan camps and stayed at them for about a moon cycle each. This satisfied their wander lust and they contributed evenly to the wellbeing of the entire Elk Clan. They taught their hunting techniques, the use of weapons and how to develop people. Their help was readily accepted and sought by all the sub-clans.

Both Quiet Rabbit and Busy Bee commented that they too enjoyed the change from sub-clan to sub-clan because it gave them a chance to contribute their skills and to develop the young women to be hunters.

Taelo created a pouch that would carry the twins. The pouch fit over the front shoulders of the mount with a pocket on each side. This provided a safe and convenient way to carry the twins.

Busy Bee used the second pouch to put food that could be use as they rode along on the mount.

Burley Bear gave his hearty laugh and commented that Taelo had solved a problem in a unique and very practical manner.

Taelo and Golden Hawk were thinking ahead to a much longer journey. They had specifically selected the mounts that would be the ones that each of the three children would ride. The mounts were young and were gentle. Once the three children could ride and control their mounts the planned journey could begin.

Burley Bear, Saber Scar and Sharp Blade followed suit and selected mounts for their young as well.

After the seasonal gathering of all the clans, Taelo and Golden Hawk followed Feather-in-the-Wind and Running Stag who had their daughter in one of the pouches that she had received as a gift.

The demonstrated ease and comfort of how the young children were carried impressed every member of the Paradise Clan.

They stayed in at the Paradise Clan site for a full moon. During this time Taelo shared the journey that he planned to undertake. Feather-in-the-Wind immediately said that she wanted to be with the team on that journey.

Quiet Rabbit agreed that when their children were seasoned mount riders they would all travel together.

The most recent cycle of a moon stay at each sub-clan ended at the Northern Elk Clan as the cold weather closed in. The youngsters were now five seasons of age. They had bonded with their mounts. Riding seemed to come naturally to them.

Taelo declared that their new journey would begin in late winter.

He was immediately inundated with volunteers wanting to be a part of the journey.

He, Quiet Rabbit, Golden Hawk and Busy Bee decided they needed a set of criteria to use to determine who would be part of the team that would be on the journey.

They easily agreed to having Floating Cloud, her mate Whistling Arrow, Lily and her mate, Slow Walker, designated as cooks and camp managers. These four ensured that the team would have great meals and camp security if the team needed to be out hunting.

Deer Chaser a young warrior that had been part of the rescued White Bear Clan was accepted as a hunter. His longtime friend White Bear reluctantly declined the position of hunter and explained that his mate was pregnant.

Long Leaper, now mated to Bashful Lark who was the person that had saved Taelo on their last journey, was overjoyed to be selected as the second hunter.

Taelo knew that Broken Spear the Seer of the Others would request the participation of some of the Others. He decided that he would accept all of Broken Spear's suggested members. He hoped that the Ancients had not sent Broken Spear a message of any major conflict. On his last journey he had wanted to include a small army of Others.

When the word spread out among the various sub-clans about Taelo's upcoming journey, another round of volunteers surfaced.

Taelo was pleased to see that Talking Wren and Little Otter did not ask but let him know that they were going to journey with him, and they would supply enough meat to take the team to the Eastern Sea.

She reminded him of the long leap he had made from the cliff to save Golden Hawk from a shark that was more than three spears in length. She joked that she would let him kill a giant shark to feed them for the next part of the journey.

Taelo made the visit to confer with Broken Spear by himself. He wanted to spend as much time with his mentor to discuss the theory that the world was like the rough round granite stone that had become the object that he used to explain how he envisioned the journey.

He was certain enough about his supposition that he was going to take his children with him. This worried him but he felt certain he was correct and that the only danger was that of the environment and the land they would travel through.

As always his greeting by the Others was overwhelming and there was a dinner and an evening session of storytelling that he and Burley Bear led. Burley Bear was an excellent storyteller and always had everyone slapping the ground in appreciation.

Taelo knew he was outclassed by Burley Bear's storytelling talent so he told stories that would engage the audience in a very different way.

For that evening's storytelling, he chose to explain the next journey that he was going to take. When he held up his stone and pointed to a black spot that he called the Cave of the Others and then ran his fingers around the stone and returned to the black spot he heard the hooting and ground slapping that far exceeded what Burley Bear had received for his story telling.

He smiled and took his bow and sat down next to Burley Bear.

Burley Bear looked at him and in the smile that always made Taelo think of an attacking bear he complimented him on telling a story that would never have entered his own mind.

The next morning as Taelo sat with Broken Spear and explained his upcoming journey, Burley Bear looked at him again and in a serious tone apologized for having made fun of the story the previous evening. He had thought it had been a story.

Taelo smile and put his hand on Burley Bear's shoulder and pointed to Broken Spear and commented that if Broken Spear laughed at the journey then that would be all it would be.

Broken Spear looked at Taelo and said the Ancients have said that you should travel toward the rising sun until you return to where you started.

Broken Spear said that it was hard for him to accept such a thing since the world seemed flat to him.

He commented that Taelo seemed to sense that there was a bend represented by the horizon that made this world like the round stone that he held.

Broken Spear then gave a signal and his choices walked to where he sat. He had selected the people that would go on the journey with him.

Taelo stood and greeted Saber Scar and Marigold, Sharp Blade, and Single Leaf.

He looked at Burley Bear and knew that his best friend, now the leader of the Others would not be going.

He was surprised when Broken Spear called out Burley Bear's and Meadow Flower's names and said that the Ancients had identified them as members of the trip.

Taelo was stunned.

The look on Burley Bear's face reflected the same look as Taelo. Meadow Flower's smile and laughter was a pleasure to see and hear.

The team had grown in size and added three more children to the journey.

Burley Bear gained his composure and stood and pointed to the other side of the cave area. He said that the travois and sled combinations had been refurbished and were as good as new. The lodge hide was new and not as heavy as the last one. He said that each sled was lighter and not as heavy in build so they could be pulled by six wolves each instead of eight.

Taelo thanked Burley Bear and set a date for the Others to come to the Northern Elk Clan village to prepare for the journey.

He met again with Broken Spear and learned that the wolves would go until the snow gave way near the mighty river and the mounts would go to the sea, but they were not to make the journey across the sea.

Taelo was to build large, long rafts that would have a cross pole that had dry wood attached at each end so the rafts would remain stable in the waves.

Taelo listened carefully and began to imaging what such a raft would be. He would share this with Golden Hawk to see what they could come up with.

Taelo asked if the Ancients had indicated how long the journey might take. Broken Spear replied that it would be short enough for Taelo to return before he, Broken Spear became an Ancient.

Taelo smiled and said that meant that it would be a long journey since he was sure that Broken Spear had a long time to wait to become an Ancient.

Taelo put his forehead on Broken Spear's and told him that he would make sure to be present before his mentor became an Ancient.

He thanked him for letting him know that his journey would be one of adventure and of success.

He talked with Burley Bear, and they agreed that in one moon cycle, Burley Bear and the rest would arrive at the Northern Elk Clan valley.

Chapter 2:Journey's Preparation

Standing at the compound wall, Taelo was thinking through his journey. The beauty of the distant waterfall, and the cloud of mist seemed to augment his thoughts as the mist was turned into fine sparkling snowflakes in the morning sunlight. He was thinking about how to handle each step of the journey that he could envision but everything beyond the far sea was an unknown.

He felt a light touch on his arm and reflexively put his arm around Quiet Rabbit. They had agreed that the journey would begin in the next few sun cycles.

The planning was complete. The children were now excellent riders. Probably better than their parents. They had a natural way of riding that seemed to make them one with their mounts.

The supplies had been accumulated and had been organized.

Burly Bear had delivered the sleds and helped to organize each sled.

The sleds and the wolves that pulled them would all be returned to at the Paradise Clan after the team had reached the mighty river. The journey from there would be on mounts and travois. The mounts would only go as far as the sea.

Feather-in-the-Wind had sent word that three of her clan would bring the sleds back to Paradise and three would accompany them to the sea and would return to Paradise Valley with the mounts.

White Swan wished them well and supplied them with all the salt that would be needed for at least three seasons.

Grey Fox Running had made them special spear heads from the giant shark teeth.

Golden Hawk and Busy Bee had spent the last moon cycle with their parents in the Valley of plenty and planned to accompany Little Otter and Talking Wren back to the Northern Elk Clan valley.

The Others would come up with them at the same time.

It was all coming together.

Taelo was focused on making sure that nothing was overlooked. The trip to the far sea had been made once before and he was clear on how that would be done.

He and Golden Hawk had talked through, and they had discussed how the rafts would be made.

He knew that the children would affect the pace of the journey and had discussed this with Quiet Rabbit, Busy Bee, and his mother.

His mother suggested that the team travel more slowly than in the past and spend time showing the children the wonders of the world around them. She pointed out that these children would be the most developed in the Clan when they returned and would likely be future cleaders.

Taelo asked her if the team could once again launch the journey from the ancient cave at the top of the falls. The drawings on the walls of each of the teams adventures had been drawn up on the walls by Quite Rabbit and Busy Bee. He wanted to have the team recall the highlights that stood out in their minds about those journeys.

He wanted them to remember that they had succeeded on each journey because they worked together as a team and had acted to ensure that all were safe.

White Swan gave him a hug and reminded him that he and Golden Hawk were the finders of the cave. They had linked the Northern Elk Clan members to a past that had become legend and that they had proved the stories of their grandparents had been the true history of the original Elk clan.

Taelo thanked her and asked that those stories be told again, and new ones would be added by his team members. It would put the team on common ground and inspire them.

Quiet Rabbit made the point that their children would be listening to their grandparents telling the stories for the first time. It would be a moment when the family bond would be reaffirmed.

Taelo agreed and commented that on their return perhaps the children could augment the drawings with what they had been a part of during the upcoming journey. They could participate in putting the next story on the wall.

Down the coast in the Valley of Plenty, Golden Hawk gave his mother, Quiet Pheasant a hug. She wished him a safe journey and to bring her granddaughter, Yellow Flower, safely back to her.

Red Oak presented him with the shark spear heads. He gave the same admonition to bring Yellow Flower back in full bloom.

Golden Hawk walked to his mount that like the other four mounts that would be leaving the Valley of Plenty would be pulling travois loaded with as much buffalo meat as could be pulled.

He watched as Little Otter and Talking Wren were going through the same departure process with their parents.

Little Otter was in the lead as they headed out of the valley. Talking Wren was second. Golden Flower was third and Busy Bee was behind her.

Golden Hawk was last. He held up his spear with the golden feather and waved it as they left.

He wondered how many moons would pass before he once again put his eyes on the Valley of Plenty.

The sea was trying to make the journey to the Cave of the Others as miserable as possible. The waves were crashing onto the beach and the wind was whipping the water into the air where it became salty snowflakes.

Little Otter was leading them up along the edge of the forest as far from the edge of the sea as possible but all of them soon looked like white bears riding on mounts.

Yellow Flower had disappeared beneath the multiple hides put on her by Busy Bee.

They all agreed that they should continue until they arrived at the cave of the Others.

When they arrived at Whale Beach they were greeted by a group of the Others. Burley Bear said that he had brought each of them a mount and that his warriors would take over the mounts pulling the travois with the meat.

He commented that they were expected for dinner and should not be late.

On arrival they all went to the hot water pool. They sat there until the cold left them. They enjoyed the white view of the valley beyond the cave opening.

The aroma of the cooking soon had them eager to dry off and get ready for the celebration meal.

The meal was more formal that usual. Golden Hawk was informed that it was a departure dinner for the members of the Others that would be leaving with him to go to the Northern Elk Clan lodge.

The meal was as always an overwhelming taste experience. It consisted of honey basted roast buffalo, grilled fish, and a clam stew. The salted roasted onions added a special taste to all the dishes.

Golden Hawk was to be the featured storyteller. He decided that he would highlight each of the members that had made past journeys with Taelo and he.

He began with Burley Bear's and Meadow Flower's experience with putting up the team compound covering and their realization how weak their Elk Clan teammates were. He pointed out how lucky they had been that Running Stag had suggested using the mounts to provide the power that the team lacked.

He then highlighted Saber Scar and how he had faced a giant lion and had miraculously survived but only because Feather-in-the-Wind had used her body like a spear and had left her knife buried in the lion's chest for him to use.

He gave Marigold recognition for having killed the most ferocious animal that could ever be imagined. She had demonstrated that when she was mad she was truly the killer of monsters. He reminded everyone that they should not harm Saber Scar and make her mad.

Finally, he highlighted Single Leaf's fall into the ice cold waters of the gorge and how Taelo jumped down and saved her. She fell because she had exerted herself and she was pregnant.

He pointed out that Sharp Blade had demonstrated that love had made him capable of out running all the Elk Clan members. He used all his strength to pick up Spear Tip to show the clan the wonder that Single Leaf had delivered.

He was greeted with palm slapping after each story. It was by far the best response to his story telling that he had experienced.

He then listened as Burley Bear told the stories about he and Busy Bee. Burley Bear lowered his voice and pointed at Golden Hawk and Busy Bee and quietly said that the best he could say was that the two had one redeeming accomplishment. He then picked her up and showed Yellow Flower off to the Clan.

He went on to claim that on every journey Golden Hawk was in constant need of being protected by one of the Others.

He even suggested that when the giant monster attacked it was Saber Scar that had been hit by the monsters tail as he saved Golden Hawk, and that most likely the noise Golden Hawk had made hunting had roused the lion that attacked Saber Scar, and his hesitation in crossing along the river gorge was likely the reason that Single Leaf fell in and if he had been a little stronger the camp cover would have gone up without a problem.

The floor slapping was louder than any that Golden Hawk had received.

Both he and Busy Bee laughed and slapped the floor along with the rest of the Clan.

He let Burley Bear know that he would practice his own story telling so that in the future he could get even in the story telling score.

That caused Burley Bear to laugh and pat him on the back and say that he was looking forward to the stories.

The next morning Burley Bear led the way north toward the valley where the Northern Elk Clan was located.

Golden Hawk brought up the rear of the procession that now had four children that were all within one season in age.

The journey though heavily loaded made very good time and they decided to push on past the lake between the mountains that was often the normal place to stop.

An eagle let out a cry and Burley Bear commented that they had made the right decision and that they would now be expected at the lodge of the Northern Elk Clan.

He commented that he and the team of Others would demonstrate how easily their new encampment covering could be set up.

He said that they had learned a lot about using their mounts and minimizing the required human strength. He gave a gruff laugh and said that even the same number of Elk Clan members would be able to raise the covering.

As Golden Hawk expected the Northern Elk Clan was out in mass. He and Burley Bear led the procession into the compound. The mounts with the meat loaded travois remained at the base of the compound area.

Once the greetings were over Burley Bear asked permission to set up the encampment covering. He was surprised when his team set a new speed record in setting it up.

He felt great when Taelo commented that Burley Bear and his clan had become the best builders of sleds and he would now add the best makers of camp coverings.

The rest of the evening was spent on a grand meal. It was not as elaborate as the one thrown for Burley Bear at his departure dinner but one that did feature story telling.

Golden Hawk took his opportunity to do some payback. He commented that Burley Bear for all his faults and his weakness in battle had lucked out when Meadow Flower took pity on him and agreed to be his mate. And that their child with a name he was sure Burley Bear had copied from he and Busy Bee, was the only talent that Burley Bear had demonstrated recently.

Golden Hawk then picked up Aristosa and pointed out that it was another name for a yellow flower and showed her off to the Northern Elk Clan members. The clan members hit the floor with sticks in appreciation of the story.

Burley Bear stood up and pointed to Golden Hawk and pounded his spear on the ground and complemented him on his improved story telling capability.

Chapter 3: Stories and Bonding

The moment arrived and Taelo signaled the entire team to move from the lodge and across the valley and then up to the top of the cliff. He declared it the first step in their much longer journey. The entire Northern Clan had come out just as the sun was breaking over the mountains to see the team off.

An eagle let out a cry and everyone stopped what they were doing.

Taelo was just getting ready to proceed when the eagle cried again.

Feather-in-the Wind, Running Stag, and their daughter Neiva came riding into the valley at top speed.

Feather-in-the-Wind said that they had come because they wanted to experience every step of the journey.

After the greetings ended, Taelo got everyone back into order and signaled that it was time to go.

This first step was a practice move to the top of the far cliff and then a night of enjoying the warm rain shower, the feasting and storytelling.

This would be the first time for all the children to enter the cave and to hear the stories of old.

They had all enjoyed the hot shower at the cave of the Others. That shower at the cave of the Others had been a gift that Golden Hawk and Taelo had given to Broken Spear. The shower in the cave, at the top of the falls was the original hot rain that many stories of old talked about.

Golden Hawk and the other members of the Northern Elk Clan had replaced all the wooden parts and it now functioned as if new.

Taelo had the Elk Clan Members set up the camp cover as Burley Bear and Meadow Flower gave the instructions. And as Burley Bear had boasted even the weak Elk Clan Members put it up with ease. The area they had chosen had been cleared of snow and four small fires strategically placed inside the cover provided all the warmth needed. The inside temperature was warm enough that only light clothing needed to be worn.

Once in the cave, the hot rain was activated, and everyone gathered around it and took turns enjoying standing under it and getting refreshed.

The kids were fascinated with the cave and the only concern was that they seemed fearless in getting too close to edge of the cliff at the opening behind the waterfall.

Quite Rabbit drew a line on the stone floor and instructed them not to get any nearer. One of the parents was always at the line to ensure that the instruction was followed.

The cooking was being done outside of the cave and soon the kids were gathered around the cooking ring enjoying snacks.

The meal was eaten inside under the camp cover. It was a slow and enjoyable meal. When it was over, and everything put away, the activity was taken back into the cave.

Grey Fox Running introduced the story tellers. White Swan would begin with the telling of the arrival of the first ancestors. Floating Cloud would tell how the entire camp that was situated along the banks of the lake below the falls was destroyed by a giant bear and how the cave was found when the hunters followed the bear back to it.

He would tell of the journey down to the salt cave, the counting stone, the test at the fishpond and of cutting the salt block and then the arduous journey up the mountain with the salt on the salt gather's back.

He went on to say that now it was time to add new stories. It was time for Taelo and his team of wanderers to tell one story for each journey they had been on.

Taelo was surprised by this request but stood up and looked at the team members and made the following suggestions.

Burley Bear and Meadow Flower to tell about the team's first male and female hunting experience and how all the current team members met their mates.

Saber Scar, Feather-in-the-Wind, and Running Stag to tell about facing the giant lion. This was a story of three team members that together had faced and defeated a huge lion.

He asked Lily and Running Stag to tell about their ordeal with being captives of the cannibals and their first time in the cave.

He asked Little Otter and Talking Wren to tell about the only mastodon that the team had killed during their first hunt.

He asked White Rabbit and Busy Bee to tell about the Journey of Discovery and to show the story that was now sketched on the cave wall.

He asked Golden Hawk to tell about the raid he had led against the Warrior Clan during their second visit to the Condor Clan territory.

He asked Single Leaf to tell the story of the Condor Clan slingers and the bravery and skill demonstrated by all the women in the Condor Clan.

Finally, he asked White Rabbit and Busy Bee to tell about the rescue of the Condor King's princess, who was now the leader of the Paradise Elk clan.

He said that he and Golden Hawk would listen and add points of interest.

The story telling went on for most of the night. The children were engaged for the entire time.

Several breaks were taken. Lily and Floating Cloud served snacks, and everyone had some of the honey drink that had been especially made for this occasion.

The sun had set, and the stars were sparkling in the sky. It was a magnificent black with all the Ancients letting them know that it was a special evening.

Once back in the in the cave the blend of the past merging with the present seemed to affect everyone and the silence allowed every word of the person telling a story to resonate throughout the cave.

It was magical. Taelo felt the presence of the Ancients. He allowed the stories to flow into his mind and felt the light that seemed to sparkle as it did in the dark of the sky.

The new stories were as vivid to Taelo and Golden Hawk as if the events had happened only a few sun cycles before.

They added a few highlights and praised the teller of the story for their role and highlighted their experience.

Taelo knew every story by heart. He enjoyed hearing it from someone else's perspective.

The grey of dawn was just lighting up the water of the falls when the final story was told.

Taelo declared the sun cycle to be a time for sleep.

Lily announced that there was a final snack available to everyone.

The entire team went to their sleeping hides and the dawn of a new day was experienced in warmth under sleeping hides.

Chapter 4: The Venture's First Step

Taelo took the lead sled and guided it out through the northern mountains. He knew the way. The weather was cold but calm and the travel was smooth. For this part of the journey, the kids were sheltered in pairs under a hide cover on the sleds. They had the space just behind a half load of some goods that would not be needed for the early part of the journey. They could talk to the two persons that were guiding the sleds and just relax and play.

Six sleds were only partially loaded so that a person or two kids could ride protected from the weather. The two larger sleds were fully loaded and had an extra pair of wolves harnessed to them. Taelo was leading with one of the larger sleds. He set a rather slow and steady tempo that kept everyone together as they navigated through the mountains.

The mounts were tied one behind the other as they went through the mountains but would later be grouped as they traveled.

Taelo cleared the last gap and could see the endless plain out ahead. The grasses were mostly buried beneath a thick layer of snow. He looked for the path that seemed to be flat, smooth and the snow not too deep.

Lasher was out front and seemed to understand and find the path that had enough but not too much snow.

Taelo let everyone know that they would only stop when it was time to make camp. Eating would have to take place as they moved along.

Lily and Floating Cloud let everyone know that they had set up their sled with all the food anyone wanted as they moved along.

Slow Walker and Whistling Arrow, riding on their mounts made the rounds and delivered food to everyone that asked for it. The kids thought it was a great way for them to get their snacks. They were Lily's best customers.

As the day neared the end. Taelo spotted a flat area that he then circled. Everyone knew what to do. The eight sleds made a perfect circle. It was large enough to set up the camp cover inside the ring and hold all the mounts on the inside of the sleds. The wolves found enough room around the inside of the circle and after getting fed, they curled up and went to sleep.

The team went out and brought back enough dried grasses for the mounts and then they fed them some grain that had been brought along.

Lilly made sure that everyone had a hearty stew. The kids were still full of energy.

Taelo watched as Quiet Rabbit, Busy Bee and Single Leaf led the kids out to see if they could get some rabbits with their slings. That venture was a big hit, and he could hear the children laughing as they went out after the rabbits.

The hunters returned with enough rabbit to feed the entire team. He later found out that most of the rabbits had been bagged by the three mothers but that each of the children had bagged at least one rabbit.

Taelo took in the camp scene and was pleased with the first sun cycle's progress.

He and the rest of the team sat quietly talking about when they would arrive at the Eastern Elk Clan's village. Taelo had made the trip many times. He knew that they had another four sun cycles. He and Golden Hawk had made sure the Clan had plenty of food on their last stay and did not plan to bring in any additional for the village.

Taelo expected to stay only one sun cycle and then move on to Paradise.

Feather-in-the-Wind made the point that Paradise was ready to host all the wolves and sleds. However, she understood that they would use the sleds all the way to the mighty river if the snow held. If the snow cover gave out before the river then they would load up travois to the mounts and travel in that fashion.

She had arranged for sled handlers from the Paradise village to accompany them as far as the river. They would return with the empty sleds.

Another three of her young warriors would go all the way to the sea and then return to Paradise with the mounts.

Golden Hawk brought up the crossing of the Mighty river. If there was ice covering it then they would need to figure out how to get across.

Taelo agreed and said that he hoped that they could cross by floating on log rafts. The water would be very cold and getting the mounts across would be the challenge. They would need to see if they could use the river current and large rafts to float the mounts across.

He said they would cross at the same location that they had crossed on their Journey of Discovery that had an island in the middle of the river. One group would hold the rope on the far side and the mounts would be put on rafts and the force of the current would do the work of swinging them across.

The discussion turned to figuring out how they would resupply themselves if they ran low on food supplies.

Taelo reminded them that on every journey they had worked as a team and had each contributed to meals that far surpassed most.

Lily and Floating cloud reminded them that on their Journey of Discovery they had eaten bear, buffalo, ground hogs, goat, fish, a giant shark, and the tail of the most gruesome monster from the swamp.

She went on to make the point that they had all complimented her repeatedly on how well they ate.

Marigold laughed and said that she had never eaten such a wonderful piece of meat as that of the tail of the monster

The kids finally fell asleep, and everyone prepared to turn in.

Taelo commented that they would need to adjust their travel to allow the children time to explore and enjoy each location. He said he wanted to have a short stay in Paradise with a trip to show the children the herds of mounts that populated that region.

He said if they saw a large herd of buffalo they would spend some time to take in the overwhelming site.

He hoped they would also see some mastodons.

He mentioned the stops the team would be making. He called out the large tree they had sheltered in on the other side of the mighty river, the treasure of honey in the giant oak by the small river, then a stop at the gorge that led through the mountains, the singing beach that he knew would fascinate the children and a stay at their shark cove as places they would take a few extra sun cycles to let the children enjoy the journey.

Talking Wren laughed and commented that the children were going to make this journey, the most enjoyable one of the journeys the team had taken.

Chapter 5: Paradise

The stop at the Eastern Elk Clan was only one sun cycle. Fierce Badger welcomed them back and said that their shelters were clean and ready for use.

Taelo thanked him but said that the entire team would set up their camp outside the village since they planned to only stay for one sun cycle.

Taelo planned to stay in Paradise for a minimum of seven sun cycles. He wanted to give the children time to enjoy the wonderful location. His and Golden Hawks children had spent several moon cycles there as they grew. However, they were now old enough that this visit would have a lasting impression.

The other children had never been at the Paradise Clan location. He knew they were in for a treat. They would get to enjoy the waterfall and the small ice covered lake.

The lodge that he and his team had built so many moons ago to survive the severe blizzard had been kept up and was now used as a recreation retreat. Burley Bear said that his team of Others would stay in the lodge.

Taelo and Quiet Rabbit had their own lodge located in a spot that gave them a panoramic view of the plains beyond. Golden Hawk and Busy Bee had their lodge next to them.

They invited the rest of the team to stay with them.

The entire Paradise Elk clan was out to greet their arrival.

Feather-in-the-Wind had set up a team to prepare a celebration meal and the aroma of what was awaiting everyone on the team made all of them get quickly situated and then go to the stream to freshen up in record time.

Feather-in-the-Wind had arranged for the storytelling to be held during the meal. The story tellers had been selected from all the people that Taelo and his team had rescued from the Cannibals, from the blizzard, and from the Blue Eyes.

Busy Bee praised her "younger sister" on having arranged this story telling trip through time and having it told by those that had experienced it directly. It added a new perspective to stories that had been told before but seldom by those directly affected.

Running Stag and Lily heard the story as it was told by Little Pearl one of the few that along with them had survived the Cannibals. It was the first time that Little Pearl had told the story.

She first introduced her mate and her two children each named after her parents that had not survived but who had been brutally killed and eaten as she watched. She made the point that she would never get that scene to leave her, but she thanked Taelo and Golden Hawk for having eliminated the Cannibals. She was able to sleep at night knowing that those horrible creatures no longer walked on the ground.

She told of how Lily had taken the opportunity to escape and had taken her and everyone else through the forest until they were overcome by the amount of snow falling during the blizzard. Lily had used the only large hide they had been able to bring along to make a lean to against a boulder. It was so cold that everyone was soon passed out.

Then a strange man that talked to his wolf saved them. He had wolves that pulled his sled. It was clear that the wolves loved him. She and her companions marveled at how he fed the wolves.

What was even more wonderful was that he could cook. He made them a soup broth from meat and salt. He only allowed them a small amount. He indicated more would make them sick.

He then put all of them on the sled and helped the wolves pull the sled.

He took them to a cave were he made them all bathe. The water came from the top like warm rain. She was overwhelmed by feeling so warm and clean. She had asked Lily whether they were still alive.

The aroma of the food this man was cooking made them eager to eat. But no, he fed his wolves first and then he again only gave them some broth. She and her companions wanted to attack the wolves and get their food.

Lily said that he was making sure that they got nourishment but did not get sick.

We were clean, we were no longer hungry, we were exhausted.

He provided sleeping hides, and we slept in warmth for the first time that we could remember.

He slept on the other side of the wolves and one in particular that is here with him today, Lasher lay at his side and every time I came awake, Lasher would open his eyes.

I knew that none of us would ever be able to do anything that would endanger this strange man who had saved us.

The next morning this man had us tell him our story. Lily and he seemed to understand each other by drawing in the sand that he had spread between them.

He understood the concept of people that ate other people. He then made a request for help in going back and attacking the cannibals. All of us except Running Stag moved back away from him and shook our heads to indicated that we would not go back and fight the cannibals.

We knew it was hopeless.

They had defeated our warriors and taken us all captive. They had brutally killed most of the warriors and had devoured their hearts, raw, in front of us.

We could not go back.

Running Stag was the youngest among us. His mother and father were still alive.

He was brave beyond his years. He said that he would go back to save anyone that was still alive. He wanted the cannibals dead.

He walked bravely up to Taelo and indicated that he would go.

Taelo departed with an empty sled except for the weapons that he had selected for his planned battle and a bag where he kept herbs and moss to treat wounds.

He took very little food.

We were sure we would never see him again. We were sure that one person with a child could never defeat the cannibals.

We later learned from Running Stag the story of how with a weapon that we had never seen or imagined, Taelo was able to kill the cannibals that were dragging his father to be eaten. They had broken his father's legs in preparation, but Taelo killed each one before they knew they were being attacked.

Taelo then went from hutch to hutch and killed anyone inside. He was confronted by one cannibal that had emerged from another hutch. Taelo had two babies, one in each hand, that he had to drop in the snow as he was attacked.

Running Stag said he aimed his weapon planning to hit the cannibal in the chest but instead hit him in the leg.

It was just enough time for Taelo to pull his shark toothed weapon from its holder and kill the attacker.

He then sent Lasher out to seek any cannibal that might have tried to escape.

He then set the leg bones of Running Stag's father. He prepared the same broth as he had given us.

Running Stag's Mother, Father, and several other people were saved.

Now when we go to the Elk Clan meetings those of us who were given a second chance in life meet for one meal where we recall and regal this strange man that we came to know as Taelo, "the claw that strikes."

He struck the Cannibals who had terrorized us. He gave us a second chance.

As at that meeting, I would like to have everyone that was saved by Taelo and later Taelo and his team to stand and raise your hands in his honor.

Taelo and team were amazed at the number of the Paradise Elk Clan that stood and raised their hands. He was also surprised that Burley Bear, Saber Scar, Feather-in-the-Wind, Single Leaf, all stood and raised their arms.

A loud cheer rose up as Little Pearl sat down. It was clear that she was overcome with emotion as she wiped away tears.

Taelo stood and thanked her for her kind words. He pointed to all of the Clan members and commented that they were all capable of doing what he and his team had done.

He then turned to the team and asked them to stand. He thanked them for their support and for saving him on more than one occasion.

He pointed to Saber Scar and Burley Bear and thanked them for having saved him when his sled was pulled into the ice crevasse. He patted Lasher on the head and said that Lasher also wanted to thank them.

He thanked the team for having nursed him back to life when the bear paw pierced his back and he had spent many hours in discussions with the Ancestors.

He thanked Marigold for her bravery and skill at killing the swamp monster that attacked him.

He pointed to Running Stag and highlighted his brave actions in the final battle with the Cannibals when he had single handedly faced three cannibals twice his size in a hand to hand battle and defeated them.

He pointed to Feather-in-the-Wind and smiled as he complimented her on being the only person he knew who had killed a hammer head shark.

That made her laugh and she stood to explain that her shark was no longer than her arm. Her entire clan hooted and pounded their spear butts to the ground.

He then told of how she had helped him kill a giant bear on the journey they now called Dangerous Journey.

He pointed at Quiet Rabbit, Busy Bee, Talking Wren, and Single Leaf and complimented them on training the Condor Clan women to be slingers that single handed defeated a superior number of Warrior Clan attackers in such a successful fashion that not one male Condor Clan warrior was involved in battle.

He ended by pointing at Golden Hawk and complimented him on always being at the right place at the right time to save him.

Taelo ended by raising his arms and then taking his spear with the golden feather and pounding the ground

The entire Paradise Clan stood and stomped their feed in unison with Taelo's beat.

Everyone finished their meals, and the evening came to a close.

The sky above was a blanket of shimmering light. The moon was full and seemed to bring a light brighter than was normally present.

Chapter 6:Mount Herd

Taelo, and most of the team sat on their mounts and watched as Feather-in-the-Wind showed the children how to ride standing on the mounts. Once they had all demonstrated their ability to stand, she rode around in a circle as she did a handstand on the back of the mount.

Quiet Rabbit commented that Feather-in-the-Wind was one of the most talented persons that she had ever known. She had been the one that had taught the team how a mount could be tamed. She had become one of the best slingers. She was the youngest Clan leader and was adored by her Clan members. Quiet Rabbit went on to say that she was glad that she and Busy Bee had been able to rescue her from the cave of a frozen Condor brides.

Taelo knew most of the kids would take falls and told everyone to get ready to console those children and make sure they were not hurt. He was glad that the riding was taking place where the snow covered grass would provide the maximum buffer to the fall.

He commented that the journey they were on would likely take a little while longer than he had planned since he wanted the experience to be one that the children enjoyed and learned new skills.

The herd of mounts just a short distance across the meadow seemed to be mesmerized by Feather-in-the-Wind's riding show as well. The leader of the herd had stopped and had actually come closer. Taelo commented that the herd seemed to be thriving and that the mounts seemed to be healthy.

Feather-in-the-Wind led the troop of children back to the rest of the team and commented that it was time to return to the village and enjoy a leisurely afternoon meal. She said that the kids were ready for some warmer place to play, and she was ready to freshen up, so she did not smell like her mount.

Running Stag commented that he could support her desire. He did not want to have a mount sleeping next to him.

The team had raised their camp cover and the inside was toasty warm. Burley Bear commented that he had decided that the cover would give everyone a place to meet away from the center of the camp.

It also provided a place where cooking could easily be done. When they returned, Lily and Floating Cloud had a warm stew ready that they served to the kids.

Taelo mentioned that the speed of travel was going to be slower than he had originally thought. He pointed to the kids and said that they should enjoy the journey and that meant that they should shorten the travel period during each sun cycle. That way there would be time to play and do casual hunting and fishing.

The discussion about the impact of having children along on a journey went on as they enjoyed their honey seasoned grilled meat and roasted vegetables.

Taelo complemented Lily and Floating Cloud on the great meal.

He smiled when they thanked him but let everyone know this was only because they had been given ample time to prepare and that on the trail it would often just be a quick stew.

The next morning was spent with the kids playing out on the frozen lake. One game was to see who could slide a stone to the edge of the ice were it opened under the waterfall. By the time the game ended there was a small wall of stones where the ice ended.

Meadow Flower made sure that none of the kids tried to retrieve any of the stones and commented that come spring all the stones would raise the lake's water level.

The team was sitting out as the sun began its journey to the far horizon when two runners came up the trail along the stream. It was Bold Walker and his friend, Long Leaper.

Feather-in-the-Wind jumped up and ran to him and jumped into his arms. She asked why he was coming to Paradise.

He explained that he had awakened a few sun cycles ago with the urge to see her. He said that when he came awake he thought she was about to do something exciting.

Feather-in-the-Wind explained that she was about to go with Taelo on a really exciting journey around mother earth.

Bold Walker gave a small laugh and said that then he would need to go along to protect his younger sister.

That brought laughter from Burley Bear who commented that his younger sister had demonstrated the capability of taking on monstrous bears and lions and surviving.

Taelo welcomed Bold Runner to the team and said he could only come along if his "younger" sister provided the additional mounts and food for him and if he did not mind the team confusing the name of a brave wolf with that of a Condor Clan member.

Bold Runner laughed and said that he would take it all in stride.

He asked Long Leaper if he would return to the Condor Clan and let them know that he would be gone for a period of time.

One evening a few sun cycles later Burley Bear commented that it was time to continue the journey if they wanted to use their sleds all the way to the mighty river.

Taelo looked around to the rest of the team and asked if everyone was ready. Their next goal would be the mighty river, but they did have one special spot where they would spend at least a couple of sun cycles.

Saber Scar ran his hand along his chest where the scars of the giant lion crossed the scars of the saber tooth lion. He smiled and commented that it was a spot that he would like to see again and that all he remembered from the last time was Quite Rabbit stitching the flesh back onto this body.

Feather-in-the-Wind said that all she remembered was the pain in the ribs that had lasted for several moon cycles. She said she would like to see that spot but hoped not to see another lion.

Running Stag commented that he remembered the place well and the fear that had overwhelmed him when he saw the giant lion attacking Feather-in-the-Wind.

Marigold jokingly commented that she remembered the great taste of the wild boar that she and Lily had prepared. She thought of it as a place of wonder. She went on to say that she had wondered whether either of the two would survive.

Quite Rabbit smiled and recalled how worried Marigold had been about Saber Scar. She had been worried too since the lion had opened four gashes across Saber Scar's chest and left marks on his rib bones.

If the lion had not been knocked aside by Feather-in-the-Wind the lion would have ripped Saber Scar's ribs out.

She had to put two layers of stiches to close each of the four gashes. She had been relieved when Saber Scar had healed enough to be pulled on a travois.

Taelo reminded everyone that this time they had children along and they would always have to keep that in mind when they were out hunting.

It was a crisp, frosty morning as the loaded sleds made their way through the Paradise Clan village and out to the flat plain that disappeared in the distant horizon.

Taelo was on the runners of the sled that held the twins who were sitting and playing under the hide covering the sled. Quite Rabbit and Busy Bee were together on the lead sled, guiding one of the two bigger supply sleds.

Lily's sled was also a larger one that was essentially thought of as the sled where the meals would be made.

Lily and Floating Cloud had devised a small four sided fire pit at the back of the sled where they could have a small fire as they went along. They always had warm stew available, but they would grill any rabbit that was handed to them.

The eight sleds made a long line. Burley Bear was on the last sled.

Bold Walker was learning how to handle a sled from Feather-in-the-Wind.

He took a ribbing for being a slow learner. He knew that his comment about protecting his younger sister would cost him a lot of ribbing.

He was so glad that he had arrived in time to join the adventure that went beyond his personal journey with his now dead friend, Mountain Runner. That journey along a river that became so large that other side could not be seen had been almost ten moon cycles long. It sounded as if this journey would be much longer than the one he had taken.

Saber Scar and Running Stag were leading the mounts and bringing up the rear.

The journey was progressing smoothly and Taelo was relaxed as he looked back at the sleds.

He thought of the next stop as the Lion's Den.

Chapter 7: The Boar

Ｔhe way to the point of the journey where the team had previously stopped and where Feather-in-the-Wind, Saber Scar and Running Stag had faced and killed the lion took the team several sun cycles.

Taelo was pacing the team. He called a halt each day when the sun was halfway down toward the horizon. Each team member had to come up with the activities in which both the children and the adults would participated.

Taelo appreciated the ingenuity of the team.

One activity that everyone enjoyed was using the sling and trying to hit a swinging target.

Another was spear throwing to see who could throw and hit a designated target.

The snowshoe race was one that turned out to be hilarious because trying to move fast was almost impossible without ending up with your nose in the snow.

All the activities provided the team with great exercise and developed all of their skills.

Riding the mounts and picking up objects from the ground was one activity that everyone also enjoyed.

Burley Bear and the rest of the Others were not as agile as the rest of the team, and they weighed at least twice as much. They stopped participation in the event when their mounts kept falling due to the weight imbalance created when one of them went to pick up something on the ground.

Taelo gave Burley Bear a ribbing about the fact that he outweighed his mount and perhaps he should carry the mount.

Burley Bear agreed that this event put the mount at risk, and they were too valuable to chance hurting them.

The wolves were very tolerant of the children and some of them enjoyed the game of fetching the sticks that the kids would throw. It was soon clear to the kids which wolves to stay clear of and which ones were willing to play.

It was obvious to Taelo that the pace that he was setting was the right one. Both the children and the adults seemed to be enjoying the journey.

The pace also allowed time for hunting.

This was often a parent, child activity. Small game was the aim for these hunts.

But mother nature did not always cooperate.

Taelo and Golden Hawk were out hunting with the Red Fox, Black Wolf, and Yellow Flower when they came across a large boar. They had surprised the boar that instead of fleeing, attacked.

The attack was directly at Golden Hawk and Yellow Flower.

Taelo rushed in from the side and with the butt of his spear he pushed the boar to the side.

Golden Hawk got Yellow Flower behind a tree with the twins and then together the two of them faced the boar that had spun around and was charging.

There was only enough time to react.

Taelo jumped to his left and Golden Hawk went right. Then the two of them attacked from each side and buried their spears just behind the front leg. The boar twisted and turned toward Taelo and continued the attack.

Taelo leaped high in the air and as he went over the boar, he used his flat shark toothed weapon to hit the boar behind his ear. The crack of the hit resounded through the forest and the boar went down on his front knees. Golden Hawk landed his war hammer between the boar's eyes and finished him.

It seemed to have been a long battle, but Taelo knew that it had been as fast as lightening.

Taelo called the twins out to look closely at one of the more dangerous animals that one could face.

He asked Golden Hawk to go back to camp and return with a mount. He would stay and prepare a travois and then they would pull the boar back to camp.

The twins wanted to stay and help. Taelo agreed and put them to work cutting some smaller saplings to make the cross members for the travois. He showed them how to strip the green bark so it could be used to bind the cross members to the main travois poles.

This was the kind learning that he wanted the children to absorb.

Golden Hawk did not return alone. Saber Scar, Burley Bear and three kids all returned on their mounts.

Burly Bear said that he figured Taelo would be too weak to put the boar on the travois, but he and Saber Scar would have no problem.

Taelo and Burley Bear always exchanged snide comments, but they were best of friends. Their exchanges were always followed with a pat on the back and a hearty laugh.

Once back in camp, Lily and White Cloud claimed the carcass and said that the evening meal would include roasted boar.

Taelo thanked them. He watched as Slow Walker and Whistling arrow began to expertly skin the boar. They were quick and efficient and had the hide off quicker than it took Taelo to walk to the stream, wash up and return.

Feather-in-the-Wind took the opportunity to tease Taelo and Golden Hawk about the "rabbit" that they had taken their children to hunt.

Taelo smiled and replied that it was smaller than the one she had hunted with Saber Scar and Running Stag. He knew that he had hit the mark reminding her of her rabbit hunting and facing a lion, as she gave a bow and took a step backward and replied that sometimes rabbits took on very dangerous shapes.

Black Wolf, Red Fox and Yellow Flower enjoyed telling the story of the attack and how their fathers had worked together to kill the boar.

Floating Cloud rewarded their story with a strip of honey roasted flank boar meat.

Burley Bear kept asking questions of the three and said he would help them improve their story telling. Soon his story telling coaching had Taelo leaping high into the sky and Golden Hawk using a war hammer the size of boulder. And the story took the angle of the poor victim boar that was given no chance at survival.

He had the kids laughing and the rest of the team helping him turn the hunt into two ruthless, ferocious hunters taking advantage of a helpless animal.

The honey roast boar dinner was among one of the best field meals that the team enjoyed.

Chapter 8: Remembering

*M*arigold, in the lead sled created the camp circle. Taelo knew she had a great eye when the sleds created the exact sized circle that allowed the camp cover to fit and still provide room for the mounts.

The camp cover went up in record time.

Taelo asked if Feather-in-the-Wind, Saber Scar and Running Stag wanted to go to where the actual lion attack had occurred. They said yes and Taelo asked who else on the team wanted to go.

Everyone raised their hand and then followed the three, who had not dismounted, to the spot where the lion had come out of the brush.

The place had not changed.

Saber Scar, Feather-in-the-Wind and Running Stag had chosen to ride their mounts into the area where they had faced the giant lion. For them this point in the journey was similar to getting back onto a mount after having been thrown off. They were again reliving their near death experience.

Saber Scar dismounted and stood in the spot where he had stood during the tiger attack.

Feather-in-the-Wind jumped down from her mount and had her sling loaded as she approached the bush from which the lion had appeared.

Her heart was racing as she relived that day.

A rabbit caused her to jump back. He raced out and in a flash, she nailed him when it zagged toward the stream.

She then backed up as she had done that sun cycle that seemed like it was just the sun cycle before this one.

Running Stag shot half his arrows into the ground and then jumped off his mount and emptied his arrow holder.

Feather-in-the-Wind did her running slide just as she had done with the lion.

Saber Scar jump down from his mount, planted his spear, then pushed it aside, spun, fell, and jabbed upward with his blade as Feather-in-the-Wind, did a flip as she flew over him and this time landed on her feet.

An eagle's cry made everyone look up.

Taelo commented that the eagle had called to her and that she now had closed the circle on the event with the lion. He made the point that she was wearing the coat made from the lions hide and both Running Stag and Saber Scar were wearing jackets made from that same hide.

Feather-in-the-Wind picked up the dead rabbit and handed it to Running Stag.

She then opened her coat to show the interior and the stripes of the lion. It had been a gift made by Marigold as a present for saving Saber Scar.

She then leaped up and mounted her mount and stood up. She looked at White Cloud and Lily and asked if there was any lion meat to eat and then led the way back to the camp.

There was no lion meat but there was rabbit, a ground hog, and deer.

Taelo led the way to the stream and shortly, he, Golden Hawk, Burley Bear and Sharp Knife returned with one fish each. Each fish was enough to feed two or three.

Almost immediately, Lily put the fish on spits and had them over the fire.

Taelo asked Feather-in-the-Wind, Saber Scar and Running Elk to tell the story of the lion attack experience on that day on the Journey of Discovery.

He listened as Saber Scar started the story about he and Running Stag complaining about the fact that like today, Feather-in-the-Wind killed almost every rabbit that moved. He and Running Stag never had a chance to do anything but open up the game bag to take the next rabbit that she put into it.

Then in a flash, things changed. Feather-in-the-Wind put up her hand and began backing away from the bush.

The attacking lion was as big as their mounts, but when it leaped out at her, Feather-in-the Wind ran toward the lion and then threw herself under it and stabbed multiple times as she slid out the back between the attacking lion's legs.

There was no time to think, Saber Scar described how he jumped down and was planning to put his spear into the lions chest. He knew he was going to die when it knocked the spear aside with one paw and was about to close its mouth on his neck.

Suddenly the lion was knocked to the side as Feather-in-the-Wind used herself and flew into the side of the lion like a spear. Her speed and her weight was enough to knock the lion to the side, but it still managed to draw its sharp claw across his chest.

He described feeling incredible pain as he slid under the lion. He used the knife that Feather-in-the-Wind had left embedded in the lion's body.

He was passing out and knew he was going to die. With all that he had left, he repeatedly stabbed the beast.

He then passed out and knew that he was on his journey to the next world. It was a journey that he had not planned to take.

He said that he later learned that Running Stag had shot all his arrows into the beast and had jumped from his mount and used his war hammer to repeatedly strike the beast between his eyes.

He then clarified that he did not recall much beyond looking into Quiet Rabbit's eyes and being told that she was going to sew him up.

He never felt a thing.

The next time he opened his eyes he was looking into Marigold's concerned eyes as she tried to give him some broth. It was then that he felt the burning pain across his chest.

Feather-in-the-Wind took up the story and made the point that only a person with Saber Scars strength would have been able to use her blade to kill the giant beast. Had it not been for his strength she knew that she and Running Stag would probably be in the next world.

Running Stag added that he had used every arrow that he had taken along, and they seemed to have no effect. He jumped down from his mount and figured that he had no chance at survival, but he planned to do as much damage as possible. He was surprised that his war hammer had an effect. He would never know if it had been the repeated head strikes or if Saber Scar had found the heart.

He was just overjoyed that the lion was dead.

He immediately rolled the lion's body off of Saber Scar and saw the bones of his ribs. He thought at first that Saber Scar was dead. His chest was a bloody mess, and the rib bones were showing. It did not seem that anyone could survive such a wound.

He was pushed aside by Quiet Rabbit. He went to Feather-in-the-Wind who claimed she was alright but as she tried to stand she passed out because of the pain of a broken rib and collar bone.

Running Stag continued as he lauded the bravery displayed by Feather-in-the-Wind and Saber Scar. He recalled only one other person with such bravery. That was the person who had saved him and had gone back to save his parents from the cannibals.

Taelo thanked Running Stag for recognizing him, but he wanted the team to know that the three were examples of how working together as a team had made their survival possible.

He went on to extol all the members of the team and to have them recall their moments when the eagle called from the sky to let the team know that they had taken the right action.

Taelo then pointed to the sky and reminded everyone that even the eagle had signaled that it too knew of the bravery that had been displayed that day. It was the day that the eagle began recognizing the entire team for taking the right action when it was called for.

Chapter 9: Mammoth

Taelo was greeted by a sky filled with glorious pink clouds as he walked down to the stream to splash cold water on his face. He stopped in the chill of the morning to absorb the beauty. He felt the hug on his legs and knew that Red Fox and Black Wolf had followed him. He reached down with each hand and gave them a hug. He then crouched down and asked them if they saw the beauty of the pink clouds.

They nodded and followed his example of splashing water on their faces.

Once back by the cooking fire they each ate a bowl of the hot savory stew.

The camp was being packed as they watched. This was the morning they were moving on toward the mighty river.

Yellow Flower and Busy Bee said good morning as they filled their bowl with stew. Busy Bee pointed to Golden Hawk and commented that he would join them as soon as he had the sled packed and loaded.

Taelo stood as Quiet Rabbit arrived and filled her bowl. He commented that he had to get their sled ready to travel.

He had to stop as the main camp cover came down. Several of the team had decided they would get it done and out of the way.

Taelo looked around and appreciated how the team flowed to the work in a natural almost unconscious way. Their actions spoke of a sharing and caring culture. He could feel it in the friendly and natural actions that everyone displayed.

The sun was halfway to its zenith when the team was finally ready to move out. The area had been cleaned and would be back to its natural state in a few sun cycles.

Burley Bear was in the lead as he crested the hill and stopped. He turned and called out that everyone should come up and to see the valley below.

Taelo recalled the view that they had experienced on their last journey. This time the sea of buffalo was much smaller but what was exciting was that a small herd of mastodon were on the far side of the valley traveling along with the buffalo.

He was prepared to lead the team down to the valley when a lioness about the size of the lion that had attacked Feather-in-the-Wind, Saber Scar and Running Stag appeared out of the brush to the teams right.

The lioness seemed surprised and stopped.

The entire team stopped what they were doing as well. They watched as Taelo and Golden Hawk slowly got off their mounts. Each had his spear in hand but made no move toward the lioness.

Taelo asked Lily for a bag of meat junks. Then he and Golden Hawk walked slowly walked toward the lioness.

Golden Hawk handed a junk of meat to Taelo.

Taelo threw her the sizeable piece of meat. When she gulped it down, he threw her another. He had his spear leaning in the crock of his left arm and was throwing the meat with his other arm. He was prepared for an attack but did not want to kill the lioness.

He told the lioness that this was her lucky day because he was not hunting her and once she had her fill she should go back the way she had come.

Burley Bear, and the rest of the team had all gathered in a group with their spears ready. The children were behind them guarded by their mothers.

The tension in the air weight like a heavy sleeping hide over the entire team.

Feather-in-the-Wind, Running Stag and Saber Scar were in a ready to attack position.

The lioness ate several more pieces of meat and then gave a growl as she seemed to shake her head and turn. She trotted back the way she had come.

It appeared that she had understood.

Silence hung in the air like the quiet before a storm.

Then the eagle cry from the sky lifted the blanket of dread that had come over the team and they let out a cheer.

Taelo heard Burley Bear tell the team that "Taelo also talked to bears and wolves and those that did not listen usually ended up as a hide."

Taelo suggested they take their sleds down into the valley and then take an excursion with their mounts and get a close look at the giant mastodon.

Once the team had reached the valley, Taelo had them circle the sleds, but they left the wolves harnessed.

He had Lasher, Arrow and Walker released from their lead position since they would go with them.

He asked for volunteers to stay with the sleds.

He was pleased Little Otter and Talking Wren volunteered to stay. Each of them commented that they had one very close at hand experience with a mastodon on their first team hunt.

Talking Wren laughed and said she had to pull her mate to safety so that he didn't end up underneath that mammoth.

Saber Scar said that he had been there to see Talking Wren rescue her mate, but he wanted Spear Tip to see the mastodon.

The rest of the team prepared their mounts. Quiet Rabbit instructed the children to stay immediately behind one of the adult riders. If they got separated they should travel in the same direction as the buffalo and then call out so that they could be helped. She stressed how dangerous it would be to ride through the herd of buffalo.

Burley Bear took the lead and Aristosa was immediately behind him, and Meadow Flower was behind her.

Quiet Rabbit took the lead, and the twins followed her. Taelo assumed the last position. He wanted to be able to respond if anything went wrong.

Single Leaf was next, then Flint followed by Sharp Blade. Feather-in-the-Wind was followed by Neiva and Running Stag was the next rider.

Floating Cloud, Whistling Arrow, Lily, and Slow Walker formed a separate group as did the six warriors from Paradise that were with them.

The buffalo seemed to ignore the mounts and the team as they went through and across to the other side.

Burley Bear slowly crossed the herd at an angle that took them slowly to the far side. A few buffalo were following behind the Mastodon, but it was now easier to approach them.

When the Mastodon were immediately in front of the team, their size overwhelmed everyone. In whispered tones they commented that the large fur covered animals were magnificent.

Taelo took the lead and guided the team to the far side of the herd. The team was able to slowly make its way forward until they reached the lead mastodon. The tusks of many mastodon were longer than the length of the mount he was riding.

Taelo quietly commented that the group of mastodon was led by a female and commented that the curved tusks reminded him of a huge scorpion tail. He said that he was sure that she would know how to use her tusks with even a more deadly effect than the scorpion.

The younger and smaller mammoths were in toward the middle where they would be protected from predators.

He had everyone ride up to see the leader and then led the team off to the side beyond the edge of the buffalo herd.

The team then spent a few moments sharing their thoughts about the wonder of the mammoths.

The children asked how long mammoths could live and why the littler ones were in the middle.

Taelo shared the stories he had listened to that told of the long lives of the mastodon that matched that of most people. He also made the point that the mastodon's were practicing protecting the younger ones, just like the team was doing with their younger ones.

He smiled when Yellow Flower laughed and said that she was not a young mastodon, but she understood.

This time Golden Hawk led the team along the side of the buffalo herd but in the opposite direction of how they had come across. He went well past where the ring of sleds were located on the other side and then entered the herd and slowly angled across in the same direction that the buffalo were moving.

When they came out of the herd almost exactly at the ring of sleds, Spear Tip asked how Golden Hawk had done that.

Saber Scar laughed and said that Golden Hawk was always lucky.

Golden Hawk explained that he had figured how long it took to cross the herd the first time and how far they had traveled during that crossing. He had traveled in the opposite direction past the camp circle the same amount of time and then had crossed at the angle they had safely done before.

Everyone gathered around the cooking ring and continued discussing what they had just witnessed.

The sun was now at it zenith.

Taelo looked out at the herd and decided to demonstrate the hunting technique that he and Golden Hawk used.

The hunt would also provide the extra meat that was needed when the sleds were taken back to Paradise.

He discussed this with the team. Taelo had decided that he wanted the children to see that both men and women could hunt.

They decided that Golden Hawk would down one buffalo and Quiet Rabbit would down the second one. Feather in the Wind would back up Golden Hawk and Talking Wren would back up Quiet Rabbit.

He, Burly Bear, Marigold would make sure that the buffalo was dead and would help to bring the animal to the nearest tree where it would be processed.

Everyone watched as Quiet Rabbit and Golden Hawk selected their animal and slowly guided them toward the forest.

Then both of them got their animal to bolt toward the edge of the forest. The two of them seemed synchronized in their run and then at the same time they both rushed past the front of the animals and placed the tip of the spear on the chest of the buffalo and placed the butt end of their spears on the ground.

Both animals ran the spear through their chest and fell to their knees dead, just short of the forest's edge.

The Golden Hawk and Quiet Rabbit came together and danced a jig.

There was nothing that the backup team needed to do.

One buffalo was designated to go back with the returning sleds, and one would be added to the food supply for the team.

Taelo declared that at the rise of the next sun they would travel as far as possible until the sun was reaching for the earth's horizon.

He made the point that everyone had enjoyed this sun cycle and they needed to reach the mighty river before they lost the snow cover.

Chapter 10: Transition

ℐt was only two sun cycles later that Taelo called a halt when the snow began to thin to the point that the sled runners were hitting the ground.

The team made camp and prepared to transition to pulling their belongings on travois. Taelo watched as the Paradise hunters that had come along to take the sleds and wolves back to Paradise loaded the food they would need to make the return trip.

These hunters would sleep in the sleds as they made their return. One of the larger sleds held the entire carcass of a buffalo.

There would be no need for those returning to hunt on the way back.

Early on the following sun cycle, Feather-in-the-Wind thanked them for having volunteered for that role. They all raised their arm in salute and said it had been a wonderful experience and they were glad to have been given the chance.

They commented that they were jealous of the three Paradise hunters that would continue to the far sea before they had to return with the mounts.

They wondered how three warriors would be able to get the mounts across the river.

Taelo nodded and agreed the three would need to be able to do that before the team would continue on the journey.

Taelo and the team watched until the sleds seemed to disappear far out on the horizon.

Taelo pointed to the edge of the forest where a pack of wolves were sitting. He commented that the wolves were his friends, who had last time escorted the team to the mighty river and appeared to be ready to do it again.

He asked Lily for enough meat scraps so that he could feed each wolf a handful. She had watched Taelo do this several times before and knew exactly how large to cut each piece of meat.

He asked Burley Bear to accompany him and carry the chunks of meat.

Then he walked towards the wolf pack.

He heard Meadow Flower explaining to the children what he was about to do.

Taelo approached the pack and talked about the last time they had provided him with an escort to the mighty river. He strategically threw the first piece to the lead wolf and then slowly proceeded to place his throws to each of the other wolves.

He had a few pieces left over that he threw to the leader and to those wolves around the leader.

Then he said that they should follow but to stay to the woods, and he would see them when the sun met the horizon.

Then he returned to the team and led the way toward the mighty river.

The going had been as slow as Taelo had anticipated. The wolves seemed to have understood his instructions and they were following slowly through the forest. At the close of each sun cycle he went out to feed them.

He shared with the children that he did so because the wolves would provide the team a warning against other predators.

He spent several conversations explaining that he did not think the wolves understood what he was saying but the tone of his voice was non-threatening and by showing no fear they saw him as the leader of the pack.

After their evening meal, as Quiet Rabbit and Busy Bee sketched in the herd of Mastodon on their record hide, Taelo inquired how many suns it was until they would reach the mighty river.

Quiet Rabbit unrolled the hide that they had made during the Journey of Discovery and pointed to where she thought they were currently camped.

Busy Bee said that she estimated that it would be four or five sun cycles to the river.

He asked them to share their two hides with the rest of the team and show the children how they were keeping track of this journey.

The kids glued on to the hide that documented the Journey of Discovery. They asked about the drawings that were on the hide.

Quiet Rabbit and Busy Bee took turns telling the experience associated with each drawing.

The children listened to each story and then asked a series of questions.

The first story was about Feather-in-the-Wind and Running Stag finding Paradise. This got many questions from Neiva and almost as many from the other kids.

The next drawing was of the lion attack and that story was still fresh on everyone's mind, but they listened again as Feather-in-the-Wind told it again,

The crossing of the mighty river and the experience of almost being swept away by the extremely strong current as the rain made it impossible to see was next.

All of the kids wondered how they would cross the river this time.

The story included finding shelter in the trunk of a giant tree. Taelo shared how in the raining downpour he had gone out to look for a place that the team could shelter. He followed Lasher who he credited with finding the huge tree that provided shelter for the entire team.

He pointed out that the rain continued for several sun cycles.

Feather-in-the-Wind then told of waking up very early and realizing that the rain had stopped. She decided to go for a walk with Bold Walker. She was going into a blackberry patch when a giant bear rose up and then chased her. She managed to climb to the top of a pine tree to escape.

She shared how Taelo arrived not long after as he followed Bold Walker back to where she was up in the tree. He had distracted the bear and had asked it to leave the clearing or die on his spear.

The swift charge of the bear caught her by surprise. Taelo's thrust his spear upward through the bottom the standing bears jaw hard enough that she saw the large sharks tooth tip of the spear come out of the bear's head. She recalled how she had scrambled down to help get the bear off of Taelo and had been relieve to see he was alive. She became alarmed when she realized that the blood she saw was coming from a wound in Taelo's back.

Quiet Rabbit worked at stopping the bleeding from his back where the bears claws had gone all the way in and badly wounded him.

She shared how she sat by where Taelo lay as they all waited for him to recover. She recalled the seven sun cycles that Taelo had mumbled as he seemed to be speaking to unseen people.

She said that she later learned that he had been speaking to the Ancients.

She felt personally guilty of having caused Taelo to be hurt. He had asked her if she had called the bear into the clearing to attack him. She understood his message but even to this day she felt that she had some responsibility for what the bear had done.

The stories had to stop when the sun slowly sank below the far horizon, but Busy Bee and Quiet Rabbit promised to tell the story of each picture in detail.

When they had originally drawn the pictures on their Journey of Discovery hide they had never imagined using it to tell their children the stories before sending them to sleep.

Feather-in-the-Wind commented that telling the stories to the kids made her get a tingly feeling about that journey. She went on to say that she cherished every experience she had as part of Taelo's team. It was the reason she had come to the Northern Elk Clan village to join the team from the very beginning of their current journey.

Running Stag commented that when, at the last moment, Feather-in-the-Wind had made up her mind to join the journey from the very beginning, they took four mounts and rode nonstop across the plains in the dead of winter. He had never expected that she would lead Neiva and he through a blizzard when in the past Feather-in-the-Wind was the person who always hid under every hide she could pile on top herself.

This time she had put on her warmest coat and the eye slits and put all the hides on Neiva. She had then led the way through a blizzard almost as strong as the one Taelo had experienced when he had saved Semper and Wan's people.

He pointed to the hide and asked if that part of the adventure could be added.

That got a laugh from everyone, but Busy Bee drew in three riders and four horses riding through the snow, as they approached the Northern Elk Clan valley.

This caused tears for Feather-in-the-Wind, and she gave both Quite Rabbit and Busy Bee a hug as she whispered that they were the best "older sister's" that she had.

It brought back the memory of the time when White Swan had made a point to call the three of them sisters. It had elevated Feather-in-the-Wind to a higher position in the Clan.

After a short time, Taelo pointed out that the going was much slower by travois, but the meals had become better.

The kids were becoming good slingers and would often get enough rabbits that each had their own.

Running Stag commented that between Feather-in-the-Wind and Single Leaf the rest of them had little chance at any small game that crossed their path within sling range.

Lily laughed and said that she would take all the rabbits and ground hogs that they bagged. Cooking was easy when all she had to do was to rub salt on the rabbits and put them on a spit and let each person cook their own.

Taelo and Golden Hawk made a set of shortened slings. They gave one to each of the children and said that they should ask their mothers how to use the sling as they rode their mounts.

The going was slow enough that walking and jogging was easy to accomplish and Taelo varied the pace so that everyone kept in shape by doing some jogging.

The estimated number of sun cycles to reach the mighty river turned out to be accurate.

Taelo complemented Busy Bee and Quiet Rabbit on the fact that their travel hide seemed to be well calibrated.

Chapter 11:The Mighty River

Taelo knew his memory and sense of direction was serving him well when they arrived at almost the exact spot along the mighty river where they had crossed the previous time.

He had the camp located in a clearing a short distance from the river. The days had been clear so he did not expect the same challenge as in the previous crossing but this time he wanted to get the mounts across in a manner that could be done by the three Paradise warriors. On their return to the river, they would have to do that by themselves.

He, Golden Hawk, Burley Bear and Talking Wren had talked through a method that would use the flow of the river to aid in moving the mounts across.

As the sun broke the horizon in the early morning, Taelo, the twins, Golden Hawk and Yellow Flower walked out to the wolf pack that was still staying in the forest.

Quiet Rabbit and Busy Bee had both been apprehensive about letting the children go with their mates. They were both standing by ready to defend them if the wolf pack attacked.

Taelo thanked them for their vigilance but said he would not be taking the children if he felt the wolves would attack. He had instructed the children that they must not show fear and must move slowly.

He then led the way out to where he could easily toss the pieces of meat and spoke to the wolves. He thanked them for their escort and let them know that he was crossing the mighty river. He let them know that they should return to their hunting grounds. He wished them all well and good hunting.

It seemed that the wolf pack leader understood. Once the feeding ended the wolf pack set out away from the river.

Taelo led the way back to the camp and let everyone know that by the time the sun hit the horizon they would be sleeping on the island.

He, Golden Hawk and Burley Bear then managed the construction of a raft the was large enough to hold one mount. It had four floats mounted on long poles out in each direction to stabilize the raft. They secured one rope to the front float pole and one to the rear float pole. They let out the rear pole rope to see how the raft performed.

The raft seemed to handle well.

On a raft built to take two people, Taelo and one of the Paradise warriors went across to the island that was about a third of the way across the river. They carried the rope connected to the front float of the horse raft with them and once on the island they found a stout tree to which they secured the rope.

The first crossing of the raft carried a second Paradise warrior as the passenger. The raft was launched and the rope on the bank where everyone stood watching, was slowly released. The pull of the river current slowly caused the raft to move toward the island. Once the raft was near, the rope in the back was held so the raft swung into the shore, corner first. This kept the floats from being damaged.

The design worked as intended and the passenger was able to step off onto dry ground.

A cheer went up from the team.

Taelo had the three warriors transfer all the mounts to the island. This gave the warriors the experience they would need on the return trip.

The three were amazed that they were able to do the task by themselves. They kept complementing Taelo on how well it worked.

Once the mounts were across, the entire team and their supplies came across next.

The team camp cover would not be used. The team would spend the night in individual sleeping hides. This kept them from having to set up a large camp site.

They would leave the next morning after the transfer raft was set up to cross the larger distance to the far bank.

This time the team would be first to cross and the mounts last.

The crossing, the next morning, was somewhat more challenging since the distance to the far bank was twice that of the day before.

Taelo and Golden Hawk were the first to cross. This time their raft had a rope on each end. This allowed them to get it pulled back so that two of the Paradise warriors could cross with the actual larger mount raft transfer rope.

Taelo wanted to make sure that these warriors had the experience in dealing with the river current and with the effort to get the rope secured on each end.

He wanted the three to transfer all the mounts once again. He did not want to risk the three not being able to cross the river when they returned.

Taelo, Golden Hawk, Burley Bear and Saber Scar did the work of getting the team and the supplies across.

The transfer across of the team went smoothly.

Taelo then turned the process of getting the mounts across to the three warriors. He was pleased that the three worked well together.

It took twice as long as the first crossing to the island, but the last mount was brought across as the sun reached the horizon.

Taelo watched as the raft for the mounts was pulled up out of the water and onto the bank.

Then the last warrior got on the smaller raft and let the current pull him across.

The three let out a whoop and danced in a circle. They were now sure they would be able to cross back when going back to Paradise.

The team had gone ahead to the tree that was hollow. There they found the poles that Taelo had put on stones and leaned up inside the hollow tree.

The campsite went up before the sun sank down below the horizon.

Lilly and Floating Cloud had a wonderful dinner of salt and honey rubbed grilled buffalo as a celebration for having crossed the mighty river. She commented that the team was getting better at crossing.

This time not even the mounts got wet.

She commented that the eagle did not have to cry, and they were all safe.

Feather-in-the-Wind commented that this time she would not go wandering by herself, but she did want to go see the place where she had met the bear that had almost taken Taelo to the land of the Ancestors.

Taelo smiled and replied that he had been with the Ancestors, but they had told him that he was not yet ready to make that journey. He too wanted to visit the site where the bear had not listened to his advice. He said he would be wearing a jacket that had been made from its hide. He suggested that they go to that clearing after the team was packed and ready to move on.

He jokingly said that they could all go to the spot where Feather-in-the-Wind had "summoned" a very large and angry bear to test his survival skills.

Once the team had reached the small clearing where Taelo had faced the bear, Feather-in-the-Wind climbed up to the limb she had been on when the bear attacked Taelo. She looked down where Taelo was standing in the same spot he had stood when attacked. She called down that the tree had grown but that Taelo looked just as small as on that fateful day.

Taelo smiled and called back and said that she looked even smaller than he remembered.

Quiet Rabbit gave Taelo a hug and told him that for her and all the team members, that the past time that now seemed so long ago had stayed on their minds. This journey gave them closure and they would now remember it as a place of wonder versus one where they had almost lost him.

Taelo hugged her and said that he was forever under her spell and that he would not become an Ancient for many cycles to come.

He looked up as the eagle gave a cry as it circled. He gave the sign of friend used by the Others. He hoped that Broken Spear was flying with the eagle and could see him.

Chapter 12: Broken Spear's First Report

Broken Spear sat enjoying the warmth of the heated pool as he watched the sun slowly clear the mountains. The valley mist, grey in the early light, slowly gave way to the light that seemed to slowly take the mist up and away.

He let the warmth of the water warm his old joints and ease the pain. He knew that he was near his end, but he was determined to fly with the eagle and absorb the beauty of the land that Taelo was traveling.

Before reaching the Paradise Elk Clan village Taelo and the team hunted three buffalo.

Broken Spear did not know when Feather-in-the-Wind had joined the team, but he now saw her with them on the hunt as she downed one of the three.

He was surprised when the eagle gave a cry when she downed her buffalo. That the eagle watched more than one individual surprised him.

He experienced the stay at Paradise in several segments. The trip out to see the mounts was one segment. It was clear that Taelo had taken the children to see the mount herd and had captured several mounts.

The eagle flew around the Paradise village for several sun cycles, and he was able to see the preparation for the next part of the journey.

He knew that the wolves and sleds were to be left behind once they reached the mighty river.

The mounts would be used on the other side to pull travois.

He wondered what all the goods might be. He knew that Burley Bear had packed heavy winter gear as well as hunting equipment. He also knew of the amount of dried goods that had been loaded onto the sleds. He was sure that the other team members had all loaded their sleds with the critical items they could think of.

He was sure that salt was one of the goods that the team had taken all that they could carry.

He was roused from his thinking by his two companions. He was helped onto his mount that Taelo had given him. The three of them rode the valley each morning. The mount had changed his life. He was able to travel and be mobile. The seat between his two companions was raised so he could see ahead.

He had made several longer trips in this manner. One to the Valley of Plenty and one to the Northern Elk Clan. They also rode together to every Elk Clan gathering after the hunting season ended.

He was impatient this morning because he wanted to get situated and see if he could connect with the eagle. He knew that Taelo was on the way to the mighty river.

When he returned from the ride, he had his morning meal and then sat where he could lean back against the wall and relax.

He was ready to fly. He was pleased to connect almost immediately.

He recognized the creek and the valley beyond. It was where Feather-in-the-Wind, Saber Scar and Running Stag had faced and killed a giant lion. This time there was no lion in the bush but when the team was getting ready to leave the area they met a female lion as they crested the hill.

He watched as Taelo walked out toward the lion. Taelo threw what Broken Spear took to be meat to the lioness. He was not sure what Taelo did other than feed her, but she turned and left the area.

The eagle continued to catch the up drafts and seemed to be waiting for something. Then Broken Spear saw the small herd of mastodon at the far side of the large buffalo herd.

Burley Bear was in the lead and guided the way through the buffalo herd to the side where the Mastodon were. Taelo then took each of the children and most of his team up alongside of the mastodon.

He enjoyed the time in the air as the team followed Golden Hawk in the opposite direction. Golden Hawk went past the location of the camp circle and then slowly crossed the buffalo herd and came out almost exactly at the camp.

Then a short time later he watched as Quiet Rabbit and Golden Hawk each downed a buffalo that was skinned, and the meat put on a separate travois.

Broken Spear knew that on every journey the team always ate well. They hunted as they traveled, and they cooked one large meal each sun cycle.

He had eaten Meadow Flower's and Marigold's cooking and knew that the team always joined in helping to do the cooking. There was always action around the cooking fire.

From the view of the eagle, it seemed to be a dance being performed by the team,

The setting sun seemed to signal the end of his flight and he opened his eyes to see the far side of the valley outside of his cave.

He was tired and hungry, but his large morning meal had carried him through the sun cycle. He was immediately offered a warm fish and vegetable soup.

He was ready for his sleeping hide.

The next sun cycle was a day similar to the one before, but he watched as the team transitioned from the wolf pulled sleds to horse drawn travois.

The eagle did many more loops in the sky because the pace of travel was now slower.

The children seemed to have mastered hunting with slings from their mounts and had become proficient at bagging many rabbits.

The portable cooking ring had been put on one of the travois and he watched both Lily and Floating Cloud take turns roasting rabbits and giving them back to the children.

He saw the mighty river long before the team reached its banks.

Once again Taelo fed the wolves and then the wolves left the area. It was clear to Broken Spear that the wolves seemed to listen to him.

Taelo floated some wood in the river and then had the team build a raft that had poles with dry wood floats out from each side. The raft stayed in balance even with a mount standing on it.

The river crossing was done utilizing only three people to manage the rafts. Broken Spear knew that Taelo had thought about how to cross the river during the winter. The cold water would have disabled the mounts as well as having made the team sick.

The team settled in on the island for the night cycle and the eagle once again left the area.

The following sun cycle Broken Spear was again with the eagle as the team let the flow of the river carry the mounts and all of them across. He was impressed that no one had to get wet during the crossing.

The giant tree was once again used and Broken Spear recognized the area where he had talked to Taelo when he was included in the Ancient's conversations with him. He remembered that Taelo thought he was dying but the Ancients told him many things about the time ahead including the fact that he would be the father of twin boys.

Broken Spear marveled as he watched Feather-in-the-Wind climb to the point in the tall pine where she had watched as Taelo faced the giant bear. This time he noted that Taelo and she exchanged words that made Taelo smile as he looked up at her.

The team left the area a short time later and continued their journey toward the rising sun.

Broken Spear was not able to fly with the eagle on the next sun cycle. He knew that he would have to wait until sometime in the near future.

The next sun cycle he sent runners with invitations to the Northern Elk Clan and to the main Elk Clan in the Valley of plenty, It was time to share the current journey with them and with the rest of his clan.

Chapter 13: The Honey Tree

Taelo recalled the last time he had left the mighty river. He had barely been able to sit on his mount. This time he was at full strength, and he alternated walking and jogging as they made their way toward the early morning sun. The twins copied him and soon he had the entire team giving their mounts breaks.

Burley Bear earned a laugh from the team when he commented that his mount had thanked him. Meadow Flower teased back that she thanked Burley Bear too since jogging would get him back into shape.

Two sun cycles later Taelo knew that the honey tree would be reached on that sun cycle. He patted Lasher on the head and said honey tree.

Lasher led the team toward the left and then kept a steady pace ahead of the team.

Yellow Flower commented that she didn't know that Lasher understood their language. Running Stag replied that he was sure that Lasher, his wolf Arrow, and her mother's wolf Bold Walker all understood more than anyone expected.

Bold Walker, the man, heard the reply and commented that Feather-in-the-Wind's wolf was the smartest one and her brother was even smarter.

Feather-in-the-Wind chuckled and commented that she knew who could leap the farthest and who had traveled the most, but she was still trying to determine which one of her two Bold Walkers was the smartest.

That brought out another team laugh.

Gentle Fern gave Bold Walker a hug and said that she knew who was not only the smartest but the best looking warrior on the team.

Taelo had been listening to the exchange and commented that he had the best team of all the clans.

Taelo was following Lasher and his memory. He knew he was close. He dismounted and jogged. He was energized and somewhat anxious. The last time, when he had followed a bee to the tree, he was still somewhat weak. This time he was feeling great.

It would be a treat to let the kids all participate in gathering the honey.

He heard Running Stag declare that it was his turn to climb up and get the honey. He had sealed the bees nest and felt that he should be the one that opened it.

Taelo agreed with him and said that he would standby with the youngsters that could climb and not be afraid of getting stung.

Taelo followed Lasher to where the massive spear wide trunk of the honey tree commanded one half of the clearing, The mounts were circled around the edge of the clearing and the team set up the camp cover inside the circle that had been formed.

They had been slowly getting to a higher elevation and knew that the night would get cold.

He watched as Lily and Floating Cloud set up the cooking ring. Golden Hawk said that he was going to see about getting a few fish and was joined by Burley Bear and Saber Scar.

They walked to the creek and went down the stream along the bank.

Lily and Floating Cloud laid out one honey sack for each person on the team. They had used the intestine of the buffalo to make one sack for each team member. They put them out on a low limb of the honey tree and let Running Stag know that his goal was to fill them.

Running Stag replied that he hoped that the bees had stored a record amount of honey since the last time that the team had harvested the nest.

He climbed the limb and Taelo asked who would like to help gather the honey. The twins and Yellow Flower immediately raised their hands. Neiva raised her hand and Feather-in-the-Wind said that she would accompany her.

Meadow Flower, Marigold, and Single leaf redirected their three to the role of sending up the empty honey sack and taking back the full ones. They knew that their young were three times heavier than the other children and would be poor climbers.

Taelo instructed the four that would climb to the nest that they should stay relaxed and not show any fear of the bees. If a bee did sting them, they would need to accept the sting and not cry out.

He was not sure that if the bees stung one of them that they would act as instructed.

He said that they would take turns being near the nest.

He watched as Running Stag use a scraping blade to remove the wax that still sealed the circular opening. The wax had hardened, and it took all the skill that Running Stag had for him to open the nest.

Running Stag commented on how well the sealing had worked.

Taelo was pleased to hear that the bees had replace all the honey cone that they had previously harvested and had added even more. He and Red Fox went up together. Red Fox pulled the first bag up to Running Stag. After a fourth of the bags were full, Black Wolf came up and took for his turn to help fill the next four.

The bees were flying all around them but were not attacking.

Yellow Flower was as steady as the first two. She hummed a song, and she thanked him for keeping her steady as she was raising or lowering the sacks.

Taelo then descended and Neiva went up with Feather-in-the-Wind, who was the only nervous person in the tree.

As the last of the honey harvesting was taking place, Taelo prepared the wax that would be used to seal the opening. He put the wax in the last pouch that went up.

He watched as Running Stag put the round piece of trunk back and expertly packed the wax back along the edges.

Running Stag commented that there seemed to be plenty of honey left for the bees.

Lily commented that the last time several of the team had questioned the care with which Taelo had the hole closed. Now they could all see the benefit of having done so.

Taelo replied that the team had left every location ready to use again even if they might never return. On this journey they had already benefited several times from their careful preservation of the things they had to create at each location.

Quiet Rabbit made the comment that their stop at the head of the small stream that allowed passage through the mountains would be the next time they would benefit.

The fishermen that had gone down stream returned, and each carried several large trout.

Golden Hawk listened as Busy Bee then commented that when they got to Shark Bay, she hoped that she would not have to watch Taelo fly from the cliff to save her mate.

Taelo replied that he was now too old to fly, and that if Golden Hawk attracted any shark he would be on his own.

Golden Hawk commented that he was not sure he would be able to go back in to collect the seaweed that he so enjoyed.

The next sunrise was one of relaxation and a time to rest. Taelo enjoyed walking down the small stream to spear fish and spend some time showing the kids how to do it. He and all the team enjoyed the outing and then as if in reward Burley Bear bagged a young boar.

Lily and Floating Cloud rubbed the boar with salt and honey. The roasted tubers and onions rounded out the meal that everyone relished as they watched the sun sink below the horizon.

They were all ready to continue their journey.

Chapter 14: Mountain Stream Passage

Taelo continued to pace the travel to allow time for the children to observe interesting animals and to play. The team was always moving forward but Quiet Rabbit or one of the other mothers would point out interesting plants and small animals. They also continued to train them on using the sling and gathering various tubers with the digging sticks.

Many rabbits and a few squirrels ended up in someone's game bag and later became part of the late dinner.

The days were warming and the snow giving way to green grasses and a myriad of flowers. The squirrels were able to follow them through the trees and often did so until some meadow or break in the forest caused them to stop.

A handful of sun cycles later they came to the site where Quiet Rabbit and Feather-in-the-Wind had successfully scouted out the way through the mountains ahead.

This time Taelo led the team to where the stream that went through the mountains began. The team setup camp.

He then described the two rafts they would build. They needed to find enough dry wood to make the rafts buoyant and able to carry all the teams supplies.

He asked Burley Bear and the Others to be the pilots of the rafts and he and the rest of the team would lead the horses along the bank. This would put the strongest of the team on the rafts.

The children had a choice of sitting on top of goods on the raft or they could ride a mount. Without exception at the beginning, they all chose to ride on the rafts.

Building the rafts took several sun cycles.

Taelo and Golden Hawk took the children spear fishing and returned with enough fish to feed the entire team.

Lily complemented them and said that she would be sure to prepare a fish for each of them.

The evening before their departure, Lily and Floating Cloud prepared a meal of honey coated buffalo meat that was praised by the entire team as another of their wonderful meals.

The two used every spice in their cooking supplies that they could find, and their various grilled meat pieces took on distinct and different flavors. Salt was the one constant that made the biggest difference, but they needed to ration it until they found a source other than the large block that was now almost the entire load of one travois.

Taelo knew that feeding his team was one of the more challenging parts of this journey. He was constantly on the lookout for food.

The fact that he had a small army of slingers eased this concern because on almost every sun cycle the team gathered in enough food to feed themselves. This left most of the food he had brought in reserve and available.

He also appreciated that Lily and Floating Cloud spent almost every sun cycle drying the various meats and putting them away for later use in stews.

He made it a point to thank the team for gathering the meat and he called out the two for their efforts in insuring that the team would eat on days where it had not been able to gather food.

The entire team turned and praised the two as the most valuable members of the team. They all agreed that it seemed that every day was another feast day.

Taelo signaled the start of the float down the stream as the sun broke over the horizon.

He was on his mount leading the way along the stream. On the first raft Burley Bear was on the long flat oar that went out behind the raft. Meadow Flower and Single leaf stood at the front of the raft and used poles to keep it in the middle of the stream. Saber Scar was on the long flat oar of the second raft and Marigold and Sharp Blade had the front positions.

The children were split with some on top of the goods on each raft.

Often the rafts would outpaced the mounts and at other times the mounts were ahead.

As the sun began its descent, Taelo decided to pick up the pace with the mounts so he could locate a place to make camp.

Not too far ahead and perhaps somewhat too early he found an opening where a stream joined the river. It was a good location, and since it was somewhat early it would allow for some hunting.

He had just finished tying off the mounts around the edge of the clearing when the rafts came into sight.

He watched as Quiet Rabbit and Busy Bee signaled the rafts to stop.

Burley Bear easily grounded his raft just before the entrance of the stream. He jumped off and held the raft in position.

Saber Scar duplicated the landing and then took the rope from the back of his raft and tied it to a small tree by the stream edge.

Burley Bear tied the back of his raft to the back of Saber Scars raft.

Taelo complemented them on their great landing and coordination and the fact that their passengers never had to step in the water.

The fishing was good and once again Taelo made the point that they called themselves hunters but that they relied more on catching fish than on hunting game.

Burley Bear laughed and said if Taelo was a better hunter then they would eat less fish. He of course was joking. He considered Taelo and Golden Hawk as the two best hunters he knew.

The next sunrise several of the children chose to ride the mounts but most stayed on the rafts.

Taelo repeated the camping procedure for two sun cycles and then they were out of the mountains. He knew that only a few more sun cycles and they would arrive at the sea.

Everything was put back on the travois and the raft material stored in case they ever returned to the area.

He and the team had talked about what they would do when they arrived at the small bay where they had stayed once before. They would need to build rafts similar to those they had taken through the mountains but at least three times as large. This would present a challenge. They would need to gather enough dry logs to make the base layer for the three rafts.

He said that the team would rest at the bay as he located where to build the rafts.

He and Burley Bear would take a trip up along the coast to see where there was enough material to build and then launch their rafts.

He knew that building the rafts would take most of two or three moon cycles.

Chapter 15:At Shark Bay

The team had dubbed the lovely bay, Shark Bay. The shark they had killed there, measuring more than four spear lengths, was the largest anyone had ever seen.

Golden Hawk recalled seeing the mouth open ready to cut him in half and the sudden change in direction as Taelo drove the spear through it just behind its head. He remembered driving his spear into the shark's mouth and having it cut in two. He had then used what was left in his hand and had driven it into the sharks eye as he pushed himself away from the gapping mouth.

He later learned that Taelo had jumped from the cliff to spear the shark. He went to see the distance that Taelo had jumped and declared that Taelo knew how to fly because no human could jump so far.

He took Bold Walker, known for his ability to leap the gorge that protected the Condor Clan village, and showed him the distance that Taelo had jumped. Bold Walker said that no one could jump so far and agreed that Taelo could fly.

Busy Bee shared her horror when she saw the shark about to eat Golden Hawk. She had fallen to her knees crying out in anguish and then had seen Taelo making his leap. She had expected him to be too late but as he entered the water she had seen his spear and his impact move the shark sideways. She had run down to the sea and had swam back across to the beach. By the time she got there Golden Hawk, Taelo, Lily and the Saber Scar were dragging the shark out of the water with a mount. Saber Scar repeatedly hit the shark with his war hammer until it was dead.

All four had sat down in exhaustion. Busy Bee saw blood everywhere and worried that it was Golden Hawks' but amazingly Taelo had more cuts than he had.

The children had been listening and asked if it was safe to swim in the bay.

Taelo said that yes it was safe as long as no sharks were swimming there as well. He then said that this time one of the team members would need to stand watch from the top of the cliff to make sure no sharks were in the bay when the children were playing in the water.

He then reminded everyone that other than the shark incident, their stay last time had been very relaxing and enjoyable. They had eaten the best fish, the best lobster, had small clam soup and had collected may berries and eggs from the small island. They had also discovered the singing sand beach where Feather-in-the-Wind and the wolves had vocalized their joy in harmony.

He suggested that this time the team stay at the bay until the raft building location was found.

This would give the children time to enjoy the area. He planned to take them and go gather the small clams that Lilly and Floating Cloud would put into their fish stew. He suggested that chives and onions be gathered and that someone try to spear a large fish.

Golden Hawk said he planned to harvest some seaweed for the stew but wanted someone to be on shark watch for him.

Taelo watched as the team seemed to naturally take up the various tasks.

Slow Walker took the shark watch and Golden Hawk took a bag to put the seaweed into and walked along the base of the cliff to the point where he would bring in the seaweed.

It took all his nerve to dive in and go out to where the seaweed was abundant. He made several trips before he felt that he had enough.

Busy Bee was standing next to the pile of seaweed when he got out. She said that she had gotten nervous and had to come out to make sure he was OK.

The children were all playing with the small waves close to the beach under the watchful eyes of Meadow Flower and Quiet Rabbit.

Taelo and several of the kids had collected some bags of the small clams and then had gone to the Island to gather birds eggs. He returned to see Busy Bee and Golden Hawk carrying the seaweed up to the cooking fire.

The kids had gotten into digging for the clams and had contributed another bag.

Burley Bear and Saber Scar had gone along the bottom of the cliff well past the point where Golden Hawk had entered the water to get the seaweed. They returned with a fish that was almost a spear in length.

Taelo asked how they had managed to spear and retrieve such a large one.

He knew he was getting his leg pulled when Burley Bear claimed to have thrown Saber Scar as far as he could, and Saber Scar had speared it as it swam by.

Saber Scar laughed and said that he had indeed speared the fish and that Burley Bear had to rescue him when he fell into the water and both he and he fish began to sink like a rock. He had almost let go of his spear when the butt of Burley Bear's spear came into sight. He had grabbed it and Burley Bear pulled both he and the fish up to the base of the cliff.

Taelo gave a laugh and said that in that case Burley Bear should get the credit for catching the fish.

Burley Bear put his arm around Taelo's shoulder and said that he agreed.

Lily said that the three of them should go wash up. She would take care of the fish and serve it both in the stew and grill some of it. It took Lily, Floating Cloud and Whistling Arrow to hand carry the fish up to the fire ring and prepare the fish.

The evening stars were starting to fill the sky as the team sat around enjoying the fish clam chowder and the grilled fish.

Taelo let the conversations flow over him as he leaned into Quiet Rabbit and looked up to the many points of light that they called the Ancients. He did not believe that to be the case but relished the fact that it let him imagine all the people that had come before him.

Quiet Rabbit pushed slightly back on him and quietly said that days such as this made the journey one that she would remember for her lifetime. She pulled Red Fox and Black Wolf to her and put a hide around all of them.

They sat there watching the light disappear and the black above sparkle with all the ancestors.

Chapter 16: Sea Going Rafts

𝒯aelo led the way through the forest and made his way up the coast. When the massive white wall of the glacier loomed ahead he turned toward the sea. He looked for a sheltered cove where the team could assemble rafts very much like the ones they had used to go down the stream through the mountains. Those had been practice for what he knew had to be much larger ones for the next part of the journey.

He envisioned a sail, the long rear guide paddle, and long poles out to each side with dry logs attached to provide stability. Talking Wren had suggested that they put one long slab down into the water to help guide the raft.

Burley Bear spotted a large fallen oak that had dried limbs to make most of the floating part of the rafts.

The green trees to make the second layer of the raft were located and marked. The number of trees needed was not clear but there was an abundant supply close at hand.

The longer trees needed to make the long arms out to each side of the raft were also located.

Taelo suggested that they spend time to organize all the needed material before returning for the rest of the team. They would then bring everyone up to help assemble the rafts and bind all the pieces together.

The cove was smaller than Shark Bay, but it had a clean beach and there seemed to be a good supply of fish.

Each sun cycle was spent in cutting down the appropriate timbers or cutting the dry logs to make the base of each raft.

Taelo pointed out that the three rafts would fit side by side on the beach. He wanted to be able to use the mounts to pull the partially assemble rafts into the water and then the platform that covered the dry logs would be put on with the rafts in the water.

The front of the raft was one third as wide as the middle of the raft. The covering timers would each be strapped to the dry log cross members below them. He had the ends of the dry logs burned to seal the wood.

The ideas on how to make the platform stable and strong were discussed and the group decided that a layer of smaller trees would be put a spear length apart on top crossing the long main second layer. This Taelo figured would help if the waves were large or if the weather turned rough.

He had floated several logs out beyond the bay and was relieved to see the current pulling them out to sea. He hoped the current would stay in that direction. It seemed to go parallel to the towering face of the glacier.

It took this part of the team seven sun cycles to get everything organized. Their work allowed Taelo to improve his estimate of how long it would take to assemble the rafts. He was now estimating it would take at least another full moon cycle.

Taelo decided that only one person needed to return to get the rest of the team back to where they were located.

He recalled his learning about sending only one person and decided to send two. He asked Golden Hawk and one of the Paradise members to go back for the rest of the team.

He knew he could count on Golden Hawk to return to Shark Bay and return with the team.

He could have sent any other member of his team and have felt the same way, but he wanted Burley Bear and the rest of the Others to stay. Their strength significantly enhanced the ability to move the large dry logs into position.

The dry logs for the three rafts were positioned on the beach, and it soon became evident that they would need at least another dry tree to make the first layer.

Taelo suggested that they spend one sun cycle going out in a radial fashion looking for another large dead tree.

Sharp Blade found the tree as the sun reached the zenith and lit a fire on which he put green leaves on to signal the rest of the team.

Getting this tree back to the shore required all the mounts and all of the team members pulling as well. The path back often had to be widened and the trees that were cut down were marked as to where they would be used on the rafts. Taelo wanted to make sure that they did not let any material go to waste.

It took two sun cycles to get the tree to the cove where it could be processed.

Taelo called for a day of spear fishing and gathering eggs or other items to eat. He went to the beach to see if the small clams were under the sand and was disappointed when he found none. He then took a swim in the small bay to see if there were any seaweeds and found that the seaweeds were thick on the bottom along the rocky cliff making up one side of the small cove. He was delighted to find the seaweed floor was full of lobsters.

He had to come out before gathering anything because the water was so cold that he was losing feeling in his arms.

The group hunting for eggs returned with several gathering bags full.

Taelo shared his findings and said that they would take turns going down and gathering lobster. Later they would gather some of the seaweed.

As the sun reached the horizon, the group had gathered forty lobsters and had them hanging on a long pole.

Taelo hoped the rest of the team would return so that Lily and Floating Cloud could prepare lobster tail with honey and process the rest for the upcoming trip across the sea.

He and the team had discussed how much food they should carry with them. They all agreed that each raft should carry as much food as the team could possibly put on it.

Taelo wanted at least three moon cycles of food on each raft.

The distinguishing feature on each raft was the ring of flat stone that was covered in clay and fired to make a cooking pit. It had holes out the side to drain any water that might get into the cooking pit. The wood for the cooking pit took up the two sides at the back of the raft and was piled up to a spear height. This was dry wood that had been saved from the dry trees. It was stacked on top of a layer of small limbs that would keep the bottom layer out of the water and then each piled stack was covered with a hide to keep the wood dry.

Taelo also made sure that a water bag was strategically placed by each cooking ring. He wanted to make sure to keep the fires small and in control and he wanted to have a way to immediately extinguish any fire that might get out of hand.

The team arrived two sun cycles later and set up the camp cover a short distance from the beach. The sound of the children had an immediate positive effect.

Taelo led Lily and Floating Cloud to what now was almost forty lobsters of various sizes that were suspended from poles positioned up in some trees.

The two said they would process the lobster. They would freeze the tails in the face of the glacier. The body parts would be used to make a lobster stew. They figured they would have at least enough to feed the team several servings of lobster stew.

They asked if their partners could dive and get more of the lobster. Taelo was pleased to have been asked because it allowed he and the rest of the team to focus on building the rafts. Taelo showed the two the best spot to dive from and to bring up the lobster.

He suggested they take turns and each time warm themselves up by a fire.

He then suggested that they also gather all the seaweed they could. This could be dried and later used in preparing various stews.

Quiet Rabbit, Busy Bee, Talking Wren showed Taelo the water bags that they had prepared. They had figured that they needed the same number of days of water as they needed for food. They had also thought about how they might capture rainwater to replenish the supply.

Taelo complimented them on having thought through the need for fresh water and showed them a small nearby stream of clear, cold water.

He walked along the shore with Golden Hawk and shared the progress that had been made. He suggested that almost every hide they currently possessed would be needed to bind the rafts together.

Golden Hawk agreed and said that what the team needed was the equivalent of a long hunt to gather more food and more hides. He also suggested that the tree bark of small green willow trees could be stripped to augment binding the parts of the rafts that would stay dry most of the time.

The days seem to pass too rapidly and Taelo was concerned about getting the rafts completed.

Golden Hawk departed to hunt. He was accompanied by Quiet Rabbit, Busy Bee, Marigold, Single Leaf, and their kids.

This left enough horsepower and the muscle power of the Others to keep the building going.

The rafts took shape. Taelo watched as Lily and Floating Cloud used each fire ring on the rafts. They came over to him and asked who the third lucky person was that would use the third ring.

Taelo decided it was time to make the assignments of which team members would go on each raft.

He named Burley Bear the person to handle the long pole rudder on one raft.

Saber Scar to handle the second raft.

Sharp Blade would handle the third raft.

He wanted to be on the raft with Burley Bear. He knew that Quiet Rabbit would want her mother, Floating Cloud to be on that raft.

He would asked Golden Hawk to be on the second raft and would see if Marigold would do the cooking.

He would ask Little Otter to be on the third raft and enjoy the meals that Lilly would prepare.

He, Golden Hawk and Little Otter would be the second person on each raft to handle the long back paddle.

Everyone agreed to these assignments and soon they were concentrating on getting their raft prepared.

Golden hawk and his team returned with every mount pulling a travois loaded with meat. The number of hides provided enough binding strips to get all the top timber layer bound to the bottom layer.

The suggestion to use willow strips went a long way toward making everything else secure.

The time for departer was near. Each of the rafts were now fully in the water and the final preparation was being done.

Taelo designated Talking Wren to lead an inspection team to check that each raft was properly built. Her keen eye found several missing bindings that were immediately corrected. She suggested that more cooking firewood should be added to each raft.

She also suggested that the downward flat blades be put on each side of the raft and that a second dry float be put on each of the long balance arms.

It was finally time to take each raft for a trial run.

Taelo had the entire team take the first raft out and sail it out for a half sun cycle and then return.

The current easily took them out, but the return took some learning and took longer that Taelo had expected.

He and Burley Bear learned to move in a zigzag pattern back toward the harbor.

He had each team member equipped with a paddle in case they would have to paddle the rafts back.

There was one immediate learning. As the raft went over a wave the front would catch the next wave and water would run across the raft.

The ability to use the wind and zigzag back toward shore was made possible by the two side downward flat blades that kept the raft going in the direction that it was pointed.

He was pleased with the rafts performance

Before taking out the next raft Talking Wren had a barrier put up at the front of the raft to prevent water from coming across the raft

Taelo went out on the next raft with only the crew for that raft. Talking Wren was on the raft as well. She was making sure the front barrier worked as she desired.

Talking Wren had suggested that the front barrier should be twice as high as it currently was. She made the point that the rafts would be more heavily loaded and would go a little deeper into the next wave. She also suggested that they cross waves in a way that it would not come down nose first but slide more sideways down the back of the wave.

Once back on shore she adjusted the front barrier and extended it farther back on the next raft to go out.

That raft went out and returned in a dry state. The modification worked and it was duplicated on the other rafts.

When the loading began, Talking Wren suggested that the load be more to the back of the raft. That would make the front ride higher.

The layout adjustments were made and soon the rafts were ready.

It was time to begin the journey across the sea.

Chapter 17: The Open Sea and the Crumbling Glacier

The final loading of each raft was quickly taking place. The firewood, the drinking water and all the food was put on board and located toward the back.

The sleeping areas were completed. They were elevated a hand's height above the top layer of the raft and covered with a hide to keep everyone inside warm and dry. The sleeping area opening was to the back of the raft. This allowed easy entry and it put the opening away from water that might come over the raft.

This area would also serve as the play area for the children when the weather kept them inside.

The majority of the food was toward the back and most of the firewood was moved from the sides to the front of the sleeping area. This was done to provide extra protection for the sleeping area.

The team had beat the estimated time to build the three rafts.

Taelo asked Talking Wren to make a final inspection of each raft and determine if everything was in order.

He felt relieved to be leaving seven sun cycles before the time he had estimated and at the same time he was now concerned about the team safety as they began what he felt was one of the most dangerous parts of their journey.

A departure dinner for the three individuals returning to Paradise with the mounts also served as the departure dinner for the team.

Early with the rising of the sun Taelo's raft took the lead with Burley Bear guiding the raft. The current and wind were all going in the same direction as the team was going so the ride was smooth.

The suggestion that Talking Wren had made on how to go over the waves had them going smoothly up the back side and then gliding slightly at an angle down the front side. It worked to make the ride smoother.

The team quickly learned that the motion made some of them sick.

Every raft team decided independently on their meals for the day, and everyone took turns to help prepare it. The wood was carefully used, and the fire put out after the cooking was complete.

The fire pits were a luxury that would allow the teams to enjoy the great cooking that they had come to expect.

They had sailed for a handful of sun cycles when all of them heard a very loud cracking, popping and crackling sound. They watched in fascination as a large part of the glacier began to slide down into the sea.

Taelo saw a huge wave form that was at least a third as high as the glacier coming out from the collapsed area. He had all the rafts, so they were moving away and in the same direction as the towering approaching wave.

He stood with Burley Bear and when the wave caught them, he put his back into helping hold the guide paddle.

Burley Bear's strength and weight seemed to make the difference.

It turned out the outgoing wave was as large as he feared and when it reached the rafts it picked each of them up in turn as if they were mere specks. The rafts were pointed steeply down and seemingly racing forward.

It took both he and Burley Bear to hold the guide paddle and keep the raft from getting misaligned.

Everyone was holding on for dear life. It was as if they were flying.

The raft groaned, creaked, popped but held together and seemed to slowly climb backwards up the face of the wave and then took a backward slide down behind the wave.

The whole experience was lightning fast and left the team wondering how they had survived.

Taelo then looked around to see if the other rafts had survived.

Burley Bear lightened the moment by laughing and saying that they had survived because every raft had been built to Talking Wren's specification and they had their best persons controlling them.

He said that he had contemplated staying at the top of the wave since they were moving so fast, but he realized that the raft was going in the wrong direction.

An eagle cry came down from above. Taelo looked up and gave it a thank you sign. He was sure that Broken Spear had seen the event. He was curious of what it might have looked like from above.

Taelo signaled the rafts to gather together to make sure everyone was alright.

The entire team cheered and shouted that they had the best rafts and the best paddle handlers, and they were doing great.

It took them the rest of the sun cycle to get back to the point where they could once again see the face of the glacier.

Taelo and his team decided that they would stay just within sight of the glacier but as far away as possible.

After the third full moon cycle Taelo began wondering how much farther it might be. He was worried about having enough food to complete the journey across.

During the next sun cycle a seagull landed on the front of the raft and Taelo knew that land was somewhere ahead. He made a point of letting the team know that they were within two sun cycles of the shore.

Floating Cloud bumped into him and quietly said that she had seen the sea gull too. She smiled and handed him a piece of lobster.

He then let Quiet Rabbit and the boys know why he was making that prediction, but he left the rest of the team in the dark.

The rest of team all wanted to know how after so many moon cycles that he could predict that land was ahead. He took out his round rock and said that he knew how large the rock was that they were on.

Two sun cycles latter as the raft mounted the wave, Burley Bear pointed and shouted out that he saw land.

There was a cheer, and everyone agreed that Taelo knew the size of the rock.

As they approached the land Taelo could tell that it was an island of substantial size but the end to the right disappeared at an angle away from the rafts. He suggested that they sail along the coast before landing.

The suggestion turned out to be a good one since a rocky coast topped with high cliffs would have made landing almost impossible.

Three sun cycles later a long sandy beach came into sight.

Taelo had two team members stand by each of the side boards. He told them that they would have to pull them up as they came into shore. He wanted to get the raft fronts to be on the very edge of the beach. The goal he said was to step off the rafts and not wet their feet.

The landing was close in achieving that goal, but they all had to step down into water halfway to their knees.

The teams then pulled the rafts so that unloading would be directly onto the dry beach.

Taelo organized three search teams to go out and find a location where the team could set up camp. He said that they would need to be able to set up the team camp cover. He was looking for a place either by a lake or close to the sea so they could replenish their food supply. They were also to keep an eye out for any game.

Sending out the teams reminded him of the time when his mother was asked to lead a team to find a place for the Elk Clan to set up a winter camp. She had returned after finding the place that he still thought of as his first true home. It was where most of the members of his current team had bonded. That was the time when Little Otter had led the first Elk Clan hunting team that had both men and women on it. Those team members bonded, and each was with him for this journey.

He turned his attention back to the rafts and recruited Talking Wren to inspect and determine what to do next.

As always Talking Wren applied her great organizing skill and commented that the deck of one raft could be used to supply all the poles for the travois needed to pull their goods.

The wood supply for cooking was close to being gone and would not need resupplying since they would collect wood as they traveled.

They had at least another ten sun cycles of food and if the game in the area was plentiful the team would resupply itself as they traveled.

Taelo commented that taking the rafts apart would be as big a task as building them. He disliked leaving them on the shore, but he did not know what to do with them.

Golden Hawk suggested that they use most of the materials from one raft. Remove the firepits from all of them and then sail the two remaining rafts away from the coast.

Taelo agreed and decided to have a landing ceremony where he and Golden Hawk would send out the two remaining rafts in such a way that they would sail away toward the setting sun as the team celebrated have used them well and the fact that the rafts had functioned as desired.

As the sun set, the pile of dry wood on each raft was ignited and the team sat eating their late dinner and watched as their rafts slowly burned. The sea turned almost as dark as the sky above and the two burning rafts were eerily visible as they slowly burnt and then each seemed to disappear.

Chapter 18: Broken Spear Out to Sea

Broken Spear knew that Taelo's theory of a round world must be right. As Taelo continued his journey, to fly with the eagle, Broken Spear had to be awake before the sun came over the horizon and when he joined the eagle the sun was just breaking the horizon where Taelo and his team were located. If it was a flat world the sun would have been seen outside his cave at the same time as the eagle saw it.

Broken Spear watched as Taelo led the team to a small clearing bordered by a small river and dominated by a huge oak tree. He could not tell exactly what the team was doing but he knew they were collecting something from inside the tree. He figured a beehive lived in the giant tree.

He was always amazed by Taelo's and Golden Hawks ability to find food treasures.

The eagle circled a few times in a circle above the clearing and then followed the small river and suddenly swooped down and captured a large fish. It flew on toward its nest.

Broken Spear was delighted to be allowed to see the two young eagles before he was shunted out of the eagles mind.

He opened his eyes to see one of his keepers holding a warm stew. He was always surprised and grateful that his two companions were always making sure that he was well fed, well rested and well exercised. They were older women who had lost their mates and had adopted him after he lost his mate. They were older but he knew that they were almost half his age. Their care made his life easier, and he was grateful for their care.

He had watched when Taelo's team reached the mighty river. He was amazed at the ingenuity that was displayed as the raft ferried each of the mounts across. The fact that it took only three people to control the raft and get each mount across spoke to the skill and innovation that the team had.

He had watched them reach the honey tree and was delighted to see the children participate in gathering the honey.

He laughed at the fact that he was slowly backing up in time and would soon be getting up in the middle of the night to fly with the eagle.

He looked out of the cave and saw the sun rising.

He was looking forward to his ride through the valley and then he would once again go to sleep early so he would be rested when he joined the eagle in the sky.

On the next flight, he caught sight of an animal that was three spear lengths high, had fierce looking claws but seemed slow. He watched as Taelo led the children in closer. Broken Spear knew then, that as ferocious as the animal appeared, that Taelo knew it was not a threat.

Once again the eagle flew a few circles and then it caught an up draft and continued its journey. Broken Spear opened his eyes to the dark of the cave. He went to his sleeping hide and went immediately to sleep.

Broken Spear did not have another flight with the eagle for several sun cycles. Then once again even later than before he felt the call to join the eagle.

On the subsequent flights, he watched as Taelo, and his team built three rafts alongside of a river.

From above he could tell that the river cut through the mountains to a valley beyond.

The teams possessions and food supplies were loaded on the rafts, but the mounts were led alongside of the river.

He watched as the children on each raft stood by the sides and tried to spear fish. Broken Spear knew that all the children on this journey would return enriched in the way they saw the world around them and would most likely be strong leaders in the Clans to which they belonged.

Once again it was a few sun cycles later before he again had a chance to fly with the eagle.

When he next joined the eagle he recalled the bay he was looking down upon. It was what Taelo's team referred to as Shark Bay. This was where they claimed that Taelo had taken wing and flown off the cliff in a dive into the sea to spear a giant shark. He had saved Golden Hawk's life and killed the largest shark the team had ever seen. Together the two were able to drag the shark to shore where the rest of the team then took over.

This time there was no shark in sight as the eagle swooped in low and skimmed the water and rose with a sizeable fish in its claws. He actually heard the team give a shout as the eagle rose and sailed back into the air took a long, graceful turn and went back inland toward the forest.

A few sun cycles later, he was again flying with the eagle when Taelo led a small part of his team away from Shark Bay up toward where, from his flying height, he could see the glacier towering above the height at which the eagle was flying.

Then for the next series of flights with the eagle, he had watched them make rafts similar to the ones they had made to float the river through the mountains. These were much larger and more strongly built.

Broken Spear was able to easily identify all the Others that were on Taelo's team as they used the mounts to pull logs to the beach. He was surprised at the number of trees and the large amount of dry wood that was needed. The length and width of the rafts were impressive. He figured they were close to fifteen spear lengths long and six spear lengths wide.

He was flying with the eagle when the rest of the team followed Golden Hawk back to the raft building area.

The camp cover went up near the forest and the work on the rafts intensified.

He watched as the dead dry wood was used to make the first layer of the raft. The logs went from side to side. Then a layer of long timbers were put from front to back on top of the dry wood. Broken Spear was impressed with the way the raft was constructed.

He noted that the living area located to the back of the raft had its floor raised about the length of his hand above the top of the raft.

He wondered who had thought through all the intricate design features. He constantly observed Talking Wren checking the raft building work and figured she would be one person who had contributed to the design.

Broken Spear knew that his flights with the eagle were giving him knowledge that he never would have achieved on his own.

Each time Broken Spear had flown with the eagle he had gotten up earlier. For the last series of flights, the time was always in the greying light of predawn. He wondered how far back into the night he would be when Taelo continued his journey.

When he flew with the eagle again, the three rafts were in the water and being loaded. He marveled at the ability that the team had to build rafts that would be able to go out to sea. These rafts were much larger than the river rafts and had long poles out to each side that Broken Spear figured were meant to stabilize them when they were in the wave dominated seas.

The eagle flew out as each raft went out to sea and then returned. Broken Spear watched as the raft was steered by a combination of side paddlers and the rear guide paddle. He was impressed by the ease that the team handled each raft. He noted that the water would often sweep over the front of the raft and run down its length.

When the rafts were back in the harbor he watched as Talking Wren supervised the construction of a shield to go around the front part of the raft.

Once the three rafts had taken their trial runs and the changes to them had been made, he watched them get loaded and the teams moved on to the rafts.

The beach was cleaned, and it was hard to tell that more than twenty people had been living there for most of two moon cycles.

The morning of departure he saw the mounts being led through the forest by three persons as they went back toward the mighty river.

The eagle flew up the coast, and he watched the three rafts going toward the glacier.

It was a few sun cycles later that he flew with the eagle for most of the sun cycle as the rafts sailed out on the sea along the glacier face that could be seen disappearing on the horizon.

The eagle let out a cry and then turned and flew back toward the shore and Broken Spear found himself looking into his own valley. It was time for his late afternoon ride.

He had not expected to fly again until Taelo had crossed the sea, but he felt the call and in the darkness of the night he joined the eagle for a flight that raised the hair on the back of his neck.

He did not know what the loud cracking and popping meant but then he watched as a huge piece of the glacier broke off from its face and fell into the sea.

A monstrous towering wave rose up and swept toward the three rafts. He was sure that doom was overtaking the rafts that were moving slowly away from the face of the glacier.

The rafts had turned and were sailing away from the wave, but the speed of the wave quickly overtook them. It was a hopeless sight.

He had to close his eyes as the wave caught up to the rafts. He was sure they would be smashed. From on high he heard the rafts groan and pop. He opened his eyes to see that the rafts were not smashed but they had survived and holding together. He then watched as they seemed to slowly rise up on the face of the giants wave and then slide down the back side.

His two aids later said that he had groaned and then had shouted out in joy.

The eagle let out a cry and then flew away back toward the coast.

Broken Spear was still recovering from the fear he had felt for the team. He went to the pool to let the hot water calm him.

He wondered how early he would need to get up to fly with the eagle when Taelo was across the sea.

He was not sure about when, but he knew it was time to share what he had seen with those closest to Taelo's team.

The next sun cycle Broken Spear sent out invitations to the Northern Elk Clan and to the Valley of Plenty Elk Clan. He let the members of the Clan of Others know that another Taelo story telling get together was on hand.

Chapter 19: Black Friends

The use of the deck timbers from one raft greatly increased the speed by which the team was able to make travois and load their possessions and food. In two sun cycles they were ready to continue their journey on land.

Taelo had send out three teams to find the best way through the forest toward the rising sun. He hoped to find a river that would make the going easier. The forest was thick but thankfully it did not have significant under growth.

The first two teams back reported that the forest continued for as far as they had traveled. Ironically, it was Feather-in-the-Wind, Quiet Rabbit and Meadow Flower who returned with the news that they had found a river that ran towards the sun.

Feather-in-the-Wind and Quiet Rabbit had been the two that had previously found the stream that went through the mountains during their Journey of Discovery.

Taelo commented that next time he would just send out the two in any direction they chose to go.

The team traveled until they reached the river and discussed the best way to travel. The forest had little underbrush and was open and had not posed the barrier that Taelo had anticipated.

After some discussion, the team decided to continue using the travois and wait to use the river if it became necessary.

Taelo commented that the team had not faced any adversaries, but they should establish their fighting diamonds and get everyone use to forming and moving in formation.

He pointed out that it would be a good way for the children to learn that their parents knew how to protect them and for them to learn how to fight.

Little Otter laughed and loudly said, "and we will do it three times" then one of us will randomly call the fighting diamonds into formation as we travel.

He got a poke in the ribs from Talking Wren and made as if she had hurt him.

Taelo took a moment to organize the teams into two fighting diamonds. He explained to the children that the fighting diamond was both a defensive formation and an offensive one when needed. He explained that if one of the members of the diamond was injured they would move into the middle of the diamond for protection and to take time to recover.

He formed the children into a small fighting diamond so they could practice along with their parents.

He, Burley Bear, Saber Scar, Sharp Knife and Golden Hawk made small spears and war hammers for the children. They presented the weapons to the children a few sun cycles later. They then spent time training them in the use of each weapon and how to use it in the position each child had in the fighting diamond.

A few sun cycles later Taelo recognized the children for their ability to get into the fighting diamond position just as quickly as the two teams made up of their parents. He let them know that he now felt confident that all of them could face an attack and they would not have to worry about them.

The journey continued and they were making good time. Taelo was now more relax. He had his feet on land and knew how to survive. The hunting was good. They had not seen any buffalo, but the deer were abundant. The rabbits were of a different variety, but they faced the same fate as the ones on the other side of the sea.

He had asked Feather-in-the-Wind to climb a tall tree and look out ahead to see what lay ahead. He was not surprised that she soon had competition. Red Fox, Black Wolf, Yellow Flower, and Neiva all periodically would climb a tree to look out ahead.

It was Yellow Flower that said she saw smoke over the next hill. Feather-in-the-Wind climbed up to her and confirmed that there were two fires sending up plumes.

Taelo instructed them to move forward slowly.

He sent Bold Walker and Deer Chaser ahead as scouts with instructions to locate the people ahead, but they should not be seen and not engage.

He instructed everyone to be quiet and move slowly through the forest.

Not long after, Bold Walker and Deer Chaser were waiting for them at the bottom of a hill. They said that there were at least ten totally black individuals sitting around two cooking fires. It looked as if they had killed an elk and were roasting meat and enjoying themselves.

Taelo called the fighting diamonds into formation. He then led the way up the hill and quietly descended toward the camp.

He was within a spears throw when someone in the camp saw them. The camp sprang to life and the spears with long sharp sparkling blades were ready to be thrown.

Taelo took in the large size and the apparent readiness of the warriors in front of him to strike.

He had his flat shark toothed weapon on his back, but his hands were empty. He raised his right hand and quietly said his name and said he was coming forward as a friend.

The person at the head of the warriors gave his spear to the person on his right and raised his hand and gave his name as "Ekoni."

He then clenched his fist and curled his right arm to flex his muscle and with his left hand he reached over to pat his muscle and then said his name again.

He pointed to his warriors and said "Lutalo."

Taelo understood that the warrior's name meant strength and that as a group of warriors were called Lutalo, a name that probably meant warriors.

He was about to explain the meaning of his name when high in the sky an eagle let out its cry. Taelo pointed to it and made his hand into a claw and acted as if he was striking.

He was pleased that the warrior seemed to understand.

Taelo walked slowly forward. He wagged his finger when one of the warriors stepped forward with a spear as if to strike.

The leader signaled for his warrior to step back.

Taelo then had to reach up with his hand to put it on the leaders left shoulder. He was at least two heads shorter than the warrior he was greeting.

The warrior returned the gesture and with a smile that seemed to flash white light, he instructed his warriors to sit down.

He then pointed up to the fighting diamonds and made his hand into a claw and acted out a strike.

He then walked over to the elk hanging in the tree and instructed one of the warriors to cut a piece and offered that to Taelo.

Taelo accepted the meat and called out to the first fighting diamond with Burley Bear in the lead to put down their weapons and come down to the campfire.

Burley Bear and the Others seemed to have a quieting effect on the black warriors. One of them came forward and pointed to a recent scar on his side and pointed to Burley Bear.

Quiet Rabbit came forward and put her hand on the scar and then went to Burley Bear and touched him. She then wagged her finger to indicate that Burley Bear had not done such a thing.

Burley Bear was as tall as most of the black warriors and much larger in body size. It was clear that he had made a lasting impression and that his kind was present in this area.

Taelo then introduced all the people in the first fighting diamond.

He then signaled the second fighting diamond to come down to the camp site and introduced them

He then called to the fighting diamond made up of the children to come down in formation.

Their appearance and display of fighting ability brought out a cheer from the black warriors. Several of them put their spears down and walked over to the fighting diamond.

Taelo instructed the children to remain calm and to not be afraid.

It was clear to him that the children had become the center of attention and that they would be well treated.

There was plenty of room in the area for the team to put up their camp.

A small stream near the camp would provide the water.

Taelo indicated to Ekoni that he wanted to make camp in the same place.

Ekoni understood and waved his arm to indicate that they should pick the place they wanted.

Taelo instructed the team to set up camp and to set up another cooking fire ring.

He watched as the travois were pulled in and the camp set up.

The travois was of immediate interest to the warriors.

The camp cover set up was even more of an attraction.

The camp cover literally pulled the black warriors in. They walked around talking as the team's possession and goods were brought in.

As Ekoni was examining the travois, Talking Wren walked over to him and tapped him on the shoulder. She then walked to the hanging body of the large elk and then back to the travois. She pointed to the travois and asked Yellow Flower to pick up the travois and indicated that Yellow Flower would be able to pull the body of the Elk.

Ekoni smiled, pointed to Yellow Flower, and then flexed his arm muscle.

Taelo was watching the camp and the reaction of the various black warriors. It was clear that they were well disciplined and adhered to Ekoni's guidance. He figured that they were on a journey similar to the ones he and Golden Hawk often took.

He observed both Golden Hawk and Running Stag practicing the language of the warriors. He knew the two would very quickly know enough to improve the simple communication between the team and the group of warriors.

He would make sure that all of the team took lessons. He remembered the positive impact of being able to communicate with the Others.

It was Lily and Floating Cloud that provided the final transition into friendship between all of them. They basted the elk meat in honey and salt as it cooked. And they topped it off with freshly grilled fish that the team caught in the stream.

The black warriors came over and smacked their lips to show Lily and Floating Cloud that they thought the food was delicious.

The smiles and conversations flowed easily, and the team worked at communicating with their new friends.

Taelo was now aware that people came in all colors, shapes, and sizes. He wondered if there were any more varieties.

He did not plan to stay at the camp for more than a few sun cycles and then his team would continue their journey.

The pleasant surprise for him would be that his team would grow to include his new friends.

Chapter 20: Treat Others

The team relaxed for a few sun cycles and got to know their new black friends. The team seemed to naturally accept their new friends and seemed to enjoy trying to learn a new language.

Ekoni asked where Taelo and his team were from. Taelo took out his round stone and held it in one hand and with his other hand he touched a spot on the stone and then patted the ground. He then took his finger and went halfway around the stone and then touched himself. He then reversed his travel by bringing his finger back to the beginning spot touched Ekoni and then touched himself and put his finger on the stone. He then touched himself and pointed to the team members and then again put his finger on the other side of the stone and slowly pulled his finger to the point at the top of the stone.

Ekoni laughed and shook his head and poured some water in his hand and then moved his hand like a wave.

Taelo replied with a similar hand motion and pointed to his team. He was glad that the moon was in the sky. He pointed to the moon and then put twelve marks on the ground. He made the sign of the wave and put four marks on the ground.

Ekoni shook his head and took the stone in his hand. He repeated the story in sign language.

Taelo nodded in the affirmative.

Ekoni talked to all his warriors and in his language once again told the story.

Taelo was surprised when they all stood up and held up their spears and gave loud roar. He knew it was a form of recognition and acceptance.

There was also a change in the atmosphere.

Taelo observed several of the warriors experimenting with the travois. It was clear that this was a tool that would be immediately accepted.

The warriors were invited to spend the night under the team's camp cover. It made the situation crowded but the nights were cold, and the team knew that the warriors had been sleeping out on the ground.

The next sun cycle Taelo observed a group of warriors sewing their hides together to make a similar camp cover.

Several sun cycles later Ekoni had his warriors set up their own camp cover. It was much smaller than the teams cover but it was large enough for them.

Quiet Rabbit pointed out that the warriors had used most of their sleeping hides to make the cover. She asked the team if they should give the warriors the extra hides that they had brought across the sea for emergency. She pointed out that the land they were now going through had plenty of game and would yield the new hides the team might need.

There was total agreement.

Quite Rabbit brought out the bear hide that she had been carrying on her Travois. She also laid out several elk hides. There were enough that all the warriors would be able to have a sleeping hide.

She presented the bear hide to Ekoni. She acted out being a bear and then she used the stone to show that it had come across the sea.

Ekoni looked surprised. He turned and said something to his second. A moment later, he turned to Quiet Rabbit and presented her with one of his spears.

It had a long black glass blade mounted on a type of black wood that she had never known. She thanked him for the spear that was at least another half-length longer than the one she used. Given its beauty, she knew it would become her ceremonial weapon.

Golden Hawk came over with his flat weapon that had been presented to him by Star Leaper, the leader of the Condor Clan. He compared the glass on his weapon to the glass on the end of the spear. They seemed to be the same.

Ekoni touched the weapon. He made a motion to indicate how it might be used.

Golden Hawk demonstrated how to use it.

Taelo pulled out his weapon. It was the one he had made with shark teeth. He had left his other blade with the glass cutting blades back at the Northern Elk Clan village.

Ekoni called his warriors over to look at both weapons. He pointed to the wood and then he touched the wood on the spear. It was clear that he was talking to them about making a similar weapon.

A few sun cycles later Taelo indicated that he and his team were planning to continue their journey.

He was pleased when Ekoni indicated that he and his warriors would like to go along.

Taelo agreed with him. He felt it would be good to have additional members in case they met a less friendly group.

Taelo noted that the warriors had made several travois to pull their camp cover and the remainder of the elk.

Ekoni pointed to Taelo and then to the travois that Taelo was pulling. He had one of his warriors take the travois.

He indicated that he wanted to talk as they walked.

Ekoni pointed to his warriors and then to the children. He indicated that he wanted the children to teach the warriors how to use the sling.

Taelo nodded in agreement. He liked the thought of the children getting such an experience.

Taelo soon noted that every one of the team members was periodically relieved. They immediately were asked to give instruction on the sling.

Taelo now understood why Ekoni was the leader and why his warriors were so loyal to him, he grew his followers.

After several sun cycles of traveling the team crested a hill and encountered a large group of Others.

Their black warriors friends were immediately ready to attack.

Taelo put up his hand and said in a level tone that they would first try friendship.

He called on the team to form the fighting diamonds.

Ekoni did not understand the words but understood the tone.

Taelo looked at Burley Bear and the rest of the Others on the team and said that it was their turn to make friends.

Taelo and Burley Bear walked down toward the group of Others that was at least twice as many as the entire team following him.

Taelo raised his hand and in the language of the Others he said he was a friend.

The surprised look on the face of the leader of this group of Others let Taelo know that at least the word friend was understood.

He watched as Burley Bear spoke in his own language and let the leader know that they were coming in friendship and that Taelo and he were leading a team on a quest for learning.

The leader pointed to the black warriors and replied that they were not friends and had engaged in a recent battle with some of his warriors.

Taelo called to Ekoni and asked for him to pull the meat loaded travois down the hill.

After some clarification by Quiet Rabbit, Ekoni complied.

Taelo pointed to the remainder of the Elk on the travois. He then told the leader of the Others that there would be no fight. They were in the land of plenty and that Ekoni was giving the elk to the Others.

Ekoni pulled the travois up to the leader and put it down.

The leader reached out and touched Ekoni and thanked him.

He walked over to Taelo and put his hand on his shoulder and said friend.

He turned to Burley Bear and did the same.

He finally turned to Ekoni and slowly put his hand on his shoulder and in a more questioning tone said friend.

Ekoni put his hand on the Other Leader's shoulder and said friend as best he could in the language of the Others.

This attempt to use the language of the Others brought a cheer from the members of the Others.

Once again, Lily and Floating Cloud changed the entire setting as they were joined by Marigold, Mayflower and Single Leaf in preparing a meal for everyone to share.

They used a portion of the elk that had been given to the new group of Others and added some of the meat they were pulling. Their honey basted meat was an instant hit.

Taelo had sitting stones arranged so the two teams could sit across from each other.

The women that were accompanying the Others joined in the cooking and the conversations and the slight variations in the exact language of the Others was causing some laughter.

It was a surprise to them that Busy Bee, Talking Wren, and Quiet Rabbit all talked in their language.

The children of the Elk Clan and those of Burley Bear and Saber Scar were readily accepted.

The meal ended with the two groups with smiles on their faces.

To Taelo the smiles of the Others always reminded him of a grimace.

The smiles of the black warriors seemed to beam white light.

They departed after enjoying a meal together and continued their journey.

A sun cycle later, when the two teams were under their camp covers, Taelo asked the members to recount what they had learned in the last few sun cycles.

He was gratified to hear Black Wolf, and Red Fox say that "treating others the way you wish to be treated" worked.

They had now met two different kinds of people and Taelo knew somewhere ahead a third kind of people with sky eyes was yet to be encountered.

Chapter 21: Broken Spear and the Others

It had been several moon cycles since Broken Spear had last flown with the eagle. He had watched the sun set on the far sea horizon. He then returned to the cave and was now relaxing before going to sleep.

Not much later, he felt the call of a faraway eagle and took up the position where he could lean back and relax.

He saw a beach and out at sea he could see rafts approaching. He knew that Taelo and his team had crossed the far sea and were now about to land on the beach.

The eagle cried out as the rafts rode the last wave in and then grounded their noses in the sand.

The eagle continued to circle.

Broken Spear was surprised when Taelo waved at the eagle and gave his palm up salute and then clapped them together. This was a sign of hello used by the Clan of Others. It warmed Broken Spear's heart to know that Taelo expected him to be watching.

The eagle seemed to give a cry of response and then Broken Spear was back in his cave. He went to sleep wondering how long it would be before he next flew with the eagle.

It came sooner than he expected. The very next night he was once again flying with the eagle. He watched as Taelo, and his team sent two empty rafts out to sea. Taelo and his team were all sitting by cooking fires as each raft was put out to sea. As each raft left shore a large fire was ignited in the center of the raft. The rafts were slowly burning themselves up. It was a scene that he had not expected. The two rafts soon looked like huge fires as they rode the current and sailed into the setting sun.

Broken Spear knew the team had built three rafts. He noted the travois and figured the burning wood on the two rafts came from the material that the team had left over from utilizing what they could from the third raft.

The eagle rode the air currents and seemed to be watching the rafts with the teams. When the rafts became small glowing specks in the red setting sun, the eagle gave a loud cry and glided back into the forest.

Broken Spear had been moved by the sight and wiped away a tear. He was thankful to have been able to see such a sight and wished he could have been there in person. He once again slept well.

His next surprise was one that he had not expected. Once again he was flying high with the eagle. He watched as Taelo, and his team met a group of people that were Black. Broken Spear watched as Taelo approached a very tall Black warrior.

He marveled at the fact that Taelo always approached new people in the spirit of friendship, but Broken Spear did not miss that his team had three fighting diamonds ready for action.

It was apparent that Taelo had organized the children to form the third fighting diamond. Broken Spear was sure that he had also made weapons and trained the children how to defend themselves.

The meeting turned out to be a friendly one and Taelo and his team set up a camp nearby and then shared a meal with their new acquaintances.

The eagle gave a loud cry and Taelo once again signaled a hello, pointed to the black warriors, and made the sign of a friend.

It was clear to Broken Spear that Taelo had continued his learning and was now proficient in the sign language of the Others and he knew Broken Spear would see him.

He was awake and flying with the eagle each of his sleep cycles. He was now sure of the theory that Taelo had shared with him about the shape of the world in which they lived.

Broken Spear was once again looking forward to sharing what he had seen with all the clans. He had become the storyteller at every Clan gathering and he continued to host the periodic gathering of the Northern Elk Clan and the Main Elk Clan at his Clan's dwelling.

Almost a moon cycle later he was once again flying with the eagle when he was again surprised. This time he saw a large group of warriors that looked exactly like the ones in his cave.

Taelo and his team accompanied by the group of black warriors had come upon a large group of Others. Broken Spear watched in wonder as this time Taelo, and Burley Bear walked down to a group of Others that were ready to fight.

Taelo stepped forward and raised his hand in friendship. He must have surprised the leader of the group because, then Burley Bear stepped forward and raised his hand in friendship. The leader responded in kind but then pointed at the tall black warrior and called one of his fighters and showed the scar on his side.

Taelo turned and called the Black Warrior forward and had him raise his hand in friendship. The black warrior did this and then stepped forward and presented the leader with an object that Broken Spear took to be spear made of black wood and that had a long shining blade. Even from on high he could see that it was a magnificent weapon. The chief accepted the spear.

The black warrior had also pulled a travois that had what looked like the body of an elk and he gave that to the chief as well.

The eagle gave a cry and Taelo pointed to him and then made the sign of the claw. The leader pointed to a nearby boulder and made a sign to show the boulder splitting. Broken Spear took the sign to mean he was called Boulder Splitter.

Boulder Splitter then pointed at Lasher and Taelo put his hand on Lasher's head and then brought the leaders hand so Lasher could smell it.

The leader looked back at his group and gave a laugh that Broken Spear could hear. He hesitantly did as he was asked, and Lasher gave his hand a lick.

The eagle stayed long enough so that Broken Spear could see that Taelo had once again made a potentially hostile group into his friends

Taelo shared the high sun meal with the Others and then proceeded to take his team toward the white topped mountains that were brightly glowing on the far horizon.

Chapter 22: "Battle Partners"

The team traveled within site of the glacier and toward mountains that appeared to be high, snow covered and impassable. The mountains nearest the glacier seemed to be trying not to get buried under it.

Taelo knew that the mountains posed a serious barrier in their travels. He knew from experience that the team still had several sun cycles to go before reaching the mountains. He wanted to find out if there was a passage through that would keep the team from having to climb over the mountains.

He discussed the need to find a passage through the mountains similar to the ones they used for the two major mountain ridges in the land that was now on the other side.

He asked whether Quiet Rabbit and Feather-in-the-Wind would be willing to go out and find that perfect river that the team could use to get through to the other side.

He pointed out that it seemed pointless to send anyone else.

The two enjoyed being singled out, challenged, and replied that they would certainly be willing to scout the mountains ahead for that river.

Ekoni volunteered two of his warrior to be part of the scouting team. He said that they would provide protection for the two women.

Taelo looked at the smile on Quiet Rabbits face and knew those two warriors were in for a challenge. He pointed out that two wolves would also be going with the team and pointed to Lasher and Brave Walker.

During the evening meal he observed Feather-in-the-Wind, Quiet Rabbit, and several others talking, laughing and obviously making plans to test their black protectors.

That night before they went to sleep Taelo asked Quiet Rabbit to go easy on the two warriors. He was sure their hearts were in the right place.

Early the next morning, after a hearty meal, Feather-in-the-Wind led the team out at a fast jog. She and Quiet Rabbit had agreed that they would keep a very brisk pace and see how the two warriors handled it.

It was not long until the two warriors started to drop back.

Quiet Rabbit called a rest stop and while they were resting she and Feather-in-the-Wind used their sling and bagged four rabbits. They planned to roast them for the high sun meal.

They then set out again at the rapid jog that they intended to keep throughout the entire scouting trip.

It was clear that the warriors were struggling and using all their energy to keep up.

Their struggles fueled Feather-in-the-Wind's legs and she kept the challenging pace.

They began their search at the base of the glacier and then headed away from it. As the sun reached its zenith, they came upon the river they were hoping to find.

They were about to celebrate the discovery and call a halt to have a meal when both Lasher and Bold Walker began to growl.

Quiet Rabbit signaled the two warriors to stop and stand still. Then she and Feather-in-the-Wind stepped forward.

Two dire wolves several times the size of Lasher and much darker in color than those that Quiet Rabbit was familiar with, came out of the woods and each gave a deep snarling growl.

The two warriors were ready to throw their spears, but Quiet Rabbit signaled them to hold their spears.

She looked at Feather-in-the-Wind and said, "Just like we hunt the buffalo but put the spear down their throat."

Then together they both took one step forward and one step away from each other. They used their slings to pelt the wolves to distract them and then they immediately prepared for the attack.

It happen so fast that neither of them had time to think.

They each thrust their spears down the throat of the wolf attacking them and then planted the butt of their spear into the ground and stepped on it to keep it from sliding.

The velocity and weight of the wolves made it look as if they were eagerly swallowing the spears.

The wolves fell to their knees.

Lasher and Bold Walker had each attacked from the side and had clamped down on the wolves' throat and did not let go until the wolves died.

The two warriors came forward and measured the two wolves. They were huge. They were both almost two of their spears long and at least as tall as Quiet Rabbit's shoulders.

They each put their hand to their chest, pointed to the wolves and drew a travois on the ground with two figures pulling it.

Quiet Rabbit smiled as she pointed at the drawing and nodded in agreement.

Originally she had planned to roast the rabbits that she and Feather-in-the-Wind had bagged but now she knew that they would not have time. It would require all their effort to get the wolf carcasses back by the time the sun went below the horizon.

Back at the camp, as the sun approached the zenith, Burley Bear suggested that he and Running Stag go out with Arrow to see if they could locate the scouting team.

Taelo said that was a great idea and that he would join them.

Running Stag talked to Arrow and asked him to find Feather-in-the-Wind.

Running Stag looked up at Taelo and told him that he had said something similar to Lasher when Taelo was out in the blizzard rescuing part of Semper's Clan. He recalled that Lasher had found him and safely brought him through the blizzard back to the Northern Clan Lodge.

Taelo replied that he well remembered that time and thanked Running Stag for having prepared Lasher so well.

Taelo had no objections when Ekoni said he wished to go along.

The four of them followed Arrow. Arrow at first seemed to go out on the trail hat the scouting team had taken but then suddenly he went out sharply toward the right and began baying.

The sun was nearing the far horizon and Taelo was glad that Arrow had connected with the scouting team.

Taelo could not hear any response, but it was clear that Arrow had. Arrow now took off at a pace that had the four of them at almost a full run.

Taelo was glad when he could hear Lasher respond.

He slowed the pace so that they would not surprise the returning scouting team.

Taelo could not help but chuckle when he saw the arrangement of the scouting team.

He noted that the two warriors were each pulling a travois. Lasher and Bold Walker were harnessed on the inside travois member and Quite Rabbit and Feather-in-the-Wind were harnessed to the outside member.

The load on the travois was immense and at first Taelo thought it was buffalo but then he recognized the two almost black animals.

He asked about the two dire wolves and listened to the brief story Quiet Rabbit shared.

It was clear to him that she was tired. Feather-in-the-Wind was sitting on the ground and was clearly exhausted.

Taelo took Quiet Rabbits position and Ekoni took Feather-in-the-Wind's position. They then followed the most direct way back to the camp.

The two warriors kept a running dialogue going with Ekoni as they all pulled the load into camp.

The team all came over to look at the two huge dire wolves.

The questions were flying.

Quiet Rabbit asked that the four of them eat first then she and the rest would tell their story.

Taelo knew that whatever had been shared with Ekoni was now common knowledge for the rest of his warriors. Each warrior made their way over to Feather-in-the-Wind and Quiet Rabbit and touched them on the shoulder and said "stryd vennoot." He later learned that it meant "battle partner" and that the two had been recognized as the equals to each of the warriors.

Ekoni was first to stand and begin telling about the killing of the two dire wolves. He first described the constant running that had worn his two warriors down to where they did not think they could throw a spear. They were tired and hungry.

He then had the two stand and tell of how Quiet Rabbit had signaled them that she and Feather-in-the-Wind would handle the two huge wolves. They described how the two had stepped toward the wolves and used their slings to hit the wolves in their snouts. It was clear that it had both angered and confused the wolves.

They had watched as the two dropped their slings, and each took a step away from the other.

The wolves made a lightning fast attacked.

The two warriors commented that they were sure the wolves would kill the two persons that they had been sent out to protect.

But the two stood their ground and thrust their spears into the wolves' mouths and then they had put the butt of the spear into the ground and stepped on it.

The two warriors both said that it seemed as if the wolves were eagerly swallowing the spears. He pointed at Lasher and Bold Walker and said that the two wolves rushed in from the side and clamped down on the throats of the dire wolves and did not let go until both were dead.

Then the two warriors walked over to Quiet Rabbit and Feather-in-the-Wind and hoisted them into the air and loudly called out, "stryd vennoot" and the entire warrior group repeated the cry.

They turned around and looked at the rest of the gathering and again called out "stryd vennoot."

This time Taelo and the rest of the team responded with the call.

Taelo then asked that Quiet Rabbit and Feather-in-the-Wind tell the story so the rest of the team could better understand why they had been hunting dire wolves and why they had just been honored by being inducted into their black warrior friend's fighting unit.

Quiet Rabbit and Feather-in-the-Wind told their version of seeking out a way through the mountains and the attack of the dire wolves. They said that they had used the same technique that Taelo had taught the team in how to down a buffalo by putting the spear tip on the buffalo's chest and then putting the butt of the spear into the ground.

She and Feather-in-the-Wind had used that approach with the two dire wolves and luckily it had worked.

She pointed and then walked over to Lasher and Bold Walker and gave them a treat of roast buffalo meat. She praised them for having given the early warning and then attacking from the side and clamping down on the throats of the dire wolves and not letting go until they were dead.

The team stood up, and in unison said "stryd vennoot" and then repeated it in their own language "battle partner."

Taelo stood up and slowly swept his hand across the entire group and called out "battle partner" in both languages.

He then asked if the team had found a way through the mountains.

Both Quiet Rabbit and Feather-in-the-Wind laughed and said that yes, the wolves were killed on the bank of a river that seemed to go through the mountains.

They had not gone any farther but suggested that the team move their camp to that point and then make sure the river was the way to go.

Chapter 23: Mountain Passage

Quiet Rabbit led the way back to the riverbank where the two dire wolves had attacked. She pointed downstream to a clearing that provided a good place to set up camp. She noted that there was a good supply of dead wood for the cooking fire and that the forest would provide timbers if it was decided that they would build rafts to float down the river.

Black Wolf commented that it was too bad that they could not have brought the rafts with which they had crossed the sea.

Taelo agreed. He laughed and said that they could have hooked up the children and had them pull it to this point.

Yellow Flower commented that sending them out to sea was a much better decision.

Taelo suggested that the team see what fresh food they could find while he and Burley Bear went along the river to see how they would proceed.

They found that the river entered the mountains, and the banks though passable were very steep on both sides. As the two continued to walk along the edge, the banks turned more into cliff than bank. It became clear that they would need to ride the river.

The only concern that Taelo had was whether there might be waterfalls that posed a danger to the team.

He would have liked to explore the entire way through, but he was not sure if doing so could be done without a great delay.

He and Burley Bear returned to the team and discussed the pros and cons of doing a full, thorough through the mountain check. It would mean that the team would most likely spend the winter at their current camp.

The team concluded that they would rather ride the river and take a chance on it not having any massive waterfalls.

The raft building began in earnest on the next rise of the sun.

Taelo had the team build four river going rafts.

Talking Wren supervised the work being done by the warriors.

The rest of the team seemed to know what to do and soon the rafts took shape. These rafts were not built like their sea going counter parts. There was no double deck. There was only the one layer of dry dead wood bound together with strips of willow bark. It did have one vertical guide made of young willow limbs down into the water to help in guiding the raft.

Building a stone and clay fire ring for each raft was one feature that Taelo made sure each raft had. He watched as Lily and Floating cloud made four small fire rings from clay. This was a skill that was new to the clan and would be a learning that the team would take back with them to their clans.

He was making sure that if they had to spend several sun cycles on the river each raft would have the ability to prepare their own meals.

The goods to be kept dry were put up on raised platforms but the water would splash up on what was the main platform.

If the team had to spend several sun cycles on the rafts they would sleep on top of their supplies.

Since this was the first experience for the warriors, Taelo asked Little Otter and Talking Wren to take charge in guiding that raft. Little Otter would control the long paddle in the back. Talking Wren would supervise the warriors with guide poles at the front.

They would be the last raft in the order of going down the river.

He invited Ekoni to ride with him on the first raft.

Burley Bear would handle the back long paddle on the first raft.

Saber Scar was handling the back long paddle on the second raft and Sharp Blade was doing it on the third raft.

Taelo had intentionally asked the strongest to handle the rear guide paddles. He had assigned two of the team to be on the front with guide poles to keep the rafts away from the edge of the river and to maneuver the raft around any boulders or rocks that might be in the river.

He instructed the rafts to keep within sight of each other but stay at least four or five raft lengths apart.

Taelo stood at the front of the raft. He was looking as far ahead as possible. He wanted to know of any danger as soon as possible. He was hoping for an problem free ride through the mountains.

Lily and Floating Cloud had prepared several sun cycles of stews and put them on each raft. They had also prepared enough dried and seasoned meat for at least five sun cycles for each raft.

Each raft also had a separate amount of food that could be used if the way through the mountains turned out to be long.

Taelo had asked the children to see if they could spear some fish.

Quiet Rabbit liked that idea and said that she, Busy Bee, and Feather in the Wind would each supervise the children and teach them how to successfully spear fish.

The warriors on the last raft were naturals at spearing fish. They shouted out that they would have enough fish for all the team members.

Taelo relaxed after they had been on the river for most of the first sun cycle. It was becoming clear that the team would spend more than one sun cycle on the river.

He then began to look for a point where the four rafts could stop for the night.

The river took a gradual bend and a rocky beach at the elbow presented such a spot where the four rafts could put up for the night.

Burly Bear took his raft in at the lowest point and each raft pulled in alongside of each other.

There was not a good place to sleep on the shore so the team would be sleeping on top of their goods.

The warriors had delivered on their promise of spearing a fish for each of the team.

The fish spearing was a success among the children as well and they said that it was fun and that they would do it again when they were back on the river.

Taelo had a common fire made up on the shore and everyone sat around and enjoyed chewing on some dry snacks and roasting the fish that had been caught.

Ekoni pointed to all the fish being roasted and thanked his warriors for being as good at spear fishing as they were in battle.

Taelo had planned for several sun cycles to make it through. It turned out that the team spent one hand worth of sun cycles riding the river before the mountains gave way to a hilly terrain.

He called a halt where the river slowed its speed, and a wide valley of grasses greeted them.

The river turned away from the direction that the team needed to travel.

Taelo declared that it was time to proceed on foot and continue on their journey toward the rising point morning sun.

Chapter 24: Sky Eyes

℔t was the season when the Elk Clan gathered. Taelo brought up the fact that the team was going to miss their second Clan gathering.

Everyone shared the fact that they hated to miss the gathering, but they countered that their current journey had so far captivated them, and they would not have wanted to miss it.

Feather-in-the-Wind was somewhat more emotional than usual as she hugged Neiva and said that this journey of Circumvention was something she was so happy to be on, with her daughter, her brother, and the most wonderful mate she could ever have wished for. She would return and have a lifetime of stories to share at future gatherings.

Quiet Rabbit agreed that having her two twins on the journey was so enriching that she was glad that Taelo had persisted with his theory that the world was round. She had at first thought her mate had been affected by the stress of being a father.

Ekoni understood the essence of the discussion and commented that he and his team were on a less ambitious journey but that meeting Taelo, and the team was a rich reward for them. They would remember and tell the stories of each of the team members.

He went on to reaffirm that he was especially pleased that Feather-in-the-Wind and Quiet Rabbit had been inducted by his warriors into their ranks.

He pointed out that he now understood why Taelo listened so closely to Talking Wren whose mind was powerful.

He put his hand on Burley Bear and said that the people of his clan were the most powerful that he had experienced, and he had learned that friendship was more powerful than doing battle.

Ekoni laughed when Red Fox said "Behandel ander soos jy behandel wil word" and then said it in the language of the team, "treat others the way you wish to be treated."

He then complimented him on having learned the language of his people. It spoke well of he and his father's team.

Yellow Flower blurted out, "Hy pronk," and in her own language she said that Red Fox was just showing off and that all the kids had learned a lot of the warriors language as well as the language of the Others.

Taelo decided to intervene and complimented all the children on the skills that they had all acquired.

They were all very good with the sling and were often providing the entire team with the evening meal.

They had learned the diamond formation and he was sure that they would be able to defeat any attackers.

They had all received praise from Lily and Floating Cloud on their cooking abilities and they had been the obest at fishing when the team had come through the mountains.

The entire team stood, pointed to the children, and gave a cheer.

The rise of the sun caught the team in its final preparation to continue their journey. Taelo and the team left the river behind as they followed the point where the sun had risen.

Two sun cycles later the team came upon a river that was running toward the glacier which at the time was not in sight. It was the first river that any of them had seen running in the direction that it was running.

Ekoni commented that where he came from there was another river that ran in that direction.

Taelo decided it was a good place to camp and it would give him a chance to talk with the team about his desire to follow the river at least to the point where it cut through the glacier.

He wondered how wide of cut the river had created. The team agreed that they too would like to see the cut into the glacier.

They followed the river for three sun cycles. They could now see that the river had seemingly created a wide split through the glacier.

They were moving along when Taelo called a halt. He had spotted smoke rising toward the sky.

He called on the team to form the diamond fighting formation and be prepared for whatever they might face.

He let them know that he expected the people in this region to be the Sky Eyed ones.

Ekoni understood the request and his team formed their two fighting diamonds.

Quiet Rabbit organized the children into their fighting diamond.

The team then moved forward, and they practiced putting down their travois and getting into the fighting diamond formation.

As Little Otter had loudly commented and was joined by Burley Bear, "And we will do this at least three times."

Taelo had laughed and said he was glad that the two had remembered because he had forgotten.

The team proceeded toward a village of substantial size.

An eagle was flying overhead which caused Taelo to wonder what they might face.

He was reminded of what Red Fox had shared a few sun cycle past and decided that they should prepare a gift for the village leader.

He stopped the team and asked what an appropriate gift might be. Ekoni held up a spear and said that it would be a very good gift. Lily held up a prize cut of buffalo meat and said that food always showed respect and was always welcome.

Busy Bee held up a pair of elk and buffalo hide boots.

Taelo thanked them for their suggestions and decided that on the initial meeting the spear and the food would be enough. If the team received a warm welcome additional gifts could be shared.

Ekoni said he was impressed with how the team on the one hand prepared for battle and on the other prepared for friendship.

The team moved forward and made their final approach to the village.

He was surprised that they were very near before they were seen. This let him know that the village was not expecting any one to attack. It told Taelo that the people in the village were most likely dominant in the region.

A person that was almost as large as Burley Bear walked toward them. He had a large number of spear carrying warriors behind him.

Taelo recognized some of them as the Sky Eyes that the team had faced in battle. He called for the team to form their fighting diamonds and move in parallel toward the oncoming group.

When they were two spear throws apart he called a halt and said he was going forward on his own.

Taelo slowly approached the village leader. He was watching the fighters behind the leader. They seemed to be waiting on the command of the leader to attack.

When Taelo was within a spears length of the leader, he raised his hand and in the language of the Blue Eyes he said, "Friend" and pointed to the eagle in the sky put his hand on his chest and gave his name as the claw that strikes.

He caught the surprised look of the leader, who pointed to the eagle put his hand on his chest and indicated with his hand that his name was Flying Eagle.

A warrior behind the leader came up and pointed at Taelo said something to the leader.

Taelo remembered the warrior and knew that he had met him in battle. He was now ready for one and took a step back.

The leader put up his hand and said friend.

He pointed at Taelo and indicated that he was welcome in the village.

Taelo called for Ekoni and Lily to bring forward the gifts they had prepared.

Ekoni brought the spear and handed it to Taelo.

Lily walked past Taelo and presented the buffalo hump meat to Flying Eagle. He had one of his warriors take it for him.

And then he accepted the spear and immediately ran his hand along the wood and touched the spear head with his finger.

He held it up, grinned and said something that Taelo interpreted as beautiful. It was clear that the spear was appreciated.

Taelo pointed to Ekoni and then to the spear to indicate that it was a gift from him.

Flying Eagle nodded his head and said friend.

He then turned and indicated that Taelo should follow him.

Taelo signaled his team to follow.

They slowly made their way into the village where they were greeted and shown where they could set up their camp.

Taelo asked the team to set up the camp cover and get settled for a short stay.

Ekoni gave similar instructions to his team.

Taelo took a rather large group with him as he was led to the center of the village where the Flying Eagle was sitting.

Taelo introduced Quiet Rabbit. He watched as the warrior sitting next to Flying Eagle said something about her. He then introduced Golden Hawk and observed that the warrior again said something to Flying Eagle. When he introduced Busy Bee, he continued and in the language of the Sky Eyes he let him know that she was one of the slingers that had decimated Angry Cougar and his fighters.

Flying Eagle nodded.

Taelo then introduced Feather-in-the-Wind and Talking Wren as the two who had commanded an army of, and he pointed at Lasher. This time the warrior again commented to Flying Eagle who nodded and pointed at Lasher and said wolf in his language.

The introduction of Burley Bear, Meadow Flower, Saber Scar, and Marigold seemed to take Flying Eagle by surprise. He made a comment that Taelo understood as fierce fighters.

Flying Eagle then stood and called forward a group of fighters and a few women. When they were assembled Flying Eagle pointed to the wounds on their faces, their legs, and their bodies.

He put his hand on his chest and pointed to the woman that had been sitting to his right and indicated that Angry Cougar was their son.

He then pointed at Taelo and indicated that Taelo should be his son.

Taelo stood and put his hand on his chest and indicated that he was honored to be called son of Flying Eagle.

Taelo had a bag of honey drink brought to the meeting. He took a drink and gave it to Flying Eagle. Taelo then gave it to Quiet Rabbit, and she walked over to Flying Eagle's mate and handed it to her. Then she handed it to Golden Hawk.

The honey drink had the impact that Taelo had hoped for.

Soon the food and drink was being shared and the atmosphere took on the feeling of a celebration.

This was the reception he would have wished for when he had first met the Sky Eyes, but that first meeting was with a renegade group of Sky Eyes.

Taelo let that memory fade and embraced the moment.

Chapter 25: Ekoni's Departure

The cordial relationship with Flying Eagle and his Clan continued. The sling was new to the Sky Eyes and the children could be seen showing their counter parts how to use it.

The rest of the team spent time interacting with the various Sky Eye Clan members and learning some of their language.

Taelo met with all the Sky Eye warriors that had faced him in battle on their previous meeting and let them know that he had tried to meet them as a friend, but that Angry Cougar had made that impossible. He let them know that he was pleased that he had the chance to now meet them as a friend.

Flying Eagle had been sitting by, listening, and let Taelo know that he had no ill feelings about what had happened to his son. He had learned that even to the last his son was trying to take advantage in his attempt to kill Taelo and that he had met the end that he earned for himself.

Several sun cycles later, Ekoni announced that it was time for he and his warriors to depart and return to their land. He praised Taelo and his team for having educated his warriors and himself in the many ways that the team had learned to manage their environment.

Taelo and the team all praised Ekoni and his warriors and called them good friends that they would miss. Lily and Floating Cloud prepared several days of meals for each of the warriors.

Ekoni and his warriors gave each of the team members small bags that had several pieces of a gold medal that was new to Taelo and his team. Ekoni explained that each bag made that person a rich person in his land. He hoped that the richness in the bags would be the richness each of Taelo's team would experience in their life's journeys.

In return, Taelo presented his personal flat, shark toothed weapon to Ekoni. He addressed Ekoni in his language, "broer" which meant brother.

Ekoni nodded and repeated that word as he accepted the weapon.

On the morning of departure, the team escorted Ekoni and his warriors along part of their starting journey. The warriors were chanting their traveling song and Taelo and his team mimicked it and joined the singing. They went with them to the top of the hill just beyond the village. There they stopped but continued their singing until Ekoni and his warriors disappeared beyond eyesight.

Then the team let out their battle cry that they knew would reach the warriors.

Very faintly they heard the corresponding cry from Ekoni and his warriors.

High in the sky an eagle let out a cry, took a long, graceful turn and then went upriver.

As the team returned to the village, they all agreed that it was time for them to also continue with their journey.

Taelo thanked Flying Eagle for the hospitality that he had extended and let him know that the team was preparing to continue their journey.

He was surprised when Flying Eagle said that there were several members of his clan that wanted to make the journey with them to where the land met the sea.

Flying Eagle pointed out that one of the persons was the person that had been his son's best friend but who had chosen to leave Angry Cougar and return and had asked to be taken back by the clan that he had left.

He introduce Rolling Stone. The scars on his face and the wolf bite marks on his legs marked him as one of the Sky Eyes that Taelo and his team had faced.

Taelo raised his hand to indicate that he was a friend.

He watched as Rolling Stone returned the sign.

Taelo indicated that he would be pleased to be guided by Rolling Stone and a few of the other people who were introduced.

There were eight in all. They were four mated couples and there were four children that would also make the trip.

Taelo returned to the team and informed them of the additional people that would accompany them.

Burley Bear and Meadow Flower commented that it seemed that people wanted both a good life and the adventure of traveling and learning the land.

They were very aware of the fact that the Sky Eyes were very aggressive but that they were basically the same as all the people that they had met.

They wondered if the harsh environment in which the Sky Eyes lived made them more aggressive in their effort to survive.

It was a handful of sun cycles later that the eagle circling in the sky let out a cry and the team left the village.

They took up their travel chant and soon had Rolling Stone and his team chanting as well.

Quiet Rabbit commented that the chanting helped in bonding the team and it seemed that their Sky Eye guides would bond with them as well.

Busy Bee agreed and commented that it was good to go from enemy to being friends.

Several sun cycles later the team reached a river that ran in the direction they were following.

Taelo had observed that Rolling Stone was following a series of stone markers. When he asked Rolling Stone about them, he learned that they had been put up as Rolling Stone returned from their battle with Taelo, with the wounded fighters. He had put the markers up so that if any other members that had stayed with Angry Cougar who chose to return had a way to do so.

Taelo complemented him on his having done so.

The river ran through a vast plane of tall grasses and seemed to be a good place for the team to set up their camp for a brief stay.

The camp cover had just been set up when it began to snow.

Taelo made sure that the edges of the camp cover were weighed down with stones and then had the team collect as much grass as they could so it could be used as fuel for the cooking fire and for small fires for the inside of the covered areas.

Rolling Stone and his team showed the team how to tightly bind the grass so that it would burn slowly.

Taelo made sure that the food supply was in good shape. The hunting had been reduced to mostly the small game that the team was downing with their slings. So far that had provided the food for each sun cycle.

The team had bagged several antelopes that Rolling Stone had called saiga. The saiga could be seen in rather large herds and Taelo and Golden Hawk had tried their hunting technique that they used on buffalo but had failed. These animals were faster and kept themselves at a distance.

They instead learned that they could surprise one of them and run along with the very fast animal and easily throw their spear and down the animal and then finish them with their war hammers.

The first hunt had resulted in a full meat carrying travois by each team.

Rolling Stone had complimented Taelo and Golden Hawk on their ability to approach the saiga and then be able to run fast enough to get close enough to throw their spear.

The snow provided the perfect time to stop and celebrate their continuing journey.

Taelo requested that each team member select a story that they would tell.

Most of the team focused on telling stories associated with the Journey they now called "Dangerous Passage" because of all the different dangerous events that had occurred. These stories culminated in the battle with the Blue Eyes and the subsequent end of Angry Cougar.

Quiet Rabbit focused her stories on the discovery of the mounts that the team called the Journey of Discovery.

Busy Bee told the Story of the first Journey to the land of the Condor and the learnings they had brought back and almost immediately put to use to establish the Northern Elk Clan.

Lily told the story of the Cannibals and Taelo's rescue.

Bold Walker and Single Leaf told the story of the second journey to the land of the Condor and the Condor Glass Slingers.

Burley Bear, Meadow Flower, Saber Scar and Meadow Gold each told stories about their experiences as members of Taelo's team.

The food and honey drink kept the team's energy up during the stories. The children were wide awake. They had heard many of the stories, but many were new or were told by someone with a different perspective.

Rolling Stone shared his story of how his lifetime friend, Angry Cougar slowly changed as he grew older. His friend earned his second name because he seemed to be angry with the world and the elders that he felt were the cause of the situation they lived in.

His friend was determined to gain power and did so in a very destructive way. He learned that by acting immediately and killing the leaders of a village that the element of surprise allowed him to take over.

He had repeatedly done this as he left his homeland until he reached the village where Taelo and his team confronted him.

He had planned to do to Taelo what he had done to all other leaders, but Taelo had reacted faster than the spear that was being thrust at him and had cut off Angry Cougar's right hand.

It was all downhill after that first encounter.

After the devastating battle on the hill where the stone slingers, the battle diamond, the wolf attacks from two sides and the rear attack of the small but very effective team from the village, Rolling Stone knew it was time to return back to his homeland and ask to be taken back by Flying Eagle.

Taelo's run through the camp to deliver the message for Angry Cougar to rescue his three surviving warriors crystalized Rolling Stone's decision and he warned Angry Cougar not to get in the way of those that wished to return to their homeland.

He pointed to Saber Scar and said he knew that he was followed by him and had his warriors put their spears into the ground blade first to show that they had withdrawn from the battle.

Taelo thanked Rolling Stone for the story and said that it was now time to let that memory be in the past and to embrace a future where everyone would allow the space for others to flourish and grow.

The entire team stomped the ground and shouted agreement.

Chapter 26: The Peka

*T*aelo had watched as the face of the glacier began to recede. He made sure that the team was going toward the point from which the sun rose over the horizon. They were on course and Rolling Stone was following a series of stone markers that he had set up when he returned from the battle on the far coast.

Rolling Stone led them to a river that he said they should follow. He said that it would be easier if they floated downriver until they got to the point where he had erected a very large marker. At that location they would take a direction that put the rising sun a spears length to their right shoulder.

The building of the river rafts was now a thing that the team could do quickly and efficiently. The challenge this time was getting enough timber together to build them. The trees were less abundant, and they were scraggly bent ones. The rafts when they were completed seemed to lack flat areas and looked more like twisted brush floating on the river.

However, they were functional. They had used several of the travois' poles to make the back guide paddles. These were the only straight timbers available.

Each of the construction teams pointed to and laughed at the construction of the other rafts.

Taelo joined the fun.

He set up a team of judges to select the raft that was,

    1.   the most twisted.
    2.   the raft that seemed to be the straightest.
    3.   the raft that had the highest twisted surface.

The prizes to be awarded to the raft building teams were,

    •   First prize - a honey roasted boar,
    •   Second prize - buffalo tail soup,
    •   Third prize - freshly roast fish.

The cook would be the leader of each raft construction team with the cooking guidance of Meadow Flower, Floating Cloud and Marigold.

The judges were the children, Yellow Flower, Red Fox, Black Wolf, Aristosa, Spear Tip, Flint, and Neiva and the four new Sky Eyes.

Taelo called the judges aside and suggested that each raft only get awarded one of the prizes.

The adult team members loved the idea and there was a great deal of teasing and laughter. Several even tried to influence the judges with small bribes.

The morning of the judging Lily and Floating Cloud made a special meal for the judges. They pointed out that they wanted the judges to be at their best and that judging the work of their elders properly and thoroughly was very important.

Taelo watched as the children embraced being the center of attention. The construction leaders of each raft made it a point to serve the meal to each of the judges and to point out the great raft that each had built.

Taelo waited until the meal was over to call for the judging.

He then asked the judges to look at all three rafts. Then go off together and decided the award for each raft and come back and let everyone know their decision.

The judges walked up to each raft as a group and looked it over. After looking at the last raft they walked down along the bank. They were laughing and enjoying their role. Aristosa seemed to take control of the group and soon they were back with their decision.

Taelo announced that the awards were to be given in the reverse order. And as the award was given, that raft would launch and stand ready to begin its journey down the river that the Blue Eyes called the Peka.

The judges would ride the first prize raft until the first stop.

The raft that Little Otter was guiding won third. That team launched as instructed and held position in the middle of the river.

The raft that Burley Bear was guiding won second and joined the third-place raft.

The raft that Sharp Blade was guiding won first. His team let out a whoop and howl as they helped the judges get on board before they pushed off.

Taelo began the travel chant and soon all three rafts were chanting in unison.

The river had a strong current and the rafts, despite their looks, functioned well. Each team member found a spot where they could get comfortable.

The ride was going well and the weather, though on the chilly side, was good.

Taelo decided that they would stop when the sun was a spear height above the horizon.

The three rafts landed, and the promised meals were prepared. The judges got the privilege of having a taste of each of the three meals.

Taelo asked each team to select a story that they would tell.

The camp cover was hoisted and the story telling began.

Taelo took note that only Black Wolf and Red Fox were still awake as the last story was coming to an end.

Rolling Stone commented that he had never experienced traveling the way he saw Taelo's team do it.

He commented that when he returned to Flying Eagle's village, he would tell some of the stories that he had now heard but he would also tell of the powerful culture that he had experienced.

Taelo thanked him for sharing his comments. He said he wished their first meeting would have been different but that this time their meeting was on friendly terms.

The team rode the river for six sun cycles until the large marker that Rolling Stone had set up was reached.

The team set up camp and talked about the next part of their journey. It would be slow going as compared to riding the river. They laughed at the fact that their distorted rafts looked great as compared to pulling travois.

Chapter 27: Change of Plan

Taelo fell asleep thinking that the team should spend a sun cycle in preparing to travel overland using their travois. He had heard and agreed to the fact that river travel was much easier than traveling across the land.

He was up early the next morning and went to the river to watch the sun break over the horizon.

The eagle in the sky immediately caught his attention. He watched it take a long, smooth gliding circle as it rode the updraft of warming air.

The sky was cloudless and turning from an early morning grey to a live bright blue. The slow transition pulled Taelo into deep thought.

Then the eagle gave a cry and continued its slide down the "Peka" towards the sea.

Burley Bear had quietly walked up besides his friend. He watched as the eagle slowly faded out of sight. He then said, "I believe we should continue our ride down the river."

Taelo smiled and put his hand on Burley Bear's shoulder and said, "I will let the team know that you feel a little weak and can only handle the stress of guiding the raft and that you have suggested that we continue riding our rafts down the river."

Burley Bear gave his guttural laugh and said that he indeed felt weak and that riding down the river sounded like a great idea.

Taelo returned to the camp where Lily and Floating Cloud greeted him.

They had seen the eagle and heard the cry and watched it fly down river toward the rising sun.

They smiled and said that riding down the river would be a great way to reach the sea.

Taelo chuckled and asked if they would let each of the team know as they came to get something to eat.

Quiet Rabbit heard the exchange and said that she had heard the cry of the eagle and knew that a change was in hand.

Golden Hawk commented on the wisdom of the eagle and how he would enjoy fishing as they continued their journey.

Rolling Stone did not understand the change and asked why Taelo was choosing to continue to ride the river. It would be a venture that he, Rolling Stone was looking forward to, but he knew nothing about what was ahead.

Taelo chose that moment to tell his Burley Bear version of why they were going downstream.

Little Otter laughed and said he had noticed that Burley Bear seemed to be having trouble handling the raft steering paddle. Then he asked if the cry he had heard was from an eagle flying in the sky.

Feather-in-the-Wind looked at Neiva and speaking in a voice that everyone could hear she explained that Taelo often got a sign from an eagle. This time the eagle had given Taelo and the team direction on how to reach the sea.

Each of the team members then gave an example of how the eagle had helped the team in their journeys.

Rolling Stone kept nodding his head and periodically saying "azta." One of the children asked him what he was saying, and he explained that it was a word expressing amazement.

Taelo added that the eagle had chosen him on his naming day when he had selected the claw of the eagle. Since then, an eagle had been present at every personal major occurrence.

Rolling Stone told the team he would share this learning with his leader, Flying Eagle, and let him know of the close bond that Taelo and the eagle shared.

Little Otter added that the team never argued with the eagle, but they often challenged Taelo.

Talking Wren hit Little Otter in the ribs and walked over to Taelo and gave him a hug.

Taelo then asked the team to get all their things back on the rafts so they could continue their journey to the sea.

Taelo was not sure how long the journey to the sea might be, but he chose to organize the team so that when they reached the sea they would be ready to construct three sea going rafts. These would be the duplicates that the team had built to cross the first sea.

The journey continued down the swiftly flowing river for three hands of sun cycles.

Lily warned that they were down to where they would only be eating the fish that they could catch.

Taelo decided that hunting should take the priority to reaching the sea.

He hoped that the deer and other animals would be like the ones he and his team were used to hunting.

He organized the team into four hunting groups. He asked Lily and Floating Cloud and their mates to remain in the camp and keep it from being damaged by animals.

Each group selected the direction they wanted to take.

Taelo had selected, Rolling Stone, Feather-in-the-Wind, Running Stag and Neiva, Golden Hawk, Busy Bee and Yellow Flower, Quiet Rabbit, Black Wolf, and Red Fox. His team was the largest and had the most children in it.

He had Burley Bear, Saber Scar and Little Otter form the other teams.

The teams all left just as the sun was breaking over the horizon.

Taelo had chosen to go toward the rising sun. The other teams each went in different directions.

He had specified that each team should hunt until the sun was passing its highest point or until the team had enough meat to load a travois.

The first animal they encountered looked like a small black bear, but it ran on four legs. Running Stag downed it with an arrow and Golden Hawk finished him off. It was the first time anyone had seen this animal. It was about a third of the size of Lasher.

Taelo silently approached a black bear that was rubbing his back against a tree and brought him down with one thrust of his spear. This was a significant kill that almost filled the travois by itself.

Quiet Rabbit and Feather-in-the-Wind had been busy bagging rabbits, two pheasant and had guided the children to use their slings to do the same.

Together they had accumulated twenty rabbits, two squirrel like animals, some pheasant and one large ground hog.

Taelo called an end to their hunt. The sun was just past the zenith. He said the team should begin their return to camp but he and Golden Hawk would run toward the sea for a short time and then return when the sun reached the point, he had instructed everyone to return to camp.

Together they ran along the edge of the river. This gave Taelo the opportunity to see what the river ahead was like and to see if the sea was near.

The white birds gliding in the sky let him know that they were near the sea. He would have liked to continue but the sun had reached the point that indicated it was time to return to camp.

On returning to camp Taelo took note that each team had been successful. They had rapidly accumulated a large supply of meat.

He let the team know that they were within a handful of sun cycles from the sea.

He wanted the team to continue to hunt and accumulate enough food to last at least two moon cycles.

There seemed to be renewed energy as the team discussed building their ocean-going rafts. The three teams that had built the river rafts challenged each other in how quickly they could get the ocean-going crafts built.

Taelo said that they would not be able to compete because there would only be one team doing the building. He laughed and told the entire team to look at the outcome of their last competition and asked if they wanted to ride a sea going version of them for two to three moon cycles.

He then named the team to be the hunt team and let the rest know that they would be on the raft building team.

Burley Bear commented that the Others were being singled out to do the hard work because of their strength.

Taelo nodded, smiled, and said that in fact he had selected them because of their superior thinking ability and that their strength was only a secondary consideration.

Chapter 28: The Other Sea

Taelo thought through the journey that he and the team had made to this point and was amazed at the learning, the people he had met and how it had changed his thinking about what his journeys had meant. From the time he was little, his experiences had expanded his thinking. He had gone from thinking about himself to embracing Golden Hawk as his equal to realizing that gender should not be a barrier. He knew that intelligence resided in all humans, and he had learned that humans came in many forms. The Others with their massive strength, the Black Warriors with stories similar his own, the Sky Eyes that were more aggressive but wanting the good life that stability offered.

He and his team needed to navigate one more challenging sea crossing to complete their current journey.

Traveling down the river allowed him to take in the terrain. The forest slowly thickened as the rafts made their way toward the sea.

He, Talking Wren, and Burley Bear were in constant discussion on how to quickly build the rafts. The rest of the team participated as well and everyone had suggestions to speed up the process. This time they had the needed hides. They had learned that the willow bark strips provided a better binding when it was wet. If they found a large stand of willows, they would harvest the bark.

Golden Hawk spent his time organizing the hunt team. He wanted to be as successful as possible and wanted to keep on the move. He decided to exclude the children. He also limited the number of hunters. He only asked Dear Chaser, Rolling Stone and his three sky eyes warriors, and Running Stag to be part of the hunt team.

Busy Bee and Quite Rabbit suggested that they organize the children into a willow gathering and bark stripping team. This would provide the quantity of bark strips and would allow the children to do something of great value.

Taelo once again took note how the team seemed to naturally flow to address the needed work.

He thanked everyone for being a team that functioned so smoothly.

Sea gulls gliding through a bright blue, cloud spotted sky caused the team to let out a cheer. They were almost at the sea.

Taelo was glad to see the forest was thickening. He hoped the hunting would go as well as the ride down the river had gone. The forest promised the materials that would be needed, and the willows were growing in abundance along the banks.

The riverbanks were forest covered all the way to the sea. The forest terminated prior to a beach to the south side. Both sides of the river were lined with willows.

The left side of the river had a rocky beach area. A sandy beach was to the right.

Taelo had the rafts beach on the right side. He then led the entire team to the edge of the sea. The water had small waves coming in. He pointed out to the land within sight and said it was a large island that was blocking the waves.

He threw in a dry piece of wood as far as he could, and it slowly drifted to his left. He knew that the rafts would move slowly in that direction. It was the direction that they needed to go.

He then declared it was time for the team to set up camp and then get started.

Talking Wren located a place near the forest to set up the camp cover. The nights were getting cold, and the camp cover had become a necessity. Stones were placed around the bottom of the hide walls and the sleeping areas inside were prepared. The food stores were all located in the center. The meat that might attract bears and other predators were tied up in the trees.

When the camp was up and functional Taelo asked that the building team find the dry dead wood to make the first layer of the rafts. He said that they should locate the trees for the second layer as close to the beach as possible.

Quiet Rabbit and Busy Bee led their team of willow gathers up along the riverbank. They chose to go past the first willows to a point where they figured would be as far as they would need to harvest.

Each of the children had their slings and spears. Quiet Rabbit and Busy Bee had their slings, spears, and war clubs. They were gathering willows, but they were at the edge of a forest where wild animals ruled.

They had warned the children about the fact that they needed to stay vigilant.

Black Wolf let his spear fly and held up a large frog by one of its hind legs. This immediately had the rest of them looking for and spearing frogs.

The cutting of willows began in earnest only to be interrupted by Red Fox Spearing a fish that took Spear Tip's and Flint's help to get it pulled out of the water.

Busy Bee suggested that she, Spear Tip, Flint, and Yellow Flower carry the fish and frogs back to camp.

Quiet Rabbit agreed and said that she and the rest of the willow gatherers would return when each had a load of willow to pull behind them.

Taelo and Talking Wren marked the spot on the beach where each raft would be built. They spaced them far enough apart so that work on one of the rafts would not interfere with the work going on, on the other.

Taelo was pleased to see part of the team that had been out looking for the dry wood pulling in a long dry pine.

The delicious smell of honey baked roast announced that Lily and Floating Cloud had set up their cooking ring and were preparing the dinner.

Taelo looked up at the sun and realized that the first sun cycle at the beach was coming to an end.

Busy Bee arrived and the fish that was brought in was added to the dinner menu. The frog legs were a pleasant surprise. These would be great treats that each person would cook on their own.

Taelo thanked the ancients for having provided such a fine arrival to the beach.

Not long after Quiet Rabbit led the rest of the willow team in with their bundles of long willow limbs.

Quiet Rabbit pulled out several rabbits to add to the dinner. She praised the Willow team for having been so successful. She hoped that all their gathering trips were as bountiful as their first one.

Golden Hawk returned with a respectable amount of meat, but it was not up to the amount needed.

He announced that they would go up along the river and see if they could be as successful as the team gathering the willow.

The last group to arrive was pulling a very long dry pine. The rest of the team joined them on pulling it out onto the beach.

Talking Wren paced the two trees and announce they had almost enough dry wood to make the first raft.

The building group let out a moan as they recognized the additional work they needed to do.

Taelo said that he and Talking Wren would join them so that there would be additional muscle to help.

Little Otter laughed and added that the supervision of the dead log finding effort would be greatly improved.

This earned him a poke in the ribs from his mate.

823

Chapter 29: Of Salt, Clams and Sea Cows

The supply of salt was almost totally depleted. The team had not found another salt supply as they traveled, and they were almost out of it. Lily's and Floating Cloud's careful use of salt had made their original supply last.

Quiet Rabbit carried good news as she crossed back across the river to the beach location where the rafts were being built. She had taken time to go to see the salt production station that Whistling Arrow, Slow Walker, her grandmother Floating Cloud and Lily had set up

They had used the concept of the clay lined fire pits made for the sea going rafts and had made two salt making stations that kept the salt clean and sand free.

Each morning they would flood the pits with a thin layer of salt water that they brought up from the sea. They would then let the sun evaporate the water. After a handful of sun cycles, they were able to scrape up a bag of salt.

They had chosen the other side of the river because there was no beach and the salt making rings stayed sand free.

Quiet Rabbit shared the news with the rest of the team that the rafts would be launched with a supply of salt that would be sufficient for the last part of the journey.

The team all gave a cheer to the salt making team for taking the initiative to produce the salt that made the difference in how food tasted.

Taelo went a step farther and gave each of the salt makers one of his remaining sharks teeth.

Talking Wren shared the good news that all the dry timbers needed for the first layer of each raft had been found and pulled to the beach. Cutting them into the cross members onto which the next layer of green pine would be lashed was in full progress.

Talking Wren had learned from the first sea voyage that the binding in the water should be something other than leather. The leather expanded when wet and had to constantly be tightened. She recommend the use of willow bark strips. This was a significant change in the construction process.

Binding the first layer together was in full progress. The main binders were the children. They had the dexterity and nimble fingers that allowed them to put the required hand finger number of turns of the willow strips around the logs and then knotting them at the top.

Golden Hawk, somewhat by default, became the inspector of the completed bound logs. He was actually responsible for selecting and getting the next layer of logs cut to the length needed for each raft. He was asked by one of the children for help in tying the top knot and from that point forward he was constantly interacting with all the children.

Talking Wren jokingly gave him guff for trying to take over her inspection role.

Each sun cycle as the evening meal was about to be served Taelo, Quiet Rabbit, Golden Hawk and Busy Bee would walk along the beach to unwind and discuss the events of the day.

Quiet Rabbit was walking out in about knee high water when she stepped on something that made her fall. Soaking wet and ready to get angry, she picked up the object that turned out to be a large, long, black clam. Already wet, she walked out a little farther and felt several more. She began picking them up with her feet and throwing them up on the beach.

This got the other three to join her and soon the beach was covered with black clams.

Black Wolf came out to see what they were doing. He let out a whoop and ran back to tell the rest of the team.

The entire team came out and joined in on harvesting black clams.

Soon the clams were being carried back and piled up near the cooking ring.

The last meal of the day was postponed, and the team spent the time gathering clams until the sun hit the horizon.

Taelo called a halt and got everyone back to the camp. He asked for everyone to have their meal and then afterward they would all take the clams out of their shells.

Lily set up hot water bags into which the clams were to be dropped so they would open. Then they could be removed from their shell. The body of the clam would then be put into holding bags. The holding bags would be either cooked and then dried or the clams would be put out on rocks to dry in the sun. Lily said she would take the ones to be dried across the river to where the salt making pits were located. But getting the clams dried in the sun would mean that someone needed to keep the hungry birds from eating all the clams.

Taelo agreed and said that he would send a couple of the team to set up a shelter for the person who was to camp on that side.

The lights of the ancestors filled the dark sky as the team continued to clean clams. Their ambitious harvest was a great add for the critically needed food, but they also needed to get some sleep to renew their energy and be able to work the next sun cycle.

Lily volunteered to finish the processing and sent the rest of the team to get some sleep.

The next morning Taelo sent a few team members to set up a camp for two people. He had again recognized the need to always have two people together for safety reasons.

The camp was up against the cliff and out of the direct wind but there was a constant breeze that kept the camp comfortable.

Whistling Arrow and Slow Walker volunteered to be the ones guarding the clams. The two moved their sleeping hides to that side of the river.

Lily and Floating Cloud kept the supply of clams growing by taking time after the morning meal to gather more clams. They gathered only the amount they could process before the late meal preparation needed to begin. Each sun cycle a fresh supply crossed over the river for drying. There would be an ample supply of dried clam meat for the crossing.

Slow Walker was walking the rocky beach to stretch his legs when he spotted a large crayfish shaped animal among the rocks. He found and caught a large lobster. He carefully carried it back to the camp and showed it to Whistling Arrow.

The two of them waded out and realized that the area was full of the lobster. They decided to begin harvesting them and getting the tails cooked.

After sharing their find with Lily and Floating Cloud they began in earnest to gather and boil the tails. It was cold enough that they put several lobster tails into bags and let them freeze. Once the tails were frozen they put the frozen tails into larger holding baskets.

They were weaving the holding baskets from the young willow trees that had the bark stripped off to be used as binding. They split the young trees lengthwise and made baby finger thick material that they then wove into baskets. The young green trees were very flexible and when they needed sharp turns they were put into warm water and then bent into the turn that was needed.

The meat supply was now made up mainly of clams and lobster tails. Red meat was now in the second position and fish in the third.

Then a few sun cycles later, Whistling Arrow noticed a large animal floating out in the water. It was not a shark, but it was very large and moved slowly among the large boulders out in the water. He let Slow Walker know that he was swimming to one of the large boulders in front of the camp.

He swam out with his spear.

He found it very hard to get on the boulder and ended up using his spear to help him get on it. He sat at the top and looked out around in the water.

There was a gathering of five of the animals. They had flat front snouts and seemed to be eating the moss and seaweed on the bottom. He stood very still and watched as they approached the boulder.

He was excited as they came up to the boulder.

He selected one of the smaller members of the pod. It was the smallest but still as large as a buffalo. He waited patiently as the pod made their way around the boulder. When the one he had selected got into position he plunged his spear straight down. He was able to drive the spear all the way through just behind the head. He knew he had been lucky to kill it immediately. The rest of the pod swam away.

He called to Slow Runner to bring a rope so they could pull the animal to shore.

Together they were able to pull it to the shallow water, but it was so large that they knew that they would need several people to help them to get it out of the water and processed.

Slow Runner went across the river and let the team know about the large animal that they had brought to shore.

Sharp Knife and Single Leaf volunteered to help get it to shore. Meadow Flower and Marigold volunteered to skin and begin the processing of the meat.

It took all six of them to pull the animal up onto the rocky shore.

The animal proved to have about a finger thick layer of fat similar to the fat on a whale. The flesh below it was a light pink in color.

Lily cooked several pieces and declared that it was a delicious tasting meat. She prepared it for the teams last meal so everyone would have a chance to sample it.

Taelo congratulated Whistling Arrow on being the person that had bagged the most meat for the team. It yielded the equivalent amount of meat as that from a large buffalo.

He was now confident that the team would have sufficient food to make the next crossing.

Now he and the team had to concentrate on finishing the rafts.

He knew that his Sky Eye friends who had been helping get the rafts built had a long trip back. It would all be on foot since there were no rivers running in the direction they would travel. He planned to send them off with as much food as they could carry.

He and Golden Hawk would go on one more hunt and see if they could return with the food that would top off the food needed for their trip.

Chapter 30: Seaworthy Rafts

𝒯aelo listened as Talking Wren instructed her team to split the three spear length pine trunk into three long sections. She was leading the construction of the side guide sections for the rafts. These would be positioned on each side of the raft. Their function was to keep the raft going in the direction that the person using the steering paddle was aiming the raft.

Little Otter was guiding the construction of the barrier for the front of the raft intended to keep the waves from washing over the deck. Talking Wren had changed the design so that the barrier leaned forward and pushed the water downward and outward away from the front of the raft. The barrier frame was made from the willow trees that had been harvested and then covered in hide.

It was soon clear that they would need more willow trees. The binding of the raft logs and the use of the willow for a variety of construction had quickly depleted the original harvest.

This time Taelo sent a team of six to gather the willow. They were to also hunt for the frogs and for large fish.

The willow gathering was a fruitful venture. Three very large fish were speared and there were enough frogs bagged that every team member got four. Taelo made sure that the Others got extra. He was aware that they always needed significantly more food to maintain themselves.

The side guide sections got built, the bow sections were constructed and the main decks for each raft was complete.

Taelo decided that the next sun cycle the rafts would be pushed into the water. They needed to be in the water to do the remainder of the work.

Talking Wren was supervising the launch of each raft. She had assigned the team members to pulling locations along each side of the raft. She had positioned Burley Bear, Saber Scar, Sharp Blade, and Little Otter to push at the back of the raft. They were to use stout poles to use as pushing levers.

She had smooth round logs put under the front of the raft.

It took all the strength the team had and the use of four of the strongest members using leveraging poles at the back of the rafts to move the raft forward.

Getting the raft movement started turned out to be a bigger effort than anyone had anticipated.

It seemed to grudgingly move forward. It seemed as if it was trying to hold on to the beach.

Finally, the front log was rolling, the raft slowly moved into the water. The back of the raft hit the sand on the beach, and it would have stopped but Talking Wren shouted for the side pullers to pull with all their strength.

The raft grudgingly and slowly moved the rest of the way into the water and finally floated free.

Talking Wren had the team move the raft into the position she wanted and then she had three team members drop the boulder off the front of the raft. The boulder had a long line attached that was tied to the front of the raft.

She had two similar sized boulders in the water at the back near the beach and ropes attached to them were tied to the back of the raft.

The sun was past its zenith, halfway to the horizon.

Taelo called for a break so the team could eat and then discuss what might make the next launch easier.

He also let the team know that they would attempt to launch the next raft on the next sun cycle.

The rest of this sun cycle should be used to relax. He knew that everyone had used a tremendous amount of their energy to get the first raft into the water.

He listened as Black Wolf suggested that the rolling log should be positioned as farther back under the raft as possible by lifting the front of the raft with the poles to be used in the back.

Taelo asked the team what they thought of the suggestion. There was support for trying it.

Yellow Flower commented that the strongest people were using the poles in the back but when the raft started to move, the poles were no longer useful, and the four strongest people were left standing and looking. She suggested that there be a pulling rope for them to grab and help move the raft into the water.

Lily showed her approval by picking up a lobster tail in each hand and presenting one to Black Wolf and one to Yellow Flower.

Taelo thanked Yellow Flower who had a beaming smile and was pulling the lobster meat from the tail.

The ideas were put into action on the next sun cycle.

They were able to launch both rafts by the time the sun was halfway past its zenith. The two ideas had made a significant difference.

Taelo made a point of again congratulating both Yellow Flower and Black Wolf for their ideas at that sun cycles late meal.

The remaining work of getting the two side floats put on each raft, constructing the sleep shelters, mounting the side guides, and setting up the center pole to mount their sail went forward in rapid order.

It was three sun cycles later, as the red sun began its descent into the far horizon, when Taelo and Talking Wren completed the inspection of each of the rafts.

They declared them ready to go to sea.

During the last meal of that sun cycle, Talking Wren announced that the rafts were ready to be sailed out for their sea test.

Taelo assigned the crew for each raft and said that they would take their rafts out and then bring them back.

They would take each raft out one at a time. He and Talking Wren would ride each raft to see how it handled. Once the raft was back to shore, the people assigned to that raft were to load the firewood, the food, the cooking rings, and their own personal possessions. Everything should get covered, tied down, and ready to sail.

The cooking rings were smaller and of better construction than the ones that had been used on their first set of sea going rafts. Lily and Floating Cloud had improved them by making them from the river clay that was a mixture of clay, sand, and small pebbles. They had formed the cooking fire rings on top of firewood and then covered them with additional firewood. They then ignited the wood. They kept the fires burning throughout the night.

The next sun cycle they washed the ash off and made sure their fire rings were solid and functional.

Taelo complemented them on having improved the fire ring. Their design made it easier to use on the rafts. He pointed out that on good days it could be moved to the front of the rafts and on stormy ones it could be moved to the back of the raft.

The sleeping shelters had also been improved. Each shelter could sleep six adults and four children. The floor was a hand height above the raft surface and had a cover that kept the cold air out. Body heat would keep the shelter comfortable even during the coldest of days. The back facing opening could be left open by putting the bottom cross pole into Y shaped holders or the bottom pole could be bound to the wall corner posts and entry was through a center overlap of two hides that were the opening cover.

The food was stacked up just behind the shelters and in front of where the person using the guide paddle stood. This put the food in a protected area and provided the guide paddle person some protection from any blowing snow or rain.

The two vertical side guides could be lowered and tied in place once the rafts were in deep enough water.

The two long poles with the floats out on the end were also adjustable. Talking Wren made the point that the two long poles would be adjusted to optimize their support based on the wave shape and action

Taelo inspected each raft. He was pleased with the work the team had done and was confident that the rafts would make it across to the far shore.

He had each raft team spend the night on their raft.

He let them know that they would depart on the rising of the sun.

Chapter 31: Broken Spear the Homebound Sea

Broken Spear was fascinated by the fact that he now had to be up in the middle of the night to fly with the eagle and see Taelo and his team as the sun made its way across the sky.

His two helpers had also adjusted their schedule and would have food available at different periods of the night. They would let him sleep during their sun cycle and when he awoke they would take him for a ride on the mount.

The Clan also took his new cycle into account and remained quiet in the area where he slept.

Broken Spear found it quite pleasant to sit in the hot water pool in the dark and look out at the countless points of light that he thought of as the Ancestors.

The ancestors had laughed at him when he had mentioned that to them. They pointed out that there were more points of light in the dark sky then their ever had been people of any kind. None the less he took comfort in his way of thinking about the twinkling lights in the dark sky.

His new hours also lent themselves to a deeper inner self inspection. He felt invigorated in flying with the eagle but each time he felt exhausted as if he had been powering the wings keeping them gliding so smoothly through the air.

Now that Taelo and the team were on land, the eagle flew almost every sun cycle to see what Taelo and his team were doing.

He was surprised that his two helpers thanked him for describing what he was seeing. He had not realized that he had started to vocalize his thoughts. The two rewarded him with a honey drink as he flew with the eagle. He now returned from his flights and had more energy.

On this flight the eagle was silent, and its glide was effortless. The up draft let it slowly glide toward the far mountains and then it would take a wide graceful turn and return to a position behind the team.

Broken Spear easily distinguished the different members of the team. He was astounded by the sharp vision that the eagle possessed.

Taelo, Burley Bear and the tall black leader all were easy to distinguish. The team was now in full winter cover, and it was hard to tell who was who but Feather-in-the-Wind stood out because she was always out on the edge of the team with her sling. She constantly put rabbits into her holding bag.

Broken Spear figured the other two figures using their slings were Quiet Rabbit and Busy Bee. Periodically Single Leaf made her presence known. She seemed to ignore rabbits, but she was always at hand when a small boar or ground hog made the mistake of being in range of her sling.

The black warriors formed a protective edge to the teams travel. It was clear that they had become an integral part of the team.

Broken Spear let out a deep breath as the eagle called it a day and changed its course as a small river came into view. The sun was close to the horizon. The eagle took a turn and returned to where the team was setting up camp and then it seemed to eject him from its mind.

Broken Spear opened his eyes and took in the small fire illuminating the area where he sat. He smiled as he was handed some honey drink and a small, salted piece of buffalo meat.

On his next flight the eagle coasted silently watching as Feather-in-the-Wind and Quiet Rabbit left camp and set a fast pace toward the mountains. Two black warriors followed but soon they were falling farther and farther back. It was evident to Broken Spear that the pace was more than they could handle.

He gave a chuckle. They must have said something to offend either Feather-in-the-Wind or Quiet Rabbit who were setting a very brisk pace.

They gave the warriors a break but then continued the same jogging pace. They approached the mountains and went toward the glacier and then as they got closer they went away from the glacier along the mountains. They arrived at a river. From his height Broken Spear could see that cut through to the other side of the mountains.

Suddenly the eagle let out a cry.

Broken Spear then saw the largest two dire wolves he had ever seen. From above they looked like massive black animals almost the size of a buffalo.

He was amazed as Quiet Rabbit and Feather-in-the-Wind stepped forward and with their slings pelted the wolves with their slings.

He at first thought they had lost their minds.

He watched Lasher go out to one side and Bold Walker go out to the right.

Suddenly the two dire wolves charged.

Quiet Rabbit and Feather-in-the-Wind took side steps away from each other, stepped back and when the wolves seemed about to hit them, they both placed their spears into the wolves mouths and planted the butt of their spears into the ground.

Broken Spear gave a cheer as he watched Lasher and Bold Walker each clamp down on the throats of the dire wolves.

The two black warriors rushed forward and hit each wolf with their war clubs.

He knew the wolves were dead when Lasher let go of the dire wolf's throat.

Quiet Rabbit and Feather-in-the-Wind both got down on their knees and gave their wolves a hug.

Then as the eagle cried, they looked up and each gave the sign of friend and danced around with each other.

The eagle circled long enough for Broken Spear to see that the wolves were so heavy that it took the warriors, the wolves, Quiet Rabbit, and Feather-in-the-Wind working together to pull the travois. Each travois had only one dire wolf on it.

When Broken Spear opened his eyes. His two companions let him know that he had shouted and cheered as he watched the dire wolves die. They laughed with him when he said that he felt that he had participated in the hunt. He knew that his heart had raced and that he felt lightheaded.

He comment that he had only had a few flights with the eagle that matched the excitement that he had just experienced.

He thanked them for the food and suggested that they all chat for while so that he could decompress and maybe get some sleep. He did not want to see those dire wolves in his sleep.

The next several flights with the eagle were short. The team was building three rafts. These Broken Spear could see were much simpler and quicker to build. He noted that there would be no cooking on the rafts and no shelter. He saw that the loads would be on a platform so they would keep dry.

The eagle flew high above and gave a loud cry as the rafts all took to the water. He saw that the children were all standing around the edges of the rafts with spears at the ready apparently looking for fish.

Lasher, Arrow, and Bold Walker each sitting at the front of their rafts made it clear that Taelo was on the lead raft and Feather-in-the-Wind and Running Stag on the second raft.

The eagle stayed briefly with the rafts for several sun cycles. Broken Spear was with it when the rafts cleared the mountains and then turned and headed away from the direction Taelo wanted to travel.

He watched as they dismantled the rafts. It was clear that the travois poles had served as part of each raft. The travois were loaded and the remaining timber from the rafts were piled on a rock base. It would be there if anyone came that way and needed poles.

Broken Spear knew that it was Taelo's desire not to waste useful resources.

The travois journey continued once again heading toward the horizon where the morning sun would crest.

Then a strange river running in the opposite direction that Broken Spear had ever experienced.

The eagle turned to follow it and gave a loud cry as it did.

Taelo and several of the team pointed to the eagle and the team turned to follow the river. It flowed between the glacier in a wide green valley. From the air it was clear that the glacier was much lower in height and seemed to end at the far horizon.

The next surprise was the smoke rising from a rather large village. Broken Spear thought the construction of the lodges resembled the top of a beaver's den.

The next surprise was that the people were very light in color. He thought that if their color was any lighter they would be white.

The village leader and a rather large number of fighters came out of the village as Taelo, and his team approached.

Taelo organized his team into fighting diamonds and then walked forward with Golden Hawk and Burley Bear. Taelo put his open hand up to indicated friend and continued to slowly approach the much larger and taller leader.

Broken Spear could see one fighter standing next to the leader. It was clear that he was pointing at Taelo and several of the other team members and speaking to the leader.

The leader nodded and stepped forward and raised his hand to indicate that he accepted Taelo's sign of friendship.

He pointed at the eagle flapped his two arms and then patted his chest. Broken Spear smiled as he learned the name of the leader was Flying Eagle.

Then he watched as Taelo pointed at the Eagle and made his hand into a claw and acted as if to strike.

A smile came across the leaders face.

The fighter came to the side of the leader and continued to talk to him. It was clear that this person had information about Taelo that he felt needed to be shared.

Then Quiet Rabbit, Busy Bee, Meadow Flower, Talking Wren, and Feather-in-the-Wind all walked forward with their slings in one hand and their other hand raised in friendship.

Quiet Rabbit walked up to the fighter and put her hand on his face and then lifted her sling and patted her chest and then in the language of the person in front of her said, "friend." This caused a looked of surprise.

Then the entire team repeated the word "friend."

The leader raised his hand and responded and then indicated that the team should follow him back into the village.

The eagle let out a cry, flew a circle around the village, and then went back upriver.

Broken Spear was once again in the dark of his cave. He now knew that people came in all colors from almost white to almost black. He wondered if there were any other colors. As he contemplated the colors of animals, he felt that he had now seen the range.

Broken Spear flew a few more sun cycles with the eagle and then he saw that the black warriors were leaving.

He saw the exchange of gifts between Taelo's team and the black warriors. Each of the black warriors were given a vest that Broken Spear was sure was made of the hide of the dire wolves. He could see that the vests were designed to be open in front and had three straps that had wolf teeth on the end of the tie that went across the chest and into a slit on the other side.

The warriors responded by giving one of their spare black wood spears to each of Taelo's team members.

Then to Broken Spear's surprise he could hear the Black Warrior's give a loud cry "Vriende" which meant friends and Taelo's team replied.

The warrior's turned and followed their leader. They were now using the travois to carry their possessions. Taelo and Team stood on the hill and watched as the warriors reached the horizon then they let out the black warrior's friendship call and followed it with Taelo's call of "friends."

From on high, Broken Spear saw both teams and knew that true friendship had been reached between them.

The eagle gave its call and then turned to go upriver, and Broken Spear was back in the dark of his cave.

It seemed only a few sun cycles later that Taelo and his team departed from the village.

They followed four Sky Eyed warriors and what Broken Spear took to be their mates and their children from the village. The trek was now across a grassy plateau, and he could see that the glacier slowly ended near the horizon.

Golden Spear could see that the glacier slowly sloped down and then stopped.

Then after several sun cycles the team came to a river where they once again built rafts.

Broke Spear marveled at the fact that the trees were bent and knurled, and the rafts ended up looking like floating brush. However, the load was high above the water.

It was clear that the most comfortable place to be, was on top of the load. The river was swift, and the rafts sped along. Even at the good speed the rafts were making more than a moon cycle passed before the river bent slightly lower along the horizon.

It appeared as if the team was going to leave the river to go in a upward direction.

The sun had just broken the horizon and Taelo was at the riverbank when the eagle gave a cry and flew down along the river.

Broken Spear could see far down the river and knew that the eagle wanted Taelo to stay to the river.

The eagle flew until he could see the vast sea then Broken Spear was once again back in the dark of his cave.

He thought back about the trip to the sea and knew that Taelo would soon reach it and then rafts to cross it would need to be built.

It was almost a moon cycle of time before Taelo, and the steam made it to the sea. The rafts were pulled up onto the small beach and the camp set up along the edge of the forest.

Broken Spear marveled at how the team seemed to work together and contribute to the progress of getting the rafts built. He saw that even the children had a vital part of getting the rafts built.

Then he watched as the team tried to move the first raft into the water. They were all pulling on ropes and Burley Bear, Saber Scar, Sharp Blade were using strong poles to leverage the back forward.

It was clear that they were all straining to get the raft to move.

Just as the sun was threatening to go below the horizon, he saw the raft float free of the beach.

The eagle was back at the next sun rise and it was clear that the team had figured out how to get the rafts into the water in a new manner. They had the other two rafts floating free before the sun reached its zenith.

The eagle followed each raft out to sea. Broken Spear could see land across the water was close at hand and he figured that the water was not that of the sea that Taelo would cross.

He watched as Talking Wren set up long poles out to the sides of the raft with wood floats on the end. She adjusted the length of the poles to balance the rafts. He then watched as she placed a long flat piece down into the water on each side of the raft. He planned to ask her later what they were for.

Each raft went out and then returned to the beach, Broken Spear watched and learned how the square hide was used to capture the wind and move the raft. He was again amazed at what the team had learned to do. It reminded Broken Spear about the time he had watched the fish swim into Taelo's fish trap and not be able to get out.

Then he watched as the rafts were loaded. He noted that the cooking ring was carried on to the raft by two people and wondered what it was made of.

He saw that the hutch for the people to sleep in and where they could get out of the weather was raised to keep the inside dry.

The front of the raft had a protective barrier that was designed to keep the water from washing over the floor of the raft.

Broken Spear wished he could experience being on the raft.

Several flights later the eagle flew out toward where the ice bridge would be.

Broken Spear was flying with it almost a moon cycle later when the looming height of the ice bridge came into sight. It rose into the sky far above the eagle.

The rafts stopped their journey towards the ice bridge and turned toward the horizon where the sun had arisen.

The eagle then landed on the front of the lead raft.

Broken Spear watched as Taelo came forward with a large piece of meat on the end of his spear and gave it to the eagle.

He heard Taelo say in the language of the Others, "We will be at your cave soon and then we can celebrate and talk about all the things you have seen."

This time when he opened his eyes, Broken Spear was smiling, and he realized that he had been granted a part of his wish. He had been on the raft.

He was now looking forward to the arrival of Taelo and the rest of his team. He would make sure that they would have the best reception that he could arrange.

Chapter 32: The Northern Glacier Seen from the Sea

The few white fluffy clouds glowed yellow as the sun broke the horizon. Burley Bear was on the guide paddle as Taelo hoisted the square sail and turned it, so the wind contributed power to the four team members using their poles to push the raft out to deeper water.

The wind caught and soon the rafts were moving single file along a relatively calm sea. Taelo sailed out toward the rising sun until he caught sight of mountains rising on the far horizon. He then knew that they were in an inner sea of substantial size but not the one that would take them to the shore of their homeland. He had the rafts turn so the rising sun was to their right.

Five sun cycles later the waves grew in size. Taelo knew that the land toward the rising sun was ending.

Talking Wren now adjusted the long float poles to stabilize the way the rafts crossed the waves. She took in the float on the top wave side and put the float on the trough side of the wave out farther so it would touch the bottom sooner. The two floats worked to keep the raft stably on the wave for long periods of time. The ride was faster and smoother.

Talking Wren instructed her float teams on the other rafts and soon all three rafts were riding the same wave.

Taelo knew their first goal was to reach the massive glacier that made up the ice bridge that marked the end of their journey. His goal was to sail his rafts into the harbor found by his mother and where he had made the giant fish trap.

Life on the rafts took on a restful, repeatable casual cycle.

The only work was to guide the raft, adjust the sail and to cook the meals.

Fishing was not as fruitful as had been anticipated. The team on the second raft speared a shark but that was the extent of fish being caught. Black Wolf, Red Fox and Aristosa found a variety of activities and seemed to entertain themselves well. Black Wolf especially liked to work with Lily to get the cooking done. Aristosa was determined to get a shark and Red Fox was interested in helping guide the raft.

Burley Bear was pleased to have someone asking to be allowed to guide the raft.

Taelo and Quite Rabbit spent much of their time on her travel hide. She was going over all the places that they had been and adding the details that she had previously not had time to sketch.

He wished the three rafts could get closer and be able to trade passengers. He planned to get the rafts together when they reached the glacier.

Reaching the glacier took longer than anyone anticipated. It was clear to Taelo that the river that had given the team a fast ride to the sea had also taken them significantly farther away from the glacier than they had anticipated

Then ahead glowing red, purple and grey in the last rays of the sun was a wall that rose as far as the eye could see. The sky beyond was just turning grey and a few Ancients were sparkling in the sky.

Taelo signaled the sails to be lowered and the rafts brought together.

Talking Wren guided each of the back rafts to bring their front in alongside of the raft in front until the long out pole reached close to the back of the raft in front.

Taelo watched as she got all the rafts bound together. The last raft became the raft to steer the entire group.

He was pleased with how stable the three rafts move forward together.

Lily set up the lead raft to serve them all the last meal of the day.

Talking Wren adjusted the floats and the three rafts seemed to ride the wave in a smooth flow.

Taelo got everyone to share their experiences on their rafts.

Every member gave Talking Wren credit for having figured out how to make the rafts sail much better than the first long crossing that they had. So far the ride had been smooth. They all hoped that the rest of the journey would be as pleasant.

Taelo and Talking Wren took the time the rafts were together to inspect and make sure that all the fastening's were holding.

They found several that needed reinforcement and Talking Wren followed up to get the fixes done.

The rafts were now sailing toward the direction of the rising sun with the wall of ice within sight.

To his surprise an eagle landed on the front barrier of his raft.

He put a large piece of the sea cow meat on the end of his spear and gave it to the eagle as he thanked it for its guidance. He also let Broken Spear know that the team would soon be at the cave of the Others.

A handful of sun cycles later, the sea began to get rough. Taelo had the rafts separate and assume their original formation.

Once again, Talking Wren had her teams adjust the outer floats to stabilize each raft.

It seemed as if after the floats were adjusted, the sky turned black, and the sea began to churn, and the waves increased in intensity.

Taelo had everything securely tied down. The sleeping area now became the area that everyone occupied. He and Burley Bear took short turns at the long guide paddle.

The cooking ring was small enough to be inside the living area. It now began to serve as a source of heat as well as the place to cook.

Taelo was sitting and getting his hands warmed when the water rushed through the floor of the sleeping area. He jumped up and rushed out to make sure Burley Bear was still handling the guide paddle.

He found Burley Bear totally soaked. The ice was already starting to form on the coat he was wearing.

He sent Burley Bear in to change and assumed the guide paddle. He saw that Burley Bear had tied the sail down and they were just riding the waves.

He noted that the floats were keeping the raft from rolling over. One float was skimming the bottom of the wave and the other was holding to the higher surface.

The waves were at least twice the sized that they had so far experienced. He also felt that they were moving faster than before.

His coat kept him comfortable. It was one that Quiet Rabbit had made from the northern buffalo that they had hunted on their last journey. He had put on the wooden slit eye covering. It helped keep the saltwater spray out of his eyes.

It was impossible to see where they were going. He opted to keep the raft going slightly toward his right. He did not want to accidently guide his raft into the glacier.

They had set up oil soaked torches to mount on the back of the two lead rafts to help keep the rafts together.

The weather did not let up for a long period of time. Taelo figured it was at least six sun cycles, but it had been hard to keep track because night was only slightly darker than the day.

Taelo was on the guide paddle when the sun broke the horizon. The sea was still rough, and the glacier was not in sight.

He turned the front of the raft back toward where he knew they would find the glacier.

Two sun cycles later, he saw not the glacier but mountains.

He knew it was time to bring the rafts together again and to have a group celebration.

He could hear the cheer from the other two rafts as he signaled for them to get together.

Chapter 33: Home Harbor

*O*nce he had the rafts together, he asked Lily to organize a celebration feast. He pointed to the mountains and then he pointed to the rock that had traveled with him and went around it with his finger and let everyone know that they had traveled around to the land that was their home.

He once again had everyone tell how they had fared since they had last all been tied together. Every one of the guide paddle holders commented on the fact that they had no way to know where they were going except for the light from the torch on the back of the raft in front of them.

They would periodically panicked when the torch in front went out.

Taelo recalled that during the worst of the storm he and Burley Bear were constantly having to get another torch fired up when they fell off a wave and the next wave would wash over the raft and extinguish the torch. He and Burley Bear fought to stay on a wave as long as possible because every time they fell into the trough between the waves they would plow into the next wave and have it flow over them.

The story telling was in full swing, the sun had yet to reach the far horizon when suddenly Aristosa began to scream for help. She was holding on to a rope that was tied to her spear. On the other end was a huge shark.

Taelo and Burley Bear both took hold of the line. Golden Hawk planted a spear vertically between two of the deck pines and tied the rope to it. Together they slowly pulled the shark closer to the raft. Saber Scar and Sharp Blade each speared the shark. When the shark was parallel with the raft, Slow Walker put a rope on the tail. He, Meadow Flower, and Marigold then pulled the shark part of the way onto the raft. Single Leave was standing by with a war hammer in her hand. She commented that she was going to take on Marigold's role of making sure the monster they were pulling on board would quickly be dead.

This brought a laugh out of Marigold and most of the team.

The team then used some of the spare timber to make a triangle stand to hoist the shark up. The skinning and processing went quickly.

Taelo complemented Aristosa on her catch of the biggest shark that he could remember.

Burley Bear commented that he had been with Taelo when he had caught and killed one as big. He then went on to share that Taelo had given everyone a shark tooth reward because they had all helped in the building of the fish trap where Taelo had caught the shark.

Taelo observed Burley Bear and Meadow Flower take Aristosa aside and talk to her.

Later the shark teeth were given to her.

The story telling resumed and the eating now included some freshly grilled shark meat.

Aristosa stood up and told her story of trying to catch a fish. The one she had speared was the first fish she had ever caught. She thanked everyone for helping bringing it up on the raft.

She then reached into her bag of sharks teeth and walked up to each of her friends and gave them a large tooth that was about the size of her hand and then two smaller ones.

She then went up to each of the adults and gave them a sharks tooth.

She made a point of giving one to Taelo and saying that she now understood why he was a hero to the Others.

To Burley Bear and Meadow Flower, she gave the largest ones.

Taelo complemented her and said that as a reward for her generosity she would be at the guide rudder when they reached their home harbor.

The rafts once again remained tied together as they sailed down the coast. The sails were up, and the current was steady.

They almost missed the harbor, but Burley Bear recognized the beach where he had chased after Red Oak when he had tried to steal the meat from him.

Taelo had the rafts split up and assume their normal sailing position. He had Aristosa join him. Burley Bear and Meadow Flower were each standing on one side. Aristosa had the guide paddle.

Taelo gave her the instruction to guide the raft as close to the huge headstone boulder that was on one side of the harbor. The long spit on the other side formed the arm that seemed to circle the huge boulder.

The raft sailed up onto the beach.

Taelo took Aristosa by the hand and had her step off first. He gave a huge shout that they had made it around the world.

Everyone was jubilant and cheering.

Lasher gave a howl as he jumped to shore and led the two other wolves on a run around the beach area and the lodge that was still there and in good shape.

They did not land on a deserted beach. The salt makers were there shouting a welcome and helping everyone come on shore.

Taelo knew that Red Oak and Quiet Pheasant would want them to come to the Valley of Plenty. He instead planned to take the entire team directly to the cave of the Others. He would invited Red Oak and Quiet Pheasant to attend as well.

Talking Wren, Little Otter, Busy Bee, and Golden Hawk all went to get some mounts from the Elk Clan in the Valley of Plenty.

The mounts and a large handful of helpers arrived soon after.

Taelo and Talking Wren supervised getting the rafts up on the sand and having small boulders put under them to keep the rafts off the sand.

Then a small caravan proceeded to go up the coast toward the cave of the Others.

Red Oak and Quiet Pheasant and the other parents of Taelo's team members were all accompanying the team.

They knew that Taelo would be greeted and treated to an long celebration.

Broken Spear had sent them all invitations.

Taelo was not surprised when he saw White Swan and Grey Fox Running standing next to Broken Spear as the entire team came up the beach to where the cave of the Others was located.

He had led a journey that he had dreamt about and had returned as proof that the land he lived on was like one huge circular rock. It had been a journey that he knew was monumental and he had thought it would be his last but now he had two more journey's in mind.

The three rafts would be used one more time on the next journey and then he would build three more for the other sea and make a similar journey there

The End

Taelo: Journey of Sages

Dedicated:

To the Wise people providing guidance to all of us around them.

Taelo: Journey of Sages

Chapter 1: Mural on the Wall

Taelo and Golden Hawk and the rest of their family were in the valley of the Northern Elk Clan. Several moons had passed since the completion of their last adventure. The rushing sound of the water falling past the opening filled the cave with the constant but pleasant sound of water rushing past the cave opening. This was the leadership cave that the two of them had found when they first entered the valley many moon cycles ago. The drawings on the walls verified the stories that they had been told, as young children, by their parents and grandparents. The valley was the very first place that their Elk Clan ancestors had settled when they arrived from the other side of the ice bridge.

The cave was high on a cliff behind a thundering waterfall with water that as it fell on its long journey to the lake below, spread out into a mist. The sun shining through the waterfall illuminated the cave with shimmering light. It provided little heat, but it made for a cheerful atmosphere.

They were all staying in the cave while the record of the Journey of Circumvention was transferred from Quiet Rabbit's and Busy Bee's travel hide to a mural on the wall. It was a story that she wanted to add to the history of the Elk Clan. He glanced at the story of each of the journeys that they had all taken.

There was their first Journey down to the south where they encountered people that had come before the Elk Clan.

There was the rescue of the new people coming in from the north.

There was the battle against the cannibals that followed after he had rescued Lily and Running Stag.

There was the Journey of Discovery when they had found the mount and had reached the other sea. They showed him jumping from a high cliff into the sea below to save Golden Hawk.

The journey north that they now referred to as the Dangerous Passage depicted the crossing of the Ice Bridge, the battle with the Sky eyes and his near death when his sled fell through the ice covering when they crossed back across the ice bridge.

The scene of the Condor Clan Slingers defeating the Warrior Clan was one of his favorites.

The air flowed in a controlled manner from the partially open entrance and was pulled out by the flow of water passing by the cave opening behind the waterfall.

The warmth was provided by the hot spring water that was directed by a hollow wooden log to where it rained down into a shallow pool in the center of the cave.

Their three children, Red Fox, Black Wolf, and Yellow Flower were frolicking under the hot rain shower. Their voices added a light personal warmth to the cave.

The three of them had been on the Journey of Circumvention and would react each time a new scene was etched on the wall by Quiet Rabbit or Busy Bee. Their reactions to and description of each scene added a richness to the drawings that were being rendered.

Taelo and Golden Hawk relaxed by the fire pit and watched. They marveled at the fact that they had circumvented the world. They now knew it was round, like the stone that Taelo had used to explain the concept of the journey.

Everyone but Golden Hawk had initially thought that the idea was crazy, but Taelo had persevered and then had been supported by Broken Spear who said that he had received direction from the Ancients to support the effort. Broken Spear had affirmed the idea and had selected the members of the Others who went on the journey.

Quiet Rabbit and Busy Bee had at first been skeptical but knowing their mates, they had given them their supported. Once on the journey, they had captured key events with drawings on a large buffalo hide. Now they were transferring the drawings onto a wall mural.

Taelo and Golden Hawk relived each step as the pictures were drawn on the wall mural. They laughed as they recalled the first time Taelo had shared the journey with a large group. At a dinner gathering of the Others, Taelo had shared his vision of the journey and had received a thunderous approval for telling the best story of the evening. Burley Bear had complimented Taelo for besting him in good story telling.

The next morning Broken Spear, seer of the Others, shared that the Ancients had advised him that the journey should be guided by the point where the sun rose each morning.

Broken Spear had then introduced the six members of the Others that would make the journey. They were Saber Scar, Marigold, Single Leaf, Sharp Blade, Burley Bear and Meadow Flower.

Burley Bear was as surprised as Taelo when he heard his name called. He then apologized for having thought Taelo was only telling a superb story the evening before.

Taelo was surprised but had been pleased that Burley Bear would be part of the team.

The final membership of the team had included Feather-in-the-Wind, Running Stag, and their daughter Neiva. Later they were joined by Bold Walker, her brother who had surprised them when they arrived at the Paradise Elk camp.

They traveled the same path, to the far sea, that they had taken on their Journey of Discovery. There they built and sailed across the sea on three rafts.

On the other side the team had met the Black warriors. They had made friends and together they had continued the journey until they met the Sky Eyes.

On the Dangerous Passage Journey, Taelo and team had bested a rogue band of Sky Eye warriors in battle. This time they met and made friends with the main Sky Eye Clan. They met some of the warriors that they had defeated in battle. One warrior and his family became their escorts to the next sea. He shared how he had been amazed by the skill with which Taelo and his greatly outnumbered team had easily defeated the Sky Eyed fighters. The defeat had been the first for the rogue Sky Eyes and had marked the end of their rogue adventure.

This meeting was friendly, and they all enjoyed the hospitality of the Sky Eye Clan. Then their black warrior friends announced their return to the land from which they had ventured. The parting of their good friends was a bittersweet moment.

As each step of the journey went up on the cave wall, Taelo and Golden Hawk recalled their memories and shared what they had learned from each event.

The three children had exited from the pool and were now helping with coloring in the figures being drawn by their mothers.

The transfer drawings of the Circumvention Journey took almost a full moon cycle. During this time, Taelo and Golden Hawk took care of the children. The three children had participated in the Journey of Circumvention and had matured beyond the age of most children their age.

They were easy to care for and they loved to hunt. This worked out well and each morning the five of them and Lasher would leave the cave and hunt for that days food. The surrounding mountains were covered with a thick layer of snow and the tall pines protruded up through the snow like porcupine needles. Taelo and Golden Hawk sunk into the deep snow. They envied the fact that the three children, wearing snowshoes, were able to scurry along on top of the snow.

Lasher had a hopping technique that kept him moving along the top layer of snow. Lasher was always ready to go out on the hunt each morning and then when they returned to the cave he would lay down and watch everyone.

When they returned, they would cook the zenith meal and make sure there was enough for the late meal.

Red Fox, Black Wolf and Yellow Flower enjoyed spending time reviewing the drawings as they were sketched. They discussed each event. They got involved in detailing some of the sketches and shared their memories of the journey.

Taelo commented that their participation putting up the wall mural added a depth and a different perspective to the journey.

One afternoon, Yellow Flower asked what the next adventure would be.

Taelo replied that they should all discuss how they could get the Sages of the three clans to participate in the next adventure. It would need to be an adventure that was very different from all the rest.

Red Fox asked what "Sages" meant.

After a brief moment of thinking, Taelo said that Broken Speer was as an example of a Sage. He then added White Swan, Grey Fox Running and Red Oak and Quiet Pheasant as additional examples.

Yellow Flower pointed out that Broken Spear was unable to walk without assistance.

Taelo agreed and asked how they would be able to go on an adventure that Broken Spear could also go on.

Everything went quiet. The only sound in the cave was the sound of falling water as it swished by the opening of the cave. Even Quiet Rabbit and Busy Bee had stopped to hear what Taelo's reply would be.

Taelo took in the mounting anticipation. He had shared his idea with Golden Hawk and now asked him how the older people could participate in the *Journey of Sages*.

Golden Hawk smiled and nodded. He then stood up and dramatically walked to the opening behind the falling water. He then turned and walked slowly back to the center of the cave.

Taelo listened as Golden Hawk pointed to the murals on the wall and made the point that Broken Spear would not have been able to make any of the journeys. The journey that he could make would require a way for him to travel in comfort and yet be able to see the wonders of nature and the world around him.

He looked at the three children and asked if they could think of a way that such a way could be arranged.

Once again the only sound was that of the waterfall.

Busy Bee finally said that she wanted to get back to the mural and she had no idea how such a journey could be achieved and would someone please tell her.

Golden Hawk nodded and said that he had felt the same way when Taelo had put the question to him. He looked at Taelo and told him that he should share the next journey with everyone.

Taelo then stood and took the same walk that Golden Hawk had taken. He turned and said that he was thinking beyond just Broken Spear and was including his two attendants, Chirping Swallow, and Sly Squirrel. He was also including White Swan, Grey Fox Running, Red Oak, Quiet Pheasant, Brave Deer, Little Pebble, Floating Cloud, Whistling Arrow, Wise Council, Golden Flower, , Quiet Fox, Little Doe, Lily, Whistling Arrow, Saber Scar, and Marigold.

He waited for a moment and then said that the next journey he was thinking about would utilize one of the rafts and the journey would be to ride the sea down the coast until the waters of the sea turned, took them across and brought them up the other side.

Quiet Rabbit asked why Saber Scar and Marigold were included in the list of names.

Taelo replied that he had include the two because he felt he would need their strength with guiding the raft and they were the ones that did not have other responsibilities.

Busy Bee commented that she would volunteer to do the cooking that would free Floating Cloud and Whistling arrow from having to go.

Taelo nodded. He said that he was sure that Floating Cloud would want to go because she was close friends of both White Swan and Quiet Pheasant, and she would have two grandchildren on the raft as well.

Black Wolf asked how long the journey would take.

Taelo replied that he was not sure, but they should plan on it taking at least as long as the Circumvention Journey.

Red Fox then asked if they would stop anywhere or would they stay on the raft the whole time.

Taelo responded by saying they would stop when they needed to replenish the food and cooking wood supply. He also wanted to stop at the point where he could take everyone to the top of the mountain where they would see the sun rise on one sea and go down on the other sea.

The final stop as they went down was when they reached the land of the Condor. There he hoped to take them all up to the Condor Clan Village and then up to see the condor nest.

Yellow Flower asked if they would be able to see the cave of the frozen princesses.

Taelo replied that he was not sure whether that was allowed but he was sure they would go and see the nest of the giant bird, the giant Condor.

Quiet Rabbit asked about what was planned for the other side of the sea.

Taelo replied that on the far side he wanted to see if they could find the cove where they had built the rafts that were now on the beach. He felt that would be an unique place to stop and renew the raft and give everyone a break. He added that there would at least be other stops to replenish the food supply.

Busy Bee looked at Quiet Rabbit and said that they had to get done with their mural quickly or they might get left behind.

Taelo laughed and said that he couldn't leave until his mural makers prepared the next hide on which to capture the upcoming journey.

Taelo was looking forward to sharing his next journey idea. He had no idea how popular it would be with those he planned to engage.

Chapter 2: The sharing of the Journey of Sages

Taelo and Golden Hawk rolled the cave door stone so that the entrance to the cave was sealed. The sky was the grey before the full morning arrived but a bright yellow streak outlining the edges of the mountains let them know that the sun would soon appear.

Taelo knew that crossing the length of the valley before the sun disappeared below the mountains on the other side of the valley was a challenge. There had been no snow when they came to the cave, so they had crossed on foot. Now he wished they had a sled and wolves to pull them swiftly across, but they were on foot.

The travel pace was set by the three children who were accompanied by their mothers. Taelo and Golden Hawk brought up the rear. They watched as periodically someone would use their sling to slay a rabbit that had made the mistake of being nearby.

Each time Lasher would retrieve the rabbit and bring it to Quiet Rabbit who then passed it back to Taelo to carry.

When the sun reached its zenith Busy Bee gave each person something to eat but they continued to walk across the valley.

Once again Taelo watched as the children, on their snowshoes, shuffled easily along the top of the snow, Quiet Rabbit and Busy Bee sank slightly, he and Golden Hawk had to raise their feet as high as possible to make each step. Even then they would sink down and have to fight their way forward.

Lasher hopped along and kept up with the children.

Taelo watched the sun as it slowly kissed the tops of the mountains and began beaming its last rays as if it was signaling the moon. He knew that they would make the last part of the trip across the valley to the lodge in the dark. To ensure they stayed together, he would tie everyone together with a rope and lead the way.

He talked to Lasher as he tied the rope to him and asked him to take them to the lodge.

He recalled the last time he had asked Lasher to do the same thing. It was the time that he, Golden Hawk, Burley Bear and Little Otter had rescued Semper and Wan and their clan from where they had been trapped in the snow. He had stayed behind with twenty of their younger members and was caught by a blizzard as he led them back on foot. He had tied them all together and had led them until he could no longer see the way.

They were all saved by Lasher's return and his ability to find the way back to the lodge.

This time it was not desperation, he could see the dim glimmers of lights from the lodges firepit.

The barking of the wolves announced their arrival. They were greeted by Grey Fox Running and a group of younger warriors all carrying their spears.

Taelo appreciated the fact that the lodge was in the defense mode and made sure to identify himself as he followed Lasher up the slope toward the lodge.

They were all escorted inside where White Swan gave each of them a hug. The surprise was that Red Oak and Quiet Pheasant had arrived the previous night and had planned to go up to the cave on the following day.

Their arrival turned the evening into a family gathering and they all sat around the central fire and enjoyed a variety of grilled meats and vegetables.

Once the mural on the cave wall was explained by Busy Bee and Quiet Rabbit who spread their hide out so everyone could view the scenes as they described them, the discussion turned to what the next journey might be.

Red Oak commented that Taelo and Golden Hawk had led journeys to the north, to the east, to the south. He asked where they would go next.

Yellow Flower got excited and jumped up and said that she knew, and she would tell them. Taelo looked around and said that a young storyteller was about to share the story of the next journey.

Taelo listened as Yellow Flower explained the trip and how it would accommodate all the Sages in the Northern Elk Clan, the Clan of Others, and the Valley of Plenty Elk Clan. She gave a small laugh and then explained that Sage was a nice word for everyone who was past being young.

Taelo spoke up to clarify that the journey was planned so Broken Spear could participate. He went on to say that the "Sages" were the wise leaders of the three Clans. He did not want to offend those that he was trying to honor.

Yellow Flower then continued to describe how they would ride on a raft on the current of the sea. They would stop whenever they needed to hunt but what she was looking forward to was the first stop where they would go to the to the top of a volcano and watch the sun rise on one sea and then set on the other sea.

Then they would again ride the raft until they came to the land of the Condor where they would visit the Condor Clan village.

She looked at Quiet Rabbit and Busy Bee and once again asked if they would be able to go to the cave of the frozen princesses. They both replied that they were not sure that it would be allowed but they were sure they would go past the cave opening when they went up to see the nest of the great Condor.

Yellow Flower then said that she knew that they would also visit the place where the raft had been built but that was all she knew.

Taelo complimented her on remembering all the details. He then looked around and asked if there were any questions.

Grey Fox Running asked if Taelo had a list of Sages.

Taelo looked around the room and then named White Swan and Grey Fox Running.

He looked at Golden Hawk and asked him for two names. He named Red Oak and Quiet Pheasant.

He looked at Quiet Rabbit and ask for her to name two Sages. She named Floating Cloud and Whistling Arrow.

He then asked Busy Bee to name her two Sages. She named Little Pebble and Brave Deer, her parents.

Taelo then went on to call out Lily and Slow Walker, Semper and Wan, Golden Flower, Wise Council and Wise Owl and his mate.

Lily smiled and replied that she was honored to be called a Sage, but she said that her council was to always cook a good meal.

Semper, Wan, Wise Council and Golden Flower all thanked Taelo for recognizing them as Sages but they preferred to stay and help run the Northern Elk Clan. They all commented that they had survived their own journey and preferred to enjoy their new home.

Taelo was pleased to hear White Swan thank them for staying in the valley and that she asked them to form a leadership team.

He looked around and asked if there were any Sages that may have been missed.

After moment he said that there were additional Sages in the Clan of Others and in the Valley of Plenty Elk Clan.

He let everyone know that he was going to go to the Clan of Others and that Golden Hawk and Busy Bee would go to the Valley of Plenty to identify the additional Sages.

Once they knew how many Sages would be on the raft and be a part of the Journey of Sages, the final preparations could be made.

Chapter 3: Broken Spear's Surprise

The Journey of Sages was eagerly accepted by the Northern Elk Clan members. Red Oak and Quiet Pheasant said that they were sure that the other Sages in the Valley of Plenty would have the same enthusiasm.

Taelo suggested that they coordinate the visit to the Others' cave and together share the concept. Taelo made the point that Broken Spear was one of the main considerations for his having thought of such a journey. Taelo had blocked the idea in his mind to keep it a secret from Broken Spear. He hoped to surprise him as he had never done before.

Broken Spear had periodically been on every journey as he flew in the mind of the eagle. He had confided to Taelo that he wished he had full use of his legs so that he could be physically a part of the journey. He was sure that being on such a journey in person would be an experience much more powerful than watching it from the view of an eagle.

Taelo planned to make sure that his wish would come true.

Golden Hawk and Busy Bee decided to make the trip back to the Valley of Plenty with Red Oak and Quiet Pheasant. They would stop at the cave of Others along with Taelo and Quiet Rabbit.

A few suns later, their two wolf drawn sleds left the Northern Elk Clan valley. They took their children with them and on their arrival at the cave of the Others they were greeted by Burley Bear and a small group of warriors.

Burley Bear said that Broken Spear had let him know of the arrival but had shared that there seemed to be a hidden reason why Taelo was coming.

Taelo chuckled and told Burley Bear that he had been blocking his mind because he wanted to surprise Broken Spear. He said he was sure it would surprise everyone.

Burley Bear nodded and then turned and led the way into the cave.

Once the sleds were put aside and the wolves fed, Taelo and Golden Hawk made their way to the heated pool where everyone was gathered.

Broken Spear was at the center of the gathering, joking with the children as he greeted them. He complimented them on being able to use his language.

During the Journey of Circumvention, the three had spent many hours conversing with the Others who were on the journey and all three were now fluent. They often drew a smile or laughter because some of the guttural sounds were hard for them to duplicate.

Taelo knelt down, gave Broken Spear a hug, and told him that he would open his mind if Broken Spear promised to arrange for an evening feast for the Clan.

This brought a cheer from everyone standing around.

Broken Spear laughed and said that he would comply so that he could find out the secret that Taelo had work so hard to keep from him.

The rest of the afternoon was spent enjoying the warm waters of the pool and in sharing stories.

Taelo continued to keep his mind blocked

The evening meal was served in the large open meeting area.

The entire clan was eagerly awaiting for Taelo to stand and share with them why he had come for a visit. The last time he had shared the story of the Circumvention. They had all laughed and pounded the ground thinking he had out done Burley Bear in storytelling. Even Burley Bear had taken it as a story until the next day when he was named by Broken Spear as one of the people going on the Journey of Circumvention.

Taelo took his time enjoying his meal. He then stood but instead of saying anything he signaled for Yellow Flower, Red Fox, and Black Wolf to join him. He knelt down and gave each a part of the story to share.

He then sat down next to Broken Spear.

Black Wolf led off and each of the three shared the concept of the Voyage of Sages in the language of the Others. They each put forward a name of one of the Sages in the clan of Others. One Sage was not mentioned.

At the end of their part, the three received a sustained ground slapping approval.

Taelo stood and said he had the name of the Sage that had been the inspiration for the journey. He turned and pointed at Broken Spear and asked whether he was ready to go on the Journey of Sages.

It was clear to all that for once Broken Spear was caught by surprise. He bent his head down for what seemed like an eternity. When he looked up it was clear he had tears in his eyes. All he could do was to nod in the affirmative. Then he bent his down again and wiped his eyes.

Taelo walked over and helped Broken Spear stand up. He held him and told the Clan of Others that Broken Spear had been his mentor and guide through many years and this time, he Taelo would be the guide that took Broken Spear on a journey in which he could participate.

The ground slapping was accompanied by a roar of the clan members. It went on until Taelo helped Broken Spear sit down.

Taelo sat down with Broken Spear and asked if he had been surprised.

It was clear to Taelo that he had. Broken Spear was still in shock and could not reply but only nodded.

The next morning Golden Hawk, Busy Bee and Yellow Flower departed to the Valley of Plenty. Yellow Flower commented that she had never seen anyone be as surprised as Broken Spear had been.

Taelo agreed and said that Broken Spear's reaction had been more than he had expected.

He spent the rest of the morning in conversation with Broken Spear who said that he had conversed with the Ancients when he found Taelo's mind closed to him. The Ancients told him that Taelo was not a Seer but sensed the essence of the environment and acted on those senses. He had the ability to block his mind from any outside linkages and he had the ability to send feelings of emotion.

Broken Spear asked if Taelo fully understood the powers of his mind.

Taelo replied that did not fully understand but that he knew that he could often influence others into taking the actions that he thought were the correct ones.

Broken Spear nodded and said that he often felt that he did not understand the gift the bear that had almost killed him had given him but that each day he took another step in trying to use the gift to make things around him better.

Taelo took a break and went on a short walk down into valley. On his return, Silver Arrow and Bending Willow, Burley Bear's parents, Broken Spear and his two attendants Chirping Swallow, Sly Squirrel and Quiet Fox and Little Doe parents of Meadow Flower and Marigold thanked Taelo for asking them to be part of the journey.

Taelo said that they were welcome and that he had two more names of the people he was inviting. He called out Saber Scar and Marigold.

Saber Scar almost knocked Taelo off his feet as he ran forward and gave Taelo a hug. He then asked why he and Marigold were being asked.

Taelo replied that he would need some strong hands at the raft guide paddle and then some strength in helping carry Broken Spear up the mountains. He joked that he would have chosen Single Leaf and Sharp Blade, but he had learned that Single Leaf would have a child in the spring. Marigold responded that she had been sad about not having a child yet but now she was ecstatic about being able to be on the next journey.

Everyone was curious what they could do to help in the preparation for the next journey.

Taelo let them know that he was going to ask Talking Wren to be in charge of refurbishing the raft that they would use. He was sure that she would be pleased to have some muscle power.

He also mentioned that they should take along the items they would take to the fall meeting of all the clans when they returned. They would be able to use it themselves and have them available as gifts.

The entire clan of Others saw him off and in a loud roar shouted, the "Golden Feather" a Sage for the ages.

This was the first time that Taelo had heard them do such a thing and he knew that he had earned a new level in the ranking of the Others.

He held up his spear with the Golden Feather that both he and Golden Hawk had been awarded by the leaders of the Elk Clan.

The Golden Feather designated both of them as members of all the Elk Clans and now he had been recognized by the Clan of Others.

Chapter 4: Raft Rebuild Plans

The twin snow covered mountains with their dark green skirt of sentinel pines came into view as Lasher led the wolve team around the bend. Taelo roused the three riding in the sled, and they let the cover down and joined him in enjoying the sight of the blue jewel of the lake nestled in the middle of a stand of pine, maple, and oak trees.

Taelo had decided to stop and take the two boys ice fishing at the lake that was nestled between the two mountains. He had carried the large cover that allowed him to use the sled to make a quick and easy shelter. He had food for the wolves, and he was sure that Quiet Rabbit would use her sling to garner a few rabbits to round out a meal of grilled buffalo meat. If luck held, he and the boys would add a couple of fish to the meal.

After setting up the camp he led the way out to the lake. By the time they were ready to go out and open a hole in the ice, Taelo saw that Quiet Rabbit already had the three rabbits he had hoped she would tag, and she was still walking slowly around the lake. Lasher had chosen to accompany her and had gathered the first rabbits.

Taelo took his war hammer and carefully broke the ice. He scooped out the chips of ice from the hole he was cutting through to the water. Taelo was glad that the ice was a full hand length thick. He felt it was safe to be out on the ice. He used small pieces of buffalo meat on the end of the bone hooks and then the three waited for the fish to find their lines. Each line was a different length, but all were closer to the bottom than the top. His was the closest to the top. He expected that longer lines to be closer to where the fish would congregate.

Black Wolf was the first to get a strike. Taelo had him keep the line tight and slowly back up. When he could see the fish. He lifted the line straight up the middle of the hole and threw the fish well away from the hole so Black Wolf could take care of it.

Just as he had thrown the fish, Red Fox cried out that he had one. Taelo repeated the process of pulling the fish from the hole and throwing it aside.

He walked over to his own line and slowly rolled it up on the stick that it was attached to.

He saw that Quiet Rabbit had made her way around the lake and that her catch bag was bulging.

He knew that two large bass and a bag full of rabbits would make a hearty late meal.

He watched as Black Wolf and Red Fox each scaled and gutted their fish and carried them to the cooking ring where Quiet Rabbit was lighting the fire.

He picked up the bag full of rabbits and walked to the edge of the camp and skinned and cleaned them. Quiet Rabbit had done well and had seven rabbits. He kept the hearts and livers of each. These would be salted and roasted over the fire as snacks as they waited for the fish and the rabbits to roast.

He followed Quiet Rabbit's lead and gave the roasted liver to Lasher but ate the heart. The boys followed suit but ate everything themselves.

The meal was delicious and afterwards they all sat wrapped up in a large hide and talked about the many spots of light up in the sky.

The next morning, they ate the remainder of the fish and the rabbit and then loaded everything and proceeded to the valley of the Northern Elk Clan.

As they approached the lodge, the gate opened, and he was able to guide the sled into the lodge gathering area. The door to the lodge opened and White Swan waved them in and said that the wolves would be tended to.

Taelo walked to the end of the team and released Lasher, gave him a treat, and then did the same for each of the wolves. He then went into the lodge with Lasher at his side.

He and Quiet Rabbit discussed how the refurbishing of the rafts would get done. They agreed that they should go to the Valley of Plenty and recruit Talking Wren to organize and manage the raft refurbishment.

A few sun cycles later the sled was loaded and ready to go when the call that an approaching sled with a huge person guiding it was coming full speed toward the lodge.

Taelo took one look and told the guard to open the gate. He knew by the size that it was Little Otter and the sled got closer Talking Wren stood up, lifted her red spear, and let out the teams war cry.

The sled came in full speed and almost hit the wall on the far side of the courtyard.

Taelo walked over and gave the two a hug. He asked what had brought the two to the Northern Elk Clan.

Talking Wren, in a super excited voice said that she had come to make sure that the Journey of Sages would have the best raft that could be built.

Taelo laughed and said that he was eager to hear what she had planned.

White Swan insisted that the first thing that they should all do was to decide what should be prepared for a celebration dinner.

Taelo laughed when Talking Wren said that dinner was secondary and what she had to share was monumental and really important.

Wan replied that breathing was the most important and eating was next. He said building a great raft was very important but could wait until after everyone was relaxed and ready to listen.

Taelo raised a flask of honey wine and passed it to Talking Wren and suggested that she think through how she would entertain everyone that evening. He again thanked her for her enthusiasm and said he was really looking forward to what she had to say.

After the dinner, the lodge filled up with all the members of the clan. The word was out that Talking Wren, the person who had laid out the Northern Elk Clan village and had designed each of the individual hutches with running water was going to be sharing her design of the raft to be used for the Journey of Sages. This was an event that all felt would be very interesting. Each family brought a snack to be shared with the other members.

White Swan introduced Talking Wren as her "daughter." This was an honor that she bestowed on Talking Wren.

Talking Wren was silent for a moment and then walked up to White Swan and gave her hug as she realized that she was being given one of the highest compliments possible.

Taelo raised his spear with the yellow feather and called out that he was ready for his "Sister" to share her design for the raft. The lodge then resounded with the slapping of hands on the floor.

Little Otter and the twins turned a stand across which a large hide was stretched. It had a series of drawings to show how the raft would be built.

Taelo scanned the different individual sketches and realized that it was not going to be a refurbishing effort but the creation of an entirely new raft design. He now had a better understanding of why Talking Wren was so excited. She had envisioned and sketched out a very much improved raft that appeared to be larger than the current ones.

Talking Wren began by explaining that the material of the three current rafts would be combined to make one larger and more stable one.

Taelo watched and listened closely as Talking Wren showed the diagram of a finished raft. He followed her explanation as she described how the raft would be lengthened and widened. It would be almost three times as long as the current ones and about twice as wide. She had added another set of out riggers and a third down fin for stability. The steering paddle was farther back and there were two square open areas to either side of the steering paddle. The paddle had been redesigned to have a shorter handle but a wider paddle area. The third stability fin was just in front of the steering paddle area.

Talking Wren then pointed to the front of the raft and highlighted the chest high raised front sloped wave deflector that now went back about a third of the way along each side of the raft. She pointed to a raised platform that she said was for Broken Spear to sit on and be able to look ahead. This got a round of ground slapping from everyone.

Taelo thanked her for thinking about Broken Spear.

Talking Wren replied that she knew why the Journey of Sages had been born and she was going to do her best to make it a success.

She then turned the focus to the living quarters. She pointed out that there was only one on the raft. She had designed it as an independent structure built in a similar fashion to the bent wooden hide covered hutches that were made for the land.

The structure was made of poles bent and secured to what appeared to be that of a bow but the string across the bow was another pole. The center of the bow was of the height of Burley Bear and the sleeping areas were divided into sections that would have hides hanging down to provide some privacy. The storage areas were along the outside edges of the lodge.

Talking Wren pointed out that the front and back of the lodge would have similar curved surfaces to the sides. This would provide the maximum protection from waves that might come over the raft.

The lodge would be similar to the back of a turtle in shape and strength.

Taelo asked where entrance to the lodge would be.

Talking Wren pointed to the left side and said that the entrance would be wide enough for Broken Spear to be carried in and that he had the center living area that had a sitting and sleeping area for him.

Removable bent poles to secure the opening was part of the design. Also, the floor made of smaller poles would be raised above the raft surface and be covered with buffalo hide. The hides on the lodge would have flaps that could be held open to control the temperature inside.

The entire structure would be made separately from the raft and then bound on to it.

Talking Wren pointed to the out riggers one located to the front of the lodge. The out riggers had a front to back off set from each other to provide a walk space between and through them.

She highlighted the two strengthening logs bound across the raft that allowed her to provide an easier way to adjust the length of the out-rigger location.

Her final feature was the new sail feature. She had enlarged the main sail and she had added a smaller sail toward the front of the raft.

The large sail would come up through the center of the lodge and had adjustments along each side of the raft. The front sail was of similar design and was located directly behind Broken Spear's sitting area.

When Talking Wren stopped, Taelo stood and praised the deep thinking that she had put into the rebuilding of the raft. He complemented her on having been able to do this so quickly.

Talking Wren replied that she had thought of these ideas as she rode the rafts on the Journey of Circumvention and that she had most of it sketched out before learning of the Journey of Sages and had only a few modifications to add.

White Swan offered that the Northern Elk Clan would provide all the help Talking Wren needed.

Talking Wren said she would need many helpers and pointed out that the children had previously participated by doing the gathering of willows and then binding the logs with the willow strips. They would be needed again. She said she was sure to need the muscle power of the Others and she would need people to gather the poles and making the amount of the rope that would be needed.

She commented that Busy Bee had volunteered to organize those who wanted to help, and that Golden Hawk had volunteered to inspect the bindings.

She ended by saying that everyone was welcome to participate. It would take the help of all three clans to accomplish what she had in mind in the time she had in mind.

Chapter 5: Rebuild Site

The snow was still holding its own against a slowly warming spring. Taelo and family arrived at the beach with Lasher leading the dog sled. They all got out and Taelo realized that the three rafts had been moved. He scanned the beach area trying to locate the rafts. Then he located several piles of logs sorted by length. It became clear that Talking Wren had dismantled the rafts as she prepared to build the new one. He then realized that Talking Wren was building everything from scratch.

A few moments later Little Otter and several helpers led his fully grown buffalo that was pulling a log longer than all the ones on the beach to where several stones had been strategically positioned. He and his helpers positioned the log on top of two flat stones. The thin end of the long log pointed toward the bay.

Taelo then saw that there were stones positioned to each side of the one that Little Otter had used. It became clear to him that the new logs would be at least twice as long as the longest ones of the old raft.

Little Otter came over and greeted them and then excused himself and said that he had more logs of similar length to pull to the beach,

Not long after Talking Wren arrived from the other side of the hill. She was followed by six helpers that were leading mounts loaded with long willow tree trunks that were about two fingers in thickness.

She came over and thanked Red Fox and Black Wolf for coming early and said that when the second long log was pulled into place, her team of bark strippers would keep them supplied with willow bark binding strips so they could bind the first two logs together. She said that her goal was to have the seven long central logs bound by the time the sun went down.

She then planned to use the poles from the previous rafts to continue building the main deck of the raft.

She let Quiet Rabbit know that the lodge on the beach was ready to be occupied. She pointed to the smaller hutch that had been Quiet Rabbit and Floating Cloud's original home and said that it had new hide covering and was also available.

She pointed to additional hutches that had been prepared to house the volunteers coming from the Northern Elk Clan and those coming from the Clan of Others.

Quiet Rabbit thanked her and complimented her on the amount of work already accomplished.

Talking Wren in turn complimented Busy Bee for having organized and assigned a small army of volunteers to dismantle the rafts and to do the other work that was now very visible. She pointed to the mounts coming over the hill into the beach area and said that they were carrying the hides that would be used in making the covering of the raft lodge. Construction on it would begin as soon as she had the raft assembly underway.

Taelo volunteered to manage the assembly, but Talking Wren said that Golden Hawk would be doing that. She asked if he would manage the construction of the raft lodge.

Taelo readily agreed and followed Talking Wren to the lodge. There he was shown the details of how the raft lodge was to be constructed. Talking Wren had a step-by-step approach to its assembly and specific binding instructions. She insisted on triple binding of the bent sections to each other and triple binding to the entire structure to the floor.

She commented that the raft lodge would take the most pounding in a storm. It had to be able to withstand the impact of huge waves. It would be the protection for all the Sages.

Taelo had learned the depth of Talking Wren's mind over the many moons that he had now know her. He was always amazed at her ability to visualize the problem that she was trying to solve and then solving it in a manner that often was beyond imagination.

He asked where on the beach she wanted the raft lodge to be built.

He followed Talking Wren to the beach where she said she would have stones positioned alongside the raft. It would be built so that the final two raft logs would be under the lodge.

Taelo understood the concept. The lodge would be heavy so having its edge over the raft would allow it to be pulled and pushed across and required the minimum lifting.

Red Fox and Black Wolf were already binding the first raft logs together when Golden Hawk and Yellow Flower arrived. He greeted everyone and then looked at the bindings that had already been done. He complemented the two. Yellow Flower joined in on doing the bindings. It was clear that the three were keeping well ahead of the logs being brought in by Little Otter and his team.

Taelo greeted him and asked where Busy Bee happened to be. Golden Hawk said that Busy Bee sent her greetings and that she would be up after the next sun cycle. She had organized the effort to dry the buffalo meat that would be taken with them on the journey and was making sure all the volunteers knew what she wanted.

Golden Hawk pointed to his personal lodge and offered it to Taelo and Quiet Rabbit. He and Busy Bee planned to return to the Valley of Plenty each evening.

Taelo thanked him and said he accepted. He knew that Floating Cloud and Whistling Arrow would prefer her old lodge.

The following Sun cycle Taelo greeted the helpers from the north that were led in by White Swan. She was accompanied by the members of the Others.

Taelo greet them and let them know that the work was going on full speed, and they would all be worn out by the time the sun set.

The number of folks doing the binding more than tripled. More weeping willows were gathered and Taelo was able to accelerate the building of the raft's lodge.

Taelo watched as Talking Wren made her rounds and inspected the quality of the work. He was pleased that the workers working on the raft lodge receive her praise for the good work getting done. After only three sun cycles they were ready to finish the lodge by putting on the hides.

He agreed with Talking Wren that the lodge should be on the raft before the hides were put on. He reassigned his workers to help with the raft construction.

The use of the mounts and the muscle power of the Others accelerated the construction significantly. Binding the logs together became the barrier.

He had some of his team build the two sail masts and put on the rigging. Two holes were dug on the beach, and the masts were set vertically, and the rigging and sails were set and tried out. Red Fox, Black Wolf, Yellow Flower, and Spear Tip each had a role in handling of the sails. Taelo was able to work with them and soon they were able to maneuver the sails.

After three hands of sun cycles the raft was complete and the raft's lodge was pulled onto the raft. Binding it to the raft took a full sun cycle.

Taelo walked around the raft and took in the space it provided. He felt a great appreciation for Talking Wren's design. He was now anxious to see how the raft would handle out on the sea.

Talking Wren supervised the mounting of the two sail masts and the construction of the new center stability panel. The new steering paddle was of a vertical design like the stability panels, but it was shorter and pivoted like the gate that Burley Bear had designed.

Taelo looked over the design and realized that it would still take significant muscle power, but he felt it would be a more effective way of controlling the raft.

Busy Bee and Quiet Rabbit supervised putting on the hides to cover the raft lodge.

Meanwhile Talking Wren had a group put together Broken Spear's sitting area at the front of the raft and also the one inside the lodge.

Taelo stood at the front of the raft and realized that the barrier to keep the waves from flowing over the raft was chest high and went back a third of the way on each side. He took the initiative to have poles put in all the way around the raft and then connected with leather rope.

He was thinking of the time Yellow Flower had fallen off the raft and had to be saved from the shark she had speared.

The rope barrier would help in preventing someone from falling from the raft.

The sun was setting when Talking Wren declared the raft was ready for its sea trial. She declared she had sent a runner to let Broken Spear know that the "Raft of Sages" would take its maiden voyage as soon as he arrived.

Taelo hoped that Broken Spear was as anxious as he to try out the raft at sea.

Chapter 6: Launch

It was the morning of the third sun cycle after the raft was completed when from the top of the Head Rock the team saw a caravan of Others coming toward them. Broken Spear was in the lead and by the numbers following him Taelo wondered if anyone was still back in the cave of the Others.

Burley Bear had brought the teams portable cover and supervised getting it up so those arriving would have a place out of the weather. It took the Others most of the morning to set up their camp.

Taelo greeted them and invited the leaders to enjoy the zenith meal up on the Head Rock. Once the camp was set up Burley Bear led Broken Spear's mount up the slope to the top of the Head Rock.

Taelo had a large cooking bag with a hot seaside stew ready. Quiet Rabbit and Busy Bee dished out the stew and also offered honey roasted buffalo and rabbit meat.

Broken Spear had a seat with his back to the beach so he could easily look out across the harbor and to the far horizon.

Talking Wren let everyone know that the raft would be pushed and pulled into the water early the following sun cycle. The first passengers would consist of all the Sages plus her team who would inspect and evaluate the raft's performance.

Then for the next five sun cycles the raft would go out with anyone who wanted to experience the ride. This would give her a chance to see how the raft handled at different times and hopefully different conditions.

White Swan said that she would send a runner to the Northern Elk clan and let them know about the raft ride.

Red Oak said that five sun cycles would not be enough time to take out all the clan members that would want to experience the raft ride. He suggested that the amount of time should be based on how many of the clan members wanted go out on the raft.

After a brief round of discussion, Taelo agreed that it would be a great experience for all the clan members and it would be a good way for he, Golden Hawk, Saber Scar and Marigold to learn how to handle the raft. Taelo pointed out that Black Wolf, Red Fox, and Yellow Flower would also get good experience in how to handle the sails.

He had just finished getting agreement when he looked up the beach and saw a team of wolves pulling a sled down the beach toward them. The Spear tied to the sled handle signaled that was Feather-in-the-Wind racing toward the Head Rock. She let out the team's war cry and guided her sled up the slope to the top of the Head Rock.

She, Running Stag and Nieva ran forward and gave everyone a hug.

Running Stag introduced the fourth person that had arrived with them as Running Brook, Nieva's grandniece who had come to Paradise to visit. Her visit was her reward for being the fastest runner in the Condor Clan Village.

Feather-in-the-Wind said that Golden Flower and Wise Council had sent a runner to Paradise with the Journey of Sages information, and she had immediately packed and come to wish everyone a good journey.

Upon learning of the raft excursions that everyone would be taking, Feather-in-the-Wind negotiated the same experience for the Paradise Elk Clan, but it would occur when the Journey of Sages was over.

The discussion continued until the sun slowly sank into the far horizon. Broken Spear commented that it had been a wonderful day and he was looking forward to watching the raft pushed into the water.

Taelo suggested that they all get a good night's sleep. He mentioned that Talking Wren and her crew were going to perform a small sunrise miracle when they removed the stones on which the raft had been built. He commented that it seemed to be an impossible task and he was very interested and planned to be out early to see how she planned to do it.

Talking Wren explained that each stone holding up the raft had a rope tied to it. She pointed to the numerous ropes that came out to each side of the raft. She explained that the four tall posts currently leaning inward on top of the raft witch were positioned in deep holes. A rope was tied from the top of each pole to the far side of the raft. Two ropes from the top of each pole would be attached to two mounts that were positioned to pull the pole upright. There were four short posts positioned to keep the raft from being pulled sideward. This would cause the far side of the raft to lift. As soon as the raft lifted a few fingers off the rocks, they would be pulled out. Each rock had two people assigned to do the pulling. and a rope was tied to each pole.

She pointed at Taelo and said that he had taught her how to use leverage when he had used the mounts to set up the super heavy covering that Burley Bear and the Others had just set up on the beach.

Taelo commented that it was an ingenious way to get the raft off the stones on which it was built and that he was glad to have thought of it.

This got a laugh from everyone.

They all proceeded down from the Head Rock.

On the following sunrise, Talking Wren had her small army of helpers ready to take the stones out from under the raft.

She signaled the lifting to begin. The ropes sang as they strained as the mounts slowly pulled the raft up. The stones were rapidly pulled out and the raft was lowered.

She then directed the set up to tilt the raft the opposite way. One side of the raft was now on the sand and the posts to keep it from sliding were positioned vertically along the side of the raft. The tall pole attachment was done, and the mounts tilted the raft in the opposite direction. The stones were pulled out and the raft lowered.

The raft was at the edge of the water sitting on the sand.

A cheer went up and Talking Wren gave a sweeping hand gesture to include all her helpers.

Talking Wren announced that the rest of the sun cycle would be spent on removing the rocks from the beach and filling in the holes that had been dug for the tall poles.

She announce that the sea launch would be on the following sunrise.

White Swan announced that the Northern Elk Clan would host the evening dinner at the top of the Head Rock for all the leaders and they would provide the same dinner to everyone else in the Main Lodge. She thanked Quiet Pheasant and Red Oak for providing the buffalo meat.

The next morning Burley Bear was at the head of the raft with a team of Others.

Talking Wren had recruited all the young men of the Others to help lift the front of the raft so that logs that would serve as rollers could be positioned under it.

Burley Bear, Saber Scar, and Sharp Blade were at the head raft and the rest of the young men of the Others were to each side. Burley Bear gave the command to lift, and the front of the raft came up almost an arm's length.

Everyone on the beach repeated Taelo's war cry when the raft was lifted. It was a feat that only the strength of the Others made possible.

The rolling transport logs were pulled under the raft by Talking Wren's crew and then Burley Bear gave the lower command, and the front of the raft was sitting on the logs.

Taelo had Red Fox and Black Wolf reward each of the Other's with a large shark tooth as he publicly thanked them for doing what no one else could.

He presented several to Talking Wren and said that she was making the Voyage of Sages possible. She held up her shark teeth and held up her red spear and gave the team's battle cry.

He and Talking Wren walked to the front of the raft. He lifted a sack filled with Honey and took a sip then handed it to Talking Wren who took a sip.

She turned to the people on the beach and said that she was naming the raft the Journey of Sages and poured some of the wine on the barge. She then turned and walked to the edge of the water and poured the rest into the sea as she asked it to protect the Journey of Sages.

The roar from the beach was deafening. It continued until everyone saw that Talking Wren was talking to her team.

She was instructing them to attach the mounts and pull the raft into the water. The raft rolled over the logs and with a large splash floated outward. The mounts then had to pull hard in the opposite direction to keep it from continuing its journey.

Talking Wren's team jumped on the raft and with poles turned it, so the bow was up on the beach. Ropes attached to two large boulders were then tied to the front of the raft.

Taelo once again let out his war cry.

High in the sky an Eagle echoed the cry.

On the ground, Lasher let out a howl.

Talking Wren waved to the crowd and then instructed her team to mount the side floats on the frame mounted on the raft. The frame was halfway back from the front of the raft, but they were off set from the front so that there was a walkway between them. This arrangement allowed the floats to be a bit longer and the frame stronger. She had made the frame waist high so it would be easier to adjust the length of the float arms. She had the team set the floats as close to the raft as possible. The length would be optimized on the first trial run.

Talking Wren then had the front mast brought on board and secured about three spears lengths back from the front. It was just behind Broken Spears sitting platform.

The frame for the mast was shaped to have four legs that were wide at the bottom and fit the mast at the frame's top. Both the mast and the stabilizing frame were thoroughly secured to the raft logs. The sail tie down pins were located along the edge of the raft. There were enough pins so that the sail could be turned to almost parallel from front to back of the raft.

The large mast was two thirds of the way back and was more difficult to erect because it went through the raft's lodge. Otherwise, it had the same arrangement as the front mast. A key difference was that the main mast stabilizing frame was large enough that it would serve as a storage area inside the lodge.

Taelo got on board and took a walk around the nearly finished raft. It still needed the covering hides and the safety ropes but otherwise it was done.

He led Talking Wren to the front of the raft and once again thanked her for the beautiful raft.

Golden Hawk handed him a spear that they had carved together. The spear tip was a huge shark's tooth, and the feathers tied just below it were blue. A small Wren that had blue waves coming from its beak was carved just below the feathers and below it were three rafts each larger than the one above.

Talking Wren had tears in her eyes as she held up her spear as the watchers on the beach let out Taelo's war cry.

The sun was now nearing the horizon. The raft was ready for its first sea trial.

Burley Bear announced that the dinner that evening would be hosted by the Clan of Others and that Broken Spear would tell one of his stories from the Top of the Head Rock.

Chapter 7: Sea Trial

Taelo had worked with Talking Wren to identify who would be the raft's sea trial crew. Red Fox, Black Wolf, Yellow Flower, and Spear Tip would be on board to learn how to handle the sails. Quiet Rabbit and Busy Bee would be shown how to adjust the side stabilizers. Saber Scar, Golden Hawk, Marigold, and he would be on board to learn how to guide the raft.

Talking Wren had a crew that would be on board to help and make any adjustments that might be required.

Before leaving the harbor, Talking Wren had the hides stretched over the front wave barrier to evaluate how it would perform.

Taelo looked up to the Head Rock and saw that Broken Spear and his two helpers were sitting and watching the preparation work. Broken Spear had shared that he was anxious to experience riding out to sea.

Taelo had responded that he wanted to hear the same enthusiasm when they had all been riding the raft for several moons.

He turned his attention back to the raft as Talking Wren had her helpers pushed the raft out into the harbor. Taelo noted that there was just enough room in front of the front water barrier for the four that pushed the raft away from shore to jump on. They then used some long poles that were attached on the side of the wave barrier and pushed the raft so that the front turned as it went farther into the harbor. Once the raft had turned two pushers went down each side and pushed the raft out toward the open sea.

Once the raft was just beyond the upper arm, Talking Wren had the front sail turned to catch the wind blowing toward the shore and the raft began moving up the coast against the current.

He and Golden Hawk had lowered the middle stabilizer while Saber Scar and Marigold held the guide paddle handle that they pulled toward the shore side.

The raft picked up some speed, but it was slowly being blown in towards the shore.

When the raft had cleared the tip of the upper arm of the harbor, Talking Wren instructed the front sail to be pivoted and that the paddle be pulled to the other side. The raft slowly turned and began to move toward the tip of the harbor spit, but it was clearly heading out to sea.

She moved the sail handlers to the larger sail and had them raise it and set the same angle as the front sail. The large sail filled, and the sail boom lines went taunt. The raft picked up speed as it began to meet the incoming waves.

Talking Wren then worked with her crew to adjust the length of the side poles holding the stabilizing floats. She pointed to an incoming wave and made the point that she wanted the stabilizer that would meet the wave first to just be at the bottom of the wave the raft was riding while the top stabilizer should be skimming close to the top of the wave they were riding. Busy Bee and Quiet Rabbit nodded their heads to indicate they understood.

Talking Wren then had Saber Scar and the four sail handlers coordinate the next turn. This time Yellow Flower and Red Fox were to handle the front sail and Black Wolf and Spear Tip were to handle the large sail. She instructed Saber Scar to give the turn command and slowly move his guide paddle while the sails were turned.

The raft slowly turned and began sailing back up the coast. Talking Wren instructed the team to hold the course until they were well past the opening of the bay and then change the sail and the guide paddle again in the opposite direction but this time the main sail was to be lowered and only the front sail would be used.

Taelo noted that the raft slowed, and the movement inward could be easily controlled.

Talking Wren pointed to a boulder at the very back of the raft that had a long rope tied to it. She asked that on her command Golden Hawk and Taelo were to push the rock off the raft and make sure the rope was smoothly fed out.

They were to slow the raft down as it came to the beach and stop it with just the tip touching the sand.

She instructed two of her team to jump to shore and secure the two front ropes to the large boulders that had been strategically placed.

She said that the next time the raft went out it would be pulled out instead of being pushed off the shore.

A loud cheer came from the top of the Head Rock where a large group had gathered.

Taelo arranged for the team of Sages to come aboard. This time Talking Wren's helpers stayed on shore, but she accompanied the Sages.

Taelo and Golden Hawk took the guide paddle and Saber Scar and Marigold pulled them out to the anchor stone. Their grunts told Taelo that he and Golden Hawk might not be able to raise the anchor stone.

The ride out and back was smooth, and this time Red Fox and Black Wolf tied the raft off to the stones on the beach.

There was time for one more run. Talking Wren wanted to see how the raft would handle with it loaded to maximum capacity, so she had five double handful of people come onto the raft. There was standing room only.

Saber Scar and Marigold had the steering paddle and he and Golden Hawk were the ones to pull up the anchor rock. They were both grunting, and their arm muscles were straining as they slowly raised the stone.

Taelo almost stopped pulling when he looked at Golden Hawks face turning purple. They managed to get the boulder onto the raft and they both sat down laughing. Golden Hawk pointed to Taelo and said that his face had turned a deep purple. This made Taelo laugh as he let Golden Hawk know that the same had happened to his face.

The sail handlers had some difficulty working around the people on the raft. The out riggers needed to be extended. The raft handle more sluggishly but it did well otherwise.

Taelo and Golden Hawk were both laughing when they re-entered the harbor and they pushed the boulder in. They then let Saber Scar and Marigold know that the two of them would be the official boulder raisers. He and Golden Hawk were the official boulder droppers.

That brought out a laugh from both of them and they said they were pleased to have an official role in operating the raft.

The raft now began giving everyone rides.

Feather-in-the-Wind was the next to get on board. She had arranged that she and Nieva, would handle the front sail and that Running Stag and Running Brook would handle the large sail. She arranged for Black Wolf to help Running Brook.

The arrangement did not escape Quiet Rabbit watchful eye and she wondered if a close friendship was forming.

Burley Bear and Meadow Flower would handle the guide paddle and coordinate the sails. Single Leaf and Sharp Blade volunteered to lift the anchor boulder.

Taelo watched as Talking Wren and Little Otter counted the number of riders. Since no supplies were yet on the raft and the hides for the lodge were not on, the raft could take extra passengers. Taking full loads gave Talking Wren the opportunity to see how it would handle.

Five Sun Cycles later everyone that wanted to experience riding the raft had gotten a ride.

Talking Wren then had her crew put the hides on the lodge.

The loading of supplies would be the next part of the preparation

Chapter 8: Departure

Taelo watched as Talking Wren supervised the loading of the raft.

The portable cooking ring was placed just behind the raft's lodge. It had an opening into the lodge that could be closed so the cooking smoke would not enter the lodge. The fire ring had sides that could be rolled up during good weather. The roof had an adjustable opening to allow the smoke to rise. The cooking ring had a small oven to one side to be used for firing pottery and could also be used to prepare various dishes.

Taelo was impressed with the design and the practicality of the cooking area. He liked the fact that it was just in front of the steering paddle area.

The wood for the fire was positioned along both sides of the raft. It stretched from the back to where the front wave guards ended. It was stacked to about chest height.

The food supplies to be used first was positioned alongside the wood stacks. The rest of the food was placed inside the lodge. It took up the space around the mast and all the spaces where the sides came down to the deck.

Talking Wren surprised Taelo when she had a wave and rain barrier positioned in front of the guide paddle area It could be left open, but it had hides that could cover the entire structure. This he knew would provide protection during severe storms.

The raft building came to an end on the third sun setting cycle.

A departure dinner hosted by the Valley of Plenty Elk Clan had been in the making during this time.

After the dinner, Red Oak announced that Talking Wren had been selected by all the leaders to guide the Elk Clan during his absence. Those "Sages" that had chosen to stay were now on the council of elders and would provide any advice and guidance that she would need.

Taelo congratulated Talking Wren and put the feather of an Eagle on her spear.

The eagle cry from above caused all to look up and then a loud cheer reverberated from the cliff walls. The eagle seemed to respond and made a low pass over the beach and then disappeared over the top edge of the cliff.

The cooking rings on the beach were surrounded by members from all three clans. The festivity continued well into the dark and the sky was emblazoned by the countless bright points of the light that they all considered the lights to be the Ancestors.

Taelo and all the Sages that would be on the raft, were at the top of the Head Rock and were able to see all the fires on the beach.

Broken Spear commented that he had flown with the eagle as it acknowledged Talking Wren and that it had specifically focused on the eagle feather being attached to her leader's spear. He was sure that Talking Wren would now have the eagle provide warning.

Talking Wren had been exceptionally quiet. She was humbled and overwhelmed by the recognition that she had received. Broken Spear's comment seemed to break her silence and she became much more talkative and went into several explanations of how the raft could be managed.

Taelo quietly told Broken Spear that it was his fault that the bird was once again singing endlessly.

Talking Wren laughed and said she had heard his comment and she would keep her knowledge of how to handle the raft to herself and he would have to find out on his own.

The night ended with all sitting around the fire and listing to one of Broken Spear's Stories about his talks with the Ancients and how they had laughed at him when he said he looked up at the sky at night and tried to count how many they were.

Taelo nodded and said that he was not sure what all the points of light were in the sky but there were too many to be the light of the people that had gone to the next life. He felt that thinking about them as Ancients was a good idea so they could remember all those that had come before them and had made their lives possible.

The next morning before the sun began to lighten the sky, Taelo and Golden Hawk did an overall examination of the raft.

On the front on each side of the wave barrier they found what they were sure were sturdy holders for the raft anchor boulders on the beach. There were ropes arranged that would tie the boulders on securely. It was clear to them that Saber Scar and Marigold would be needed to move the boulders onto any beach they brought the raft to.

On the very back they found a small raft that had a torch holder mounted on it and it was attached to a long coil of rope. One end of the rope was tied to the main raft and the other to the small raft.

Taelo pointed to it, gave a light laugh and the two of them agreed they should ask Talking Wren how it was to be used.

They were confident the raft was ready and that it was the best raft they had been on so far.

Floating Cloud and Lily came on board and started a fire in the cooking ring. They said they were going to prepare a morning fish stew that would be enough for everyone. They commented that they were excited to prepare a meal that they would all share as they left the protection of the harbor and began their journey.

Taelo complemented them for thinking ahead and that he was looking forward to his first meal on the raft.

Quiet Rabbit and Busy Bee boarded. They were followed by three sleepy kids who were eager to get into the raft's lodge to try out their sleeping area. They had all put their travel things on the raft the night before and were ready to ride the raft.

Quiet Rabbit and Busy Bee went to the cooking ring and joined in the preparation of the first meal. They chatted with Lily and Floating Cloud and asked how they could help.

Saber Scar, Marigold and Spear Tip got on next. Saber Scar and Marigold joined them at the steering paddle area. Saber Scar laughed when he was told that he and Marigold had the honor of pulling the raft out into the harbor. He replied that he knew Taelo was not as weak as he claimed to be because he had watched Taelo lift Single Leaf up over his shoulders and then hold her by her legs when he had saved her from drowning.

Taelo replied that that strength had come from fear, and he countered that he was giving the two the honor of starting the Journey of Sages.

The stream of "Sages" boarded. Taelo had arranged for Broken Spear to be the last to board. He was helped into his observation seat in the front.

The sun broke over the mountains and the incoming waves glistened and flashed on their way into the harbor. It was as if the ocean was greeting them and inviting them to travel its realm.

Talking Wren came on board and gave a small laughed when Taelo asked where the torches were for the small raft with the torch holder.

She walked over to a woven box and lifted the lid. It was filled with torches made of tightly bound sea moss saturated with hardened fat.

She took one out and put into the holder on the raft. She asked if there were any other questions.

Taelo knew that she was dragging out her explanation about the use of the raft to get even with his comment the night before about the singing wren to make her point. He pointed at the small raft and asked if it was the place to put anyone that misbehaved.

Talking Wren laughed again and said she had instructed Quiet Rabbit about placing him on it when he disagreed with her.

Quiet Rabbit heard the interaction and told the two to leave her out of it.

Taelo finally asked how the small raft was to be use.

Talking Wren then explained that once out on the sea, the raft was to be pulled behind the raft and used as a way to guide the raft. When the small raft was directly behind, the main raft was going straight. When the steering paddle was moved toward one side of the main raft, the small raft would swing out to the other side. How far it went out was determined by how far the steering paddle was moved. Once the steering paddle was back to center the small raft would come back and be directly behind the main raft.

She made the point that it would be most useful during cloudy night travel when the points of light could not be seen. The torch would provide a useful reference for those handling the steering paddle.

Taelo nodded and thanked her for having thought of making the small raft. He listened as Talking Wren explained that she had taken his idea when they were coming across the sea, and he had kept a torch lit on his lead raft and the other two raft had lined up behind him. He had saved them from the storm by keeping his torch lit.

Talking Wren gave him a hug. She went to each person and gave them all hugs and wished them a good journey.

Taelo waited for her to jump to the beach. He asked Saber Scar and Marigold to bring the anchor boulders and place them in the holders.

Once they were on board Taelo let out his war cry.

He asked Saber Scar and Marigold to handle the guide paddle and he and Golden Hawk would pull up the anchor rock.

Saber Scar knew that Taelo had just elevated his and Marigold's stature. He was pleased and made sure that the launch was flawless and that the raft turned smoothly and followed the streaming rays of the sun out into the open sea.

Taelo stood at the back of the raft and let out his war cry.

The spectators on the beach gave him a thunderous war cry in return.

High in the sky the eagle let out its cry and Lasher responded with a howl of his own.

The Journey of Sages had begun.

Chapter 9: Organized

As the raft took to the waves Taelo and Golden Hawk began to practice guiding it and trying to ride the waves.

Taelo called to Red Fox and Black Wolf to raise the large sail. He had them adjust the angle to the point that the wind both pushed the raft a little faster and seemed to hold it on the wave.

Once he felt that he had the raft in control. He called to Quiet Rabbit to shorten the stabilizing float at the bottom of the wave, so it was just short of the trough. He then asked her to trim the top float, so it was just below the wave crest.

The raft handling became easier, and it rode each wave for a longer time.

Broken Spear sent word back that the exhilarating feeling he was experiencing took him back to his childhood when he went sliding down long hillsides on the snow. He raised his hand and let out a long whoop.

Taelo asked Saber Scar to launch the small raft. He laughed as he watched the small raft skipping along and holding to the top of the wave. This meant that it was not directly behind the larger raft. He would have to tell Talking Wren that the raft would only provide good guidance on calm, flat water.

He then thought about it and decided that it would be a good indicator of the raft staying on the wave and it would provide some stability information.

Red Oak, Grey Fox Running, Slow Walker, and Whistling Arrow had been standing by watching and listening. Grey Fox Running let Taelo know that they all wanted to learn how to handle the raft and then take turns doing it as they traveled. This would give them something to do, and it would relieve Taelo, Golden Hawk, Saber Scar and Marigold.

Taelo and Golden Hawk both said that having their help would be great. They agreed to do the training as soon as they felt that the two of them and Saber Scar and Marigold were themselves qualified.

Marigold agreed that they had some learning to do. Marigold suggested that Red Oak and Grey Fox Running should partner with she and Saber Scar, and that Slow Walker and Whistling Arrow should partner with Taelo and Golden Hawk. She pointed out that this would speed up all of their qualification.

She also suggested that they should all qualify on handling the sails and setting up the outriggers.

They all agreed.

Taelo asked Marigold to share her concept and enroll all the Sages. He felt that it would be a great experience for everyone, and it would ensure that the skill required during an emergency was present.

Marigold received enthusiastic agreement from all the Sages, and she also got enthusiastic agreement from all the young riders.

Busy Bee and Quiet Rabbit took the opportunity to put forward the idea of having everyone take a turn to prepare the main meal of the day.

Taelo then asked them to list the other opportunities that they had thought through. He made the point that the raft would be the place where everyone would spend most of their time. It would be a great opportunity to learn and grow.

Quiet Rabbit pointed to Floating Cloud and said that pottery making would be done following her guidance and those that were interested should let her know.

She pointed at Golden Hawk and said that he would hold language classes at the bow every morning.

He spoke up and said that he would train everyone in the basics of the Condor Clan language and Broken Spear would sharpen everyone's knowledge of the Other's language. He said that the language lessons would alternate sun cycles with Taelo's exercise classes.

She then pointed to Little Doe and Marigold and said that they had partnered with White Swan and Quiet Pheasant to teach the art of leather finishing. Making leather goods and clothing would be included.

She then pointed to Saber Scar and Taelo and said they would focus on weapon and tool making.

Taelo noted an immediate improvement in everyone as they each let the activity leaders know about their interest.

Taelo organized the raft handling training. He and the first set of sages to qualify to handle the raft gathered together and discussed what qualification meant. Taelo listened as Grey Fox Running explained that every condition that the raft might face should be thought through and the actions required should be listed and then practiced.

Taelo laughed as Saber Scar, imitated Little Otter's voice as he announced, "and then practiced each condition three times."

As the sun threatened to sink below the horizon, Taelo guided the raft as close to shore as possible. The size of the waves decreased, the raft slowed down, and the small tailing steering raft was now almost directly behind.

Taelo asked Whistling Arrow to pull it in and put a lighted torch into the torch holder and the set the raft with the lighted torch back out.

He was pleased that Talking Wren's idea seemed to be working. He asked Marigold and Saber Scar to look ahead and pick the point as far forward as possible that he should point the main raft.

Once he had the raft pointed to their satisfaction and he got the feel of how quickly the raft was being pushed toward the shore he adjusted the direction slightly away from the target. He then tied the steering paddle in place and began to monitor the position of the small raft trailing behind.

The sun sank below the horizon and the sky above filled with countless points of light. He was also pleased that the moon was providing enough light to create a black outline of the shore. This allowed him to monitor the drift toward or away from it as they sailed forward.

He looked up to see if there was a point of light high in the sky to the front of the raft that he could also use as a reference.

He, Golden Hawk, Saber Scar, Marigold, Red Oak, Grey Fox Running, Whistling Arrow, and Slow Walker spent time discussing their situation and how well the raft was sailing and moving.

When the torch on the small raft began to flicker Taelo suggested that the next steering team get some sleep and that he and his team would wake them when it was their turn.

Taelo took a walk around the deck and found that almost everyone was still out and enjoying the early part of the evening.

He stopped where Broken Spear was sitting. Broken Spear had a hide over his shoulders and his two helpers were sitting on each side.

He listened as Broken Spear shared that it had been a great sun cycle and that he looked forward to many more.

Taelo agreed. He let the three know that if they needed help to get into the lodge they should let the steering team know.

Chapter 10: Qualification

The idea of qualifying on using the sails, trimming the length of the stabilizing floats, and operating the guide paddle was enthusiastically embraced. Teams of two had been identified. Taelo insisted that four teams made up of Grey Fox Running, Red Oak, Whistling Arrow, Slow Walker, Saber Scar, Marigold, Golden Hawk, and he would spend the upcoming five sun cycles with their own qualifications. Then they would qualify each additional team as the raft made its way down the coast.

He asked Quiet Rabbit and Busy Bee to organize the Sages into operating guide paddle pairs.

The initial teams identified and designed the qualification process. They concluded that they could practice every qualification process except handling the raft in a storm.

As each sun cycle passed, they took turns holding the raft on a wave, adjusting the stabilizing floats for the various wave sizes, using the small raft to guide the steering during the night, raising and setting each sail and optimizing the angle based on the wind and the direction of the coastline.

They had mastered each of the tasks when the weather took a turn for worse, and the sea changed. The waves grew dramatically higher. Staying close to the shore became more dangerous. The sails needed to be reduced in size. The stabilizing floats need to be adjusted to be farther out. Holding the raft on a wave became a challenge and the small guide raft could not be used.

They commented that the hardest part of their qualification was at hand.

Taelo and Golden Hawk led in trying out and determining the settings for the sails and on how to best set the stabilizing floats. They practiced with the guide paddle to determine the best technique for keeping the raft on a wave. They were closely watched by the other three pairs. Slow Walker and Whistling Arrow were at their side but only observing. Saber Scar and Marigold were their shadows and practiced his and Golden Hawk's every action. Red Oak and Grey Fox Running were at their side but also only observing.

The storm was with them for at least three sun cycles. Every one of the first teams were able to experience handling the raft in a storm. They all felt capable and able to manage the raft.

Because the sky remained dark it was hard to keep track of day or night. By the end of the second sun cycle, they were taking turns at every position.

Taelo was confident that they all qualified at handling every condition that they and the raft might face. He knew that they might face even more fierce storms but the one they were experiencing was a great qualification.

He had kept a close eye on the behavior of everyone on the raft. It seemed that being out in the open was preferred to remaining in the raft lodge. Several of the members were noticeably sick and were at the sides of the raft heaving. It was clear they were miserable. He was glad that he was not one of them.

Broken spear and his two helpers had a large hide over them and sat at his bow chair. He expressed his amazement at how well the raft went through the sea and how much he was enjoying it.

Taelo agreed and said he would complement Talking Wren on the strength and quality of the raft she had built.

The storm subsided. Taelo watched as the shoreline seemed to end. He realized that the next shoreline was far toward the east and that they would need to guide the raft toward the rising sun. He remembered the path that he had traveled twice on land and that it turned toward the rising sun. Even though all land disappeared from view, he felt confident in the direction they were heading.

The waves settled down but were generally going in the desired direction. The point of the raft needed to be more parallel to the wave crest. He had the trough stabilizer set out to it longest and the crest stabilizer set to its shortest length.

Then he began qualifying all the additional Sage teams.

Busy Bee introduced him to the future Sage teams made up of Yellow Flower paired with Spear Tip and the twins working together.

It took ten sun cycles before the shore again became visible. During this time everyone on the raft qualified on every operating station.

When the shore came into sight, there was a small celebration and Lilly and Floating Cloud prepared honey glazed roasted buffalo, deer, and rabbit. The chatter on the raft was noticeably up and several asked if they were stopping at the oncoming shore.

Taelo deflected the questions by announcing that it was time for everyone to begin doing their other activities. He planned to walk the raft and do a different exercise after every ten paces. He shared that he would do this every other sun cycle, and everyone interested could participate.

His announcement caused each activity leader to identify their activity and invite any interested Sage to join them.

Golden Hawk was the person that had everyone wanting to join his Condor language lessons. He said he would run his class from the front of the raft and would do so on the days that Taelo was not leading an exercise session.

The rest of the activities all had a good following.

Taelo thanked Quiet Rabbit and Busy Bee for having organized all the activities. He was especially pleased that everyone would take a turn being in charge of the food preparation for the sun zenith meal.

He chuckled when Broken Spear commented that he would be very active in two events but that he thought the zenith meal preparation would be better than the language lessons.

The Sun sank behind them and Taelo had the small raft with a lighted torch set into the water.

The bright lights twinkling above, lighting the blackness surrounding them and the moon rising in front set a peaceful mood that seemed to embrace everyone on the raft. Everyone was out on the deck, and many slept there as well.

Taelo and Golden Hawk were on station for the first steering session and were expertly keeping the raft on the wave. It turned out that the small raft with the torch worked to guide them, but it required that they periodically needed to drop back off the wave lined up with one of the spots of light in the sky and then get up on the next wave.

The skill of the main teams at handling the raft became obvious and they were often complimented at making the ride enjoyable.

Chapter Site 11: Sun Rise, Sun Set

Grey mist lay like a gray wolf hide ahead of the raft. Taelo was counting on Broken Spear and his two helpers to give warning of any obstruction that might lay ahead. He had the sails only half opened and he had turned away from the direction of the shore.

There was an earie quiet that had engulfed the raft. The breeze came from the back and seemed to sweep along the raft surface and raised swirls of fog that reminded Taelo of the dust bunnies that he had seen in the desert

Suddenly Broken Spear said that he had encountered a new mind. It was beaming a bright light into his mind, and he was able to see under the clear waters of the sea. He said that it was very different than flying with the eagle and that the mind he was encountering was powerful and controlled his vision.

Broken Spear said that when he thought about the shore, the mind he was in turned to his left as if expecting the raft to follow.

Taelo turned the paddle so the head of the raft pointed to where he thought the shore would be and waited for Broken Spear to confirm the direction.

Broken Spear called back and said that the mind he was in had brightened the light. He was certain that they were now going in the right direction.

Taelo could feel the presence of the mind and the goodwill that seemed to emanate from it. He had experienced this same presence when he had gone swimming with the dolphins on his return trip from the land of the Condor. He could not see where the raft was heading but felt sure that it was not in danger.

Quiet Rabbit asked what she should say to all the Sages that remained worried about going through the grey mist and not knowing where they were.

Taelo smiled and told her that some old friends were guiding them safely toward the shore and she should tell the Sages that Broken Spear was not flying with an eagle but swimming with a powerful friend, the Dolphin. They should prepare a zenith celebration meal and have Broken Spear share his experience.

The raft seemed to come out from under the grey wolf like mist into the bright sunlight. Taelo looked back and saw the mist's edge that looked like the edge of the stone slabs on the Northern Elk Clan lodge. He was glad to have followed the mind that had guide the raft in toward shore.

Chirping Swallow stood up from her seat and pointed to the horizon. She shouted out that she saw land.

Taelo did not see what she was pointing at but was confident that she was right. The others had much better long-range vision than he or anyone in the Elk Clan.

He had the sails opened full and adjusted so that the raft headed toward shore.

He asked Saber Scar and Marigold to go up front with Broken Spear and see if they could locate the mountain from where they could see the sun rise on one sea and then watch it set on the other sea.

The land ahead was a lush bright green that was sandwiched between the light blue of the sky and the darker blue green of the sea. It seemed that the raft was sliding slowly toward a bright green line.

Broken Spear called back and said that his connection was guiding him more to the left and Taelo needed to turn the front of the raft that way.

As Taelo turned the raft both Marigold and Saber Scar pointed toward the shore and shouted they thought that the peak that seemed to be far into the green of the shore was the one that they were seeking.

Taelo shouted back that he thought that they had found the right mountain. He was now almost certain that the dolphin was guiding him into the same beach where he had first met them.

The sun hit its zenith and Broken Spear had almost every Sage surrounding him during the zenith meal. They eagerly waited for him to share his experience of swimming with the dolphin.

Taelo listened as Broken Spear told everyone that the dolphin remembered Taelo and that the telling had been done by showing a second light on the raft. He was one bright light and Taelo was another.

Broken Spear went on to share that it seemed that there were five fainter lights that the dolphin had encountered before.

Taelo commented that Quiet Rabbit, Golden Hawk, Busy Bee, Saber Scar and Marigold had all swam with the dolphins. It amazed him that the dolphin could indicate their presence. It gave him new respect for the minds of an animal that at one time he had thought of as a source of food. He wondered if there were other animals that had such powerful minds.

Broken Spear described some of what he experienced was similar to walking through a dark area where the light reflected back off of dark objects that could then be avoided. During the time he was in the bright mind the dark areas where below and it seemed that the dolphin was making sure the depth of the sea was adequate.

As the raft approached the shore, Taelo had the main sail lowered, the stabilizing arms adjusted to their shortest length and the guide boards raised up halfway. When they approached the shore, they would be raised the rest of the way.

He asked everyone but Broken Spear to stand on the back third of the raft. He wanted the front to be up as high as possible so that he could match the beach angle.

Saber Scar and Marigold were ready to drop the anchor boulder at his command. Golden Hawk, Red Oak, Grey Fox running, Slow Walker and Whistling Arrow were ready to slow the raft's approach to the beach by slowly letting the anchor rope out.

Taelo asked Broken Spear to call out the number of spear lengths to the beach.

He had the main sail lowered.

He had Red Fox, Black Wolf, Spear Tip and Yellow Flower standing at the small sail ready to take it down at his command.

Broken Spear called back that he was getting flashes in his mind as they neared the shore and that the flashes were increasing the closer, they got.

The beach seemed to cautiously approach the raft like an alert deer approaches the edge of the forest.

When the distance was ten spear lengths, Taelo had the anchor boulder pushed over and the front sail taken down and the guide boards pull up all the way.

Broken Spear called back that the blinking yellow light in his mind was now a solid light.

Taelo had the anchor rope tightened and called out cadence for slowly letting it out. He felt the raft slowly touch the beach and go ever so slightly forward as it came to a complete stop.

Saber Scar and Marigold carried the two front anchor boulders to the beach and then made sure they were equally spaced to each side of the raft and the ropes taunt.

Red Oak and Grey Fox Running each pounded a stake at each boulder to keep it from being pulled toward the sea.

Taelo asked that everyone remain on board until he and Golden Hawk scouted the area to make sure they were safe from any Warrior Clan that might be present.

He asked Red Oak and Grey Fox Running to set up a defense perimeter.

White Swan and Quiet Pheasant made sure all their weapons were at the ready and distributed to the Sages.

As he and Golden Hawk scouted the area, they discussed how everyone would be able to make the journey to the top of the volcano.

Taelo said that he had an idea how the raft could remain with no one on board and still be secured from random pilfering.

After a safe landing, Taelo turned and walked out into the ocean and hit the top of the water with his hand. He watched as several fins appeared above the water and smoothly came in towards him.

He let his mind think warm thoughts as he thanked his old friends for helping him. He kept his hand out as each dolphin swam by him and let him slide his hand along them. They all flashed a light in his mind and then swam off.

Chapter 12: Finding the Way

Golden Hawk took charge of setting up the beach defenses. He had confronted and defeated many of the Warrior Clan members but knew that they were fierce fighters. He was not expecting to be confronted but planned to be ready. He set up three hidden watch stations that would provide warning if any intruders were discovered.

Red Oak complemented him on his skill at setting up the watch and of organizing the Sages into fighting diamonds and holding practices on the beach. This was the first time that the Sages were part of a fighting diamond, and they were surprised at how efficient and effective that formation happened to be. They enjoyed the practices that Golden Hawk trained them on.

Quiet Rabbit, Busy Bee, and Marigold each took command of one of the fighting diamonds and helped practice the moves that they all had experienced in actual battle.

Taelo and Saber Scar set off to find the way to the top of the volcano. They had stayed long enough to help get the fighting diamonds set up and seeing several of the practices they both felt better about their departure to locate the mountain. They knew that any assault on the beach would be devastating to the attackers.

Saber Scar set the pace as they jogged along. Taelo had chosen Saber Scar to go with him in case his strength was needed. The pace for him was relatively slow but it gave him time to mark the path they were taking. Mark may have been an overstatement. He knew that only someone who knew what they were looking for would notice his "markings."

For two sun cycles their travel was quiet and uneventful. On the zenith of their third sun cycle, they heard laughter and chatter ahead. They both slowed and went silently forward. They approached a small lake where they saw some young women and younger children frolicking in the water. They were all clearly there to enjoy themselves.

Taelo spotted three young men standing by with spears and war clubs. They were there to protect the frolickers from any lions or leopards that might come to the lake.

A series of small structures let him know that the frolickers were staying for a few sun cycles. He looked around and figured the area provided a place to relax that was not too far from their village.

Taelo took a wide berth as he led the way around to the other side and then they once again set off. When the sun met the far horizon and the lights above emblazoned the sky, they stopped, had something to eat and then took turns sleeping.

Taelo fell asleep thinking that they should be very close to the volcano.

The next sunrise outlined the mountains and the two examined them to see if they could discern the one, they though was the volcano. A slight grey plume spiraled up into the morning light and they both pointed to it at the same time. There was no doubt about which peak they were looking at.

Taelo remembered that the way up that they had taken the first time he and his team had gone up would be too difficult to carry Broken Spear and it would also be very difficult for the older Sages.

At that time, they had found an easier way down and now he was looking for it. The jungle made locating it a challenge. The plants all grew much faster in this climate than in the forests in the north and that growth constantly transformed the environment. It took them a full sun cycle of travel around the base of the volcano before they found the way up.

Taelo led the way up toward the top. Along the way he and Saber Scar cleared boulders and fallen limbs from the path in preparation for bringing Broken Spear up. They also identified the best places to stop to rest.

Once at the top, they took a quick look to ensure that everything was as they thought it should be and then turned and made their way back down and set off for the beach.

Back on the beach the Sages enjoyed walking the shore, gathering seaweed, and doing some spear fishing. The fresh fish made great treats. A small freshwater stream was located nearby and the fresh water for the raft was resupplied.

Floating Cloud and Lilly made some drying racks, and the excess fish were placed on it and dried.

A few of the Sages had chosen to sleep at the edge of the forest but a regular late sun cycle shower soon convinced them to move back to the raft. The hides on the sides were lifted and the ocean breeze kept the lodge cool and comfortable. It also served to protect everyone from the rain.

Golden Hawk moved his language lessons to the beach and Quiet Rabbit led a walk along the beach at each sunset.

Everyone was waiting for Taelo's and Saber Scar's return.

Taelo and Saber Scar made a return that kept them away from the lake where they had seen some of the Warrior Clan members.

He and Saber scar did take a quick detour to see if there were any people at the lake and were relieved to find no one there.

Taelo carefully and almost invisibly marked the path back to the volcano. He had selected a common fern that grew along the entire way and had broken a stem of the plant every hand full of paces. This had slowed his return trip, but it would make is much easier to lead the way back. It also kept him away from the lake where the swimmers from the Warrior Clan had been spotted.

Their return took them three sun cycles. In total they had spent ten sun cycles to locate the volcano.

Taelo knew that taking everyone up would take twice as long.

They received a cheer on their return to the beach. A dinner was held, and everyone wanted to hear about the way to the top of the volcano and when they could all go.

Golden Hawk waved his hand to indicate all the Sages and loudly said that they were all qualified in using the fighting diamond and that Broken Spear would be at the center of one of the diamonds.

Golden Hawk let out the war cry and the fighting diamonds were formed.

Taelo noted that Silver Arrow was at the head of the fighting diamond that surrounded Broken Spear. The rest of the diamond was made up of Others. He was sure no attacker would ever touch Broken Spear.

Taelo asked Golden Hawk if the carrying chair for Broken Spear was ready.

Golden Hawk pointed to the seat that Broken Spear was sitting on and replied that two long carrying poles were ready to be tied to it. Broken Spear would ride to the top of the Volcano like the king of the Warrior Clan or that of the Condor Clan.

Taelo jokingly announced that Broken Spear was the King of the Sages and got a round of ground thumping from the Others and a cheer from the rest of the group.

Taelo suggested that everyone spend the next sun cycle organizing the things that they would need for a ten-sun cycle trip. He suggested they travel as light as possible.

He pulled the teams that operated the raft together and told them that they would take it out a good distance from shore and anchor it.

Lily and Floating Cloud volunteered to stay with the raft. Marigold and Saber Scar said that they would also stay but wanted Spear Tip to go.

They all said that they had been to the top and would miss experiencing the amazement that the Sages would have but they felt that the safety of the raft was of greater importance.

Taelo thanked them and let them know how good it felt to have them volunteer. It made the worry about bad weather taking the raft less of a concern.

He said that he and Quiet Rabbit would take good care of Spear Tip.

Saber Scar joked that it was the only way he knew of as a way to get out of carrying Broken Spear up to the top of the volcano. He received a hug from Marigold and the praise about her having such a smart mate.

The next morning Taelo watched as the four of them slowly took the raft offshore and anchored it.

When he got the "all clear" signal from the raft, he led the way toward the volcano.

<u>Chapter 13 To the Top</u>

*O*nce the procession was on the way to the volcano, he pointed out his markings to Golden Hawk and the rest. He gave them warning about the Warrior Clan and that if they met any of them he would call for the fighting diamond formation.

Once at the base of the volcano, he called for a stop for the rest of the sun cycle. He noted an eagle flying circles overhead and he felt reassured that there was no cry.

Everyone randomly selected a place to sleep.

He set up the safety watch and positioned them strategically around the camp and gave the instructions that if they became sleepy they should awaken their replacements.

Lasher was laying by where Quiet Rabbit had set up their sleeping area.

Taelo had called for a cold camp with no fires. The weather was very warm and the humidity high. No one complained about not having a fire.

Taelo was treating all the Sages in the same manner as he did any teammate. He was surprised at how well that approach was received.

He made the carrying assignments and was pleasantly surprised by an outpour of volunteers.

White Swan spoke for all of them. She said that they might only be able to carry Broken Spear for a short distance but if each of them put in their short carrying distance, together they would achieve a long distance. This she pointed out would let those doing most of the carrying have a break.

He knew that by the time they all reached the top they would all be worn out. He hoped that the older Sages could make it all the way on their own.

Red Fox spoke up and said that he, Spear Tip, Yellow Flower, and Black Wolf volunteered that together they would carry the front of the chair. He smiled and said that then those carrying the back would think they were going downhill and have more energy.

Taelo thanked everyone and suggested that the extra help would be used at the bottom of the Volcano and as they neared the top, he wanted everyone to help each other make it to the very top.

The way up was as difficult as he had expected. He held frequent breaks and made sure to cycle the volunteer Sages after short carries.

The sun was at its zenith when he called for a longer break. He suggested drinking a large amount of water but only eating a few bites.

Taelo was not surprised when White Swan let him know that she and Quiet Pheasant were going to stop carrying and instead help some of the older Sages.

Taelo agreed with her and suggested that they have the struggling Sages walk backwards up the trail.

Taelo then took Red Fox, Black Wolf, Yellow Flower, and Speer Tip aside and asked them to work with White Swan in helping the older Sages.

He then had the two front persons that carried Broken Spear face forward but had those in the back walk backwards. There were only two permanent teams left to do the carrying. Sly Squirrel, Chirping Swallow insisted that they could continue to give short periods of carrying help.

Taelo thanked them. It gave him a way to rotate the main carriers.

Taelo kept everyone moving but the pace was slow. He worried that they would not make it to the top.

He asked White Swan to set the pace for the Sages and let her know that he was going to make a push for the top with Broken Spear.

He discussed this with Grey Fox Running and Red Oak. They agreed that they needed to make it to the top before the sun hit the horizon.

The carrying became like a dance with each first pair walking forward then changing position and walking backwards.

They agreed that the backward walk relieved their strained muscles.

The pace was twice as fast as before and when they made it to the top they let out a war cry. The eagle above let out a cry and Lasher let out a howl.

After a brief rest. Taelo said he was going down to help those that might be struggling.

When they all said the same thing, he instructed Lasher to stay, and guard Broken Spear.

Taelo was pleased with the progress that the Sages had made.

He had six of them tie ropes to their waists. He tied it to his waist then pulled them up with the rope. He watched as Golden Hawk, Red Oak, and Grey Fox Running did the same.

Taelo began his travel chant and soon everyone joined in.

The chant seemed to energize everyone and soon they all reached the top

The sun was just kissing the far horizon as they got to the area to set up camp.

Taelo had his carriers pick Broken Spear up and then still chanting he had them all jogging toward the southern edge of the Volcano.

Everyone more or less collapsed where they would spend the night.

Taelo lit a small cooking fire, cut off several pieces of meat, and put them on the grill. He soon handed a piece to Broken Spear. Then he gave one to Quiet Rabbit and continued grilling and handing out grilled meat.

He then took out a large pouch filled with a honey wine and passed it around and congratulated everyone on having made it to the top.

The sun chose that moment to wink below the horizon. The eagle let out a short screech and flew away.

Taelo said that he was ready for a good night of sleep but that he would be up early to watch the sun rise.

Taelo, Quite Rabbit, Golden Hawk and Busy Bee, Yellow Flower, Red Fox, Black Wolf, and Spear Tip were all sitting together the next morning as the sun was threatening to come up over the far horizon.

Broken Spear, Sly Squirrel and Chirping Swallow were next to them.

The rest of the Sages had arranged themselves along the edge of the volcano edge.

The light on the far horizon created a white light between the dark ocean water and the lighter greyish sky. The suns orb broke the horizon, and everyone gave a cheer.

Everyone gathered around the cooking ring for their morning meal.

The breeze came from the valley below and kept the fumes of the volcano from overcoming everyone.

Quick excursions were made to see the volcano's bubbling lava, but the fumes made it impossible to stay for long.

However, even a brief visit left the visitor smelling like a rotten egg which resulted in a round robin of teasing.

The day was spent chatting and walking around the edge of the volcano. Everyone was trying to work out their sore muscles.

The sun's approach to the far horizon once again drew everyone to the volcano's edge. The sun was a giant golden ball sinking slowly into the water. When it went down there seemed to be a flicker and the grey of evening made its way around all of them.

Sleep came easily and the camp grew quiet.

Taelo and Golden Hawk were the last to lay down. They had agreed that because of the effort to come up had taxed all of them the way down would be as hard or perhaps harder than the way up.

Chapter 14: Out to Sea

The way down was as tough as Taelo had described. He was walking down backwards to relieve his leg muscles by the time they were almost down. Most of the Sages were also doing the same.

Once they reached the base of the volcano, White Swan suggested they go by the freshwater lake where Taelo had seen the Warrior Clan enjoying themselves. She suggested that she and Quiet Pheasant scout ahead and make sure the lake was clear.

Everyone agreed that a sun cycle at the lake would give them all a chance to wash off the smell of rotten eggs.

Taelo agreed. The odor of rotten eggs was very strong. He would lead the way.

High overhead an eagle let out a cry. Broken Spear said that he was in the eagle's mind and would follow them.

Taelo led the way and made his way back toward where he had the lake located in his mind. It turned out that his mental map was accurate and within the sun cycle the three of them were at the edge of the forest on the banks of the lake.

The three of them made their way around the lake to make sure there were no Warrior Clan members present.

Taelo returned to get the rest of the Sages and White Swan and Quiet Pheasant stayed to select the site by the lake.

Golden Hawk had the Sages most of the way to the lake when Taelo met up with him. He said that he was following Broken Spear's direction as seen from the eagle.

They all arrived as the sun was giving way to the night.

The next morning, they all enjoyed the fresh water of the lake. One fighting diamond team was always at the ready while the rest enjoyed themselves and all their clothes got washed. The smell of pine needles and scent rose flower that accompanied the use of the oils they used took the place of the smell of rotten eggs.

Everyone agreed that they would rather exude the smell of a rose even if it alerted any of the Warrior Clan members.

Taelo was in the lead at the rise of the sun. He led the procession at a brisk pace. He made sure that everyone was keeping pace and that those carrying Broken Spear could keep up.

When they arrived at the beach, he spotted the raft resting much closer to the beach in the wave shadow made by a spit of rocks that protruded out into the ocean.

The raft immediately hoisted the front sail and made its way to the beach. Marigold was the first one off and took one of the front anchor rocks and put it on the beach.

She then took Spear Tip into her arms and gave him a hug. He began to immediately share the experience he had at the top of the volcano. It was clear that it had made a lasting impression.

Taelo was surprised that it was the bubbling lava not the rise and setting of the sun that was more exciting to him. He learned that many of the members felt the same way about the bubbling lava.

Saber Scar joined Marigold and gave Spear Tip a hug.

He explained that they had relocated the raft closer to the beach to escape the pounding of the waves. The closer position had also allowed them to come to shore each sun cycle to walk the beach and to hunt for clams.

Lily and Floating Cloud made their welcoming rounds and then set up their shore-based cooking ring.

The returning Sages all went on the raft and prepared their areas.

They spent the rest of the evening walking the beach and sharing stories of their volcano adventure.

The raft sailed out the next morning as the sun's rays broke over the jungle's far horizon.

Taelo and Golden Hawk were at the guide paddle. Taelo first worked with the small sail team to do the initial optimization. Then the large sail was set. The final adjustment was to set the position of the side floats.

Taelo praised the sail and trim crew as they all did minor final adjustments.

The raft smoothly rode the waves, and the small trailing guide raft assumed its place and the journey settled in.

The raft activities were once again in full swing. Condor Clan language lessons were now a focus for everyone. They all had a goal to be able to interact with the Condor Clan as effectively as possible.

Taelo's exercise session now encompassed everyone. Even Broken Spear insisted that he make at least three rounds of the raft twice a day.

Taelo also engaged in using the glazing oven as he made jewelry as gifts for the Condor Clan.

He watched as Marigold demonstrated her pottery making skill that featured the scenes from the legends of the Others. She made a set that featured the Condor Clan Slingers in battle action against the Warrior Clan. She got requests for additional sets from Busy Bee, Quiet Rabbit, Floating Cloud and Lily.

He listened as they agreed to make this one of their projects after their visit to the Condor Clan.

Their activities triggered he, Saber Scar and Golden Hawk to think about a unique gift they could make for their arrival at the Condor Clan.

For Bold Walker, who had led in pole vaulting over the great chasm that protected the Condor Clan Village, they design a pole that they labeled the Condor Mountain Pole.

This would be a gag gift that was almost as long as the raft and decorated with the various battle scenes when they had faced the Warrior Clan. It would be presented to Bold Walker so he could leap mountain to mountain.

Saber Scar had several large conch shells that he suggested get designs carved on them and be given as signal horns to Star Leaper and Nieva.

Taelo and the three set up a daily session as they prepared their gifts. They put in extra time when they attended to their guide paddle duties.

The routine lasted a full moon cycle and then they saw a plume of white smoke.

Taelo was certain as he guided his raft toward the plume that he would be greeted by Bold Walker and members of the Condor Clan.

They had made good time and it was clear that they had been expected and had been watched for.

Chapter 15: Condor Clan Greeting

Taelo guided the raft toward the plume on the beach. When the raft was within hailing distance, he saw Bold Walker signaling to him to go down the beach. Then he saw the white smoke rising from behind what appeared to be a stone walled area. As he guided the raft along the beach an opening that was almost invisible appeared and two Condor Clan members were signaling for him to enter.

It was a tight fit. He had the side floats pulled all the way in and the three stabilizing guides raised. The side floats came within a half a spear of the lava stone walls at the entrance.

Once he made it by the entrance, it was clear to him that the small bay was an ideal place to keep the raft. The ocean waves hit the entrance at an angle and the water in the bay had only a slight ripple.

Taelo had the rear anchor dropped and the crew had to pole the raft up to the beach. The two front anchors were put out along the small beach.

Bold Walker, his father and mother, Star Leaper and Nieva were with him. They were accompanied by a small army of helpers.

Taelo and the members that had been with him when the Condor Clan Slingers had defeated the Warrior Clan were all greeted with great enthusiasm. The Sages took note of the high stature that Taelo's team held with the Condor Clan.

Taelo introduced each of the Sages that were with him. Nieva paid special attention to the children. She had brought them honey sweets and other treats.

She gave White Swan and Quiet Pheasant big hugs and praised how well they had raised their children.

Taelo took in the cordial greeting that was being given and then he was surprised by a small army of Llama's that were brought to the beach to carry the personal goods that would be needed for a stay at the Condor Clan village.

Bold Walker looked over the carrying poles for Broken Spear and talked with one of the Llama handlers. Four Llamas were harnessed to the poles and Broken Spear was hoisted into his seat. Two Llamas in front and two in back would be ample Llama power.

After making sure the band of warriors that would stay with the raft understood how to take care of it, Bold Walker led the way back up a narrow trail that was just wide enough for everyone to go single file.

The way to the top took a short time. Once there, it was clear to Taelo that they could go back down to the beach were the first signal fire had been, but if you went to the right, the path went upward toward the mountains in the far distance.

They went only a short distance and arrived at a camp that had several cooking fires going. All around them were hide covered enclosures. It was clear to Taelo that Bold Walker had somehow learned the exact number of Sages that were on the journey. He knew that Feather-in-the-Wind had no doubt sent word of the journey and had let her Brother know the count.

Star Leaper let everyone know that he was also now a Sage and that Bold Walker had assumed the leadership of the Condor Clan. He went on to say that the entire Condor Clan would celebrate the visit of their friends from the north for the entire time of their visit. It would be a continuous celebration; abundant eating and they had entertainment planned for every day of their stay.

White Swan let Taelo know how proud she felt about the high esteem that the Condor Clan displayed for him and his team. She pointed out that Nieva had especially singled out Quiet Rabbit and Busy Bee for saving Feather-in-the-Wind from becoming a frozen bride of the Condor.

Taelo was somewhat taken aback at the way he and the team were being celebrated. He had looked forward to the visit but had not expected the situation he found themselves in.

Floating Cloud commented that she felt a little overwhelmed by how they were being heralded. She remembered well fighting the Warrior Clan and rescuing Busy Bee and Quiet Rabbit. The sight of Taelo running with the speed of a mad man as he ran to save Quiet Rabbit was a vision that was as clear at the moment as when it had happened. She remembered watching Taelo rotate his spear and throw it backward with all his might. She had thought he had made a mistake until she saw the spear hit the war priest in the chest and knock him backwards as his blade came down to take off Quiet Rabbits head. She got tears in her eyes as she thought of that moment and of Taelo leaping over Quiet Rabbit and bringing his shark toothed flat weapon down to sever the priest's neck to the point that his head was hanging from only some skin.

She reached down and patted Lasher as she remembered that he had crushed the wrist of the priest's hand that held the blade meant for Quiet Rabbit. Lasher was barely able to walk, and it took several weeks for him to recover from wounds he had received when Quiet Rabbit was captured. She always wondered how Lasher had been able to climb the mountain to make it in time to help save Quiet Rabbit.

She and her team had surrounded Quiet Rabbit who had insisted on carrying Lasher. They had made a fighting retreat from the battle. She remembered Bold Walker and a score of other warrior's leaping over the crevasse that protected the Condor Clan Village and participate in driving the Warrior Clan fighters up the side of the valley.

She and Lily sat around the firepit and recalled those events and the ones that followed before the Condor Clan Slingers decimated the Warrior Clan fighters using the sling and the glass shards that were brought down from the mountain. They recalled how the Slingers would step forward and hit the oncoming Warriors in the face with the glass shards.

The slingers credited Single Leaf, Busy Bee, and Quiet Rabbit for teaching them their skill. And they heralded Nieva for standing at the front calling out the cadence and keeping the slingers moving forward in a slow and steady pace.

Taelo relaxed as Bold Walker led the way back toward the Condor Clan village. It was a new experience for him and clearly for every one of the Sages. They were all riding on Llamas as they made their way to the village.

Taelo was impressed that the Llama were able to carry them.

Bold Walker laughed when he heard Taelo make the comment about the strength of the Llamas and said that he had personally selected the strongest ones he could find. He knew how heavy Taelo was, and he knew that the Others were even heavier.

Taelo was no bigger than Bold Walker and knew that he was joking about the weight but not about that of the Others.

Each sun cycle they arrived at the next site that had specifically been prepared ahead of time.

Taelo asked how many sites there were before they would reach the village and learned that there were five in all.

After they left the fifth site Taelo began to recognize the terrain.

Then he watched as Bold Walker blew into a conch shell and a few moments later a reply could be heard.

As they went over the next rise, the sight of the village built into the face of the mountain came into view.

The Sages stopped and commented on the beauty of the sight.

Then when they reached the crevasse and the foot bridge that crossed over there was complete silence.

Taelo was not surprised. He remembered the first crossing over the crevasse. Burley Bear had asked whether it would hold his weight. On the way across he had dropped a large stone expecting to hear it hit bottom. No sound ever returned. It was a very deep crevasse.

Taelo led the way. Broken Spear was carried across on his seat by four of the Condor Clan members. He remained very still as the bridge swayed slightly. When he was across he let out his breath and thanked his carriers for not dropping him. His carriers laughed and said that he was as light as a feather. They then continued on to the villa were they would all stay.

Taelo turned and suggested that the Sages look straight ahead at where he was standing as they crossed over into the stronghold of the Condor Clan.

Each Sage was accompanied by a Condor Clan member who took the lead. They had the Sage place their hand on their shoulder.

Taelo took note that the gender of the Condor Clan member was the same as the Sage.

The children all came across escorted by Condor Clan Children. They came across laughing and enjoying themselves.

Chapter 16: The Cave of the Condor Princesses

On the following sunrise Bold Walker announced that it was the start of a celebration that would last for several sun cycles.

Taelo his team and a few of the Sages set out on their morning run around the large plateau just after sunrise. He was somewhat surprised at the number of Condor Clan members that joined to follow. He spotted Bold Walker and his mate, Gentle Fern in the lead of the followers. Seeing Gentle Fern with Bold Walker took him back to the time he was fighting off a sneak attack by Angry Cougar of the Sky Eyes. Gentle Fern's cousin Gentle Cub had taken down one of his attackers and most likely saved his life. For the rest of the run, he relived the battle with the Sky Eyes and the confrontation with Angry Cougar. He knew that he owned his life to Golden Hawk and Gentle Cub. Golden Hawk had wounded one of the three attackers that were helping Angry Cougar. Gentle Fern had finished him off.

When they returned to their villa, the crowd let out the Condor Battle cry and dispersed.

Bold Walker and Gentle Fern joined them at the Villa. Bold Walker said that he had to limit the number of villagers wanting to follow but that each day Taelo would have Condor Clan members following him. He looked around and addressed White Swan, and Quiet Pheasant and let them know that a group of the village women were extending an invitation for them to attend a zenith meal. He said that the women insisted they meet the mothers of their heroes.

He looked at Red Oak and Grey Fox Running and commented that his father and several of the other leaders wished to walk the valley with them. They were sure they would hit on topics that would help them be better leaders.

He took in the rest with a wave of his hand and said that each evening, there would be refreshments and the meeting area would be filled with villagers wishing to meet and converse with all of them.

He complemented the Sages on the positive impression they had already made by greeting everyone in the Condor Clan language.

He then let them know that on the next sun cycle they would begin the climb up to the top of Condor Mountain. They were to prepare their things, but they would not have to carry anything. He let them know that the people carrying up the load for them thought of it as a reward. The village had to set a limit on the number that could go up. He said that he had never seen so many of their younger clan members be so eager to participate.

Yellow Flower asked about the cave of the princesses and if they would be allowed in.

Bold Walker looked around and said that this would be the first time that he would see the cave of the princesses that had been sacrificed to the Condor King as brides for him. He had convinced the Condor Clan's Seer to let those that had ended the ritual of sacrificing one young woman each season cycle see what more than one hundred season cycles had created.

He looked at Quiet Rabbit and Busy Bee and thanked them for saving his sister from that fate. He looked at White Swan and thanked her for taking Feather-in-the-Wind under her wing and giving her a vision of what she could be. He looked at Taelo and thanked him for developing his sister into the finest person he could envision and for working the politics to make her the Clan leader of the Paradise Elk Clan.

He went on to say that she was now more Elk Clan than Condor Clan and he was himself now tied to the Elk Clan through his mate who insisted that she would always be Elk Clan.

Taelo thanked Bold Walker for his praise and for his compliments.

He then addressed everyone and suggested they all rest up because the way up, even with others carrying their things would be much harder than the climb up the volcano. He related the difficulty breathing he had experienced the last time Bold Walker took them up to see the condor nest.

As the sun was halfway past its zenith Taelo once again went out on his run. Bold Walker ran besides Taelo, and Long Leaper, Bold Walker's close friend led a large contingent of Condor Clan runners behind them.

Bold Walker commented that he had made Long Leaper his leadership advisor. He would soon replace the current advisor that was also the ceremonial priest.

Taelo commented that it was good to have such a good friend to count on.

The next morning, Taelo ate the robust breakfast that Lily and Floating Cloud had prepared. He saw that everyone was doing the same. He knew that by the time the sun reached its zenith they would only be half of the way to the cave of the Condor Princesses.

He also knew that many of the Sages would be very tired.

He asked Bold Walker about the possibility of having a few helpers to look after the older Sages.

Bold Walker smiled and replied that he even had a helper for his old friend and went on to say that each visitor would have someone attending to them all the way up and down.

He shared the fact that everyone in the village wanted to make the trip and that he had promised the village that small teams of visitors would be allowed to make the trip each moon cycle until everyone had gotten an opportunity to see the Condor clan's nest area.

Taelo responded that as an old friend he thanked him and would try to make the climb on his own.

Bold Walker insisted on having Quiet Rabbit and Busy Bee lead the way. Two young women accompanied them and were constantly trying to help them.

Quiet Rabbit, in the Condor Clan language, quietly and politely asked the two to relax and enjoy themselves and if either she or Busy Bee needed anything they would ask.

She then shared how in the dark of night she and Busy Bee had jogged up the trail and had at the last moment climbed up into a crack to let the two returning ceremonial priests pass by.

Taelo smiled as the two escorts asked if Quiet Rabbit could recall the crack in the hill side and point it out to them. Not long after, Quiet Rabbit looked at Busy Bee and asked if the crack they were approaching could be the one.

Busy Bee jogged ahead and climbed in. She called back that she had found the comb she had dropped the last time they had been there.

Bold Walker called for a rest, and everyone took a turn looking into the crack and many of them climbed in to get the feel of being in the crack.

Taelo watched as stones were arranged to mark the crack. It was clear to him that this crack would be visited by many of the Condor Clan members.

He looked back along the trail and lost count of the many similar cracks. He looked ahead and saw many more. He wondered how Busy Bee could possibly have found the one that she and Quiet Rabbit had used. She had never before said a word about having lost her comb.

He looked over at where Quiet Rabbit and Busy Bee were sitting and instinctively knew that Busy Bee had randomly selected the crack. He saw that the comb she was holding was one that Golden Hawk had carved from the ivory that they had brought back from their Journey of Circumvention.

He looked at Golden Hawk and knew that they both had come to the same conclusion that Busy Bee had pulled off her latest prank.

He commented to Golden Hawk that he had selected a devious mate. Golden Hawk commented that Taelo had been lucky that Quiet Rabbit had out run Busy Bee when the selection of hunting partners had occurred otherwise she would have been Taelo's mate.

Bold Walker asked what they were talking about, and they both commented that they were just discussing having such marvelous mates.

They smiled as Bold Walker said that he agreed and then called for the procession to continue up the mountain.

Broken Spear had been watching everything going on. He asked Busy Bee to see her comb.

Taelo knew that Broken Spear had seen through the prank. He watched as Broken Spear put the comb in one of his pouches.

The procession arrived at the cave of the Condor Princesses. The flat area around the entrance and along the trail that went towards the condor clan nest served as the area for the camp and cookfire to be set up.

Taelo noted that everyone had a good meal but then immediately retired to their sleeping hides.

Taelo claimed that he had no idea what Quiet Rabbit was talking about when she thanked him for not saying anything about the crack that Busy Bee had selected as the one where they had hidden.

The next morning the camp was left set up. Bold Walker let them know that they would all go to the condor nest area and then return before the dark of night replaced the sun.

Taelo was pleased that once again he was able to see several young condors as well as their parents. Lasher took a spot between him and Quiet Rabbit. Taelo's hand found Quiet Rabbits as they both stroked Lasher behind his ears. He looked over and gave her hand a squeeze.

As each group concluded their observations they took leave and returned to the camp. Taelo and the Sages were back in time for a Zenith meal and then had time to discuss what they had seen and time to walk to the edge of the cliff outside of the cave and look across the valley and the mountains beyond.

Taelo commented that the jungle ruled the valley's, but the cold and snow ruled the top of the mountains. He pointed to two peaks that had a small amount of snow at the very top.

After the late dinner, Bold Walker explained that once the camp was packed and everyone was ready to go back down the mountain the Condor Princesses' cave would be opened and everyone would take a slow walk to the back and then come out. He explained that nothing was to be touched. His father Star Leaper would lead, and he would be the last in line. Each of the visitors would be accompanied by a Condor Clan member.

Taelo thanked Bold Walker for making the arrangement. He would learn later that one of the frozen Princesses was to have been Bold Walker's mate.

He had wondered why Bold Walker had chosen a mate from the Elk Clan and learning about the frozen Princess gave the choice new meaning.

Gentle Fern was with him for the walk through the cave and nodded as she passed the frozen Princess.

Chapter 17: Sailing On

The trip down the mountain was almost as hard as the trip up. The Sages were walking backwards for much of the time.

The procession stopped at the crack that Busy Bee had picked as the one that she and Quiet Rabbit had used. Most of the Condor Clan members went to the crack and either climbed in or stood and looked in.

Star Leaper complimented Busy Bee on her excellent memory and being able to find the one that she and Quiet Rabbit had used, and he was glad that she had found her comb.

Taelo was sure that Star Leaper had seen through the ruse.

The departure from the Condor Clan village occurred a sun cycle after the trip down from the cave of the Condor Princesses. The departure was trumpeted by many of the Condor Clan villagers blowing on conch shells.

Taelo responded by getting the departing group chanting the traveling refrain that his team had developed during their Journey of Circumvention. It had a rhythm that caused everyone to begin an easy jog as they traveled down the mountain.

Broken Spear said that he felt that he was riding his mount as the Llamas carrying his seat kept pace.

Star Leaper replied that he felt as if he had the energy of a young man.

Nieva assured him that he was still the oldest in the family.

Bold Walker laughed and said he would have to thank Taelo for accepting his parents on the voyage of Sages so he could have a time to enjoy the Condor Clan kingdom on his own.

Two sun cycles later, Taelo and Quiet Rabbit were both resting against a large boulder as the sun went slowly below the horizon when Running Stag sat quietly down next to them.

This was a surprise that neither had expected.

He quickly explained that Feather-in-the-Wind was already on the raft. He let them know that she had decided that she would accompany her father and mother on the Journey of Sages. He would return to the Paradise Elk Clan and await her return.

He then wished them a safe journey and then he disappeared into the dark of the night before either of them could react.

Taelo looked over at Quiet Rabbit and asked if it really had been Running Stag that had just added two persons to the journey.

Quiet Rabbit replied that it was, and it certainly would be something she expected Feather-in-the-Wind to do. She pointed out that she hoped that Feather-in-the-Wind would not be discovered.

Taelo replied that he was certain that she would stay hidden until he exposed her.

The next sun cycle the procession arrived at the beach where the raft was safeguarded as the sun kissed the far horizon. The Condor Clan members who had stayed to guard it shared that all had been calm and the raft was as it had been left.

Taelo thanked them and awarded each of them a spear that he and Golden Hawk had previously made.

He asked Quiet Rabbit and Busy Bee to get everyone situated on board since he planned to launch the raft when the sun once again came over the horizon.

He went on board to see where Feather-in-the-Wind had hidden herself.

Feather-in-the-Wind and Nieva were comfortably laying under Broken Spear's elevated seating area. She had put a leather skirt around the seat base and made a comfortable sleeping area.

Taelo sat where Broken Spear normally sat and greeted her. He told her that he would let her out once they were out of sight of all those on shore. He would then announce her presence. He gave a laugh and added that then he was going to make her cook the zenith meal for the entire raft population.

Feather-in-the-Wind asked if a Condor Queen should take orders from a common eagle's claw.

Taelo knew that her mother would be overjoyed by having her daughter and granddaughter on the raft. It would be a moment of joy for the Condor Clan Sages and a surprise for everyone.

As the sun rose, Marigold and Saber Scar placed the two front boulders into their holders, helped to push the raft off and then climbed on board.

Red Oak and Grey Fox Running pulled the raft out to the offshore anchor boulder and Taelo called for the small front sail to be hoisted.

Saber Scar and Marigold lowered the stabilizing boards and Taelo pointed the raft out of the cove and navigated the narrow passage.

He waited until the raft caught the first wave and then asked Quiet Rabbit and Busy Bee to adjust the two side floats.

He turned over the raft to Saber Scar who then called for the main sail to be raised. The raft caught the wind, mounted a wave, and glided smoothly forward.

Taelo walked to the front of the raft and announced that he had a surprise to share. He then lifted the hide that surrounded the elevated seat that Broken Spear was sitting on and helped Feather-in-the-Wind and Nieva out.

Everyone had an instant reaction. Nieva, the grandmother rushed forward and lifted her granddaughter into the air and then pulled Feather-in-the-Wind into her arms. Star Leaper came forward and gave them all a bear hug.

White Swan came forward laughing at the fact that her youngest "daughter" had once again demonstrated why she had become the Paradise Elk Clan Leader.

Taelo laughingly announced that all stowaways had to fix the zenith meal for the next handful of sun cycles. He knew that Feather-in-the-Wind would have plenty of help as she fulfilled the price of stowing away.

Golden Hawk and Busy Bee watched as Yellow Flower led Nieva, her best friend, around the raft and explained how it worked and how they could be partners for the rest of the trip. They had been together for three season cycles for the entire Circumvention Journey.

Taelo turned to Quiet Rabbit and told her that he was pleased with Feather-in-the-Wind's decision to join the journey.

Not long after, the two Nievas, Star Leaper and Feather-in-the-Wind were at the guide paddle and following the instructions of Saber Scar and Marigold.

They would be one of the teams to qualify on all raft operating positions.

Taelo watched as they caught a wave and held it for a long ride and then caught the next one. He looked at the coastline and then went back to leading his walking session.

Chapter 18: Counter Current Endeavor

The coast, though stunning in its beauty ended at the sea with towering cliffs that millions of birds swooped from down to the sea for a meal and then returned to the roost that they had swooped from. Everyone on board agreed that it looked as if the birds were synchronized, and the swooping made a wave that traveled along the cliff.

A large number of sandy beaches dotted the base of the cliffs, but they would have been impossible to reach for someone on the shore.

Taelo made a note of the beaches and looked for protected ones in case a storm appeared.

The weather had been very warm, but the sea breeze kept the raft conditions comfortable.

The sailing was smooth and uneventful until Red Fox and Black Wolf called Taelo to the steering paddle. They pointed to the waves that were coming toward them and then to the sail that was puffed in the opposite direction from what it normally did. They made the point that the sea had changed directions.

Taelo verified what they had pointed out. He looked to the shore and saw where a freshwater stream running from a small valley came out to the beach. He had the raft turned and pointed toward it and to a beach on which to land.

He let everyone know that they would land and make camp. Then he and the raft handlers would investigate the change in the direction of the sea waves.

Just passed the opening to the sea, the small valley opened up to an area covered with a pine like tree forest and some brush and other smaller plants,

Taelo asked White Swan to supervise building several hutches for everyone to sleep in. He asked Grey Fox Running to supervise setting up a fish trap in the small river and asked Lily to set up the fish processing.

He shared that he thought figuring out what came next would take about five sun cycles. He thought that the raft had sailed past the current that they would ride across the great sea. He and the sailing crew would find where the current left the shore and then return to pick everyone up.

He pointed to the river and said he was sure it would yield a good catch. He pointed to the forest and suggested that it should hold abundant game, but the hunters should beware of any animals like lions or tigers.

He made the point that the journey across would be as long as the journey had been up to this point and that everyone should enjoy themselves.

Broken Spear pointed out that without his mount, he would be bound to sit in his chair and watch everyone else. He asked to go on the raft and be the lookout. Chirping Swallow and Sly Squirrel could be the cooks and help him as well.

Taelo said that he could use Broken Spear's help. Chirping Swallow and Sly Squirrel, helping him and providing the cooking would make things easier on all of them.

He made sure that Saber Scar and Meadow Flower knew that he needed them. He did not plan to take anyone else. Marigold said that she was fine with that and that she had already asked Quiet Rabbit to care for Spear Tip.

He conferred with Golden Hawk, Quiet Rabbit, and Busy Bee to make sure they were onboard with his plan and that they would manage the Sages while he was gone.

He said his major concern was that the kids, though well trained and capable of defending themselves might let their guard down and take too much of a risk as they played in the river or went into the woods.

Quiet Rabbit replied that she, Busy Bee, Feather-in-the-Wind, and the grandmothers had already organized themselves to take care of his concern. They planned to take turns, in pairs and be on watch during the day.

He nodded and thanked them for taking a worry off his mind.

Just before the sun broke over the horizon, Saber Scar and Marigold carried Broken Spear on board and placed him on the seat at the front of the raft.

Chirping Swallow and Sly Squirrel lit the cooking fire and arranged a series of meat that they put on a spit so that they could offer each person a morning snack.

Taelo took up the rope tied to the back of the raft and was already pulling it off the beach as Marigold and Saber Scar jumped back on board.

Saber Scar came to the back to help, and Marigold stayed up front ready to hoist the front sail.

As they cleared the beach, Saber Scar lowered the three stabilizing boards and then turned to help Taelo lift the large bolder on board.

Taelo then took the steering paddle in hand and call to Marigold to hoist the sail.

The raft turned slowly, and the front sail caught the wind. They were underway.

Saber Scar and Marigold stood at the ready and when Taelo signaled they hoisted the main sail.

Then they stood by the out riggers waiting for the raft to board the first wave.

Broken Spear pointed to the sky. An eagle was flying overhead. He said that he was flying with the eagle.

The mouth-watering aroma of the grilling meat seemed to cap the beginning of a good morning.

Taelo accepted his spit of meat chunks.

He made a point of riding the wave for as long as possible.

The sun had just passed the zenith when Broken Spear called out that from on high he could see what he thought were two opposing flows of water meeting and then turning and flowing away from the cliffs like twin rivers flowing together. He said that there was even a difference in the color of each stream. The one from the south was darker than the one from the north.

Taelo felt the change in the flow and turned the raft and adjusted the sails. He was not planning to go too far but wanted to get the feel of the two currents flowing together and what the flow of air into the sails would be. As the sight of land began to sink down into the trailing horizon, he called for the sails to be turned and he brought the raft around.

As he had expected he had to zigzag his way back towards the cliffs. It was going to take the rest of the sun cycle to make it back. He did not want to risk sailing at night so he asked Broken Spear to look for a beach where they could bring the raft in for the night.

As the sun set behind him, Taelo looked ahead at black cliffs with the top outlined by the sun's rays.

He agreed with Saber Scar's comment that they seemed to be a frightening opening to a world of dark and death, but he then countered that the cliffs would shelter them and provide for a comfortable night. He patted Saber Scar on the shoulder and suggested he eat another of the wonderful sticks of skewered meat that Sly Squirrel and Chirping Swallow had prepared.

Marigold joined in and suggested that the cliffs looked like the dawning of night as opposed to the dawning of the morning. She said she saw rest and relaxation ahead.

Taelo said he liked her version much better than Saber Scar's description and that she should reward herself with a skewer of meat as well.

Broken Spear called back that the small beach that was just to the right of the large crack in the face to the cliff looked to be the best place to bring the raft in.

The eagle gave a piercing cry and Saber Scar replied that they all agreed with him.

Taelo asked Broken Spear to call out the distance to the beach.

At ten spears length, Taelo pushed the back anchor over and had Saber Scar and Marigold pull up the guide boards. At the same time, he called to Sly Squirrel and Chirping Swallow to lower the large sail.

He used the rudder and the pull of the small sail and the momentum of the raft to slowly take the raft toward the shore.

Marigold and Saber Scar were standing on the front of the raft ready to take the front anchor boulders up on the beach.

Saber Scar jumped out and was almost up to his shoulders in the water. The small beach had a steep incline that made it difficult to get the anchor boulders to the shore.

Marigold saw what had happened to Saber Scar and chose to carry her boulder to the very front of the raft. Saber Scar took that boulder and positioned it on the beach.

Taelo took a pole, gaged the depth of the water, and found that it was deep enough so that the guide boards could have remained down.

He hoped for a quiet sea because if it got rough, he feared that there would be little protection for the raft.

The late meal was a hearty stew and after some small talk they all retired for the night.

Taelo had set a watch schedule for he, Marigold, and Saber Scar to ensure they would be ready to respond to the sea if necessary.

It was a calm night and Taelo watched the sun break over the top of the cliff and illuminated the water behind the raft.

At first Taelo was not sure what he was seeing. The water seemed to have a grey layer a half spear length below the water. He then realized that it was a layer of fish that seemed to be gathered at the back of and below the raft.

He took out his spear and using the same technique that he had used at the salt gatherers pond he speared a fish and threw it up onto the deck of the raft. The difference was that this fish was at least ten times the size of the ones found in the pond and the strength required was also ten times more.

The fish was the ugliest fish he had ever seen. The size of the teeth would rival that of any land carnivore. Its teeth were jagged and twisted. It made for a crazy looking fish.

He filleted the fish and asked Sly Squirrel to season it and see if it was worth harvesting more of the fish.

She cooked a piece and offered it to him after commenting that it was the best fish that she had ever eaten.

The rest had gathered around, and she then offered it to them.

The general consensus was that it was truly worth getting as many of the fish as possible.

Taelo suggested that they set up a fish processing system. He suggested that he, Marigold, and Saber Scar would spear a fish, bring it up on the raft and gut it. They would then pass it on to Chirping Swallow to cut off the head. She would then pass it to Sly Squirrel to cut the meat off the bone and then throw the meat into the basket.

Broken Spear spoke up and suggested that both Chirping Swallow and Sly Squirrel cut off the head and the meat of the bone. He would take the head, guts and any other pieces of fish and push if off the raft.

Taelo agreed to the adjustments and said they should try one round to make sure everyone was in the right place.

After minor adjustments they got into a rhythm that produced a constant flow of large fish being process.

By the time the sun reached its Zenith, Taelo was exhausted. He realized that he was the weakest of the team and that his shoulder and back muscles would be hurting the next day.

He said that three large baskets would feed all the Sages for two handful of sun cycles. It was time to quit.

There seemed to be an immediate response by the school of fish that seemed to immediately disappear.

The eagle cry from above had an immediate effect on everyone on the raft. They looked around for what the threat might be.

They were on the alert but still totally surprised by the huge gapping jaw that clamped down on the raft. It was so close to Broken Spear that Taelo pushed him aside as he drove his spear into the shark.

Saber Scar repeatedly pounded the shark in the head and Marigold drove a spear through its body.

Saber Scar then drove his spear into the shark and repeated the pounding on the skull.

He then threw a rope over the shark and using his spear to brace himself he used a crooked piece of wood to pull the rope around the shark.

Once it was tied off just behind the dorsal fin he stood up and began to pull up on the rope.

Sly Squirrel and Chirping Swallow joined him on the pulling as Taelo used his spear to pull the shark forward and Marigold used her spear to help lift the shark out of the water.

Every time the shark wiggled; Saber Scar would take the time to pound its head several more times.

When the shark was on board Taelo realized that they had caught a shark that was almost as wide as the raft.

They pulled the shark to the front of the raft and pulled it over the front barrier and tied it so that it had its mouth open. They got off the raft and agreed that it looked as if the shark was ready to attack anyone standing in front of the raft.

Taelo declared that it was time to sail for the beach where the Sages were camping.

He wanted to get there and get help in processing the shark.

They had been successful in finding the crossing current and they were returning with enough meat to feed everyone for a full moon cycle.

Taelo told everyone that they were coming back from a very successful endeavor.

Chapter 19: The Sage's Riches

The sailing against the oncoming waves was more of a challenge than Taelo had expected. However, by the time the sun was just past its zenith he had reached the small beach by the side of the river.

Everyone on shore seemed to be waiting for the raft.

Golden Hawk was the first to greet them back as he stood and pointed his spear at the mouth of the shark and gave the battle cry.

There was an enthusiastic organic response of everyone giving the battle cry and running forward with their spears raised.

They all agreed that the raft looked as threatening as it could possibly look.

Almost everyone participated in getting the shark off the boat and up on the beach. Lily, Slow Walker, Floating Cloud and Whistling arrow volunteered to skin it and begin the meat drying preparation.

Quiet Pheasant volunteered to get a group to gather wood to smoke the shark meat.

Taelo pointed to the four large baskets of fish still on the raft and said that they were full of fish that needed salting and drying as well.

He suggested that a large departure celebration meal be prepared for the next sun cycle and that everything had to be on the raft ready for departure by the third sun cycle. This meant that much of the drying would be done by the sun as they travel westward on the raft.

Golden Hawk pointed to the three deer that were hanging in the tree and White Swan took him to see the rows of fish being smoke dried.

The evening meal was fresh shark meat grilled over the open fire, rubbed with salt, and sprinkled with honey. Everyone was enjoying a relaxing evening on the beach.

Taelo asked Broken Spear to explain to everyone the fact that two currents, one from the south and one from the north, met and then together went westward. This would be the way they would cross to the other side where once again there would be land.

Broken Spear described that from the eagles view he could see the difference in the watercolor between the current coming down from the north and the current coming up from the south. He said that the combined flow was greater than either one was on its own.

He then described returning to the cliff base where thousands of fish gathered under and behind the raft. He held up the head of one of the fish and declared it as the ugliest fish he had ever seen. The head was passed around and everyone agreed how ugly it looked. They all commented that the taste of the fish made up for its ugliness.

Broken Spear then described how the shark had attacked the raft at the point where he had been pushing the fish scraps over the side. The mouth he looked into was the most frightening sight that he could remember. Even the bear that had ruined his body had not frightened him as much as looking down into the sharks open mouth as it bit into the raft less than a foot from him.

He credited Taelo, Saber Scar and Marigold with their quick action in killing the shark and on the getting it on board. He gave Chirping Swallow and Sly Squirrel recognition for helping get the shark on board as well. He smiled and said that they had kept up their strength by always carrying him around.

Golden Hawk then shared his experience in leading the hunt in the forest. He shared how the hunt team had gone out and circled a large part of the forest and then worked their way inward towards each other.

Red Oak looked at Grey Fox running and commented that he thought they knew the hunting technique very well and that his son had learned how to use it as well.

Golden Hawk credited the hunters for bagging several animals that looked like ground hogs and in downing the three deer. He described the surprise toward the end of the hunt when a large lion was spotted. He had declared the end of the hunt and had the line break to allow the lion to go its way.

They had all been relieved that the lion chose to depart and not engage them.

Taelo thanked everyone for contributing to making the journey enjoyable and one that would not be short on food.

He took a moment to thank all the Sages for having trained their children so well and he was pleased that they accepted being a part of this journey. He said that to him it was a way that he and his team could contribute some new understanding that would enrich the knowledge that they had bestowed on him and his team.

He then pointed at the those in the next generation and made the point that they would soon contribute to the wellbeing of the clans as well.

Star Leaper stood and looked around. He then described how in the Condor Kingdom, Taelo and all his team members were the stuff of legend.

He pointed to Feather-in-the-Wind and made the point that she would have been a Condor Ice princess but for the brave action of Taelo's team.

He described how Quiet Rabbit and Busy Bee had made their way up the trail that they had all now climbed in the dead of night and rescued Feather-in-the-Wind and carried her down that same trail.

He looked at Busy Bee and complimented her on her being able to pick the exact crack along the trail that she had chosen in the dead of night so many moons before. He assured her that that crack would be visited by everyone that went up that trail.

He thanked the Elk Clan Sages for having recognized the courage, strength and leadership of his daughter and elevating her into the position of the Paradise Elk Clan leader. He went on to emotionally describe how happy he and Neiva were to meet their granddaughter for the first time and to embrace their daughter once again.

Taelo stood and made the point that strong Sages developed strong Sages to be, and he hoped that young Nieva would be as strong as her mother.

As the sun was touching the water on the far horizon Taelo announced that he would like Broken Spear, Sly Squirrel, and Chirping Swallow to each accept three large shark teeth.

He asked that they then select three teeth for Saber Scar and Marigold. He held up some very large shark teeth and he gave three to Golden Hawk, Busy Bee, and Quiet Rabbit.

He then asked the Sages to come forward and select two teeth each.

Once everyone had selected their shark teeth he handed each of the children two teeth as well.

There was still a pile of teeth left that he put in a bag and said that he would keep them in case they met other people with whom they would need to trade and if they had some left on their return to their land they would share them with their Clans.

White Swan looked at Quiet Pheasant and commented that their son's generous nature was once again on display and that they had done the same thing back on the beach of Head Rock Cove when they had caught a similar huge shark.

Quiet Pheasant smiled and recalled Floating Cloud's comment that their two sons were turning out just as the two of them had planned.

Chapter 20: The Current Across

Taelo took the raft out and caught the northward current. He then asked Black Wolf and Red Fox, who had been at the guide paddle when they had discovered the change of currents, to take over. He thanked them for discovering the change in currents and now they would be the first to catch the combined currents that would take them across the mighty sea.

The eagle on high gave a loud cry as the raft reached the combined currents and the raft seemed to pick up speed.

Broken Spear, who was flying with the eagle, called out that the raft was exactly in the middle.

Taelo watched as the sails both bulged with the wind and the raft once again sped up. He was sure it was the fastest the raft had sailed.

The land disappeared and they were surrounded by an expanse of sea that seemed to form a continuous circle horizon.

Taelo looked back and the small guide raft was directly in back. There was nothing to do but sail. The sun was directly in front of them. He hoped that once again he could find a light in the sky that would help him guide the raft through the night.

By the tenth sun cycle all the guide paddle control teams had experienced both sailing in the day as well as holding the course through the night.

Life on the raft took on a pattern where everyone had an activity that kept them busy but there were many periods where everyone just relaxed and enjoyed the breeze.

The raft was ripe with the sweet salty smell of the drying and dried fish. It was rather strong and overpowering as it hit everyone's nasal cavity in musky sticky waves. Everyone was glad to experience the slowly diminishing smell as the drying ended.

The smell of the dried fish being cooked in a stew attracted everyone and the drying process was forgotten. Everyone commented about the magic that Lily and Floating Cloud had done in making such a wonderful stew.

Taelo felt that they had all been fortunate that the beginning of the way across had been sunny and pleasant. Then as he looked ahead he knew that things were about to change. It looked like the cliffs they left behind them were dead ahead. The sky ahead was black foreboding and went up into the sky as far as he could see.

The lightening between the black clouds and the horizon below warned Taelo that the weather was going to take a dramatic turn. He had everyone secure their possessions and make sure that the hides of the lodge were tied down.

He had extra wood placed where it could be used for cooking without having anyone needing to go out to get it.

He had the hides put up to protect the guide paddle area stretched tight.

He went around the raft tying everything that might be damaged down to the deck itself.

The waves rose to the point that the guide control paddle handlers had to use all their skill to ride farther back so that they could keep the nose of the raft from falling into the wave trough. Taelo feared the raft would not survive such a fall.

Taelo reduced the teams to three; He and Marigold, Saber Scar and Golden Hawk and Red Oak and Grey Fox Running. The teams would double up and one team would always be in reserve to come out to help in an emergency.

He made sure that everyone inside the lodge secured themselves in their positions so they would not be tossed around if large waves hit them.

He and everyone on the raft were as prepared as they could be when the storm rolled over them in full force. The sails had been rolled down and the raft was moving on the current only, but Taelo was not sure that the raft was doing anything but getting pounded by the continuous stream of waves.

The waves seemed to continuously engulf them as they rolled over the raft. Those at the guide paddle had tied themselves off to the beams on the raft floor to keep from being swept off.

Taelo kept thanking Talking Wren for the extra log bindings that she had insisted on using to give the raft and all its structure extra strength. The raft seemed to cry like a wart hog being gored while fighting a stronger rival. The groaning and rubbing sounds had everyone on edge.

Then a cracking sound warned Taelo that the main mast was breaking. He rushed and tied the guide robes to the deck and just managed to get back to the guide paddle area as a wave finished the act of ripping the top half of the mast off, Taelo was able to wrap the mast rigging to the raft to keep the broken portion from being washed overboard.

He felt Marigolds iron grip pull him back into the guide paddle protection.

It was impossible to talk. Taelo and Golden Hawk took over and sent the others to shelter in the raft's lodge. They turned the raft to ride the waves that were being driven by the storm.

It was impossible to tell day from night and time seemed to stand still.

It was one continuous fight to keep the raft from being torn apart.

Lily kept time by how many of the same size logs she burned in her small cooking fire that she somehow managed from being consumed by the water washing around her.

She knew that on a regular day she normally consumed six logs. She kept count and finally when she counted all her fingers and her toes, the storm passed, and the sun once again cast its rays on a battered but on a raft that had withstood the pounding.

Taelo did a quick inspection and found that the raft was structurally sound. The protection barrier at the front of the raft required extensive repairs and Broken Spear's sitting area had been battered and needed to be replaced.

The main mast posed the most serious damage. There was no main mast replacement on the raft. Taelo and Saber Scar tied small willow tree stems to form an area around the break to the top half to make a tube. They then had to set up a structure that allowed them to lift the top half up and drop in onto the bottom half. Once that had been accomplished they were able to tie the bottom of the tube to the lower part of the mast. Then additional small willow limbs were added to strengthen the broken area.

Broken Spear said that the repair looked like the repair that had been put on his leg when he had been mauled by the bear. He said he hoped that the repair was better than the one that had been done to his legs.

Once the mast was repaired, Taelo had the main sail hoisted and the raft once again caught the wind and proceeded to make its westward way.

He was sure that his decision to run with the storm versus to continue to face it head on had saved the raft, but he was also sure that they had lost the ten-sun cycle distance they had previously achieved.

Chapter 21: Sea Gulls

The winds and the current settled into the previous pattern and Taelo once again had the raft of Sages smoothly riding the waves. He was at the guide paddle when he spotted a lone sea gull gliding through the air. He announced that there was land ahead.

Everyone perked up and began looking ahead. A few took up their fishing spots and tried their luck.

Broken Spear announced that everyone should relax and that he and his two keepers would let them know when they saw land. He said that he sensed dolphins nearby and as he finished saying it, three dolphins came along side and rode the small wave created by the nose of the raft.

Broken Spear let everyone know that he could not understand the dolphins, but he was getting the feeling of sunshine and warmth in his mind and was sure it was being sent by one of the dolphins.

Taelo replied that he too felt the sunshine.

Once again everyone came out on the raft and watched the dolphins and looked ahead. They all commented that they envied Broken Spear's and Taelo's gift of being able to sense the dolphins.

Taelo gave Quiet Rabbit a hug and told her that he always sensed her heart and got a hug back from her.

The land came into view as the sun hit its crest. The sky was a light blue and the land of high mountains ahead stood out in an almost black contrast.

It was clear to Taelo that they were approaching a series of islands by the way the blue of the water split between the towering black peaks to meet the light blue of the sky that lay beyond.

Taelo asked Broken Spear to select the opening ahead that they should take.

Broken Spear conferred with Chirping Swallow and Sly Squirrel and together they selected an opening that was among the narrowest but that suggested there were beaches that might allow the raft to land.

Taelo went back to the team guiding the raft and pointed out the opening. It was easily spotted because beyond the opening between the islands the dark grey plumes of a volcano was rising like a signal plume.

As the raft approached the opening, the sun seemed to be setting just beyond the two islands and behind the volcano.

Taelo and Golden Hawk were at the guide paddle when Broken Spear pointed to a small cove with a sandy beach that seemed protected from the sea waves and the wind. They guided the raft toward the beach. Taelo had Red Fox and Black Wolf bring the main sail down.

Red Oak and Grey Fox Running were at the back ready to drop the back anchor stone and Marigold and Saber Scar were at the front.

When they were in position, Taelo told Red Oak to drop the back stone. It went down but did not hit bottom. Grey Fox Running let all the rope out and still the stone did not hit.

Taelo immediately called for Spear Tip and Yellow Flower to lower the front sail.

Taelo called out to Saber Scar and Marigold that he was going to let the raft go up on the beach and that they should make sure they jumped on the beach as far as possible to drop the front anchor stones.

He asked everyone to come to the back of the raft.

The front of the raft seemed to kiss the sandy beach and slide smoothly up and then stop. About a third of the raft was up on the beach and the back stone was still not touching bottom.

Taelo and Golden Hawk pulled the back stone up and put it into its holder.

Saber Scar looked down into the water and wondered out loud how deep it might be.

Lily set up a cooking ring on the beach and everyone contributed some driftwood that they picked up along the beach.

Red Oak and Grey Fox Running returned from the far end of beach dragging what turned out to be a huge crab that they had captured and that was holding on to a branch they had teased it with.

Marigold used her war hammer and killed it and then broke off each leg and took it over to the cooking ring and gave them to Lily to roast. The front claws were cracked open, and each half was put by the fire to roast.

Taelo declared a crab dinner celebration for having survived the successful crossing of the great sea.

Yellow Flower asked about going swimming.

Broken Spear, sitting with his back to a black glass like stone, pointed out to a large fin in the water that seemed to be slowly gliding by, and said that Yellow Flower would only be a small bite for a shark of that size that seemed to be looking for dinner.

Yellow Flower sat down next to Broken Spear and thanked him for the warning and said that she would be much happier just watching.

Taelo brought up the need to find a replacement for the main sail mast. He said that he would feel fortunate to find two masts. One to put up and one to hold in reserve in case they faced another fierce storm.

Golden Hawk agreed with Taelo and pointed out the fact that they also needed to resupply the raft with firewood and that many of the hides had seen better days and needed repair or replacement.

Lily spoke up and suggested that they hunt for some fresh meat and catch some fish.

Taelo agreed with her and made the point that fishing should now once again be reasonable since they would be sailing close to land.

The next morning it took all the Sages to push the raft into the water. Once it was floating free, everyone quickly boarded. Saber Scar and Marigold put the shore boulders into their holders and once they were on board they tied them down and the with long poles they pushed the raft away from the beach.

The raft slowly glide backward until the wind caught the front sail and Taelo was able to line the front of the raft up with the island that Broken Spear pointed out.

Once the wind filled the small sail, Taelo had the main sail raised and then adjusted so that he could guide the raft toward the island.

They passed the rumbling and smoldering volcano to their right. He hoped to get as far away as possible. He did not want to be near when it erupted.

Chapter 22: People on the Beach

The wind filled the sails and Taelo urged the raft forward as fast as possible. The rumbling from the volcano behind him made him nervous. He wanted to be as far away as possible in the event of an eruption. He was focused on maximizing the forward motion of the raft when Broken Spear pointed toward the island ahead and said there were people on the beach.

Taelo asked Saber Scar and Marigold to take over at the guide paddle. He went to the front of the raft to get a better look ahead.

He asked everyone to get into their fighting diamond groups and to lay out their weapons. He said that when they landed he would like to have White Swan's diamond in front of the raft. Saber Scar's diamond to the left and Red Oaks diamond to the right. He would step to the front of them all and greet the people on the beach.

Everyone else should remain on the raft but be prepared to join the fight if there was a confrontation.

He asked Broken Spear to keep his seat but gave him a shield in case a fight ensued. Taelo asked him to act as a grand master. He would be on the beach but would turn and point to Broken Spear who then would raise his open hand and give a friendly greeting.

High in the sky a large brown eagle let out a cry. Broken Spear closed his eyes and concentrated on the eagle. He then spoke and said he was now flying with a cousin of Taelo's white-headed totem.

He said that he could now clearly see the people gathered on the beach. They looked much like everyone on the raft. Their attention seemed to be on the rumbling volcano, and they had not yet seen the raft approaching. They all seemed to be carrying a spear, but their spears did not have stone or shark tooth tips. A few had wooden clubs, but none had a stone war hammer. And none had the flat shark toothed weapon that everyone on the raft now possessed.

Taelo asked White Swan's diamond to gather on the very front of the raft so they could immediately take their position and be ready to protect Saber Scar and Marigold as they placed the beach anchor stones.

They were within hailing distance when the gathering on the beach finally took notice of the raft.

Broken Spear raised his right arm with an open hand and, in the three languages represented on the raft, he called out that they came as friends.

As the raft kissed the beach, Saber Scar and Marigold took the two beach anchors and proceeded to place them.

White Swan and her team were immediately in position and she raised her empty hand and called out friend in all three languages.

Taelo walked to the front and raised his right hand and said friend and slowly walked forward. He had his flat blade weapon on his back, but he had nothing in his hands.

A cry came from the sky, and everyone looked up to see an eagle that was mostly brown but had bright golden neck feathers.

Taelo pointed to the sky, tapped his chest, and made his hand like a claw and tapped his chest again.

An older member of those on the beach approached and tapped his chest and made the sign of a swimming fish and then the act of biting.

Taelo took his action to mean his name was Shark. Taelo took out one of the shark teeth he had in his vest pocket and handed it to the person who had introduced himself.

The smile and the universal shaking of one's head up and down confirmed Taelo's guess at the name.

The smile seemed to message the friendliness Taelo had hoped for.

Shark pointed at the raft and shook his head back and forth and pointed to the smoldering volcano. He pointed to his right and indicated that Taelo should take the raft around the island away from the beach area.

As if the volcano was listening it increased its rumbling and the ground on the beach seemed to shake and the beach rose and undulated. A sand wave traveled down the beach toward the raft

Taelo turned and shouted for everyone to get back on board. He called out to get the raft out into the water.

Saber Scar and Marigold had their anchors in place in record time and Grey Fox running and Red Oak were pulling the raft out as fast as they could.

Taelo called out for everyone to be storm ready.

The front sail team had their sail up in record time.

Marigold and Saber Scar were almost as fast with the main sail.

Taelo and Golden Hawk were at the guide paddle keeping the raft as close to shore as they dared.

Suddenly the sky seemed to shake and the wind that hit the sails tried to rip them off. Taelo could hear the mast cracking as if it would once again break but this time it held.

The cry from the sky added to natures drama as suddenly a huge black plume seem to rise from the top of the volcano and an ear-splitting boom followed. Almost immediately a red pulsing stream of lava followed the rising black plume as if it was chasing it off. The red plum then began a slow descent and as the raft went behind the island Taelo could see the red plume hitting the water and sending a huge wave outward towards the island.

Several dolphins had followed the raft and Broken Spear said they had been urging the raft on.

Taelo looked ahead for a place to take the raft back to shore. He saw a person waving him in toward a small beach.

As he got closer he could see an opening that led into an enclosed area that had several large wooden boats that carved out of a large trees.

The area was just large enough for the raft.

Taelo took the raft in and followed the normal landing procedure. This time only a few of the people of the island were at hand.

Taelo asked everyone to remain on the raft until he had time to determine what the arrangements would be.

Star Leaper ask to accompany Taelo. He said that he thought he had heard some words that were similar to his language. The origin stories of the Condor Clan told of their people having crossed the seas for many moons and finally finding a new land. He was very curious if the words he thought he had heard were the old language of the Condor Clan.

Taelo agreed that he should come along and see if these were some of his ancestors.

Chapter 23: Ancestors

The sun seemed to be shining through a grey mist. A light grey ash was falling and coating everything.

Taelo suggested everyone stay in the raft's lodge and try not to breath the ash.

He followed the guide up the winding path. They arrived at the opening of a large cave. There seemed to be about ten hands of people standing at the cave opening.

Taelo greeted the person that had spoken to him on the beach.

The response of friend and welcome seemed to almost be of the Condor Clan language.

Star Leaper replied, "I am pleased to meet you and glad to see that you seem to be doing well" in the Condor Clan language.

He got a surprised look from the person standing in front of them who then looked over his shoulder and shouted to the people at the mouth of the cave that a long-lost brother had returned.

Star Leaper understood most of what was said and replied that he was from the land across the ocean.

He turned to Taelo and told him that the Condor Clan had stories of having crossed the ocean and making the Condor land their new home.

They were invited to sit on some stones positioned so that they faced the sea toward where the sun was faintly shining through the ash as it slowly made its way to the far horizon.

They were offered an unfamiliar drink that Taelo learned was made from the coconut. It was immediately clear that it was fermented and had a significant kick. He took sparing sips as they sat and talked.

Taelo let Star Leaper do most of the talking as he watched the two excitedly tell stories of the past. He was amazed that they had crossed the sea and found what seemed to be the origin of the people of the Condor Clan.

He was sure that Star Leaper was as amazed as he.

The leader said that he was known as Shark Fin and that his people were known as the Sea Wave Clan to a handful of other clans on the other islands.

After a snack of some grilled fish, Shark Fin extended an invitation for the people on the raft to come up to the cave to spend the night.

Star Leaper thanked Shark Fin for the invitation and responded that the plan was to hold a celebration feast on the beach and stay on the raft. He extended an invitation for Shark Fin and his people to join in on the celebration.

On the way back to the raft, Star Leaper commented that he had made up the celebration as a way to stay out of the cave. He said that the bad odor made it hard enough to sit outside without making a face.

Taelo agreed and complemented him on finding a friendly way to stay out of the cave.

On return to the beach, Taelo shared what had happened on at the meeting with the leader of the Sea Wave People.

He also complemented Star Leaper for having deflected an invitation for all of them to sleep at the cave that smelled worse than any he had ever been to.

He let them know that Star Leaper had declared that they were all having a celebration feast and that they needed to start preparing it for all of them and all of the Sea Wave people that had been invited.

Lily and Floating Cloud suggested they share the last of the buffalo meat prepared in a stew and offer grilled fish as a second meat dish.

Saber Scar pointed to a large pile of coconuts that he had gathered and said that there was sweet water inside that they could offer as a drink. He said that he was sure the Sea Wave people would know what it was.

He said he had already loaded the raft with a huge number of them to augment the water supply.

The sun was low on the horizon when the Sea Wave people came down to the beach.

Quiet Rabbit and Busy Bee had recruited many of the Sages to sweep the ash off the beach using the leaves from the trees that the coconuts grew on. Once that was done they all took a quick swim to rinse the ash off themselves.

The clean beach was a surprise to the Sea Wave people, and they thanked their friends for taking the ash off.

They were also surprised when they found out that all the Sages and even the children all spoke the language that was almost the same as theirs. There was a constant chatter and much laughter when the communication failed because of words that were used were not understood.

Taelo took the opportunity to show Shark Fin the broken main mast. He went on the raft and used a stick to tap on the broken part of the mast. He returned to the beach and asked if there were any trees that could be used to replace it.

Shark Fin talked to one of his men. He ran off and returned with a spear made of black wood and handed it to Shark Fin who then showed it to Taelo and then pointed to the mast.

Taelo took the spear and ran his hand along dark brown wood. He nodded to indicate that it would be a good wood.

Shark Fin indicated that at the rising of the sun he would take Taelo to where ten trees that could make masts could be found.

Taelo thanked him and then offered him a sip of honey wine. It got the smile and favorable nod that he had expected. It was probably as potent as the fermented coconut drink he had sipped outside of the cave but much smoother.

As the islanders left the beach Taelo led a discussion of what needed to get done before they once again set off on their journey.

He would go and get two masts. Those remaining on the beach needed to restock, repair, fish and enjoy their time on shore.

Chapter 24: Masts

Taelo had spent the night out on the beach and was up when the sun broke over the mountain. He was enjoying some of the coconut drink and walking along the shore when a young member of the Sea Wave Clan came to guide him to the place where the masts for the raft were located.

Golden Hawk came along and the two of them talked to their young guide. Golden Hawk had the better command of the Condor Clan language and he and the guide kept up a constant dialogue.

He learned that far toward where the sun set there were other people that were fierce warriors and were not friendly but often came and tried to take over his clan. His clan never fought with them directly but went into hiding and repeatedly harassed them until they left the island.

Taelo complemented the young man for taking the better way to face superior fighters.

They were joined by Shark Fin when they reached the top of the trail. Then they continued around the mountain until a long valley nestled between the mountain they were on and the next two mountains. The valley looked like a lush green lake in the middle of the island.

The valley had a small freshwater stream meandering through a forest of tall trees with grayish brown fibrous bark that had shallow longitudinal fissures.

Taelo and Golden Hawk walked among the trees and picked out two that appeared to be the right height and diameter. He commented on the look of the leaves whose upper surface were rough and the lower surface covered in yellowish hair. He pointed to the new young red leaves and the dark green mature ones.

Taelo was showing Golden Hawk the seeds from the tree and Shark Fin explained that the seeds had many uses. He explained that by boiling them and drinking the water constipation could be taken care of. He also said that by grinding the seed and mixing it with water it could be spread on the skin to cure burns or some infections. He indicated that it was also useful in stopping itching.

Shark Fin had several of his young men begin to cut down the trees that had been selected. A light smell of leather seemed to waft into the air.

Taelo commented on the pleasant scent and Shark Fin said that fresh branches were often brought to the cave to improve the odor there.

Taelo took in the golden-brown color and dense close grained smooth grain and texture of the wood that had a strange waxy texture seemed seemed to be a faint smell of leather.

He learned from Shark Fin that they called the tree Technitona. He pointed to the color of the wood at the base of the fallen tree and then at the much darker color of his wooden walking stick.

He indicated that the wood darkened as it aged.

Taelo watched as the limbs were removed and the bark taken off the tree. The leaves were put into a large bag and the limbs bundled together. It was clear to him that every part of the tree would be used, and the forest floor would be cleared.

Each tree required six people to carry it. He and Golden Hawk picked the trunk end of one of the trees and followed behind the group carrying the first tree. He looked behind and saw that all the branches had been bundled and were being pulled along as well. The area around the base of the two trees had been cleared and other than the two stumps there was no indication of the area having been disturbed.

Going back to the cave meant an uphill climb followed by a long level trail. They reached the cave just after the sun's zenith.

Shark Fin invited them to have something to eat.

Both he and Golden Hawk accepted. They were drinking from a young coconut as they watched a group of young men and women carry the two logs down the trail toward the beach.

Taelo smiled and pointed to them. He took the bag tied to his vest and picked out a large shark tooth and handed it to Shark Fin. Then he took out a shark tooth for each person who had helped to harvest the two trees.

Shark Fin nodded and thanked Taelo then he called to a young man standing nearby. The young man listened and walked back into the cave. He returned with two walking sticks that Shark Fin presented to Taelo and Golden Hawk.

After their meal and a drink of the fermented coconut water Taelo stood up and brandishing his new walking stick led the way down the trail.

He arrived at the beach just as the group that had carried the masts down were on their way back up the trail.

Everyone was gathered around the two masts and the pile of limbs that had also been brought down.

White Swan commented on the leather like smell of the tree and the fine grain of the wood.

Red Oak commented on the quality of the two masts.

Grey Fox asked where the extra mast was going to be kept.

Taelo had been thinking about how to handle the extra mast. He asked Saber Scar to make an opening at the bottom of the front wave guard and make sure the area under Broken Spear's seat was clear.

He then recruited Red Oak, Grey Fox Running, and Saber Scar to help lift the tree he had chosen to be the spare mast. He and Golden Hawk together with the rest lifted the tree and guided it to the opening that had been made. When the trunk was about halfway on the raft he went on board to make sure it stopped well short of the two out rigger stations.

After some minor adjustment he asked Marigold, to show Spear Tip, Black Wolf, Red Fox, Yellow Flower, and Neiva how to tie the mast to the floor of the raft.

They all laughed and said that they were expert at tying logs together and could do it with their eyes closed.

Taelo then asked for some help in removing the main mast. He had the sail and rigging set aside and then proceeded to cut the bindings from the bottom of the main mast. Once it was loose he had Saber Scar and Marigold each hold of a pair of poles with a rope between them and he and Golden Hawk pushed the mast into the middle of the two poles.

They then helped Marigold and Saber Scar to lower the main mast between the outrigger stands. Once it was down, Red Oak and Grey Fox Running joined in to lift the mast and drop it over the side into the water. The mast was pulled ashore and was broken up and made into a large pile that would be burned that evening.

The new mast towered higher into the air and the sail was lengthened about a half a spear's length.

Everyone had pitched in, and the raft was once again seaworthy and sported a better new mast and a larger sail.

For a second evening the Sea Wave Clan came down to the beach. This time they brought a young boor that had been roasted on a spit to share. They explained that it had been seasoned with a mix of young white coconut flesh and salt and roasted over the fire for the entire day.

Taelo lit the bonfire that was fueled by the remains of the old mast, and they all sat around or walked the beach talking and sharing stories in the language of the Condor Clan.

Chapter 25: Sea Attack

The Sea Wave Clan were all on the beach to wish the Sages off. Everyone exchanged their farewells and then the raft was pushed off by Sea Wave Clan members as the rest of the clan chanted what Star Leaper explained was their traveling chant.

As the raft turned toward the sunset horizon they waved goodbye to the people that Star Leaper was sure were those of his ancestral roots. It had been an eventful meeting that would be a story that he would share with the Condor Clan on his return.

He made the point that the Journey of Sages had filled in a part of the Condor Clan's history that had been thought of as legend but in fact had been a description of their true history.

They sailed toward the setting sun for two sun cycles when Broken Spear called out that a large number of boats were approaching them.

Taelo could barely make them out but had everyone prepare for the encounter. He warned everyone to be ready to defend the raft. He asked the younger members to go into the raft lodge and build themselves a second barrier from the goods stored inside.

He told them they could leave the sides of the lodge open but to stay down if fighting began.

He asked Broken Spear for additional reports and learned that the oncoming boats seemed to be warriors that were planning to fight.

Taelo wondered if the volcano's explosion had caused them to come toward it and the encounter they were about to have was pure coincidence.

He asked that Broken Spear go into the lodge and supervise the younger group and asked that Chirping Swallow and Sly Squirrel provide protection for everyone in the lodge.

He then had White Swan's fighting diamond take the front position, Saber Scar's take the right side and Marigold's to take the left side.

The wind was full in the sails and Taelo had no intension of slowing down. He tied the steering paddle off and he and Golden Hawk laid their weapons out. If there was a fight he would be as deadly as was possible.

The raft was sailing smoothly forward as the flotilla of canoes rapidly came at them. When they were within a spear's throw, Taelo went to the front of the raft and raised his hand and in the local language he called out that they were friends.

The spear he had to avoid was the reply and the shouting of the warriors in the oncoming flotilla rose to a roar.

Taelo let out his war cry and everyone on the raft echoed it.

He returned to his position in the back.

One warrior took hold of the mast that was out front and began climbing on board.

White Swan waited until his foot touched the raft. She gave out the war cry and then pushed him off with the tip of her spear.

The canoes swarmed each side of the raft and as the warriors tried to climb on board they were met with war hammers smashing their heads in and the flat shark toothed weapon cutting down from above and nearly decapitating them.

The fighting diamond members gave out a war cry with every blow.

It was a short-lived battle and the warriors in the canoes were decimated.

Taelo watched as the canoes regrouped and then began to paddle to catch the raft.

White Swan reported that no one on the raft had been wounded and none of the attackers had made it onboard.

Taelo thanked everyone and warned them that the second attack would most likely be a hail of spears.

He asked Quiet Rabbit to organize the slingers on each side of the boat. Two groups would sling directly towards the back and two would cover any canoe that tried to come to the sides.

Every person on board was a capable slinger. They had an ample supply of glass shards that had been given to them by the Condor Clan. Quiet Rabbit set up four slinging stations that had two rotating slingers and one glass supplier at each station.

She suggested that the slingers aim for the chest and arms. If that did not slow down the attack then she would call out a command to aim at the face.

Taelo waited until the warrior in the lead canoe was raising his spear to throw it and then called out for the slingers to sling.

The warrior was hit dead center in the chest by Feather-in-the-Wind and he fell backwards into the canoe.

The rotation of the slingers and their effectiveness caused an immediate stop of the canoes. Loud shouting and spear waving followed but the pursuit stopped.

The raft sailed on and the brief encounter with the attackers was over.

Once Broken Spear was back in his bow seat, Taelo asked him to keep a lookout for any other canoes or people on beaches.

They sailed out toward the open sea. The islands slowly diminished in the horizon behind them as the sun ahead threatened to sink below the open sea horizon.

There was no land ahead in sight.

Taelo decided that he would turn the raft to his right. The sun ahead set three spear lengths from the tip of his spar mast to the left.

He then made sure each of the guide paddle teams understood what he had done and that they should keep the small guide raft with the torch sailing directly behind the raft.

Lily and Floating Cloud passed out roast shark meat and congratulated everyone for having defeated their attackers.

White Swan let out Taelo's war cry and was then echoed by everyone on board.

Taelo listened and took in the fact that the battle had invigorated all the Sages and was being talked about by the next generation.

He told Golden Hawk that he could not have planned a better situation if he had wanted to and that the Journey of Sages was in fact turning out to meet his expectations.

Chapter 26: Replenishment

The currents turned toward the north and Taelo guided the raft as close to land as possible while keeping far enough off the coast to allow him from traveling into small harbors or other inlets. He did not want to add time to the journey by following too close to the coastline.

Broken Spear, using his long-range vision to highlight land that seemed to indicate the coast was going northward but coming out towards the east into the sea, became key. Then he pointed out what seemed to be either a huge inlet harbor or they were approaching a very large island which had a very wide channel to the west.

Taelo decided that they would stay to the eastern side and see if there was a good place to land. He made the point that they were in need of replenishing their supplies. He asked Quiet Rabbit, Busy Bee, and Feather-in-the-Wind to organize the work of renewing everything on the raft. He asked Red Oak and Grey Fox Running to organize three hunting teams.

He laughed when Feather-in-the-Wind asked what he would be doing and replied that he planned to sit with Broken Spear and do a little fishing.

The fish he had in mind were the sharks that seemed to be patrolling the beach area. He pointed out the sharks that seemed to be feeding as they went back and forth along the beach. He asked Golden Hawk, Whistling Arrow, and Slow Walker if they cared to join him in trying to spear one of the sharks.

He asked them to help carry Broken Spear up toward a spit of black rock that jutted out into the sea. He then led the way along a shallow area that was knee deep to a large craggy boulder that appeared to be lava that had rolled into the sea and had solidified.

Once out on the rock, he tied his barbed spear off to the boulder.

Everyone followed his lead, and they stood along the rock waiting for a shark to come near enough to spear.

Taelo looked down on a series of turtles that were feeding on the moss and fern growing off the boulder. Just beyond them a good sized school of fish were hovering in the ebb and flow of the incoming waves.

Taelo watched as a huge shark seemed to glide in toward the boulder as if it was going to hit on one of turtles. Then as it turned toward the school of fish Taelo threw his spear with all his might and watched as it hit just behind the head and went through to the other side.

Almost at the same time another spear hit the shark about two feet back on the body.

The shark took a swift turn and tried to swim away. Taelo was sure the ropes were going to snap as they sang when they hit the end. The two ropes held, and the shark headed back toward the rock. The shark appeared to be getting ready to leap out of the water and everyone took a step back from the edge.

Taelo and Golden Hawk both wrapped the lose rope around the tie off point. The shark was now constrained and could not take another run.

Whistling Arrow speared the shark about halfway back toward the tail and Slow Walker threw his spear another two feet back.

They both pulled their ropes tight. Taelo and Golden Hawk both pulled their ropes farther in.

Taelo gave his war cry and then announced that all the four of them had to do was to be able to wrestle the shark to the shore and kill it.

Taelo led off keeping his rope tight and staying well ahead of the head of the shark. Golden Hawk followed but stayed behind the head of the shark and pulled in sideward so it could not position itself to strike Taelo.

Slow Walker pulled the tail toward him, and Whistling arrow pulled his rope toward the shore.

The shark's thrashing did not diminish. It increased as the four dragged it halfway out of the water toward where Broken Spear was sitting.

Sly Squirrel and Chirping Swallow both came out carrying their war hammers.

Taelo called for everyone to hold tight to their ropes and asked the two to be like Saber Scar or Marigold when they had smashed the heads of the shark and the alligator.

They both laughed, they knew those stories well and they both took turns hitting the shark's head until it finally stopped thrashing.

Taelo announced that he would have to tell the story of the two and how they had subdued the largest shark that had ever been caught.

"Don't make us mad they both shouted," and held up their war hammers.

Taelo organized everyone and they pulled the shark all the way from the water.

He watched as Lily and Floating Cloud took over the skinning of the shark.

Saber Scar and Marigold and their hunt team had returned. Their team was pulling two bears, a deer, and several smaller animals on a travois.

They came over to see what was happening. They both laughed when Lily told them about Sly Squirrel and Chirping Swallow taking the place of the two and claiming no one should make them mad.

Taelo had turned Broken Spear's seat so the two could sit and watch the shark get skinned.

Broken Spear pointed to Slow Walker as he measured the size of the shark. He counted and gave an exclamation as the measuring spear was flipped over for the sixth time.

He commented that every shark seemed to be bigger and that the next shark would be so large that it would be longer than the raft.

As the hunt teams returned, the beach became the scene of bears, deer and a variety of animals getting skinned.

Star Leaper came over to where Broken Spear was sitting and commented about the success of all the teams. He said that he had learned why the Elk Clan was so rich in food. The hunting technique that was used was new to him and he was impressed by the way the hunters could select which animals to let go and which ones to take.

Whistling Arrow and Slow Walker spent the afternoon taking the teeth from the shark's mouth and jaw.

They had sorted and put them in size order in front of Broken Spear's seat. Taelo stood up and called everyone together. He took the first three teeth and gave them to Broken Spear and praised him for being a top Sage that had given him the good advice not to kill any sharks that were larger than the length of the raft.

He then gave three to Sly Squirrel and Chirping Swallow for being so brave as to get in the water with the shark.

He then gave four each to Whistling Arrow, Slow Walker, and Golden Hawk. He took four and gave them to Quiet Rabbit to hold for him.

The rows of teeth seemed to be undiminished. He pointed to them and declared that the Sages line up by age and pick up the next two until they all had two. Then the Sages to be would all get two. If there were any remaining they would go into the shark tooth bag and be used as bartering goods.

White Swan quietly shared that Taelo had been generous with the wealth that could have been mostly his since he, Golden Hawk and Burley Bear had killed the first of the giant sharks so many seasons ago at the Head Rock Bay.

Floating Cloud repeated what she had said then, "Isn't this how you raised them and planned for them to turn out?"

She remembered well learning that Taelo had been the one that had made sure that she and Quiet Rabbit always had food throughout their first winter with the Elk Clan.

She felt very lucky for it to have had turned out how she had desired it would.

Chapter 27: Northward Bound

Taelo's generosity lifted the energy of everyone on the journey. It was clear to all that they had all become closer and seemed to enjoy being together. They all had a better understanding of why Taelo and Golden Hawk had such devoted and faithful friends. The two displayed an aura of confidence, friendliness and an inner confidence that seemed to fill the air. They were generous and they were constantly seeking to enrich those around them.

They also learned that the two were constantly teasing and joking with each other.

Before harvesting the seaweed that he had found growing along the base of the cliff towering over a rocky seashore, Golden Hawk approached Taelo and pointed to the very top of the cliff and suggested that Taelo stand at the top and watch for any sharks that might attack so that he could jump down with his spear and save any Sage that was threatened.

That was a reference to Taelo's amazing jump from a cliff to save Golden Hawk from a giant shark on their Journey of Discovery. This was a well-known story among most of the Sages and after they looked at the height of the cliff, they all laughed.

White Swan explained the joke to Star Leaper and Neiva who then joined in on urging Taelo to climb the cliff.

Taelo joined in and said that he had planned to climb up, but he had already accepted Broken Spear's invitation to sit with him to watch the seaweed harvest from the shore and he did not want to disappoint the wisest Sage on the journey.

It was a bountiful seaweed harvest and was put on the drying racks on the raft along with all the meat that needed to be dried.

The firewood was replenished and tied down securely.

The food supply was put on board.

Everyone arranged their belongings for the continuing journey.

The Journey of Sages was once again ready to leave shore and head northward.

Broken Spear looked ahead and suggested the landmark that should be the first goal as the raft sailed along the shore.

Taelo agreed and had the outrigger floats adjusted so that the raft held to a wave and had the sails turned to catch the wind. He felt the raft surge forward as it held steady and seamed to eagerly take to the sea.

Life on the raft once again seemed to flow naturally.

The hides being processed, dried fish was bundled and put in baskets and the seaweed was put into bags. Spears, hand axes and other tools were repaired and renewed.

Language was being taught and Taelo once again led the exercise sessions.

A favorite activity was making bowls and other clay objects in the glazing furnace that was part of the cooking ring.

With fresh shark, bear, and deer meat available, everyone took turns sitting at the fire ring grilling snacks to eat.

Lily commented that she liked having everyone enjoying grilling their own food and sitting around the cooking ring. It was one constant that everyone seemed to gravitate to. The chatter and laughter seemed to warm the atmosphere on the raft.

Spear fishing was excellent, and the fish brought back to the cooking ring went directly onto grilling sticks.

Feather-in-the-Wind got accused of having a hollow leg. She seemed to consistently be grilling and eating. Young Neiva seemed to have the same capacity as her mother.

Even Lasher seemed to gravitate to the cooking ring. He seemed to be part of the exercise group, or by the cooking ring or he would nap under Broken Spear's sitting area.

Yellow Flower was the one that first spotted the location where the three rafts that had been built in the Journey of Circumvention. She climbed up on the rafts front wave protector and pointed to the cliffs that graced the northern side of the river as she excitedly announced that they had come to where she had been before.

Taelo guided the raft to the southern edge of the river's mouth and had the back anchor dropped and the guide boards lifted as the raft came up to the beach.

He announced that they would spend two sun cycles at this location before once again going northward to the great ice bridge.

The weather was cooling, and the stop allowed everyone to prepare for the colder weather they would face as they continued their journey northward.

Whistling Arrow and Slow Walker remembered the large crabs that they had harvested on the north side of the river. They soon returned with a bag full and then led several of the Sages to where the crabs were easily harvested from a shallow rocky area.

The crab meat would be added to the rafts well stocked food supply and would be added to the grilling at the fire ring.

The wood supply was replenished and the black clams that populated the shallow waters along the beach were harvested and added to the meat supply.

Taelo was relieved that food would not be an issue for the remainder of the journey.

His only remaining concern was the weather they might face in crossing back toward the east as they went along the ice bridge back to Head Cove.

The cool mornings and the nip in the air seemed to signal a change in the weather. It was clear to everyone that the weather would continue to get colder as they proceeded. Everyone took out their cold weather clothes and laid them out in the sun to refresh them.

Taelo and Lasher took a long walk along the shore and returned with a series of shells and sand dollars that he planned to use to make items that he could trade at the clan meeting.

He let everyone know that he expected to arrive back in time for them to attend the upcoming clan meeting and that they should be prepared to show their wealth and goods they had to trade.

Nieva and Star Leaper asked about the Elk Clan meeting and announced that they would love to attend, and they were eager to do the trading that everyone seemed to be preparing for. Nieva pointed out that she had a good supply of glazed pottery and eating utensils. Star Leaper said that he would concentrate on making decorative spears and hand axes and that he was looking forward to be part of the Elk Clan event.

Chapter 28: The Eagle's Cry

Taelo was leading his exercise walking class when the cry of the eagle caused him to stop and look up. He approached Broken Spear who held up his hand and said softly that he was flying with the eagle.

The eagle was flying toward a white plume of smoke rising from a beach that was not yet in sight. Broken Spear commented that there was a group of fighters with their backs to the sea facing a large group attacking them.

Taelo called out for the fighting diamonds to form. He asked each diamond if they had any reservations of engaging in battle. He asked Spear Tip, Black Wolf, Red Fox, Yellow Flower, Young Neiva to stay on board and guard Broken Spear.

Saber Scar and Marigold were sailing the raft toward the white plume.

The eagle cried again as the raft approached the beach.

The warrior's on the beach formed two lines. One facing the sea and one facing the forest at the edge of the beach.

Taelo surveyed the situation and asked Quiet Rabbit to take her diamond to the left, and Busy Bee to take the right. Then he asked White Swan to take left center and Feather-in-the-Wind to take right center.

He let them know that he, Golden Hawk, Saber Scar, Marigold, Red Oak, and Grey Fox Running would form a small fighting triangle in front of all of them.

He turned the raft over to Red Fox and Black Wolf and told them that they, Yellow Flower, Spear Tip and Young Nieva should stay on the raft and keep everyone away.

He was already in the water as Marigold and Saber Scar positioned the front boulders on the beach.

He took his position at the front of all the fighting diamonds and repeated the word friend in the language of the White Bear Clan.

He heard Broken Spear also calling out friend in that language.

The leader on the beach approached and pointed to the sky and said, "the cry of the eagle let us know that the "claw that strikes," our friend, Taelo was on the way.

We remember you well from our battle with the Sky Eyes. I see that you have arrived with a small army to aid us once again in our time of peril.

We are losing our fight with the cannibal people. They have taken some of our people as hostages and for food. We were making our last stand when the eagle called on us to light a signal fire.

Taelo gave a brief greeting and then organized the warriors on the beach. He had the Sage's fighting diamonds take the front position to guard the beach while he organized the White Bear Clan warriors.

Taelo explained the fighting diamond formation and the role each person in the diamond played. He moved three experienced people from the Sage's fighting diamond to take the front three positions of each of four fighting diamonds made up of the White Bear Clan warriors. The Sage's fighting diamonds were augmented with warriors from the beach. These warriors took positions in the rear and were given instructions by each diamond leader what their role was to be.

Taelo positioned the nine fighting diamonds in a wide V that resembled the formation that geese form when flying in the air.

He had been surprised by Lily's insistence that she would be his left side slinger. He turned to find Floating Cloud taking the slinging position to his right.

He had made sure that each fighting diamond had three top slingers at the front and that every member carried a bag of glass shards for the slingers.

He made his instructions clear. There would be no taking of prisoners and no cannibals should be allowed to launch a spear. He emphasized that this was a battle of absolute annihilation. These instructions were very different than any he had ever given to the fighting diamonds.

White Swan commented to her fighting diamond that she had never been with Taelo when he had assumed such authority and such an uncompromising position. She had heard some stories from Lily and some of the other survivors of their experiences as captives of the cannibals, but they had always praised Taelo for his fairness.

Quiet Pheasant who had taken the lead position of the fighting diamond next to White Swan's added that she had talked with Golden Hawk who had been part of the battles with the cannibals and learned that Taelo had taken the same position when fighting those battles. He made the point that Taelo had saved the infants, but no cannibal parent had survived.

Quiet Rabbit took note of Lily and her grandmother who had taken up positions as slingers in Taelo's fighting diamond. She was somewhat surprised but pleased that they had taken those two spots. She knew her grandmother was a true believer in Taelo, and that Lily would do anything for him.

Nieva had the fighting diamond next to her and she made a point that only three fighting diamonds had a male at point. One was up front and the other two were in back.

Taelo walked the formation of fighting diamonds and made sure each diamond was ready and knew their role and knew to stay in their assigned position.

He let the back of the diamonds know that they would be asked to turn and face the sea and bring the two outer diamonds to form a closed back for the formation if the cannibals tried to get around and behind them.

He left two handful of warriors in a diamond formation with instructions to guard the raft. They were to give a blast on their seashell horn if they were attacked.

The eagle let out a cry.

Lasher who had taken a position next to Quiet Rabbit let out a howl.

Taelo blew on a seashell horn and let out his war cry.

Each step forward was accompanied by the blast of horns and the chorus of battle cries.

The cannibals rushed forward. They never reached spear throw distance before they were hit in the face with the shards of glass. The forward marching diamonds finished each cannibal off as instructed. The trail of dead cannibals outlined the path of the moving fighting diamonds.

Saber Scar called out the attack from the rear and the back of the V fighting diamond formation closed and the back fighting diamonds began a backward walk as the battle continued.

Not one spear made it to any fighting diamond.

Taelo called a halt to the forward movement and turned all the diamonds back toward the sea.

He positioned each of the fighting diamonds within sight of each other but in an arch that extended the length of the beach.

He shared that he had counted five double handful of dead cannibal warriors.

He then shared that he would lead one fighting diamond and attack the camp of the cannibals and rescue any White Bear prisoners.

He thanked the White Bear warriors that volunteered to accompany him but rejected their help.

He asked Golden Hawk, Saber Scar, Red Oak, Grey Fox Running to accompany him.

Lily once again surprised him when she insisted that she would be needed to reassure those he rescued that they were friends.

She nodded and said that it was her time to be as brave as Running Stag had been when he was just a young boy. She held up her spear and announced that she had grown brave by watching two of the bravest, Golden Hawk and Taelo.

Everyone on the beach gave cheer.

Chapter 29: Annihilation

In the dark of the night, Taelo led the five from the beach. He had Lasher with him and watched for signs of Lasher sensing the cannibals. Lasher would stop, point to a location, and give a low hardly audible growl.

Each time Taelo led the team silently by. His goal was the rear camp where supplies, weapons and camp followers were located.

He had laid out the plan in two steps. The first action would be to rescue the White Bear prisoners. Then when these prisoners were free and on the way to the beach, Taelo said that he would return and deal with the cannibals remaining in the camp.

Taelo turned down the help that each of the team offered.

But Lily and Golden Hawk insisted that they be part of the confrontation with the camp members.

He agreed but said that it would affect them for many seasons to come. It would not be a battle. It would be a slaughter and no mercy would be shown.

The camp was situated on the same river where Taelo and his team had camped when they were returning with a good number of the White Bear Clan members during their journey that they now called Dangerous Passage.

He and Golden Hawk knew the area well. He approached the camp from the south knowing that the prison cage would be located the farthest from the cooking ring that he anticipated would be close to the river.

The White Bear Prisoners were huddled in the center of the cage trying to stay warm.

Lily crawled up to the cage and quietly let those inside know that they were being rescued.

Taelo crawled up to where two guards were sitting around a small fire. He stood up and still undetected he slit the throat of one guard and drove a stake through the other guard's eye. Neither of the guards made a sound.

He looked around to make sure that he had not been detected.

There were twenty-three prisoners. Taelo gave the weapons that the guards had carried to the two warriors he knew had participated in the battle against the Sky Eyes. He asked them all to quietly follow Grey Fox running back to the beach.

He then prepared to eliminate the rest of the cannibals. He was surprised to see that Saber Scar had stayed but that Lily had gone with the freed prisoners.

They had learned from the prisoners that some of the young White Bear women had been taken to individual hutches and were still there.

This complicated the situation and added another level of risk. Each time they entered a hutch they called out White Bear Clan and then based on the reaction of the women they took the necessary action. The male warriors in any hutch died immediately, the women had time to identify themselves before action was taken based on their response.

The immediate attack of the cannibal women made the decision a clear choice.

Six young White Bear women were rescued from the encampment.

Taelo layered all the cannibal bodies with wood between the bodies and lit a huge fire. He then led the group of young women back toward the beach.

He let Saber Scar know that he and Golden Hawk were going to eliminate the remaining warriors and that he should lead the young women to the beach.

The dark of night allowed the two of them to approach each group and ruthlessly eliminate them.

Lasher was their silent partner and more than once Lasher bit down on the wrist holding a war club enabling either Golden Hawk or Taelo to strike first.

Taelo looked down at the bodies of the last group of cannibal warriors. He and Golden Hawk had left ten groups of dead bodies. There were no survivors.

Taelo led the way back to the beach and walked silently past everyone and waded out into the sea. He, Golden Hawk and Lasher swam out and then returned to dry off.

They were met by Saber Scar who had stayed in the shallows were he could stand. The three of them stood together and commented that it would be a night that would long be remembered. Taelo commented that it would be a sad but also joyous memory. They had saved more than thirty White Bear Clan members.

Quiet Rabbit, Busy Bee and Marigold met them on the beach with dry outfits and some grilled shark meat.

They then led them to the central fire ring where all the people they had saved gave them a cheer and thanked them. Several warriors that had fought in the fighting diamonds were also at the fire ring and made a point of thanking everyone for saving one of their friends or relatives. Several had sisters that had been held captive.

One young warrior stood with one of the six young women who Taelo, Golden Hawk and Saber Scar had rescued from the cannibal hutches and thanked them for saving his mate.

Everyone looked up into the morning sky as the eagle let out a cry.

Broken Spear said he was flying with the eagle and there were two cannibal survivors that were going south away from the area.

Taelo stood up and said he had an errand to run. He asked Broken Spear where the two retreating warriors were located.

He took a spear and his flat blade and was ready to leave the camp when he was joined by Golden Hawk, Quiet Rabbit, and Busy Bee.

They all simply stated that they were going with him.

Taelo set a fast pace and they all left in the direction that Broken Spear had identified.

Soon they were racing through a long valley of tall grass. They were travelling single file behind Taelo.

The cry of the eagle warned Taelo that their quarry was close.

He had his spear in hand at the ready, but he did not want to kill these two. He wanted to give them a message to take back to their cannibal clan.

The message was, "all your companions are dead, only death awaits your clan when it comes up into this territory. Stay away."

Chapter 30: Northern Ice Wall

The White Bear Clan stood in fighting diamond formation on the beach and let out the war cry they had learned from Taelo. They had invited him to return whenever he chose, and they would celebrate once again the greatness of the Elk Clan.

Taelo had agreed to Feather-in-the-Wind's request to let her bring the young women that had been violated by the cannibals back to the Paradise Elk Clan.

He took the raft out and guided it out toward the northern sea and onward to the ice wall that would signal a turn toward the east. He was experiencing the mild weather he had hoped for.

Life on the raft had taken on another hue. The young women that Feather-in-the-Wind had brought on board became a focus for all the Sages. One young woman had come on board with her mate who had asked to make the trip with her.

Feather-in-the-Wind had commended him for standing by his mate and agreed to have both of them join her Paradise Clan.

Neiva, her mother complimented her on what she saw as a very generous gesture to all the young women who had been the victims of the cannibals. She invited the young women to participate in making and firing a variety of clay objects.

Lily recruited them to participate in cooking a variety of dishes.

Quiet Rabbit and Busy Bee spent time showing them how to hoist the sails and adjust the outriggers.

The young man, Bear Claw, which had come on board with his mate, turned out to be the younger brother of White Bear who had returned with Taelo on the Dangerous Passage journey.

Taelo integrated them all into the teams that controlled the guide paddle. He knew that staying active was the best way to erase the worst of the bad memories. He also knew that as Lily often reminded them that the bad memories were always there, but they became the beacon fire that made the new memories seem bright.

Feather-in-the-Wind felt a personal passion to help heal the six abused young women. She identified with their feelings of guilt and shame. She had experience feelings of guilt at having been saved from being a frozen offering to the Condor King. It had been Taelo and his team that had saved her. She felt it her duty to help in the recovery of the young women.

She also took note of how Taelo, Golden Hawk and Saber Scar seemed to intensify their activities. She was sure they were working through their feelings at the extermination of all the warriors and all the women that had accompanied them.

Running Stag had shared his feelings about how he had felt about his battle against the cannibals and about Taelo's aggressive nonnegotiable actions to save his parents.

They both thought of Taelo as a wise leader and developer of the people around him.

This was the first time she had seen him personally struggling with the actions he had taken.

Taelo spent time with Golden Hawk and Saber Scar discussing the difference between the battle against the cannibals that had captured Lily and Running Stag and the one they had just gone through. He likened it to a battle versus a straight execution. In a battle one defended themselves. Their actions had not been one of self-defense but one of delivering death. No matter how much they might justify their actions, they had not given the other person any chance at survival.

Quiet Rabbit and Busy Bee had both faced death when they were captured by the Warrior Clan. They were saved by the aggressive actions of Bold Walker of the Condor Clan and Taelo.

They reminded the three that they had taken the right action and should let the feelings of guilt go and embrace the fact that they had saved the captives and had guided everyone to a battle victory that had freed the White Bear Clan from being the victims.

Floating Cloud reminded Taelo that as long as she had known him, he had always taken the right action at the right time.

Lily didn't say anything but gave the three hugs as tears ran down her cheek.

The exchange was capped by the six young women who expressed their gratitude for having been rescued and for having been brought aboard the raft.

White Swan and Quiet Pheasant talked about the situation and agreed that the brutal actions of what their sons had taken were the right ones. They agreed with all the perspectives that had been shared and they felt it would be better if they kept their opinion to themselves.

The discussion had transpired over several sun cycles and had been the talk of everyone on the raft.

The overhead cry of the eagle caught everyone's attention.

Broken Spear said that he was flying with the eagle and could see the towering ice wall ahead.

Taelo began the turn of the raft when the wall came into view. His previous experience when a section of the wall fell into the sea and sent out a huge wave made him want to stay as far away as possible while still keeping it in sight.

He asked Broken Spear, Sly Squirrel, and Chirping Swallow to keep the raft sailing parallel to the wall but at the limit of their vision.

He declared the journey was on the last leg before they would all be traveling to the end of the season Elk Clan gathering.

The waves seemed to accept the raft at their crest and grudgingly pass beneath it and seemingly let the raft softly slide into the trough of the next wave.

Taelo was pleased with this action and instructed all the guide paddle teams to hold to that pattern. He pointed out that it made for a smooth, gentle ride.

Two moon cycles past and the raft continued to enjoy a sea that had been mostly calm. There had been a few sun cycles of rougher, white capped waves but overall, it was the calmest crossing the raft had experienced.

Broken Spear announced that he could see white capped mountains far ahead.

A cheer went up on the raft.

Taelo knew that everyone was ready to put their feet on the ground and ready to be back home in their own environment. He felt the same.

Chapter 31: Head Rock Bay Surprise

The mountains ahead seemed to stay on the horizon and resist getting closer. Taelo had experienced this visual phenomenon several times. The higher the mountains the longer it seemed that it took to reach them.

Finally, the shore came into view. It was time to turn the raft and follow the sea current toward the south.

Taelo had the rescued young women organized into two guide paddle control teams. He had them guiding the raft as it made its way toward Head Rock Bay. He wanted them to feel in control as they approached their new land.

The six of them and the faithful mate of one of them had spent many sun cycles learning the language of the Elk Clan and the language of the Others.

Golden Hawk and Quiet Rabbit had been the main teachers and Lily had been the person who cleared up the nuances of the different languages.

Lily's willingness to share her personal experiences as a captive of the cannibals had made a huge difference. The young women seemed to overcome most of the trauma that had initially affected them.

The raft seemed to sense that it was close to the end of the voyage of Sages and held the front edge of the southern flowing waves and made the most of the wind in the sails.

The fresh roasting salmon that were speared by the now eager fishers became a constant snack. Everyone was energized.

Red Oak and Quiet Pheasant volunteered the Valley of Plenty as a stopover before everyone dispersed. Quiet Fox and Little Doe thanked them but said that they planned on making a quick stop at their cave and then proceed to the Clan gathering. Broken Spear said that he would accompany Quiet Fox.

White Swan accepted her sister's invitation. Taelo knew that Quiet Rabbit and Floating Cloud would also accept the invitation.

Lily commented that some buffalo meat in the Valley of Plenty would be a great way to celebrate the end of the Journey of Sages. She made sure that the six young women would also stay.

She had talked with Taelo and was able to promise to take them to a cave where the water was hot, and the view of the Valley was amazing.

Head Rock Bay came into view, and everyone came out on deck to observe the entry. They were surprised to see the beach full of people.

Burley Bear and Meadow Flower were in front of a large contingent of Others and Talking Wren and Little Otter stood in front of the contingent from the Valley of Plenty.

The lone figure of Running Stag standing between the two groups was the big surprise.

Taelo wondered how all of them could be there to greet the returning Sages.

A cheer rose up from those on the beach as the raft came to rest on the sand and Marigold and Saber Scar put the anchor stones in place.

High in the sky the cry of the eagle announced the arrival as well.

Lasher gave a loud howl as he jumped to shore and ran to the cliff and then to the freshwater stream for a drink.

The raft quickly emptied, and everyone went about greeting each other.

Burley Bear said that he had responded to the cry of the eagle a few sun cycles ago and had organized his group to come to welcome home the Sages.

Talking Wren added that the eagle had cried out a sun cycle ago and that the Others had arrived at the Valley of Plenty the sun cycle before.

They had all been surprised when Running Stag had ridden in on his mount leading a dozen mounts to be traded at the Elk Clan gathering.

He said that the Paradise Clan was being led to the meeting valley by one Bold Walker that said that the Condor and the Eagle had flown over the Condor Clan Village, and he had interpreted that the Voyage of Others was returning.

Taelo again looked up as the eagle came in low over the beach and let out a cry.

Taelo gave his version of the eagles cry, and a cheer went up from the gathering on the beach.

Talking Wren informed everyone that the Valley was prepared to celebrate their return. The Valley of Plenty Elk Clan had departed for the Elk Clan meeting two sun cycles ago, but a small contingent had remained and had prepared a celebration dinner for everyone and there was plenty of space to have every one spend a few sun cycles resting before proceeding to the Elk Clan gathering.

Red Oak and Quiet Pheasant complimented Talking Wren on her preparation and said that the Sages were rested and as soon as Taelo and Golden Hawk bagged the buffalo that they wanted to take to the gathering, everyone was ready to go to the Elk Clan gathering.

Lily commented that she wanted to take their new members up to the warm water cave to spend the night. They would join the feast but leave before it got too dark to climb up to the cave.

Broken Spear's carrying chair was put on two mounts and the entire group made their way into the Valley of Plenty.

It was clear to Taelo that the celebration would last well into the night.

He and Golden Hawk led Lily and the young women to the cave. They asked the Bear Claw, White Bear's younger brother to return with them and then go hunting with them in the morning. It was their way of making the stay in the cave for the young women something that they would have for themselves, and it would allow he and Golden Hawk a chance to see if Bear Claw was fast enough to outrun a buffalo.

The celebration was in full swing when they returned to the Valley of Plenty lodge.

The stories and the honey wine was flowing. The three of them grabbed a grilled buffalo rib and a bag of the honey wine and joined in the festivities.

It was a good night for all three.

Chapter 32: Elk Clan Gathering

Taelo had gone out for three buffalo. Quiet Rabbit, Golden Hawk and Busy Bee all participated in taking down the first two. While Saber Scar, Marigold, Burley Bear and Meadow Flower provided the back up.

A large number of the Sages had come out to observe the technique used by Taelo.

He had situated the observers in a location to where he would guide the selected buffalo.

He and Golden Hawk selected the first two buffalo and guided them toward the observers.

Bear Claw and his mate Running Fox ran along with Quiet Rabbit and Busy Bee in preparation for them participating in getting the third buffalo. They carried the spears that they would use. They both proved to be fast enough and had enough endurance to hunt the third buffalo.

This was the first time for Broken Spear to be personally present for such a hunt. It was also a first for Star Leaper and Neiva. They were astonished by the ability of Taelo and Golden Hawk to accelerate and pass the buffalo.

For the third buffalo, Taelo ran along with Bear Claw and Quiet Rabbit ran along with Running Fox. Taelo waited until the buffalo was almost to the edge of the woods and then signaled for Running Fox to place his spear. The buffalo fell to its knees and slid next to the tree where it would be hoisted after getting skinned.

Bear Claw and Running Fox danced a jig that reminded Taelo of him and Quiet Rabbit doing many similar dancing celebrations a few seasons before.

Everyone congratulated the two for having demonstrated their skill and Taelo welcomed them as hunters of the Elk Clan. He let them know that he would present them to all the Elk Clan members as qualified buffalo hunters.

The buffaloes were skinned, the meat wrapped in the buffalo hide and put on travois.

It was time to travel to the Elk Clan meeting.

Talking Wren, Little Otter, Burley Bear, and Running Stag all rode at the front of the procession of Sages.

Everyone was riding a mount and the travel was easy for most of them.

When Star Leaper complained about the pain in his lower back Taelo nodded and said he understood the problem.

Taelo dropped down from his mount and jogged alongside of his mount and said that the jogging would relieve the back pain.

Star Leaper laughed and said that he was sure that he would end up with his legs and back competing for his attention by the time they got to the meeting valley.

A few mornings later, when they reached the crest overlooking the meeting valley Burley Bear signaled a halt.

The view reminded Taelo of the time when as a young boy he had stood between White Swan and Grey Fox Running and watched the pink tinted campfire smoke twist slowly as it rose into the sky.

This morning the rising smoke was bending with the light breeze and rising tinted both pink and grey with an edging of black. It reminded him of a gathering of snakes warning the sky to keep its distance.

Everyone commented on the beauty of the landscape and how the meeting place seemed nestled by the surrounding mountains and guarded by the tall green pines that surrounded the valley.

The small crystal-clear lake reflecting the yellow leaves of the willow and the tall mountains above it seemed to be a second sky.

An eagle cried overhead, and a white swan crested the valley to their right and came honking loudly but made a long smooth landing on the lake.

White Swan knew that her totem had arrived to greet her and that Taelo's totem had greeted him.

A horn sound in the valley and all the various Elk Clans came out to greet their returning Sages.

Talking Wren had rearranged the camp so that the returning Sages had the center camp by the edge of the lake.

Once the Sages were situated in their individual huts, the Elk Clan meeting was officially open.

The trading and bargaining began.

Food and snacks were shared.

Old friends reconnected with each other.

Mothers were introducing daughters and sons to each other with the goal of lighting the mating urge.

Feather-in-the-Wind made sure that the young White Bear Clan women were introduced to all the mothers of young men.

Lily made a point of being the mother for all six of the eligible White Bear Clan women.

The pottery that all the Sages had brought was in great demand.

Star Leapers walking sticks were soon gone.

Taelo's jewelry and other decorative items lasted less than a day.

Finally, the evening of stories to be told arrived. Broken Spear would be the main storyteller and at this meeting all the younger members that had made the Journey of Sages would be his voice. Taelo remembered well the evening that was so vivid in his mind when he and his team had been the loud voice for Broken Spear.

The Sages were situated around the edge of those sitting and listening. They were roasting and handing out the buffalo meat that they had brought as snacks for those sitting and listening.

This display of humility and of generosity did not go unnoticed. It was this attitude among the leaders that held the Elk Clans together and made the Clan meeting such a looked forward to event.

Taelo kicked off the session by introducing the newest members of the Elk Clan. He made sure to let all the young men know that the young ladies were eligible. He then introduced Bear Claw and Running Fox as two new and qualified hunters of the Paradise Elk Clan.

He then made the point that he was turning the evening over to the Sage of Sages, Broken Spear.

The Journey of Sages was over, but the journey of the Elk Clan would continue.

The End

About the Author

Ronald E. Mueller
remwriter95@gmail.com

Ron grew up in what is now Flint River State Park in Southeast Iowa. The 170-year-old house Ron lived in is built into a hillside. It faces a 125-foot-high cliff towering over the little Flint River. The house and the land talked to him about the passing of time, the struggle to conquer the land, the struggles people faced and the wonder of nature.

He climbed the cliffs, crawled into the caves, dove from the swimming rock, collected clams from the bottom of the pond, gigged and skinned frogs for their legs. He trapped muskrats for fur, hunted raccoon in the dead of night, and hunted rabbits in the dead of winter with only a stick. His young life was outdoors, and nature tested him. He walked to a one room: stone schoolhouse uphill both ways. It was a great way to grow up.

His experiences inter-twined with snippets of fantasy lend themselves to the adventures Taelo leads the reader through.

Ron has told many similar stories to impart life values and influence the thinking of his children and now grandchildren. He feels stories are a wonderful means for parents and their children to engage in meaningful discussions about behavior and fundamental values and principles.

<u>Character names and Roles</u>

Taelo	Elk Clan Main Character through all series
White Swan	Taelo's Mother
Grey Fox Running	Taelo's Father
Golden Hawk,	Taelo's cousin and best friend
Quiet Pheasant,	Golden Hawks mother
Red Oak	Husband to Quiet Pheasant
Quiet Rabbit	Eventually Taelo's mate
Fast Skimmer	Quiet Rabbit's father
Silent Pool	Quiet Rabbit's mother
Floating Cloud	Quiet Rabbits Grandmother
Busy Bee	Eventually Golden Hawk's mate
Brave Deer	Busy Bee's Father
Little Otter	first long hunt leader for the Taelo team
Talking Wren	Eventual mate to Little Otter
Little Pebble	Busy Bees Mother
Wise Owl	Elk Hide Clan leader, Council Leader.
Grey Weaver	Elk Hide Clan, storyteller.
Silent Hawk	Initial Leader of the Elk Clan
Sharp Beaver	Hunter in Brave Deer's team
Soft Down	Minor character when the elk clan reach the beach.
Fierce Badger	Leader of the Eastern Elk Clan
Whistling Wind	Hunter of the Eastern Elk Clan

<u>The Others</u>

Broken Spear	Seer of the Others was Long Spear.
Tall Fern	Broken Spear's early mate
Quiet Fox	Leader of the Others
Little Doe	Wife of the Others Leader
Burley Bear	Of, the Others Taelo's protector and friend
Meadow Flower	Burley Bear's mate
Saber Scar	Rolling Stone new name when scared by a saber tooth.
Marigold	Saber Scar's mate
Single Leaf	friend of Meadow Flower
Sharp Blade	Mate to Single Leaf

<u>Warrior Clan</u> (Southern Mexico)

Tough Hide	Co-leader of the Warrior Clan
Storm Wind	youngest son of Tough Hide
Strong Sinew	eldest son of Tough Hide
Sharp Stone	Co-leader of the Warrior Clan - bad guy

<u>Rescued People from Snow pit</u>

Semper	leader of the rescued people from snow pit
Wan	mate to Semper
Lani	Young Mother with a baby

<u>Rescued people from Cannibals</u>

Lily	led the escape group.
Slow Walker	Lily's Mate
Mayflower	member of escape group
White Pearl	member of escape group
Gentle Fern	member of escape group
Little Pearl	member of escape group
Running Stag	member of escape group

<u>Sky Eyes</u>

Flying Eagle	River Clan Leader
Running Fox	Mate of Flying Eagle, mother of Angry Cougar
Angry Cougar	Son of Flying Eagle
Rolling Stone	Friend and confident of Angry Cougar
Sharp Claw	Advisor to Flying Eagle

<u>White Bear Clan</u>

White Bear	Young Warrior friend to Deer Chaser
Deer Chaser	Young Warrior, friend to White Bear
Whistling Arrow	White Bear Clan elder-only one to survive
Gentle Cub	Young woman, fast runner
Bending Willow	Young woman, fast runner
Bubbling Brook	Young woman, fast runner

<u>Andes Condor Clan</u>

Star Leaper	Leader of the Andes Clan
Neiva	Wife of the leader.
Bold Walker	Feather-in-the-Wind's older brother
Feather in the Wind	Was a sacrifice to the Condor King (bird)
Wolf Bold Walker	Name of Feather-in-the-Wind's wolf
Mountain Runner	Close friend of Bold Walker
Long Leaper	Brother to Mountain Runner
Sharp Claws	Leader of one of the raiding teams
Dark Night	New Leader of the Warrior Clan
Tough Hide	Leader Killed by Dark Night
Strong Sinew	Son of Tough Hide
Storm Wind	Son of Tough Hide
Sharp Stone	Warrior Clan leader killed by Taelo

QR Links to
ATWP.US web site

www.ingramcontent.com/pod-product-compliance
Lightning Source LLC
Chambersburg PA
CBHW070659100726
47907CB00001B/2